TOR BOOKS BY V. E. SCHWAB

STANDALONES
The Invisible Life of Addie LaRue

THE VILLAINS SERIES
Vicious
Vengeful

THE SHADES OF MAGIC SERIES
A Darker Shade of Magic
A Gathering of Shadows
A Conjuring of Light

Praise for the Shades of Magic series

"Schwab has given us a gem of a tale that is original in its premise and compelling in its execution. This is a book to treasure."
—Deborah Harkness, *New York Times* bestselling author, on *A Darker Shade of Magic*

"Feels like a priceless object, brought from another, better world of fantasy books." —*io9* on *A Darker Shade of Magic*

"Compulsively readable . . . Her characters make the book."
—NPR on *A Darker Shade of Magic*

"This is how fantasy should be done."
—*Publishers Weekly* (starred review) on *A Gathering of Shadows*

"Addictive and immersive, this series is a must-read."
—*Entertainment Weekly*

"Desperate gambits, magical battles, and meaningful sacrifice make this a thrilling read." —*Kirkus Reviews* (starred review) on *A Conjuring of Light*

"Flawless prose . . . This bittersweet conclusion is a fitting one for a fantastic, emotionally rich series that redefines epic."
—*Publishers Weekly* (starred review) on *A Conjuring of Light*

Praise for *The Invisible Life of Addie LaRue*

"For someone damned to be forgettable, Addie LaRue is a most delightfully unforgettable character, and her story is the most joyous evocation of unlikely immortality."
—Neil Gaiman, *New York Times* bestselling author

"A book perfectly suspended between darkness and light, myth and reality. [This novel] is—ironically—unforgettable."
—Alix E. Harrow, Hugo Award–winning author of *The Ten Thousand Doors of January*

"*The Invisible Life of Addie LaRue* is the kind of book you encounter only once in a lifetime. . . . A defiant, joyous rebellion against time, fate, and even death itself—and a powerful reminder that the only magic great enough to conquer all of it is love."
—Peng Shepherd, author of *The Book of M*

"Schwab's page-turner is an achingly poignant romantic fantasy about the desperate desire to make one's mark on the world."
—*Oprah Daily,* Best LGBTQ Books of 2020

"One of the most propulsive, compulsive, and captivating novels in recent memory."
—*The Washington Post*

A CONJURING OF LIGHT

V. E. SCHWAB

TOR PUBLISHING GROUP
NEW YORK

This is a work of fiction. All of the characters, organizations, and events portrayed in this novel are either products of the author's imagination or are used fictitiously.

A CONJURING OF LIGHT

Copyright © 2017 by Victoria Schwab

All rights reserved.

A Tor Book
Published by Tom Doherty Associates / Tor Publishing Group
120 Broadway
New York, NY 10271

www.tor-forge.com

Tor® is a registered trademark of Macmillan Publishing Group, LLC.

The Library of Congress has cataloged the hardcover edition as follows:

Names: Schwab, Victoria, author.
Title: A conjuring of light / V. E. Schwab.
Description: First edition. | New York : Tor, a Tom Doherty Associates book, 2017.
Identifiers: LCCN 2017299702 (print) | ISBN 9780765387462 (hardcover) | ISBN 9780765387486 (ebook)
Subjects: LCSH: Magicians—Fiction. | Space and time—Fiction. | Magic—Fiction. | Quantum theory—Fiction. | London (England)—Fiction. | LCSHAC: Magicians—Fiction. | Other subjects: FANTASY. | FICTION / Fantasy / Historical. | Magic. | Magicians. | Quantum theory. | Space and time. | Magicians—Fiction. | Magic—Fiction. | Quantum theory—Fiction. | England—London. | London (England)—Fiction. | LCGFT: Fantasy fiction. | Fiction. | Science fiction.
Classification: LCC PS3619.C4848 C66 2017 (print) | DDC 813/.6—dc23
LC record available at https://lccn.loc.gov/2017299702

ISBN 978-1-250-89124-2 (second trade paperback)

Our books may be purchased in bulk for promotional, educational, or business use. Please contact your local bookseller or the Macmillan Corporate and Premium Sales Department at 1-800-221-7945, extension 5442, or by email at MacmillanSpecialMarkets@macmillan.com.

Second Tor Paperback Edition: 2023

Printed in the United States of America

0 9 8 7 6 5 4 3 2

For the ones who've found their way home

Pure magic has no self. It simply is, *a force of nature, the blood of our world, the marrow of our bones. We give it shape, but we must never give it soul.*

—MASTER TIEREN,
head priest of the London Sanctuary

ONE

WORLD IN RUIN

I

Delilah Bard—always a thief, recently a magician, and one day, hopefully, a pirate—was running as fast as she could.

Hold on, Kell, she thought as she sprinted through the streets of Red London, still clutching the shard of stone that had once been part of Astrid Dane's mouth. A token stolen in another life, when magic and the idea of multiple worlds were new to her. When she had only just discovered that people could be possessed, or bound like rope, or turned to stone.

Fireworks thundered in the distance, met by cheers and chants and music, all the sounds of a city celebrating the end of the *Essen Tasch,* the tournament of magic. A city oblivious to the horror happening at its heart. And back at the palace, the prince of Arnes—Rhy—was dying, which meant that somewhere, a world away, so was Kell.

Kell. The name rang through her with all the force of an order, a plea.

Lila reached the road she was looking for and staggered to a stop, knife already out, blade pressing to the flesh of her arm. Her heart pounded as she turned her back on the chaos and pressed her bloody palm—and the stone still curled within it—to the nearest wall.

Twice before Lila had made this journey, but always as a passenger.

Always using Kell's magic.

Never her own.

And never alone.

But there was no time to think, no time to be afraid, and certainly no time to wait.

Chest heaving and pulse high, Lila swallowed and said the words, as boldly as she could. Words that belonged only on the lips of a blood magician. An *Antari*. Like Holland. Like Kell.

"As Travars."

The magic sang up her arm, and through her chest, and then the city lurched around her, gravity twisting as the world gave way.

Lila thought it would be easy or, at least, *simple*.

Something you either survived, or did not.

She was wrong.

II

A world away, Holland was drowning.

He fought to the surface of his own mind, only to be forced back down into the dark water by a will as strong as iron. He fought, and clawed, and gasped for air, strength leaching out with every violent thrash, every desperate struggle. It was worse than dying, because dying gave way to death, and this did not.

There was no light. No air. No strength. It had all been taken, severed, leaving only darkness and, somewhere beyond the crush, a voice shouting his name.

Kell's voice—

Too far away.

Holland's grip faltered, slipped, and he was sinking again.

All he had ever wanted was to bring the magic back—to see his world spared from its slow, inexorable death—a death caused first by the fear of another London, and then by the fear of his own.

All Holland wanted was to see his world restored.

Revived.

He knew the legends—the dreams—of a magician powerful enough to do it. Strong enough to breathe air back into its starved lungs, to quicken its dying heart.

For as long as Holland could remember, that was all he'd wanted.

And for as long as Holland could remember, he had wanted the magician to be *him*.

Even before the darkness bloomed across his eye, branding him with the mark of power, he'd wanted it to be him. He'd stood on the banks of the Sijlt as a child, skating stones across the frozen surface, imagining that he would be the one to crack the ice. Stood in the Silver Wood as a grown man, praying for the strength to protect his home. He'd never wanted to be *king,* though in the stories the magician always was. He didn't want to rule the world. He only wanted to save it.

Athos Dane had called this arrogance, that first night, when Holland was dragged, bleeding and half conscious, into the new king's chambers. Arrogance and pride, he'd chided, as he carved his curse into Holland's skin.

Things to be broken.

And Athos had. He'd broken Holland one bone, one day, one order at a time. Until all Holland wanted, more than the ability to save his world, more than the strength to bring the magic back, more than *anything,* was for it to end.

It was cowardice, he knew, but cowardice came so much easier than hope.

And in that moment by the bridge, when Holland lowered his guard and let the spoiled princeling Kell drive the metal bar through his chest, the first thing he felt—the first and last and *only* thing he felt—was relief.

That it was finally over.

Only it wasn't.

It is a hard thing, to kill an *Antari.*

When Holland woke, lying in a dead garden, in a dead city, in a dead world, the first thing he felt then was pain. The second thing was freedom. Athos Dane's hold was gone, and Holland was alive—broken, but alive.

And stranded.

Trapped in a wounded body in a world with no door at the mercy of another king. But this time, he had a *choice.*

A chance to set things right.

He'd stood, half dead, before the onyx throne, and spoken to the king carved in stone, and traded freedom for a chance to save his London, to see it bloom again. Holland made the deal, paid with his own body and soul. And with the shadow king's power, he had finally brought the magic back, seen his world bloom into color, his people's hope revived, his city restored.

He'd done everything he could, given up everything he had, to keep it safe.

But it still was not enough.

Not for the shadow king, who always wanted more, who grew stronger every day and craved chaos, magic in its truest form, power without control.

Holland was losing hold of the monster in his skin.

And so he'd done the only thing he could.

He'd offered Osaron another vessel.

"*Very well . . .* " said the king, the demon, the god. *"But if they cannot be persuaded, I will keep your body as my own."*

And Holland agreed—how could he not?

Anything for London.

And Kell—spoiled, childish, headstrong Kell, broken and powerless and snared by that damned collar—had still refused.

Of course he had refused.

Of course—

The shadow king had smiled then, with Holland's own mouth, and he had fought, with everything he could summon, but a deal was a deal and the deal was done and he felt Osaron surge up—that single, violent motion—and Holland was shoved down, into the dark depths of his own mind, forced under by the current of the shadow king's will.

Helpless, trapped within a body, within a deal, unable to do anything but watch, and feel, and drown.

"Holland!"

Kell's voice cracked as he strained his broken body against the frame, the way *Holland* had once, when Athos Dane first bound him. Broke him. The cage leached away most of Kell's power; the collar around his throat cut off the rest. There was a terror in Kell's eyes, a desperation that surprised him.

"Holland, you bastard, fight back!"

He tried, but his body was no longer his, and his mind, his tired mind, was sinking down, down—

Give in, said the shadow king.

"Show me you're not weak!" Kell's voice pushed through. "Prove you're not still a slave to someone else's will!"

You cannot fight me.

"Did you really come all the way back to lose like this?"

I've already won.

"Holland!"

Holland hated Kell, and in that moment, the hatred was almost enough to drive him up, but even if he wanted to rise to the other *Antari*'s bait, Osaron was unyielding.

Holland heard his own voice, then, but of course it wasn't his. A twisted imitation by the monster wearing his skin. In Holland's hand, a crimson coin, a token to another London, Kell's London, and Kell was swearing and throwing himself against his bonds until his chest heaved and his wrists were bloody.

Useless.

It was all useless.

Once again he was a prisoner in his own body. Kell's voice echoed through the dark.

You've just traded one master for another.

They were moving now, Osaron guiding Holland's body. The door closed behind them, but Kell's screams still hurled themselves against the wood, shattering into broken syllables and strangled cries.

Ojka stood in the hall, sharpening her knives. She looked up, revealing the crescent scar on one cheek, and her two-toned eyes, one yellow, the other black. An *Antari* forged by their hands—by their mercy.

"Your Majesty," she said, straightening.

Holland tried to rise up, tried to force his voice across their—*his*—lips, but when speech came, the words were Osaron's.

"Guard the door. Let no one pass."

A flicker of a smile across the red slash of Ojka's mouth. "As you wish."

The palace passed in a blur, and then they were outside, passing the statues of the Dane twins at the base of the stairs, moving swiftly beneath a bruised sky through a garden now flanked by trees instead of bodies.

What would become of it, without Osaron, without *him*? Would the city continue to flourish? Or would it collapse, like a body stripped of life?

Please, he begged silently. *This world needs me.*

"*There is no point,*" said Osaron aloud, and Holland felt sick to be the thought in their head instead of the word. "*It is already dead,*" continued the king. "*We will start over. We will find a world worthy of our strength.*"

They reached the garden wall and Osaron drew a dagger from the sheath at their waist. The bite of steel on flesh was nothing, as if Holland had been cut off from his very senses, buried too deep to feel anything but Osaron's grip. But as the shadow king's fingers streaked through the blood and lifted Kell's coin to the wall, Holland struggled up one last time.

He couldn't win back his body—not yet—not all of it—but perhaps he didn't need everything.

One hand. Five fingers.

He threw every ounce of strength, every shred of will, into that one limb, and halfway to the wall, it stopped, hovering in the air.

Blood trickled down his wrist. Holland knew the words to break a body, to turn it to ice, or ash, or stone.

All he had to do was guide his hand to his own chest.

All he had to do was shape the magic—

Holland could feel the annoyance ripple through Osaron. Annoyance, but not rage, as if this last stand, this great protest, was nothing but an itch.

How tedious.

Holland kept fighting, even managed to guide his hand an inch, two.

Let go, Holland, warned the creature in his head.

Holland forced the last of his will into his hand, dragging it another inch.

Osaron sighed.

It did not have to be this way.

Osaron's will hit him like a wall. His body didn't move, but his mind slammed backward, pinned beneath a crushing pain. Not the pain he'd felt a hundred times, the kind he'd learned to exist beyond, outside, the kind he might escape. This pain was rooted in his very core. It lit him up, sudden and bright, every nerve burning with such searing heat that he screamed and screamed and screamed inside his head, until the darkness finally—mercifully—closed over him, forcing him under and down.

And this time, Holland didn't try to surface.

This time, he let himself drown.

III

Kell kept throwing himself against the metal cage long after the door slammed shut and the bolt slid home. His voice still echoed against the pale stone walls. He had screamed himself hoarse. But still, no one came. Fear pounded through him, but what scared Kell most was the loosening in his chest—the unhinging of a vital link, the spreading sense of loss.

He could hardly feel his brother's pulse.

Could hardly feel anything but the pain in his wrists and a horrible numbing cold. He twisted against the metal frame, fighting the restraints, but they held fast. Spell work was scrawled down the sides of the contraption, and despite the quantity of Kell's blood smeared on the steel, there was the collar circling his throat, cutting off everything he needed. Everything he had. Everything he *was*. The collar cast a shadow over his mind, an icy film over his thoughts, cold dread and sorrow and, through it all, an absence of hope. Of strength. *Give up*, it whispered through his blood. *You have nothing. You are nothing. Powerless.*

He'd never been powerless.

He didn't know how to be powerless.

Panic rose in place of magic.

He had to get out.

Out of this cage.

Out of this collar.

Out of this world.

Rhy had carved a word into his own skin to bring Kell home, and he'd turned around and left again. Abandoned the prince, the crown, the city. Followed a woman in white through a door in the world because she told him he was needed, told him he could help, told him it was his fault, that he had to make it right.

Kell's heart faltered in his chest.

No—not *his* heart. Rhy's. A life bound to his with magic he no longer *had*. The panic flared again, a breath of heat against the numbing cold, and Kell clung to it, pushing back against the collar's hollow dread. He straightened in the frame, clenched his teeth and *pulled* against his cuffs until he felt the crack of bone inside his wrist, the tear of flesh. Blood fell in thick red drops to the stone floor, vibrant but useless. He bit back a scream as metal dragged over—and into—skin. Pain knifed up his arm, but he kept pulling, metal scraping muscle and then bone before his right hand finally came free.

Kell slumped back with a gasp and tried to wrap his bloody, limp fingers around the collar, but the moment they touched the metal, a horrible pins-and-needles cold seared up his arm, swam in his head.

"*As Steno,*" he pleaded. *Break.*

Nothing happened.

No power rose to meet the word.

Kell let out a sob and sagged against the frame. The room tilted and tunneled, and he felt his mind sliding toward darkness, but he forced his body to stay upright, forced himself to swallow the bile rising in his throat. He curled his skinned and splintered hand around his still-trapped arm, and began to pull.

It was minutes—but it felt like hours, years—before Kell finally tore himself free.

He stumbled forward out of the frame, and swayed on his feet. The metal cuffs had cut deep into his wrists—too deep—and the pale stone beneath his feet was slick with red.

Is this yours? whispered a voice.

A memory of Rhy's young face twisted in horror at the sight of Kell's ruined forearms, the blood streaked across the prince's chest. *Is this all yours?*

Now the collar dripped red as Kell frantically pulled on the metal.

His fingers ached with cold as he found the clasp and clawed at it, but still it held. His focus blurred. He slipped in his own blood and went down, catching himself with broken hands. Kell cried out, curling in on himself even as he screamed at his body to rise.

    He had to get up.

    He had to get back to Red London.

    He had to stop Holland—stop *Osaron*.

    He had to save Rhy.

    He had to, he had to, he had to—but in that moment, all Kell could do was lie on the cold marble, warmth spreading in a thin red pool around him.

IV

The prince collapsed back against the bed, soaked through with sweat, choking on the metal taste of blood. Voices rose and fell around him, the room a blur of shadows, shards of light. A scream tore through his head, but his own jaw locked in pain. Pain that was and wasn't his.

Kell.

Rhy doubled over, coughing up blood and bile.

He tried to rise—he had to get up, had to find his brother—but hands surged from the darkness, fought him, held him down against silk sheets, fingers digging into shoulders and wrists and knees, and the pain was there again, vicious and jagged, peeling back flesh, dragging its nails over bone. Rhy tried to remember. Kell—arrested. His cell—empty. Searching the sun-dappled orchard. Calling his brother's name. Then, out of nowhere, pain, sliding between his ribs, just as it had that night, a horrible, severing thing, and he couldn't breathe.

He couldn't—

"Don't let go," said a voice.

"Stay with me."

"Stay . . ."

Rhy learned early the difference between want and need.

Being the son and heir—the only heir—of the Maresh family, the light of Arnes, the future of the empire, meant that he had never (as a nursery minder once informed him, before being removed from the royal service) experienced true *need*. Clothes, horses, instruments, fineries—all he had to do was ask for a thing, and it was given.

And yet, the young prince *wanted*—deeply—a thing that could not be fetched. He wanted what coursed in the blood of so many low-born boys and girls. What came so easily to his father, to his mother, to Kell.

Rhy wanted *magic*.

Wanted it with a fire that rivaled any need.

His royal father had a gift for metals, and his mother an easy touch with water, but magic wasn't like black hair or brown eyes or elevated birth—it didn't follow the rules of lineage, wasn't passed down from parent to child. It chose its own course.

And already at the age of nine, it was beginning to look as though magic hadn't chosen him at all.

But Rhy Maresh refused to believe that he'd been passed over entirely; it *had* to be there, somewhere within him, that flame of power waiting for a well-timed breath, a poker's nudge. After all, he was a prince. And if magic would not come to him, he'd go to *it*.

It was that logic that had brought him here, to the stone floor of the Sanctuary's drafty old library, shivering as the cold leached through the embroidered silk of his pant legs (designed for the palace, where it was always warm).

Whenenver Rhy complained about the chill in the Sanctuary, old Tieren would crinkle his brow.

Magic makes its own warmth, he'd say, which was well and good if you were a magician, but then, Rhy wasn't.

Not yet.

This time he hadn't complained. Hadn't even told the head priest he was here.

The young prince crouched in an alcove at the back of the library, hidden behind a statue and a long wooden table, and spread the stolen parchment on the floor.

Rhy had been born with light fingers—but of course, being royal, he almost never had to use them. People were always willing to offer things freely, indeed leaping at the ready to deliver, from a cloak on a chilly day to a frosted cake from the kitchens.

But Rhy hadn't asked for the scroll; he'd lifted it from Tieren's desk, one of a dozen tied with the thin white ribbon that marked a priest's spell. None of them were all that fancy or elaborate, much to Rhy's chagrin. Instead they focused on utility.

Spells to keep the food from spoiling.

Spells to protect the orchard trees from frost.

Spells to keep a fire burning without oil.

And Rhy would try every single one until he found a spell that he could do. A spell that would speak to the magic surely sleeping in his veins. A spell that could *wake it up*.

A breeze whipped through the Sanctuary as he dug a handful of red *lin* from his pocket and weighted the parchment to the floor. On its surface, in the head priest's steady hand, was a map—not like the one in his father's war room that showed the whole kingdom. No, this was a map of a spell, a diagram of magic.

Across the top of the scroll were three words in the common tongue.

Is Anos Vol, read Rhy.

The Eternal Flame.

Beneath those words was a pair of concentric circles, linked by delicate lines and dotted with small symbols, the condensed shorthand favored by the spell-makers of London. Rhy squinted, trying to make sense of the scrawl. He had a knack for languages, picking up the airy cadence of the Faroan tongue, the choppy waves made by each Veskan syllable, the hills and valleys of Arnes's own border dialects—but the words on the parchment seemed to shift and blur before his eyes, sliding in and out of focus.

He chewed his lip (it was a bad habit, one his mother was always warning him to break because it wasn't *princely*), then planted his hands on either side of the paper, fingertips brushing the outer circle, and began the spell.

He focused his eyes on the center of the page as he read, sounding out each word, the fragments clumsy and broken on his tongue.

His pulse rose in his ears, the beat at odds with the natural rhythm of the magic. But Rhy held the spell together, pinned it down with sheer force of will, and as he neared the end a tingling of heat started in his hands; he could feel it trickling through his palms, into his fingers, brushing the circle's edge, and then . . .

Nothing.

No spark.

No flame.

He said the spell once, twice, three more times, but the heat in his hands was already fading, dissolving into an ordinary prickle of numbness. Dejected, he let the words trail off, taking the last of his focus with them.

The prince sagged back onto the cold stones. "*Sanct,*" he muttered, even though he knew it was bad form to swear, and worse to do it *here.*

"What are you doing?"

Rhy looked up and saw his brother standing at the mouth of the alcove, a red cloak around his narrow shoulders. Even at ten and three quarters, Kell's face had the set of a serious man, down to the furrow between his brows. Kell's red hair glinted even in the grey morning light, and his eyes—one blue, the other black as night—made people look down, away. Rhy didn't understand why, but he always made a point of looking his brother in the face, to show Kell it didn't matter. Eyes were eyes.

Kell wasn't *really* his brother, of course. Even a passing look would mark them as different. Kell was a mixture, like different kinds of clay twined together; he had the fair skin of a Veskan, the lanky body of a Faroan, and the copper hair found only on the northern edge of Arnes. And then, of course, there were his eyes. One natural, if not particularly Arnesian, and the other *Antari,* marked by magic itself as *aven.* Blessed.

Rhy, on the other hand, with his warm brown skin, his black hair and amber eyes, was all London, all Maresh, all royal.

Kell took in the prince's high color, and then the parchment spread out before him. He knelt across from Rhy, the fabric of his cloak pooling on the stones around him. "Where did you get this?" he asked, a prickle of displeasure in his voice.

"From Tieren," said Rhy. His brother shot him a skeptical look, and Rhy amended, "From Tieren's study."

Kell skimmed the spell and frowned. "An eternal flame?"

Rhy absently plucked one of the *lin* from the floor and shrugged. "First thing I grabbed." He tried to sound as if he didn't care about the stupid spell, but his throat was tight, his eyes burning. "Doesn't matter," he said, skipping the coin across the ground as if it were a pebble on water. "I can't make it work."

Kell shifted his weight, lips moving silently as he read over the priest's scrawl. He held his hands above the paper, palms cupped as if cradling a flame that wasn't even there yet, and began to recite the spell. When Rhy had tried, the words had fallen out like rocks, but on Kell's lips, they were poetry, smooth and sibilant.

The air around them warmed instantly, steam rising from the penned lines on the scroll before the ink drew in and up into a bead of oil, and lit.

The flame hovered in the air between Kell's hands, brilliant and white.

He made it look so easy, and Rhy felt a flash of anger toward his brother, hot as a spark—but just as brief.

It wasn't Kell's fault Rhy couldn't do magic. Rhy started to rise when Kell caught his cuff. He guided Rhy's hands to either side of the spell, pulling the prince into the fold of his magic. Warmth tickled Rhy's palms, and he was torn between delight at the power and knowledge that it wasn't his.

"It isn't right," he murmured. "I'm the crown prince, the heir of Maxim Maresh. I should be able to light a blasted candle."

Kell chewed his lip—Mother never chided *him* for the habit—and then said, "There are different kinds of power."

"I would rather have magic than a crown," sulked Rhy.

Kell studied the small white flame between them. "A crown is a sort of magic, if you think about it. A magician rules an element. A king rules an empire."

"Only if the king is strong enough."

Kell looked up, then. "You're going to be a good king, if you don't get yourself killed first."

Rhy blew out a breath, shuddering the flame. "How do you know?"

At that, Kell smiled. It was a rare thing, and Rhy wanted to hold fast to it—he was the only one who could make his brother smile, and he wore it like a badge—but then Kell said, "Magic," and Rhy wanted to slug him instead.

"You're an arse," he muttered, trying to pull away, but his brother's fingers tightened.

"Don't let go."

"Get off," said Rhy, first playfully, but then, as the fire grew brighter and hotter between his palms, he repeated in earnest, "Stop. You're hurting me."

Heat licked his fingers, a white-hot pain lancing through his hands and up his arms.

"Stop," he pleaded. "Kell, *stop*." But when Rhy looked up from the glowing fire to his brother's face, it wasn't a face at all. Nothing but a pool of darkness. Rhy gasped, tried to scramble away, but his brother was no longer flesh and blood but stone, hands carved into cuffs around Rhy's wrists.

This wasn't right, he thought, it had to be a dream—a nightmare—but the heat of the fire and the crushing pressure on his wrists were both so real, worsening with every heartbeat, every breath.

The flame between them went long and thin, sharpening into a blade of light, its tip pointed first at the ceiling, and then, slowly, horribly, at Rhy. He fought, and screamed, but it did nothing to stop the knife as it blazed and buried itself in his chest.

Pain.

Make it stop.

It carved its way across his ribs, lit his bones, tore through his heart. Rhy tried to scream, and retched smoke. His chest was a ragged wound of light.

Kell's voice came, not from the statue, but from somewhere else. Somewhere far away and fading. *Don't let go.*

But it hurt. It hurt so much.
Stop.
Rhy was burning from the inside out.
Please.
Dying.
Stay.
Again.

For a moment, the black gave way to streaks of color, a ceiling of billowing fabric, a familiar face hovering at the edge of his tear-blurred sight, stormy eyes wide with worry.

"Luc?" rasped Rhy.

"I'm here," answered Alucard. "I'm here. Stay with me."

He tried to speak, but his heart slammed against his ribs as if trying to break through.

It redoubled, then faltered.

"Have they found Kell?" said a voice.

"Get away from me," ordered another.

"Everyone *out*."

Rhy's vision blurred.

The room wavered, the voices dulled, the pain giving way to something worse, the white-hot agony of the invisible knife dissolving into cold as his body fought and failed and fought and failed and failed and—

No, he pleaded, but he could feel the threads breaking one by one inside him until there was nothing left to hold him up.

Until Alucard's face vanished, and the room fell away.

Until the darkness wrapped its heavy arms around Rhy, and buried him.

V

Alucard Emery wasn't used to feeling powerless.

Mere hours earlier, he'd won the *Essen Tasch* and been named the strongest magician in the three empires. But now, sitting by Rhy's bed, he had no idea what to do. How to help. How to save him.

The magician watched as the prince curled in on himself, deathly pale against the tangled sheets, watched as Rhy cried out in pain, attacked by something even Alucard couldn't see, couldn't fight. And he would have—would have gone to the end of the world to keep Rhy safe. But whatever was killing him, it wasn't here.

"What is *happening*?" he'd asked a dozen times. "What can I *do*?"

But no one answered, so he was left piecing together the queen's pleas and the king's orders, Lila's urgent words and the echoes of the royal guards' searching voices, all of them calling for Kell.

Alucard sat forward, clutching the prince's hand, and watched the threads of magic around Rhy's body fray, threatening to snap.

Others looked at the world and saw light and shadow and color, but Alucard Emery had always been able to see more. Had always been able to see the warp and weft of power, the pattern of magic. Not just the aura of a spell, the residue of an enchantment, but the tint of true magic circling a person, pulsing through their veins. Everyone could see the Isle's red light, but Alucard saw the entire world in streaks of vivid color. Natural wells of magic glowed crimson. Elemental magicians were cloaked in green and blue. Curses stained purple. Strong spells burned gold. And *Antari*? They alone shone with a dark but iridescent light—not one color, but every color folded together, natural and unnatural, shimmering threads that wrapped like silk around them, dancing over their skin.

Alucard now watched those same threads fray and break around the prince's coiled form.

It wasn't right—Rhy's own meager magic had always been a dark green (he'd told the prince once, only to watch his features crinkle in distaste—Rhy had never liked the color).

But the moment he'd set eyes on Rhy again, after three years away, Alucard had known the prince was different. *Changed.* It wasn't the set of his jaw, the breadth of his shoulders, or the new shadows beneath his eyes. It was the magic bound to him. Power lived and breathed, was meant to move in the current of a person's life. But this new magic around Rhy lay still, threads wrapped tight as rope around the prince's body.

And each and every one of them shone like oil on water. Molten color and light.

That night, in Rhy's chamber, when Alucard slid the tunic aside to kiss the prince's shoulder, he'd seen the place where the silvery threads knitted into Rhy's skin, woven straight into the scarred circles over his heart. He didn't have to ask who'd made the spell—only one *Antari* came to mind—but Alucard couldn't see *how* Kell had done it. Normally he could pick apart a piece of magic by looking at its threads, but the strands of the spell had no beginning, no end. The threads of Kell's magic plunged into Rhy's heart, and were lost—no, not lost, *buried*—the spellwork stiff, unshakeable.

And now, somehow, it was crumbling.

The threads snapped one by one under an invisible strain, every broken cord eliciting a sob, a shuddering breath from the half-conscious prince. Every fraying tether—

That's what it was, he realized. Not just a spell, but a kind of *link*. To Kell.

He didn't know *why* the prince's life was bound to the *Antari*'s. Didn't want to imagine—though he now saw the scar between Rhy's trembling ribs, as wide as a dagger's edge, and the understanding reached him anyway, and he felt sick and helpless—but the link was breaking, and Alucard did the only thing he could.

He held the prince's hand, and tried to pour his own power into the fraying threads, as if the storm-blue light of his magic could fuse with Kell's iridescence instead of wicking uselessly away. He prayed to every power in the world, to every saint and every priest and every blessed figure—the ones he believed in and the ones he didn't—for strength. And when they didn't answer, he spoke to Rhy instead. He didn't tell him to hold on, didn't tell him to be strong.

Instead, he spoke of the past. *Their* past.

"Do you remember, the night before I left?" He fought to keep the fear from his voice. "You never answered my question."

Alucard closed his eyes, in part so he could picture the memory, and in part because he couldn't bear to watch the prince in so much pain.

It had been summer, and they'd been lying in bed, bodies tangled and warm. He'd drawn a hand along Rhy's perfect skin, and when the prince had preened, he'd said, "One day you will be old and wrinkled, and I will still love you."

"I'll never be old," said the prince with the certainty mustered only by the young and healthy and terribly naive.

"So you plan to die young, then?" he'd teased, and Rhy had given an elegant shrug.

"Or live forever."

"Oh, really?"

The prince had swept a dark curl from his eyes. "Dying is so mundane."

"And how, exactly," said Alucard, propping himself on one elbow, "do you plan to live forever?"

Rhy had pulled him down, then, and ended their conversation with a kiss.

Now he shuddered on the bed, a sob escaping through clenched teeth. His black curls were matted to his face. The queen called for a cloth, called for the head priest, called for Kell. Alucard clutched his lover's hand.

"I'm sorry I left. I'm sorry. But I'm here now, so you can't die," he said, his voice finally breaking. "Don't you see how rude that would be, when I've come so far?"

The prince's hand tightened as his body seized.

Rhy's chest hitched up and down in a last, violent shudder.

And then he stilled.

And for a moment, Alucard was relieved, because Rhy was finally resting, finally asleep. For a moment, everything was all right. For a moment—

Then it shattered.

Someone was screaming.

The priests were pushing forward.

The guards were pulling him back.

Alucard stared down at the prince.

He didn't understand.

He *couldn't* understand.

And then Rhy's hand slipped from his, and fell back to the bed.

Lifeless.

The last silver threads were losing their hold, sliding off his skin like sheets in summer.

And then *he* was screaming.

Alucard didn't remember anything after that.

VI

For a single horrifying moment, Lila ceased to exist.

She felt herself unravel, breaking apart into a million threads, each one stretching, fraying, threatening to snap as she stepped out of the world, out of life—and into nothing. And then, just as suddenly, she was staggering forward onto her hands and knees in the street.

She let out a short, involuntary cry as she landed, limbs shaking, head ringing like a bell.

The ground beneath her palms—and there *was* ground, so that at least was a good sign—was rough and cold. The air was quiet. No fireworks. No music. Lila dragged herself back to her feet, blood dripping from her fingers, her nose. She wiped it away, red dots speckling the stone as she drew her knife and shifted her stance, putting her back to the icy wall. She remembered the last time she'd been here, in this London, the hungry eyes of men and women starved for power.

A splash of color caught her eye, and she looked up.

The sky overhead was streaked with sunset—pink and purple and burnished gold. Only, White London didn't *have* color, not like this, and for a terrible second, she thought she'd crossed into yet *another* city, another world, had trapped herself even farther from home— wherever that was now.

But no, Lila recognized the road beneath her boots, the castle rising to gothic points against the setting sun. It was the same city, and yet entirely changed. It had only been four months since she'd set foot here, four months since she and Kell had faced the Dane twins. Then it had been a world of ice and ash and cold white stone. And now . . .

now a man walked past her on the street, and he was *smiling*. Not the rictus grin of the starving, but the private smile of the content, the blessed.

This was wrong.

Four months, and in that time she'd learned to sense magic, its presence if not its intent. She couldn't *see* it, not the way Alucard did, but with every breath she took, she tasted power on the air as if it were sugar, sweet and strong enough that it was cloying. The night air shimmered with it.

What the hell was going on?

And where was Kell?

Lila knew where *she* was, or at least where she'd chosen to pass through, and so she followed the high wall around a corner to the castle gates. They stood open, winter ivy winding through the iron. Lila dragged to a stop a second time. The stone forest—once a garden filled with bodies—was gone, replaced by an actual stretch of trees, and by guards in polished armor flanking the castle steps, all of them alert.

Kell had to be inside. A tether ran between them, thin as thread, but strangely strong, and Lila didn't know if it was made by their magic or something else, but it drew her toward the castle like a weight. She tried not to think about what it meant, how much farther she would have to go, how many people she'd have to fight, to find him.

Wasn't there a locator spell?

Lila wracked her mind for the words. *As Travars* had carried her between worlds, and *As Tascen,* that was the way to move between different places in the *same* world, but what if she wanted to find a person, not a place?

She cursed herself for not knowing, never asking. Kell had told her once, of finding Rhy after he'd been taken as a boy. What had he used? She dragged her memory—something Rhy had made. A wooden horse? Another image sprang to mind, of the kerchief—her kerchief—clenched in Kell's hand when he first found her at the Stone's Throw. But Lila didn't have anything of his. No tokens. No trinkets.

Panic welled, and she fought it down.

So she didn't have a charm to guide her. People were more than what they owned, and surely objects weren't the only things that held a mark. They were made of pieces, words . . . memories.

And Lila had those.

She pressed her still-bloody hand to the castle gate, the cold iron biting at her palm as she squeezed her eyes shut, and summoned Kell. First with the memory of the night they'd met, in the alley when she'd robbed him, and then later, when he'd walked through her wall. A stranger tied to her bed, the taste of magic, the promise of freedom, the fear of being left behind. Hand in hand through one world, and then another, pressed together as they hid from Holland, faced down sly Fletcher, fought the not-Rhy. The horror at the palace and the battle in White London, Kell's blood-streaked body wrapped around hers in the rubble of the stone forest. The broken pieces of their lives cast apart. And then, returned. A game played behind masks. A new embrace. His hand burning on her waist as they danced, his mouth burning against hers as they kissed, bodies clashing like swords on the palace balcony. The terrifying heat, and then, too soon, the cold. Her collapse in the arena. His anger hurled like a weapon before he turned away. Before she let him go.

But she was here to take him back.

Lila steeled herself again, jaw clenched against the expectation of the pain to come.

She held the memories in her mind, pressed them to the wall as if they were a token, and said the words.

"As Tascen Kell."

Against her hand, the gate shuddered and the world fell away as Lila staggered through, out of the street and into the pale polished chamber of a castle hallway.

Torches burned in sconces along the walls, footsteps sounded in the distance, and Lila allowed herself the briefest moment of satisfaction, maybe even relief, before realizing Kell wasn't here. Her head was pounding, a curse halfway to her lips when, beyond a door to her left, she heard a muffled scream.

Lila's blood went cold.

Kell. She reached for the door's handle, but as her fingers closed around it, she caught the low whistle of metal singing through air. She cut to the side as a knife buried itself in the wood where Lila had been a moment before. A black cord drew a path from the hilt back through the air, and she turned, following the line to a woman in a pale cloak. A scar traced the other woman's cheekbone, but that was the only ordinary thing about her. Darkness filled one eye and spilled over like wax, running down her cheek and up her temple, tracing the line of her jaw and vanishing into hair so red—redder than Kell's coat, redder even than the river in Arnes—it seemed to singe the air. A color too bright for this world. Or, at least, too bright for the world it had been. But Lila felt the wrongness here, and it was more than vivid colors and ruined eyes.

This woman reminded her not of Kell, or even of Holland, but of the stolen black stone from months ago. That strange pull, a heavy beat.

With a flick of the wrist, a second knife appeared in the stranger's left hand, hilt tethered to the cord's other end. A swift tug, and the first knife freed itself from the wood and went flying back into the fingers of her right. Graceful as a bird gliding into formation.

Lila was almost impressed. "Who are you supposed to be?" she asked.

"I am the messenger," said the woman, even though Lila knew a trained killer when she saw one. "And you?"

Lila drew two of her own knives. "I am the thief."

"You cannot go in."

Lila put her back to the door, Kell's power like a dying pulse against her spine. *Hold on,* she thought desperately and then aloud, "Try and stop me."

"What is your name?" asked the woman.

"What's it to you?"

She smiled, then, a murderous grin. "My king will want to know who I've—"

But Lila didn't wait for her to finish.

Her first knife flew through the air, and as the woman's hand moved to deflect it, Lila struck with the second. She was halfway to meeting flesh when the corded blade came at her and she had to dodge, diving out of the way. She spun, ready to slash again, only to find herself parrying another scorpion strike. The cord between the knives was elastic, and the woman wielded the blades the way Jinnar did wind, Alucard water, or Kisimyr earth, the weapons wrapped in will so that when they flew, they had both the force of momentum and the elegance of magic.

And on top of it all, the woman moved with a disturbing grace, the fluid gestures of a dancer.

A dancer with two very sharp blades.

Lila ducked, the first blade biting through the air beside her face. Several strands of dark hair floated to the floor. The weapons blurred with speed, drawing her attention in different directions. It was all Lila could do to dodge the glinting bits of silver.

She'd been in her fair share of knife fights. Had started most of them herself. She knew the trick was to find the guard and get behind it, to force a moment of defense, an opening for attack, but this wasn't hand-to-hand combat.

How was she supposed to fight a woman whose knives didn't even stay in her hands?

The answer, of course, was simple: the same way she fought anyone else.

Quick and dirty.

After all, the point wasn't to look good. It was to stay alive.

The woman's blades lashed out like vipers, striking forward with sudden, terrifying speed. But there was a weakness: they couldn't change course. Once a blade flew, it flew straight. And that was why a knife in the hand was better than one thrown.

Lila feinted right, and when the first blade came, she darted the other way. The second followed, charting another path, and Lila dodged again, carving a third line while the blades were both trapped in their routes.

"Got you," she snarled, lunging for the woman.

And then, to her horror, the blades *changed course.* They veered midair, and plunged, Lila taking frantic flight as both weapons buried themselves in the floor where she'd been crouched a second earlier.

Of course. A metal worker.

Blood ran down Lila's arm and dripped from her fingers. She'd been fast, but not quite fast enough.

Another flick of a wrist, and the knives flew back into the other woman's hands. "Names are important," she said, twirling the cord. "Mine is Ojka, and I have orders to keep you out."

Beyond the doors, Kell let out a scream of frustration, a sob of pain.

"My name is Lila Bard," she answered, drawing her favorite knife, "and I don't give a damn."

Ojka smiled, and attacked.

When the next strike came, Lila aimed not at flesh, or blade, but the cord between. Her knife's edge came down on the stretched fabric and bit in—

But Ojka was too fast. The metal barely grazed the cord before it snapped back toward the fighter's fingers.

"*No,*" growled Lila, catching the material with her bare hand. Surprise flashed across Ojka's face, and Lila let out a small, triumphant sound, right before pain lanced up her leg as a *third* blade—short and viciously sharp—buried itself in her calf.

Lila gasped, staggered.

Blood speckled the pale floor as Lila pulled the knife free and straightened.

Beyond that door, Kell screamed.

Beyond this world, Rhy died.

Lila didn't have time for this.

She dragged her knives together and they sparked, caught fire. The air seared around her, and this time when Ojka threw her blade, the burning edges of Lila's own met the length of cord, and the fire caught. It wicked along the tether, and Ojka hissed as she pulled herself back. Halfway to her hand, the cord snapped, and the knife faltered, missing its return to her fingers. A dancer, off cue. The assassin's face burned with anger as she closed the distance to her opponent, now armed with only a single blade.

Despite that, Ojka still moved with the terrifying grace of a predator, and Lila was so focused on the knife in the woman's hand that she forgot the room was filled with other weapons for a magician to use.

Lila dodged a flash of metal and tried to leap back, but a low stool caught her behind the knees and she stumbled, balance lost. The fire in her hands went out, and the red-haired woman was on her before she hit the floor, blade already arcing down toward her chest.

Lila's arms came up to block the knife as it slashed down, their hilts crashing together in the air above her face. A wicked smile flashed across Ojka's lips as the weapon in her hand suddenly extended, metal thinning into a spike of steel that drove toward Lila's eyes—

Her head snapped sideways as metal struck glass and the sound of a sharp crack reverberated through her skull. The knife, having skidded off her false eye, made a deep scratch across the marble floor. A droplet of blood ran down her cheek where the blade had sliced skin, a single crimson tear.

Lila blinked, dismayed.

The bitch had tried to drive a knife through her eye.

Fortunately, she'd picked the wrong one.

Ojka stared down, caught in an instant of confusion.

And an instant was all Lila needed.

Her own knife, still raised, now slashed sideways, drawing a crimson smile across the woman's throat.

Ojka's mouth opened and closed in a mimicry of the parted skin at her neck as blood spilled down her front. She fell to the floor beside Lila, fingers wrapped around the wound, but it was wide and deep—a killing blow.

The woman twitched and stilled, and Lila shuffled backward out of the spreading pool of blood, pain still singing through her wounded calf, her ringing head.

She got to her feet, cupping one hand against her shattered eye.

Her lost second blade jutted from a sconce, and she pried it free, trailing a line of blood in her wake as she stumbled over to the door. It had gone quiet beyond. She tried the handle, but found it locked.

There was probably a spell, but Lila didn't know it, and she was too tired to summon air or wood or anything else, so instead she simply summoned the last of her strength and kicked the door in.

VII

Kell stared up at the ceiling, the world so far above, and getting farther with every breath.

And then he heard a voice—*Lila's* voice—and it was like a hook, wrenching him back to the surface.

He gasped and tried to sit up. Failed. Tried again. Pain shuddered through him as he got to one knee. Somewhere far away, he heard the crack of a boot on wood. A lock breaking. He made it to his feet as the door swung open, and there she was, a shadow traced in light, and then his vision slid away and she became a blur, rushing toward him.

Kell managed a halting step forward before his boots slipped in the pool of blood, and shock and pain plunged him briefly into black. He felt his legs buckling, then warm arms snaking around his waist as he fell.

"I've got you," said Lila, sinking with him to the floor. His head slumped against her shoulder, and he whispered hoarsely into her coat, trying to form the words. When she didn't seem to understand, he dragged his bloody, broken hands and numbed fingers once more around the collar at his throat.

"Take it . . . off," choked Kell.

Lila's gaze—was there something wrong with her eyes?—flicked over the metal for an instant before she wrapped both hands around the collar's edge. She hissed when her fingers met the metal, but didn't let go, grimacing as she cast her hands around until she found the clasp at the base of Kell's neck. It came free, and she hurled the collar across the room.

Air rushed back into Kell's lungs, heat pouring though his veins. For an instant, every nerve in his body sang, first with pain and then power as the magic returned in an electric surge. He gasped and doubled over, chest heaving and tears running down his face as the world around him pulsed and rippled and threatened to catch fire. Even Lila must have felt it, leaping back out of the way as Kell's power surfaced, settled, every stolen drop reclaimed.

But something was still missing.

No, thought Kell. *Please, no.* The echo. The second pulse. He looked down at his ruined hands, wrists still dripping blood and magic, and none of it mattered. He tore at his chest, tunic ripping over the seal, which was still there, but beneath the scars and the spellwork, only one heart beat. Only one—

"Rhy—" he said, the word a sob. A plea. "I can't . . . he's . . ."

Lila grabbed him by the shoulders. "Look at me," she said. "Your brother was still alive when I left. Have a little faith." Her words were hollow, and his own fear ricocheted inside them, filling the space. "Besides," she added, "you can't help him from here."

She looked around the room at the metal frame, cuffs slick with red, at the table beside it, littered with tools, at the metal collar lying on the floor before her attention returned to him. There *was* something wrong with her eyes—one was its usual brown, but the other was full of cracks.

"Your eye—" he started, but Lila waved her hand.

"Not now." She rose. "Come on, we have to go."

But Kell knew he was in no shape to go anywhere. His hands were broken and bruised, blood still running in ropes from his wrists. His head spun every time he moved, and when she tried to help him up, he only made it halfway to his feet before his body swayed and buckled again. He let out a strangled gasp of frustration.

"This isn't a good look on you," she said, pressing her fingers to a gash above her ankle. "Hold still, I'm going to patch you up."

Kell's eyes widened. "Wait," he said, twitching back from her touch.

Lila's mouth quirked. "Don't you trust me?"

"No."

"Too bad," she said, pressing her bloody hand against his shoulder. "What's the word, Kell?"

The room rocked as he shook his head. "Lila, I don't—"

"What's the fucking word?"

He swallowed and answered shakily. *"Hasari. As Hasari."*

"All right," she said, tightening her grip. "Ready?" And then, before he could answer, she cast the spell. *"As Hasari."*

Nothing happened.

Kell's eyes fluttered in relief, exhaustion, pain.

Lila frowned. "Did I do it ri—"

Light exploded between them, the force of the magic hurling them in opposite directions, like shrapnel from a blast.

Kell's back hit the floor, and Lila's thudded against the nearest wall.

He lay there, gasping, so dazed that for a second he couldn't tell if it had actually worked. But then he flexed his fingers and felt the wreckage of his hands and wrists knitting back together, skin smooth and warm beneath the trails of blood, felt the air move freely in his lungs, the emptiness filled, the broken made whole. When he sat up, the room didn't spin. His pulse pounded in his ears, but his blood was back inside his veins.

Lila was slumped at the base of the wall, rubbing the back of her head with a low groan.

"Fucking magic," she muttered as he knelt beside her. At the sight of him intact, she flashed a triumphant smirk.

"Told you it would wor—"

Kell cut her off, taking her face in his stained hands and kissing her once, deeply, desperately. A kiss laced with blood and panic, pain and fear and relief. He didn't ask her how she'd found him. Didn't berate her for doing it, only said, "You are *mad*."

She managed a small, exhausted smile. "You're welcome."

He helped her to her feet and retrieved his coat, which sat crumpled on the table where Holland—Osaron—had dropped it.

Again Lila scanned the room. "What happened, Kell? Who did this to you?"

"Holland."

He saw the name land like a fist, imagined the images filling her mind, the same ones that had filled his when he found himself face-to-face with the new White London king and saw not a stranger at all, but a familiar foe. The *Antari* with the two-toned eyes, one emerald, the other black. The magician bound to serve the Dane twins. The one he'd slain and pushed into the abyss between worlds.

But Kell knew that Lila had another image in her mind: of the man who'd killed Barron and thrown the bloodstained watch at her feet as a taunt.

"Holland's dead," she said icily.

Kell shook his head. "No. He survived. He came back. He's—"

Shouts sounded beyond the door.

Footsteps pounding on stone.

"Dammit," snarled Lila, gaze flicking to the hall. "We really have to go."

Kell spun toward the door, but she was a step ahead, a Red London *lin* in one bloody hand as she reached for his and brought her other down on the table.

"*As—*" she started.

Kell's eyes went wide. "Wait, you can't just—"

"*—Travars.*"

The guards burst in as the room dissolved, the floor gave way, and they were falling.

Down through one London and into another.

Kell braced himself, but the ground never caught them. It wasn't there. The castle became the night, the walls and floor replaced by nothing but cold air, the red light of the river and the bustling streets and the steepled roofs reaching for them as they fell.

There were rules when it came to making doors.

The first—and, in Kell's opinion, *most* important—was that you could either move between two places in the same world, or two worlds in the same place.

The same *exact* place.

Which was why it was so important to make sure that your feet were on the ground, and not on, say, the floor of a castle chamber two stories up, because chances were there would be no castle floor a world away.

Kell had tried to tell Lila this, but it was too late. The blood was already on her hand, the token already in her palm, and before he could get the words out, before he could say more than "don't," they were falling.

They plunged down through the floor, through the world, and through several feet of winter night, before hitting the slanted roof of a building. The tiles were half frozen, and they skidded down another few feet before finally catching themselves against the drain. Or rather—Kell caught himself. The metal beneath Lila's boots buckled sharply, and she would have tumbled over the side if he hadn't grabbed her wrist and hauled her back up onto the shingles beside him.

For a long moment, neither spoke, only lay back against the angled roof, huffing unsteady plumes of breath into the night.

"In the future," said Kell finally, "do make sure you're standing *on the street*."

Lila exhaled a shaky cloud. "Noted."

The cold roof burned against his flushed skin, but Kell didn't move, not right away. He couldn't—couldn't think, couldn't feel, couldn't bring himself to do anything but look up and focus on the stars. Delicate dots of light against a blue-black sky—*his* sky—lined with clouds, their edges tinged red from the river, everything so normal, untouched, oblivious, and suddenly he wanted to scream because even though Lila had healed his body, he still felt broken and terrified and hollow and all he wanted to do was close his eyes and sink again, to find that dark and silent place beneath the surface of the world, the place where Rhy—Rhy—Rhy—

He forced himself to sit up.

He had to find Osaron.

"Kell," started Lila, but he was already pushing himself forward off the roof, dropping to the street below. He could have summoned the wind to ease the fall, but he didn't, barely felt the pain lancing up his shins when he landed on the stones. A moment later he heard the soft whoosh of a second body, and Lila landed in a crouch beside him.

"Kell," she said again, but he was already crossing to the nearest wall, digging his knife from his coat pocket and carving a fresh line in his newly healed skin.

"Dammit, Kell—" She caught his sleeve, and there he was again, staring into those brown eyes—one whole, the other shattered. How could he have known? How could he have *not*?

"What do you mean, *Holland's back*?"

"He—" Something splintered inside him, and Kell was back in the courtyard with the red-haired woman—*Ojka*—following her through a door in the world, into a London that made no sense, a London that should have been broken but wasn't, a London with too much color— and there stood the new king, young and healthy, but unmistakable. Holland. Then, before Kell could process the *Antari*'s presence—the horrible cold of the spelled collar, the stunning pain of being torn away from himself, away from everything, the metal cage cutting into his wrists. And the look on Holland's face as it became someone else's, the jagged sound of Kell's own voice pleading as the second heart failed within his chest and the demon turned away and—

Kell recoiled suddenly. He was back in the street, blood dripping from his fingers, and Lila was inches from his face, and he couldn't tell if she'd kissed him or struck him, only knew his head was ringing and something deep inside him was screaming still.

"It's him," he said, hoarsely, "but it's not. It's—" He shook his head. "I don't know, Lila. Somehow Holland made it to Black London, and something got inside. It's like Vitari but worse. And it's . . . *wearing* him."

"So the real Holland is dead?" asked Lila as he drew a sigil on the stones.

"No," said Kell, taking her hand. "He's still in there somewhere. And now they're here."

Kell pressed his bloody palm flat to the wall, and this time when he said the spells, the magic rose effortlessly, mercifully, to his touch.

VIII

Emira refused to leave Rhy's side.

Not when his screams gave way to hitching sobs.

Not when his fevered skin went pale, his features slack.

Not when his breathing stopped and his pulse failed.

Not when the room went still, and not when it exploded into chaos, and the furniture shook, and the windows cracked, and the guards had to force Alucard Emery from the bed, and Maxim and Tieren tried to draw her hands away from his body, because they didn't understand.

A queen could leave her throne.

But a mother *never* leaves her son.

"Kell will not let him die," she said in the quiet.

"Kell will not let him die," she said in the noise.

"Kell will not let him die," she said, over and over to herself when they stopped listening.

The room was a storm, but she sat perfectly still beside her son.

Emira Maresh, who saw the cracks in beautiful things, and moved through life afraid of making more. Emira Nasaro, who hadn't wanted to be queen, hadn't wanted to be responsible for legions of people, their sorrows, their follies. Who'd never wanted to bring a child into this dangerous world, who now refused to believe that her strong and beautiful boy . . . her heart . . .

"He is dead," said the priest.

No.

"He is dead," said the king.

No.

"He is dead," said every voice but hers, because they didn't understand that if Rhy was dead, then so was Kell, and that wouldn't happen, that *couldn't* happen.

And yet.

Her son wasn't moving. Wasn't breathing. His skin, so newly cool, had taken on a horrible grey pallor, his body skeletal and sunken, as if he'd been gone for weeks, months, instead of minutes. His shirt lay open, revealing the seal against his chest, the ribs so wrongly visible beneath his once-brown skin.

Her eyes blurred with tears, but she wouldn't let them fall, because crying would mean grieving and she wouldn't grieve her son because he *was not dead*.

"Emira," pleaded the king as she bowed her head over Rhy's too-still chest.

"Please," she whispered, and the word wasn't for fate, or magic, the saints or the priests or the Isle. It was for Kell. "Please."

When she dragged her eyes up, she could *almost* see a glint of silver in the air—a thread of light—but with every passing second, the body on the bed bore less resemblance to her son.

Her fingers moved to brush the hair from Rhy's eyes, and she fought back a shudder at the brittle locks, the papery skin. He was falling apart before her eyes, the silence punctuated only by the dry crack of settling bones, the sound like embers in a dying fire.

"Emira."

"Please."

"Your Majesty."

"Please."

"My queen."

"Please."

She began to hum—not a song, or a prayer, but a spell, one she learned when she was just a girl. A spell she'd sung to Rhy a hundred times when he was young. A spell for sleep. For gentle dreams.

For release.

She was nearly to the end when the prince gasped.

IX

One moment Alucard was being dragged from the prince's room, and the next he was forgotten. He didn't notice the sudden absence of weight on his arms. Didn't notice anything but the glitter of luminescent threads and the sound of Rhy's breath.

The prince's gasp was soft, almost inaudible, but it rippled through the room, picked up by every body, every voice as the queen and the king and the guards inhaled in shock, in wonder, in relief.

Alucard braced himself in the doorway, his legs threatening to give.

He'd *seen* Rhy die.

Seen the last threads vanish into the prince's chest, seen the prince go still, seen the impossible, immediate decay.

But now, as he watched, it was undone.

Before his eyes, the spell returned, a flame coaxed suddenly back from embers. No, from ash. The threads surged up like water over a broken levy before wrapping fierce, protective arms around Rhy's body, and he breathed a second time, and a third, and between every inhale and exhale, the prince's corpse returned to life.

Flesh grew taut over bone. Color flooded into hollow cheeks. As quickly as the prince had decayed, he now revived, all signs of pain and strain smoothed into a mask of calm. His black hair settled on his brow in perfect curls. His chest rose and fell with the gentle rhythm of deep sleep.

And as Rhy calmly slept, the room around him was plunged into a new kind of chaos. Alucard staggered forward. Voices spoke over one another, layered into meaningless sound. Some shouted and others whispered words of prayer, blessings for what they'd just seen, or protection from it.

Alucard was halfway to Rhy's side when King Maxim's voice cut through the noise.

"No one is to speak of this," he said, his voice unsteady as he drew himself to full height. "The winner's ball has started, and it must finish."

"But, sir," started a guard as Alucard reached Rhy's bed.

"The prince has been ill," the king cut in. "Nothing more." His gaze landed hard on each of them. "There are too many allies in the palace tonight, too many potential enemies."

Alucard did not care about the ball or the tournament or the people beyond this room. He only wanted to touch the prince's hand. To feel the warmth of his skin and assure his own shaking fingers, his own aching heart, that it was not some horrible trick.

The room emptied around him, the king first, and then the guards and priests, until only the queen and Alucard stood, silently, staring at the prince's sleeping form.

Alucard reached out, then, his hand closing over Rhy's, and as he felt the pulse flutter in the prince's wrist, he didn't dwell on the impossibility of what he'd seen, didn't wonder at what forbidden magic could be strong enough to bind life to the dead.

All that mattered—all that would *ever* matter—was this.

Rhy was alive.

X

Kell staggered out of the street and into his palace chamber, caught by the sudden light, the warmth, the impossible normalcy. As if a life hadn't shattered, a world hadn't broken. Gossamer billowed from the ceiling and a massive, curtained bed stood on a dais on one wall, the furniture dark wood, trimmed in gold, and overhead, he could hear the sounds of the winner's ball on the roof.

How could it still be happening?

How could they not *know*?

Of *course* the king would have the winner's ball go on as planned, Kell thought bitterly. Hide his own son's situation from the prying eyes of Vesk and Faro.

"What do you mean Holland's here?" demanded Lila. "Here as in London, or here as in *here*?" She trailed in his wake, but Kell was already to his chamber doors and through. Rhy's room stood at the end of the hall, rosewood-and-gold doors shut fast.

The space between their rooms was littered with men and women, guards and *vestra* and priests. They turned sharply at the sight of Kell, bare-chested beneath his coat, hair plastered and skin streaked with blood. In their eyes he read the shock and horror, surprise and fear.

They moved, some toward him and others away, but all in his path, and Kell summoned a gust of wind, forcing them aside as he surged through the mass to the prince's doors.

He didn't want to go in.

He *had* to go in.

The screaming in his head was worsening with every step as Kell threw open the doors and skidded into the room, breathless.

The first thing he saw was the queen's face, blanched with grief.

The second was his brother's body, stretched out on the bed.

The third, and last, was the slow rise and fall of Rhy's chest.

At that small, blessed movement, Kell's own chest lurched.

The storm in his head, held so brittly at bay, now broke, the sudden violent flush of fear and grief and relief and hope giving way to jarring calm.

His body folded with relief; Rhy was alive. Kell simply hadn't felt the faint return of Rhy's heart through the raging and erratic pulse of his own. Even now, it was too soft to sense. But Rhy was alive. He was alive. He was *alive*.

Kell sank to his knees, but before they hit the floor, she was there—not Lila this time, but the queen. She didn't stop him from falling, but sank gently with him. Her fingers clutched at his front, tightened in the folds of his coat, and Kell braced himself for the words, the blow. He had left. He had failed her son. He had nearly lost Rhy—again.

Instead, Emira Maresh bent her head against his bare and bloodstained chest, and cried.

Kell knelt there, frozen, before lifting his tired arms and wrapping them gingerly around the queen.

"I prayed," she whispered, over and over and over as he helped her to her feet.

The king was there, then, in the doorway, breathless, as if he'd run the length of the palace, Tieren at his side. Maxim stormed forward, and again Kell braced himself for the attack, but the king said nothing, only folded Kell and Emira both into a silent hug.

It was not a gentle thing, that embrace. The king held on to Kell as if he were the only stone structure in a violent storm. Held so hard it hurt, but Kell didn't pull away.

When at last Maxim withdrew, taking Emira with him, Kell went to his brother's bed. To Rhy. Brought a hand to the prince's chest just to feel the beat. And there it was, steady, impossible, and as his own heart finally began to slow, he felt Rhy's again behind his ribs, nestled against his, an echo, still distant but growing nearer with every beat.

Kell's brother did not look like a man close to death.

The color was high in Rhy's cheeks, the hair curling against his brow a glossy black, rich, at odds with the mussed cushions and wrinkled sheets that spoke of suffering, of struggle. Kell ducked his head and pressed his lips to Rhy's brow, willing him to wake and make some tease about damsels in distress, or spells and magic kisses. But the prince didn't stir. His eyelids didn't flutter. His pulse didn't lift.

Kell squeezed his brother's shoulder gently, but still the prince didn't wake, and he would have shaken Rhy if Tieren hadn't touched Kell's wrist, guided his hand away.

"Be patient," said the *Aven Essen,* gently.

Kell swallowed and turned back toward the room, suddenly aware of how quiet it was, despite the presence of the king and queen, the growing audience of priests and guards, including Tieren and Hastra, the latter now in common clothes. Lila hung back in the doorway, pale with exhaustion and relief. And in the corner stood Alucard Emery, whose reddened eyes had turned storm-dark irises to sunset blue.

Kell couldn't bear to ask what had happened, what they'd seen. The whole room wore the pall of the haunted, the too-still features of the shocked. It was so quiet Kell could hear the music of the damned winner's ball still trilling on overhead.

So quiet he could—finally—hear Rhy's breathing, soft and steady.

And Kell so badly wished they could stay in this moment, wished he could lie down beside the prince and sleep and avoid the explanations, the accusations of failure and betrayal. But he could see the questions in their eyes as they looked from Lila to him, taking in his sudden return, his bloody state.

Kell swallowed and began to speak.

XI

The boundary between the worlds gave way like silk beneath a sharpened blade.

Osaron met no resistance, nothing but shadow and a step, a moment of nothing—that narrow gap between the end of one world and the beginning of the next—before Holland's boot—*his* boot—found solid ground again.

The way between his London and Holland's had been hard, the spells old but strong, the gates rusted shut. But like old metal, there were weaknesses, cracks, and in those years of questing from his throne, Osaron had found them.

That doorway had resisted, but this one gave.

Gave onto something marvelous.

The castle was gone, the cold less brittle, and everywhere he looked was the pulse of magic. It trailed in lines before his eyes, rising off the world like steam.

So much power.

So much *potential*.

Osaron stood in the middle of the street and smiled.

This was a world worth shaping.

A world that worshipped magic.

And it would worship *him*.

Music drifted on the breeze, as faint as far-off chimes, and all around was light and life. Even the darkest shadows here were shallow pools compared to his world, to Holland's. The air was rich with the scent of flowers and winter wine, the hum of energy, the heady pulse of power.

The coin hung from Osaron's fingers, and he tossed it away, drawn toward the blooming light at the center of the city. With every step he felt himself grow stronger, magic flooding his lungs, his blood. A river glowed red in the distance, its pulse so strong, so vital, while Holland's voice was a fading heartbeat in his head.

"*As Anasae,*" it whispered over and over, trying to dispel Osaron as if he were a common curse.

Holland, he chided, *I am not a piece of spellwork to be undone.*

A scrying board hung nearby, and as his fingers brushed it, they snagged the threads of magic and the spellwork shuddered and transformed, the words shifting into the *Antari* mark for darkness. For shadow. For *him.*

As Osaron passed lantern after lantern, the fires flared, shattering glass and spilling into night while the street beneath his boots turned smooth and black, darkness spreading like ice. Spells unraveled all around him, elements morphed from one into another as the spectrum tilted, fire into air, air into water, water into earth, earth into stone, stone into magic magic *magic—*

A shout went up behind him, and the clatter of hooves as a carriage reared. The man clutching the reins spat at him in a language he'd never heard, but words were threaded together just like spells, and the letters unraveled and rewove in Osaron's head, taking on a shape he knew.

"Get out of the way, you fool!"

Osaron narrowed his eyes, reaching for the horse's reins.

"*I'm not a fool,*" he said. "*I am a god.*"

His grip tightened on the leather straps.

"*And gods should be worshipped.*"

Shadow spread up the reins as fast as light. It closed over the driver's hands, and the man gasped as Osaron's magic slid under skin and into vein, wrapped around muscle and bone and heart.

The driver didn't fight the magic, or if he did, it was a battle quickly lost. He half leaped, half fell from the carriage seat to kneel at the shadow king's feet, and when he looked up, Osaron saw the smoky echo of his own true form twining in the man's eyes.

Osaron considered him; the threads of power running beneath his own command were dull, weak.

So, he thought, *this is a strong world, but not all are strong within it.*

He would find a use for the weak. Or weed them out. They were kindling, dry but thin, quick to burn, but not enough to keep him burning long.

"*Stand,*" he commanded, and when the man clambered to his feet, Osaron reached out and wrapped his fingers loosely around the driver's throat, curious what would happen if he poured more of himself into such a modest shell. Wondering how much it could hold.

His fingers tightened, and the veins beneath them bulged, turning black and fracturing across the man's skin. Hundreds of tiny fissures shone as the man began to *burn* with magic, his mouth open in a silent, euphoric scream. His skin peeled away, and his body flickered ember red and then black before he finally *crumbled*.

Osaron's hand fell away, ash trailing through the night air.

He was so caught up in the moment that he *almost* didn't notice Holland trying once again to surface, to claw his way through the gap in his attention.

Osaron closed his eyes, turning his focus inward.

You're becoming unpleasant.

He wrapped the threads of Holland's mind around his fingers and pulled until, deep in his head, the *Antari* let out a guttural scream. Until the resistance—*and the noise*—finally crumbled like the driver in the road, like every mortal thing that tried to stand in the way of a god.

In the ensuing quiet, Osaron turned his attention back to the beauty of his new kingdom. The streets, alive with people. The sky, alive with stars. The palace, alive with light—Osaron marveled at this last, for it was not a squat stone castle like in Holland's world, but an arcing structure of glass and gold that seemed to pierce the sky, a place truly fit for a king.

The rest of the world seemed to blur around the dazzling point of that palace as he made his way through the streets. The river came into view, a pulsing red, and the air caught in his chest.

Beautiful. Wasted.

We could be so much more.

A market burned in shades of crimson and gold along the riverbank, and ahead, the palace stairs were strewn with bouquets of frost-laced flowers. As his boots hit the first step, a row of flowers lost their icy sheen and blossomed back into vivid color.

Too long, he'd been holding back.

Too long.

With every step, the color spread; the flowers grew wild, blossoms bursting and stems shining with thorns, all of it spilling down the stairs in carpets of green and gold, white and red.

And all of it thrived—*he* thrived—in this strange, rich world, so ripe and ready for taking.

Oh, he would do such wondrous things.

In his wake, the flowers changed again, and again, and again, petals turning now to ice, now to stone. A riot of color, a chaos of form, until finally, overcome by their euphoric transformation, they went black and smooth as glass.

Osaron reached the top of the stairs, and came face-to-face with a huddle of men waiting for him before the doors. They were speaking to him, and for a moment he simply stood and let the words spill tangled into the air, nothing but inelegant sounds cluttering his perfect night. Then he sighed and gave them shape.

"I said *stop*," one of the guards was warning.

"Don't come any closer," ordered a second as he drew a sword, its edge glinting with spellwork. To weaken magic. Osaron almost smiled, though the gesture still felt stiff on Holland's face.

There was only one word for *stop* in his tongue—*anasae*—and even that meant only to unravel, undo. One word for ending magic, but so many to make it *grow, spread, change.*

Osaron lifted one hand, a casual gesture, power spiraling down around his fingers toward these men in their thin metal shells, where it—

An explosion tore through the sky above.

Osaron craned his neck and saw, over the crown of the palace, a sphere of colored light. And then another, and another, in bursts of red and gold. Cheers reached him on the wind, and he felt the resonant beat of bodies overhead.

Life.

Power.

"Stop," said the men in their clumsy tongue.

But Osaron was just getting started.

The air swirled around his feet, and he rose up into the night.

TWO

CITY IN SHADOW

I

Kisimyr Vasrin was a little drunk.

Not unpleasantly so, just enough to dull the edges of the winner's ball, smooth the faces on the roof, and blur the mindless chatter into something more enjoyable. She could still hold her own in a fight—that was how she judged it, not by how many glasses she'd gone through, but how quickly she could turn the contents of her glass into a weapon. She tipped the goblet, poured the wine straight out, and watched it freeze into a knife before it landed in her other hand.

There, she thought, leaning back against the cushions. *Still good.*

"You're sulking," said Losen from somewhere behind the couch.

"Nonsense," she drawled. "I'm celebrating." She tipped her head back to look at her protégé and added dryly, "Can't you tell?"

The young man chuckled, eyes alight. "Suit yourself, *mas arna.*"

Arna. Saints, when had she gotten old enough to be called a mistress? She wasn't even thirty. Losen swept away to dance with a pretty young noble, and Kisimyr drained her glass and settled back to watch, gold tassels jingling in her ropes of hair.

The rooftop was a pretty enough place for a party—pillars rising into pointed crowns against the night sky, spheres of hearth fire warming the late winter air, and marble floors so white they shone like moonlit clouds—but Kisimyr had always preferred the arena. At least in a fight, she knew how to act, knew the point of the exercise. Here in society, she was meant to smile and bow and, even worse, *mingle.* Kisimyr hated mingling. She wasn't *vestra,* or *ostra,* just old-fashioned

London stock, flesh and blood and a good turn of magic. A good turn honed into something more.

All around her, the other magicians drank and danced, their masks mounted like brooches on their shoulders or worn like hoods thrown back atop their hair. The faceless ones registered as ornament, while the more featured cast unnerving expressions on the backs of heads and cloaks. Her own feline mask sat beside her on the couch, dented and singed from so many rounds in the ring.

Kisimyr wasn't in the mood for a party. She knew how to feign grace, but inside she was still seething from the final match. It had been close—there was that much.

But of all the people to lose to, it had to be that obnoxious prettyboy noble, Alucard Emery.

Where was the bastard, anyway? No sign of him. Or the king and queen, for that matter. Or the prince. Or his brother. Strange. The Veskan prince and princess were here, roaming as if in search of prey, while the Faroan regent held his own small court against a pillar, but the Arnesian royal family was nowhere to be seen.

Her skin prickled in warning, the way it did the instant before a challenger made their move in the ring. Something was off.

Wasn't it?

Saints, she couldn't tell.

A servant in red and gold swept past, and she plucked a fresh drink from the tray, spiced wine that tickled her nose and warmed her fingers before it touched her tongue.

Ten more minutes, she told herself, and she could go.

She was, after all, a victor, even if she hadn't won this year.

"Mistress Kisimyr?"

She looked up at the young *vestra,* beautiful and tan, eyelids painted gold to match his sash. She cast a look around for Losen, and sure enough found her protégé watching, looking smug as a young cat offering up a mouse. "I'm Viken Rosec—" started the noble.

"And I'm not in the mood to dance," she cut in.

"Perhaps, then," he said coyly, "I could keep your company here."

He didn't wait for permission—she could feel the sofa dip beside her—but Kisimyr's attention had already drifted past him, to the figure standing at the roof's edge. One minute that stretch was empty, dark, and then the next, as a last firework lit the sky, he was there. From here, the man was nothing but a silhouette against the darker night, but the way he looked around—as if taking in the rooftop for the first time—set her on edge. He wasn't a noble or a tournament magician, and he didn't belong to any of the entourages she'd seen throughout the *Essen Tasch*.

Curiosity piqued, she rose from the couch, leaving her mask on the cushions beside Viken as the stranger stepped forward between two pillars, revealing skin as fair as a Veskan's, but hair blacker than her own. A midnight blue half cloak spilled over his shoulders, and on his head, where a magician's mask might be, was a silver crown.

A royal?

But she'd never seen him before. Never caught this particular scent of power, either. Magic rippled off him with every step, woodsmoke and ash and fresh-turned earth, at odds with the flowered notes that filled the roof around them.

Kisimyr wasn't the only one to notice.

One by one the faces at the ball turned toward the corner.

The stranger's own head was bowed slightly, as if considering the marble floor beneath his polished black boots. He passed a table on which someone had left a helmet, and drew a finger almost absently along the metal jaw. As he did, it crumbled to ash—no, not ash, but sand, a thousand glittering specks of glass.

A cold breeze brushed them away.

Kisimyr's heart quickened.

Without thinking, her own feet carried her forward, matching him step for step as he crossed the roof until they both stood at opposite edges of the broad polished circle used for dancing.

The music stopped abruptly, broke off into half-formed chords and then silence as the strange figure strode into the center of the floor.

"*Good evening,*" said the stranger.

As he spoke, he raised his head, black hair shifting to reveal two all-black eyes, shadows twisting in their depths.

Those close enough to meet his gaze tensed and recoiled. Those farther afield must have felt the ripple of unease, because they too began to edge away.

The Faroans watched, gems dancing in their darkened faces as they tried to understand if this was some kind of show. The Veskans stood stock still, waiting for the stranger to draw a weapon. But the Arnesians roiled. Two guards peeled away to send word through the palace below.

Kisimyr held her ground.

"*I hope I haven't interrupted,*" he continued, his voice becoming two—one soft, the other resonant, one scattered on the air like that pile of sand, the other crystal clear inside her head.

His black eyes tracked over the roof. "*Where is your king?*"

The question rang through Kisimyr's skull, and when she tried to force his presence back, the stranger's attention flicked toward her, landing like a stone.

"*Strong,*" he mused. "*Everything here is strong.*"

"Who are you?" demanded Kisimyr, her own voice sounding thin by comparison.

The man seemed to consider this a moment and then said, "*Your new king.*"

That sent a ripple through the crowd.

Kisimyr stretched out one arm, and the nearest pitcher of wine emptied, its contents sailing toward her fingers and hardening into an icy spear.

"Is that a threat?" she said, trying to focus on the man's hands instead of those eerie black eyes, that resonant voice. "I am a high magician of Arnes. A victor of the *Essen Tasch*. I bear the favored sigil of the House of Maresh. And I will not let you harm my king."

The stranger cocked his head, amused. "*You are strong, mage,*" he said, spreading his arms as if to welcome her embrace. His smile widened. "*But you are not strong enough to stop me.*"

Kisimyr spun her spear once, almost idly, and then lunged.

She made it two steps before the marble floor splashed beneath her feet, stone one instant and water the next, and then, before she could reach him, stone again. Kisimyr gasped, her body shuddering to a halt as the rock hardened around her ankles.

Losen was starting toward her, but she held a hand up without taking her gaze off the stranger.

It wasn't possible.

The man hadn't even moved. Hadn't touched the stone, or said anything to change its shape. He'd simply willed it, out of one form, and into another, as if it were nothing.

"*It* is *nothing*," he said, words filling the air and slinking through her head. *"My will is magic. And magic is my will."*

The stone began to climb her shins as he continued forward, crossing to her in long, slow strides.

Behind him, Jinnar and Brost moved to attack. They made it to the edge of the circle before he sent them back with a flick of his wrist, their bodies crashing hard into pillars. Neither rose.

Kisimyr growled and summoned the other facet of her power. The marble rumbled at her feet. It cracked, and split, and still the stranger came toward her. By the time she staggered free, he was there, close enough to kiss. She didn't even feel his fingers until they were already circling her wrist. She looked down, shocked by the touch, at once feather-light and solid as stone.

"*Strong*," he mused again. *"But are you strong enough to hold me?"*

Something passed between them, skin to skin, and then deeper, spreading up her arm and through her blood, strange and wonderful, like light, like honey in her veins, sweet and warm and—

No.

She pushed back, trying to force the magic away, but his fingers only tightened, and suddenly the pleasant heat became a burn, the light became a fire. Her bones went hot, her skin cracked, every inch of her ablaze, and Kisimyr began to scream.

II

Kell told them everything.

Or, at least, everything they needed to know. He didn't say that he'd gone with Ojka *willingly,* still fuming from his imprisonment and his fight with the king. He didn't say that he'd condemned the prince's life and his own rather than agreeing to the creature's terms. And he didn't say that, at some point, he'd given up. But he did tell the king and queen of Lila, and how she'd saved his life—and Rhy's—and brought him home. He told them of Holland's survival, and Osaron's power, of the cursed metal collar, and the Red London token in the demon's hand.

"Where is this monster now?" demanded the king.

Kell sagged. "I don't know." He needed to say more, to warn them of Osaron's strength, but all he could manage was, "I promise, Your Majesty, I will find him." His anger didn't rage—he was too tired for that—but it burned coldly in his veins.

"And I will kill him."

"You will stay here," said the king, gesturing to the prince's bed. "At least until Rhy wakes."

Kell started to protest, but Tieren's hand settled again on his shoulder, and he felt himself sway beneath the priest's influence. He sank into a chair beside his brother's bed as the king left to summon his guards.

Beyond the windows, the fireworks had begun, showering the sky in red and gold.

Hastra, who hadn't taken his eyes from the sleeping prince, stood against the wall nearby, whispering softly. His brown curls were touched with gold in the lamplight, and he was turning something over and over in his fingers. A coin. And at first Kell thought the words were some spell for calm, remembering that Hastra had once been destined for the Sanctuary, but soon the words registered as simple Arnesian. It was a prayer, of sorts, but he was asking for, of all things, forgiveness.

"What's wrong?" asked Kell.

Hastra reddened. "It's my fault she found you," whispered his former guard. "My fault she took you."

She. Hastra meant *Ojka.*

Kell rubbed his eyes. "It's not," he said, but the youth just shook his head stubbornly, and Kell couldn't bear the guilt in his eyes, too close a mirror of his own. He glanced instead at Tieren, who now stood with Lila, her chin in his hand as he tilted her head to see the damage to her eye, not even the hint of surprise in his own.

Alucard Emery still lurked, half in shadow, in the corner beyond the royal bed, his gaze leveled not on Kell or the rest of the room, but on Rhy's chest as it rose and fell. Kell knew of the captain's gift, his ability to see the threads of magic. Now Alucard stood, perfectly still, only his eyes following some invisible specter as it wove around the prince.

"Give him time," murmured the captain, answering a question Kell hadn't yet asked. Kell took a breath, hoping to say something civil, but Alucard's attention flicked suddenly to the balcony doors.

"What is it?" asked Kell as the man pushed off the wall, peering out into the red-tinged night.

"I thought I saw something."

Kell tensed. "Saw what?"

Alucard didn't answer. He brushed his hand along the glass, clearing the steam. After a moment, he shook his head. "Must have been a trick of the—"

He was cut off by a scream.

Not in the room, not in the palace at all, but overhead.

On the roof. The winner's ball.

Kell was on his feet before he knew if he could stand. Lila, always the faster, had her knife out, even though no one had seen to her wounds.

"Osaron?" she demanded as Kell surged toward the door.

Alucard was on his heels, but Kell spun, and forced him back with a single, vicious shove. "No. Not you."

"You can't expect me to stay—"

"I expect you to watch over the prince."

"I thought that was your job," snarled Alucard.

The blow landed, but Kell still barred the captain's path. "If you go upstairs, you will die."

"And you won't?" he challenged.

Behind Kell's eyes, the image flared, of the darkness swarming in Holland's eyes. The hum of power. The horror of a curse noose-tight around his neck. Kell swallowed. "If I *don't* go, *everyone* will die."

He looked to the queen, who opened her mouth and closed it several times as if searching for an order, a protest, but in the end, she said only, "Go."

Lila hadn't waited around for permission.

She was halfway up the stairs when he caught her, and he wouldn't have if not for her injured leg.

"How did he get up there?" muttered Kell.

"How did he get out of Black London?" countered Lila. "How did he cut off your power? How did he—"

"Fine," growled Kell. "Point taken."

They shoved past the mounting guards, launching themselves up flight after flight.

"Just so we're clear," said Lila. "I don't care if Holland's still in there. If I get a chance, I'm not sparing him."

Kell swallowed. "Agreed."

When they reached the rooftop doors, Lila grabbed his collar, hauling his face toward hers. Her eyes bore into his, one smooth, the other fractured into shadow and light. Beyond the doors, the scream had stopped.

"Are you strong enough to win?" she asked.

Was he? This wasn't a tournament magician. Wasn't even a sliver of magic like Vitari. Osaron had destroyed an entire world. Changed another on a whim.

"I don't know," he said honestly.

Lila flashed a glimmer of a smile, sharp as glass.

"Good," she answered, pushing open the door. "Only fools are certain."

Kell didn't know what he expected to find on the roof.

Blood. Bodies. A sick version of the stone forest that had once stretched at the feet of White London's castle, with its petrified corpses.

What he saw instead was a crowd caught between confusion and terror, and at its center, the shadow king. Kell felt the blood drain from his face, replaced by cold hatred for the figure in the middle of the roof—the monster wearing Holland's skin—as he turned in a slow circle, considering his audience. Surrounded by the most powerful magicians in the world, and not a hint of fear in those black eyes. Only amusement, and the sharp edge of want threaded through it. Standing there, in the center of the marble circle, Osaron seemed the center of the world. Unmovable. Invincible.

The scene shifted, and Kell saw Kisimyr Vasrin lying on the ground at Osaron's feet. At least—what was left of her. One of the strongest magicians in Arnes, reduced to a scorched black corpse, the metal rings in her hair now melted down to dots of molten light.

"*Anyone else?*" asked Osaron in that sick distortion of Holland's voice, silky and wrong and somehow everywhere at once.

The Veskan royals crouched behind their sorcerers, a pair of frightened children cowering in silver and green. Lord Sol-in-Ar, even for his lack of magic, did not retreat, though his Faroan entourage could be seen urging him behind a pillar. At the marble platform's edge, the rest of the magicians gathered, their elements summoned—flame swirled around fingers, shards of ice held like knives—but no one struck. They were tournament fighters, used to parading around a ring, where the greatest thing at risk was pride.

What had Holland said to Kell, so many months ago?
Do you know what makes you weak?
You've never had to be strong.
You've certainly never had to fight for your life.

Now Kell saw that flaw in these men and women, their unmasked faces pale with fear.

Lila touched his arm, a knife ready in her other hand. Neither spoke, but neither needed to. In palace balls and tournament games they were mismatched, awkward, but they understood each other here and now, surrounded by danger and death.

Kell nodded, and without a word, Lila slipped thief-smooth into the shadows around the roof's edge.

"*No one?*" goaded the shadow king.

He brought a boot to rest on Kisimyr's remains, and they gave way like ash beneath his step. "*For all your strength, you surrender so easily.*"

Kell took a single breath and forced himself forward, out of the shelter at the circle's edge, and into the light. When Osaron saw him, he actually smiled.

"*Kell,*" said the monster. "*Your resilience surprises me. Have you come to kneel before me? Have you come to beg?*"

"I've come to fight."

Osaron tipped his head. "*The last time we met, I left you screaming.*"

Kell's limbs shook, not with fear but anger. "The last time we met, I was in chains." The air around him sang with power. "Now I'm free."

Osaron's smile widened. "*But I have seen your heart, and it is bound.*"

Kell's hands curled into fists. The marble beneath his feet trembled and began to splinter. Osaron flicked his wrist, and the night came crashing down on Kell. It crushed the air from his lungs, forcing him toward his knees. It took all his strength to stay upright under the weight, and after a horrible second he realized it wasn't the air straining against him—Osaron's will pressed against his very bones. Kell was *Antari*. No one had ever managed to will his body against him. Now his joints ground together, his limbs threatening to crack.

"*I will see you kneel before your king.*"

"No."

Kell tried again to summon the marble floor, and the stone trembled as will clashed against will. He kept his feet, but realized by the almost bored expression on the other *Antari*'s face that the shadow king was toying with him.

"Holland," Kell snarled, trying to subdue the horror. "If you are in there, fight. Please—fight."

A sour look crossed Osaron's face, and then something crashed behind Kell, armor against wood as more guards barreled onto the roof, Maxim at their center.

The king's voice boomed through the night. "How dare you set foot in my palace?"

Osaron's attention flicked to the king, and Kell gasped, suddenly free from the weight of the creature's will. He staggered a step, already freeing his knife and drawing blood, red drops falling to the pale stone.

"How dare you claim to be king?"

"I have more claim than you."

Another twitch of those long fingers, and the king's crown sailed from his head—or it would have if Maxim hadn't snatched it from the air with terrifying speed. The king's eyes glowed, as if molten, as he crushed the crown between his hands, and drew it out into a blade. A single, fluid gesture that spoke of days long past, when Maxim Maresh had been the Steel Prince instead of the Golden King.

"Surrender, demon," he ordered, "or be slain."

At his back, the royal guards raised their swords, spellwork scrawled along the edges. The sight of the king and his guards seemed to shake the other magicians from their stupor. Some began to retreat, ushering their own royals off the roof or simply fleeing, while a few were bold enough to advance. But Kell knew they were no match. Not the guards, not the magicians, not even the king.

But the king's appearance had bought Kell something.

An advantage.

With Osaron's attention still on Maxim, Kell sank into a crouch. His blood had spread in brittle fractures across the stone floor, thin lines of red that reached and wrapped around the monster's boot.

"*As Anasae,*" he ordered. *Dispel.* The words had been enough, once, to purge Vitari from the world. Now, they did nothing. Osaron shot him a pitying glance, shadows twisting in his pitch black eyes.

Kell didn't retreat. He forced his hands flat. "*As Steno*," he ordered, and the marble floor shattered into a hundred shards that rose and hurled themselves at the shadow king. The first one found home, burying itself in Osaron's leg, and Kell's hopes rose before he realized his mistake.

He hadn't gone for the kill.

That first stone blade was the only one to land. With nothing but a look, the rest of the shards faltered, slowed, stopped. Kell pushed with all his force, but his own body was one thing to will, and a hundred makeshift blades another, and Osaron quickly won, turning the stone fragments outward like the spokes on a wheel, the dazzling edges of a sun.

Osaron's hands drifted lazily up, and the shards trembled, like arrows on taut strings, but before he could unleash them on the guards and the king and the magicians on the roof, something passed through him.

A flinch. A shudder.

The shadows in his eyes went green.

Somewhere deep inside his body, Holland was fighting back.

The fragments of stone tumbled to the ground as Osaron stood frozen, all his attention focused inward.

Maxim saw the chance, and signaled.

The royal guards struck, a dozen men falling on one distracted god.

And for an instant, Kell thought it would be enough.

For an instant—

But then Osaron looked up, flashing black eyes and a defiant smile. And let them come.

"Wait!" shouted Kell, but it was too late.

The instant before the guards fell on the shadow king, the monster abandoned its shell. Darkness poured from Holland's stolen body, as thick and black as smoke.

The *Antari* collapsed, and the shadow that was Osaron moved, serpentine, across the roof. Hunting for another form.

Kell spun, looking for Lila, but couldn't see her through the crowd, the smoke.

And then, suddenly, the darkness turned on *him*.

No, thought Kell, who had already refused the monster once. He couldn't fathom another collar. The cold horror of a heartbeat stopping in his chest.

The darkness surged toward him, and Kell took an involuntary step back, bracing himself for an assault that never came. The shadow brushed his blood-streaked fingers, and pulled back, not so much repelled as considering.

The darkness *laughed*—a sickly sound—and began to draw itself together, to coalesce into a column, and then into a man. Not flesh and blood, but layered shadow, so dense it looked like fluid stone, some edges sharp and others blurred. A crown sat atop the figure's head, a dozen spires thrust upward like horns, their points faded into smoke.

The shadow king, in his true form.

Osaron drew in a breath, and the molten darkness at his center flared like embers, heat rippling the air around him. And yet he seemed solid as stone. As Osaron considered his hands, the fingers tapering less to fingertips than points, his mouth stretched into a cruel smile.

"It has been a long time since I was strong enough to hold my own shape."

His hand shot toward Kell's throat, but was stopped short as steel came singing through the air. Lila's knife caught Osaron in the side of the head, but the blade didn't lodge; it passed straight through.

So he wasn't real, wasn't *corporeal*. Not yet.

Osaron spared a glance at Lila, who was already drawing another blade. She slammed to a stop under his gaze, her body clearly straining against his hold, and Kell stole his chance once more, pressing his bloodstained palm to the creature's chest. But the shape turned to smoke around Kell's fingers, recoiling from his magic, and Osaron twisted back, annoyance etched across his stone features. Freed once more, Lila reached him, a guard's short sword in one hand, and swung the weapon in a vicious arc, carving down and across and through his body, shoulder to hip.

Osaron parted around the blade, and then he simply *dissolved*.

There one moment, and gone the next.

Kell and Lila stared at each other, breathless, stunned.

The guards were hauling an unconscious Holland roughly to his feet, his head lolling as, all around the roof, the men and woman stood as if under a spell, though it might have simply been shock, horror, confusion.

Kell met King Maxim's eyes across the roof.

"You have so much to learn."

He spun toward the sound, and found Osaron re-formed and standing, not in the broken center of the roof, but atop the railing at its edge, as if the spine of metal were solid ground. His cloak billowed in the breeze. A specter of a man. A shadow of a monster.

"You do not slay a god," he said. *"You worship him."*

His black eyes danced with dark delight.

"Do not worry. I will teach you how. And in time . . ."

Osaron spread his arms.

"I will make this world worthy of me."

Kell realized too late what was about to happen.

He started running just as Osaron tipped backward off the railing, and fell.

Kell sprinted, and got there just in time to see the shadow king hit the water of the Isle far below. His body struck without a splash, and as it broke the surface and sank, it began to plume like spilled ink through the current. Lila pressed against him, straining to see. Shouts were going up over the roof, but the two of them stood and watched in silent horror as the plume of darkness grew, and grew, and grew, spreading until the red of the river turned black.

III

Alucard paced the prince's room, waiting for news.

He hadn't heard anything since that single scream, the first shouts of guards in the hall, the steps above.

Rhy's lush curtains and canopies, his plush carpets and pillows, all created a horrible insulation, blocking out the world beyond and shrouding the room in an oppressive silence.

They were alone, the captain and the sleeping prince.

The king was gone. The priests were gone. Even the queen was gone. One by one they'd peeled away, each casting a glance at Alucard that said, *Sit, stay.* As if he would have left. He would have gladly abandoned the maddening quiet and the smothering questions, of course, but not Rhy.

The queen had been the last to leave. For several seconds she'd stood between the bed and the doors, as if physically torn.

"Your Majesty," he'd said. "I will keep him safe."

Her face had changed, then, the regal mask slipping to reveal a frightened mother. "If only you could."

"Can *you*?" he'd asked, and her wide brown eyes had gone to Rhy, lingering there for a long moment before at last she'd turned and fled.

Something drew his attention to the balcony. Not movement exactly, but a change in the light. When he approached the glass doors, he saw shadow spilling down the side of the palace like a train, a tail, a curtain of glossy black that shimmered, solid, smoke, solid, as it ran from the riverbank below all the way to the roof.

It had to be magic, but it had no color, no light. If it followed the warp and weft of power, he could not see the threads.

Kell had told them about Osaron, the poisonous magic from another London. But how could a magician do *this*? How could anyone?

"It's a demon," Kell had said. "A piece of living, breathing magic."

"A piece of magic that thinks itself a man?" asked the king.

"No," he'd answered. "A piece of magic that thinks itself a *god*."

Now, staring out at the column of shadow, Alucard understood—this *thing* wasn't obeying the lines of power at all. It was stitching them from nothing.

He couldn't look away.

The floor seemed to tilt, and Alucard felt like he was tipping forward toward the glass doors and the curtain of black beyond. If he could get closer, maybe he could see the threads. . . .

The captain lifted his hands to the balcony doors, about to push them open, when the prince shifted in his sleep. A soft groan beyond him, the subtle hitch of breath, and that was all it took to make Alucard turn back, the darkness beyond the glass momentarily forgotten as he crossed to the bed.

"Rhy," he whispered. "Can you hear me?"

A crinkle between the prince's brows. A ghost of strain along his jaw. Small signs, but Alucard clung to them, and brushed the dark curls from Rhy's brow, trying to brush away the image of the prince desiccating atop the royal sheets.

"Please wake up."

His touch trailed down the prince's sleeve, coming to rest on his hand.

Alucard had always loved Rhy's hands, smooth palms and long fingers, meant for touching, for talking, for music.

He didn't know if Rhy played anymore, but he had once, and when he did, he played the way he spoke a language. Fluently.

A ghost of memory behind his eyes. Nails dancing over skin.

"Play me something," Alucard had said, and Rhy had smiled his dazzling smile, the candlelight turning his amber eyes to gold as his fingers drifted, chords flitting over shoulder, ribs, waist.

"I'd rather play you."

Alucard threaded his fingers through the prince's, now, relieved to find them warm, relieved again when Rhy's hand tightened, ever so slightly, on his own. Carefully, Alucard climbed into the bed. Cautiously, he stretched himself beside the sleeping prince.

Beyond the glass, the darkness began to splinter, spread, but Alucard's eyes were on Rhy's chest as it rose and fell, a hundred silver threads knitting slowly, slowly back together.

IV

At last, Osaron was *free*.

There had been an instant on the roof—the space between a breath in and a breath out—when it felt as if the pieces of himself might scatter in the wind without flesh and bone to hold them in. But he did *not* scatter. Did not dissolve. Did not cease to be.

He'd grown strong over the months in that other world.

Stronger over the minutes in this one.

And he was free.

A thing so strange, so long forgotten, he hardly knew it.

How long had he sat on that throne at the center of a sleeping city, watching the pulse of his world go still, watching until even the snow stopped falling and hung suspended in the air and there was nothing left to do but sleep and wait and wait and wait and wait . . .

To be free.

And now.

Osaron smiled, and the river shimmered. He laughed, and the air shook. He flexed, and the world shuddered.

It welcomed him, this world.

It *wanted* change.

It knew, in its marrow, in its bones, that it could be *more*.

It whispered to him, *Make, make, make.*

This world burned with promise, the way his own had burned so long ago, before it went to ash. But he had been a young god then, too eager to give, to be loved.

He knew better now.

Humans did not make good rulers. They were children, servants, subjects, pets, food, fodder. They had a place, just as he had a place, and he would be the god they needed, and they would love him for it. He would show them how.

He would feed them power. Just enough to keep them bound. A taste of what could be. What *they* could be. And as he wove around them, through them, he would draw a measure of their strength, their magic, their potential, and it would feed him, stoke him, and they would give it freely, because he was theirs, and they were his, and together they would make something extraordinary.

I am mercy, he whispered in their ears.

I am power.

I am king.

I am god.

Kneel.

And all over the city—his new city—they *were* kneeling.

It was a natural thing, to kneel, a matter of gravity, of letting your weight carry you down. Most of them *wanted* to do it; he could feel their submission.

And those who didn't, those who refused—

Well, there was no place for them in Osaron's kingdom.

No place for them at all.

V

"Two cheers to the wind..."
"And three to the women..."
"And four to the splendid sea."

The last word trailed off, dissolving into the coarser sounds of glasses knocking against tables, ale splashing onto floor.

"Is that really how it goes?" asked Vasry, tipping his head back against the booth. "I thought it was *wine,* not *wind.*"

"Wouldn't be a sea shanty without the wind," said Tav.

"Wouldn't be a shanty without the wine," countered Vasry, slurring his words. Lenos didn't know if it was for effect or because the sailor—the entire crew for that matter—was soused.

The entire crew, that was, except for Lenos. He'd never been big on the stuff (didn't like the way it muddled everything and left him feeling ill for days), but nobody seemed to notice whether or not he actually drank, so long as he had a glass in his hand for toasting. And he always did. Lenos had a glass when the crew toasted their captain, Alucard Emery, the victor of the *Essen Tasch,* and had it still when they kept on toasting him every half hour or so, until they lost track.

Now that the tournament was done, most of the pennants sat soaking up ale on tabletops, and the silver-and-blue flame on Alucard's banner was looking muddier by the round.

Their illustrious captain was long gone, probably toasting himself up at the winner's ball. If Lenos strained, he could hear the occasional echo of fireworks over the rattle of the crowd in the Wandering Road.

There'd be a proper parade in the morning, and a final wave of celebration (and half of London still in their cups), but tonight, the palace was for the champions, the taverns for the rest.

"Any sign of Bard?" asked Tav.

Lenos looked around, scanning the crowded inn. He hadn't seen her, not since the first round of drinks. The crew teased him for the way he was around her, mistaking his skittishness for shyness, attraction, even fear—and maybe it was fear, at least a little, but if so, it was the smart kind. Lenos feared Lila the way a rabbit feared a hound. The way a mortal feared lightning after a storm.

A shiver ran through him, sudden and cold.

He'd always been sensitive to the balance of things. Could have been a priest, if he'd had a bit more magic. He knew when things were right—that wonderful feeling like warm sun on a cool day—and he knew when they were *aven*—like Lila, with her strange past and stranger power—and he knew when they were wrong.

And right now, something was wrong.

Lenos took a sip of ale to steady his nerves—his reflection a frowning amber smudge on its surface—and got to his feet. The *Spire*'s first mate caught his eye, and rose as well. (Stross knew about his *moments,* and unlike the rest of the crew, who called him odd, superstitious, Stross seemed to believe him. Or, at least, not disbelieve him outright.)

Lenos moved through the room in a kind of daze, caught up in the strange spell of the feeling, the cord of wrongness like a rope tugging him along. He was halfway to the door when the first shout came from the tavern window.

"There's something in the river!"

"Yeah," Tav called back, "big floating arenas. Been there all week."

But Lenos was still moving toward the tavern's entrance. He pushed open the door, unmoved by the sudden cut of cold wind.

The streets were emptier than usual, the first heads just poking out to see.

Lenos walked, Stross on his heels, until he rounded the corner and saw the edge of the night market, its crowd shifting to the riverbanks, tilting toward the red water like loose cargo on a ship.

His heart thudded in his chest as he pushed forward, his slim body slipping through where Stross's broad form lodged and stuck. There, ahead, the crimson glow of the Isle, and—

Lenos stopped.

Something was spreading along the river's surface, like an oil slick, blotting out the light, replacing it with something black, and glistening, and wrong. The darkness slipped onto the bank, sloshing up against the dead winter grass, the stone walk, leaving an iridescent streak with every lapping wave.

The sight tugged at Lenos's limbs, that same downward pull, easy as gravity, and when he felt himself stepping forward, he tore his gaze away, forced himself to stop.

To his right, a man stumbled forward to the river's edge. Lenos tried to catch his sleeve, but the man was already past him, with a woman following close behind. All around, the crowd was torn between staggering back and jostling forward, and Lenos, unable to move *away,* could only fight to hold his ground.

"Stop!" called a guard as the man who'd swept past Lenos sank to one knee and reached out, as if to touch the river's surface. Instead, the river touched *him,* stretched out a hand made of blackish water and wrapped its fingers around the man's arm, and pulled him in. Screams went up, swallowing the splash, the instant of struggle before the man went under.

The crowd recoiled as the oily sheen began to smooth, went silent as it waited for the man—or his body—to surface.

"Stand aside!" demanded another guard, forcing his way forward. He was almost to the bank when the man reappeared. The guard stumbled back in shock as the man came up, not gasping for air, or struggling against the river's hold, but calm and slow, as if rising from a bath. Gasps and murmurs as the man climbed out of the river and onto the bank, oblivious to the waterlogged clothes weighing him down. Dripping from his skin, the water looked clean, clear, but when it pooled on the stones, it glistened and moved.

Stross's hand was on Lenos's shoulder, straining, but he couldn't take his eyes from the man on the bank. There was something wrong with him. Something very wrong. Shadows swirled in his eyes, coiling like wisps of smoke, and his veins stood out against his tan skin, darkening to threads of black. But it was the rictus smile more than anything that made Lenos shiver.

The man spread his arms, streaming water, and announced boldly, "The king has come."

He threw his head back and began to laugh as the darkness climbed the banks around him, tendrils of black fog that reached like fingers, clawing their way forward into the street. The crowd was thrown into panic, the ones close enough to see now scrambling to get away, only to be penned in by those behind. Lenos turned, looking for Stross, but the man was nowhere to be seen. Down the bank, another scream. Somewhere in the distance, an echo of the man's words, now on a woman's lips, now a child's.

"The king has come."

"The king has come."

"The king has come," said an old man, eyes shining, "and he is *glorious*."

Lenos tried to get away, but the street was a roiling mass of bodies, crowded in by the shadow's reach. Most fought to get free, but dotting the crowd were those who couldn't tear their eyes from the black river. Those who stood, stiff as stone, transfixed by the glistening waves, the gravity of the spell pulling them down.

Lenos felt his own gaze drawn back into the murk and madness, stammered a prayer to the nameless saints even as his long limbs took a single step forward.

And then another.

His boots sank into the loamy soil of the riverbank, his thoughts quieting, vision narrowing to that mesmerizing dark. At the edge of his mind, he heard the rumble of hooves, like thunder, and then a voice, cutting through the chaos like a knife.

"Get back!" it shouted, and Lenos blinked, stumbling away from the reaching river right before a royal horse could crush him underfoot.

The massive steed reared up, but it was the figures mounted on top that held Lenos's attention now.

The *Antari* prince sat astride the horse, disheveled, his crimson coat open to reveal bare skin, a streak of blood, a detailed scar. And behind the black-eyed prince, clinging to him for dear life, was Lila Bard.

"Fucking beast," she muttered, nearly falling as she tried to free herself from the saddle. Kell Maresh—*Aven Vares*—hopped easily down, coat billowing around him, one hand resting on Bard's shoulder, and Lenos couldn't tell if the man was seeking balance or offering it. Bard's eyes scanned the crowd—one of them was decidedly *wrong,* a starburst of glassy light—before landing on Lenos. She managed a quick, pained smile before someone screamed.

Nearby a woman collapsed, a tendril of shadow wrapping itself around her leg. She clawed at it, but her fingers went straight through. Lila spun toward her, but the *Antari* prince got there first. He tried to force the fog back with a gust of wind, and when that didn't work, he produced a blade and carved a fresh line across his palm.

He knelt, hand hovering over the shadows that ran between the river and the woman's skin.

"*As Anasae,*" he ordered, but the substance only parted around the blood. The air itself seemed to vibrate with laughter as the shadows seeped into the woman's leg, staining skin before sinking into vein.

The *Antari* swore, and the woman shuddered, clutching at his sliced hand in fear. Blood streaked her fingers and, as Lenos watched, the shadows suddenly let go, recoiled from their host.

Kell Maresh was staring down at the place where his hand met hers.

"Lila!" he called, but she'd already seen, already had her own knife out. Blood welled across her skin as she shot toward a man on the bank, grabbing him a breath before the shadows could. Again, they recoiled.

The *Antari* and—no, the two *Antari,* thought Lenos, for that was what Bard was, that was what she had to be—began to grab everyone in reach, brushing stained fingers over hands and cheeks. But the blood did nothing to those already poisoned—they only snarled, and wiped it away, as if it were filth—and for every one they marked, two more fell before they could.

The royal *Antari* spun, breathless, taking in the scope, the scale. Instead of running from body to body, he held up his hands, palms a span apart. His lips moved and his blood pooled in the air, gathering itself into a ball. It reminded Lenos of the Isle itself, its red glow, an artery of magic, pulsing and vibrant.

With a single surging motion, the sphere rose above the panicked crowds and—

That was all Lenos saw before the shadows came for *him*.

Fingers of night snaked toward him, serpent fast. There was nowhere to go—the *Antari* was still casting his spell, and Lila was too far away—so Lenos held his breath and began to pray, the way he'd learned back in Olnis, when the storms got rough. He closed his eyes and prayed for calm as the shadows broke against him. For balance as they washed—hot and cold at once—over his skin. For stillness as they murmured soft as shoretide in his head.

Let me in, let me in, let me—

A drop of rain landed on his hand, another on his cheek, and then the shadows were retreating, taking their whispers with them. Lenos blinked, let out a shaky breath, and saw that the rain was red. All around him, dew-fine drops dotted faces, and shoulders, settled in mist along coats and gloves and boots.

Not rain, he realized.

Blood.

The shadows in the street dissolved beneath the crimson mist, and Lenos looked at the *Antari* prince in time to see the man sway from the effort. He'd carved a slice of safety, but it wasn't enough. Already the dark magic was shifting focus, form, dividing from a fist into an open hand, fingers of shadow surging inland.

"*Sanct*," cursed the prince as hooves pounded down the street. A wave of royal guards reached the river and dismounted, and Bard moved quick as light between the armored men, brushing bloodied fingertips against the metal of their suits.

"Round up the poisoned," ordered Kell Maresh, already moving toward his horse.

The afflicted souls didn't flee, didn't attack, simply stood there, grinning and saying things about a shadow king who whispered in their ears, who told them of the world as it could be, would be, who played their souls like music and showed them the true power of a king.

The *Antari* prince swung up onto his mount.

"Keep everyone away from the banks," he called. Lila Bard hoisted herself up beside him with a grimace, arms wrapped tight around his waist, and Lenos was left standing there, dazed, as the prince kicked the horse into motion and the two vanished into the streets of London.

VI

They had to split up.

Kell didn't want to, that much was obvious, but the city was too big, the fog too fast.

He took the horse, because she refused it—plenty of other ways to die tonight.

"Lila," he'd said, and she'd expected him to chastise her, to order her back to the palace, but he'd only caught her by the arm and said, "Be careful." Tipped his forehead against hers and added, almost too low to be heard, "Please."

She'd seen so many versions of him in the past few hours. The broken boy. The grieving brother. The determined prince. This Kell was none of those and all of them, and when he kissed her, she tasted pain and fear and desperate hope. And then he was gone, a streak of pale skin against the night as he rode for the night market.

Lila took off on foot, heading for the nearest cluster of people.

The night should have been cold enough to keep them inside, but the last day of the tournament meant the last night of celebration, and the entire city had been in the taverns, ushering out the *Essen Tasch* in style. Crowds were spilling out into streets, some drawn by the chaos at the river's edge, and others still oblivious, drinking and humming and stumbling over their own feet.

They didn't notice the lack of red light at the city's heart, or the spreading fog, not until it was nearly upon them. Lila dragged the knife down her arm as she raced between them, pain lost beneath panic as blood pooled in her palm and she flicked her wrist, pricks of red lancing like needles through the air, marking skin. Revelers stiffened, shocked and searching for the source of the assault, but Lila didn't linger.

"Get inside," she called, racing past. "Lock the doors."

But the poisoned night didn't care about locked doors and shuttered windows, and soon Lila found herself pounding on houses, trying to beat the darkness in. A distant scream as someone fought back. A laugh as someone fell.

Her mind raced, even as her head spun.

Her Arnesian wasn't good enough, and the more blood she lost, the worse it got, until her speech dissolved from, "There's a monster in the city, moving in the fog, let me help. . . ." to simply, "Stay."

Most stared at her, wide-eyed, though she didn't know if it was the blood or the shattered eye or the sweat streaming down her face. She didn't care. She kept going. It was a lost cause, all of it, an impossible task when the shadows moved twice as fast as she could, and part of her wanted to give up, to pull back, to save what strength she had—only a fool fought when they *knew* they couldn't win—but somewhere out there, Kell was still trying, and she wouldn't give up until he did, so she forced herself on.

She rounded the corner and saw a woman lying in the road, pale dress pooling on the cold stones as she curled in on herself and clutched her head, fighting whatever monstrous force had clawed inside. Lila ran, hand outstretched, and was nearly to her when the woman went suddenly still. The fight went out of her limbs, and her breath clouded in the air above her face as she stretched out lazily against the cold stones, oblivious to the biting cold, and smiled.

"I can hear his voice," she said, full of rapture. "I can see his beauty." She turned her head toward Lila. Shadows slid through her eyes like a cloud over a field. "Let me show you."

Without warning, the woman sprang, lunging for Lila, fingers wrapping around her throat, and for an instant, she felt the press of searing heat and burning cold as Osaron's black magic tried to get in.

Tried—and failed.

The woman recoiled violently as if scorched, and Lila struck her hard across the face.

The woman crumpled to the ground, unconscious. It was a good sign. If she'd truly been possessed, a blade wouldn't have stopped her, let alone a fist.

Lila straightened, aware of the magic as it swept and curled around her. She couldn't shake the feeling that the darkness had eyes, and it was watching.

Intently.

"Come out, come out," she called softly, twirling her knife. The shadows wavered. "What's the matter, Osaron? Feeling shy? A little bare without a body?" She turned in a slow circle. "I'm the one who killed Ojka. I'm the one who stole Kell back." She spun the blade between her fingers, exuding a calm she didn't feel as the darkness shuddered around her and began to pull itself together, thickening into a column before it grew limbs, a face, a pair of eyes as black as ice at night and—

Somewhere nearby, a horse whinnied.

A shout went up—not the strangled cry of those fighting the spelled fog, but the simple, guttural sound of frustration. A voice she knew too well.

The shadows collapsed as Lila cut through them, racing toward the sound.

Toward Kell.

She found his horse first. Abandoned and galloping down the street toward her, a shallow slice along one flank.

"Dammit," she swore, trying to decide whether to bar the horse's path or dive out of the way. In the end she dove, letting the beast barrel past, then sprinted in the direction it had come. She followed the scent of his magic—rose and soil and leaves—and found Kell on the ground, surrounded, not by Osaron's fog, but by men, three of them with weapons dangling from their hands. A knife. An iron bar. A plank of wood.

Kell was on his feet at least, gripping one shoulder, his face ghostly pale. He didn't look like he had the blood left to stand, let alone strike back at the attackers. It wasn't until she got closer that she recognized one of the men as Tav, her shipmate from the *Night Spire,* and another as the man who'd played Kamerov at the Banner Night before the tournament. A third was dressed in the cloak and arms of a royal guard, his half sword held at the ready.

"Listen to me," Kell was saying. "You are stronger than this. You can fight back."

The men's faces contorted in glee, surprise, confusion. They spoke in their own voices, not the echoing two-speak Osaron had used on the roof, and yet there was a lilting cadence to their words, a singsong quality that chilled her.

"The king wants you."

"The king will have you."

"Come with us."

"Come and kneel."

"Come and beg."

Kell stiffened, jaw set. "You tell your king he will not take this city. You tell him—"

The man with the scrap of wood struck out, swinging at Kell's stomach. He caught the beam, wood lighting and burning to ash in his hands. The circle collapsed, Tav raising the iron bar, the guard stepping forward, but Lila was already kneeling, palms pressed to the cold ground. She remembered the words Kell had used. Summoned what was left of her strength.

"*As Isera,*" she said. *Freeze.*

Ice shot from beneath her hands, gliding along the ground and up men's bodies in a breath.

Lila didn't have Kell's control, couldn't tell the ice where to go, but he saw it coming and leaped back out of the spell's path, and when the frozen edge met his boots, it melted, leaving him untouched. The other men stood, encased in ice, the shadows still swimming in their eyes.

Lila straightened, and the night tilted dangerously beneath her feet, the spell stealing the last power from her veins.

Somewhere, another scream, and Kell took a step toward it, one knee nearly giving way before he caught himself against the wall.

"Enough," said Lila. "You can barely stand."

"Then you can heal me."

"With *what*?" she rasped, gesturing to her bruised and battered form. "We can't keep this up. We could both bleed ourselves dry and still not mark a fraction of this city." She let out an exhausted, humorless laugh. "You know I'm all for steep odds, but it's too much. Too many."

It was a lost cause, and if he couldn't see it—but he did, of course. She saw in his eyes, the set of his jaw, the lines in his face, that he knew it too. Knew it, and couldn't let it be. Couldn't surrender. Couldn't retreat.

"Kell," she said, gently.

"This is my city," he said, shaking visibly. "My home. If I can't protect it . . ."

Lila's fingers inched toward a loose rock in the street. She wouldn't let him kill himself, not like this. Not after everything. If he wouldn't listen to reason—

Hooves sounded against stone, and a moment later four horses rounded the bend, mounted by royal guards.

"Master Kell!" called the one at the front.

Lila recognized the man as one of the guards assigned to Kell. He was older, and he shot a look at Lila, and then, obviously not knowing how to address her, pretended she wasn't there. "The priests have warded the palace, and you are to return at once. King's orders."

Kell looked like he was about to curse the king. Instead he shook his head. "Not yet. We're marking the citizens wherever we can, but we haven't found a way to contain the shadows, or shield the city against—"

"It's too late," cut in the guard.

"What do you mean?" demanded Kell.

"Sir," said another voice, and the man at the back took off his helmet. Lila knew him. Hastra. The younger of Kell's guard. When he spoke, his voice was gentle, but his face was tight. "It's over, sir," he said. "The city has fallen."

VII

The city has fallen.

Hastra's words followed Kell through the streets, up the palace steps, through the halls. They couldn't be right.

Couldn't be true.

How could a city fall when so many were still fighting?

Kell burst into the Grand Hall.

The ballroom glittered, ornate, extravagant, but the mood had altered entirely. The magicians and nobles from the rooftop gala now huddled in the center of the room. The queen and her entourage carried bowls of water and pouches of sand to the priests drawing amplifiers on the polished marble floor and warding spells along each wall. Lord Sol-in-Ar stood with his back against a pillar, features grim but unreadable, and Prince Col and Princess Cora sat on the stairs, looking shell-shocked.

He found King Maxim by the platform where musicians in gold leaf had played each night, conferring with Master Tieren and the head of his guard.

"What do you mean, the city has fallen?" demanded Kell, storming across the marble floor. Between his bloodstained hands and his bare chest on display beneath his open coat, he knew he looked insane. He didn't care. "Why did you call me back?" Tieren tried to block his path, but Kell pushed past. "Do you have a plan?"

"My plan," said the king calmly, "is to stop you from getting yourself killed."

"It was *working*," Kell snarled.

"What was working?" asked Maxim. "Opening a vein over London?"

"If my blood can shield them—"

"How many did you shield, Kell?" demanded the king. "Ten? Twenty? A hundred? There are tens of *thousands* in this city."

Kell felt like he was back in White London, the steel noose cinching around his neck. Helpless. Desperate. "It is *something*—"

"It is *not enough*."

"Do you have a better idea?"

"Not yet."

"Then, *Sanct,* let me do what I can!"

Maxim took him by the shoulders. "Listen to me," the king said, voice low. "What are Osaron's strengths? What are his weaknesses? What is he doing to our people? Can it be undone? How many questions have you failed to ask because you were too busy being valiant? You have no plan. No strategy. You have not found a crack in your enemy's armor, a place to slide your knife. Instead of devising an attack, you are out there, slashing blindly, not even able to land a blow because you're spending every drop of precious blood protecting others from an enemy we don't know how to best."

Everything in Kell tightened at that. "I was out there trying to protect *your people*."

"And for every one you shielded, a dozen more were taken by the dark." There was no judgment in Maxim's voice, only grim resolve. "The city has fallen, Kell. It will not rise again without your help, but that does not mean you can save it alone." The king tightened his grip. "I will not lose my sons to this."

Sons.

Kell blinked, shaken by the words as Maxim released his hold, his anger deflating. "Has Rhy woken?" he asked.

The king shook his head. "Not yet." His attention slid past Kell. "And you."

Kell turned and saw Lila, hair falling over her shattered eye as she scraped blood from under her nails. She looked up at the summons.

"Who are you?" demanded the king.

Lila frowned, started to answer. Kell cut her off.

"This is Miss Delilah Bard."

"A friend to the throne," said Tieren.

"I've already saved your city," added Lila. "*Twice.*" She cocked her head, shifting the dark curtain of hair to reveal the starburst of her shattered eye. Maxim, to his credit, didn't startle. He simply looked at Tieren.

"Is this the one you told me of?"

The head priest nodded, and Kell was left wondering what exactly the *Aven Essen* had said, and how long Tieren had known what she was. The king considered Lila, his gaze moving from her eyes to her bloodstained fingers, before coming to a decision. Maxim raised his chin slightly, and said, "Mark everyone here."

It was not a request, but the order of a king to a subject.

Lila opened her mouth, and for a second Kell thought she might say something awful, but Tieren's hand came down on her shoulder in the universal sign for *Be quiet,* and for once, Lila listened.

Maxim stepped back, voice rising a measure so that others in the hall could overhear. And they *were* listening, Kell realized, several heads already turned carefully to catch the words as the king addressed his *Antari.*

"Holland has been taken to the cells." Only hours before, *Kell* had been the one imprisoned below the palace. "I would have you speak with him. Learn everything you can about the force we're facing." Maxim's expression darkened. "By whatever means."

Kell stiffened.

The cold press of steel.

A collar around his throat.

Skin shredding against a metal frame.

"Your Majesty," said Kell, striving for the proper tone. "It will be done."

Kell's boots echoed on the prison stairs, each step carrying him away from the light and heat of the palace's heart.

Growing up, Rhy's favorite place to hide had been the royal cells. Located directly beneath the guards' hall, carved into one of the massive stone limbs that held the palace up over the river, the cells were rarely filled. They had once been in frequent use, according to Tieren, back when Arnes and Faro were at war, but now they sat abandoned. The royal guards made use of them occasionally, saints knew for what, but whenever Rhy ran off with nothing but a laugh, or a note—*come find me*—Kell started by going to the cells.

They were always cold, the air heavy with the smell of damp stone, and his voice would echo as he called for Rhy—*come out, come out, come out.* Kell had always been better at finding than Rhy was at hiding, and the games usually dissolved into the two boys tucked into a cell, eating stolen apples and playing hands of Sanct.

Rhy always loved coming down here, but Kell thought that what his brother really loved was the going back upstairs afterward, the way he could simply shrug off his surroundings when he was done and trade the dank underbelly for lush robes and spiced tea, having been reminded how lucky he was to be a prince.

Kell had never been fond of the cells back then.

Now he hated them.

Revulsion rose in him with every step, revulsion for the memory of his imprisonment, revulsion for the man now sitting in his place.

Lanterns cast pale light over the space. It glinted where it struck metal, fanned against stone.

Four guards in full armor stood across from the largest cell. The same one Kell had occupied a few hours before. They had their weapons ready, eyes fixed on the shape beyond the bars. Kell took in the way the guards looked at Holland, the venom in their glares, and knew it was the way some wanted to look at *him*. All the fear and anger, none of the respect.

The White *Antari* sat on the stone bench at the back of the cell, shackled hand and foot to the wall behind him. A black blindfold was cinched tight over his eyes, but Kell could tell by the subtle shift of his limbs, the incline of his head, that Holland was awake.

It had been a short trip from the roof to the cell, but the guards had not been gentle. They'd stripped him to the waist to search for weapons, and fresh bruises blossomed along his jaw and across his stomach and chest, the fair skin revealing every abuse, though they'd taken care to clean the blood away. Several fingers looked broken, and the faint stutter of his chest hinted at cracked ribs.

Standing across from Holland, Kell was again taken aback by the changes in the man. The breadth of Holland's shoulders, the lean muscle wrapping his waist, the emotionless set of his mouth, those were all still there. But the newer things—the color in Holland's cheeks, the flush of youth—Osaron had taken those with him when he fled. The *Antari*'s skin looked ashen where it wasn't bruised, and his hair was no longer the glossy black he'd briefly had as king, or even the faded charcoal Kell was more accustomed to—now it was threaded with silver.

Holland looked like someone caught between two selves, the effect eerie, disconcerting.

His shoulders rested against the icy stone wall, but if he felt the cold, he didn't let it show. Kell took in the remains of Athos Dane's control spell, carved into the *Antari*'s front—and ruined by the steel bar Kell himself had driven through his chest—before noticing the web of scars that lined Holland's skin. There was order to the mutilations, as if whoever'd done them had done them carefully. Methodically. Kell knew from experience how easily *Antari* healed. To leave these kinds of scars, the wounds would have to have been very, very deep.

In the end, Holland was the one to break the silence. He couldn't *see* Kell, not through the blindfold, but he must have known it was him, because when the older *Antari* spoke, his voice was laced with disdain. "Come to get your revenge?"

Kell took a slow breath, steadying himself.

"Leave," he said, gesturing to the guards.

They hesitated, eyes flicking between the two *Antari*. One retreated without hesitation, two had the decency to grow nervous, and the fourth looked loath to miss the scene.

"King's orders," warned Kell, and at last they withdrew, taking with them the clank of armor, the echo of boots.

"Do they know?" asked Holland, flexing his ruined fingers. His voice had none of Osaron's echo, only that familiar, gravelly tone. "That you abandoned them? Came to my castle of your own free will?"

Kell flicked his wrist, and the chains around Holland tightened, forcing him back against the cell wall. The gesture earned him nothing—Holland's tone remained cold, unflinching.

"I'll take that as a no."

Even through the blindfold, Kell could *feel* Holland's gaze, the black of his left eye scraping against the black of Kell's right.

He summoned the king's tone as best he could.

"You will tell me everything you know about Osaron."

A gleam of bared teeth. "And then you'll let me go?" sneered Holland.

"What is he?"

A heavy pause, and Kell thought Holland would force him to drag the answers out. But then he answered. "An *oshoc*."

Kell knew that word. It was Mahktan for *demon,* but what it really meant was a piece of *incarnated* magic. "What are his weaknesses?"

"I do not know."

"How can he be stopped?"

"He can't." Holland twitched the chains. "Does this make us even?"

"*Even?*" snarled Kell. "If I could yet discount the atrocities you committed during the rule of the Danes, it would not change the fact that *you* are the one who set that *oshoc* free. *You* plotted against Red London. *You* lured me into your city. *You* bound me, tortured me, purposefully severed me from my magic, and in so doing *you* nearly killed my brother."

A tilt of the chin. "If it's worth anything—"

"It isn't," snapped Kell. He began to pace, torn between exhaustion and fury, his body aching but his nerves alight.

And Holland, so maddeningly calm. As if he weren't chained to the wall. As if they were standing together in a royal chamber instead of separated by the iron bars of a prison cell.

"What do you want, Kell? An apology?"

He felt his fraying temper finally snap. "What do I *want*? I want to destroy the demon *you've* unleashed. I want to protect my family. I want to save my home."

"So did I. I did what I had to—"

"No," snarled Kell. "When the Danes ruled, they may have forced your hand, but this time, *you* chose. You chose to set Osaron free. You chose to be his vessel. You chose to give him—"

"Life isn't made of choices," said Holland. "It's made of trades. Some are good, some are bad, but they all have a cost."

"You traded away *my* world's safety—"

Holland strained forward suddenly against his chains, and even though his voice didn't rise, every muscle in him tightened. "What do you think *your* London did, when the darkness came? When Osaron's magic consumed his world, and threatened to take ours with it? *You* traded away *our* world's safety for your own, locked the doors and trapped us between the raging water and the rocks. How does it feel now?"

Kell wrapped his will around Holland's skull and forced it back against the wall. The slightest clench in Holland's jaw and the flare of his nostrils were the only signs of pain.

"Hatred is a powerful thing," continued Holland through gritted teeth. "Hold on to it."

And in that moment, Kell *wanted* to. He wanted to keep going, wanted to hear the crack of bone, wanted to see if he could break Holland the way Holland had broken *him* in White London.

But Kell knew he couldn't break Holland.

Holland was already broken. It showed, not in the scars, but in the way he spoke, the way he held himself in the face of pain, too well acquainted with its shape and scale. He was a man hollowed out long before Osaron, a man with no fear and no hope and nothing to lose.

For an instant, Kell tightened his grip anyway—in anger, in spite—and felt Holland's bones groan under the strain.

And then he forced himself to let go.

THREE

FALL OR FIGHT

I

Alucard had been dreaming of the sea when he heard the door open. It wasn't a loud sound, but it was so out of place, at odds with the ocean spray and the summer gulls.

He rolled over, lost for a moment in the haze of sleep, his body aching from the abuse of the tournament and his head full of silk. And then, a step, wooden boards groaning underfoot. The sudden, very real presence of another person in the room. *Rhy's* room. And the prince, still unconscious, unarmed, beside him.

Alucard rose in a single, fluid movement, the water from the glass beside the bed rising up and freezing into a dagger against his palm.

"Show yourself."

He held the shard in a fighting stance, ready to strike as the intruder continued his slow march forward. The room around them was dim, a lamp burning just behind the intruder's back, casting him in shadow.

"Down, dog," said an unmistakable voice.

Alucard let out a low curse and slumped back against the side of the bed, heart pounding. "Kell."

The *Antari* stepped forward, light illuminating his grim mouth and narrowed eyes, one blue, the other black. But what caught Alucard's attention, what held it in a vice, was the sigil scrawled over his bare chest. A pattern of concentric circles. An exact replica of the mark over Rhy's heart, the one woven through with iridescent threads.

Kell flicked his fingers, and Alucard's frozen blade flew from his hand, melting back into a ribbon of water as it returned to its glass.

Kell's gaze shifted to the bed, sheets rumpled where Alucard had been lying moments before. "Taking your task seriously, I see."

"Quite."

"I told you to keep him safe, not cuddle."

Alucard spread his hands behind him on the sheets. "I'm more than capable of multitasking." He was about to continue when he registered the pallor of Kell's skin, the blood staining his hands. "What happened?"

Kell looked down at himself, as if he'd forgotten. "The city is under attack," he said hollowly.

Alucard suddenly remembered the pillar of dark magic beyond the window, fracturing across the sky. He spun back toward the balcony, and stiffened at the sight. There was no familiar red light against the clouds. No glow from the river below. When he reached for the door, Kell caught his wrist. Fingers ground against bone.

"Don't," he ordered in his imperious way. "They're warding the palace, to keep it out."

Alucard pulled free, rubbing at the smudge left by Kell's grip. *"It?"*

The *Antari* looked past him. "The infection, or poison, spell, I don't know . . ." He lifted a hand, as if to rub his eyes, then realized it was stained and let it fall. "Whatever it is. Whatever he's done . . . doing. Just stay away from the doors and windows."

Alucard looked at him, incredulous. "The city is being attacked, and we're just going to hole up in the palace and let it happen? There are people out there—"

Kell's jaw clenched. "We cannot save them all," he said stiffly. "Not without a plan, and until we have one—"

"My *crew's* out there. My family, too. And you expect me to just sit and watch—"

"No," snapped Kell. "I expect you to make yourself useful." He pointed at the door. "Preferably somewhere else."

Alucard's eyes went to the bed. "I can't leave Rhy."

"You've done it before," said Kell.

It was a cheap shot, but Alucard still flinched. "I told the queen I'd—"

"Emery," cut in Kell, closing his eyes, and it was only then that he realized how close the magician was to falling over. His face was grey, and it looked like sheer will was keeping him on his feet, but he was beginning to sway. "You're one of the best magicians in this city," said Kell, wincing as if the admission hurt. "Prove it. Go and help the priests. Help the king. Help someone who needs it. You cannot help my brother any more tonight."

Alucard swallowed, and nodded. "All right."

He forced himself to cross the chamber, glancing back only once, to see Kell half sinking, half falling into the chair beside the prince's bed.

The hall beyond Rhy's room was strangely empty. Alucard made it to the stairs before he saw the first servants hurrying past, their arms full of cloth and sand and water basins. Not the tools for binding wounds, but the ones needed for making wards.

A guard rounded the corner, his helmet under his arm. There was a line of blood across his forehead, but he didn't appear wounded, and the mark was too deliberate to be the weary wiping of a brow.

Through a set of wooden doors, Alucard saw the king surrounded by members of his guard, all of them bent over a large map of the city. Runners carried word of new attacks, and with every one, King Maxim placed a black coin atop the parchment.

As Alucard moved through halls, down flights of stairs, he felt like he'd woken from a dream into a nightmare.

Hours before, the palace had brimmed with life. Now the only motions were nervous, halting. The faces masked by shock.

In a trance, his feet found the Grand, the palace's largest ballroom, and stopped cold. Alucard Emery rarely felt helpless, but now he stood in stunned silence. Two nights before, men and women had danced here in pools of light as music played from the gold dais. Two nights before, Rhy had stood here, dressed in red and gold, the shining centerpiece of the ball. Two nights before, this had been a place of laughter and song, crystal glasses and whispered conversation. Now *ostra* and *vestra* huddled together in shock, and white-robed priests stood at every window, hands pressed flat against glass as they wove spells around the palace, shielding it against the poisonous night. He could see their magic, pale and shimmering, as it cast its net over the windows and the walls. It looked fragile compared with the heavy shadows that pushed against the glass, wanting in.

Standing there, at the mouth of the ballroom, Alucard's ears caught slices of information, too thin, and all confused, tangling with one another until he couldn't pick the news apart, sort the real from the fabulous, the truth from the fear.

The city was under attack.

A monster had come to London.

A fog was poisoning the people.

Invading their minds.

Driving them mad.

It was like the Black Night all over again, they said, but worse. That plague had taken twenty, thirty, and passed by touch. This, it seemed, moved on the air itself. It had taken hundreds, maybe even thousands.

And it was spreading.

The tournament magicians stood in clusters, some speaking in low, urgent tones while others simply stared out through the gallery's vaulting windows as tendrils of dark fog wrapped around the palace, blotting out the city in streaks of black.

The Faroans gathered around Lord Sol-in-Ar in tight formation as their general spoke in his serpentine tongue, while the Veskans stood in sullen silence, their prince staring into the night, their princess surveying the room.

The queen caught sight of Alucard and frowned, pulling away from the knot of *vestra* around her.

"Is my son awake?" she said under her breath.

"Not yet, Your Majesty," he answered. "But Kell is with him now."

A long silence, and then the queen nodded, once, attention already shifting away.

"Is it true?" he asked. "That Rhy . . ." He didn't want to shape the words, didn't want to give them life and weight. He'd picked up fragments in the chaos of Rhy's collapse, seen the matching spellwork on Kell's chest.

Someone has wounded you, he'd said nights before, offering to kiss the seal above the prince's heart. But someone had done worse than that.

"He will recover now," she said. "That is what matters."

He wanted to say something else, to tell her he was worried, too (he wondered if she knew—how *much* she knew—about his summer with her son, how much he cared), but she was already moving away, and he was left with the words going sour on his tongue.

"All right then, who's next?" said a familiar voice nearby, and Alucard turned again to see his thief surrounded by palace guards. His pulse quickened until he realized Bard wasn't in any danger.

The guards were *kneeling* around her, and Lila Bard of all people was touching each of their foreheads, as if bestowing a blessing. Head bowed, she almost looked like a saint.

If a saint dressed all in black and carried knives.

If a saint blessed using blood.

He went to her as the guards peeled away, each anointed with a line of red.

Up close, Bard looked pale, shadows like bruises beneath her eyes, jaw clenched as she wrapped a cut in linen.

"Keep some of that in your veins, if you can," he said, reaching out to help her tie the knot.

She looked up, and he stiffened at the unnatural glint in her gaze. The glass surface of her right eye, once a brown that *almost* matched her left, was shattered.

"Your eye," he said dumbly.

"I know."

"It looks . . ."

"Dangerous?"

"Painful." His fingertips drifted to the dried blood caught like a tear in the outer corner of the ruined eye, a nick where a knife had grazed the skin. "Long night?"

She let out a single stifled laugh. "And getting longer."

Alucard's gaze tracked from the guards' marked skin to her stained fingers. "A spell?"

Bard shrugged. "A blessing." He raised a brow. "Haven't you heard?" she added absently. "I'm *aven*."

"You're certainly something," he said as a crack snaked up the nearest window and a pair of older priests rushed toward the novice working to ward the glass. He lowered his voice. "Have you been outside?"

"Yes," she said, features hardening. "It's . . . it's not . . . good . . ." She trailed off. Bard had never been chatty, but he didn't think he'd ever seen her at a loss for words. She took a moment, squinting at the odd gathering that they faced here, and began again, her voice low. "The guards are keeping the people in their homes, but the fog—whatever's *in* the fog—is poisonous. Most fall within moments of contact. They aren't rotting the way they did in the Black Night," she added, "so it's not possession. But they're not themselves, either. And those who fight the hold, they fall to something worse. The priests are trying to learn more, but so far . . ." She blew out a breath, shifting her hair over her damaged eye. "I caught sight of Lenos in the crowd," she added, "and he looked all right, but Tav . . ." She shook her head.

Alucard swallowed. "Has it reached the northern bank?" he asked, thinking of the Emery estate. Of his sister. When Bard didn't answer, he twisted toward the door. "I have to go—"

"You can't," she said, and he expected a reprimand, a reminder there was nothing he could do, but this was Bard—his Bard—and *can't* meant something simple. "The guards are on the doors," she explained. "They've strict orders not to let anyone in or out."

"You never let that stop *you*."

The ghost of a smile. "True." And then, "I could stop you."

"You could try."

And she must have seen the steel in his eyes, because the smile flickered and went out. "Come here."

She tangled her fingers in his collar and pulled his face toward hers, and for a strange, disorienting second he thought she meant to kiss him. The memory of another night flared in his mind—a point made with bodies pressed together, an argument punctuated with a kiss—but now she simply pressed her thumb to his forehead and drew a short line above his brows.

He lifted a hand to his face, but she swatted it away. "It's supposed to shield you," she said, nodding at the windows, "from whatever's out there."

"I thought that's what the palace was for," he said darkly.

Lila cocked her head. "Perhaps," she said, "but only if you plan to stay inside."

Alucard turned to go.

"God be with you," said Bard dryly.

"What?" he asked, confused.

"Nothing," she muttered. "Just try to stay alive."

II

Emira Maresh stood in the doorway to her son's chamber and watched the two of them sleep.

Kell was slumped in a chair beside Rhy's bed, his coat cast off and a blanket around his bare shoulders, his head resting on folded arms atop the bedsheets.

The prince lay stretched out on the bed, one arm draped across his ribs. The color was back in his cheeks, and his eyelids fluttered, lashes dancing the way they did when he dreamed.

In sleep, they both looked so peaceful.

When they were children, Emira used to slip from room to room like a ghost after they'd gone to bed, smoothing sheets and touching hair and watching them fall asleep. Rhy wouldn't let her tuck him in—he claimed it was undignified—and Kell, when she'd tried, had only stared at her with those large inscrutable eyes. He could do it himself, he'd insisted, and so he had.

Now Kell shifted in his sleep, and the blanket began to slip from his shoulders. Emira, unthinking, reached to resettle it, but when her fingers brushed his skin, he started and shot upright as if under attack, eyes bleary, face contorted with panic. Magic was already singing across his skin, flushing the air with heat.

"It's only me," she said softly, but even as recognition settled in Kell's face, his body didn't loosen. His hands returned to his sides, but his shoulders stayed stiff, his gaze landing on her like stones, and Emira's escaped to the bed, to the floor, wondering why he was so much harder to look at when he was awake.

"Your Majesty," he said, reverent, but cold.

"Kell," she said, trying to find her warmth. She meant to go on, meant his name to be the beginning of a question—*Where did you go? What happened to you? To my son?*—but he was already on his feet, already taking up his coat.

"I didn't mean to wake you," she said.

Kell scrubbed at his eyes. "I didn't mean to sleep."

She wanted to stop him, and couldn't. Didn't.

"I'm sorry," he said from the doorway. "I know it's my fault."

No, she wanted to say. And *yes.* Because every time she looked at Kell, she saw Rhy, too, begging for his brother, saw him coughing up blood from someone else's wound, saw him still as death, no longer a prince at all but a body, a corpse, a thing long gone. But he'd come back, and she knew it was Kell's spell that had done it.

She had seen now what Kell had given the prince, and what the prince was without it, and it *terrified* her, the way they were bound, but her son was lying on the bed, alive, and she wanted to cling to Kell and kiss him and say *Thank you, Thank you, thank you.*

She forgave him nothing.

She owed him everything.

And before she could say so, he was gone.

When the door shut behind him, Emira sank into Kell's abandoned seat. Words waited in her mouth, unsaid. She swallowed them, wincing as though they scratched on the way down.

She leaned forward, resting one hand gently over Rhy's.

His skin was smooth and warm, his pulse strong. Tears slid down her cheek and froze as they fell, tiny beads of ice landing in her lap only to melt again into her dress.

"It's all right," she finally managed, though she didn't know if the words were for Kell, or Rhy, or herself.

Emira had never wanted to be a mother.

She'd certainly never planned on being queen.

Before she married Maxim, Emira had been the second child of Vol Nasaro, fourth noble line from the throne behind the Maresh and the Emery and the Loreni.

Growing up, she was the kind of girl who broke things.

Eggs and glass jars, porcelain cups and mirrors.

"You could break a stone," her father used to tease, and she didn't know if she was clumsy or cursed, only that in her hands, things always fell apart. It had seemed a cruel joke when her element proved to be neither steel nor wind, but water—*ice*. Easily made. Easily ruined.

The idea of children had always terrified her—they were so small, so fragile, so easily broken. But then came Prince Maxim, with his solid strength, his steel resolve, his kindness like running water under heavy winter snow. She knew what it meant to be a queen, what it *entailed*, though even then she'd secretly hoped it wouldn't happen, couldn't happen.

But it did.

And for nine months, she'd moved as if cupping a candle in a very strong wind.

For nine months, she'd held her breath, buoyed only by the knowledge that if anyone came for her son, they would have to go through her.

For nine months, she'd prayed to the sources and the nameless saints and the dead Nasaro to lift her curse, or stay its hand.

And then Rhy was born, and he was perfect, and she knew she would spend the rest of her life afraid.

Every time the prince tumbled, every time he fell, she was the one fighting tears. Rhy would spring up with a laugh, rubbing bruises away like dirt, and be off again, charging toward the next catastrophe, and Emira would be left standing there, hands still outstretched as if to catch him.

"Relax," Maxim would say. "Boys don't break so easily. Our son will be as strong as forged steel and thick ice."

But Maxim was wrong.

Steel rusted and ice was only strong until a crack sent it shattering to the ground. She lay awake at night, waiting for the crash, knowing it would come.

And instead came Kell.

Kell, who carried a world of magic in his blood.

Kell, who was unbreakable.

Kell, who could protect her son.

"At first, I *wanted* to raise you as brothers."

Emira didn't know when she had started talking instead of thinking, but she heard her voice echo gently through the prince's chamber.

"You were so close in age, I thought it would be nice. Maxim had always wanted more than one, but I—I couldn't bring myself to have another." She leaned forward. "I worried, you know, that you might not get along; Kell was so quiet and you so loud, like morning and midnight, but you were thick as vines from the start. And it was well enough, when the only danger came from slick stairs and bruised knees. But then the Shadows came and stole you away, and Kell wasn't there because you two were playing one of your games. And after that, I realized you didn't need a brother. You needed a guardian. I tried to raise Kell as a ward, then, not a son. But it was too late. You were inseparable. I thought that maybe as you aged, you would drift, Kell to magic, and you to the crown. You're so different, I hoped that time would carve some space between you. But you grew together instead of apart. . . ."

A flutter of movement on the bed, the shift of legs against sheets, and she was up, brushing the dark curls from his cheek, whispering, "Rhy, Rhy."

His fingers curled in the sheets, his sleep growing shallow, restless. A word escaped his lips, little more than an exhale, but she recognized the sound and shape of Kell's name, before, at last, her son woke up.

III

For a moment, Rhy was caught between sleep and waking, impenetrable darkness and a riot of color. A word sat on his tongue, the echo of something already said, but it melted away, thin as a wafer of sugar.

Where was he?

Where had he been?

In the courtyard, searching for Kell, and then falling, straight through the stone floor and into the dark place, the one that reached for him every time he slept.

It was dark here, too, but the subtle layered dark of a room at night. The red cushions of his bed, with their honeyed trim, were cast in variant shades of grey, the bedsheets mussed beneath him.

Dreams clung to Rhy like cobwebs—dreams of pain, of strong hands holding him up, holding him down, dreams of ice-cold collars and metal frames, of blood on white stone—but he couldn't hold on to their shape.

His body hurt with the memory of hurting, and he collapsed back against the pillows with a gasp.

"Easy," said his mother. "Easy." Tears were spilling down her cheeks, and he reached out to catch one, marveling at the crystal of ice quickly melting in his palm.

He didn't think he'd ever seen her cry.

"What's wrong?"

She let out a stifled sound, something caught between a laugh and a sob and verging on hysterical.

"What's wrong?" she echoed with a shudder. "You left. You were *gone*. I sat here with your *corpse*."

Rhy shivered at that word, the darkness catching, trying to drag his mind back down into the memory of that place without light, without hope, without life.

His mother was still shaking her head. "I thought . . . I thought he healed a wound. I thought he brought you back. I didn't realize he was the only thing keeping you here. That you were . . . that you had really . . ." Her voice hitched.

"I'm here now," he soothed, even though part of him still felt caught somewhere else. He was pulling free of that place, moment by moment, inch by inch. "And where is Kell?"

The queen tensed and pulled away.

"What happened?" pressed Rhy. "Is he safe?"

Her face hardened. "I watched you die because of him."

Frustration hit Rhy in a wave, and he didn't know if it was only his or Kell's as well, but the force was rocking. "I am *alive* again because of him," he snapped. "How can you hate Kell, after all of this?"

Emira rocked back as if struck. "I do not hate him, though I wish I could. You have a blindness when it comes to each other, and it terrifies me. I don't know how to keep you safe."

"You don't have to," said Rhy, getting to his feet. "Kell has done it for you. He's given his life, and saints know what else, to save—to *salvage*—me. Not because I am his prince. But because I am his brother. And I will spend every day of this borrowed life trying to repay him for it."

"He was meant to be your shield," she murmured. "Your shelter. You were never meant to be his."

Rhy shook his head, exasperated. "Kell isn't the only one you fail to understand. My bond with him didn't start with this curse. You wanted him to kill for me, die for me, protect me at all costs. Well, Mother, you got your wish. You simply failed to realize that that kind of love, that bond, it goes both ways. I would kill for him, and I would die for him, and I will protect him however I am able, from Faro and Vesk, from White London, and Black London, and from you."

Rhy went to the balcony doors and threw open the curtains, intending to shower the room in the Isle's red light. Instead, he was met with a wall of darkness. His eyes went wide, anger dissolving into shock.

"What's happened to the river?"

IV

Lila rinsed the blood from her hands, amazed that she had any left. Her body was a patchwork of pain—funny, how it still found ways to surprise her—and under that, a hollowness she knew from hungry days and freezing nights.

She stared down into the bowl, her focus sliding.

Tieren had seen to her calf, where Ojka's knife had gone in; her ribs, where she'd hit the roof; her arm, where she'd drawn blood after blood after blood. And when he was done, he'd touched his fingers to her chin and tipped it up, his gaze a weight, solid but strangely welcome.

"Still in one piece?" he'd asked, and she remembered her ruined eye.

"More or less."

The room had swayed a little, then, and Tieren had steadied her.

"You need to rest," he'd said.

She'd knocked his hand away. "Sleep is for the rich and the bored," she'd said. "I am neither, and I know my limits."

"You might have known them before you came here," he lectured, "before you took up magic. But power has its own boundaries."

She'd brushed him off, though in truth she was tired in a way she'd rarely known, a tired that went down far past skin and muscle and even bone, dragged its fingers through her mind until everything rippled and blurred. A tired that made it hard to breathe, hard to think, hard to be.

Tieren had sighed and turned to go as she dug the stone shard of

Astrid's cheek from her coat pocket. "I guess I've answered the question."

"When it comes to you and questions, Miss Bard," said the priest without looking back, "I think we've only just begun."

Another drop of blood hit the water, clouding the basin, and Lila thought of the mirror in the black market at Sasenroche, the way it had nicked her fingers, taken blood in trade for a future that could be hers. On one side, the promise, on the other, the means. How tempting it had been, to turn the mirror over. Not because she wanted what she'd seen, but simply because there was power in the knowing.

Blood swirled in the bowl between her hands, twisting into almost-shapes before dissolving into a pinkish mist.

Someone cleared their throat, and Lila looked up.

She'd nearly forgotten the boy standing by the door. Hastra. He'd led her here, given her a silver cup of tea—which sat abandoned on the table—filled the basin, then taken up his place by the door to wait.

"Are they afraid I'll steal something, or run away?" she'd asked when it was clear he'd been assigned to mind her.

He'd flushed, and after a moment said bashfully, "Bit of both, I think."

She'd nearly laughed. "Am I a prisoner?" she'd asked, and he'd looked at her with those wide earnest eyes and said, in an English softened by his smooth Arnesian accent, "We are all prisoners, Miss Bard. At least for tonight."

Now he fidgeted, looking toward her, then away, then back again, eyes snagging now on the reddening pool, now on her shattered eye. She'd never met a boy who wore so much on his face. "Something you want to ask me?"

Hastra blinked, cleared his throat. At last, he seemed to find the nerve. "Is it true, what they say about you?"

"What is it they say?" she asked, rinsing the final cut.

The boy swallowed. "That you're the third *Antari*." It gave her a shiver to hear the words. "The one from the *other* London."

"No idea," she said, wiping her arm with a rag.

"I do hope you're like him," the boy pressed on.

"Why's that?"

His cheeks flushed. "I just think Master Kell shouldn't be alone. You know, the only one."

"Last time I checked," said Lila, "you have another in the prison. Maybe we could start bleeding *him* instead." She wrung the rag, red drops falling to the bowl.

Hastra flushed. "I only meant . . ." He pursed his lips, looking for the words, or perhaps the way to say them in her tongue. "I'm glad that he has you."

"Who says he does?" But the words had no bite. Lila was too tired for games. The ache in her body was dull but persistent, and she felt bled dry in more ways than one. She stifled a yawn.

"Even *Antari* need sleep," said Hastra gently.

She waved the words away. "You sound like Tieren."

His face lit up as if it were praise. "Master Tieren is wise."

"Master Tieren is a nag," she shot back, her gaze drifting again to the reflection in the clouded pool.

Two eyes stared up, one ordinary, the other fractured. One brown, the other just a starburst of broken light. She held her gaze—something she'd never been keen to do—and found that, strangely, it was easier now. As if this reflection were somehow closer to the truth.

Lila had always thought of secrets like gold coins. They could be hoarded, or put to use, but once you spent them, or lost them, it was a beast to get your hands on more.

Because of that, she'd always guarded her secrets, prized them above any take.

The fences back in Grey London hadn't known she was a street rat.

The street patrols hadn't known she was a girl.

She herself didn't know what had happened to her eye.

But no one knew it was fake.

Lila dragged her fingers through the water one last time.

So much for that secret, she thought.

And she was running out of ones to keep.

"What now?" she asked, turning toward the boy. "Do I get to

inflict wounds on someone else? Make some trouble? Challenge this Osaron to a fight? Or shall we see what Kell is up to?"

As she ticked off the options, her fingers danced absently over her knives, one of which was missing. Not lost. Simply loaned.

Hastra held the door for her, looking balefully back at the abandoned cup.

"Your tea."

Lila sighed and took up the silver cup, its contents long cold.

She drank, cringing at the bitter dregs before setting it aside, and following Hastra out.

V

Kell didn't realize he was looking for Lila, not until he collided with someone who *wasn't* her.

"Oh," said the girl, resplendent in a green-and-silver dress.

He caught her, steadying them both as the Veskan princess leaned into him instead of away. Her cheeks were flushed, as if she'd been running, her eyes glassy with tears. At only sixteen, Cora still had the long-limbed gait of youth and the body of a young woman. When he first saw her, he'd been struck by that contrast, but now, she looked all child, a girl playing dress-up in a world she wasn't ready for. He still couldn't believe that this was the one Rhy had been afraid of.

"Your Highness."

"Master Kell," she answered breathlessly. "What is going on? They won't tell us anything, but the man on the roof, and that awful fog, now the people in the streets—I saw them, through the window, before Col pulled me away." She spoke quickly, her Veskan accent making her trip over every few words. "What will happen to the rest of us?"

She was flush against him now, and he was grateful he'd stopped at his own room to put on a shirt.

He eased her back gently. "So long as you stay in the palace, you will be safe."

"Safe," she echoed, gaze slanting toward the nearest doors, glass panes frosted with winter chill and streaked with shadow. "I think I'd only feel safe," she added, "with you beside me."

"How romantic," said a dry voice, and Kell turned to see Lila leaning against the wall, Hastra a few strides behind. Cora stiffened in Kell's arms at the sight of them.

"Am I interrupting?" asked Lila.

Cora said "yes" at the same time Kell said "no." The princess shot him a wounded look, then turned her annoyance on Lila. "Leave," she ordered in the imperious tone peculiar to royalty and spoiled children.

Kell cringed, but Lila only raised a brow. "What was that?" she asked, strolling forward. She was half a head taller than the Veskan royal.

To her credit, Cora didn't retreat. "You are in the presence of a princess. I suggest you learn your place."

"And where is that, *Princess*?"

"Beneath me."

Lila smiled at that, one of those smiles that made Kell profoundly nervous. The kind of smile usually followed by a weapon.

"*Sa'tach,* Cora!" Her brother, Col, rounded the corner, his face tight with anger. At eighteen, the prince had none of his sister's childlike features, none of her lithe grace. The last traces of youth lingered in his darting blue eyes, but in every other way he was an ox, a creature of brute strength. "I told you to stay in the gallery. This isn't a game."

A storm cloud crossed Cora's face. "I was looking for the *Antari*."

"And now you have found him." He nodded once at Kell, then took his sister's arm. "Come."

Despite the difference in size, Cora wrenched free, but that was the sum of her defiance. She shot Kell an embarrassed look, and Lila a venomous one, before following her brother out.

"Don't kill the messenger," said Lila when the two were gone, "but I think the princess is trying to get into your"—her gaze trailed Kell up and down—"good graces."

He rolled his eyes. "She's just a child."

"Baby vipers still have fangs. . . ." Lila trailed off, swaying on her feet, the gentle rock of a body trying to find balance. She braced herself against the wall.

"Lila?" He reached to steady her. "Have you slept?"

"Not you, too," she snapped, flicking a hand dismissively at him and then back toward Hastra. "What I need is a stiff drink and a solid plan." The words tumbled out in their usual acerbic way, but she didn't look well. Blood dotted her cheekbones, but it was her eyes—again her eyes—that caught him. One warm and brown, the other a burst of jagged lines.

It looked wrong, and yet right, and Kell couldn't tear his gaze away.

Lila didn't even try. That was the thing about her. Every glance was a test, a challenge. Kell closed the gap between them and brought his hand to her face, the beat of her pulse and power strong against his palm. She tensed at the touch, but didn't pull away.

"You don't look well," he whispered, his thumb tracing her jaw.

"All things considered," she murmured, "I think I'm holding my own. . . ."

Several feet away, Hastra looked like he was trying to melt into the wall.

"Go on," Kell told him without taking his eyes from Lila. "Get some rest."

Hastra shifted. "I can't, sir," he said. "I'm to escort Miss Bard—"

"I'll take that charge," cut in Kell. Hastra bit his lip and retreated several steps.

Lila let her forehead come to rest against his, her face so close the features blurred. And yet, that fractured eye shone with frightening clarity.

"You never told me," he whispered.

"You never noticed," she answered. And then, "Alucard did."

The blow landed, and Kell started to pull away when Lila's eyelids fluttered and she swayed dangerously.

He braced her. "Come on," he said gently. "I have a room upstairs. Why don't we—"

A sleepy flicker of amusement. "Trying to get me into bed?"

Kell mustered a smile. "It's only fair. I've spent enough time in yours."

"If I remember correctly," she said, her voice dreamy with fatigue, "you were on *top* of the bed the entire time."

"And tied to it," observed Kell.

Her words were soft at the edges. "Those were the days...." she said, right before she fell forward. It happened so fast Kell could do nothing but throw his arms around her.

"Lila?" he asked, first gently, and then more urgently. *"Lila?"*

She murmured against his front, something about sharp knives and soft corners, but didn't rouse, and Kell shot a glance at Hastra, who was still standing there, looking thoroughly embarrassed.

"What have you done?" demanded Kell.

"It was just a tonic, sir," he fumbled, "something for sleep."

"You *drugged* her?"

"It was Tieren's order," said Hastra, chastised. "He said she was mad and stubborn and no use to us dead." Hastra lowered his voice when he said this, mimicking Tieren's tone with startling accuracy.

"And what do you plan to do when *she wakes back up?*"

Hastra shrank back. "Apologize?"

Kell made an exasperated sound as Lila nuzzled—actually *nuzzled*—his shoulder.

"I suggest," he snapped at the young man, "you think of something better. Like an escape route."

Hastra paled, and Kell swept Lila up into his arms, amazed at her lightness. She took up so much space in the world—in *his* world—it was hard to imagine her being so slight. In his mind, she was made of stone.

Her head lolled against his chest. He realized then that he'd never seen her sleep—without the edge to her jaw, the crease in her brow, the glint in her glare, she looked startlingly young.

Kell swept through the halls until he reached his room and lowered Lila onto the couch.

Hastra handed him a blanket. "Shouldn't you take off her knives?"

"There's not enough tonic in the world to risk it," said Kell.

He started to drape the blanket over her, then paused, frowning at the holsters that lined Lila's arms and legs.

One of them was empty.

It was probably nothing, he told himself, tucking her in, but the prickle of doubt followed him to his feet, a nagging worry that faded to a whisper as he stepped into the hall.

Probably nothing, he thought as he sagged against the door and scrubbed the dregs of sleep from his eyes.

He hadn't meant to fall asleep earlier, in Rhy's room, had only wanted a moment of quiet, a second to catch his breath. To steady himself for all that was to come.

Now he heard someone clear their throat and looked up to see Hastra, one hand still turning a coin over and over between his fingers.

"Let it go," said Kell.

"I can't," said the former guard.

Kell willed the coin from Hastra's fingers into his. The guard made a small yelp, but didn't try to take it back.

Up close Kell saw it wasn't an ordinary coin. It was of White London make, a wooden disk with the remains of a control spell etched into its face.

What had Hastra said?

It's my fault she found you.

So this was how Ojka had done it.

This was why Hastra blamed himself.

Kell closed his hand over the coin and summoned fire, letting the flames devour the coin. "There," he said, tipping ash from his palm. He pushed himself off the floor, but Hastra's gaze stayed, stuck to the tiles.

"Is the prince truly alive?" he whispered.

Kell pulled back as if struck. "Of course. Why would you ask—"

Hastra's wide brown eyes were tight with worry. "You didn't see him, sir. The way he was, before he came back. He wasn't just gone. It was like he'd . . . *been* gone. Gone for a long time. Like he'd never come back." Kell stiffened, but Hastra kept talking, his voice low but urgent, the color high in his cheeks. "And the queen, she wouldn't leave his body, she kept saying over and over that he would come back, because *you* would come back, and I know you two have the same scar, I know you're bound together, somehow, life to life, and, well, I know it's not my place, I know it's not, but I have to ask. Is it some cruel illusion? Is the real prince—"

Kell brought his hand to the guard's shoulder, and felt the quiver in it, the genuine fear for Rhy's life. For all his foolishness, these people loved his brother.

He pointed down the hall.

"The real prince," he said firmly, "sleeps beyond that door. His heart beats as strongly in his chest as my heart does in mine, and it will until the day I die."

Kell was pulling away when Hastra's voice drew him back, soft, but insistent. "There is a saying in the Sanctuary. *Is aven stran.*"

"*The blessed thread,*" translated Kell.

Hastra nodded eagerly. "Do you know what it means?" His eyes brightened as he spoke. "It's from one of the myths, the Origin of the Magician. Magic and Man were brothers, you see, only they had nothing in common, for each's strength was the other's weakness. And so one day, Magic made a blessed thread, and tied itself to Man, so tightly that the thread cut into their skin. . . ." Here he turned his hands up, flexing his wrists to show the veins, "and from that day, they shared their best and worst, their strength and weakness."

Something fluttered in Kell's chest. "How does the story end?" he asked.

"It doesn't," Hastra said.

"Not even if they part?"

Hastra shook his head. "There's no 'they' anymore, Master Kell. Magic gave so much to Man, and Man so much to Magic, that their edges blurred, and their threads all tangled, and now they can't be pulled apart. They're bound together, you see, life to life. Halves of a whole. If anyone tried to part them, they'd both unravel."

VI

Alucard knew the Maresh palace better than he should have.

Rhy had shown him a dozen ways in and out; hidden doors and secret halls, a curtain pulled aside to reveal a stairwell, a door set flush with the wall. All the ways a friend could sneak into a room, or a lover into a bed.

The first time Alucard had snuck into the palace, he'd been so turned around he'd nearly walked in on *Kell* instead. He *would* have, if the *Antari* had actually been in his rooms, but the chamber was empty, the candlelight dancing over a bed still made, and Alucard had shuddered and slipped back the way he'd come, and fallen into Rhy's arms several minutes later, laughing with relief until the prince pressed a palm over his mouth.

Now he raked his mind, trying to remember the nearest escape. If the doors had been made by—or cloaked with—magic, he'd have seen the threads, but the palace portals were simple, wood and stone and tapestry, forcing him to find his way by touch and memory instead of sight.

A hidden door led from the first floor down into the undercarriage of the palace. Six pillars held the massive structure up, solid bases from which the ethereal arch of the Maresh residence vaulted up against the sky. Six pillars of hollowed rock with a network of tunnels where they met the palace floor.

It was simply a matter of remembering which one to take.

He descended into what he thought was the old sanctuary, and found it converted into a kind of training chamber. The concentric circles of a meditation ring were still set into the floor, but the surfaces bore the scorches and stains befitting a sparring hall.

A lone torch with its enchanted white fire cast the space in shades of grey, and in the colorless haze, Alucard saw weapons scattered on one table and elements on another, bowls of water and sand, shards of stone. Amid them all, a small white flower was growing in a bowl of earth, its leaves spilling over the sides of the pot, a tame thing gone wild.

Alucard took the stairwell on the opposite side of the room, pausing only when he reached the door at the top. Such a thin line, he thought, between inside and out, safe and exposed. But his family, his crew, waited on the other side. He touched the wood, summoning his strength, and the door opened with a groan onto darkness.

Darkness, and before it, a web of light.

Alucard hesitated, face to face with the fabric of the priests' protection spell. It looked like spider silk, but when he passed through, the veil didn't tear; it simply shuddered, and settled back into shape.

Alucard stepped forward into the fog, half expecting it to fold around him. And yet, the shadows wicked off his coat, washed up against his boots and sleeves and collar only to fall away, rebuffed. Retreating with every step, but not far, never far.

His forehead itched, and he remembered Lila's touch, the streak of blood, now dry, across his brow.

It was a thin protection, the shadows trying again and again to find their way in.

How long would it last?

He pulled his jacket close and quickened his pace.

Osaron's magic was *everywhere,* but instead of the threads of spellwork, Alucard saw only heavy shadow, charcoal streaked across the city, the stark *absence* of light like spots across his vision. The darkness *moved* around him, every shadow swaying, dipping, and rolling the way a room did after too many drinks, and woven through it all, the colliding scents of wood fire and spring blossom, snowmelt and poppy, pipe smoke and summer wine. At turns sickly sweet and bitter, and all of it dizzying.

The city was something out of a dream.

London had always been made of sound as much as magic, the music drifting on the air, the singing glass and laughing crowds, the carriages and the bustle of the market.

The sounds he heard now were all wrong.

The wind was up, and on it he heard the hooves of guards on horseback, the clank of metal and the multitude of ghostly voices, an echo of words that all broke down before they reached him, forming a terrible music. Voices, or maybe one voice repeating, looping over and under itself until it seemed like a chorus, the words just out of reach. It was a world of whispers, and part of Alucard wanted to lean in, to listen, to strain until he could make out what it was saying.

Instead, he said the names.

Names of everyone who needed him and everyone he needed and everyone he couldn't—*wouldn't*—lose.

Anisa. Stross. Lenos. Vasry. Jinnar. Rhy. Delilah . . .

The tournament tents sat empty, the fog reaching inside for signs of life. The streets were abandoned, the citizens forced into their homes, as if wood and stone would be enough to stop the spell. Maybe it would. But Alucard doubted it.

Down the road, the night market was on fire. A pair of guards worked furiously to put out the blaze, summoning water from the lightless Isle while two more tried to wrangle a group of men and women. The dark magic scrawled itself across their bodies, smudging out Alucard's vision, engulfing the light of their own energy, blues and greens and reds and purples swallowed up with black.

One of the women was crying.

Another was laughing at the flames.

A man kept making for the river, arms outstretched, while another knelt silently, head tipped back toward the sky. Only the guards' mounts seemed immune to the magic. The horses snorted and flicked their tails, whinnying and stamping hooves at the fog as if it were a snake.

Berras and Anisa waited across the river, the *Night Spire* bobbed in its berth, but Alucard felt himself moving toward the burning market and the guards as a man rushed toward one of them, a metal rod in his hands.

"*Ras al!*" called Alucard, ripping the pole from the man's grip right before it met the guard's neck. It went skittering away, but the sight of it had given the others an idea.

Those on the ground began to rise, their movements strangely fluid, almost coordinated, as if guided by the same invisible hand.

The guard shot toward his horse, but there wasn't time. They were on him, hands tearing blindly at the armor as Alucard surged toward them. A man was beating the guard's helmeted head against the stones, saying, "Let him in, let him in, let him in."

Alucard tore the man off, but instead of letting go, tumbling away, the man held fast to Alucard's arm, fingers digging in.

"Have you met the shadow king?" he asked, eyes wide and swirling with fog, veins edging toward black. Alucard drove his boot into the man's face, tearing himself free.

"Get inside," ordered the second guard, "quickly, before—"

His voice was cut off by the scrape of metal and the wet sound of a blade finding flesh. He looked down at the royal half sword, *his* sword, protruding from his chest. As he slumped to his knees, the woman holding the sword's hilt flashed Alucard a dazzling smile.

"Why won't you let him in?" she asked.

The two guards lay dead on the ground, and now a dozen pairs of poisoned eyes swiveled toward him. Darkness webbed across their skin. Alucard scrambled to his feet and began to back away. Fire was still tearing through the market tents, exposing the metal cords that kept the fabric taut, the steel turning red with heat.

They came at him in a wave.

Alucard swore, and flicked his fingers, and the metal snapped free as they fell on him. The cords snaked through the air, first toward his hands, and then, sharply away. It caught the men and women in its metal grip, coiling around arms and legs, but if they felt its bite or burn, it didn't show.

"The king will find you," snarled one as Alucard lunged for the guard's mount.

"The king will get in," said a second, as he swung up and kicked the horse into motion.

Their voices trailed in his wake.

"All hail the shadow king...."

"Berras?" called Alucard as he rode through unlocked gates. "Anisa?"

His childhood home loomed before him, lit like a lantern against the night.

Despite the cold, Alucard's skin was slick with sweat from riding hard. He'd crossed the Copper Bridge, held his breath for the full stretch as the oily slick of poisoned magic roiled on the surface of the river below. He'd hoped—desperately, dumbly—that the sickness, whatever it was, hadn't reached the northern bank, but the moment his mount's hooves touched solid earth, those hopes crumbled. More chaos. The people moved in mobs, the marked from the *shal* alongside the nobles in their winter fineries, still done up from the last of the tournament balls, all searching out those who hadn't fallen to the spell, and dragging them under.

And through it all, the same haunting chant.

"Have you met the king?"

Anisa. Stross. Lenos.

Alucard spurred the horse on.

Vasry. Jinnar. Rhy. Delilah . . .

Alucard swung down from the borrowed horse and hurried up the steps.

The front door was ajar.

The servants were gone.

The front hall sat empty, save for the fog.

"Anisa!" he called again, moving from the foyer into the library, the library into the dining room, the dining room into the salon. In every room, the lamps were lit, the fires burned, the air stifling with heat. In every room, the low fog twisted around table legs and through chairs, crept the walls like trellis vines. "Berras!"

"For saints' sake, be still," growled a voice behind him.

Alucard spun to find his older brother, one shoulder tipped against the door. A wineglass hung as it always did from his fingers, and his chiseled face held its usual disdain. Berras, ordinary, impertinent Berras.

Relief knocked the air from Alucard's lungs.

"Where are the servants? Where is Anisa?"

"Is that how you greet me?"

"The city is under attack."

"Is it?" Berras asked absently, and Alucard hesitated. There was something wrong with his voice. It held a lightness, bordering on amusement. Berras Emery was never amused.

He should have known then that it was wrong.

All wrong.

"It isn't safe here," said Alucard.

Berras shifted forward. "No, it isn't. Not for you."

The light caught his brother's gaze, snagging on the ropes of fog that shimmered in his eyes, turning them glassy, the beads of sweat beginning to pool in the hollows of his face. Beneath his tan skin, his veins were edging black, and if Berras Emery had had more than an ounce of magic to start with, Alucard would have seen it winking out, smothered by the spell.

"Brother," he said slowly, though the word tasted wrong in his mouth.

Once, Berras would have knocked the term aside. Now he didn't even seem to notice.

"You're stronger than this," said Alucard, even though Berras had never been the master of his temper or his moods.

"Come to claim your laurels?" continued Berras. "One more title to add to the stack?" He lifted his glass and then, discovering it empty, simply let it fall. Alucard caught it with his will before it could shatter against the inlaid floor.

"Champion," drawled Berras, ambling toward him. "Nobleman. Pirate. Whore." Alucard tensed, the last word finding its mark.

"You think I didn't know all along?"

"Stop," he whispered, the word lost beneath his brother's steps. In that moment, Berras looked so much like their father. A predator.

"I'm the one who told him," said Berras, as if reading his mind. "Father wasn't even surprised. Only *disgusted*. 'What a *disappointment,*' he said."

"I'm glad he's dead," snarled Alucard. "I only wish I could have been in London when it happened."

Berras's look darkened, but the lightness in his voice, a hollow ease, remained.

"I went to the arena, you know," he rambled. "I stayed to watch you fight. Every match, can you believe it? I didn't carry your pennant, of course. I didn't come to see you win. I just hoped that someone would beat you. That they would *bury* you."

Alucard had learned how to take up space. He had never felt small, except here, in this house, with Berras, and despite years of practice, he felt himself retreating.

"It would have been worth it," continued Berras, "to see someone knock that smug look off your face—"

A muffled sound from upstairs, the thud of a weight hitting the floor.

"Anisa!" called Alucard, taking his eyes off Berras for an instant.

It was a foolish thing to do.

His brother slammed him back into the nearest wall, a mountain of muscle and bone. Growing up without magic, his brother knew how to use his fists. And he used them well.

Alucard doubled over, the air rushing from his lungs as knuckles cracked into ribs.

"Berras," he said with a gasp. "Listen to—"

"No. You listen to *me,* little brother. It's time to set things straight. I'm the one Father wanted. I'm already the heir of House Emery, but I could be so much *more*. And I will be, once you're gone." His meaty fingers found Alucard's throat. "There is a new king rising."

Alucard had never been one to fight dirty, but he'd spent enough time recently watching Delilah Bard. He brought his hands up swiftly, palm crunching into the base of his brother's nose. A blinder, she'd called that move.

Tears and blood spilled down Berras's face, but he didn't even flinch. His fingers only tightened around Alucard's throat.

"Ber—ras—" gasped Alucard, reaching for glass, for stone, for water. Even *he* wasn't strong enough to call an object to hand without seeing it, and with Berras blocking his way, and his vision tunneling, Alucard found himself reaching futilely for anything and everything. The whole house trembled with the pull of Alucard's power, his carefully honed precision lost in the panic, the struggle for air.

His lips moved, silently summoning, pleading.

The walls shook. The windows shattered. Nails jerked free of boards and wood cracked as it peeled up from the floor. For one desperate instant, nothing happened, and then the world came hurtling in toward a single point.

Tables and chairs, artwork and mirrors, tapestries and curtains, pieces of wall and floor and door all crashed into Berras with blinding force. The massive hands fell away from Alucard's throat as Berras was driven back by the whirlwind of debris twining around his arms and legs, dragging him down.

But still he fought with the blind strength of someone severed from thought, from pain, until at last the chandelier came down, tearing long cracks in the ceiling as it fell and burying Berras in iron and plaster and stone. The whirlwind fell apart and Alucard gasped, hands on his knees. All around him, the house still groaned.

From overhead, nothing. Nothing. And then he heard his sister scream.

He found Anisa in an upstairs room, tucked in a corner with her knees drawn up, her eyes wide with terror. Terror, he soon realized, at something that wasn't there.

She had her hands pressed over her ears, her head buried against her knees, whispering over and over, "I'm not alone, I'm not alone, I'm not alone."

"Anisa," he said, kneeling before her. Her face flushed, veins climbing her throat, darkness clouding her blue eyes.

"Alucard?" Her voice was thin. Her whole body shook. "Make him stop."

"I did," he said, thinking she meant Berras, but then she shook her head and said, "He keeps trying to get in."

The shadow king.

He scanned the air around her, could see the shadows tangling in the green light of her power. It looked like a storm was trapped in the unlit room, the air flickering with mottled light as her magic fought against the intruder.

"It hurts," she whispered, curling in on herself. "Don't leave me. Please. Don't leave me alone with him."

"It's all right," he said, lifting his little sister into his arms. "I'm not going anywhere, not without you."

The house groaned around them as he carried Anisa through the hall.

The walls fissured, and the stairs began to splinter beneath his feet. Some deep damage had been done to the house, a mortal wound he couldn't see but felt with every tremor.

The Emery Estate had stood for centuries.

And now it was coming down.

Alucard *had* ruined it, after all.

It took all his strength to hold the structure up around them, and by the time they crossed the threshold, he was dizzy from the effort.

Anisa's head lolled against his chest.

"Stay with me, Nis," he said. "Stay with me."

He mounted his horse with the aid of a low wall, and kicked the beast into motion, riding through the gate as the rest of the estate came tumbling down.

FOUR

WEAPONS AT HAND

I

White London

Nasi stood before the platform and did not cry.

She was nine winters old, for crow's sake, and had long ago learned to look composed, even if it was fake. Sometimes you had to pretend, everyone knew that. Pretend to be happy. Pretend to be brave. Pretend to be strong. If you pretended long enough, it eventually came true.

Pretending not to be sad was the hardest, but looking sad made people think you were weak, and when you were already a foot too short and a measure too small, and a girl on top of that, you had to work twice as hard to convince them it wasn't true.

So even though the room was empty, save for Nasi and the corpse, she didn't let the sadness show. Nasi worked in the castle, doing whatever needed to be done, but she knew she wasn't supposed to be in here. Knew the northern hall was off limits, the private quarters of the king. But the king was missing, and Nasi had always been good at sneaking, and anyway, she hadn't come to snoop, or steal.

She'd only come to see.

And to make sure the woman wasn't lonely.

Which Nasi knew was ridiculous, because dead people probably didn't feel things like cold, or sad, or lonely. But she couldn't be sure, and if it was her, she would have wanted someone there.

Besides, this was the only quiet room left in the castle.

The rest of the place was plunging into chaos, everyone shouting and searching for the king, but not in here. In here, candles burned, and the heavy doors and walls held in all the quiet. In here, at the center of the chamber, on a platform of beautiful black granite, lay Ojka.

Ojka, laid out in black, hands open at her sides, a blade resting in each palm. Vines, the first things to bloom in the castle gardens, were wound around the platform's edge, a dish of water at Ojka's head and a basin of earth at her feet, places for the magic to go when it left her body. A black cloth was draped over her eyes, and her short red hair made a pool around her head. A piece of white linen had been wrapped tight around her neck, but even in death a line of blackish-red stained through where someone had cut her throat.

Nobody knew what had happened. Only that the king was missing, and the king's chosen knight was dead. Nasi had seen the king's prisoner, the red-haired man with his own black eye, and she wondered if it was his fault, since he was missing, too.

Nasi clenched her hands into fists, and felt the sudden bite of thorns. She'd forgotten about the flowers, wild things plucked from the edge of the castle yard. The prettiest ones hadn't blossomed yet, so she'd been forced to dig up a handful of pale buds studded with vicious thorns.

"*Nijk shöst,*" she murmured, setting the bundle of flowers on the platform, the tail of her braid brushing Ojka's arm as she leaned forward.

Nasi used to wear her hair loose so it covered the scars on her face. It didn't matter that she could barely see through the pale curtain, that she was always tripping and stumbling. It was a shield against the world.

And then one day Ojka passed her in the corridor, and stopped her, and told her to pull the hair off her face.

She hadn't wanted to, but the king's knight stood there, arms crossed, waiting for her to obey, and so she had, cringing as she tied back the strands. Ojka surveyed her face, but didn't ask her what had happened, if she'd been born that way (she hadn't) or caught off-turn in the *Kosik* (she had). Instead, the woman had cocked her head and said, "Why do you hide?"

Nasi could not bring herself to answer Ojka, to tell the king's knight that she hated her scars when Ojka had darkness spilling down one side of her face and a silver line carving its way from eye to lip on the other. When she didn't speak, the woman crouched in front of her and took her firmly by the shoulders.

"Scars are not shameful," said Ojka, "not unless you let them be." The knight straightened. "If you do not wear them, they will wear you." And with that, she'd walked away.

Nasi had worn her hair back ever since.

And every time Ojka had passed her in the halls, her eyes, one yellow, the other black, had flicked to the braid, and she'd nodded in approval, and everything in Nasi had grown stronger, like a starving plant fed water drop by drop.

"I wear my scars now," she whispered in Ojka's ear.

Footsteps sounded beyond the doors, the heavy tread of the Iron Guard, and Nasi pulled back hastily, nearly tipping over the bowl of water when she snagged her sleeve on the vines coiled around the platform.

But she was only nine winters old, and small as a shadow, and by the time the doors opened, she was gone.

II

In the Maresh dungeons, sleep eluded Holland.

His mind drifted, but every time it began to settle, he saw London—*his* London—as it crumbled and fell. Saw the colors fade back to gray, the river freeze, and the castle . . . well, thrones did not stay empty. Holland knew this well. He pictured the city searching for its king, heard the servants calling out his name before new blades found their throats. Blood staining white marble, bodies littering the forest as boots crushed everything he'd started like new grass underfoot.

Holland reached out automatically for Ojka, his mind stretching across the divide of worlds, but found no purchase.

The prison cell he currently occupied was a stone tomb, buried somewhere deep in the bones of the palace. No windows. No warmth. He had lost track of the number of stairs when the Arnesian guards dragged him in, half conscious, mind still gutted from Osaron's intrusion and sudden exit. Holland barely processed the cells, all empty. The animal part of him had struggled at the touch of cold metal closing around his wrists, and in response, they'd slammed his head against the wall. When he'd surfaced, everything was black.

Holland lost track of time—tried to count, but without any light, his mind skipped, stuttered, fell too easily into memories he didn't want.

Kneel, whispered Astrid in one ear.
Stand, goaded Athos in the other.
Bend.
Break.

Stop, he thought, trying to drag his mind back to the cold cell. It kept slipping.

Pick up the knife.

Hold it to your throat.

Stay very still.

He'd tried to will his fingers, of course, but the binding spell held, and when Athos had returned hours—sometimes days—later, and plucked the blade from Holland's hand, and given him permission to move again, his body had folded to the floor. Muscles torn. Limbs shaking.

That is where you belong, Athos had said. *On your knees.*

"*Stop.*" Holland's growl vibrated through the quiet of the prison, answered only by its echo. For a few breaths, his mind was still, but soon, too soon, it all began again, the memories seeping in through the cold stone and the iron cuffs and the silence.

The first time someone tried to kill Holland, he was barely nine years old.

His eye had turned black the year before, pupil widening day by day until the darkness overtook the green, and then the white, slowly poisoning him lash to lid. His hair was long enough to hide the mark, as long as he kept his head down, which Holland always did.

He woke to the hiss of metal, lunged to the side in time to *almost* miss the blade.

It grazed his arm before burying itself in the cot. Holland tumbled to the floor, hitting his shoulder hard, and rolled, expecting to find a stranger, a mercenary, someone marked with the brand of thieves and killers.

Instead, he saw his older brother. Twice his size, with their father's muddy green eyes and their mother's sad mouth. The only blood Holland had left.

"Alox?" he gasped, pain burning up his injured arm. Bright red drops flecked the floor of their room before Holland managed to press his hand over the weeping wound.

Alox stood over him, the veins on his throat already edging toward black. At fifteen, he had taken on a dozen marks, all to help bend will and bind escaping magic.

Holland was on his back on the floor, blood still spilling between his fingers, but he didn't cry out for help. There was no one to cry out *to*. Their father was dead. Their mother had disappeared into the *sho* dens, drowned herself in smoke.

"Hold still, Holland," muttered Alox, dragging the blade free of the cot. His eyes were red with drink or spellwork. Holland didn't move. Couldn't move. Not because the blade was poisoned, though he feared it was. But because every night he'd dreamed of would-be attackers, given them a hundred names and faces, and none of them had ever been Alox.

Alox, who told him stories when he couldn't sleep. Tales of the someday king. The one with enough power to bring the world back.

Alox, who used to let him sit on makeshift thrones in abandoned rooms and dream of better days.

Alox, who had first seen the mark in his eye, and promised to keep him safe.

Alox, who now stood over him with a knife.

"*Vosk,*" pleaded Holland now. *Stop.*

"It isn't right," his brother slurred, intoxicated by the knife, the blood, the nearness of power. "That magic isn't *yours*."

Holland's bloody fingers went swiftly to his eye. "But it chose me."

Alox shook his head slowly, ruefully. "Magic doesn't *choose,* Holland." He swayed. "It doesn't belong to those who *have*. It belongs to those who *take*."

With that, Alox brought the knife down.

"*Vosk!*" begged Holland, bloody hands outstretched.

He caught the blade, pushing back with every ounce of strength, not on the weapon itself but on the air, the metal. It still bit in, blood ribboning down his palms.

Holland stared up at Alox, pain forcing the words across his lips.

"*As Staro.*"

The words surfaced on their own, rising from the darkness of his mind like a dream suddenly remembered, and with them, the magic surged up through his torn hands, and around the blade, and wrapped around his brother. Alox tried to pull away, but it was too late. The spell had rolled over his skin, turning flesh to stone as it spread over his stomach, climbed his shoulders, wrapped around his throat.

A single gasp escaped, and then it was over, body to stone in the time it took a drop of blood to hit the floor.

Holland lay there beneath the precarious weight of his brother's statue. With Alox frozen on one knee, Holland could look his brother in the eyes, and he found himself staring up into his brother's face, his mouth open and his features caught between surprise and rage. Slowly, carefully, Holland slid free, inching his body out from beneath the stone. He got to his feet, dizzy from the sudden use of magic, shaking from the attack.

He didn't cry. Didn't run. He simply stood there, surveying Alox, searching for the change in his brother as if it were a freckle, a scar, something he should have seen. His own pulse was settling and something else, something deeper, was beginning to steady, too, as if the spell had turned part of *himself* to stone as well.

"Alox," he said, the word barely an exhale as he reached out and touched his brother's cheek, only to recoil from the hardness. His fingers left a rust-red smear against the marble face.

Holland leaned forward to whisper in his brother's stone ear.

"This magic," he said, putting his hand on Alox's shoulder, "is mine."

He pushed, letting gravity tip the statue until it fell and shattered on the floor.

Footsteps sounded on the prison stairs, and Holland straightened, his senses snapping back to the cell. At first, he assumed the visitor would be Kell, but then he counted the footfalls—three sets.

They were speaking Arnesian, running the words together so Holland couldn't catch them all.

He forced himself still as the lock ground free and his cell door swung open. Forced himself not to lash out when an enemy hand wrapped around his jaw, pinning his mouth shut.

"Let's see . . . eyes . . ."

Rough fingers tangled in his hair and the blindfold came free, and for an instant, the world was gold. Lantern light cast haloes over everything before the man forced his face up.

"Should we carve . . ."

"Doesn't look . . . to me."

They weren't wearing armor, but all three had the stature of palace guards.

The first let go of Holland's jaw and started rolling up his sleeves.

Holland knew what was coming, even before he felt the vicious pull on the chains, shoulders straining as they hauled him to his feet. He held the guard's eyes, right up until the first punch landed, a brutal blow between his collar and his throat.

He followed the pain like a current, tried to ground it.

It really was nothing he hadn't felt before. Athos's cold smile surfaced in Holland's mind. The fire of that silver whip.

No one suffers . . .

He staggered as his ribs cracked.

. . . as beautifully as you.

Blood filled Holland's mouth. He could have spat it in their faces and used the same breath to turn them to stone, leave them broken on the floor. Instead, he swallowed.

He would not kill them.

But he would not give them the satisfaction of display, either.

And then, a glint of steel—unexpected—as a guard drew out a knife. When the man spoke, it was in the common tongue of kings.

"This is from Delilah Bard," he said, driving the dagger toward Holland's heart.

Magic rose in him, sudden and involuntary, the dampening chains too weak to stop the flood as the knife plunged toward his bare chest. The guard's body slowed as Holland forced his will against metal and bone. But before he could stop the blade, it flew from the guard's hand, out of Holland's own control, and landed with a snap against Kell's palm.

The guard spun, shock quickly replaced by fear as he took in the man at the base of the stairs, the black coat blending into shadow, the red hair glinting in the light.

"What is this?" asked the other *Antari,* his voice sharp.

"Master Ke—"

The guard went flying backward and struck the wall between two lanterns. He didn't fall, but hung there, pinned, as Kell turned toward the other two. Instantly they let go of Holland's chains, and he half sat, half fell back against the bench, locking his teeth against the jolt of pain. Kell released his hold on the first guard, and the man went crashing to the floor.

The air in the room was frosting over as Kell considered the knife in his hand. He brought the tip of his finger to the point of the blade and pressed down, drawing a single bead of red.

The guards recoiled as one, and Kell glanced up, as if surprised. "I thought you wanted blood sport."

"*Solase,*" said the first guard, rising to his feet. "*Solase, mas vares.*" The others bit their tongues.

"Go," ordered Kell. "The next time I see any of you down here, you will not leave."

They fled, leaving the cell door open as they went.

Holland, who had said nothing since the first footsteps drew him from reverie, leaned his head back against the stone wall. "My hero."

The blindfold hung around his neck, and for the first time since the roof, their eyes met as Kell reached out and swung the cell door closed between them.

He nodded at the stairs. "How many times has that happened?"

Holland said nothing.

"You didn't fight back."

Holland's swollen fingers curled around the chains as if to say, *How could I?,* and Kell raised a brow as if to say, *Those make a difference?* Because they both knew the simple truth: a prison could not hold an *Antari* unless he let it.

Kell turned his attention back to the blade, clearly recognizing the make. "Lila," he muttered. "Should have realized sooner . . ."

"Miss Bard does not care for me."

"Not since you killed her only family."

"The man in the tavern," said Holland, thoughtfully. "She killed him when she took what wasn't hers. When she led me to her home. If she'd been a better thief, perhaps he would still be alive."

"I'd keep that opinion to yourself," said Kell, "if you want to keep your tongue."

A long silence. In the end, Holland was the one to break it.

"Have you finished sulking?"

"You know," snapped Kell, "you're very good at making enemies. Have you ever tried to make a *friend*?"

Holland cocked his head. "What use are those?" Kell gestured to the cells. Holland didn't rise to the bait. He changed course. "What is happening beyond the palace?"

Kell pressed a palm between his eyes. When he was tired, his composure slipped, the cracks on display. "Osaron is free," he said.

Holland listened, brows drawn, as Kell went on about the blackened river, the poisoned fog. When he was done, he stared at Holland, waiting for some answer to a question he'd never asked. Holland said nothing, and at last Kell made an exasperated sound.

"What does he *want*?" demanded the young *Antari*, clearly resisting the urge to pace.

Holland closed his eyes and remembered Osaron's rising temper, his echo of *more, more, more, we could do more, be more*.

"More," he said simply.

"What does that mean?" demanded Kell.

Holland weighed the words before he spoke. "You asked what he wants," he said. "But for Osaron, it's not about *want* so much as *need*. Fire needs air. Earth needs water. And Osaron needs chaos. He feeds on it, the energy of entropy." Every time Holland had found steady ground, every time things had begun to settle, Osaron had forced them back into motion, into change, into chaos. "He's much like you," he added as Kell paced. "He cannot bear to be still."

The cogs were turning behind Kell's eyes, thoughts and emotions flickering across his face like light. Holland wondered if he knew how much he showed.

"Then I must find a way to *make* him still," said the young *Antari*.

"If you can," said Holland. "That alone won't stop him, but it will force him to be reckless. And if reckless humans make mistakes, then so will reckless gods."

"Do you truly believe that he's a god?"

Holland rolled his eyes. "It doesn't matter what someone is. Only what they *think* they are."

A door ground open overhead, and Holland tensed reflexively, hating the subtle but traitorous rattle of his chains, but Kell didn't seem to notice.

Moments later a guard appeared at the base of the stairs. Not one of Holland's attackers, but an older man, temples silver.

"What is it, Staff?" asked Kell.

"Sir," answered the man gruffly. He held no love for the *Antari* prince. "The king has summoned you."

Kell nodded, and turned to leave. He hesitated at the edge of the room. "Do you care so little for your own world, Holland?"

He stiffened. "My world," he said slowly, "is the *only* thing I care about."

"Yet you stay here. Helpless. Useless." Somewhere deep in Holland, someone—the man he used to be, before Osaron, before the Danes—was screaming. Fighting. He held still, waited for the wave to pass.

"You told me once," said Kell, "that you were either magic's master or its slave. So which are you now?"

The screaming died in Holland's head, smothered by the hollow quiet he'd trained to take its place.

"That's what you don't understand," said Holland, letting the emptiness fold over him. "I have only ever been its slave."

III

The royal map room had always been off limits.

When Kell and Rhy were young, they'd played in every palace chamber and hallway—but never here. There were no chairs in this room. No walls of books. No hearth fire or cells, no hidden doors or secret passages. Only the table with its massive map, Arnes rising from the surface of the parchment like a body beneath a taut sheet. The map spanned the table edge to edge, in full detail, from the glittering city of London at its center to the very edges of the empire. Tiny stone ships floated on flat seas, and tiny stone soldiers marked the royal garrisons stationed at the borders, and tiny stone guards patrolled the streets in troops of rose quartz and marble.

King Maxim told them that the pieces on this board had consequences. That to move a chalice was to make war. To topple a ship was to doom the vessel. To play with the men was to the play with lives.

The warning was a sufficient deterrent—whether or not it was *true,* neither Rhy nor Kell dared chance it and risk Maxim's anger and their own guilt.

The map *was* enchanted, though—it showed the empire as it was; now the river glistened like a streak of oil; now tendrils of fog thin as pipe smoke drifted through the miniature streets; now the arenas stood abandoned, darkness rising like steam off every surface.

What it didn't show were the fallen roaming the streets. It didn't show the desperate survivors pounding on the doors of houses, begging to be let in. It didn't show the panic, the noise, the fear.

King Maxim stood at the map's southern edge, hands braced against the table, head bent over the image of his city. To one side stood Tieren, looking like he'd aged ten years in the course of a single night. To the other stood Isra, the captain of the city guard, a broad-shouldered Londoner with cropped black hair and a strong jaw. Women might be rare in the guard, but if someone questioned Isra's standing, they only did it once.

Two of Maxim's *vestran* council, Lord Casin and Lady Rosec, commanded the map's eastern side, while Parlo and Lisane, the *ostra* who'd organized and overseen the *Essen Tasch,* occupied the west. Each and every one of them looked out of place, still dressed for a winner's ball and not a city under siege.

Kell forced himself up to the map's northern edge, stopping directly across from the king.

"We cannot make sense of it," Isra was saying. "There appear to be two kinds of attack, or rather, two kinds of victim."

"Are they possessed?" asked the king. "During the Black Night, Vitari took multiple hosts, spreading himself like a plague between them."

"This isn't possession," interjected Kell. "Osaron is too strong to take an ordinary host. Vitari ate through every shell he found, but it took hours. Osaron would burn through a shell in seconds." He thought of Kisimyr on the roof, her body cracking and crumbling under Osaron's boot. "There's no point trying to possess them."

Unless, he thought, *they are* Antari.

"Then, by saints," demanded Maxim, "what *is* he doing?"

"It seems like some kind of sickness," said Isra.

The *ostra,* Lisane, shuddered. "He's infecting them?"

"He is creating puppets," said Tieren grimly. "Invading their minds, corrupting them. And if that fails . . ."

"He's taking them by force," said Kell.

"Or killing them in the process," added Isra. "Thinning the pack, weeding out resistance."

"Any wards?" asked the king, looking to Kell. "*Besides Antari* blood?"

"Not yet."

"Survivors?"

A long silence.

Maxim cleared his throat.

"We've no word from either House Loreni or House Emery," started Lord Casin. "Can't your men be mustered—"

"My men are doing everything they can," snapped Maxim. Beside him, Isra shot the lord a cold glare.

"We've sent scouts to follow the fog's line," she continued evenly, "and there *is* a perimeter to Osaron's magic. Right now the spell ends seven measures beyond the city's edge, carving out a circle, but our reports show that it is spreading."

"He's drawing power from every life he claims." Tieren's voice was quiet, but authoritative. "If Osaron is not stopped soon, his shadow will cover Arnes."

"And then Faro," cut in Sol-in-Ar, storming through the doorway. The captain's hand twitched toward her sword, but Maxim stayed her with a look.

"Lord Sol-in-Ar," said the king coolly. "I did not call for you."

"You should have," countered the Faroan as Prince Col appeared at his heels. "Since this matter concerns not only Arnes."

"Do you think this darkness will stop at your borders?" added the Veskan prince.

"If we stop it first," said Maxim.

"And if you do not," said Sol-in-Ar as his dark eyes fell on the map, "it will not matter who fell first."

Who fell first. An idea flickered at the edge of Kell's mind, fighting to take shape amid the noise. The feel of Lila's body sagging against his. Staring at the empty cup cradled in Hastra's hand.

"Very well," said the king. He nodded at Isra to continue.

"The jails are full of those who've fallen," reported the captain. "We've commandeered the plaza, and the port cells, but we're running out of places to put them. We're already using the Rose Hall for those with fever."

"What about the tournament arenas?" offered Kell.

Isra shook her head. "My men won't go onto the river, sir. Not safe. A few tried, and they didn't come back."

"The blood sigils are not lasting," added Tieren. "They fade within hours, and the fallen seem to have discovered their purpose. We've already lost a portion of the guards."

"Call the rest back at once," said the king.

Call the rest.

There it was. "I have an idea," said Kell, softly, the threads of it still drawing together.

"We are caged in," said the Faroan general, sweeping a hand over the map. "And this creature will pick over our bones unless we find a way to fight back."

Make him still. Force him to be reckless.

"I have an idea," said Kell again, louder. This time the room went quiet.

"Speak," said the king.

Kell swallowed. "What if we take away the people?"

"Which people?"

"All of them."

"We can't evacuate," said Maxim. "There are too many poisoned by Osaron's magic. If they were to leave, they'd simply spread the illness faster. No, it must be contained. We still don't know if those lost can be regained, but we must hope it is a sickness and not a sentence."

"No, we can't evacuate them," confirmed Kell. "But every waking body is a potential weapon, and if we want a chance at defeating Osaron, we need him disarmed."

"Speak plainly," ordered Maxim.

Kell drew breath, but was cut off by a voice from the door.

"What's this? No vigil by my bed? I'm offended."

Kell spun to see his brother standing in the doorway, hands in his pockets and shoulder tipped casually against the frame as if nothing were wrong. As if he hadn't spent the better part of the night trapped between the living and the dead. None of it showed, at least, not on the surface. His amber eyes were bright, his hair combed, the ring of burnished gold back where it belonged atop his curls.

Kell's pulse surged at the sight of him, while the king hid his relief *almost* as well as the prince hid his ordeal.

"Rhy," said Maxim, voice nearly betraying him.

"Your Highness," said Sol-in-Ar slowly, "we heard you were hurt in the attack."

"We heard you fell victim to the shadow fog," said Prince Col.

"*We* heard you'd taken ill before the winner's ball," added Lord Casin.

Rhy managed a lazy smile. "Goodness, the rumors fly when one is indisposed." He gestured to himself. "As you can see . . ." A glance at Kell. "I'm surprisingly resilient. Now, what have I missed?"

"Kell was just about to tell us," said the king, "how to defeat this monster."

Rhy's eyes widened even as a ghost of fatigue flitted across his face. He'd only just returned. *Is this going to hurt?* his gaze seemed to ask. Or maybe even, *Are we going to die?* But all he said was, "Go on."

Kell fumbled for his thoughts. "We can't evacuate the city," he said again, turning toward the head priest. "But could we put it to sleep?"

Tieren frowned, knocking his bony knuckles on the table's edge. "You want to cast a spell over London?"

"Over its people," clarified Kell.

"For how long?" asked Rhy.

"As long as we must," retorted Kell, turning back toward the priest. "Osaron has done it."

"He's a god," observed Isra.

"No," said Kell sharply. "He's not."

"Then what exactly *are* we facing?" demanded the king.

"It's an *oshoc*," said Kell, using Holland's word. Only Tieren seemed to understand.

"A kind of *incarnation*," explained the priest. "Magic in its natural form has no self, no consciousness. It simply *is*. The Isle river, for instance, is a source of immense power, but it has no identity. When magic gains a self, it gains motive, desire, will."

"So Osaron is just a piece of magic with an ego?" asked Rhy. "A spell gone awry?"

Kell nodded. "And according to Holland, he feeds on chaos. Right now Osaron has ten thousand sources. But if we took them all away, if he had nothing but his own magic—"

"Which is still considerable—" cut in Isra.

"We could lure him into a fight."

Rhy crossed his arms. "And how do you plan to fight him?"

Kell had an idea, but he couldn't bring himself to voice it, not yet, when Rhy had just recovered.

Tieren spared him. "It could be done," said the priest thoughtfully. "In a fashion. We'll never be able to cast a spell that broad, but we could make a network of many smaller incantations," he rambled, half to himself, "and with an anchor, it could be done." He looked up, pale eyes brightening. "But I'll need some things from the Sanctuary."

A dozen eyes flicked to the map room's only window, where the fingers of Osaron's spell still scratched to get in, despite the morning light. Prince Col stiffened. Lady Rosec fixed her gaze on the floor. Kell started to offer, but a look from Rhy made him pause. The look wasn't refusal. Not at all. It was permission. Unflinching trust.

Go, it said. *Do whatever you must.*

"What a coincidence," said a voice from the door. They turned as one to see Lila, hands on her hips and very much awake. "*I* could use some fresh air."

IV

Lila made her way down the hall, an empty satchel in one hand and Tieren's list of supplies in the other. She'd had the luxury of seeing Kell's shock and Tieren's displeasure register at the same time, for whatever that was worth. Her head was still aching dully from whatever she'd been slipped, but the stiff drink had done its part, and the solid plan—or at least a step—had done the rest.

Your tea, Miss Bard.

It wasn't the first time she'd been drugged, but most of her experience had been of a more . . . investigative nature. She'd spent a month aboard the *Spire* collecting powder for the tapers and ale she intended to take onto the *Copper Thief,* enough to bring down an entire crew. She'd inhaled her share, at first by accident, and then with a kind of purpose, training her senses to recognize and endure a certain portion because the last thing she needed was to faint in the middle of the task.

This time, she'd tasted the powder in the tea the moment it hit her tongue, even managed to spit most of it back into the cup, but by then her senses were going numb, winking out like lights in a strong wind, and she knew what was coming—the shallow, almost pleasant slide before the drop. One minute she'd been in the hall with Kell, and the next her balance was going, floor tipping like a ship in a storm. She'd heard the lilt of his voice, felt the heat of his arms, and then she was gone, down, down, down, and the next thing she knew she was bolting upright on a couch with a headache and a wide-eyed boy watching from the wall.

"You shouldn't be awake," Hastra had stammered as she'd thrown the covers off.

"Is that really the first thing you want to say?" she'd asked, staggering toward the sideboard to pour herself a drink. She hesitated, remembering the bitter tea, but after a few searching sniffs, she found something that burned her nose in a familiar way. She downed two fingers, steadied herself against the counter. The drug was still clinging to her like cobwebs, and she was left trying to drag the edges of her mind back into order, squinting until the blurred lines all hardened into sharp ones.

Hastra was shifting his weight from foot to foot.

"I'm going to do you the favor," she said, setting aside the empty glass, "of assuming this wasn't your idea." She turned on him. "And you're going to do yourself the favor of staying out of my way. And next time you mess with my drink"—she drew a knife, twirled it on her fingers, and brought it up beneath his chin—"I'll pin you to a tree."

The sound of steps hurrying toward her returned Lila to the present.

She spun, knowing it would be him. "Was it your idea?"

"What?" stammered Kell. "No. Tieren's. And what have you done with Hastra?"

"Nothing he won't recover from."

A deep furrow formed between Kell's eyes. Christ, he was an easy mark.

"Come to stop me, or to see me off?"

"Neither." His features smoothed. "I came to give you this." He held out her missing knife, knuckled hilt first. "I believe it's yours."

She took the blade, examining the edge for blood. "Too bad," she murmured, as she slid it back into the sheath.

"While I understand the urge," said Kell, "killing Holland was *not* a helpful notion. We need him."

"Like a dose of poison," muttered Lila.

"He's the only one who knows Osaron."

"And why does he know him so well?" she snapped. "Because he made a *deal* with him."

"I know."

"He let that creature into his head—"

"I know."

"—into his world, and now into yours—"

"I *know*."

"Then *why*?"

"Because it could have been me," said Kell darkly. The words hung between them. "It almost was."

The image came back to her, of Kell lying on the floor before the broken frame, blood pooling rich and red around his wrists. What had Osaron said to him? What had he offered? What had he *done*?

Lila found herself reaching for Kell, and stopped. She didn't know what to say, how to smooth the line between his eyes.

The satchel slipped on her shoulder. The sun was up. "I should go."

Kell nodded, but when she turned away, he caught her hand. The touch was slight, but it pinned her like a knife. "That night on the balcony," he said. "Why did you kiss me?"

Lila's chest tightened. "It seemed like a good idea."

Kell frowned. "That's all?" He started to let go, but she didn't. Their hands hung between them, intertwined.

Lila let out a short, breathless laugh. "What do you want, Kell? A declaration of my affection? I kissed you because I wanted to and—"

His hand tightened around hers, pulling her into him, her free hand splayed against his chest for balance.

"And now?" he whispered. His mouth was inches from her own, and she could feel his heart hammering against his ribs.

"What?" she said with a sly grin. "Do I *always* have to take the lead?" She started to lean in, but he was already there, already kissing her. Their bodies crashed together, the last of the distance disappearing as hips met hips and ribs met ribs and hands searched for skin. Her body sang like a tuning fork against his, like finding like.

Kell's grip tightened, as if he thought she would disappear, but Lila wasn't going anywhere. She could have walked away from almost anything, but she wouldn't have walked away from this. And that itself was terrifying—but she didn't stop, and neither did he. Sparks lit across her lips, and heat burned through her lungs, and the air around them churned as if someone had thrown all the doors and windows open.

The wind rustled their hair, and Kell *laughed* against her.

A soft, dazzling sound, too brief, but wonderful.

And then, too soon, the moment ended.

The wind died away, and Kell pulled back, his breath ragged.

"Better?" she asked, the word barely a hush.

He bowed his head, then let his forehead fall against hers. "Better," he said, and almost in the same moment, "Come with me."

"Where are we going?" she asked as he pulled her up the stairs and into a bedroom. *His* bedroom. Gossamer billowed from the high ceiling in the Arnesian style, a cloudlike painting of night. A sofa spilled cushions, a mirror gleamed in its gold trim, and on a dais stood a bed, dripping with silks.

Lila felt her face go hot.

"This really isn't the time," she started, but then he was pulling her past the fineries to a door and, beyond, into the alcove lined with books, and candles, and a few spare trinkets. Most were too battered to be anything but sentimental. In here, the air smelled less like roses than polished wood and old paper, and Kell spun her around to face the door. There she saw the markings on the wood—a dozen symbols drawn in the ruddy brown of dried blood, each simple but distinct. She'd almost forgotten about his shortcuts.

"This one," he said, tapping a circle quartered by a cross. Lila drew a knife, and nicked her thumb, tracing over the mark in blood.

When she was done, Kell put his hand over hers. He didn't tell her to be safe. He didn't tell her to be careful. He simply pressed his lips to her hair and said, "*As Tascen,*" and then he was gone—the room was gone, the world was gone—and Lila was tipping forward once more into darkness.

V

Alucard rode hard for the docks, Anisa shivering against him.

His sister slid in and out of consciousness, her skin slick and hot to the touch. He couldn't take her to the palace, that much he knew. They'd never let her in now that she was infected. Even though she was fighting it. Even though she hadn't fallen—*wouldn't* fall, Alucard was sure of it.

He had to take her home.

"Stay with me," he told her as they reached the line of ships.

The Isle's current was up, leaving oily streaks against the dock walls and splashing over onto the banks. Here at the river's edge, the magic rolled off the water's surface like steam.

Alucard dismounted, carrying Anisa up the ramp and onto the *Spire*'s deck.

He didn't know if he hoped to find anyone aboard, or feared it, since only the mad and the sick and the fallen seemed to be in the city now.

"Stross?" he called. "Lenos?" But no one answered, and so Alucard took her below.

"Come back," whispered Anisa as the night sky disappeared, replaced by the low wood ceiling of the hold.

"I'm right here," said Alucard.

"Come back," she pleaded again as he lowered her onto his bed, pressed a cold compress to her cheeks. Her eyes drifted open, focused, found his. "Luc," she said, her voice suddenly crisp, clear.

"I'm here," he said, and she smiled, fingers brushing his brow. Her eyes began to flutter shut again, and fear rippled through him, sudden, sharp.

"Hey, Nis," he said, squeezing her hand. "Do you remember the story I used to tell you?" She shivered feverishly. "The one about the place where shadows go at night?"

Anisa curled in toward him, then, the way she used to when he told her tales. A flower to the sun, that's what their mother used to say. Their mother, who'd died so long ago, and taken most of the light with her. Only Anisa held a candle to it. Only Anisa had her eyes, her warmth. Only Anisa reminded Alucard of kinder days.

He lowered himself to his knees beside the bed, holding her hand between his. "A girl was once in love with her shadow," he began, voice slipping into the low, melodic tone befitting stories, even as the *Spire* swayed and the world beyond the window darkened. "All day they couldn't be parted, but when night fell, she was left alone, and she always wondered where her shadow went. She would check all the drawers, and all the jars, and all the places where she liked to hide, but no matter where she looked, she couldn't find it. Until finally the girl lit a candle, to help her search, and there her shadow was."

Anisa murmured incoherently. Tears slipped down her hollowed cheeks.

"You see"—Alucard's fingers tightened around hers—"it hadn't really left. Because our shadows never do. So you see, you're never alone"—his voice cracked—"no matter where you are, or when, no matter if the sun is up, or the moon is full, or there's nothing but stars in the sky, no matter if you have a light in hand, or none at all, you know . . . Anisa? Anisa, stay with me . . . please . . ."

Over the next hour, the sickness burned through her, until she called him father, called him mother, called him Berras. Until she stopped speaking altogether, even in her fevered sleep, and sank deeper, to somewhere dreamless. The shadows hadn't won, but the spring green light of Anisa's own magic was fading, fading, like a fire burning itself out, and all Alucard could do was watch.

He got to his feet. The cabin swayed beneath him as he went to the mantel to pour himself a drink.

Alucard caught his reflection in the ruddy surface of the wine and frowned, tipping the glass. The smudge over his brow, where Lila had streaked a bloody finger across his skin, was gone. Rubbed away by Anisa's fevered hand, or maybe Berras's attack.

How strange, he thought. He hadn't even noticed.

The cabin swayed again before Alucard realized it wasn't the floor tipping.

It was him.

No, thought Alucard, just before the voice slid inside his head.

Let me in, it said as his hands began to tremble. The glass slipped and shattered on the cabin floor.

Let me in.

He braced himself against the mantel, eyes squeezed shut against the creeping vines of the curse as they wound through him, blood and bone.

Let me in.

"No!" he snarled aloud, slamming the doors of his mind and forcing the darkness back. Until then, the voice had been a whisper, soft, insistent, the pulse of magic a gentle but persistent guest knocking at the door. Now, it forced its way in with all its might, prying open the edges of Alucard's mind until the cabin fell away and he was back in the Emery Estate, their father before him, the man's hands brimming with fire. Heat burned along Alucard's cheek from the first lingering blow.

"A disgrace," snarled Reson Emery, the heat of his anger and magic both forcing Alucard back against the wall.

"Father—"

"You've made a fool of yourself. Of your name. Of your house." His hand wrapped around the silver feather that hung from Alucard's neck, flame licking his skin. "And it ends now," he rumbled, tearing the sigil of House Emery from Alucard's throat. It melted in his grip, drops of silver hitting the floor like blood, but when Alucard looked up again, the man standing before him was and was not his father. The image of Reson Emery flickered, replaced by a man made of darkness from head to toe, if darkness were solid and black and caught the light like stone. A crown glittered on the outline of his head.

"I can be merciful," said the dark king, "if you beg."

Alucard straightened. *"No."*

The room rocked violently, and he stumbled forward onto his knees in a cold stone cell, held down as his manacled wrists were forced onto the carved iron block. Embers crackled as the matching poker prodded the fire, and smoke burned Alucard's lungs when he tried to breathe. A man pulled the poker from the coals, its end a violent red, and again Alucard saw the carved features of the king.

"Beg," said Osaron, bringing the iron to rest against the chains.

Alucard clenched his teeth, and would not.

"Beg," said Osaron, as the chains grew hot.

As the heat peeled away flesh, Alucard's refusal became a single, drawn-out scream.

He tore backward, suddenly free, and found himself standing in the hall again, no king, no father, only Anisa, barefoot in a nightgown, holding a burned wrist, their father's fingers like a cuff circling her skin.

"Why would you leave me in this place?" she asked.

And before he could answer, Alucard was dragged back into the cell, his brother Berras now holding the iron and smiling while his brother's skin burned. "You should never have come back."

Around and around it went, memories searing through flesh and muscle, mind and soul.

"Stop," he pleaded.

"Let me in," said Osaron.

"I can be true," said his sister.

"I can be merciful," said his father.

"I can be just," said his brother.

"If you only *let us in*."

VI

"Your Majesty?"

The city was falling.

"Your Majesty?"

The darkness was spreading.

"Maxim."

The king looked up and saw Isra, clearly waiting for an answer to a question he hadn't heard. Maxim turned his attention to the map of London one last time, with its spreading shadows, its black river. How was he supposed to fight a god, or a ghost, or whatever this *thing* was?

Maxim growled, and pushed forcefully away from the table. "I cannot stand here, safe within my palace, while my kingdom dies." Isra barred his way.

"You cannot go out there, either."

"Move aside."

"What good will it do your kingdom, if you die with it? Since when is solidarity a victory of any kind?" Few people would speak to Maxim Maresh with such candor, but Isra had been with him since before he was king, had fought beside him on the Blood Coast so many years ago, when Maxim was a general and Isra his second, his friend, his shadow. "You are thinking like a soldier instead of a king."

Maxim turned away, raking a hand through his coarse black hair.

No, he was thinking *too much* like a king. One who'd been softened by so many years of peace. One whose battles were now fought in ballrooms and in stadium seats with words and wine instead of steel.

How would they have fought Osaron back on the Blood Coast?

How would they have fought him if he were a foe of flesh and blood? With cunning, thought Maxim.

But that was the difference between magic and men—the latter made *mistakes*.

Maxim shook his head.

This monster was magic with a mind attached, and minds could be tricked, bent, even broken. Even the best fighters had flaws in their stance, chinks in their armor . . .

"Move aside, Isra."

"Your Majesty—"

"I've no intention of walking out into the fog," he said. "You know me better than that," he added. "If I fall, I will fall fighting."

Isra frowned but let him pass.

Maxim left the map room, turning not toward the gallery, but away, through the palace and up the stairs to the royal chambers. He crossed the room without pausing to look at the welcoming bed, the grand wood desk with its inlaid gold, the basin of clear water and the decanters of wine.

He'd hoped, selfishly, to find Emira here, but the room was empty.

Maxim knew that if he called for her, she would come, would help in any way she could to ease the burden of what he had to do next—whether that meant working the magic with him, or simply pressing her cool hands to his brow, sliding her fingers through his hair the way she had when they were young, humming songs that worked like spells.

Emira was the ice to Maxim's fire, the cool bath in which to temper his steel. She made him stronger.

But he did not call her.

Instead, he crossed alone to the far wall of the royal chamber where, half hidden by swaths of gossamer and silk, there stood a door.

Maxim brought all ten fingertips to the hollow wood and reached for the metal laid within. He rotated both hands against the door and felt the shift of cogs, the clunk of pins sliding free, others sliding home. It was no simple lock, no combination to be turned, but Maxim Maresh had built this door, and he was the only one who ever opened it.

He'd caught Rhy trying once, when the prince was just a boy.

The prince had a fondness for discovering secrets, whether they belonged to a person or a palace, and the moment he discovered that the door was locked he must have gone and found Kell, dragged the black-eyed boy—still new to his benign breed of mischief—back up into the royal chamber. Maxim had walked in on the two, Rhy urging Kell on as the latter lifted wary fingers to the wood.

Maxim had crossed the room at the sound of sliding metal and caught the boy's hand before the door could open. It wasn't a matter of ability. Kell was getting stronger by the day, his magic blooming like a spring tree, but even the young *Antari*—perhaps the young *Antari* most of all—needed to know that power had its limits.

That rules were meant to be obeyed.

Rhy had sulked and stormed, but Kell had said nothing as Maxim ushered them out. They had always been like that, so different in temper, Rhy's hot and quick to burn, Kell's cold and slow to thaw. Strange, thought Maxim, unlocking the door, in some ways Kell and the queen were so alike.

There was nothing *forbidden* about the chamber beyond. It was simply private. And when you were king, privacy was precious, more so than any gem.

Now Maxim descended the short stone flight into his study. The room was cool and dry and traced with metal, the shelves lined with only a few books, but a hundred memories, tokens. Not of his life in the palace—Emira's gold wedding rose, Rhy's first crown, a portrait of Rhy and Kell in the seasons courtyard—those were all kept in the royal chamber. There were relics of another time, another life.

A half-burned banner and a pair of swords, long and thin as stalks of wheat.

A gleaming helm, not gold, but burnished metal, traced with bands of ruby.

A stone arrowhead Isra had freed from his side in their last battle on the Blood Coast.

Suits of armor stood sentry against the walls, faceless masks tipped down, and in this sanctuary, Maxim threw off the elegant gold-and-crimson cloak, unfastened the chalice pins that held his tunic cuffs, set aside his crown. Piece by piece he shed his kingship, and called up the man he'd been before.

An Tol Vares, they'd called him.

The Steel Prince.

It had been so long since Maxim Maresh had worn that mantle, but there were tasks for kings and tasks for soldiers, and now the latter rolled up his sleeves, took up a knife, and began to work.

VII

The difference of a single day, thought Rhy, standing alone before the windows as the sun rose. One day. A matter of hours. A world of change.

Two days ago, Kell had disappeared, and Rhy had carved five letters into his arm to bring him home. *Sorry.* The cuts were fresh on his skin, the word still burned with movement, and yet it felt like a lifetime ago.

Yesterday his brother had come home, and been arrested, and the prince had fought to see Kell freed, only to lose him again, to lose himself, to lose everything.

And wake to this.

We heard, we heard, we heard.

In darkness, the change was hard to see, but the thin winter light revealed a terrifying scene.

Only hours before, London had brimmed with the cheers of the *Essen Tasch,* the rippling pennants of the final magicians as they fought in the central arena.

Now, all three stadiums floated like sullen corpses on the blackened river, the only sound the steady chant of morning bells coming from the Sanctuary. Bodies bobbed like apples on the surface of the Isle, and dozens—hundreds—more knelt along the riverbank, forming an eerie border. Others moved in packs through the streets of London, searching for those who hadn't fallen, hadn't knelt before the shadow king. The difference of a single day.

He felt his brother coming.

Strange, the way that worked. He'd always been able to tell when Kell was near—sibling intuition—but these days he felt his brother's presence like a cord in reverse, drawing tight instead of slack whenever they were close.

Now the tension thrummed.

The echo in Rhy's chest grew stronger as Kell stepped into the room. He paused in the doorway.

"Do you want to be alone?"

"I am never alone," said the prince absently, and then, forcing himself to brighten, "but I *am* still alive." Kell swallowed, and Rhy could see the apology climbing his brother's throat. "Don't," he said, cutting him off. His attention went back to the world beyond the glass. "What happens, after we put them all to sleep?"

"We force Osaron to face us. And we beat him."

"How?"

"I have a plan."

Rhy raised his fingertips to the glass. On the other side, the fog drew itself into a hand, brushed the window, and then pulled away, collapsing back into mist.

"Is this how a world dies?" he asked.

"I hope not."

"Personally," said Rhy with sudden, hollow lightness, "I'm rather done with dying. It's begun to lose its charm."

Kell shrugged out of his coat and sank into a chair. "Do you know what happened?"

"I know what Mother told me, which means I know what you told her."

"Do you want to know the truth?"

Rhy hesitated. "If it will help you to say it."

Kell tried to smile, failed, and shook his head. "What do you remember?"

Rhy's gaze danced over the city. "Nothing," he said, though in truth, he remembered the pain, and the absence of pain, the darkness like still water folding over him, and a voice, trying to pull him back.

You cannot die . . . I've come so far.

"Have you seen Alucard?"

Kell shrugged. "I assume he's in the gallery," he answered, in a way that said he really didn't care.

Rhy's chest tightened. "You're probably right."

But Rhy knew he wasn't. He had already scanned the Grand Hall as he passed through, searching, searching. The foyer, the ballrooms, the library. Rhy had scoured every room for that familiar shine of silver and blue, the sun-kissed hair, the glint of a sapphire, and found a hundred faces, some known and others foreign, and none of them Alucard.

"He'll turn up," added Kell absently. "He always does."

Just then a shout went up, not from outside, but from within the palace. The crash of doors bursting open somewhere below, a Veskan accent clashing with an Arnesian one.

"*Sanct,*" snarled Kell, shoving himself to his feet. "If the darkness doesn't kill them, their tempers will."

His brother plunged out of the room without looking back, and Rhy stood alone for a long moment, shadows whispering against the glass, before he grabbed Kell's coat, found the nearest hidden door, and slipped through.

The city—*his* city—was full of shadows.

Rhy pulled Kell's coat close about his shoulders and wrapped a scarf around his nose and mouth, the way one might before braving a fire, as if a strip of cloth could keep the magic out. He held his breath as he plunged forward into the sea of fog, but when his body met the shadows, they recoiled, granting Rhy a berth of several feet.

He looked around and, for a moment, felt as if he were a man expecting to drown, only to find the water two feet deep.

And then Rhy stopped thinking altogether, and ran.

Chaos blossomed all around him, the air a tangled mess of sound and fear and smoke. Men and women were trying to drag their neighbors toward the black stretch of the river. Some people staggered and fell, attacked by invisible foes, while others hid behind bolted doors and tried to ward the walls with water, earth, sand, blood.

Still, Rhy moved like a ghost among them. Unseen. Unsensed. No footsteps followed him through the streets. No hands sought to drag him into the river. No mobs tried to sicken him with shadow.

The poisoned fog parted for the prince, slipped around him like water around a stone.

Was it Kell's life shielding him from harm? Or was it the absence of Rhy's own? The fact that there was nothing left for the darkness to claim?

"Get inside," he called to the fevered, but they could not hear him.

"Get back," he shouted at the fallen, but they did not listen.

The madness surged around him, and Rhy tore himself away from the breaking city and turned his sights again to his quest for the captain of the *Night Spire*.

There were only two places Alucard Emery would go: his family estate or his ship.

Logic said he'd go to the house, but something in Rhy's gut sent him in the opposite direction, toward the docks.

He found the captain on his cabin floor.

One of the chairs by the hearth had been toppled, a table knocked clean of glasses, their glittering shards scattered in the rug and across the wooden floor. Alucard—decisive, strong, beautiful Alucard—lay curled on his side, shivering with fever, his warm brown hair matted to his cheeks with sweat. He was clutching his head, breath escaping in ragged gasps as he spoke to ghosts.

"Stop . . . please . . ." His voice—that even, clear voice, always brimming with laughter—broke. "Don't make me . . ."

Rhy was on his knees beside him. "Luc," he said, touching the man's shoulder.

Alucard's eyes flashed open, and Rhy recoiled when he saw them filled with shadows. Not the even black of Kell's gaze, but instead menacing streaks of darkness that writhed and coiled like snakes through his vision, storm blue irises flashing and vanishing behind the fog.

"*Stop*," snarled the captain suddenly. He struggled up, limbs shaking, only to fall back against the floor.

Rhy hovered over him, helpless, unsure whether to hold him down or try to help him up. Alucard's eyes found his, but looked straight through him. He was somewhere else.

"Please," the captain pleaded with the ghosts. "Don't make me go."

"I won't," said Rhy, wondering who Alucard saw. What he saw. How to free him. The captain's veins stood out like ropes against his skin.

"He'll never forgive me."

"Who?" asked Rhy, and Alucard's brow furrowed, as if he were trying to see through the fog, the fever.

"Rhy—" The sickness tightened its hold, the shadows in his eyes streaking with lines of light like lightning. The captain bit back a scream.

Rhy ran his fingers over Alucard's hair, took his face in his hands. "Fight it," he ordered. "Whatever's holding you, *fight it*."

Alucard folded in on himself, shuddering. "I can't. . . ."

"Focus on me."

"Rhy . . ." he sobbed.

"I'm here." Rhy Maresh lowered himself onto the glass-strewn floor, lay on his side so they were face-to-face. "I'm here."

He remembered, then. Like a dream flickering back to the surface, he remembered Alucard's hands on his shoulders, his voice cutting through the pain, reaching out to him, even in the dark.

I'm here now, he'd said, *so you can't die.*

"I'm here now," echoed Rhy, twining his fingers through Alucard's. "And I'm not letting go, so don't you dare."

Another scream tore from Alucard's throat, his grip tightening as the lines of black on his skin began to glow. First red, then white. Burning. He was burning from the inside out. And it hurt—hurt to watch, hurt to feel so helpless.

But Rhy kept his word.

He didn't let go.

VIII

Kell stormed toward the western foyer, following the sounds of a brewing fight.

It was only a matter of time before the mood in the palace turned. Before the magicians refused to sit and wait and watch the city fall. Before someone took it in their head to act.

He threw open the doors and found Hastra standing before the western entrance, royal short sword clutched in both hands, looking like a cat facing down a line of wolves.

Brost, Losen, and Sar.

Three of the tournament's magicians—two Arnesians and a Veskan—competitors now aligned against a common foe. Kell expected as much from Brost and Sar, two fighters with tempers to match their size, but Kisimyr's protégé, Losen, was built like a willow, known for his looks as much as his budding talent. Gold rings jingled in his black hair, and he looked out of place between the two oaks. But bruises stained the skin beneath his dark eyes, and his face was grey from grief and lack of sleep.

"Get out of the way," demanded Brost.

Hastra stood resolute. "I cannot let you pass."

"On whose orders?" snapped Losen, his voice hoarse.

"The royal guard. The city guard. The king."

"What is this?" demanded Kell, striding toward them.

"Stay out of it, *Antari*," snarled Sar without turning. She stood even taller than Brost, her Veskan form filling the hall, a pair of axes strapped to her back. She'd fallen to Lila in the opening round, spent the rest of the tournament sulking and drinking, but now her eyes were full of fire.

Kell stopped at their backs, relying on their fighters' instincts to make them turn. It worked, and through the forest of their limbs, he saw Hastra slump back against the doors.

Kell took in Losen first. "It won't bring Kisimyr back."

The young magician flushed with indignation. Sweat prickled on his brow, and he swayed a little when he spoke. "Did you see what that monster did to her?" he said, voice slurring. "I have to—"

"No you don't," said Kell.

"Kisimyr would have—"

"Kisimyr tried, and lost," said Kell grimly.

"You can stay here, hiding in your palace," growled Brost, "but our friends are out there! Our families!"

"And your bravado cannot help them."

"Veskans do not sit idly by and wait for death," boomed Sar.

"No," said Kell, "your pride carries you right to it."

She bared her teeth. "We will not hide like cowards in this place."

"This place is the only thing keeping you safe."

The air was beginning to shimmer with heat around Brost's clenched hands. "You cannot keep us here."

"Believe me," said Kell, "there are a dozen other people I'd rather keep, but you were the only ones lucky enough to be in the palace when the curse fell."

"And now our city needs us," roared Brost. "We're the best it has."

Kell curled his hand, pricking the base of his palm with the point of metal he kept against his wrist. He felt the sting, the heat of blood welling on his skin.

"You're show ponies," he said. "Meant to prance in a ring, and if you think that's the same thing as battling magic, you're sorely mistaken."

"How dare you—" started Brost.

"Master Kell could fell you all with a single drop of blood," announced Hastra from behind them.

Kell stared at the young man with bald surprise.

"I've heard the royal *Antari* has no teeth," cut in Sar.

"We don't want to hurt you, little prince," said Brost.

"But we will," muttered Losen.

"Hastra," said Kell evenly, "leave."

The young man hesitated, torn between abandoning Kell and defying him, but in the end, he obeyed. The eyes of the magicians flicked toward him as he passed, and in that instant, Kell moved.

A breath, and he was behind them, one hand raised to the outer doors.

"*As Staro,*" he said. The locks within the door fell with a heavy clank, and fresh steel bars spread back and forth over the wood, sealing the doors shut.

"Now," said Kell, holding out his bloodied hand, palm up, as if to offer it. "Go back to the gallery."

Losen's eyes widened, but Brost's temper was too high, and Sar was lusting for a fight. When none of them moved, Kell sighed. "I want you to remember," he said, "that I gave you a chance."

It was over quickly.

Within moments, Brost sat on the floor, clutching his face, Losen slumped against the wall, holding bruised ribs, and Sar was out cold, the tails of her blond braids singed black.

The hall was a little worse for wear, but Kell had managed to keep most of the damage confined to the bodies of the three magicians.

Drawn by the noise, the inner doors flew open, and the doorway filled with people—some magicians, others nobles, all straining to see into the foyer. Three magicians laid out, and Kell standing at their center. Just what he needed. A scene. The whispers were starting, and Kell could feel the weight of eyes and words as they landed on him.

"Do you yield?" he asked the crumpled forms, unsure which exactly he was addressing.

A huddle of Faroans looked rather amused as Brost struggled to his feet, still clutching his nose.

A pair of Veskans went to rouse Sar, and while most of the Arnesians hung back, Jinnar, the wind mage with the silver hair, went straight to Losen and helped the grieving youth to his feet.

"Come on," he said, his voice slower and softer than Kell had ever heard it. Tears were streaming silently down Losen's cheeks, and Kell knew they didn't stem from bruised ribs or wounded pride.

"I didn't reach for her on the roof," he murmured. "I didn't . . ."

Kell knelt to clean a drop of blood from the marble floor before it stained, and heard the king's heavy steps before he saw the crowd part around him, Hastra on his heels.

"Master Kell," said Maxim, sweeping his gaze over the scene. "I'll thank you not to bring down the palace." But Kell could sense the approval lacing the king's words. Better a show of strength than a tolerance of weakness.

"Apologies, Your Majesty," said Kell, bowing his head.

The king turned on his heel, and that was that. A mutiny subdued. An instant of chaos restored to order.

Kell knew as well as Maxim how important that was right now, with the city clinging to every shred of power, every sign of strength. As soon as the magicians had been led or carried out, and the hall emptied of spectators, he slumped into a chair along the wall, its cushion still smoking faintly from the incident. He patted it out, then looked up to find his former guard still standing there, warm eyes wide beneath his cap of sun-kissed hair.

"No need to thank me," said Kell, waving his hand.

"It's not that," said Hastra. "I mean, I'm grateful, sir, of course. But . . ."

Kell had a sickening feeling in his stomach. "What is it now?"

"The queen is asking for the prince."

"Last time I checked," said Kell, "that wasn't me."

Hastra looked to the floor, to the wall, to the ceiling, before mustering the courage to look at him again. "I know, sir," he said slowly. "But I can't *find* him."

Kell had felt the blow coming, but it still struck. "You've searched the palace?"

"Pillar to spire, sir."

"Is anyone else missing?"

A hesitation, and then, "Captain Emery."

Kell swore under his breath.

Have you seen Alucard? Rhy had asked, staring out the palace windows. Would he know if the prince had been infected? Would he feel the dark magic swarming in his blood?

"How long?" asked Kell, already moving toward the prince's chambers.

"I'm not certain," said Hastra. "An hour, maybe a little more."

"*Sanct.*"

Kell burst into Rhy's rooms, taking up the prince's gold pin from the table and jabbing it into his thumb, harder than necessary. He hoped that wherever Rhy was, he felt the prick of metal and knew that Kell was coming.

"Should I tell the king?" asked Hastra.

"You came to me," said Kell, "because you have more sense than that."

He knelt, drawing a circle in blood on Rhy's floor, and pressed his palm flat, the gold pin between flesh and polished wood. "Guard the door," he said, and then, to the mark itself, and the magic within, "*As Tascen Rhy.*"

The floor fell away, the palace vanished, replaced by an instant of darkness and then, just as swiftly, by a room. The ground rocked gently beneath his feet, and Kell knew before taking in the wooden walls, the portal windows, that he was on a ship.

He found the two of them lying on the floor, foreheads pressed together and fingers intertwined. Alucard's eyes were closed, but Rhy's were open, gaze fixed on the captain's face.

Anger rose in Kell's throat.

"Sorry to interrupt," he snapped, "but this is hardly the time for a lover's—"

Rhy silenced Kell with a look. The amber in his eyes was shot with red, and that's when Kell noticed how pale the captain was, how still.

For a second, he thought Alucard Emery was dead.

Then the captain's eyes drifted wearily open. Bruises stood out beneath them, giving him the gaunt look of a person who'd been ill for a very long time. And something was wrong with his skin. In the low cabin light, silver—not molten bright, but the dull shine of scarred flesh—ribboned at his wrists, his collar, his throat. It traced paths up his cheeks like tears, flashed at his temples. Threads of light that traced the paths where the blue of veins should be, had been.

But there was no curse in his eyes.

Alucard Emery had survived Osaron's magic.

He was alive—and when he spoke, he was still his infuriating self.

"You could have knocked," he said, but his voice was hoarse, his words weak, and Kell saw the darkness in Rhy's expression—not the product of any spell, only fear. How bad had it gotten? How close had he been?

"We have to go," said Kell. "Can Emery stand, or . . ." His voice trailed off as his eyesight sharpened. Across the cabin, something had moved.

A shape, piled on the captain's bed, sat up.

It was a girl. Dark hair fell around her face in sleep-messed waves, but it was her eyes that stilled him. They were not curse-darkened. They were nothing. They were empty.

"Anisa?" started Alucard, struggling to get to his feet. The name stirred something in Kell. A memory of reading scrolls, tucked next to Rhy, in the Maresh library.

Anisa Emery, twelfth in line to the throne, the third child of Reson, and Alucard's younger sister.

"Stay back," ordered Kell, barring the captain's path but keeping his gaze on the girl.

Kell had seen death before, witnessed the moment when a person ceased to be a person and became simply a body, the flame of life extinguished, leaving only a shell. It was as much a feeling as a sight, the sense of missing.

Staring at Anisa Emery, Kell had the horrible sense that he was already looking at a corpse.

But corpses didn't stand.

And she did.

The girl swung her legs out of bed, and when her bare feet hit the floor, the wooden boards began to petrify, color leaching out of the timber as it withered, decayed. Her heart glowed through her chest like a coal.

When she tried to speak, no sound came out, only the crackling of embers, as the thing in her continued to burn.

Kell knew that the girl was already gone.

"Nis?" said her brother again, stepping toward her. "Can you hear me?"

Kell caught the captain's arm and hauled him back just as the girl's fingers brushed Alucard's sleeve. The fabric greyed under her touch. Kell shoved Alucard into Rhy's arms and turned back toward Anisa, reaching out to hold her at bay with his will, and when that didn't work—it wasn't *her* will he was fighting, not anymore, but the will of a monster, a ghost, a self-made god—he bent the ship around them, wood peeling away from the cabin walls to bar her path. She was disappearing from them, board by board, and then suddenly Kell realized he was warring with a second will—Alucard's.

"Stop!" shouted the captain, struggling against Rhy's grip. "We can't leave her, I can't leave her, not again—"

Kell turned and punched Alucard Emery in the stomach.

The captain doubled over, gasping, and Kell knelt before them, quickly drew a second circle on the cabin floor.

"Rhy, now," said Kell, and as soon as the prince's hand met his shoulder, he said the words. The burning girl vanished, the cabin fell away, and they were back in Rhy's room, crouched on the prince's inlaid floors.

Hastra wilted in relief at the sight of them, but Alucard was already fighting to his feet, Rhy straining to hold him back, murmuring "*Solase, solase, solase*" over and over.

I'm sorry, I'm sorry, I'm sorry.

Alucard grabbed Kell by the collar, eyes wide and desperate. "Take me back."

Kell shook his head. "There's no one left on that ship."

"My sister—"

He gripped Alucard's shoulders hard. "Listen to me," he said. "There's *no one left*."

It must have finally registered, because the fight went out of Alucard Emery. He slumped back onto the nearest sofa, shaking.

"Kell—" started Rhy.

He rounded on his brother. "And you. You're a fool, do you know that? After everything we've been through, you just walked outside? You could have been killed. You could have been poisoned. It's a miracle you didn't fall ill."

"No," said Rhy slowly, "I don't think it is."

Before Kell could stop him, the prince was at the balcony, unlatching the doors. Hastra surged forward, but it was too late. Rhy threw open the doors and stepped out into the fog, Kell reaching him just in time to see the shadows meet the prince's skin—and pull away.

Rhy reached toward the nearest one, and it recoiled from his touch. Kell did the same. Again, the tendrils of Osaron's magic retreated.

"My life is yours," said Rhy softly, thoughtfully. "And yours is mine." He looked up. "It makes sense."

Footsteps, and then Alucard was there beside them. Kell and Rhy both turned to stop him from stepping out, but the shadows were already pulling away.

"You must be immune," said Rhy.

Alucard looked down at his hands, considering the scars that traced his veins. "And to think, all I had to give up were my good looks."

Rhy managed a ghost of a smile. "I rather like the silver."

Alucard raised a brow. "Do you? Maybe it will start a trend."

Kell rolled his eyes. "If you two are done," he said, "we should show the king."

IX

There were moments when Lila wondered how the hell she'd gotten here.

Which steps—and missteps—she'd taken. A year ago she'd been a thief in another London. A month ago she'd been a pirate, sailing on the open seas. A week ago she'd been a magician in the *Essen Tasch*. And now she was this. *Antari*. Alone, and not alone. Severed, but not adrift. There were too many lives tangled up in hers. Too many people to care about, and once again, she didn't know whether to stay or to run—but the choice would have to wait, because this city was dying and she wanted to save it. And maybe that was a sign she'd already chosen. For now.

Lila looked around the Sanctuary cell, with nothing but its cot and the symbols on the floor. Lila had been here once before, a dying prince draped around her shoulders. The Sanctuary had seemed cold and remote even then, but it was colder now. The hall beyond, once quiet, sat deathly still, her breath the only motion in the air. Pale light burned in sconces along the walls with a steadiness she'd come to recognize as spelled. A gust tore through, strong enough to rustle her coat, but the wind barely stirred the torches. The priests were all gone, most taking refuge while holding up the wards at the palace, and the rest scattered through the city, lost in the fog. Strange, she thought, that they weren't immune, but she supposed that being closer to magic wasn't always a good thing. Not when magic played the devil as well as god.

The Sanctuary's silence felt unnatural—she'd spent years slipping through crowds, carving out privacy in tight quarters. Now, she moved alone through a place meant for dozens, hundreds, a church of sorts that felt wrong without its worshippers, without the soft and steady warmth of their combined magic.

Only stillness, and the voice—voices?—beyond the building urging her to *Come out, come out, or let me in.*

Lila shivered, unnerved, and began to sing beneath her breath as she made her way up the stairs.

"How do you know that the Sarows is coming. . . ."

At the top, the main hall, with its vaulting ceilings and stone pillars, all of it carved from the same flecked stone. Between the columns sat large basins carved from smooth white wood, each brimming with water, flowers, or fine sand. Lila ran her fingers through the water as she walked by, an instinctive benediction, a buried memory from a childhood a world away.

Her steps echoed in the cavernous space, and she cringed, shifting her stride back into that of a thief, soundless even on the stone. The hair bristled on the back of her neck as she crossed the hall and—

A thud, like stone against wood. It came once, and then again, and again.

Someone was knocking on the Sanctuary door.

Lila stood there, uncertain what to do.

"Alos mas en," cried a voice. *Let me in.* Through the heavy wood, she couldn't tell if it belonged to a man or a woman, but either way, they were making too much noise. She'd seen the riots in the streets, the mobs of shadow-eyed men and women attacking those who hadn't fallen, those who tried to fight, drawn to their struggle like cats to mice. And she didn't need them coming *here.*

"Dammit," she growled, storming toward the doors.

They were locked, and she had to lean half her weight on the iron to make it move, knife between her teeth. When the bolt finally slid free and the Sanctuary doors fell open, a man scrambled in, falling to his knees on the stone floor.

"Rensa tav, rensa tav," he stammered breathlessly as Lila forced the doors shut again behind him and spit the blade back into her palm.

She turned, bracing for a fight, but he was still kneeling there, head bowed, and apologizing to the floor.

"I shouldn't have come," he said.

"Probably not," said Lila, "but you're here now."

At the sound of her voice, the intruder's head jerked up, his hood tumbling back to reveal a narrow face with wide eyes unspelled.

Her knife fell back to her side. *"Lenos?"*

The *Spire*'s second mate stared up at her. "Bard?"

Lila half expected Lenos to scramble away in fear—he'd always treated her like an open flame, something that might burn him at any moment if he got too close—but his face was merely a mask of shock. Shock, and gratitude. He let out a sob of relief, and didn't even recoil when she hauled him to his feet, though he stared at the place where their hands met even as he said, *"Tas ira . . ."*

Your eye.

"It's been a long night. . . ." Lila glanced at the light streaming in through the windows. "Day. How did you know I was here?"

"I didn't," he said, head ticking side to side in his nervous way. "But when the bells rang, I thought that maybe one of the priests . . ."

"Sorry to disappoint."

"Is the captain safe?"

Lila hesitated. She hadn't seen Alucard, not since marking his forehead, but before she could say as much, the knocking came again at the door. Lila and Lenos spun.

"Let me in," said a new voice.

"Were you alone?" she whispered.

Lenos nodded.

"Let me in," it continued, strangely steady.

Lila and Lenos took a step away from the doors. They were solid, the bolts strong, the Sanctuary supposedly warded against dark magic, but she didn't know how long any of that would hold without the priests.

"Let's go," she said. Lila had a thief's memory, and Tieren's map unfolded in her mind in full detail, revealing the halls, the cells, the study. Lenos followed close at her heels, his lips moving soundlessly in some kind of prayer.

He'd always been the religious one aboard the ship, praying at the first sign of bad weather, the start and end of every journey. She had no idea what or who he was praying *to*. The rest of the crew indulged him, but none of them seemed to put much stock in it, either. Lila assumed that magic was to people here what God was to Christians, and she'd never believed in God, but even if she had, she thought it pretty foolish to think He had time to lend a hand to every rocking ship. And yet . . .

"Lenos," she said slowly, "how are you all right?"

He looked down at himself, as if he wasn't entirely sure. Then he drew a talisman from beneath his shirt. Lila stiffened at the sight of it—the symbol on the front was badly worn, but it had the same curling edges as the sigil on the black stone, and looking at it gave her the same hot-and-cold feeling. In the very center of the talisman, trapped in a bead of glass, hung a single drop of blood.

"My grandmother," he explained, "Helina. She was—"

"*Antari,*" cut in Lila.

He nodded. "Magic doesn't get passed on," he said, "so her power's never done me much good." He looked down at the necklace. "Until now." The knocking continued, growing softer as they walked. "The pendant was supposed to go to my older brother, Tanik, but he didn't want it, said it was just a useless trinket, so it went to me."

"Perhaps the gods of magic favor you after all," she said, scanning the halls to either side.

"Perhaps," said Lenos, half to himself.

Lila took the second left and found herself at the doors to the library. They were closed.

"Well," she said, "you're either lucky or blessed. Take your pick."

Lenos cracked a nervous smile. "Which would *you* choose?"

Ear to the wood, she listened for signs of life. Nothing.

"Me?" she said, pushing open the doors. "I'd choose clever."

The doors gave way onto rows of tables, books still open on top, pages rustling faintly in the drafty room.

At the back of the library, beyond the final set of shelves, she found Tieren's study. A towering pile of scrolls sat on the desk. Pots of ink and books lined the walls. A cabinet stood open, showing shelf after shelf of glass jars.

"Watch the door," she said, her fingers tripping over the tinctures and herbs as she squinted at the names, written in a kind of shorthand Arnesian she couldn't read. She sniffed one that looked like it held oil before tipping the mouth of the bottle against the pad of her thumb.

Tyger, Tyger, she sang to herself, stirring the power in her veins, unsheathing it the way she would a knife. She snapped her fingers, and a small flame burst to life in her hand. In its flickering light, Lila scanned the list of supplies, and got to work.

"I think that's it," she said, shouldering the canvas bag. Scrolls threatened to spill out, and vials clattered softly inside, bottles of blood and ink, herbs and sand and other things the names of which made no sense. In addition to Tieren's list, she'd nicked a flask of something called "sleep sweet" and a tiny ampule marked "seer's tea," but she'd left the rest, feeling quite impressed with her restraint.

Lenos stood by the doors, one hand against the wood, and she didn't know if he needed support or was simply listening, the way a sailor sometimes did to a coming storm, not with sound but touch.

"Someone is still knocking," he said softly. "And I think there are more of them now."

Which meant they couldn't go out, not the way they'd come, not without trouble. Lila stepped into the hall and looked around at the branching paths, summoning to mind the map and wishing she'd had time to study more than her own intended path. She snapped her fingers. Fire came to life in her palm, and she held her breath as the flame settled, then began to dance subtly. Lila took off, Lenos on her heels as she followed the draft.

Behind them came the short sound of something rolling from a high shelf.

Lila spun, fire flaring in her hand, in time see the stone orb shatter on the floor.

She braced for an attack that never came. Instead, only a pair of familiar amethyst eyes caught the light.

"Esa?"

Alucard's cat crept forward, hackles raised, but the moment she made toward it, the creature shied away, obviously spooked, and darted through the nearest open door. Lila swore under her breath. She thought of letting it go—she hated the cat, and she was pretty sure the feeling was mutual—but maybe it knew another way out.

Lila and Lenos followed the cat through one door and then a second, the rooms around them turning cold enough to frost. Beyond the third open door they found a kind of cloister, open to the morning air. A dozen arches led onto a garden, not groomed like the rest of the Sanctuary, but wild—a tangle of trees, some winter dead and others summer green. It reminded her of the palace courtyard where she'd found Rhy the day before, only without a shred of order. Flowers bloomed and vines snaked across the path, and beyond the garden—

But beyond the garden, there was *nothing*.

No arches. No doors. The cloisters faced the river, and somewhere beyond the wild foliage, the garden simply ended, dropping away into shadow.

"Esa?" she called, but the cat had darted between hedges and was nowhere to be seen. Lila shivered and swore at the sudden, cutting cold. She was already turning back toward the doors, but she could see the question in Lenos's eyes. The whole crew knew how much the stupid cat meant to Alucard. He'd once jokingly told her that it was a talisman he kept his heart inside, but he'd also confessed that Esa was a gift from his beloved younger sister. Maybe in a way, both were true.

Lila swore and slung the satchel into Lenos's arms. "Stay here."

She turned her collar up against the cold and stormed into the garden, stepping over wild vines and ducking low branches. It was probably some kind of metaphor for the chaos of the natural world—she could almost hear Tieren lecturing her on treading lightly as she drew her sharpest knife and hacked an obnoxious vine aside.

"Here, Esa," she called. She was halfway through the garden when she realized she could no longer see the path ahead. Or behind. It was as though she'd stepped out of London entirely, into a world made of nothing but mist.

"Come back, kitty," she muttered, reaching the garden's edge, "or I swear to god I will throw you into the . . ." Lila trailed off. The garden ended abruptly in front of her, roots trailing onto a platform of pale stone. And at the platform's edge, just as she'd thought, there was no wall, no barrier. Only a sheer drop into the black slick of the Isle below.

"Haven't you heard?"

Lila spun toward the voice and found a girl no taller than her waist standing between her and the garden's edge. A novice dressed in white Sanctuary robes, her dark hair pulled cleanly back into a braid. Her eyes swirled with Osaron's magic, and Lila's fingers tightened on her blade. She didn't want to kill the girl. Not if there was some part of her still inside, trying to get out. She didn't want to, but she would.

The little novice craned her head, staring up at the pale sky. Bruised skin ringed her fingernails and drew dark lines up her cheeks. "The king is calling."

"Is that so?" asked Lila, cheating a step toward the garden.

The mist was thickening around them, swallowing the edges of the world. And then, out of nowhere, it began to snow. A flake drifted down, landing on her cheek, and—

Lila winced as a tiny blade of ice nicked her skin.

"What the hell . . ."

The novice giggled as Lila wiped her cheek with the back of her sleeve as all around her, snowflakes sharpened into knifepoints and came raining down. The fire was in Lila's hands before she thought to call it, and she ducked her head as the heat swept around her in a shield, ice melting before it met her skin.

"Nice trick," she muttered, looking up.

But the novice was gone.

An instant later a small, icy hand slid around Lila's wrist.

"Got you!" said the girl, her voice still filled with laughter as shadow poured from her fingers, only to recoil from Lila's skin. The girl's face fell.

"You're one of *them*," she said, disgusted. But instead of letting go, her hand vised tighter. The girl was strong—inhumanly strong—black veins coursing over her skin like ropes, and she dragged Lila away from the garden, toward the place where the Sanctuary ended and the marble fell away. Far below, the river stretched in a still black plane.

"Let go of me," warned Lila.

The novice did not. "He's not happy with you, Delilah Bard."

"Let *go*."

Lila's boots skidded on the slick stone surface. Four strides to the edge of the platform. Three.

"He heard what you said about setting Kell free. And if you don't let him in"—another giggle—"he'll drown you in the sea."

"Well, aren't you creepy," snarled Lila, trying one last time to wrench free. When that didn't work, she drew a knife.

It was barely out of its sheath when another hand, this one massive, caught her wrist and twisted viciously until she dropped the weapon. When Lila turned, trapped now between the two, she found a royal guard, broader than Barron, with a dark beard and the ruined remains of *her* mark on his forehead.

"Have you met the shadow king?" he boomed.

"Oh hell," said Lila as a third figure strode out of the garden. An old woman, barefoot and dressed in nothing but a shimmering nightgown.

"Why won't you let him in?"

Lila had had enough. She threw up her hands and *pushed,* the way she had in the ring so recently. Bodily. Will against will. But whatever these people were made of now, it didn't work. They simply bent around the force. It moved right through them like wind through wheat, and then they were dragging her again toward the precipitous drop.

Two strides.

"I don't want to hurt you," she lied. At that moment, she wanted to hurt them all quite badly, but it wouldn't stop the monster pulling their strings. She scrambled to think of something.

One stride, and she was out of time. Lila's boot connected with the little girl's chest and sent the novice stumbling away. She then flicked her fingers, producing a second knife, and drove it between the joints of the guard's armor at the knee. Lila expected the man to buckle, to scream, to at least *let go*. He did none of those things.

"Oh, come on," she growled as he pushed her half a step toward the edge, the novice and the woman barring her escape.

"The king wants you to pay," said the guard.

"The king wants you to beg," said the girl.

"The king wants you to kneel," said the old woman.

Their voices all had the same horrible singsong quality, and the ledge was coming up against her heels.

"Beg for your city."

"Beg for your world."

"Beg for your life."

"I don't *beg*," growled Lila, slamming her foot into the blade embedded in the guard's knee. At last his leg buckled, but when he went down, he took her with him. Luckily he fell *away* from the ledge, and she rolled free and came up again, the woman's thin arms already winding around her throat. Lila threw her off, into the approaching novice, and danced back several feet from the edge.

Now, at least, she had the garden behind her and not the stone cliff.

But all three attackers were upright again, their eyes full of shadows and their mouths full of Osaron's words. And if Lila ran, they would simply follow.

Her blood sang with the thrill of the fight and her fingers itched to summon fire, but fire only worked if you cared about getting burned. A body without fear would never slow in the face of flame. No, what Lila needed was something of substance. Of weight.

She looked down at the broad stone platform.

It could work.

"He wants me to kneel?" she said, letting her legs fold beneath her, the cold stone hitting her knees. The fallen watched darkly as she pressed both palms to the marble floor and scoured her memory for a piece of Blake—something, anything to center her mind—but then, suddenly Lila realized she didn't *need* the words. She felt for the pulse in the rock and found a steady thrum, like a plucked string.

The fallen were starting toward her again, but it was too late.

Lila caught hold of the threads and pulled.

The ground shook beneath her. The girl and the guard and the old woman looked down as fissures formed like deep roots in the stone floor. A vicious crack ran edge to edge, severing the ledge from the garden, the fallen souls from Delilah Bard. And then it broke, and the three went tumbling down into the river below with a crash and a wave and then nothing.

Lila straightened, breathless, a defiant smile cracking across her lips as a few last bits of rock tumbled free and fell clattering out of sight. Not the most elegant solution, she knew, but effective.

Within the garden, someone was calling her name.

Lenos.

She turned toward him just as a tendril of darkness wrapped around her leg, and *pulled*.

Lila hit the ground hard.

And kept falling.

Sliding.

Shadow was coiled around her ankle like a stubborn vine—no, like a *hand,* dragging her toward the edge. She skidded over the broken ground, scrambling for something, anything to hold on to as the edge came nearer and nearer, and then she was over, and falling, nothing but black river below.

Lila's fingers caught the edge. She held on with all her strength.

The darkness held on too, pulling her down as the broken edge of the stone platform cut into her palms, and blood welled, and only then, when the first drops fell, did the darkness recoil, and let go.

Lila hung there, gasping, forcing her gashed hands to take her weight as she hauled herself up, hooked one boot on the jagged lip and dragged her body up and over.

She rolled onto her back, hands throbbing, gasping for breath.

She was still lying there when Lenos finally arrived.

He looked around at the broken platform, the streaks of blood. His eyes went saucer wide. "What *happened*?"

Lila dragged herself to a sitting position. "Nothing," she muttered, getting to her feet. Blood was still sliding in fat drops down her fingers.

"This is nothing?"

Lila rolled her neck. "Nothing I couldn't handle," she amended.

That's when she noticed the fluffy white mass in his arms. Esa.

"She came when I called," he said shyly. "And I think we found a way out."

FIVE

ASH AND ATONEMENT

I

"Fascinating," said Tieren, turning Alucard's hands over, tracing a bony finger through the air above his silver-scarred wrists. "Does it hurt?"

"No," said Alucard slowly. "Not anymore."

Rhy watched from his perch on the back of the couch, fingers laced to keep them from shaking.

The king and Kell studied Tieren as Tieren studied the captain, spotting the heavy silence with questions that Alucard tried to answer, even though he was clearly still suffering.

He wouldn't say what it was like, only that he'd been delirious, and in that fevered state, the shadow king had tried to get inside his mind. And Rhy did not betray him by saying more. His hands still ached from clenching Alucard's, his body stiff from his time on the *Spire* floor, but if Kell felt that pain, he said nothing of it, and for that, amid so many things, Rhy was grateful.

"So Osaron *does* need permission," said Tieren.

Alucard swallowed. "Most people, I imagine, give it without knowing. The sickness came on fast. By the time I realized what was happening, he was already inside my head. And the moment I tried to resist . . ." Alucard trailed off. Met Rhy's gaze. "He twists your mind, your memories."

"But now," cut in Maxim, "his magic cannot touch you?"

"So it seems."

"Who found you?" he demanded.

Kell shot a look at Hastra, who stepped forward. "I did, Your Majesty," lied the former guard. "I saw him go, and—"

Rhy cut him off. "Hastra didn't find Captain Emery. *I* did."

His brother sighed, exasperated.

His mother went still.

"Where?" demanded Maxim in a voice that had always made Rhy shrink. Now, he held his ground.

"On his ship. By the time I arrived, he was already ill. I stayed with him to see if he'd survive, and he did—"

His father had flushed red, his mother pale. "You went out there, alone," she said. "Into the fog?"

"The shadows did not touch me."

"You put yourself at risk," chided his father.

"I am in no danger."

"You could have been taken."

"You don't get it!" snapped Rhy. "Whatever part of me Osaron could take, it's already gone."

The room went still. He couldn't bring himself to look at Kell. He could feel the quickening of his brother's pulse, the weight of his stare.

And then the door burst open, and Lila Bard stormed in, trailed by a thin, nervous-looking man holding, of all things, a *cat*. She saw—or felt—the tension humming through the room and stopped. "What did I miss?"

Her hands were bandaged, a deep scratch ran along her jaw, and Rhy watched his brother move toward her as naturally as if the world had simply tipped. For Kell, apparently, it had.

"*Casero,*" said the man trailing behind her, his gaunt eyes lighting up at the sight of Alucard. He'd clearly come from beyond the palace, but he showed no signs of harm.

"Lenos," said the captain as the cat leaped down and went to curl around his boot. "Where . . . ?"

"Long story," cut in Lila, tossing the satchel to Tieren, and then, registering the silver scars on Alucard's face: "What happened to *you*?"

"Long story," he echoed.

Lila went to the sideboard to pour herself a drink. "Aren't they all at this point?"

She said it lightly, but Rhy noticed her fingers shaking as she brought the amber liquid to her lips.

The king was staring at the thin and rather scraggly looking sailor. "How did you get into the palace?" he demanded.

The man looked nervously from king to queen to Kell.

"He's my second mate, Your Majesty," answered Alucard.

"That doesn't answer my question."

"We found each other—" started Lila.

"He can speak for himself," snapped the king.

"Maybe if you bothered questioning your people in their own language," she shot back. The room quieted. Kell raised a brow. Rhy, despite himself, almost laughed.

A guard appeared in the doorway and cleared his throat. "Your Majesty," he said, "the prisoner wishes to speak."

Lila stiffened at the mention of Holland. Alucard sank heavily into a chair.

"Finally," said Maxim, starting toward the door, but the guard ducked his head, embarrassed.

"Not with you, Your Majesty." He nodded at Kell. "With him."

Kell looked to Maxim, who nodded brusquely. "Bring me answers," he warned, "or I will find another way to get them."

A shadow crossed Kell's face, but he only bowed and left.

Rhy watched his brother go, then turned to his father. "If Alucard survived, there must be others. Let me—"

"Did you know?" demanded Maxim.

"What?"

"When you left the safety of this palace, did you *know* you were immune to Osaron's magic?"

"I suspected," said Rhy, "but I would have gone either way."

The queen took hold of his arm. "After everything—"

"Yes, after everything," said Rhy, pulling free. "*Because* of everything." He turned to his parents. "You taught me that a ruler suffers with his people. You taught me that he is their strength, their stone. Don't you see? I will never have magic, but finally I have a *purpose*."

"Rhy—" started his father.

"No," he cut in. "I will not let them think the Maresh have abandoned them. I will not hide within a warded palace when I can walk without fear through those streets. When I can remind our people that they are not alone, that I am fighting with them, *for* them. When I may be struck down but rise again and in so doing show them the immortality of hope. That is what I can do for my city, and I will gladly do it. You need not shield me from the darkness. It cannot hurt me anymore. Nothing can."

Rhy felt suddenly wrung out, empty, but in that emptiness lay a kind of peace. No, not peace exactly. Clarity. Resolve.

He looked to his mother, who was clutching her hands together. "Would you have me be your son, or the prince of Arnes?"

Her knuckles went white. "You will always be both."

"Then I will succeed at neither."

He met the king's gaze, but it was the head priest who spoke.

"The prince is right," said Tieren in his soft, steady way. "The royal and city guard are cut in half, and the priests are at their limits trying to keep the palace wards up. Every man and woman immune to Osaron's magic is an ally we cannot forfeit. We need every life we can save."

"Then it's settled," said Rhy. "I will ride out—"

"Not alone," cut in his father, and again, before Rhy could protest, "*No one* goes alone."

Alucard looked up from his seat, pale, exhausted. His hands tightened on the chair, and he started to rise when Lila stepped forward, finishing her drink. "Lenos, put the captain to bed," she said, and then, turning to the king, "I'll go with His Highness."

Maxim frowned. "Why should I trust *you* with my son's safety?"

She tilted her head when she spoke, shifting her dark hair so it framed her shattered eye. In that single defiant gesture, Rhy could see why Kell liked her so.

"Why?" she echoed. "Because the shadows can't touch me, and the fallen won't. Because I'm good with magic, and better with a blade, and I've got more power in my blood than you've got in this whole damned palace. Because I've no qualms about killing, and on top of it all, I've got a knack for keeping your sons—*both* of them—alive."

If Kell had been there, he would have turned white.

As it was, the king went nearly purple.

Alucard let out a small, exhausted sound that might have been a laugh.

The queen stared blankly at the strange girl.

And Rhy, despite everything, smiled.

The prince had only a single suit of armor.

It had never seen battle, never seen anything but a sculptor's eye, cast for the small stone portrait in his parents' chamber, a gift from Maxim to Emira on their tenth anniversary. Rhy had worn the armor just the once—he'd planned to wear it again on the night of his twentieth birthday, but nothing about that night had gone as planned.

The armor was light, too light for a real fight, but perfect for posing, a soft hammered gold with pearl-white trim and a cream-colored cape, and it made the faintest chime whenever he moved, a pleasant sound like a far-off bell.

"Not very subtle, are you?" said Lila when she saw him striding through the palace foyer.

She'd been standing in the doorway, her eyes on the city and the fog still shifting in the late morning light, but at the gentle sound of Rhy's approach, she'd turned, and nearly laughed out loud. And he supposed she had reason to. After all, Lila was dressed in her worn boots and her black high-collared coat, looking with her bandaged hands like a pirate after a hard night, and there *he* was, practically glowing in polished gold, a full complement of silvered guards behind him.

"I've never been fond of subtle," he said.

Rhy imagined Kell shaking his head, exasperation warring with amusement. Perhaps he looked foolish, but Rhy *wanted* to be seen, wanted his people—if they were out there, if they were *in* there—to know their prince was not hiding. That he was not afraid of the dark.

As they descended the palace stairs, Lila's expression hardened, her wounded hands curled into loose fists at her sides. He didn't know what she'd seen at the Sanctuary, but he could tell it hadn't been pleasant, and for all her jaunty posturing, the look on her face now threw him.

"You think this is a bad idea," he said. It wasn't a question. But it sparked something in Lila, rekindled the fire in her eyes and ignited a grin.

"Without a doubt."

"Then why are you smiling?"

"Because," she said, "bad ideas are my favorite kind."

They reached the plaza at the base of the stairs, the flowers that usually lined the steps now sculptures of black glass. Smoke rose from a dozen spots on the horizon, not the simple trails from hearth fires, but the too-dark plumes of burning buildings. Rhy straightened. Lila pulled her jacket close. "Ready?"

"I don't need a chaperone."

"Good thing," she said, setting off. "I don't need a prince tripping on my heels."

Rhy started. "You told my father—"

"That I could you keep alive," she said, glancing back. "But you don't need me to."

Something in Rhy loosened. Because of all the people in his life, his brother and his parents and his guards and even Alucard Emery, Lila was the first—the only—person to treat him like he didn't need saving.

"Guards," he called, hardening his voice. "Split up."

"Your Highness," started one. "We're not to lea—"

He turned on them. "We've too much ground to cover, and last time I checked, we all had a pair of working eyes"—he shot a look at Lila, realizing his error, but she only shrugged—"so put them to use, and *find me my survivors*."

It was a grim pursuit.

Rhy found too many bodies, and worse, the places where bodies *should* have been but where only a tatter of fabric and a pile of ash were left, the rest blown away by the winter wind. He thought of Alucard's sister, Anisa, burning from the inside out. Thought of what happened to those who lost their battle with Osaron's magic. And what of the fallen? The thousands of people who had *not* fought against the shadow king, but had given in, given way. Were they still in there, prisoners of their own minds? Could they be saved? Or were they already lost?

"*Vas ir,*" he murmured over the bodies he found, and the ones he didn't.

Go in peace.

The streets were hardly empty, but he moved through the masses like a ghost, their shadowed eyes passing over him, through him. He walked in gleaming gold, and still they did not notice. He called to them, but they did not answer. Did not turn.

Whatever part of me Osaron could take, it's already gone.

Did he really believe that?

His boot slid a little on the ground, and, looking down, he saw that a piece of the street had *changed,* from stone to something else, something glassy and black, like the flowers on the stairs.

He knelt, brushing his gloved hand against the smooth patch. It wasn't cold. Wasn't warm, either. Wasn't wet like ice. It wasn't *anything.* Which made no sense. Rhy straightened, perplexed, and kept looking for something, *someone,* he could help.

Silvers, that's what some were calling them, those who'd been burned by Osaron's magic and survived. The priests, it turned out, had discovered a handful already, most rising from the fever beds that lined the Rose Hall.

But how many more waited in the city?

In the end, Rhy didn't find the first silver.

The silver found him.

The young boy came stumbling toward him out of a house and sank to his knees at Rhy's feet. Lines danced like light over his skin, his black hair falling over fever-bright eyes. *"Mas vares."*

My prince.

Rhy knelt in his armor, scratching the plate as gold met stone. "It's all right," he said as the boy sobbed, tears tracing fresh tracks over the silver on his cheeks.

"All alone," he murmured, breath hitching. "All alone."

"Not anymore," said the prince.

He rose and started toward the house, but small fingers caught his hand. The boy shook his head, and Rhy saw the ash dusting the boy's front, and understood. There was no one else inside the house.

Not anymore.

II

Lila went straight for the night market.

The city around her wasn't empty. It would have been less chilling if it were. Instead, those who'd fallen under Osaron's spell moved through the streets like sleepwalkers carrying out remembered tasks while deep within their dreams.

The night market was a shadow of its former self, half of it burned, and the rest carrying on in that dazed and ghostly way.

A fruit vendor hawked winter apples, his eyes swimming with shadows, while a woman carried flowers, their edges frosting black. The whole thing had a haunted air, a sea of puppets, and Lila kept squinting at the air around them as if looking for the strings.

Rhy moved through the city like a specter, but Lila was like an unwelcome guest. The people looked at her when she passed, their eyes narrowing, but the cuts on her palms were still fresh, and the blood kept them at bay, even as their whispers trailed her through the streets.

Scattered throughout the market, as if someone had splashed inky water onto the ground and let it freeze, were patches of black ice. Lila stepped around them with a thief's sure footing and a fighter's grace.

She was making her way toward Calla's familiar green tent at the end of the market when she saw a man pitch a basin of flaming stones into the river. He was broad and bearded, silver scars tracing his hands and throat.

"You couldn't get me, you monster!" he was screaming. "You couldn't hold me down."

The basin hit the river with a crash, rippling the half-frozen water and sending up a plume of hissing steam.

And just like that, the illusion shattered.

The man selling apples and the woman with flowers and every other fallen in the marketplace broke off and turned toward the man, as if waking from a dream. Only they weren't waking. Instead, it was like the darkness rose inside them, Osaron rousing and turning his head, looking through their eyes. They moved as a single body, one that wasn't theirs.

"Idiot," muttered Lila, starting toward him, but the man didn't seem to notice. Didn't seem to *care*.

"Face me, you coward!" he bellowed as part of the nearest tent tore free and lifted into the air beside him.

The crowd hummed in displeasure.

"How dare you," said a merchant, eyes shining dully as he drew a knife.

"The king will not stand for this," said a second, twining rope between her hands.

The air shook with the sudden urge for violence, and realization struck Lila like a blow—Osaron gained obedience from the fallen, and energy from the fevered. But he had no use for the ones who'd fought free of his spell. And what he couldn't use . . .

Lila ran.

Her injured leg throbbed as she sprinted toward him.

"Look out!" she shouted, her first blade already flying. It caught the nearest attacker in the chest, buried to the hilt, but the merchant's own knife had left his hand before he fell.

Lila tackled the scarred man to the ground as metal sang over their heads.

The stranger looked up at her in shock, but there wasn't time. The fallen were circling them, weapons raised. The man slammed a fist into the ground, and a piece of road as wide as a market stall tipped up into a shield.

He raised another makeshift wall and turned, clearly intending to summon a third, but Lila had no desire to be entombed. She dragged the man to his feet, sprinting into the nearest tent before a steel kettle thudded against the heavy canvas side.

"Keep moving," she called, carving her way through a second tent wall and then a third before the man hauled her to a stop.

"Why did you do that?"

Lila wrenched free. "A thank-you would be nice. I lost my fifth favorite knife out—"

He forced her back against the tent pole. "Why?" he snarled, eyes wide. They were a shocking green, flecked with black and gold.

A swift kick to the ribs with the bottom of her boot, and he went stumbling backward, though not as far as she'd hoped. "Because you were shouting your head off at nothing but shadow and mist. A tip: don't start a fight like that if you want to live."

"I didn't *want* to live." His voice shook as he looked down at his silver-scarred hands. "I didn't want *this*."

"A lot of people would love to trade places."

"That monster took everything. My wife. My father. I fought through it because I thought someone would be waiting for me. But when I woke—when I—" He made a strangled sound. "You should have let me die."

Lila frowned. "What's your name?"

"What?"

"You have a name. What is it?"

"Manel."

"Well, Manel. Dying doesn't help the dead. It doesn't find the lost. A lot of people have fallen. But some of us are still standing. So if you want to give up, walk out that curtain. I won't stop you. I won't save you again. But if you want to put your second chance to better use, come with me."

She turned on her heel and slashed the next tent wall, stepping through, only to slam to a stop.

She'd found Calla's tent.

"What is it?" asked Manel behind her. "What's wrong?"

"This is the last tent," she said slowly. "Go out the flap, and head for the palace."

Manel spat. "The *palace*. The royals hid inside their palace while my family died. The king and queen sat safe on their thrones while London fell and that spoiled prince—"

"Enough," snarled Lila. "That spoiled prince is searching the streets for men like you. He's hunting for the living and burying the dead and doing everything he can to keep one from becoming the other, so you can either help or disappear, but either way, get out."

He looked at her long and hard, then swore beneath his breath and vanished through the tent's flap, bells jingling in his wake.

Lila turned her attention back to the empty shop.

"Calla?" she called, hoping the woman was there, hoping she wasn't. The lanterns that hung in the corners were unlit, the hats and scarves and hoods on the walls casting strange shapes in the dark. Lila snapped her fingers, and the light sparked in her hand, unsteady but bright as she crossed the small tent, searching for any sign of the merchant. She wanted to see the woman's kind smile, wanted to hear Calla's teasing words. She wanted Calla to be far, far away, wanted her to be safe.

Something cracked beneath Lila's boot.

A glass bead, like the ones in the trunk Lila had brought ashore. The box of gold thread and ruby clasps and a dozen other tiny, beautiful things she'd given Calla to pay for the coat, and the mask, and the kindness.

The beads were scattered across the floor in a messy trail that vanished beneath the hem of a second curtain hung near the back of the stall. The light slid beneath, struck gem, and rug, and something solid.

Delilah Bard never read many books.

The few she did had pirates and thieves, and always ended with freedom and the promise of more stories. Characters sailed away. They lived on. Lila always imagined people that way, a series of intersections and adventures. It was easy when you moved through life—through worlds—the way she did. Easy when you didn't care, when people came onto the page and walked away again, back to their own stories, and you could imagine whatever you wanted for them, if you cared enough to write it in your head.

Barron had walked into her life and refused to walk back out, and then he'd gone and died and she had to keep remembering that over and over instead of letting him live on in some version without her.

She didn't want that for Calla.

She didn't want to look behind the curtain, didn't want to know the end of this story, but her hand reached out of its own traitorous accord and pulled the fabric back.

She saw the body on the floor.

Oh, thought Lila dully. *There she is.*

Calla, who had drawn the *i*'s of Lila's name into *e*'s, and always sounded on the verge of laughing.

Calla, who had simply smiled when Lila walked in one night and asked for a man's coat instead of a woman's dress.

Calla, who'd thought Lila was in love with a black-eyed prince, even before Lila really had been. Calla, who wanted Kell to be happy just as a man, not as an *aven*. Who wanted *her*—*Lila*—to be happy.

The box of trinkets Lila had once brought home for the merchant now lay open on its side, spilling a hundred spots of light onto the floor around the woman's head.

Calla was lying on her side, her short, round body curled in on itself, one hand beneath her cheek. But the other hand was pressed over her ear, as if trying to block something out, and for a moment, Lila thought—hoped—she was sleeping. Thought—hoped—she could kneel down and shake the woman gently, and she would get up.

Of course, Calla wasn't a woman anymore. She wasn't even a body. Her eyes—what was left of those warm eyes—were open, the same ruined shade as the rest of her, the chalky grey of hearth ash after the fire's gone and cooled.

Lila's throat closed.

This is why I run.

Because caring was a thing with claws. It sank them in, and didn't let go. Caring hurt more than a knife to the leg, more than a few broken ribs, more than anything that bled or broke and healed again. Caring didn't break you clean. It was a bone that didn't set, a cut that wouldn't close.

It was better not to care—Lila *tried* not to care—but sometimes, people got in. Like a knife against armor, they found the cracks, slid past the guard, and you didn't know how deep they were buried until they were gone and you were bleeding on the floor. And it wasn't fair. Lila hadn't asked to care about Calla. She hadn't wanted to let her in. So why did it still hurt this much?

Lila felt the tears spilling down her cheeks.

"Calla."

She didn't know why she said it that way, soft, as if a soft voice could wake the dead.

She didn't know why she said it at all.

But she didn't have time to wonder. As Lila took a step forward, a gust of winter air cut through the tent, and Calla simply . . . blew apart.

Lila let out a strangled cry and lunged for the curtain, but it was too late.

Calla was already gone.

Nothing but a collapsing pile of ash, and a hundred bits of silver and gold.

Something folded in Lila, then. She sank to the ground, ignoring the bite of the glass beads where they cut into her knees, fingers digging into the threadbare rug.

She didn't mean to summon fire.

It wasn't until the smoke tickled her lungs that Lila realized the tent was catching. Half of her wanted to let it burn, but the rest couldn't bear the thought of Calla's store burning away like her life, nothing left. Never to be seen again.

Lila pressed her hands together, smothering the fire.

She wiped the tears away and got up.

III

Kell stood before Holland's cell, waiting for the man to speak.

He didn't. Didn't even raise his gaze to meet Kell's own. The man's eyes were fixed on something in the distance, beyond the bars, beyond the walls, beyond the city. A cold anger burned in them, but it seemed directed inward as much as out, at himself and the monster who had poisoned his mind, stolen his body.

"You summoned *me*," said Kell at last. "I assumed you had something to say."

When Holland still didn't answer, he turned to go.

"One hundred and eighty-two."

Kell glanced back. "What?"

Holland's attention was still pointedly somewhere else. "That is the number of people killed by Astrid and Athos Dane."

"And how many killed by *you*?"

"Sixty-seven," answered Holland without hesitation. "Three before I became a slave. Sixty-four before I became a king. And none since." At last, he looked at Kell. "I value life. I've issued death. You were raised a prince, Kell. I watched my whole world wither, day by day, season by season, year by year, and the only thing that kept me going was the hope that I was *Antari* for a reason. That I could do something to help."

"I thought the only thing that kept you going was the binding spell branded into your skin."

Holland cocked his head. "By the time *you* met me, the only thing that kept me going was the thought of killing Athos and Astrid Dane. And then you took that from me."

Kell scowled. "I won't apologize for depriving you of your revenge."

Holland said nothing. Then, "When I asked you what you would have had me do upon waking in Black London, you told me that I should have stayed there. That I should have died. I thought about it. I knew that Athos Dane was dead. I could feel that much." The chains rattled as he reached to tap the ruined branding on his chest. "But *I* wasn't. I didn't know why, but I thought of who'd I'd been, those years before they stripped me down to hate, of what I'd wanted for my world. That's what drove me home. Not fear of death—death is gentle, death is kind—but the hope that I was still capable of something more. And the idea of being free—" He blinked, as if he'd drifted.

The words rang through Kell's chest, echoing chords.

"What will happen to me now?" There was no fear in his voice. There was *nothing* at all.

"I assume you will be tried—"

Holland was shaking his head. "No."

"You're in no place to make demands."

Holland sat forward as far as the chains would let him.

"I don't want a trial, Kell," he said firmly. "I want an execution."

IV

The words landed, as Holland knew they would.

Kell was staring at him, waiting for the twist, the turn.

"An execution?" he said, shaking his head. "Your penchant for self-destruction is impressive, but—"

"It's a matter of practicality," said Holland, letting his shoulders graze the wall, "not atonement."

"I don't follow."

You never do, he thought bleakly.

"How is it done here?" he asked, a false lightness in his voice, as if they were talking of a meal or a dance, and not an execution. "By blade or by fire?"

Kell stared at him blankly, as if he'd never even seen one.

"I imagine," said the other *Antari* slowly, "it would be done by the blade." So Holland was right, then. "How was it done in *your* city?"

Holland had witnessed his first execution on his brother's shoulders. Had followed Alox to the square for years. He remembered the arms forced wide, deep cuts and broken bones and fresh blood caught in basins. "Executions in my London were slow, and brutal, and very public."

Distaste washed across Kell's face. "We don't glorify death with displays."

The chains rattled as Holland sat forward. "This one *needs* to be public. Something out in the open where he can see."

"What are you getting at?"

"Osaron needs a body. He cannot take this world without one."

"Is that so?" challenged Kell. "Because he's doing an impressive job of it so far."

"It's clumsy, broad strokes," said Holland dismissively. "This isn't what he wants."

"You would know."

Holland ignored the jab. "There is no glory in a crown he cannot wear, even if he has not realized it yet. Osaron is a creature of potential. He will never be satisfied with what he has, not for long. And for all his power, all his conjuring, he cannot craft flesh and blood. Not that it will stop him from trying, and poisoning every soul in London in search of a pawn or vessel, but none will do."

"Because he needs an *Antari*."

"And he has only three options."

Kell stiffened. "You knew about Lila?"

"Of course," said Holland evenly. "I'm not a fool."

"Fool enough to play into Osaron's hands," said Kell through clenched teeth. "Fool enough to call for your own execution. To what end? Reduce his options from three to two, and he still—"

"I plan to give him what he wants," said Holland grimly. "I plan to kneel and beg and invite him in. I plan to grant him his vessel." Kell stared in bald disgust. "And then I plan to let you kill me."

Kell's disgust turned to shock, then confusion.

Holland smiled, a cold, rueful twitch of the lips.

"You should learn to guard your feelings."

Kell swallowed, made a thin attempt to mask his features. "As much as I'd like to kill you, Holland, doing so won't kill *him*. Or have you forgotten that magic does not die?"

"Perhaps not, but it can be contained."

"With what?"

"As Tosal."

Kell flinched reflexively at the sound of a blood command, then paled as the realization dawned. "No."

"So you do know the spell?"

"I could turn you to stone. It would be a kinder end."

"I'm not looking for kindness, Kell." Holland tilted his chin up, attention settling on the cell's high ceiling. "I'm looking to finish what I started."

The *Antari* ran a hand through his copper hair. "If Osaron doesn't take the bait. If he doesn't come, then you'll die."

"Death comes for us all," said Holland evenly. "I would simply have mine mean something."

The second time someone tried to kill Holland, he was eighteen, walking home with a loaf of coarse bread in one hand and a bottle of *kaash* in the other.

The sun was going down, the city taking on another shape. It was a risk, to walk with both hands full, but Holland had grown into his frame, long limbs corded with muscle, shoulders broad and straight. He no longer wore his black hair down over his eye. He no longer tried to hide.

Halfway home, he realized he was being followed.

He didn't stop, didn't turn around, didn't even quicken his pace.

Holland didn't go looking for fights, but still they came to him. Trailed him through the streets like strays, like shadows.

He kept walking, now, letting the soft clink of the bottle and the steady tread of his boot form a backdrop for the sounds of the alley around him.

The shuffle of steps.

The soft exhale before a weapon's release.

A blade whistling out of the dark.

Holland dropped the bread and turned, one hand raised. The knife stopped an inch from his throat and hung there in the air, waiting to be plucked. Instead, he twirled his hand and the blade spun on its edge, reversing course. With a flick of his finger, he flung the metal back into the dark, where it found flesh. Someone screamed.

Three more men came out of the shadows. Not by choice—Holland was dragging them forward, their faces contorted as they fought their own bones, his will on their bodies stronger than their own.

He could feel their hearts racing, blood pounding through their veins.

One of the men tried to speak, but Holland willed his mouth shut. He didn't care what they had to say.

All three were young, though a little older than Holland himself, with tattoos already staining their wrists and lips and temples. Blood and word, the sources of power. He had half a mind to walk away and leave them pinned in the street, but this was the third attack in less than a month, and he was getting tired.

He loosened a single pair of jaws.

"Who sent you?"

"Ros . . . Ros Vortalis," stammered the youth through still-clenched teeth.

It wasn't the first time he'd heard the name. It wasn't even the first time he'd heard the name from one of the would-be killers following him home. Vortalis was a thug from the *shal,* a nobody trying to carve a piece of power from a place with too little to spare. A man trying to get Holland's attention in all the wrong ways.

"Why?" he demanded.

"He told us . . . to bring him . . . your head."

Holland sighed. The bread was still on the ground. The wine was beginning to frost. "Tell this *Vortalis* that if he wants my head, he'll have to come for it himself."

With that, he flicked his fingers, and the men went flying backward, just like the knife, slamming into the alley walls with a solid thud. They fell and didn't get back up, and Holland took up the bread, stepped over their bodies—chests still rising—and continued home.

When he got there, he pressed his palm to the door, felt the locks slide free within the wood, and eased it open. There was a slip of paper on the floor, and he was halfway to it when he heard the padding rush of steps, and looked up just in time to catch the girl. She threw her arms around his neck, and when he spun with the weight of her, the skirts of her dress fanned like petals, the edges stained from dancing.

"Hello, Hol," she said sweetly.

"Hello, Tal," he answered.

It had been nine years since Alox attacked him. Nine years trying to survive in a city out for blood, weathering every storm, every fight, every sign of trouble, all the while waiting for something better.

And then, something better came.

And her name was Talya.

Talya, a spot of color in a world of white.

Talya, who carried the sun with her wherever she went.

Talya, so fair that when she smiled, the day grew brighter.

Holland saw her in the market one night.

And next he saw her in the square.

And after that, he saw her everywhere he looked.

She had scars in the corners of her eyes that winked silver in the light, and a laugh that took his breath away.

Who could laugh like that, in a world like this?

She reminded him of Alox. Not the way he'd disappear for hours, or days, come home with blood caking his clothes, but the way her presence could make him forget about the darkness, the cold, the dying world outside their door.

"What's wrong?" she asked as he set her down.

"Nothing," he said, kissing her temple. "Nothing at all."

And perhaps that wasn't strictly true, but there was a startling truth beneath the lie: for the first time in his life, Holland was something like happy.

He stoked the fire with a glance, and Talya pulled him onto the cot they shared, and, then, tearing off pieces of bread and sipping cold wine, she told him the stories of the someday king. Just the way Alox had. The first time, Holland had flinched at the words, but didn't stop her because he liked the way she told them, so full of energy and light. The stories were her favorite—and so he let her talk.

By the third or fourth telling, he'd forgotten why the stories sounded so familiar.

By the tenth, he'd forgotten that he'd first heard them from someone else.

By the hundredth time, he'd forgotten about that other life.

That night, they lay wrapped in blankets, and she ran her fingers through his hair, and he felt himself drifting from the rhythm of the touch and the heat of the fire.

That was when she tried to cut his heart out.

She was fast, but he was faster, the knife's tip sinking only an inch before Holland came to his senses and forced her bodily away. He was up, on his feet, clutching his chest as blood leaked between his fingers.

Talya just stood there in the middle of their tiny room, their *home,* the blade hanging from her fingers.

"Why?" he asked, stunned.

"I'm sorry, Hol. They came to me in the market. Said they'd pay in silver."

He wanted to ask when, ask who, but he never got the chance.

She lunged at him again, tightly, swiftly, all her dancer's grace, and the knife whistled sweetly toward him. It happened so fast. Without thinking, Holland's fingers twitched, and her knife twisted in her grip, freezing in the air even as the rest of her kept moving forward. The blade sank smoothly between her own ribs.

Talya looked at him then with such surprise and indignation, as if she'd thought he'd let her kill him. As if she'd thought he'd simply surrender.

"Sorry, Tal," he said as she tried to breathe, to speak, and couldn't.

She tried to take a step and Holland caught her as she fell, all that dancer's grace gone out of her limbs at the end.

Holland stayed there till she died, then laid her carefully on the floor, got to his feet, and left.

V

"He wants *what*?" said the king, looking up from the map.

"An execution," repeated Kell, still reeling.

As Tosal, those had been Holland's words.

"It must be a trick," said Isra.

"I don't think so," started Kell, but the guard wasn't listening.

"Your Majesty," she said, turning to Maxim. "Surely he wants to draw Osaron in so he can escape. . . ."

As Tosal.

To confine.

Kell had used the blood spell only once in his life, on a bird, a small sunflit he'd caught in the Sanctuary gardens. The sunflit had gone perfectly still in his hands, but it hadn't died. He could feel its heart beating frantically beneath its feathered breast while it lay motionless, as if paralyzed, trapped inside its own body.

When Tieren had found out, the *Aven Essen* was furious. Blood spell or not, Kell had broken the cardinal rule of power: he had used magic to harm a living creature, to alter its life. Kell had apologized profusely, and said the words to dispel what he'd done, to heal the damage, but to his shock and horror, the commands had no effect. Nothing he said seemed to work.

The bird didn't revive.

It just lay there, still as death, in his hands.

"I don't understand."

Tieren shook his head. "Things are not so simple, when it comes to life and death," he'd said. "With minds and bodies, what is done cannot always be undone." And then he'd taken up the sunflit, and brought it to his chest, and broken its neck. The priest had set the lifeless bird back in Kell's hands.

"That," said Tieren grimly, "was a kinder end."

He had never tried the spell again, because he'd never learned the words to undo it.

"*Kell.*"

The king's voice jarred him out of the memory.

Kell swallowed. "Holland did what he did to save his world. I believe that. Now he wants it to be over."

"You're asking us to *trust* him?" challenged Isra.

"No," said Kell, holding the king's gaze, "I'm asking you to trust *me*."

Tieren appeared in the doorway.

Ink stained his fingers, and fatigue hollowed out his cheeks. "You called for me, Maxim?"

The king exhaled heavily. "How long until your spell is ready?"

The *Aven Essen* shook his head. "It is not a simple matter, putting an entire city to sleep. The spell must be broken down into seven or eight smaller ones and then positioned around the city to form a chain—"

"How *long*?"

Tieren made an exasperated sound. "Days, Your Majesty."

The king's gaze returned to Kell. "Can you end it?"

Kell didn't know if Maxim was asking if he had the will or the strength to kill another *Antari*.

I'm not looking for kindness, Kell. I'm looking to finish what I started.

"Yes," he answered.

The king nodded and swept his hand over the map. "The palace wards do not extend to the balconies, do they?"

"No," said Tieren. "It is all we can do to keep them up around the walls, windows, and doors."

"Very well," said the king, letting his knuckles fall to the table's edge. "The north courtyard, then. We'll raise a platform overlooking the Isle, and hold the ritual at dawn, and whether or not Osaron comes . . ." His dark eyes landed on Kell. "Holland dies by your hand."

The words followed Kell into the hall.

Holland dies by your hand.

He sank back against the map room doors, exhaustion winding around his limbs.

It's rather hard to kill an Antari.

By the blade.

A kinder end.

As Tosal.

He pushed off the wood and started for the stairs.

"Kell?"

The queen was standing at the end of the hall, looking out a pair of balcony doors at the shadow of her city. Her eyes met his in the reflection in the glass. There was a sadness in them, and he found himself taking a step toward her before he stopped. He didn't have the strength.

"Your Majesty," he said, bowing before he turned and walked away.

VI

All day Rhy had searched the city for survivors.

In ones and sometimes twos, he found them—shaken, fragile, but alive. Most were startlingly young. Only a few were very old. And just like the magic in their veins, there was no common factor. No bond of blood, or gender, or means. He found a noble girl from House Loreni, still dressed for a tournament ball, an older man in threadbare clothes tucked in an alleyway, a mother in red mourning silks, a royal guard whose mark had failed or simply faded. All now left with the silver veins of a survivor.

Rhy stayed with them only long enough to show they weren't alone, long enough to lead them to the palace steps for shelter, and then he was off again, back into the city, in search of more.

Before dusk, he returned to the *Spire*—he'd known it was too late, but had to see—and found all that was left of Anisa: a small pile of ashes, smoldering on the floor of Alucard's cabin, beyond the cage of warped planks. A few drops of silver from her House Emery ring.

Rhy was crossing the deck in numbed silence when he caught the glint of metal and saw the woman sitting on the deck with her back to a crate and a blade in her hand.

His boots hit the wooden dock with a thud.

The woman didn't move.

She was dressed like a man, like a *sailor,* a black-and-red captain's sash across her front.

At first glance, he could tell she was from the borderlands, the coast where Arnes looked onto Vesk. She had the build of a northerner and the coloring of a local, her rich brown hair worn in two massive braids that coiled like a mane around her face. Her eyes were open, unblinking, but they looked ahead with an intensity that said she was still there, and thin lines of silver shone against her sea-tanned face.

The knife in her hand was slick with blood.

It didn't appear to be hers.

A dozen warnings echoed in Rhy's head—all of them in Kell's voice—as he knelt beside her.

"What's your name?" he asked in Arnesian.

Nothing.

"Captain?"

After several long seconds, the woman blinked, a slow, final gesture.

"Jasta," she said, her voice hoarse, and then, as if the name had sparked something in her, she added, "He tried to drown me. My first mate, Rigar, tried to drag me into that whispering river." She didn't take her eyes off the ship. "So I killed him."

"Are there any others on board?" he asked.

"Half of them are missing," she said. "The others . . ." She trailed off, dark eyes dancing over the vessel.

Rhy touched her shoulder. "Can you stand?"

Jasta's face drifted toward his. She frowned. "Has anyone told you that you look like the prince?"

Rhy smiled. "Once or twice." He held out his hand and helped her to her feet.

VII

The sun had gone down, and Alucard Emery was trying to get drunk.

So far it wasn't working, but he was determined to see it through. He'd even made a little game:

Every time his mind drifted to Anisa—her bare feet, her fevered skin, her small arms around his neck—he took a drink.

Every time he thought of Berras—his brother's cutting tone, the hateful smile, the hands around his throat—he took a drink.

Every time his nightmares rose like bile, or his own screams echoed in his head, or he had to remember his sister's empty eyes, her burning heart, he took a drink.

Every time he thought of Rhy's fingers laced through his, of the prince's voice telling him to *hold on, hold on, hold on to me,* he took a very, very long drink.

Across the room, Lila seemed to be playing her own game; his quiet thief was on her third glass. It took a great deal to shake Delilah Bard, that much he knew, but still, something had shaken her. He might never be able to read the secrets in her face, but he could tell she was keeping them. What had she seen beyond the palace walls? What demons had she faced? Were they strangers or friends?

Every time he asked a question Delilah Bard would never answer, he took a drink, until the pain and grief finally began to blur into something steady.

The room rocked around him, and Alucard Emery—the last surviving Emery—slumped back in the chair, fingering the inlaid wood, the fine gold trim.

How strange it was, to be here, in Rhy's rooms. It had been strange enough when Rhy was stretched out on his bed, but then the details, the room, everything but Rhy himself, had gone out of focus. Now, Alucard took in the glittering curtains, the elegant floor, the vast bed, now made. All signs of struggle smoothed away.

Rhy's amber gaze kept swinging toward him like a pendulum on a heavy rope.

He took another drink.

And then another, and another, in preparation for the ache of want and loss and memory washing over him, a small boat pitching miserably against the waves.

Hold on to me.

That's what Rhy had said, when Alucard was burning from the inside out. When Rhy was lying there beside him in the ship's cabin, hoping desperately that his hands could keep Alucard there, and whole and safe. Keep him from vanishing again, this time forever.

Now that Alucard was alive and more or less upright, Rhy couldn't bring himself to look at his lover, and couldn't bear to look away, so he ended up doing both and neither.

It had been so long since Rhy'd been able to study his face. Three summers. Three winters. Three years, and the prince's heart still cracked along the lines Alucard had made.

They were in the conservatory, Rhy and Alucard and Lila.

The captain sat slumped in a tall-backed chair, silver scars and sapphire stud both winking in the light. A glass hung from one hand, and a fluffy white cat named Esa curled beneath his seat, and his eyes were open but far away.

Over at the sideboard, Lila was pouring herself another drink. (Was this her fourth? Rhy felt he wasn't the one to judge.) However, she was pouring a little too liberally and spilled the last of Rhy's summer wine onto his inlaid floor. There was a time when he would have cared about the stain, but it was gone, that life. It had fallen between the boards like a bit of jewelry, and now lay somewhere out of reach, vaguely remembered but easily forgotten.

"Steady, Bard."

It was the first thing Alucard had said in an hour. Not that Rhy had been waiting.

The captain was pale, his thief ashen, and the prince himself was pacing, his armor cast off like a broken shell onto a corner chair.

By the end of the first day, they'd found twenty-four silvers. Most were being kept in the Rose Hall, treated by the priests. But there were more. He knew there were more. There had to be. Rhy wanted to keep looking, to carry the search into the night, but Maxim had refused. And worse, the remaining royal guards had put him under an unyielding watch.

And what troubled Rhy as much as his own confinement when there were souls still trapped in the city was the sight of the rot spreading through London. A blackness like ice on top of the street stones and splashed across the walls, a film that wasn't a film at all, but a *change*. Rock and dirt and water all being swallowed up, replaced by something that wasn't an element at all, a glossy, dark nothing, a presence and an absence.

He'd told Tieren, pointed out a lone spot at the courtyard's edge, just outside their wards, where the void was spreading like frost. The old man's face had gone pale.

"Magic and nature exist in balance," he'd said, brushing fingers through the air above the pool of black. "This is what happens when that balance fails. When magic overwhelms nature."

The world was *decaying,* he'd explained. Only instead of going soft, like felled branches on a forest floor, it was going hard, calcifying into something like stone that wasn't stone at all.

"Would you stand still?" snapped Lila now, watching Rhy pace. "You're making me dizzy."

"I suspect," said a voice from the door, "that's the wine."

Rhy turned, relieved to see his brother. "Kell," he said, trying to summon something like humor as he tipped his glass at the four guards framing the door. "Is this what you feel like all the time?"

"Pretty much," said Kell, lifting the drink from Lila's hand and taking a long sip. Amazingly, she let him.

"How maddening," said Rhy with a groan. And then, to the men, "Could you at least sit down? Or are you trying to look like coats of armor on my walls?"

They didn't answer.

Kell returned the drink to Lila's hand and then frowned as he noticed Alucard. His brother pointedly ignored the captain's presence and poured himself a very large glass. "What are we drinking to?"

"The living," said Rhy.

"The dead," said Alucard and Lila at the same time.

"We're being thorough," added Rhy.

His attention swung back to Alucard, who was looking out at the night. Rhy realized he wasn't the only one watching the captain. Lila had followed Alucard's gaze to the glass.

"When you look at the fallen," she said, "what do you see?"

Alucard squinted dully, the way he always had when he was trying to picture something. "Knots," he said simply.

"Care to expand?" said Kell, who knew of the captain's gift, and cared for it about as much as he cared for the rest of him.

"You wouldn't understand," murmured Alucard.

"Maybe if you chose the right words."

"I couldn't make them short enough."

"Oh, for Christ's sake," snapped Lila. "If you two could stop bickering for a moment."

Alucard leaned forward in his chair and set the once-more-empty glass on the floor beside his boot, where his cat sniffed it. "This *Osaron*," he said, "is siphoning energy from everyone he touches. His magic, it feeds on ours by . . . *infecting* it. It gets in among the strings of our power, our life, and gets tangled up in our threads until everything is in knots."

"You're right," said Kell after a moment. "I have no idea what you're talking about."

"It must be maddening," said Alucard, "to know I have a power you don't."

Kell's teeth clicked together, but when he spoke, he kept his voice civil, smooth. "Believe it or not, I relish our smallest differences. Besides, I may not be able to see the world the way *you* do, but I can still recognize an asshole."

Lila snorted.

Rhy made an exasperated sound. "Enough," he said, and then, to Kell, "What did our prisoner have to say?"

At the mention of Holland, Alucard's head snapped. Lila sat forward, a glint in her eyes. Kell downed his drink, wincing, and said, "He's to be executed in the morning. A public display."

For a long moment, no one spoke.

And then Lila raised her glass.

"Well," she said cheerfully, "I'll toast to *that*."

VIII

Emira Maresh drifted through the palace like a ghost.

She heard what people said about her. They called her distant, distracted. But in truth, she was simply listening. Not only to them, but to everyone and everything beneath the gilded spires of the roof. Few people noticed the pitchers by every bed, the basins on every table. A bowl of water was a simple thing, but with the right spell, it could carry sound. With the right spell, Emira could make the palace speak.

Her fear of breaking things had taught her well to watch her step, to listen close. The world was a fragile place, full of cracks that didn't always show. One misstep, and they might fissure, break. One wrong move, and the whole of it could come crashing down, a tower of Sanct cards burned to cinders.

It was Emira's job to make sure that her world stayed strong, to shore the fractures, to listen for fresh cracks. It was her duty to keep her family safe, her palace whole, her kingdom well. It was her calling, and if she was careful enough, sharp enough, then nothing bad would happen. That is what Emira told herself.

Only *she had been wrong.*

She'd done everything she could, and Rhy had nearly died. A shadow had fallen on London. Her husband was hiding something. Kell would not look at her.

She hadn't been able to stop the cracks, but now she turned her focus on the rest of the palace.

As she walked the halls, she could hear the priests in the sparring room, the crinkle of scrolls, the drag of ink, the soft murmur as they prepared their spell.

She could hear the heavy tread of guards in armor moving through the lower levels, the deep, guttural voices of Veskans and the sibilant melody of the Faroan tongue in the eastern hall, the murmur of the nobles in the gallery as they sat up still, whispering over tea. Talking about the city, the curse, the king. What was he doing? What *could* he do? Maxim Maresh, gone soft with age and peace. Maxim Maresh, a man against a monster, against a god.

From the Rose Hall, Emira heard the toss and turn of the fevered bodies still trapped in burning dreams, and when she turned her ear to the palace's east wing she heard her son's similarly fitful sleep, echoed in turn by Kell's own restless turnings.

And through it all, the steady whisper against the windows, against the walls, words muffled by the wards, breaking down into the rise and fall and hush of the wind. A voice trying to get in.

Emira heard so many things, but she also heard the absences where sound should be, and wasn't. She heard the muffled hush of those trying too hard to be quiet. In a corner of the ballroom, a pair of guards summoning their courage. In an alcove, a noble and a magician tangled up like string. And in the map room, the sound of a single man standing alone before the table.

She went toward him, but drawing closer, she realized it wasn't her husband.

The man in the map room stood with his back to the door, head bent over the city of London. Emira watched as he reached out a single, dark finger and brought it to rest on the quartz figurine of a royal guard before the palace.

The figurine fell onto its side with the tiny clatter of stone on stone. Emira winced, but the statue did not break.

"Lord Sol-in-Ar," she said evenly.

The Faroan turned, the white gold gems embedded in his profile catching the light. He showed neither surprise at her presence nor guilt at his own.

"Your Majesty."

"Why are you here alone?"

"I was looking for the king," answered Sol-in-Ar in his smooth, susurrant way.

Emira shook her head, eyes darting around the room. It felt askew without Maxim. She scanned the table, as if something might be missing, but Sol-in-Ar had already righted the fallen piece and taken up another from the table's edge. The chalice and sun. The marker of the House Maresh.

The sigil of Arnes.

"I hope it is not out of line," he said, "to say I believe we are alike."

"You and my husband?"

A single shake of the head. "You and I."

Emira's face warmed even as the temperature in the room fell. "How so?"

"We both know much, and say little. We both stand at the side of kings. We are the truth whispered in their ears. The reason."

She said nothing, only inclined her head.

"The darkness is spreading," he added softly, though the words were full of edges. "It must be contained."

"It will be," answered the queen.

Sol-in-Ar nodded once. "Tell the king," he said, "that we can help. If he will let us."

The Faroan started toward the door.

"Lord Sol-in-Ar," she called after him. "Our standard."

He looked down at the carved figure in his hand as if he'd forgotten about it entirely. "Apologies," he said, setting the piece back on the board.

Emira finally found her husband in their chamber, though not in their bed. He'd fallen asleep at her writing desk, slumped forward on the carved wooden table, his head on folded arms atop a ledger, the scent of ink still fresh.

Only the first line was legible beneath his wrinkled sleeve.

To my son, the crown prince of Arnes, when it is time . . .

Emira drew in a sharp breath at the words, then steadied herself. She did not wake Maxim. Did not pull the book from its place beneath his head. She padded silently to the sofa, took up a throw, and settled the blanket over his shoulders.

He stirred briefly, arms shifting beneath his head, the small change revealing not only the next line—*know that a father lives for his son, but a king lives for his people*—but the bandage wrapped around his wrist. Emira stilled at the sight of it, lines of blood seeping through the crisp white linen.

What had Maxim done?

What was he yet planning to do?

She could hear the workings of the palace, but her husband's mind was solid, impenetrable. No matter how hard she listened, all she heard was his heart.

IX

As night fell, the shadows bloomed.

They ran together with the river and the mist and the moonless sky until they were everywhere. *Osaron* was everywhere. In every heartbeat. In every breath.

Some had escaped. For now. Others had been reduced already to dust. It was a necessary thing, like the razing of a forest, the clearing of ground so that new things—*better* things—could grow. A process as natural as the passing of the seasons.

Osaron was the fall, and the winter, and the spring.

And all across the city, he heard the voices of his loyal servants.

How can I serve you?

How can I worship?

Show me the way.

Tell me what to do.

He was in their minds.

He was in their bodies. He whispered in their heads and coursed through their blood. He was in every one of them, and bound to none.

Everywhere, and nowhere.

It was enough.

And it was *not* enough.

He wanted *more*.

SIX

EXECUTION

I

Grey London

Ned Tuttle woke to a very bad feeling.

He'd recently moved out of his family's house in Mayfair and into the room above the tavern—*his* tavern—that magical place once called the Stone's Throw, and rechristened the Five Points.

Ned sat up, listening intently to the silence. He could have sworn someone was speaking, but he couldn't hear the voice anymore, and, as the moments ticked past, he couldn't be sure if it had ever been real, or simply the dregs of sleep clinging to him, the urge to listen to an echo of some peculiar dream.

Ned had always had vivid dreams.

So vivid he couldn't always tell when something had truly happened or when he'd simply dreamed it. Ned's dreams had always been strange, and sometimes they were wonderful, but lately, they'd grown . . . disturbing, skewing darker, more menacing.

Growing up, his parents had written off his dreams as simply an effect of his reading too many novels, disappearing for hours—sometimes days—into fictional and fantastical worlds. In his youth, he'd seen the dreams as a sign of his sensitivity to the *other*, that aspect of the world most people couldn't see—the one even *Ned* couldn't see—but that he believed in, fervently, determinedly, doggedly, right up until the day he met Kell and learned for certain that the *other* was real.

But tonight, Ned had been dreaming of a forest made of stone. Kell was in the dream, too, had been at one point but wasn't anymore, and now Ned was lost, and every time he called out for help, the whole forest echoed like an empty church, but the voices that came back weren't his. Some of them were high and others low, some young and sweet, and others old, and there at the center, a voice he couldn't quite make out, one that bent around his ears the way light sometimes bent around a corner.

Now, sitting up in the stiff little bed, he had the strangest urge to call out, the way he had in the forest, but some small—well, not as small as he'd like—part of him feared that just like in the forest, someone *else* would call back.

Perhaps the sound had come from the tavern downstairs. He swung his long legs over the side of the bed, slid his feet into his slippers, and stood, the old wooden floor groaning beneath his toes.

He moved in silence, only that *creak-creak-creak* following him across the room, and then the *oomph* as he ran into the dresser, the *eek* of the metal lantern rocking, almost tipping, then *humph*ing back into place, followed by the *shhhh* of tapers rolling of the table.

"Bugger," muttered Ned.

It would have been dreadfully handy, he thought, if he could simply snap his fingers and summon a bit of fire, but in four straight months of trying, he'd barely managed to shift the pieces in Kell's kit of elements, so he fumbled on his robe in the dark and stepped out onto the stairs.

And shivered.

Something was most certainly strange.

Ordinarily Ned loved strange things, lived in the hope of spying them, but this was a type of strange bordering on *wrong*. The air smelled of roses and woodsmoke and dying leaves, and when he moved it felt like he was wading through a warm spot in a cold pool, or a cold spot in a warm one. Like a draft in a room when all the doors were shut, the windows latched.

He knew this feeling, had sensed it once before in the street outside the Five Points, back when it was the Stone's Throw and he was still waiting for Kell to return with his promised dirt. Ned had seen a cart crash, heard the driver rant about a man he'd crushed. Only there was no body left behind, no man, only smoke and ash and the faint frisson of magic.

Bad magic.

Black magic.

Ned returned to his room and fetched his ceremonial dagger—he'd bought it from a patron the week before, the handle etched with runes around a pentagram of inlaid onyx.

My name is Edward Archibald Tuttle, he thought, gripping the dagger, *I am the third of that name, and I am not afraid.*

The *creak-creak-creak* followed him down the warping stairs, and when he reached the bottom, standing in the darkened tavern with only the *thud-thud* of his heart, Ned realized where that feeling of strangeness was coming from.

The Five Points was too quiet.

A heavy, muffled, *unnatural* quiet, as if the room were filled with wool instead of air. The last embers in the hearth smoldered behind their grate, the wind blew through the boards, but none of it made any sound.

Ned went to the front door and threw back the bolt. Outside, the street was empty—it was the darkest hour, that time before the first streaks of dawn—but London was never truly still, not this close to the river, and so he was instantly greeted by the *clop-clop* of carriages, the distant trills of laughter and song. Somewhere near the Thames, the scrape of a fiddle, and much closer, the sound of a stray cat, yowling for milk or company or whatever stray cats wanted. A dozen sounds that made up the fabric of his city, and when Ned closed the door again, the noises followed him, sneaking in through the crack beneath the door, around the sill. The pressure ebbed, the air in the tavern thinning, the spell broken.

Ned yawned, the sense of strangeness already slipping away as he climbed the stairs. Back in his room, he cracked the window despite the cold, and let the sounds of London drift in. But as he crawled back into bed and pulled the covers up, and the world settled into silence, the whispers came again. And as he sank back into that place between waking and sleep, those elusive words finally took shape.

Let me in, they said.

Let me in.

II

Voices rang out past Holland's cell just after midnight.

"You're early," said the guard nearest the bars.

"Where's your second?" asked the one on the wall.

"The king needs men on the steps," answered the interloper, "what with the scarred fellows coming in." His voice was muffled by his helm.

"We've got orders."

"So do I," said the new guard. "And we're running thin."

A pause, and in that pause, Holland felt a strange thing happen. It was like someone took the air—the energy in the air—and pulled on it. Shallowly. A tug of will. A shifting of scales. A subtle exertion of control.

"Besides," the new guard was saying absently, "what would you rather be doing? Staring at this piece of filth, or saving your friends?"

The balance tipped. The men roused from their places. Holland wondered if the new guard knew what he'd done. It was the kind of magic forbidden in this world, and worshipped in his own.

The new guard watched the others climb the stairs, and swayed ever so slightly on his feet. When they were gone, he leaned back against the wall facing Holland's cell, the metal of his armor scraping stone, and drew a knife. He toyed with it absently, fingertips on the tip, tossing and catching and tossing it again. Holland felt himself being studied, and so he studied in return. Studied the way the new guard tipped his head, the speed of his fingers on the knife, the scent of another London wafting in his blood.

Her blood.

He should have recognized that voice, even through the stolen helm. Maybe if he'd slept—how long had it been?—maybe if he wasn't bloody and broken and behind bars. He still should have known.

"Delilah," he said evenly.

"Holland," she answered.

Delilah Bard, the *Antari* of Grey London, set her helmet on the table beneath a hook holding the jailer's keys. Her fingers danced absently across their teeth. "Your last night . . ."

"Did you come to say farewell?"

She made a humming sound. "Something like that."

"You're a long way from home."

Her gaze flicked toward him, quick and sharp as a sliver of steel. "So are you." One of her eyes had the glassy sheen that came with too much drink. The other, the false one, had been shattered. It hung together by a shell of glass, but the inside was a starburst of color and cracks.

Lila's knife vanished back into its sheath. She pulled off the gauntlets, one by one, and set them on the table, too. Even drunk, she moved with the fluid grace of a fighter. She reminded him of Ojka.

"Ojka," she echoed, as if reading his mind.

Holland stilled. "What?"

Lila tapped her cheek. "The redhead with the scar and the face leaking black. She did this—tried to drive a knife into my eye—right before I cut her throat."

The words were a dull blow. Just a small flame of hope flickering out inside his chest. Nothing left. Ash over embers. "She was following orders," he said hollowly.

Lila lifted the keys from their hook. "Yours or Osaron's?"

It was a hard question. When had they been different? Had they ever been the same?

He heard the clang of metal, and Holland blinked to find the cell door falling open, Lila stepping in. She pulled the door shut behind her, snapped the lock back into place.

"If you came to kill me—"

"No," she sneered. "That can wait till morning."

"Then why are you here?"

"Because good people die, and bad people live, and it doesn't seem very fair, does it, Holland?" Her face crinkled. "Of all the people you could kill, you chose someone who actually mattered to me."

"I had to."

Her fist hit him like a brick, hard enough to crack his head sideways and make the world go momentarily white. When his vision cleared, she was standing over him, knuckles bleeding.

She tried to strike him again, but this time Holland caught her wrist.

"Enough," he said.

But it wasn't. Her free hand swung up, fire dancing across her knuckles, but he caught that, too.

"Enough."

She tried to pull free, but his hands vised tighter, finding the tender place where bones met. He pressed down, and a guttural sound escaped her throat, low and animal.

"It does nothing to dwell on what's been taken from you," he snarled. *"Nothing."*

Over seven years, Holland's life had been distilled to one desire. To see Athos and Astrid Dane suffer. And Kell had stolen that from him. Stolen the look in Astrid's eyes as he drove the dagger through her heart. Stolen Athos's expression as he took him apart piece by piece.

No one suffers as beautifully as you do.

Seven years.

Holland shoved Lila back. She stumbled, her shoulders hitting the bars. For a moment, the cell was filled with only the sounds of ragged breathing as they stared at one another across the narrow space, two beasts caged together.

And then, slowly, Lila straightened, flexing her hands.

"If you want your revenge," he said, "take it."

One of us should have it, he thought, closing his eyes. He took a steadying breath and began to count his dead, starting with Alox and ending with Ojka.

But when he opened his eyes again, Delilah Bard was gone.

They came to collect him just after dawn.

In truth, he didn't know the hour, but he could feel the palace stirring overhead, the subtle warming of the world beyond the prison's pillar. With so many years of cold, he'd learned to sense the smallest shifts in warmth, knew how to mark the passing of a day.

The guards came and freed Holland from the wall, and for a moment, he was bound by nothing but two hands before they wrapped the chains around his wrists, his shoulders, his waist. The heavy metal was hobbling, and it took all his strength to keep his feet, to climb the stairs, his stride reduced to a halting step.

"*On vis och*," he told himself.

Dawn to dusk. A phrase that meant two things in his native tongue.

A fresh start. A good end.

The guards marched Holland up and through the palace halls, where men and women gathered to watch him pass. They led him out onto a balcony, a large space stripped bare except for a broad wooden platform, freshly constructed, and on it, a block of stone.

On vis och.

Holland felt the change as soon as he stepped outside, the prickling magic of the palace wards giving way to nothing but crisp air and light so bright it stung his eyes.

The sun was rising on a frigid day, and Holland, still stripped to the waist beneath the chains, felt the icy air bite viciously into his skin. But he had long ago learned not to give others the satisfaction of his suffering. And though he knew he stood at the center of a performance—had in fact orchestrated it himself—Holland could not bring himself to shiver and beg. Not in front of these people.

The king was present, and the prince, as well as four more guards, their foreheads marked with blood, and a handful of magicians, similarly stained—a young, silver-haired man, the wind jostling around his limbs; a pair of dark-skinned twins, their faces set with gems; a blond man built like a wall. There, beside them, his skin scarred by silver lines, stood an almost-familiar man with a blue gem above one eye; an old man in white robes, a drop of crimson on his brow; Delilah Bard, her shattered brown eye catching the light.

And last—just there, on the platform, beside the stone block—stood Kell, a long sword in his hands, its broad point resting on the ground.

Holland's steps must have slowed, because one of the guards drove a gauntlet into his back, forcing him forward, up the two short steps onto the newly built dais. He came to a stop and straightened, looking out at the darkened river beyond the balcony.

So like Black London.

Too like Black London.

"Second thoughts?" asked Kell, gripping the sword.

"No," said Holland, staring past him. "Just taking a moment to enjoy the view."

His gaze flicked to the young *Antari,* took in the way he held the sword, one hand around the hilt and the other resting on the blade, pressing down just hard enough to draw a line of blood.

"If he does not come—" started Holland.

"I'll make it quick."

"Last time, you missed my heart."

"I won't miss your head," answered Kell. "But I hope it doesn't come to that."

Holland started to speak but forced the words down.

They served no purpose.

Still, he thought them.

I hope it does.

The king's voice thundered through the cold morning.

"Kneel," ordered the ruler of Arnes.

Holland stiffened at the word, his mind stuttering into another day, another life, cold steel and Athos's smooth voice—but he let the weight of the memories, as well as the present weight of chains, pull him down. He kept his eyes on the river, the darkness moving just beneath the surface, and when he spoke, his voice was low, the words meant not for the crowd on the balcony, or for Kell, but for the shadow king.

"Help me."

The words were nothing but a breath of fog. To the gathered crowd, it might have looked like a prayer, given to whatever gods they thought he worshipped. And in a way, it was.

"*Antari*," said the king, addressing him not by name, or even title, only by what he was, and Holland wondered if Maxim Maresh even knew his given name.

Vosijk, he almost said. *My name is Holland Vosijk.*

But it didn't matter now.

"You are guilty of grievous sins against the empire, guilty of practicing forbidden magic, of inciting chaos and ruin, of bringing war...."

The king's words washed around him as Holland tipped his head back toward the sky. Birds flew high overhead, while shadows threaded through the low clouds. Osaron was there. Holland gritted his teeth and forced himself to speak, not to the men around him, not to the king or Kell, but to the presence lurking, listening.

"Help me."

"You are sentenced to death by the blade for your crimes, your body committed to fire...."

He could feel the *oshoc*'s magic weaving through his hair, brushing against his skin, but still it did not come.

"If you have any words, speak them now, but know that your fate is sealed."

He heard a new voice, then, like a vibration in the winter air.

Beg.

Holland went still.

"Have you nothing to say?" demanded the king.

Beg.

Holland swallowed, and did something he'd never done, not in seven years of slavery and torture.

"Please," he begged, first softly, and then louder. "Please. I will be yours."

The darkness laughed but did not come.

Holland's pulse began to race, the chains suddenly too tight.

"*Osaron,*" he called out. "This body is yours. This life—what's left of it—is yours—"

The guards were on either side of him now, gauntleted fists forcing Holland's head forward onto the block.

"Osaron," he growled, fighting their grip for the first time.

The laughter continued, ringing through his head.

"Gods don't need bodies, but kings do! How will you rule without a head for your crown?"

Kell was beside him now, both hands on the sword's hilt.

"End it," ordered the king.

Wait, thought Holland.

"Kill him," said Lila.

"Be still," demanded Kell.

Holland's vision narrowed to the wood of the platform.

"Osaron!" he bellowed as Kell's sword sang upward.

It never came down.

A shadow swept over the balcony. One moment the sun was there, and the next, they were plunged into shade, and everyone looked up in time to see the wave of black water crest overhead and come crashing down.

Holland twisted sideways, still clinging to the stone block as the river slammed onto the platform. One of the guards was knocked over the edge, down into the roiling surf below, while the other held on to Holland.

The icy torrent knocked the blade from Kell's hands and sent him backward across the dais, a shard of ice pinning his sleeve to the floor as the guards dove to cover the king and prince. The wave hit the steps between the platform and the balcony and splashed up, swirling first into a column, before its edges smoothed and pulled together into the shape of a man.

A king.

Osaron smiled at Holland.

"*Do you see?*" he said in his echoing way. "*I can be merciful.*"

Someone was moving across the balcony. The silver-haired magician came surging forward, the air like knives around him.

Osaron didn't take his eyes off Holland, but he flicked his watery fingers and a spike of ice materialized, launching toward the magician's chest. The man actually smiled as he spun around the shard, the movement light as air before shattering it with a single sharp gust.

Silver hair and swirling robes danced again toward Osaron, a blur, and then the magician slashed, one hand surrounded by a blade of wind. Osaron's watery form parted around the magician's wrist, then vised closed. The airborne magician slammed to a stop, pinned in the icy core of Osaron's form. Before he could break free, the shadow king drove his own hand through the magician's chest.

His fingers went clean through, icy black points glistening with streams of red.

"Jinnar!" screamed someone as the wind suddenly died atop the platform, and the magician collapsed, lifeless, to the ground.

Osaron shook the blood from his fingers as he climbed the steps.

"*Tell me, Holland,*" he said. "*Do I look in need of a body?*"

Using their distraction, Kell tore the icy shard free of his sleeve and threw it hard at the shadow king's back. Holland was grudgingly, fleetingly, impressed—but it passed right through Osaron's watery form. He turned, as if amused, to face Kell.

"*It will take more than that,* Antari."

"I know," said Kell, and Holland saw the ribbon of blood swirling in the column of water that formed Osaron's chest the moment before Kell said, "*As Isera.*"

And just like that, Osaron *froze.*

It happened in an instant, the shadow king replaced by a statue rendered in ice.

Holland met Kell's gaze through the frozen surface of Osaron's torso.

He saw it first, relief turning to horror as the dead magician—Jinnar—rose to his feet. His eyes were black—not shadowed, but solid—his skin already beginning to burn with the strength of his new host. And when he spoke, a smooth, familiar voice poured out.

"*It will take more than that,*" said Osaron again, silver hair steaming.

Bodies were rising around him, and Holland understood too late. The wave. The water. "Kell!" he shouted. "The blood marks—"

He was cut off by a fist as the nearest guard drove a gauntleted hand into his ribs, the crimson smear on his helmet washed away by the first swell of the river. "Kneel before the king."

The silver-scarred man and the Maresh prince both surged forward, but Kell stopped them with a jagged slash of his arm, a wall of ice surging up and cutting them off from the platform and Osaron.

Osaron, who now stood between Holland and Kell in his stolen host, his skin flaking away like curls of burning paper.

Holland forced himself up despite the weight of chains. "What a poor substitute you've chosen," he said, drawing the *oshoc*'s attention as Kell shifted forward, blood dripping from his fingers. "How quickly it crumbles." His voice was low amid the surge of chaos, dripping with disdain. "It is not a body for a king."

"*You would still offer yours instead,*" mused Osaron. His shell was dying fast, lit by a bloodred glow that cracked along his skin.

"I do," said Holland.

"*Tempting,*" said Osaron. His black eyes burned inside his skull. In a flash, he was at Holland's side. *"But I'd rather watch you fall."*

Holland felt the push before he saw the hand, felt the force against his chest and the sudden weight of gravity as the world shifted and the platform disappeared, and the chains pulled him over the edge and down, down, down into the river below.

III

Kell saw Holland fall.

One moment the *Antari* was there, at the edge, and the next he was gone, plunging down into the river with no magic at hand, only the cold, dead weight of the spelled iron around him. The balcony was chaos, one guard on his knees, fighting the fog, while Lila and Alucard squared off against the animated corpse of Jinnar, who was now nothing more than charred bone.

There wasn't time to think, to wonder, to question.

Kell dove.

The drop was farther than it seemed.

The impact knocked the air from Kell's lungs, jarring his bones, and he gasped as the river closed over him, ice-cold and black as ink.

Far below, almost out of sight, a pale form sank to the bottom of the tainted water.

Kell swam down toward Holland, lungs aching as he fought the press of the river—not only the weight of water, but Osaron's magic, leaching heat and focus as it tried to force its way in.

By the time he reached Holland, the man was on his knees on the river floor, his lips moving faintly, soundlessly, his body weighed down by the shackles at his wrists and the steel chains around his waist and legs. The *Antari* struggled to his feet but couldn't manage any further. After a brief struggle he lost his battle with gravity and sank back to his knees, driving up a cloud of silt as the irons hit the riverbed.

Kell hovered in front of him, his own coat heavy with water, its weight enough to keep him under. He drew his dagger, slicing skin before he realized the futility—the instant the blood welled, it vanished, dissipated by the current. Kell swore, sacrificing a thin stream of air as Holland struggled to hold on to the last of his own. Holland's black hair floated in the water around his face, his eyes closed, a resignation to his posture, as if he would rather drown than return to the world above.

As if he meant to end his life here, at the bottom of the river.

But Kell couldn't let him do that.

Holland's eyes flashed open as Kell took hold of his shoulders, crouching to reach his wrists where they were weighted to the river floor. The *Antari* shook his head minutely, but Kell didn't let go. His whole body ached from the cold and the lack of air, and he could see Holland's chest stuttering as he fought the urge to breathe in.

Kell wrapped his hands around the iron shackles and pulled, not with muscle but with magic. Iron was a mineral, somewhere between stone and earth on the spectrum of elements. He couldn't unmake it, but he could—with enough effort—change its shape.

Transmuting an element was no small feat, even in a workroom with ample time and focus; doing it underwater surrounded by dark magic while his chest screamed and Holland slowly drowned was something else entirely.

Focus, Master Tieren chided in his head. *Unfocus.*

Kell squeezed his eyes shut and tried to remember Tieren's instructions.

Elements are not whole unto themselves, the Aven Essen *had said, but parts, each a knot on the same, ever-circling rope, one giving way onto the next and the next. There is a natural pause, but no seam.*

It had been years since he'd learned to do this; ages since he'd stood in the head priest's study with a glass in each hand, following the lines of the element spectrum as he poured the contents back and forth, turning a cup of water into sand, sand into rock, rock into fire, fire into air, air into water. On and on, slowly, painstakingly, the action never as natural as the theory. The priests could do it—they were so attuned to the subtleties of magic, the boundaries between elements porous in their hands—but Kell's magic was too loud, too bright, and half the time he faltered, shattering the glass or spilling contents that were now half rock, half glass.

Focus.

Unfocus.

The iron was cold under his hands.

Unyielding.

Knots on a rope.

Holland was dying.

The watery world swirled darkly.

Focus.

Unfocus.

Kell's eyes flashed open. He met Holland's gaze, and as the metal began to soften in his hands, something flashed across the magician's face, and Kell realized suddenly that Holland's resignation had been a mask, veiling the panic beneath. The cuffs gave way beneath Kell's desperate fingers, turning from iron to sand, silt that formed a cloud and then dissolved in the river's current.

Holland lurched forward in the sudden absence of chains. He rose up, the need for air propelling him toward the surface.

Kell pushed off the river floor to follow.

Or tried to.

He lifted a few feet, only to be wrenched back down, held fast by a sudden, unseen force. The last of Kell's air escaped in a violent stream as he fought the water's hold. The force tightened around his legs, tried to crush the strength from his limbs, his chest, dragging his arms out to his sides in a gruesome echo of the steel frame in the White London castle.

The water before Kell shifted and swirled, the current bending around the outlines of a man.

Hello again, Antari.

Too late, Kell understood. That last moment on the balcony, when Osaron had looked not at Holland, but at him. Pushing Holland into the river, knowing Kell would save him. They'd set a trap for the shadow king, and he'd set one for them. For *him*.

After all, Kell was the one who'd resisted, the one who'd refused to yield.

Now will you kneel?

The invisible bonds forced Kell to the river floor. His lungs flamed as he tried to push back against the river. Tried, and failed. Panic tore through him.

Now will you beg?

He closed his eyes and tried to fight against the need for air that screamed through his chest, drowning his senses. His vision flickered with spots of white light and hollow black.

Now will you let me in?

IV

Lila saw Kell vanish over the balcony's edge.

At first, she thought he must have been knocked over, that surely he wouldn't have *willingly* jumped into the black water, not for Holland, but then she remembered his words—*it could have been me*—and she realized, with icy clarity, that Kell hadn't told her the truth. The execution was a farce. Holland was never supposed to die.

It had all been a trap, and Osaron hadn't taken the bait, and now Holland was sinking to the bottom of the Isle, and Kell was going with him.

"Fucking hell," muttered Lila, shrugging out of her coat.

On the balcony, Jinnar had collapsed, body crumbling to muddy ash, while those who'd fallen to Osaron's spell were being subdued. A pair of silver-scarred guards fought to regain order while a third fought the fever raging through him. The king shoved past his own guard, scouring the balcony, while Alucard shielded Rhy, who had one hand to his chest as if he couldn't breathe.

Because, of course, he *couldn't* breathe. Kell wasn't the only one drowning.

Lila turned, mounted the balcony edge, and jumped.

The water cut like knives. She sputtered, shocked by the pain and the cold, and she was going to *kill* someone when this was over.

Without the weight of her coat, her body rebelled, trying with every stride to lift her toward the surface, toward air, toward life. Instead she swam down, lungs burning, icy water stinging her open eyes, toward the shape on the river floor. She expected it to be Holland, weighed down by chains. But the figure was thrashing freely, his hair a tangled cloud.

Kell.

Lila kicked toward him when a hand caught her arm. She twisted around behind her to see Holland, now free of chains.

She brought up her boot to kick him away, but the water gripped it and his fingers tightened as he forced her back around to face the struggling figure on the river floor.

For a sick, frozen moment she thought he wanted her to watch Kell die.

But then she saw it, the faint outline of something—*someone*—hovering in the water before him.

Osaron.

Holland pointed at himself and then the shadow king. He pointed at her and then Kell. And then he let go, and she understood.

They dove as one, but Holland reached the bottom first, landing in a plume of silt that caught the edges of the shadow king like dust catching light.

Lila reached Kell's side in the cover of the clouded water and tried to pull him up, pull him free, but Osaron's will held firm. She flung a desperate hand toward Holland, a speechless plea, and the magician spread his arms and *shoved.*

The river recoiled, flung away in every direction, carving out a column of air with Kell and Lila at its center. Kell and Lila, but not Holland.

Lila drew in a deep breath, lungs aching, while Kell collapsed to the river floor, gasping and heaving up water.

Get him out, mouthed Holland, hands trembling from the force of holding the river—and *Osaron*—at bay.

With what? Lila wanted to say. They might be able to breathe, but they were still standing at the bottom of the river, Kell only half conscious and Lila with all her strength but none of his skill. She couldn't craft wings of air, couldn't sculpt a set of stairs from ice. Her gaze went to the silt floor.

The column of air swayed around them.

Holland was losing his hold.

Shadows grew, curling in the water around the faltering *Antari,* like roaming limbs, fingers, mouths.

She wanted to leave him, but Kell had brought them here, to this point, all for Holland's bloody life. *Leave him. Save him. Damn him.* Lila snarled and, keeping one hand on Kell's sleeve, thrust the other out toward the column, widening the circle until Holland staggered forward, safely within.

Safe being a relative thing.

Holland drew in ragged breaths, and Kell, finally recovering his senses, pressed his palms to the damp river floor. It began to rise, a disk of earth beneath their feet surging toward the surface as the column collapsed below.

They broke the surface and scrambled onto the riverbank beneath the palace, dropping to the ground soaked and half frozen, but alive.

Holland was the first to recover, but before he was even halfway to his feet, Lila had a knife against his throat.

"Steady now," she said, her own limbs shaking.

"Wait—" Kell began to speak, but the king and his men were already on them, the guards forcing Holland back to his knees on the icy bank. When they realized he was no longer chained, half of them lunged forward, blades drawn, the other half away. But Holland made no move to strike. Lila kept her knife out all the same until the king's men had hauled their prisoner back toward the cells. In their wake, Rhy came storming down the riverbank. The prince's jaw was set, his cheeks red, as if he'd almost drowned. Because, of course, he had.

Kell saw him coming.

"Rhy—"

The prince slammed his fist into his brother's face.

Kell staggered backward to the ground, and the prince reeled back in mirrored pain, cradling his own cheek.

Rhy grabbed Kell by the soaking collar of his coat. "I've made my peace with death," he said, jabbing a finger at Holland's retreating form. "But I refuse to die for *him.*"

With that, Rhy shoved his brother away again. Kell's mouth opened and closed, a fleck of blood at the corner of his lip, but the prince turned and marched back toward the palace.

Lila brushed herself off.

"You had that coming," she said before leaving Kell on the bank, soaked and shivering and alone.

V

"Gods don't need bodies, but kings do."

Osaron *seethed* at the words echoing through his mind. Weeds to be torn out at the root. After all, he was a god. And a god did not need a body. A shell. A *cage*. A god was everywhere.

The river rippled, and from it rose a drop, a shimmering black bead that stretched and lengthened until it had a form, limbs, fingers, a face. Osaron stood on the surface of the water.

Holland was *wrong*.

A body was merely a tool, a thing to be used, discarded, but it was never *needed*.

Osaron had wanted to kill Holland slowly, to tear out his mortal heart—a heart he *knew*, a heart he'd listened to for months.

He had given Holland so much—a second chance, a city reborn—and all he'd asked for in return was *cooperation*.

They'd made a deal.

And Holland would pay for breaking it.

The insolence of these Antari.

As for the *other* two—

He hadn't decided yet how to use them.

Kell was a temptation.

A gift given, and then lost, a body to break in—or simply break.

And the girl. Delilah. Strong and sharp. So much fight. So much promise. So much *more* that she could be.

He wanted—

No.

But then—

It was a different thing, for a god to want, and a human to need.

He didn't *need* these playthings, these shells.

Did not need to be *confined*.

He was everywhere.

(It was enough.)

It was—

Osaron looked down at his form sculpted of dark water, and was reminded of another body, another world.

Missing—

No.

But something *was* missing.

He drifted up from the surface of the water, rose into the air to survey the city that would become *his* city, and frowned. It was midday, and yet London sulked in shadow. The mists of his power shimmered, twisted, coiled, but beneath their blanket, the city looked *dull*.

The world—his world—should be beautiful, bright, filled with the light of magic, the song of power.

It *would* be, once the city stopped fighting. Once they all bowed, all kneeled, all recognized him as king, then he could make the city what it would be, what it *should* be. Progress was a process, change took time, a winter before every spring.

But in the meantime—

Missing—

What was missing—

He spun in place, and there it was.

The royal palace.

Somewhere inside, the defiant huddled, hiding behind their wards as if wards would outlast *him*. And they would fall, in time, but it was the palace itself that shone in his gaze, rising above the blackened river like a second sun, casting its spokes of reddish light into the sky even now, its echo dancing on the mirror-dark surface of the river.

Every ruler needed a palace.

He'd had one once, of course, at the center of his first city. A beautiful thing sculpted from want and will and sheer potential. Osaron had told himself he would not repeat that place, would not make the same mistakes—

But that was the wrong word.

He'd been young, learning, and though the city had fallen, it wasn't the *palace's* doing. Wasn't *his* doing. It was theirs, the people's, with their flawed minds, their brittle shapes—and yes, he'd given them the power, but he knew better now, knew the power must be his and his alone, and it had been *such* a splendid palace. The dark heart of his kingdom.

It would do better here.

Right here.

Then, perhaps, this place would feel like home.

Home.

What a strange idea.

But still. Here. This.

Osaron had risen high into the air now, far above the shimmering black expanse of the river, the lifeless arenas, hulking skeletons of stone and wood topped with their lions and serpents and birds of prey, their bodies empty, their banners still whipping in the breeze.

Right here.

He spread his hands and pulled on the strings of this world, on the threads of power in the stadium stones and the water below, and the massive silhouettes began to draw together, groaning as they came free from their bridges and holds.

In his mind, the palace took shape, smoke and stone and magic prying loose, rearranging into something else, something more. And, as in his mind, so in the world below. His new palace lengthened like a shadow, rising up instead of out, tendrils of mist climbing the sides like vines, smoothing into polished black stone like new flesh over old bones. Overhead, the stadium banners rose like smoke before hardening into a crown of glossy spires above his creation.

Osaron smiled.

It was a start.

VI

Kell had always been a fan of silence.

He craved those too-rare moments when the world calmed and the chaos of life in the palace gave way to easy, comfortable stillness.

This was *not* that kind of silence.

No, this silence was a hollow, sulking thing, a heavy quiet broken only by the drip of river water hitting the polished floor, and the fire crackling in the hearth, and the shuffle of Rhy's restless steps.

Kell sat in one of the prince's chairs, a cup of scalding hot tea in one hand, his bruised jaw in the other, his hair a mess of damp red streaks, beads of river water trickling down his neck. While Tieren tended to his bruised lungs, Kell took stock of the damage—two guards were dead, as well as another Arnesian magician. Holland was back in the cells, the queen was in the gallery, and the king stood across the room by the prince's hearth, his face shadowed, gaunt. Hastra was by the doors, Alucard Emery—a shade Kell seemingly couldn't be rid of—sat on the couch with a glass of wine, while his shipmate, Lenos, hovered like a shadow at his back. Blood and ash still stained Alucard's front. Some of it was his, but the rest belonged to Jinnar.

Jinnar—who'd taken it upon himself to fight, and failed.

The single best wind worker in Arnes, reduced to a burning puppet, a pile of ash.

Lila was lounging on the floor, her back against Alucard's sofa, and the sight of her sitting there—near the damned privateer instead of Kell—stoked the fire in Kell's aching chest.

The minutes ticked past, and his damp hair finally began to dry, yet no one spoke. Instead the air hummed with the frustration of things unsaid, of fights gone dormant.

"Well," said the prince at last, "I think it's safe to say that didn't go as planned."

The words broke the seal, and suddenly the room was filled with voices.

"Jinnar was my *friend*," said Alucard, glaring at Kell, "and he's dead because of you."

"Jinnar is dead because of himself," said Kell, shaking off Tieren's attentions. "No one forced him onto that balcony. No one told him to attack the shadow king."

Lila scowled. "You should have let Holland drown."

"Why didn't you?" interjected Rhy.

"After all," she went on, "wasn't it supposed to be an *execution*? Or did you have other plans? Ones you didn't share with us."

"Yes, Kell," chimed Alucard. "Do enlighten us."

Kell shot the captain a frigid look. "Why are you here?"

"Kell," said the king in a low, stern way. "Tell them."

Kell ran a hand through his frizzing hair, frustrated. "Osaron needs permission to take an *Antari* shell," he said. "The plan was for Holland to let Osaron in, and for me to then kill Holland."

"I knew it," said Lila.

"So did Osaron, it seems," said Rhy.

"During the execution," continued Kell, "Holland was trying to draw Osaron in. When Osaron appeared, I assumed it had worked, but then when he pushed Holland into the river . . . I didn't think—"

"No," snapped Rhy, "you didn't."

Kell held his ground. "He *might* have let Holland drown, *or* he might have simply been trying to get him away from us before claiming his shell, and if you think Osaron is bad without a body, you should have seen him in Holland's. I didn't realize he was after *me* until it was too late."

"It was the right thing to do," said the king. Kell looked at him, stunned. It was the closest Maxim had come to taking Kell's side in *months*.

"Well," said Rhy peevishly, "Holland is still alive, and Osaron is still free, and we still have no idea how to stop him."

Kell pressed his palms to his eyes. "Osaron still needs a body."

"He doesn't seem to think so," said Lila.

"He'll change his mind," said Kell.

Rhy stopped pacing. "How do you know?"

"Because right now, he can afford to be stubborn. He has too many options." Kell looked to Tieren, who had remained silent, still as stone. "Once you put the city to sleep, he'll run out of bodies to play with. He'll get restless. He'll get angry. And then we'll have his attention."

"And what do we do *then*?" said Lila, exasperated. "Even if we can convince Osaron to take the body we give him, we have to be fast enough to trap him in it. It's like trying to catch lightning."

"We need another way to contain him," said Rhy. "Something better than a body. Bodies come with minds, and those, as we know, can be manipulated." He plucked a small silver sphere off a shelf, and stretched it out between his fingers. The sphere was made of fine metal cords woven in such a way that they drew apart, expanding into a large orb of delicate filaments, and folded back together, collapsing into a dense ball of tightly coiled silver. "We need something stronger. Something permanent."

"We would need an Inheritor," said Tieren softly.

The room looked to the *Aven Essen,* but it was Maxim who spoke. He was turning red. "You told me they didn't exist."

"No," said Tieren. "I told you I would not help you *make* one."

The priest and the king locked stares for long enough that Rhy spoke up. "Anyone want to explain?"

"An Inheritor," said Tieren slowly, addressing the room, "is a device that transfers magic. And even if it could be made, it is by its very nature corrupt, an outright defiance of cardinal law and an *interference*"—Maxim stiffened at this—"with the natural order of magical selection."

The room went quiet. The king's face was rigid with anger, Rhy's own features set but pale, and understanding settled in Kell's chest. A device to transfer magic would be able to grant it to those without.

What wouldn't a father do for a son born without power? What wouldn't a king do for his heir?

When the prince spoke, his voice was careful, even. "Is that really possible, Tieren?"

"In *theory*," answered the priest, crossing to an ornate desk that stood in the corner of the room. He pulled a piece of parchment from the drawer, produced a pencil from one of the many folds of his white priest robes, and began to draw.

"Magic, as you know, does not follow blood. It chooses the strong and the weak as it will. As is *natural*," he added, casting a stern look at the king. "But some time ago, a nobleman named Tolec Loreni wanted a way to pass on not only his land and his titles, but also his power to his beloved eldest son." The sketch on the page began to take shape. A metal cylinder shaped like a scroll, the length embossed with spellwork. "He designed a device that could be spelled to take and hold a person's power until the next of kin could lay claim to it."

"Hence, *Inheritor*," said Lila.

Rhy swallowed. "And it actually worked?"

"Well, no," said Tieren. "The spell killed him instantly. But"—he brightened—"his niece, Nadina, had a rather brilliant mind. She perfected the design, and the first Inheritor was made."

Kell shook his head. "Why have I never heard of this? And if they worked, why aren't they still used?"

"Power does not like being forced into lines," said Tieren pointedly. "Nadina Loreni's Inheritor worked. But it worked on *anyone. For* anyone. There was no way to control *who* claimed the contents of an Inheritor. Magicians could be *persuaded* to relinquish the entirety of their power to the device, and once it was surrendered to the Inheritor, it was anyone's to claim. As you can imagine, things got . . . messy. In the end, most of the Inheritors were destroyed."

"But if we could find the Loreni designs," said Lila, "if we could re-create one—"

"We don't need to," said Alucard, speaking up at last. "I know exactly where to find one."

VII

"What do you mean you *sold* it?" Kell snapped at the captain.

"I didn't know what it *was*."

This had been going on for several minutes now, and Lila poured herself a fresh drink as the room around her hummed with Kell's anger, the king's frustration, Alucard's annoyance.

"I didn't recognize the magic," Alucard was saying for the third time. "I'd never seen anything like it before. I knew it was rare, but that was all."

"You *sold* an *Inheritor*," repeated Kell, drawing out the words.

"Technically," said Alucard, defensively, "I didn't *sell* it. I offered it in trade."

Everyone groaned at that.

"Who did you give it to?" demanded Maxim. The king didn't look well—dark bruises stood out beneath his eyes, as though he hadn't slept in days. Not that any of them had, but Lila liked to think she wore fatigue rather well, given her sheer amount of practice.

"Maris Patrol," answered Alucard.

The king reddened at the name. No one else seemed to notice. Lila did. "You know them."

The king's attention snapped toward her. "What? No. Only by reputation."

Lila knew a lie, especially a bad one, but Rhy cut in.

"And what reputation is that?"

The king wasn't the one to answer. Lila noticed that, too.

"Maris runs the *Ferase Stras*," said Alucard.

"The Going Waters?" translated Kell, assuming Lila didn't know the words. She did. "I've never heard of it," he added.

"I'm not surprised," said the captain.

"*Er an merst . . .*" started Lenos, speaking up for the first time. *It's a market.* Alucard shot the man a look, but the shipmate kept going, his voice soft, the accent rural Arnesian. "It caters to sailors of a special sort, looking to trade in . . ." He finally caught the captain's look and trailed off.

"You mean a black market," offered Lila, tipping her drink toward the captain. "Like Sasenroche."

The king raised a brow at that.

"Your Majesty," started Alucard. "It was before I served the crown—"

The king held up a hand, clearly not interested in excuses. "You believe the Inheritor is still there?"

Alucard nodded once. "The head of the market took a shine to it. Last I saw, it was around Maris's neck."

"And where is this *Ferase Stras*?" asked Tieren, pushing a piece of parchment toward them. On it, he'd outlined a rough map of the empire. No labels, just the drawn borders of land. The sight tickled something in the back of Lila's mind.

"That's the thing," said Alucard, running a hand through his messy brown curls. "It moves around."

"Can you find it?" demanded Maxim.

"With a pirate's cipher, sure," answered Alucard, "but I don't have one anymore. On the honor of Arnes, I swear—"

"You mean it was confiscated when you were arrested," said Kell.

Alucard shot him a venomous look.

"A pirate's cipher?" asked Lila. "Is that a kind of sea map?"

Alucard nodded. "Not all sea maps are made equal, though. They all have the ports, the paths to avoid, the best places and times for making deals. But a pirate's cipher is designed to keep secrets. To the passing eye, the cipher's practically useless, nothing but lines. Not even a city named." He glanced at Tieren's rough map. "Like that."

Lila frowned. There it was again, that tickle, only now it took shape.

Behind her eyes, another room in another London in another life. A map with no markings spread across the table in the attic of the Stone's Throw, weighted down by the night's take.

She must have lowered her guard, let the memory show in her face, because Kell touched her arm. "What is it?"

She drew a finger around the rim of her glass, trying not to betray the emotion in her voice. "I had a map like that once. Nicked it from a shop when I was fifteen. Didn't even know what it was—the parchment was all rolled up, bound with string—but it just kind of . . . *pulled* at me, so I took it. Weird thing was, after all that, I never thought to sell the thing. I suppose I liked the idea of a map with no names, no places, nothing but land and sea and promise. My map to anywhere, that's what I called it. . . ."

Lila realized the room had gone quiet. They were all staring at her, the king and the captain, the magician and the priest and the prince. "What?"

"Where is it now," said Rhy, "this map to anywhere?"

Lila shrugged. "Back in Grey London, I suspect, in a room at the top of the Stone's Throw."

"No," said Kell gently. "It's not there anymore."

The knowledge hit her like a blow. A last door slamming closed. "Oh . . ." she said, a little breathless, "well . . . I should have figured someone would—"

"I took it," cut in Kell. And then, before she could ask him why, he added, hurriedly, "It just caught my eye. It's like you said, Lila, the map has a kind of pull to it. Must be the spellwork."

"Must be," said Alucard dryly.

Kell scowled at the captain, but went to fetch the map.

While he was gone, Maxim lowered himself into a chair, fingers gripping the cushioned arms. If anyone else noticed the strain in the monarch's dark eyes, they said nothing, but Lila watched as Tieren moved too, taking up a place behind the king's chair. One hand came to rest on Maxim's shoulder, and Lila saw the king's features softening, some pain or malady eased by the priest's touch.

She didn't know why the sight made her nervous, but she was still trying to shake the prickle of unease when Kell returned, map in hand. The room gathered around the table, all but the king, while Kell unfurled his prize, weighting the edges. One side was stained with long-dry blood. Lila's fingers drifted toward the stain, but she stopped herself and shoved her hands instead in the pockets of her coat, fingers curling around her timepiece.

"I went back once," said Kell softly, head tipped toward hers. "After Barron . . ."

After Barron, he said. As if Barron had been a simple thing, a marker in time. As if Holland hadn't cut his throat.

"Nick anything else?" she asked, voice tight. Kell shook his head. "I'm sorry," he said, and she didn't know if he was sorry for taking the map, or for not taking more, or for simply reminding Lila of a life—a death—she wanted so badly to forget.

"Well," asked the king, "*is* it a cipher?"

Alucard, on the other side of the table, nodded. "It appears to be."

"But the doors were sealed centuries ago," said Kell. "How would an Arnesian pirate's cipher even come to *be* in Grey London?"

Lila blew out a breath. "Honestly, Kell."

"What?" he snapped.

"You weren't the first *Antari,*" she said, "and I'll bet you weren't the first to break the rules, either."

Alucard raised a brow at the mention of Kell's past crimes, but had the sense for once to say nothing. He kept his attention fixed on the map, running his fingers back and forth as if searching for a clue, a hidden clasp.

"Do you even know what you're doing?" asked Kell.

Alucard made a sound that was neither a yes nor a no, and might have been a curse.

"Spare a knife, Bard?" he said, and Lila produced a small, sharp blade from the cuff of her coat. Alucard took the weapon and briskly pierced his thumb, then pressed the cut to the corner of the paper.

"Blood magic?" she asked, sorry she'd never known how to unlock the map's secrets, never even known it had secrets to unlock.

"Not really," said Alucard. "Blood is just the ink."

Under his hand, the map was *unfolding*—that was the word that came to mind—crimson spreading in thin lines across the paper, illuminating everything from ports and cities to the serpents marking the seas and a decorative band around the edge.

Lila's pulse quickened.

Her map to anywhere became a map to *everywhere*—or, at least, everywhere a pirate might want to go.

She squinted, trying to decipher the blood-drawn names. She picked out *Sasenroche*—the black market carved into the cliffs at the place where Arnes and Faro and Vesk all met—and a town on the cliffs named *Astor,* as well as a spot at the northern edge of the empire marked only by a small star and the word *Is Shast.*

She remembered that word from the tavern in town, with its twofold meaning.

The Road, or *the Soul.*

But nowhere could she find the *Ferase Stras.*

"I don't see it."

"Patience, Bard."

Alucard's fingers skimmed the edge of the map, and that's when she saw that the border wasn't simply a design, but three bands of small, squat numbers trimming the paper. As she watched, the numbers seemed to *move*. It was a fractional progress, slow as syrup, but the longer she stared, the more certain she was—the first and third lines were shifting to the left, the middle to the right, to what end she didn't know.

"*This,*" said Alucard proudly, tracing the lines, "is the pirate's cipher."

"Impressive," said Kell, voice dripping with skepticism. "But can you *read* it?"

"You'd better hope so."

Alucard took up a quill and began the strange alchemy of transmuting the shifting symbols of the map's trim into something like coordinates: not one set, or two, but three. He did this, keeping up a steady stream of conversation not with the room, but with himself, the words too low for Lila to hear.

By the hearth, the king and Tieren fell into muted conversation.

By the windows, Kell and Rhy stood side by side in silence.

Lenos perched nervously on the sofa's edge, fiddling with his medallion.

Only Lila stayed with Alucard and watched him translate the pirate's cipher, all the while thinking she had so much left to learn.

VIII

It took the better part of an hour for the captain to crack the code, the air in the room growing tenser with every minute, the quiet taut as sails in a strong wind. It was a thief's quiet, coiled, lying in wait, and Lila kept having to remind herself to exhale.

Alucard, who could usually be counted on to disrupt any silence before it grew oppressive, was busy scratching numbers on a slip of paper and snapping at Lenos whenever the man began to hover.

Tieren had left shortly after the captain started, explaining that he had to help his priests with their spell, and King Maxim had risen to his feet several minutes later looking like a corpse revived.

"Where are you going?" Rhy asked as his father turned toward the door.

"There are other matters to attend to," he said in a distracted way.

"What could be more—"

"A king is not one man, Rhy. He does not have the luxury of valuing one direction and ignoring the rest. This Inheritor, *if* it can be found, is but a single course. It is my task to chart them all." The king left with only the short command to summon him when the damned business of the map was done.

Rhy now sprawled across the couch, one arm over his eyes, while Kell seemed to be sulking against the hearth and Hastra stood at attention with his back to the door.

Lila tried to focus on these men, their slow movements like ticking cogs, but her own attention kept flicking back to the window, to those tendrils of fog that coiled and uncoiled beyond the glass, taking shape and falling apart, cresting, then crashing like waves against the palace.

She stared at the fog, searching for shapes in the shadows the way she sometimes did in clouds—a bird, ship, a pile of gold coins—before she realized that the shadows were indeed taking the shape of something.

Hands.

The revelation was unsettling.

Lila watched as the darkness drew together into a sea of fingers. Mesmerized, she lifted her own hand to the cold glass, the warmth of her touch steaming the window around her fingertips. Just beyond the window, the nearest shadows drew into a mirror image, palm pressed to hers, the seam of glass suddenly too thin, humming as wall and ward strained and shuddered between them.

Her brow furrowed as she flexed her fingers, the shadow hand mimicking with a child's slow way, close but not in time, a fraction off the beat.

She moved her hand back and forth.

The shadows followed.

She tapped her fingers soundlessly on the glass.

The other hand echoed.

She was just beginning to curl her fingers into a rude gesture when she saw the greater darkness—the one beyond the wave of hands, the one that rose from the river, blanketed the sky—begin to move.

At first, she thought they were coalescing into a column, but soon that column began to grow wings. Not the kind you found on a sparrow or a crow. The kind of wings that formed on a *castle*. Buttresses, towers, turrets, unfolding like a flower in sudden, violent bloom. As she watched, the shadows shimmered and hardened into glassy black stone.

Lila's hand fell away from the glass. "Am I losing my wits," she said, "or is there another palace floating on the river?"

Rhy sat up. Kell was at her shoulder in an instant, peering out through the fog. Parts of it were still blossoming, others dissolving into mist, caught in a never-ending process of being made and remade. The whole thing seemed at once very real and utterly impossible.

"*Sanct*," swore Kell.

"That fucking monster," growled the prince, now at Lila's other side, "is playing blocks with my arenas."

Lenos hung back, his eyes wide with either horror or awe as he stared at the incredible palace, but Hastra abandoned his place by the door, surging forward to see.

"By the nameless saints . . ." he whispered.

Lila called over her shoulder. "Alucard, come see this."

"A little busy," muttered the captain without looking up. Judging by the crease between his brows, the cipher wasn't proving quite as simple as he'd hoped. "Blasted numbers, sit *still*," he muttered, leaning closer.

Rhy kept shaking his head. "Why?" he said sadly. "Why did he have to use the arenas?"

"You know," said Kell, "that's really not the most important aspect of this situation."

Alucard made a triumphant sound and set the quill aside. "There."

Everyone turned back toward the table except for Kell. He stayed by the window, visibly appalled by the shift in focus. "Are we just going to ignore the shadow palace, then?" he asked, sweeping his hand at the specter beyond the glass.

"Not at all," said Lila, glancing back. "In fact, shadow palaces are where I draw the line. Which is why I'm keen to find this Inheritor." She took in the map. Frowned.

Lenos looked down at the parchment. "*Nas teras*," he said softly. *I don't see it.*

The prince cocked his head. "Neither do I."

Lila leaned in. "Maybe you should draw an *X*, for dramatic effect."

Alucard blew out an indignant breath. "You're quite an ungrateful bunch, you know that?" He took up a pencil and, plucking a very expensive-looking book from a shelf, used its spine to draw a line across the map's surface. Kell finally drifted over as Alucard drew a second, and a third, the lines intersecting at odd angles until they formed a small triangle. "There," he said, adding a little *X* with a flourish at the center.

"I think you've made a mistake," said Kell dryly. The *X* was, after all, not on the coast, or inland, but in the Arnesian Sea.

"Hardly," said Alucard. "*Ferase Stras* is the largest black market *on water*."

Lila broke into a smile. "It's not a market, then," she said. "It's a *ship*."

Alucard's eyes were bright. "It's both. And now," he added, tapping the paper, "we know where to find it."

"I'll summon my father," said Rhy as the others pored over the map. According to Alucard's calculations, the market wasn't far this time of year, sitting somewhere between Arnes and the northwest edge of Faro.

"How long to reach it?" asked Kell.

"Depends on the weather," said Alucard. "A week, perhaps. Maybe less. Assuming we don't run into trouble."

"What kind of trouble?"

"Pirates. Storms. Enemy ships." And then, with a sapphire wink: "It is the sea, after all. Do try to keep up."

"We still have a problem," said Lila, nodding at the window. "Osaron has a hold on the river. His magic is keeping the ships in their berths. Nothing in London is likely to sail, and that includes the *Night Spire*."

She saw Lenos straighten at this, the man's thin form shifting from foot to foot.

"Osaron's strength isn't infinite," Kell was saying. "His magic has limits. And right now, his power is still focused largely on the city."

"Well, then," sniped Alucard. "Can't you magic the *Spire* out of London?"

Kell rolled his eyes. "That's not how my power works."

"Well what good are you, then?" muttered the captain.

Lila watched Lenos duck out of the room. Neither Kell nor Alucard seemed to notice. They were too busy bickering.

"Fine," said Alucard, "I'll need to get beyond Osaron's sphere, and *then* find a ship."

"You?" said Kell. "I'm not leaving the fate of this city in *your* hands."

"I'm the one who found the Inheritor."

"And you're the one who lost it."

"A trade isn't the same thing as a—"

"I'm not letting you—"

Alucard leaned across the desk. "Do you even know how to sail, *mas vares*?" The honorific was said with serpentine sweetness. "I didn't think so."

"How hard can it be," snarled Kell, "if they let someone like you do it?"

A glint of mischief flashed in the captain's eyes. "I'm rather good with hard things. Just ask—"

The blow caught Alucard across the cheek.

Lila hadn't even seen Kell move, but the captain's jaw was marked with red.

It was an insult, she knew, for one magician to strike another with a bare fist.

As if they weren't worth the use of power.

Alucard flashed a feral grin, blood staining his teeth.

The air hummed with magic and—

The doors swung open, and they all turned, expecting the king or the prince returning. Instead there was Lenos, holding a woman by the elbow, which made a strange picture, since the woman was twice his weight and didn't look the type to be easily led. Lila recognized her as the captain who'd greeted them on the docks before the tournament.

Jasta.

She had to be half Veskan, broad as she was. Her hair plumed in two massive braids around her face, dark eyes threaded with gold, and despite the winter cold she wore nothing but trousers and a light tunic rolled to the elbows, revealing the silver lines of fresh scars along her skin. She'd survived the fog.

Alucard and Kell trailed off at the sight of her.

"*Casero Jasta Felis*," said the woman, by way of grudging introduction.

"*Van nes,*" said Lenos, nudging the captain forward. *Tell them.*

She shot him a look Lila recognized—one she'd doled out a dozen times. A look that said, quite simply, that the next time the sailor laid a hand on her, he'd lose a finger.

"*Kers la?*" demanded Kell.

Jasta crossed her arms, scars flashing in the light. "Some of us are wanting to leave the city." She spoke the common tongue, and her accent had the rumble of a big cat, dropping letters and slurring syllables so that Lila missed every third word if she wasn't careful. "I might have mentioned something about a ship, down in the gallery. Your fellow heard me, and now I am here."

"The ships in London will not sail," said the king, appearing behind her, Rhy at his side. He spoke the captain's tongue like a man who'd mastered Arnesian but did not relish the taste. Jasta took a formal step to the side, bowing her head a fraction. "*Anesh,*" she said, "but then, my ship is not here. It is docked at Tanek, Your Majesty."

Alucard and Lila both straightened at that. Tanek was the mouth of the Isle, the last port before the open sea.

"Why wouldn't you sail it into London?" asked Rhy.

Jasta shot the prince a wary look. "She is a sensitive skiff. Private-like."

"A pirate ship," said Kell, bluntly.

Jasta flashed a sharp-toothed grin. "Your words, Prince, not mine. My ship, she carries all kinds. Fastest skiff on the open seas. To Vesk and back in nine days flat. But if you are asking, no, she does not sail the red and gold."

"Now she does," said the king pointedly.

After a moment, the captain nodded. "It is dangerous, but I could lead them to the ship...." She trailed off.

For a moment Maxim looked irritated. Then his gaze narrowed and his demeanor cooled. "What is it you want?"

Jasta gave a short bow. "The favor of the crown, Your Majesty ... and a hundred *lish.*"

Alucard hissed through his teeth at the sum, and Kell glowered, but the king was evidently not in the mood to negotiate. "Done."

The woman raised a brow. "I should have asked for more."

"You should have asked for none," said Kell. The pirate ignored him, dark eyes sweeping the room. "How many will go?"

Lila wasn't about to miss this. She raised her hand.

So did Alucard and Lenos.

And so did *Kell*.

He did this while holding the king's gaze, as if daring the monarch to say no. But the king said nothing, and neither did Rhy. The prince only stared at his brother's raised hand, his face unreadable. Across the room, Alucard folded his arms and scowled at Kell.

"This can't possibly go wrong," he muttered.

"You could stay behind," snapped Kell.

Alucard snorted, Kell seethed, Jasta watched, amused, and Lila poured herself another drink.

She had a feeling she was going to need it.

IX

Rhy heard Kell coming.

One moment he was alone, staring out at the ghostly mirage of the shadow palace—the strange impostor of his *home*—and the next he found his brother's reflection in the glass. Kell's coat was no longer royal red but black and high-collared, silver buttons running down the front. It was the coat he wore whenever he carried messages to other Londons. A coat meant for traveling. For leaving.

"You always wanted to travel beyond the city," said Rhy.

Kell ducked his head. "This isn't what I had in mind."

Rhy turned toward him. Kell was standing before the mirror, so Rhy could see his own face repeated. He tried—and failed—to force his features smooth, tried—and failed—to keep the sadness from his voice. "We were supposed to go together."

"And one day we will," said Kell, "but right now, I can't stop Osaron by sitting here, and if there's a chance that he's after the *Antari* instead of the city, if there's a chance we can draw him away—"

"I know," said Rhy, in a way that said *Stop*. In a way that said *I trust you*. He slumped into a chair. "I know you thought it was just a line, but I had it all planned out. We could have left after the season's end, toured the island first, gone from the mist-strewn valleys up to Orten and down through the Stasina forests to the cliffs at Astor, then taken a ship over to the mainland." He leaned back, let his gaze escape to the ceiling with its folds of color. "Once we landed, we'd have hit Hanas first, then gone by carriage to Linar—I heard the capital there will one day rival London—and the market in Nesto, near the Faroan border, is said to be made of glass. I figured we'd pick up a ship there, stop at the point of Sheran, where the water's barely a seam between Arnes and Vesk—so narrow you can walk across it—and we'd be back in time for the dawn of summer."

"Sounds like quite an adventure," said Kell.

"You're not the only restless soul," said Rhy, getting to his feet. "I suppose it's time now?"

Kell nodded. "But I brought you something." He dug a hand into his pocket and came up with two gold pins, each emblazoned with the chalice and rising sun of the House Maresh. The same pins they'd worn during the tournament—Rhy with pride, and Kell under duress. The same pin Rhy had used to carve a word into his arm, its twin the one Kell had used to bring Rhy and Alucard back from the *Night Spire*.

"I've done my best to spell the two together," explained his brother. "The bond should hold, no matter the distance."

"I thought my way was rather clever," said Rhy, rubbing his forearm, where he'd carved the word into his skin.

"This one requires far less blood." Kell came forward, and fastened the pin over his brother's heart. "If something worrisome happens, and you need me to come back, simply take hold of the pin and say 'tol.'"

Tol.

Brother.

Rhy managed a rueful smile. "And what if I get lonely?"

Kell rolled his eyes, pinning the second pendant to the front of his coat.

Rhy's chest tightened.

Don't go, he wanted to say, even though that wasn't fair, wasn't right, wasn't princely. He swallowed. "If you don't come back, I'll have to save the day without you and steal all the glory for myself."

A short laugh, a ghost of a smile, but then Kell brought a hand to Rhy's shoulder. It was so light. So heavy. He could feel the tether tighten, the shadows lap at his heels, the darkness whisper through his head.

"Listen to me," said his brother. "Promise me you won't go after Osaron. Not until we're back."

Rhy frowned. "You can't expect me to hide in the palace until it's over."

"I don't," said Kell. "But I expect you to be smart. And I expect you to trust me when I say I have a plan."

"It would help if you shared it."

Kell chewed his lip. A dreadful habit. Hardly princely. "Osaron can't see us coming," he said. "If we go storming in, demanding a fight, he'll know we've got a card to play. But if we come to save one of ours—"

"I'm to be a lure?" said Rhy, pretending to be aghast.

"What?" teased Kell. "You've always liked people fighting for you."

"Actually," said the prince, "I prefer people fighting *over* me."

Kell's grip tightened on his sleeve, and the humor died on the air. "Four days, Rhy. We'll make it back in that. And then you can get yourself into trouble, and—"

Behind them someone cleared their throat.

Kell's eyes narrowed. His hand fell from Rhy's arm.

Alucard Emery was waiting in the doorway, his hair pinned back, a blue traveling cloak fastened around his shoulders. Rhy's body ached at the sight of him. Standing there, Alucard didn't look like a nobleman, or a triad magician, or even the captain of a ship. He looked like a stranger, like someone who could slip into a crowd, and disappear. *Is this what he looked like that night?* wondered Rhy. *When he snuck out of my bed, out of the palace, out of the city?*

Alucard stepped forward into the room, those thin silver scars dancing in the light.

"Are the horses ready?" asked Kell coolly.

"Almost," answered the captain, plucking at his gloves.

A brief silence fell as Kell waited for Alucard to leave, and while Alucard did not.

"I was hoping," the captain said at last, "to have a word with the prince."

"We need to go," said Kell.

"I won't be long."

"We don't—"

"Kell," said Rhy, giving his brother a short, gentle nudge toward the door. "Go on. I'll be here when you get back."

Kell's arms were a sudden circle around Rhy's shoulders, and then, just as quickly, they were gone, and Rhy was left dizzy from their weight, and then the loss of it. A flutter of black fabric, and the door was swinging shut behind Kell. A strange, irrational panic rose in Rhy's throat, and he had to fight the urge to call his brother back or run after him. He held his ground.

Alucard was watching the place where Kell had been as if the *Antari* had left his shadow behind. Some visible trace now lingering between them.

"I always hated how close you two were," he murmured. "Now I suppose I should be thankful for it."

Rhy swallowed, dragging his gaze from the door. "I suppose I should be, too." His attention fell on the captain. For all their time together in the last few days, they'd hardly spoken. There was Alucard's delirium aboard the ship, and the flickering memories of Alucard's hand, his voice a tether in the dark. The *Essen Tasch* had been a flurry of witty quips and stolen looks, but the last time they'd been together in this room, *alone* in this room, Rhy's back had been up against the mirror, the captain's lips against his throat. And before that . . . before that . . .

"Rhy—"

"Leaving?" he cut in, straining to keep the words light. "At least this time you came to say good-bye."

Alucard winced at the jab, but didn't retreat. Instead, he closed the gap between them, Rhy fighting back a shiver as the captain's fingers found his skin. "You were with me, in the dark."

"I was returning a favor." Rhy held his gaze. "I believe we're even now."

Alucard's eyes were searching his face, and Rhy felt himself flush, his body singing with the urge to pull Alucard's mouth to his, to let the world beyond this room disappear.

"You'd better go," he said breathlessly.

But Alucard didn't pull away. A shadow had crossed the captain's face, something like sadness in his eyes. "You haven't asked me."

The words sank like a stone in Rhy's chest, and he staggered under the weight. A too-heavy reminder of what had happened three summers ago. Of going to bed in Alucard's arms, and waking up alone. Alucard gone from the palace, from the city, from his life.

"What?" he said, his voice cool, but his face burning. "You want me to ask you why you left? Why you chose the open sea over my bed? A criminal's brand over my touch? I didn't ask you, Alucard, because I don't want to hear them."

"Hear what?" asked Alucard, cupping Rhy's cheek.

He knocked the hand away. "The excuses." Alucard drew breath to speak, but Rhy cut him off. "I know what I was to you—a piece of fruit to be picked, a summer fling."

"You were more than that. You *are*—"

"It was only a season."

"That's not—"

"*Stop*," said Rhy with all the quiet force of a royal. "Just. Stop. I've never cared for liars, Luc, and I care even less for fools, so don't make me feel like more of one. You caught me off guard on the Banner Night. What happened between us, happened . . ." Rhy tried to steady his breathing, then sliced a hand through the air dismissively. "But now it's done."

Alucard caught Rhy's wrist, head bowed to hide those storm blue eyes as he said, under his breath, "What if I don't want it to be done?"

The words landed like a blow, the air leaving his lungs in a jagged exhale. Something burned through him, and it took Rhy a moment to realize what it was. *Anger.*

"What right have you," he said softly, imperiously, "to want *anything* of me?"

His hand splayed across Alucard's chest, a touch once warm, now full of force as he pushed Alucard away. The captain caught himself and looked up, startled, but made no motion to advance. Alucard was standing on the wrong side of the line. He might have been a noble, but Rhy was a prince, untouchable unless he *wanted* to be touched, and he'd just made it clear that he didn't.

"Rhy," Alucard said, clenching his fists, all playfulness gone. "I didn't want to leave."

"But you did."

"If you would only listen—"

"No." Rhy was fighting back another deep, internal tremor. The tension between love and loss, holding on and letting go. "I am not a toy anymore. I am not a foolish youth." He forced the waver from his words. "I am the crown prince of Arnes. The future king of this empire. And if you want another audience with me, a chance to explain yourself, then you must earn it. Go. Bring me back this Inheritor. Help me save my city. Then, Master Emery, I will consider your request."

Alucard blinked rapidly, obviously stricken. But after a long moment, he drew himself up to his full height. "Yes, Your Highness." He turned and crossed the room with steady strides, his boots echoing Rhy's heart as it pounded in his chest. For the second time, he watched someone precious walk away. For the second time, he held his ground. But he could not help the urge to soften the blow. For both of them.

"And, Alucard," he called, when the captain had reached the door. Alucard glanced back, his features pale but set as Rhy said, "Do try not to kill my brother."

A small, defiant smile flickered across the captain's face. Laced with humor, with hope.

"I'll do my best."

SEVEN

SETTING SAIL

I

No wonder Lila hated good-byes, thought Kell. It would have been so much easier to simply *go*. His brother's heart still echoed in his chest as he descended the inner palace stairs, but the threads between them slackened a little with every step. What would it feel like when they were cities apart? When days and leagues stretched between them? Would he still know Rhy's heart?

The air went suddenly cold around him, and Kell looked up to find Emira Maresh barring his path. Of course, it had been too simple. After all this, the king would grant him leave, but the queen would not.

"Your Majesty," he said, expecting accusations, a rebuke. Instead, the queen's gaze fell on him, not a glancing blow, but something soft, solid. They were a cyclone of green and gold, those eyes, like leaves caught in a fall breeze. Eyes that had not held his in weeks.

"You are leaving, then," she said, the words caught between question and observation.

Kell held his ground. "I am, for now. The king has given me permission—"

Emira was already shaking her head, an inward gesture as if trying to clear her own mind. There was something in her hands, a piece of fabric twisted in her grip. "It is poor luck," she said, holding out the cloth, "to leave without a piece of home."

Kell stared at the offering. It was a square of crimson, the kind stitched to children's tunics, embroidered with two letters: *KM*.

Kell Maresh.

He'd never seen it before, and he frowned, confused by that second initial. He'd never considered himself a Maresh. Rhy's brother, yes, and once upon a time, their adopted son, but never this. Never family.

He wondered if it was some kind of peace offering, newly fashioned, but the fabric looked old, worn by someone else's touch.

"I had it made," said Emira, fumbling in a way she rarely did, "when you first came to the palace, but then I couldn't . . . I didn't think it was . . ." She trailed off, and tried again. "People break so easily, Kell," she said. "A hundred different ways, and I was afraid . . . but you have to understand that you are . . . have always been . . ."

This time, when she trailed off, she didn't have the strength to start again, only stood there, staring down at the swatch of cloth, thumb brushing back and forth across the letters, and he knew this was the moment to reach out, or walk away. It was his choice.

And it wasn't fair—he shouldn't *have* to choose—she should have come to him a dozen times, should have listened, should have, should have, but he was tired, and she was sorry, and in that moment, it was enough.

"Thank you," said Kell, accepting the square of cloth, "my queen."

And then, to his surprise, she reached out and placed her other hand against his face, the way she had so many times, when he'd returned from one of his trips, a silent question in her eyes. *Are you all right?*

But now, the question altered, *Will we be all right?*

He nodded once, leaning into her touch.

"Come home," she said softly.

Kell found her gaze again. "I will."

He was the first to pull away, the queen's fingers slipping from his jaw to his shoulder to his sleeve as he left. *I will come back,* he thought, and for the first time in a long time, he knew it was the truth.

Kell knew what he had to do next.

And knew Lila wouldn't be happy about it.

He headed toward the royal cells, and was nearly there when he felt the gentle smoothing of his pulse, the blanket of calm around his shoulders that came with the priest's presence. Kell's steps faltered but didn't stop as Tieren fell in step beside him. The *Aven Essen* said nothing, and the silence dragged like water around Kell's limbs.

"It's not what you think," he said. "I'm not running away."

"I never said you were."

"I'm not doing this because I want to go," continued Kell. "I would never—" He stumbled over the words—there was a time when he would have, when he *had*. "If I thought the city would be safer with me in it—"

"You're hoping to lure the demon away." It wasn't a question.

At last, Kell's steps dragged to a stop. "Osaron *wants,* Tieren. It is his nature. Holland was right about that. He wants change. He wants power. He wants whatever *isn't*. We made an offering, and he scorned it, tried to claim my life instead. He doesn't want what he has, he wants to *take* what he doesn't."

"And if he chooses not to follow you?"

"Then you put the city to sleep." Kell set off again, determined. "Deprive him of every puppet, every person, so that when we return with the Inheritor, he has no choice but to face us."

"Very well. . . ." said Tieren.

"Is this where you tell me to be safe?"

"Oh," said the priest, "I think the time for that is gone."

They walked together, Kell stopping only when he reached the door that led down into the prison. He brought his hand to the wood, fingers splayed across the surface.

"I keep wondering," he said softly, "if all of it is my fault. Where does it start, Tieren?" He looked up. "With Holland's choice, or with mine?"

The priest looked at him, eyes bright within his tired face, and shook his head. For once, the old man didn't seem to have the answer.

II

Delilah Bard did *not* like horses.

She'd never liked them, not when she only knew them for their snapping teeth, and their flicking tails, and their stomping hooves, and not when she found herself on the back of one, the night racing past so fast it blurred around her, and not now as she watched a pair of silver-scarred guards saddle up three for their ride to the port.

As far as she was concerned, nothing with so little brain should have so much force.

Then again, she could say the same about half the tournament magicians.

"If you look at animals like that," said Alucard, clapping her on the shoulder, "it's no wonder they hate you."

"Yes, well, then the feeling is mutual." She glanced around. "No Esa?"

"My cat dislikes horses almost as much as you do," he said. "I left her in the palace."

"God help them all."

"Chatter chatter," said Jasta in Arnesian, her mane of hair pulled back beneath a traveling hood. "Do you always prattle on in that high tongue?"

"Like a songbird," preened Alucard, looking around. "Where's His Highness?"

"I'm right here," said Kell, without rising to the jab. And when Lila turned toward him, she saw why. He wasn't alone.

"*No,*" she snarled.

Holland stood a step behind Kell, flanked by two guards, his hands bound in iron beneath a grey half cloak. His eyes met hers, one a dazzling green, the other black. "Delilah," he said by way of greeting.

Beside her, Jasta went still as stone.

Lenos turned white.

Even Alucard looked uncomfortable.

"*Kers la?*" growled Jasta.

"What is he doing here?" echoed Lila.

Kell's brow furrowed. "I can't leave him in the palace."

"Of course you can."

"I won't." And with those two words, she realized it wasn't only the *palace's* safety he was worried about. "He comes with us."

"He's not a pet," she snapped.

"See, Kell," said Holland evenly. "I told you she wouldn't like it."

"*She's* not the only one," muttered Alucard.

Jasta snarled something too low and slurred for her to hear.

"We're wasting time," said Kell, moving to unlock Holland's manacles.

Lila had a knife out before key touched iron. "He stays chained."

Holland held up his cuffed hands. "You do realize, Delilah, that these won't stop me."

"Of course not," she said with a feral grin. "But they'll slow you down long enough that *I* can."

Holland sighed. "As you wish," he said, just before Jasta slammed her fist into his cheek. His head snapped sideways and his boots slid back a step, but he didn't fall.

"Jasta!" called Kell as the other *Antari* flexed his jaw and spit a mouthful of blood into the dirt.

"Anyone else?" asked Holland darkly.

"I wouldn't mind a go—" started Alucard, but Kell cut him off.

"Enough," he snapped, the ground rumbling faintly with the order. "Alucard, since you volunteered, Holland can ride with you."

The captain sulked at the assignment, even as he hauled the chained *Antari* up onto the horse.

"Try anything . . ." he growled.

"And you'll kill me?" finished Holland dryly.

"No," said Alucard with a vicious smile. "I'll let Bard have you."

Lenos saddled up with Jasta, this pairing just as comical, her massive frame making the sailor seem even smaller and more skeletal. He hinged forward and patted the horse's flank as Kell swung up into his own saddle. He was infuriatingly elegant on horseback, with the regal posture that only came, Lila expected, from years of practice. It was one of those moments that reminded her—as if she could ever forget—that Kell was in so many ways a prince. She made a mental note to tell him sometime, when she was next particularly cross.

"Come on," he said, holding out his hand. And this time, when he pulled her up, he seated her before him instead of behind, one arm wrapping protectively around her waist.

"Don't stab me," he whispered in her ear, and she wished it were full night so no one could see the color rising in her cheeks.

She cast a last look up at the palace, the dark, distorted echo stretching like a shadow at its side.

"What if Osaron follows us?" she asked.

Kell glanced back. "If we're lucky, he will."

"You've an odd notion of luck," said Jasta, kicking her horse into motion.

Lila's own mount lurched forward beneath her, and so did her stomach. *This is not how I die,* she told herself as, in a thunder of hooves and fogging breath, the horses plunged into the night.

III

It was a palace fit for a king.

Fit for a *god*.

A place of promise, potential, power.

Osaron strode through the great hall of his newest creation, his steps landing soundlessly on polished stone. The floor flickered beneath each stride, grass and blossom and ice born with every step, fading behind him like footsteps on sand.

Columns rose up from the floor, growing more like trees than marble pillars, their stone limbs branching up and out, flowering with dark-hued glass and fall leaves and beads of dew, and in their shining columns he saw the world as it could be. So many possible transformations, such infinite potential.

And there, at the heart of the great hall, his throne, its base throwing roots, its back surging into crownlike spires, its arms spread like an old friend waiting to be embraced. Its surface shone with an iridescent light, and as Osaron climbed the steps, mounted the platform, took his seat, the whole palace sang with the rightness of his presence.

Osaron sat at the center of this web and felt the strings of the city, the mind of each and every servant tethered to his by threads of magic. A tug here, a tremor there, thoughts carrying like movement along a thousand lines.

In each devoted life, a fire burned. Some flames were dull and small, barely kindling, while others shone bright and hot, and those he summoned now, called them forward from every corner of the city.

Come, he thought. *Kneel at my feet like children, and I will raise you. As men. As women. As chosen.*

Beyond the palace walls, bridges began to bloom like ice over the river, hands extended to usher them in.

My king, they said, rising from their tables.

My king, they said, turning from their work.

Osaron smiled, savoring the echo of those words, until a new chorus interrupted them.

My king, whispered his subjects, *the bad ones are leaving.*

My king, they said, *the bad ones are fleeing.*

The ones who dared to refuse you.

The ones who dare defy you.

Osaron steepled his fingers. The *Antari* were leaving London.

All of them? he asked, and the echo came.

All of them. All of them. All of them.

Holland's words came back to him, an unwelcome intrusion.

"*How will you rule without a head for your crown?*"

Words quickly swallowed by his clamoring servants.

Shall we chase them?

Shall we stop them?

Shall we drag them down?

Shall we bring them back?

Osaron rapped his fingers on the arm of the throne. The gesture made no sound.

Shall we?

No, thought Osaron, his command rippling through the minds of thousands like a vibration along a string. He sat back in his sculpted throne. *No. Let them go.*

If it was a trap, he would not follow.

He did not need them.

He did not need their minds, or their bodies.

He had *thousands*.

The first of those he'd summoned was entering the hall, a man striding toward him with a proud jaw and a head held high. He came to a stop before the throne, and knelt, dark head bowed.

"*Rise*," commanded Osaron, and the man obeyed. *"What is your name?"*

The man stood, broad shouldered and shadow eyed, a silver ring in the shape of a feather circling one thumb.

"My name is Berras Emery," said the man. "How may I serve you?"

IV

Tanek came into sight shortly after dark.

Alucard didn't like the port, but he knew it well. For three years, it was as close to London as he'd dared to come. In many ways it was *too* close. The people here knew the name Emery, had an idea of what it meant.

It was here he learned to be someone else—not a nobleman, but the jaunty captain of the *Night Spire*. Here he first met Lenos and Stross, at a game of Sanct. Here he was reminded, again and again and again, of how close—how far—he was from home. Every time he returned to Tanek, he saw London in the tapestries and trappings, heard it in the accents, smelled it in the air, that scent like woods in spring, and his body ached.

But right now, Tanek seemed nothing like London. It was bustling in a surreal way, oblivious to the danger lurking inland. The berths were filled with ships, the taverns with men and women, the greatest danger a pickpocket or a winter chill.

In the end, Osaron hadn't taken their halfhearted bait, and so the shadow of his power had ended an hour back, the weight of it lifting like the air after a storm. The strangest thing, thought Alucard, was the *way* it stopped. Not suddenly, but slowly, over the course of a click, the spellwork tapering so that by the end of its reach, the few people they met had no shadows in their eyes, nothing but a bad feeling, an urge to turn back. Several times they passed travelers on the road who seemed lost, when in fact they'd simply waded to the edge of the spell, and stopped, repelled by a thing they couldn't name, couldn't remember.

"Don't say anything," Kell had warned when they'd passed the first bunch. "The last thing we need is panic spreading beyond the capital."

A man and woman stumbled past now, arm in arm and laughing drunkenly.

Word clearly hadn't reached the port.

Alucard hauled Holland down from the horse, setting him roughly on the ground. The *Antari* hadn't said a word since they'd left, and the silence made Alucard nervous. Bard didn't talk much either, but hers was a different kind of quiet, present, inquisitive. Holland's silence hung in the air, made Alucard want to speak just to break it. Then again, maybe it was the man's magic that set him on edge, silver threads splintering the air like lightning.

They handed the horses off to a stablehand whose eyes widened at the royal emblem blazoned on the harnesses.

"Keep your heads down," said Kell as the boy led the mounts away.

"We are hardly inconspicuous," said Holland finally, his voice like rough-hewn rock. "Perhaps, if you unchained me—"

"Not likely," said Lila and Jasta, the same words overlapping in different tongues.

The air had warmed a fraction despite the thickening dark, and Alucard was looking around for the source of that warmth when he heard the approach of armored boots and caught the gleam of metal.

"Oh, look," he said. "A welcome party."

Whether it was because of the royal horses or the sight of the strange entourage, a pair of soldiers was heading straight toward them.

"Halt!" they called in Arnesian, and Holland had the sense to fold his cuffed hands beneath his cloak; but at the sight of Kell, the two men paled, one bowing deeply, the other murmuring what might have been a blessing or a prayer, too low for him to make out.

Alucard rolled his eyes at the display as Kell adopted an imitation of his usual arrogance, explaining that they were here on royal business. Yes, everything was well. No, they did not need an escort.

At last, the men retreated to their post, and Lila gave her own mocking bow in Kell's direction.

"*Mas vares,*" she said, then straightened sharply, the humor gone from her face. With a gesture that was at once casual and frighteningly quick, she freed a knife from her belt.

"What is it?" asked Kell and Alucard at once.

"Someone's been following us," she said.

Kell's brows went up. "You didn't think to mention that before?"

"I could have been wrong," she said, twirling the blade in her fingers, "but I'm not."

"Where are—"

Before Kell could finish, she spun, and threw.

The knife sang through the air, eliciting a yelp as it embedded itself in a post a few inches above a crop of brown curls threaded with gold. A boy stood, back pressed to the post and empty hands raised in immediate surrender. On his forehead was a mark in blood. He was dressed in ordinary clothes, no red and gold trim, no symbols of the House Maresh emblazoned on his coat, but Alucard still recognized him from the palace.

"Hastra," said Kell darkly.

The young man ducked out from under Lila's blade. "Sir," he said, dislodging the knife.

"What are you doing here?"

"Tieren sent me."

Kell groaned, and muttered under his breath, "Of course he did." Then, louder, "Go home. You have no business here."

The boy—and he really was just a boy, in manner as well as age—straightened at that, puffing up his narrow chest. "I'm your guard, sir. What is that worth if I don't guard you?"

"You're not my guard, Hastra," said Kell. "Not anymore."

The boy flinched but held his ground. "Very well, sir. But if I am not a guard, then I am a priest, and my orders come from the *Aven Essen* himself."

"Hastra—"

"And he's really very hard to please, you know—"

"Hastra—"

"And you do owe me a favor, sir, since I did stand by you, when you snuck out of the palace and entered the tournament—"

Alucard's head whipped around. "You did *what*?"

"Enough," cut in Kell, waving his hand.

"*Anesh*," said Jasta, who hadn't been following the conversation and didn't seem to care. "Come, go, I don't care. I'd rather not stand here on display. Bad for my reputation to be seen with black-eyed princes and royal guards and nobles playing dress-up."

"I'm a privateer," said Alucard, affronted.

Jasta only snorted and started toward the docks. Hastra hung back, his wide brown eyes still leveled expectantly on Kell.

"Oh, come on," said Lila. "Every ship needs a pet."

Kell threw up his hands. "Fine. He can stay."

"Who were you?" demanded Alucard as they walked along the docks, passing ships of every size and color. The thought of *Kell* entering the tournament—his tournament—was madness. The thought that Alucard had had the chance to fight him—that maybe he *had*—was maddening.

"It doesn't matter," said Kell.

"Did we fight?" But how could they have? Alucard would have seen the silver thread, would have known—

"If we had," said Kell pointedly, "I would have won."

Annoyance flared through Alucard, but then he thought of Rhy, the tether between the two, and anger swallowed indignation.

"Do you have any idea how foolish that was? How dangerous for the prince?"

"Not that it's any of your business," said Kell, "but the whole thing was Rhy's idea." That two-toned gaze cut his way. "I don't suppose you tried to stop *Lila*?"

Alucard glanced over his shoulder. Bard brought up the rear of the party, Holland a pace ahead of her. The other *Antari* was looking at the ships the way Lila had looked at the horses, with a mixture of discomfort and disdain.

"What's the matter," she was saying, "can't swim?"

Holland's lips pursed. "It is a little harder with chains on." His attention went back to the boats, and Alucard understood. He recognized the look in his eyes, a wariness bordering on fear.

"You've never been on a ship, have you?"

The man didn't answer. He didn't need to.

Lila let out a small, malicious laugh. As if she'd known half a thing about ships when Alucard first took her on.

"Here we are," said Jasta, coming to a stop beside something that might—in certain places—qualify as a ship, the way some cottages might qualify as mansions. Jasta patted the boat's side the way a rider might a horse's flank. Its name ran in silver stenciling along the white hull. *Is Hosna. The Ghost.*

"She's a bit small," said the captain, "but whip fast."

"A bit small," echoed Lila dryly. The *Ghost* was half the length of the *Night Spire,* with three short sails and a Faroanesque hull, narrow and feather sharp. "It's a *skiff.*"

"It's a runner," clarified Alucard. "They don't hold much, but there are few things faster on the open sea. It won't be a cozy ride, by any stretch, but we'll reach the market quickly. Especially with three *Antari* keeping wind in our sails."

Lila looked longingly at the ships to either side, towering vessels with dark wood and gleaming sails.

"What about that one?" she said, pointing to a proud ship two berths down.

Alucard shook his head. "It isn't ours."

"It *could* be."

Jasta shot her a look, and Lila rolled her eyes. "Kidding," she said, even though Alucard knew she wasn't. "Besides," she added, "wouldn't want something *too* pretty. Pretty things tend to draw greedy eyes."

"Speaking from experience, Bard?" he teased.

"Thank you, Jasta," cut in Kell. "We'll bring her back in one piece."

"Oh, I'll be making sure of it," said the captain, striding up the boat's narrow ramp.

"Jasta—"

"My vessel, my rules," she said, arms akimbo. "I can get you wherever you're going in half the time, and if you're on some mission to save the kingdom, well, it is my kingdom, too. And I wouldn't mind having the crown on my side next time *I'm* in troubled waters."

"How do you know our motives are so honorable?" said Alucard. "We could just be fleeing."

"*You* could be," she said, and then, jabbing a finger at Kell, "but *he* isn't." With that she stomped onto the deck and they had little choice but to follow her aboard.

"Three *Antari* get on a boat," singsonged Alucard, as if it were the beginning of a tavern joke. He had the added delight of seeing both Kell and Holland try to balance as the deck bobbed under the sudden weight. One looked uncomfortable, the other ill, and Alucard could have assured them that it wouldn't be so bad once they were out at sea, but he wasn't feeling generous.

"Hano!" called Jasta, and a young girl's head appeared above a stack of crates, her black hair pulled into a messy bun.

"*Casero!*" She swung up onto the crate, legs dangling over the edge. "You're back early."

"I have some cargo," said Jasta.

"*Sha!*" said Hano delightedly.

There was a thud and a muffled curse from somewhere on board, and a moment later an old man shuffled out from behind another crate, rubbing his head. His back was bent like a hook, his skin dark and his eyes a milky white.

"*Solase,*" he mumbled, and Alucard couldn't tell if he was apologizing to them or to the crates he'd thudded into.

"That's Ilo," said Jasta, nodding at the blind man.

"Where's the rest of your crew?" asked Kell, looking around.

"This is it," said Jasta.

"You let a little girl and a blind man guard a ship full of stolen merchandise," said Alucard.

Hano giggled and held up a purse. *Alucard's* purse. A moment later Ilo held up a blade. It was Kell's.

The magician flicked his fingers, and the blade snapped hilt first back into his hand, a display that earned him an approving clap from the girl. Alucard reclaimed his purse with a similar flourish and went so far as to let the leather retie itself onto his belt. Lila patted herself down, making sure she still had all her knives, and smiled in satisfaction.

"The map," prompted Jasta. Alucard handed it over.

The captain unfurled the paper, clicking her tongue. "Going Waters, then," she said. It was no surprise to anyone that Jasta, given her particular interests, was familiar with the market.

"What's in these boxes?" asked Kell, resting a hand on one lid.

"A little of this, a little of that," said the captain. "Nothing that will bite."

Hastra and Lenos were already unwinding the ropes, the young guard cheerfully following the sailor's lead.

"Why are you in chains?" asked Hano. Alucard hadn't seen the girl hop down from her perch, but now she stood directly in front of Holland, hands on her hips in a mimic of Jasta's own stance, her black bun coming roughly to the *Antari*'s ribs. "Did you do a bad thing?"

"Hano!" called Jasta, and the girl flitted away again without waiting for an answer. The boat came unmoored, rocking beneath them. Bard smiled, and Alucard felt his balance shift, and then return.

Holland, meanwhile, tipped his head back and drew a deep, steadying breath, eyes up to the sky as if that would keep him from being ill.

"Come on," said Kell, taking the other *Antari*'s arm. "Let's find the hold."

"I don't like that one," said Alucard as Bard came to stand at his side.

"Which one?" she asked dryly, but she cut him a glance, and must have seen something in his face because she sobered. "What do you see when you look at Holland?"

Alucard drew in a breath, and blew it out in a cloud. "This is what magic looks like," he said twirling his fingers through the plume. Instead of dispersing, the pale air twisted and coiled into thin ribbons of mist against the seamless stretch of night and sea.

"But Holland's magic is . . ." He splayed his fingers, and the ribbons of fog splintered, frayed. "He isn't weaker for it. If anything, his light is brighter than yours or Kell's. But the light is uneven, unsteady, the lines all broken, re-formed, like bones that didn't set. It's . . ."

"Unnatural?" she guessed.

"Dangerous."

"Splendid," she said, folding her arms against the cold. A yawn escaped, like a silent snarl through clenched teeth.

"Get some rest," he said.

"I will," said Bard, but she didn't move.

Alucard turned automatically toward the wheel before remembering he wasn't the captain of this ship. He hesitated, like a man who's gone through a door to fetch something, only to forget what he'd come for. At last, he went to help Lenos with the sails, leaving Bard at the ship's rail.

When he looked back ten, fifteen, twenty minutes later, she was still there, eyes trained on the line where water met sky.

V

Rhy rode out as soon as they were gone.

There were too many souls to find, and the thought of staying in the palace another minute made him want to scream. Soon the dark would be upon them, upon him, the fall of night and the confinement. But for now, there was still light, still time.

He took two men, both silvers, and set out into the city, trying to keep his attention from drifting to the eerie palace floating next to his, the strange procession of men and women climbing its steps, trying to keep himself from dwelling on the strange black substance that turned stretches of road into glossy, icelike streaks and climbed bits of wall like ivy or frost. *Magic overwhelming nature.*

He found a couple hunkered down in the back of their house, too afraid to leave. A girl wandering, dazed and coated in the ash of someone else, family or friend or stranger, she wouldn't say. On the third trip, one of the guards came galloping toward him.

"Your Highness," called the man, blood mark smearing with the sweat on his brow as he reined in his horse. "There's something you need to see."

They were in a tavern hall.

Two dozen men, all dressed in the gold and red of the royal guard. And all sick. All dying. Rhy knew each and every one, by face if not by name. Isra had said that some of them were missing. That the blood marks had failed. But they hadn't vanished. They were *here.*

"Your Highness, wait!" called the silver as Rhy plunged forward into the hall, but he was not afraid of the smoke or the sickness. Someone had pushed the tables and chairs out of the way, cleared the space, and now his father's men—his men—were lying on the floor in rows, spaces here and there where a few had risen up, or fallen forever.

Their armor had been stripped off and set aside, propped like a gallery of hollow spectators along the walls as, on the floor, the guards sweated and writhed and fought demons he couldn't see, the way Alucard had aboard the *Spire*.

Their veins stood out black against their throats, and the whole hall smelled vaguely of burning skin as the magic scorched its way through them.

The air was thick with something like dust.

Ash, realized Rhy.

All that was left of those who'd burned.

One man was slumped against the wall by the doors, sweat sheening his face, the sickness just beginning to set in.

His beard was trimmed short, his hair streaked with grey, and Rhy recognized him at once. Tolners. A man who'd served his father before he was king. A man assigned to serve *Rhy*. He'd seen the guard this morning in the palace, safe and well within the wards.

"What have you done?" he asked, grabbing the guard by the collar. "Why did you leave the palace?"

The man's vision slid in and out of focus. "Your Majesty," he rasped. Trapped in the fever's hold, he mistook Rhy for his father. "We are—the royal guard. We—do not hide. If we are not—strong enough—to brave the dark—we do not—deserve to serve—" he broke off, wracked by a sudden, violent chill.

"You fool," snapped Rhy, even as he eased Tolners back into his chair and pulled the man's coat close around his shivering form. Rhy turned on the room of dying guards, raking an ash-slicked hand through his hair, feeling furious, helpless. He couldn't save these men. Could only watch as they fought, failed, died.

"We are the royal guard," murmured a man on the floor.

"We are the royal guard," echoed two more, taking it up as a chant against whatever darkness fought to take them.

Rhy wanted to yell, to curse, but he couldn't, because he knew the things he had done in the name of strength, knew what he was doing even now, walking the cursed streets, combing the poisoned fog, knew that even if Kell's magic hadn't shielded him, he would have gone again, and again, for his city, his people.

And so Rhy did what he had done for Alucard on the *Spire* floor.

He did the only thing he could.

He *stayed*.

Maxim Maresh knew the value of a single *Antari*.

He had stood before the windows and watched *three* ride away from the palace, the city, the monster poisoning its heart. He had weighed the odds, known it was the right decision, the strategy with the highest odds, and yet he could not help but feel that his best weapons were suddenly out of reach. Worse, that he had loosened his grip, let them fall, and now stood facing a foe without a blade.

His own wasn't ready—it was still being forged.

Maxim's reflection hung suspended in the glass. He did not look well. He felt worse. One hand rested against the window, shadows contouring to his fingers in a ghostly mimic, a morbid echo.

"You let him leave," said a gentle voice, and the *Aven Essen* materialized in the glass behind him, a specter in white.

"I did," said Maxim. He had seen his son's body on the bed, chest still, cheeks hollow, skin grey. The image was burned like light against his eyes, an image he would never forget. And he understood, now more than ever, that Kell's life was Rhy's, and if he could not guard it himself, he would see it sent away. "I tried to stop Kell once. It was a mistake."

"He might have stayed this time," said Tieren carefully, "if you'd asked instead of ordered."

"Perhaps." Maxim's hand fell away from the glass. "But this city is no longer safe."

The priest's blue eyes were piercing. "The world might prove no safer."

"I cannot do anything about the dangers in the world, Tieren, but I can do something about the monster here in London."

He began to cross the room, and made it three steps before it tipped violently beneath him. For a terrible instant his vision dimmed, and he thought he would fall.

"Your Majesty," said Tieren, catching his arm. Beneath his tunic, the fresh line of cuts ached, the wounds deep, flesh and blood carved away. A necessary sacrifice.

"I'm well," he lied, pulling free.

Tieren gave him a scornful look, and he regretted showing the priest his progress.

"I cannot stop you, Maxim," said Tieren, "but this kind of magic has consequences."

"When will the sleeping spell be ready?"

"If you are not careful—"

"When?"

"It is difficult to make such a spell, harder still to stretch it over a city. The very nature of it toes the line of the obscene, to put a body and mind to rest is still a manipulation, an exertion of one's will over—"

"*When?*"

The priest sighed. "Another day. Maybe two."

Maxim straightened, nodded. They would last that long. They had to. When he began to walk again, the ground held firm beneath his feet.

"Your Majesty—"

"Go and finish your own spell, Tieren. And let me finish mine."

VI

By the time Rhy returned to the palace, the light was gone and his armor was painted grey with ash. More than half of the men in the hall had died; the surviving few now marched in his wake, helms beneath their arms, faces gaunt from fever and lit by lines of silver that trailed like tears down this cheeks.

Rhy climbed the front steps in exhausted silence.

The silvered guards stationed at the palace doors said nothing, and he wondered if they'd known—they *had* to have known, letting so many of their own pass through into the fog. They wouldn't meet their prince's gaze, but they met one another's, exchanging a single nod that might have been pride or solidarity, or something else Rhy couldn't read.

His second guard, Vis, was standing in the front hall, clearly waiting for word of Tolners. Rhy shook his head and pushed past him, past everyone, heading for the royal baths, needing to be clean, but as he walked his armor seemed to tighten around him, cutting into his throat, binding his ribs.

He couldn't breathe, and for an instant he thought of the river, of Kell trapped beneath the surface while he'd gasped for air above, but this wasn't an echo of his brother's suffering. His own chest was heaving itself against the armor plate, his own heart pounding, his own lungs coated with the ash of dead men. He had to be rid of it.

"Your Highness?" said Vis as he fought to strip off the armor. The pieces tumbled to the floor, clanging and sending up plumes of dust.

But his chest was still lurching, and his stomach, too, and he barely reached the nearest basin before he was sick.

He clutched the edges of the bowl, dragging in ragged breaths as his heart finally slowed. Vis stood nearby, holding the discarded helmet in his hands.

"It's been a long day," said Rhy shakily, and Vis didn't ask what was wrong, didn't say anything, and for that, Rhy was grateful. He wiped his mouth with a shaking hand, straightened, and continued toward the royal baths.

He was already unbuttoning his tunic when he reached the doors and saw that the room beyond wasn't empty.

Two servants draped in silver and green stood along the far wall, and Cora perched on the stone rim of the large bath set into the floor, dipping a comb into the water and running it through her long, loose hair. The Veskan princess was wearing only a robe, open at the waist, and Rhy knew her people weren't prudish when it came to bodies, but still he blushed at the sight of so much fair skin.

His shirt still half buttoned, his hands slid back to his sides.

Cora's blue eyes drifted up.

"*Mas vares,*" she said in halting Arnesian.

"*Na ch'al,*" he responded hoarsely in Veskan.

The comb came to rest in her lap as she took in his ash-streaked face. "Do you want me to go?"

He honestly didn't know. After hours of holding his head up, of being strong while other men fought and died, he couldn't put on another show, couldn't pretend that everything was all right, but the thought of being alone with his thoughts, with the shadows, not the ones outside the palace walls, but the ones that came for *him* at night . . .

Cora was starting to rise when he said, "*Ta'ch.*"

Don't.

She sank back to her knees as two of his own servants came forward and began to undress him with quick, efficient motions. He expected Cora to look away, but she watched steadily, a curious light in her eyes as they freed the last of his armor, unlaced his boots, unfastened the buttons at cuff and collar with hands steadier than his. The servants peeled away the tunic, exposing his bare, dark chest, smooth except for the line at his ribs, the swirling scar over his heart.

"Clean the armor," he said softly. "Burn the cloth."

Rhy stepped forward, then, a silent command that he'd see to the rest himself.

He left his trousers on and padded barefoot straight down the beautiful inlaid steps and into the bath, the warm water embracing his ankles, his knees, his waist. The clear pool fogged around him, a clouded train of ash in his wake.

He waded to the center of the bath and went under, folding to his knees on the basin floor. His body tried to rise, but he forced all the air from his lungs and dug his fingertips into the grate on the bath floor, and held on until it hurt, until the water smoothed around him, and the world began to tunnel, and no more ash came off his skin.

And when at last he rose, breaking the surface with a ragged gasp, Cora was there, robe discarded on the edge of the bath, her long blond hair held up by some deft motion of the comb. Her hands floated from the surface of the bath like lilies.

"Can I help?" she asked, and before he could answer, she was kissing him, her fingertips brushing his hips beneath the water. Heat flared through him, simple and physical, and Rhy fought to keep his senses as the girl's hands caught the laces of his trousers and began to drag them loose.

He tore his mouth free.

"I thought you had a fondness for my brother," he rasped.

Cora flashed a mischievous smile. "I have a fondness for many things," she said, pulling him close again. Her hand slid over him, and he felt himself rising as she pressed into him, her mouth soft and searching against his, and part of Rhy wanted to let her, to take her, to lose himself the way he had so many times after Alucard left, to hold off the shadows and the nightmares with the simple, welcome distraction of another body.

His hands drifted up to her shoulders.

"*Ta'ch,*" he said, easing her back.

Her cheeks colored, hurt crossing her face before indignation. "You do not want me."

"No," he said gently. "Not like this."

Her gaze flicked down to the place where her fingers still rested against him, her expression coy. "Your body and your mind seem to disagree, my prince."

Rhy flushed and took a step back through the water. "I'm sorry." He continued to retreat until his back hit the stone side of the bath. He sank onto a bench.

The princess sighed, letting her arms drift absently through the water in a childlike way, as if those fingers hadn't just been questing deftly across his skin. "So it's true," she mused, "what they say about you?"

Rhy tensed. He had heard most of the rumors, and all of the truths, heard men speak about his lack of powers, about whether he deserved to be king, about who shared his bed, and who didn't, but still he forced himself to ask. "What do they say, Cora?"

She drifted toward him—wisps of blond hair escaping her bun in the bath's heat—and came to rest beside him on the bench, legs tucked up beneath her. She crossed her arms on the edge of the bath, and leaned her head on top, and just like that, she seemed to shed the last of her seduction and become a girl again.

"They say, Rhy Maresh, that your heart is taken."

He tried to speak, but he didn't know what to say. "It's complicated," he managed.

"Of course it is." Cora trailed her fingers through the water. "I was in love once," she added, as if it were an afterthought. "His name was Vik. I loved him the way the moon loves the stars—that is what we say, when a person fills the world with light."

"What happened?"

Her pale blue eyes drifted up. "You are the sole heir to your throne," she said. "But I am one of seven. Love is not enough."

The way she said it, as if it were a simple, immutable truth, made his eyes burn, his throat tighten. He thought of Alucard, not the way he'd been when Rhy sent him away, or even as he was on the Banner

Night, but the Alucard who'd lingered in his bed that first summer, lips playing against his skin as he whispered the words.

I love you.

Cora's fingers stilled, splaying on the water's surface, and Rhy noticed the deep scratches circling her wrist, the bruised skin. She caught him looking and flicked her hand, a motion of dismissal.

"My brother has a temper," she said absently. "Sometimes he forgets his strength." And then, a small, defiant smile. "But he always forgets mine."

"Does it hurt?"

"It is nothing that won't heal." She shifted. "Your scars are far more interesting."

Rhy's fingers went to the mark over his heart, but he said nothing, and she asked nothing, and they settled into an easy quiet, steam rising in tendrils around them, the patterns swirling in the mist. Rhy felt his mind drifting, to shadows, and dying men, to blades between ribs, and cold, dark places slick with blood, and beyond, beyond, the silence, thick as cotton, heavy as stone.

"Do you have the gift?"

Rhy blinked, the visions dissolving back into the baths. "What gift?"

Cora's fingers curled through the steam. "In my country, there are those who look into the fog and see things that are not there. Things that haven't happened yet. Just now, you looked like you were seeing something."

"Not seeing," said Rhy. "Just remembering."

They sat for ages in the bath, eager to leave neither the warmth nor the company. They perched side by side on the stone bench at the basin's edge, or on the cooler tile of its rim, and spoke—not about the past, or their respective scars. Instead, they shared the present. Rhy told her about the city beyond the walls, about the curse cast over London, its strange and spreading transmutation, about the fallen, and the silvers. And Cora told him about the claustrophobic palace with its maddening nobles, the gallery where they gathered to worry, the corners where they huddled to whisper.

Cora had the kind of voice that rang out through a room, but when she spoke softly, there was a music to it, a melody that he found lulling. She wove stories about this lord and that lady, calling them by their clothes since she didn't always know their names. She spoke of the magicians, too, with their tempers and their egos, recounted whole conversations without a stutter or a stop.

Cora, it seemed, had a mind like a gem, sharp and bright, and buried beneath childish airs. He knew why she did it—it was the same reason he played a rake as much as a royal. It was easier, sometimes, to be underestimated, discounted, dismissed.

". . . And then he actually did it," she was saying. "Swallowed a glass of wine and lit a spark, and poof, burned half his beard off."

Rhy laughed—it felt easy, and wrong, and so very needed—and Cora shook her head. "Never dare a Veskan. It turns us stupid."

"Kell said he had to knock one of your magicians out cold to keep her from charging into the fog."

Cora cocked her head. "I haven't seen your brother all day. Where has he gone?"

Rhy leaned his head back against the tiles. "To find help."

"He's not in the palace?"

"He's not in the city."

"Oh," she said thoughtfully. And then her smile was back, lazy on her lips. "And what about this?" she asked, producing Rhy's royal pin.

He shot upright. "Where did you get that?"

"It was in your trouser pocket."

He reached for it, and she pulled playfully out of reach.

"Give it *back*," he demanded, and she must have heard the warning in his voice, the sudden, shocking cold of the command, because she didn't resist, didn't play any games. Rhy's hand closed over the water-warmed metal. "It's late," he said, rising out of the bath. "I should go."

"I didn't mean to upset you," she said, looking genuinely hurt.

He ran a hand through damp curls. "You didn't," he lied as a pair of servants appeared, wrapping a robe around his bare shoulders. Anger burned through him, but only at himself for letting his guard slip, letting his focus drift. He should have left long ago, but he hadn't wanted to face the shadows that came with sleep. Now his body ached, his mind blurring with fatigue. "It's been a long day, and I'm tired."

Sadness washed across Cora's face.

"Rhy," she mewed, "it was only a game. I wouldn't have kept it."

He knelt on the bath's tiled edge, tipped her chin, and kissed her once on the forehead. "I know," he said.

He left her sitting alone in the bath.

Outside, Vis was slumped in a chair, weary but awake.

"I'm sorry," said Rhy as the guard rose beside him. "You shouldn't have waited. Or I shouldn't have stayed."

"It's all right, sir," said the man groggily, falling into step behind him.

The palace had gone quiet around them, only the murmur of the guards on duty filling the air as Rhy climbed the stairs, pausing outside Kell's room before remembering he wasn't there.

His own chamber stood empty, the lamps lit low, casting long shadows on every surface. A collection of tonics glittered on the sideboard—Tieren's concoctions for nights when it got bad—but the warmth of the bath still clung to his limbs and dawn was only a few hours away, so Rhy set his pin on the table and fell into the bed.

Only to be assaulted by a ball of white fur.

Alucard's cat had been sleeping on his pillow, and gave an indignant chirp when Rhy landed on the sheets. He didn't have the energy to evict the cat—its violet eyes were daring him to try—so Rhy slumped back, content to share the space. He threw an arm over his eyes and was surprised to feel the soft weight of a paw prodding his arm before curling up against his side. He slid his fingers absently through the creature's fur, letting the soft rumble of its purr and the faint, lingering scent of the captain—all sea breeze and summer wine—pull him down into sleep.

VII

There was a moment, when a ship first put out to sea.

When the land fell away and the world stretched wide, nothing but water and sky and freedom.

It was Lila's favorite time, when anything could happen and nothing yet had. She stood on the deck of the *Ghost* as Tanek parted around them, and the wild night opened its arms.

When she finally went below, Jasta was waiting at the base of the stairs.

"*Avan*," said Lila casually.

"*Avan*," rumbled Jasta.

It was a narrow hall, and she had to sidestep the captain in order to get by. She was halfway past when Jasta's hand shot out and closed around her throat. Lila's feet left the floor and then she was hanging, pinned roughly against the wall. She scrambled for purchase, too stunned to summon magic or reach her blade. By the time she finally freed the one she kept strapped to her ribs, the captain's hand had withdrawn and Lila was sagging back against the wall. One leg buckled before she managed to catch herself.

"What the everloving hell was that for?"

Jasta just stood there, looking down at Lila as if she hadn't just tried to strangle her. "That," said the captain, "was for insulting my ship."

"You've got to be kidding me," she snarled.

Jasta simply shrugged. "That was a warning. Next time, I throw you over."

With that, the captain held out her hand. It seemed a bad idea to take it, but a worse idea to refuse. Before Lila could decide, Jasta reached down and hauled her upright, gave her a sturdy pat on the back, and walked away, whistling as she went.

Lila watched the woman go, rocked by the sudden violence, the fact that she hadn't seen it coming. She holstered her blade with shaking fingers, and went to find Kell.

He was in the first cabin on the left.

"Well, this is cozy," she said, standing in the doorway.

The cabin was half the size of a closet, and about as welcoming. With just enough space for a single cot, it reminded Lila a bit too much of the makeshift coffin she'd been buried in by a bitter Faroan during the tournament.

Kell was sitting on the cot, turning a royal pin over in his fingers. When he saw her, he tucked it in his pocket.

"Room for another?" she asked, feeling like a fool even as she said it. There were only four cabins, and one was being used as a cell.

"I think we can make do," said Kell, rising to his feet. "But if you'd rather . . ."

He took a step toward the door, as if to go. She didn't want him to.

"Stay," she said, and there it was, that flickering smile, like an ember, coaxed with every breath.

"All right."

A single lantern hung from the ceiling, and Kell snapped his fingers, pale fire dancing above his thumb as he reached up to light the wick. Lila turned in a careful circle, surveying the cubby. "A bit smaller than your usual accommodations, *mas vares*?"

"Don't call me that," he said, pulling her back toward him, and she was about to say it again just to tease him when she saw the look in his eyes and relented, running her hands along his coat.

"All right."

He pulled her close, brushing his thumb against her cheek, and she knew he was looking at her eye, the spiral of fractured glass.

"You really didn't notice?"

Color spread across his fair cheeks, and she wondered, absently, if his skin freckled in the summer. "I don't suppose you'd believe me if I said I was distracted by your charm?"

Lila let out a low, sharp laugh. "My knives, perhaps. My quick fingers. But not my charm."

"Wit, then. Power."

She flashed a wicked smile. "Go on."

"I was distracted by everything about you, Lila. I still am. You're maddening, infuriating, incredible." She'd been teasing, but he clearly wasn't. Everything about him—the set of his mouth, the crease in his brow, the intensity in that blue eye—was dead serious. "I have never known what to make of you. Not since the day we met. And it terrifies me. You terrify me." He cupped her face in both hands. "And the idea of you walking away again, vanishing from my life, that terrifies me most of all."

Her heart was racing, banging out that same old song—*run, run, run*—but she was tired of running, of letting things go before she had the chance to lose them. She pulled Kell closer.

"Next time I walk away," she whispered into his skin, "come with me." She let her gaze drift up to his throat, his jaw, his lips. "When this is all over, when Osaron is gone and we've saved the world again, and everyone else gets their happily ever after, come with me."

"Lila," he said, and there was so much sadness in his voice, she suddenly realized she didn't want to hear his answer, didn't want to think of all the ways their story could end, of the chance that none of them would make it out alive, intact. She didn't want to think beyond this boat, this moment, so she kissed him, deeply, and whatever he was going to say, it died on his lips as they met hers.

VIII

Holland sat on the cot with his back against the cabin wall.

Beyond the wooden boards, the sea splashed against the ship's hull, and the rocking of the floor beneath him made him dizzy every time he moved. The iron cuff around Holland's wrist wasn't helping—the manacles been spelled to dampen magic, the effect like a wet cloth over a fire, not enough to douse his flame, but enough to make it smoke, like a cloud smothering his senses.

He was kept off balance by the second cuff, no longer around his wrist but clamped to a hook in the cabin wall.

And worse, he wasn't alone.

Alucard Emery was leaning in the doorway with a book in one hand and a glass of wine in the other (the thought of both made Holland ill) and every now and then his dark blue eyes flicked up, as if to make sure the *Antari* was still there, safely tethered to the wall.

Holland's head ached. His mouth was dry. He wanted air. Not the stale air of the cabin cell, but the fresh air above, whistling across the deck.

"If you set me free," he said, "I could help propel the ship."

Alucard licked his thumb and turned a page. "If I set you free, you could kill us all."

"I could do that from here," said Holland casually.

"Words that do not help your cause," said the captain.

A small window was embedded in the wall above Holland's head. "You could at least open that," he said. "Give us both some air."

Alucard looked at him long and hard before finally tucking the book under his arm. He downed the last of the wine, set the empty glass on the ground, and came forward, leaning over him to unlock the hatch.

A gust of cold air spilled in, and Holland filled his lungs as a spray of water sloshed against the hull and through the open window, spilling into the cabin.

Holland braced for the icy spray, but it never hit him.

With a flick of his wrist and a murmur of words, the water sprang up, circling Alucard's fingers once before hardening into a thin but vicious blade. His hand tightened on the hilt as he brought the knife's ice edge to rest against Holland's throat.

He swallowed, testing the blade's bite as he met Alucard's gaze.

"It would be a foolish thing," he said slowly, "to draw my blood."

Flexing his wrist, Holland felt the splinter of wood he'd slipped under the manacle, point digging into the base of his palm. It wouldn't take much pressure. A drop, a word, and the cuffs would melt away. But it wouldn't set him free.

Alucard's smile sharpened, and the knife dissolved back into a ribbon of water dancing in the air around him.

"Just remember something, *Antari*," he said, twirling his fingers and the water with them. "If this ship sinks, you will sink with it." Alucard straightened, shooing the sea spray back out the open window. "Any other requests?" he asked, the picture of hospitality.

"No," said Holland coolly. "You've already done so much."

Alucard cracked an icy smile and opened his book again, obviously content with his post.

The third time Death came for Holland, he was on his knees.

He crouched beside the stream, blood dripping from his fingertips in fat red drops as the Silver Wood rose around him. Twice a year he went there, a place up the river where the Sijlt branched off through a grove of trees growing up from the barren ground in shades of burnished metal—neither wood nor stone nor steel. Some said the Silver Wood had been made by a magician's hand, while others said it was the place where magic made its final stand before withdrawing from the surface of the world.

It was a place where, if you stood still, and closed your eyes, you could smell the echoes of summer. A memory of natural magic worn into the wood.

Holland bowed his head. He didn't pray—didn't know who to pray to, or what to say—only watched the frosted waters of the Sijlt swirl beneath his outstretched hand, waiting to catch each drop as it fell. A dash of crimson, a cloud of pink, and then gone, the pale surface of the stream returning to its usual whitish grey.

"What a waste of blood," said a voice behind him casually.

Holland didn't startle. He'd heard the steps coming from the edge of the grove, boots landing on dry grass. A short, sharp knife lay on the bank beside him, and Holland's fingers drifted toward it, only to find it wasn't there. He rose to his feet, then, and turned to find the stranger holding his weapon in both hands. The man was half a head shorter than Holland, and two decades older, dressed in a faded grey that almost passed for black, with dusty brown hair and dark eyes flecked with amber.

"Nice blade," said the intruder, testing its tip. "Gotta keep them sharp."

Blood dripped from Holland's palm, and the man's eyes flicked to the vivid red before smiling broadly. "*Sot*," he said easily, "I didn't come looking for trouble."

He sank onto a petrified log and drove the knife into the hard earth at his feet before lacing his fingers and leaning forward, elbows on his knees. One hand was covered in binding spells, an element scrawled along each finger. "Nice view."

Holland still said nothing.

"I come here sometimes, to think," continued the man, drawing a rolled paper from behind his ear. He looked at the end, unlit, then held it toward Holland.

"Help a friend out?"

"We're not friends," said Holland.

The man's eyes danced with light. "Not yet."

When Holland didn't move, the man sighed and flicked his own fingers, producing a small coin-sized flame that danced above his thumb. It was no small feat, this display of natural magic, even with the spellwork scrawled on his skin. He took a long drag. "My friends call me Vor."

The name settled like a stone in Holland's chest. "Vortalis."

The man brightened. "You remember," he said. Not *you've heard of me,* or *you know,* but you *remember.*

And Holland did. Ros Vortalis. He was a legend in the Kosik, a story in the streets and the shadows, a man who used his words as much as his weapons, and one who always seemed to get his way. A man known across the city as the Hunter, named for tracking down whoever and whatever he wanted, and for never leaving without his quarry. A man who had been hunting *Holland* for years.

"You have a reputation," said Holland.

"Oh," said Vortalis, exhaling, "we both have those. How many men and women walk the streets of London without weapons at hand? How many end fights without lifting a finger? How many refuse to join the gangs or the guard—"

"I'm not a thug."

Vortalis cocked his head. His smile vanished. "What are you, then? What's the point of you? All the magic in that little black eye, and what do you use it for? Emptying your veins into a frozen river? Dreaming of a nicer world? Surely there are better uses."

"My power has never brought me anything but pain."

"Then you're using it wrong." With that he stood and put the end of his taper out against the nearest tree.

Holland frowned. "This is a sacred—"

He didn't get the chance to finish the admonition, for that was when Vortalis moved, so fast it had to be a spell, something scrawled somewhere beneath his clothes—but then again, spells only *amplified* power. They didn't make it from scratch.

His fist was inches from Holland's face when Holland's will ground against flesh and bone, forcing Vortalis to a stop. But it wasn't enough. The man's fist trembled in the air, warring with the hold, and then it came crashing through, like a brick through glass, and slammed into Holland's jaw. The pain was sudden, bright, Vortalis beaming as he danced backward out of Holland's range. Or tried to. The stream shot up behind him and surged forward. But just before it caught Vortalis in the back, he moved again, sidestepping a blow he couldn't have seen before Holland finally lost patience and sent two spears of ice careening toward the man from opposite sides.

He dodged the first, but the second took him in the stomach, the spear spinning on its axis so it shattered broadside across the man's ribs instead of running him through.

Vortalis fell backward with a groan.

Holland stood, waiting to see if the man would get back up. He did, chuckling softly as he rocked forward to his knees.

"They told me you were good," said Vortalis, rubbing his ribs. "I've a feeling you're even better than they know."

Holland's fingers curled around his drying blood. Vortalis picked up a shard of ice, handling it less like a weapon than an artifact. "As it is, you could have killed me."

And Holland could have. Easily. If he hadn't turned the spear, it would have gone straight through flesh and muscle, broken against bone, but there was Alox in his head, stone body shattering against the floor, and Talya, slumping lifeless against her own knife.

Vortalis got to his feet, holding his side. "Why didn't you do it?"

"You weren't trying to kill *me*."

"The men I sent were. But you didn't kill them, either."

Holland held his gaze.

"You got something against killing?" pressed Vortalis.

"I've taken lives," answered Holland.

"That's not what I asked."

Holland fell silent. He clenched his fists, focused on the line of pain along his palm. At last, he said, "It's too easy."

"Killing? Of course it is," said Vortalis. "Living with it, that's the hard part. But sometimes, it's worth it. Sometimes, it's *necessary*."

"It wasn't necessary for me to kill your men."

Vortalis raised a brow. "They could have come after you again."

"They didn't," said Holland. "You just kept sending new ones."

"And you kept letting them live." Vortalis stretched, wincing faintly at his injured ribs. "I'd say you have a death wish, but you don't seem all that keen to die." He walked to the edge of the grove, his back to Holland as he looked out over the pale expanse of the city. He lit another taper, stuck the end between his teeth. "You know what I think?"

"I don't care—"

"I think you're a romantic. One of those fools waiting for the someday king to come. Waiting for the magic to return, for the world to wake up. But it doesn't work like that, Holland. If you want change, you have to make it." Vortalis waved dismissively at the stream. "You can empty your veins into that water, but it won't change a thing." He held out his hand. "If you really want to save this city, help me put that blood to better use."

Holland stared at the man's spell-covered hand. "And what use would that be?"

Vortalis smiled. "You can help me kill a king."

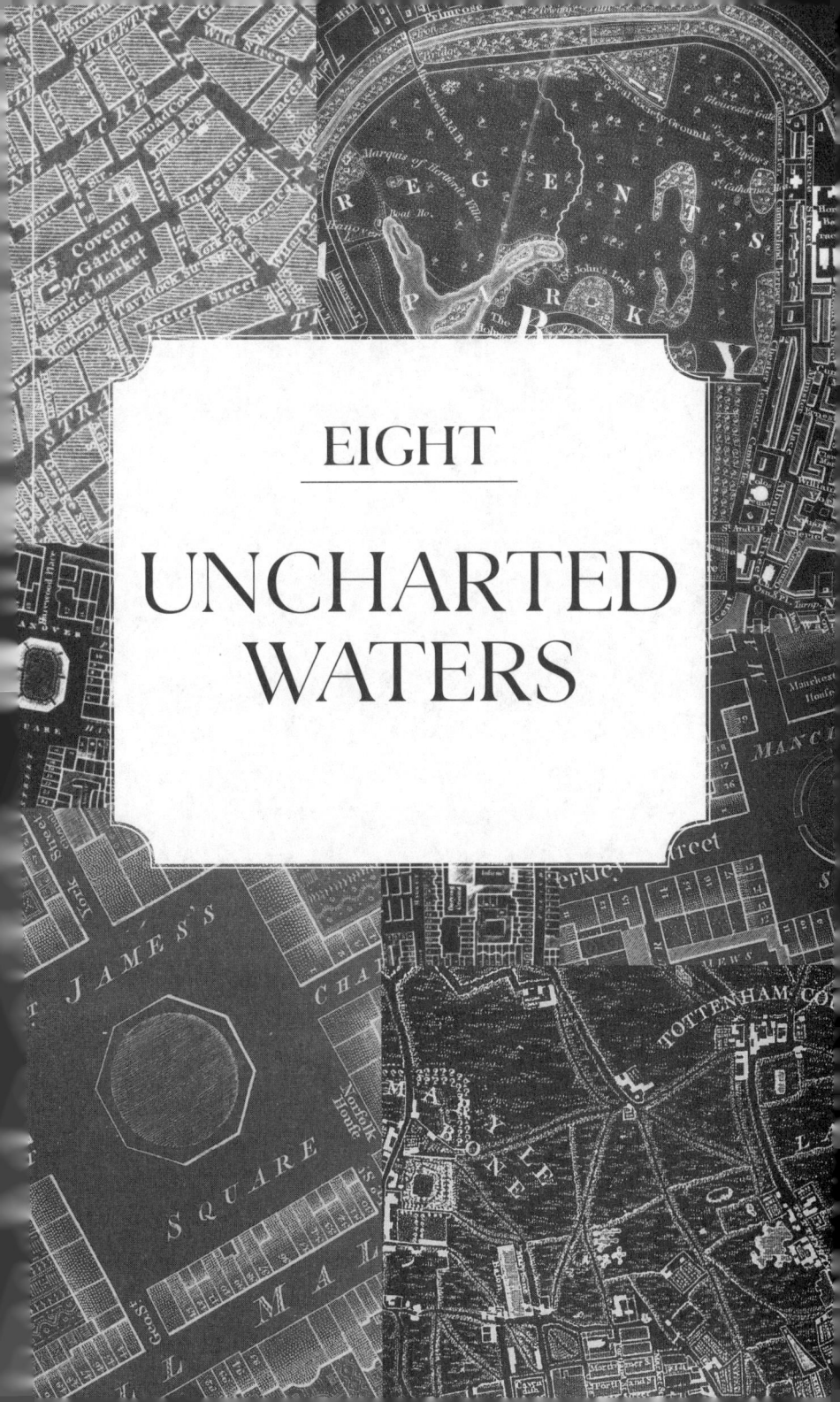

EIGHT

UNCHARTED WATERS

I

The coffee tasted like muck, but it kept Alucard's hands warm.

He hadn't slept, nerves sharpened to knife points by the foreign ship and the traitor magician and the fact that every time he closed his eyes, he saw Anisa burning, saw Jinnar crumbling to ash, saw himself reaching out as if there were a damned thing he could do to save his sister, his friend. Anisa had always been so bright, Jinnar had always been so strong, and it had meant nothing in the end.

They were still dead.

Alucard climbed the steps to the deck and took another swig, forgetting how bad the brew really was. He spit the brown sludge over the rail and wiped his mouth.

Jasta was busy tying off a rope against the mainmast. Hastra and Hano were sitting on a crate in the shade of the mainsail, the young guard cross-legged and the sailor girl perched like a crow, leaning forward to see something cupped in his hands. It looked, of all things, like the leafy green beginnings of an acina blossom. Hano made a delighted sound as the thing slowly unfurled before her eyes. Hastra was surrounded by the thin white threads of light particular to those rare few who held the elements in balance. Alucard wondered briefly why the young guard was not instead a priest. The air around Hano was a nest of dark blue spirals: a wind magician in the making, like Jinnar—

"Careful, now," said a voice. "A sailor's no good without a full set of fingers."

It was Bard. She was standing near the prow, teaching Lenos a trick with one of her knives. The sailor watched, eyes wide, as she took the blade between her fingertips and flipped it up into the air, and by the time she caught it handle side, the knife's edge was on fire. She gave a bow, and Lenos actually flashed a nervous smile.

Lenos, who'd come to Alucard on her first night aboard the *Spire* and warned that she was an omen. As if Alucard didn't already know.

Lenos, who'd named her the Sarows.

The first time Alucard had seen Delilah Bard, she'd been standing on his ship, bound at the wrists and frizzing the air with silver. He'd only ever met one magician who glowed like that, and that one had a black eye and an air of general disdain that spoke louder than any words. Lila Bard, however, had two average brown eyes, and nothing to say for herself, nothing to say for the corpse of Alucard's crewmember, stretched out there on the plank. Had offered a single broken sentence:

Is en ranes gast.

I am the best thief.

And as he'd stood there, taking in her dagger smile, her silver lines of light, Alucard had thought, *Well, you're certainly the strangest.*

The first bad decision he'd made was taking her aboard.

The second was letting her stay.

From there, the bad decisions seemed to multiply like drinks during a game of Sanct.

That first night, in his cabin, Lila sat across from Alucard, her magic tangled, a snarled knot of power never used. And when she asked him to teach her, he'd nearly choked on his wine. Teach an *Antari* magic? But Alucard had. He'd groomed the coil of power, smoothed it as best he could, and watched the magic flow through clear channels, brighter than anything he'd ever seen.

He'd had his moments of clarity, of course.

He'd thought of selling her to Maris at the *Ferase Stras*.

Thought of killing her before she decided to kill him.

Thought of leaving her, betraying her, dreamed up a dozen ways to wash his hands of her. She was trouble—even the crew knew it, and they couldn't see the word written in knotted silver above her head.

But for all of that, he *liked* her.

Alucard had taken a dangerous girl and made her positively lethal, and he knew that combination was likely to be the end of him, one way or another. So when she'd betrayed him, attacking a competitor before the *Essen Tasch,* stealing their place even though she had to know what it would mean for *him, his crew,* his *ship* . . . Alucard hadn't truly been surprised. If anything, he'd been a bit relieved. He'd always known *Antari* were selfish, bullheaded magicians. Lila was simply proving his instinct right.

He thought it would be easy then, to be rid of her, to take back his ship, his order, his life. But nothing about Bard was easy. That silver light had snagged him, gotten his own blue and green all tangled up.

"You *knew.*"

Alucard hadn't heard Kell coming, hadn't noticed the silver stirring the air outside his thoughts, but now the other magician stood beside him, following his gaze to Bard. "We look different to you, don't we?"

Alucard crossed his arms. "Everyone looks different to me. No two threads of magic are the same."

"But you knew what she was," said Kell, "from the moment you saw her."

Alucard tipped his head. "Imagine my surprise," he said, "when a cutpurse with a silver cloud killed one of my men, joined up with my crew, and then asked *me* to teach *her* magic."

"So it's *your* fault she entered the *Essen Tasch.*"

"Believe it or not," said Alucard, echoing Kell's words about Rhy from the night before, "it was her idea. And I tried to stop her. Valiantly, but it turns out she's rather stubborn." His gaze flicked toward Kell. "Must be an *Antari* trait."

Kell gave a grunt of annoyance and turned away. Always storming off. That was definitely an *Antari* habit.

"Wait," said Alucard. "Before you go, there's something—"

"No."

Alucard bristled. "You don't even know what I was going to say."

"I know it was probably about Rhy, so I know I don't want to hear it, because if you say one more thing about how my brother was in bed, I'm going to break your jaw."

Alucard laughed softly, sadly.

"Is that *funny*?" snarled Kell.

"No . . ." said Alucard, trailing off. "You're just so easy to rile. You really can't fault me for doing it."

"No more than you will be able to fault me for hitting you when you go too far."

Alucard raised his hands. "Fair enough." He began to rub the old scars that circled his wrists. "Look, all I wanted to say was—that I never meant to hurt him."

Kell gave him a disparaging look. "You treated him like a fling."

"How would you know?"

"Rhy was in love with you, and you *left* him. You made him think . . ." An exasperated sigh. "Or have you forgotten, that you ran from London long before I ever tried to cast you out?"

Alucard shook his head, eyes escaping to the steady blue line of the sea. His jaw locked, body revolting against the truth. The truth had claws, and they were sunk into his chest. It would be easier to let it go unsaid, but when Kell turned again to go, he forced it up.

"I *left*," he said, "because *my* brother found out where I was spending my nights—who I was spending them *with*."

Alucard kept his eyes on the water, but he heard Kell's steps drag to a stop. "Believe it or not, not all families are willing to put aside propriety to indulge a royal's taste. The Emerys have old notions. Strict ones." He swallowed. "My brother, Berras, told my father, who beat me until I couldn't stand. Until he broke my arm, my shoulder, my ribs. Until I blacked out. And then he had Berras put me out to sea. I woke up in a ship's hold, the captain ten *rish* richer with the order not to return to London until his crew had *set me right*. I made it off that ship the first time it docked, with three *lin* in my pocket and a fair bit of magic in my veins, and no one to welcome me home, so no, I didn't turn back. And that's my fault. But I didn't know what I meant to him." He tore his gaze from the sea and met Kell's eyes.

"I never wanted to leave," he said. "And if I'd known Rhy loved me then as much as I love him, I would never have stayed away."

They stood surrounded by the sea spray and the crack of sails.

For a long minute, neither spoke.

At last, Kell sighed. "I still can't stand you."

Alucard laughed with relief. "Oh, don't worry," he said. "The feeling's mutual."

With that, the captain left the *Antari* and made his way to his thief. Lenos had left her standing alone at the rail, and she was now using her blade to scrape dirt from beneath her nails, gaze trained on something distant.

"Coin for your thoughts, Bard."

She glanced his way, and a smile touched the corner of her mouth.

"I never thought we'd ever share a deck again."

"Well, the world is full of surprises. And shadow kings. And curses. Coffee?" Alucard asked, offering the cup. She took one look at the brown sludge and said, "I'll pass."

"Don't know what you're missing, Bard."

"Oh, I do. I made the mistake of trying some this morning."

Alucard made a sour face and tipped the rest of the drink out over the side. Ilo was making the *Spire*'s usual cook look like a palace chef. "I need a real meal."

"I'm sorry," teased Lila, "when did someone exchange my stalwart captain for a whining noble?"

"When did someone exchange my best thief for a thorn in the ass?"

"Ah," she said, "but I've always been one of those."

Lila tipped her face toward the sun. Her hair was getting long, the dark strands brushing her shoulders, her glass eye winking in the crisp winter light.

"You love the sea," he said.

"Don't you?"

Alucard's hand tightened on the rail. "I love pieces of it. The air on the open water, the energy of a crew working together, the chance for adventure and all that. But . . ." He sensed her attention sharpening, and stopped. For months they'd walked a careful line between outright lie and truth by omission, caught in a stalemate, neither willing to tip their hand. They'd doled out truths like precious currency, and only ever in trade.

Just now, he'd almost gone and told her something for free.

"But?" she prodded with a thief's light touch.

"Do you ever get tired of running, Bard?"

She cocked her head. "No."

Alucard's gaze went to the horizon. "Then you haven't left enough behind."

A chill breeze cut through, and Lila crossed her arms on the rail and looked down at the water below. She frowned. "What is that?"

Something bobbed on the surface, a piece of driftwood. And then another. And another. The boards floated past in broken shards, the edges burned. An unpleasant chill went through Alucard.

The *Ghost* was sailing through the remains of a ship.

"That," said Alucard, "is the work of Sea Serpents."

Lila's eyes widened. "Please tell me you're talking about mercenaries and not giant ship-eating snakes."

Alucard raised a brow. "Giant ship-eating snakes? Really?"

"What?" she challenged. "How am I supposed to know where to draw the line in this world?"

"You can draw it well before giant ship-eating snakes. . . . You see this, Jasta?" he called.

The captain squinted in the direction he was pointing. "I see it. Looks maybe a week old."

"Not old enough," muttered Alucard.

"You wanted the fastest route," she called, turning back to the wheel as a large piece of hull floated past, part of the name still painted on its side.

"So what are they, then," asked Lila, "these Sea Serpents?"

"Swords for hire. They sink their own ships right before they attack."

"As a distraction?" asked Lila.

He shook his head. "A message. That they won't be needing them anymore, that once they're done killing everyone aboard and dumping the bodies in the sea, they'll take their victims' boat instead and sail away."

"Huh," said Lila.

"Exactly."

"Seems like a waste of a perfectly good ship."

He rolled his eyes. "Only you would mourn the vessel instead of the sailors."

"Well," she said matter-of-factly, "the ship certainly didn't do anything wrong. The *people* might have deserved it."

II

When Kell was young and couldn't sleep, he'd taken to wandering the palace.

The simple act of walking steadied something in him, calmed his nerves and stilled his thoughts. He'd lose track of time, but also space, look up and find himself in a strange part of the palace with no memory of getting there, his attention turned inward instead of out.

He couldn't get nearly as lost on the *Ghost*—the whole of the ship was roughly the size of Rhy's chambers—but he was still surprised when he looked up and realized he was standing outside Holland's makeshift cell.

The old man, Ilo, was propped in a chair in the doorway, silently whittling a piece of black wood into the shape of a ship by feel alone, and doing a rather decent job. He seemed lost in his task, the way Kell had been moments before, but now Ilo rose, sensing his presence and reading in it a silent dismissal. He left the small wooden carving behind on the chair. Kell glanced into the small room, expecting to see Holland staring back, and frowned.

Holland was sitting on the cot with his back to the wall, his head resting on his drawn-up knees. One hand was cuffed to the wall, the chain hanging like a leash. His skin had taken on a greyish pallor—the sea clearly wasn't agreeing with him—and his black hair, Kell realized, was streaked with new bright silver, as if shedding Osaron had cost him something vital.

But what surprised Kell most was the simple fact that Holland was *asleep*.

Kell had never seen Holland lower his guard, never seen him relaxed, let alone unconscious. And yet, he wasn't entirely *still*. The muscles in the other *Antari*'s arms twitched, his breath hitching, as though he were trapped in a bad dream.

Kell held his breath as he lifted the chair out of the way and stepped into the room.

Holland didn't stir when Kell neared, nor when he knelt in front of the bed.

"Holland?" said Kell quietly, but the man didn't shift.

It wasn't until Kell's hand touched Holland's arm that the man woke. His head snapped up and he pulled suddenly away, or tried to, his shoulders hitting the cabin wall. For a moment his gaze was wide and empty, his body coiled, his mind somewhere else. It lasted only a second, but in that sliver of time, Kell saw fear. A deep, trained fear, the kind beaten into animals who'd once bitten their masters, Holland's careful composure slipping to reveal the tension beneath. And then he blinked, once, twice, eyes focusing.

"Kell." He exhaled sharply, his posture shifting back into a mimicry of calm, control, as he wrestled with whatever demons haunted his sleep. "*Vos och?*" he demanded brusquely in his own tongue. *What is it?*

Kell resisted the urge to retreat under the man's glare. They'd hardly spoken since he had arrived in front of Holland's cell and told him to get up. Now he said only, "You look ill."

Holland's dark hair was plastered to his face with sweat, his eyes feverish. "Worried for my health?" he said hoarsely. "How touching." He began to fiddle absently with the manacle around his wrist. Beneath the iron, his skin looked red, raw, and before Kell had fully decided, he was reaching for the metal.

Holland stilled. "What are you doing?"

"What does it look like?" said Kell, producing the key. His fingers closed around the cuff, and the cold metal with its strange numbing weight made him think of White London, of the collar and the cage and his own voice screaming—

The chains fell away, manacle hitting the floor hard and heavy enough to mark the wood.

Holland stared down at his skin, at the place where the metal cuff had been. He flexed his fingers. "Is that a good idea?"

"I suppose we'll see," said Kell, retreating to sit in the chair against the opposite wall. He kept his guard up, hand hovering over a blade even now, but Holland made no motion to attack, only rubbed his wrist thoughtfully.

"It's a strange feeling, isn't it?" said Kell. "The king had me arrested. I spent some time in that cell. In those chains."

Holland raised a single dark brow. "How long did you spend in chains, Kell?" he asked, voice dripping with scorn. "Was it a few hours, or an entire day?"

Kell went silent, and Holland shook his head ruefully, a mocking sound caught in his throat. The *Ghost* must have caught a wave, because it rocked, and Holland paled. "Why am I on this ship?" When Kell didn't answer, he went on. "Or perhaps the better question is, why are *you* on this ship?"

Kell still said nothing. Knowledge was a weapon, and he had no intention of arming Holland, not yet. He expected the other magician to press the issue, but instead he settled back, face tipped to the open window.

"If you listen, you can hear the sea. And the ship. And the people on it." Kell tensed, but Holland continued. "That Hastra, he has the kind of voice that carries. The captains, too, both of them like to talk. A black market, a container for magic . . . it won't be long before I've pieced it all together."

So he wasn't dropping it.

"Enjoy the challenge," said Kell, wondering why he was still there, why he'd come in the first place.

"If you're planning an attack against Osaron, then let me *help*." The other *Antari*'s voice had changed, and it took Kell a moment to realize what he heard threaded through it. Passion. Anger. Holland's voice had always been as smooth and steady as a rock. Now, it had fissures.

"Help requires trust," said Kell.

"Hardly," countered Holland. "Only mutual interest." His gaze burned through Kell. "Why did you bring me?" he asked again.

"I brought you along so you wouldn't cause trouble in the palace. And I brought you as bait, in the hopes that Osaron would follow us." It was a partial truth, but the telling of it and the look in Holland's eyes loosened something in Kell. He relented. "That container you heard about—it's called an Inheritor. And we're going to use it to contain Osaron."

"How?" demanded Holland, not incredulous, but intense.

"It's a receptacle for power," explained Kell. "Magicians used them once to pass on the entirety of their magic by transferring it into a container."

Holland went quiet, but his eyes were still fever bright. After a long moment he spoke again, his voice low, composed. "If you want me to use this Inheritor—"

"That isn't why I brought you," cut in Kell, too fast, unsure if Holland's guess was too far from or too close to the truth. He'd already considered the dilemma—in fact, had tried to think of nothing else since leaving London. The Inheritor required a sacrifice. It would be one of them. It had to be. But he didn't trust it to be Holland, who'd fallen once before, and he didn't want it to be Lila, who didn't fear anything, even when she should, and he knew Osaron had his sights set on *him,* but he had Rhy, and Holland had no one, and Lila had lived without power, and he would rather die than lose his brother, himself . . . and around and around it went in his head.

"Kell," said Holland sternly. "I own my shadows, and Osaron is one of them."

"As Vitari was mine," replied Kell.

Where does it start?

He got to his feet before he could say more, before he seriously began to entertain the notion. "We can argue over noble sacrifices when we have the device in hand. In the meantime . . ." He nodded at Holland's chains. "Enjoy the taste of freedom. I'd give you leave to walk the ship, but—"

"Between Delilah and Jasta, I wouldn't make it far." Holland rubbed his wrists again. Flexed his fingers. He didn't seem to know what to do with his hands. At last he crossed his arms loosely over his chest, mimicking Kell's own stance. Holland closed his eyes, but Kell could tell he wasn't resting. His guard was up, his hackles raised.

"Who were they?" Kell asked softly.

Holland blinked. "What?"

"The three people you killed before the Danes."

Tension rippled through the air. "It doesn't matter."

"It mattered enough for you to keep track," said Kell.

But Holland's face had retreated back behind its mask of indifference, and the room filled with silence until it drowned them both.

III

Vortalis had always wanted to be king—not the *someday* king, he told Holland, but the *now* king. He didn't care about the stories. Didn't buy into the legends. But he knew the city needed order. Needed strength. Needed a leader.

"Everyone wants to be king," said Vortalis.

"Not me," said Holland.

"Well, then you're either a liar or a fool."

They were sitting in a booth at the Scorched Bone. The kind of place where men could talk of regicide without raising any brows. Now and then the attention drifted toward them, but Holland knew it had less to do with the topic and more to do with his left eye and Vortalis's knives.

"A pretty pair we make," the man had said when they first entered the tavern. "The *Antari* and the Hunter. Sounds like one of those tales you love," he'd added, pouring the first round of drinks.

"London *has* a king," said Holland now.

"London *always* has a king," countered Vortalis. "Or queen. And how long has that ruler been a tyrant?"

They both knew there was only one way the throne changed hands—by force. A ruler wore the crown as long as they could keep it on their head. And that meant every king or queen had been a killer first. Power required corruption, and corruption rewarded power. The people who ended up on that throne had always paved the way with blood.

"It takes a tyrant," said Holland.

"But it doesn't have to," argued Vortalis. "You could be my might, my knight, my power, and I could be the law, the right, the order, and together, we could more than take this throne," he said, setting down his cup. "We could *hold* it."

He was a gifted orator, Holland would give him that. The kind of man who stoked passion the way an iron did coals. They had called him the Hunter, but the longer Holland was in his presence, the more he thought of him as the Bellows—he'd told him once, and the man had chuckled, said he was indeed full of air.

There was an undeniable charm about the man, not merely the youthful airs of one who hadn't seen the worst the world has to offer, but the blaze of someone who managed to believe in change, in spite of it.

When Vortalis spoke to Holland, he always met both eyes, and in that flecked gaze, Holland felt like he was being *seen*.

"You know what happened to the last *Antari*?" Vortalis was saying now, leaning forward into Holland's space. "I do. I was there in the castle when Queen Stol cut his throat and bathed in his blood."

"What were you doing in the castle?" wondered Holland.

Vortalis gave him a long, hard look. "That's what you take away from my story?" He shook his head. "Look, our world needs every drop of magic, and we've got kings and queens spilling it like water so they can have a taste of power, or maybe just so it can't rise against them. We got where we are because of fear. Fear of Black London, fear of magic that wasn't ours to control, but that's no way forward, only down. I could have killed you—"

"You could have tried—"

"But the world *needs* power. And men who aren't afraid of it. Think what London could do with a leader like that," said Vortalis. "A king who cared about his people."

Holland ran a finger around the rim of his glass, the ale itself untouched, while the other man drained his second cup. "So you want to kill our current king."

Vortalis leaned forward. "Doesn't everyone?"

It was a valid question.

Gorst—a mountain of a man who'd carved his way to the throne with an army at his back and turned the castle into a fortress, the city into a slum. His men rode the streets, taking everything they could, everything they wanted, in the name of a king who pretended to care, who claimed he could resurrect the city even while he drained it dry.

And every week, King Gorst opened throats in the blood square, a tithe to the dying world, as if that sacrifice—a sacrifice that wasn't even his—could set the world to rights. As if the spilling of *their* blood was proof of *his* devotion to his cause.

How many days had Holland stood at the edge of that square, and watched, and thought of cutting Gorst's throat? Of offering *him* back to the hungry earth?

Vortalis was giving him a weighted look, and Holland understood. "You want *me* to kill Gorst." The other man smiled. "Why not kill him yourself?"

Vortalis had no problem killing—he hadn't earned his nickname by abstaining from violence—and he was really very good at it. But only a fool walked into a fight without his sharpest knives, Vortalis explained, leaning closer, and Holland was uniquely suited to the task. "I know you're not fond of the practice," he'd added. "But there's a difference between killing for purpose and killing for sport, and wise men know that some must fall so others can rise."

"Some throats are meant to be opened," said Holland dryly.

Vortalis flashed a cutting grin. "Exactly. So you can sit around waiting for a storybook ending, or you can help me write a real one."

Holland rapped his fingers on the table. "It won't be easy to do," he said thoughtfully. "Not with his guard."

"Like rats, those men," said Vortalis, producing a tightly rolled paper. He lit the end in the nearest lantern. "No matter how many I kill, more scurry out to take their place."

"Are they loyal?" asked Holland.

Smoke poured from the man's nostrils in a derisive snort. "Loyalty is either bought or earned, and as far as I can tell, Gorst has neither the riches nor the charm to merit his army. These men, they fight for him, they die for him, they wipe his ass. They have the blind devotion of the cursed."

"Curses die with their makers," mused Holland.

"And so we return to the point. The death of a tyrant and a curse-maker, and why you're so suited for the job. According to one of the few spies I've managed, Gorst keeps himself at the top of the palace, in a room guarded on all four sides, locked up like a prize in his own treasure chest. Now, is it true," Vortalis said, his eyes dancing with light, "that the *Antari* can make doors?"

Three nights later, at the ninth bell, Holland walked through the castle gate, and disappeared. One step took him across the threshold, and the next landed in the middle of the royal chamber, a room brimming with cushions and silks.

Blood dripped from the *Antari*'s hand, where he still clutched the talisman. Gorst wore so many, he hadn't even noticed it was missing, pinched by Vortalis's spy within the castle. Three simple words—*As Tascen Gorst*—and he was in.

The king sat before a blazing fire, gorging himself on a feast of fowl and bread and candied pears. Across the city, people wasted away, but Gorst's bones had long been swallowed up by his constant feasting.

Occupied by his meal, the king hadn't noticed Holland standing there behind him, hadn't heard him draw his knife.

"Try not to stab him in the back," Vortalis had advised. "After all, he *is* the king. He deserves to see the blade coming."

"You have a very odd set of principles."

"Ah, but I do have them."

Holland was halfway to the king when he realized Gorst was not dining alone.

A girl, no more than fifteen, crouched naked at the king's side like an animal, a pet. Unlike Gorst, she had no distraction, and her head drifted up at the movement of Holland's steps. At the sight of him, she began to scream.

The sound cut off sharply as he pinned the air in the girl's lungs, but Gorst was already rising, his massive form filling the hearth. Holland didn't wait—his knife went whipping toward the king's heart.

And Gorst *caught* it.

The king plucked the weapon from the air with a sneer while the girl still clawed at her throat. "Is that all you have?"

"No," said Holland, bringing his palms together around the brooch.

"*As Steno,*" he said, opening his hands as the brooch shattered into a dozen shards of metal. They flew through the air, fast as light, driving through cloth and flesh and muscle.

Gorst let out a groan as blood blossomed against the white of his tunic, stained his sleeves, but still he did not fall. Holland forced the metal deeper, felt the pieces grind against bone, and Gorst sank to his knees beside the girl.

"You think it is that easy—to kill—a king?" he panted, and then, before Holland could stop him, Gorst lifted Holland's knife, and used it to slit the girl's throat.

Holland staggered, letting go of her voice as blood splashed onto the floor. Gorst was running his fingers through the viscous pool. He was trying to write a spell. Her life had been worth nothing more than the meanest ink.

Anger flared in Holland. His hands splayed out, and Gorst was wrenched back and up, a puppet on strings. The tyrant let out a guttural roar as his arms were forced wide.

"You think you can rule this city?" he rasped, bones straining against Holland's hold. "You try, and see—how long—you last."

Holland whipped the fire from the hearth, a ribbon of flame that wrapped around the king's throat in a burning collar. At last, Gorst began to keen, screams dragging into whimpers. Holland stepped forward, through the wasted girl's blood, until he was close enough that the heat of the burning coil was licking his skin.

"It's time," he said, the words lost beneath the sounds of mortal anguish, "for a new kind of king."

"*As Orense,*" said Holland when it was done.

The flames had died away, and the chamber doors fell open one after the other, Vortalis striding into the room, a dozen men in his wake. Across the front of their dark armor they already bore his chosen seal—an open hand with a circle carved into its palm.

Vortalis himself wasn't dressed for battle. He wore his usual dark grey, the only spots of color the spectrum of his eyes and the blood he tracked like mud into the room.

The bodies of Gorst's guards littered the hall behind him.

Holland frowned. "I thought you said the curse would lift. They wouldn't have to die."

"Better safe than sorry," said Vortalis, and then, seeing Holland's face, "I didn't kill the ones that begged."

He took one look at Gorst's body—the bloody wounds, the burn around his neck—and whistled under his breath. "Remind me never to cross you."

Gorst's meal still sat before the hearth and Vortalis took up the dead king's glass, dumped the contents in the fire with a hiss, and poured himself a fresh drink, swishing the wine to cleanse the vessel.

He raised the glass to his men. "*On vis och,*" he said. "The castle is ours. Take down the old banners. By dawn, I want the whole city to know the tyrant no longer sits on the throne. Take his stores, and this shitty wine, and see it spread from the *das* to the Kosik. Let the people know there's a new king in London, and his name is Ros Vortalis."

The men erupted into cheers, pouring out through the open doors, past and around and over the bodies of the old guard.

"And find somebody to clean up that mess!" Vortalis called after them.

"You're in a fine mood," said Holland.

"You should be too," chided Vortalis. "This is how change happens. Not with a whisper and a wish like in those tales of yours, but with a well-executed plan—and, yes, a bit of blood, but that's the way of the world, isn't it? It's our turn now. I will be this city's king, and you can be its valiant knight, and together we will build something better." He raised the glass to Holland. *"On vis och,"* he said again. "To new dawns, and good ends, and loyal friends."

Holland folded his arms. "I'm amazed you have any left, after sending so many after me."

Vortalis laughed. Holland hadn't heard a laugh like that since Talya, and even then, her laugh had been the sweet of poison berries, and Vortalis's was the open rolling of the sea.

"I never sent you friends," he said. "Only enemies."

IV

Lenos was standing at the *Ghost*'s stern, toying with one of the little carved ships Ilo left everywhere, when a bird flew past.

He looked up, worried. The sudden appearance could only mean one thing—they were approaching land. Which wouldn't be a problem if they weren't meant to be heading straight for Maris's market, in the middle of the sea. The sailor hurried to the prow as the *Ghost* glided serenely toward a port that rose on the shoreline.

"Why are we docking?"

"It is easier to chart the course from here," said Jasta. "Besides, supplies are low. We left in a hurry."

Lenos cast a nervous glance at Alucard, who was climbing the steps. "Aren't we still in a hurry?" asked Lenos,

"Won't take long," was all Jasta said.

Lenos shielded his eyes against the sun—it had already passed its apex and was now sinking toward the horizon—and squinted at the line of ships tethered to the docks.

"Port of Rosenal," offered Alucard. "It's the last stop of any interest before the northern bay."

"I don't like this," grumbled the *Antari* prince as he joined them on deck. "Jasta, we—"

"We unload the crates and restock," insisted the captain as she and Hano uncoiled the ropes and threw them over. "One hour, maybe two. Stretch your legs. We'll be out of port by nightfall, and to the market by late morning."

"I for one could use a meal," said Alucard, unhitching the ramp. "No offense meant, Jasta, but Ilo cooks about as well as he sees."

The ship drifted to a stop as two dock hands caught the ropes and tied them off. Alucard set off down the ramp without a backward glance, Bard on his heels.

"*Sanct,*" muttered Jasta under her breath. Kell and Lenos both turned toward her. Something was wrong, Lenos felt it in his gut.

"You coming?" called Lila, but Kell called back, "I'm staying on the ship." And then he spun on Jasta. "What is it?"

"You need to get off," said the *Ghost*'s captain. *"Now."*

"Why?" asked Kell, but Lenos had already seen the trio headed their way down the dock. Two men and a woman, all in black, and each with a sword hanging at their waist. A nervous prickle ran through him.

Kell finally noticed the strangers. "Who are they?"

"Trouble," spat Jasta, and Lenos turned to warn Alucard and Bard, but they were already halfway down the dock, and the captain must have seen the danger, too, because he threw his arm casually around Lila's shoulder, angling her away.

"What's going on?" demanded Kell as Jasta spun on her heel and started for the hold.

"They shouldn't be here, not this early in the year."

"Who *are* they?" demanded Kell.

"This is a private port," said Lenos, his long legs easily keeping pace, "run by a man named Rosenal. Those are his swords. Normally they don't dock until summer, when the weather holds and the sea is full. They are here to check the cargo, search for contraband."

Kell shook his head. "I thought this ship *dealt* in contraband."

"It does," said Jasta, descending the steps in two strides and taking off down the hold. "Rosenal's men take a cut. Convenient, too, since the only ships that come here do not fly royal colors. But they are early."

"I still don't understand why we have to *go*," said Kell. "Your cargo is your problem—"

Jasta turned on him, her form filling the hall. "Is it? Not in London anymore, princeling, and not everyone outside the capital is friend to the crown. Out here, coin is king, and no doubt Rosenal's men would love to ransom a prince, or sell *Antari* parts to the *Ferase Stras*. If you want to make it there intact, get the traitor magician and go."

Lenos saw the other man go pale.

Steps sounded on deck, and Jasta snarled and took off again, leaving Kell to snag a pair of caps from the hooks in the hall and pull one down over his copper hair. Holland couldn't have heard Jasta's warning through the floor, but the stomping must have said enough, because he was already on his feet when they arrived.

"I assume there's a problem." Lenos's stomach cramped with worry at the sight of him free, but Kell just pushed the second cap into the *Antari*'s hands.

"Jasta?" called a new voice overhead.

Holland tugged the cap down, his black eye lost beneath the brim's shadow as the captain nudged them both out of the cabin toward the window at the back of the ship. She threw it open, revealing a short ladder that plunged toward the water below.

"Go. Now. Come back in an hour or two." Jasta was already turning away as one of the figures reached the stairs leading down into the hold. A pair of black boots came into sight and Lenos threw his narrow frame in front of the window.

Behind him, Kell climbed through.

He waited for the splash, but heard nothing but a rush of breath, an instant of silence, and then the muted thud of boots hitting dock. Lenos glanced over his shoulder to see Holland leap from the ladder and land in an elegant crouch beside Kell just before Rosenal's sellswords came stomping into the hold.

"What's this now?" said the woman when she saw Lenos, limbs spread across the opening. He managed an awkward smile.

"Just airing out the hold," he said, turning to swing the window shut. The sellsword caught his wrist and shoved him aside.

"That so?" Lenos held his breath as she stuck her head out the window, scanning the water and the docks.

But when she drew back into the hold, he saw the answer in her bored expression and sagged with relief.

She'd seen nothing strange.

The *Antari* were gone.

V

Lila had a bad feeling about Rosenal.

She didn't know if it was the port town itself that disturbed her, or the fact that they were being followed. Probably the latter.

At first, she thought it might be nothing, an echo of nerves from that close call back on the docks, but as she climbed the hill to the town, the certainty settled like a cloak around her shoulders, awareness scratching at her neck.

Lila had always been good at knowing when she wasn't alone. People had a presence, a weight in the world. Lila had always been able to sense it, but now she wondered if maybe it was the magic in their blood she'd been hearing all along, ringing like a plucked string.

And by the time they reached the rise, Kell either sensed it, too, or he simply felt her tensing beside him.

"Do you think we're being followed?" he asked.

"Probably," offered Holland blandly. The sight of him loose, unchained, turned her stomach.

"I always assume I'm being followed," she said with false cheer. "Why do you think I have so many knives?"

Kell's brow furrowed. "You know, I honestly can't tell if you're joking."

"Some towns have fog," offered Alucard, "and some have bad feelings. Rosenal simply has a bit of both."

Lila slid her arm free of Kell's, senses pricking. The town overlooking the port was a tight nest of streets, squat buildings huddled against the icy wind. Sailors hurried from doorway to doorway, hoods and collars up against the cold. The town was riddled with alleys, the dregs of light thin and the shadows deep enough to swallow the places where a person might wait.

"Gives it a strange kind of charm," continued the captain, "that sense of being watched..."

Her steps slowed before the mouth of a winding street, the familiar weight of a knife falling into her grip. The bad feeling was getting worse. Lila knew the way a heart raced when it was chasing someone, and the way it stuttered when it was being chased, and right now her heart felt less like predator and more like prey, and she didn't like it. She squinted into the lidded dark of the alley but saw nothing.

The others were getting ahead of her, and Lila was just turning to catch up when she saw it. There, in the hollow where the road curved away—the shape of a man. The sheen of rotting teeth. A shadow wrapped around his throat. His lips were moving, and when the wind picked up it carried the broken edge of a melody.

A song she'd hummed a hundred times aboard the *Spire*.

How do you know when the Sarows is coming?

Lila shivered and took a step forward, drawing her fingertip along the oil-slicked edge of her knife.

Tyger, Tyger—

"Bard!"

Alucard's voice cut through the air, scattering her senses. They were waiting, all of them, at the top of the road, and by the time Lila looked back at the alley, the road was empty. The shadow was gone.

Lila slumped back in the rickety old chair and folded her arms. Nearby a woman climbed into the lap of her companion, and three tables down a fight broke out, Sanct cards spilling onto the floor as a table overturned between the brawling men. The tavern was all stale liquor and jostling bodies and cluttered noise.

"Not the most savory lot," observed Kell, sipping his drink.

"Not the worst, either," said the captain, setting down a round of drinks and a heaping tray of food.

"Do you really plan to eat all that?" asked Lila.

"Not by myself, I don't," he said, nudging a bowl of stew her way. Her stomach growled and she took up the spoon, but focused her gaze on Holland.

He was sitting in the back of the booth, and Lila on the outside edge, as far from him as possible. She couldn't shake the feeling he was watching her beneath that brimmed cap, even though every time she checked, his attention was leveled on the tavern behind her head. His fingers traced absent patterns in a pool of spilled ale, but his green eye twitched in concentration. It took her several long seconds to realize he was counting the bodies in the room.

"Nineteen," she said coolly, and Alucard and Kell both looked at her as if she'd spoken out of turn, but Holland simply answered, "Twenty," and despite herself, Lila swiveled in her seat. She did a swift count. He was right. She'd missed one of the men behind the bar. Dammit.

"If you have to use your eyes," he added, "you're doing it wrong."

"So," said Kell, frowning at Holland before turning toward Alucard. "What do you know about this floating market?"

Alucard took a swig of his ale. "Well, it's been around about as long as its owner, Maris, which is to say a long damn time. There's a running line that the same way magic never dies, it never really disappears, either. It just ends up in the *Ferase Stras*. It's a bit of a legend among the seaborne—if there's something you want, the Going Waters has it. For a price."

"And what did you buy," asked Lila, "the last time you were there?"

Alucard hesitated, lowering the glass. It always amazed her, the things he chose to guard.

"Isn't it obvious?" said Kell. "He bought his sight."

Alucard's eyes narrowed. Lila's widened. "Is that true?"

"No," said her captain. "For your information, Master Kell, I've always had this gift."

"Then what?" pressed Lila.

"I bought my father's death."

The table went still, a pocket of silence in the noisy room. Kell's mouth hung open. Alucard's clenched shut. Lila stared.

"That's not possible," murmured Kell.

"These are open waters," said Alucard, pushing to his feet. "Anything is possible. And on that note . . . I've got an errand to run. I'll meet you back at the ship."

Lila frowned. There were a hundred shades between a truth and lie, and she knew them all. She could tell when someone was being dishonest, and when they were only saying one word for every three.

"*Alucard,*" she pressed. "What are you—"

He turned, hands in his pockets. "Oh, I forgot to mention—you'll each need a token to enter the market. Something valuable."

Kell set his cup down with a crack. "You could have told us this before we left London."

"I could have," said Alucard. "It must have slipped my mind. But don't worry, I'm sure you'll think of *something*. Perhaps Maris will settle for your coat."

Kell's knuckles were white on the handle of his cup as the captain strode away. By the time the door swung shut, Lila was already on her feet.

"Where are *you* going?" snapped Kell.

"Where do you think?" She didn't know how to explain—they had a deal, she and Alucard, even if they would never say it. They watched each other's back. "He shouldn't go alone."

"Leave him," muttered Kell.

"He has a way of getting lost," she said, buttoning her coat. "I'm—"

"I said *stay*—"

It was the wrong thing to say.

Lila bristled. "Funny thing, Kell," she said coldly. "That sounded like an order." And before he could say anything else, Lila turned up her collar against the wind and marched out.

Within minutes, Lila lost him.

She didn't want to admit it—she'd always prided herself on being a clever tail, but the streets of Rosenal were narrow and winding, full of hidden breaks and turns that made it too easy to lose sight—and track—of whoever you were trying to follow. It made sense, she supposed, in a town that catered mostly to pirates and thieves and the sort who didn't like to be tracked.

Somewhere in that maze, Alucard had simply disappeared. Lila had given up any attempts at stealth after that, let her steps fall loud, even called his name, but it was no use; she couldn't find him.

The sun was setting fast over the port, the last light quickly giving way to shadow. In the twilight, the edges between light and dark began to blur, and everything was rendered in flattened layers of grey. Dusk was the only time Lila truly felt the absence of her second eye.

If it had been a little darker, she would have hauled herself up onto the nearest roof and scanned the town that way, but there was just enough daylight to turn the act into display.

She stopped at the intersection of four alleys, certain she'd already come this way, and was about to give up—to turn back toward the tavern and her waiting drink—when she heard the voice.

That *same* voice, its melody carrying on the breeze.

How do you know when the Sarows is coming . . .

A flick of her wrist, and a knife dropped into her palm, her free hand already reaching for the one beneath her coat.

Footsteps sounded, and she turned, bracing for the attack.

But the alley was empty.

Lila started to straighten just as a weight hit the ground behind her—boots on stone—and she spun, jumping back as a stranger's blade sang through the air, narrowly missing her stomach.

Her attacker smiled that rotting grin, but her eyes went to the tattoo of the dagger across his throat.

"Delilah Bard," he growled. "Remember me?"

She twirled her blades. "Vaguely," she lied.

In truth, she did. Not his name, that she'd never caught, but she knew the tattoo worn by the cutthroats of the *Copper Thief.* They had sailed under Baliz Kasnov, a ruthless pirate she'd murdered—somewhat carelessly—weeks before, as part of a bet with the crew of the *Night*

Spire. They'd scoffed at the idea that she could take an entire ship herself.

She'd proven them wrong, won the bet, even spared most of the Thieves.

Now, as two more men dropped from the rooftops behind him, and a third emerged from the lengthening shadows, she decided that act of mercy had been a mistake.

"Four on one hardly seems fair," she said, putting her back to the wall as two more men slunk toward her, tattoos like dark and jagged wounds beneath their chins.

That made six.

She'd counted them once before, but then she'd been counting down instead of up.

"Tell you what," said the first attacker. "If you beg, we'll make it quick."

Lila's blood sang the way it always did before a fight, clear and bright and hungry. "And why," she said, "would I want to rush your deaths?"

"Cocky bitch," growled the second. "I'm gonna fu—"

Her knife hissed through the air and embedded itself in his throat. Blood spilled down his front as he clawed at his neck and toppled forward, and she made it under the next man's guard before the body hit the ground, driving her serrated blade up through his chin before the first blow caught her, a fist to the jaw.

She went down hard, spitting blood into the street.

Heat coursed through her limbs as a hand grabbed her by the hair and hauled her to her feet, a knife under her chin.

"Any last words?" asked the man with the rotting teeth.

Lila held up her hands, as if in surrender, before flashing a vicious smile.

"*Tyger, Tyger*," she said, and the fire roared to life.

VI

Kell and Holland sat across from each other, swathed in a silence that only thickened as Kell tried to drown his annoyance in his drink. Of all the reasons for Lila to leave, of all the people for her to go with, it had to be Emery.

Across the room a group of men were deep in their cups and singing a sea shanty of some kind.

" . . . *Sarows is coming, is coming, is coming aboard* . . . "

Kell finished his glass, and reached for hers.

Holland was drawing his fingers through a spill on the table, the glass in front of him untouched. Now that they were back on solid ground, the color was returning to his face, but even dressed down in winter greys with a cap pulled over his brow, there was something about Holland that drew the eye. The way he held himself, perhaps, mixed with the faintest scent of foreign magic. Ash and steel and ice.

"Say something," Kell muttered into his drink.

Holland's attention flicked toward him, then slid pointedly away. "This Inheritor . . ."

"What about it?"

"I should be the one to use it."

"Perhaps." Kell's answer was simple, blunt. "But I don't trust you." Holland's expression hardened. "And I'm certainly not letting Lila try her hand. She doesn't know how to *use* her power, let alone how to survive getting rid of it."

"That leaves you."

Kell looked down into the last of his ale. "That leaves me."

If the Inheritor worked as Tieren suggested, the device absorbed a person's magic. But Kell's magic was all that bound Rhy's life to his. He'd learned that from the collar, the horrible severing of power from body, the stutter of Rhy's failing heart. Would it be like that? Would it hurt that much? Or would it be easy? His brother had known what he would do, had given his assent. He'd seen it in Rhy's eyes when they parted. Heard it in his voice. Rhy had made his peace long before he said good-bye.

"Stop being selfish."

Kell's head snapped up. "What?"

"Osaron is *mine*," said Holland, finally taking up his drink. "I don't give a damn about your self-sacrificing notions, your need to be the hero. When the time comes for one of us to destroy that monster, it is going to be *me*. And if you try to stop me, Kell, I'll remind you the hard way which of us is the stronger *Antari*. Do you understand?"

Holland met Kell's eyes over the glass, and beyond the words and the bravado, he saw something else in the man's gaze.

Mercy.

Kell's chest ached with relief as he said, "Thank you."

"For what?" said Holland coldly. "I'm not doing this for *you*."

In the end, Vortalis had named himself the Winter King.

"Why not summer," Holland asked, "or spring?"

Vortalis snorted. "Do you feel warmth on the air, Holland? Do you see the river running blue? We are not in the spring of this world, and certainly not in the summer. Those are the seasons for your someday king. This is winter, and we must survive it."

They were standing side by side on the castle balcony while the banners—the open hand turned out on its dark field—snapped in the wind. The gates stood open, the grounds filling edge to edge as people gathered to see the new king, and waited for the castle doors to open so they could make their cases and their claims. The air buzzed with excitement. Fresh blood on the throne meant new chances for the streets. The hope that *this* ruler would succeed where so many had failed before him, that he would be the one to restore what was lost—what began to die when the doors first closed—and breathe life back into the embers.

Vortalis wore a single ring of burnished steel in his hair to match the circle on his banner. Beyond that, he looked like the same man who'd come to Holland months ago, deep in the Silver Wood.

"The outfit suits you," said the Winter King, gesturing to Holland's half cloak, the silver pin bearing Vortalis's seal.

Holland took a step back from the balcony's edge. "Last time I checked, *you* are king. So why am *I* on display?"

"Because, Holland, ruling is a balance between hope and fear. I may have a *way* with people, but you have a way of *frightening* them. I draw them like flies, but you keep that at bay. Together we are a welcome and a warning, and I would have each and every one of them know that my black-eyed knight, my sharpest sword, stands firmly beside me." He shot Holland a sidelong glance. "I'm quite aware of our city's penchant for regicide, including the bloody pattern we continued in order to stand here today, but, selfish as it seems, I'm not keen to go out as Gorst did."

"Gorst didn't have *me*," said Holland, and the king broke into a smile.

"Thank the gods for that."

"Am I supposed to call you king now?" asked Holland.

Vortalis blew out a breath. "You are supposed to call me friend."

"As you wish . . ." A smile stole across Holland's lips at the memory of their meeting in the Silver Wood. "Vor."

The king smiled at that, a broad, bright gesture so at odds with the city around them. "And to think, Holland, all it took was a crown and—"

"Köt Vortalis," cut in a guard behind them.

Vor's face closed, the open light replaced by the hardened planes befitting a new king. "What is it?"

"There is a boy requesting an audience."

Holland frowned. "We haven't opened the doors yet."

"I know, sir," said the guard. "He didn't come by the door. He just . . . *appeared*."

The first thing Holland noticed was the boy's red coat.

He was standing in the throne hall, craning his head toward the vaulted bones of the castle ceiling, and that coat—it was such a vivid color, not a faded red like the sun at dusk, or the fabrics worn in summer, but a vibrant crimson, the color of fresh blood.

His hair was a softer shade, like autumn leaves, muted, but not faded by any stretch, and he wore crisp black boots—true black, as dark as winter nights—with gold clasps that matched his cuffs, every inch of him sharp and bright as a glare on new steel. Even stranger than his appearance was the scent that drifted off him, something sweet, almost cloying, like crushed blossoms left to rot.

Vortalis gave a low whistle at the sight of him, and the boy turned, revealing a pair of mismatched eyes. Holland stilled. The boy's left eye was a light blue. The right was solid black. Their gazes met, and a strange vibration lanced through Holland's head. The stranger couldn't be more than twelve or thirteen, with the unmarked skin of a royal and the imperious posture to match, but he was undeniably *Antari*.

The boy stepped forward and started speaking briskly, in a foreign tongue, the accent smooth and lilting. Vortalis bore a translation rune at the base of his throat, the product of times abroad, but Holland bore nothing save an ear for tone, and at the blankness in his gaze the boy stopped and started again, this time in Holland's native tongue.

"Apologies," he said. "My Mahktahn is not perfect. I learned it from a book. My name is Kell, and I come bearing a message from my king."

His hand went into his coat, and across the room the guards surged forward, Holland already shifting in front of Vor, when the boy drew out, of all things, a *letter*. That same sweet scent drifted off the envelope.

Vortalis looked down at the paper and said, "I am the only king here."

"Of course," said the boy *Antari*. "*My* king is in another London."

The room went still. Everyone knew, of course, about the other Londons, and the worlds that went with them. There was the one far away, a place where magic held no sway. There was the broken one, where magic had devoured everything. And then there was the cruel one, the place that had sealed its doors, forcing Holland's world to face the dark alone.

Holland had never been to this other place—he knew the spell to go there, had found the words buried in his mind like treasure in the months after he'd turned Alox to stone—but travel needed a token the way a lock needed a key, and he'd never had anything with which to cast the spell, to buy his way through.

And yet, Holland had always assumed that other world was like *his*. After all, both cities had been powerful. Both had been vibrant. Both had been cut off when the doors sealed. But as Holland took in this *Kell*, with his bright attire, his healthy glow, he saw the hall as the boy must—dingy, coated with the film of frost-like neglect, the mark of years fighting for every drop of magic, and felt a surge of anger. Was *this* how the other London lived?

"You are a long way from home," said Vor coolly.

"A long way," said the boy, "and a single step." His gaze kept flicking back toward Holland, as if fascinated by the sight of another *Antari*. So they were rare in his world, too.

"What does your king want?" asked Vor, declining to take the letter.

"King Maresh wishes to restore communication between your world and mine."

"Does he wish to open the doors?"

The boy hesitated. "No," he said carefully. "The doors cannot be opened. But this could be the first step in rebuilding the relationships—"

"I don't give a damn about relationships," snapped the Winter

King. "I am trying to rebuild a *city*. Can this *Maresh* help me with that?"

"I do not know," said Kell. "I am only the messenger. If you write it down—"

"Hang the message." Vortalis turned away. "You found your way in," he said. "Find it back out."

Kell lifted his chin. "Is that your final answer?" he asked. "Perhaps I should return in a few weeks, when the *next* king takes the throne."

"Careful, boy," warned Holland.

Kell turned his attention—and those unnerving eyes, so strange and so familiar—toward him. He produced a coin, small and red, with a gold star at the center. A token. A key. "Here," he said. "In case your king changes his mind."

Holland said nothing, but flexed his hand, and the coin whipped out of the boy's grip and into his own, his fingers closing silently over the metal.

"It's *As Travars*," added Kell. "In case you didn't know."

"Holland," said Vortalis from the door.

Holland was still holding Kell's gaze. "Coming, my *king*," he said pointedly, breaking away.

"Wait," called the boy, and Holland could tell by his tone that the words were meant not for Vor, but for him. The *Antari* jogged toward him, steps ringing like bells from his gold clasps.

"What?" demanded Holland.

"It's nice," said Kell, "to meet someone like me."

Holland frowned. "I am not like you," he said, and walked away.

VII

For a while, Lila held her own.

Flame and steel against blind strength, a thief's cunning against a pirate's might.

She might have even been winning.

And then, quite suddenly, she wasn't.

Six men became four, but four was still a good deal more than one.

A knife slid along her skin.

A hand wrapped around her throat.

Her back slammed against the wall.

No, not a wall, she realized, a *door*. She had hit it hard enough to crack the wood, bolts and pins jangling in their grooves. An idea. She threw up her hands, and the nails shuddered free. Some struck only air or stone, but others found flesh, and two of the Copper Thieves staggered back, clutching their arms, stomachs, heads.

Without its pins, the door gave way behind her, and Lila tumbled backward, rolling into a crouch inside a shabby hall and heaving the door back up before pressing her blood-slicked fingers to the wood.

"*As Steno,*" she said, thinking that was the word Kell had taught her for *seal,* but she was wrong. The whole door *shattered* like a pane of glass, wooden splinters raining down, and before she could summon them back up, she was hauled into the street. Something hit her in the stomach—a fist, a knee, a boot—and the air left her lungs in a violent breath.

She summoned the wind—it tore through the alley and whipped around her, forcing the men back as she took a running step, pushed off the wall, and leaped for the edge of the roof.

She almost made it, but one of them caught her boot and jerked her back. She fell, hitting the street with brutal force. Something cracked inside her chest.

And then they fell on her.

Holland was proving horrible company.

Kell had tried to keep the conversation alive, but it was like stoking coals after a bucket of water had been poured on them, nothing but fragile wisps of smoke. He'd finally given up, resigned himself to the uncomfortable quiet, when the other *Antari* met his gaze across the table.

"At the market tomorrow," he said. "What will you offer?"

Kell raised a brow. His own mind had just been drifting over the question.

"I was thinking," he said, "of offering you."

It was said in jest, but Holland only stared at him, and Kell sighed, relenting. He'd never been very good at sarcasm.

"It depends," he answered honestly, "on whether Maris cares for cost or worth." He patted down his pockets, and came up with a handful of coins, Lila's kerchief, his royal pin. The look on Holland's face mirrored the worry in Kell's gut—none of these things were good enough.

"You *could* offer the coat," said Holland.

But the thought made Kell's chest hurt. It was *his,* one of the only things in his life not bestowed by the crown, or bartered for, not given because of his position, but won. Won in a simple game of cards.

He put the trinkets away, and instead dug the cord out from under his shirt. On the end hung the three coins, one for each world. He unknotted the cord and slid the last coin out onto his palm.

His Grey London token.

George III's profile was on the front, his face rubbed away from use.

Kell had given the king a new *lin* with every visit, but he still had the same shilling George had given him on his very first trip. Before the age and the madness wore him away, before his son buried him in Windsor.

It cost almost nothing, but it was worth a great deal to him.

"I hate to interrupt whatever reverie you're having," said Holland, nodding at the window, "but your friend has returned."

Kell turned in his seat, expecting Lila, but instead he found Alucard strolling past. He had a vial in his hand, and was holding it up to the light of a lantern. The contents glittered faintly like white sand, or finely broken glass.

The captain looked their way and flashed an impatient summons that a little too closely resembled a rude gesture.

Kell sighed, shoving to his feet.

The two *Antari* left the tavern, Alucard a block ahead, his stride brisk as he headed for the docks. Kell frowned, scanning the streets.

"Where's Lila?" called Kell.

Alucard turned, brows raised. "Bard? I left her with you."

Dread coiled through him. "And she followed *you* out."

Alucard started shaking his head, but Kell was already doubling back, heading up the rise, Holland and the captain close on his heels.

"Split up," said Alucard as they reached the maze of streets. He took off down the first one, but when Holland started down another, Kell caught his sleeve.

"Wait." His mind spun, torn between duty and panic, reason and fear.

Letting the White London *Antari* out of his chains was one thing.

Letting him out of Kell's sight was another.

Holland looked down at the place where the younger *Antari* gripped him. "Do you want to find her or not?"

Rhy's voice echoed in Kell's head, those warnings about the world beyond the city, the value of a black-eyed prince. An *Antari*. He'd told Kell what the Veskans thought of him, and the Faroans, but he hadn't said enough about their own people, and Kell, fool that he was, hadn't thought about the risk of ransom. Or worse, knowing Lila.

Kell snarled, but let go. "Don't make me regret this," he said, taking off at a run.

VIII

Lila sagged against the wall, gasping for breath. She was out of knives, and blood was running into her eye from a blow to the temple, and it hurt to breathe, but she was still on her feet.

It would take more than that, she thought, shoving off the wall and stepping over the bodies of the six men now lying dead in the street.

There was a hollow feeling in her veins, like she'd used up everything she had. The ground swayed beneath her and she braced herself against the alley wall, leaving a smear of red as she went. One foot in front of the other, every breath a jagged tear, her pulse heavy in her ears, and then something that wasn't her pulse.

Footsteps.

Someone was coming.

Lila dragged her head up, wracking her tired mind for a spell as the steps echoed against the alley walls.

She heard a voice calling her name, somewhere far behind her, and turned just in time to watch someone drive a knife between her ribs.

"This is for Kasnov," snarled the seventh Thief, forcing the weapon in to the hilt. It tore through her chest and out her back and for a moment—only a moment—she felt nothing but the warmth of the blood. But then her body caught up, and the pain swallowed everything.

Not the brisk bright pain of grazed skin but something deep. Severing.

The knife came free, and her legs folded beneath her.

She tried to breathe, choked as blood rose in her throat. Soaked her shirt.

Get up, she thought as her body slumped to the ground.

This isn't how I die, she thought, *this isn't—*

She retched blood into the street.

Something was wrong.

It hurt.

No.

Kell.

Get up.

She tried to rise, slipped in something slick and warm.

No.

Not like this.

She closed her eyes, tried desperately to summon magic.

There wasn't any left.

All she had was Kell's face. And Alucard's. Barron's watch. A ship. The open sea. A chance at freedom.

I'm not done.

Her vision slipped.

Not like this.

Her chest rattled.

Get up.

She was on her back now, the Thief circling like a vulture. Above him, the sky was turning colors like a bruise.

Like the sea before a . . . what?

He was getting closer, crouching down, burying a knee in her wounded chest and she couldn't breathe and this wasn't how it happened, and—

A blur of motion, quick as a knife, at the edge of her sight, and the man was gone. The beginnings of a shout cut off, the distant sound of a weight hitting something solid, but Lila couldn't raise her head to see, couldn't . . .

The world narrowed, the light slipping from the sky, then blotted out altogether by the shadow kneeling over her, pressing a hand to her ribs.

"Hold on," said a low voice as the world darkened. Then: "Over here! Now!"

Another voice.

"Stay with me."

She was so cold.

"Stay . . ."

It was the last thing she heard.

IX

Holland knelt over Lila's body.

She was deathly pale, but he had been quick enough; the spell had taken hold in time. Kell was at Lila's other side, distraught, face pale under crimson curls, checking her wounds as if he doubted Holland's work.

If he'd gotten there first, he could have healed her himself.

Holland hadn't thought it wise to wait.

And now there were more pressing problems.

He'd caught the slow-moving shadows flitting over the wall at the end of the alley. He rose to his feet.

"Stay with me," Kell was murmuring to Lila's bloody form, as if that would do any good. "Stay with—"

"How many blades do you have?" Holland cut in.

Kell's eyes never left Lila, but his fingers went to the sheath on his arm. "One."

Holland rolled his eyes. "Brilliant," he said, pressing his palms together. The gash he'd made in his hand wept a fresh line of red.

"*As Narahi,*" he murmured.

Quicken.

Magic flared at his command, and he moved with a speed he rarely showed and had certainly never seen fit to show *Kell*. It was a hard piece of magic under any circumstances, and a grueling spell when done to one's self, but it was worth it as the world around him *slowed*.

He became a blur, pale skin and grey cloak knifing through the dark. By the time the first man crouching on the roof above had drawn his knife, Holland was behind him. The man looked wide eyed at the place where his target had been as Holland lifted his hands and, with an elegant motion, snapped the man's neck.

He let the limp body fall to the alley stones and followed quickly after, putting his back to Kell—who'd finally caught the scent of danger—as three more shadows, glinting with weapons, dropped from the sky.

And just like that, their fight began.

It didn't last long.

Soon three more bodies littered the ground, and the winter air around the two *Antari* surged with exhaustion and triumph. Blood ran from Kell's lip, and Holland's knuckles were raw, and they'd both lost their hats, but otherwise they were intact.

It was strange, fighting beside Kell instead of against him, the resonance of their styles, so different but somehow in sync—unnerving.

"You've gotten better," he observed.

"I had to," said Kell, wiping the blood from his knife before he sheathed it. Holland had the strange urge to say more, but Kell was already moving to Lila's side again as Alucard appeared at the mouth of the alley, a sword in one hand and a curl of ice in the other, clearly ready to join the fight.

"You're late," said Holland.

"Did I miss all the fun?" asked the magician, but when he saw Lila in Kell's arms, her limp body covered in blood, every trace of humor left his face. *"No."*

"She'll live," said Holland.

"What happened? Saints, Bard. Can you hear me?" said Alucard as Kell took up his useless chant again, as if it were a spell, a prayer.

Stay with me.

Holland leaned against the alley wall, suddenly tired.

Stay with me.

He closed his eyes, memories rising like bile in his throat.

Stay with me.

NINE

TROUBLE

I

Tieren Serense had never been able to see the future.

He could only see himself.

That was the thing so many didn't understand about scrying. A man could not gaze into the stream of life, the heart of magic, and read it as if it were a book. The world spoke its own language, as indecipherable as the chirping of a bird, the rustling of leaves. A tongue meant not even for priests.

It is an arrogant man that thinks himself a god.

And an arrogant god, thought Tieren, looking to the window, that thinks himself a man.

So when he poured the water into the basin, when he took up the vial of ink and tipped three drops into the water, when he stared into the cloud that bloomed beneath the surface, he was not trying to see the future. He wasn't looking out at all, but in.

A scrying dish, after all, was a mirror for one's mind, a way to look in at one's self, to pose questions that only the self could answer.

Tonight Tieren's questions revolved around Maxim Maresh. Around the spell his king was weaving, and how far the *Aven Essen* should let him go.

Tieren Serense had served Nokil Maresh when he was king, had watched his only son, Maxim, grow, had stood beside him when he married Emira, and been there to usher Rhy into the world, and Kell into the palace. He had spent his life serving this family.

Now, he did not know how to save it.

The ink spread through the basin, turning the water grey, and in the shudder of its surface, he felt the queen before he saw her. A blush of cold in the room behind him.

"I hope you won't mind, Your Majesty," he said softly. "I borrowed one of your bowls."

She was standing there, arms folded across her front as if chilled, or guarding something fragile behind her ribs.

Emira, who never confided in him, never sought out his waiting ear, no matter how many times he offered. Instead, he'd learned of her through Rhy, through Maxim, through Kell. He'd learned of her through watching her watch the world with those wide, dark eyes that never blinked for fear of missing something.

Now those wide, dark eyes went to the shallow bowl between his hands. "What did you see?"

"I see what all reflections show," he answered wearily. "Myself."

Emira bit her lip, a gesture he'd seen Rhy make a hundred times. Her fingers tightened around her ribs. "What is Maxim doing?"

"What he believes is right."

"Aren't we all?" she whispered.

Thin tears slid down her cheeks, and she dashed them away with the back of her hand. It was only the second time he'd ever seen Emira cry.

The first had been more than twenty years ago, when she was new to the palace.

He'd found her in the courtyard, her back up against a winter tree, arms wrapped around herself as if she were cold, even though two rows away the summer was in bloom. She stood perfectly still, save for the silent shudder of her chest, but he could see the storm behind her eyes, the strain in her jaw, and he remembered thinking, then, that she looked old for one so young. Not aged, but worn, weary from the weight of her own mind. Fears, after all, were heavy things. And whether or not Emira voiced them, Tieren could feel them on the air, thick as rain right before it falls.

She wouldn't tell him what was wrong, but a week later Tieren heard the news, watched Maxim's face glow with pride while Emira stood at his side, steeling herself against the declaration as if it were a sentence.

She was pregnant.

Emira cleared her throat, eyes still trained on the clouded water. "May I ask you something, Master Tieren?"

"Of course, Your Highness."

Her gaze shifted toward him, two dark pools that hid their depths. "What do you fear most?"

The question took him by surprise, but the answer rose to meet it. "Emptiness," he said. "And you, my queen?"

Her lips quirked into a sad smile. "Everything," she said. "Or so it feels."

"I do not believe that," said Tieren gently.

She thought. "Loss, then."

Tieren curled a finger around his beard. "Love and loss," he said, "are like a ship and the sea. They rise together. The more we love, the more we have to lose. But the only way to avoid loss is to avoid love. And what a sad world that would be."

II

Lila opened her eyes.

At first all she saw was sky. That same bruised sunset she'd been staring at a moment before. Only the moment was gone, and the colors had bled away, leaving a heavy blanket of night. The ground was cold beneath her but dry, a coat bunched up beneath her head.

"It shouldn't take this long," a voice was saying. "Are you sure—"

"She'll be fine."

Her head spun, fingers drifting over her ribs to the place where the blade had gone in. Her shirt was sticky with blood, and she cringed reflexively, expecting pain. The *memory* of pain sang through her, but it was nothing but an echo, and when she took a testing breath, crisp air filled her lungs instead of blood.

"Fucking Copper Thieves," said a third voice. "Should have killed them months ago, and stop pacing, Kell, you're making me dizzy."

Lila closed her eyes, swallowed.

When she blinked, vision sliding in and out of focus, Kell was kneeling over her. She looked up into his two-toned eyes, and realized they weren't his eyes at all. One was black. The other emerald green.

"She's awake." Holland straightened, blood dripping from a gash along his palm.

A copper tang still filled her mouth, and she rolled over and spit onto the stones.

"Lila," said Kell, so much emotion in her name, and how could she ever have thought that cold, steady voice belonged to him? He crouched beside her, one hand beneath her back—she shivered at the sudden visceral memory of the blade scraping over bone, jutting out beneath her shoulder blade—as he helped her sit up.

"I told you she'd be fine," said Holland, folding his arms.

"She still looks pretty rough," said Alucard. "No offense, Bard."

"None taken," she said hoarsely. She looked up into their faces—Kell pale, Holland grim, Alucard tense—and knew it must have been a near thing.

Leaning on Kell, she got to her feet.

Ten Copper Thieves lay sprawled on the alley floor. Lila's hands shook as she took in the scene, and then kicked the nearest corpse as hard as she could. Again and again and again, until Kell took her by the arms and pulled her in, the breath leaving her lungs in broken gasps, even though her chest was healed.

"I miscounted," she said into his shoulder. "I thought there were six. . . ."

Kell brushed the tears from her cheek. She hadn't realized she was crying.

"You were only at sea for four months," he said. "How many enemies did you *make*?"

Lila laughed, a small, jagged hiccup of a laugh, as he pulled her closer.

They stood there like that for a long moment, while Alucard and Holland walked among the dead, freeing Lila's knives from chests and legs and throats.

"And what have we learned from this, Bard?" asked the captain, wiping a blade on a corpse's chest.

Lila looked down at the bodies of the men she'd once spared aboard the *Copper Thief*.

"Dead men can't hold grudges."

They made their way back to the ship in silence, Kell's arm around her waist, though she no longer needed him for support. Holland walked in front with Alucard, and Lila kept her eyes on the back of his head.

He hadn't had to do it.

He could have let her bleed out in the street.

He could have stood and watched her die.

That's what she would have done.

She told herself that's what she would have done.

It isn't enough, she thought. *It doesn't make up for Barron, for Kell, for me. I haven't forgotten.*

"*Tac,*" said Jasta as they made their way up the dock. "What happened to *you?*"

"Rosenal," said Lila blandly.

"Tell me we're ready to sail," said Kell.

Holland said nothing, but made his way straight toward the hold. Lila watched him go.

I still don't trust you, she thought.

As if he could feel the weight of her gaze, Holland glanced back over his shoulder.

You do not know me, his gaze seemed to say.

You do not know me at all.

III

"I've been thinking about the boy," said Vor.

They were sitting at a low table in the king's room, he and Holland, playing a round of Ost. It was a game of strategy and risk, and it was Vortalis's favorite way to unwind, but no one would play him anymore—the guards were tired of losing the game, and their money—so Holland always ended up across the board.

"Which boy?" he asked, rolling the chips in his palm.

"The messenger."

It had been two years since that visit, two long years spent trying to rebuild a broken city, to carve a shelter in the storm. Trying—and failing. Holland kept his voice even. "What of him?"

"Do you still have the coin?" asked Vor, even though they both knew he did. It sat in his pocket always, the metal worn from use. They did not speak of Holland's absences, of the times he disappeared, only to return smelling too sweetly of flowers instead of ash and stone. Holland never stayed, of course. And he was never gone long. He hated those visits, hated seeing what his world could have been, and yet he couldn't keep himself from going, from seeing, from knowing what was on the other side of the door. He couldn't look away.

"Why?" he asked now.

"I think it's time to send a letter."

"Why now?"

"Don't play the fool," said Vor, letting his chips fall to the table. "It doesn't suit you. We both know the stores are thinning and the days grow shorter. I make laws, and people break them, I make order and they turn it into chaos." He ran a hand through his hair, fingers snagging on the ring of steel. His usual poise faltered. With a snarl he flung the crown across the room. "No matter what I do, the hope is rotting, and I can hear the whispers starting in the streets. New blood, they call. As if that will fix what is broken, as if shedding enough will bring the magic in this world to heel."

"And you would fix this with a *letter*?" demanded Holland.

"I would fix it any way I can," countered Vor. "Perhaps their world was once like ours, Holland. Perhaps they know a way to *help*."

"They're the ones who sealed us off, who live in splendor while we rot, and you would go begging—"

"I would do anything if I thought it would truly help my world," snapped Vortalis, "and so would you. That is why you're here beside me. Not because you are my sword, not because you are my shield, not because you are my friend. You are here with me because we will *both* do whatever we can to keep our world alive."

Holland looked hard at the king then, hard, took in the grey threading his dark hair, the permanent furrow between his brows. He was still charming, still magnetic, still smiled when something delighted him, but the act now drew deep lines in his skin, and Holland knew the spells across Vor's hands weren't enough to bind the magic anymore.

Holland set a chip on the board, as though they were still playing. "I thought I was here to keep your head on your shoulders."

Vortalis managed a strained laugh, a farce of humor. "That, too," he said, and then, sobering: "Listen to me, Holland. Of all the ways to die, only a fool chooses pride."

A servant entered with a loaf of bread, a bottle of *kaash,* a pile of thin cigars. Despite the crown, the castle, Vor was still a man of habit.

He took up a tightly rolled paper, and Holland snapped his fingers, offering the flame.

Vor sat back and examined the burning end of the taper. "Why didn't you want to be king?"

"I suppose I'm not arrogant enough."

Vor chuckled. "Maybe you're a wiser man than I am." He took a long drag. "I'm beginning to think that thrones make tyrants of us all."

He blew out the smoke, and coughed.

Holland frowned. The king smoked ten times a day, and never seemed to suffer for it.

"Are you well?"

Vor was already waving the question away, but as he leaned forward to pour himself a drink, he put too much weight on the table's edge and it upset, the Ost chips raining down onto the stone floor as he fell.

"Vortalis!"

The king was still coughing, a deep, wracking sound, clawing at his chest with both hands as Holland folded over him. On the floor nearby, the cigar still burned. Vor tried to speak, but managed only blood.

"*Kajt,*" swore Holland as he clutched a shard of glass until it bit into his hand, blood welling as he tore open Vor's tunic and pressed his palm against the king's chest, and commanded him to *heal.*

But the toxin had been too fast, the king's heart too slow. It wasn't working.

"Hold on, Vor. . . ." Holland splayed both hands against his friend's heaving chest, and he could feel the poison in his blood, because it wasn't poison after all but a hundred tiny slivers of spelled metal, tearing the king apart from within. No matter how fast Holland tried to heal the damage, the shards made more.

"Stay with me," the *Antari* ordered, with all the force of a spell, while he drew the metal shards free, his king's skin soaking first with sweat and then blood as the metal slivers pierced vein and muscle and flesh before rising in a dark red mist into the air above Vor's chest.

"*As Tanas,*" said Holland, closing his fist, and the shards drew together into a cloud of steel before fusing back into a solid piece, cursework scrawled along its surface.

But it was too late.

He was too late.

Beneath the spelled steel, beneath Holland's hand, the king had gone still. Blood matted his front, flecked his beard, shone in his open, empty eyes.

Ros Vortalis was dead.

Holland staggered to his feet, the cursed steel falling from his fingers, landing among the abandoned Ost chips. It didn't roll, but splashed softly in the pool of blood. Blood that already slicked Holland's hands, misted his skin.

"Guards," he said once, softly, and then, raising his voice in a way he never did, "*Guards!*"

The room was too still, the castle too quiet.

Holland called again, but no one came. Part of him knew they weren't coming, but shock was singing him, tangled up with grief, making him clumsy, slow.

He forced himself up, turned from Vor's body, drawing the blade his king—his friend—had given him the day they stood on the balcony, the day Vor became the Winter King, the day Holland became his knight. Holland left his king and stormed through the doors, into an eerily silent castle.

He called out to the guards again, but of course they were already dead.

Bodies slumped forward on tables and against walls, halls empty and the world reduced to the *drip drip drip* of blood and wine on pale stone floors. It must have happened in minutes. Seconds. The time it took to light a cigarette, to draw a breath, exhale a plume of cursed smoke.

Holland didn't see the spell written on the floor.

Didn't feel the room slow around him until he'd crossed the line of magic, his body dragging suddenly as if through water instead of air.

Somewhere, echoing off the castle walls, someone laughed.

It was a laugh so unlike Talya's, so unlike Vor's. No sweetness, no richness, no warmth. A laugh as cold and sharp as glass.

"Look, Athos," said the voice. "I've caught us a prize."

Holland tried to turn, dragging his body toward the sound, but he was too slow, and the knife came from behind, a barbed blade that sank deep into his thigh. Pain lit his mind like light as he staggered to one knee.

A woman danced at the edges of his sight. White skin. White hair. Eyes like ice.

"Hello, pretty thing," she said, twisting the knife until Holland actually screamed. A sound that rang out through the too-quiet castle, only to be cut off by a flash of silver, a slash of pain, a whip closing around his throat, stealing air, stealing everything. A swift tug, and Holland was forced forward, onto his hands and knees, his throat on fire. He couldn't breathe, couldn't speak, couldn't spell the blood now dripping to the floor beneath him.

"Ah," said a second voice. "The infamous Holland." A pale shape strode forward, winding the handle of the whip around his fingers. "I was hoping you would survive."

The figure stopped at the edge of the spell, and sank onto his haunches in front of Holland's buckled form. Up close, his skin and hair were the same white as the woman's, his eyes the same frigid blue.

"Now," said the man with a slow smile. "What to do with *you*?"

Alox was dead.

Talya was dead.

Vortalis was dead.

But Holland wasn't.

He was strapped into a metal frame, his skin fever-hot and his limbs splayed like a moth mid-flight. Blood dripped to the stone floor, a dark red pool beneath his feet.

He could have cast a hundred spells, with all that blood, but his jaw was strapped shut. He'd woken with the vice around his head, teeth forced together so hard the only thing he could manage was a guttural sound, a groan, a sob of pain.

Athos Dane swam in his vision, those cold blue eyes and that curled mouth, a smile lurking beneath the surface like a fish under thin ice.

"I want to hear your voice, Holland," said the man, sliding the knife under his skin. "Sing to me." The blade sank deeper, probing for nerves, biting into tendons, slipping between bones.

Holland shuddered against the pain, but didn't scream. He never did. It was small consolation in the end, some quicksilver hope that if he didn't break, Athos would give up and simply kill him.

He didn't *want* to die. Not in the beginning. For the first few hours—days—he'd fought back, until the metal frame had cut into his skin, until the pool of blood was large enough to see himself in, until the pain became a blanket, and his mind blurred, deprived of food, of sleep.

"Pity," mused Athos when Holland made no sound. He turned to a table that held, among so many gruesome things, a bowl of ink, and dipped his bloodstained knife, coating the crimson steel black.

Holland's stomach turned at the sight of it. Ink and blood, these were the stuff of *curses*. Athos returned to him and splayed a hand over Holland's ribs, clearly savoring the hitching breath, the stuttering heart, the smallest tells of terror.

"You think you know," he said quietly, "what I have planned for you." He lifted the knife, brought the tip to the pale, unbroken skin over Holland's heart, and smiled. "You have no idea."

When it was done, Athos Dane took a step back to admire his work.

Holland slumped in the metal frame, blood and ink spilling down his ruined chest. His head buzzed with magic, even though some vital part of him had been stripped away.

No, not stripped away. Buried.

"Are you finished?"

The voice belonged to the other Dane. Holland dragged his head up.

Astrid was standing in the doorway behind her brother, arms folded lazily across her front.

Athos, with his sated smile, flicked his blade as if it were a brush. "You cannot rush an artist."

She clicked her tongue, that icy gaze raking over Holland's mutilated chest as she drew near, boots clicking sharply over stone.

"Tell me, brother," she said, playing her cool fingers up Holland's arm. "Do you think it wise to keep this pet?" She traced a nail along his shoulder. "He might bite."

"What good is a beast that *cannot*?"

Athos slid his knife along Holland's cheek, slicing the leather strap of the vice around his mouth. Pain sang through his jaw as it slackened, teeth aching. Air rushed into his lungs, but when he tried to speak, to summon the spells he'd kept ready on his tongue, they froze in his throat so suddenly he choked on them and nearly retched.

One wrist came free of its cuff, and then another, and Holland staggered forward, his screaming limbs nearly buckling beneath the sudden weight while Athos and Astrid stood there, simply *watching*.

He wanted to kill them both.

Wanted to, and could not.

Athos had carved the lines of the curse one by one, sunk the rules of the spell into his skin with steel and ink.

Holland had tried to close his mind to the magic, but it was already inside him, burning through his chest, driven like a spike through flesh and mind and soul.

The chains of the spell were stiff, articulated things. They coiled through his head, weighed heavy as iron around every limb.

Obey, they said, not to his mind, his heart—only his hands, his lips.

The command was written on his skin, threaded through his bones.

Athos cocked his head and gestured absently.

"Kneel."

When Holland made no motion to obey, a block of stone struck him in the shoulders, a sudden, vicious, invisible weight forcing him forward. He fought to keep his feet, and the binding spell crackled through his nerves, ground against his bones.

His vision went white, and something too close to a scream escaped his aching mouth before his legs finally folded, shins meeting the cold stone floor.

Astrid clapped her hands once, pleased.

"Shall we test it?"

A sound, half curse, half cry, rang through the room as a man was dragged in, hands bound behind his back. He was bloody, beaten, his face more broken than not, but Holland recognized him as one of Vor's. The man staggered, was righted. The moment he saw Holland, something shifted in him. Fell. His mouth opened.

"Traitor."

"Cut his throat," instructed Athos.

The words rippled through Holland's limbs.

"No," he said hoarsely. It was the first word he'd managed in days, and it was useless, his fingers moving even before his mind could register. Red blossomed at the man's throat and he went down, his last words drowned in blood.

Holland stared at his own hand, the knife's edge crimson.

They left the body where it fell.

And brought another in.

"No," snarled Holland at the sight of him. A boy from the kitchens, hardly fourteen, who looked at him with wide, uncertain eyes. "Help," he begged.

Then they brought another.

And another.

One by one, Athos and Astrid paraded the remains of Vor's life before Holland, instructing him again and again to cut their throats. Every time, he tried to fight the order. Every time, he failed. Every time, he had to look them in their eyes and see the hatred, the betrayal, the anguished confusion before he cut them down.

The bodies piled. Athos watched. Astrid grinned.

Holland's hand moved on its puppet string.

And his mind screamed until it finally lost its voice.

IV

Lila couldn't sleep.

The fight kept spinning through her head, dark alleys and sharp knives, her heart racing until she was sure the sound would wake Kell. Halfway through the night she shoved up from the cot, crossed the tiny cabin in two short strides, and sank against the opposite wall, one blade resting on her knee, a small but familiar comfort.

It was late, or early, that dense dark time before the first shreds of day, and cold in the cabin—she pulled her coat down from its hook and shrugged it on, shoving her free hand in her pocket for warmth. Her fingers brushed stone, silver, silver, and she thought of Alucard's words.

You'll need a token to enter. Something valuable.

She searched her meager possessions for something precious enough to buy her entrance. There was the knife she'd taken from Fletcher, with its serrated blade and knuckled hilt, and then the one she'd won from Lenos, with its hidden catch that split one blade into two. There was the bloodstained shard of white marble that had once been part of Astrid Dane's face. And last, a warm and constant weight in the bottom of her pocket, there was Barron's timepiece. Her only tether to the world she'd left. The life she'd left. Lila knew, with bone-deep certainty, that the knives wouldn't be enough. That left her key to White London, and her key to Grey. She closed her eyes, clutching the two tokens until it hurt, knowing which was useless, and which would buy her passage.

Behind her eyes, she saw Barron's face the night she returned to the

Stone's Throw, the smoke from the burning ship still rising at her back. Heard her own voice offering the stolen watch up as payment. She felt the heavy warmth of his hand as he closed her fingers over the timepiece, told her to keep it. She'd left it behind, though, the night she followed Kell, more a token of gratitude than anything, the only good-bye she could manage. But the watch had come back to her at Holland's hands, stained with Barron's blood.

It was a part of her past now.

And holding on to it wouldn't bring him back.

Lila returned the tokens to her coat and let her head fall back against the cabin wall.

On the cot, Kell shifted in his sleep.

Overhead, the muffled sound of someone walking on the deck.

The gentle slosh of the sea. The rock of the ship.

Her eyes were just drifting shut when she heard a short, pained gasp. She jerked forward, alert, but Kell was still asleep. It came again and she was on her feet, knife at the ready as she followed the sound across the narrow corridor to the cabin where they were keeping Holland.

He was on his back on the cot, not chained, not even guarded, and dreaming—badly, it seemed. His teeth were clenched, his chest rising and falling in a staccato way. His whole body shuddered, fingers digging into the thin blanket beneath him. His mouth opened and a breath hitched in his throat. The nightmare wracked him like a chill, but he never made a sound.

Lying there, trapped within his dreams, Holland looked . . . exposed.

Lila stood, watching. And then she felt herself step into the room.

The boards beneath her creaked, and Holland tensed in his sleep. Lila held her breath, hovering for an instant before she crossed the narrow space and reached out and—

Holland shot forward, his fingers vising around her wrist. Pain shot up Lila's arm. There was no electricity, no magic, only skin on skin and the grind of bones.

His eyes were feverish as they found hers in the dark.

"What do you think you're doing?" The words hissed out like wind through a crack.

Lila pulled free. "You were having a bad dream," she snapped, rubbing her wrist. "I was going to wake you up."

His eyes flicked to the knife in her other hand. She'd forgotten it was there. She forced herself to sheath it.

Now that he was awake, Holland's face was a mask of calm, his stress betrayed only by the rivulet of sweat that slid down his temple, tracing a slow line along cheek and jaw. But his eyes followed her as she retreated to the doorway.

"What?" she said, crossing her arms. "Afraid I'll kill you in your sleep?"

"No."

Lila watched him. "I haven't forgotten what you did."

At that, Holland closed his eyes. "Neither have I."

She hovered, unsure what to say, what to do, tethered by the inability to do either. She had a feeling Holland wasn't trying to sleep, wasn't trying to dismiss her, either. He was giving her a chance to attack him, testing her resolve not to do it.

It was tempting—and yet somehow it wasn't, and that angered her more than anything. Lila huffed and turned to go.

"I did save your life," he said softly.

She hesitated, turned back. "It was one time."

The slight arching of one brow, the only movement in his face. "Tell me, Delilah, how many times will it take?"

She shook her head in disgust. "The man in the Stone's Throw," she said. "The one with the watch. The one whose throat you cut, he didn't deserve to die."

"Most people don't," said Holland calmly.

"Did you ever consider sparing his life?"

"No."

"Did you even hesitate before you killed him?"

"No."

"Why not?" she snarled, the air trembling with her anger.

Holland held her gaze. "Because it was easier."

"I don't—"

"Because if I stopped I would think, and if I thought, I would remember, and if I remembered, I would—" He swallowed, the smallest rise in his throat. "No, I did not hesitate. I cut his throat, and added his death to the ones I count every day when I wake." His eyes hardened on her. "Now tell me, Delilah, how many lives have you ended? Do you know the number?"

Lila started to answer, then stopped.

The truth—the infuriating, maddening, sickening truth—was that she didn't.

Lila stormed back to her own cabin.

She wanted to sleep, wanted to fight, wanted to quell the fear and anger rising in her throat like a scream. Wanted to banish Holland's words, carve out the memory of the knife between her ribs, smother the terrible instant that reckless energy of danger turned to cold fear.

She wanted to forget.

Kell was halfway to his feet, coat in one hand, when she came in.

Wanted to feel . . .

"There you are," he said, his hair mussed from sleep. "I was just coming to look for—"

Lila caught him by the shoulders and pressed her mouth against his.

"—*you*," he finished, the word nothing but a breath between her lips.

. . . This.

Kell returned the kiss. Deepened it. That current of magic like a spark across her lips.

And then his arms were folding around her, and in that small gesture, she understood, felt it down to her bones, that draw, not the electric pulse of power but the thing beneath it, the weight she'd never understood. In a world where everything rocked and swayed and fell away, this was solid ground.

Safe.

Her heart was beating hard against her ribs, some primal part of her saying *run,* and she *was* running, just not away. She was tired of running away. So she was running into Kell.

And he caught her.

His coat fell to the floor, and then they were half stepping, half stumbling back through the tiny room. They missed the bed, but found the wall—it wasn't that far—and when Lila's back met the hull of the ship, the whole thing seemed to rock beneath them, pressing Kell's body into hers.

She gasped, less from the sudden weight than from the sense of him against her, one leg between hers.

Her hand slid beneath his shirt with all the practiced grace of a thief. But this time she *wanted* him to feel her touch, her palms gliding over his ribs and around his back, fingertips digging into his shoulder blades.

"Lila," he rasped into her ear as the ship righted, swung the other way, and they tumbled back onto the cot. She pulled his body down with hers, and he caught himself on his elbows, hovering over her. His lashes were strands of copper around his black and blue eyes. She'd never noticed before. She reached up and brushed the hair out of his face. It was soft—feathery—where the rest of him was sharp. His cheekbone scraped against her palm. His hips cut into hers. Their bodies sparked against each other, the energy electric across their skin.

"Kell," she said, the word something between a whisper and a gasp.

And then the door burst open.

Alucard stood in the doorway, soaking wet, as if he'd just been dumped in the sea, or the sea had been dumped over him. *"Stop fucking with the ship."*

Kell and Lila stared at him in stunned silence, and then burst into laughter as the door slammed shut.

They fell back against the cot, the laughter trailing off, only to rise again out of the silence full force. Lila laughed until her body ached, and even when she thought she was done, the sound came on like hiccups.

"Hush," Kell whispered in her hair, and that nearly set her off again as she rolled toward him on the narrow cot, squeezing in so she wouldn't fall off. He made room, one arm beneath his head and the other wrapped around her waist, pulling her in against him.

He smelled like roses.

She remembered thinking that, the first time they met, and even now, with the salty sea and the damp wood of the ship, she could smell it, the faint, fresh garden scent that was his magic.

"Teach me the words," she whispered.

"Hm?" he asked sleepily.

"The blood spells." She propped her head on her hand. "I want to know them."

Kell sighed in mock exhaustion. "Now?"

"Yes, now." She rolled onto her back, eyes trained on the wooden ceiling. "What happened in Rosenal—I don't plan on letting it happen again. Ever."

Kell lifted himself onto one elbow above her. He looked down at her for a long, searching moment, and then a mischievous grin flickered across his face.

"All right," he said. "I'll teach you."

His copper lashes sank low over his two-toned eyes. "There's *As Travars,* to travel between worlds."

She rolled her eyes. "I know that one."

He lowered himself a fraction, bringing his lips to her ear.

"And *As Tascen,*" he continued, breath warm. "To move within a world."

She felt a shiver of pleasure as his lips brushed her jaw. "And *As Hasari,*" he murmured. "To heal."

His mouth found hers, stealing a kiss before he said, "*As Staro.* To seal." And she would have let him linger there, but his mouth continued downward.

"*As Pyrata.*"

A breath against the base of her throat.

"To burn."

His hands sliding beneath the fabric of her shirt.

"*As Anasae.*"

A blossom of heat between her breasts.

"To dispel."

Above her navel.

"As Steno."

One hand unlacing the ties of her slacks.

"To break."

Guiding them off.

"As Orense."

His teeth skimming her hip bone.

"To open . . ."

Kell's mouth came to rest between her legs, and she arched against him, fingers tangling in his auburn curls as heat rolled through her. Sweat prickled across her skin. She blazed inside, and her breath grew ragged, one hand clenched in the sheets over her head as something like magic rose inside her, a tide that swelled and swelled until she couldn't hold it in.

"Kell," she moaned as his kiss deepened. Her whole body trembled with the power, and when she finally let go, it crashed down in a wave at once electric and sublime.

Lila collapsed back against the sheets with something between a laugh and a sigh, the whole cabin buzzing in the aftermath, the sheets singed where she'd gripped them.

Kell rose, fitting himself beside her once again.

"Was that a good enough lesson?" he asked, his own breath still uneven.

Lila grinned, and then rolled on top of him, straddling his waist. His eyes widened, his chest rising and falling beneath her. "Well," she said, guiding his hands over his head. "Let's see if I remember it all."

They lay pressed together in the narrow cot, Kell's arm looped around her. The heat of the moment was gone, replaced by a pleasant, steady warmth. His shirt was open, and she brought her fingertips to the scar over his heart, tracing the circles absently until his eyes drifted shut.

Lila knew she wouldn't sleep. Not like this, body to body in the bed. She usually slept with her back to a wall.

Usually slept with a knife on her knee.

Usually slept *alone*.

But soon, the ship was quiet, the small skiff rocking gently on the current, and Kell's breathing was low and even, his pulse a lulling beat against her skin, and for the first time in as long as she could remember, Lila fell well, and truly, and soundly, asleep.

V

"*Sanct,*" muttered Alucard, "it's getting *worse.*"

He spit Ilo's latest batch of dawn coffee over the side of the ship. Jasta called out from the wheel, her words lost on the breeze, and he wiped his mouth with the back of his hand and looked up to see the Going Waters take shape on the horizon.

First only a specter, and then, slowly, a ship.

When he'd first set out for Maris's infamous vessel, he'd done so expecting to find something like the port of Sasenroche or London's night market, only set at sea. *Is Feras Stras* was neither. It was indeed a ship—or rather, several, growing together like coral atop the crisp blue sea. Squares of canvas stretched here and dipped there, turning the network of decks and masts into something that resembled a nest of tents.

The whole thing looked unstable, a house of cards waiting to fall, swaying and bobbing in the winter breeze. It had the worn air of something that had lasted a very long time, that only grew, not torn down and rebuilt by whim or by wind, but added to in layers like paint.

But there was a strange elegance to the madness, an order to the chaos, made more severe by the quiet shrouding the ship. There were no shouts from any of the decks. No layered voices echoing on the breeze. The whole affair sat silently atop the waves, a ramshackle estate bathing in the sun.

It had been nearly two years since Alucard had last seen Maris's craft, and the sight of it still left him strangely awed.

Bard appeared beside him at the rail.

She let out a low whistle, her eyes wide with the same hungry light.

A low boat was already drawn up beside the floating market, and as the *Ghost* slowed, Alucard could make out a man, skeletal thin and leathered by the sun and the sea, being escorted from Maris's ship.

"Wait!" he was saying. "I paid my due. Let me keep looking. I'll find something else!"

But the men on his arms seemed oblivious to his pleas and protestations as they heaved him bodily overboard. He fell several feet before landing on the deck of his own small craft, groaning in pain.

"A word of advice," said Alucard lightly. "When Maris says leave, you leave."

"Don't worry," said Bard. "I'll be on my best behavior."

It wasn't a comforting notion. As far as he could see, she only had one kind of behavior, and it usually ended with several dead bodies.

In Jasta's hands, the *Ghost* slowed, drawing up beside the *Ferase Stras*. A plank was shifted into place between the *Ghost* and the brim of the floating market, which led onto a covered platform with a simple wooden door. They crossed the plank one at a time, Jasta in the front, then Lila and Kell, with Alucard bringing up the rear. After an hour's disagreement, the decision was made to leave Holland behind with Hastra and Lenos.

The remaining *Antari* was cuffed again, but some silent accord must have been struck between Holland and Kell, because he'd been granted freedom to move aboard the ship—Alucard had walked into the galley that morning and seen the magician sitting at the narrow table holding a cup of *tea*. Now Holland stood on the deck, leaning against the mast in the shadow of the mainsail, arms crossed as much as his chains would allow, head tipped toward the sky.

"Do we knock?" asked Lila, grinning at Alucard, but before she could reach out and rap her knuckles on the door, it swung open and a man stepped forward, dressed in trim white clothes. That, more than anything, made the scene surreal. Life at sea was a painting done primarily in muted shades—the sun and salt leached color, the sweat and grime wore whites to grey. Yet the man stood in the midst of the sea spray and mid-morning light, spotless in his milk-colored slacks and spotless tunic.

On his head, the man wore something between a headscarf and a helm. It circled his head and swept down over his brow and across his high cheeks. The gap between showed his eyes, which were the lightest shade of brown, fringed by long black lashes. He was lovely. Had always been lovely.

At the sight of Alucard, the figure cocked his head. "Didn't I just get rid of you?"

"Good to see you, too, Katros," he said cheerfully.

The man's gaze swept past Alucard to the others, pausing an instant on each before he held out a tan hand. "Your tokens."

They gave them up: Jasta, a small metal sphere full of holes that whistled and whispered; Kell, a Grey London coin; Lila, a silver watch; and Alucard, the vial of dreamsquick he'd picked up at Rosenal. Katros vanished behind the door, and the four stood in silence on the platform for several long minutes before he returned to let them in.

Kell passed through the door first, vanishing into the shadowed space beyond, followed by Bard with her brisk, soundless step, and then Jasta—but as the captain of the *Ghost* started forward, Katros blocked her way.

"Not this time, Jasta," he said evenly.

The woman scowled. "Why not?"

Katros shrugged. "Maris chooses."

"My gift was good."

"Perhaps," was all he said.

Jasta let out something that might have been a curse, or merely a growl, too low for Alucard to parse. They were roughly the same size, she and Katros, even counting the helm, and Alucard wondered what would happen if she tried to force her way through. He doubted it would end well for any of them, so he was relieved when she threw up her hands and skulked back onto the *Ghost*.

Katros turned toward him, a wry smile nocked like an arrow on his lips. "Alucard," he said, weighing the captain with those light eyes. And then, at last, "Come in."

VI

Kell stepped into the room, and drew up short.

He'd expected a contradiction of space, an interior as strange and mysterious as the ship's facade.

Instead, he found a room roughly the same size of Alucard's cabin aboard the *Night Spire,* though far more cluttered. Cabinets bulged with trinkets, cases brimmed with books, and massive chests hugged every wall, some locked and others open (and one trembling as if something inside was both alive and wanted to get out). There were no windows, and with so much clutter, Kell would have expected the room to smell stuffy, moth-eaten, but he was surprised to find the air crisp and clear, the only scent a faint but pleasant one, like old paper.

A broad table sat in the center of the room with a large white hound—though really it looked less like a dog and more like a pile of books shoved under a shaggy rug—snoring gently beneath it.

And there, behind the table, sat Maris.

The king of the floating market, who turned out to be a *queen.*

Maris was old, old as anyone Kell had ever seen, her skin dark even by Arnesian standards, its surface cracked into a hundred lines like tree bark. But like the sentry at the door, her clothing—a crisp white tunic laced to the throat—lacked even the smallest crease. Her long silver hair was pulled back off her weathered face and spilled between her shoulders in a narrow sheet of metal. She wore silver in both ears, and on both hands, one of which held their tokens while the other curled its bony fingers around the silver head of a cane.

And around her neck—along with three or four other silver chains—hung the Inheritor. It was the size of a small scroll, just as Tieren had said, not a cylinder exactly, but a thing of six or eight sides—he couldn't tell from here—all short and flat and shaped to form a column, each facet intricately patterned and its base tapered to a spindle's point.

When they were all there—all save Jasta, who'd apparently been turned back—Maris cleared her throat.

"A pocket watch. A coin. And a vial of sugar." Her voice held none of the frailty of age—it was rich and low and scornful. "I must admit, I'm disappointed."

Her gaze lifted, revealing eyes the color of sand. "The watch isn't even spelled, though I do suppose that's half the charm. And is this blood? Well, that's the other half for you. Though I do enjoy an object with a story. As for the coin, yes, I can tell it's not from here, but rather worn out, isn't it? As for the dreamsquick, Captain Emery, at least you remembered, needless as it is two years after the point. But I must say, I expected more from two *Antari* magicians and the victor of the *Essen Tasch*—yes, I know, word does travel quickly, and Alucard, I suppose I owe you a congratulations, though I doubt you've had much time to celebrate, what with the shadows looming over London."

All of this was said without a pause, or, as far as Kell could tell, the need for breath. But that wasn't what unnerved him most. "How do you know about the state of London?"

Maris's attention drifted toward him, and she began to answer, then squinted. "Ah," she said, "it seems you've found my old coat." Kell's hands rose defensively to his collar, but Maris waved it away. "If I wanted it back, I wouldn't have lost it. Thing's got a mind of its own, I think the spellwork must be fraying. Still eating coins and spitting out lint? No? It must like you."

Kell never got a word in edgewise, as Maris seemed more than content to carry on her conversations without a partner. He wondered if the old woman was a little daft, but her pale eyes flicked from target to target with all the speed and accuracy of a well-thrown knife.

Now that attention landed on Lila. "Aren't you a trinket," said Maris.

"But I'm betting a devil to hold on to. Has anyone told you, you've something in your eye?" Her hand tipped, letting the tokens tumble roughly to the table. "The watch must be yours, my darling traveler. It smells of ash and blood instead of flowers."

"It's the most precious thing I own," said Lila through gritted teeth.

"*Owned*," corrected Maris. "Oh, don't look at me like that, dearie. *You* gave it up." Her fingers tightened on the cane, eliciting a crackle of ligament and bone. "You must want something more. What brings a prince, a noble, and a stranger to my market? Have you come with a single prize in mind, or are you here to browse?"

"We only want—" started Kell, but Alucard clapped a hand on his shoulder.

"To help our city," said the captain.

Kell shot him a confused look but had the sense to say nothing.

"You're right, Maris," continued Alucard. "A shadow has fallen over London, and nothing we have can stop it."

The old woman rapped her nails on the table. "And here I thought London wanted nothing to do with *you*, Master Emery."

Alucard swallowed. "Perhaps," he said, casting a dark look Kell's way. "But I still care for it."

Lila's attention was still leveled on Maris. "What are the rules?"

"This is a black market," she said. "There are no rules."

"This is a ship," countered Lila. "And every ship has rules. The captain sets them. Unless, of course, you're *not* the captain of this ship."

Maris flashed her teeth. "I am captain and crew, merchant and law. Everyone aboard works for me."

"They're family, aren't they?" said Lila.

"Stop talking, Bard," warned Alucard.

"The two men who threw the other overboard, they take after you, and the one guarding the door—Katros, was it?—has your eyes."

"Perceptive," said Maris, "for a girl with only one of her own." The woman stood, and Kell expected to hear the creak and pop of old bones settling. Instead, he heard only a soft exhale, the rustle of cloth as it settled. "The rules are simple enough: your token buys you access to this market; it buys you nothing more. Everything aboard has a price, whether or not you elect to pay it."

"And I assume we can only choose one thing," said Lila.

Kell recalled the man thrown overboard, the way he'd called out for another chance.

"You know, Miss Bard, there *is* such a thing as being sharp enough to cut yourself."

Lila smiled, as if it were a compliment.

"Lastly," continued Maris with a pointed look her way, "the market is warded five ways to summer against acts of magic and theft. I encourage you not to try and pocket anything before it's yours. It will not go well."

With that, Maris took her seat, opened a ledger, and began to write.

They stood there, waiting for her to say more, or to excuse them, but after several uncomfortable moments, during which the only sound was the rattling of one trunk, the slosh of the sea, and the scratch of her quill, Maris's bony fingers drifted to a second door set between two stacks of boxes.

"Why are you still here?" she said without looking up, and that was all the dismissal they got.

"Why are we even bothering with the ship?" asked Kell as soon as they were through the door. "Maris has the only thing we need."

"Which is the last thing you're going to *tell* her," snapped Alucard.

"The more you want something from someone," added Lila, "the less they'll want to part with it. If Maris finds out what we actually *need,* we'll lose what power we have to bargain." Kell crossed his arms and looked about to counter, but she pressed on. "There are three of us, and only one Inheritor, which means the two of you need to find something else to buy." Before either of the men could protest, she cut them off. "Alucard, you can't ask for the Inheritor back, you're the one who gave it to her, and Kell, no offense, but you tend to make people angry."

Kell's brow furrowed. "I don't see how that—"

"Maris is a *thief*," said Lila, "and a bloody good one by the look of this ship, so she and I have something in common. Leave the Inheritor to me."

"And what are *we* supposed to do?" asked Kell, gesturing to himself and the captain.

Alucard made a sweeping gesture across the market, the sapphire twinkling above his eye. "Shop."

VII

Holland still hated being at sea—the dip and swell of the ship, the constant sense of imbalance—but moving around helped, somewhat. The manacles still emitted their dull, muffling pressure, but the air on deck was crisp and fresh, and if he closed his eyes, he could almost imagine he was somewhere else—though where he'd be, Holland didn't really know.

His stomach panged, still hollowed out from his first hours aboard, and he reluctantly made his way back down into the hold.

The old man, Ilo, stood at the narrow counter in the galley, rinsing potatoes and humming to himself. He didn't stop when Holland entered, didn't even soften his tune, just carried on as if he didn't know the magician was there.

A bowl of apples sat in the center of the table, and Holland reached out, chains scraping the wood. Still the cook didn't move. So the gesture was pointed, thought Holland, turning to go.

But his way was blocked.

Jasta stood in the doorway, half a head taller than Holland, her dark eyes leveled on him. There was no kindness in that gaze, and no sign of the others behind her.

Holland frowned. "That was fast. . . ."

He trailed off at the sight of the blade in her hand. One manacled wrist leaned on the table, the apple in his other hand, a short length of chain between. He'd lost the splinter he'd kept between metal and skin, but a paring knife sat on the counter nearby, its handle within reach. He didn't move toward it, not yet.

It was a narrow room, and Ilo was still washing and humming as if nothing were amiss, pointedly ignoring the rising tension.

Jasta held her blade loosely, with a comfort that gave Holland pause.

"Captain," he said carefully.

Jasta looked down at her knife. "My brother is dead," she said slowly, "because of you. Half my crew is gone because of you."

She stepped toward him.

"My city is in peril because of you."

He held his ground. She was close now. Close enough to use the blade before he could stop her without things getting messy.

"Perhaps two *Antari* will be enough," she said, bringing the tip of the knife to rest against his collar. Her gaze held his as she pressed down, testing, the knife sinking just enough to draw blood before a new voice echoed down the hall. Hastra. Followed by Lenos. Steps tumbling briskly down the stairs.

"Perhaps," she said again, stepping back, "but I'm not willing to risk it."

She turned and stormed out. Holland rocked back against the counter, wiping the blood from his skin as Hastra and Lenos appeared and Ilo took up another song.

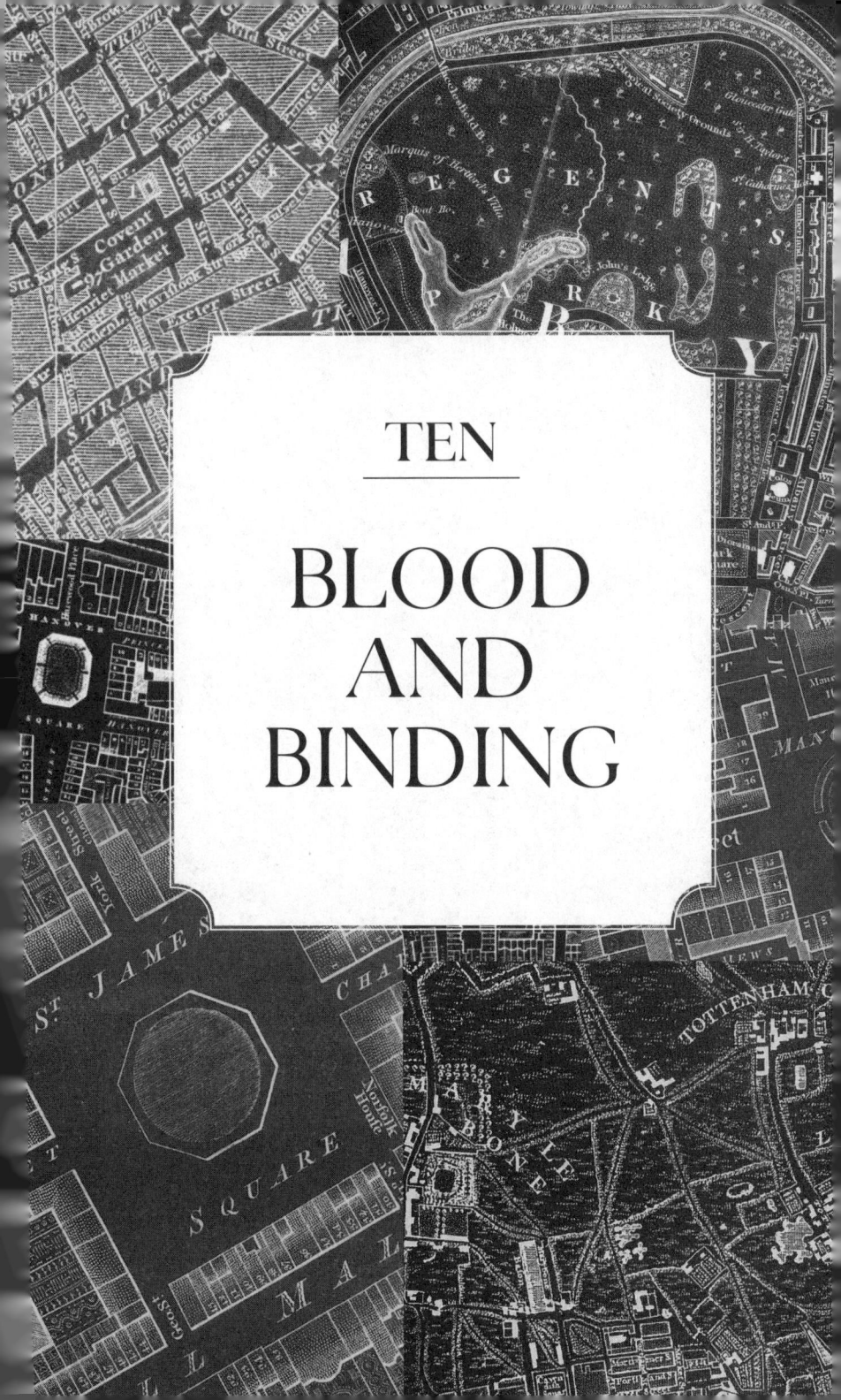

TEN

BLOOD AND BINDING

I

Grey London

Ned Tuttle woke to the sound of someone knocking.

It was late morning, and he'd fallen asleep at a table in the tavern, the grooves of the table's pentagram now etched like sheet folds into the side of his face.

He sat up, lost for a moment between where he was and where he'd been.

The dreams were getting stranger.

Every time, he found himself somewhere else—on a bridge overlooking a black river, looking up at a palace of marble and crimson and gold—and every time he was lost.

He'd read about men who could walk through dreams. They could project themselves into other places, other times—but when they walked, they were able to speak to people, and learn things, and they always came away wiser. When *Ned* dreamt, he just felt more and more alone.

He moved like a ghost through crowds of men and women who spoke languages he'd never heard, whose eyes swam with shadows and whose edges burned with light. Sometimes they didn't seem to see him, and other times they did, and those were worse, because then they'd reach for him, claw at him, and he'd have to run, and every time he ran, he ended up lost.

And then he'd hear that particular voice; the murmur and the susurrus, low and smooth and steady as water over rocks, the words muffled by some unseen veil between them. A voice that reached just like those shadow hands, wrapping fingers around his throat.

Ned's temples were pounding in time with the door as he reached for the glass on the table that had so recently served as his bed. Realizing the glass was empty, he swore and took up the bottle just beyond his fingers, swigging in a way that would have earned him a reproach if he were still at home. The table itself was scattered with parchment, ink, the elemental kit he'd bought from the gentleman who'd bought it from Kell. This last item rattled sporadically as if possessed (and it *was*, the bits of bone and stone and drops of water trying to get out). Ned thought groggily that it might have been the source of the knocking, but when he put his hand firmly on the box, the sound still echoed from the door.

"Coming," he called hoarsely, pausing a moment to steady his aching head, but when he rose and turned toward the tavern door, his jaw dropped.

The door was knocking *itself,* rocking forward and back in its frame, straining against the bolt. Ned wondered if there was a strong wind outside, but when he threw the shutters, the tavern sign hung still as death in the early morning light.

A shiver passed through him. He had always known this place was special. He'd heard the rumors from patrons back when he was one of them, and now they'd lean forward on their stools and ask *him,* as if he knew any more than they.

"Is it true . . ." they'd start, followed by a dozen different questions.

"That this place is haunted?"

"That it's built on a ley line?"

"That it sits in two worlds?"

"That it belongs to neither?"

Is it true, is it true, and Ned only knew that whatever it was, it had drawn him, and now it was drawing something else.

The door kept up its phantom knocking as Ned stumbled up the stairs and into his room, searching through the drawers until he found his biggest bundle of sage and his favored book of spells.

He was halfway down the stairs again when the noise stopped.

Ned returned to the tavern, crossing himself for good measure, and set the book on the table, turning through the pages until he found one to banish negative forces.

He went to the hearth, stoked the last embers of the night's fire, and touched the end of the sage bundle until it caught.

"I banish the darkness," he intoned, sweeping the sage through the air. "It is not welcome," he went on, tracing the windows and doors. "Begone foul spirits, and demons, and ghosts, for this is a place of . . ."

He trailed off as the smoke from the sage curled through the air around him and began to make *shapes*. First mouths, and then eyes, nightmarish faces drawing themselves in the pale plumes around him.

That wasn't supposed to happen.

Ned fumbled for a piece of chalk and dropped to his knees, drawing a pentagram on the tavern floor. He climbed inside, wishing he had a bit of salt, too, but unwilling to venture out behind the bar as all around him the grotesque faces swelled and fell apart and swelled again, their mouths yawning wide, as if laughing, or screaming—but the only sound that came out was *that voice*.

The one from his dream.

It was up close and far away, the kind of voice that seemed to be coming from the other room and another world at once.

"What are you?" Ned demanded, voice trembling.

"*I am a god,*" it said. "*I am a king.*"

"What do you want?" he said, because everyone knew that spirits had to tell the truth. Or was that fae? Christ . . .

"*I am just,*" said the voice. "*I am merciful. . . .*"

"What is your name?"

"*Worship me, and we will do great things. . . .*"

"Answer me."

"*I am a god. . . . I am a king. . . .*"

That's when Ned realized that, whatever it was, *wherever* it was, the voice wasn't talking to *him*. It was reciting its lines, repeating the words as one might a spell. Or a summoning.

Ned began to back out of the pentagram, his foot slipping on something smooth. Looking down, he saw a small patch of black on the old wooden floor, the size of a large coin. He thought at first that he had missed a spill, the remnants of someone's drink frozen in the recent cold snap. But the room wasn't really cold enough, and when Ned touched the strange dark slick, neither was it. He tapped it once with his nail and it sounded almost like glass, and then, before his eyes, the patch began to *spread*.

The knocking started up again, but this time a very human voice beyond the door called out, "Oy, Tuttle! Open up!"

Ned looked from the door, to the thinning smoke faces still hanging in the air, to the patch of creeping darkness on the floor, and called back, "We're closed!"

The words were met by a grumbled curse and the scuff of boots, and as soon as the man was gone, Ned was up, propping a chair against the locked door for good measure before he returned to the open book and started looking for a stronger spell.

II

It didn't matter that Alucard had been to the market once before. And it didn't matter that he had a compass in his head from years at sea, and a knack for learning paths. Within minutes, Alucard Emery was lost. The floating market was a maze of stairs and cabins and corridors, all of them empty of people and full of treasure.

There were no merchants here, calling out their wares. This was a private collection, a pirate's hoard on display. Only the rarest and strangest and most forbidden objects in the world made it onto Maris's ship.

It was a marvel nothing had ever been lost—or lifted, though not, he'd heard, for lack of trying. Maris had a fearful reputation, but a reputation carried only so far, and inevitably, drunk either on power or cheap wine, a thief would get it in their head to try to steal from the queen of the *Ferase Stras*.

As she'd warned, it never ended well.

Most of the stories involved missing limbs, though a few of the more outlandish tales involved entire crews scattered over land and sea in pieces so small no one ever found more than a thumb, a heel.

It made sense—when you had a wealth of black magic at your fingertips, you also had a wealth of ways to keep it safe. The market wasn't simply warded against light fingers. It was warded, he knew, against *intent*. You couldn't draw a knife. Couldn't reach for a thing you didn't mean to purchase. Some days, when the wards were fickle, you couldn't even think about stealing.

Unlike most magicians, Alucard was fond of Maris's wards, the way they muted everything. Without the noise of other magic, the treasures shone—his eyes could pick out the strands of power clinging to each artifact, the signatures of the magicians who'd spelled them. In a place without merchants to tell him what an object *did,* his sight came in handy. A spell was, after all, a kind of tapestry, woven from the threads of magic itself.

But it didn't stop him from getting lost.

In the end, it had taken Alucard half an hour to find the room of mirrors.

He stood there, surrounded by artifacts of every shape and size—some made of glass, and others polished stone, ones that reflected his own face, and ones that showed him other times and other places and other people—scanning the spellwork until he found the right one.

It was a lovely, oval thing with an onyx rim and two handles like a serving tray. Not an ordinary mirror, by any stretch, but not strictly forbidden, either. Only very rare. Most reflective magic showed what was in your mind, but a mind could invent almost anything, so a reflector could be fooled into showing a tale instead of the truth.

Reaching into the past—reflecting things not as they were remembered, or rewritten, but as they *were,* as they'd really happened—that was a very special kind of magic.

He slid the mirror into its case, a sleeve like a sheath but made of delicately carved onyx, and went to face Maris.

He was on his way back to the captain's chamber when his eyes snagged on the familiar threads of *Antari* magic. At first he thought he was simply catching sight of Kell, whose iridescence always trailed behind him like a coat, but when he rounded the corner, the magician was nowhere to be seen. Instead, the threads of magic were spilling from a table where they wrapped around a ring.

It was old, the metal fogged with age, and wide, the length of one full knuckle, and it sat on a table with a hundred others, each in an open box—but where the rest were woven with threads of blue and green, gold and red, this one was knotted with that unsteady color, like oil and water, that marked an *Antari.*

Alucard took it up, and went to find Kell.

III

Despite a wealth of natural magic, and years of rigorous study alongside the *Aven Essen,* Kell didn't know everything there was to know about spells. He *knew* that, but it was still disconcerting to be surrounded by so much *evidence* in support of the fact. In Maris's market, Kell didn't even *recognize* half the objects, let alone the enchantments woven through them. When the spellwork was written on an object's surface, he could usually make it out, but most of the talismans bore nothing but a design, a flourish. Now and then he could *feel* their intent, not a specific purpose so much as a general sense, but that was all.

He could tell the *Feras Stras* was a place where most people came with an object in mind, a goal, and the longer he wandered without one, the more he began to feel lost.

Which was likely why he found the room of knives so comforting. It was the kind of place Lila would gravitate to; the smallest weapon was no longer than his palm, the largest greater than the spread of his arms.

He knew Maris didn't deal in ordinary weapons, but as he squinted at the spellwork shorthand carved into the hilts and blades—every magician had their own dialect—he was still taken aback by the variety.

Swords to cut wounds that would not heal.

Knives to bleed truth instead of blood.

Weapons that channeled power, or stole it, or killed with a single stroke, or—

A low whistle behind him as Alucard appeared at the entrance.

"Picking out a gift?" asked the captain.

"No."

"Good, then take this." He dropped a ring into Kell's hand.

Kell frowned. "I'm flattered, but I think you're asking the wrong brother."

An exasperated sound escaped the man's throat. "I don't know what it *does,* but it's . . . like you. And I don't mean pompous and infuriating. The magic surrounding that ring—it's *Antari.*"

Kell straightened. "Are you sure?" He squinted at the band. It bore no seals, no obvious spellwork, but the metal hummed faintly against his skin, resonating. Up close, the silver was grooved, not in patterns but in rings. Tentatively, Kell slipped it onto his finger. Nothing happened—not that anything would, of course, since the ship was warded. He let the band slide back off into his palm.

"If you want it, buy it yourself," he said, handing it to Alucard. But the captain shied away.

"I can't," he said. "There's something else I need."

"What could you possibly need?"

Alucard looked purposefully away. "Time is wasting, Kell. Just take it."

Kell sighed and lifted the ring again, holding it between both hands and turning it slowly in search of markings or clues. And then, the strangest thing happened. He pulled gently, and part of the ring *came away* in his hand.

"Just perfect," said Alucard, looking around, "now you've gone and broken it."

But Kell didn't think he had. Instead of holding two broken pieces of one ring, he was now holding two *rings,* the original somehow unchanged, as if it hadn't given up half of itself to make the second, which was an exact replica of its brother. The two bands both thrummed in his hands, singing against his skin. Whatever they were, they were strong.

And Kell knew they'd need every drop of strength they could muster.

"Come on," he said, sliding both rings into his pocket. "Let's go see Maris."

They found Lila still standing outside the woman's door. Kell could tell it had taken a feat of self-restraint for her to stay put, with so many treasures strewn across the ship. She fidgeted, hands in the pockets of her coat.

"Well?" asked Alucard. "Did you get it?"

She shook her head. "Not yet."

"Why not?"

"I'm saving the best for last."

"Lila," chided Kell, "we only have one chance—"

"Yes," she said, straightening. "So I guess you'll have to trust me."

Kell shifted his weight. He wanted to trust her. He *didn't,* but he wanted to. For the moment, it would have to be enough.

At last, she flashed a small, sharp smile. "Hey, want to make a bet?"

"No," said Kell and Alucard at the same time.

Lila shrugged, but when he held the door for her, she didn't follow.

"Trust," she said again, leaning on the rail as if she had nowhere else to be. Alucard cleared his throat, and Maris was waiting, and finally Kell had no choice but to leave Lila there, staring hungrily out at the market.

Inside, Maris was sitting at her desk, paging through the ledger. They stood there, silently waiting for her to look up at them. She didn't.

"Go on, then," she said, turning the page.

Alucard went first. He stepped forward and produced, of all things, a *mirror.*

"You've got to be joking," growled Kell, but Maris only smiled.

"Captain Emery, you always have had a knack for finding rare and precious things."

"How do you think I found you?"

"Flattery is no payment here."

The sapphire above Alucard's eye winked. "And yet, like coin, it never hurts."

"Ah," she countered, "but like coin, I have no interest in it, either." She put down the ledger and held one hand out, across the table, but to the side, her fingers drifting toward a large sphere in a stand beside the desk. At first, Kell had taken the object for a globe, its surface raised and dented with impressions that could have been land and sea. But now he saw that it was something else entirely.

"Five years," she said.

Alucard let out a small, audible gasp, as if he'd taken a blow to the ribs. "Two."

Maris steepled her fingers. "Do I look like the kind of person who haggles?"

The captain swallowed. "No, Maris."

"You're young enough to bear the cost."

"Four."

"Alucard," she warned.

"A lot can be done with a year," he countered. "And I have already lost three."

She sighed. "Very well. Four."

Kell still didn't understand, not until Alucard set the mirror on the desk's edge and went to the sphere. Not until he placed his hands in the grooves on either side as the dial turned, ticking up from zero to four.

"Do we have a deal?" she asked.

"Yes," answered Alucard, bowing his head.

Maris reach out and pulled a lever on the sphere's stand, and Kell watched in horror as a shudder wracked the captain's body, shoulders hunched against the strain. And then it was done. The device let go, or he did, and the captain took up his bounty and retreated, cradling the mirror against his chest.

His face had altered slightly, the hollows in his cheeks deepening, the faintest creases showing at the corners of his eyes. He'd aged a fraction.

Four *years*.

Kell's attention snapped back to the sphere. It was, like the Inheritor around Maris's neck, like so many things here, a forbidden kind of magic. Transferring power, transferring *life,* these things contradicted nature, they—

"And you, princeling?" said Maris, her pale eyes dancing in her dark face.

Kell tore his gaze from the sphere and dug the rings from his coat pocket, and came up with one instead of two. He froze, afraid he'd somehow dropped the second, or worse, that the coat had eaten it the way it sometimes did with coins, but Maris didn't seem concerned.

"Ah," she said as he placed the object on the desk, "*Antari* binding rings. Alucard, your little *talent* is quite a nuisance sometimes."

"How do they work?" asked Kell.

"Do I look like a set of instructions?" She sat back. "Those have been sitting in my market for a very long time. Fickle things, they take a certain touch, and you could say that touch has all but died off, though between my boat and yours, you've managed quite a collection." Shock rattled through him. Kell started to speak, but she waved a hand. "The third *Antari* means nothing to me. My interests are bounded by this ship. But as for your purchase." She steepled her fingers. "Three."

Three years.

It could have been more.

But it could have been less.

"My life is not my own," he said slowly.

Maris raised a brow, the small gesture causing the wrinkles to multiply like cracks across her face. "That is your problem, not mine."

Alucard had gone silent behind him, his eyes open but vacant, as if his mind were somewhere else.

"What good is this to you," pressed Kell, "if no one else can use it?"

"Ah, but *you* can use it," she countered, "and therein lies its worth."

"If I refuse, we both end up empty-handed. As you said, Maris, I am a dying breed."

The woman considered him over her fingertips. "Hm. Two for making a valid point," she said, "and one for annoying me. The cost stays at three, Kell Maresh." He started to back away when she added, "It would be wise of you to take this deal."

And there was something in her gaze, something old and steady, and he wondered if she saw something he couldn't. He hesitated, then moved to the sphere and placed his fingers in the grooves.

The dial ticked down from four to three.

Maris pulled the lever.

It did not hurt, not exactly. The orb seemed to suddenly bind to his hands, holding them in place. His pulse surged in his head, and there was a short, dull ache in his chest, as if someone were drawing the air from his lungs, and then it was done. Three years, gone in three seconds. The sphere released him, and he closed his eyes against a shallow wave of dizziness before taking up the ring, now rightfully his. Bought and paid for. He wanted to be free of this room, this ship. But before he could escape, Maris spoke again, voice heavy as stone.

"Captain Emery," she said. "Give us the room."

Kell turned to see Alucard vanish through the door, leaving him alone with the ancient woman who'd just robbed him of three years of life.

She rose from the table, knuckles whitening on her cane as she used it to lever her old body up, then crossed behind the sphere.

"Captain?" he prompted, but she didn't speak, not yet. He watched as the old woman splayed one hand across its top. She murmured a few words, and the surface of the metal glowed, a tracery of light that withdrew line by line beneath her fingers. When it was gone, Maris exhaled, shoulders loosening as if a weight had been lifted.

"*Anesh*," she said, wiping her hands. There was a new ease to her motions, a straightness to her spine. "Kell Maresh," she said, turning the name over on her tongue. "The prize of the Arnesian crown. The *Antari* raised as royalty. We've met before, you and I."

"No, we haven't," said Kell, even though the sight of her tickled something in his mind. Not a memory, he realized, but the absence of one. The place where a memory should be. The place where it was *missing*.

He'd been five years old when he was given to the royal family, deposited at the palace with nothing but a sheathed knife, the letters *KL* carved into its hilt, and a memory spell burned into the crook of his arm, his short life before that moment erased.

"You were young," she said. "But I thought by now you might remember."

"You knew me before?" His head spun at the thought. "How?"

"I deal in rare things, *Antari*. There are few things rarer than you. I met your parents," continued Maris. "They brought you here."

Kell felt dizzy, ill. "Why?"

"Perhaps they were greedy," she said absently. "Perhaps they were afraid. Perhaps they wanted what was best. Perhaps they wanted only to be rid of you."

"If you know the answer—"

"Do *you* really want to know?" she cut in.

He started to say *yes,* the word automatic, but it stuck in his throat. How many years had he lain awake in bed, thumb brushing the scar at his elbow, wondering who he was, who he'd *been,* before?

"Do you want to know the last thing your mother said? What the initials stand for on your father's knife? Do you want to know who your true family was?"

Maris rounded her desk and took her seat with a slow precision that belied her age. She took up a quill and scribbled something on a slip of parchment, folding it twice into a small, neat square. She held it out between two aged fingers.

"To remove the spell I put on you."

Kell stared at the paper, his vision sliding in and out. He swallowed. "What is the price?"

A smile played across the woman's old mouth. "This one, and this one alone, is free. Call it a debt now paid, a kindness, or a closing door. Call it whatever you want, but expect nothing more."

He willed his body forward, willed his hand not to tremble as it reached for the paper.

"You still have that crease between your eyes," she said. "Still the same sad-faced boy you were that day."

Kell closed his fist around the slip of paper. "Is that all, Maris?"

A sigh escaped like steam between her lips. "I suppose." But her voice followed him through the door. "Strange thing about forgetting spells," she added as he hovered on the threshold, caught between shadow and sharp light. "Most will fade on their own. Stuck on at first, sure as stone. But over time, they slide right off. Unless we don't *want* to let them go...."

With that, a gust of wind cut through, and the door to Maris's market swung shut behind him.

IV

The market called to Delilah Bard.

She couldn't see the threads of magic like Alucard, couldn't read the spells like Kell, but the pull was there all the same, enticing as new coins, fine jewels, sharp weapons.

Temptation: that was the word for it, the urge to let herself look, touch, take.

But that shine, that unspoken promise—of strength, of power— reminded Lila of the sword she'd found back in Grey London, the way Vitari's magic had called to her through the steel, singing of promise. Almost everything in her life had changed since that night, but she still didn't trust that kind of blind, bottomless want.

So she waited.

Waited until the sounds beyond the door had stopped, waited until Kell and Alucard were gone, waited until there was no one and nothing left to stop her, until Maris was alone, and the want in Lila's chest had cooled into something hard, sharp, usable.

And then she went in.

The old woman was at her desk, cupping Lila's watch in one gnarled hand as if it were a piece of ripened fruit as she drew a nail across the crystal surface.

It is not Barron, Lila told herself. *That watch is not him. It's just a thing, and things are meant to be used.*

The dog heaved a sigh beneath Maris's feet, and it must have been a trick of the light, because the queen of the market looked . . . younger. Or, at least, a few wrinkles shy of ancient.

"Nothing strike your fancy, dearie?" she said without looking up.

"I know what I want."

Maris set the watch down, then, with a surprising degree of care. "And yet, your hands are empty."

Lila pointed at the Inheritor hanging from the woman's throat. "That's because you're wearing my prize."

Maris's hand drifted up. "This old piece?" she demurred, twirling the Inheritor between her fingers as if it were a simple pendant.

"What can I say?" said Lila casually. "I have a weakness for antiquated things."

A smile split the old woman's face, the innocence shed like a skin. "You know what it is."

"A smart pirate keeps her best treasure close."

Maris's sandy eyes drifted back to the silver watch. "A valid point. And if I refuse?"

"You said everything had a price."

"Perhaps I lied."

Lila smiled and said without malice, "Then perhaps I'll just cut it from your wrinkled neck."

A gravelly laugh. "You wouldn't be the first to try, but I don't think that would go well for either of us." She traced the hem of her white tunic. "You wouldn't believe how hard it is to get blood out of these clothes." Maris took up the watch again, weighing it in her palm. "You should know, I don't often take things without power, but then few people realize that memory casts its own spell, that it writes itself on an object just like magic, waiting to be picked over—or picked apart—by clever fingers. Another city. Another home. Another life. All bound up in something as simple as a cup, a coat, a silver watch. The past is a powerful thing, don't you think?"

"The past is the past."

A withering look. "Lies don't write themselves on me, Miss Bard."

"I'm not lying," said Lila. "The past is the past. It doesn't live in any one thing. It certainly doesn't live in something that can be given away. If it did, I would have just handed you everything I was, everything I am. But you can't have that, not even for a look around your market."

Lila tried to slow her heartbeat before continuing. "What you *can* have is a silver watch."

Maris's gaze held hers. "A pretty speech." She lifted the Inheritor over her head and set it on the desk beside the timepiece. Her face betrayed no strain, but when the object hit the wood, it made a solid sound, as if it weighed a great deal more than it seemed, and the woman's shoulders seemed lighter for the lack of it. "What will you give me?"

Lila cocked her head. "What do you *want*?"

Maris leaned back and crossed her legs, one white boot resting on the dog's back. It didn't seem to mind. "You'd be surprised how rarely people ask. They come here assuming I'll want their money or power, as if I've any need for either."

"Why run this market, then?"

"Someone has to keep an eye on things. Call it a passion, or a hobby. But as to the question of payment . . ." She sat forward. "I'm an old woman, Miss Bard—older than I look—and I really want only one thing."

Lila lifted her chin. "And what is that?"

She spread her hands. "Something I don't already have."

"A tall order, by the looks of this place."

"Not really," said Maris. "You want the Inheritor. I'll sell it to you for the price of an eye."

Lila's stomach turned. "You know," she said, fighting to keep her tone airy, "I need the one I have."

Maris chuckled. "Believe it or not, dearie, I'm not in the business of blinding my customers." She held out her hand. "The broken one will do."

Lila watched the lid of the small black box close over her glass eye.

The cost had been higher, the loss greater, than she realized when she first agreed. The eye had always been useless, its origins as strange and lost to her as the accident that took her real one. She'd wondered about it, of course—the craftwork so fine it must have been stolen—but for all that, Lila wasn't sentimental. She'd never been particularly attached to the ball of glass, but the moment it was gone, she felt suddenly wrong, exposed. A deformity on display, an absence made visible.

It is only a thing, she told herself again, *and things are meant to be used.*

Her fingers tightened on the Inheritor, relishing the pain as it cut into her palm.

"The instructions are written on the side," Maris was saying. "But perhaps I should have mentioned that the vessel is empty." The woman's expression went coy, as if she'd managed a trick. As if she thought Lila was after the remains of someone else's power instead of the device itself.

"Good," she said simply. "That's even better."

The woman's thin lips curled with amusement, but if she wanted to know more, she didn't ask. Lila started toward the door, combing the hair over her missing eye.

"A patch will help," said Maris, setting something on the table. "Or perhaps this."

Lila turned back.

The box was small and white and open, and at first, it looked empty, nothing but a swatch of crushed black velvet lining its sides. But then the light shifted and the object caught the sun, glinting faintly.

It was a sphere roughly the size and shape of an eye.

And it was solid black.

"Everyone knows the mark of an *Antari*," explained Maris. "The all-black eye. There was a fashion, oh, about a century ago—those who'd lost an eye in battle or by accident and found themselves in need of a false one would don one of blackened glass, passing themselves off as more than they were. The fashion ended, of course, when those ambitious, misguided few discovered that an *Antari* is much more than a marking. Some were challenged to duels they could not win, some were kidnapped or murdered for their magic, and some simply couldn't stand the pressure. As such, these eyes became quite rare," said Maris. "Almost as rare as you."

Lila didn't realize she'd crossed the room until she felt her fingers brush the smooth black glass. It seemed to sing beneath her touch, as if wanting to be held. "How much?"

"Take it."

Lila looked up. "A gift?"

Maris laughed softly, the sound of steam escaping a kettle. "This is the *Ferase Stras*," she said. "Nothing is free."

"I've already given you my left eye," growled Lila.

"And while an eye for an eye is enough for some—for this," she said, nudging the box toward Lila, "I'll need something more precious."

"A heart?"

"A favor."

"What kind of favor?"

Maris shrugged. "I suppose I'll know when I need it. But when I call you, you will come."

Lila hesitated. It was a dangerous deal, she knew, the kind villains coaxed from maidens in fairy tales, and devils from lost men, but she still heard herself answer, a single binding word.

"Yes."

Maris's smile cracked wider. "*Anesh,*" she said. "Try it on."

When she had it in, Lila stood before the mirror, blinking fiercely at her changed appearance, the startling difference of a shadow cast across her face, a pit of darkness so complete it registered as absence. As if a piece of her were missing—not an eye, but an entire self.

The girl from Grey London.

The one who picked pockets and cut purses and froze to death on winter nights with only pride to keep her warm.

The one without a family, without a world.

This new eye looked startlingly strange, wrong, and yet right.

"There," said Maris. "Isn't that better?"

And Lila smiled, because it was.

V

The slip of paper Maris had given Kell still blazed against his palm, but he kept his fist closed tight around it as he and Alucard stood, waiting, beyond the door.

He was worried that if they crossed the platform and left the ship, they wouldn't be allowed back on, and given Lila's tendency for trouble, Kell wanted to stay close.

But then the door swung open and Lila stepped through, the Inheritor clutched in her hand. And yet it wasn't the scroll-like device that caught his attention. It was Lila's smile, a dazzling, happy smile, and just above, a sphere of glossy black where shattered brown had been. Kell sucked in a breath.

"Your eye," he said.

"Oh," said Lila with a smirk, "you noticed."

"Saints, Bard," said Alucard. "Do I want to know how much *that* cost?"

"Worth every penny," she said.

Kell reached out and tucked the hair behind Lila's ear so he could see it better. The eye looked stark and strange and utterly right. His own gaze didn't clash against it, the way it did with Holland's, and yet, now that it was there, her eyes divided into brown and black, he couldn't imagine ever thinking she was ordinary. "It suits you."

"Not to interrupt . . ." said Alucard behind them.

Lila tossed him the Inheritor as if it were a mere coin, a simple token instead of the entire goal of their mad mission, their best—and maybe only—chance of saving London. Kell's stomach dropped, but Alucard snatched the talisman from the air just as easy.

He crossed the plank between the market and the *Ghost,* Lila falling in step behind him, but Kell lingered. He looked down at the paper in his hand. It was nothing but parchment, yet it could have weighed more than stone, the way it rooted him to the wooden floor.

Your true family.

But what did that mean? Was family the ones you were born to, or the ones who took you in? Did the first years of his life weigh more than the rest?

Strange thing about forgetting spells.

Rhy was his brother.

They fade on their own.

London was his home.

Unless we don't let go.

"Kell?" called Lila, looking over her shoulder with those two-toned eyes. "You coming?"

He nodded. "I'm right behind you."

His fingers closed over the paper, and with a brush of heat, it caught fire. He let it burn, and when the note was nothing but ashes, he tipped them over the side, letting the wind catch them before they ever hit the sea.

The crew stood on deck, gathered around a wooden crate—the makeshift table where Kell had set the bounty for which he'd paid three years.

"Tell me again," said Lila, "why, with a ship full of shiny things, you bought yourself a ring."

"It's not just a ring," he protested with far more certainty than he felt.

"Then what is it?" asked Jasta, arms crossed, still clearly bitter from being turned away.

"I don't exactly know," he said, defensively. "Maris called it a *binding* ring."

"No," corrected Alucard. "Maris called it binding *rings*."

"There's more than one?" asked Holland.

Kell took up the loop of metal and pulled, the way he had before, one ring becoming two the way Lila's knives did, only these had no hidden clasp. It wasn't an illusion. It was magic.

He set the newly made second ring back atop the crate, wondering at the original. Perhaps two was the limit of its power, but he didn't think it was.

Again Kell held the ring in both hands, and again he pulled, and again it came apart.

"That one never gets smaller," noted Lila, as Kell tried to make a fourth ring. It didn't work. There was no resistance, no rebuff. The refusal was simple and solid, as if the ring simply had no more to give.

All magic has limits.

It was something Tieren would say.

"And you're sure it's *Antari*-made?" asked Lenos.

"That's what *Alucard* said," said Kell, cutting him a look.

Alucard threw up his hands. "*Maris* confirmed it. She called them *Antari* binding rings."

"All right," said Lila. "But what do they *do*?"

"That she wouldn't say."

Hastra took up one of the spell-made rings and squinted through it, as if expecting to see something beside Kell's face on the other side.

Lenos poked at the second with his index finger, startling a little when it rolled away, not a specter, but a solid band of metal.

It tumbled right off the crate, and Holland caught it as it fell, his chains rattling against the wood.

"Would you take these foolish things off?"

Kell looked to Lila, who frowned back but didn't threaten mutiny. He slipped the original ring on his finger so he wouldn't drop it as he undid the manacles. They fell away with a heavy thud, everyone on deck tensing at the sudden sound, the knowledge that Holland was free.

Lila plucked the third ring from Hastra's grip.

"A little plain, aren't they?" She started to put it on, then cut a look at Holland, who was still considering the band of metal in his palm. Her eyes narrowed in distrust—they were *binding* rings, after all—but the moment Holland returned his ring to the crate, Lila flashed Kell a wicked grin.

"Shall we see what they do?" she asked, already sliding the silver band onto her finger.

"Lila, wait—" Kell started tugging his own ring off, but he was too late. The moment the band crossed her knuckle, it hit him like a blow.

Kell let out a short, breathless cry and doubled over, bracing himself against the crate as the deck tilted violently beneath him. It wasn't pain, but something just as deep. As if a thread in the very center of his being had pulled suddenly tight, and his whole self thrummed with the sudden tension of the cord.

"*Mas vares,*" Hastra was saying, "what's wrong?"

Nothing was *wrong*. Power coursed through him, so bright it lit the world, every one of his senses singing with the strain. His vision blurred, overwhelmed by the sudden surge, and when he managed to focus, to look at Lila, he could almost *see* the threads running between them, a metallic river of magic.

Her eyes were wide, as if she saw it, too.

"Huh," said Alucard, gaze flicking along the lines of power. "So that's what Maris meant."

"What is it?" asked Jasta, unable to see.

Kell straightened, the threads humming beneath his skin. He wanted to try something, so he reached, not with his hands, but with his will, and drew a fraction of Lila's magic toward him. It was like drinking light, warm and lush and startlingly bright, and suddenly anything felt possible. Was this what the world looked like to Osaron? Was this how it *felt* to be invincible?

Across the deck, Lila frowned at the shifting balance.

"That's mine," she said, wrenching the power back. As quick as it had come, the magic was gone, not just Lila's borrowed stake but his natural well, and, for a terrifying moment, Kell's world went black. He staggered and fell to his hands and knees on the deck. Nearby, Lila let out a sound that was part shock, part triumph, as she claimed his power as her own.

"Lila," he said, but his voice was unsteady, weak, swallowed by the whipping wind and the rocking ship and that sudden, gutting absence of strength, too like the cursed collar and the metal frame. Kell's whole body shook, his vision flickered, and through the spotted dark he saw her bring her hands together and, with nothing but a smile, summon an arc of flame.

"*Lila, stop,*" he gasped, but she didn't seem to hear him. Her gaze was empty, elsewhere, her attention consumed by the gold-red light of the fire as it grew and grew around her, threatening to brush the wooden boards of the *Ghost,* rising toward the canvas sail. A shout went up. Kell tried to rise, but couldn't. His hands tingled with heat, but he couldn't pull the ring from his finger. It was stuck, fused in place by whatever spellwork bound the two of them together.

And then, as sudden as the gain of Lila's magic, the loss of his, a new wave of magic surged through his veins. It wasn't coming from Lila, who still stood at the burning center of her own world. It was a third source, sharp and cold but just as bright. Kell's vision focused and he saw *Holland,* the final ring on his hand, its presence flooding the paths between them with fresh magic.

Kell's own power came back like air into starved lungs as the other *Antari* peeled away thread after thread of Lila's magic, the fire in her hands shrinking as the power was drawn away, divided between them, the air around Holland's hands dancing with tendrils of stolen flame.

Lila blinked rapidly, waking from the power's thrall. Startled, she dragged the ring from her finger, and nearly toppled over from the sudden spike and subsequent loss of power. As soon as the band was free of her hand, it melted away, first dissolving into a ribbon of silver mist and then—nothing.

Without her presence, the connection shuddered and shortened, drawing taut between Kell and Holland, the light of their collective power dimming a fraction. Again Kell tried to wrench the ring from his finger. Again he couldn't. It wasn't until *Holland* withdrew his own band, the echo of Kell's original, that the spell broke and his ring came free, tumbling to the wooden deck and rolling several feet before Alucard stopped it with the toe of his boot.

For a long moment, no one spoke.

Lila was leaning heavily against the rail, the deck scorched beneath her feet. Holland braced one hand against the mast for balance. Kell shivered, fighting the urge to be sick.

"What—" gasped Lila, "—the bloody hell—just happened?"

Hastra whistled softly to himself as Alucard knelt and retrieved the abandoned ring. "Well," he mused. "I'd say that was worth three years."

"Three years of what?" asked Lila, swaying as she tried to straighten. Kell glared at the captain, even as he sagged back against a stack of crates.

"No offense, Bard," continued Alucard, scuffing his boot where Lila had scorched the deck. "But your form could use some work."

Kell's head was pounding so loudly, it took him a moment to realize Holland was talking, too.

"This is how we do it," he was saying quietly, his green eye fever-bright.

"Do what?" asked Lila.

"This is how we catch Osaron." Something crossed Holland's face. Kell thought it *might* have been a smile. "This is how we *win*."

VI

Rhy sat atop his mount, squinting through the London fog for signs of life.

The streets were too still, the city too empty.

In the last hour, he hadn't found a single survivor. He'd hardly seen anyone at all, for that matter. The cursed, who'd moved like echoes through the beat of their lives, had withdrawn into their homes, leaving only the shimmering mist and the black rot spreading inch by inch over the city.

Rhy looked to the shadow palace, sitting like oil atop the river, and for a moment he wanted to spur his horse up the icy bridge to the doors of that dark, unnatural place. Wanted to force his way in. To face the shadow king himself.

But Kell had said to wait. *I have a plan,* he'd said. *Do you trust me?*

And Rhy did.

He turned the horse away.

"Your Highness," said the guard, meeting him at the mouth of the road.

"Have you found any more?" asked Rhy, heart sinking when the man shook his head.

They rode back toward the palace in silence, only the sound of their horses ringing through the deserted streets.

Wrong, said his gut.

They reached the plaza, and he slowed his horse as the palace steps came into view. There at the base of the stairs stood a young woman with a bunch of flowers in her hand. Winter roses, their petals frosty white. As he watched, she knelt and placed the bouquet on the steps. It was such an ordinary gesture, the kind of thing a commoner would have done on a normal winter day, an offering, a thanks, a prayer, but it wasn't a normal winter day, and everything about it was out of place against the backdrop of fog and barren streets.

"*Mas vares?*" said the guard as Rhy dismounted.

Wrong, beat his heart.

"Take the horses and get inside," he ordered, starting forward on foot across the plaza. As he drew near, he could see the darkness splashed like paint across the other flowers, dripping onto the pale polished stone beneath.

The woman didn't look up, not until he was nearly at her side, and then she rose and tipped her chin to the palace, revealing eyes that swirled with fog, veins traced black with the shadow king's curse.

Rhy stilled, but didn't retreat.

"All things rise and all things fall," she said, her voice high and sweet and lilting, as if reciting a bit of song. "Even castles. Even kings."

She didn't notice Rhy—or so he thought, until her hand shot out, thin fingers clutching the armor plate of his forearm so hard it buckled. "He sees you now, hollow prince."

Rhy tore free, stumbling back against the steps.

"Broken toy soldier."

He got to his feet again.

"Osaron will cut your threads."

Rhy kept his back to the palace as he retreated up, one step, two.

But on the third stair, he stumbled.

And on the fourth, the shadows came.

The woman gave a manic little laugh, wind rippling her skirts as Osaron's puppets poured from the houses and the shops and the alleys, ten, twenty, fifty, a hundred. They appeared at the edge of the palace plaza, holding iron bars, axes, and blades, fire and ice and rock. Some were young and others old, some tall and others little more than children, and all of them under the shadow king's spell.

"There can be only one castle," called the woman, following Rhy as he scrambled up the stairs. "There can be only one—"

An arrow took her in the chest, loosed by a guard above. The young woman staggered a step before wrapping those same delicate fingers around the arrow's shaft and ripping it free. Blood spilled down her front, more black than red, but she dragged herself after him another few steps before her heart failed, her limbs folded, her body died.

Rhy reached the landing and spun back to see his city.

The first wave of the assault had reached the base of the palace steps. He recognized one of the men at the front—thought, for a terrifying second, that it was Alucard, before Rhy realized it was the captain's older brother. Lord Berras.

And when Berras saw the prince—and he *did* see him now—those curse-dark eyes narrowed and a feral, joyless smile spread across his face. Flame danced around one hand.

"Tear it down," he boomed in a voice lower and harder than his brother's. "Tear it *all* down."

It was more than a rally—it was a general's command, and Rhy stared in shock and horror as the mass surged up the stairs. He drew his sword as something blazed in the sky above, a comet of fire launched by another, unseen foe. A pair of guards hauled him backward into the palace a breath before the blast struck the wards and shattered in a blaze of light, blinding but futile.

The guards slammed the doors, the nightmarish view beyond the palace replaced suddenly by dark wood and the muted resonance of strong magic, and then, sickeningly, by the sound of bodies striking stone, wood, glass.

Rhy staggered back from the doors and hurried to the nearest bay of windows.

Until that day, Rhy had never seen what happened when a forbidden body threw itself against an active ward. At first, it was simply repelled, but as it tried again and again and again, the effect was roughly that of steel against thick ice, one chipping away at the other while also ruining itself. The wards on the palace shuddered and cracked, but so did the cursed. Blood ran from their noses and ears as they threw element and spell and fist against the walls, clawed at the foundation, threw themselves against the doors.

"What is going on?" demanded Isra, storming into the foyer. When the head of the royal guard saw the prince, she recoiled a step and bowed. "Your Highness."

"Find the king," said Rhy as the palace shook around him. "We are under attack."

At this rate, the wards wouldn't hold. Rhy didn't need a gift for magic to see that. The palace gallery shook with the force of the bodies throwing themselves against the wood and stone. They were on the banks. They were on the steps. They were on the river.

And they were killing themselves.

The *shadow king* was killing them.

All around priests scrambled to draw fresh concentration rings on the gallery floor. Spells to focus magic. To bolster the wards.

Where was Kell?

Light flared against the glass with every blow, the spellwork straining to hold under the strength of the attack.

The royal palace was a shell. And it was cracking.

The walls trembled, and several people screamed. Nobles huddled together in corners. Magicians barred the doors, braced for the palace to break. Prince Col stood before his sister like a human shield while Lord Sol-in-Ar instructed his entourage in a rapid stream of Faroan.

Another blast, and the wards fractured, light webbing across the windows. Rhy lifted his hand to the glass, expecting it to shatter.

"Get back," ordered his mother.

"Every magician stand within a circle," ordered his father. Maxim had appeared in the first moments of the attack looking drawn but determined. Blood flecked his cuff, and Rhy wondered, dazedly, if his father had been fighting. Tieren was at his side. "I thought you said the wards would hold," snapped the king.

"Against Osaron's spell," replied the priest, drawing another circle on the floor. "Not against the brute force of three hundred souls."

"We have to stop them," said Rhy. He hadn't worked so hard and saved so few only to watch the rest of his people break themselves against these walls.

"Emira," ordered the king, "get everyone else into the Jewel."

The Jewel was the ballroom at the very center of the palace, the farthest from the outer walls. The queen hesitated, eyes wide and lost as she looked from Rhy to the windows.

"Emira, *now*."

At that moment, a strange transformation happened in his mother. She seemed to wake from a trance; she drew herself up and began to speak in crisp, clear Arnesian. "Brost, Losen, with me. You can hold up a circle, yes? Good. Ister," she said, addressing one of the female priests, "come and set the wards."

The walls shook, a deep, dangerous rattle.

"They will not hold," said the Veskan prince, drawing a blade as if the foe were flesh and blood, a thing that could be cut down.

"We need a plan," said Sol-in-Ar. "Before this sanctuary becomes a cage."

Maxim spun on Tieren. "The sleeping spell. Is it ready?"

The old priest swallowed. "Yes, but—"

"Then, for saint's sake," cut in the king, "*do it now*."

Tieren stepped in, lowering his voice. "Magic of this size and scale requires an anchor."

"What do you mean?" asked Rhy.

"A magician to hold the spell in place."

"One of the priests, then—" started Maxim.

Tieren shook his head. "The demands of such a spell are too steep. The wrong mind will break. . . ."

Understanding hit Rhy.

"No," he said, "not you—" even as his father's order came down: "See it done."

The *Aven Essen* nodded. "Your Majesty," said Tieren, adding, "once it's started, I won't be able to help you with—"

"It's all right," interrupted the king. "I can finish it myself. Go."

"Stubborn as ever," said the old man, shaking his head. But he didn't argue, didn't linger. Tieren turned on his heel, robes fluttering, and called to three of his priests, who fell into his wake. Rhy hurried after them.

"Tieren!" he called. The old man slowed but didn't stop. "What is my father talking about?"

"The king's business is his own."

Rhy stepped in front of him. "As the royal prince, I demand to know what he is doing."

The *Aven Essen* narrowed his eyes, then flicked his fingers, and Rhy felt himself forced physically out of the way as Tieren and his three priests filed past in a flurry of white robes. He brought a hand to his chest, stunned.

"Don't stand there, Prince Rhy," called Tieren, "when you could help to save us all."

Rhy pushed off the wall and hurried after them.

Tieren led the way to the guards' hall, and into the sparring room.

The priests had stripped the space bare, all of the armor and weapons and equipment cleared save for a single wooden table on which sat scrolls and ink, empty vials lying on their sides, the dustlike contents glittering in a shallow bowl.

Even now, with the walls trembling, a pair of priests were hard at work, steady hands scrawling symbols he couldn't read across the stone floor.

"It's time," said Tieren, stripping off his outer robe.

"*Aven Essen*," said one of the priests, looking up. "The final seals aren't—"

"It will have to do." He undid the collars and cuffs of his white tunic. "I will anchor the spell," he said, addressing Rhy. "If I stir or die, it will break. Do not let that happen, so long as Osaron's own curse holds."

It was all happening too fast. Rhy reeled. "Tieren, please—"

But he stilled as the old man turned and brought his weathered hands to Rhy's face. Despite everything, a sense of calm washed through him.

"If the palace falls, get out of the city."

Rhy frowned, focusing through the sudden peace. "I will *not* run."

A tired smile spread across the old man's face. "That is the right answer, *mas vares*."

With that, his hands were gone, and the wave of calm vanished. Fear and panic surged, raging anew through Rhy's blood, and when Tieren crossed into the circle of the spell, the prince fought the urge to pull him back.

"Remind your father," said the *Aven Essen,* "that even kings are made of flesh and bone."

Tieren sank to his knees in the center of the circle and Rhy was forced to retreat as the five priests began their work, moving with smooth, confident motions, as if the palace weren't threatening to collapse around them.

One took up a bowl of spelled sand and poured the grainy contents around the traced white line of the circle. Three others took up their places as the last held a burning taper out to Rhy and explained what to do.

He cradled the small flame as if it were a life while the five priests joined hands, heads bowed, and began to recite a spell in a language Rhy himself couldn't speak. Tieren closed his eyes, lips moving in time with the spell, which began to echo against the stone walls, filling the room like smoke.

Beyond the palace, another voice whispered through the cracks in the wards. *"Let me in."*

Rhy knelt, as he'd been told to do, and touched the taper to the sand line that traced the circle.

"Let me in."

The others continued the spell, but as the sand's end lit like a fuse, Tieren's lips stopped moving. He drew a deep breath, and then the old priest began to exhale slowly, emptying his lungs as the flameless fire burned its way around the circle, leaving a charred black line in its wake.

"Let me in," snarled the voice, echoing in the room as the final inches of sand burned away and the last of the air left the priest's lungs.

Rhy waited for Tieren to breathe again.

He didn't.

The *Aven Essen*'s kneeling form slumped sideways, and the other priests were there to catch him before he hit the floor. They lowered his body to the stone, laying him out within the circle as if he were a corpse, cushioning his head, lacing his fingers. One took the taper from Rhy's hands and nested it in the old man's.

The flickering flame went suddenly steady.

The whole room held its breath as the palace shuddered a final time, and then went still.

Beyond the walls, the whispers and the shouts and the pounding of fists and bodies all . . . stopped, a heavy silence falling like a sheet over the city.

The spell was done.

VII

"Give me the ring," said Holland.

Lila raised a brow. It wasn't a question or a plea. It was a *demand*. And considering that the speaker had spent most of the trip chained in the hold, it struck her as a fairly audacious one.

Alucard, who was still cradling the silver band, started to refuse him, but Holland rolled his eyes and flicked his fingers, and the ring shot out of the captain's hand. Lila lunged for it, but Kell caught her arm and the ring landed in Holland's waiting palm.

He turned the band between his hands.

"Why should we let him have it?" she snarled, pulling free.

"Why?" echoed Holland as a sliver of silver came flying toward her. She plucked the second ring out of the air. A moment later, Kell caught the third. "Because I'm the strongest."

Kell rolled his eyes.

"Want to prove it?" growled Lila.

Holland was considering his ring. "There is a difference, Miss Bard, between power and strength. Do you know what that difference is?" His eyes flicked up. "Control."

Indignation flared like a match, not just because she hated Holland, hated what he was insinuating, but because she knew he was right. For all her raw power, it was just that, raw. Unformed. Wild.

She *knew* he was right, but her fingers still itched for a knife.

Holland sighed. "Your distrust is all the more reason to let me do it."

Lila frowned. "How do you figure?"

"The original ring is the anchor." He slipped it onto his thumb. "As such, it is bound to its copies, not the other way around."

Lila didn't follow. It wasn't a feeling she relished. The only thing she relished *less* was the look in Holland's eyes, the smug look of someone who *knew* she was lost.

"The rings will bind our power," he said slowly. "But *you* can break the connection whenever you want, whereas *I* will be tethered to the spell."

A cruel smile cut across Lila's face. She clicked her tongue. "Can't go a day without chaining yourself to someone, can y—"

He was on her in an instant, his fingers wrapped around her throat and her knife against his. Kell threw up his hands in exasperation, Jasta called out a warning about getting blood on her ship, and a second blade came to rest below Holland's jaw.

"Now, now," said Alucard casually, "I know, I've thought of killing you *both,* but in the interest of the greater good, let's try to keep this civil."

Lila lowered her knife. Holland let go of her throat.

They each took a single step back. Annoyance burned through Lila, but so did something else. It took her a second to recognize it. *Shame.* It sat, a cold weight, steaming in her stomach. Holland stood there, features carefully set as if the blow hadn't landed, but it clearly had.

She swallowed, cleared her throat. "You were saying . . . ?"

Holland held her gaze.

"I'm willing to be the anchor of our spell," he said carefully. "As long as we three are bound, my power will be yours."

"And until we choose to break that bond," she countered, "*our* power will be *yours.*"

"It is the only way," pressed Holland. "One *Antari*'s magic wasn't enough to entice Osaron, but together . . ."

"We can lure him in," finished Kell. He looked down at the ring in his hand, then slid it on. Lila saw the moment their powers met. The shudder that passed like a chill between them, the air humming with their combined power.

Lila looked down at her own silver band. She remembered the

power, yes, but also the terrifying sense of being exposed, and yet trapped, laid bare and subject to someone else's will.

She wanted to help, but the idea of binding herself to another—

A shadow crossed her vision as Holland stepped toward her. She didn't look up, didn't want to see his expression, filled with disdain, or worse, whatever was now visible through the crack she'd made.

"It's not easy, is it? To chain yourself to someone else?" A chill ran through her as he threw the words back in her face. She clenched her fist around the ring. "Even when it's for a higher cause," he went on, never raising his voice. "Even when it could save a city, heal a world, change the lives of everyone you know . . ." Her eyes flicked to Kell. "It's a hard choice to make."

Lila met Holland's gaze, expecting—maybe even hoping—to find that cold, implacable calm, perhaps tinged with disgust. Instead, she found shades of sadness, loss. And somehow, strength. The strength to go on. To try again. To trust.

She put on the ring.

ELEVEN

DEATH AT SEA

I

To the Nameless Saints who soothe the winds and still the restless sea . . .

Lenos turned his grandmother's talisman between his hands as he prayed.

I beg protection for this vessel—

A sound shuddered through the ship, followed by a swell of cursing. Lenos looked up as Lila got to her feet, steam rising from her hands.

—and those who sail aboard it. I beg kind waters and clear skies as we make our way—

"If you break my ship, I will kill you all," shouted Jasta.

His fingers tightened around the pendant.

—our way into danger and darkness.

"Damned *Antari*," muttered Alucard, storming up the steps to the landing where Lenos stood, elbows on the rail.

The captain slumped down against a crate and produced a flask. "This is why I drink."

Lenos pressed on.

I beg this as a humble servant, with faith in the vast world, in all its power.

He straightened, tucking the necklace back under his collar.

"Did I interrupt?" asked Alucard.

Lenos looked from the singe marks on the deck to Jasta bellowing from the wheel as the ship tipped suddenly sideways under the force of whatever magic the three *Antari* were working, and at last to the man who sat drinking on the floor.

"Not really," said Lenos, folding his long limbs in beside him.

Alucard offered Lenos the flask, but he declined. He'd never been much of a drinker. Never thought the during was much worth the after.

"How do you know they're listening?" asked Alucard, taking another sip. "These saints you pray to?"

The captain wasn't a spiritual man, as far as Lenos could tell, and that was fine. Magic was a river carving its course, picking who to flow through and who to bend around, and for those it bent around, well, there was a reason for that, too. For one thing, they tended to have a better view of the water from the bank. Lenos shrugged, searching for the words. "It's not . . . really . . . a conversation."

Alucard raised a brow, his sapphire glittering in the dying light. "What then?"

Lenos fidgeted. "More like . . . an offering."

The captain made a sound that might have been understanding. Or he might have simply been clearing his throat.

"Always were an odd one," mused Alucard. "How did you even end up on my ship?"

Lenos looked down at the talisman still cradled in one palm. "Life," he said, since he didn't believe in luck—it was the absence of design, and if Lenos believed one thing, it was that everything had an order, a reason. Sometimes you were too close to see it, sometimes too far away, but it was there.

He thought about that, then added, "And Stross."

After all, it had been the *Spire*'s gruff first mate who ran into Lenos in Tanek when he was fresh off the boat from Hanas, who'd taken a shine to him, for one reason or another, and marched him up onto the deck of a new ship, its hull shining, its sails a midnight blue. There an odd lot had gathered, but oddest to Lenos was the man perched atop the wheel.

"Taking in strays, are we?" the man had asked when he caught sight of Lenos. He had an easy way about him, the kind of smile that made you want to smile too. Lenos stared—the sailors in his village had all been sun scorched and scraggly. Even the captains looked like they'd been left out for a summer and a winter and a spring. But this man was young and strong and striking, dressed in crisp black with silver trim.

"The name's Alucard Emery," he'd said, and a murmur had gone through the gathered men, but Lenos didn't have a clue what an Emery was, or why he was supposed to care. "This here's the *Night Spire,* and you're here because she needs a crew. But you're not my crew. Not yet."

He nodded at the nearest man, a towering figure, muscles wound like coarse ropes around his frame. "What can you do?"

A chuckle went through the group.

"Well," said the broad man. "I'm decent at lifting."

"Can read any map," offered another.

"A thief," said a third. "The best you'll find."

Each and every man aboard was more than a sailor. They each had a skill—some had several. And then Alucard Emery had looked at Lenos with that storm-dark gaze.

"And you?" he'd said. "What can *you* do?"

Lenos had looked down at his too-thin form, ribs protruding with every breath, his hands roughened only by a childhood playing on rocky banks. The truth was, Lenos had never been very good at anything. Not natural magic or pretty women, feats of strength or turns of phrase. He wasn't even terribly skilled at sailing (though he could tie a knot and wasn't afraid of drowning).

The only thing Lenos had a knack for was sensing danger—not reading it in a darkened dish, or spotting it in lines of light, but simply *feeling* it, the way one might a tremor underfoot, a coming storm. Sensing it, and steering to avoid it.

"Well?" prompted Alucard.

Lenos swallowed. "I can tell you when there's trouble."

Alucard had raised a brow (there was no sapphire winking from it, then, not until their first outing in Faro).

"Captain," Lenos had added hastily, misreading the man's surprise for insult.

Alucard Emery had flashed another kind of smile. "Well, then," he'd said, "I'll hold you to it."

That was another night, another time, another ship.

But Lenos had always kept his word.

"I've got a bad feeling," he whispered now, looking out to sea. The water was calm, the skies were clear, but there was a weight in his chest like a breath held too long.

"Lenos." Alucard chuckled thinly and got to his feet. "A piece of magic is parading as a god, a poisoned fog is destroying London, and three *Antari* are sparring aboard our ship," said the captain. "I'd be worried if you *didn't*."

II

Bloody hell, thought Lila, as she doubled over on the deck.

After hours of practice, she was dizzy and Kell's skin was slick with sweat, but Holland barely looked winded. She fought the urge to hit him in the stomach before Hano called out from the crow's nest. The ship needed a breeze.

She slumped back onto a crate as the others went to help. She felt like she'd gone three rounds in the *Essen Tasch,* and lost every single one. Every inch of her body—flesh down to bone—ached from using the rings. How the other two *Antari* had the energy left to put wind in the sails, she had no idea.

But the training seemed to be working.

As the ship sailed through the first fingers of dusk, they'd reached a kind of equilibrium. They were now able to balance and amplify their magic without over-drawing from each other. It was such a strange sensation, to be stronger and weaker at the same time, so much power but so hard to wield, like an off-weighted gun.

Even still, the world blazed with magic, the threads of it tracing the air like light, lingering every time Lila blinked. She felt as if she could reach out and pluck one and make the world sing.

She held her hand before her eyes, squinting at the silver ring still wrapped around her middle finger.

It was control. It was balance. It was everything she wasn't, and even now Lila was tempted to chuck it in the sea.

She'd never been one for moderation. Not when she was just a street rat with a quick temper and a quicker knife, and certainly not now that she'd struck flint against the magic in her veins. She knew this about herself, she *liked* it, was convinced it had kept her alive. Alive, but also alone—hard to keep an eye on others when you were keeping both out for yourself.

Lila shivered, the sweat long cold along her scalp.

When had the stars come out?

She dragged herself upright, hopped down from the crate, and was halfway to the hold when she heard the singing. Her body ached, and she wanted a drink, but her feet followed the sound, and soon she found its source. Hastra sat cross-legged with his back against the rail, something cupped in his hands.

Even in the low light, Hastra's brown curls were threaded with gold. He looked young, even younger than she was, and when he saw her standing there, he didn't shy away like Lenos. Instead, Hastra grinned. "Miss Bard," he said warmly. "I like your new eye."

"So do I," she said, sliding to the floor. "What's in your hands?"

Hastra uncurled his fingers to reveal a small blue egg. "I found it on the docks in Rosenal," he said. "You're supposed to sing to eggs, did you know that?"

"To make them hatch?"

Hastra shook his head. "No, they'll do that anyway. You sing to them so they hatch happy."

Lila raised a brow. They were roughly the same age, but there was something *boyish* about Hastra—he was young in a way she'd never been. And yet, the air was always warm around him, the same way it was with Tieren, calm sliding through her mind like silk, like snow. "Kell tells me you should have been a priest."

Hastra's smile saddened. "I know I didn't make a very good guard."

"I don't think he meant it as an insult."

He ran his thumb over the brittle shell. "Are you as famous in your world as Kell is here?"

Lila thought of the wanted posters lining *her* London. "Not for the same reasons."

"But you've decided to stay."

"I think so."

His smile warmed. "I'm glad."

Lila blew out a breath, ruffling her hair. "I wouldn't be," she said. "I tend to make a mess of things."

Hastra looked down at the little blue egg. "Life is chaos. Time is order."

Lila drew her knees up to her chest. "What's that supposed to mean?"

He blushed. "I'm not certain. But Master Tieren said it, so it sounded wise."

Lila started to laugh, then cut off as her body crackled with pain. She really needed that drink, so she left Hastra to his egg and his songs and made her way down into the hold.

The galley wasn't empty.

Jasta sat at the narrow table, a glass in one hand and a deck of cards in the other. Lila's stomach growled, but the room smelled like Ilo had tried (and failed) to make a stew, so she went for the shelf instead, pouring herself a cup of whatever Jasta was already having. Something strong and dark.

She could feel the captain's gaze on her.

"This new eye," mused Jasta, "it suits you."

Lila tipped the cup her way. "Cheers."

Jasta set down her glass and shuffled the deck between both hands. "Sit with me. Play a hand."

Lila scanned the table, which was covered in the remains of a game, empty glasses piled to one side and cards to the other.

"What happened to your last opponent?"

Jasta shrugged. "He lost."

Lila smiled thinly. "I think I'll pass."

Jasta gave a soft grunt. "You won't play because you know you will lose."

"You can't goad me into playing."

"*Tac,* maybe you are not a pirate after all, Bard. Maybe you are just pretending, like Alucard, playing dress-up in clothes that do not fit. Maybe you belong in London, not out here, on the sea."

Lila's smile sharpened. "I belong wherever I choose."

"I think you are a thief, not a pirate."

"A thief steals on land, a pirate at sea. The last time I checked, I was both."

"That is not the true difference," said Jasta. "The true difference is *tarnal*." Lila didn't know the word. The woman must have seen, because she searched for several long seconds and then said, in English, "Fearless."

Lila's eyes narrowed. She didn't realize Jasta spoke anything but Arnesian. Then again, sailors had a way of snatching words up like coins, pocketing them for later.

"You see," continued Jasta, cutting the deck, "a thief plays the game only when they think they'll win. A pirate plays the game even when they think they'll lose."

Lila downed her drink and swung a leg over the bench, her limbs leaden. She rapped her knuckles on the table, her new ring glinting in the lantern light. "All right, Jasta. Deal me in."

The game was Sanct.

"You lose, you drink," said Jasta, dealing the cards. They hissed across the tabletop, face down. Their backs were black and gold. Lila took up her cards and scanned them absently. She knew the rules well enough to know it was less about knowing how to play and more about knowing how to cheat.

"Now tell me," continued the captain, stacking her own hand, "what do you want?"

"That's a broad question."

"And an easy one. If you don't know the answer, you don't know yourself."

Lila paused, thinking. She threw down two cards. A specter and a queen. "Freedom," she said. "And you?"

"What do I want?" mused Jasta. "To win."

She threw down a pair of saints.

Lila swore.

Jasta smiled crookedly. "Drink."

"*How do you know when the Sarows is coming?*" hummed Lila as she made her way down the ship's narrow hall, fingertips skimming either wall for balance.

Right about then, Alucard's warning about Jasta was coming back in full force.

"Never challenge that one to a drinking contest. Or a sword fight. Or anything else you might lose. Because you will."

The boat rocked beneath her feet. Or maybe she was the one rocking. Hell. Lila was slight, but not short of practice, and even so, she'd never had so much trouble holding her liquor.

When she got to her room, she found Kell hunched over the Inheritor, examining the markings on its side.

"Hello, handsome," she said, bracing herself in the doorway.

Kell looked up, a smile halfway to his lips before it fell away. "You're drunk," he said, giving her a long, appraising look. "And you're not wearing any shoes."

"Your powers of observation are astonishing." Lila looked down at her bare feet. "I lost them."

"How do you lose shoes?"

Lila crinkled her brow. "I bet them. I lost."

Kell rose. "To who?"

A tiny hiccup. "Jasta."

Kell sighed. "Stay here." He slipped past her into the hall, a hand alighting on her waist and then, too soon, the touch was gone. Lila made her way to the bed and collapsed onto it, scooping up the discarded Inheritor and holding it up to the light. The spindle at the cylinder's base was sharp enough to cut, and she turned the device carefully between her fingers, squinting to make out the words wrapped around it.

Rosin, read one side.

Cason, read the other.

Lila frowned, mouthing the words as Kell reappeared in the doorway. "*Give—and Take,*" he translated, tossing her the boots.

She sat up too fast, winced. "How did you manage that?"

"I simply explained that she couldn't have them—they wouldn't have fit—and then I gave her mine."

Lila looked down at Kell's bare feet, and burst into laughter. Kell was leaning over her then, pressing a hand over her mouth—*You'll wake the boat*—a ghost of whisper, a caress of air—and she fell back onto the cot, taking him down with her.

"Dammit, Lila." He caught himself just before he slammed his head against the wall. The bed really wasn't big enough for two. "How much did you have to drink?"

Lila's laughter died away. "Never used to drink in company," she mused aloud. Odd to feel herself speaking even though she didn't think to do it. The words just spilled out. "Didn't want to get caught unawares."

"And now?"

That flickering grin. "I think I could take you."

He lowered himself until his hair brushed Lila's temple. "Is that so?" But then something caught his eye through the port window. "There's a ship out there."

Lila's head spun. "How can you see it in the dark?"

Kell frowned. "Because it's burning."

Lila was up in an instant, the world tipping beneath her bare feet. She dug her nails deep into her palms, hoping the pain would clear her head. Danger would have to do the rest.

"What does it mean?" Kell was asking, but she was already sprinting up the stairs.

"Alucard!" she called as she reached the deck.

For a brief, terrible second, the *Ghost* stretched quiet around her, the deck empty, and Lila thought she was too late, but there were no corpses, and a second later the captain was there, Hastra, too, still cradling his egg. Lenos appeared, rubbing the sleep from his eyes, shoulders tensed like he'd woken from bad dreams. Kell caught up, barefoot as he tugged on his coat.

In the distance, the ship burned, a flare of red and gold against the night.

Alucard came to a halt beside her.

"*Sanct,*" he swore, the flames reflected in his eyes.

"*Mas aven . . .*" started Lenos.

And then he made a strange sound, like a hiccup caught in his throat, and Lila turned in time to see the barbed blade protruding from his chest before he was wrenched back over the side, and the Sea Serpents boarded the *Ghost*.

III

For months, Kell had trained alone beneath the royal palace, leaving his sweat and blood to stain the Basin floors. There he'd faced a hundred enemies and fought a hundred forms, sharpened his mind and his magic, learned to use anything and everything at hand, all of it preparing—not for the tournament, which he'd never thought of entering—but for this very moment. So that when death came for him again, he would be ready.

He had trained for a fight in the palace.

Trained for a fight in the streets.

Trained for a fight in daylight and in darkness.

But Kell hadn't thought to train for a fight at sea.

Without Alucard's power filling the sails, the canvases collapsed, twisting the *Ghost* so the water struck sidelong, rocking the ship as the mercenaries spilled onto the deck.

All that was left of Lenos, after the short and fleeting splash, were the drops of blood dappling the wood. A square of calm in a night turned wild—water and wind in Kell's ears, wood and steel beneath his feet, all of it pitching and rolling as if caught in a storm. It was so much louder and sharper than those imagined battles in the Basin, so much more terrifying than those games in the *Essen Tasch,* that for an instant—*only an instant*—Kell froze.

But then the first shout cut the air, and a flash of water surged into ice as Alucard drew a blade from the dark sea, and there was no time to think, no time to plan, no time to do anything but *fight.*

Kell lost sight of Lila within moments, relying on the threads of her magic—the persistent hum of her power in his veins—to tell him she remained alive as the *Ghost* plunged into chaos.

Hastra was grappling with a shadow, his back to the mast, and Kell flicked his wrist, freeing the slivers of steel he kept sheathed within his cuff as the first two killers came for him. His steel nails flew as they had in the Basin so many times, but now they pierced hearts instead of dummies, and for every shadow he killed, another came.

Steel whispered behind him, and Kell turned in time to dodge an assassin's knife. It still found flesh, but sliced his cheek instead of his throat. Pain registered as a distant thing, sharpened only by sea air as his fingers brushed the cut and then caught the assassin's wrist. Ice blossomed up his arm, and Kell let go just as another shadow caught him around the waist and slammed him sideways into the ship's rail.

The wood broke beneath the force, and the two went crashing down into the sea. The surface was a frozen wall, knocking the air from Kell's lungs, icy water flooding in as he grappled with the killer, the churning darkness broken only by the light of the burning ship somewhere above. Kell tried to will the water calm, or at least clear it from his eyes, but the ocean was too big, and even if he'd drawn on Holland and Lila both it wouldn't have been enough. He was running out of air, and he couldn't stomach the thought of Rhy, a London away, gasping for breath again. He had no choice. The next time the killer slashed with a curved knife, Kell let the blow land.

A gasp escaped in a stream of air as the blade sliced his coat sleeve and bit deep into his arm. Instantly the water began to cloud with blood.

"*As Steno,*" he said, the words muffled by the water, his last expelled breath, but still audible and brimming with intent. The mercenary went rigid as his body turned from human flesh to stone and plummeted down toward the sea floor. Kell surged urgently upward in reflected movement and broke through the surface of the waves. From where he was, he could see the attackers' shallow rafts, handholds spelled from wood and steel leading up from the water to the *Ghost*'s deck.

Kell climbed, his arm throbbing and his waterlogged clothes weighing him down with every upward step, but he made it, hauling himself over the side.

"Sir, look out!"

Kell spun as the killer came at him, but the man was drawn up short by Hastra's sword slashing through his back. The assassin folded, and Kell found himself staring into the young guard's terrified eyes. Blood splattered Hastra's face and hands and curls. He looked unsteady on his feet.

"Are you hurt?" asked Kell urgently.

Hastra shook his head. "No, sir," he said, his voice trembling.

"Good," said Kell, retrieving the assassin's knife. "Then let's take back this ship."

IV

Holland was sitting on his cot, studying the band of silver on his thumb, when he heard Lila storming up the stairs, heard the splash of something heavy breaking water, the tread of too many feet.

He rose, and was halfway to the door when the floor tilted and his vision plunged into black, all of his power bottoming out for a sudden, lurching moment.

He scrambled for strength, felt his knees hit the floor, his body a thing severed from his power as someone else pulled on his magic as if it were a rope.

For a terrifying instant, there was nothing, and then, just as suddenly, the room was back, resolving just as it had been before, only now there were shouts overhead, and a burning ship beyond the window, and someone was coming down the steps.

Holland forced himself up, his head still spinning from the shortness of magic.

He tore the abandoned chains from the wall, wrapped them around his hands, and staggered out into the corridor.

Two strangers were coming toward him.

"*Kers la?*" said one as he let himself stumble, fall.

"A prisoner," said a second, seeing the glint of metal and assuming—wrongly—that Holland was still bound.

He heard the hiss of blades sliding free from sheaths as he drew his borrowed power back in like a breath.

Holland's blood sang, magic flooding his veins anew as the

intruder's hand tangled in his hair, wrenching his head back to expose his throat. For a single beat, he let them think they'd won, let them think it would be so easy, and could almost feel their guard lower, their tension ebb.

And then he sprang, twisting up and free in a smooth, almost careless motion and wrapping the chains around his foe's throat before turning the vise from iron to stone. He let go and the man toppled forward, clawing uselessly at his neck as Holland drew the blade from his hip and sliced the second man's throat.

Or tried to.

The killer was fast, dodging back one step, two, dancing around the blade the way Ojka used to, but Ojka never stumbled, and the killer did, erring just long enough for Holland to knock him over and drive the sword down through his back, skewering the man to the floor.

Holland stepped over the writhing bodies and toward the steps.

The scythe came out of nowhere, singing in its special way.

If Athos and Astrid hadn't favored the vicious curls of steel, if Holland hadn't dreamed of using the curved blades to cut their throats—he would have never recognized the tone, would not have known how and when to duck.

He dropped to a knee as the scythe embedded in the wall above his head, and turned just in time to catch a second blade with his bare hands. The steel cut quick and deep, even as he fought to cushion the blow, willing metal and air and bone. The killer leaned into the blade, and Holland's blood dripped thickly to the floor, triumph turning to fear on the man's face as he realized what he'd done.

"*As Isera,*" said Holland, and ice surged out from his ruined palms, swallowing blade and skin in the space of a breath.

The scythe slipped from frozen fingers, Holland's own hands singing with pain. The cuts were deep, but before he could bind them, before he could do anything, a cord wrapped around his throat. His hands went for his neck, but two more cords came out of nowhere, cinching each wrist and forcing his arms wide.

"Hold him," ordered an assassin, stepping over and around the few bodies littering the corridor. In one hand she held a hook. "They want the eye intact."

Holland didn't lash out. He went still, taking stock of their weapons and counting the lives he'd add to his list.

As the killer stalked toward him, his hands began to prickle with unfamiliar heat. The echo of someone else's magic.

Lila.

Holland smiled, wrapped his fingers around the ropes, and pulled—not on the cords themselves, but on the other *Antari*'s spell.

Fire erupted down the ropes.

The twisted threads snapped like bones, and Holland was free. With a slash of his hand, the lanterns shattered, the corridor went dark, and he was on them.

V

The Sea Serpents were good.

Frighteningly good.

Certainly better than the Copper Thieves, better than all the pirates Lila had come across in those months at sea.

The Serpents fought like it mattered.

Fought like their lives were on the line.

But so did she.

Lila ducked as a curved blade embedded itself in the mast behind her, spun away from a sword as it cut the air. Someone tried to loop a cord around her throat, but she caught it, twisted free, and slid her knife between a stranger's ribs.

Magic thudded through her veins, drawing the ship in lines of life. The Serpents moved like shadows, but to Lila, they shone with light. Her blades slipped under guards, found flesh, freed blood.

A fist caught her jaw, a knife grazed her thigh, but she didn't stop, didn't slow. She was humming with power, some of it hers and some of it borrowed and all of it blazing.

Blood ran into Lila's good eye, but she didn't care because every time she took a life, she saw Lenos.

Lenos, who'd feared her.

Lenos, who'd been kind despite that.

Lenos, who'd called her a portent, a sign of change.

Lenos, who'd seen her, before she knew to recognize herself.

Lenos, who'd died with a barb in his chest and the same sad confusion she'd felt in the alley at Rosenal, the same horrible understanding scrawled across his face,

She could feel Kell and Holland fighting too, on opposite sides of the ship, feel the flex and pull of their magic in her veins, their pain a phantom limb.

If the Serpents had magic, they weren't using it. Perhaps they were just trying to avoid damaging the *Ghost,* since they'd already sunk their own ship, but Lila would be damned if she went down trying to spare this shitty little craft. Fire flared in her hands. The floorboards groaned as she pulled on them. The ship tipped violently beneath her.

She would sink the whole fucking boat if she had to.

But she didn't get the chance. A hand shot out and grabbed her by the collar, hauling her behind a crate. She freed the knife from her hidden arm sheath, but the attacker's other hand—so much larger than her own—caught her wrist and pinned it back against the wood beside her head.

It was Jasta, towering over her, and for a moment Lila thought the captain was trying to help, trying for some reason to pull her out of harm's way, to spare her from the fight. Then she saw the body slumped on the deck.

Hano.

The girl's eyes shone in the dark, open, empty, a clean cut across her throat.

Anger rolled through Lila as understanding struck. Jasta's insistence on steering the *Ghost,* on going with them to the floating market. The sudden danger on the docks at Rosenal. The drinking game, earlier this evening, with its too-strong drink.

"You're with them."

Jasta didn't deny it. Only flashed a ruthless smile.

Lila's will ground against the turncoat captain's, and the other woman was forced back, away. "Why?"

The woman shrugged. "Out here, coin is king."

Lila lunged, but Jasta was twice as fast as she looked, and just as strong, and a second later Lila was being slammed back into the side of the ship, the rail catching her in the ribs hard enough to knock the air from her lungs.

Jasta stood exactly where she'd been before, looking almost bored.

"My orders are to kill the Arnesian princeling," she said, freeing a blade from her hip. "No one ever told me what to do with you."

Cold hatred surged through Lila's veins, overtaking even the heat of power. "If you wanted to kill me, you should have done it already."

"But I do not *have* to kill you," said Jasta as the ship continued to swarm with menacing shadows. "You are a thief and I am a pirate, but we are both knives. I see it in you. You know you don't belong. Not here, with them."

"You're wrong."

"You can pretend all you like," sneered Jasta. "Change your clothes. Change your language. Change your face. But you will always be a knife, and knives are good for one thing and one thing only: cutting."

Lila let her hands fall back to her side, as if considering the traitor's words. Blood dripped from her fingers, and her lips moved slowly, almost imperceptibly, the words—As Athera—lost beneath Jasta's preening and the clash of metal to every side.

Lila raised her voice. "Maybe you're right."

Jasta's smile widened. "I know how to spot a knife, always have. And I can teach you—"

Lila clenched her fist, pulling on the wood, and the crates behind Jasta slammed forward. The woman spun, tried to dodge, but Lila's whispered magic had worked—As Athera, to grow—and the ship boards had branched up over Jasta's boots while she was gloating. She went crashing to the deck beneath the heavy boxes.

Jasta let out a strangled curse in a language Lila didn't speak, her leg pinned beneath the weight, the snap of bone hanging on the air.

Lila squatted in front of her.

"Maybe you're right," she said again, lifting her blade to Jasta's throat. "And maybe you're wrong. We don't choose what we are, but we choose what we do." The knife was poised to bite in.

"Make sure you cut deep," goaded Jasta as blood welled around the tip, spilling in thin lines down her throat.

"No," said Lila, withdrawing.

"You won't kill me?" she sneered.

"Oh, I will," said Lila. "But not until you tell me everything."

VI

The ship was blood and steel and death.

And then it wasn't.

There was no in between.

The last body crumpled to the deck at Kell's feet, and it was over. He could tell by the silence, and the sudden stilling of the threads that ran between him and Holland and Lila.

Kell swayed from exhaustion as Holland strode up the stairs, stepping over a shining pool of wetness, his hands a mess of torn flesh. In the same moment, Alucard appeared, cradling one arm against his chest. Someone had torn the sapphire from his brow, and blood ran into his eye, turning the storm grey a violent blue.

Nearby, Hastra sagged onto a crate, still shaking and pale. Kell touched the young guard's shoulder.

"Was this the first time you took a life?"

Hastra swallowed, nodded. "I always knew that life was fragile," he said hoarsely. "Keeping something alive is hard enough. But ending it . . ." He trailed off, and then, quite abruptly, turned and retched onto the deck.

"It's all right," said Kell, kneeling over him, his own body screaming from a dozen minor wounds as well as the hollowness that always followed a fight.

After a few seconds Hastra straightened, wiping his mouth on his sleeve. "I think I'm ready to be a priest. Do you think Tieren will take me back?"

Kell squeezed the boy's shoulder. "We can talk to him," he said, "when we get home."

Hastra managed to smile. "I'd like that."

"Where's Bard?" cut in Alucard.

Lila appeared a moment later, hauling the massive, hobbled form of the *Ghost*'s captain behind her.

Kell stared in shock as Lila forced Jasta to her knees on the deck. The woman's face was swollen and streaked with blood, her hands bound with coarse rope, one leg clearly broken.

"Lila, what are you—"

"Why don't you tell them?" said Lila, nudging Jasta with her boot. When the woman only snarled, Lila said, "It was her."

Alucard made a disgusted sound. "*Tac,* Jasta. The Sea Serpents?"

It was the woman's turn to sneer. "We can't all be crown pets."

Kell's tired mind turned. It was one thing to be attacked by pirates. It was another to be made bounty. "Who hired you?"

"I found these on her," said Lila, producing a pouch of blue gems. Not just any kind, but the small oval chips used to adorn a Faroan's face.

"Sol-in-Ar," muttered Kell. "What was your task?"

When Jasta answered by spitting on the deck, Lila drove her boot down into the woman's wounded leg. A snarl escaped her throat.

"Killing the traitor would have been a perk," she growled. "I was hired to slaughter the black-eyed prince." Her gaze drifted up to meet Kell's. "And a Serpent doesn't stop until the job is done."

The knife came out of nowhere.

One moment Jasta's hands were empty, and the next, her last, hidden piece of steel was free and flying toward Kell's heart. His mind caught up before his limbs, and his hands rose, too slow, too late.

He would wonder for weeks, months, years, if he could have stopped it.

If he could have summoned the strength to will the steel away.

But in that moment, he had nothing left to give.

The blade struck home, embedding to the hilt.

Kell staggered back, braced for a pain that never came.

Hastra's curls floated up before his eyes, touched with gold even in the dark. The boy had moved like light, lunging between Kell and the knife, his arms not up to block the blade, but out, as if to catch it.

It took him in the heart.

An animal sound tore from Kell's throat as Hastra—Hastra, who made things grow, who would have been a priest, who could have been anything he wanted and chose to be a guard, *Kell's* guard—staggered, and fell.

"No!" he cried, catching the young man's body before it hit the deck. He was already so quiet, so still, already gone, but Kell had to say something, had to do something. What was the use of so much power if people still kept dying?

"As Hasari," he pleaded, pressing his palm to Hastra's chest, even as the last rhythms of a pulse faded beneath Kell's hands.

It was too late.

He had been too late.

Even magic had its limits.

And Hastra was already gone.

Curls tumbled back from eyes that had once—*just*—been lit with life, that now sat dark, still, open.

Kell lowered Hastra's body, dragging the knife free of his guard's chest as he rose. His chest was heaving, ragged breaths tearing free. He wanted to scream. He wanted to sob.

Instead he crossed the deck, and cut Jasta's throat.

VII

Rhy groaned in pain.

It wasn't a sudden, lancing blow, but the deep ache of muscles pushed too far, of energy drained. His head pounded and his heart raced as he sat up, trying to ground himself in the silk sheets, the warmth of the fire still smoldering in the hearth.

You are here, he told himself, trying to disentangle his mind from the nightmare.

In the dream, he had been drowning.

Not the way he'd almost drowned on the balcony, just hours—days?—ago when Kell had followed Holland into the river. No, this was slower. Rhy's dream-self had been sinking, deeper and deeper into a wave-wracked grave, the pressure of the water crushing the air from his lungs.

But the pain Rhy felt now hadn't followed him out of the dream.

It didn't belong to him at all.

It belonged to Kell.

Rhy reached for the royal pin on the table, wishing he could see what was happening to his brother instead of only feeling the effects. Sometimes he thought he did, in glimpses and dreams, but nothing stuck, nothing ever stayed.

Rhy curled his fingers around the spelled circlet of gold, waiting to feel the heat of Kell's summons, and only then did he realize how helpless he truly was. How useless to Kell. He could summon his brother, but Kell wouldn't—or couldn't—ever summon him.

Rhy slumped back against the pillows, clutching the pin to his chest.

The pain was already fading, an echo of an echo, a tide receding, leaving only dull discomfort and fear in its wake.

He'd never get back to sleep.

The decanters on the sideboard glinted in the low firelight, calling, and he rose to pour himself a drink, adding a single drop of Tieren's tonic to the amber liquid. Rhy raised the glass to his lips, but didn't swallow. Something else had caught his eye. His armor. It lay stretched like a sleeping body on his sofa, gauntleted arms folded on its chest. There was no need of it now, not with the city fast asleep, but it still called to him, louder than the tonic, louder even than the darkness—always worst before dawn.

Rhy set the glass aside, and took up the golden helm.

VIII

Myths do not happen all at once.

They do not spring forth whole into the world. They form slowly, rolled between the hands of time until their edges smooth, until the saying of the story gives enough weight to the words—to the memories—to keep them rolling on their own.

But all stories start somewhere, and that night, as Rhy Maresh walked through the streets of London, a new myth was taking shape.

This was the story of a prince who watched over his city as it slept. Who went on foot, for fear of trampling one of the fallen, who wove his way between the bodies of his people.

Some would say he moved in silence, with only the gentle clang of his golden-armored steps echoing like distant bells through the silent street.

Some would say he spoke, that even in the far-off darkness, the sleeping heard him whisper, over and over, "You are not alone."

Some would say it never happened at all.

Indeed, there was no one there to see.

But Rhy *did* walk among them, because he was their prince, and because he could not sleep, and because he knew what it was like to be held by a spell, to be dragged into darkness, to be bound to something and yet feel utterly alone.

A sheen of frost was settling over his people, making them look more like statues than men and women and children. The prince had seen fallen trees slowly swallowed by moss, pieces of the world slowly reclaimed, and as he moved through the crowd of fallen, he wondered what would happen if London stayed under this spell a month, a season, a year.

Would the world climb up over the sleeping bodies?

Would it claim them, inch by inch?

It began to snow in earnest (strange, close as they were to spring, but not the strangest thing befalling London, then), and so Rhy brushed the ice from still cheeks, tore canvas down from the ghostly bones of the night market, and took blankets from homes now haunted only with the memories of breath. And patiently, the prince covered each and every person he found, though they did not seem to feel the cold beneath their shrouded safety of spellwork and sleep.

The chill ate at the prince's fingers. It seeped through armor and into aching skin, but Rhy did not turn back, did not break his vigil until the first light of day broke the shell of darkness and the dawn thinned the frost. Only then did the prince return to the palace, and fall into bed, and sleep.

TWELVE

BETRAYAL

I

Dawn broke in silence over the *Ghost*.

They'd dumped the bodies overboard—Hano, with her throat cut, and Ilo, whom they'd found dead below, Jasta, who'd betrayed them all, and every last one of the Serpents.

Hastra alone had been wrapped in a blanket. Kell fastened the fabric carefully around the boy's legs, waist, shoulders, sparing his face—the shy smile gone, the glossy curls now lank—as long as possible.

Sailors went into the sea, but Hastra wasn't a sailor. He was a royal guard.

If they'd had flowers on the ship, Kell would have laid one on the rent over Hastra's heart—that was the custom, in Arnes, to mark a mortal wound.

He thought of the blossom waiting back in the Basin, the one Hastra had made for Kell that day, coaxing life from a clod of dirt, a drop of water, a seed, the sum more than its parts, a sliver of light in a darkening world. Would it still be there, when they returned home? Or had it already withered?

If Lenos were there, he could have said something, sent a prayer to the nameless saints, but Lenos was gone too, lost to the tide, and Kell didn't have any flowers, didn't have any prayers, didn't have anything but the hollow anger swimming in his heart.

"*Anoshe,*" he murmured as the body went over the side.

They should have cleaned the deck, but there seemed no point. The *Ghost*—what was left of it—would reach Tanek within the day.

His body swayed with fatigue.

He hadn't slept. None of them had.

Holland was focused on keeping wind in the sails while Alucard stood numbly at the wheel—power was precious, but Lila had insisted on healing the captain's wounds. Kell supposed he couldn't fault her. Alucard Emery had done his share to keep the ship afloat.

Lila herself stood nearby, tipping the Faroan gems from hand to hand, staring down at the blue chips, her brow furrowed in thought.

"What is it?" he asked.

"I killed a Faroan once," she mused, tipping the gems back into her first hand. "During the tournament."

"You *what*?" started Kell, hoping he'd misheard, that he wouldn't feel compelled to mention this to Rhy—or worse, Maxim—once they docked. "When would you have—"

"That's not the point of the story," she chided, letting the gems tumble between her fingers. "Have you ever seen a Faroan part with these? Ever seen one trade in anything but coin?"

Kell frowned a little. "No."

"That's because the gems are set into their skin. Couldn't pluck one off if you wanted to, not without a knife."

"I hadn't noticed."

Lila shrugged, holding her hand out over a crate. "It's the kind of thing you think about, when you're a thief."

She tipped her hand, and the gems clattered onto the wooden top. "And when I killed that Faroan, the gems in his face came free. Fell away, like whatever was holding them in place was gone."

Kell's eyes widened. "You don't think these came from a Faroan."

"Oh, I'm sure they did," said Lila, taking up a single gem. "But I doubt they had a choice."

II

Maxim finished his spell sometime after dawn.

He slumped back against the table and admired his work, the faceless men standing in formation, their armored chests locked over steel hearts. Twelve deep cuts ran along the inside of the king's arm, some healing and others fresh. Twelve pieces of steel-clad spellwork bound together before him, forged and welded and made whole.

The strain of binding the magic was grueling, a constant pull on his power, amplifying with every added shell. His body trembled faintly with the weight, but it would not take long, once the task was started. Maxim would manage.

He straightened—the room spun dangerously for several seconds before it settled—and went downstairs to share a last meal with his wife, his son. A farewell without the words. Emira would understand, and Rhy, he hoped, would forgive him. The book would help.

As Maxim walked, he imagined sitting with them in the grand salon, the table covered in pots of tea and fresh-baked bread. Emira's hand on his. Rhy's laughter spilling over. And Kell, where he had always been, sitting at his brother's side.

Maxim let his tired mind live within this dream, this memory, let it carry him forward.

Just one last meal.

One last time.

"Your Majesty!"

Maxim sighed, turning. His last dream died at the sight of the royal guards holding a man between them. The captive wore the purple-and-white wraps of the Faroan entourage, silver veins running like molten metal between the gems on his dark skin. Sol-in-Ar stormed down the hall after the men, closing the distance with every stride.

"Unhand him," ordered the Faroan lord.

"What is the meaning of this?" asked Maxim, fatigue wearing down every muscle, every bone.

One of the guards held out a letter. "We stopped him, Your Majesty, trying to slip out of the palace."

"A messenger?" demanded Maxim, rounding on Sol-in-Ar.

"Are we not permitted to send letters?" challenged the Faroan lord. "I did not realize we were prisoners here."

Maxim moved to tear the letter open, but Sol-in-Ar caught his wrist.

"Do not make an enemy of allies," he warned in his sibilant way. "You have enough of the former already."

Maxim drew his wrist free and sliced open the letter in a single, fluid gesture, eyes flitting over the Faroan script. "You called for reinforcements."

"We are in *need* of them," said Sol-in-Ar.

"No." Maxim's head pounded. "You will only draw more lives into the fray—"

"Perhaps if you had *told* us about your priests' spell—"

"—more lives for Osaron to claim and use against us *all*."

The Veskan prince had arrived by now, and Maxim turned his ire on him, too. "And you? Have the Veskans sent word beyond the city, too?"

Col paled. "And risk their lives as well? Of course not."

Sol-in-Ar glared at the Veskan prince. "You are lying."

Maxim didn't have the energy for this. He didn't have the time.

"Confine Lord Sol-in-Ar and his entourage to their rooms."

The Faroan stared at him, aghast. "King Maresh—"

"You have two choices," cut in Maxim, "your rooms, or the royal prison. And for your sake, and ours, I hope you only sent one man."

When Maxim's men led Sol-in-Ar away, he didn't protest, didn't fight. He said only one thing, the words soft, strained.

"You're making a mistake."

The Maresh family wasn't sitting in the grand salon. The chairs stood empty. The table hadn't been set—it wouldn't be for hours, he realized. The sun wasn't even up.

Maxim's body was beginning to shake.

He didn't have the strength to keep searching, so he returned to the royal chambers, hoping vainly that Emira would be there, waiting for him. His heart sank when he found the room empty, even as some small part of him exhaled, relieved at being spared the drawn-out pain of parting.

With trembling hands, he began setting his affairs in order. He finished dressing, cleared his desk, set the text he'd written for his son in the center.

The spell was pulling on Maxim with every breath, every heartbeat, threads of magic drawn taut through walls and down stairs, leaching energy with every unused moment.

Soon, the king promised the spell. Soon.

He penned three letters, one to Rhy, one to Kell, and the last to Emira, all too long and far too short. Maxim had always been a man of action, not words. And time was running out.

He was just blowing on the ink when he heard the door open.

His heart quickened, hope rising as he turned, expecting to find his wife.

"My dearest . . ." He trailed off at the sight of the girl, fair and blond and dressed in green, a crown of silver in her hair and crimson splashed like paint across her front.

The Veskan princess smiled. She had four polished blades between her fingers, thin as needles and each dripping blood, and when she spoke, her voice was easy, bright, as if she weren't trespassing in the royal chamber, as if there were no bodies in the hall behind her, no blood smeared on her brow.

"Your Majesty! I was hoping you'd be here."

Maxim held his ground. "Princess, what are you—"

Before he could finish, the first blade came sailing through the air, and by the time the king had his hand up, magic rising to turn the blow, a second knife was driving down through his boot, pinning his foot to the floor.

A growl of pain escaped as Maxim attempted to pivot, even so, to avoid a third blade, only to take a fourth through the arm. This one hadn't flown—it was still in his attacker's hand as she drove the steel in deep above his elbow, pinning his arm back against the wall.

It had taken less than a full breath.

The Veskan princess was standing on tiptoes as if she meant to kiss him. She was so young, to seem so old.

"You don't look well," she said.

Maxim's head pounded. He'd given too much of himself to the spell. Had too little strength left to summon magic for a fight. But there was still the blade sheathed at his hip. Another on his calf. His fingers twitched, but before he could grab either, one of Cora's discarded blades sailed back into her fingers.

She brought it to rest against his throat.

Maxim's arm and foot were going numb—not from pain alone, but something else.

"Poison," he growled.

Her head bobbed. "It won't kill you," she said cheerfully. "That's my job. But you've been a lovely host."

"What have you done? You foolish girl."

Her smile sharpened into a sneer. "This foolish girl will bring glory to her name. This foolish girl will take your palace and hand your kingdom to her own."

She leaned in close, voice slipping from sweet to sensual. "But first, this foolish girl will cut your throat."

Through the open door, Maxim saw the fallen bodies of his guards littering the hall, their armored arms and legs sprawled motionless across the carpet.

And then he saw the streak of dark skin, the shine of gems like tears catching the light.

"You are out of your depth, Princess," he said as the numbness spread through his limbs and the Faroans slipped silently forward, Sol-in-Ar in the lead. "Killing a king grants you only one thing."

"And what is that?" she whispered.

Maxim met her eyes. "A slow death."

Cora's blade bit in as the Faroans flooded the room.

In a flash, Sol-in-Ar had the murderous girl back against him, one arm around her throat.

She spun the needlelike knife in her hand, moved to drive the point into the Faroan's leg, but the others were on her fast, holding her arms, forcing her to her knees before Maxim.

The king tried to speak, and found his tongue heavy in his mouth, his body fighting too many foes between the poison and the cost of spent magic.

"Find the Arnesian guards!" ordered Sol-in-Ar.

Cora fought then, viciously, violently, all the girlish humor stripped away as they divested her of blades.

Maxim finally wrenched the knife free of his arm with half-numbed fingers and unpinned his foot, blood squelching in his boot as he moved with uneven steps to the sideboard.

He found the tonics Tieren kept mixed for him, those for pain and those for sleep, and one, just one, for poison, and poured himself a glass of the rosy liquid, as if he were simply thirsty and not fighting back death.

His fingers shook but he drank deeply, and set the empty glass aside as the feeling returned in a flush of heat, bringing pain with it. A new wave of guards appeared in the doorway, all of them breathless and armed, Isra at the front.

"Your Majesty," she said, scanning the room and paling at the sight of the slight Veskan princess pinned to the floor, the Faroan lord giving orders instead of bound to his palace wing, the discarded knives and bloody trail of steps.

Maxim forced himself to straighten. "See to your guards," he ordered.

"Your wounds," started Isra, but the king cut her off.

"I am not so easily dispatched." He turned to Sol-in-Ar. It had been a near thing, and they both knew it, but the Faroan lord said nothing.

"I am in your debt," said Maxim. "And I will repay it." Fearing he might fall over if he lingered long, Maxim turned his attention to the Veskan girl kneeling on his floor. "You failed, little princess, and it will cost you."

Cora's blue eyes were bright. "Not as much as you," she said, her mouth splitting into a cold smile. "Unlike me, my brother Col has *never* missed his marks."

Maxim's blood ran cold as he spun on Isra and the other guards. "Where is the queen?"

III

Rhy hadn't gone looking for his mother.

He found her entirely by accident.

Before the nightmares, he had always slept late. He'd lie in bed all morning, marveling at the way his pillows felt softest after sleep, or the way light moved against the canopied ceiling. For the first twenty years of his life, Rhy's bed had been his favorite place in the palace.

Now he couldn't wait to be rid of it.

Every time his body sank into the cushions, he felt the darkness reaching up, folding its arm around him. Every time his mind slid toward sleep, the shadows were there to meet him.

These days Rhy rose early, desperate for the light.

It didn't matter that he'd spent the better part of the night holding vigil in the streets, didn't matter that his head was cloudy, his limbs stiff and sore and aching with the echo of someone else's fight. The lack of sleep worried him less than what he found in his dreams.

The sun was just cresting the river as Rhy woke, the rest of the palace still likely folded in their troubled sleep. He could have called a servant—there were always two or three awake—but instead he dressed himself, not in the princely armor or in the formal red-and-golds, but in the soft black cut he sometimes wore within the interior rooms of the palace.

It was almost an afterthought, the sword, the weapon at odds with the rest of his attire. Maybe it was Kell's absence. Maybe it was Tieren's sleep. Maybe it was the way his father grew paler by the day, or maybe he'd simply grown used to wearing it. Whatever the reason, Rhy took up his royal short sword, fastened the belt around his hips.

He made his way absently to the salon, his sleep-starved mind half expecting to find the king and queen taking breakfast, but of course it was empty. From there he wandered toward the gallery, but turned back at the first sounds of voices, low and worried and wondering questions to which he didn't have the answers.

Rhy retreated, first to the training rooms, filled with the exhausted remains of the royal guard, and then to the map room, in search of his father, who wasn't there. Rhy went to ballroom after ballroom, looking for peace, for quiet, for a shred of normalcy, and finding silvers, nobles, priests, magicians, questions.

By the time he wandered into the Jewel, he just wanted to be alone.

Instead, Rhy Maresh found the queen.

She was standing at the center of the massive glass chamber, her head bowed as if in prayer.

"What are you doing, Mother?" The words were said softly, but his voice echoed through the hollow room.

Emira raised her head. "Listening."

Rhy looked around, as if there might be something—or someone—he hadn't noticed. But they were alone in the vast chamber. Beneath his feet, the floor was marked with half-finished circles, the beginnings of spells made when the palace was under attack and abandoned once Tieren's spell had taken hold, and the ceiling rose high overhead, blossoms winding around thin crystal columns.

His mother reached out and ran her fingers along the nearest one.

"Do you remember," she said, her voice carrying, "when you thought the spring blossoms were all edible?"

His steps sounded on the glass floor, causing the room to sing faintly as he moved toward her. "It was Kell's fault. He's the one who insisted they were."

"And you believed him. You made yourself so sick."

"I got him back, though, remember? When I challenged him to see who could eat the most summer cakes. He didn't realize until the first bite the cooks had made them all with lime." A soft laugh escaped at the memory of Kell resisting the urge to spit it out, and getting ill into a marble planter. "We got into a fair amount of mischief."

"You say that as though you ever stopped." Emira's hand fell away from the column. "When I first came to the palace, I hated this room." She said it absently, but Rhy knew his mother—knew that nothing she said or did was ever without meaning.

"Did you?" he prompted.

"What could be worse, I thought, than a ballroom made of glass? It was only a matter of time before it broke. And then one day, oh, I was so angry at your father—I don't remember why—but I wanted to break something, so I came in here, to this fragile room, and pounded on the walls, the floor, the columns. I beat my hands on the crystal and the glass until my knuckles were raw. But no matter what I did, the Jewel would not break."

"Even glass can be strong," said Rhy, "if it is thick enough."

A flickering smile, there and then gone, and there again, the first one real, the second set. "I raised a smart son."

Rhy ran a hand through his hair. "You raised *me*, too."

She frowned at that, the way she had at his quips so many times before. Frowned in a way that reminded him of Kell, not that he would ever say so.

"Rhy," she said. "I never meant—"

Behind them, a man cleared his throat. Rhy turned to find Prince Col standing in the doorway, his clothing wrinkled and his hair mussed, as though he'd never been to bed.

"I hope I am not interrupting?" said the Veskan, a subtle tension in his voice that set the prince on edge.

"No," answered the queen coolly at the same time Rhy said, "Yes."

Col's blue eyes flicked between them, clearly registering their discomfort, but he didn't withdraw. Instead he stepped forward into the Jewel, letting the doors swing shut behind him.

"I was looking for my sister."

Rhy remembered the bruises around Cora's wrist. "She isn't here."

The Veskan prince gave the room a sweeping look. "So I see," he said, ambling toward them. "Your palace really is magnificent." He moved at a casual pace, as if admiring the room, but his eyes kept flicking back toward Rhy, toward the queen. "Every time I think I've seen it all, I find another room."

A sword hung at his hip, a jeweled hilt marking the blade for show, but Rhy's hackles still rose at the sight of it, at the prince's carriage, his very presence. And then Emira's attention flicked suddenly upward, as if she'd heard something Rhy couldn't.

"Maxim."

His father's name was a strangled whisper on the queen's lips, and she started toward the doors, only to come up short as Col drew his weapon free.

In that one gesture, everything about the Veskan changed. His youthful arrogance evaporated, the casual air replaced by something grim, determined. Col may have been a prince, but he held his sword with the calm control of a soldier.

"What are you doing?" demanded Rhy.

"Isn't it obvious?" Col's grip tightened on the blade. "I'm winning a war before it starts."

"Lower your blade," ordered the queen.

"Apologies, Your Highness, but I can't."

Rhy searched the prince's eyes, hoping to see the shadow of corruption, to find a will twisted by the curse beyond the palace walls, and shuddered when he found them green and clear.

Whatever Col was doing, he was doing it by choice.

Somewhere beyond the doors, a shout went up, the words smothered, lost.

"For what it's worth," said the Veskan prince, raising his blade. "I really only came for the queen."

His mother spread her arms, the air around her fingers shimmering with frost. "Rhy," she said, her voice a plume of mist. "*Run.*"

Before the word was fully out, Col was surging forward.

The Veskan was fast, but Rhy was faster, or so it seemed as the queen's magic weighted Col's limbs. The icy air wasn't enough to stop the attack, but it slowed Col long enough for Rhy to throw himself in front of his mother, the blade meant for her driving instead into *his* chest.

Rhy gasped at the savage pain of steel piercing skin, and for an instant he was back in his rooms, a dagger thrust between his ribs and blood pouring between his hands, the horrible sear of torn flesh quickly giving way to numbing cold. But this pain was real, was hot, was giving way to nothing.

He could feel every terrible inch of metal from the entry wound just beneath his sternum to the exit wound below his shoulder. He coughed, spitting blood onto the glass floor, and his legs threatened to fold beneath him, but he managed to stay on his feet.

His body screamed, his mind screamed, but his heart kept beating stubbornly, *defiantly,* around the other prince's blade.

Rhy drew in a ragged breath, and raised his head.

"How . . . dare you," he growled, mouth filling with the copper taste of blood.

The victory on Col's face turned to shock. "Not possible," he stammered, and then, in horror, "*What are you?*"

"I am—Rhy Maresh," he answered. "Son to Maxim and Emira—brother to Kell—heir to this city—and the future king of Arnes."

Col's hands fell from the weapon. "But you should be *dead.*"

"I know," said Rhy, dragging his own blade from its sheath and driving the steel into Col's chest.

It was a mirror wound, but there was no spell to shield the Veskan prince. No magic to save him. No life to bind his own. The blade sank in. Rhy expected to feel guilt—or anger, or even triumph—as the blond boy collapsed, lifeless, but all he felt was relief.

Rhy dragged in another breath and wrapped his hands around the hilt of the sword still embedded in his chest. It came free, its length stained red.

He let it fall to the floor.

Only then did he hear the small gasp—a soundless cry—and feel his mother's cold fingers tightening on his arm. He turned toward her. Saw the red stain spreading across the front of her dress where the sword had driven in. Through him. Through her. There, just above her heart. The too-small hole of a too-great wound. His mother's eyes met his.

"Rhy," she said, a small, disconcerted crease between her brows, the same face she'd made a hundred times whenever he and Kell got into trouble, whenever he shouted or bit his nails or did anything that wasn't princely.

The furrow deepened, even as her eyes went glassy, one hand drifting toward the wound, and then she was falling. He caught her, stumbled as the sudden weight tore against his open, ruined chest.

"No, no, no," he said, sinking with her to the prismed floor. No, it wasn't fair. For once, he'd been fast enough. For once, he'd been strong enough. For once—

"Rhy," she said again, so gently—too gently.

"No."

Her bloody hands reached for his face, tried to cup his cheek, and missed, streaking red along his jaw.

"Rhy . . ."

His tears spilled over her fingers.

"No."

Her hand fell away, and her body slumped against him, still, and in that sudden stillness, Rhy's world narrowed to the spreading stain, the lingering furrow between his mother's eyes.

Only then did the pain come, folding over him with such sudden force, such horrible weight, that he clutched his chest and began to scream.

IV

Alucard stood at the ship's wheel, attention flicking between the three magicians on deck and the line of the sea. The *Ghost* felt wrong under his hands, too light, too long, a shoe made for someone else's foot. What he wouldn't have given for the steady bulk of the *Spire*. For Stross, and Tav, and Lenos—each name a shard of wood under his skin. And for Rhy—that name an even deeper wound.

Alucard had never longed so much for London.

The *Ghost* was making good time, but even with the cool, clear day and three recovering *Antari* keeping wind in the sails, someone still had to chart a course, and for all his posturing, Kell Maresh didn't know the first thing about steering ships, Holland could barely keep his food down, and Bard was a quick study but would always be a better thief than a sailor—not that he'd ever say so to her face. Thus the task of getting the *Ghost* to Tanek and the crew—what few were left—to London fell to him.

"What does it mean?" Bard's voice drifted up from the lower deck. She was standing close to the *Antari* prince while the latter held the Inheritor up to the sun.

Alucard winced, remembering what he'd gone through to get the blasted thing. The tip-off in Sasenroche. The boat to the cliffs at Hanas. The unmarked grave and the empty coffin and that was just the beginning, but it all made for a good story, and for Maris that was half the price.

And everyone paid. First timers most of all. If Maris didn't know you, she didn't trust you, and a modest prize was like to earn you a swift departure with no invitation to return, so Alucard had paid. Dug up that Inheritor and taken it all the way to Maris, and now here they were, and here it was, with him again.

Rhy's brother (Alucard discovered that he hated Kell a little less when he thought of him that way) was turning the device gingerly between his fingers while Bard leaned over him.

Holland was watching the others in silence, and so Alucard watched him. The third *Antari* didn't often speak, and when he did, his words were dry, disdainful. He had all the airs of someone who knew his own strength, and knew it went unequaled, at least in present company. Alucard might have liked him if he were a little less of an asshole. Or maybe a little more. He might have liked him, anyway, if he weren't a traitor. If he hadn't summoned the monster that now raged like a fire through London. The same monster that had killed Anisa.

"*Give* and *Take*," said Kell, squinting.

"Right," pressed Bard. "But how does it *work*?"

"I imagine you pierce your hand against the point," he explained.

"Give it here."

"This isn't a toy, Lila."

"And I'm not a child, Kell."

Holland cleared his throat. "We should all be familiar with it."

Kell rolled his eyes and took a last studying look before offering up the Inheritor.

Holland reached to take it when Kell gasped suddenly and let go. The cylinder tumbled from his fingers as he doubled over, a low groan escaping his throat.

Holland caught the Inheritor and Bard caught Kell. He'd gone white as a sail, one hand clutching his chest.

Alucard was on his feet, racing toward them, one word pounding through his head, his heart.

Rhy.
Rhy.
Rhy.

Magic flared in his vision as he reached Kell's side, scanning the silvery lines that coiled around the *Antari*. The knot at Kell's heart was still there, but the threads were glowing with a fiery light, pulsing faintly at some invisible strain.

Kell fought back a cry, the sound whistling through his clenched teeth.

"What is it?" demanded Alucard, barely able to hear his own words over that panicked echo in his blood. "What's happening?"

"The prince," Kell managed, his breath ragged.

I know that, he wanted to scream. "Is he alive?" Alucard realized the answer even before Kell scowled at him.

"Of course he's alive," snapped the *Antari,* fingers digging into his front. "But—he's been attacked."

"By who?"

"I don't know," growled Kell. "I'm not psychic."

"My money's on Vesk," offered Bard.

Kell let out a small hiccup of pain as the threads flared, singeing the air before dimming back to their usual silver glow.

Holland pocketed the Inheritor. "If he can't die, then there's no reason to worry."

"Of course there's a *reason,*" Kell shot back, forcing himself up. "Someone just tried to *murder* the prince of Arnes." He drew a royal pin from the pocket of his coat. "We have to go. Lila. Holland."

Alucard stared. "What about *me*?" His pulse was steadying, but his whole body still hummed with the animal panic, the need to act.

Kell pressed his thumb to the pin's tip, drawing blood. "You can stay with the ship."

"Not a chance," snarled Alucard, casting his gaze at the meager crew left on board.

Holland was just standing there, watching, but when Lila made as if to go to Kell's side, his pale fingers caught her arm. She glared at him, but he didn't let go, and Kell didn't look back, didn't wait to see if they were following as he brought the token to the wall.

Holland shook his head. "That won't work."

Kell wasn't listening. *"As Tascen—"*

The rest of the spell was cut off by a crack splitting the air, accompanied by the sudden pitch of the ship and Kell's stunned yelp as his body was forcefully hurled backward across the deck.

To Alucard's eyes, it looked like a Saint's Day firework had gone off in the middle of the *Ghost*.

A crackle of light, a sputter of energy, the silver of Kell's magic crashing against the blues and greens and reds of the natural world. Rhy's brother tried to stand up, holding his head, clearly surprised to find himself still on the ship.

"What in the ever-loving hell was that?" asked Bard.

Holland took a slow step forward, casting a shadow over Kell. "As I was saying, you cannot make a door on a moving craft. It defies the rules of transitional magic."

"Why didn't you tell me sooner?"

The other *Antari* raised a brow. "Obviously, I assumed you knew."

The color was coming back into Kell's face, the pained furrows fading, replaced by a hot flush.

"Until we reach land," continued Holland, "we're no better than ordinary magicians."

The disdain in his voice raked on Alucard's nerves. No wonder Bard was always trying to kill him.

Lila made a sound then, and Alucard turned in time to see Kell on his feet, hands lifted in the direction of the mast. The current of magic filled his vision, power tipping toward Kell like water in a glass. A second later the gust of wind hit the ship so hard its sails snapped and the whole thing made a low wooden groan.

"Careful!" shouted Alucard, sprinting toward the wheel as the ship banked hard beneath the sudden gale.

He got the *Ghost* back on course as Kell drove it on with a degree of focus—of concentrated force—he'd never seen the *Antari* use. A level of strength reserved not for London, or the king and queen, not for Rosenal, or Osaron himself.

But for Rhy, thought Alucard.

The same force of love that had broken the laws of the world and brought a brother back to life.

Threads of magic drew taut and bright as Kell forced his strength into the sails, Holland and Lila bracing themselves as he drew past the limits of his power and leaned on theirs.

Hold on, Rhy, thought Alucard, as the ship skated forward, rising until it skimmed the surface of the water, sea spray misting the air around them as the *Ghost* surged anew for London.

V

Rhy descended the prison stairs.

His steps were slow, bracing. It hurt to breathe, a pain that had nothing to do with the wound to his chest, and everything to do with the fact that his mother was dead.

Bandages wove around his ribs and over his shoulder, too tight, the skin beneath already closed. *Healed*—if that was the word for it. But it wasn't, because Rhy Maresh hadn't *healed* in months.

Healing was natural, healing took *time*—time for muscle to fuse, for bones to set, for skin to mend, time for scars to form, for the slow recession of pain followed by the return of strength.

In all fairness, Rhy had never known the long suffering of convalescence. Whenever he'd been injured as a child, Kell had always been there to mend him. Nothing worse than a cut or bruise ever lasted more than the time it took to find his brother.

But even that had been different.

A choice.

Rhy remembered falling from the courtyard wall when he was twelve and spraining his wrist. Remembered Kell's quickness to draw blood, Rhy's quickness to stop him, because he could bear the pain more than he could bear Kell's face when the blade sank in, the knowledge that he'd feel dizzy and ill the rest of the day from the magic's strain. And because, secretly, Rhy wanted to know he had a choice.

To heal.

But when Astrid Dane had driven the blade between his ribs, when the darkness had swallowed him, and then receded like a tide, there'd been no choice, no chance to say no. The wound was already closed. The spell already done.

He'd stayed in bed for three days in a mimicry of convalescence. He'd felt weak and ill, but it had less to do with his mending body than the new hollowness inside it. The voice in his head that whispered *wrong, wrong,* with every pulse.

Now he did not heal. A wound was a wound and then it wasn't.

A shudder went through him as he reached the bottom step.

Rhy did not want to do this.

Did not want to face her.

But someone had to handle the living, as much as someone had to handle the dead, and the king had already laid claim to the latter. His father, who was dealing with his grief as though it were an enemy, something to defeat, subdue. Who had ordered every Veskan in the palace rounded up, put under armed guard, and confined to the southern wing. His father, who had laid out his dead wife on the stone grieving block with such peculiar care, as if she were fragile. As if anything could touch her now.

In the gloom of the prison, a pair of guards stood watch.

Cora was sitting cross-legged on the bench at the back of her cell. She wasn't chained to the wall, as Holland had been, but her delicate wrists were bound in iron so heavy her hands had to rest on the bench before her knees, making her look as though she were leaning forward to whisper a secret.

Blood dappled her face like freckles, but when she saw Rhy, she actually smiled. Not the rictus grin of the mad, or the rueful smirk of the guilty. It was the same smile she'd given him as they perched in the royal baths telling stories: cheerful, innocent.

"Rhy," she said brightly.

"Was it your idea, or Col's?"

She pursed her lips, sulking at the lack of preamble. But then her eyes went to the bandage that peeked through Rhy's stiffened collar. It should have been a killing blow. It had been.

"My brother is one of the best swordsmen in Vesk," said Cora. "Col has never missed his mark."

"He didn't," said Rhy simply.

Cora's brow crinkled, then smoothed. Expressions flitted across her face like pages flipping in a breeze, too fast to catch.

"There are rumors, in my city," she said. "Rumors about Kell, and rumors about you. They say you di—"

"Was it your idea, or his?" demanded Rhy, fighting to keep his voice even, to hold his grief at bay, the way his father did, sadness kept behind a dam.

Cora rose to her feet despite the weight of the manacles. "My brother has a gift for swords, not strategies." She curled her fingers around the bars, metal sounding against metal like a bell. The cuff slipped down, and again Rhy saw the bruised skin circling her wrist. There was something unnatural about those marks, he realized now, something inhuman.

"That wasn't your brother, was it?"

She caught him looking, chuckled. "Hawk," she admitted. "Beautiful birds. Easy to forget that they have claws."

He could see it now, the curve of talons he'd mistaken for fingers, the prick of the creature's nails.

"I'm sorry about your mother," said Cora, and what he hated most was that she sounded sincere. He thought of the night they'd spent together, the way she'd made him feel less alone. The ease of her presence, the realization that she was just a child, a girl pretending, playing at games she didn't fully understand. Now, he wondered about that innocence, if it had all been an illusion. If he should have been able to tell. If it would have changed anything. If, if, if.

"*Why* did you do it?" he asked, his resolve threatening to break. She cocked her head, perplexed, like a hooded bird of prey.

"I'm the sixth of seven children. What future is there for me? In what world would I ever rule?"

"You could have killed your *own* family instead of mine."

Cora leaned in, that cherubic face pressed against the cell bars. "I thought about it. I suppose one day I might."

"No, you won't." Rhy turned to go. "You'll never see the outside of this cell."

"I'm like you," she said softly.

"No." He shoved her words away.

"I have hardly any magic," she pressed on. "But we both know there are other kinds of power." Rhy's steps slowed. "There's charm, cunning, seduction, strategy."

"Murder," he said, rounding on her.

"We use what we have. We make what we don't. We're truly not so different," said Cora, gripping the bars. "We both want the same thing. To be seen as strong. The only difference between you and me is the number of siblings standing in our way to the throne."

"That's not the only difference, Cora."

"Does it drive you mad, to be the weaker one?"

He wrapped his hand around hers, pinning them to the bars of the cell. "I am alive because my brother is strong," he said coldly. "You are alive only because yours is dead."

VI

Osaron sat on his throne and waited.

Waited for the impostor's palace to fall.

Waited for his subjects to return.

Waited for word of his victory.

For any word at all.

Thousands of voices had whispered in his head—determined, weeping, crowing, pleading, triumphant—and then, in a single moment, they were gone, the world suddenly still.

He reached out again and plucked the threads, but no one answered.

No one came.

They couldn't all have perished throwing themselves against the palace wards. Couldn't all have vanished so easily from his power, from his will.

He waited, wondering if the silence itself was some kind of trick, a ruse, but when it stretched, his own thoughts loud and echoing in the hollow space, Osaron rose.

The shadow king walked toward his palace doors, the smooth dark wood dissolving to smoke before him and taking shape again in his wake, parting as the world should for a god.

Against the sky, the impostor's palace of stone stood, its wards cracked but not broken.

And there, littering the steps, the banks, the city, Osaron saw the bodies of his puppets, their strings cut.

Everywhere he looked, he saw them. Thousands. Dead.

No, not dead.

But not entirely *alive*.

Despite the cold, each had the essential glow of life, the faint, steady rhythm of a heart still beating, the sound so soft it couldn't crack the silence.

That silence, that horrible, deafening silence, so like the world—his world—when the last life had ebbed and all that was left was a shred of power, a withered sliver of the magic that had once been Osaron. He'd paced for days through the dead remains of his city, every inch gone black, until even he had stilled, too weak to move, too weak to do anything but exist, to beat stubbornly on like these sleeping hearts.

"*Get up,*" he ordered his subjects now.

No one answered.

"*Get up,*" he screamed into their minds, into their very cores, pulling on every string, reaching into memory, into dream, into bone.

Still, no one rose.

A servant lay curled at the god's feet, and Osaron knelt, reached into the man's chest, and wrapped his fingers around his heart.

"*Get up,*" he ordered. The man did not move. Osaron tightened his grip, pouring more and more of himself into the shell, until the form simply—fell apart. Useless. Useless. All of them, useless.

The shadow king straightened, ash blowing in the wind as he turned his gaze on that *other* palace, that seat of *redundant* royalty, the threads of spellwork spooling from its spires. So they had done this, they had stolen his servants, silenced his voice.

It did not matter.

They could not stop him.

Osaron would conquer this city, this world.

And first, he would tear the palace down himself.

VII

People spoke of love as if it were an arrow. A thing that flew quick, and always found its mark. They spoke of it as if it were a pleasant thing, but Maxim had taken an arrow once, and knew it for what it was: excruciating.

He had never wanted to fall in love, never wanted to welcome that pain, would have happily faked an arrow's bite.

And then he met Emira.

And for a long time, he thought the arrow had played its cruelest trick, had struck him and missed *her*. He thought she'd stepped around the point, the way she stepped around so many things she did not like.

He'd spent a year trying to free the barb from his own chest before he realized he didn't want to. Or maybe, he couldn't. Another year before he realized she was injured, too.

It had been a slow pursuit, like melting ice. A kinship of hot and cold, of strong forces equally opposed, of those who did not know how to soften, how to soothe, and found the answer in each other.

That arrow's barb had so long healed. He'd forgotten the pain entirely.

But now.

Now he felt the wound, a shaft driven through his ribs. Scraping bone and lung with every ragged breath, and loss the hand twisting the arrow, trying to rend it free before it killed and doing so much damage in the process.

Maxim wanted to be with her. Not the body laid out in the Rose Hall, but the woman he loved. He wanted to be with her, and instead he stood in the map room across from Sol-in-Ar, forced to bind up a mortal wound, to fight through the pain, because the battle wasn't yet won.

His spell was beating against the inside of his skull, and he tasted blood with every swallow, and as he lifted the crystal cut glass to his lips, his hand shook.

Sol-in-Ar stood on the other side of the map, the two of them divided by the wide expanse of the Arnesian empire on the table, the city of London rising at its center. Isra waited by the door, head bowed.

"I am sorry for your loss," said the Faroan lord, because it was a thing that had to be said. Both men knew the words fell short, would always fall short.

The part of Maxim that was king knew it wasn't right to mourn a single life more than a city, but the part of Maxim that had set the rose on his wife's heart was still breaking inside.

When was the last time he'd seen her? What was the last thing he'd said? He didn't know, couldn't recall. The arrow twisted. The wound ached. He fought to remember, remember, remember.

Emira, with her dark eyes that saw so much, and her lips that guarded smiles as if they were secrets. With her beauty, and her strength, her hard shell around her fragile heart.

Emira, who'd taken down her walls long enough to let him in, who'd built them twice as high when Rhy was born, so nothing could get in. Whose trust he'd fought for, whose trust he'd failed when he promised over and over and over again that he would keep them safe.

Emira, gone.

Those who thought death looked like sleep had never seen it.

When Emira slept, her lashes danced, her lips parted, her fingers twitched, every part of her alive within her dreams. The body in the Rose Hall was not his wife, not his queen, not the mother of his heir, not anyone at all. It was empty, the intangible presence of life and magic and personhood gutted like a candle, leaving only cooling wax behind.

"You knew it was the Veskans," said Maxim, dragging his mind back to the map room.

Sol-in-Ar's features were grim, set, the white gold accents on the lord's face strangely steady in the light. "I suspected."

"How?"

"I do not have magic, Your Majesty," Sol-in-Ar answered in slow but even Arnesian, the edges smoothing with his accent, "but I do have sense. The treatise between Faro and Vesk has become strained in recent months." He gestured at the map. "Arnes sits squarely between our empires. An obstacle. A wall. I have been watching the prince and princess since my arrival, and when Col answered you that he had not sent word to Vesk, I knew that he was lying. I knew this because you housed their gift in the chamber below mine."

"The hawk," said Maxim, recalling the Veskans' offering—a large grey predator—before the *Essen Tasch*.

Sol-in-Ar nodded. "I was surprised by their gift. A bird like that does not enjoy a cage. The Veskans use them to send missives across the harsh expanses of their territory, and when they are confined, they caw in a low and constant way. The one beneath my room fell silent two days ago."

"*Sanct,*" muttered Maxim. "You should have said something."

Sol-in-Ar raised a single dark brow. "Would you have listened, Your Majesty?"

"I apologize," said the king, "for distrusting an ally."

Sol-in-Ar's gaze was steady, his pale beads pricks of light. "We are both men of war, Maxim Maresh. Trust does not come easily."

Maxim shook his head and refilled his glass, hoping the liquid would quelch the lingering taste of blood and steady his hands. He hadn't meant to hold his spell aloft for this long, had only meant to—to see Emira, to say good-bye. . . .

"It has been a long time," he said, forcing his thoughts back, "since I was at war. Before I was king, I led command at the Blood Coast. That was the nickname my soldiers and I had for the open waters that ran between the empires. That gap of terrain where pirates and rebels and anyone who refused to recognize the peace went to make a little war."

"*Anastamar,*" said Sol-in-Ar. "That was our name for it. It means *the Killing Strait.*"

"Fitting," mused Maxim, taking a long sip. "The peace was new enough to be fragile, then—though I suppose peace is always fragile—and I had only a thousand men to hold the entire coast. Though I had another title. Not one given by court, or my father, but by my soldiers."

"The Steel Prince," said Sol-in-Ar, and then, reading Maxim's expression: "It surprises you, that the tales of your exploits reach beyond your own borders?" The Faroan's fingers grazed the edge of the map. "The Steel Prince, who tore the heart from the rebel army. The Steel Prince, who survived the night of knives. The Steel Prince, who slayed the pirate queen."

Maxim finished his drink and set the glass aside. "I suppose we never know the scale of our life's stories. Which parts will survive, and which will die with us, but—"

He was cut off by a sudden tremor, not in his limbs, but in the room itself. The palace gave a violent shudder around them, the walls trembling, the stone figures on the map threatening to tip. Maxim and Sol-in-Ar both braced themselves as the tremor passed.

"Isra," ordered Maxim, but the guard was already moving down the hall. He and Sol-in-Ar followed.

The wards were still weak in the aftermath of the attack, but it shouldn't have mattered, because everyone beyond the palace doors was asleep.

Everyone—but Osaron.

Now the creature's voice rumbled through the city, not the smooth, seductive whisper in Maxim's mind, but an audible, thunderous thing.

"This palace is mine."
"This city is mine."
"These people are mine."

Osaron knew about the spell, must have known too that it was coming from within the walls. If Tieren woke, the enchantment would shatter. The fallen would revive.

It was time, then.

Maxim forced himself toward the front of the palace, carrying the weight of his spell with every step, even as his heart called for Rhy. If only his son were there. If only Maxim could see him one last time.

As if summoned by the thought, the prince appeared in the doorway, and suddenly Maxim wished he hadn't been so selfish. Grief and fear were painted across Rhy's features, making him look young. He *was* young.

"What's going on?" asked the prince.

"Rhy," he said, the short word leaving him breathless. Maxim didn't know how to do this. If he stopped moving, he would never start again.

"Where are you going?" demanded his son as Osaron's voice shook the world.

"Face me, false king."

Maxim tugged on the threads of his power and felt his spell pull tight, cinching like armor around him as steel hearts came to life within steel breasts.

"Father," said Rhy.

"Surrender, and I will spare those within."

The king summoned his steel men, felt them marching through the halls.

"Refuse, and I will tear this place apart."

He kept walking.

"Stop!" demanded Rhy. "If you go out there, you will die."

"There is no shame in death," said the king.

"You are no god."

"You can't do this," said Rhy, barring his path as they reached the front hall. "You're walking right into his trap."

Maxim stopped, the weight of the spell and his son's stricken face threatening to drag him down. "Stand aside, Rhy," he ordered gently.

His son shook his head furiously. "Please." Tears were brimming on his dark lashes, threatening to spill. Maxim's heart ached. The palace trembled. The steel guard was coming. They reached the front hall, a dozen suits of armor spelled into motion with blood and will and magic. Royal short swords hung at their waists, and through their helmets, the soft light of their spelled hearts burned like coal. They were ready. He was ready.

"Rhy Maresh," said Maxim steadily, "I will ask you as your father, but if I must, I will command you as your king."

"*No,*" said Rhy, grabbing him by the shoulders. "I won't let you do this."

The arrow in his chest drove deep.

"Sol-in-Ar," Maxim said, and, "Isra."

And they understood. The two came forward and seized Rhy's arms, pulling him away. Rhy fought viciously against them, but at a nod from the king, Isra drove her gauntleted fist into the prince's ribs and Rhy doubled, gasping, "*No, no . . .* "

"*Sosora nastima,*" said Sol-in-Ar. "*Listen to your king.*"

"Watch, my prince," added Isra. "Watch with pride."

"Open the doors," ordered Maxim.

Tears spilled down Rhy's face. "Father—"

The heavy wood parted. The doors swung back. At the base of the palace stairs stood the shadow, a demon masquerading as a king.

Osaron lifted his chin.

"*Face me.*"

"Let me go!" cried Rhy.

Maxim strode through the doors. He didn't look back, not at the steel guard marching in his wake, not at his son's face, the eyes so like Emira's, now red with anguish.

"*Please,*" begged Rhy. "Please, let me go. . . ."

They were the last words Maxim heard before the palace doors fell shut.

VIII

The first time Rhy saw his father's map room, he was eight years old.

He hadn't been allowed past the golden doors, had only glimpsed the stone figures arrayed across the sprawling table, the scenes moving with the same slow enchantment of the pictures on the city's scrying boards.

He'd tried to sneak back in, of course, but Kell wouldn't help him, and there were other places in the palace to explore. But Rhy couldn't forget the strange magic of that room, and that winter, when the weather turned and the sun never seemed to come out, he built his own map, crafting the palace from a golden three-tiered cake stand, the river from a stretch of gossamer, a hundred tiny figures from whatever he could get his hands on. He made *vestra* and *ostra*, priests and royal guards.

"This one's you," he told Kell, holding up a fire-starter with a red top, a dab of black paint for an eye. Kell wasn't impressed.

"This one's you," he told his mother, brandishing the queen he'd fashioned from a glass tonic vial.

"This one's you," he told Tieren, proudly showing him the bit of white stone he'd dug out of the courtyard.

He'd been working on the set for more than a year when his father came to see. He'd never found the stuff to make the king. Kell—who didn't usually want to play—had offered up a rock with a dozen little grooves that *almost* made a ghoulish face, if the light was right, but Rhy thought it looked more like the royal cook, Lor.

Rhy was crouched over the board before bed one night when Maxim entered. He was a towering man draped in red and gold, his dark beard and brows swallowing his face. No wonder Rhy couldn't find the piece to play him. Nothing felt *large* enough.

"What's this?" asked his father, sinking to one knee beside the makeshift palace.

"It's a game," said Rhy proudly, "just like yours."

That was when Maxim took him by the hand, and led him down the stairs and through the palace, bare feet sinking into the plush carpet. When they reached the golden doors, Rhy's heart leapt, half in dread, half in excitement, as his father unlocked the doors.

Memory often bends a thing, makes it even more marvelous. But Rhy's own memory of the map room paled in comparison to the truth. Rhy had grown two inches that year, but instead of seeming smaller, the map was just as grand, just as sweeping, just as magical.

"This," said his father sternly, "is not a game. Every ship, every soldier, every bit of stone and glass—the lives of this kingdom hang in the balance of this board."

Rhy stared in wonder at the map, made all the more magical for his father's warning. Maxim stood, arms crossed, while Rhy circled the table, examining every facet before turning his attention to the palace.

It was no kettle, no cake tray. This palace shone, a perfect miniature—sculpted in glass and gold—of Rhy's home.

Rhy stood on his toes, peering into the windows.

"What are you searching for?" asked his father.

Rhy looked up, eyes wide. "You."

At last, a smile broke through that trimmed beard. Maxim pointed to a slight rise in the cityscape, a plaza two bridges down from the palace where a huddle of stone guards sat on horseback. And at their center, no larger than the rest, was a figure set apart only by the gold band of a crown.

"A king," said his father, "belongs with his people."

Rhy reached a hand into the pocket of his bedclothes and pulled out a small figure, a boy prince spun from pure sugar and stolen from his last birthday cake. Now, carefully, Rhy set the figure on the map beside his father.

"And the prince," he said proudly, "belongs with his king."

Rhy screamed, and thrashed, and fought against their grip.

A king belongs with his people.

He begged, and pleaded, and tried to tear free.

A prince belongs with his king.

The doors were closed. His father had vanished, swallowed up by wood and stone.

"Your Highness, please."

Rhy threw a punch, catching Isra hard across the jaw. She let go, and he made it a single step before Sol-in-Ar locked him in a viciously efficient hold, one arm twisted up behind his back.

"Your Highness, no."

Pain flared through him when he tried to fight, but pain was nothing to Rhy now and he wrenched free, tearing something in his shoulder as he threw his elbow back into the Faroan's face.

More guards were arriving now, blocking the door as Isra shouted orders through bloodstained teeth.

"Stand aside," he demanded, voice breaking.

"Your Highness—"

"Stand aside."

Slowly, reluctantly, the guards stepped away from the doors, and Rhy surged forward, grasping for the handle just before Isra pinned his hand to the wood.

"Your Highness," she snarled, "don't you *dare*."

A king belongs with his people.

"Isra," he pleaded. "A prince belongs with his king."

"Then be with him," said the guard. "By honoring his last request."

The weight of Isra's hand retreated, and Rhy was left alone before the broad wood doors. Somewhere on the other side, so close and yet so far . . .

He felt something tear inside him, not flesh but something so much deeper. He splayed his hands across the wood. Rhy squeezed his eyes shut, pressed his forehead to the door, his whole body shaking with the urge to throw them open, to run after his father.

He didn't.

His legs gave way, body sinking to the floor, and if the world had chosen that moment to swallow him whole, Rhy would have welcomed it.

THIRTEEN

A KING'S PLACE

I

Maxim Maresh had forgotten about the fog.

The moment he stepped through the palace wards, he felt Osaron's poison lacing the air. It was too late to hold his breath. It forced its way in, filling his lungs as the curse whispered through his head.

Kneel before the shadow king.

Maxim resisted the fog's hypnotic pull, nerves crackling as he forced its hold away, focused instead on the sound of the steel guard marching in his wake and the rippling figure waiting at the base of the palace stairs.

Without a body, the shadow king looked less like a man and more like smoke trapped within a darkened glass, the presence shifting within its false shell like a trick of the light. Only its eyes seemed solid, the glossy black of polished stone.

Like Kell's, thought Maxim, and then he revoked the thought. *No, not like Kell's at all.*

Kell's gaze had the warmth of a flame, while Osaron's eyes were sharp and cold and utterly inhuman.

At the sight of Maxim descending the stairs, the shadow king's face flickered, mouth twisting into a smile.

"False king."

Maxim forced his body down step after step as his vision blurred and his skin pricked with the beginnings of fever. When his boots struck the stone of the plaza floor, the twelve men of his final guard fanned out, taking up their places around the two kings like points on a clock. Each drew a steel short sword, its blade spelled to sever magic.

Osaron barely seemed to notice the figures in their steel trappings, the way they moved together like fingers on a hand, the way the shadows bent and swirled around their armor and their blades, never touching.

"Have you come to kneel?" asked the shadow king, the words echoing through Maxim's skull, ringing against his bones. *"Have you come to beg?"*

Maxim lifted his head. He wore no armor, no helm, nothing but a single sword at his hip and the gold crown resting in his hair. Still, he looked straight into those onyx eyes and said, "I've come to destroy you."

The darkness chuckled, a sound like low thunder.

"You've come to die."

Maxim's balance almost faltered, not from fear, but from fever. Delirium. The night danced before his eyes, memories transposing themselves on top of truth. Emira's body. Rhy's screams. Pain lanced jaggedly through Maxim's chest as he resisted the shadow king's magic. Sickness quickened his heart, Osaron's curse straining his mind as his own spell strained his body.

"Shall I make your own men kill you?"

Osaron's hand twitched, but the steel guard circling them did not move. No sword hands lifted to attack. No boots shifted obediently forward.

A frown crossed the shadow king's face like a passing cloud as he realized the guards weren't real, only puppets on clumsy strings, the armor nothing but a hollow enchantment, a last effort to spare Maxim's own men from this grim task.

"What a waste."

Maxim straightened, sweat sliding down the nape of his neck. "You'll have to face me yourself."

With that, the Arnesian king drew his sword, spelled like the others to break the threads of magic, and slashed at the shadowy mass before him. Osaron did not duck or dodge or strike. He did not move at all. He simply *parted* around Maxim's blade and re-formed a few feet to the left.

Again, Maxim attacked.

Again, Osaron dissolved.

With every lunge, every swing, Maxim's fatigue and fever rose, a tide threatening to overtake him.

And then, on the fifth or the sixth or the tenth attack, Osaron finally fought back. This time, when he took shape again, it was inside Maxim's guard.

"*Enough,*" said the monster with a flickering grin.

He reached out an insubstantial hand, fingers splayed, and Maxim felt his body stall mid-stride, felt the bones beneath his skin groan and grind, pain lighting up his nerves as he was pinned like a doll against the night.

"*So fragile,*" chided Osaron.

A twitch of that hand—more fog than fingers—and Maxim's wrist shattered. His short sword clattered to the ground, the metallic scrape of metal on stone drowning out his pained gasp.

"*Beg,*" said the shadow king.

Maxim swallowed. "No, I—"

His collarbone snapped with the vicious crack of a stick over a knee. A strangled scream broke through his clenched teeth.

"*Beg.*"

Maxim shuddered, his ribs shaking beneath the force of Osaron's will as it tap-tap-tapped like fingers over his bones.

"No."

The shadow king was teasing, toying, drawing it out. And Maxim let him, hoping all the while that Rhy was safe inside the palace, far from the windows, far from the door, far from this. His steel guards trembled in their places, gauntlets gripping swords. Not yet. Not yet. Not yet.

"I am the king . . . of this empire—"

Something cracked in his chest, and Maxim spasmed, blood rising in his throat.

"*This is what passes for a king in this world?*"

"My people will never—"

At that, Osaron's hand—not flesh and bone or smoke at all, but something dense and cold and *wrong*—wrapped around Maxim's jaw. *"The insolence of mortal kings."*

Maxim looked into the swirling darkness of the creature's gaze. "The . . . insolence of . . . fallen . . . gods."

Osaron's face broke into a terrible smile. *"I will wear your body through the streets until it burns."*

In those black eyes, Maxim saw the warped reflection of the palace, the *soner rast,* the beating heart of his city.

His home.

He pulled the final strings, and the guards finally stepped forward. Twelve faceless men drew their swords.

"I am the head . . . of the House Maresh," said Maxim, ". . . seventh king of that name . . . and you are not fit . . . to wear my skin."

Osaron cocked his head. *"We shall see."*

The darkness forced its way in.

It was not a wave, but an ocean, and Maxim felt his will give way beneath the weight of Osaron's power. There was no air. No light. No surface.

Emira. Rhy. Kell.

The arrows drove deep, the pain an anchor, but Maxim's mind was already breaking apart, and his body tore further as he pulled with the last of his strength on his steel guards. Gauntlets tightened and a dozen short swords rose into the air, points turning toward the center of their circle as Osaron poured himself like molten metal into the body of Maxim Maresh.

And the king began to *burn*.

His mind guttered, his life failed, but not before a dozen steel points sang through the air, driving toward the source of their spell.

Toward Maxim's body.

His heart.

He stopped fighting. It was like setting down a heavy weight, the dazzling relief of letting go. Osaron's voice laughed through his head, but he was already falling, already gone, when the blades found home.

II

Across the city of London, the darkness began to thin.

The deep gloom drew back, and the shining black pane of the river cracked, giving way, here and there, to violent ribbons of red as Osaron's hold faltered, slipped.

Maxim Maresh's body knelt in the street, a dozen swords driven in to the hilt. Blood pooled beneath him in a rich red slick, and for a few long moments, the body did not move. The only sound came from the drip-drip-drip of the dead king's blood hitting stone, the whistle of wind through the sleeping streets.

And then, after a long moment, Maxim's corpse rose.

It shuddered, like a curtain in a breeze, and then a sword drew itself free of the ruined chest and clattered to the ground. And then another, and another, one by one until all twelve blades were out, lengths of crimson steel lying in the street. Smoke began to leak in thin tendrils from every wound before drawing together into a cloud, then a shadow, and then, at last, something like a man. It took several tries, the darkness collapsing back into smoke again and again before finally managing to hold its shape, its edges wavering unsteadily as its chest rose and fell in smoldering breaths.

"*I am king,*" snarled the shadow as the whorls of red in the river vanished, and the mist thickened.

But the nightmare's hold was not quite as strong as it had been.

Osaron let out a growl of anger as his limbs dissolved, reformed. The spellwork etched into those swords still ran like ice through the veins of his power, stamping out heat and smothering flame. Such a stupid little spell, driven in so deep.

Osaron scowled down at the king's corpse, finally kneeling before him.

"*All men bow.*"

Shadowy fingers flicked, once, and the body toppled, lifeless, to the ground.

Insolent mortal, thought the shadow king as he turned and stormed back across the sleeping city and up the bridge and into his palace, fuming as he struggled with every step to hold his shape. When his hand grazed a column, it went straight through as if he were *nothing.*

But the false king was dead, and Osaron lived on. It would take more than spelled metal, more than one man's magic, to kill a god.

The shadow king climbed the stairs to his throne and sat, smoking hands curled around the arms of his seat.

These mortals thought they were strong, thought they were clever, but they were nothing but children in this world—Osaron's world—and he had lived long enough to take their measure.

They had *no idea* what he was capable of.

The shadow king closed his eyes and opened his mind, reaching past the palace, past the city, past the world, to the very edges of his power.

Just as a tree might know itself, from deepest root to topmost leaf, Osaron knew every inch of his magic. And so he reached, and reached, and reached, grasping in the dark until he felt her there. Or rather, felt what was left of him inside her.

"*Ojka.*"

Osaron knew, of course, that she was dead. Gone, blown away as all things were in time. He had felt the moment when it happened, even that small death rippling his psyche, the sudden sense of loss pale but palpable.

And yet—Osaron still ran through her. He was in her blood. That blood might no longer *flow,* but he still lived in it, his will a filament, a thread of wire woven through her straw body. Her consciousness was gone, her own will forfeit, but her form was still a form. A vessel.

And so Osaron filled the silence of her mind, and wrapped his will around her limbs.

"*Ojka,*" he said again. *"Get up."*

III

White London

Nasi always knew when something was wrong.

It was a gut knowing, come from years of watching faces, hands, reading all the little tells a person made before they did a bad thing.

It wasn't a person going wrong now.

It was a world.

A chill was back in the air, the castle windows frosting at the corners. The king was gone, still gone, and without him, London was getting bad again, getting *worse*. The world felt like it was unraveling around her, all the color and life bleeding out the way it must have done the first time, all those years ago. Only according to the stories that was slow, and this was quick, like a snake shedding a skin.

And Nasi knew she wasn't the only one who felt it.

All of London seemed to sense the wrongness.

A few members of the king's Iron Guard, those still loyal to his cause, were doing their best to keep things from getting out of hand. The castle was under constant watch. Nasi hadn't been able to sneak out again, so she didn't have fresh flowers—not that many had survived the sudden chill—to lay near Ojka's body.

But she came anyway, in part because of the quiet, and in part because the rest of the world was getting scary, and if something happened, Nasi wanted to be near the king's knight, even if she was dead.

It was early morning—that time before the world woke up all the way, and she was standing beside the woman's head, saying a prayer, for power, for strength (they were the only prayers she knew). She was running out of words when, on the table, Ojka's fingers *twitched*.

Nasi startled, but even as her eyes widened and her heart skipped, she was talking herself down, the way she had done when she was little, and every little shadow had a way of becoming a monster. It could have been a trick of the light, probably was, so she reached out and tentatively touched the knight's wrist, feeling for a pulse.

Sure enough, Ojka was still cold. Still dead.

And then, abruptly, the woman sat up.

Nasi staggered back as the black cloth tumbled away from Ojka's face.

She didn't blink, didn't turn her head, or even seem to notice Nasi or the death table or the candlelit room. Her eyes were wide and flat and empty, and Nasi remembered the soldiers who used to guard Astrid and Athos Dane, hollowed out and spelled into submission.

Ojka looked like them.

She was real, and yet not real, alive and still very, very dead.

The wound at her neck was there and deep as ever, but now Ojka worked her jaw. When she tried to speak, a low hiss came from her ruined throat. The knight pursed her lips, and swallowed, and Nasi watched as tendrils of shadow and smoke wove over and around her neck, almost like a fresh bandage.

She leapt down from the table, upsetting the vines and bowls that Nasi had laid so carefully around her corpse. They fell to the floor with a clang and a crash.

Ojka had always been so graceful, but now her steps had the stilted quality of a colt, or a puppet, and Nasi backed up until her shoulder hit the pillar. The knight looked straight at the girl, shadows swimming through her pale eye. Ojka didn't speak, only stared, the drip of spilled water tapping on the stones behind her. Her hand had begun to drift toward Nasi's cheek when the doors swung open and two members of the Iron Guard stormed in, drawn by the crash.

They saw the dead knight standing upright and froze.

Ojka's hand fell away from Nasi as she spun toward them with returning grace. The air around her shimmered with magic, something from the table—a dagger—sailing into Ojka's hand.

The guards were shouting now, and Nasi should have run, should have done something, but she was frozen against the pillar, pinned by something as heavy as the strongest magic.

She didn't want to see what happened next, didn't want to see the king's knight die a second time, didn't want to see the last of Holland's guard fall to a ghost, so she crouched, squeezed her eyes shut, and pressed her hands over her ears. The way she used to when things got bad in the castle. When Athos Dane played with people until they broke.

But even through her hands, she heard the voice that came from Ojka's throat—not Ojka's at all, but someone else's, hollow and echoing and rich—and the guards must have been afraid of ghosts and monsters too, because when Nasi finally opened her eyes, there was no sign of Ojka or the men.

The room was empty.

She was all alone.

IV

The *Ghost* was almost back to Tanek when Lila felt the vessel drag to a sudden stop.

Not the smooth coasting of a ship losing current, but a jarring halt, unnatural at sea.

She and Kell were in their cabin when it happened, packing up their few belongings, Lila's hand drifting repeatedly to her pocket—the absence of her watch its own strange weight—while Kell's kept going to his chest.

"Does it still hurt?" she'd asked, and Kell had started to answer when the ship stuttered harshly, the groan of wood and sail cut off by Alucard calling them up. His voice had the peculiar lightness it took on when he was either drunk or nervous, and she was pretty sure he hadn't been drinking at the ship's wheel (though it wouldn't surprise her if he had).

It was a grey day above, mist clouding the world beyond the boat. Holland was already on deck, staring out into the fog.

"Why have you stopped?" demanded Kell, a crease between his brows.

"Because we have a problem," said Alucard, nodding ahead.

Lila scanned the horizon. The fog was heavier than it should have been given the hour, sitting like a second skin above the water. "I can't see anything."

"That's the idea," said Alucard. His hands splayed, his lips moved, and the mist he'd conjured thinned a little before them.

Lila squinted, and at first she saw nothing but sea, and then—

She went still.

It wasn't land ahead.

It was a line of ships.

Ten hulking vessels with pale wood bodies and emerald flags that cut the fog like knives.

A Veskan fleet.

"Well," said Lila slowly. "I guess that answers the question of who paid Jasta to kill us."

"And Rhy," added Kell.

"How far to land?" asked Holland.

Alucard shook his head. "Not far, but they're standing directly between us and Tanek. The nearest coast is an hour's sail to either side."

"Then we go around."

Alucard shot Kell a look. "Not in this," he said, gesturing at the *Ghost,* and Lila understood. The captain had maneuvered the ship so that its narrow prow faced the fleet's spine. As long as the fog lingered, as long as the *Ghost* held still, it *might* go unnoticed, but the moment it moved closer, it would be a target. The *Ghost* wasn't flying flags, but neither were the three small vessels bobbing like buoys beside the fleet, each running the white banner of a captured boat. The Veskans were clearly holding the pass.

"Should we attack?" asked Lila.

That drew looks from Kell, Alucard, *and* Holland.

"What?" she said.

Alucard shook his head, dismayed. "There are probably *hundreds* aboard those ships, Bard."

"And we're *Antari.*"

"*Antari,* not immortal," said Kell.

"We don't have time to battle a fleet," said Holland. "We need to get to land."

Alucard's gaze shifted back to the line of ships. "Oh, you can make it to the coast," he said, "but you'll have to *row.*"

Lila thought Alucard must be joking.

He wasn't.

V

Rhy Maresh kept his eyes on the light.

He stood at the edge of the spell circle where Tieren lay, and focused on the candle cradled in the priest's hands with its steady, unwavering flame.

He wanted to wake the *Aven Essen* from his trance, wanted to bury his head in the old man's shoulder and sob. Wanted to feel the calm of his magic.

In the last few months, he had become intimately acquainted with pain, and with death, but grief was new. Pain was bright, and death was dark, but grief was grey. A slab of stone resting on his chest. A toxic cloud stripping him of breath.

I can't do this alone, he thought.

I can't do this—

I can't—

Whatever his father had been trying to achieve, it hadn't worked.

Rhy had seen the river lighten, the shadows begin to withdraw, had glimpsed his city of red and gold like a specter through the fog.

But it hadn't lasted.

Within minutes, the darkness had returned.

He'd lost his father for what?

A moment?

A breath?

They'd recovered the king's body from the base of the palace steps.

His father, lying in a pool of cooling blood.

His father, now laid out beside his mother, a pair of sculptures, shells, their eyes closed, their bodies suddenly aged by death. When had his mother's cheeks grown hollow? When had his father's temples gone grey? They were impostors, gross imitations of the people they'd been in life. The people Rhy had loved. The sight of them—what was left of them—made him ill, and so he'd fled to the only place he could. The only person.

To Tieren.

Tieren, who slept with a stillness that might have passed for death if Rhy hadn't just seen it, hadn't pressed hands to his father's unmoving ribs, hadn't clutched his mother's stiffened shoulder.

Come back—
Come back—
Come back—

He did not say the words aloud, for fear of rousing the priest, some deep feeling that no matter how softly he might speak, the sadness would still be loud. The other priests knelt, their heads bowed, as if themselves in a trance, brows furrowed in concentration while Tieren's face bore the same smooth pallor of the men and women sleeping in the streets. Rhy would have given anything to hear the *Aven Essen*'s voice, to feel the weight of arms around his shoulders, to see the understanding in his eyes.

He was so close.

He was so far.

Tears burned Rhy's eyes, threatened to spill over, and when they did, they hit the floor an inch from the ashen edge of the binding circle. His fingers ached from where he'd struck Isra, shoulder throbbing where he'd twisted free of Sol-in-Ar's grip. But these pains were little more than memory, shallow wounds compared to the tearing in his chest, the absence where two people had been carved out, torn away.

His arms hung heavy at his sides.

In one hand, his own crown, the circle of gold he'd worn since he was a boy, and in the other, the royal pin capable of reaching Kell.

He had thought of summoning his brother, of course. Gripped the pin until the emblem of the chalice and sun had cut into his palm, even though Kell said blood wasn't necessary. Kell was wrong. Blood was always necessary.

One word, and his brother would come.

One word, and he wouldn't be alone.

One word—but Rhy Maresh couldn't bring himself to do it.

He had failed himself so many times. He wouldn't fail Kell, too.

Someone cleared their throat behind him. "Your Majesty."

Rhy let out a shuddering breath and stepped back from the edge of Tieren's spell. Turning, he found the captain of his father's city guard, a bruise blossoming along Isra's jaw, her own eyes lidded with grief.

He followed her out of the silent chamber and into the hall where a messenger stood waiting, breathless, his clothing slick with sweat and mud, as if he'd ridden hard. This was one of his father's scouts, sent to monitor the spread of Osaron's magic beyond the city, and for an instant, Rhy's tired mind couldn't process why the messenger had come to *him*. Then he remembered: there was no one else—and there it was again, worse than a knife, the sudden assault of memory, a raw wound reopened.

"What is it?" asked Rhy, his voice hoarse.

"I bring word from Tanek," said the messenger.

Rhy felt ill. "The fog has reached that far?"

The messenger shook his head. "No, sir, not yet, but I met a rider on the road. He spotted a fleet at the mouth of the Isle. Ten ships. They fly the silver-and-green banners of Vesk."

Isra swore beneath her breath.

Rhy closed his eyes. What was it his father said, that politics was a dance? Vesk was trying to set the tempo. It was time for Rhy to take the lead. To show that he was king.

"Your Majesty?" prompted the messenger.

Rhy opened his eyes.

"Bring me two of their magicians."

He met them in the map room.

Rhy would have preferred the Rose Hall, with its vaulted stone ceilings, its dais, its throne. But the king and queen were laid out there, so this would have to do.

He stood in his father's place behind the table, hands braced on the lip of the wood, and it must have been a trick of the senses, but Rhy thought he could feel the grooves where Maxim Maresh's fingers had pressed into the table's edge, the wood still lingering with warmth.

Lord Sol-in-Ar stood against the wall to his left, flanked on either side by a member of his retinue.

Isra and two members of the guard lined the wall to his right.

The Veskan magicians came, Otto and Rul, massive men led in by a pair of armored guards. On Rhy's orders, their manacles had been removed. He wanted them to realize that they weren't being punished for the actions of their crown.

Not yet.

In the tournament ring, Rul "the Wolf" had howled before every match.

Otto "the Bear" had beaten his chest.

Now, the two stood silent as pillars. He could tell by their faces that they knew of their rulers' treason, of the queen's murder, the king's sacrifice.

"We are sorry for your loss," said Rul.

"Are you?" asked Rhy, masking his sorrow with disdain.

While Kell had spent his childhood studying magic, Rhy had studied people, learned everything he could about his kingdom, from *vestra* and *ostra* down to commoner and criminal, and then he'd moved on to Faro and Vesk. And while he knew that a world couldn't truly be learned from a book, it would have to be a start.

After all, knowledge was a kind of power, a breed of strength. And Veskans, he'd been taught, respected anger and joy, even envy, but not grief.

Rhy gestured at the map. "What do you see?"

"A city, sir," answered Otto.

Rhy nodded at the line of figurines he'd placed at the mouth of Arnes. Small stone ships stained emerald green and flying grey banners. "And there?"

Rul frowned at the row. "A fleet?"

"A *Veskan* fleet," clarified Rhy. "Before your prince and princess attacked my king and queen, they sent word to Vesk and summoned a fleet of ten warships." He looked to Otto, who had stiffened at the news—not in guilt, he thought, but shock. "Has your kingdom grown so tired of our peace? Does it wish for war?"

"I . . . I am only a magician," said Otto. "I do not know my queen's heart."

"But you know your empire. Are you not a part of it? What does *your* heart say?"

The Veskans, Rhy knew, were a proud and stubborn people, but they were not fools. They savored a good fight, but did not go looking for war.

"We do not—"

"Arnes may be the battlefield," cut in Sol-in-Ar, "but if Vesk covets war, they will find it with Faro, too. Say the word, Your Majesty, and I will bring a hundred thousand soldiers to meet your own."

Rul had gone red as embers, Otto white as chalk.

"We did not *do* this," growled Rul.

"We knew nothing of this deceit," added Otto tightly. "We do not want—"

"*Want?*" snarled Rhy. "What does want have to do with it? Do I want my people to suffer? Do I want to see my kingdom plunged into war? The masses pay for the choices of a few, and if your royals had come to you and asked for your aid, can you say you would not have given it?"

"But they did not," said Otto coldly. "With respect, Your Majesty, a ruler does not follow her people, but a people must follow her rule. You are right, many pay for the choices of a few. But *royals* are the ones who choose, and we are the ones who pay for it."

Rhy fought the urge to cringe in the face of the words. Fought the urge to look to Isra or Sol-in-Ar.

"But you ask my heart," continued Otto, "and my heart has a family. My heart has a life and a home. My heart enjoys the fields of play, not war."

Rhy swallowed and took up one of the ships.

"You will write two letters," he said, weighing the marker in his palm. "One to the fleet, and one to the crown. You will tell them of the prince and princess's cold-blooded treason. You will tell them that they can withdraw now and we will take the actions of two royals to be their own. They can withdraw, and spare their country a war. But if they advance even a measure toward this city, they do so knowing they face a king who is very much alive, and an empire allied against them. If they advance, they will have signed the deaths of thousands."

His voice slipped lower as he spoke, the way his father's always had, the words humming like fresh-drawn steel.

"Kings need not raise their voices to be heard."

One of Maxim's many lessons.

"And what about this shadow king?" asked Rul icily. "Shall we write of him as well?"

Rhy's fingers tightened around the small stone ship. "My city's weakness will become yours if those ships cross into London. My people will sleep, but yours will die. For their sakes, I suggest you be as persuasive as possible." He set the marker back on the table. "Do you understand?" he said, the words more order than question.

Otto nodded. So did Rul.

As the doors closed behind them, the strength went out of Rhy's shoulders. He slumped back against the map room wall.

"How was that?" he asked.

Isra bowed her head. "Handled like a king."

There was no time to relish it.

The Sanctuary bells had gone silent with the rest of the city, but here in the palace, a clock began to chime. No one else stirred, because no one else had been counting time, but Rhy straightened.

Kell had been gone four days.

"Four days, Rhy. We'll make it back in that. And then you can get yourself into trouble. . . ."

But trouble had come and gone and come again without any sign of his brother. He had promised Kell he would wait, but Rhy had waited long enough. It was only a matter of time before Osaron recovered his strength. Only a matter of time before he turned his sights back on the palace. The city's last defense. It sheltered every waking body, every silver, every priest, guarded Tieren and the spell that kept the rest asleep. And if it fell, there would be nothing.

He'd made Kell a promise, but his brother was late, and Rhy could not stay here, entombed with the bodies of his parents.

He would not hide from the shadows when the shadows could not touch him.

He had a choice. And he would make it.

He would face the shadow king himself.

Once again, the captain of the guard barred his path.

Isra was his father's age, but where Maxim was—had been—broad, she was lean, wiry. And yet she was the most imposing woman he'd ever met, straight backed and severe, one hand always resting on the hilt of her sword.

"Stand aside," instructed Rhy, fastening the red-and-gold cape around his shoulders.

"Your Majesty," said the guard. "I was always honest with your father, and I will always be honest with you, so forgive me when I speak freely. How much blood must we feed this monster?"

"I will feed him every drop I have," said Rhy, "if it will sate him. Now, stand aside. That is an order from your king." The words scorched his throat as he said them, but Isra obeyed, stepping out of the way.

Rhy's hand was on the door when the woman spoke again, her voice low, insistent. "When these people wake," she said, "they will need their king. Who will lead them if you die?"

Rhy held the woman's gaze. "Haven't you heard?" he said, pushing open the door. "I am already dead."

VI

The *Ghost* had exactly one dinghy, a shallow little thing roped against the ship's side. It had one seat and two oars, meant to carry a single person between vessels, or perhaps between the vessel and the coast, if it either couldn't dock, or didn't want to.

The dinghy didn't look like it would hold four, let alone get them all to shore without sinking, but they didn't have much choice.

They lowered it to the water, and Holland went down first, steadying the little craft against the side of the *Ghost*. Kell had one leg over, but when Lila moved to follow, she saw Alucard still in the middle of the deck, attention trained on the distant fleet.

"Come on, Captain."

Alucard shook his head. "I'll stay."

"Now's not the time for grand acts," said Lila. "This isn't even your ship."

But for once Alucard's gaze was hard, unyielding. "I am the victor of the *Essen Tasch,* Bard, and one of the strongest magicians in the three empires. I cannot stop a fleet of ships, but if they decide to move, I'll do what I can to slow them down."

"And they'll kill you," said Kell, swinging his leg back onto deck.

The captain offered only a dry smile. "I've always wanted to die in glory."

"Alucard—" started Lila.

"The mist is my doing," he said, looking between them. "It should give you cover."

Kell nodded, and then after a moment, offered his hand. Alucard looked at it as if it were a hot iron, but he took it.

"*Anoshe,*" said Kell.

Lila's chest tightened at the word. It was what Arnesians said when they parted. Lila said nothing, because good-byes in any language felt like surrenders, and she wasn't willing to do that.

Even when Alucard wrapped his arms around her shoulders.

Even when he pressed a kiss to her forehead.

"You're my best thief," he whispered, and her eyes burned.

"I should have killed you," she muttered, hating the waver in her voice.

"Probably," he said, and then, so soft his words were lost to everyone but her, "Keep him safe."

And then his arms were gone, and Kell was pulling her toward the boat, and the last thing she saw of Alucard Emery was the line of his broad shoulders, his head held high as he stood alone on the deck, facing the fleet.

Lila's boots hit the dinghy floor, rocking it in a way that made Holland grip the side.

The last time she'd been in a boat this small, she'd been sitting in the middle of the sea with her hands tied and a barrel of drugged ale between her knees. That had been a bet. This was a gamble.

The dinghy pushed away, and within moments Alucard's mist was swallowing the *Ghost* from view.

"Sit down," said Kell, taking up an oar.

She did, reaching numbly for the second pole. Holland sat at the back of the little boat, casually rolling up his cuff.

"A little help?" said Lila, and his green eye narrowed at her as he produced a small blade and pressed it to his palm.

Holland brought his bleeding hand to the boat's side and said a phrase she'd never heard before—*As Narahi*—and the small craft lurched forward in the water, nearly throwing Kell and Lila from their bench.

Mist sprayed up into her eyes, salty and cold, the wind whipping around her face, but as her vision cleared she realized the dinghy was racing forward, skimming the surface of the water as if propelled by a dozen unseen oars.

Lila looked to Kell. "You didn't teach me this one."

His jaw was slack. "I . . . I didn't know it."

Holland gave them both a bland look. "Amazing," he said dryly. "There are still things you haven't learned."

VII

The streets were filled with bodies, but Rhy felt entirely alone.

Alone, he left his home.

Alone, he moved through the streets.

Alone, he climbed the icy bridge that led to Osaron's palace.

The doors swung open at his touch, and Rhy stilled—he'd half expected to find a grim replica of his own palace, but found instead a specter, a skeletal body hollowed out and filled in again with something less substantial. There were no grand hallways, no staircases leading up to other floors, no ballrooms or balconies.

Only a cavernous space, the bones of the arenas still visible here and there beneath the veneer of shadow and magic.

Pillars grew up from the floor like trees, branching toward a ceiling that gave way here and there to open sky, an effect that made the palace seem at once a masterpiece and a ruin.

Most of the light came from that broken roof, the rest from within, a glow that suffused every surface like fire trapped behind thick glass. Even that thin light was being swallowed up, blotted out by the same black slick he'd seen spreading through the city, magic voiding nature.

Rhy's boots echoed as he willed himself forward through the vast hall, toward the magnificent throne waiting at its center, as natural and unnatural as the palace around it. Ethereal, and empty.

The shadow king stood several paces to the side, examining a corpse.

The corpse itself was on its feet, held up by ribbons of darkness that ran like puppet strings from head and arms up toward the ceiling.

Threads that not only propped the body up, but seemed to be stitching it back together.

It was a woman, he could tell that much, and when Osaron twitched his fingers, the threads pulled tight, lifting her face toward the watery light. Her red hair—redder even than Kell's—hung lank against her hollow cheeks, and below one closed eye, black spilled down her face as if she'd been weeping ink.

Without a shell, Osaron himself looked as spectral as his palace, a half-formed image of a man, the light shining through him every time he moved. His cloak billowed, caught by some imaginary wind, and his whole form rippled and shuddered, as if it couldn't quite hold itself together.

"*What are you?*" said the shadow king, and though he faced the corpse, Rhy knew the words were meant for *him*.

Alucard had warned Rhy of Osaron's voice, the way it echoed through a person's head, snaked through their thoughts. But when he spoke, Rhy heard nothing but the words themselves ringing against stone.

"I am Rhy Maresh," he answered, "and I am king."

Osaron's shadowy fingers slipped back to his sides. The woman slumped a little on her strings.

"*Kings are like weeds in this world.*" He turned, and Rhy saw a face made of layered shadow. It flickered with emotions, there and gone and there and gone, annoyance and amusement, anger and disdain. "*Has this one come to beg, or kneel, or fight?*"

"I've come to see you for myself," said Rhy. "To show you the face of this city. To let you know that I am not afraid." It was a lie—he was indeed afraid, but his fear paled against the grief, the anger, the need to act.

The creature gave him a long, searching look. "*You are the empty one.*"

Rhy shivered. "I am not empty."

"*The hollow one.*"

He swallowed. "I am not hollow."

"*The dead one.*"

"I am not dead."

The shadow king was coming toward him now, and Rhy fought the urge to retreat. *"Your life is not your life."*

Osaron reached out a hand, and Rhy stepped back, then, or tried to, only to find his boots bound to the floor by a magic he couldn't see. The shadow king brought his hand to Rhy's chest, and the buttons on his tunic crumbled, the fabric parting to reveal the concentric circles of the seal scarred over his heart. Slivers of cold pierced the air between shadow and skin.

"My magic." Osaron made a gesture, as if to tear the seal away, but nothing happened. *"And not my magic."*

Rhy let out a shaky breath. "You have no hold on me."

A smile danced across Osaron's lips, and the darkness tightened around Rhy's boots. Fear grew louder then, but Rhy fought hard to smother it. He was not a prisoner. He was here by choice. Drawing Osaron's attention, his wrath.

Forgive me, Kell, he thought, leveling his gaze on the shadow king.

"Someone took my body from me once," he said. "They took my will. Never again. I am not a puppet, and there is *nothing* you can make me do."

"You are wrong." Osaron's eyes lit up like a cat's in the dark. *"I can make you suffer."*

Cold knifed up Rhy's shins as the bindings around his ankles turned to ice. He caught his breath as it began to spread, not up his limbs, but around his entire body, a curtain, a column, devouring first his vision of the shadow king and his dead puppet, and then the throne, and finally the entire chamber, until he was trapped inside a shell of ice. Its surface was so smooth, he could see his own reflection, distorted by the warp of the ice as it thickened. Could see the shadow of the creature on the other side. He imagined Osaron grinning.

"Where is the Antari *now?"* A ghostly hand came to rest against the ice. *"Shall we send him a message?"*

The column of ice shivered, and then, to Rhy's horror, it began to grow spikes. He tried to retreat, but there was nowhere to go.

Rhy bit back a scream as the first point pierced his calf.

Pain flared through him, hot and bright, but fleeting.

I am not empty, he told himself as a second spike cut into his side. A muffled cry as another shard drove through his shoulder, sliding in and out of his collar with terrible ease.

I am not hollow.

The air caught in his chest as ice pierced a lung, his back, his hip, his wrist.

I am not dead.

He had seen his mother run through, his father killed by a dozen steel blades. And he could not save them. Their bodies were their own. Their lives, their own.

But Rhy's was not. It was not a weakness, he realized now, but a strength. He could suffer, but it could not break him.

I am Rhy Maresh, he told himself as blood slicked the floor.

I am the king of Arnes.

And I am unbreakable.

VIII

They were nearly to the coast when Kell started to shiver.

It was a cold day, but the chill had come on from somewhere else, and just as he realized it for what it was—an echo—the pain caught up. Not a glancing blow, but sudden and violent and sharp as knives.

Not again.

It lanced through his leg, his shoulder, his ribs, opening into a full-blown assault against his nerves.

He gasped, bracing himself against the side of the boat.

"Kell?"

Lila's voice was distant, drowned out by the pulse raging in his ears.

He *knew* his brother couldn't die, but it didn't douse the fear, didn't stop the simple, animal panic that pounded in his blood, crying out for help. He waited for the pain to pass, the way it always had before, fading with every heartbeat like a rock thrown into a pond, the crash giving way to smaller ripples before finally smoothing.

But the pain didn't pass.

Every breath brought a new rock, a new crash.

Lila's hands hovered in the air. "Can I heal you?"

"No," said Kell, breath jagged. "It's not . . . his body isn't . . ." His mind spun.

"Alive?" offered Holland.

Kell scowled. "Of course it's *alive*."

"But that life is not his," countered Holland calmly. "He's just a shell. A vessel for your power."

"Stop."

"You've cut strings from your magic and made a puppet."

The water surged around the small boat with Kell's temper.

"*Stop.*" This time the word was coming from Lila. "Before he sinks us."

But Kell heard the question in her voice, the same one he'd asked himself for months.

Was something truly alive if it couldn't be killed?

A week after Kell had bound his brother's life to his, he'd woken with a sudden pain searing across his palm, white hot, as if the skin were burning. He'd stared down at the offending hand, certain the flesh would be blistered, charred, but it wasn't. Instead, he'd found his brother sitting in his rooms before a low table with a candle on it, eyes distant as he held his hand over the flame. Kell had snatched Rhy's fingers away, pressing a damp rag to the red and peeling skin as his brother slowly came back to his senses.

"I'm sorry," Rhy had said, a now tiring refrain. "I just needed . . . to know."

"Know what?" he'd snapped, and his brother's eyes had gone lost.

"If I'm real."

Now Kell shuddered on the floor of the small boat, the echo of his brother's pain fierce, unyielding. This didn't feel like a self-inflicted wound, no candle flame or word scrawled on skin. This pain was deep and piercing, like the blade to the chest but worse, because it was coming from everywhere.

Bile filled Kell's mouth. He thought he'd already been sick.

He tried to remember that pain was only terrifying because of what it signaled—danger, death—that without those things, it was nothing . . .

His vision blurred.

. . . just another sense . . .

His muscles screamed.

. . . a tether . . .

Kell shivered violently, and registered Lila's arms circling him, thin but strong, the warmth of her narrow body like a candle against the cold. She was saying something, but he couldn't make out the words.

Holland's voice came in and out, reduced to short bursts of incoherent sound.

The pain was smoothing—not easing, exactly, just evening into something horrible but steady. He dragged his thoughts together, focused his vision, and saw the coast approaching. Not the port at Tanek, but a stretch of rocky beach. It didn't matter. Land was land.

"Hurry," he murmured thickly, and Holland shot him a dark look.

"If this boat goes any faster, it will catch fire before we have a chance to crash upon those rocks." But he saw the magician's fingertips go white with force, felt the world part around his power.

One moment the jagged shore was rising in the distance, and the next, it was nearly upon them.

Holland rose to his feet, and Kell managed to uncoil his aching body, his mind clearing enough to think.

He had his token in hand—the swatch of fabric the queen had given him, *KM* stitched on the silk—and fresh blood streaked the cloth as the dinghy drew precariously close to the rocky shore. Their coats were soaked with icy water by the time they drew near enough to disembark.

Holland stepped off first, steadying himself atop sea-slicked rocks.

Kell started to follow, and slipped. He would have crashed down into the surf, had Holland not been there to catch his wrist and haul him up onto the shore. Kell turned back for Lila, but she was already beside him, her hand in his and Holland's on his shoulder as Kell pressed the swatch of cloth to the rock wall and said the words to take them home.

The freezing mist and the jagged coast instantly vanished, replaced by the smooth marble of the Rose Hall, with its vaulted ceiling, its empty thrones.

There was no sign of Rhy, no sign of the king and queen, until he turned and saw the wide stone table in the middle of the hall.

Kell stilled, and somewhere behind him, Lila drew in a short, shocked breath.

It took him a moment to process the shapes that lay on top, to understand that they were bodies.

Two bodies, side by side atop the stone, each draped with crimson cloth, the crowns still shining in their hair.

Emira Maresh, with a white rose, edged in gold, laid over her heart.

Maxim Maresh, the petals of another rose scattered across his chest.

The cold settled in Kell's bones.

The king and queen were dead.

IX

Alucard Emery had imagined his death a hundred times.

It was a morbid habit, but three years at sea had given him too much time to think, and drink, and dream. Most of the time his dreams started with Rhy, but as the nights lengthened and the glasses emptied, they invariably turned darker. His wrists would ache and his thoughts would fog, and he'd wonder. When. How.

Sometimes it was glamorous and sometimes it was gruesome. A battle. A stray blade. An execution. A ransom gone wrong. Choking on his own blood, or swallowing the sea. The possibilities were endless.

But he never imagined death would look like this.

Never imagined that he would face it alone. Without a crew. Without a friend. Without a family. Without even an enemy, save the faceless masses that filled the waiting ships.

Fool, Jasta would have said. *We all face death alone.*

He didn't want to think of Jasta. Or Lenos. Or Bard.

Or *Rhy*.

The sea air scratched at the scars on Alucard's wrists, and he rubbed at them as the ship—it wasn't even *his* ship—rocked silently in the surf.

The Veskans' green and silver were drawn in, the ships floating grimly, resolutely, a mountainous line along the horizon.

What were they waiting for?

Orders from Vesk?

Or from within the city?

Did they know about the shadow king? The cursed fog? Was that what held them at bay? Or were they simply waiting for the cover of night to strike?

Sanct, what good was it to speculate?

They hadn't moved.

Any minute they *could* move.

The sun was sinking, turning the sky a bloody red, and his head was pounding from the strain of holding the mist for as long as he had. It was beginning to thin, and there was nothing he could do but wait, wait, and try to summon the strength to—

To do what? challenged a voice in his head. *Move the sea?*

It wasn't possible. That wasn't just a line he'd fed Bard to keep her from doing herself in. Everything had limits. His mind raced, the way it had been racing for the last hour, stubbornly, doggedly, as if it might finally round a corner and find an idea—not a mad notion parading as a plan, but an *actual* idea—waiting for him.

The sea. The ships. The sails.

Now he was just listing things.

No. Wait. The *sails*. Perhaps he could find a way to—

No.

Not from this distance.

He would have to move the *Ghost,* sail her right up to the ass end of the Veskan fleet and then—what?

Alucard rubbed his eyes.

If he was going to die, he could at least think of a way to make it count.

If he was going to die—

But that was the problem.

Alucard didn't *want* to die.

Standing there on the prow of the *Ghost,* he realized with startling clarity that death and glory didn't interest him nearly as much as living long enough to go home. To make sure Bard was alive, to try to find any remaining members of the *Night Spire.* To see Rhy's amber eyes, press his lips to the place where his collar curved into his throat. To kneel before his prince, and offer him the only thing Alucard had ever held back: the truth.

The mirror from the floating market sat in its shroud on a nearby crate.

Four years for a gift that would never be given.

Movement in the distance caught his eye.

A shadow gliding across the twilit sky—now a bruised blue instead of bloody red. His heart lurched. It was a bird.

It plunged down onto one of the Veskan ships, swallowed up by the line of mast and net and folded sail, and Alucard held his breath until his chest ached, until his vision spotted. This was it. The order to move. He didn't have much time.

The sails . . .

If he could damage the sails . . .

Alucard began to gather every piece of loose steel aboard the ship, ransacked the crates and the galley and the hold for blades and pots and silverware, anything he could fashion into something capable of cutting. Magic thrummed in his fingers as he willed the surfaces sharp, molded serrated edges into the sides.

He lined them up like soldiers on the deck, three dozen makeshift weapons that could rend and tear. He tried to ignore the fact that the sails were down, tried to smother the knowledge that even *he* didn't have the ability control this many things at once, not with any delicacy.

But brute force was better than nothing.

All he had to do was bring the *Ghost* in range to strike. He was lifting his attention to his own sails when he saw the Veskan sails draw taut.

It happened in a wave, green and silver blossoming out from the masts at the center ship, and then the ones to either side, on and on until the whole fleet was ready to sail.

It was a gift, thought Alucard, readying his weapons, pulling on the air with the remains of his strength as the first ship began to move.

Followed by a second.

And a third.

Alucard's jaw went slack. The last of his strength faltered, died.

The wind dissolved, and he stood there, staring, a makeshift blade tumbling from his fingers, because the Veskan ships weren't sailing toward Tanek and the Isle and the city of London.

They were sailing *away*.

The fleet's formation dissolved as they pivoted back toward open sea.

One of the ships passed close enough for him to see the men aboard, and a Veskan soldier looked his way, broad face unreadable beneath his helm. Alucard lifted a hand in greeting. The man didn't wave back. The ship continued on.

Alucard watched them go.

He waited for the waters to still, for the last colors to fade from the sky.

And then he folded to his knees on the deck.

X

Kell stared, numbly, at the bodies on the table.

His king and queen. His father and his mother . . .

He heard Holland say his name, felt Lila's fingers curl around his arm. "We have to find Rhy."

"He's not here," said a new voice.

It was Isra, the head of the city guard. Kell had taken the woman for a statue with her full armor and bowed head, had forgotten the rules of mourning—the dead were never left alone.

"Where?" he managed. "Where is he?"

"The palace, sir."

Kell started for the doors that led back into the royal palace, when Isra stopped him.

"Not that one," said the woman wearily. She pointed to the massive front doors of the Rose Hall, the ones that led out to the city street. "The *other* one. On the river."

Kell's pulse pounded madly in his chest.

The *shadow* palace.

His head spun.

How long had they been gone?

Three days?

No, four.

Four days, Rhy.

Then you can get yourself into trouble.

Four days, and the king and queen were dead, and Rhy hadn't waited any longer.

"You just let him go?" snapped Lila, accosting the guard.

Isra bristled. "I had no choice." She met Kell's eyes. "As of today, Rhy Maresh is the king."

The reality landed like a blow.

Rhy Maresh, young royal, flirtatious rake, resurrected prince.

The boy always looking for places to hide, who moved through his own life as if it were a piece of theatre.

His brother, who had once accepted a cursed amulet because it promised strength.

His brother, who now carved apologies into his skin and held his hands over candle flames to feel alive.

His brother was king.

And his first act?

To march straight into Osaron's palace.

Kell wanted to wring Rhy's neck, but then he recalled the pain he'd felt, wave after wave rocking him in the boat, crashing through him even now, a current of suffering. *Rhy.* Kell's feet carried him past Isra, past row after row of large stone basins to the doors of the Rose Hall and out into the thin London light.

He heard their steps behind him, Lila's thief-soft and quick, Holland's sure, but he didn't look back, didn't look down at the sea of spelled bodies lying in the street, kept his eyes trained on the river, and the impossible shadow stretching up against the sky.

Kell had always thought of the royal palace like a second sun caught in perpetual rise over the city. If that was true, Osaron's palace was an eclipse, a piece of perfect darkness, only its edges rimmed with reflected light.

Somewhere behind him, Holland drew a weapon from a fallen man's sheath, and Lila swore softly as she wove through the bodies, but neither strayed far from his side.

Together, the three *Antari* climbed the onyx incline of the palace bridge.

Together, they reached the polished black glass of the palace doors.

The handle gave under Kell's touch, but Lila caught his wrist and held it firm.

"Is this really the best plan?" she asked.

"It's the only one we have," said Kell as Holland drew the Inheritor over his head and slipped the device into his pocket. He must have sensed Kell staring, because he looked up, met his gaze. One eye green and one black, and both as steady as a mask.

"One way or another," said Holland, "this ends."

Kell nodded. "It ends."

They looked to Lila. She sighed, freeing Kell's fingers.

Three silver rings caught the dying light—Lila's and Kell's the narrower echoes of Holland's band—all of them singing with shared power as the door swung open, and the three *Antari* stepped through into the dark.

FOURTEEN

ANTARI

I

As Kell's boot crossed the threshold, the pain flared in his chest. It was as if the walls of Osaron's palace had muted the connection, and now, without the boundaries, the cord drew tight, and every step brought Kell closer to Rhy's suffering.

Lila had two knives already out, but the palace was empty around them, the hall clear. Tieren's magic had worked, stripped the monster of his many puppets, but Kell still felt Lila's nervous tension in his own limbs, saw that same unease reflected again in Holland's inscrutable face.

There was a wrongness to this place, as if they'd stepped out of London, out of time, out of life entirely, and into somewhere that didn't quite exist. It was magic without balance, power without rule, and it was dying, every surface slowly taking on the glossy black pall of nature burned to nothing.

But in the center of the vast chamber, Kell felt it.

A pulse of life.

A beating heart.

And then, as Kell's eyes adjusted to the low light, he saw Rhy.

His brother hung several feet off the floor, suspended within a web of ice, held up by a dozen sharpened points that drove in and through the prince's body, their frosted surfaces slick with red.

Rhy was alive, but only because he could not die.

His chest stuttered and heaved, tears frozen on his cheeks. His lips moved, but his words were lost, his blood a broad dark pool beneath him.

Is this yours? Rhy had asked when they were young, and Kell had cut his wrists to heal him. *Is all this yours?*

Now Rhy's blood splashed under Kell's boots, the air metallic in his mouth as he raced forward.

"Wait!" called Lila.

"Kell," warned Holland.

But if it was a trap, they'd already been caught. Caught the moment they entered the palace.

"Hold on, Rhy."

Rhy's lashes fluttered at the sound of Kell's voice. He tried to raise his head, but couldn't.

Kell's hand was already wet with his own blood when he reached his brother's side. He would have melted the ice with a single touch, a word, if he'd had the chance.

Instead his fingers stopped an inch above the ice, barred by someone else's will. Kell fought against the magic's hold as a voice spilled from the shadows behind the throne.

"That is mine."

The voice came from nowhere. Everywhere. And yet, it was contained. No longer a hollow construction of shadow and magic, but bounded by lips and teeth and lungs.

She walked into the light, red hair rising into the air around her face as if caught up in some imaginary wind.

Ojka.

Kell had *followed* her.

Listened to her lies in the palace courtyard—the words mixing with doubt and anger into something poisonous—and let her lead him through a door in the world and into a trap.

And when he saw Ojka now, he shivered.

Lila had *killed* her.

Faced her in the hall with Kell screaming beyond the door and Rhy dying a world away and no choice but to fight, losing a glass eye before she cut the woman's throat.

And when she saw Ojka now, she smiled.

Holland had *made* her.

Plucked her from the streets of the Kosik, the alleys that had shaped his own past so many years before, and given her the chance Vortalis had given him, the chance to do more, to be more.

And when he saw Ojka now, he stilled.

II

Ojka, the assassin—

Ojka, the messenger—

Ojka, the *Antari*—

—wasn't Ojka anymore.

"*My king,*" she'd called Holland so many times, but her voice had always been low, sultry, and now it resonated through the hall and in his head, familiar and strange, just as this place was familiar and strange. Holland had faced Osaron in an echo of this palace when the shadow king was nothing but glass and smoke and the dying ember of magic.

And now he faced him again, in his newest shell.

Ojka once had yellow eyes, but now they both shone black. A crown perched in her hair, a dark and weightless ring that thrust up spikes like icicles into the air above her head. Her throat was wrapped in black ribbon, her skin at once luminous with power and unmistakably dead. She never drew breath, and her dark veins stood out on her skin, parched, empty.

The only signs of life, impossibly, came from those black eyes—*Osaron's* eyes—which danced with light and swirled with shadows.

"*Holland,*" said the shadow king, and anger burned in him to hear the monster form the word with Ojka's lips.

"I killed you," mused Lila, crouched at Holland's left side, her knives at the ready.

Ojka's face contorted with amusement.

"*Magic does not die.*"

"Let my brother go," demanded Kell, stepping in front of the other two *Antari,* his voice imperious, even now.

"Why should I?"

"He has no power," said Kell. "Nothing for you to use, nothing for you to *take.*"

"And yet he lives," mused the corpse. *"How curious. All life has strings. So where are his?"*

Ojka's chin tipped up, and the ice spearing Rhy's body splayed like fingers, drawing from the prince a stifled cry. The color drained from Kell's face as he fought back a mirrored scream, pain and defiance warring in his throat. The ring sang on Holland's fingers as their shared power hummed between them, trying to tip toward Kell in his distress.

Holland held it steady.

Ojka's hands, delicate but strong, rose, palms up. *"Have you finally come to beg,* Antari? *To kneel?"* Those swimming black eyes went to Holland. *"To let me in?"*

"Never again," said Holland, and it was true, though the Inheritor hung heavy in his pocket. Osaron had a talent for sliding through one's mind, turning over its thoughts, but Holland had more practice than most at hiding his. He forced his mind away from the device.

"We've come to stop you," said Lila.

Ojka's hands fell back to her sides. *"Stop me?"* said Osaron. *"You cannot stop time. You cannot stop change. And you cannot stop me. I am inevitable."*

"You," said Lila, "are nothing but a demon masquerading as a god."

"And you," said Osaron smoothly, *"will die slowly."*

"I killed that body once," she countered. "I think I can do it again."

Holland was still staring at Ojka's corpse. The bruises on her skin. The cloth wrapped tight around her throat. As if Osaron felt the weight of that gaze, he turned his stolen face toward Holland. *"Are you not happy to see your knight?"*

Holland's anger had never burned hot. It was forged cold and sharp, and the words were a whetstone along its edge. Ojka had been loyal, not to Osaron, but to *him.* She had served him. Trusted him. Looked at him and seen not a god, but a king. And she was dead—like Alox, like Talya, like Vortalis.

"She did not let you in."

A tip of the head. A rictus grin. *"In death, none can refuse."*

Holland drew a blade—a scythe, taken from a body in the square. "I will cut you from that body," he said. "Even if I have to do it one piece at a time."

Fire sparked across Lila's knives.

Blood dripped from Kell's fingers.

They had shifted slowly around the shadow king, circling, caging.

Just as they'd planned.

"No one offers," instructed Kell. "No matter what Osaron says or does, no matter what he promises or threatens, *no one* lets him in."

They were sitting in the *Ghost*'s galley, the Inheritor between them.

"So we're just supposed to play coy?" said Lila, spinning a dagger point-down on the wooden table.

Holland started to speak, but the ship gave a sudden sway and he had to stop, swallow. "Osaron covets what he does not have," he said when the wave of illness had passed. "The goal is not to *give* him a body, but to force him into needing one."

"Splendid," said Lila dryly. "So all we have to do is defeat an incarnation of magic strong enough to ruin worlds."

Kell shot her a look. "Since when do you shy from a fight?"

"I'm not shying," she snapped. "I just want to be sure we can *win*."

"We win by being stronger," said Kell. "And with the rings, we just might be."

"*Might* be," echoed Lila.

"Every vessel can be emptied," said Holland, twisting the silver binding ring around his thumb. "Magic can't be killed, but it can be weakened, and Osaron's power might be vast, but it is by no means infinite. When I found him in Black London, he was reduced to a statue, too weak to hold a moving form."

"Until *you* gave him one," muttered Lila.

"Exactly," said Holland, ignoring the jab.

"Osaron has been feeding on my city and its people," added Kell. "But if Tieren's spell has worked, he should be running out of sources."

Lila dislodged her dagger from the table.

"Which means he should be good and ready for a fight."

Holland nodded. "All we have to do is give him one. Make him weak. Make him desperate."

"And then what?" demanded Lila.

"*Then*," said Kell, "and only then, do we give him a host." Kell nodded at Holland when he said it, the Inheritor hanging around the *Antari*'s neck.

"And what if he doesn't pick *you*?" she snarled. "It's well and good to offer, but if he gives *me* a shot, I'm going to take it."

"Lila," started Kell, but she cut him off.

"So will you. Don't pretend you won't."

Silence settled over them.

"You're right," said Kell at last, and to Holland's surprise—though it shouldn't have surprised him anymore—Lila Bard cracked a smile. It was hard and humorless.

"It's a race, then," she said. "May the best *Antari* win."

Osaron moved with a fraction of Ojka's grace, but twice as much speed. Twin swords blossomed from her hands in plumes of smoke and became real, their surfaces shining as they sliced the air where Lila had been a moment before.

But Lila was already airborne, pushing off the nearest pillar as Holland willed a gust of wind through the hall with blinding force, and Kell's steel shards flew on the gust like heavy rain.

Ojka's hands came up, stilling the wind and the steel within as Lila plummeted down toward Ojka's body, carving a path down her back.

But Osaron was too quick, and Lila's knife barely grazed the shoulder of his host. Shadow poured from the wound like steam before stitching the dead skin closed.

"*Not fast enough, little* Antari," he said, backhanding her across the face.

Lila fell sideways, knife tumbling from her grip even as she rolled up into a fighting crouch. She flicked her fingers and the fallen blade sang through the air, burying itself in Ojka's leg.

Osaron growled as more smoke spilled out of the wound, and Lila flashed a cold smile. "I learned that one from her," she said, a fresh blade appearing in her fingers. "Right before I cut her throat."

Ojka's mouth was a snarl. "*I will make you—*"

But Holland was already moving, electricity dancing along his scythe as it cut the air. Osaron turned and blocked the blow with one sword, driving the other up toward Holland's chest. He spun out of the way, the blade grazing his ribs as Kell attacked from the other side, ice curled around his fist.

It shattered against Ojka's cheek, slicing through to bone. Before the wound could heal, Lila was there, blade glowing red with heat.

They moved like pieces of the same weapon. Danced like Ojka's knives—back when *she* had wielded them—every push and pull conveyed through the tether between them. When Lila moved, Holland felt her path. When Holland feinted, Kell knew where to strike.

They were blurs of motion, shards of light dancing around a coil of darkness.

And they were winning.

III

Lila was running out of knives.

Osaron had turned three of them to ash, two to sand, and a sixth—the one she'd won from Lenos—had vanished entirely. She had only one left—the knife she'd nicked from Fletcher's shop her first day in Red London—and she wasn't keen on losing it.

Blood ran into her good eye, but she didn't care. Smoke was seeping from Ojka's body in a dozen places as Kell and Holland and the demon clashed. They'd made their mark.

But it wasn't enough.

Osaron was still on his feet.

Lila swiped a thumb along her bloody cheek and knelt, pressing her hand against the stone, but when she tried to summon it, the rock resisted. The surface hummed with magic, yet rang hollow.

Because, of course, it wasn't *real*.

A dream thing, dead inside, just like—

The floor began to soften, and she leapt back an instant before it turned to tar. Another one of Osaron's traps.

She was sick of playing by the shadow king's rules.

Surrounded by a palace only he could will.

Lila's gaze swept the chamber, and then went up—up past the walls to the place where the sky shone through. She had an idea.

Lila reached out with all her strength—and part of Holland's, part of Kell's—and *pulled,* not on the air, but on the Isle.

"You cannot will the ocean," Alucard had told her once.

But he never said anything about a river.

Blood trickled down Lila's throat as she pressed the kerchief to her nose.

Alucard was sitting across from her, chin in one hand. "I'm honestly not sure how you've lived this long."

Lila shrugged, her voice muffled by the cloth. "I'm hard to kill."

The captain shoved to his feet. "Stubborn's not the same thing as infallible," he said, pouring himself a drink, "and I've told you three times you cannot move the fucking ocean, no matter how hard you try."

"Maybe *you're* not trying hard *enough*," she muttered.

Alucard shook his head. "Everything has a scale, Bard. You cannot will the sky, you cannot move the sea, you cannot shift the whole continent beneath your feet. Currents of wind, basins of water, patches of earth, that is the breadth of a magician's reach. That is the circumference of their power."

And then, without warning, he lobbed the wine bottle at her head.

She was quick enough to catch it, but just barely, fumbling the cloth from her bloody nose. "What the hell, Emery?" she snapped.

"Can you fit your hand around it?"

She looked down at the bottle, her fingers wrapped around the glass, their tips a breath away from touching.

"Your hand is your hand," said Alucard simply. "It has limits. So does your power. It can only hold so much, and no matter how hard you stretch your fingers around that glass, they will never touch."

She shrugged, spun the bottle in her hand, and shattered it against the table.

"And now?" she said.

Alucard Emery groaned. He pinched the bridge of his nose the way he did when she was being particularly maddening. She'd taken to counting the number of times a day she could make him do it.

Her current record was seven.

Lila sat forward in her seat. Her nose had stopped bleeding, though she could still taste the copper on her tongue. She willed the broken shards up into the air between them, where they formed a cloud in the vague shape of a bottle.

"You're a brilliant magician," she said, "but there's something you just don't get."

He slumped back into his chair. "What's that?"

Lila smiled. "The trick to winning a fight isn't strength, but strategy."

Alucard raised his brows. "Who said anything about fighting?"

She ignored him. "And *strategy* is just a fancy word for a special kind of common sense, the ability to see options, to make them where there were none. It's not about knowing the rules."

Her hand fell away, and the bottle crumbled again, falling in a rain of glass.

"It's about knowing how to break them."

IV

It wasn't enough, thought Holland.

For every blow they landed, Osaron avoided three, and for every one they dodged, Osaron landed three in turn. Blood began to dot the floor.

It spilled down Kell's cheek. Dripped from Lila's fingers. Slicked the cloth at Holland's side.

His head spun as the other two *Antari* drew on his power.

Kell was busy summoning a force of wind while Lila had gone very still, her head tipped back toward the place where the bones of the ceiling met the sky.

Osaron saw the opening and moved toward her, but Kell's wind whipped through the throne room, trapping the shadow king within a tunnel of air.

"We have to do something," he called over the wind as Osaron slashed at the column. Holland knew it wouldn't hold, and sure enough, moments later, the cyclone shattered, slamming Kell and Holland both backward in the blast. Lila staggered, but stayed on her feet, a trickle of red running from her nose as the pressure in the palace rose and darkness blacked the windows to either side.

Kell was just finding his feet when Osaron sprang toward her again, too fast for Kell to catch. Holland touched the gash across his ribs.

"*As Narahi,*" he said, the words thundering through him.

Quicken.

It was a hard piece of magic under the best circumstances, and a grueling one now, but it was worth it as the world around him *slowed*.

To his right, Lila still looked up. To his left, Kell was drawing his hands apart against the massive force of time, a fire sparking in slow motion between his palms. Only Osaron still moved with any semblance of speed, black eyes shifting his way as Holland spun the scythe and lunged.

They clashed together, apart, together again.

"I will make you bend."

Weapon against weapon.

"I will make you break."

Will against will.

"You were mine, Holland."

His back hit a pillar.

"And you will be mine again."

The blade raked his arm.

"Once I hear you beg."

"Never," Holland snarled, slashing the scythe. It should have met Osaron's swords, but at the last instant the weapons disappeared and he caught Holland's blade with Ojka's bare hands, letting the steel cut deep. Blood—dead, black, but still *Antari*—leaked around the blade, and Osaron's stolen face split into a grim, triumphant smile.

"As Ste—"

Holland gasped, letting go of the scythe before the spell was out.

It was a mistake. The weapon turned to ash in Osaron's grip, and before Holland could dodge, the demon wrapped one bloody hand around his face and pinned him back against the pillar.

Overhead, a shadow was blotting out the sky. Holland's hands wrapped around Osaron's wrists, trying to pry them loose, and for an instant the two were locked in a strange embrace, before the shadow king leaned in and whispered in his ear.

"As Osaro."

Darken.

The words echoed through his head and became shadow, became night, became a black cloth cinching over Holland's sight, blotting out Osaron, and the palace, and the wave of water cresting overhead, and plunging Holland's world into black.

Blood was dripping from Lila's nose as the wave of black water curled over the palace—

Too big—

Far too big—

And then it *fell*.

Lila let go of the river, head spinning as it came crashing down onto the palace hall. She threw her hands up to block the crushing weight, but her magic was slow—too slow—in the conjuring's wake.

The pillar shielded Holland from the worst of the blow, but the water slammed Ojka's body down into the floor with an audible crack. Lila dove for cover but found none, and only Kell's quick reflexes spared them both the same fate. She felt her power dip as Kell pulled it close to his and cast it back in a shield above her head. The river fell like heavy rain, spilling in curtains around her.

Through the veil she saw Ojka's body twitch and flex, broken pieces already knitting back together as Osaron forced the puppet up.

Nearby, Holland was on his hands and knees, fingers splayed on the flooded floor as if searching for something he'd dropped.

"Get up!" shouted Lila, but when Holland's head swiveled toward her, she recoiled. His eyes were wrong. Not black, but shuttered, blind.

There was no time.

Osaron was up and Holland wasn't and she and Kell were both racing forward, boots splashing in the shallow water as it spun up around them into weapons.

A sword spilled from nothing into Osaron's hand as Holland struggled, empty-eyed. His fingers wrapped around the shadow king's ankle, but before he could issue a spell he was being sent backward with a vicious kick, skidding across the flooded ground.

Kell and Lila ran, but they were too slow.

Holland was on his knees in front of the shadow king with his raised sword.

"I told you I would make you kneel."

Osaron brought the blade down, and Kell slowed the weapon in a cloud of frost as Lila dove for Holland, tackling him out of the way the instant before the metal struck stone.

Lila spun up, throwing off water into shards of ice that sang through the air. Osaron flung up a hand, but he wasn't fast enough, wasn't *strong* enough, and several slivers of ice found flesh before he could will them away.

There was no time to relish the victory.

With a single sweep of his arm, every drop of river water she'd summoned came together and swirled up into a column before turning to dark stone. Just another pillar in his palace.

Osaron pointed at Lila. *"You will—"*

She sprang at him, shocked when the now-dry floor splashed beneath her feet. The stone pooled around her ankles, one moment liquid and the next solid again, pinning her the way the floor had pinned Kisimyr on the palace roof.

No.

She was trapped, and she had the last knife out and in her hand, fire starting in the other as she braced herself for an attack that never came.

Because Osaron had turned.

And he was heading for *Kell.*

Kell had only a stolen moment as Lila fought Osaron, but he sprinted for the prison of ice.

Hold on, Rhy, he pleaded, slashing his blade at the frozen cage, only to be rebuffed by the shadow king's will.

He tried again and again, a frustrated sob clawing up his throat.

Stop.

He didn't know if he heard Rhy's voice, or only felt it as he tried to reach him. His brother's head was bowed, blood running into his amber eyes and turning them gold.

Kell—

"Kell!" shouted Lila, and he looked up, catching Ojka's reflection in the column of ice as it surged toward him. He spun, drawing the crimson-stained water at his feet up into a spear, and lifting the weapon an instant before the shadow king struck.

Osaron's twin blades came singing down, shattering the spear in Kell's hands before lodging in the walls of Rhy's prison. The ice cracked, but didn't break. And in that moment, when Osaron's weapons were trapped, his stolen shell caught between attack and retreat, Kell drove the broken shard of ice into Ojka's chest.

The shadow king looked down at the wound, as if amused by the feeble attempt, but Kell's hand was a mess from gripping the shattered spear, blood slicking hand and ice alike, and when he spoke, the spell rang through the air.

"As Steno."

Break.

The magic tore through Ojka's body, warring with Osaron's will as her bones broke and mended, shattered and set, a puppet being torn apart in one breath, patched together in the next. Fighting—and failing—to hold its shape, the shadow king's stolen shell began to look grotesque, pieces peeling, the whole thing knit together more by magic than sinew.

"That body will not hold," snarled Kell as broken hands forced him up against his brother's cage.

Osaron smiled a ruined grin. *"You are right,"* he said, as an icy spike drove through Kell's back.

V

Someone screamed.

A single, agonized note.

But it wasn't Kell.

He *wanted* to scream, but Ojka's ruined hand was wrapped around his jaw, forcing his mouth closed. The frozen blade had pierced above his hip and come out his side, its tip coated with vivid red blood.

Beyond Osaron, Lila was trying to tear herself free, and Holland was on his hands and knees, searching the ground for something lost.

A groan escaped Kell's throat as the shadow king prodded the tear in his side.

"*This is not a mortal wound,*" said Osaron. "*Not yet.*"

He felt the monster's voice sliding through his mind, weighing him down.

"*Let me in,*" it whispered.

No, thought Kell viscerally, violently.

That darkness—the same darkness that had caught him when he fell into White London so recently—wrapped around his wounded body, warm, soft, welcoming.

"*Let me in.*"

No.

The column of ice burned cold against his spine.

Rhy.

Osaron echoed in his mind. Said, "*I can be merciful.*"

Kell felt the shards of ice slide free—not from his own body but his brother's—pain withdrawing limb by limb. He heard the short gasp, the soft, wet sound of Rhy collapsing to the blood-slicked floor, and relief surged through him even as the cold took root again, branched, flowered.

"Let me in."

In the corner of Kell's vision, something flashed on the floor. A shard of metal, near Holland's searching hand.

The Inheritor.

Kell's mind was slipping with the pain as he called it toward him, but as the cylinder rose into the air, his power failed, suddenly, completely. As if severed, stolen.

Snatched away by a thief.

Lila couldn't move.

The floor gripped her legs in a stone embrace, bones threatening to break with every motion. Across the chamber Kell was trapped and bleeding, and she couldn't reach him, not with her hands, couldn't force Osaron away. But she could draw him to her. She pulled on the tether between them, stealing Kell's magic, and Osaron's attention with it. Power flared like light before Lila's eyes, and the demon spun toward her, a moth drawn to a flame.

Look at me, she wanted to say as Osaron abandoned Kell. *Come to me.*

But as soon as those black eyes leveled on her, she would have given everything to get loose. To be free.

Kell was horribly pale, his fingers slipping over the blade of ice driven through his side. Holland clutched at a pillar and struggled to his feet. The Inheritor sat on the ground nearby, but before Lila could summon it, Osaron was there, one mangled hand knotted in her hair and a blade against her throat.

"*Let go,*" he whispered, and whether he meant her knife or her will, she didn't know. But at least she had his attention now. She let the weapon fall with a clatter to the floor.

He forced her face toward his, her gaze toward his, felt him sliding through her mind, probing thoughts, memories.

"So much potential."

She tried to pull away, but she was pinned, the floor gripping her ankles and Osaron her scalp and the blade still at her throat.

"*I am what you saw in the mirror at Sasenroche,*" said the shadow king. "*I am what you dream of being. I can make you unstoppable. I can set you free.*"

Across the throne room, Kell had finally summoned the strength to break free. The ice shattered around him and he collapsed to the floor. Osaron didn't turn. His attention was on her, eyes dancing hungrily in the light of her power.

"Free," she said softly, as if pondering the word.

"*Yes,*" whispered the shadow king.

In the black of his eyes, she saw it, that version of herself.

Unbeatable.

Unbreakable.

"*Let me in, Delilah Bard.*"

It was tempting, even now. Her hand drifted up to Ojka's arm. A dancer's embrace. Bloody fingers digging into ruined flesh.

Lila smiled. "*As Illumae.*"

Osaron wrenched back, but he was too late.

Ojka's body began to burn.

The blade slashed blindly at Lila's throat but she dodged, and then it was gone, tumbling from Ojka's hand as the corpse went up in flames.

Smoke poured from the thrashing body, first the acrid stuff of burning flesh, and then the dark fog of Osaron's power as it was finally forced to flee its shell.

The palace shuddered with the sudden loss of his power, his control. The floor loosened around her boots and Lila stumbled forward, free, as Osaron struggled to find form.

The shadows swirled, fell apart, swirled again.

The Osaron that took shape was a ghost of himself.

A brittle facade, transparent and flat. His edges bled and blurred, and through his spectral center she could see Kell clutching the wound across his front. Rhy, struggling to rise.

This was it.

Her chance.

Their chance.

She flexed her fingers, reaching for the Inheritor. It trembled on the ground and rose toward her.

And then it fell, tumbled back to the floor as her strength vanished. It was like being swallowed by a wave in reverse. All the power flooding suddenly, violently, away. Lila gasped as the world tilted beneath her, legs buckling, her vision dim.

Magic was such a new thing that the absence of it shouldn't have hurt so much, but Lila felt gutted as every last ounce of power was wrenched away. She cast about for Kell, certain that he had stolen her strength, but Kell was still on the ground, still bleeding.

The shadow king loomed over her, hands splayed, and the air began to coil around Lila's throat, tightening until she couldn't speak, couldn't breathe.

And there, behind him, in a halo of silver light, stood Holland.

Holland couldn't see.

The darkness was everywhere, raging around him like a storm, swallowing the world. But he could hear. And so he heard Kell being stabbed, heard Ojka burn, heard the Inheritor as Lila called it from the ground, and knew it was his chance. And when he drew on the binding ring, and pulled the magic of the other two *Antari* to him, he found a kind of sight. The world took shape not in light and dark, but in ribbons of power.

The strands glowed, flowing around and through Lila's kneeling form, and Kell's, and Rhy's, all of it drawn in silver light.

And there, right in front of him, the absence.

A man in the shape of a void.

A void in the shape of a man.

No longer a puppet. Just a piece of rotten magic, smooth and black and empty.

And when the shadow king spoke, it was his own voice, liquid, susurrant.

"*I know your mind, Holland,*" said the darkness. "*I lived inside it.*"

The shadow king came toward him, and Holland took a single, final step back, his shoulders meeting the pillar as his fingers tightened on the metal cylinder.

He could feel Osaron's hunger.

His need.

"*Do you want to see your world? How it crumbles without you in it?*"

A cold hand, not flesh and blood but shadow and ice, came to rest against Holland's heart.

I am tired, he thought, knowing Osaron would hear. *Tired of fighting. Of losing. But I will never let you in.*

He felt the darkness smile, sickly and triumphant.

"*Have you forgotten?*" whispered the shadow king. "*You never cast me out.*"

Holland exhaled. A shuddering breath.

To Osaron, it might have sounded like fear.

To Holland, it was simply relief.

It ends, he thought as the darkness wrapped itself around him, and sank in.

VI

Lila was on her knees when it happened.

Osaron returned to Holland, like steam into a pot, and his body went rigid. His back arched. His mouth opened in a silent scream, and for an awful moment, Lila thought it was too late, thought he'd been too slow, hadn't had the time, or the strength, or the will to hold on—

And then Holland slammed the Inheritor's point into his palm and said a word through gritted teeth.

"*Rosin.*"

Give.

An instant later, the shadow palace exploded into light.

Lila gasped as something began to tear inside her and she remembered the binding ring. She closed her hand into a fist and smashed the band against the stone floor, severing the connection before the Inheritor could pull her in as well.

But Kell wasn't fast enough.

A scream escaped his throat and Lila scrambled up, stumbling toward him as he curled in, clawing at the ring with blood-slicked fingers.

Rhy reached him first.

The prince was shuddering, his body slipping between life and death, whole and unmade and whole again as he knelt over Kell, his ghostly fingers wrapped around his brother's hand. The ring came free. It skated across the floor, bouncing once before dissolving into smoke.

Kell collapsed against Rhy, ashen and still, and Lila fell to her knees beside them, smearing blood on Kell's cheek as she felt his face, ran a hand through his hair, the copper parted by a streak of silver.

He was alive, he had to be alive, because Rhy was still there, leaning over him, eyes empty and full at the same time, soaked in blood, but breathing.

In the center of the room, Holland was a sphere of light, a million silver threads laced with black, all of it visible, all of it unraveling into the air around him in silence that wasn't silent at all but ringing in her ears.

And then, suddenly, the light was gone.

And Holland's body folded to the floor.

VII

Kell opened his eyes and saw the world falling apart.

No, not the world.

The palace.

It was crumbling, not like a building made of steel and stone, but like embers burning, rising up instead of down. That was the way the shadow palace fell. It simply broke apart, the imagined dissolving, leaving only the real behind, bit by bit, stone by stone, until he was lying on the floor not of a palace, but in the ruined remains of the central arena, the seats empty, the silver-and-blue banners still drifting in the breeze.

Kell tried to sit up, and gasped, forgetting he'd been stabbed.

"Easy," said Rhy with a wince. His brother was kneeling beside him, covered in blood, his clothing torn in a dozen places where the ice had run him through. But he was alive, the skin beneath the cloth already knitting, though the ghost of pain lingered in his eyes.

Holland's words came back to Kell.

"You've cut strings from your magic and made a puppet."

Holland. He dragged himself slowly upright, and found Lila crouching over the other *Antari*.

Holland was lying on his side, curled up as if he'd simply gone to sleep. But the only time Kell had seen him sleep, everything about him had been tense, wracked by nightmares, and now his features were smooth, his sleep dreamless.

Only three things broke the image of peace.

His charcoal hair, which had turned a shocking white.

His hands, which still clutched the Inheritor, its point driven through his palm.

And the device itself, which had taken on an eerie but familiar darkness. An absence of light. A void in the world.

Holland had done it.

He had trapped the shadow king.

VIII

In myths, the hero survives.
    The evil is vanquished.
    The world is set right.
    Sometimes there are celebrations, and sometimes there are funerals.
    The dead are buried. The living move on.
    Nothing changes.
    Everything changes.
    This is a myth.
    This is not a myth.
    The people of London still lay in the streets, wrapped tight within the cloth of sleep. Had they woken at that very moment, they would have seen the light flare within the spectral palace, like a dying star, banishing the shadows.

They would have seen the illusion crumble, the palace collapsing back into the bones of the three arenas, banners still waving overhead.

If they had gotten to their feet, they would have seen the oily darkness on the river crack like ice, giving way to red, the mist thinning the way it does in the morning, before the market opens.

If they had looked long enough, they would have seen the figures picking their way out of the rubble—the prince (now their king) staggering down the crumbling bridge with his arm around his brother, and they might have wondered who was leaning on whom.

They would have seen the girl standing where the palace doors had been, not the collapsed entrance to the stadium. Would have seen her cross her arms against the cold and wait until the royal guards came.

Would have seen them carrying the body out, with its hair the same white as that dying star.

But the people in the street didn't wake. Not just yet.

They didn't see what happened.

And so they never knew.

And none who had been within the shadow palace—which was not a palace anymore but the bones of something dead, something ruined, something broken—said anything of that night, save that it was over.

A myth without a voice is like a dandelion without a breath of wind.

No way to spread the seeds.

FIFTEEN

ANOSHE

I

The king of England did not like to be kept waiting.

A goblet of wine hung from his fingers, sloshing precariously as he paced the room, prevented from spilling over only by his constant sips. George IV had left the party—a party in *his* honor (as were most of those he bothered to attend)—to make this monthly meeting.

And Kell was late.

He had been late before—his arrangement, after all, had been with George's father, and as the old man failed in health, Kell had made a point of being late to spite him, George was sure—but the messenger had never been *this* late.

The agreement was clear.

The trade of letters scheduled for the fifteenth of every month.

By six in the evening, and no later than seven.

But as the clock against the wall struck *nine,* George was forced to refill his own glass because he'd dismissed everyone else. All to please his guest. A guest who was absent now.

A letter bulged on the table. Not only a missive—the time for idle correspondence was passed—but a set of demands. Instructions, really. One artifact of magic per month in exchange for England's best technology. It was more than fair. The seeds of magic for the seeds of might. Power for power.

The clock chimed again.

Half past nine.

The king sank onto the sofa, buttons straining against his not inconsiderable form. His father had only been in the ground six weeks, and already Kell was proving a problem. Their relationship would have to be corrected. The rules defined. He was not a daft old man, and he would not stand for the messenger's temper, magic or no.

"Henry," called George.

He did not shout the name—kings need not need raise their voices to be heard—but a moment later the door opened and a man came through.

"Your Majesty," he said with a bow.

Henry Tavish was an inch or two taller than George himself—a detail that irked the king—with a heavy mustache and dark, trim hair. A handsome fellow with the rather unhandsome job of conducting business the crown wouldn't—couldn't—do itself.

"He's late," said the king.

Henry knew of his visitor's name and station.

George had been careful, of course, hadn't gone about spreading the word of this other London, much as he'd have liked to. He knew what would happen if word got out too soon. Some might see eye to eye, but woven in with the wonder, there would be a poisonous thread of skepticism.

"Such tales," they'd say. "Perhaps troubled minds run in the family."

Revolutionaries were too easily mistaken for madmen.

And George would not have that. No, when he revealed magic to this world—*if* he revealed it—it would not be a whisper, a rumor, but a demonstrable, undeniable threat.

But Henry Tavish was different.

He was essential.

He was a *Scotsman,* and every good Englishman knew that a Scotsman had few qualms about getting his hands dirty.

"No sign of him as yet," said the man in his gruff but lilting way.

"You checked the Stone's Throw?"

King George was no fool. He'd been having the foreign "ambassador" followed since before he was crowned, had his fair share of men reporting that they'd lost sight of the strange man in the stranger coat, that he had simply disappeared—*apologies, Your Majesty, so sorry, Your*

Majesty—but Kell never left London without a visit to the Stone's Throw.

"It's called the Five Points now, sir," said Henry. "Run by a rather squirrelly fellow named Tuttle after the death of its old owner. Gruesome thing, according to authorities, but—"

"I don't need a history lesson," cut in the king, "only a straight answer. Did you check the tavern?"

"Aye," said Henry, "I went by, but the place was closed up. Strange thing, though, as I could hear someone in there, scurrying around, and when I told Tuttle to open up, he said he couldn't. Not wouldn't, mind, couldn't. Struck me as suspicious. You're either in or you're out, and he sounded even more wound up than normal, like something had him spooked."

"You think he was hiding something."

"I think he was *hiding*," amended Henry. "It's a known thing that that pub caters to occultists, and Tuttle's a self-proclaimed magician. Always thought it was a scam, even with your telling me about this Kell—I went inside once, nothing but some curtains and crystal balls—but maybe there's a reason your traveler frequented that place. If he's up to something, perhaps this Tuttle knows what. And if your traveler's got a mind to stand you up, well, maybe he'll still show there."

"The insolence of it," muttered George. He set his cup on the table and hauled himself to his feet, snatching up the letter from the table.

It appeared there were still some things a king must do himself.

It was getting worse.

Much worse.

Ned had tried banishing spells in three different languages, one of which he didn't even *speak*. He'd burned all the sage he had stockpiled, and then half the other herbs he kept in the kitchen, but the voice was getting louder. Now his breath fogged no matter how high the hearth was stoked, and that black spot on the floor had grown first to the size of a book, then a chair, and it was now larger than the table he'd hurriedly pushed against the doors.

He had no choice.

He had to summon Master Kell.

Ned had never successfully summoned anyone, unless you counted his great-aunt when he was fourteen, and he still wasn't entirely sure it was her, since the kettle had been overfilled, and the cat quick to spook. But desperate times.

There was, of course, the problem of Kell's being in another world. But then, so was this creature, it seemed, and *it* was reaching through, so perhaps Ned could whisper back. Perhaps the walls were thinner here. Perhaps there was a draft.

Ned lit five candles around the element kit and the coin Kell had gifted him on his last visit, a makeshift altar in the center of the tavern's most auspicious table. The pale smoke, which was spreading even in the absence of the sage, seemed to bend around the offering, which Ned took as a very good sign.

"All right, then," he said to no one and to Kell and the darkness in between. He sat, elbows on the table and palms up, as if waiting for someone to reach out and take his hands.

Let me in, whispered that ever-present voice.

"I summon Kell—" Ned paused, realizing he didn't know the other man's full name, and began again. "I summon the traveler known as Kell, from London far away."

Worship me.

"I summon a light against the dark."

I am your new king.

"I summon a friend against an enemy I do not know."

Goose bumps broke out along Ned's arm—another good sign, at least, he hoped. He pressed on.

"I summon the stranger with the many mantles."

Let me in.

"I summon the man with eternity in his eye, and magic in his blood."

The candles shivered.

"I summon *Kell.*"

Ned closed his hands into fists, and the quivering flames went out.

He held his breath as five tendrils of thin white smoke trailed into the air, forming five faces with five yawning mouths.

"Kell?" he ventured, voice trembling.

Nothing.

Ned sank back into his chair.

Any other night, he would have been over the moon to extinguish the candles, but it wasn't enough.

The traveler hadn't come.

Ned reached out and took up the foreign coin with the star at its center and the lingering scent of roses. He turned it over in his fingers.

"Some magician," he muttered to himself.

Beyond the bolted door, he heard the heavy clomp of a coach and four drawing up, and a moment later, a fist pounded on the wood.

"Open up!" bellowed a deep voice.

Ned sat up straight, pocketing the coin. "We're closed!"

"Open this door!" ordered the man again, "by orders of His Majesty the King!"

Ned held his breath as if he could starve the moment out with lack of air, but the man kept knocking and the voice kept saying *Let me in* and he didn't know what to do.

"Break it down," ordered a second voice, this one smooth, pompous.

"Wait!" called Ned, who really couldn't afford to lose the front door, not when that slab of wood was one of the only things keeping the darkness from spilling out.

He slid the bolt, opened the door a crack, just enough to see a man with a sleek handlebar mustache filling the step.

"I'm afraid there's been a leak, sir, not fit for—"

The mustached man shoved the door inward with a single push, and Ned stumbled backward as George the Fourth strode into his pub.

The man wasn't dressed as the king, of course, but a king was a king whether they wore silk and velvet or burlap. It was in his bearing, his haughty look, and, of course, the fact that his face was on the newly minted coin in Ned's pocket.

But even a king would still be in danger.

"I beg of you," said Ned. "Leave this place at once."

The king's man snorted, while George himself sneered. "Did you just issue an order to the king of England?"

"No, no, of course not, but, Your Majesty—" His gaze darted nervously around the room. "It isn't safe."

The king crinkled his nose. "The only thing poised to cause me ill is the state of this place. Now where is Kell?"

Ned's eyes widened. "Your Majesty?"

"The traveler known as Kell. The one who's frequented this pub once a month without fail for the last seven years."

The shadows were beginning to draw together behind the king. Ned swore to himself, half curse, half prayer.

"What was that?"

"Nothing, Your Majesty," stammered Ned. "I haven't seen Master Kell this month, I swear it, but I could send word—" The shadows had faces now. The whispers were growing. "—Send word if he comes around. I know your address." A nervous laugh. The shadows leered. "Unless you'd rather I make it out to—"

"What the devil are you looking at?" demanded the king, glancing back over his shoulder.

Ned couldn't see His Majesty's face, so he couldn't gauge the expression that crossed it when the king saw the ghosts with their gaping mouths and their scornful eyes, their silent commands to *kneel,* to *beg,* to *worship.*

Could they hear the voices, too? wondered Ned. But he never got the chance to ask.

The king's man crossed himself, turned on his heel, and left the Five Points without a backward glance.

The king himself went very still, jaw working up and down without making any sound.

"Your Majesty?" prompted Ned as the ghosts yawned and collapsed into smoke, into mist, into nothing.

"Yes . . ." said George slowly, smoothing his coat. "Well, then . . ."

And without another word, the king of England drew himself up very straight, and walked very briskly out.

II

It was raining when the hawk returned.

Rhy was standing on an upper balcony, under the shelter of the eaves, watching as freights hauled the remains of the tournament arenas from the river. Isra waited just inside the doorway. Once the captain of his father's city guard, now the captain of *his* royal one. She was a statue dressed in armor, while Rhy himself wore red, as was the custom for those in mourning.

Veskans, he'd read, streaked their faces with black ash, while Faroans painted their gems white for three days and three nights, but Arnesian families celebrated loss by celebrating life, and that they did by wearing red: the color of blood, of sunrise, of the Isle.

He felt the priest come through the door behind him, but did not turn, did not greet him. He knew that Tieren was grieving, too, but he couldn't bear the sadness in the old man's eyes, couldn't bear the calm, cold blue. The way he'd listened to the news of Emira, of Maxim, his features still, as if he'd known, before the spell was done, that he would wake to find the world changed.

And so they stood in silence beneath the curtain of rain, alone with their thoughts.

The royal crown sat heavy in Rhy's hair, much larger than the golden band he'd worn for most of his life. That band had grown with him, the metal drawn out every year to fit his changing stature. It should have lasted him another twenty years.

Instead, it had been stripped away, stored for a future prince.

Rhy's new crown was too great a weight. A constant reminder of his loss. A wound that wouldn't close.

The rest of his wounds *did* heal—far too fast. Like a pin driven into clay, the damage absorbed as soon as the weapon was gone. He could still summon the feelings, like a memory, but they were distant, fading, leaving that horrible question in their wake.

Was it real?

Am I real?

Real enough to ache with grief. Real enough to reach out a hand and savor the spring rain as it dripped coolly on his skin. To step out of the palace's shelter and let it soak him to the bone.

And real enough to feel his heart quicken when the streak of darkness slid past against the pale sky.

He recognized the bird at once, knew it came from Vesk.

The foreign fleet had retreated from the mouth of the Isle, but the crown had yet to answer for its crimes. Col was dead, but Cora sat in the royal prisons, waiting to learn her fate. And here it was, strapped to the ankle of a hawk.

Word of Col and Cora's treason had spread with the waking of the city, and London was already calling for Rhy to take the empire to war. The Faroans had pledged their aid—a little too quickly for his tastes—and Sol-in-Ar had returned to Faro in the name of diplomacy, which Rhy feared meant readying his soldiers.

Sixty-five years of peace, he thought grimly, ruined by a pair of bored, ambitious children.

Rhy turned and made his way downstairs, Isra and Tieren falling into step beside him. Otto was waiting in the foyer.

The Veskan magician shook the rain from his coarse blond hair, a scroll—its seal already broken—clutched in his hand.

"Your Majesty. I bring news from my crown."

"What news?" asked Rhy.

"My queen does not court war."

It was a hollow phrase. "But her children do."

"She wishes to make amends."

Another empty promise. "How?"

"If it pleases the Arnesian king, she will send a year's worth of winter wine, seven priests, and her youngest son, Hok, whose gift for stone magic is unsurpassed in all of Vesk."

My mother is dead, Rhy wanted to scream, *and you would give me drink and danger.* Instead he said only, "And what of the princess? What will the queen give me for her?"

Otto's expression hardened. "My queen wants nothing of her."

Rhy frowned. "She is her blood."

Otto shook his head. "The only thing we despise more than a traitor is a failure. The princess went against her queen's command for peace. She set her own mission, and then she failed to see it through. My queen grants Your Majesty leave to do with Cora as he will."

Rhy rubbed his eyes. Veskans did not look at mercy and see strength, and he knew the only solution the queen sought, the only one she would *respect,* was Cora's death.

Rhy resisted the urge to pace, to chew his nails, to do a dozen different things that were not *kingly.* What would his father say? What would his father *do?* He resisted the urge to look at Isra, or Tieren, to defer, to escape.

"How do I know the queen won't use her daughter's execution against me? She could claim I broke the final strands of peace, slaughtered Cora in the name of revenge."

Otto said nothing for a long moment and then, "I do not know my queen's mind, only her words."

It could all be a trap, and Rhy knew it. But he could see no other choice.

His father had told him so many things about peace and war, had compared it to a dance, a game, a strong wind, but the words that rose in Rhy's mind now were some of the first.

War against an empire, Maxim had said, was like a knife against a well-armored man. It may take three strikes or thirty, but if the hand was determined, the blade would eventually find its way in.

"Like your queen," he said at last, "I do not covet war. Our peace has been made fragile, and a public execution could either quell my city's anger or inflame it."

"Something need not be a demonstration to be an act," said Otto. "So long as the right eyes see it done."

Rhy's hand drifted to the hilt of the gold short sword at his hip. It was meant to be decorative, another piece of his elaborate mourning garb, but it had been sharp enough to cut down Col. It would do the same for Cora.

At the sight of the gesture, Isra stepped forward, speaking for the first time.

"I will do it," she offered, and Rhy wanted to let her, wanted to shed the business of killing. There had been enough blood.

But he shook his head, forced himself toward the prison cell.

"The death is mine," he said, trying to infuse the words with an anger he didn't feel—wished he felt, for it would have burned hot where grief ran cold.

Tieren did not follow—priests were made for life, not death—but Otto and Isra fell in step behind him.

Rhy wondered if Kell could feel his racing heart, if he would come running—the king wondered, but didn't wish it. His brother had his own chapters to close.

As soon as Rhy's boots hit the stairs, he knew something was wrong. Instead of being met by Cora's lilting voice, he was met by silence and the metal tang of blood on his tongue. He plunged down the last few steps into the prison, taking in the scene.

There were no guards.

The princess's cell was still locked.

And Cora lay inside, stretched out on the stone bench, her fingers trailing limply along the floor, nails swallowed by the shining slick of blood.

Rhy rocked back.

Someone must have slipped her a blade. Had it been a mercy or a taunt? Either way, she'd slashed her arms from elbow to wrist and written a single Veskan word on the wall above the bench.

Tan'och.

Honor.

Otto stared in silence, but Rhy rushed forward to open the cell, to what end, he didn't know. Cora of Vesk was dead. And even though he'd come to kill her, the sight of her lifeless body, her empty gaze, still made him sick. And then—shamefully—relieved. Because he hadn't known if he could do it. Hadn't wanted to find out.

Rhy unlocked the cell and stepped inside.

"Your Majesty—" started Isra as blood stained his boots, splashed up onto his clothes, but Rhy didn't care.

He knelt, brushing the limp blond hair from Cora's face before he forced himself upright, forced his voice steady. Otto's gaze was trained not on the body but the bloody word painted on the wall, and Rhy sensed the danger in it, the call to action.

When the Veskan's blue eyes swung back to Rhy's, they were flat, steady.

"A death is a death," said Otto. "I will tell my queen it's done."

III

Ned was drooping with fatigue. He hadn't slept more than a handful of hours in the past three days, and then not at all since the king's visit. The shadows had stopped sometime before dawn, but Ned didn't trust the silence any more than he had the sound, so he kept the windows boarded and the door locked, and stationed himself at a table in the center of the room with a glass in one hand and his ceremonial dagger in the other.

His head was beginning to loll when he heard the voices coming from the front step. He stumbled to his feet, nearly overturning the chair as the locks on the tavern door began to *move*. He watched in abject horror as the three bolts slid free one by one—drawn back by some invisible hand—and then the handle shuddered, the door groaning as it opened inward.

Ned took up the nearly empty bottle in his free hand, wielding it like a bat, oblivious to the last few drops that spilled into his hair and down his collar as two shadows crossed the threshold, their edges rimmed with mist.

He moved to strike, only to find the bottle stripped from his fingers. A second later it struck the wall and shattered.

"*Lila,*" said a familiar—and exasperated—voice.

Ned squinted, eyes adjusting to the sudden light. "Master Kell?"

The door swung shut again, plunging the room back into a lidded dark as the magician came forward. "Hello, Ned."

He had his black coat on, the collar turned up against the cold. His eyes shone in their magnetic way, one blue, the other black, but a streak of silver now marred the copper of his hair, and there was a new gauntness to his face, as though he'd been long ill.

Beside him, the woman—Lila—cocked her head. She was rakishly thin, with dark hair that brushed her jaw and trailed across her eyes—one brown, the other black.

Ned stared at her with open awe. "You're like him."

"No," said Kell dryly, striding past him. "She's one of a kind."

Lila winked at that. She was holding a small chest between her hands, but when Ned offered to take it from her, she pulled back, setting it instead on the table, one hand resting protectively on its lid.

Master Kell was making a circle of the room, as if looking for intruders, and Ned started, remembering his manners.

"What can I do for you?" he asked. "Have you come for a drink? I mean, of course you haven't just come for a drink, unless you have, and then I'm truly flattered, but . . ."

Lila made a decidedly unladylike noise, and Kell shot her a look before offering Ned a tired smile. "No, we haven't come for a drink, but perhaps you'd better pour one."

Ned nodded, ducking behind the bar to fetch a bottle.

"Bit gloomy, isn't it?" mused Lila, taking a slow turn.

Kell took in the shuttered windows, the spell book and the ash-strewn floor. "What's happened here?"

Ned needed no further encouragement. He launched into the story of the nightmares and the shadows and the voices in his head, and to his surprise, the two magicians listened, their drinks untouched, his own glass emptying twice before the tale was done.

"I know it sounds like lunacy," he finished, "but—"

"But it doesn't," said Kell.

Ned's eyes widened. "Did you see the shadows too, sir? What were they? Some kind of echo? It was dark magic, I'll tell you that. I did everything I could here, blockaded the pub, burned every bit of sage and tried a dozen different ways to clear the air, but they just kept coming. Until they stopped, quick as you like. But what if they come again, Master Kell? What am I to do?"

"They won't come again," said Kell. "Not if I have your help."

Ned started, certain he'd misheard. He'd dreamed a hundred times of this moment, of being wanted, being needed. But it was a dream. He always woke up. Beneath the counter's edge, he pinched himself hard, and didn't wake.

Ned swallowed. "*My* help?"

And Kell nodded. "The thing is, Ned," he said, eyes trailing to the chest on the table. "I've come to ask a favor."

Lila, for one, thought it was a bad idea.

Admittedly, she thought anything involving the Inheritor was a bad idea. As far as she was concerned, the thing should be sealed in stone and locked inside a chest and dropped down a hole to the center of the earth. Instead, it was sealed in stone and locked inside a chest and brought here, to a tavern in the middle of a city without magic.

Entrusted to a man, *this* man, who looked a bit like a pigeon, with his large eyes and his flitting movements. The strange thing was, he reminded her a little of Lenos—the nervous air, the fawning looks, even if they were geared at Kell instead of her. He seemed to teeter on the line between wonder and fear. She watched as Kell explained the chest's contents, not entirely, but enough—which was probably too much. Watched as this Ned fellow nodded so fast his head looked hinged, eyes round as a child's. Watched as the two carried the chest down into the cellar.

They would bury it there.

She left them to it, drifting through the tavern, feeling the familiar creak of boards under her feet. She scuffed her boot on a small, smooth patch of black, the same suspicious slick that lingered in the streets of Red London, places where magic had rotted through. Even with Osaron gone, the damage stayed done. Not everything, it seemed, could be fixed with a spell.

In the hall, she found the narrow stairs that led up to a landing, then up again to the small green door. Her feet moved without her, climbing the worn steps one by one until she reached Barron's room. The door stood ajar, giving way to a space that was no longer his. She averted her gaze, unsure if she would ever be ready to see it, and continued up, Kell's voice fading by the time she reached the top. Beyond the small green door, her room sat untouched. Part of the floor was dark, but not smooth, the faintest trace of fingers in the ruddy stain where Barron had died.

She crouched, brought her hand to the marks. A drop of water hit the floor, like the first sign of a London rainfall. Lila wiped her cheek brusquely and stood up.

Scattered across the floor, like tarnished stars, were beads of shot from Barron's gun. Her fingers twitched, the magic humming in her blood, and the metal rose into the air, drawing together like a blast rewound until the beads gathered, fused, formed a single sphere of steel that fell into her outstretched palm. Lila slipped the ball into her pocket, savoring the weight as she went downstairs.

They were back in the tavern, Ned and Kell, Ned chattering and Kell listening indulgently, though she could see the strain in his eyes, the fatigue. He hadn't been well, not since the battle and the ring, and he was a fool if he thought she hadn't noticed. But she didn't say anything, and when their eyes met, the strain faded, replaced by something gentle, warm.

Lila drew her fingertips along a wooden tabletop, the surface branded with a five-point star. "Why did you change the name?"

Ned's head swiveled toward her, and she realized it was the first time she'd spoken to him.

"It was just a thought," he said, "but you know, I've had the worst luck since I did it, so I'm thinking it's a sign I should change it back."

Lila shrugged. "It doesn't matter what you call it."

Ned was squinting at her now, as if she were out of focus.

"Have we met?" he asked, and she shook her head, even though she'd seen him in this place a dozen times, back when it was called the Stone's Throw, back when Barron had been the one behind the bar, serving watered-down drinks to men seeking a taste of magic, back when she came and went like a ghost.

"If your king comes around again," Kell was saying, "you give him this letter. *My* king would like him to know that it will be the last. . . ."

Lila slipped out the front door and into the grey day. She looked up at the sign over the entrance, the dark clouds beyond, threatening rain.

The city always looked drab this time of year, but it looked even bleaker now that she had come to know Red London and the world that surrounded it.

Lila tipped her head back against the cool bricks, and heard Barron as if he were standing there beside her, a cigar between his lips.

"Always looking for trouble."

"What's life without a little trouble?" she said softly.

"Gonna keep looking till you find it."

"I'm sorry it found you."

"Do you miss me?" His gravelly tone seemed to linger in the air.

"Like an itch," she murmured.

She felt Kell come up beside her, felt him trying to decide if he should touch her arm or give her space. In the end, he hovered there, half a step behind.

"Are you sure about him?" she asked.

"I am," he said, his voice so steady she wanted to lean against it. "Ned's a good man."

"He'd cut off a hand to make you happy."

"He believes in magic."

"And you don't think he'll try to use it?"

"He'll never get the box open, and even if he did, no. I don't think he will."

"Why's that?"

"Because I asked him not to."

Lila snorted. Even after all they'd seen and done, Kell still had faith in people. She hoped, for all their sakes, he was right. Just this once.

All around them, carriages clattered and people jogged and strolled and stumbled by. She'd forgotten the simple solidity of this city, this world.

"We could stay awhile, if you want?" offered Kell.

She took a long breath, the air on her tongue stale and full of soot instead of magic. There was nothing for her here, not anymore.

"No." She shook her head, reaching for his hand. "Let's go home."

IV

The sky was a crisp blue sheet, drawn tight behind the sun. It stretched, cloudless and bare, save for a single black-and-white bird that soared overhead. As it crossed into the sphere of light, the bird became a flock, shattering like a prism when it meets the sun.

Holland craned his neck, mesmerized by the display, but every time he tried to count their number, his vision slid out of focus, strained by the dappled light.

He didn't know where he was.

How he'd gotten here.

He was standing in a courtyard, the high walls covered in vines that threw off blossoms of lush purple—such an impossible hue, but their petals solid, soft. The air felt like the cusp of summer, a hint of warmth, the sweet scent of blossoms and tilled earth—which told him where he *wasn't,* where he couldn't be.

And yet—

"Holland?" called a voice he hadn't heard in years. Lifetimes. He turned, searching for the source, and found a gap in the courtyard wall, a doorway without a door.

He stepped through, and the courtyard vanished, the wall solid behind him and the narrow road ahead crowded with people, their clothes white but their faces full of color. He *knew* this place—it was in the Kosik, the worst part of the city.

And yet—

A pair of muddy green eyes cut his way, glinting from a shadow at the end of the lane.

"Alox?" he called, starting after his brother, when a scream made him reel around.

A small girl raced past, only to be swept up into the arms of a man. She let out another squeal as the man spun her around. Not a scream at all.

A short, delighted laugh.

An old man tugged on Holland's sleeve and said, "The king is coming," and Holland wanted to ask what he meant, but Alox was slipping away, and so Holland hurried after him, down the road, around the corner, and—

His brother was gone.

As was the narrow lane.

All at once, Holland was in the middle of a busy market, stalls overflowing with brightly colored fruits and fresh-baked bread.

He knew this place. It was the Grand Square, where so many had been cut down over the years, their blood given back to the angry earth.

And yet—

"Hol!"

He spun again, searching for the voice, and saw the edge of a honey-colored braid vanish through the crowd. The twirl of a skirt.

"Talya?"

There were three of them dancing at the edge of the square. The other two dancers were dressed in white, while Talya was a blossom of red.

He pushed through the market toward her, but when he broke the edge of the crowd, the dancers were no longer there.

Talya's voice whispered in his ear.

"The king is coming."

But when he spun toward her, she was gone again. So was the market, and the city.

All of it had vanished, taking the bustle and noise with it, the world plunged back into a quiet broken only by the rustle of leaves, the distant caw of birds.

Holland was standing in the middle of the Silver Wood.

The trunks and branches still glinted with their metallic sheen, but the ground beneath his boots was rich and dark, the leaves overhead a dazzling green.

The stream snaked through the grove, the water thawed, and a man crouched at the edge to run his fingers through, a crown sitting in the grass beside him.

"Vortalis," said Holland.

The man rose to his feet, turned toward Holland, and smiled. He started to speak, but his words were swallowed by a strong and sudden wind.

It cut through the woods, rustling the branches and stripping the leaves. They began to fall like rain, showering the world with green. Through the downpour, Holland saw Alox's clenched fists, Talya's parted lips, Vortalis's dancing eyes. There and gone, there and gone, and every time he took a step toward one, the leaves would swallow them up, leaving only their voices to echo through the woods around him.

"The king is coming," called his brother.

"The king is coming," sang his lover.

"The king is coming," said his friend.

Vortalis reappeared, striding through the rain of leaves. He held out his hand, palm up.

Holland was still reaching for it when he woke up.

Holland could tell where he was by the plushness of the room, red and gold splashed like paint on every surface.

The Maresh royal palace.

A world away.

It was late, the curtains drawn, the lamp beside the bed unlit.

Holland reached absently for his magic before remembering it wasn't there. The knowledge hit like loss, leaving him breathless. He stared at his hands, plumbing the depths of his power—the place where his power had always been, where it should be—and finding nothing. No hum. No heat.

A shuddering exhale, the only outward sign of grief.

He felt hollow. He *was* hollow.

Bodies moved beyond the door.

The shuffle of weight, the subtle clang of armor shifting, settling.

Haltingly, Holland drew himself upright, unearthing his body from the bed's thick blankets, its cloudlike mass of pillows. Annoyance flickered through him—who could possibly sleep in such a state?

It was kinder, perhaps, than a prison cell.

Not as kind as a quick death.

The act of rising took too much, or perhaps there was simply too little left to give; he was out of breath by the time his feet met the floor.

Holland leaned back against the bed, gaze traveling over the darkened room, finding a sofa, a table, a mirror. He caught his reflection there, and stilled.

His hair, once charcoal—then briefly, vibrantly black—was now a shock of white. An icy shroud, sudden as snowfall. Paired with his pale skin, it rendered him nearly colorless.

Except for his eyes.

His eyes, which had so long marked his power, defined his life. His eyes, which had made him a target, a challenge, a king.

His eyes, *both* of which were now a vivid, almost *leafy* green.

V

"Are you sure about this?" asked Kell, looking out at the city.

He thought—no, he *knew*—it was a terrible idea, but he also knew the choice wasn't his.

A single deep crease cut Holland's brow. "Stop asking."

They were on a rise overlooking the city, Kell on his feet and Holland on a stone bench, recovering his breath. It had clearly taken all of his strength to make the climb, but he had insisted on doing it, and now that they were here, he was insisting on this as well.

"You could stay here," offered Kell.

"I don't want to stay here," Holland answered flatly. "I want to go home."

Kell hesitated. "Your home isn't exactly kind to those without power."

Holland held his gaze. Against his pale complexion and shock of newly white hair, his eyes were an even more vivid shade of green, and all the more startling now that they both were. And yet, Kell still felt like he was looking at a mask. A smooth surface behind which Holland—the *real* Holland—was hiding even now. Would always hide.

"It's still my home," he said. "I was born in that world. . . ."

He didn't finish. Didn't need to. Kell knew what he would say.

And I will die there.

In the wake of his sacrifice, Holland didn't look *old,* only tired. But it was an exhaustion that ran deep, a place once filled with power now hollowed out, leaving the empty shell behind. Magic and life were intertwined in everyone and everything, but in *Antari* most of all. Without it, Holland clearly wasn't whole.

"I'm not certain this will work," said Kell, "now that you're—"

Holland cut him off. "*You've* nothing to lose by trying."

But that wasn't strictly true.

Kell hadn't told Holland—hadn't told anyone but Rhy, and only then out of necessity—the true extent of the damage. That when the binding ring had lodged on his finger and Holland had poured his magic—and Osaron's, and nearly Kell's—into the Inheritor, something had torn inside of him. Something vital. That now, every time he summoned fire, or willed water, or conjured anything from blood, it pained him.

Every single time, it hurt, a wound at the very center of his being. But unlike a wound, it refused to heal.

Magic had always been a part of Kell, as natural as breathing. Now, he couldn't catch his breath. The simplest acts took not only strength, but will. The will to suffer. To be hurt.

Pain reminds us that we're alive.

That's what Rhy had said to him, when he first woke to find their lives tethered. When Kell caught him with his hand over the flame. When he learned of the binding ring, the cost of its magic.

Pain reminds us.

Kell dreaded the pain, which seemed to worsen every time, felt ill at the thought of it, but he would not deny Holland this last request. Kell owed him that much, and so he said nothing.

Instead, he looked around at the rise, the city beneath them. "Where are we now, in your world? Where will we be, once we step through?"

A flicker of relief crossed Holland's face, quick as light on water.

"The Silver Wood," he said. "Some say it was the place where magic died." After a moment he added, "Others think it's nothing, has never been anything but an old grove of trees."

Kell waited for the man to say more, but he just rose slowly to his feet, leaning ever so slightly on a cane, only his tense white knuckles betraying how much it took for him to stand.

Holland put his other hand on Kell's arm, signaling his readiness, and so Kell drew his knife and cut his free hand, the discomfort so simple compared to the pain that waited. He pulled the White London token from around his neck, staining the coin red, and reached out to rest his hand on the bench.

"*As Travars,*" he said, Holland's voice echoing softly beneath his as they both stepped through.

Pain reminds us . . .

Kell clenched his teeth against the spasm, reaching out to brace himself against the nearest thing, which was not a bench or a wall but the trunk of a tree, its bark smooth as metal. He leaned against the cool surface, waiting for the wave to pass, and when it did, he dragged his head up to see a small grove, and Holland, a few feet away, alive, intact. A stream cut into the ground before him, little more than a ribbon of water, and beyond the grove, White London rose in stony spires.

In Holland's absence—and Osaron's—the color had begun to leach back out of the world. The sky and river were a pale grey once more, the ground bare. This was the White London Kell had always known. That other version—the one he'd glimpsed in the castle yard, in the moments before Ojka closed the collar around his throat—was like something from a dream. And yet Kell's heart ached to see it lost, and to see Holland bear that loss, the smooth planes of his mask finally cracking, the sadness showing through.

"Thank you, Kell," he said, and Kell knew the words for what they were: a dismissal.

Yet he felt rooted to the spot.

Magic made everything feel so impermanent, it was easy to forget that some things, once changed, could never be undone. That not everything was either changeable or infinite. Some roads kept going, and others had an end.

For a long moment the two men stood in silence, Holland unable to move forward, Kell unable to step back.

At last, the earth released its hold.

"You're welcome, Holland," said Kell, dragging himself free.

He reached the edge of the grove before he turned back, looking at Holland for a last time, the other *Antari* standing there at the center of the Silver Wood, his head tipped back, his green eyes closed. The winter breeze tousled white hair, ruffled ash-black clothes.

Kell lingered, digging in the pockets of his many-sided coat, and when at last he turned to go, he set a single red *lin* on a tree stump. A reminder, an invitation, a parting gift, for a man Kell would never see again.

VI

Alucard Emery paced outside the Rose Hall, dressed in a blue so dark it registered as black until it caught the light just so. It was the color of the sails on his ship. The color of the sea at midnight. No hat, no sash, no rings, but his brown hair was washed and pinned back with silver. His cuffs and buttons shone as well, polished to beads of light.

He was a summer sky at night, speckled with stars.

And he had spent the better part of an hour assembling the outfit. He couldn't decide between Alucard, the captain, and Emery, the noble. In the end, he had chosen neither. Today he was Alucard Emery, the man courting a king.

He'd lost the sapphire above his eye and gained a new scar in its place. It didn't wink in the sun, but it suited him anyway. The silver threads that traced over his skin, relics of the shadow king's poison, shone with their own faint light.

I rather like the silver, Rhy had said.

Alucard rather liked it, too.

His fingers felt bare without his rings, but the only absence that mattered was the silver feather he'd worn wrapped around his thumb. The mark of House Emery.

Berras had survived the fog unscathed—which was to say he'd fallen to it—and woken in the street with the rest, claiming he had no memory of what he'd said or done under the shadow king's spell. Alucard didn't believe a word of it, had kept his brother's company only long enough to tell him of the estate's destruction and Anisa's death.

After a long silence, Berras had said only, "To think, the line comes down to us."

Alucard had shaken his head, disgusted. "You can have it," he'd said, and walked away. He didn't throw the ring at his brother, as good as that would have felt. Instead he simply dropped it in the bushes on his way out. The moment it was gone, he felt lighter.

Now, as the doors to the Rose Hall swung open, he felt *dizzy*.

"The king will see you," said the royal guard, and Alucard forced himself forward, the velvet bag hanging from his fingers.

The hall wasn't full, but it wasn't empty, either, and Alucard suddenly wished he'd requested a private meeting with the prince—the *king*.

Vestra and *ostra* were gathered, some waiting for an audience, others simply waiting for the world to return to normal. The Veskan entourage was still confined to its quarters, while the Faroan assembly had divided, half sailing home with Lord Sol-in-Ar, the others lingering in the palace. Councilors, once loyal aides to Maxim, stood ready to advise, while members of the royal guard lined the hall and flanked the dais.

King Rhy Maresh sat on his father's throne, his mother's empty seat beside him. Kell stood at his side, head bowed over his brother in quiet conversation. Master Tieren was at Rhy's other side, looking older than ever, but his pale blue eyes were sharp among the hollows and wrinkles of his face. He rested a hand on Rhy's shoulder as he spoke, the gesture simple, warm.

Rhy's own head was tipped down as he listened, the crown a heavy band of gold in his hair. There was sadness in his shoulders, but then Kell's lips moved, and Rhy managed a fleeting smile, like light through clouds.

Alucard's heart lifted.

He scanned the room quickly and saw Bard leaning against one of the stone planters, cocking her head the way she always did when she was eavesdropping. He wondered if she'd picked any pockets yet this morning, or if those days were over.

Kell cleared his throat, and Alucard was startled to realize that his feet had carried him all the way to the dais. He met the king's amber eyes, and saw them soften briefly with, what—happiness? concern?—before Rhy spoke.

"Captain Emery," he said, his voice the same, and yet different, distant. "You requested an audience."

"As you promised I might, Your Majesty, if I returned"—Alucard's gaze flicked to Kell, the shadow at the king's shoulder—"without killing your brother."

A murmur of amusement went through the hall. Kell scowled, and Alucard immediately felt better. Rhy's eyes widened a fraction—he'd realized where this was going, and he had obviously assumed Alucard would request a *private* meeting.

But what they'd had—it was more than stolen kisses between silk sheets, more than secrets shared only by starlight, more than a youthful dalliance, a summer fling.

And Alucard was here to prove it. To lay his heart bare before Rhy, and the Rose Hall, and the rest of London.

"Nearly four years ago," he began, "I left your . . . court, without explanation or apology. In doing so, I fear I wounded the crown and its estimation of me. I have come to make amends with my king."

"What is in your hand?" asked Rhy.

"A debt."

A guard stepped forward to retrieve the parcel, but Alucard pulled away, looking back to the king. "If I may?"

After a moment, Rhy nodded, rising as Alucard approached the dais. The young king descended the steps and met him there before the throne.

"What are you doing?" asked Rhy softly, and Alucard's whole body sang to hear *this* voice, the one that belonged not to the king of Arnes, but to the prince he'd known, the one he'd fallen in love with, the one he'd lost.

"What I promised," whispered Alucard, gripping the mirror in both hands and tipping its surface toward the king.

It was a *liran*.

Most scrying dishes could share the contents of one's mind, ideas and memories projected on the surface, but a mind was a fickle thing—it could lie, forget, rewrite.

A *liran* showed only the truth.

Not as it had been remembered, not as one *wanted* to remember it, but as it had happened.

It was no simple magic, to sift truth from memory.

Alucard Emery had traded four years of his future for the chance to relive the worst night of his past.

In his hands, the mirror's surface went dark, swallowing Rhy's reflection and the hall behind him as another night, another room, took shape in the glass.

Rhy stiffened at the sight of his chamber, of *them,* tangled limbs and silent laughter in his bed, his fingers trailing over Alucard's bare skin. Rhy's cheeks colored as he reached out and touched the mirror's edge. As he did, the scene flared to life. Mercifully, the sound of their pleasure didn't echo through the throne room. It stayed, caught between them, as the scene unspooled.

Alucard, rising from Rhy's bed, trying to dress while the prince playfully undid every clasp he fastened, unlaced every knot. Their final parting kiss and Alucard's departure through the maze of hidden halls and out into the night.

What Rhy couldn't see—then or now—in the mirror's surface was Alucard's happiness as he made his way across the copper bridge to the northern bank, his racing heart as he climbed the front steps to the Emery estate. Couldn't feel the sudden horrible stutter of that heart when Berras stood waiting in the hall.

Berras, who had followed him to the palace.

Berras, who *knew.*

Alucard had tried to play it off, feigning drunkenness, letting himself tip casually back against the wall as he rattled off the taverns he'd been to, the fun he'd had, the trouble he'd gotten himself into over the course of that long night.

It didn't work.

Berras's disgust had hardened into stone. So had his fists.

Alucard didn't want to fight his brother, had even dodged the first blow, and the second, only to be caught upside the head by something sharp and silver.

He went down, world ringing. Blood dripped into his eyes.

His father was standing over him, his cane glinting in his grip.

Back in the Rose Hall, Alucard closed his eyes, but the images played on in his mind, scorched into memory. His fingers tightened on the mirror, but he didn't let go, not when his brother called him a disgrace, a fool, a whore. Not when he heard the snap of bone, his own muffled scream, silence, and then the sickening slosh of a ship.

Alucard would have let the memory play on, let it run through those first horrific nights at sea, and his escape, all the way to the prison and the iron cuffs and the heated rod, his forced return to London and the warning in his brother's eyes, the hurt in the prince's, the hatred in Kell's.

He would have let it play on as long as Rhy wanted, but something weighed suddenly against the mirror's surface, and he opened his eyes to see the young king standing very close, one hand splayed across the glass as if to block out the images, the sounds, the memories.

Rhy's amber eyes were bright, his brow knitted with anger and sadness.

"Enough," he said, voice trembling.

Alucard *wanted* to speak, tried to find the words, but Rhy was already letting go—too soon—turning away—too soon—and retaking his throne.

"I have seen enough."

Alucard let the mirror fall back to his side, the world around him dragging into focus. The room around him had gone still.

The young king gripped the edges of his throne and spoke in hushed tones with his brother, whose expression flickered between surprise and annoyance before finally settling into something more resigned. Kell nodded, and when Rhy turned toward the room and spoke again, his voice was even.

"Alucard Emery," he said, his tone soft, but stern. "The crown appreciates your honesty. *I* appreciate it." He looked to Kell one last time before continuing. "As of right now, you have been stripped of your title as privateer."

Alucard nearly folded under the sentence. "Rhy . . ." The name was out before he realized his error. The impropriety. "Your Majesty . . ."

"You will no longer sail for the crown on the *Night Spire,* or any vessel."

"I do not—"

The king's hand came up in a single silencing gesture.

"My brother wishes to travel, and I have granted him permission." Kell's expression soured at the word, but did not interrupt. "As such," continued Rhy, "I require an ally. A proven friend. A powerful magician. I require you here in London, Master Emery. With me."

Alucard stiffened. The words were a blow, sudden, but not hard. They teased the line between pleasure and pain, fear that he'd misheard and hope that he hadn't.

"That is the first reason," continued Rhy evenly. "The second is more personal. I have lost my mother, and my father. I have lost friends, and strangers who might one day have been friends. I have lost too many of my people to count. And I will not suffer losing you."

Alucard's gaze cut to Kell. The *Antari* met his eyes, and he found a warning in them, but nothing more.

"Will you obey the will of the crown?" asked Rhy.

It took Alucard several stunned seconds to summon his faculties enough to bow, enough to form the three simple words.

"Yes, Your Majesty."

The king came to Alucard's room that night.

It was an elegant chamber in the western wing of the palace, fit for a noble. A royal. There were no hidden doors to be found. Only the broad entrance with its inlaid wood, its golden trim.

Alucard was perched on the edge of the sofa, rolling a glass between his hands, when the knock came. He had hoped, and he had not dared to hope.

Rhy Maresh entered the room alone. His collar was unbuttoned, his crown hanging from his fingers. He looked tired and sad and lovely and lost, but at the sight of Alucard, something in him brightened. Not a light Alucard could see in the molten threads that coiled around him, but a light behind his eyes. It was the strangest thing, but Rhy seemed to become *real* then, solid in a way he hadn't been before.

"*Avan,*" said the prince who was no longer a prince.

"*Avan,*" said the captain who was no longer a captain.

Rhy looked around the room.

"Does it suit?" he asked, drawing his hand absently along a curtain, long fingers tangling in red and gold.

Alucard's smile tilted. "I suppose it will do."

Rhy let the crown fall to the sofa as he came forward, and his fingers, now freed from their burden, traced Alucard's jaw, as if assuring himself that Alucard was here, was real.

Alucard's own heart was racing, even now threatening to run away. But there was no need. Nowhere to go. No place he'd rather be.

He had dreamed of this, every time the storms raged at sea. Every time a sword was drawn against him. Every time life showed its frailty, its fickleness. He had dreamed of this, as he stood on the bow of the *Ghost,* facing death in a line of ships.

Now he reached to draw Rhy in against him, only to be rebuffed.

"It is not right for you to do that," he reprimanded softly, "now that I am king."

Alucard withdrew, trying to keep hurt and confusion from his face. But then Rhy's dark lashes sank over his eyes, and his lips slid into a coy smile. "A king should be allowed to *lead.*"

Relief flooded through him, followed by a wave of heat as Rhy's hand tangled in his hair, mussing the silver clasps. Lips brushed his throat, warmth grazed his jaw.

"Don't you agree?" breathed the king, nipping at Alucard's collarbone in a way that stole the air from his chest.

"Yes, Your Majesty," he managed, and then Rhy was kissing him, long and slow and savoring. The room moved beneath his tripping feet, the buttons of his shirt coming undone. By the time Rhy drew back, Alucard was against the bedpost, his shirt open. He let out a small, dazed laugh, resisting the urge to drag Rhy toward him, to press him down into the sheets.

The longing left him breathless.

"Is this how it's to be now?" he asked. "Am I to be your bedmate as well as your guard?"

Rhy's lips split into a dazzling smile. "So you admit it, then," he said, closing the last of the distance to whisper in Alucard's ear, "that you are mine."

And with that, the king dragged him down onto the bed.

VII

Arnesians had a dozen ways to say *hello,* but no word for *good-bye.*

When it came to parting ways, they sometimes said *vas ir,* which meant *in peace,* but more often they chose to say *anoshe—until another day.*

Anoshe was a word for strangers in the street, and lovers between meetings, for parents and children, friends and family. It softened the blow of leaving. Eased the strain of parting. A careful nod to the certainty of today, the mystery of tomorrow. When a friend left, with little chance of seeing home, they said *anoshe.* When a loved one was dying, they said *anoshe.* When corpses were burned, bodies given back to the earth and souls to the stream, those left grieving said *anoshe.*

Anoshe brought solace. And hope. And the strength to let go.

When Kell Maresh and Lila Bard had first parted ways, he'd whispered the word in her wake, beneath his breath, full of the certainty—the hope—they'd meet again. He'd known it wasn't an end. And this wasn't an end, either, or if it was, then simply the end of a chapter, an interlude between two meetings, the beginning of something new.

And so Kell made his way up to his brother's chambers—not the rooms he'd kept beside Kell's own (though he still insisted on sleeping there), but the ones that had belonged to his mother and father.

Without Maxim and Emira, there were so few people for Kell to say good-bye *to.* Not the *vestra* or the *ostra,* not the servants or the guards who remained. He would have said farewell to Hastra, but Hastra, too, was dead.

Kell had already gone to the Basin that morning, and come across the flower the young guard had coaxed to life that day, withering in its pot. He'd carried it up to the orchard, where Tieren stood between the rows of winter and spring.

"Can you fix it?" asked Kell.

The priest's eyes went to the shriveled little flower. "No," he said gently, but when Kell started to protest, Tieren held up a gnarled hand. "There's nothing to fix. That is an acina. They aren't meant to last. They bloom a single time, and then they're gone."

Kell looked down helplessly at the withered white blossom. "What do I do?" he asked, the question so much bigger than the words.

Tieren smiled a soft, inward smile and shrugged in his usual way. "Leave it be. The blossom will crumble, the stem and leaves, too. That's what they're *for*. Acina strengthen the soil, so that other things can grow."

Kell reached the top of the stairs, and slowed his step.

Royal guards lined the hall to the king's chamber, and Alucard stood outside the doors, leaning back against the wood and flipping through the pages of a book.

"This is your idea of guarding him?" said Kell.

The man pointedly turned a page. "Don't tell me how to do my job."

Kell took a steadying breath. "Get out of my way, Emery."

Alucard's storm-dark eyes flicked up from the book. "And what is your business with the king?"

"Personal."

Alucard held up a hand. "Perhaps I should have you searched for weapo—"

"Touch me and I'll break your fingers."

"Who says I have to touch you?" His hand twitched, and Kell felt the knife on his sleeve shudder before he shoved the man back against the wood.

"Alucard!" called Rhy through the door. "Let my brother in before I have to find *another* guard."

Alucard smirked, and gave a sweeping bow, and stepped aside.

"Ass," muttered Kell as he shoved past him.

"Bastard," called the magician in his wake.

Rhy waited on the balcony, leaning his elbows on the rail.

The air still held a chill, but the sun was warm on his skin, rich with the promise of spring. Kell came storming through the room.

"You two are getting along well, then?" asked Rhy.

"Splendidly," muttered his brother, stepping through the doors and slumping forward over the rail beside him. A reflection of his own pose.

They stood like that for some time, taking in the day, and Rhy almost forgot that Kell had come to say good-bye, that he was leaving, and then a breeze cut through, sudden and biting, and the darkness whispered from the back of his mind, the sorrow of loss and the guilt of survival and the fear that he would keep outliving those he loved. That this borrowed life would be too long or too short, and there forever was the inevitable cusp, blessing or curse, blessing or curse, and the feeling of leaning forward into a gust of wind as it tried with every step to force him back.

Rhy's fingers tightened on the rail.

And Kell, whose two-toned eyes had always seen right through him, said, "Do you wish I hadn't done it?"

He opened his mouth to say *Of course not,* or *Saints no,* or any of the other things he should have said, *had* said a dozen times, with the mindless repetition of someone being asked how he is that day, and answering *Fine, thank you,* regardless of his true temperament. He opened his mouth, but nothing came out. There were so many things Rhy hadn't said since his return—wouldn't *let* himself say—as if giving the words voice meant giving them weight, enough to tip the scale and crush him. But so many things had tried, and here he was, still standing.

"Rhy," said Kell, his gaze heavy as stone. "Do you wish I hadn't brought you back?"

He took a breath. "I don't know," he said. "Ask me in the morning, after I've spent hours weighed down by nightmares, drugged beyond reason just to hold back the memories of dying, which was not so bad as coming back, and I'd say yes. I wish you'd let me die."

Kell looked ill. "I—"

"But ask me in the afternoon," cut in Rhy, "when I've felt the sun cutting through the cold, or the warmth of Alucard's smile, or the steady weight of your arm around my shoulders, and I would tell you it was worth it. It *is* worth it."

Rhy turned his face to the sun. He closed his eyes, relishing the way the light still reached him. "Besides," he added, managing a smile, "who doesn't love a man with shadows? Who doesn't want a king with scars?"

"Oh, yes," said Kell dryly. "That's really the reason I did it. To make you more appealing."

Rhy felt his smile slip. "How long will you be gone?"

"I don't know."

"Where are you going?"

"I don't know."

"What will you do?"

"I don't know."

Rhy bowed his head, suddenly tired. "I wish I could go with you."

"So do I," said Kell, "but the empire needs its king."

Softly, Rhy said, "The king needs his brother."

Kell looked stricken, and Rhy knew he could make him stay, and he knew he couldn't bear to do it. He let out a long, shuddering sigh and straightened. "It's about time you did something selfish, Kell. You make the rest of us look bad. Try to shrug that saint's complex while you're away."

Across the river, the city bells began to ring the hour.

"Go on," said Rhy. "The ship is waiting." Kell took a single step back, hovering in the doorway. "But do us a favor, Kell."

"What's that?" asked his brother.

"Don't get yourself killed."

"I'll do my best," said Kell, and then he was going.

"And come back," added Rhy.

Kell paused. "Don't worry," he said. "I will. Once I've seen it."

"Seen what?" asked Rhy.

Kell smiled. "Everything."

VIII

Delilah Bard made her way toward the docks, a small bag slung over one shoulder. All she had in the world that wasn't already on the ship. The palace rose behind her, stone and gold and ruddy pink light.

She didn't look back. Didn't even slow.

Lila had always been good at disappearing.

Slipping like light between boards.

Cutting ties as easily as a purse.

She never said good-bye. Never saw the point. Saying good-bye was like strangling slowly, every word tightening the rope. It was easier to just slip away in the night. Easier.

But she told herself he would have caught her.

So in the end, she'd gone to him.

"Bard."

"Captain."

And then she'd stalled. Hadn't known what to say. This was why she hated good-byes. She looked around the palace chamber, taking in the inlaid floor, the gossamer ceiling, the balcony doors, before she ran out of places to look and had to look at Alucard Emery.

Alucard, who'd given her a place on his ship, who'd taught her the first things about magic, who'd—her throat tightened.

Bloody good-byes. Such useless things.

She picked up her pace, heading for the line of ships.

Alucard had leaned back against the bedpost. "Silver for your thoughts?"

And Lila had cocked her head. "I was just thinking," she'd said, "I should have killed you when I had the chance."

He'd raised a brow. "And I should have tossed you in the sea."

An easy silence had settled, and she knew she'd miss it, felt herself shrink from the idea of missing before heaving out a breath and letting it fall, settle. There were worse things, she supposed.

Her boots sounded on the wooden dock.

"You take care of that ship," he'd said, and Lila had left with only a wink, just like the ones Alucard had always thrown her way. He'd had a sapphire to catch the light, and all she had was a black glass eye, but she could feel his smile like sun on her back as she strode out and let the door swing shut behind her.

It wasn't a good-bye, not really.

What was the word for parting?

Anoshe.

That was it.

Until another day.

Delilah Bard knew she'd be back.

The dock was full of ships, but only one caught her eye. A stunning rig with a polished dark hull and midnight-blue sails. She climbed the ramp to the deck, where the crew were waiting, some old, some new.

"Welcome to the *Night Spire,*" she said, flashing a smile like a knife. "You can call me Captain Bard."

IX

Holland stood alone in the Silver Wood.

He had listened to the sounds of Kell's departure, those few short strides giving way to silence. He tipped his head back and took a deep breath, squinting into the sun.

A spot of black streaked through the clouds overhead—a bird, just like in his dream—and his tired heart quickened, but there was only one, and there was no Alox, no Talya, no Vortalis. Voices long silent. Lives long lost.

With Kell gone, and no one left to see, Holland sagged back against the nearest tree, the icy surface of its side like cold steel against his spine. He let himself sink, lowering his tired body to the dead earth.

A gentle breeze blew through the barren grove, and Holland closed his eyes and imagined he could almost hear the rustle of leaves, could almost feel the feathery weight of them falling one by one onto his skin. He didn't open his eyes, didn't want to lose the image. He just let the leaves fall. Let the wind blow. Let the woods whisper, shapeless sounds that threaded into words.

The king is coming, it seemed to say.

The tree was beginning to warm against his back, and Holland knew, in a distant way, that he was never getting up.

It ends, he thought—no fear, only relief, and sadness.

He had tried. Had given everything he could. But he was so tired.

The rustle of leaves in his ears was getting louder, and he felt himself sinking against the tree, into the embrace of something softer than metal, darker than night.

His heart slowed, winding down like a music box, a season at its end.

The last air left Holland's lungs.

And then, at last, the world breathed in.

X

Kell wore a coat that billowed in the wind.

It was neither royal red, nor messenger black, nor tournament silver. This coat was a simple, woolen grey. He wasn't quite sure if it was new or old or something in between, only that he'd never seen it before. Not until that morning when, turning his coat past black and red, he'd come across a side he didn't recognize.

This new coat had a high collar, and deep pockets, and sturdy black buttons that ran down the front. It was a coat for storms, and strong tides, and saints knew what else.

He planned to find out, now that he was free.

Freedom itself was a dizzying thing. With every step, Kell felt unmoored, as if he might drift away. But no, there was the rope, invisible but strong as steel, running between his heart and Rhy's.

It would stretch.

It would reach.

Kell made his way down the docks, passing ferries and frigates, local vessels, the Veskan impounds, and Faroan skiffs, ships of every size and shape as he searched for the *Night Spire*.

He should have known she'd choose that one, with its dark hull and its blue sails.

He made it all the way to the boat's ramp without looking back, but there at last he faltered, and turned, taking in the palace one last time. Glass and stone, gold and light. The beating heart of London. The rising sun of Arnes.

"Having second thoughts?"

Kell craned his neck to see Lila leaning on the ship's rail, spring wind tousling her short dark hair.

"Not at all," he said. "Just enjoying the view."

"Well, come on, before I decide to sail without you." She spun away, shouting orders at the ship's crew like a true captain, and the men aboard all listened and obeyed. They leapt to action with a smile, threw off ropes and drew up anchor as if they couldn't wait to set sail. He couldn't blame them. Lila Bard was a force to be reckoned with. Whether her hands were filled with knives or fire, her voice low and coaxing or lined with steel, she seemed to hold the world in her hands. Maybe she did.

After all, she'd already taken two Londons as her own.

She was a thief, a runaway, a pirate, a magician.

She was fierce, and powerful, and terrifying.

She was still a mystery.

And he loved her.

A knife struck the docks between Kell's feet, and he jumped.

"Lila!" he shouted.

"Leaving!" she called from the deck. "And bring me back that knife," she added. "It's my favorite one."

Kell shook his head, and freed the blade from where it had lodged in the wood. "They're *all* your favorite."

When he climbed aboard, the crew didn't stop, didn't bow, didn't treat him as anything but another pair of hands, and soon the *Spire* pushed away from the docks, sails catching the morning breeze. His heart was thudding in his chest, and when he closed his eyes, he could feel a twin pulse, echoing his own.

Lila came to stand beside him, and he handed back her knife. She said nothing, slipping the blade into some hidden sheath, and leaning her shoulder into his. Magic ran between them like a current, a cord, and he wondered who she would have been if she'd stayed in Grey London. If she'd never picked his pocket, never held the contents ransom for adventure.

Maybe she would never have discovered magic.

Or maybe she would have simply changed her world instead of his.

Kell's eyes went to the palace one last time, and he thought he could almost make out the shape of a man standing alone on a high balcony. At this distance, he was little more than a shadow, but Kell could see the band of gold glinting in his hair as a second figure came to stand beside the king.

Rhy raised his hand, and so did Kell, a single unspoken word between them.

Anoshe.

Read on for a preview of the first book
in V. E. Schwab's Villains series

Available now from Tor Books

Copyright © 2013 by Victoria Schwab

I.

LAST NIGHT
MERIT CEMETERY

VICTOR readjusted the shovels on his shoulder and stepped gingerly over an old, half-sunken grave. His trench billowed faintly, brushing the tops of tombstones as he made his way through Merit Cemetery, humming as he went. The sound carried like wind through the dark. It made Sydney shiver in her too big coat and her rainbow leggings and her winter boots as she trudged along behind him. The two looked like ghosts as they wove through the graveyard, both blond and fair enough to pass for siblings, or perhaps father and daughter. They were neither, but the resemblance certainly came in handy since Victor couldn't very well tell people he'd picked up the girl on the side of a rain-soaked road a few days before. He'd just broken out of jail. She'd just been shot. A crossing of fates, or so it seemed. In fact, Sydney was the only reason Victor was beginning to believe in fate at all.

He stopped humming, rested his shoe lightly on a tombstone, and scanned the dark. Not with his eyes so much as with his skin, or rather with the thing that crept beneath it, tangled in his pulse. He might have stopped humming, but the sensation never did, keeping on with a faint electrical buzz that only he could hear and feel and read. A buzz that told him when someone was near.

Sydney watched him frown slightly.

"Are we alone?" she asked.

Victor blinked, and the frown was gone, replaced by the even calm he always wore. His shoe slid from the gravestone. "Just us and the dead."

They made their way into the heart of the cemetery, the shovels tapping softly on Victor's shoulder as they went. Sydney kicked a loose rock that had broken off from one of the older graves. She could see that there were letters, parts of words, etched into one side. She wanted to know what they said, but the rock had already tumbled into the weeds, and Victor was still moving briskly between the graves. She ran to catch up, nearly tripping several times over the frozen ground before she reached him. He'd come to a stop, and was staring down at a grave. It was fresh, the earth turned over and a temporary marker driven into the soil until a stone one could be cut.

Sydney made a noise, a small groan of discomfort that had nothing to do with the biting cold. Victor glanced back and offered her the edge of a smile.

"Buck up, Syd," he said casually. "It'll be fun."

Truth be told, Victor didn't care for graveyards, either. He didn't like dead people, mostly because he had no effect on them. Sydney, conversely, didn't like dead people because she had such a marked effect on them. She kept her arms crossed tightly over her chest, one gloved thumb rubbing the spot on her upper arm where she'd been shot. It was becoming a tic.

Victor turned and sunk one of the spades into the earth. He then tossed the other one to Sydney, who unfolded her arms just in time to catch it. The shovel was almost as tall as she was. A few days shy of her thirteenth birthday, and even for twelve and eleven twelfths, Sydney Clarke was small. She had always been on the short side, but it certainly didn't help that she had barely grown an inch since the day she'd died.

Now she hefted the shovel, grimacing at the weight.

"You've got to be kidding me," she said.

"The faster we dig, the faster we get to go home."

Home wasn't home so much as a hotel room stocked only with Sydney's stolen clothes, Mitch's chocolate milk, and Victor's files, but that wasn't the point. At this moment, home would have been any place that *wasn't* Merit Cemetery. Sydney eyed the grave, tightening her fingers on the wooden grip. Victor had already begun to dig.

"What if...," she said, swallowing, "... what if the other people accidentally wake up?"

"They won't," cooed Victor. "Just focus on *this* grave. Besides..." He looked up from his work. "Since when are *you* afraid of bodies?"

"I'm not," she snapped back, too fast and with all the force of someone used to being the younger sibling. Which she was. Just not *Victor's*.

"Look at it this way," he teased, dumping a pile of dirt onto the grass. "If you do wake them up, they can't go anywhere. Now dig."

Sydney leaned forward, her short blond hair falling into her eyes, and began to dig. The two worked in the dark, only Victor's occasional humming and the thud of the shovels filling the air.

Thud.

Thud.

Thud.

II

TEN YEARS AGO
LOCKLAND UNIVERSITY

VICTOR drew a steady, straight, black line through the word *marvel*.

The paper they'd printed the text on was thick enough to keep the ink from bleeding through, so long as he didn't press down too hard. He stopped to reread the altered page, and winced as one of the metal flourishes on Lockland University's wrought-iron fence dug into his back. The school prided itself on its country-club-meets-Gothic-manor ambience, but the ornate railing that encircled Lockland, though *striving* to evoke both the university's exclusive nature and its old-world aesthetic, succeeded only in being pretentious and suffocating. It reminded Victor of an elegant cage.

He shifted his weight and repositioned the book on his knee, wondering at the sheer size of it as he twirled the Sharpie over his knuckles. It was a self-help book, the latest in a series of five, by the world-renowned Drs. Vale. The very same Vales who were currently on an international tour. The very same Vales who had budgeted just enough time in their busy schedules—even back before they were best-selling "empowerment gurus"—to produce Victor.

He thumbed back through the pages until he found the beginning of his most recent undertaking and began to read. For the first time he wasn't effacing a Vale book simply for pleasure. No, this was for credit. Victor couldn't help but smile. He took an immense pride in paring down his parents' works, stripping the expansive chapters on empowerment down to simple, disturbingly effective messages. He'd been blacking them out for more than a decade now, since he was ten, a painstaking but satisfying affair, but until last week he'd never been able to count it for anything as useful as school credit. Last week, when he'd accidentally left his latest project in the art studios over lunch—Lockland University had a mandatory art credit, even for budding doctors and scientists—he'd come back to his teacher poring over it. He'd expected a reprimand, some lecture on the cultural cost of defacing literature, or maybe the material cost of paper. Instead, the teacher had taken the literary destruction as art. He'd practically supplied the explanation, filled in any blanks using terms such as *expression, identity, found art, reshaping.*

Victor had only nodded, and offered a perfect word to the end of the teacher's list—*rewriting*—and just like that, his senior art thesis had been determined.

The marker hissed as he drew another line, blotting out several sentences in the middle of the page. His knee was going numb from the weight of the tome. If *he* were in need of self-help, he would search for a thin, simple book, one whose shape mimicked its promise. But maybe some people needed more. Maybe some people scanned the shelves for the heftiest one, assuming that more pages meant more emotional or psychological aid. He skimmed the words and smiled as he found another section to ink out.

By the time the first bell rang, signaling the end of Victor's art elective, he'd turned his parents' lectures on how to start the day into:

Be lost. Give up. give In. in the end It would be better to surrender before you begin. be lost. Be lost And then you will not care if you are ever found.

He'd had to strike through entire paragraphs to make the sentence perfect after he accidentally marked out *ever* and had to go on until he found another instance of the word. But it was worth it. The pages of black that stretched between *if you are* and *ever* and *found* gave the words just the right sense of abandonment.

Victor heard someone coming, but didn't look up. He flipped through to the back of the book, where he'd been working on a separate exercise. The Sharpie cut through another paragraph, line by line, the sound as slow and even as breathing. He'd marveled, once, that his parents' books were in fact self-help, simply not in the way they'd intended. He found their destruction incredibly soothing, a kind of meditation.

"Vandalizing school property again?"

Victor looked up to find Eli standing over him. The library-plastic cover crinkled beneath his fingertips as he tipped the book up to show Eli the spine, where VALE was printed in bold capital letters. He wasn't about to pay $25.99 when Lockland's library had such a suspiciously extensive collection of Vale-doctrine self-help. Eli took the book from him and skimmed.

"Perhaps . . . it is . . . in . . . our . . . best interest to . . . to surrender . . . to give up . . . rather than waste . . . words."

Victor shrugged. He wasn't done yet.

"You have an extra *to*, before *surrender*," said Eli, tossing the book back.

Victor caught it and frowned, tracing his finger through the makeshift sentence until he found his mistake, and efficiently blotted out the word.

"You've got too much time, Vic."

"You must make time for that which matters," he recited, "for that which defines you: your passion, your progress, your pen. Take it up, and write your own story."

Eli looked at him for a long moment, brow crinkling. "That's awful."

"It's from the introduction," said Victor. "Don't worry, I blacked it out." He flipped back through the pages, a web of thin letters and fat black lines, until he reached the front. "They totally murdered Emerson."

Eli shrugged. "All I know is that book is a sniffer's dream," he said. He was right, the four Sharpies Victor had gone through in converting the book to art had given it an incredibly strong odor, one which Victor found at once entrancing and revolting. He got enough of a high from the destruction itself, but he supposed the smell was an unexpected addition to the project's complexity, or so the art teacher would spin it. Eli leaned back against the rail. His rich brown hair caught the too bright sun, bringing out reds and even threads of gold. Victor's hair was a pale blond. When the sunlight hit him, it didn't bring out any colors, but only accentuated the *lack* of color, making him look more like an old-fashioned photo than a flesh-and-blood student.

Eli was still staring down at the book in Victor's hands.

"Doesn't the Sharpie ruin whatever's on the other side?"

"You'd think," said Victor. "But they use this freakishly heavy paper. Like they want the weight of what they're saying to sink in."

Eli's laugh was drowned by the second bell, ringing out across the emptying quad. The bells weren't buzzers, of course—Lockland was too civilized—but they *were* loud, and almost ominous, a single deep church bell from the spiritual center that sat in the middle of campus. Eli cursed and helped Victor to his feet, already turning toward the huddle of science buildings, faced in rich red brick to make them seem less sterile. Victor took his time. They still had a minute before the final bell sounded, and even if they were late, the teachers would never mark them down. All Eli had to do was smile. All Victor had to do was lie. Both proved frighteningly effective.

VICTOR sat in the back of his Comprehensive Science Seminar—a course designed to reintegrate students of various scientific disciplines for their senior theses—learning about research methods. Or at least being *told* about research methods. Distressed by the fact that the class relied on laptops, and since striking through words on a screen hardly gave him the same satisfaction, Victor had taken to watching the other students sleep, doodle, stress out, listen, and pass digital notes. Unsurprisingly, they failed to hold his interest for long, and soon his gaze drifted past them, and past the windows, and past the lawn. Past everything.

His attention was finally dragged back to the lecture when Eli's hand went up. Victor hadn't caught the question, but he watched his roommate smile his perfect all-American-political-candidate smile before he answered. Eliot—Eli—Cardale had started out as a predicament. Victor had been none too happy to find the lanky, brown-haired boy standing in the doorway of his dorm a month into sophomore year. His first roommate had experienced a change of heart in the first week (through no fault of Victor's, of course) and had promptly dropped out. Due either to a shortage of students or perhaps a filing error made possible by fellow sophomore Max Hall's penchant for any Lockland-specific hacking challenge, the student hadn't been replaced. Victor's painfully small double was converted into a much more adequate single room. Until the start of October when Eliot Cardale—who, Victor had immediately decided, smiled too much—appeared with a suitcase in the hall outside.

Victor had initially wondered what it would take to recover his bedroom for a second time in a semester, but before he put any plans into motion, an odd thing happened. Eli began to . . . grow on him. He was precocious, and frighteningly charming, the kind of guy who got away with everything, thanks to good genes and quick wits. He was born for the sports teams and the clubs, but he surprised everyone, especially Victor, by showing no inclination whatsoever to join either. This small defiance of social norm earned him several notches in Victor's estimation, and made him instantly more interesting.

But what fascinated Victor *most* was the fact that something about Eli was decidedly *wrong*. He was like one of those pictures full of small errors, the kind you could only pick out by searching the image from every angle, and even then, a few always slipped by. On the surface, Eli seemed perfectly normal, but now and then Victor would catch a crack, a sideways glance, a moment when his roommate's face and his words, his look and his meaning, would not line up. Those fleeting slices fascinated Victor. It was like watching two people, one hiding in the other's skin. And their skin was always too dry, on the verge of cracking and showing the color of the thing beneath.

"Very astute, Mr. Cardale."

Victor had missed the question *and* the answer. He looked up as Professor Lyne turned his attention to the rest of his seniors, and clapped his hands once, with finality.

"All right. It's time to declare your thesis."

The class, composed mostly of pre-med students, a handful of aspiring physicists, and even an engineer—not Angie, though, she'd been assigned a different section—gave a collective groan, on principle.

"Now, now," said the professor, cutting off the protest. "You knew what you were getting into when you signed up."

"We didn't," observed Max. "It's a mandatory course." The remark earned him a ripple of encouragement from the class.

"My sincerest apologies then. But now that you're here, and seeing as there's no time like the present—"

"Next week would be better," called out Toby Powell, a broad-shouldered surfer, pre-med, and the son of some governor. Max had only earned a murmur, but this time the other students laughed at a level proportionate to Toby's popularity.

"Enough," said Professor Lyne. The class quieted. "Now, Lockland encourages a certain level of . . . industriousness where theses are concerned, and offers a proportionate amount of freedom, but a word of warning from *me*. I've taught this thesis seminar for seven years. You will do yourselves no favors by making a safe selection and flying under the radar; *however,* an ambitious thesis will win no points on the grounds of ambitiousness alone. Your grade is contingent upon execution. Find a topic close enough to your area of interest to be productive without selecting one you already consider yourselves expert on." He offered Toby a withering smile. "Start us off, Mr. Powell."

Toby ran his fingers through his hair, stalling. The professor's disclaimer had clearly shaken his confidence in whatever topic he'd been about to declare. He made a few noncommittal sounds while scrolling through his notes.

"Um . . . T helper 17 cells and immunology." He was careful not to let his voice wander up at the end into a question. Professor Lyne let him hang for a moment, and everyone waited to see if he would give Toby "the look"—the slight lift of his chin and the tilt of his head that he had become famous for; a look that said, *perhaps you'd like to try again*—but finally he honored him with a small nod.

His gaze pivoted. "Mr. Hall?"

Max opened his mouth when Lyne cut in with, "No tech. Science yes, tech no. So choose wisely." Max's mouth snapped shut a moment as he considered.

"Electrical efficacy in sustainable energy," he said after a pause.

"Hardware over software. Admirable choice, Mr. Hall."

Professor Lyne continued around the room.

Inheritance patterns, equilibriums, and radiation were all approved, while effects of alcohol/cigarettes/illegal substances, the chemical properties of methamphetamines, and the body's response to sex all earned "the look." One by one the topics were accepted or retooled.

"Next," ordered Professor Lyne, his sense of humor ebbing.

"Chemical pyrotechnics."

A long pause. The topic had come from Janine Ellis, whose eyebrows hadn't fully recovered from her last round of research. Professor Lyne gave a sigh, accompanied by "the look," but Janine only smiled and there wasn't much Lyne could say. Ellis was one of the youngest students in the room and had, in her freshman year, discovered a new and vibrant shade of blue that firework companies across the world now used. If she was willing to risk her eyebrows, that was her own business.

"And you, Mr. Vale?"

Victor looked at his professor, narrowing down his options. He'd never been strong in physics, and while chemistry was fun, his real passion lay in biology—anatomy and neuroscience. He'd like a topic with the potential for experimentation, but he'd also like to keep his eyebrows. And while he wanted to hold his rank in the department, offers from med schools, graduate programs, and research labs had been coming in the mail for weeks (and under the table for months). He and Eli had been decorating their entry hall with the letters. Not the offers, no, but the letters that preceded them, all praise and charm, batting lashes and handwritten postscripts. Neither one of them needed to move worlds with their papers. Victor glanced over at Eli, wondering what he would choose.

Professor Lyne cleared his throat.

"Adrenal inducers," said Victor on a lark.

"Mr. Vale, I've already turned down a proposal involving intercourse—"

"No," Victor said, shaking his head. "Adrenaline and its physical and emotional inducers and consequences. Biochemical thresholds. Fight or flight. That kind of thing."

He watched Professor Lyne's face, waiting for a sign, and Lyne eventually nodded.

"Don't make me regret it," he said.

And then he turned to Eli, the last person to answer. "Mr. Cardale."

Eli smiled calmly. "EOs."

The whole class, which had devolved more and more into muffled conversation as students declared their topics, now stopped. The background chatter and the sound of typing and the fidgeting in chairs went still as Professor Lyne considered Eli with a new look, one that hung between surprise and confusion, tempered only by the understanding that Eliot Cardale was consistently top of the class, top of the entire pre-medical department, even—well, alternating with Victor for first and second spot, anyway.

Fifteen pairs of eyes flicked between Eli and Professor Lyne as the moment of silence lasted and became uncomfortable. Eli wasn't the kind of student to propose something as a joke, or a test. But he couldn't possibly be serious.

"I'm afraid you'll have to expand," said Lyne slowly.

Eli's smile didn't falter. "An argument for the theoretical feasibility of the existence of ExtraOrdinary people, deriving from laws of biology, chemistry, and psychology."

Professor Lyne's head tilted and his chin tipped, but when he opened his mouth, all he said was, "Be careful, Mr. Cardale. As I warned, no points will be given for ambition alone. I'll trust you not to make a mockery of my class."

"Is that a yes, then?" asked Eli.

The first bell rang.

One person's chair scraped back an inch, but no one stood up.

"Fine," said Professor Lyne.

Eli's smile widened.

Fine? thought Victor. And, reading the looks of every other student in the room, he could see everything from curiosity to surprise to envy echoed in their faces. It was a joke. It had to be. But Professor Lyne only straightened, and resumed his usual composure.

"Go forth, students," he said. "Create change."

The room erupted into movement. Chairs were dragged, tables knocked askew, bags hoisted, and the class emptied in a wave into the hall, taking Victor with it. He looked around the corridor for Eli and saw that he was still in the room, talking quietly, animatedly, with Professor Lyne. For a moment the steady calm was gone and his eyes were bright with energy, glinting with hunger. But by the time he broke away and joined Victor in the hall, it was gone, hidden behind a casual smile.

"What the hell was that?" Victor demanded. "I know the thesis doesn't matter much at this point, but still—was that some kind of joke?"

Eli shrugged, and before the matter could be pressed, his phone broke out into electro-rock in his pocket. Victor sagged against the wall as Eli dug it out.

"Hey, Angie. Yeah, we're on our way." He hung up without even waiting for a response.

"We've been summoned." Eli slung his arm around Victor's shoulders. "My fair damsel is hungry. I dare not keep her waiting."

ABOUT THE AUTHOR

VICTORIA "V. E." SCHWAB is the #1 *New York Times* bestselling author of more than a dozen books, including the acclaimed novel *The Invisible Life of Addie LaRue,* the Shades of Magic series, the Villains series, *This Savage Song,* and *Our Dark Duet.* Her work has received critical acclaim, been featured in the *New York Times, Entertainment Weekly, The Washington Post,* and more; been translated into more than a dozen languages; and has been optioned for television and film. When she's not haunting Paris streets or trudging up English hillsides, she lives in Edinburgh, Scotland, and is usually tucked into the corner of a coffee shop, dreaming up monsters.

Praise for the Shades of Magic series

"Addictive and immersive, this series is a must-read."
—*Entertainment Weekly*

"Schwab has given us a gem of a tale that is original in its premise and compelling in its execution. This is a book to treasure."
—Deborah Harkness, *New York Times* bestselling author, on *A Darker Shade of Magic*

"Feels like a priceless object, brought from another, better world of fantasy books." —*io9* on *A Darker Shade of Magic*

"Compulsively readable . . . A world worth getting lost in."
—NPR

"This is how fantasy should be done. . . . A series that redefines epic." —*Publishers Weekly* (starred review)

"If you haven't picked up the Shades of Magic series before, do so. *A Darker Shade of Magic* is good; *A Gathering of Shadows* is better; *A Conjuring of Light* blows them both away." —*Culturess*

Praise for V. E. Schwab and *The Invisible Life of Addie LaRue*

"The most joyous evocation of unlikely immortality."
—Neil Gaiman, *New York Times* bestselling author

"Completely absorbed me enough to make me forget the real world." —Jodi Picoult, *New York Times* bestselling author

"One of the most propulsive, compulsive, and captivating novels in recent memory." —*The Washington Post*

"This evocative and clever tale will leave you smiling, filled with love and longing for more magical moments in everyday life."
—CNN, Best Books of October 2020

"Schwab is simply one of the most skilled writers working in her genre." —*Tor.com*

TOR BOOKS BY V. E. SCHWAB

STANDALONES
The Invisible Life of Addie LaRue

THE VILLAINS SERIES
Vicious
Vengeful

THE SHADES OF MAGIC SERIES
A Darker Shade of Magic
A Gathering of Shadows
A Conjuring of Light

A GATHERING OF SHADOWS

V. E. SCHWAB

TOR PUBLISHING GROUP
NEW YORK

This is a work of fiction. All of the characters, organizations, and events portrayed
in this novel are either products of the author's imagination
or are used fictitiously.

A GATHERING OF SHADOWS

Copyright © 2016 by Victoria Schwab

All rights reserved.

A Tor Book
Published by Tom Doherty Associates / Tor Publishing Group
120 Broadway
New York, NY 10271

www.tor-forge.com

Tor® is a registered trademark of Macmillan Publishing Group, LLC.

The Library of Congress has cataloged the hardcover edition as follows:

Names: Schwab, Victoria, author.
Title: A gathering of shadows / V. E. Schwab.
Description: First edition. | New York : Tor, 2016. | "A Tom Doherty
    Associates book."
Identifiers: LCCN 2015031510 (print) | ISBN 9780765376473 (hardcover) |
    ISBN 9780765376497 (ebook)
Subjects: Other subjects: FICTION / Fantasy / General. | FICTION / Fantasy /
    Historical. | LCGFT: Fantasy fiction. | Science fiction.
Classification: LCC PS3619.C4848 G38 2016 (print) | DDC 813/.6—dc23
LC record available at https://lccn.loc.gov/2015031510

ISBN 978-1-250-89123-5 (second trade paperback)

Our books may be purchased in bulk for promotional, educational, or business use.
Please contact your local bookseller or the Macmillan Corporate and Premium
Sales Department at 1-800-221-7945, extension 5442, or by email at
MacmillanSpecialMarkets@macmillan.com.

Second Tor Paperback Edition: 2023

Printed in the United States of America

0 9 8 7 6 5 4 3

For the ones who fight their way forward

Magic and magician must between them balance. Magic itself is chaos. The magician must be calm. A fractured self is a poor vessel for power, spilling power without focus or measure from every crack.

—TIEREN SERENSE,
head priest of the London Sanctuary

ONE

THIEF AT SEA

I

The Arnesian Sea.

Delilah Bard had a way of finding trouble.

She'd always thought it was better than letting trouble find *her,* but floating in the ocean in a two-person skiff with no oars, no view of land, and no real resources save the ropes binding her wrists, she was beginning to reconsider.

The night was moonless overhead, the sea and sky mirroring the starry darkness to every side; only the ripple of water beneath the rocking boat marked the difference between up and down. That infinite reflection usually made Lila feel like she was perched at the center of the universe.

Tonight, adrift, it made her want to scream.

Instead, she squinted at the twinkle of lights in the distance, the reddish hue alone setting the craft's lanterns apart from the starlight. And she watched as the ship—*her* ship—moved slowly but decidedly *away.*

Panic crawled its way up her throat, but she held her ground.

I am Delilah Bard, she thought as the ropes cut into her skin. *I am a thief and a pirate and a traveler. I have set foot in three different worlds, and lived. I have shed the blood of royals and held magic in my hands. And a ship full of men cannot do what I can. I don't need any of you.*

I am one of a damned kind.

Feeling suitably empowered, she set her back to the ship, and gazed out at the sprawling night ahead.

It could be worse, she reasoned, just before she felt cold water licking her boots and looked down to see that there was a hole in the boat. Not a large hole by any stretch, but the size was little comfort; a small hole could sink a boat just as effectively, if not as fast.

Lila groaned and looked down at the coarse rope cinched tight around her hands, doubly grateful that the bastards had left her legs free, even if she was trapped in an abominable *dress*. A full-skirted, flimsy green contraption with too much gossamer and a waist so tight she could hardly breathe and *why in god's name* must women *do* this to themselves?

The water inched higher in the skiff, and Lila forced herself to focus. She drew what little breath her outfit would allow and took stock of her meager, quickly dampening inventory: a single cask of ale (a parting gift), three knives (all concealed), half a dozen flares (bequeathed by the men who'd set her adrift), the aforementioned dress (damn it to hell), and the contents of that dress's skirts and pockets (necessary, if she was to prevail).

Lila took up one of the flares—a device like a firework that, when struck against any surface, produced a stream of colored light. Not a burst, but a steady beam strong enough to cut the darkness like a knife. Each flare was supposed to last a quarter of an hour, and the different colors had their own code on the open water: yellow for a sinking ship, green for illness aboard, white for unnamed distress, and red for pirates.

She had one of each, and her fingers danced over their ends as she considered her options. She eyed the rising water and settled on the yellow flare, taking it up with both hands and striking it against the side of the little boat.

Light burst forth, sudden and blinding. It split the world in two, the violent gold-white of the flare and the dense black nothing around it. Lila spent half a minute cursing and blinking back tears at the brightness as she angled the flare up and away from her face. And then she began to count. Just as her eyes were finally adjusting, the flare faltered, flickered, and went out. She scanned the horizon for a ship but saw none, and the water in the boat continued its slow but steady rise up the calf of her boot. She took up a second flare—white for distress—and struck it on the wood, shielding her eyes. She counted the minutes as they ticked by, scouring the night beyond the boat for signs of life.

"Come on," she whispered. "Come on, come on, come on . . ." The words were lost beneath the hiss of the flare as it died, plunging her back into darkness.

Lila gritted her teeth.

Judging by the level of the water in the little boat, she had only a quarter of an hour—one flare's worth of time—before she was well and truly in danger of sinking.

Then something snaked along the skiff's wooden side. Something with teeth.

If there is a god, she thought, *a celestial body, a heavenly power, or anyone above—or below—who might just like to see me live another day, for pity's or entertainment's sake, now would be a good time to intercede.*

And with that, she took up the red flare—the one for pirates—and struck it, bathing the night around her in an eerie crimson light. It reminded her for an instant of the Isle River back in London. Not *her* London—if the dreary place had ever been hers—or the terrifyingly pale London responsible for Athos and Astrid and Holland, but *his* London. Kell's London.

He flashed up in her vision like a flare, auburn hair and that constant furrow between his eyes: one blue, one black. *Antari.* Magic boy. Prince.

Lila stared straight into the flare's red light until it burned the image out. She had more pressing concerns right now. The water was rising. The flare was dying. Shadows were slithering against the boat.

Just as the red light of the pirate's flare began to peter out, she saw it.

It began as nothing—a tendril of mist on the surface of the sea—but soon the fog drew itself into the phantom of a ship. The polished black hull and shining black sails reflected the night to every side, the lanterns aboard small and colorless enough to pass for starlight. Only when it drew close enough for the flare's dying red light to dance across the reflective surfaces did the ship come into focus. And by then, it was nearly on top of her.

By the flare's sputtering glow, Lila could make out the ship's name, streaked in shimmering paint along the hull. *Is Ranes Gast.*

The Copper Thief.

Lila's eyes widened in amazement and relief. She smiled a small, private smile, and then buried the look beneath something more fitting—an expression somewhere between grateful and beseeching, with a dash of wary hope.

The flare guttered and went out, but the ship was beside her now, close enough for her to see the faces of the men leaning over the rail.

"*Tosa!*" she called in Arnesian, getting to her feet, careful not to rock the tiny, sinking craft.

Help. Vulnerability had never come naturally, but she did her best to imitate it as the men looked down at her, huddled there in her little waterlogged boat with her bound wrists and her soggy green dress. She felt ridiculous.

"*Kers la?*" asked one, more to the others than to her. *What is this?*

"A gift?" said another.

"You'd have to share," muttered a third.

A few of the other men said less pleasant things, and Lila tensed, glad that their accents were too full of mud and ocean spray for her to understand all the words, even if she gleaned their meaning.

"What are you doing down there?" asked one of them, his skin so dark his edges smudged into the night.

Her Arnesian was still far from solid, but four months at sea surrounded by people who spoke no English had certainly improved it.

"*Sensan,*" answered Lila—*sinking*—which earned a laugh from the gathering crew. But they seemed in no hurry to haul her up. Lila held her hands aloft so they could see the rope. "I could use some help," she said slowly, the wording practiced.

"Can see that," said the man.

"Who throws away a pretty thing?" chimed in another.

"Maybe she's all used up."

"Nah."

"Hey, girl! You got all your bits and pieces?"

"Better let us see!"

"What's with all the shouting?" boomed a voice, and a moment later a rail-thin man with deep-set eyes and receding black hair came into sight at the side of the ship. The others shied away in deference as he took hold of the wooden rail and looked down at Lila. His eyes raked over her, the dress, the rope, the cask, the boat.

The captain, she wagered.

"You seem to be in trouble," he called down. He didn't raise his voice, but it carried nonetheless, his Arnesian accent clipped but clear.

"How perceptive," Lila called back before she could stop herself. The insolence was a gamble, but no matter where she was, the one thing she knew was how to read a mark. And sure enough, the thin man smiled.

"My ship's been taken," she continued, "and my new one won't last long, and as you can see—"

He cut her off. "Might be easier to talk if you come up here?"

Lila nodded with a wisp of relief. She was beginning to fear they'd sail on and leave her to drown. Which, judging by the crew's lewd tones and lewder looks, might actually be the better option, but down here she had nothing and up there she had a chance.

A rope was flung over the side; the weighted end landed in the rising water near her feet. She took hold and used it to guide her craft against the ship's side, where a ladder had been lowered; but before she could hoist herself up, two men came down and landed in the boat beside her, causing it to sink *considerably* faster. Neither of them seemed bothered. One proceeded to haul up the cask of ale, and the other, much to Lila's dismay, began to haul up *her*. He threw her over his shoulder, and it took every ounce of her control—which had never been plentiful—not to bury a knife in his back, especially when his hands began to wander up her skirt.

Lila dug her nails into her palms, and by the time the man finally set her down on the ship's desk beside the waiting cask ("Heavier than she looks," he muttered, "and only half as soft . . .") she'd made eight small crescents in her skin.

"Bastard," growled Lila in English under her breath. He gave her a wink and murmured something about being soft where it mattered, and Lila silently vowed to kill him. Slowly.

And then she straightened and found herself standing in a circle of sailors.

No, not sailors, of course.

Pirates.

Grimy, sea stained and sun bleached, their skin darkened and their clothes faded, each and every one of them with a knife tattooed across his throat. The mark of the pirates of the *Copper Thief*. She counted seven surrounding her, five tending to the rigging and sails, and assumed another half dozen below deck. Eighteen. Round it up to twenty.

The rail-thin man broke the circle and stepped forward.

"*Solase,*" he said, spreading his arms. "What my men have in balls, they lack in manners." He brought his hands to the shoulders of her green dress. There was blood under his nails. "You are shaking."

"I've had a bad night," said Lila, hoping, as she surveyed the rough crew, that it wasn't about to get worse.

The thin man smiled, his mouth surprisingly full of teeth. "*Anesh*," he said, "but you are in better hands now."

Lila knew enough about the crew of the *Copper Thief* to know that was a lie, but she feigned ignorance. "Whose hands would those be?" she asked, as the skeletal figure took her fingers and pressed his cracked lips to her knuckles, ignoring the rope still wound tightly around her wrists. "Baliz Kasnov," he said. "Illustrious captain of the *Copper Thief*."

Perfect. Kasnov was a legend on the Arnesian Sea. His crew was small but nimble, and they had a penchant for boarding ships and slitting throats in the darkest hours before dawn, slipping away with their cargo and leaving the dead behind to rot. He may have looked starved, but he was an alleged glutton for treasure, especially the consumable kind, and Lila knew that the *Copper Thief* was sailing for the northern coast of a city named Sol in hopes of ambushing the owners of a particularly large shipment of fine liquor. "Baliz Kasnov," she said, sounding out the name as if she'd never heard it.

"And you are?" he pressed.

"Delilah Bard," she said. "Formerly of the *Golden Fish*."

"Formerly?" prompted Kasnov as his men, obviously bored by the fact she was still clothed, began to tap into the cask. "Well, Miss Bard," he said, linking his arm through hers conspiratorially. "Why don't you tell me how you came to be in that little boat? The sea is no place for a fair young lady such as yourself."

"*Vaskens*," she said—*pirates*—as if she had no idea the word applied to present company. "They stole my ship. It was a gift, from my father, for my wedding. We were meant to sail toward Faro—we set out two nights ago—but they came out of nowhere, stormed the *Golden Fish* . . ." She'd practiced this speech, not only the words but the pauses. "They . . . they killed my husband. My captain. Most of my crew." Here Lila let herself lapse into English. "It happened so fast—" She caught herself, as if the slip were accidental.

But the captain's attention snagged, like a fish on a hook. "Where are you from?"

"London," said Lila, letting her accent show. A murmur went through the group. She pressed on, intent on finishing her story. "The *Fish* was small," she said, "but precious. Laden down with a month's supplies. Food, drink . . . money. As I said, it was a gift. And now it's gone."

But it wasn't really, not yet. She looked back over the rail. The ship was a smudge of light on the far horizon. It had stopped its retreat and seemed to be waiting. The pirates followed her gaze with hungry eyes.

"How many men?" asked Kasnov.

"Enough," she said. "Seven? Eight?"

The pirates smiled greedily, and Lila knew what they were thinking. They had more than twice that number, and a ship that hid like a shadow in the dark. If they could catch the fleeing bounty . . . she could feel Baliz Kasnov's deep-set eyes scrutinizing her. She stared back at him and wondered, absently, if he could do any magic. Most ships were warded with a handful of spells—things to make their lives safer and more convenient—but she had been surprised to find that most of the men she met at sea had little inclination for the elemental arts. Alucard said that magical proficiency was a valued skill, and that true affinity would usually land one gainful employment on land. Magicians at sea almost always focused on the elements of relevance— water and wind—but few hands could turn the tide, and in the end most still favored good old-fashioned steel. Which Lila could certainly appreciate, having several pieces currently hidden on her person.

"Why did they spare you?" asked Kasnov.

"Did they?" challenged Lila.

The captain licked his lips. He'd already decided what to do about the ship, she could tell; now he was deciding what to do about her. The Copper Thieves had no reputation for mercy.

"Baliz . . ." said one of the pirates, a man with skin darker than the rest. He clasped the captain's shoulder and whispered in his ear. Lila could only make out a few of the muttered words. *Londoners. Rich.* And *ransom.*

A slow smile spread across the captain's lips. "*Anesh,*" he said with a nod. And then, to the entire gathered crew, "Sails up! Course south by west! We have a golden fish to catch."

The men rumbled their approval.

"My lady," said Kasnov, leading Lila toward the steps. "You've had a hard night. Let me show you to my chamber, where you'll surely be more comfortable."

Behind her, she heard the sounds of the cask being opened and the ale being poured, and she smiled as the captain led her belowdecks.

Kasnov didn't linger, thank god.

He deposited her in his quarters, the rope still around her wrists, and vanished again, locking the door behind him. To her relief, she'd only seen three men belowdecks. That meant fifteen aboard the *Copper Thief.*

Lila perched on the edge of the captain's bed and counted to ten, twenty, then thirty, as the steps sounded above and the ship banked toward her own fleeing vessel. They hadn't even bothered to search her for weapons, which Lila thought a bit presumptuous as she dug a blade from her boot and, with a single practiced gesture, spun it in her grip and slashed the ropes. They fell to the floor as she rubbed her wrists, humming to herself. A shanty about the Sarows, a phantom said to haunt wayward ships at night.

How do you know when the Sarows is coming?
(Is coming is coming is coming aboard?)

Lila took the waist of her dress in two hands, and ripped; the skirt tore away, revealing close-fitting black pants—holsters pinning a knife above each knee—that tapered into her boots. She took the blade and slid it up the corset at her back, slicing the ribbons so she could breathe.

When the wind dies away but still sings in your ears,
(In your ears in your head in your blood in your bones.)

She tossed the green skirt onto the bed and slit it open from hem to tattered waist. Hidden among the gossamer were half a dozen thin sticks that passed for boning and looked like flares, but were neither. She slid her blade back into her boot and freed the tapers.

When the current goes still but the ship, it drifts along,
(Drifts on drifts away drifts alone.)

Overhead, Lila heard a thud, like dead weight. And then another, and another, as the ale took effect. She took up a piece of black cloth, rubbed charcoal on one side, and tied it over her nose and mouth.

When the moon and the stars all hide from the dark,
(For the dark is not empty at all at all.)
(For the dark is not empty at all.)

The last thing Lila took from deep within the folds of the green skirt was her mask. A black leather face-piece, simple but for the horns that curled with strange and menacing grace over the brow. Lila settled the mask on her nose and tied it in place.

How do you know when the Sarows is coming?
(Is coming is coming is coming aboard?)

A looking glass, half-silvered with age, leaned in the corner of the captain's cabin, and she caught her reflection as footsteps sounded on the stairs.

Why you don't and you don't and you won't see it coming,
(You won't see it coming at all.)

Lila smiled behind the mask. And then she turned and pressed her back against the wall. She struck a taper against the wood, the way she had the flares—but unlike flares, no light poured forth, only clouds of pale smoke.

An instant later, the captain's door burst open, but the pirates were too late. She tossed the pluming taper into the room and heard footsteps stumble, and men cough, before the drugged smoke brought them down.

Two down, thought Lila, stepping over their bodies.
Thirteen to go.

II

No one was steering the ship.

It had banked against the waves and was now breaching, being hit sidelong instead of head-on in a way that made the whole thing rock unpleasantly beneath Lila's feet.

She was halfway to the stairs before the first pirate barreled into her. He was massive, but his steps were slowed a measure and made clumsy by the drug dissolved in the ale. Lila rolled out of his grip and drove her boot into his sternum, slamming him back into the wall hard enough to crack bones. He groaned and slid down the wooden boards, half a curse across his lips before the toe of her boot met his jaw. His head snapped sideways, then lolled forward against his chest.

Twelve.

Footsteps echoed overhead. She lit another taper and threw it up against the steps just as three more men poured belowdecks. The first saw the smoke and tried to backtrack, but the momentum of the second and third barred his retreat, and soon all three were coughing and gasping and crumpling on the wooden stairs.

Nine.

Lila toed the nearest with her boot, then stepped over and up the steps. She paused at the lip of the deck, hidden in the shadow of the stairs, and watched for signs of life. When she saw none, she dragged the charcoal cloth from her mouth, dragging in deep breaths of crisp winter air before stepping out into the night.

The bodies were strewn across the deck. She counted them as she walked, deducting each from the number of pirates aboard.

Eight.
Seven.
Six.
Five.
Four.
Three.
Two.

Lila paused, looking down at the men. And then, over by the rail, something moved. She drew one of the knives from its sheath against her thigh—one of her favorites, a thick blade with a grip guard shaped into metal knuckles—and strode toward the shuffling form, humming as she went.

How do you know when the Sarows is coming?
(Is coming is coming is coming aboard?)

The man was crawling on his hands and knees across the deck, his face swollen from the drugged ale. At first Lila didn't recognize him. But then he looked up, and she saw it was the man who'd carried her aboard. The one with the wandering hands. The one who'd talked about finding her soft places.

"Stupid bitch," he muttered in Arnesian. It was almost hard to understand him through the wheezing. The drug wasn't lethal, at least not in low doses (she hadn't exactly erred on the side of caution with the cask), but it swelled the veins and airways, starving the body of oxygen until the victim passed out.

Looking down at the pirate now, with his face puffy and his lips blue and his breath coming out in ragged gasps, she supposed she might have been too liberal in her measurements. The man was currently trying—and failing—to get to his feet. Lila reached down, tangled the fingers of her free hand in the collar of his shirt, and helped him up.

"What did you call me?" she asked.

"I said," he wheezed, "stupid . . . bitch. You'll pay . . . for this. I'm gonna—"

He never finished. Lila gave him a sharp shove backward, and he toppled over the rail and crashed down into the sea.

"Show the Sarows some respect," she muttered, watching him flail briefly and then vanish beneath the surface of the tide.

One.

She heard the boards behind her groan, and she managed to get her knife up the instant before the rope wrapped around her throat. Coarse fibers scraped her neck before she sawed herself free. When she did, she staggered forward and spun to find the captain of the *Copper Thief,* his eyes sharp, his steps sure.

Baliz Kasnov had not partaken of the ale with his crew.

He tossed the pieces of rope aside, and Lila's grip tightened on her knife as she braced for a fight, but the captain drew no weapon. Instead, he brought his hands out before him, palms up.

Lila tilted her head, the horns of the mask tipping toward him. "Are you surrendering?" she asked.

The captain's dark eyes glittered, and his mouth twitched. In the lantern light the knife tattoo across his throat seemed to glint.

"No one takes the *Copper Thief,*" he said.

His lips moved and his fingers twitched as flames leaped across them. Lila looked down and saw the ruined marking at his feet, and knew what he was about to do. Most ships were warded against fire, but he'd broken the spell. He lunged for the nearest sail, and Lila spun the blade in her hand, then threw. It was ill weighted, with the metal guard on the hilt, and it struck him in the neck instead of the head. He toppled forward, his hands thrown out to break his fall, the conjured fire meeting a coil of ropes instead of sail.

It caught hold, but Kasnov's own body smothered most of it when he fell. The blood pouring from his neck extinguished more. Only a few tendrils of flame persisted, chewing their way up the ropes. Lila reached out toward the fire; when she closed her fingers into a fist, the flames died.

Lila smiled and retrieved her favorite knife from the dead captain's throat, wiping the blood from the blade on his clothes. She was sheathing it again when she heard a whistle, and she looked up to see her ship, the *Night Spire,* drawing up beside the *Copper Thief.*

Men had gathered along the rail, and she crossed the width of the *Thief* to greet them, pushing the mask up onto her brow. Most of the men were frowning, but in the center, a tall figure stood, wearing a black sash and an amused smile, his tawny brown hair swept back and a sapphire in his brow. Alucard Emery. Her captain.

"*Mas aven,*" growled the first mate, Stross, in disbelief.

"Not fucking possible," said the cook, Olo, surveying the bodies scattered across the deck.

Handsome Vasry and Tavestronask (who went simply by Tav) both applauded, Kobis watched with crossed arms, and Lenos gaped like a fish.

Lila relished the mixture of shock and approval as she went to the rail and spread her arms wide. "Captain," she said cheerfully. "It appears I have a ship for you."

Alucard smiled. "It appears you do."

A plank was laid between the two vessels, and Lila strode deftly across it, never once looking down. She landed on the deck of the *Night Spire* and turned toward the lanky young man with shadows beneath his eyes, as if he'd never slept. "Pay up, Lenos."

His brow crinkled. "Captain," he pleaded, with a nervous laugh.

Alucard shrugged. "You made the bet," he said. "You and

Stross," he added, nodding to his first mate, a brutish man with a beard. "With your own heads and your own coin."

And they had. Sure, Lila had boasted that she could take the *Copper Thief* herself, but they'd been the ones to bet she couldn't. It had taken her nearly a month to buy enough of the drug for the tapers and ale, a little every time her ship had docked. It was worth it.

"But it was a trick!" countered Lenos.

"Fools," said Olo, his voice low, thunderous.

"She clearly planned it," grumbled Stross.

"Yeah," said Lenos, "how were we supposed to know she'd been *planning* it?"

"You should have known better than to gamble with Bard in the first place." Alucard met her gaze and winked. "Rules are rules, and unless you want to be left with the bodies on that ship when we're done, I suggest you pay my thief her due."

Stross dragged the purse from his pocket. "How did you do it?" he demanded, shoving the purse into her hands.

"Doesn't matter," said Lila, taking the coin. "Only matters that I did."

Lenos went to forfeit his own purse, but she shook her head. "That's not what I bet for, and you know it." Lenos proceeded to slouch even lower than usual as he unstrapped the blade from his forearm.

"Don't you have enough knives?" he grumbled, his lip thrust forward in a pout.

Lila's smile sharpened. "No such thing," she said, wrapping her fingers around the blade. *Besides,* she thought, *this one is special*. She'd been coveting the weapon since she first saw Lenos use it, back in Korma.

"I'll win it back from you," he mumbled.

Lila patted his shoulder. "You can try."

"*Anesh!*" boomed Alucard, pounding his hand on the plank. "Enough standing around, Spires, we've got a ship to sack. Take it all. I want those bastards left waking up with nothing in their hands but their own cocks."

The men cheered, and Lila chuckled despite herself.

She'd never met a man who loved his job more than Alucard Emery. He relished it the way children relish a game, the way men and women relish acting, throwing themselves into their plays with glee and abandon. There was a measure of theatre to everything Alucard did. She wondered how many other parts he could play. Wondered which, if any, were *not* a part, but the actor beneath.

His eyes found hers in the dark. They were a storm of blue and grey, at times bright and at others almost colorless. He tipped his head wordlessly in the direction of his chambers, and she followed.

Alucard's cabin smelled as it always did, of summer wine and clean silk and dying embers. He liked nice things, that much was obvious. But unlike collectors or boasters who put their fineries on display only to be seen and envied, all of Alucard's luxuries looked thoroughly enjoyed.

"Well, Bard," he said, sliding into English as soon as they were alone. "Are you going to tell me how you managed it?"

"What fun would that be?" she challenged, sinking into one of the two high-backed chairs before his hearth, where a pale fire blazed, as it always did, and two short glasses sat on the table, waiting to be filled. "Mysteries are always more exciting than truths."

Alucard crossed to the table and took up a bottle, while his white cat, Esa, appeared and brushed against Lila's boot. "Are you made of anything *but* mysteries?"

"Were there bets?" she asked, ignoring both him and the cat.

"Of course," said Alucard, uncorking the bottle. "All kinds of small wagers. Whether you'd drown, whether the *Thief* would actually pick you up, whether we'd find anything left of you if they *did* . . ." He poured amber liquid into the glasses and held one out to Lila. She took it, and as she did, he plucked the horned mask off her head and tossed it onto the table between them. "It was an impressive performance," he said, sinking into his own chair. "Those aboard who didn't fear you before tonight surely do now."

Lila stared into the glass, the way some stared into fire. "There were some aboard who didn't fear me?" she asked archly.

"Some of them still call you the Sarows, you know," he rambled on, "when you're not around. They say it in a whisper, as if they think you can hear."

"Maybe I can." She rolled the glass between her fingers.

There was no clever retort, and she looked up from her glass and saw Alucard watching her, as he always did, searching her face the way thieves search pockets, trying to turn something out.

"Well," he said at last, raising his glass, "to what should we toast? To the Sarows? To Baliz Kasnov and his copper fools? To handsome captains and elegant ships?"

But Lila shook her head. "No," she said, raising her glass with a sharpened smile. "To the best thief."

Alucard laughed, soft and soundless. "To the best thief," he said.

And then he tipped his glass to hers, and they both drank.

III

Four Months Ago.
Red London.

Walking away had been easy.

Not looking back was harder.

Lila had felt Kell watching as she strode away, stopping only when she was out of sight. She was alone, again. *Free.* To go anywhere. Be anyone. But as the light ebbed, her bravado began to falter. Night dragged itself across the city, and she began to feel less like a conqueror and more like a girl alone in a foreign world with no grasp of the language and nothing in her pockets save for Kell's parting gift (an element set), her silver watch, and the handful of coins she'd nicked from a palace guard before she left.

She'd had less, to be sure, but she'd also had more.

And she knew enough to know she wouldn't make it far, not without a ship.

She clicked the pocket watch open and closed and watched the outlines of the crafts bob on the river, the Isle's red glow more marked in the settling dark. She had her eyes on one ship in particular, had been watching, coveting, all day. It was a gorgeous vessel, its hull and masts carved from dark wood and trimmed in silver, its sails shifting from midnight blue to black, depending on the light. A name ran along its hull—*Saren Noche*—and she would later learn that it meant *Night Spire*. For now she only knew that she wanted it. But she couldn't simply storm a fully manned craft and claim it as her own. She was good, but she wasn't *that* good. And then there was the grim fact that Lila didn't *technically* know how to sail. So she leaned against a smooth stone wall, her black attire blending into the shadows, and watched, the gentle rocking of the boat and the noise of the Night Market farther up the bank drawing her into a kind of trance.

A trance that broke when half a dozen men stomped off the ship's deck and down the plank in heavy boots, coins jingling in their pockets, raucous laughter in their throats. The ship had been preparing for sea all day, and the men had a manic enthusiasm that spoke of a last night on land. They looked eager to enjoy it. One kicked up a shanty, and the others caught it, carrying the song with them toward the taverns.

Lila snapped the pocket watch closed, pushed off the wall, and followed.

She had no disguise, only her clothes, which were a man's cut, and her dark hair, which fell into her eyes, and her own features, which she drew into sharp lines. Lowering her voice, she hoped she could pass for a slender young man. Masks could be worn in darkened alleys and to masquerade balls, but not in taverns. Not without drawing more attention than they were worth.

The men ahead disappeared into an establishment. It had no obvious name, but the sign above the door was made of metal, a shimmering copper that twisted and curled into waves around a silver compass. Lila smoothed her coat, turned up its collar, and went inside.

The smell hit her at once.

Not foul or stale, like the dockside taverns she'd known, or flower scented like the Red royal palace, but warm and simple and filling, the aroma of fresh stew mixing with tendrils of pipe smoke and the distant salt of sea.

Fires burned in corner hearths, and the bar stood not along

one wall but in the very center of the room, a curved metal circle that mimicked the compass on the door. It was an incredible piece of craftsmanship, a single piece of silver, its spokes trailing off toward the four hearth fires.

This was a sailors' tavern unlike any she'd ever seen, with hardly any bloodstains on the floors or fights threatening to spill out onto the street. The Barren Tide, back in Lila's London—no, not hers, not anymore—had serviced a far rougher crowd, but here half the men wore royal colors, clearly in the service of the crown. The rest were an assortment, but none bore the haggard look and hungry eyes of desperation. Many—like the men she'd followed in—were sea tanned and weather worn, but even their boots looked polished and their weapons well sheathed.

Lila let her hair fall in front of her blind eye, wrangled a quiet arrogance, and sauntered up to the counter.

"*Avan*," said the bartender, a lean man with friendly eyes. A memory hit her—Barron back at the Stone's Throw, with his stern warmth and stoic calm—but she got her guard up before the blow could land. She slid onto the stool and the bartender asked her a question, and even though she didn't know the words, she could guess at their meaning. She tapped the near-empty glass of a beverage beside her, and the man turned away to fetch the drink. It appeared an instant later, a lovely, frothing ale the color of sand, and Lila took a long, steadying sip.

A quarter turn around the bar, a man was fiddling absently with his coins, and it took Lila a moment to realize he wasn't actually touching them. The metal wound its way around his fingers and under his palms as if by magic, which of course it was. Another man, around the other side, snapped his fingers and lit his pipe with the flame that hovered at the tip of his thumb. The gestures didn't startle her, and she wondered at that; only a week in this world, and it seemed more natural to her than Grey London ever had.

She turned in her seat and picked out the men from the *Night*

Spire now scattered around the room. Two talking beside a hearth, one being drawn by a well-endowed woman into the nearest shadow, and three settling in to play a card game with a couple of sailors in red and gold. One of those three caught Lila's eye, not because he was particularly good-looking—he was in fact, quite ugly, from what she could see through the forest of hair across his face—but because he was cheating.

At least, she *thought* he was cheating. She couldn't be certain, since the game seemed to have suspiciously few rules. Still, she was certain she'd seen him pocket a card and produce another. His hand was fast, but not as fast as her eye. She felt the challenge tickle her nerves as her gaze trailed from his fingers to his seat on a low stool, where his purse rested on the wood. The purse was tethered to his belt by a leather strap, and looked heavy with coins. Lila's hand drifted to her hip, where a short, sharp knife was sheathed. She drew it free.

Reckless, whispered a voice in her head, and she was rather disconcerted to find that where once the voice had sounded like Barron, it now sounded like Kell. She shoved it aside, her blood rising with the risk, only to halt sharply when the man turned and looked straight at her—no, not at her, at the barkeep just behind her. He gestured to the table in the universal signal of *more drinks.*

Lila finished her drink and dropped a few coins on the counter, watching as the barkeep loaded the round of drinks onto a tray and a second man appeared to carry the order to its table.

She saw her chance, and got to her feet.

The room swayed once in the wake of the ale, the drink stronger than she was used to, but it quickly settled. She followed the man with the tray, her eyes fixed on the door beyond him even as her boot caught his heel. He stumbled, and managed to save his own balance, but not the tray's; drinks and glasses tumbled forward onto the table, sweeping half the cards away on a crest of spilled ale. The group erupted, cursing and shouting and pushing to their feet, trying to salvage coin and cloth, and by the time the sorry servant could turn to see who'd tripped him, the hem of Lila's black coat was already vanishing through the door.

Lila ambled down the street, the gambler's stolen purse hanging from one hand. Being a good thief wasn't just about fast fingers. It was about turning situations into opportunities. She hefted the purse, smiling at its weight. Her blood sang triumphantly.

And then, behind her, someone shouted.

She turned to find herself face to face with the bearded fellow she'd just robbed. She didn't bother denying it—she didn't know enough Arnesian to try, and the purse was still hanging from her fingers. Instead, she pocketed the take and prepared for a fight. The man was twice her size across, and a foot taller, and between one step and the next a curved blade appeared in his hands, a miniature version of a scythe. He said something to her, a low grumble of an order. Perhaps he was giving her a chance to leave the stolen prize and walk away intact. But she doubted his wounded pride would allow that, and even if it did, she needed the money enough to risk it. People survived by being cautious, but they got ahead by being bold.

"Finders keepers," she said, watching surprise light up the man's features. *Hell.* Kell had warned her that English had a purpose and a place in this world. It lived among royals, not pirates. If she was going to make it at sea, she'd have to mind her tongue until she learned a new one.

The bearded man muttered something, running a hand along the curve of his knife. It looked very, very sharp.

Lila sighed and drew her own weapon, a jagged blade with a handle fitted for a fist, its metal knuckles curved into a guard. And then, after considering her opponent again, she drew a second blade. The short, sharp one she'd used to knick the purse.

"You know," she said in English, since there was no one else around to hear. "You can still walk away from this."

The bearded man spat a sentence at her that ended with *pilse*. It was one of the only Arnesian words Lila knew. And she knew it wasn't nice. She was still busy being offended when the man lunged. Lila leaped back and caught the scythe with both blades, the sound of metal on metal ringing shrilly through the street. Even with the slosh of the sea and the noise of the taverns, they wouldn't be alone for long.

She shoved off the blade, fighting to regain her balance, and jerked away as he slashed again, this time missing her throat by a hair's breadth.

Lila ducked, and spun, and rose, catching the scythe's newest slash with her main knife, the weapons sliding until his blade fetched up against her dagger's guard. She twisted the knife free and came over the top of the scythe, slamming the metal knuckles of her grip into the man's jaw. Before he could recover, she came under with the second blade and buried it between his ribs. He coughed, blood streaking his beard, and went to slash at her with his remaining strength, but Lila forced the assaulting weapon up, through organ and behind bone, and at last the man's scythe tumbled away and his body went slack.

For an instant, another death flashed in her mind, another body on her blade, a boy in a castle in a bleak, white world. Not her first kill, but the first that stuck. The first that hurt. The memory flickered and died, and she was back on the docks again, the guilt bleeding out with the man's life. It had happened so fast.

She pulled free and let him collapse to the street, her ears still ringing from the clash of blades and the thrill of the fight. She took a few steadying breaths, then turned to run, and found herself face to face with the five other men from the ship.

A murmur passed through the crew.

Weapons were drawn.

Lila swore beneath her breath, her eyes straying for an instant to the palace arcing over the river behind them, as a weak thought flickered through her—she should have stayed, *could* have stayed, would have been safe—but Lila tamped it out and clutched her knives.

She was Delilah Bard, and she would live or die on her own damn—

A fist connected with her stomach, shattering the train of thought. A second collided with her jaw. Lila went down hard in the street, one knife skittering from her grip as her vision was shattered by starbursts. She fought to her hands and knees, clutching the second blade, but a boot came down hard on her wrist. Another met her ribs. Something caught her in the side of the head, and the world slipped out of focus for several long moments, shuddering back into shape only as strong hands dragged her to her feet. A sword came to rest under her chin, and she braced herself, but her world didn't end with a bite of the blade.

Instead, a leather strap, not unlike the one she'd cut to free the purse, was wrapped around her wrists and cinched tight, and she was forced down the docks.

The men's voices filled her head like static, one word bouncing back and forth more than the rest.

Casero. She didn't know what it meant.

She tasted blood, but she couldn't tell if it was coming from her nose or her mouth or her throat. It wouldn't matter, if they were planning to dump her body in the Isle (unless that was sacrilegious, which made Lila wonder what people here did with their dead), but after several moments of heated discussion, she was marched up the plank onto the ship she'd spent all afternoon watching. She heard a thud and looked back to see a man set the bearded corpse on the plank. *Interesting,* she thought, dully. *The men didn't carry it aboard.*

All the while, Lila held her tongue, and her silence only

seemed to rattle the crew. They shouted at each other, and at her. More men appeared. More calls for *casero*. Lila wished she'd had more than a handful of days to study Arnesian. Did *casero* mean trial? Death? Murder?

And then a man strode across the deck, wearing a black sash and an elegant hat, a gleaming sword and a dangerous smile, and the shouting stopped, and Lila understood.

Casero meant *captain*.

The captain of the *Night Spire* was striking. And strikingly young. His skin was sea tanned but smooth; his hair, a rich brown threaded with brass, was pinned back with an elegant clasp. His eyes, a blue so dark they were almost black, went from the body on the plank, to the crowd of gathered men, to Lila. A sapphire glittered in his left brow.

"*Kers la?*" he asked.

The five who'd dragged Lila on board broke into noise. She didn't even try to follow along and pick out words as they railed on around her. Instead she kept her eyes on the captain, and though he was obviously listening to their claims, he kept his eyes on her. When they'd burned themselves out, the captain began to interrogate her—or at least ramble at her. He didn't seem particularly angry, simply put out. He pinched the bridge of his nose and spoke very fast, obviously unaware of the fact she didn't know more than a few words of Arnesian. Lila waited for him to realize, and eventually he must have recognized the emptiness in her stare for lack of comprehension, because he trailed off.

"*Shast,*" he muttered under his breath, and then started up again, slowly, trying out several other languages, each either more guttural or more fluid than Arnesian, hoping to catch the light of understanding in her eyes, but Lila could only shake her head. She knew a few words of French, but that probably wouldn't help her in this world. There *was* no France here.

"*Anesh,*" said the captain at last, an Arnesian word that as far as Lila could tell was a general sound of assent. "*Ta . . .*" He pointed at her. "*. . . vasar . . .*" He drew a line across his throat. "*. . . mas . . .*" He pointed at himself. "*. . . eran gast.*" With that, he pointed at the body of the man she'd gutted.

Gast. She knew that word already. *Thief.*

"*Ta vasar mas eran gast.*"

You killed my best thief.

Lila smiled despite herself, adding the new words to her meager arsenal.

"*Vasar es,*" said one of the men, pointing at Lila. *Kill her.* Or perhaps, *Kill him,* since Lila was pretty sure they hadn't figured out yet that she was a girl. And she had no intention of informing them. She might have been a long way from home, but some things didn't change, and she'd rather be a man, even if that meant a dead one. And the crew seemed to be gunning for that end, as a murmur of approval went through the group, punctuated by *vasar.*

The captain ran a hand over his hair, obviously considering it. He raised a brow at Lila as if to say, *Well? What would you have me do?*

Lila had an idea. It was a very stupid idea. But a stupid idea was better than no idea, at least in theory. So she dragged the words into shape and delivered them with her sharpest smile. "*Nas,*" she said, slowly. "*An to eran gast.*"

No. I am your best thief.

She held the captain's gaze when she said it, her chin high and proud. The others grumbled and growled, but to her they didn't matter, didn't exist. The world narrowed to Lila and the captain of the ship.

His smile was almost imperceptible. The barest quirk of his lips.

Others were less amused by her show. Two of them advanced on her, and in the time it took Lila to retreat a matching step, she had another knife in hand. Which was a feat, considering the leather strap that bound her wrists. The captain whistled, and she couldn't tell if it was an order for his men, or a sound of approval. It didn't matter. A fist slammed into her back and she staggered forward into the captain, who caught her wrists and pressed a groove between her bones. Pain shot up her arm, and the knife clattered to the deck. She glared up into the captain's face. It was only inches from her own, and when his eyes bore into hers, she felt them searching.

"*Eran gast?*" he said. "*Anesh* . . ." And then, to her surprise, the captain let her go. He tapped his coat. "*Casero* Alucard Emery," he said, drawing out the syllables. Then he pointed at her with a questioning look.

"Bard," she said.

He nodded, once, thinking, and then turned to his waiting crew. He began addressing them, the words too smooth and fast for Lila to decipher. He gestured to the body on the plank, and then to her. The crew did not seem pleased, but the captain was the captain for a reason, and they listened. And when he was finished, they stood, still and sullen. Captain Emery turned and made his way back across the deck to a set of stairs that plunged down into the ship's hull.

When his boot touched the first step, he stopped and looked back with a new smile, this one sharp.

"*Nas vasar!*" he ordered. *No killing.*

And then he gave Lila a look that said, *Good luck,* and vanished belowdecks.

The men wrapped the body in canvas and set it back on the dock.

Superstition, she guessed, about bringing the dead aboard.

A gold coin was placed on the man's forehead, perhaps as payment for disposal. From what Lila could tell, Red London wasn't a particularly religious place. If these men worshipped anything, they worshipped magic, which she supposed would be heresy back in Grey London. But then again, Christians worshipped an old man in the sky, and if Lila had to say which one seemed more real at the moment, she'd have to side with magic.

Luckily, she'd never been devout. Never believed in higher powers, never attended church, never prayed before bed. In fact, the only person Lila had ever prayed to was herself.

She considered nicking the gold coin, but god or not, that seemed wrong, so she stood on the deck and watched the proceedings with resignation. It was hard to feel bad about killing the man—he would have killed her—and none of the other sailors seemed terribly broken up over the loss itself . . . but then again, Lila supposed she was in no place to judge a person's worth by who would miss them. Not with the closest thing she'd had to family rotting a world away. Who had found Barron? Who had buried him? She shoved the questions down. They wouldn't bring him back.

The huddle of men trudged back aboard. One of them walked straight up to Lila, and she recognized her knuckle-hilted dagger in his grip. He grumbled something under his breath, then raised the knife and buried its tip in a crate beside her head. To his credit, it wasn't *in* her head, and to hers, she didn't flinch. She brought her bound wrists around the blade and pulled down in a single sharp motion, freeing herself from the cord.

The ship was almost ready to set sail, and Lila appeared to have earned a place on it, though she wasn't entirely sure if it was as prisoner, cargo, or crew. A light rain began to fall, but she stayed on deck and out of the way as the *Night Spire* cast off, her heart racing as the ship drifted out into the middle of the Isle and turned its back on the glittering city. Lila gripped the rail at the *Spire*'s stern and watched Red London shrink in the distance.

She stood until her hands were stiff with cold, and the madness of what she was doing settled into her bones.

Then the captain barked her name—"Bard!"—and pointed at a group struggling with the crates, and she went to lend a hand. Just like that—only not just like that, of course, for there were many taut nights and fights won, first against and then beside the other men, and blood spilled and ships taken—Lila Bard became a member of the *Night Spire*'s crew.

IV

Once aboard the *Night Spire,* Lila barely said a word (Kell would have been thrilled). She spent every moment trying to learn Arnesian, cobbling together a vocabulary—but as fast as she was on the uptake, it was still easier to simply listen than engage.

The crew spent a fair amount of time tossing words her way, trying to figure out her native tongue, but it was Alucard Emery who found her out.

Lila had only been on board a week when the captain stumbled across her one night cussing at Caster, her flintlock, for being a waterlogged piece of shit with its last bullet jammed in the barrel.

"Well, this is a surprise."

Lila looked up and saw Alucard standing there. At first she thought her Arnesian must be improving, because she understood his words without thinking, but then she realized he wasn't speaking Arnesian. He was speaking *English*. Not only that, but his accent had the crisp enunciation and smooth execution of someone fluent in the royal tongue. Not like the court-climbers who fumbled over words, offering them up like a party trick. No, like Kell, or Rhy. Someone who had been raised with it balanced on their lips.

A world away, in the grey streets of Lila's old city, that fluency would mean little, but here, it meant neither of them were simple sailors.

In a last-ditch effort at salvaging her secret, Lila pretended not to understand him. "Oh don't go dumb on me now, Bard," he said. "You're just becoming interesting."

They were alone on the stretch of ship, tucked beneath the lip of the upper deck. Lila's fingers drifted to the knife at her waist, but Alucard held up a hand.

"Why don't we take this conversation to my chambers?" he asked, eyes glinting. "Unless you want to make a scene."

Lila supposed it would be better *not* to slit the captain's throat in plain sight.

No, it could be done in private.

The moment they were alone, Lila spun on him. "You speak Eng—" she started, then caught herself. "High Royal." That was what they called it here.

"Obviously," said Alucard before sliding effortlessly into Arnesian. "But it is not *my* native tongue."

"*Tac*," countered Lila in the same language. "Who says it is mine?"

Alucard gave her a playful grin and returned to English. "First, because your Arnesian is awful," he chided. "And second, because it's a law of the universe that all men swear in their native tongue. And I must say, your usage was quite colorful."

Lila clenched her teeth, annoyed at her mistake as Alucard led her into his cabin. It was elegant but cozy, with a bed in a nook along one wall and a hearth along the other, two high-backed chairs before a pale fire. A white cat lay curled on a dark wooden desk, like a paperweight atop the maps. It flicked its tail at their arrival and opened one lavender eye as Alucard crossed to the desk, riffling through some papers. He scratched the cat absently behind the ears.

"Esa," he said, by way of introduction. "Mistress of my ship."

His back was to Lila now, and her hand drifted once more

to the knife at her hip. But before she could reach the weapon, Alucard's fingers twitched and the blade jumped from its sheath and flew into his hand, hilt striking against palm. He hadn't even looked up. Lila's eyes narrowed. In the week she'd been aboard, she hadn't seen anyone do magic. Alucard turned toward her now with an easy grin, as if she hadn't been about to assault him. He tossed the knife casually onto the desk (the sound made Esa flick her tail again).

"You can kill me later," he said, gesturing to the two chairs before the fire. "First, let's talk."

A decanter sat on a table between the chairs, along with two glasses, and Alucard poured a drink the color of berries and held it out to Lila. She didn't take it.

"Why?" she asked.

"Because I'm fond of High Royal," he said, "and I miss having someone to speak it with." It was a sentiment Lila understood. The sheer relief of talking after so long silent was like stretching muscles after poor sleep, working the stiffness out. "I wouldn't want it to rust while I'm out at sea."

He sank into one of the chairs and downed the drink himself, the gem in his brow glinting in the hearth light. He tipped the empty glass at the other chair and Lila considered him, and her options, then lowered herself into it. The decanter of purple wine sat on the table between them. She poured herself a glass and leaned back, imitating Alucard's posture, her drink braced on the arm of the chair, legs stretched out, boots crossed at the ankle. The picture of nonchalance. He twisted one of his rings absently, a silver feather curled into a band.

For a long moment, they considered each other in silence, like two chess players before the first move. Lila had always hated chess. Never had the patience for it.

Alucard was the first to move, the first to speak. "Who are you?"

"I told you," she said simply. "My name is Bard."

"*Bard,*" he said. "There's no noble house by that name. Which family do you truly hail from? The Rosec? The Casin? The Loreni?"

Lila snorted soundlessly but didn't answer. Alucard was making an assumption, the only assumption an Arnesian *would* make: that because she spoke English, or High Royal—she must be noble. A member of the court, taught to flash English words like jewels, intent on impressing a royal, claiming a title, a crown. She pictured the prince, Rhy, with his easy charm and his flirtatious air. She could probably have kept his attention, if she'd wanted to. And then her thoughts drifted to Kell, standing like a shadow behind the flamboyant heir. Kell, with his reddish hair and his black eye and his perpetual frown.

"Fine," cut in Alucard. "An easier question. Do you have a first name, Miss Bard?" Lila raised a brow. "Yes, yes, I know you're a woman. You might actually pass for a very pretty boy back at court, but the kind of men who work on ships tend to have a bit more . . ."

"Muscle?" she ventured.

"I was going to say facial hair."

Lila smirked despite herself. "How long have you known?"

"Since you came aboard."

"But you let me stay."

"I found you curious." Alucard refilled his glass. "Tell me, what brought you to my ship?"

"Your men."

"But I saw you that day. You *wanted* to come aboard."

Lila considered him, then said, "I liked your ship. It looked expensive."

"Oh, it is."

"I was going to wait for the crew to go ashore, and then kill you and take the *Spire* as my own."

"How candid," he drawled, sipping his wine.

Lila shrugged. "I've always wanted a pirate ship."

At that, Alucard laughed. "What makes you think I'm a pirate, Miss Bard?"

Lila's face fell. She didn't understand. She'd seen them take a ship just the day before, even though she'd been confined to the *Spire,* had watched from the nest as they fought, and raided, and sailed on with a fresh bounty. "What else would you be?"

"I'm a *privateer,*" he explained, lifting his chin. "In the service of the good Arnesian crown. I sail by the permission of the Maresh. I monitor their seas and take care of any trouble I find on them. Why do you think my High Royal is so polished?"

Lila swore under her breath. No wonder the men had been welcome in that tavern with the compass. They were proper sailors. Her heart sank a little at the idea.

"But you don't fly royal colors," she said.

"I suppose I could. . . ."

"Then why don't you?" she snapped.

He shrugged. "Less fun, I suppose." He offered her a new smile, a wicked one. "And as I said, I *could* fly royal colors, *if* I wanted to be attacked at every turn, or scare away my prey. But I'm quite fond of the vessel, and I don't care to see it sunk, nor do I care to lose my post for lack of anything to show. No, the Spires prefer a more subtle form of infiltration. But we are not pirates." He must have seen Lila deflate, because he added, "Come now, don't look so disappointed, Miss Bard. It doesn't matter what you call it, *piracy* or *privateering,* it's just a difference of letters. The only thing that really matters is that I'm *captain* of this ship. And I intend to keep my post, and my life. Which begs the question of what to do with *you.*

"That man you knifed on the first night, Bels . . . the only thing that saved your skin was the fact that you killed him on land and not at sea. There are rules on ships, Bard. If you'd spilled his blood aboard mine, I'd have had no choice but to spill yours."

"You still could have," she observed. "Your men certainly wouldn't have objected. So why did you spare me?" The question had been eating at her since that first night.

"I was curious," he said, staring into the calm white light of the hearth fire. "Besides," he added, his dark eyes flicking back toward her, "I'd been looking for a way to get rid of Bels myself for months—the treacherous scum was stealing from me. So I suppose you did me a favor, and I decided to return it. Lucky for you, most of the crew hated the bastard anyhow."

Esa appeared beside his chair, her large purple eyes staring—or glaring—at Lila. She didn't blink. Lila was pretty sure cats were supposed to blink.

"So," Alucard said, straightening, "you came aboard intending to kill me and steal my ship. You've had a week, so why haven't you tried?"

Lila shrugged. "We haven't been ashore."

Alucard chuckled. "Are you always this charming?"

"Only in my native tongue. My Arnesian, as you pointed out, leaves something to be desired."

"Odd, considering that I've never met someone who could speak the court tongue, but not the common one. . . ."

He trailed off, obviously wanting an answer. Lila sipped her wine and let the silence thicken.

"I'll tell you what," he said, when it was clear she wouldn't follow him down that path. "Spend the nights with me, and I'll help improve your tongue."

Lila nearly choked on the wine at that, then glowered at Alucard. He was laughing—it was an easy, natural sound, though it made the cat ruffle her fur. "I didn't mean it like that," he said, regaining his composure. Lila felt as though she were the color of the liquor in her glass. Her face burned. It made her want to punch him.

"Come keep me company," he tried again, "and I'll keep your secret."

"And let the crew think you're *bedding* me?"

"Oh, I doubt they'll think that," he said with a wave of his hand. Lila tried not to feel insulted. "And I promise, I want only the pleasure of your conversation. I'll even help you with your Arnesian."

Lila rapped her fingers on the arm of the chair, considering. "All right," she said. She got to her feet and crossed to his desk, where her knife still sat atop the maps. She thought of the way he'd plucked it out of her grip. "But I want a favor in return."

"Funny, I thought the favor was allowing you to remain on my ship, despite the fact you're a liar, a thief, and a murderer. But please, do go on."

"Magic," she said, returning the blade to its holster.

He raised the sapphire-studded brow. "What of it?"

She hesitated, trying to choose her words. "You can do it."

"And?"

Lila pulled Kell's gift from her pocket and set it on the table. "And I want to learn." If she was going to have a chance in this new world, she needed to learn its *true* language.

"I'm not a very good teacher," said Alucard.

"But I'm a fast learner."

Alucard tipped his head, considering. Then he took up Kell's box and released the clasp, letting it fall open in his palm. "What do you want to know?"

Lila returned to the chair and leaned forward, her elbows on her knees. "Everything."

V

The Arnesian Sea.

Lila hummed as she made her way through the belly of the ship. She shoved one hand in her pocket, fingers closing around the shard of white stone she kept there. A reminder.

It was late, and the *Night Spire* had sailed on from the picked-over bones of the *Copper Thief.* The thirteen pirates she hadn't killed would be waking soon, only to find their captain dead and their ship sacked. It could be worse; their throats could have been slit along those inked blades. But Alucard preferred to let the pirates live, claiming that catch and release made the seas more interesting.

Her body was warm from wine and pleasant company, and as the ship swayed gently beneath her feet, the sea air wrapping around her shoulders, and the waves murmuring their song, that lullaby she'd wanted for so long, Lila realized she was happy.

A voice hissed in her ear.

Leave.

Lila recognized that voice, not from the sea, but from the streets of Grey London—it belonged to her, to the girl she'd been for so many years. Desperate, distrustful of anything that wasn't hers, and hers alone.

Leave, it urged. But Lila didn't want to.

And *that* scared her more than anything.

She shook her head and hummed the Sarows song as she reached her own cabin, the chords like a ward against trouble, even though she hadn't found any aboard her own ship in months. Not that it was *her* ship, not exactly, not yet.

Her cabin was small—barely big enough for a cot and a trunk—but it was the only place on the ship where she could be truly alone, and the weight of her persona slid from her shoulders like a coat as she closed the door.

A single window interrupted the wooden boards of the far wall, moonlight reflecting against the ocean swells. She lifted a lantern from the trunk's top and it lit in her hand with the same enchanted fire that filled Alucard's hearth (the spell wasn't hers, and neither was the magic). Hanging the light on a wall hook, she shucked her boots as well as her weapons, lining them up on the trunk, all save the knuckled knife, which she kept with her. Even though she now had a room of her own, she still slept with her back to the wall and the weapon on her knee, the way she had in the beginning. Old habits. She didn't mind so much. She hadn't had a good nights' sleep in years. Life on the Grey London streets had taught her how to rest without ever really sleeping.

Beside her weapons sat the small box Kell had given her that day. It smelled like him, which was to say it smelled like Red London, like flowers and freshly turned soil, and every time she opened it some small part of her was relieved that the scent was still there. A tether to the city, and to him. She took it with her onto the cot, sitting cross-legged and setting the object on the stiff blanket before her knees. Lila was tired, but this had become part of her nightly ritual, and she knew she wouldn't sleep well—if at all—until she did it.

The box was made of dark, notched wood and held shut by a small silver clasp. It was a fine thing, and she would have been able to sell it for a bit of coin, but Lila kept it close. Not out of sentimentality, she told herself—her silver pocket watch was the only thing she couldn't bring herself to sell—but because it was useful.

She slid the silver clasp, and the game board fell open in front of her, the elements in their grooves—earth and air, fire and water and bone—waiting to be moved. Lila flexed her fingers. She knew that most people could only master a single element, maybe two, and that she, being of another London, shouldn't be able to master any.

But Lila never let odds get in her way.

Besides, that old priest, Master Tieren, had told her that she had power somewhere in her bones. That it only needed to be nurtured.

Now she held her hands above either side of the drop of oil in its groove, palms in as if she could warm herself by it. She didn't know the words to summon magic. Alucard insisted that she didn't need to learn another tongue, that words were more for the user than the object, meant to help one focus, but without a proper spell, Lila felt silly. Nothing but a mad girl talking to herself in the dark. No, she needed something, and a poem, she had figured, was kind of like a spell. Or at least, it was more than just its words.

"*Tyger Tyger, burning bright . . .*" she murmured under her breath.

She didn't know many poems—stealing didn't lend itself to literary study—but she knew Blake by heart, thanks to her mother. Lila didn't remember much of the woman, who was more than a decade dead, but she remembered this—nights drawn to sleep by *Songs of Innocence and of Experience.* The gentle cadence of her mother's voice, rocking her like waves against a boat.

The words lulled Lila now, as they had back then, quieted the storm that rolled inside her head, and loosened the thief's knot of tension in her chest.

"*In the forests of the night . . .*"

Lila's palms warmed as she wove the poem through the air. She didn't know if she was doing it right, if there *was* such a thing as right—if Kell were here, he would probably insist there was, and nag her until she did it, but Kell wasn't here, and Lila figured there was more than one way to make a thing work.

"In what distant deeps or skies . . ."

Perhaps power had to be tended, like Tieren said, but not all things grew in gardens.

Plenty of plants grew wild.

And Lila had always thought of herself more as a weed than a rose bush.

"Burnt the fire of thine eyes?"

The oil in its groove sparked to life: not white like Alucard's hearth, but gold. Lila grinned triumphantly as the flame leaped from the groove into the air between her palms, dancing like molten metal, reminding her of the parade she'd seen that first day in Red London, when elementals of every kind danced through the streets, fire and water and air like ribbons in their wake.

The poem continued in her head as the heat tickled her palms. Kell would say it was impossible. What a useless word, in a world with magic.

What are you? Kell had asked her once.

What am I? She wondered now, as the fire rolled across her knuckles like a coin.

She let the fire go out, the drop of oil sinking back into its groove. The flame was gone, but Lila could feel the magic lingering in the air like smoke as she took up her newest knife, the one she'd won off Lenos. It was no ordinary weapon. A month back, when they'd taken a Faroan pirate ship called the *Serpent* off the coast of Korma, she'd seen him use it. Now she ran her hand along the blade until she found the hidden notch, where the metal met the hilt. She pushed the clasp, and it released, and the knife performed a kind of magic trick. It separated in her hands, and what had been one blade now became two, mirror images as thin as straight-edged razors. Lila touched the bead of oil and ran her finger along the backs of both knives. And then she balanced them in her hands, crossed their sharpened edges—*Tyger Tyger, burning bright*—and struck.

Fire licked along the metal, and Lila smiled.

This she hadn't seen Lenos do.

The flames spread until they coated the blades from hilt to tip, burning with golden light.

This she hadn't seen *anyone* do.

What am I? One of a kind.

They said the same thing about Kell.

The Red messenger.

The black-eyed prince.

The last *Antari*.

But as she twirled the fire-slicked knives in her fingers, she couldn't help but wonder . . .

Were they really one of a kind, or two?

She carved a fiery arc through the air, marveling at the path of light trailing like a comet's tail, and remembered the feeling of his eyes on her back as she walked away. Waiting. Lila smiled at the memory. She had no doubt their paths would cross again.

And when they did, she would *show* him what she could do.

TWO

PRINCE AT LARGE

I

Red London.

Kell knelt in the center of the Basin.

The large circular room was hollowed out of one of the bridge pillars that held up the palace. Set beneath the Isle's current, the faintest red glow from the river permeated the glassy stone walls with eerie light. A concentration circle had been etched into the stone floor, its pattern designed to channel power, and the whole space, wall and air alike, hummed with energy, a deep resonant sound like the inside of a bell.

Kell felt the power welling in him, wanting out—felt all the energy and the tension and the anger and the fear clawing for escape—but he forced himself to focus on his breathing, to find his center, to make a conscious act of the process that had become so natural. He wound back the mental clock until he was ten again, sitting on the floor of the monastic cell in the London Sanctuary, Master Tieren's steady voice in his head.

Magic is tangled, so you must be smooth.
Magic is wild, so you must be tame.
Magic is chaos, so you must be calm.
Are you calm, Kell?

Kell rose slowly to his feet, and raised his head. Beyond the concentration circle, the darkness twisted and the shadows loomed. In the flickering torchlight, sparring forms seemed to take the faces of enemies.

Tieren's soothing voice faded from his head, and Holland's cold tone took its place.

Do you know what makes you weak?

The *Antari*'s voice echoed in his head.

Kell stared into the shadows beyond the circle, imagining a flutter of cloak, a glint of steel.

You've never had to be strong.

The torchlight wavered, and Kell inhaled, exhaled, and struck.

He slammed into the first form, toppling it. By the time the shadow fell, Kell was already turning on the second one at his back.

You've never had to try.

Kell threw out his hand; water leaped to circle it and then, in one motion, sailed toward the figure, turning to ice the instant before it crashed into the form's head.

You've never had to fight.

Kell spun and found himself face to face with a shadow that took the shape of Holland.

And you've certainly never had to fight for your life.

Once he would have hesitated—once he *had* hesitated—but not this time. With a flick of his hand, metal spikes slid from the sheath at his wrist and into his palm. They rose into the air and shot forward, burying themselves in the specter's throat, his heart, his head.

But there were still more shadows. Always more.

Kell pressed himself against the Basin's curved wall and raised his hands. A small triangle of sharpened metal glinted on the back of his wrist; when he flexed his hand down it became a point, and Kell sliced his palm across with it, drawing blood. He pressed his hands together, then pulled them apart.

"*As Osoro*," he told the blood.

Darken.

The command rang out, echoing through the chamber, and between his palms the air began to thicken and swirl into shadows as thick as smoke. It billowed forth, and in moments the room was engulfed in darkness.

Kell sagged back into the cold stone wall of the room, breathless and dizzy from the force of so much magic. Sweat trickled into his eyes—one blue, the other solid black—as he let the silence of the space settle over him.

"Did you kill them all?"

The voice came from somewhere behind him, not a phantom but flesh and blood, and threaded with amusement.

"I'm not sure," said Kell. He collapsed the space between his palms, and the veil of darkness dissolved instantly, revealing the room for what it was: an empty stone cylinder clearly designed for meditation, not combat. The sparring forms were scattered, one burning merrily, another shot full of metal lances. The others—bashed, battered, broken—could hardly be called training dummies anymore. He closed his hand into a fist, and the fire on the burning dummy went out.

"Show-off," muttered Rhy. The prince was leaning in the arched entryway, his amber eyes caught like a cat's by the torchlight. Kell ran a bloody hand through his copper hair as his brother stepped forward, his boots echoing on the stone floor of the Basin.

Rhy and Kell were not actually brothers, not by blood. One year Rhy's senior, Kell had been brought to the Arnesian royal family when he was five, with no family and no memory. Indeed, with nothing but a dagger and an all-black eye: the mark of an *Antari* magician. But Rhy was the closest thing to a brother Kell had ever known. He would give his life for the prince. And—very recently—he had.

Rhy raised a brow at the remains of Kell's training. "I always thought being an *Antari* meant you didn't need to practice, that it all came"—he gestured absently—"naturally."

"The *ability* comes naturally," replied Kell. "The *proficiency* takes work. Just as I explained during every one of your lessons."

The prince shrugged. "Who needs magic when you look this good?"

Kell rolled his eyes. A table stood at the mouth of the alcove, littered with containers—some held earth, others sand and oil—and a large bowl of water; he plunged his hands into the latter and splashed his face before his blood could stain the water red.

Rhy passed him a cloth. "Better?"

"Better."

Neither was referring to the refreshing properties of the water. The truth was, Kell's blood pulsed with a restless beat, while the thing that coursed within it longed for activity. Something had been roused in him, and it didn't seem intent on going back to sleep. They both knew Kell's visits down to the Basin were increasing, both in frequency and length. The practice soothed his nerves and calmed the energy in his blood, but only for a little while. It was like a fever that broke, only to build again.

Rhy was fidgeting now, shifting his weight from foot to foot, and when Kell gave him a once-over, he noticed that the prince had traded his usual red and gold for emerald and grey, fine silk for wool and worn cotton, his gold-buckled boots replaced by a pair of black leather.

"What are you supposed to be?" he asked.

There was a glint of mischief in Rhy's eyes as he bowed with a flourish. "A commoner, of course."

Kell shook his head. It was a superficial ruse. Despite the clothing, Rhy's black hair was glossy and combed, his fingers dotted with rings, his emerald coat clasped with pearlescent buttons. Everything about him registered as royal. "You still look like a prince."

"Well, obviously," replied Rhy. "Just because I'm in disguise, doesn't mean I don't want to be recognized."

Kell sighed. "Actually," he said. "That's exactly what it means. Or *would* mean, to anyone but you." Rhy only smiled, as if it were a compliment. "Do I want to know *why* you are dressed like that?"

"Ah," said the prince. "Because we're going out."

Kell shook his head. "I'll pass." All he wanted was a bath and a drink, both of which were available in the peace of his own chambers.

"Fine," said Rhy. "*I'm* going out. And when I'm robbed and left in an alley, *you* can tell our parents what happened. Don't forget to include the part where you stayed home instead of ensuring my safety."

Kell groaned. "Rhy, the last time—"

But the prince waved off *the last time* as if it hadn't involved a broken nose, several bribes, and a thousand lin in damages.

"This will be different," he insisted. "No mischief. No mayhem. Just a drink at a place befitting our station. Come on, Kell, for me? I can't spend another minute cooped up planning tournaments while Mother second guesses my every choice, and Father worries about Faro and Vesk."

Kell didn't trust his brother to stay out of trouble, but he could see in the set of Rhy's jaw and the glint in his eyes, he was going out. Which meant *they* were going out. Kell sighed and nodded at the stairs. "Can I at least stop by my rooms and change?"

"No need," said Rhy cheerfully. "I've brought you a fresh tunic." He produced a soft shirt the color of wheat. Clearly he meant to usher Kell out of the palace before he could change his mind.

"How thoughtful," muttered Kell, shrugging out of his shirt. He saw the prince's gaze settle on the scar scrawled across his chest. The mirror image of the one over Rhy's own heart. A piece of forbidden, irreversible magic.

My life is his life. His life is mine. Bring him back.

Kell swallowed. He still wasn't used to the design—once black, now silver—that tethered them together. Their pain. Their pleasure. Their lives.

He pulled on the fresh tunic, exhaling as the mark disappeared beneath the cotton. He slicked his hair back out of his face and turned to Rhy. "Happy?"

The prince started to nod, then stopped. "Almost forgot," he said, pulling something from his pocket. "I brought hats." He placed a pale grey cap gingerly on his black curls, taking care to set it at a slight angle so the scattering of green gems shone across the brim.

"Wonderful," grumbled Kell as the prince reached out and deposited a charcoal-colored cap over Kell's reddish hair. His coat hung from a hook in the alcove, and he fetched it down and shrugged it on.

Rhy tutted. "You'll never blend in looking like that," he said, and Kell resisted the urge to point out that with his fair skin, red hair, and black eye—not to mention the word *Antari* following him wherever he went, half prayer and half curse—he would never blend in anywhere.

Instead he said, "Neither will you. I thought that was the point."

"I mean the coat," pressed Rhy. "Black isn't the fashion this winter. Haven't you got something indigo or cerulean hidden away in there?"

How many coats do you suppose there are inside that one?

The memory caught him like a blow. Lila.

"I prefer this one," he said, pushing the memory of her away, a pickpocket's hand swatted from the folds of a coat.

"Fine, fine." Rhy shifted his weight again. The prince had never been skilled at standing still, but Kell thought he'd gotten worse. There was a new restlessness to his motions, a taut energy that mirrored Kell's. And yet, Rhy's was different. Manic. Dangerous. His moods were darker and their turn sharper, cutting the span of a second. It was all Kell could do to keep up. "Are we ready, then?"

Kell glanced up the stairs. "What about the guards?"

"Yours or mine?" asked the prince. "Yours are standing by the upper doors. Helps that they don't know there's another way out of this place. As for my own men, they're probably still outside my room. My stealth really is in fine form today. Shall we?"

The Basin had its own route out of the palace, a narrow staircase that curled up one of the structure's supports and onto the bank; the two made their way up, lit only by the reddish dark and the pale lanterns that hung sparsely, burning with eternal flames.

"This is a bad idea," said Kell, not because he expected to change Rhy's mind, but simply because it was his job to say it, so that later he could tell the king and queen he'd tried.

"The best kind," said Rhy, looping his arm around Kell's shoulders.

And with that the two stepped out of the palace, and into the night.

II

Other cities slept away the winter months, but Red London showed no signs of retreat. As the two brothers walked the streets, elemental fires burned in every hearth, steam drifting from the chimneys, and through his clouded breath, Kell saw the haloed lights of the Night Market lining the bank, the scent of mulled wine and stew drifting on the steam, and the streets bustling with scarf-wrapped figures in jewel-toned cloaks.

Rhy was right: Kell was the only one dressed in black. He pulled the cap down over his brow, to shield him less from the cold than the inevitable looks.

A pair of young women strolled past, arm in arm, and when one cut a favoring glance at Rhy, nearly tripping over her skirts, he caught her elbow.

"*An, solase, res naster,*" she apologized.

"*Mas marist,*" replied Rhy in his effortless Arnesian.

The girl didn't seem to notice Kell, who still hung a step back, half in the bank's shadow. But her friend did. He could feel her eyes hanging on him, and when he finally met her gaze, he felt a grim satisfaction at her indrawn breath.

"*Avan,*" said Kell, his voice little more than fog.

"*Avan,*" she said, stiffly, bowing her head.

Rhy pressed his lips to the other girl's gloved fingers, but Kell didn't take his eyes off the one watching him. There had been a time when Arnesians worshipped him as blessed, fell over themselves trying to bow low enough; while he never relished that display, this was worse. There was a measure of reverence in her eyes, but also fear and, worse, distrust. She looked at him as if he were a dangerous animal. As if any sudden movement might cause him to strike. After all, as far as she knew, he was to blame for the Black Night that had swept the city, the magic that made people's eyes turn as black as his own as it ate them from the inside out. And no matter what statements the king and queen issued, no matter how many rumors Rhy tried to spread to the contrary, everyone believed it was Kell's doing. His fault.

And in a way, of course, it was.

He felt Rhy's hand on his shoulder and blinked.

The girls were walking away, arm in arm, whispering furiously.

Kell sighed and looked back at the royal palace arcing over the river. "This was a bad idea," he said again, but Rhy was already off, heading away from the Night Market and the glow of the Isle.

"Where are we going?" asked Kell, falling into step behind the prince.

"It's a surprise."

"Rhy," warned Kell, who had come to hate surprises.

"Fear not, Brother. I promised you an elegant outing, and I plan to deliver."

Kell hated the place the moment he saw it.

It was called Rachenast.

Splendor.

Ruinously loud and riotously colorful, Splendor was a leisure palace where the city's *ostra*—their elite—could stave off the coldest months by simply denying their presence. Beyond the silver-plated doors, the winter night evaporated. Inside, it was a summer day, from the fire lanterns burning sun-bright overhead to the artificial arbor, shading everyone beneath a dappled canopy of green.

Stepping from the icy night with its curtain of dark and fog into the expansive, well-lit field, Kell felt suddenly—horribly—exposed. He couldn't believe it, but he and Rhy were actually *under*dressed. He wondered if Rhy *wanted* to cause a scandal or a scene, to have his presence challenged. But the attendants at the doors either recognized the royal prince or Kell himself (and by extension Rhy, since saints knew no one else could drag the *Antari* to such a fête), because the two were welcomed in.

Kell squinted at the onslaught of activity. Banquet tables were piled with fruit and cheese and pitchers of chilled summer wine, and couples twirled across a blue stone platform made to resemble a pond, while others lounged on pillows beneath the enchanted trees. Wind chimes sang, and people laughed—the high, bright laugh of aristocrats—and toasted their companions with crystal cups, their wealth, like the landscape, on display.

Perhaps the whole charade would have been enchanting if it weren't so frivolous, so gaudy. Instead, Kell found it insufferable. Red London might have been the jewel of the Arnesian empire, but it still had poor people, and suffering—and yet, here in Splendor, the *ostra* could play pretend, craft utopias out of money and magic.

On top of it all, Rhy was right: no one else was wearing black, and Kell felt like a stain on a clean tablecloth (he thought of changing his coat, trading out the black for something brighter, but couldn't bring himself to wear any of the peacock shades so in fashion this winter) as the prince put a hand on his shoulder and ushered him forward. They passed a banquet table, and Rhy took up two flutes of summer wine. Kell kept his hat on, surveying the room from between the brim of the cap and the rim of the glass Rhy pressed into his hands.

"Do you think they've seen through my disguise yet," mused

the prince, keeping his head bowed, "or are they all too busy preening?"

Kell was surprised by the hint of judgment in his brother's tone. "Give it time," he said, "we've only just arrived." But he could feel the knowledge moving like a tremor through the room as Rhy led them toward a sofa beneath a tree.

The prince sank into the cushions and cast off his hat. His black curls shone, and even without the usual circlet of gold in his hair, everything about him—his posture, his perfect smile, his self-possession—registered as regal. Kell knew he couldn't mimic any of those things; he'd tried. Rhy tossed his hat onto the table. Kell hesitated, fingering the brim of his own, but kept it on, his only armor against prying eyes.

He sipped his drink and, having little interest in the rest of Splendor, considered his brother. He still didn't understand Rhy's half-hearted disguise. Splendor was a haunt for the elite, and the elite knew the prince's company better than anyone in the city. They spent months learning the royal tongue just so they could talk their way into his graces (even though Kell knew Rhy found that habit uncomfortable and unnecessary). But the clothes weren't the only thing that bothered him. Everything about the prince was in its place, and yet . . .

"Am I really that good-looking?" asked Rhy without meeting his gaze, while glassy laughter chimed through the room.

"You know you are," answered Kell, dragging his attention to the carpet of grass beneath their feet.

No one approached their couch save for an attendant, a young woman in a white dress, who asked if there was anything she could do to make their evening more enjoyable. Rhy flashed his smile and sent her in search of stronger drink and a flower.

Kell watched as the prince stretched his arms along the back of the sofa, his pale gold eyes glittering as he surveyed the room.

This was Rhy at his most understated, and it was still dreadfully conspicuous.

The attendant returned holding a decanter of ruby liquor and a single dark blue blossom; Rhy accepted the drink and tucked the flower behind her ear with a smile. Kell rolled his eyes. Some things didn't change.

As Rhy filled his glass, Kell caught a swell of whispers as more eyes wandered their way. He felt the inevitable weight as the collective gaze shifted from the prince to his companion. Kell's skin crawled under the attention, but instead of ducking his head, he forced himself to meet their eyes.

"This would be a good deal more fun," observed Rhy, "if you'd stop scowling at everyone."

Kell gave him a withering look. "They fear me."

"They worship you," said Rhy with a wave of his hand. "The majority of this city thinks you're a *god*."

Kell cringed at the word. *Antari* magicians were rare—so rare that they were seen by some as divine, chosen. "And the rest think I'm a devil."

Rhy sat forward. "Did you know that in Vesk, they believe you turn the seasons and control the tide, and bless the empire?"

"If you're appealing to my ego—"

"I'm simply reminding you that you will always be singular."

Kell stilled, thinking of Holland. He told himself that a new *Antari* would be born, or found, eventually, but he wasn't sure if he believed it. He and Holland had been two of a disappearing kind. They had always been rare, but they were rapidly approaching *extinct*. What if he really was the last one?

Kell frowned. "I would rather be normal."

Now it was Rhy's turn to wear the withering look. "Poor thing. I wonder what it feels like, to be put on a pedestal."

"The difference," said Kell, "is that the people *love* you."

"For every ten who love me," said Rhy, gesturing at the sprawling room, "one would like to see me dead."

A memory surfaced, of the Shadows, the men and women who had tried to take Rhy's life six years before, simply to send a message to the crown that they were wasting precious resources on frivolous affairs, ignoring the needs of their people. Thinking of Splendor, Kell could almost understand.

"My *point*," continued Rhy, "is that for every ten who worship you, one wants to see you burn. Those are simply the odds when it comes to people like us."

Kell poured himself a drink. "This place is horrible," he mused.

"Well . . ." said Rhy, emptying his own glass in one swallow and setting it down with a *click* on the table, "we could always leave."

And there it was, in Rhy's eye, that glint, and Kell suddenly understood the prince's outfit. Rhy wasn't dressed for Splendor because it wasn't his true destination. "You chose this place on purpose."

A languorous smile. "I don't know what you're talking about."

"You chose it because you *knew* I would be miserable here and more likely to cave when you offered to take me someplace else."

"And?"

"And you greatly underestimate my capacity for suffering."

"Suit yourself," said the prince, rising to his feet with his usual lazy grace. "*I'm* going to take a turn around the room."

Kell glowered but did not rise. He watched Rhy go, trying to emulate the prince's practiced nonchalance as he sat back with his glass.

He watched his brother maneuver through the field of people, smiling cheerfully, clasping hands and kissing cheeks and occasionally gesturing to his outfit with a self-deprecating laugh; despite his earlier remark, the fact was, Rhy fit in effortlessly. *As he should,* Kell supposed.

And yet, Kell loathed the greedy way the *ostra* eyed the prince.

The women's batting lashes held too little warmth and too much cunning. The men's appraising looks now held too little kindness and too much hunger. One or two shot a glance toward Kell, a ghost of that same hunger, but none were brave enough to approach. Good. Let them whisper, let them look. He felt the strange and sudden urge to make a scene, to watch their amusement harden into terror at the sight of his true power.

Kell's grip tightened on his glass, and he was about to rise when he caught the edge of conversation from a nearby party.

He didn't mean to eavesdrop; the practice just came naturally. Perhaps the magic in his veins gave him strong ears, or perhaps he'd simply learned to tune them over the years. It became habit, when you were so often the topic of whispered debate.

". . . I could have entered," said a nobleman, reclining on a hill of cushions.

"Come," chided a woman at his elbow, "even if you had the skills, which you do not, you're too late by a measure. The roster has been set."

"Has it now?"

Like most of the city, they were talking of the *Essen Tasch*—the Element Games—and Kell paid them little mind at first, since the *ostra* were usually more concerned with the balls and banquets than the competitors. And when they did speak of the magicians, it was in the way people talked of exotic beasts.

"Well, of course, the list hasn't been *posted*," continued the woman in a conspiratorial tone, "but my brother has his methods."

"Anyone we know?" asked another man in an airy, unconcerned way.

"I've heard the victor, Kisimyr, is in again."

"And what of Emery?"

At that, Kell stiffened, his grip going knuckles-white on his glass. *Surely it is a mistake,* he thought at the same time a woman said, "*Alucard* Emery?"

"Yes. *I've* heard he's coming back to compete."

Kell's pulse thudded in his ears, and the wine in his cup began to swirl.

"That's nonsense," insisted one of the men.

"You *do* have an ear for gossip. Emery hasn't set foot on London soil in three years."

"That may be," insisted the woman, "but his name is on the roster. My brother's friend has a sister who is messenger to the *Aven Essen,* and she said—"

A sudden pain lanced through Kell's shoulder, and he nearly fumbled the glass. His head snapped up, searching for the source of the attack as his hand went to his shoulder blade. It took him a moment to register that the pain wasn't actually his. It was an echo.

Rhy.

Where was Rhy?

Kell surged to his feet, upsetting the things on the table as he scanned the room for the prince's onyx hair, his blue coat. He was nowhere to be seen. Kell's heart pounded in his chest, and he resisted the urge to shout Rhy's name across the lawn. He could feel eyes shifting toward him, and he didn't care. He didn't give a damn about any of them. The only person in this place—in this *city*—he cared about was somewhere nearby, and he was in pain.

Kell squinted across the too-bright field of Splendor. The sun lanterns were glaring overhead, but in the distance, the afternoon light of the open chamber tapered off into hallways of darker forest. Kell swore and plunged across the field, ignoring the looks from the other patrons.

The pain came again, this time in his lower back, and Kell's knife was out of its sheath as he stormed into the shadowed canopy, cursing the dense trees, the star-lights in the branches the only source of light. The only other things in these woods were couples entwined.

Dammit, he cursed, his pulse raging as he doubled back.

He'd learned to keep one of Rhy's tokens on him, just in case, and he was about to draw blood and summon a finding spell when his scar throbbed in a way that told him the prince was close. He twisted around and could hear a muffled voice through the nearest copse, one that might be Rhy's; Kell shoved through, expecting a fight, and found something else entirely.

There, on a mossy slope, a half-dressed Rhy was hovering over the girl in white, the blue flower still in her hair, his face buried in her shoulder. Across his bare back, Kell could see scratch marks deep enough to draw blood, and a fresh echo of pain blossomed near Kell's hips as her nails dug into Rhy's flesh.

Kell exhaled sharply, in discomfort and relief, and the girl saw him standing there and gasped. Rhy dragged his head up, breathless, and had the audacity to smile.

"You bastard," hissed Kell.

"Lover?" wondered the girl.

Rhy sank back onto his heels, and then twisted with a languid grace, reclining on the moss. "Brother," he explained.

"Go," Kell ordered the girl. She looked disconcerted, but she gathered her dress around her and left all the same, while Rhy got unsteadily to his feet and cast about for his shirt. "I thought you were being attacked!"

"Well . . ." Rhy slipped the tunic gingerly over his head. "In a way, I was."

Kell found Rhy's coat slung over a low branch and thrust it at him. And then he led the prince back through the woods and across the field, past the silver doors, and out into the night. It was a silent procession, but the moment they were free of Splendor, Kell spun on his brother.

"What were you *thinking*?"

"Must you ask?"

Kell shook his head in disbelief. "You are an incomparable ass."

Rhy only chuckled. "How was I to know she would be so rough with me?"

"I'm going to kill you."

"You can't," said Rhy simply, spreading his arms. "You made sure of it."

And for an instant, as the words hung in the cloud of his winter breath, the prince seemed genuinely upset. But then the smile was back. "Come on," he said, slinging an arm around Kell's shoulders. "I'd had enough of Splendor anyway. Let's find somewhere more agreeable to drink."

A light snow began to fall around them, and Rhy sighed. "I don't suppose you thought to grab my hat?"

III

"Saints," cursed Rhy, "do *all* the Londons get this cold?"

"As cold," said Kell as he followed the prince away from the bright beating heart of the city, and down a series of narrower roads. "And colder still."

As they walked, Kell imagined this London ghosted against the others. Here, they would be coming upon Westminster. There, the stone courtyard where a statue of the Danes once stood.

Rhy's steps came to a halt ahead, and Kell looked up to see the prince holding open a tavern door. A wooden sign overhead read IS AVEN STRAS.

The Blessed Waters.

Kell swore under his breath. He knew enough about this place to know that they shouldn't be here. *Rhy* shouldn't be here. It wasn't as bad as the Three of Knives in the heart of the *shal,* where the black brands of limiters shone on almost every wrist, or the Jack and All, which had caused so much trouble on their last outing, but the Waters had its own rowdy reputation.

"*Tac,*" chided Kell in Arnesian, because this wasn't the kind of place to speak High Royal.

"What?" asked Rhy innocently, snatching the cap off Kell's head. "It isn't Rachenast. And I have business here."

"What kind of business?" demanded Kell as Rhy settled the

hat over his curls, but the prince only winked and went in, and Kell had no choice but to freeze or follow.

Inside, the place smelled of sea and ale. Where Splendor had been open, with bold colors and bright light, the Waters was made of dark corners and low-burning hearths, tables and booths sprawled like bodies across the room. The air was thick with smoke and loud with raucous laughter and drunken threats.

At least this place is honest with itself, thought Kell. No pretense. No illusion. It reminded him of the Stone's Throw, and the Setting Sun, and the Scorched Bone. Fixed points in the world, places where Kell had done business back when his business was less savory. When he'd traded in trinkets from faraway places, the kind only he could reach.

Rhy tugged the brim of the cap down over his light eyes as he approached the bar. He signaled to a shadow behind the barkeep, and slid a slip of paper and a single silver lish across the wood. "For the *Essen Tasch*," said the prince under his breath.

"Competitor?" asked the shadow with a voice like stones.

"Kamerov Loste."

"To win?"

Rhy shook his head. "No. Only to the nines." The shadow gave him a wary look, but he took the bet with a flick of his fingers and retreated into the corner of the bar.

Kell shook his head in disbelief. "You came here to place a bet. On the tournament *you're* running."

There was a glint in Rhy's eye. "Indeed."

"That's hardly legal," said Kell.

"Which is why we're *here*."

"And remind me why we couldn't have *started* the night here?"

"Because," said Rhy, flagging down the barkeep, "you were in an ornery mood when I dragged you from that palace—which is nothing unusual, but still—and you were determined to despise the first destination of the night on principle. I merely came prepared."

The barkeep came over, but he kept his gaze on the glass he was polishing. If he registered Kell's red hair, his black eye, he didn't show it.

"Two Black Sallies," said Rhy in Arnesian, and he was wise enough to pay in petty lin instead of lish or the gold rish carried by nobles. The barkeep nodded and served up two glasses of something thick and dark.

Kell lifted the glass—it was too dense to see through—and then took a cautious drink. He nearly gagged, and a handful of men down the bar chuckled. It was rough stock, syrupy but strong, and it clung to Kell's throat as it filled his head.

"That is vile," he choked out. "What's in it?"

"Trust me, Brother, you don't want to know." Rhy turned back toward the barkeep. "We'll take two winter ales as well."

"Who drinks this?" Kell coughed.

"People who want to get drunk," said Rhy, taking a long, pained sip.

Kell felt his own head swim as he shoved his glass away. "Slow down," he said, but the prince seemed determined to finish the draft, and he slammed the empty glass down with a shudder. The men at the end of the bar banged their own cups in approval, and Rhy gave an unsteady bow.

"Impressive," muttered Kell, at the same time that someone behind them spat, "If you ask me, the prince is a spoiled shit."

Kell and Rhy both tensed. The man was slumped at a table with two others, their backs to the bar.

"Watch yer tone," warned the second. "That's royalty yer smearing." But before Kell could feel any relief, they all burst into laughter.

Rhy gripped the counter, knuckles white, and Kell squeezed his brother's shoulder hard enough to feel the pain echo in his own. The last thing he needed was the crown prince involved in a brawl at the Blessed Waters. "What was it you said," he hissed in the Rhy's ear, "about the ones who wanted to watch us burn?"

"They say he hasn't got a lick of magic in him," continued the first man, obviously drunk. No sober man would speak such things so loudly.

"Figures," muttered the second.

"S'unfair," said the third. " 'Cause you know if he weren't up in that pretty palace, he'd be beggin' like a dog."

The sickening thing was, the man was probably right. This world was *ruled* by magic, but power followed no clear line or lineage; it flowed thick in some and thin in others. And yet, if magic denied a person power, the people took it as a judgment. The weak were shunned, left to fend for themselves. Sometimes they took to the sea—where elemental strength mattered less than simple muscle—but more often they stayed, and stole, and ended up with even less than they'd had to start with. It was a side of life Rhy had been spared only by his birth.

"What right's he got to sit up on that throne?" grumbled the second.

"None, that's what . . ."

Kell had had enough. He was about to turn toward the table when Rhy held out a hand. The gesture was relaxed, the touch unconcerned. "Don't bother," he said, taking up the ales and heading for the other side of the room. One of the men was leaning back in his chair, two wooden legs off the floor, and Kell tipped the balance as he passed. He didn't look back, but relished the sound of the body crashing to the floor.

"Bad dog," whispered Rhy, but Kell could hear the smile in his voice. The prince wove through the tables to a booth on the far wall, and Kell was about to follow him in when something across the tavern caught his eye. Or rather, some*one*. She stood out, not simply because she was one of the only women, but because he knew her. They had only met twice, but he recognized her instantly, from the catlike smile to the black hair twisted into coiling ropes behind her head, each woven through with gold. It was a bold thing, to wear such precious metal in a place of thugs and thieves.

But Kisimyr Vasrin was bolder than most.

She was also the reigning champion of the *Essen Tasch,* and the reason the tournament was being held in London. The Games weren't for a fortnight, but there she was, holding court in a corner of the Blessed Waters, surrounded by her usual handsome entourage. The fighter spent most of the year traveling the empire, putting on displays and mentoring young magicians, if their pockets were deep enough. She'd first earned a spot on the coveted roster when she was only sixteen, and over the last twelve years and four tournaments, she'd climbed the ranks to victor.

At only twenty-eight, she might even do it again.

Kisimyr tugged lazily at a stone earring, one of three in each ear, a wolfish smile on her face. And then her gaze drifted up, past her table and the room, and landed on Kell. Her eyes were a dozen colors, and some insisted she could see inside a person's soul. While Kell doubted her unique irises endowed her with any extraordinary powers (then again, who was he to talk, with the mark of magic drawn like ink across one eye?), the gaze was still unnerving.

He tipped his chin up and let the tavern light catch the glossy black of his right eye. Kisimyr didn't even look surprised. She simply toasted him, an almost imperceptible motion as she brought a glass of that pitch-black liquid to her lips.

"Are you going to sit," asked Rhy, "or stand sentry?"

Kell broke the gaze and turned toward his brother. Rhy was stretched across the bench, his feet up, fingering the brim of Kell's hat and muttering about how much he'd liked his own. Kell knocked the prince's boots aside so he could sit.

He wanted to ask about the tournament roster, about Alucard Emery—but even unspoken, the name left a sour taste in his mouth. He took a long sip of ale, but it did nothing to clear the bile.

"We should go on a trip," said Rhy, dragging himself upright. "Once the tournament is over."

Kell laughed.

"I'm serious," insisted the prince, his words slurring slightly.

He knew Rhy was, but he also knew it would never happen. The crown didn't let Kell travel beyond London, even when he ventured to different worlds. They claimed it was for his own safety—and maybe it was—but he and Rhy both knew that wasn't the only reason.

"I'll talk to Father. . . ." said Rhy, trailing off as if the subject were already fading from his mind. And then he was up again, sliding out of the booth.

"Where are you going?" asked Kell.

"To fetch us another round."

Kell looked down at Rhy's discarded glass, and then his own, still half-full.

"I think we've had enough," said Kell. The prince spun on him, clutching the booth.

"So now you speak for both of us?" he snapped, eyes glassy. "First body, now will?"

The barb struck, and Kell felt suddenly, horribly tired. "Fine," he growled. "Poison us both."

He rubbed his eyes and watched his brother go. Rhy had always had a penchant for consumption, but never with the sole intent of being too drunk to be useful. Too drunk to think. Saints knew, Kell had demons of his own, but he knew he couldn't drown them. Not like this. Why he kept letting Rhy try, he didn't know.

Kell felt in the pockets of his coat and found a brass clip with three slim cigars.

He'd never been much of a smoker—then again, he'd never

been much of a drinker, either—and yet, wanting to take back at least a measure of control over what he put in his body, he snapped his fingers and lit the cigar with the small flame that danced above his thumb.

Kell inhaled deeply—it wasn't tobacco, like in Grey London, or the horrible char they smoked in White, but a pleasant spiced leaf that cleared his head and calmed his nerves. Kell blew the breath out, his eyes sliding out of focus in the plume of smoke.

He heard steps and looked up, expecting Rhy, only to find a young woman. She bore the marks of Kisimyr's entourage, from the coiled dark hair to the gold tassels to the cat's-eye pendant at her throat.

"*Avan,*" she said, with a voice like silk.

"*Avan,*" said Kell.

The woman stepped forward, the knees of her dress brushing the edge of the booth. "Mistress Vasrin sends her regards, and wishes me to pass on a message."

"And what message is that?" he asked, taking another drag.

She smiled, and then before he could do anything—before he could even exhale—she reached out, took Kell's face in her hand, and kissed him. The breath caught in Kell's chest, heat flushed his body, and when the girl pulled back—not far, just enough to meet his gaze—she blew out a breath of smoke. He almost laughed. Her lips curled into a feline smile, and her eyes searched his, not with fear or even surprise, but with something like excitement. Awe. And Kell knew this was the part where he should feel like an impostor . . . but he didn't.

He looked past her to the prince, still standing at the bar.

"Was that all she said?" asked Kell.

Her mouth twitched. "Her instructions were vague, *mas aven vares.*"

My blessed prince.

"No," he said, frowning. "Not a prince."

"What, then?"

He swallowed. "Just Kell."

She blushed. It was too intimate—societal norms dictated that even if he shed the royal title, he should be addressed as *Master* Kell. But he didn't want to be that, either. He just wanted to be himself.

"Kell," she said, testing the word on her lips.

"And your name?" he asked.

"Asana," she whispered, the word escaping like a sound of pleasure. She guided him back against the bench, the gesture somehow forward and shy at the same time. And then her mouth was upon his. Her clothes were cinched at the waist in the current fashion, and he tangled his fingers in the bodice lacings at the small of her back.

"Kell," someone whispered in his ear.

Only it wasn't Asana, but Delilah Bard. She did that, crept into his thoughts and robbed him of focus, like a thief. Which was exactly what she was. What she'd *been,* before he let her out of her world, and into his. Saints knew what—or where—she was these days, but in his mind she would always be the thief, stealing through at the most inopportune moments. *Get out,* he thought, his grip tightening on the girl's dress. Asana kissed him again, but he was being dragged somewhere else, outside, on the path in the cool October night, and another set of lips was pressing against his, there and then gone, a ghost of a kiss.

"What was that for?"

A knife's edge smile. "For luck."

He groaned in frustration, and pulled Asana against him, kissing her deeply, desperately, trying to smother Lila's intrusion as Asana's lips brushed his throat.

"*Mas vares,*" she breathed against his skin.

"I'm not . . ." he began, but then her mouth was on his again, stealing the argument along with his air. His hand had vanished somewhere in her mane of hair. There it was now, at the nape of her neck. Her own hand splayed against his chest, and then her fingers were running down over his stomach and—

Pain.

It glanced across jaw, sudden and bright.

"What is it?" asked Asana. "What's wrong?"

Kell ground his teeth. "Nothing." *I am going to kill my brother.* He turned his thoughts from Rhy to Asana, but just as his mouth found hers again, the pain returned, raking over his hip.

For a single, hazy moment, Kell wondered if Rhy had simply found himself another enthusiastic conquest. But then the pain came a third time, this time against his ribs, sharp enough to knock his breath away, and the possibility withered.

"*Sanct,*" he swore, dragging himself from Asana's embrace and out of the booth with murmured apologies. The room swayed as he stood too fast, and he braced himself against the booth and searched the room, wondering what kind of trouble Rhy had gotten himself into now.

And then he saw the table near the bar, where the three men had sat talking. They were gone. Two doors to the Blessed Waters: the front and the back. He chose the second set, and guessed right, bursting out into the night with a speed that quite frankly surprised him, given how much he—and Rhy—had had to drink. But pain and cold were sobering things, and as he skidded to a stop in an alley dusted with snow, he could feel the magic already rushing hotly through his veins, ready for the fight.

The first thing Kell saw was the blood.

Then the prince's knife on the cobblestones.

The three men had Rhy cornered at the end of the alley. One of them had a gash on his forearm. Another along his cheek. Rhy must have gotten in a few slashes before he'd lost the weapon, but now he was doubled over, one arm wrapped around his ribs and blood running from his nose. The men obviously didn't know who he was. It was one thing to speak ill of a royal, but to lay hands on him. . . .

"Teach you to cut up my face," growled one.

"An improvement," grumbled Rhy through gritted teeth. Kell couldn't believe it: Rhy was *goading* them on.

". . . looking for trouble."

"Sure to find it."

"Wouldn't . . . be so sure . . ." The prince coughed.

His head drifted up past the men to Kell. He smiled thinly and said through bloody teeth, "Well, hello there," as if they'd just chanced upon one another. As if he weren't getting the shit kicked out of him behind the Blessed Waters. And as if, at this moment, Kell didn't have the urge to let the men have at Rhy for being stupid and self-destructive enough to pick this fight in the first place (because Kell had no doubt that the prince had started it). The urge was compounded by the fact that, though the thugs didn't know it, they couldn't actually *kill* him. That was the thing about the spell scorched into their skin. *Nothing* could kill Rhy. Because it wasn't *Rhy's* life that held him together anymore. It was *Kell's*. And as long as Kell lived, so would the prince.

But they could hurt him, and Kell wasn't angry enough to let that happen.

"Hello, Brother," he said, crossing his arms.

Two of the men turned toward Kell.

"*Kers la?*" taunted one. "A pet dog, come to nip at our heels?"

"Don't look like he's got much bite," said the other.

The third didn't even bother turning around. Rhy had said something to insult him—Kell didn't catch the words—and now he angled a kick at the prince's stomach. It never connected. Kell clenched his teeth and the man's boot froze in midair, the bones in his leg willed still.

"What the—"

Kell wrenched with his mind, and the man went flying sideways into the nearest wall. He collapsed to the ground, groaning, and the other two looked on with surprise and horror.

"You can't—" one grumbled, though the fact that Kell *could* was less shocking than the fact that he *had*. Bone magic was a rare and dangerous skill, forbidden because it broke the cardinal law: that none shall use magic, mental or physical, to control another person. Those who showed an affinity were strongly encouraged to *unlearn* it. Anyone caught doing it was rewarded with a full set of limiters.

An ordinary magician would never risk the punishment.

Kell wasn't an ordinary magician.

He tipped his chin up so the men could see his eyes, and took a measure of grim satisfaction as the color bled from their faces. And then footsteps sounded, and Kell turned to find more men pouring into the alley. Drunk and angry and armed. Something stirred in him.

His heart raced, and magic surged through his veins. He felt something on his face, and it took him a moment to realize that he was *smiling*.

He drew his dagger from the hidden sheath against his arm and with a single fluid motion cut his palm. Blood fell to the street in heavy red drops.

"*As Isera,*" he said, the words taking shape in his blood and on the air at the same time. They vibrated through the alley.

And then, the ground began to *freeze*.

It started at the drops of blood and spread out fast like frost over the stones and underfoot until a moment later everyone in the alley was standing atop a single solid pane of ice. One man took a step, and his feet went out from under him, arms flailing for balance even as he fell. Another must have had better boots on, because he took a sure step forward. But Kell was already moving. He crouched, pressed his bloody palm to the street stones, and said, "*As steno.*"

Break.

A cracking sound split the night, the quiet shattering with the pane of glassy ice. Cracks shot out from Kell's hand, fissuring the ground to every side, and as he stood, the shards came with him. Every piece not pinned by boot or body rose into the air and hung there, knifelike edges facing out from Kell like wicked rays of light.

Suddenly everyone in the alley grew still, not because he was willing the bones in their bodies, but because they were afraid. As they should be. He didn't feel drunk now. Didn't feel cold.

"Hey now," said one, his hands drifting up. "You don't have to do this."

"It's not fair," growled another softly, a blade of ice against his throat.

"Fair?" asked Kell, surprised by the steadiness in his voice. "Is three against one fair?"

"He started it!"

"Is eight against two fair?" continued Kell. "Looks to me like the odds are in *your* favor."

The ice began to inch forward through the air. Kell heard hisses of panic.

"We were just defending ourselves."

"We didn't know."

Against the back wall, Rhy had straightened. "Come on, Kell. . . ."

"Be still, Rhy," warned Kell. "You've caused enough trouble."

The jagged shards of ice hovered to every side, and then drifted on the air with slow precision until two or three had found each man, had charted a course for throat and heart and gut. The shards and the men that faced them waited with wide eyes and held breath to see what they would do.

What *Kell* would do.

A flick of his wrist, that's all it would take, to end every man in the alley.

Stop, a voice said, the word almost too soft to hear.

Stop.

And then suddenly, much louder, the voice was Rhy's, the words tearing from his throat. *"KELL, STOP."*

And the night snapped back into focus and he realized he was standing there holding eight lives in his hand, and he'd almost ended them. Not to punish them for attacking Rhy (the prince had probably provoked them) and not because they were bad men (though several of them might have been). But just because he *could,* because it felt good to be in control, to be the strongest, to know that when it came down to it, he would be the one left standing.

Kell exhaled and lowered his hand, letting the shards of ice crash to the cobblestones, where they shattered. The men gasped, and swore, and stumbled back as one, the spell of the moment broken.

One sank to the ground, shaking.

Another looked like he might vomit.

"Get out of here," said Kell quietly.

And the men listened. He watched them run.

They already thought he was a monster, and now he'd gone and given the fears weight, which would just make everything worse. But it didn't matter; nothing he did seemed to make it better.

His steps crackled on the broken ice as he trudged over to where Rhy was sitting on his haunches against the wall. He looked dazed, but Kell thought it had less to do with the beating and more to do with the drink. The blood had stopped falling from his nose and lip, and his face was otherwise unhurt; when Kell quested through his own body in search of echoing pain, he felt only a couple of tender ribs.

Kell held out his hand and helped Rhy to his feet. The prince took a step forward, and swayed, but Kell caught him and kept him upright.

"There you go again," murmured Rhy, leaning his head on Kell's shoulder. "You never let me fall."

"And let you take me down with you?" chided Kell, wrapping the prince's arm around his shoulders. "Come on, Brother. I think we've had enough fun for one night."

"Sorry," whispered Rhy.

"I know."

But the truth was, Kell couldn't forget the way he'd felt during the fight, the small defiant part of him that had undeniably *enjoyed* it. He couldn't forget the smile that had belonged to him and yet to someone else entirely.

Kell shivered, and helped his brother home.

IV

The guards were waiting for them in the hall.

Kell had gotten the prince all the way back to the palace and up the Basin steps before running into the men: two of them Rhy's, the other two his, and all four looking put out.

"Vis, Tolners," said Kell, feigning lightness. "Want to give me a hand?"

As if he were carrying a sack of wheat, and not the royal prince of Arnes.

Rhy's guards looked pale with anger and worry, but neither stepped forward.

"Staff, Hastra?" he said, appealing to his own men. He was met with stony silence. "Fine, get out of the way, I'll carry him myself."

He pushed past the guards.

"Is that the prince's blood?" asked Vis, pointing at Kell's sleeve, which he'd used to wipe Rhy's face clean.

"No," he lied. "Only mine."

Rhy's men relaxed considerably at that, which Kell found disconcerting. Vis was a nervous sort, hackles always raised, and Tolners was utterly humorless, with the set jaw of an officer. They had both served King Maxim himself before being assigned to guard the young royal, and they took the prince's defiance with far less nonchalance than Rhy's previous men. As for Kell's own guards, Hastra was young and eager, but Staff hardly ever said a word, either to Kell's face or in his company. For the first month, Kell hadn't been sure if the guard hated him, or feared him, or both. Then Rhy told him the truth—that Staff's sister had died in the Black Night—so Kell knew that it was likely both.

"He's a good guard," said Rhy when Kell asked why they would assign him such a man. And then added grimly, "It was Father's choice."

Now, as the party reached the royal hall the brothers shared, Tolners produced a note and held it up for Kell to read. "This isn't funny." Apparently Rhy had had the grace to pin the note to his door, in case anyone in the palace should worry.

> *Not kidnapped.*
> *Out for a drink with Kell.*
> *Sit tight.*

Rhy's room was at the end of the hall, marked by two ornate doors. Kell kicked them open.

"Too loud," muttered Rhy.

"Master Kell," warned Vis, following him in. "I must insist you cease these—"

"I didn't force him out."

"But you *allowed*—"

"I'm his brother, not his *guard*," snapped Kell. He knew he'd been raised as Rhy's protection as much as his companion, but it was proving no small task, and besides, hadn't he done enough?

Tolners scowled. "The king and queen—"

"Go away," said Rhy, rousing himself. "Giving me a headache."

"Your Highness," started Vis, reaching for Rhy's arm.

"*Out*," snapped the prince with sudden heat. The guards shied away, then looked uncertainly at Kell.

"You heard the prince," he grumbled. "Get out." His gaze went to his own men. "All of you."

As the doors closed behind him, Kell half guided, half dragged Rhy into his bed. "I think I'm growing on them," he muttered.

Rhy rolled groggily onto his back, an arm cast over his eyes.

"I'm sorry . . . sorry . . ." he said softly, and Kell shuddered, remembering that horrific night, the prince bleeding to death as he and Lila tried to drag him to safety, the soft *I'm sorry*s fading horribly into silence and stillness and—

". . . all my fault . . ." Rhy's voice dragged him back.

"Hush," said Kell, sinking into a chair beside the bed.

"I just wanted . . . like it was before."

"I know," said Kell, rubbing his eyes. "I know."

He sat there until Rhy fell quiet, safely wrapped in sleep, and then pushed himself back to his feet. The room rocked faintly, and Kell steadied himself for a moment on the carved bedpost before making his way back to his own rooms. Not via the hall and its contingent of guards, but the hidden corridor that ran between their chambers. The lanterns burned to life as Kell entered, the magic easy, effortless, but the light didn't make the room feel more like home. The space had always felt strangely foreign. Stiff, like an ill-fitting suit.

It was a room for a royal. The ceiling was lined with billowing fabric, the colors of night, and an elegant desk hugged one wall. A sofa and chairs huddled around a silver tea set, and a pair of glass doors led onto a balcony now coated with a thin layer of snow. Kell shrugged off his coat and turned it inside out a few times, returning it to its royal red before draping it over an ottoman.

Kell missed his little room at the top of the stairs in the Ruby Fields, with its rough walls and its stiff cot and its constant noise, but the room and the inn and the woman who ran it had all been burned to nothing by Holland months before, and Kell could not bring himself to seek out another. The room had been a secret, and Kell had promised the crown—and Rhy—that he would stop keeping secrets.

He missed the room, and the privacy that came with it, but there was something to the missing. He supposed he deserved it. Others had lost far more because of him.

So Kell remained in the royal chambers.

The bed waited on a raised platform, a plush mattress with a sea of pillows, but Kell slumped down into his favorite chair instead. A battered thing by comparison, dragged from one of the palace's studies, it faced the balcony doors and, beyond, the warm red glow of the Isle. He snapped his fingers, and the lanterns dimmed and then went dark.

Sitting there with only the river's light, his tired mind drifted, as it invariably did, back to Delilah Bard. When Kell thought of her, she was not one girl, but three: the too-skinny street thief who'd robbed him in an alley, the blood-streaked partner who'd fought beside him, and the impossible girl who'd walked away and never looked back.

Where are you, Lila, he mused. *And what kind of trouble are you getting into?*

Kell dragged a kerchief from his back pocket: a small square of dark fabric first given to him by a girl dressed as a boy in a darkened alley, a sleight of hand so she could rob him. He'd used it to find her more than once, and he wondered if he could do it again, or if it now belonged more to him than to her. He wondered where it would take him, if it worked.

He knew with a bone-deep certainty that she was alive—had to be alive—and he envied her, envied the fact that this Grey London girl was out there somewhere, seeing parts of the world that Kell—a Red Londoner, an *Antari*—had never glimpsed.

He put the kerchief away, closed his eyes, and waited for sleep to drag him under.

When it did, he dreamed of her. Dreamed of her standing on his balcony, goading him to come out and play. He dreamed of her hand tangling in his, a pulse of power twining them together. He dreamed of them racing through foreign streets, not the London ones they'd navigated, but crooks and bends in places he'd never been, and ones he might never see. But there she was, at his side, pulling him toward freedom.

V

White London.

Ojka had always been graceful.

Graceful when she danced. Graceful when she killed.

Sunlight spilled across the stone floor as she spun, her knives licking the air as they arced and dipped, tethered to her hands and to one another by a single length of black cord.

Her hair, once pale, now shone red, a shock of color against her still porcelain skin, bold as blood. It skimmed her shoulders as she twirled, and bowed, a bright streak at the center of a deadly circle. Ojka danced, and the metal kept pace, the perfect partner to her fluid movements, and the entire time, she kept her eyes closed. She knew the dance by heart, a dance she'd first learned as a child on the streets in Kosik, in the worst part of London. A dance she'd mastered. You didn't stay alive in this city on luck alone. Not if you had any promise of power. The scavengers would sniff it out, slit your throat so they could steal whatever dregs were in your blood. They didn't care if you were little. That only made you easier to catch and kill.

But not Ojka. She'd carved her way through Kosik. Grown up and stayed alive in a city that managed to kill off everyone. Everything.

But that was another life. That was before. This was after.

Ojka's veins traced elegant black lines over her skin as she moved. She could feel the magic thrumming through her, a second pulse twined with hers. At first it had burned, so hot she feared it would consume her, the way it had the others. But then she let go. Her body stopped fighting, and so did the power. She embraced it, and once she did, it embraced her, and they danced together, burned together, fusing like strengthened steel.

The blades sang past, extensions of her hands. The dance was almost done.

And then she felt the summons, like a flare of heat inside her skull.

She came to a stop—not suddenly, of course, but slowly—winding the black cord around her hands until the blades snapped against her palms. Only then did her eyes drift open.

One was yellow.

The other was black.

Proof that she had been chosen.

She wasn't the first, but that was all right. That didn't matter. What mattered was that the others had been too weak. The first had only lasted a few days. The second had scarcely made it through the week. But Ojka was different. Ojka was strong. She had survived. She *would* survive, so long as she was worthy.

That was the king's promise, when he had chosen her.

Ojka coiled the cord around the blades and slid the weapon back into the holster at her hip.

Sweat dripped from the ends of her crimson hair, and she wrung it out before shrugging on her jacket and fastening her cloak. Her fingers traced the scar that ran from her throat up over her jaw and across her cheek, ending just below the king's mark.

When the magic brought strength to her muscles, warmth to her blood, and color to her features, she feared it would wipe away the scar. She'd been relieved when it didn't. She'd earned this scar, and every other one she bore.

The summons flared again behind her eyes, and she stepped outside. The day was cold but not bitter, and overhead, beyond the clouds, the sky was streaked across with blue. *Blue*. Not the frosty off-white she'd grown up with, but true blue. As if the sky itself had thawed. The water of the Sijlt was thawing, too, more and more every day, ice giving way to green-grey water.

Everywhere she looked, the world was waking.

Reviving.

And Ojka's blood quickened at the sight of it. She'd been in a shop once, and had seen a chest covered in dust. She remembered running her hand across it, removing the film of grey and revealing the dark wood beneath. It was like that, she thought. The king had come and swept his hand across the city, brushed away the dust.

It would take time, he said, but that was all right. Change was coming.

Only a single road stood between her quarters and the castle walls, and as she crossed the street, her gaze flicked toward the river, and the other half of the city beyond. From the heart of Kosik to the steps of the castle. She'd come a long way.

The gates stood open, new vines climbing the stone walls to either side, and she reached out and touched a small purple bud as she stepped through onto the grounds.

Where the Krös Mejkt had once sprawled, a graveyard of stone corpses at the feet of the castle, now there was wild grass, creeping up despite the winter chill. Only two statues remained, flanking the castle stairs, both commissioned by the new king, not as a warning, but as a reminder of false promises and fallen tyrants.

They were likenesses of the old rulers, Athos and Astrid Dane, carved in white marble. Both figures were on their knees. Athos Dane stared down at the whip in his hands, which coiled like a snake around his wrists, his face twisted in pain, while Astrid clutched the handle of a dagger, its blade buried in her chest, her mouth stretched in a soundless, immortal scream.

The statues were grisly, inelegant things. Unlike the new king.

The new king was perfect.

The new king was chosen.

The new king was god.

And Ojka? She saw the way he looked at her with those beautiful eyes, and she knew he saw the beauty in her, too, now, more and more every day.

She reached the top of the stairs and passed through into the castle.

Ojka had heard tales of the hollow-eyed guards who had served under the Danes, men robbed of minds and souls, rendered nothing but shells. But they were gone now, and the castle stood open, and strangely empty. It had been raided, taken, held, and lost in the weeks after the Danes first fell, but there were no signs of the slaughter now. All was calm.

There were attendants, men and women appearing and disappearing, heads bowed, and a dozen guards, but their eyes weren't vacant. If anything, they moved with a purpose, a devotion that Ojka understood. This was the resurrection, a legend brought to life, and they were all a part of it.

No one stopped her as she moved through the castle.

In fact, some knelt as she passed, while others whispered blessings and bowed their heads. When she reached the throne room, the doors were open, and the king was waiting. The vaulted ceiling was gone, massive walls and columns now giving way to open sky.

Ojka's steps echoed on the marble floor.

Was it really once made of bones, she wondered, *or is that just a legend?* (All Ojka had were rumors; she'd been smart, kept to Kosik, and avoided the Danes at all costs during their rule. Too many stories surrounded the twins, all of them bloody.)

The king stood before his throne, gazing down into the glossy surface of the scrying pool that formed a smooth black circle before the dais. Ojka found its stillness almost as hypnotic as the man reflected in it.

Almost.

But there was something he had that the black pool lacked. Beneath the surface of his calm surged energy. She could feel it from across the room, rippling from him in waves. A source of power.

Life might have been taking root in the city, but in the king, it had already blossomed.

He was tall and strong, muscles twining over his sculpted body, his strength apparent even through his elegant clothes. Black hair swept back from his face, revealing high cheekbones and a strong jaw. The bow of his lips pursed faintly, and the faintest crease formed between his brows as he considered the pool, hands clasped behind his back. His hands. She remembered that day, when those hands had come to rest against her skin, one pressed against the nape of her neck, the other splayed over her eyes. She'd felt his power even then, before it passed between them, pulsing beneath his skin, and she wanted it, needed it, like air.

His mouth had been so close to her ear when he spoke. "Do you accept this power?"

"I accept it," she'd said. And then everything was searing heat and darkness and pain. Burning. Until his voice came again, close, and said, "Stop fighting, Ojka. Let it in."

And she had.

He had chosen her, and she would not let him down. Just like in the prophecies, their savior had come. And she would be there at his side.

"Ojka," he said now without looking up. Her name was a spell on his lips.

"Your Majesty," she said, kneeling before the pool.

His head drifted up. "You know I'm not fond of titles," he said, rounding the pool. She straightened and met his eyes: one green, the other black. "Call me Holland."

THREE

CHANGING TIDES

I

Red London.

The nightmare started as it always did, with Kell standing in the middle of a public place—sometimes the Stone's Throw, or the statue garden in front of the Danes' fortress, or the London Sanctuary—at once surrounded and alone.

Tonight, he was in the middle of the Night Market.

It was crowded, more crowded than Kell had ever seen it, the people pressed shoulder to shoulder along the riverbank. He thought he saw Rhy at the other end, but by the time he called his brother's name, the prince had vanished into the crowd.

Nearby he glimpsed a girl with dark hair cut short along her jaw, and called out—"Lila?"—but as soon as he took a step toward her, the crowd rippled and swallowed her again. Everyone was familiar, and everyone was a stranger in the shifting mass of bodies.

And then a shock of white hair caught his eye, the pale figure of Athos Dane sliding like a serpent through the crowd. Kell growled and reached for his knife, only to be interrupted by cold fingers closing over his.

"Flower boy," cooed a voice in his ear, and he spun to find Astrid, covered in cracks as if someone had pieced her shattered body back together. Kell staggered back, but the crowd was getting even thicker now, and someone shoved him from behind. By the time he regained his balance, both the Danes were gone.

Rhy flickered again in the distance. He was looking around as if searching for someone, mouthing a word, a name Kell couldn't hear.

Another stranger bumped into Kell hard. "Sorry," he murmured. "Sorry . . ." But the words echoed and the people kept pushing past him as if they didn't see him, as if he wasn't there. And then, as soon as he thought it, everybody stopped midstride and every face turned toward him, features resolving into gruesome masks of anger and fear and disgust.

"I'm sorry," he said again, holding up his hands, only to see his veins turning black.

"No," he whispered, as the magic traced lines up his arms. "No, please, no." He could feel the darkness humming in his blood as it spread. The crowd began to move again, but instead of walking away, they were all coming toward him. "Get back," he said, and when they didn't he tried to run, only to discover that his legs wouldn't move.

"Too late," came Holland's voice from nowhere. Everywhere. "Once you let it in, you've already lost."

The magic forced its way through him with every beat of his heart. Kell tried to fight it back, but it was in his head now, whispering in *Vitari*'s voice.

Let me in.

Pain shot jaggedly through Kell's chest as the darkness hit his heart, and in the distance, Rhy collapsed.

"*No!*" Kell shouted, reaching toward his brother, uselessly, desperately, but as his hand brushed the nearest person, the darkness leaped like fire from his fingers to the man's chest. He shuddered, and then collapsed, crumbling to ash as his body struck the street stones. Before he hit the ground, the people on either side of him began to fall as well, death rippling in a wave through the crowd, silently consuming everyone. Beyond them, the buildings began to crumble too, and the bridges, and the palace, until Kell was standing alone in an empty world.

And then in the silence, he heard a sound: not a sob, or a scream, but a *laugh*.

And it took him a moment to recognize the voice.

It was his.

Kell gasped, lurching forward out of sleep.

Light was filtering through the patio doors, glinting off a fresh dusting of snow. The shards of sun made him cringe and look away as he pressed his palm to his chest and waited for his heart to slow.

He'd fallen asleep in his chair, fully clothed, his skull aching from his brother's indulgences.

"Dammit, Rhy," he muttered, pushing himself to his feet. His head was pounding, a sound matched by whatever was going on outside his window. The blows he—well, *Rhy*—had sustained the night before were a memory, but the aftereffect of the drinks was compounding, and Kell decided then and there that he vastly preferred the sharp, short pain of a wound to the dull, protracted ache of a hangover. He felt like death, and as he splashed cold water on his face and throat and got dressed, he could only hope that the prince felt worse.

Outside his door, a stiff-looking man with greying temples stood watch. Kell winced. He always hoped for Hastra. Instead he usually got Staff. The one who hated him.

"Morning," said Kell, walking past.

"*Afternoon,* sir," answered Staff—or Silver, as Rhy had nicknamed the aging royal guard—as he fell in step behind him. Kell wasn't thrilled by the appearance of Staff *or* Hastra in the aftermath of the Black Night, but he wasn't surprised, either. It wasn't the guards' fault that King Maxim no longer trusted his *Antari*. Just like it wasn't Kell's fault that the guards couldn't always keep track of him.

He found Rhy in the sunroom, a courtyard enclosed by glass, having lunch with the king and queen. The prince seemed to be managing his own hangover with surprising poise, though Kell could feel Rhy's headache throbbing alongside his own, and Kell noted that the prince sat with his back to the panes of glass and the glinting light beyond.

"Kell," Rhy said brightly. "I was beginning to think you'd sleep all day."

"Sorry," said Kell pointedly. "I must have indulged a little too much last night."

"Good afternoon, Kell," said Queen Emira, an elegant woman with skin like polished wood and a circlet of gold resting atop her jet-black hair. Her tone was kind but distant, and it felt like it had been weeks since she'd last reached out and touched his cheek. In truth, it had been longer. Nearly four months, since the Black Night, when Kell had let the black stone into the city, and *Vitari* had swept through the streets, and Astrid Dane had plunged a dagger into Rhy's chest, and Kell had given a piece of his life to bring him back.

Where is our son? the queen had demanded, as if she had only one.

"I hope you're well rested," said King Maxim, glancing up from the sheaf of papers in front of him.

"I am, sir." Fruit and bread were piled on the table, and as Kell slid into the empty chair a servant appeared with a silver pitcher and poured him a steaming cup of tea. He finished the cup in a single, burning swallow, and the servant considered him then left the pitcher, a small gesture for which Kell was immeasurably grateful.

Two more people were seated at the table: a man and a woman, both dressed in shades of red and each with a gold pin of the

Maresh seal—the chalice and rising sun—fastened to their shoulder. The pin marked the figures as friends of the crown; it permitted them full access to the palace and instructed any servants and guards to not only welcome but assist them.

"Parlo, Lisane," said Kell in greeting. They were the *ostra* selected to help organize the tournament, and Kell felt like he had seen more of them in the past few weeks than he had the king and queen.

"Master Kell," they said in unison, tipping their heads with practiced smiles and calculated propriety.

A map of the palace and surrounding grounds was spread across the table, one edge tucked beneath a plate of tarts, another under a tea cup, and Lisane was gesturing to the south wing. "We've arranged for Prince Col and Princess Cora to stay here, in the emerald suite. Fresh flowers will be grown there the day before they arrive."

Rhy made a face at Kell across the table. Kell was too tired to try to read it.

"Lord Sol-in-Ar, meanwhile," continued Lisane, "will be housed in the western conservatory. We've stocked it with coffee, just as you instructed, and . . ."

"And what of the Veskan queen?" grumbled Maxim. "Or the Faroan king? Why do *they* not grace us with their presence? Do they not trust us? Or do they simply have better things to do?"

Emira frowned. "The emissaries they've chosen are appropriate."

Rhy scoffed. "Queen Lastra of Vesk has *seven* children, Mother; I doubt it's much of an inconvenience for her to loan us two. As for the Faroans, Lord Sol-in-Ar is a known antagonist who's spent the last two decades stirring up discontent wherever he goes, hoping it will spark enough conflict to dethrone his brother and seize control of Faro."

"Since when are you so invested in imperial politics?" asked Kell, already on his third cup of tea.

To his surprise, Rhy shot him a scowl. "I'm invested in my *kingdom,* Brother," he snapped. "You should be, too."

"*I'm* not their prince," observed Kell. He was in no mood for Rhy's attitude. "I'm just the one who has to clean up his *messes.*"

"Oh, seeing as you've made none of your own?"

They held each other's gazes. Kell resisted the urge to stab a fork into his own leg just to watch his brother wince.

What was happening to them? They'd never been cruel to each other before. But pain and pleasure weren't the only things that seemed to transfer with the bond. Fear, annoyance, anger: all plucked at the binding spell, reverberating between them, amplifying. Rhy had always been fickle, but now Kell *felt* his brother's ever-shifting temperament, the constant oscillation, and it was maddening. Space meant nothing. They could be standing side by side or Londons apart. There was no escape.

More and more, the bond felt like a chain.

Emira cleared her throat. "I think the *eastern* conservatory would be better for Lord Sol-in-Ar. It gets better light. But what about the attendants? The Veskans always travel with a full compliment. . . ."

The queen soothed the table, guiding the conversation deftly away from the brothers' rising moods, but there were too many unspoken things in the air, making it stuffy. Kell pushed himself to his feet and turned to leave.

"Where are you going?" asked Maxim, handing his papers to an attendant.

Kell turned back. "I was going to oversee the construction on the floating arenas, Your Highness."

"Rhy can handle that," said the king. "You have an errand to run." With that, he held out an envelope. Kell didn't realize how eager he was to go—to escape not only the palace but this city, this world—until he saw that slip of paper.

It bore no address, but he knew exactly where he was meant to take it. With the White London throne empty and the city plunged into crown warfare for the first time in seven years, communication had been suspended. Kell had gone only once, in the weeks after the Dane twins fell, and had nearly lost his life to the violent masses—after which it was decided that Kell would let White London alone for a time, until things settled.

That left only Grey London. The simple, magicless realm, all coal smoke and sturdy old stone.

"I'll go now," said Kell, crossing to the king's side.

"Mind the prince regent," warned the king. "These correspondences are a matter of tradition, but the man's questions have grown prodding."

Kell nodded. He had often wanted to ask King Maxim what he thought of the Grey London leader and wondered about the contents of his letters, whether the prince regent asked as many questions of his neighboring crown as he did of Kell.

"He inquires often about magic," he told the king. "I do my best to dissuade him."

Maxim grunted. "He is a foolish man. Be careful."

Kell raised a brow. Was Maxim actually worried for his safety? But then, as he reached for the letter, he saw the flicker of distrust in the king's eyes, and his spirits sank. Maxim kept grudges like scars. They faded by degrees but always left a mark.

Kell knew he'd brought it on himself. For years, he'd used his expeditions as royal liaison to transport forbidden items between the worlds. If he hadn't developed his reputation as a smuggler, the black stone would never have found its way into his hands, would never have killed men and women and brought havoc to Red London. Or perhaps the Danes would still have found a way, but they wouldn't have used *Kell* to do it. He'd been a pawn, and a fool, and now he was paying for it—just as Rhy was forced to pay for his own part, for the possession charm that had let Astrid Dane take up residence in his body. In the end, they were both to blame. But the king still loved Rhy. The queen could still look at him.

Emira held out a second, smaller envelope. The note for King George. A courtesy more than anything else, but the fragile king clung to these correspondences, and so did Kell. The ailing king had no idea how short they were getting, and Kell had no intention of letting him know. He'd taken to elaborating, spinning intimate yarns about the Arnesian king and queen, the prince's exploits, and Kell's own life in the palace. Perhaps this time he'd tell George about the tournament. The king would love that.

He took the notes and turned to go, already pulling together what he'd say, when Maxim stopped him. "What about your point of return?"

Kell stiffened imperceptibly. The question was like a short tug, a reminder that he was now being kept on a leash. "The door will be at the mouth of Naresh Kas, just off the southern edge of the Night Market."

The king glanced at Staff, who hung back by the door, to make sure he'd heard, and the guard nodded once.

"Don't be late," ordered Maxim.

Kell turned away and left the royal family to their talk of tournament visitors and fresh linens and who preferred coffee or wine or strong tea.

At the sunroom doors, he cast a glance back, and found Rhy looking at him with an expression that might have been *I'm sorry,* but also could have been *fuck off,* or at the very least *we'll talk later.* Kell let the matter go and escaped, slipping the letters into the pocket of his coat. He walked briskly through the palace halls ,back to his chambers, and through to the smaller second room beyond, closing the door behind him. Rhy probably would have used such an alcove to hold boots, or coat pins, but Kell had transformed the space into a small but well-stocked library, holding the texts he'd collected on magic. They were as much philosophical as practical, many gifted by Master Tieren or borrowed from the royal library, as well as some journals of his own, scribbled with thoughts on *Antari* blood magic, about which so little was known. One slim black volume he'd dedicated to *Vitari,* the black magic he'd grasped—awakened—destroyed—the year before. That journal held more questions than answers.

On the back of the library's wooden door were half a dozen hand-drawn symbols, each simple but distinct, shortcuts to other places in the city, carefully drawn in blood. Some were faded from disuse, others fresh. One of the symbols—a circle with a pair of crossed lines drawn through it—led to Tieren's sanctuary on the opposite bank. As Kell traced his fingers over the mark, he vividly remembered helping Lila haul a dying Rhy through the door. Another mark had once led to Kell's private chamber at the Ruby Fields, the only place in London that had been truly his. Now it was nothing more than a smudge.

Kell scanned the door until he found the symbol he was looking for: a star made of three intersecting lines.

This mark came with its own memories, of an old king in a cell of a room, his gnarled fingers curled around a single red coin as he murmured about fading magic.

Kell drew his dagger from its place under the cuff of his coat, and grazed his wrist. Blood welled, rich and red, and he dabbed the cut and drew the mark fresh. When it was done, he pressed his hand flat against the symbol and said, *"As Tascen." Transfer.*

And then he stepped forward.

The world softened and warped around his hand, and he passed from the darkened alcove into sunlight, crisp and bright enough to revive the fading ache behind his eyes. Kell was no longer in his makeshift library, but standing in a well-appointed courtyard. He wasn't in Grey London, not yet, but in an *ostra*'s garden in an elegant village called Disan, significant not because of its fine fruit trees or glass statues, but because it occupied the same ground in Red London that Windsor Castle did in Grey.

The same *exact* ground.

Traveling magic only worked two ways. Kell could either transfer between two different places in one world, or travel between the same place in different ones. And because they kept the English king at Windsor, which sat well outside the city of London, he had to make his way first to *ostra* Paveron's garden. It was a bit of clever navigation on Kell's part . . . not that anyone knew enough of *Antari* magic to appreciate it. Holland might have, but Holland was dead, and he'd likely had a network of acrosses and betweens intricate enough to make Kell's own attempts look childish. The winter air whipped around him, and he shivered as he drew the letters out of his pocket with his unbloodied hand, then turned the coat inside out and outside in until he found the side he was looking for: a black knee-length garment with a hood and velvet lining. Fit for Grey London, where the cold always felt colder, bitter and damp in a way that seeped through cloth and skin.

Kell shrugged the new coat on and tucked the letters deep into one of the pockets (they were lined with softened wool instead of silk), blew out a plume of warm breath, and marked the icy wall with the blood from his hand. But then, as he was reaching for the cord of tokens around his neck, something tugged at his attention. He paused and looked around, considering the garden. He was alone, truly alone, and he found himself wanting to savor it. Aside from one trip north when he and Rhy were boys, this was the farthest Kell ever strayed from the city. He'd always been watched, but he'd felt more confined in the past four months than in the nearly twenty years he'd served the crown. Kell used to feel like a possession. Now he felt like a prisoner.

Perhaps he should have run when he'd had the chance.

You could still run, said a voice in his ear. It sounded suspiciously like Lila.

In the end, she had escaped. Could he? He didn't have to run to another world. What if he simply . . . walked away? Away from the garden and the village, away from the city. He could take a coach, or a boat to the ocean, and then . . . what? How far would he make it with almost no money of his own and an eye that marked him as an *Antari*?

You could take what you need, said the voice.

It was a very big world. And he'd never even seen it.

If he stayed in Arnes, he would eventually be found. And if he fled into Faro, or Vesk? The Faroans saw his eye as a mark of strength, nothing more, but Kell had heard his name paired with a Veskan word—*crat'a*—*pillar*. As if he alone held up the Arnesian empire. And if either empire got their hands on him . . .

Kell stared down at his blood-streaked hand. Saints, how could he actually consider running away?

It was madness, the idea that he could—that he *would*—abandon his city. His king and queen. His brother. He'd betrayed them once—well, one crime, albeit committed many times—and it had nearly cost him everything. He wouldn't forsake them again, no matter what restlessness had been awakened in him.

You could be free, insisted the voice.

But that was the thing. Kell would *never* be free. No matter how far he fled. He'd given up freedom with his life, when he handed it to Rhy.

"Enough," he said aloud, silencing the doubts as he dug the proper cord out from under his collar and tugged it over his head. On the strap hung a copper coin, the face rubbed smooth from years of use. *Enough,* he thought, and then he brought his bloody hand to the garden wall. He had a job to do.

"*As travars.*"

Travel.

The world began to bend around the words and the blood and the magic, and Kell stepped forward, hoping to leave behind his troubles with his London, trade them for a few minutes with the king.

But as soon as his boots settled on the castle carpet, he realized that his problems were just beginning. Instantly, Kell knew that something was wrong.

Windsor was too quiet. Too dark.

The bowl of water that usually waited for him in the antechamber was empty, the candles to either side unlit. When he listened for the sound of steps, he heard them, distantly, in the halls behind him, but from the chamber ahead he was met with silence.

Dread crept in as he made his way into the king's sitting room, hoping to see his withered frame sleeping in his high-backed chair, or hear his frail, melodic voice. But the room was empty. The windows were fastened shut against the snow, and there was no fire going in the hearth. The room was cold and dark in a closed-up way.

Kell went to the fireplace and held out his hands, as if to warm them, and an instant later flames licked up across the empty grate. The fire wouldn't last long, fueled by nothing more than air and magic, but in its light Kell crossed through the space, searching for signs of recent occupation. Cold tea. A cast-off shawl. But the room felt abandoned, un-lived-in.

And then his gaze caught on the letter.

If it could be called a letter.

A single piece of crisp cream paper, folded and propped on the tray before the fire, with his name written on the front in the prince regent's steady, confident script.

Kell took up the note, knowing what he would find before he unfolded the page, but he still felt ill as the words danced in the enchanted fire's light.

The king is dead.

II

The four words hit him like a blow.

The king is dead.

Kell reeled; he wasn't accustomed to loss. He feared death—he always had—now more than ever, with the prince's life bound to his, but until the Black Night, Kell had never lost someone he knew. Someone he *liked*. He had always been fond of the ailing king, even in his later years, when madness and blindness stole most of his dignity and all of his power.

And now the king was gone. A sum returned to parts, as Tieren would say.

Below, the prince regent had added a postscript.

Step into the hall. Someone will bring you to my rooms.

Kell hesitated, looking around at the empty chamber. And then, reluctantly, he closed his hand into a fist, plunging the fire in the hearth back into nothing and the room back into shadow, and left. Out past the antechamber into the hallways beyond.

It was like stepping into another world.

Windsor wasn't as opulent as St. James, but it wasn't nearly so grim as the old king's chamber made it out to be. Tapestries and carpets warmed the halls. Gold and silver glinted from candlestick and plate. Lamps burned in wall sconces and voices and music carried like a draft.

Someone cleared their throat, and Kell turned to find a well-dressed attendant waiting.

"Ah, sir, very good, this way," said the man with a bow, and then, without waiting, he set off down the hall.

Kell's gaze wandered as they walked. He had never explored the halls beyond the king's rooms, but he was sure they hadn't always been like this.

Fires burned high in the hearths of every room they passed, rendering the palace uncomfortably warm. The rooms themselves were all occupied, and Kell couldn't help but feel like he was being put on display, led past murmuring ladies and curious gentlemen. He clenched his fists and lowered his gaze. By the time he was deposited in the large sitting room, his face was flushed from heat and annoyance.

"Ah. Master Kell."

The prince regent—the *king,* Kell corrected himself—was sitting on a sofa, flanked by a handful of stiff men and giggling women. He looked fatter and more arrogant than usual, his buttons straining, the points of his nose and chin thrust up. His companions fell silent at the sight of Kell, standing there in his black traveling coat.

"Your Majesty," he said, tipping his head forward in the barest show of deference. The gesture resettled the hair over his blackened eye. He knew that his next words should express condolence, but looking at the new king's face, Kell felt the more stricken of the two. "I would have come to St. James if I'd—"

George waved a hand imperiously. "I didn't come here for you," he said, getting to his feet, albeit ungracefully. "I'm spending a fortnight at Windsor, tying up odds and ends. Putting matters to rest, so to speak." He must have seen the distaste that contorted Kell's face because he added, "What is it?"

"You don't seem saddened by the loss," observed Kell.

George huffed. "My father has been dead three weeks, and should have had the decency to die years ago, when he first grew ill. For his sake, as well as mine." A grim smile spread across the new king's face like a ripple. "But I suppose for you the shock is fresh." He crossed to a side bar to pour himself a drink. "I always forget," he said, as amber liquid sloshed against crystal, "that as long as you are in your world, you hear nothing of ours."

Kell tensed, his attention flicking to the aristocrats that peppered the vast room. They were whispering, eying Kell with interest over their glasses.

Kell resisted the urge to reach out and grab the royal's sleeve. "How much do these people know?" he demanded, fighting to keep his voice low, even. "About me?"

George waved his hand. "Oh, nothing troublesome. I believe I told them you were a foreign dignitary. Which is true, in the strictest sense. But the problem is, the less they know, the more they gossip. Perhaps we should simply introduce you—"

"I would pay my respects," cut in Kell. "To the old king." He knew they buried men in this world. It struck him as strange, to put a body in a box, but it meant the king—what was left of him—would be here, somewhere.

George sighed, as if the request were both expected and terribly inconvenient. "I figured as much," he said, finishing the drink. "He's in the chapel. But first . . ." He held out a hand, heavily adorned with rings. "My letter." Kell withdrew the envelope from the pocket of his coat. "And the one for my father."

Reluctantly, Kell retrieved the second note. The old king had always taken such care with the letters, instructing Kell not to mar the seal. The new king took up a short knife from the side bar and slashed the envelope, drawing out the contents. He hated the idea of George seeing the sparse note.

"You came all the way out here to read him this?" he asked, scornfully.

"I was fond of the king."

"Well, you'll have to make do with me now."

Kell said nothing.

The second letter was significantly longer, and the new king lowered himself onto a couch to read it. Kell felt decidedly uncomfortable, standing there while George looked over the letter and the king's entourage looked over *him*. When the king had read it through three or four times, he nodded to himself, tucked the letter away, and got to his feet.

"All right," he said. "Let's get this over with."

Kell followed George out, grateful to escape the room and all the gazes in it.

"Bloody cold out," the king said, bundling himself into a lush coat with a fur collar. "Don't suppose you could do something about that?"

Kell's eyes narrowed. "The weather? No."

The king shrugged, and they stepped out onto the palace grounds, shadowed by a huddle of attendants. Kell pulled his coat close around his body; it was a bitter February day, the wind high and the air wet and biting cold. Snow fell around them, if it could be called falling. The air caught it up and twisted the drifts into spirals so that little ever touched the frozen ground. Kell pulled up his hood.

Despite the chill, his hands were bare inside their pockets; his fingertips were going numb, but *Antari* relied on their hands and their blood to do magic, and gloves were cumbersome, an obstacle to quick-drawn spells. Not that he feared an attack on Grey London soil, but he'd rather be prepared. . . .

Then again, with George, even simple conversation felt a bit like a duel, the two possessing little love and less trust for one another. Plus, the new king's fascination with magic was growing. How long before George had Kell attacked, just to see if and how he would defend himself? But then, such a move would forfeit the communication between their worlds, and Kell didn't think the king was *that* foolish. At least he hoped not; as much as Kell hated George, he didn't want to lose his one excuse to travel.

Kell's hand found the coin in his pocket, and he turned it over and over absently to keep his fingers warm. He assumed they were walking toward a graveyard, but instead the king led him to a church.

"St. George's Chapel," he explained, stepping through.

It was impressive, a towering structure, full of sharp edges. Inside, the ceiling vaulted over a checkered stone floor. George handed off his outer coat without looking; he simply assumed someone would be there to take it, and they were. Kell looked up at the light pouring in through the stained-glass windows, and thought absently that this wouldn't be such a bad place to be buried. Until he realized that George III hadn't been laid to rest up here, surround by sunlight.

He was in the vault.

The ceiling was lower, and the light was thin, and that, paired with the scent of dusty stone, made Kell's skin crawl.

George took an unlit candelabrum from a shelf. "Would you mind?" he asked. Kell frowned. There was something hungry in the way George asked. Covetous.

"Of course," said Kell. He reached out toward the candles, his fingers hovering above before continuing past them to a vase of long-stemmed matches. He took one, struck it with a small, ceremonial flourish, and lit the candles.

George pursed his lips, disappointed. "You were all too eager to perform for my father."

"Your father was a different man," said Kell, waving the match out.

George's frown deepened. He obviously wasn't used to being told no, but Kell wasn't sure if he was upset at being denied in general, or being denied magic specifically. Why was he so intent on a demonstration? Did he simply crave proof? Entertainment? Or was it more than that?

He trailed the man through the royal vault, suppressing a shudder at the thought of being buried here. Being put in a box in the ground was bad enough, but being *entombed* like this, with layers of stone between you and the world? Kell would never understand the way these Grey-worlders sealed away their dead, trapping the discarded shells in gold and wood and stone as if some remnant of who they'd been in life remained. And if it did? What a cruel punishment.

When George reached his father's tomb, he set the candelabrum down, swept the hem of his coat into his hand, and knelt, head bowed. His lips moved silently for a few seconds, and then he drew a gold cross from his collar and touched it to his lips. Finally he stood, frowning at the dust on his knees and brushing it away.

Kell reached out and rested his hand thoughtfully on the tomb, wishing he could feel something—anything—within. It was silent and cold.

"It would be proper to say a prayer," said the king.

Kell frowned, confused. "To what end?"

"For his soul, of course." Kell's confusion must have showed. "Don't you have God in your world?" He shook his head. George seemed taken aback. "No higher power?"

"I didn't say that," answered Kell. "I suppose you could say we worship magic. That is our highest power."

"That is heresy."

Kell raised a brow, his hand slipping from the tomb's lid. "Your Majesty, you worship a thing you can neither see nor touch, whereas I worship something I engage with every moment of every day. Which is the more logical path?"

George scowled. "It isn't a matter of logic. It is a matter of faith."

Faith. It seemed a shallow substitution, but Kell supposed he couldn't blame the Grey-worlders. Everyone needed to believe in *something,* and without magic, they had settled for a lesser god. One full of holes and mystery and made-up rules. The irony was that they had abandoned magic long before it abandoned them, smothered it with this almighty God of theirs.

"But what of your dead?" pressed the king.

"We burn them."

"A pagan ritual," he said scornfully.

"Better than putting their bodies in a box."

"And what of their *souls*?" pressed George, seeming genuinely disturbed. "Where do you think they go, if you don't believe in heaven and hell?"

"They go back to the source," said Kell. "Magic is in everything, Your Majesty. It is the current of life. We believe that when you die, your soul returns to that current, and your body is reduced again to elements."

"But what of *you*?"

"*You* cease to be."

"What is the point, then?" grumbled the king. "Of living a good life, if there is nothing after? Nothing earned?"

Kell had often wondered the same thing, in his own way, but it wasn't an afterlife he craved. He simply didn't want to return to nothing, as if he'd never been. But it would be a cold day in Grey London's hell before he agreed with the new king on anything. "I suppose the point is to live well."

George's complexion was turning ruddy. "But what stops one from committing sins, if they have nothing to fear?"

Kell shrugged. "I've seen people sin in the name of god, *and* in the name of magic. People misuse their higher powers, no matter what form they take."

"But no afterlife," grumbled the king. "No eternal soul? It's unnatural."

"On the contrary," said Kell. "It is the most natural thing in the world. Nature is made of cycles, and we are made of nature. What is unnatural is believing in an infallible man and a nice place waiting in the sky."

George's expression darkened. "Careful, Master Kell. That is blasphemy."

Kell frowned. "You've never struck me as a very pious man, Your Majesty."

The king crossed himself. "Better safe than sorry. Besides," he said, looking around, "I am the King of England. My legacy is divine. I rule by the grace of that God you mock. I am His servant, as this kingdom is mine at His grace." It sounded like a recitation. The king tucked the cross back beneath his collar. "Perhaps," he added, twisting up his face, "I would worship your god, if I could see and touch it as you do."

And here they were again. The old king had regarded magic with awe, a child's wonder. This new king looked at it the way he looked at everything. With lust.

"I warned you once, Your Majesty," said Kell. "Magic has no place in your world. Not anymore."

George smiled, and for an instant he looked more like a wolf than a well-fed man. "You said yourself, Master Kell, that the world is full of cycles. Perhaps our time will come again." And then the grin was gone, swallowed up by his usual expression of droll amusement. The effect was disconcerting, and it made Kell wonder if the man was really as dense and self-absorbed as his people thought, or if there was something there, beneath the shallow, self-indulgent shell.

What had Astrid Dane said?

I do not trust things unless they belong to me.

A draft cut through the vault, flickering the candlelight. "Come," said George, turning his back on Kell and the old king's tomb.

Kell hesitated, then drew the Red London lin from his pocket, the star glittering in the center of the coin. He always brought one for the king; every month, the old monarch claimed that the magic in his own was fading, like heat from dying coals, so Kell would bring him one to trade, pocket-warm and smelling of roses. Now Kell considered the coin, turning it over his fingers.

"This one's fresh, Your Majesty." He touched it to his lips, and then reached out and set the warm coin on top of the cold stone tomb.

"*Sores nast,*" he whispered. *Sleep well.*

And with that, Kell followed the new king up the stairs, and back out into the cold.

Kell fought not to fidget while he waited for the King of England to finish writing his letter.

The man was taking his time, letting the silence in the room thicken into something profoundly uncomfortable, until Kell found himself wanting to speak, if only to break it. Knowing that was probably the point, he held his tongue and stood watching the snow fall and the sky darken beyond the window.

When the letter was finally done, George sat back in his chair and took up a wine cup, staring at the pages as he drank. "Tell me something," he said, "about magic." Kell tensed, but the king continued. "Does everyone in your world possess this ability?"

Kell hesitated. "Not all," he said. "And not equally."

George tipped the glass from side to side. "So you might say that the powerful are chosen."

"Some believe that," said Kell. "Others think it is simply a matter of luck. A good hand drawn in cards."

"If that's the case, then you must have drawn a *very* good hand."

Kell considered him evenly. "If you've finished your letter, I should—"

"How many people can do what you do?" cut in the king. "Travel between worlds? I'd wager not many, or else I might have seen them instead. Really," he said, getting to his feet, "it's a wonder your king lets you out of his sight."

He could see the thoughts in George's eyes, like cogs turning. But Kell had no intention of becoming part of the man's collection.

"Your Majesty," said Kell, trying to keep his voice smooth, "if you are feeling the urge to keep me here, thinking it might gain you something, I would *strongly* discourage the attempt, and remind you that any such gesture would forfeit future communication with my world." *Please don't do this,* he wanted to add. *Don't even try it.* He couldn't bear the thought of losing his last escape. "Plus," he added for good measure, "I think you would find I am not easily kept."

Thankfully the king raised his ringed hands in mock surrender. "You mistake me," he said with a smile, even though Kell did not think he'd been at all mistaken. "I simply don't see why our two *great* kingdoms shouldn't share a closer bond."

He folded his letter, and sealed it with wax. It was long—several pages longer than usual, judging by the way the paper bulged and its weight when Kell took it.

"For years these letters have been riddled with formalities, anecdotes instead of history, warnings in place of explanation, useless bits of information when we could be sharing *real* knowledge," pressed the king.

Kell slipped the letter into the pocket of his coat. "If that's all . . ."

"Actually, it's not," said George. "I've something for you."

Kell cringed as the man set a small box on the table. He didn't reach for it. "That is kind of you, Your Majesty, but I must decline."

George's shallow smile faded. "You would refuse a gift from the *King of England*?"

"I would refuse a gift from anyone," said Kell, "especially

when I can tell it's meant as payment. Though I know not for what."

"It's simple enough," said George. "The next time you come, I would have you bring *me* something in return."

Kell grimaced inwardly. "Transference is treason," he said, reciting a rule he'd broken so many times.

"You would be well compensated."

Kell pinched the bridge of his nose. "Your Majesty, there was a time when I might have considered your request." *Well, not yours,* he thought, *but* someone's. "But that time has passed. Petition my king for knowledge if you will. Ask of *him* a gift, and if he concedes, I shall bring it to you. But I bear nothing of my own free will." The words hurt to say, a wound not quite healed, the skin still tender. He bowed and turned to go, even though the king had not dismissed him.

"Very well," said George, standing, his cheeks ruddy. "I will see you out."

"No," said Kell, turning back. "I would not inconvenience you so," he added. "You have guests to attend to." The words were cordial. Their tone was not. "I will go back the way I came."

And you will not follow.

Kell left George red-faced beside the desk, and retraced his steps to the old king's chamber. He wished he could lock the door behind him. But of course, the locks were on the outside of this room. Another reminder that this room had been more prison than palace.

He closed his eyes and tried to remember the last time he'd seen the man alive. The old king hadn't looked well. He hadn't looked well at all, but he'd still known Kell, still brightened at his presence, still smiled and brought the royal letter to his nose, inhaling its scent.

Roses, he'd murmured softly. *Always roses.*

Kell opened his eyes. Part of him—a weary, grieving part—simply wanted to go home. But the rest of him wanted to get out of this blasted castle, go someplace where he wouldn't be a royal messenger or an *Antari,* a prisoner or a prince, and wander the streets of Grey London until he became simply a shadow, one of thousands.

He crossed to the far wall, where heavy curtains framed the window. It was so cold in here that the glass hadn't frosted over. He drew the curtain back, revealing the patterned wallpaper beneath, the design marred by a faded symbol, little more than a smudge in the low light. It was a circle with a single line through it, a transfer mark leading from Windsor to St. James. He shifted the heavy curtain back even farther, revealing a mark that would have been lost long ago, if it hadn't been shielded entirely from time and light.

A six-pointed star. One of the first marks Kell had made, years ago, when the king had been brought to Windsor. He'd drawn the same mark on the stones of a garden wall that ran beside Westminster. The second mark had been long lost, washed away by rain or buried by moss, but it didn't matter. It had been drawn once, and even if the lines were no longer visible, a blood sigil didn't fade from the world as quickly as it did from sight.

Kell pushed up his sleeve and drew his knife. He carved a shallow line across the back of his arm, touched his fingers to the blood, and retraced the symbol. He pressed his palm to it and cast a last glance back at the empty room, at the light seeping beneath the door, listening to the far-off sounds of laughter.

Damned kings, thought Kell, leaving Windsor once and for all.

III

The Edge of Arnes.

Lila's boots hit land for the first time in months.

The last time they'd docked had been at Korma three weeks past, and Lila had drawn the bad lot and been forced to stay aboard with the ship. Before that, there was Sol, and Rinar, but both times Emery insisted she keep to the *Spire*. She probably wouldn't have listened, but there was something in the captain's voice that made her stay. She'd stepped off in the port town of Elon, but that had been for half a night more than two months ago.

Now she scuffed a boot, marveling at how solid the world felt beneath her feet. At sea, everything moved. Even on still days when the wind was down and the tide even, you stood on a thing that stood on the water. The world had give and sway. Sailors talked about sea legs, the way they threw you, both when you first came aboard, and then later when you disembarked.

But as Lila strode down the dock, she didn't feel off-balance. If anything, she felt centered, grounded. Like a weight hung in the middle of her being, and nothing could knock her over now.

It made her want to pick a fight.

Alucard's first mate, Stross, liked to say she had hot blood—Lila was pretty sure he meant it as a compliment—but in truth, a fight was just the easiest way to test your mettle, to see if you'd gotten stronger, or weaker. Sure, she'd been fighting at sea all winter, but land was a different beast. Like horses that were trained on sand, so they'd be faster when they ran on packed earth.

Lila cracked her knuckles and shifted her weight from foot to foot.

Looking for trouble, said a voice in her head. *You're gonna look till you find it.*

Lila cringed at the ghost of Barron's words, a memory with edges still too sharp to touch.

She looked around; the *Night Spire* had docked in a place called Sasenroche, a cluster of wood and stone at the edge of the Arnesian empire. The *very* edge.

Bells rang out the hour, their sound diffused by cliff and fog. If she squinted, she could make out three other ships, one an Arnesian vessel, the other two foreign: the first (she knew by the flags) was a Veskan trader, carved from what looked like a solid piece of black wood; the second was a Faroan glider, long and skeletal and shaped like a feather. Out at sea, canvas could be stretched over its spindly barbs in dozens of different ways to maneuver the wind.

Lila watched as men shuffled about on the deck of the Veskan ship. Four months on the *Spire,* and she had never traveled into foreign waters, never seen the people of the neighboring empires up close. She'd heard stories, of course—sailors lived on stories as much as sea air and cheap liquor—of the Faroans' dark skin, set with jewels; of the towering Veskans and their hair, which shone like burnished metal.

But it was one thing to hear tell, and another to see them with her own eyes.

It was a big world she'd stumbled into, full of rules she didn't know and races she'd never seen and languages she didn't speak. Full of *magic.* Lila had discovered that the hardest part of her charade was pretending that everything was old hat when it was all so new, being forced to feign the kind of nonchalance that only comes from a lifetime of knowing and taking for granted. Lila was a quick study, and she knew how to keep up a front; but behind the mask of disinterest, she took in *everything*. She was a sponge, soaking up the words and customs, training herself to see something once and be able to pretend she'd seen it a dozen—a hundred—times before.

Alucard's boots sounded on the wooden dock, and she let her attention slide off the foreign ships. The captain stopped beside her, took a deep breath, and rested his hand on her shoulder. Lila still tensed under the sudden touch, a reflex she doubted would ever fade, but she didn't pull away.

Alucard was dressed in his usual high style, a silvery blue coat accented with a black sash, his brassy brown hair pinned back with its black clasp beneath an elegant hat. He seemed as fond of hats as she was of knives. The only thing out of place was the satchel slung across his shoulder.

"Do you smell that, Bard?" he asked in Arnesian.

Lila sniffed. "Salt, sweat, and ale?" she ventured.

"Money," he answered brightly.

Lila looked around, taking in the port town. A winter mist swallowed the tops of the few squat buildings, and what showed through the evening fog was relatively unimpressive. Nothing about the place screamed money. Nothing about it screamed anything, for that matter. Sasenroche was the very definition of unassuming. Which was apparently the idea.

Because officially, Sasenroche didn't even exist.

It didn't appear on any land maps—Lila learned early on that there were two kinds of maps, land and sea, and they were as different as one London from another. A land map was an ordinary thing, but a sea map was a special thing, showing not only the open sea but its secrets, its hidden islands and towns, the places to avoid and the places to go, and who to find once you got there. A sea map was never to be taken off its ship. It couldn't be sold or traded, not without word getting back to a seafarer, and the punishment was steep; it was a small world, and the prize wasn't worth the risk. If any man of the waters—or any man who wished to keep his head on his shoulders—saw a sea map on land, he was to burn it before it burned him.

Thus Sasenroche was a well-guarded secret on land, and a legend at sea. Marked on the right maps (and known by the right sailors) as simply the Corner, Sasenroche was the only place where the three empires physically touched. Faro, the lands to the south and east, and Vesk, the kingdom to the north, apparently grazed Arnes right here in this small, unassuming port town. Which made it a perfect place, Alucard had explained, to find foreign things without crossing foreign waters, and to be rid of anything you couldn't take home.

"A black market?" Lila had asked, staring down at the *Spire*'s own sea map on the captain's desk.

"The blackest on land," said Alucard cheerfully.

"And what, pray tell, are we doing here?"

"Every good privateering ship," he'd explained, "comes into possession of two kinds of things; the ones it can turn over to the crown, and the ones it cannot. Certain artifacts have no business being in the kingdom, for whatever reason, but they fetch a pretty sum in a place like this."

Lila gasped in mock disapproval. "That hardly sounds legal."

Alucard flashed the kind of smile that could probably charm snakes. "We act on the crown's behalf, even when it does not know it."

"And even when we profit?" Lila challenged wryly.

Alucard's expression shifted to one of mock offense. "These services we render to keep the crown clean and the kingdom safe go unknown, and thus uncompensated. Now and then we must compensate ourselves."

"I see. . . ."

"It's dangerous work, Bard," he'd said, touching a ringed hand to his chest, "for our bodies and our souls."

Now, as the two stood together on the dock, he flashed her that coy smile again, and she felt herself starting to smile, too, right before they were interrupted by a crash. It sounded like a bag of rocks being dumped out on the docks, but really it was just the rest of the *Night Spire* disembarking. No wonder they all thought of Lila as a wraith. Sailors made an ungodly amount of noise. Alucard's hand fell from Lila's shoulder as he turned to face his men.

"You know the rules," he bellowed. "You're free to do as you please, but don't do anything dishonorable. You are, after all, men of Arnes, here in the service of your crown."

A low chuckle went through the group.

"We'll meet at the Inroads at dusk, and I've business to discuss, so don't get too deep in your cups before then."

Lila still only caught six words out of ten—Arnesian was a fluid tongue, the words running together in a serpentine way—but she was able to piece together the rest.

A skeleton crew stayed aboard the *Spire* and the rest were dismissed. Most of the men went one way, toward the shops and taverns nearest the docks, but Alucard went another, setting off alone toward the mouth of a narrow street, and quickly vanishing into the mist.

There was an unspoken rule that where Alucard went, Lila followed. Whether he invited her or not made little difference. She had become his shadow. "Do your eyes ever close?" he'd asked her back in Elon, seeing how intently she scanned the streets.

"I've found that watching is the quickest way to learn, and the safest way to stay alive."

Alucard had shaken his head, exasperated. "The accent of a royal and the sensibilities of a thief."

But Lila had only smiled. She'd said something very similar

once, to Kell. Before she knew he *was* a royal. And a thief, for that matter.

Now, the crew dispersing, she trailed the captain as he made his winding way into Sasenroche. And as she did, Sasenroche began to *change*. What seemed from the sea to be a shallow town set against the rocky cliffs turned out to be much deeper, streets spooling away into the outcropping. The town had burrowed into the cliffs; the rock—a dark marble, veined with white—arched and wound and rose and fell everywhere, swallowing up buildings and forming others, revealing alleys and stairways only when you got near. Between the town's coiled form and the shifting sea mists, it was hard to keep track of the captain. Lila misplaced him several times, but then she'd spot the tail of his coat or catch the clipped sound of his boot, and she'd find him again. She passed a handful of people, but their hoods were up against the cold, their faces lost in shadow.

And then she turned a corner, and the fog-strewn dusk gave way to something else entirely. Something that glittered and shone and smelled like magic.

The Black Market of Sasenroche.

IV

The market rose up around Lila, sudden and massive, as if she'd stepped inside the cliffs themselves and found them hollow. There were dozens upon dozens of stalls, all of them nested under the arched ceiling of rock, the surface of which seemed strangely . . . alive. She couldn't tell if the veins in the stone were actually glowing with light, or only reflecting the lanterns that hung from every shop, but either way, the effect was striking.

Alucard kept a casual, ambling pace ahead of her, but it was obvious that he had a destination. Lila followed, but it was hard to keep her attention on the captain instead of the stalls themselves. Most held things she'd never seen before, which wasn't that special, in and of itself—she hadn't seen most of what this world had to offer—but she was beginning to understand the basic order, and many of the things she saw here seemed to break it. Magic had a pulse, and here in the Black Market of Sasenroche, it felt erratic.

And yet, most of the things on display seemed, at first glance, fairly innocuous. Where, she wondered, did Sasenroche hide its truly dangerous treasures? Lila had learned firsthand what forbidden magic could do, and while she hoped to never come across a thing like the Black London stone again, she couldn't stifle her curiosity. Amazing, how quickly the magical became mundane; only months ago she hadn't known magic was real, and now she felt the urge to search for stranger things.

The market was bustling, but eerily quiet, the murmur of a dozen dialects smoothed by the rock into an ambient shuffle of sound. Ahead, Alucard finally came to a stop before an unmarked stall. It was tented, wrapped in a curtain of deep blue silk that he vanished behind. Lila would lose all pretense of subtlety if she followed him in, so she hung back and waited, examining a table with a range of blades, from short sharp knives to large crescents of metal.

No pistols, though, she noted grimly.

Her own precious revolver, Caster, sat unused in the chest by her bed. She'd run out of bullets, only to find that they didn't use guns in this world, at least not in Arnes. She supposed she could take the weapon to a metalworker, but the truth was, the object had no place here, and transference was considered treason (look what had happened to Kell, smuggling items in; while one of those items had been her, another had been the black stone), so Lila was a little loath to introduce another weapon. What if it set off some kind of chain reaction? What if it changed the way magic was used? What if it made this world more like hers?

No, it wasn't worth the risk.

Instead, Caster stayed empty, a reminder of the world she'd left behind. A world she'd never see again.

Lila straightened and let her gaze wander through the market, and when it landed, it was not on weapons, or trinkets, but on herself.

The stall just to her left was filled with mirrors: different shapes and sizes, some framed and some simply panes of coated glass.

There was no vendor in sight, and Lila stepped closer to consider her reflection. She wore a fleece-lined short cloak against the cold, and one of Alucard's hats (he had enough to spare), a tricorne with a feather made of silver and glass. Beneath the hat, her brown eyes stared back at her, one lighter than the other and useless, though few ever noticed. Her dark hair now skimmed her shoulders, making her look more like a girl than she cared to (she'd let it grow for the con aboard the *Copper Thief*), and she made a mental note to cut it back to its usual length along her jaw.

Her eyes traveled down.

She still had no chest to speak of, thank god, but four months aboard the *Night Spire* had effected a subtle transformation. Lila had always been thin—she had no idea if it was natural, or the product of too little food and too much running for too many years—but Alucard's crew worked hard and ate well, and she'd gone from thin to lean, bony to wiry. The distinctions were small, but they made a difference.

She felt a chill prickle through her fingers, and she looked down to find her hand touching the cold surface of the mirror. Odd, she didn't remember reaching out.

Glancing up, she found her reflection's gaze. It considered her. And then, slowly, it began to shift. Her face aged several years, and her coat rippled and darkened into Kell's, the one with too many pockets and too many sides. A monstrous mask sat atop her head, like a beast with its mouth wide, and flame licked up her reflection's fingers where they met the mirror, but it did not burn. Water coiled like a snake around her other hand, turning to ice. The ground beneath her reflection's feet began to crack and split, as if under a weight, and the air around her reflection shuddered. Lila tried to pull her hand away, but she couldn't, just as she couldn't tear her gaze from her reflection's face, where her eyes—*both* of them—turned black, something swirling in their depths.

The image suddenly let go, and Lila wrenched backward, gasping. Pain scored her hand, and she looked down to see tiny cuts, drops of blood welling on each of her fingertips.

The cuts were clean, the line made by something sharp. Like glass.

She held her hand to her chest, and her reflection—now just a girl in a tricorne hat—did the same.

"The sign says *do not touch*," came a voice behind her, and she turned to find the stall's vendor. He was Faroan, with skin as black as the rock walls, his entire outfit made from a single piece of white silk. He was clean-shaven, like most Faroans, but wore only two gems set into his skin, one beneath each eye. She knew he was the stall's vendor because of the spectacles on his nose, their glass not simply glass, but mirrors, reflecting her own pale face.

"I'm sorry," she said, looking back to the glass, expecting to see the place where she'd touched it, where it had *cut* her, but the blood was gone.

"Do you know what these mirrors do?" he asked, and it took her a moment to realize that even though his voice was heavily accented, he was speaking *English*. Except that no, he wasn't, not exactly. The words he spoke didn't line up with the ones she heard. A talisman shone at his throat. At first she'd taken it as some kind of fabric pin, but now it pulsed faintly, and she understood.

The man's fingers went to the pendant. "Ah, yes, a handy thing, this, when you're a merchant at the corner of the world. Not strictly legal, of course, what with the laws against deception, but . . ." He shrugged, as if to say, *What can you do?* He seemed fascinated by the language he was speaking, as if he knew its significance.

Lila turned back to the mirrors. "What do they do?"

The vendor considered the glass, and in his spectacles she saw the mirror reflected and reflected and reflected. "Well," he said, "one side shows you what you want."

Lila thought of the black-eyed girl and suppressed a shudder. "It did not show me what I want," she said.

He tipped his head. "Are you certain? The form, perhaps not, but the idea, perhaps?"

What was the idea behind what she'd seen? The Lila in the mirror had been . . . *powerful*. As powerful as Kell. But she'd also been different. Darker.

"Ideas are well and good," continued the merchant, "but actualities can be . . . less pleasant."

"And the other side?" she asked.

"Hmm?" His mirrored spectacles were unnerving.

"You said that *one side* shows you what you want. What about the other?"

"Well, if you still want what you see, the other side shows you how to get it."

Lila tensed. Was that what made the mirrors forbidden? The Faroan merchant looked at her, as if he could see her thoughts as clearly as her reflection, and went on. "Perhaps it does not seem so rare, to look into one's own mind. Dream stones and scrying boards, these things help us see inside ourselves. The first side of the mirror is not so different; it is almost ordinary. . . ." Lila didn't think she'd ever see *this* kind of magic as ordinary. "Seeing the threads of the world is one thing. Plucking at them is another. Knowing how to make music from them, well . . . let us say this is not a simple thing at all."

"No, I suppose it's not," she said quietly, still rubbing her wounded fingers. "How much do I owe you, for using the first side?"

The vendor shrugged. "Anyone can see themselves," he said. "The mirror takes its tithe. The question now, Delilah, is do you want to see the second side?"

But Lila was already backing away from the mirrors and the mysterious vendor. "Thank you," she said, noting that he hadn't named the price, "but I'll pass."

She was halfway back to the weapons stall before she realized she'd never told the merchant her name.

Well, thought Lila, pulling her cloak tight around her shoulders, *that was unsettling.* She shoved her hands in her pockets—half to keep them from shaking, and half to make sure she didn't accidentally touch anything else—and made her way back to the weapons stall. Soon she felt someone draw up beside her, caught the familiar scent of honey and silver and spiced wine.

"Captain," she said.

"Believe it or not, Bard," he said, "I am more than capable of defending my own honor."

She gave him a sideways look and noted that the satchel was gone. "It's not your honor that concerns me."

"My health, then? No one's killed me yet."

Lila shrugged. "Everyone's immortal until they're not."

Alucard shook his head. "What a delightfully morbid outlook, Bard."

"Besides," continued Lila, "I'm not particularly worried about your honor *or* your life, Captain. I was just looking out for my cut."

Alucard sighed and swung his arm around her shoulders. "And here I was beginning to think you cared." He turned to consider the knives on the table in front of them, and chuckled.

"Most girls covet dresses."

"I am not most girls."

"Without question." He gestured at the display. "See anything you like?"

For a moment, the image in the mirror surged up in Lila mind, sinister and black-eyed and thrumming with power. Lila shook it away, looked over the blades, and nodded at a dagger with a jagged blade.

"Don't you have enough knives?"

"No such thing."

He shook his head. "You continue to be a most peculiar creature." With that, he began to lead her away. "But keep your money in your pockets. We *sell* to the Black Market of Sasenroche, Bard. We don't buy from it. *That* would be very wrong."

"You have a skewed moral compass, Alucard."

"So I've been told."

"What if I stole it?" she asked casually. "Surely it can't be wrong to *steal* an item from an illegal market?"

Alucard choked on a laugh. "You could try, but you'd fail. And you'd probably lose a hand for your effort."

"You have too little faith in me."

"Faith has nothing to do with it. Notice how the vendors don't seem particularly concerned about guarding their wares? That's because the market has been warded." They were at the edge of the cavern now, and Lila turned back to consider it. She squinted at the stalls. "It's strong magic," he continued. "If an object were to leave its stall without permission, the result would be . . . unpleasant."

"What, did you try to steal something once?"

"I'm not that foolish."

"Maybe it's just a rumor then, meant to scare off thieves."

"It's not," said Alucard, stepping out of the cavern and into the night. The fog had thickened, and night had fallen in a blanket of cold.

"How do you know?" pressed Lila, folding her arms in beneath her cloak.

The captain shrugged. "I suppose . . ." He hesitated. "I suppose I've got a knack for it."

"For what?"

The sapphire glinted in his brow. "Seeing magic."

Lila frowned. People spoke of *feeling* magic, of *smelling* it, but never of *seeing* it. Sure, one could see the effects it had on things, the elements it possessed, but never the magic itself. It was like the soul in a body, she supposed. You could see the flesh, the blood, but not the thing it contained.

Come to think of it, the only time Lila had ever *seen* magic was the river in Red London, the glow of power emanating from it with a constant crimson light. A source, that's what Kell had called it. People seemed to believe that that power coursed through everyone and everything. It had never occurred to her that someone could see it out in the world.

"Huh," she said.

"Mm," he said. He didn't offer more.

They moved in silence through the stone maze of streets, and soon all signs of the market were swallowed by the mist. The dark stone of the tunnels tapered into wood as the heart of Sasenroche gave way again to its facade.

"What about me?" she asked as they reached the port.

Alucard glanced back. "What about you?"

"What do you see," she asked, "when you look at me?"

She wanted to know the truth. Who was Delilah Bard? *What* was she? The first was a question she thought she knew the answer to, but the second . . . she'd tried not to bother with it, but as Kell had pointed out so many times, she shouldn't be here. Shouldn't be alive, for that matter. She bent most of the rules. She broke the rest. And she wanted to know why. How. If she was just a blip in the universe, an anomaly, or something *more*.

"Well?" she pressed.

She half expected Alucard to ignore the question, but at last he turned, squaring himself to her.

For an instant, his face crinkled. He so rarely frowned that the expression looked wrong on him. There was a long silence, filled only by the thud of Lila's pulse, as the captain's dark eyes considered her.

"Secrets," he said at last. And then he winked. "Why do you think I let you stay?"

And Lila knew that if she wanted to know the truth, she'd have to give it, and she wasn't ready to do that yet, so she forced herself to smile and shrug. "You like the sound of your own voice. I assumed it was so you'd have someone to talk to."

He laughed and put an arm around her shoulders. "That, too, Bard. That, too."

V

Grey London.

The city looked positively bleak, shrouded in the dying light, as if everything had been painted over with only black and white, an entire palette dampened to shades of grey. Chimneys sent up plumes of smoke and huddled forms hurried past, shoulders bent against the cold.

And Kell had never been so happy to be there.

To be invisible.

Standing on the narrow road in the shadow of Westminster, he drew a deep breath, despite the hazy, smoke-and-cold-filled air, and relished the feeling. A chill wind cut through and he thrust his hands in his pockets and began to walk. He didn't know where he was going. It didn't matter.

There was no place to hide in Red London, not anymore, but he could still carve out space for himself here. He passed a few people on the streets, but no one knew him. No one balked or cringed away. Sure, there had been rumors once, in certain circles, but to most passersby, he was just another stranger. A shadow. A ghost in a city filled with—

"It's *you*."

Kell tensed at the voice. He slowed, but didn't stop, assuming that the words weren't meant for him, or if they were, then said by mistake.

"Sir!" the voice called again, and Kell glanced around—not for the source, but for anyone else it might be speaking to. But there was no one nearby, and the word was said with recognition, with *knowing*.

His rising mood shuddered and died as he dragged himself to a stop and turned to find a lanky man clutching an armful of papers and staring directly at him, eyes as large as coins. A dark scarf hung around the man's shoulders, and his clothes weren't shabby, but they didn't fit him well; he looked like he'd been stretched out, his face and limbs too long for his suit. His wrists protruded from the cuffs, and on the back of one Kell saw the tail edge of a tattoo.

A power rune.

The first time Kell had seen it, he remembered thinking two things. The first was that it was inaccurate, distorted the way a copy of a copy of a copy might be. The second was that it belonged to an Enthusiast, a Grey-worlder who fancied himself a magician.

Kell *hated* Enthusiasts.

"Edward Archibald Tuttle, the third," said Kell drily.

The man—Ned—burst into an awkward grin, as if Kell had just delivered the most spectacular news. "You remember me!"

Kell did. He remembered everyone he did business (or chose *not* to do business) with. "I don't have your dirt," he said, recalling his half-sarcastic promise to bring the man a bag of earth, if he waited for Kell.

Ned waved it away. "You came back," he said, hurrying forward. "I was beginning to think you wouldn't, after everything, that is to say, after the horrible business with the pub's owner—dreadful business—I waited, you know, before it happened, and then after, of course, and still, and I was beginning to wonder, which isn't the same thing as doubting, mind you, I hadn't begun to doubt, but no one had seen you, not in months and months, and now, well, you're back. . . ."

Ned finally trailed off, breathless. Kell didn't know what to say. The man had done enough talking for both of them. A sharp wind cut through, and Ned nearly lost his papers. "Bloody hell, it's cold," he said. "Let me get you a drink."

He nodded at something behind Kell when he said it, and Kell turned to see a tavern. His eyes widened as he realized where his treacherous feet had taken him. He should have known. The feeling was there, in the ground itself, the subtle pull that only belonged to a fixed point.

The Stone's Throw.

Kell was standing only a few strides from the place where he'd done business, the place where Lila had lived and Barron had died. (He had been back once, when it was all over, but the doors were locked. He'd broken in, but Barron's body was already gone. He climbed the narrow stairs to Lila's room at the top, found nothing left but a dark stain on the floor and a map with no markings. He'd taken the map with him, the last trinket he'd ever smuggle. He hadn't been back since.)

Kell's chest ached at the sight of the place. It wasn't *called* the Stone's Throw anymore. It looked the same—*felt* the same, now that Kell was paying attention—but the sign that hung above the door said THE FIVE POINTS.

"I really shouldn't . . ." he said, frowning at the name.

"The tavern doesn't open for another hour," insisted Ned. "And there's something I want to show you." He pulled a key from his pocket, fumbling one of his scrolls in the process. Kell reached out and caught it, but his attention was on the key as Ned slid it into the lock.

"You *own* this place?" he said incredulously.

Ned nodded. "Well, I mean, I didn't always, but I bought it up, after all that nasty business went down. There was talk of razing it, and it just didn't seem right, so when it came up for sale, well, I mean, you and I, we both know this place isn't *just* a tavern, that's to say it's special, got that aura of"—he lowered his voice—"*magic*..."—and then spoke up again—"about it. And besides, I knew you'd come back. I just *knew*...."

Ned went inside as he rambled, and Kell didn't have much choice but to follow—he could have walked away and left the man prattling, but Ned had waited, had bought the whole damn tavern so he could *keep* waiting, and there was something to be said for stubborn resolve, so he followed the man in.

The place was impenetrably dark, and Ned set his scrolls on the nearest table and made his way, half by feel, to the hearth to stoke a fire.

"The hours are different here now," he said, piling a few logs into the grate, "because my family doesn't know, you see, that I've taken up the Points, they just wouldn't understand, they'd say it wasn't a fitting profession for someone in my position, but they don't know me, not really. Always been a bit of a stray cat, I suppose. But you don't care about that, sorry, I just wanted to explain why it was closed up. Different crowd nowadays, too...."

Ned trailed off, struggling with a piece of flint, and Kell's gaze drifted from the half-charred logs in the hearth to the unlit lanterns scattered on tabletops and hung from ceiling beams. He sighed, and then, either because he was feeling cold or indulgent, he snapped his fingers; the fire in the hearth burst to life, and Ned staggered back as it crackled with the bluish-white light of enchanted flames before settling into the yellows and reds of more ordinary fire.

One by one, the lanterns began to glow as well, and Ned straightened and turned, taking in the spreading light of the self-igniting lamps as if Kell had summoned the stars themselves into his tavern.

He made a sound, a sharp intake of breath, and his eyes went wide: not with fear, or even surprise, but with adoration. With *awe*. There was something to the man's unguarded fascination, his unbridled delight at the display, that reminded Kell of the old king. His heart ached. He'd once taken the Enthusiast's interest as hunger, greed, but perhaps he'd been mistaken. He was nothing like the new King George. No, Ned had the childlike intensity of someone who *wanted* the world to be stranger than it was, someone who thought they could *believe* magic into being.

Ned reached out and rested his hand on one of the lanterns. "It's warm," he whispered.

"Fire generally is," said Kell, surveying the place. With the infusion of light, he could see that while the outside had stayed the same, inside the Five Points was a different place entirely.

Curtains had been draped from the ceiling in dark swaths, rising and falling above the tables, which were arranged like spokes on a wheel. Black patterns had been drawn—no, *burned*—into the wooden tabletops, and Kell guessed they were meant to be symbols of power—though some looked like Ned's tattoo, vaguely distorted, while others looked entirely made up.

The Stone's Throw had always been a place of magic, but the Five Points *looked* like one. Or at least, like a child's idea of one.

There was an air of mystery, of performance, and as Ned shrugged out of his overcoat, Kell saw that he was wearing a black high-collared shirt with glossy onyx buttons. A necklace at his throat bore a five-pointed star, and Kell wondered if that was where the tavern had gotten its name, until he saw the drawing framed on the wall. It was a schematic of the box Kell had had with him when he and Ned first met. The element game with its five grooves.

Fire, water, earth, air, bone.

Kell frowned. The diagram was shockingly accurate, down to the grain in the wood. He heard the sound of clinking glasses and saw Ned behind the counter, pulling bottles from the wall. He poured two draughts of something dark, and held one out in offering.

For a moment, Kell thought of Barron. The bartender had

been as broad as Ned was narrow, as gruff as the youth was exuberant. But he'd been as much a part of this place as the wood and stone, and he was dead because of Holland. Because of Kell.

"Master Kell?" pressed Ned, still holding out the glass.

He knew he should be going, but he found himself approaching the counter, willing the stool out a few inches before he sat down.

Show-off, said a voice in his head, and maybe it was right, but the truth was, it had been so long since anyone had looked at him the way Ned did now.

Kell took up the drink. "What is it you want to show me, Ned?"

The man beamed at the use of the nickname. "Well, you see," he said, drawing a box from beneath the bar, "I've been *practicing.*" He set the box on the counter, flicked open the lid, and drew out a smaller parcel from within. Kell had his glass halfway to his lips when he saw what Ned was holding, and promptly set the drink down. It was an element set, just like the one Kell had traded here four months ago. No, it was the same *exact* element set, from the dark wood sides down to the little bronze clasp.

"Where did you get that?" he asked.

"Well, I bought it." Ned set the magician's board reverently on the counter between them, and slid the clasp, letting the board unfold to reveal the five elements in their grooves. "From that gentleman you sold it to. Wasn't easy, but we came to an agreement."

Great, thought Kell, his mood suddenly cooling. The only thing worse than an ordinary Enthusiast was a wealthy one.

"I tried to make my own," Ned continued. "But it wasn't the same, I've never been much good with that kind of thing, you should have seen the chicken scratch of that drawing, before I hired—"

"Focus," said Kell, sensing that Ned could wander down mental paths all night.

"Right," he said, "so, what I wanted to show you"—he cracked his knuckles dramatically—"was this."

Ned tapped the groove containing water, and then brought his hands down flat on the counter. He squinted down at the board, and Kell relaxed as he realized where this was going: nowhere.

Still, something was different. The last time Ned had tried this, he'd gestured in the air, and spoken some nonsense over the water, as if the words themselves had any power. This time his lips moved, but Kell couldn't hear what he was saying. His hands stayed flat, splayed on the counter to either side of the board.

For a moment, as predicted, nothing happened.

And then, right as Kell was losing his patience, the water *moved*. Not much, but a bead seemed to rise slightly from the pool before falling back, sending tiny ripples through the water.

Sanct.

Ned stepped back, triumphant, and while he managed to keep his composure, it was clear he wanted to thrust his arms in the air and cheer.

"Did you see it? Did you see it?" he chanted. And Kell had. It was hardly a dangerous capacity for magic, but it was far more than he had expected. It should have been impossible—for Ned, for *any* Grey-worlder—but the past few months made him wonder if anything was truly out of bounds. After all, Lila had come from Grey London, and she was . . . well, but then she was something else entirely.

Magic has no place in your world, he'd told the king. *Not anymore.*

The world is full of cycles. Perhaps our time will come again.

What was happening? He'd always thought of magic as a fire, each London sitting farther and farther from its heat. Black London had burned up, so near it was to the flame, but Grey London had gone to coals long ago. Was there still somehow a spark? Something to be kindled? Had he accidently blown on the dying flames? Or had Lila?

"That's all I've been able to manage," said Ned excitedly. "But with proper training . . ." He looked at Kell expectantly as he said that, and then quickly down again. "That is, with the right teacher, or at least some guidance . . ."

"Ned," Kell started.

"Of course, I know you must be busy, in demand, and time is precious . . ."

"Edward—" he tried again.

"But I have something for you," pressed the man.

Kell sighed. Why was everyone suddenly so keen to give him gifts?

"I tried to think about what you said, last time, about how you were only interested in things that mattered, and it took me some time but I think I've found something worthy. I'll go get it."

Before Kell could tell him to stop, could explain that whatever it was, he couldn't take it, the man was out from behind the bar and hurrying into the hall, taking the steps upstairs two at a time.

Kell watched him go, wishing he could stay.

He missed the Stone's Throw, no matter its name, missed the simple solidity of this place, this city. Did he have to go home? And that was the problem, right there. Red London was *home*. Kell didn't belong here, in this world. He was a creature of magic—Arnesian, not English. And even if this world still had any power (for Tieren said no place was truly without it), Kell couldn't afford to stoke it, not for Ned, or the king, or himself. He'd already disrupted two worlds. He wouldn't be to blame for a third.

He raked a hand through his hair and pushed up from the stool, the footsteps overhead growing fainter.

The game board still sat open on the counter. Kell knew he should take it back, but then what? He'd just have to explain its presence to Staff and Hastra. No, let the foolish boy keep it. He set the empty glass down and turned to leave, shoving his hands in his pockets.

His fingers brushed something in the very bottom of his coat.

His hand closed over it, and he drew out a second Red London lin. It was old, the gold star worn smooth by hands and time, and Kell didn't know how long it had languished in his pocket. It might have been one of the coins he'd taken from the old king, exchanged for one new and pocket-worn. Or it might have been a stray piece of change, lost in the wool-lined pocket. He considered it for a moment, then heard the sound of a door shutting overhead, and footsteps on the stairs.

Kell set the coin on the counter by his empty glass, and left.

VI

Sasenroche.

Growing up, Lila had always hated taverns.

She seemed bound to them by some kind of tether; she would run as hard as she could, and then at some point she'd reach the end of the line and be wrenched back. She'd spent years trying to cut that tie. She never could.

The Inroads stood at the end of the docks, its lanterns haloed by the tendrils of the sea fog that crept into the port. A sign above the door was written in three languages, only one of which Lila recognized.

The familiar sounds reached her from within, the ambient noise of scraping chairs and clinking glass, of laughter and threats and fights about to break out. They were the same sounds she'd heard a hundred times at the Stone's Throw, and it struck her as odd that those sounds could exist here, in a black market town at the edge of an empire in a magical world. There was, she supposed, a comfort to these places, to the fabric that made them, the way that two taverns, cities apart—*worlds* apart— could feel the same, look the same, sound the same.

Alucard was holding the door open for her. "*Tas enol,*" he said, sliding back into Arnesian. *After you.*

Lila nodded and went in.

Inside, the Inroads looked familiar enough; it was the *people* who were different. Unlike the black market, here the hoods and hats had all been cast off, and Lila got her first good look at the crews from the other ships along the dock. A towering Veskan pushed past them, nearly filling the doorway as he went, a massive blond braid falling down his back. He was bare-armed as he stepped out into the winter cold.

A huddle of men stood just inside the door, talking in low voices with smooth foreign tongues. One glanced at her, and she was startled to see that his eyes were gold. Not amber, like the prince's, but bright, almost reflective, their metallic centers flecked with black. Those eyes shone out from skin as dark as the ocean at night, and unlike the Faroan she'd seen in the market, this man's face was studded with dozens of pieces of pale green glass. The fragments traced lines over his brows, followed the curve of his cheek, trailed down his throat. The effect was haunting.

"Close your mouth," Alucard hissed in her ear. "You look like a fish."

The light in the tavern was low, shining up from tables and hearths instead of down from the ceiling and walls, casting faces in odd shadow as the candles glanced off cheeks and brows.

It wasn't terribly crowded—she'd only seen four ships in the port—and she could make out the *Spire*'s men, scattered about and chatting in groups of two or three.

Stross and Lenos had snagged a table by the bar and were playing cards with a handful of Veskans; Olo watched, and broad-shouldered Tav was deep in conversation with an Arnesian from another ship.

Handsome Vasry was flirting with a Faroan-looking barmaid—nothing unusual there—and a wiry crewman named Kobis sat at the end of a couch, reading a book in the low light, clearly relishing the closest thing he ever found to peace and quiet.

A dozen faces turned as Lila and Alucard moved through the room, and she felt herself shrink toward the nearest shadow before she realized none of them were looking at her. It was the captain of the *Night Spire* who held their attention. Some nodded, others raised a hand or a glass, a few called out a greeting. He'd obviously made a few friends during his years at sea. Come to think of it, if Alucard Emery had made *enemies,* she hadn't met one yet.

An Arnesian from the other rig waved him over, and rather than trail after, Lila made her way to the bar and ordered some kind of cider that smelled of apple and spice and strong liquor. She was several sips along before she turned her attention to the Veskan man a few feet down the bar.

The *Spire* crew called Veskans *"choser"*—giants—and she was beginning to understand why.

Lila tried not to stare—that is, she tried to stare without looking like she was staring—but the man was *massive,* even taller than Barron had been, with a face like a block of stone circled by a rope of blond hair. Not the bleached whitish blond of the Danc twins, but a honey color, rich in a way that matched his skin, as though he'd never spent a day in the shade.

His arms, one of which leaned on the counter, were each the size of her head; his smile was wider than her knife, but not nearly as wicked; and his eyes, when they shifted toward her, were a cloudless blue. The Veskan's hair and beard grew together around his face, parting only for his wide eyes and straight nose, and made his expression hard to read. She couldn't tell if she was merely being sized up, or challenged.

Lila's fingers drifted toward the dagger at her hip, even though she honestly didn't want to try her hand against a man who looked more likely to *dent* her knife than be impaled on it.

And then, to her surprise, the Veskan held up his glass.

"*Is aven,*" she said, lifting her own drink. *Cheers.*

The man winked, and then began to down his ale in a single, continuous gulp, and Lila, sensing the challenge, did the same. Her cup was half the size of his, but to be fair, he was more than twice the size of her, so it seemed an even match. When her empty mug struck the counter an instant before his own, the Veskan laughed and knocked the table twice with his closed fist while murmuring appreciatively.

Lila set a coin on the bar and stood up. The cider hit her like a pitching deck, as if she were no longer on solid ground but back on the *Spire* in a storm.

"Easy now." Alucard caught her elbow, then swung his arm around her shoulders to hide her unsteadiness. "That's what you get for making friends."

He led her to a booth where most of the men had gathered, and she sank gratefully into a chair on the end. As the captain took his seat, the rest of the crew drifted over, as if drawn by an invisible current. But of course, the current was Alucard himself.

Men laughed. Glasses clanked. Chairs scraped.

Lenos cheated a glance at her down the table. He was the one who'd started the rumors, about her being the Sarows. Was he still afraid of her, after all this time?

She drew his knife—now hers—from her belt and polished it on the corner of her shirt.

Her head spun from that first drink, and she let her ears and attention drift through the crew like smoke, let the Arnesian words dissolve back into the highs and lows, the melodies of a foreign tongue.

At the other end of the table, Alucard boasted and cheered and drank with his crew, and Lila marveled at the way the man shifted to fit his environment. She knew how to adapt well enough, but Alucard knew how to *transform*. Back on the *Spire*, he was not only captain but king. Here at this table, surrounded by his men, he was one of them. Still the boss, always the boss, but not so far above the rest. This Alucard took pains to laugh as loud as Tav and flirt almost as much as Vasry, and slosh his ale like Olo, even though Lila had seen him fuss whenever she spilled water or wine in his cabin.

It was a performance, one that was entertaining to watch. Lila wondered for perhaps the hundredth time which version of Alucard was the real one, or if, somehow, they were all real, each in its own way.

She also wondered where Alucard had found such an odd group of men, when and how they'd been collected. Here, on land, they seemed to have so little in common. But on the *Spire*, they functioned like friends, like *family*. Or at least, how Lila imagined family would act. Sure they bickered, and now and then even came to blows, but they were also fiercely loyal.

And Lila? Was she loyal, too?

She thought back to those first nights, when she'd slept with her back to the wall and her knife at hand, waiting to be attacked. When she'd had to face the fact that she knew almost nothing about life aboard a ship, and grappled every day to stay on her feet, clutching at scraps of skill and language and, on the occasion it was offered, help. It seemed like a lifetime ago. Now they treated her more or less as if she was one of them. As if she *belonged*. A small, defiant part of her, the part she'd done her best to smother on the streets of London, fluttered at the thought.

But the rest of her felt ill.

She wanted to push away from the table and walk out, walk away, break the cords that tied her to this ship and this crew and this life, and start over. Whenever she felt the weight of those bonds, she wished she could take her sharpest knife and cut them free, carve out the part of her that wanted, that cared, that warmed at the feeling of Alucard's hand on her shoulder, Tav's smile, Stross's nod.

Weak, warned a voice in her head.

Run, said another.

"All right, Bard?" asked Vasry, looking genuinely concerned.

Lila nodded, fixing a sliver of a smile back on her face.

Stross slid a fresh drink her way, as if it was nothing.

Run.

Alucard caught her eye and winked.

Christ, she should have killed him when she had the chance.

"All right, Captain," shouted Stross over the noise. "You've got us waiting. What's the big news?"

The table began to quiet, and Alucard brought his stein down. "Listen up, you shabby lot," he said, his voice carrying in a wave. The group fell to murmurs and then silence. "You can have the night on land. But we sail at first light."

"Where to next?" asked Tav.

Alucard looked right at Lila when he said it. "To London."

Lila stiffened in her seat.

"What for?" asked Vasry.

"Business."

"Funny thing," called Stross, scratching his cheek. "Isn't it about time for the tournament?"

"It might be," said Alucard with a smirk.

"You *didn't*," gasped Lenos.

"Didn't what?" asked Lila.

Tav chuckled. "He's gone and entered the *Essen Tasch*."

Essen Tasch, thought Lila, trying to translate the phrase. *Element . . . something.* What was it? Everyone else at the table seemed to know. Only Kobis said nothing, simply frowned down into his drink, but he didn't look confused, only concerned.

"I don't know, Captain," said Olo. "You think you're good enough to play that game?"

Alucard chuckled and shook his head. He brought his glass to his lips, took a swig, and then slammed the stein down on the table. It shattered, but before the cider could spill, it sprang into the air, along with the contents in every other glass at the table, liquid freezing as it surged upward. The frozen drinks hung for a moment, then tumbled to the wooden table, some lodging sharp-end down, others rolling about. Lila watched the frozen spear that had once been her cider fetch up against her glass. Only the icicle that had been Alucard's drink stayed up, hovering suspended above his ruined glass.

The crew whooped and applauded.

"Hey," growled a man behind the bar. "You pay for everything you break."

Alucard smiled and lifted his hands, as if in surrender. And then, as he flexed his fingers, the shards of glass strewn across the table trembled and drew themselves back together into the shape of a stein, as if time itself were beginning to reverse. The stein formed in one of Alucard's hands, the cracks blurring and then vanishing as the glass re-fused. He held it up, as if to inspect it, and the shard of frozen cider still hovering in the air above his head liquefied and spilled back into the unbroken glass. He took a sip and toasted the man behind the bar, and the crew burst into a raucous cheer, hammering the table, their own drinks forgotten.

Only Lila sat motionless, stunned by the display.

She'd seen Alucard do magic, of course—he'd been teaching her for months. But there was a difference—a chasm, a world—between levitating a knife and *this*. She hadn't seen anyone handle magic like this. Not since Kell.

Vasry must have read her surprise, because he tipped his head toward hers. "Captain's one of the best in Arnes," he said. "Most magicians only got a handle on one element. A few are duals. But Alucard? He's a *triad*." He said the word with awe. "Doesn't go around flashing his power, because great magicians are rare out on the water, rarer than a bounty, so they're likely to be caught and sold. Of course that wouldn't be the first coin on his head, but still. Most don't leave the cities."

Then why did he? she wondered.

When she looked up, she saw Alucard's gaze leveled on her, sapphire winking above one storm-dark eye.

"You ever been to an *Essen Tasch,* Vasry?" she asked.

"Once," said the handsome sailor. "Last time the Games were in London."

Games, thought Lila. So that's what *Tasch* meant.

The Element Games.

"Only runs every three years," continued Vasry, "in the city of the last victor."

"What's it like?" she pried, fighting to keep her interest casual.

"Never been? Well you're in for a treat." Lila liked Vasry. He wasn't the sharpest man, not by a long stretch; he didn't read too much into the questions, didn't wonder how or why she didn't know the answers. "The *Essen Tasch* has been going for more than sixty years now, since the last imperial war. Every three years they get together—Arnes and Faro and Vesk—and put up their best magicians. Shame it only lasts a week."

"S'the empires' way of shaking hands and smiling and showing that all is well," chimed in Tav, who had leaned in conspiratorially.

"*Tac,* politics are boring," said Vasry, waving his hand. "But the duels are fun to watch. And the *parties*. The drinking, the betting, the beautiful women . . ."

Tav snorted. "Don't listen to Vasry, Bard," he said. "The duels are the best part. A dozen of the greatest magicians from each empire going head to head." *Duels.*

"Oh, and the masks are pretty, too," mused Vasry, eyes glassy.

"Masks?" asked Lila, interest piqued.

Tav leaned forward with excitement. "In the beginning," he said, "the competitors wore helmets, to protect themselves. But over time they began to embellish them. Set themselves apart. Eventually, the masks just became part of the tournament." Tav frowned slightly. "I'm surprised you've never been to an *Essen Tasch,* Bard."

Lila shrugged. "Never been in the right place at the right time."

He nodded, as if that answer was good enough, and let the

matter lie. "Well, if Alucard's in the ranks, it'll be a tournament to remember."

"Why do men do it?" she asked. "Just to show off?"

"Not just men," said Vasry. "Women, too."

"It's an honor, being chosen to compete for your crown—"

"Glory's well and good," said Vasry, "but this game is winner take all. Not that the captain needs the money."

Tav shot him a warning look.

"A pot that large," said Olo, chiming in, "even the king himself is sore to part with it."

Lila traced her finger through the cider that was beginning to melt on the table, half listening to the crew as they chatted. Magic, masks, money . . . the *Essen Tasch* was becoming more and more interesting.

"Can anyone compete?" she wondered idly.

"Sure," said Tav, "if they're good enough to get a spot."

Lila stopped drawing her finger through the cider, and no one noticed that the spilled liquid kept moving, tracing patterns across the wood.

Someone set a fresh drink in front of her.

Alucard was calling for attention.

"To London," he said, raising his glass.

Lila raised her own.

"To London," she said, smiling like a knife.

FOUR

LONDONS CALLING

I

Red London.

The city was under siege.

Rhy stood on the uppermost balcony of the palace and watched the forces assemble. The cold air bit at his cheeks and tugged on his half cloak, catching it up like a golden flag behind him.

Far below, structures collided, walls rose, and the sounds of stoked fires and hammer on steel echoed like weapons struck together in a barrage of wood and metal and glass.

It would surprise most to know that when Rhy thought of himself as king, he saw himself like this: not on a throne, or toasting friends at lavish dinners, but overseeing armies. And while he had never seen an *actual* battlefront—the last true war was more than sixty years past, and his father's forces always smothered the border flares and civil skirmishes before they could escalate—Rhy was blessed with enough imagination to compensate. And at first glance, London *did* appear to be under attack, though the forces were all his own.

Everywhere Rhy looked, the city was being overtaken, not by enemy soldiers but by masons and magicians, hard at work constructing the platforms and stages, the floating arenas and bankside tents that would house the *Essen Tasch* and its competitors.

"The view from up here," said a man behind him, "it is . . . magnificent." The words were High Royal, but their edges were smoothed out by the *ostra*'s Arnesian accent.

"It is indeed, Master Parlo," said Rhy, turning toward the man. He had to bite back a smile. Parlo looked positively miserable, half frozen and obviously uncomfortable with the distance between the balcony and the red river far below, clutching the scrolls to the flowery pattern of his vest as if they were a rope. Almost as bad as Vis; the guard stood with his armored back pressed against the wall, looking pale.

Rhy was tempted to lean back against the railing, just to make the *ostra* and the guard nervous. It was something Kell would do. Instead he stepped away from the edge, and Parlo gratefully mirrored his action by retreating a pace into the doorway.

"What brings you to the roof?" asked Rhy.

Parlo drew a roll of parchment from under his arm. "The arrangements for the opening ceremonies, Your Highness."

"Of course." He accepted the plans but didn't unroll them. Parlo still stood there, as if waiting for something—a tip? a treat?—and Rhy finally said, "You can go now."

The *ostra* looked wounded, so Rhy dredged up his most princely smile. "Come now, Master Parlo, you've been excused, not banished. The view up here may be magnificent, but the weather is not, and you look in need of tea and a fire. You'll find both in the gallery downstairs."

"I suppose that does sound nice . . . but the plans . . ."

"Hopefully I won't need help deciphering a scheme I made myself. And if I do, I know where to find you."

After a moment, Parlo finally nodded and retreated. Rhy sighed and set the plans on a small glass table by the door. He unrolled the parchment, wincing as sunlight made the page glow white, his head still throbbing dully from the night before. The nights had grown harder for Rhy. He'd never been afraid of the dark—even after the Shadows came and tried to kill him in the night—but that was because the dark itself *used* to be empty. Now it was not. He could feel it, whatever *it* was, hovering in the air around him, waiting until the sun went down and the world got quiet. Quiet enough to *think*. Thoughts, those were the waiting things, and once they started up, he couldn't seem to silence them.

Saints, how he tried.

He poured himself a glass of tea and dragged his attention back to the plans, setting weights at the corners against the wind. And there it was, laid out before him, the thing he focused on in a desperate attempt to keep the thoughts at bay.

Is Essen Tasch.

The Element Games.

An international tournament between the three empires—Vesk, Faro, and, of course, Arnes. It was no modest affair. The *Essen Tasch* was made up of thirty-six magicians, a thousand wealthy spectators willing to make the journey, and of course, the royal guests. The prince and princess from Vesk. The king's brother from Faro. By tradition, the tournament was hosted by the capital of the previous winner. And thanks to Kisimyr Vasrin's prowess, and Rhy's vision, London would be the dazzling centerpiece of this year's games.

And at the center, Rhy's crowning achievements: the first ever floating arenas.

Tents and stages blossomed all across the city, but Rhy's deepest pride was reserved for those three stages being erected not on the banks, but on the river itself. They were temporary, yes, and would be torn down again when the tournament was over. But they were also *glorious,* works of art, statues on the scale of stadiums. Rhy had commissioned the best metal- and earth-workers in the kingdom to build his magnificent arenas. Bridges and walkways were being crafted around the palace, and from above they resembled golden ripples across the Isle's red water. Each stadium was an octagon, canvas stretched like sails over a skeleton of stone. On top of this body, the arenas were covered: the first in sculpted scales, the second in fabric feathers, the third in grassy fur.

As Rhy watched, massive dragons carved of ice were being lowered into the river to circle the eastern arena, while canvas birds flew like kites above the central one, caught in a perpetual wind. And to the west, eight magnificent stone lions marked the stadium's posts, each caught in a different pose, a captured moment in the narrative of predator and prey.

He could have simply numbered the platforms, Rhy supposed, but that would have been woefully predictable. No, the *Essen Tasch* demanded more.

Spectacle.

That's what everyone expected. And spectacle was certainly something Rhy knew how to deliver. But this wasn't just about putting on a show. Kell could tease all he liked, but Rhy *did* care about his kingdom's future. When his father put him in charge of the tournament, he'd been insulted. He'd thought the *Essen Tasch* a glorified party, and as good as Rhy was at entertaining, he'd wanted more. More responsibility. More power. And he'd told the king as much.

"Ruling is a delicate affair," his father had chided. "Every gesture carries purpose and meaning. This tournament is not only a game. It helps to maintain peace with our neighboring empires, and it allows us to show them our resources without implying any threat." The king had laced his fingers. "Politics is a dance until the moment it becomes a war. And we control the music."

And the more Rhy thought on it, the more he understood.

The Maresh had been in power for more than a hundred years. Since before the War of the Empires. The *ostra* elite loved them, and none of the royal *vestra* were bold enough to challenge their reign, solid as it was. That was the benefit of ruling for more than a century; none could remember what life was like before the Maresh came to power. It was easy to believe the dynasty would never end.

But what of the other empires? No one spoke of war—no one ever spoke of war—but whispers of discontent reached like fog across the borders. With seven children, the Veskans were reaching for power, and the king's brother was hungry; it was only a matter of time before Lord Sol-in-Ar muscled his way onto the Faroan throne, and even if Vesk and Faro had their sights on each other, the fact remained that Arnes sat squarely between them.

And then there was Kell.

As much as Rhy joked with his brother about his reputation, it was no joke to Faro or Vesk. Some were convinced Kell was the keystone of the Arnesian empire, that it would crumble and fall without him at its center.

It didn't matter if it was true—their neighbors were always searching for a weakness, because ruling an empire was about *strength*. Which was really the *image* of strength. The *Essen Tasch* was the perfect pedestal for such a display.

A chance for Arnes to shine.

A chance for *Rhy* to shine, not only as a jewel, but as a sword. He had always been a symbol of wealth. He wanted to be a symbol of *power*. Magic was power, of course, but it wasn't the *only* kind. Rhy told himself he could still be strong without it.

His fingers tightened on the balcony's rail.

The memory of Holland's gift flickered through his mind. Months ago he had done something foolish—so foolish, it had nearly cost him and his city everything—just to be strong in the way Kell was. His people would never know how close he'd come to failing them. And more than anything else, Rhy Maresh wanted to be what his people needed. For a long time he thought they needed the cheerful, rakish royal. He wasn't ignorant enough to think that his city was free of suffering, but he used to think—or perhaps he only *wanted* to think—that he could bring a measure of happiness to his people by being happy himself. After all, they loved him. But what befitted a prince would not befit a king.

Don't be morbid, he thought. His parents were both in good health. But people lived and died. That was the nature of the world. Or at least, that was how it should be.

The memories rose like bile in his throat. The pain, the blood, the fear, and finally the quiet and the dark. The surrender of letting go, and being dragged back, the force of it like falling, a terrible, jarring pain when he hit the ground. Only he wasn't falling down. He was falling up. Surging back to the surface of himself, and—

"Prince Rhy."

He blinked and saw his guard, Tolners, standing in the doorway, tall and stiff and official.

Rhy's fingers ached as he pried them from the icy railing. He opened his mouth to speak, and tasted blood. He must have bitten his tongue. *Sorry, Kell,* he thought. It was such a peculiar thing, to know your pain was tethered to someone else's, that every time you hurt, they felt it, and every time they hurt, it was because of you. These days, Rhy always seemed to be the source of Kell's suffering, while Kell himself walked around as if the world were suddenly made of glass, all because of Rhy. It wasn't even in the end, wasn't balanced, wasn't fair. Rhy held Kell's *pain* in his hands, while Kell held Rhy's *life* in his.

"Are you all right?" pressed the guard. "You look pale."

Rhy took up a glass of tea—now cold—and rinsed the metallic taste from his mouth, setting the cup aside with shaking fingers.

"Tell me, Tolners," he said, feigning lightness. "Am I in so much danger that I need not one but *two* men guarding my life?" Rhy gestured to the first guard, who still stood pressed against the cold stone exterior. "Or have you come to relieve poor Vis before he faints on us?"

Tolners looked to Vis, and jerked his head. The other guard gratefully ducked back through the patio doors and into the safety of the room. Tolners didn't take up a spot along the wall, but stood before Rhy at attention. He was dressed, as he always was, in full armor, his red cape billowing behind him in the cold wind, gold helmet tucked under his arm. He looked more like a statue than a man, and in that moment—as in many moments—Rhy missed his old guards, Gen and Parrish. Missed their humor and their casual banter and the way he could make them forget that he was a prince. And sometimes, the way they could make *him* forget, too.

Don't be contrary, thought Rhy. *You cannot be the symbol of power and an ordinary man at the same time. You have to choose. Choose right.*

The balcony suddenly felt crowded. Rhy freed the blueprints from the table and retreated into the warmth of his chambers. He dumped the papers on a sofa, and he was crossing to the sideboard for a stronger drink when he noticed the letter sitting on the table. How long had it been there?

Rhy's gaze flicked to his guards. Vis was standing by the dark wood doors, busying himself with a loose thread on his cape. Tolners was still on the balcony, looking down at the tournament construction with a faint crease between his brows.

Rhy took up the paper and unfolded it. The message scrawled in small black script wasn't in English or Arnesian, but Kas-Avnes, a rare border dialect Rhy had been taught several years before.

He'd always had a way with languages, as long as they belonged to men and not magic.

Rhy smiled at the sight of the dialect. As clever as using code, and far less noticeable.

The note read:

Prince Rhy,

I disapprove wholeheartedly, and maintain the hope, however thin, that you will both regain your senses. In the event that you do not, I've made the necessary arrangements—may they not come to haunt me. We will discuss the cost of your endeavors this afternoon. Maybe the steams will prove clarifying. Regardless of your decision, I expect a substantial donation will be made to the London Sanctuary when this is over.

Your servant, elder, and Aven Essen,
Tieren Serense

Rhy smiled and set the note aside as bells chimed through the city, ringing out from the sanctuary itself across the river.

Maybe the steams will prove clarifying.

Rhy clapped his hands, startling the guards.

"Gentlemen," he said, taking up a robe. "I think I'm in the mood for a bath."

II

The world beneath the water was warm and still.

Rhy stayed under as long as he could, until his head swam, and his pulse thudded, and his chest began to ache, and then, and only then, he surfaced, filling his lungs with air.

He loved the royal baths, had spent many languorous afternoons—evenings, mornings—in them, but rarely alone. He was used to the laughter of boisterous company echoing off the stones, the playful embrace of a companion, kisses splashing on skin, but today the baths were silent save for the gentle drip of water. His guards stood on either side of the door, and a pair of attendants perched, waiting with pitchers of soap and oil, brushes, robes, and towels while Rhy strode through the waist-high water of the basin.

It took up half the room, a wide, deep pool of polished black rock, its edges trimmed in glass and gold. Light danced across the arched ceilings and the outer wall broken only by high, thin windows filled with colored glass.

The water around him was still sloshing from his ascent, and he splayed his fingers across the surface, waiting for the ripples to smooth again.

It was a game he used to play when he was young, trying to see if he could still the surface of the water. Not with magic, just with patience. Growing up, he'd been even worse at waiting than he was at summoning elements, but these days, he was getting better. He stood in the very center of the bath and slowed his breathing, watched the water go still and smooth as glass. Soon his reflection resolved in its surface, mirror-clear, and Rhy considered his black hair and amber eyes before his gaze invariably drifted down over his brown shoulders to the mark on his chest.

The circles wound together in a way that was both intuitive and foreign. A symbol of death and life. He focused and became aware of the pulse in his ears, the echo of Kell's own, both beats growing louder and louder, until Rhy expected the sound to ruin the glassy stillness of the water.

A subtle aura of peace broke the mounting pulse.

"Your Highness," said Vis from his place at the door. "You have a—"

"Let him pass," said the prince, his back to the guard. He closed his eyes and listened to the hushed tread of bare feet, the whisper of robes against stone: quiet, and yet loud enough to drown out his brother's heart.

"Good afternoon, Prince Rhy." The *Aven Essen*'s voice was a low thrum, softer than the king's but just as strong. Sonorous.

Rhy turned in a slow circle to face the priest, a smile alighting on his face. "Tieren. What a pleasant surprise."

The head priest of the London Sanctuary was not a large man, but his white robes hardly swallowed him. If anything, he grew to fill them, the fabric swishing faintly around him, even when he stood still. The air in the room changed with his presence, a calm settling over everything like snow. Which was good, because it counteracted the visible discomfort most seemed to feel around the man himself, shying away as if Tieren could see through them, straight past skin and bone to thought and want and soul. Which was probably why Vis was now studying his boots.

The *Aven Essen* was an intimidating figure to most—much

like Kell, Rhy supposed—but to him, Master Serense had always been *Tieren*.

"If this is a bad time . . ." the priest began, folding his hands into his sleeves.

"Not at all," said Rhy, ascending the glass stairs that lined the bath on every side. He could feel the eyes in the room drift to his chest: not only the symbol seared into the bronze skin, but the scar between his ribs, where his knife—Astrid's knife—had gone in. But before the cool air could settle or the eyes could linger, an attendant was there, draping him in a plush red robe. "Please leave us," he said, addressing the rest of the room. The attendants instantly began to withdraw, but the guard lingered. "You too, Vis."

"Prince Rhy," he began, "I'm not supposed to . . ."

"It's all right," said Rhy drolly. "I don't think the *Aven Essen* means me any harm."

Tieren's silver brows inched up a fraction. "That remains to be seen," said the priest evenly.

Vis was halfway through a step back, but stopped again at the words. Rhy sighed. Ever since the Black Night, the royal guards had been given strict instructions when it came to their kingdom's heir. And its *Antari*. He didn't know the exact words his father had used, but he was fairly sure they included *don't let them* and *out of your sight* and possibly *on pain of death*.

"Vis," he said slowly, trying to summon a semblance of his father's stony command. "You insult me, and the head priest, with your enduring presence. There is one door in and out of this room. Stand on the other side with Tolners, and *guard it*."

The impression must have been convincing, because Vis nodded and reluctantly withdrew.

Tieren lowered himself onto a broad stone bench against the wall, his white robes pooling around him, and Rhy came to sit beside him, slumping back against the stones.

"Not much humor in this bunch," said Tieren when they were alone.

"None at all," complained Rhy, rolling his shoulders. "I swear, sincerity is its own form of punishment."

"The tournament preparations are coming along?"

"Indeed," said Rhy. "The arenas are almost ready, and the empire tents are positively decadent. I almost envy the magicians."

"Please tell me *you're* not thinking of competing, too."

"After all the trouble Kell went to, to keep me alive? That would be sore thanks."

The smallest frown formed between Tieren's eyes. On anyone else it would have been imperceptible, but on the *Aven Essen*'s calm face, it registered as discontent (though he claimed that Kell and Rhy were the only ones who managed to draw out that particular forehead crease).

"Speaking of Kell . . ." said Rhy.

Tieren's gaze sharpened. "Have you reconsidered?"

"Did you really think I would?"

"A man can hope."

Rhy shook his head. "Anything we should be worried about?"

"Besides your own foolish plans? I don't believe so."

"And the helmet?"

"It will be ready." The *Aven Essen* closed his eyes. "I'm getting too old for subterfuge."

"He needs this, Tieren," pressed Rhy. And then, with a coy smile, "How old *are* you?"

"Old enough," answered Tieren. "Why?" One eye opened. "Are my grey hairs showing?"

Rhy smiled. Tieren's head had been silver for as long as he could remember. Rhy loved the old man, and he suspected that, against Tieren's better judgment, he loved Rhy, too. As the *Aven Essen,* he was the protector of the city, a gifted healer, and a very close friend to the crown. He'd mentored Kell as he came into his powers, and nursed Rhy back to health whenever he was sick, or when he'd done something foolish and didn't want to get caught. He and Kell had certainly kept the old man busy over the years.

"You know," said Tieren slowly, "you really should be more careful about who sees your mark."

Rhy flashed him a look of mock affront. "You can't expect me to remain clothed *all* the time, Master Tieren."

"I do suppose that would be too much to ask."

Rhy tipped his head back against the stones. "People assume it's just a scar from that night," he said, "which is exactly what it is, and as long as *Kell* remains clothed—which, let's be honest, is a *much* easier demand—no one will realize it's anything more."

Tieren sighed, his universal signal for discontent. The truth was that the mark unsettled Rhy, more than he wanted to admit, and hiding it only made it feel more like a curse. And, strangely, it was all he had. Looking down at his arms, his chest, Rhy saw that aside from the silvery burst of spell work, and the knife wound that looked so small and pale beneath, he bore very few scars. The seal wasn't pleasant, but it was a scar he'd earned. And one he needed to live with.

"People whisper," observed Tieren.

"If I make a point of hiding it any more than I do, they will just whisper *more*."

What would have happened, wondered Rhy, *if I had gone to Tieren with my fears of weakness, instead of accepting Holland's gift for strength? Would the priest have known what to say? How to help?* Rhy had confessed to Tieren, in the weeks after the incident. Told him about accepting the talisman—the possession charm—expecting one of the old man's reprimands. Instead Tieren had listened, speaking only when Rhy was out of words.

"Strength and weakness are tangled things," the *Aven Essen* had said. "They look so much alike, we often confuse them, the way we confuse magic and power."

Rhy had found the response flip, but in the months that

followed, Tieren had been there, at Rhy's side, a reminder and a support.

When he looked over at Tieren now, the man was staring at the water, past it, as if he could see something there, reflected in the surface, or the steam.

Maybe Rhy could learn to do that. Scry. But Tieren told him once it wasn't so much about looking out as looking in, and Rhy wasn't sure he wanted to spend any more time than necessary doing that. Still, he couldn't shake the feeling—the hope—that everyone was born with the ability to do *something,* that if he just searched hard enough he would find it. His gift. His *purpose.*

"Well," said Rhy, breaking the silence, "do you find the waters to your liking?"

"Why won't you leave me in peace?"

"There's too much to do."

Tieren sighed. "As it seems you will not be dissuaded . . ." He drew a scroll from the folded sleeves of his robes. "The final list of competitors."

Rhy straightened and took the paper.

"It will be posted in the next day or two," explained the priest, "once we receive the lists from Faro and Vesk. But I thought you'd want to see it first." There was something in his tone, a gentle caution, and Rhy undid the ribbon and uncoiled the scroll with nervous fingers, unsure of what he'd find. As the city's *Aven Essen,* it was Master Tieren's task to select the twelve representatives of Arnes.

Rhy scanned the list, his attention first landing on *Kamerov Loste*—he felt a thrill at seeing the name, an invention, a fiction made real—before a name farther down snagged his gaze, a thorn hidden among roses.

Alucard Emery.

Rhy winced, recoiled, but not before the name drew blood. "How?" he asked, his voice low, almost hollow.

"Apparently," said Tieren, "you're not the only one capable of pulling strings. And before you get upset, you should know that Emery broke *far* fewer rules than you have. In fact, he technically broke none. He auditioned for me in the fall, when the *Spire* was docked, and as far as I'm concerned, he's the strongest one in the ranks. Two weeks ago his sister came to me, to refresh my memory and to petition his place, though I think she simply wants him to come home. If that's not enough, there's the matter of the loophole."

Rhy tried to keep himself from crumpling the paper. "What loophole?"

"Emery was formally invited to compete three years ago, but . . ." Tieren hesitated, looking uncomfortable. "Well, we both know that certain circumstances prevented that. He's entitled to a spot."

Rhy wanted to climb back into the bath and vanish beneath the water. Instead he slowly, methodically rolled the paper up and retied it with string.

"And here I thought you might be happy," said Tieren. "The mystery and madness of youth is clearly lost on me."

Rhy folded forward, rubbing his neck, and then his shoulder. His fingers found the scar over his heart, and he traced the lines absently, a recent habit. The skin was silvery and smooth, just barely raised, but he knew that the seal went all the way through, flesh and bone and soul.

"Let me see," said Tieren, standing.

Rhy was grateful for the change of focus. He tipped his head out of the way and let the man examine his shoulder, pressing one cool, dry hand to the front, and one to the back. Rhy felt a strange warmth spreading through him along the lines of the spell. "Has the bond weakened?"

Rhy shook his head. "If anything, it seems to be growing stronger. At first, the echoes were dull, but now . . . it's not just pain, either, Tieren. Pleasure, fatigue. But also anger, restlessness. Like right now, if I clear my head, I can feel Kell's"—he hesitated, reaching for his brother—"weariness. It's exhausting."

"That makes sense," said Tieren, hands falling away. "This isn't simply a physical bond. You and Kell are sharing a life force."

"You mean I'm sharing *his*," corrected Rhy. His own life had been cut off by the dagger driven into his chest. What he had, he was siphoning off Kell. The heat of the bath had vanished, and Rhy was left feeling tired and cold.

"Self-pity is not a good look on you, Your Highness," said Tieren, shuffling toward the door.

"Thank you," Rhy called after him, holding up the scroll. "For this."

Tieren said nothing, only crinkled his brow faintly—there it was again, that line—and vanished.

Rhy sank back against the bench, and considered the list again, Kamerov's name so close to Alucard's.

One thing was certain.

It was going to be one hell of a tournament.

III

The guards met Kell at the mouth of the Naresh Kas, as planned.

Staff with his barrel chest and silvering temples and beard, and Hastra, young and cheerful, with a sun-warmed complexion and a crown of dark curls. *At least he's pretty,* Rhy had said months ago, on seeing the new guards. The prince had been sulking because his own set, Tolners and Vis, had neither looks nor humor.

"Gentlemen," said Kell as his coat settled around him in the alley. The guards looked cold, and he wondered how long they'd been waiting for him.

"I would have brought you a hot drink, but . . ." He held up his empty hands as if to say, *rules.*

"S'okay, Master Kell," said Hastra through clenched teeth, missing the jab. Staff, on the other hand, said nothing.

They had the decency not to search him then and there, but rather turned and fell silently in step behind him as he set off in the direction of the palace. He could feel the eyes drifting toward their small procession, any chance at blending in ruined by the presence of the royal guards flanking him in their gleaming armor and red cloaks.

Kell would have preferred subterfuge, the suspicion of being followed, to the actuality, but he straightened his shoulders and held his head high and tried to remind himself that he looked like a royal, even if he felt like prisoner.

He hadn't even done anything wrong, not today, and saints knew he'd had the chance. *Several* chances.

At last they reached the palace steps, strewn even now with frost-dusted flowers.

"The king?" Kell asked as they strode through the entryway.

Staff led the way to a chamber where King Maxim stood near a blazing hearth, in conversation with several *ostra*. When he saw Kell, he dismissed them. Kell kept his head up, but none of the attendants met his gaze. When they were gone, the king nodded him forward.

Kell continued into middle of the room before spreading his arms for Staff and Hastra in a gesture that was as much challenge as invitation.

"Don't be dramatic," said Maxim.

The guards had the decency to look uncertain as they came forward.

"Rhy must be rubbing off on me, Your Majesty," said Kell grimly as Staff helped him out of his coat, and Hastra patted down his shirt and trousers, and ran a hand around the lip of his boots. He didn't have anything on his person, and they wouldn't be able to find anything in his coat, not unless he wanted it to be found. He sometimes worried that the coat had a mind of its own. The only other person who'd ever managed to find what they wanted in its pockets was Lila. He'd never found out how she'd done that. Traitorous coat.

Staff withdrew the Grey London letter from one of the pockets, and delivered it to the king before handing the coat back to Kell.

"How was the king?" asked Maxim, taking the letter.

"Dead," said Kell. That caught the man off guard. He recounted his visit, and the Prince Regent's—now George IV's—renewed interest in magic. He even mentioned that the new king had tried to bribe him, taking care to emphasize the fact that he'd *declined* the offer.

Maxim stroked his beard and looked troubled, but he said nothing, only waved a hand to show Kell that he was dismissed. He turned, feeling his mood darken, but as Staff and Hastra moved to follow, Maxim called them back.

"Leave him be," he said, and Kell was grateful for that small kindness as he escaped to his rooms.

His relief didn't last. When he reached the doors to his chamber, he found two more guards standing outside them. The men were Rhy's.

"Saints, I swear you just keep multiplying," he muttered.

"Sir?" said Tolners.

"Nothing," grumbled Kell, pushing past them. There was only one reason Tolners and Vis would be stationed outside *his* door.

He found Rhy standing in the middle of his room, his back to Kell as he considered himself in a full-length mirror. From this angle, Kell couldn't see Rhy's face, and for a moment, a memory surged into his mind, of Rhy waiting for him to wake—only it hadn't been Rhy, of course, but Astrid wearing his skin, and they were in Rhy's chambers then, not his. But for an instant the details blurred and he found himself searching Rhy for any pendants or charms, searching his floor for blood, before the past crumbled back into memory.

"About time," said Rhy, and Kell was secretly relieved when the voice that came from Rhy's lips was undoubtedly his brother's.

"What brings you to my room?" he asked, relief bleeding into annoyance.

"Adventure. Intrigue. Brotherly concern. Or," continued the prince lazily, "perhaps I'm just giving your mirror something to look at besides your constant pout."

Kell frowned, and Rhy smiled. "Ah, there it is! That famous scowl."

"I don't scowl," grumbled Kell.

Rhy shot a conspiratorial look at his own reflection. Kell sighed and tossed his coat onto the nearest couch before heading for the alcove off his chamber.

"What are you doing?" Rhy called after.

"Hold on," Kell called back, shutting the door between them. A single candle flickered to life, and by its light he saw the symbols drawn on the wood. There, amid the other marks and fresh with blood, was the doorway to Disan. The way to Windsor Castle. Kell reached out and rubbed at the mark until it was obscured, and then gone.

When Kell returned, Rhy was sitting in Kell's favorite chair, which he'd dragged around so it was facing the room instead of the balcony doors. "What was that about?" he asked, head resting in his hand.

"That's my chair," said Kell flatly.

"Battered old thing," said Rhy, knowing how fond Kell was of it. The prince had mischief in his pale gold eyes as he got to his feet.

"I'm still nursing a headache," said Kell. "So if you're here to force me on another outing—"

"That's not why I'm here," said Rhy, crossing to the sideboard. He started to pour himself a drink, and Kell was about to say something very unkind when he saw that it was simply tea.

He nodded at one of the sofas. "Sit down."

Kell would have stood out of spite, but he was weary from the trip, and he sank onto the nearest sofa. Rhy finished fixing his tea and sat down opposite.

"Well?" prompted Kell.

"I thought Tieren was supposed to teach you patience," chided Rhy. He set the tea on the table and drew a wooden box from underneath. "I wanted to apologize."

"For what?" asked Kell. "The lying? The drinking? The fighting? The relentless—" But something in Rhy's expression made him stop.

The prince raked the black curls from his face, and Kell realized that he looked older. Not *old*—Rhy was only twenty, a year and a half younger than Kell—but the edges of his face had sharpened, and his bright eyes were less amazed, more intense. He'd grown up, and Kell couldn't help but wonder if it was all natural, the simple, inevitable progression of time, or if the last dregs of his youth had been stripped away by what had happened.

"Look," said the prince, "I know things have been hard. Harder these past months than ever. And I know I've only made it worse."

"Rhy—"

The prince held up his hand to silence him. "I've been difficult."

"So have I," admitted Kell.

"You really have."

Kell found himself chuckling, but shook his head. "One life is a hard thing to keep hold of, Rhy. Two is . . ."

"We'll find our stride," insisted the prince. And then he shrugged. "Or you'll get us both killed."

"How can you say that with such levity?" snapped Kell, straightening.

"Kell." Rhy sat forward, elbows on his knees. "I was dead."

The words hung in the air between them.

"I was *dead*," he said again, "and you brought me back. You have already given me something I shouldn't have." A shadow flashed across his face when he said it, there and then gone. "If it were lost again," he went on, "I would still have lived twice. This is all borrowed."

"No," said Kell sternly, "it is bought and paid for."

"For how long?" countered Rhy. "You cannot measure out what you have purchased. I am grateful for the life you've bought me, though I hate the cost. But what do you plan to do, Kell? Live forever? I don't want that."

Kell frowned. "You would rather die?"

Rhy looked tired. "Death comes for us all, Brother. You cannot hide from it forever. We *will* die one day, you and I."

"And that doesn't frighten you?"

Rhy shrugged. "Not nearly as much as the idea of wasting a perfectly good life in fear of it. And to that end . . ." He nudged the box toward Kell.

"What is it?"

"A peace offering. A present. Happy birthday."

Kell frowned. "My birthday's not for another month."

Rhy took up his tea. "Don't be ungrateful. Just take it."

Kell drew the box onto his knees and lifted the lid. Inside, a face stared up at him.

It was a helmet, made of a single piece of metal that curved from the chin over the top of the head and down to the base of the skull. A break formed the mouth, an arch the nose, and a browlike visor hid the wearer's eyes. Aside from this subtle shaping, the mask's only markings were a pair of decorative wings, one above each ear.

"Am I going into battle?" asked Kell, confused.

"Of a sort," said Rhy. "It's your mask, for the tournament."

Kell nearly dropped the helmet. "The *Essen Tasch*? Have you lost your mind?"

Rhy shrugged. "I don't think so. Not unless you've lost yours . . ." He paused. "Do you think it works that way? I mean, I suppose it—"

"I'm an *Antari*!" Kell cut in, struggling to keep his voice down. "I'm the adopted son of the Maresh crown, the strongest magician in the Arnesian empire, possibly in the *world*—"

"Careful, Kell, your ego is showing."

"—and you want me to compete in an inter-empire tournament."

"Obviously the great and powerful *Kell* can't compete," said Rhy. "That would be like rigging the game. It could start a war."

"*Exactly.*"

"Which is why you'll be in disguise."

Kell groaned, shaking his head. "This is insane, Rhy. And even if you were crazy enough to think it could work, Tieren would never allow it."

"Oh, he didn't. Not at first. He fought me tooth and nail. Called it madness. Called us fools—"

"It wasn't even my idea!"

"—but in the end he understood that approving of something and allowing it are not always the same thing."

Kell's eyes narrowed. "Why would Tieren change his mind?"

Rhy swallowed. "Because I told him the truth."

"And what's that?"

"That you needed it."

"Rhy—"

"That *we* needed it." He grimaced a little when he said it.

Kell hesitated, meeting his brother's gaze. "What do you mean?"

Rhy shoved himself up from the chair. "You're not the only one who wants to crawl out of their skin, Kell," he said, pacing. "I see the way this confinement is wearing on you." He tapped his chest. "I *feel* it. You spend hours training in the Basin with no one to fight, and you have not been at peace a single day since Holland, since the Danes, since the Black Night. And if you want the honest truth, unless you find some release"—Rhy stopped pacing—"I'll end up strangling you myself."

Kell winced, and looked down at the mask in his lap. He ran his fingers over the smooth silver. It was simple and elegant, the silver polished to such a shine that it was nearly a mirror. His reflection stared back at him, distorted. It was madness, and it frightened him, how badly he wanted to agree to it. But he couldn't.

He set the mask on the sofa. "It's too dangerous."

"Not if we're careful," insisted his brother.

"We're tethered to each other, Rhy. My pain becomes your pain."

"I'm well aware of our condition."

"Then you know I can't. I *won't*."

"I am not only your brother," said Rhy. "I am your prince. And I command it. You will compete in the *Essen Tasch*. You will burn off some of this fire before it spreads."

"And what about our bond? If I get hurt—"

"Then I will share your pain," said Rhy levelly.

"You say that now, but—"

"Kell. My greatest fear in life isn't dying. It's being the source of someone else's suffering. I know you feel trapped. I know I'm your cage. And I can't—" His voice broke, and Kell could feel his brother's pain, everything he tried to smother until dark and drown until morning. "You *will* do this," said Rhy. "For me. For both of us."

Kell held his brother's gaze. "All right," he said.

Rhy's features faltered, and then he broke into a smile. Unlike the rest of his face, his grin was as boyish as ever. "You will?"

Kell felt a thrill go through him as he took up the mask again. "I will. But if I'm not competing as myself," he said, "then who will I be?"

Rhy reached into the box and withdrew from among the wrappings a scroll of paper Kell hadn't noticed. He held it out, and when Kell unfurled it he saw the Arnesian roster. Twelve names. The men and women representing their empire.

There was Kisimyr, of course, as well as Alucard (a thrill ran through Kell at the thought of having an excuse to fight him). He skimmed past them, searching.

"I picked out your name myself," said Rhy. "You'll be competing as—"

"Kamerov Loste," answered Kell, reading the seventh name aloud.

Of course.

K. L.

The letters carved into the knife he wore on his forearm. The only things that had come with him from his previous life, whatever it was. Those letters had become his name—*KL, Ka-El, Kell*—but how many nights had he spent wondering what they stood for? How many nights had he dreamed up names for himself?

"Oh, come on," chided Rhy, misreading Kell's tension for annoyance. "It's a good name! Rather princely, if I do say so."

"It'll do," said Kell, fighting back a smile as he set the scroll aside.

"Well," said Rhy, taking up the helmet and holding it out to Kell. "Try it on."

Kell hesitated. The prince's voice was light, the invitation casual, but there was more to the gesture, and they both knew it. If Kell put on the mask, this would cease to be a stupid, harmless idea and become something more. Something real. He reached out and took the helmet.

"I hope it fits," said Rhy. "You've always had a big head."

Kell slipped the helmet on, standing as he did. The inside was soft, the fit made snug by the padding. The visor cut all the way from ear to ear, so his vision and hearing were both clear.

"How do I look?" he asked, his voice muffled slightly by the metal.

"See for yourself," said Rhy, nodding at the mirror. Kell turned toward the glass. It was eerie, the polished metal creating an almost tunneling reflection, and the cut of the visor hid his gaze so that even though he could see fine, no one would be able to see that one of his eyes was blue and the other black.

"I'm going to stand out," he said.

"It's the *Essen Tasch*," said Rhy. "Everyone stands out."

And while it was true that everyone wore *masks* and it was part of the drama, the tradition, this wasn't just a mask. "Most competitors don't dress as though they're going to war."

Rhy crossed his arms and gave him an appraising look. "Yes, well, most competitors don't truly *need* to maintain their anonymity, but your features are . . . unique."

"Are you calling me ugly?"

Rhy snorted. "We both know you're the prettiest boy at the ball."

Kell couldn't stop cheating glances in the mirror. The silver helmet hovered over his simple black clothes, but something was missing. . . .

His coat was still draped on the back of the couch. He took it up and shook it slightly as he turned it inside out, and as he did, his usual black jacket with silver buttons became something else. Something new.

"I've never seen that one before," said Rhy. Neither had Kell, not until a few days earlier, when he'd gotten bored and decided to see what other sides the coat had tucked away (now and then, unused outfits seemed to disappear, new ones turning up in their place).

Kell had wondered at the sudden appearance of this one, so unlike the others, but now, as he shrugged it on, he realized that was because this coat didn't belong to him.

It belonged to *Kamerov*.

The coat was knee-length and silver, trimmed in a patterned border of black and lined with bloodred silk. The sleeves were narrow and the bottom flared, the collar high enough to reach the base of his skull.

Kell slipped the coat on, fastening the clasps, which cut an asymmetrical line from shoulder to hip. Rhy had gone rooting around in Kell's closet, and now he reemerged with a silver walking stick. He tossed it, and Kell plucked it out of the air, his fingers curled around the black lion's head that shaped the handle.

And then he turned back to his reflection.

"Well, Master Loste," said Rhy, stepping back, "you do look splendid."

Kell didn't recognize the man in the mirror, and not simply because the mask hid his face. No, it was his posture, too, shoulders straight and head up, his gaze level behind the visor.

Kamerov Loste was an impressive figure.

A breeze wove gently around him, ruffling his coat. Kell smiled.

"About that," said Rhy, referring to the swirling air. "For obvious reasons, Kamerov can't be an *Antari*. I suggest you pick an element and stick with it. Two if you must—I've heard there are quite a few duals this year—but triads are rare enough to draw attention. . . ."

"Mmhmm," said Kell, adjusting his pose.

"While I'm sympathetic to your sudden bout of narcissism," said Rhy, "this is important, Kell. When you're wearing that mask, you cannot be the most powerful magician in Arnes."

"I understand." Kell tugged the helmet back off and struggled to smooth his hair. "Rhy," he said, "are you certain . . . ?" His heart was racing. He wanted this. He shouldn't want this. It was a terrible idea. But he wanted it all the same. Kell's blood sang at the idea of a fight. A good fight.

Rhy nodded.

"All right, then."

"So you've come to your senses?"

Kell shook his head, dazed. "Or lost my mind." But he was smiling now, so hard he felt his face might crack.

He turned the helmet over and over in his hands.

And then, as suddenly as his spirits had soared, they sank.

"*Sanct*," he cursed, sagging back onto the couch. "What about my guards?"

"Silver and Gold?" asked Rhy, his pet names for the men. "What about them?"

"I can't exactly ditch Staff and Hastra for the entire length of the tournament. Nor can I conveniently misplace them for each and every bout."

"I'm sorry, I thought you were a master magician."

Kell threw up his hands. "It has nothing to do with my skill, Rhy. There's suspicious, and then there's obvious."

"Well, then," said the prince, "we'll just have to tell them."

"And they'll tell the king. And do you want to guess what the king will do? Because I'm willing to bet he won't risk the stability of the kingdom so I can let off some steam."

Rhy pinched the bridge of his nose. Kell frowned. That gesture, it didn't suit the prince; it was something *he* would do, had done a hundred times.

"Leave it to me," he said. He crossed to Kell's doors and swung them open, leaning against the frame. Kell hoped the guards had truly stayed behind when he left King Maxim, but they must have only granted him a berth, because Rhy called them in, closing the door before his own guards could follow.

Kell rose to his feet, unsure what his brother meant to do.

"Staff," said Rhy, addressing the man with silver temples. "When my father assigned you to shadow Kell, what did he say?"

Staff looked from Kell to Rhy, as if it were a trap, a trick question. "Well . . . he said we were to watch, and to keep him from harm, and to report to His Majesty if we saw Master Kell doing anything . . . suspicious."

Kell scowled, but Rhy flashed an encouraging smile. "Is that so, Hastra?"

The guard with dark gold hair bowed his head. "Yes, Your Highness."

"But if you were informed about something in advance, then it wouldn't be suspicious, would it?"

Hastra looked up. "Um . . . no, Your Highness?"

"Rhy," protested Kell, but the prince held his hand up.

"You both swore your lives to this family, this crown, and this empire. Does your oath hold?"

Both men bowed their heads and brought their hands to their

chests. "Of course, Your Highness," they said, almost in unison. *What on earth is Rhy getting at?* wondered Kell.

And then, the prince's countenance changed. The easiness fell away, as did his cheerful smile. His posture straightened and his jaw clenched, and in that moment he looked less like a prince than a future king. He looked like *Maxim*.

"Then understand this," he said, his voice now low and stern. "What I'm about to tell you regards the safety and security of not only our family, but of the Arnesian empire."

The men's eyes went wide with concern. Kell's narrowed.

"We believe there is a threat in the tournament." Rhy shot Kell a knowing look, though Kell honestly had no idea where he was going with this. "In order to determine the nature of this threat, Kell will be competing in the *Essen Tasch*, disguised as an ordinary entrant, Kamerov Loste."

The guards frowned, cheating looks toward Kell, who managed a stiff nod. "The secrecy of my identity," he cut in, "is paramount. If either Faro or Vesk discovers my involvement, they'll assume we've rigged the game."

"My father already knows of Kell's inclusion," added Rhy. "He has his own matters to attend to. If you see anything during the tournament, you will tell Kell himself, or me."

"But how are we supposed to guard him?" asked Staff. "If he's pretending to be someone else?"

Rhy didn't miss a beat. "One of you will pose as his second—every competitor needs an attendant—and the other will continue to guard him from a safe distance."

"I've always wanted to be in a plot," whispered Hastra. And then, raising his voice, "Your Highness, could I be the one in disguise?" His eagerness was a barely contained thing.

Rhy looked to Kell, who nodded. Hastra beamed, and Rhy brought his hands together in a soft, decisive clap. "So it's settled. As long as Kell is Kell, you will guard him with your usual attentiveness. But when dealing with Kamerov, the illusion must be flawless, the secret held."

The two guards nodded solemnly and were dismissed. *Saints,* thought Kell as the doors swung shut. *He's actually done it.*

"There," said Rhy, slouching onto the couch. "That wasn't so hard."

Kell looked at his brother with a mixture of surprise and awe. "You know," he said, taking up the mask, "if you can rule half as well as you can lie, you're going to make an incredible king."

Rhy's smile was a dazzling thing. "Thank you."

IV

Sasenroche.

It was late by the time Lila made her way back to the *Night Spire*. Sasenroche had quieted, and it had started to sleet, an icy mix that turned to slush on the deck and had to be swept away before it froze solid.

Back in her London—*old* London—Lila had always hated winter.

Longer nights meant more hours in which to steal, but the people who ventured out usually didn't have a choice, which made them poor marks. Worse than that, in winter, everything was damp and grey and bitter cold.

So many nights in her past life, she had gone to bed shivering. Nights she couldn't afford wood or coal, so she'd put on every piece of clothing she owned and huddled down and froze. Heat cost money, but so did food and shelter and every other blasted thing you needed to survive, and sometimes you had to choose.

But here, if Lila practiced, she could summon fire with her fingertips, could keep it burning on nothing but magic and will. She was determined to master it, not just because fire was useful or dangerous, but because it was *warm,* and no matter what happened, Lila Bard never wanted to be cold again.

That was why Lila favored fire.

She blew out a puff of air. Most of the men stayed behind to enjoy the night on land, but Lila preferred her room on the ship, and she wanted to be alone so she could think.

London. Her pulse lifted at the thought. It had been four months since she first boarded the *Night Spire.* Four months since she said good-bye to a city she didn't even know, its name the only tether to her old life. She'd planned to go back, of course. Eventually. What would Kell say, when he saw her? Not that *that* was her first thought. It wasn't. It was sixth, or maybe seventh, somewhere below all the ones about Alucard and the *Essen Tasch.* But it was still *there,* swimming in her head.

Lila sighed, her breath clouding as she leaned her elbows on the ship's slush-covered rail and looked down at the tide as it sloshed up against the hull. Lila favored fire, but it wasn't her only trick.

Her focus narrowed on the water below, and as it did, she tried to push the current back, away. The nearest wave stuttered, but the rest kept coming. Lila's head had begun to hurt, pounding in time with the waves, but she gripped the splintered rail, determined. She imagined she could *feel* the water—not only the shudder traveling up the boat, but the energy coursing through it. Wasn't magic supposed to be the thing in all things? If that was true, then it wasn't about moving the water, it was about moving the *magic.*

She thought of "The Tyger," the poem she used to focus her mind, with its strong and steady beat . . . but it was a song for fire. No, she wanted something else. Something that flowed.

"Sweet dreams," she murmured, summoning a line from another Blake poem, trying to get the feeling right. *"Of pleasant streams . . . "* She said the line over and over again until the water filled her vision, until the sound of the sloshing waves was all she could hear, and the beat of them matched the beat of her pulse and she could feel the current in her veins, and the water up and down the dock began to still, and . . .

A dark drop hit the rail between her hands.

Lila lifted her fingers to her nose; they came away stained with blood.

Someone *tsk*ed, and Lila's head snapped up. How long had Alucard been standing at her back?

"Please tell me you didn't just try to exert your will on the *ocean*," he said, offering her a kerchief.

"I almost did it," she insisted, holding the cloth to her face. It smelled like him. His magic, a strange mixture of sea air and honey, silver and spice.

"Not that I doubt your potential, Bard, but that's not possible."

"Maybe not for *you*," she jabbed, even though in truth she was still unnerved by what she'd seen him do back in the tavern.

"Not for *anyone*," said Alucard, slipping into his teacher's voice. "I've told you: when you control an element, your will has to be able to encompass it. It has to be able to reach, to surround. That's how you shape an element, and that's how you command it. No one can stretch their mind around an ocean. Not without tearing. Next time, aim sma—"

He cut off as a clod of icy slush struck the shoulder of his coat. "Agh!" he said, as bits slipped down his collar. "I know where you sleep, Bard."

She smirked. "Then you know I sleep with knives."

His smile faltered. "Still?"

She shrugged and turned back to the water. "The way they treat me—"

"I've made my orders very clear," he said, obviously assuming she'd been misused. But that wasn't it.

"—like I'm one of them," she finished.

Alucard blinked, confused. "Why shouldn't they? You're part of the crew."

Lila cringed. *Crew.* The very word referred to more than one. But belonging meant caring, and caring was a dangerous thing. At best, it complicated everything. At worst, it got people killed. People like Barron.

"Would you rather they try to knife you in the dark?" asked the captain. "Toss you overboard and pretend it was an accident?"

"Of course not," said Lila. But at least then she'd know how to react. Fights she recognized. Friendship? She didn't know what to do with that. "They're probably too scared to try it."

"Some of them may fear you, but all of them respect you. And don't let on," he added, nudging her shoulder with his, "but a few may even *like* you."

Lila groaned, and Alucard chuckled.

"Who are you?" he asked.

"I'm Delilah Bard," she said calmly. "The best thief aboard the *Night Spire*."

Normally Alucard left it at that, but not tonight. "But who *was* Delilah Bard before she came aboard my ship?"

Lila kept her eyes on the water. "Someone else," she said. "And she'll be someone else again when she leaves."

Alucard blew out a puff of air, and the two stood there, side by side on deck, staring out into the fog. It sat above the water, blurring the line between sea and sky, but it wasn't entirely still. It shifted and twisted and curled, the motions as faint and fluid as the rocking of the water.

The sailors called it scrying fog—supposedly, if you stared at it long enough, you began to see things. Whether they were visions or just a trick of the eye depended on who you asked.

Lila squinted at the coiling mist, expecting nothing—she'd never had a particularly vivid imagination—but after a moment she thought she saw the fog began to shift, begin to *change*. The effect was strangely entrancing, and Lila found she couldn't look away as tendrils of ghostly mist became fingers, and then a hand, reaching toward her through the dark.

"So." Alucard's voice was like a rock crashing through the vision. "London."

She exhaled, the cloud of breath devouring the view. "What about it?"

"I thought you'd be happy. Or sad. Or angry. In truth, I thought you'd be *something*."

Lila cocked her head. "And why would you think that?"

"It's been four months. I figured you left for a reason."

She gave him a hard look. "Why did *you* leave?"

A pause, the briefest shadow, and then he shrugged. "To see the world."

Lila shrugged. "Me, too."

They were both lies, or at best, partial truths, but for once, neither challenged the other, and they turned away from the water and crossed the deck in silence, guarding their secrets against the cold.

V

White London.

Even the stars burned in color now.

What he'd always taken for white had become an icy blue, and the night sky, once black, now registered as a velvet purple, the deepest edge of a bruise.

Holland sat on the throne, gazing up past the vaulting walls at the wide expanse of sky, straining to pick out the colors of his world. Had they always been there, buried beneath the film of failing magic, or were they new? Forest-green vines crept, dark and luscious, around the pale stone pillars that circled the throne room, their emerald leaves reaching toward silver moonlight as their roots trailed across the floor and into the still, black surface of the scrying pool.

How many times had Holland dreamed of sitting on this throne? Of slitting Athos's throat, driving a blade into Astrid's heart, and taking back his life. How many times . . . and yet it hadn't been his hand at all, in the end.

It had been Kell's.

The same hand that had driven a metal bar through Holland's chest, and pushed his dying body into the abyss.

Holland rose to his feet, the rich folds of his cape settling around him as he descended the steps of the dais, coming to a stop before the black reflective pool. The throne room stood empty around him. He'd dismissed them all, the servants and the guards, craving solitude. But there was no such thing, not anymore. His reflection stared up from the glassy surface of the water, like a window in the dark, his green eye a gem floating on the water, his black eye vanishing into the depths. He looked younger, but of course even in youth, Holland had never looked like *this*. The blush of health, the softness of a life without pain.

Holland stood perfectly still, but his reflection moved.

A tip of the head, the edge of a smile, the green eye devoured in black.

We make a fine king, said the reflection, words echoing in Holland's head.

"Yes," said Holland, his voice even. "We do."

Black London.
Three months ago.

Darkness.
    Everywhere.
    The kind that stretched.
    For seconds and hours and days.
    And then.
    Slowly.
    The darkness lightened into dusk.

The nothing gave way to something, pulled itself together until there was ground, and air, and a world between.

A world that was impossibly, unnaturally still.

Holland lay on the cold earth, blood matted to his front and back where the metal bar had passed through. Around his body, the dusk had a strange permanence to it, no lingering tendrils of daylight, no edge of approaching night. There was a heavy quiet to this place, like shelves beneath long-settled dust. An abandoned house. A body without breath.

Until Holland gasped.

The dusty world shuddered around him in response, as if by breathing, he breathed life into it, set the time stuttering forward into motion. Flecks of dirt—or ash, or something else—that had been hanging in the air above him, the way motes seemed to do when caught in threads of sunlight, now drifted down, settling like snow on his hair, his cheeks, his clothes.

Pain. Everything was pain.

But he was alive.

Somehow—impossibly—he was alive.

His whole body hurt—not just the wound in his chest, but his muscles and bones—as if he'd been lying on the ground for days, weeks, and every shallow breath sent spikes through his lungs. He should be dead. Instead he braced himself, and sat up.

His vision swam for a moment, but to his relief, the pain in his chest didn't worsen. It remained a heavy ache, pulsing in time with his heart. He looked around and discovered he was sitting in a walled garden, or at least, what might have once been a garden; the plants had long since withered, and what still stood of vine and stem looked ready to crumble to ash at a touch.

Where was he?

Holland searched his memory, but the last image he had was of Kell's face, set in grim determination even as he struggled against the water Holland had used to bind him, Kell's eyes narrowing in focus, followed by the spike of pain in Holland's back, the metal rod tearing through flesh and muscle, shattering ribs and rending the scar on his chest. So much pain, and then surrender, and then nothing.

But that fight had been in another London. This place held none of that city's floral odor, none of its pulsing magic. Nor was it *his* London—this Holland knew with equal certainty, for though it shared the barren atmosphere, the colorless palette, it lacked the bitter cold, the scent of ash and metal.

Vaguely, Holland recalled lying in the Stone Forest, numb to everything but the slow fading of his pulse. And after, the drag of the abyss. A darkness he assumed was death. But death had rejected him, delivering him to this place.

And it could only be one place.

Black London.

Holland had stopped bleeding and his fingers drifted absently, automatically, not to the wound but to the silver circle that had fastened his cloak—the mark of the Danes' control—only to discover it was gone, as was the cloak itself. His shirt was ripped, and the skin beneath, once scarred silver by Athos's seal, was now a mess of torn flesh and dried blood. Only then, with his fingers hovering over the wound, did Holland feel the change. It had been overshadowed by the shock and pain and strange surroundings, but now it prickled across his skin and through his veins, a lightness he hadn't felt in seven years.

Freedom.

Athos's spell had been broken, the binding shattered. But how? The magic was bound to soul, not skin—Holland knew, had tried to cut it away a dozen times—and could only be broken by its caster.

Which could only mean one thing.

Athos Dane was *dead*.

The knowledge shuddered through Holland with unexpected intensity, and he gasped, and gripped the desiccated ground beneath him. Only it wasn't desiccated anymore. While the world to every side had the bleak stillness of a winter landscape, the ground beneath Holland, the place where his blood had soaked into the soil, was a rich and waking green.

Beside him on the grass sat the black stone—*Vitari*—and he tensed before he realized it was hollow. Empty.

He patted himself down for weapons. He'd never been particularly concerned with them, preferring his own sharp talents to the clumsier edge of a blade, but his head was swimming and, considering how much strength it was taking just to stay upright, he honestly wasn't sure he had any magic to summon at the moment. He'd lost his curved blade back in the other London, but he found a dagger against his shin. He pressed the tip to the hard ground and used it to help push himself to his knees, then his feet.

Once he was up—he bit back a wave of dizziness and a swell of pain—Holland saw that the greenery wasn't entirely confined to his impression on the ground. It trailed away from him, forging a kind of path. It was little more than a thread of green, woven through the barren earth, a narrow strip of grass and weed and wildflower, disappearing through the walled arch at the far end of the garden.

Haltingly, Holland followed.

His chest throbbed and his body ached, his veins still starved of blood, but the ribs he knew were broken had begun to heal, and the muscles held, and slowly Holland found a semblance of his old stride.

Years under the cruelty of Athos Dane had taught him to bear his pain in silence, and now he gritted his teeth and followed the ribbon of life as it led him beyond the garden wall and into the road.

Holland's breath caught in his chest, sending a fresh spike through his shoulder. The city sprawled around him, a version of London at once familiar and entirely *other*. The buildings were elegant, impossible structures, carved out of glassy stone, their shapes drifting toward the sky like smoke. They reflected what little light was left as the dusk thickened into twilight, but there was no other source of light. No lanterns on hooks or fires in hearths. Holland had keen eyes, so it wasn't the pressing dark that bothered him, but what it meant. Either there was no one here to *need* the light, or what remained preferred the darkness.

Everyone assumed Black London had consumed itself, destroyed itself, like a fire starved of fuel and air. And while that seemed to be true, Holland knew that assumptions were made to take the place of facts, and the stretch of green at Holland's feet made him wonder if the world was truly dead, or merely *waiting*.

After all, you can kill people, but you cannot kill magic.

Not truly.

He followed the thread of new growth as it wove through the ghostly streets, reaching out here and there to brace himself against the smooth stone walls, peering as he did into windows, and finding nothing. No one.

He reached the river, the one that went by several names but ran through every London. It was black as ink, but that disturbed Holland less than the fact that it wasn't flowing. It wasn't frozen, like the Isle; being made of water, it couldn't have decayed, petrified with the rest of the city. And yet, there was no current. The impossible stillness only added to the unnerving sensation that Holland was standing in a piece of time rather than a place.

Eventually, the green path led him to the palace.

Much like the other buildings, it rose like smoke to the sky, its black spires disappearing into the haze of twilight. The gates hung open, their weight sagging on rusted hinges, the great steps cracked. The grassy thread continued, undeterred by the landscape. If anything, it seemed to thicken, braiding into a rope of vine and blossom as it climbed the broken stairs. Holland climbed with it, one hand pressed to his aching ribs.

The palace doors swung open beneath his touch, the air inside still and stagnant as a tomb, the vaulted ceilings reminiscent of White London's churchlike castle, but with smoother edges. The way the glassy stone continued inside and out, without sign of forge or seam, made it seem ethereal, impossible. This entire place had been made with magic.

The path of green persisted in front of him, winding over stone floors and beneath another pair of doors, massive panes of tinted glass with withered flowers trapped inside. Holland pushed the doors open, and found himself staring at a king.

His breath caught, before he realized the man before him,

cast in shadows, wasn't made of flesh and blood, but glassy black stone.

Just a statue seated on a throne.

But unlike the statues that filled the Stone Forest in front of the Danes' palace, this one was *clothed*. And the clothes seemed to *move*. The cloak around the king's shoulders fluttered, as if caught by a wind, and the king's hair, though *carved,* seemed to rustle gently in the breeze (even though there *was* no breeze in the room). A crown sat atop the king's head, and a wisp of grey a shade lighter than the stone itself swirled in the statue's open eyes. At first Holland thought it was simply part of the rock, but then the swirl of grey twitched, and moved. It coiled into pupils that drifted until they found Holland, and stopped.

Holland tensed.

The statue was *alive*.

Not in the way of men, perhaps, but alive all the same, in a simple, enduring way, like the grass at his feet. Natural. And yet entirely unnatural.

"*Oshoc,*" murmured Holland. A word for a piece of magic that broke away, became something more, something with a mind of its own. A will.

The statue said nothing. The wisps of grey smoke watched him from the king's face, and the thread of green trailed up the dais, wound itself around the *oshoc*'s throne and over one sculpted boot. Holland found himself stepping forward, until his shoes grazed the bottom of the throne's platform.

And then, at last, the statue spoke.

Not out loud, but in Holland's mind.

Antari.

"Who are you?" asked Holland.

I am king.

"Do you have a name?"

Again, the illusion of movement. The faintest gesture: a tightening of fingers on the throne, a tipping of the head, as if this were a riddle. *All things have names.*

"There was a stone found in my city," continued Holland, "and it called itself *Vitari*."

A smile seemed to flicker like light against the creature's petrified face. *I am not* Vitari, *he said smoothly.* But Vitari *was me.* Holland frowned, and the creature seemed to relish his confusion. *A leaf to a tree,* he said, indulgently.

Holland stiffened. The idea that the stone's power was a mere leaf compared to the thing that sat before him—the *thing* with its stone face and its calm manner and its eyes as old as the world . . .

My name, said the creature, *is Osaron.*

It was an old word, an *Antari* word, meaning *shadow.*

Holland opened his mouth to speak, but his air was cut off as another spasm of pain lurched through his chest. The grey smoke twisted.

Your body is weak.

Sweat slid down Holland's cheek, but he forced himself to straighten.

I saved you.

Holland didn't know if the *oshoc* meant that he'd saved his life once, or that he was still saving it. "Why?" he choked.

I was alone. Now we are together.

A shiver went through him. This was the *thing* that had feasted on an entire world of magicians. And now, somehow, Holland had woken it.

Another spasm of pain, and he felt one knee threaten to buckle.

You live because of me. But you are still dying.

Holland's vision slid in and out of focus. He swallowed, and tasted blood. "What happened to this world?" he asked.

The statue looked at him levelly. *It died.*

"Did you kill it?" Holland had always assumed that the Black London plague was something vast and un-fightable, that it was born from weakness and greed and hunger. It had never occurred to him that it could be a thing, an entity. An *oshoc*.

It died, repeated the shadow. *As all things do.*

"*How*?" demanded Holland. "*How* did it die?"

I . . . did not know, it said, *that humans were such fragile things. I have learned . . . how to be more careful. But . . .*

But it was too late, thought Holland. *There was no one left.*

I saved you, it said again, as if making a point.

"What do you want?"

To make a deal. The invisible wind around Holland picked up, and the statue of Osaron seemed to lean forward. *What do you want, Antari?*

He tried to steel his mind against the question, but answers poured through like smoke. To live. To be free. And then he thought of his world, starving for power, for life. Thought of it dying—not like this place, but slowly, painfully.

What do you want, Holland?

He wanted to save his world. Behind his eyes, the image began to change as London—*his* London—came back to life. He saw himself on the throne, staring up through a roofless palace at a bright blue sky, the warmth of the sun against his skin, and—

"No," he snapped, digging his hand into his wounded shoulder, the pain shocking him out of the vision. It was a trick, a trap.

All things come with a cost, said Osaron. *That is the nature of the world. Give and take. You can stay here and die for nothing while your world dies, too. Or you can save it. The choice is yours.*

"What do *you* want?" asked Holland.

To live, said the shadow. *I can save your life. I can save your world. It is a simple deal,* Antari. *My power for your body.*

"And whose mind?" challenged Holland. "Whose *will*?"

Ours, purred the king.

Holland's chest ached. Another binding. Would he never be free?

He closed his eyes, and he was back on that throne, gazing up at that wondrous sky.

Well, asked the shadow king. *Do we have a deal?*

FIVE

ROYAL WELCOME

I

The Arnesian Sea.

"Dammit, Bard, you're going to set the cat on fire."

Lila's head snapped up. She was perched on the edge of a chair in Alucard's cabin, holding a flame between her palms. Her attention must have slipped, because she'd lowered her hands without thinking, letting the fire between them sink toward the floor, and Esa, who'd been sitting there watching with feline intensity.

She sucked in a breath and brought her palms together quickly, extinguishing the flame in time to spare the tip of Esa's fluffy white tail.

"Sorry," she muttered, slouching back in the chair. "Must have gotten bored."

In truth, Lila was exhausted. She had slept even less than usual since Alucard's announcement, spending every spare moment practicing everything he'd taught her, and a few things he hadn't. And when she actually *tried* to sleep, her thoughts invariably turned to London. And the tournament. And Kell.

"Must have," grumbled Alucard, hoisting Esa up under his arm and depositing her safely on his desk.

"What do you expect?" She yawned. "I was holding that flame for ages."

"Forty-three minutes by the clock," he said. "And the whole *point* of the exercise is to keep your mind from drifting."

"Well then," she said, pouring herself a drink, "I suppose I'm just distracted."

"By my intoxicating presence, or our impending arrival?"

Lila swirled the wine and took a sip. It was rich and sweet, heavier than the usual sort he kept decanted on the table. "Have you ever fought a Veskan before?" she asked, dodging his question.

Alucard took up his own glass. "Behind a tavern, yes. In a tournament, no."

"What about a Faroan?"

"Well," he said, lowering himself into the opposite chair, "if their battle manner is anything like their bed manner . . ."

"You jest," she said, sitting forward, "but won't you have to fight both, in the *Essen Tasch*?"

"Assuming I don't lose in the first round, yes."

"Then what do you know about them?" she pressed. "Their skill? Their fighting style?"

The sapphire glittered as he raised his brow. "You're awfully inquisitive."

"I'm naturally curious," she countered. "And believe it or not, I'd rather not have to go looking for a new captain when this is over."

"Oh, don't worry, few competitors actually *die*." She gave him a hard look. "As for what I know? Well, let's see. Aside from Veskans growing like trees and Faroans taking my facial fashion choices to an extreme, they're both rather fascinating when it comes to magic."

Lila set the drink aside. "How so?"

"Well, we Arnesians have the Isle as a source. We believe that magic runs through the world the way that river runs through our capital, like a vein. Similarly, the Veskans have their mountains, which they claim bring them closer to their gods, each of which embodies an element. They are strong people, but they rely on physical force, believing that the more like mountains they are, the closer to power."

"And the Faroans? What is their source?"

Alucard sipped. "That's the thing. They don't have one. The Faroans believe instead that magic is everywhere. And in a sense they're right. Magic is technically in everything, but they claim they can tap into the heart of the world simply by walking on it. The Faroans consider themselves a blessed race. A bit on the arrogant side, but they're *powerful*. Perhaps they *have* found a way to make themselves into vessels. Or perhaps they use those jewels to bind magic to them." His voice colored with distaste when he said this, and Lila remembered Kell telling her about White Londoners, the way they used tattoos to bind power, and the way Red Londoners saw the practice as disgraceful. "Or maybe it's all for show."

"It doesn't bother you, that everyone believes different things?"

"Why should it?" he asked. "We all believe the same thing really, we simply give it different names. Hardly a crime."

Lila snorted. If only people in her world took such a forgiving stance. "The *Essen Tasch* is itself a kind of lesson," continued Alucard, "that it doesn't matter what you call magic, so long as you can believe."

"Do you really think you can win the tournament?" she asked.

He scoffed. "Probably not."

"Then why bother?"

"Because fighting's half the fun," he said, and then, reading her skepticism, "don't pretend that's a concept lost on you, Bard. I've seen the way you lunge into trouble."

"It's not that. . . ."

And it wasn't. She was just trying to picture Alucard in a magical duel. It was hard, because Lila had never seen the captain *fight*. Sure, she'd seen him hold a sword and make grand gestures with it, but he usually stood around looking pretty; before his display back in Sasenroche, she'd had no idea how good he was at magic. But the effortless way he'd performed at the Inroads... She couldn't help but wonder what he'd look like fighting. Would he be a torrent of energy, or a breeze, or would he be like Kell, who was somehow both at once?

"I'm surprised," said Alucard, "that you've never seen the tournament yourself."

"Who says I haven't?"

"You've been questioning my men for days. Did you think I wouldn't notice?"

Obviously, she thought.

"So I've never been." Lila shrugged, taking up her drink again. "Not everyone spends their winters in the city."

His smug expression faltered. "You could have simply asked *me*."

"And endured your speculation, your answers that are questions, your constant probing?"

"I've been told my probing is quite pleasant." Lila snorted into her cup at this. "You cannot fault a captain for wanting to know about his crew."

"And you cannot fault a thief for keeping secrets out of reach."

"You have trouble with trust, Delilah Bard."

"Your powers of observation are astonishing." She smiled and finished her drink. Her lips tingled and her throat burned. It really was stronger than usual. Lila didn't usually drink much; she'd spent too many years needing every faculty she had to stay alive. But here, in Alucard Emery's cabin, she realized something: she wasn't afraid. She wasn't running. Sure, it was a balancing act every time they spoke, but she knew how to keep her footing.

Alucard offered her a lazy, inebriated smile. Drunk or sober, he was always smiling. So unlike Kell, who always frowned.

Alucard sighed, and closed his eyes, tipping his head back

against the plush chair. He had a nice face, soft and sharp at the same time. She had the strangest urge to reach out and trace the lines of it with her fingers.

Lila really should have killed him, back when they first met. Back before she could know him. Back before she could like him so much.

His eyes drifted open. "Silver and gold for your thoughts," he said softly, lifting his glass to his lips.

Esa brushed against Lila's chair, and she twined the cat's tail around her fingers. "I was just wishing I'd killed you months ago," she said with easy cheer, relishing the way Alucard nearly choked on his wine.

"Oh, Bard," he teased, "does that mean you've since developed a fondness for me?"

"Fondness is weakness," she said automatically.

At that, Alucard stopped smiling, and set his glass aside. He leaned forward and considered her for a long moment, and then he said, "I'm sorry." He sounded so . . . earnest, which made Lila instantly suspicious. Alucard was many things, but genuine wasn't usually one of them.

"For growing on me?" she asked.

He shook his head. "For whatever happened to you. For whoever hurt you so deeply that you see things like friends and fondness as weapons instead of shields." Lila felt the heat rising to her cheeks.

"It's kept me alive, hasn't it?"

"Perhaps. But life is pointless without pleasure."

Lila's bristled at that, and got to her feet. "Who says I don't feel pleasure? I feel pleasure when I win a bet. Pleasure when I conjure fire. Pleasure when—"

Alucard cut her off. Not with a word, but with a kiss. He closed the space between them in one single, fluid motion, and then one of his hands was on her arm, the other against the nape of her neck, and his mouth was on hers. Lila didn't pull away.

She told herself after that it was surprise that stopped her, but that might have been a lie. Maybe it was the wine. Maybe it was the warmth of the room. Maybe it was the fear that he was right about her, about pleasure, about life. Maybe, but in that moment all she knew was that Alucard was kissing her, and then she was kissing him back. And then, suddenly, his mouth was gone from hers, his smile floating in front of her face.

"Tell me," he whispered, "was that better than winning a bet?"

She was breathless. "You make a valid argument."

"I'd love to press the point," he said, "but first . . ." He cleared his throat, and looked down at the knife she had resting against the inside of his leg.

"Reflex," she said with a smirk, returning the weapon to its sheath.

Neither one of them moved. Their faces were so close, nose to nose, lip to lip, and lash to lash, and all she could see were his eyes, storm blue, and the faint laugh lines that creased their corners, the way Kell's creased the space between. Opposites. Alucard's thumb brushed her cheek, and then he kissed her again, and this time there was no attack in the gesture, no surprise, only slow precision. His mouth grazed hers, and as she leaned forward into it, he drew playfully back. Measure for measure, like a dance. He wanted her to want him, wanted to prove himself right—the logical part of her knew all that, but the logical part was getting lost beneath her pounding heart. Bodies were traitorous things, she realized, as Alucard's lips grazed her jaw, and began to trail down her throat, causing her to shiver.

He must have felt the tremor, because he smiled against her skin, that perfect, serpent-charming smile. Her back arched. His hand was at the base of her spine, pulling her against him as he teased his way along her collarbone. Heat blossomed across her body where his hands found her skin. Lila knotted her fingers in his hair and pulled his mouth back to hers. They were a tangle of limbs and want, and she didn't think it was *better* than freedom or money or magic, but it was certainly close.

Alucard was the first to come up for air.

"Lila," he whispered against her, breath jagged.

"Yes," she said, the word half answer and half question.

Alucard's half-lidded eyes were dancing. "What are you running from?"

The words were like cold water, jarring her out of the moment. She shoved him away. His chair caught him behind the knees and he tumbled gracefully into it with something half laugh, half sigh.

"You are a *bastard*," she snapped, blushing fiercely.

He tilted his head lazily. "Without question."

"All that, whatever *that* was"—she waved her hand—"just so I'd tell you the truth."

"I wouldn't say that. I'm more than capable of multitasking."

Lila took up her wine glass and threw it at him. Both wine and cup hurtled through the air, but before they reached his head they just . . . stopped. The glass hung in the air between them, beads of purple wine floating, as if weightless.

"That," he said, reaching out to pluck the goblet from the air, "is a *very* expensive vintage."

The fingers of his other hand made a swirling motion, and the wine became a ribbon, spilling back into his glass. He smiled. And so did Lila, just before she snatched the bottle from the table and hurled it into the fire. This time Alucard wasn't fast enough, and the hearth crackled and flared as it devoured the wine.

Alucard let out an exasperated sound, but Lila was already storming out, and the captain had enough sense not to follow.

II

Red London.

The bells were ringing, and Rhy was late.

He could hear the distant sounds of music and laughter, the clatter of carriages and dancing. People were waiting for him. They'd had a fight, he and his father, about how he didn't take things seriously. How he *never* took things seriously. How could he be king when he couldn't even be bothered to arrive on time?

The bells stopped ringing and Rhy cursed, trying to fasten his tunic. He kept fumbling with the top button.

"Where *is* he?" he could hear his father grumbling.

The button slipped again, and Rhy groaned and crossed to his mirror, but when he stepped in front of it, he froze.

The world got quiet in his ears.

He stared into the glass, but *Kell* stared back.

His brother's eyes were wide with alarm. Rhy's room was reflected behind him, but Kell acted as though he were trapped in a box, his chest rising and falling with panic.

Rhy reached out, but a horrible chill went through him when he touched the glass. He wrenched back.

"Kell," he said. "Can you hear me?"

Kell's lips moved, and Rhy thought for an instant that the

impossible reflection was just repeating his own words, but the shapes Kell's mouth made were different.

Kell pressed his hands against the mirror, and raised his voice, and a single muffled word came through.

"*Rhy...*"

"Where are you?" demanded Rhy, as the room behind Kell began to darken and swirl with shadows, the chamber dissolving into black. *"What's going on?"*

And then, on the other side of the glass, Kell clutched his chest and *screamed*.

A horrible, gut-wrenching sound that tore through the room and raised every hair on Rhy's body.

He shouted Kell's name and beat his fists against the mirror, trying to break the spell, or the glass, trying to reach his brother, but the surface didn't even crack. Rhy didn't know what was wrong. He couldn't feel Kell's pain. He couldn't feel *anything*.

Beyond the glass, Kell let out another sobbing cry, and doubled over before crumpling to his knees.

And then Rhy saw the blood. Kell was pressing his hands to his chest, and Rhy watched, horrified and helpless, as blood poured between his brother's fingers. So much. Too much. A life's worth. *No, no, no,* he thought, *not this.*

He looked down and saw the knife buried between his ribs, his own fingers curled around the golden hilt.

Rhy gasped and tried to pull the blade free, but it was stuck.

Beyond the glass, Kell coughed blood.

"*Hold on,*" cried Rhy.

Kell was kneeling in a pool of red. A room. A sea. So much red. His hands fell away.

"Hold on," pleaded Rhy, pulling at the knife with all his strength. It didn't move.

Kell's head slumped forward.

"Hold on."

His body crumpled.
The knife came free.

Rhy wrenched forward out of sleep.

His heart was pounding, and the sheets were soaked with sweat. He pulled a pillow into his lap and buried his face in it, dragging in ragged breaths as he waited for his body to realize the dream wasn't real. Sweat ran down his cheek. His muscles twitched. His breath hitched, and he looked up, hoping to find morning light spilling in through the balcony doors, but was met with darkness, tempered only by the Isle's pale red glow.

He bit back a sob of frustration.

A glass of water sat beside his bed, and he gulped it down with shaking fingers while he waited to see if his brother would come barging in, convinced the prince was under attack, the way he had those first few nights.

But when it came to nights and mornings and the dreams between, Rhy and Kell had quickly developed a silent understanding. After a bad night, one would give the other a small, consoling look, but it seemed crucially important that nothing actually be *said* about the nightmares that plagued them both.

Rhy pressed his palm flat against his chest, lessening the pressure with the inhalation, increasing with the exhalation, just as Tieren had taught him to do years before, after he'd been taken by the Shadows. It wasn't the abduction that gave him nightmares in the months that followed, but the sight of Kell crouched over him, eyes wide and skin pale, the knife in his hand and the rivers of blood streaming from his severed veins.

It's all right, Rhy told himself now. *You're all right. Everything's all right.*

Feeling steadier, he threw off the sheets and stumbled up.

His hands itched to pour a drink, but he couldn't bear the

thought of going back to sleep. Besides, it was closer to dawn than dusk. Better to just wait it out.

Rhy pulled on a pair of silk trousers and a robe—the latter plush and heavy in a simple, comforting way—and threw open the balcony, letting the night's icy chill dispel any dregs of sleep.

Below, the floating arenas were nothing more than shadows blotting out the river's glow. The city was speckled here and there with lights, but his attention drifted to the docks, where even now ships were sailing sleepily into port.

Rhy squinted, straining to pick out one ship in particular.

A dark-wood vessel with silver trim and blue-black sails.

But there was no sign of the *Night Spire*.

Not yet.

III

The Arnesian Sea.

Lila stormed across the *Spire*'s deck, glaring at anyone who chanced to look her way. She'd left her coat in Alucard's cabin, and the night wind hit her like a wall, piercing sleeves and skin. It bit and burned, but Lila didn't turn back; instead she welcomed the sobering shock of the cold air as she crossed to the ship's stern, and slumped against the rail.

Bastard, she grumbled at the water below.

She was used to being the thief, not the mark. And she'd nearly fallen for it, focused on the hand in front of her face while the other tried to pick her pocket. She gripped the rail with bare fingers and stared out at the open sea, furious: at Alucard, at herself, at this stupid ship, the edges of which were so fixed, and so small.

What are you running from? he'd asked.

Nothing.

Everything.

Us. This.

Magic.

The truth was, there had been an instant, staring into the hissing fire, when it had stared back, hot and fierce, and listening, and she knew she could have made it grow, could have torched the whole cabin in a moment's temper, burned the ship, and herself and everyone on it.

She was starting to understand that magic wasn't just something to be accessed, tapped into when needed. It was always there, ready and waiting. And that frightened her. Almost as much as the way Alucard had been able to play her, toy with her, twist her distraction to his advantage. She'd let her guard slip, a mistake she wouldn't make again.

Bastard.

The cold air helped cool the fire in her cheeks, but the energy still surged beneath her skin. She glared at the sea, and imagined reaching out and shoving the water with all her strength. Like a child in a bath.

She didn't bother summoning any poems, didn't expect the desire to actually take shape, but a second later she felt energy flood through her, and the water bucked and surged, the ship tilting violently on a sudden wave.

Cries of concern went up across the *Spire* as the men tried to figure out what had happened, and Lila smirked viciously, hoping that down below she'd toppled a few more of Alucard's finest wines. And then it hit her, what she'd done. She'd moved the ocean—or at least a ship-sized piece of it. She touched a hand to her nose, expecting to find blood, but there was none. She was fine. Unharmed. She let out a small, dazed chuckle.

What are you?

Lila shivered, the cold having finally reached her bones. She was suddenly tired, and she didn't know if it was the backlash of expended magic or simply her frustration burning out.

What was it Barron used to say?

Something about tempers and candles and powder kegs.

The fact that she couldn't remember the exact words hit her like a dull blow to the chest. Barron was one of her only tethers, and he was gone now. And what right did she have to mourn? She'd wanted to be free of him, hadn't she? And this was why. People could only hurt you if you cared enough to let them.

Lila was about to turn away from the rail when she heard a muffled sniff, and realized she wasn't alone. Of course, no one was ever truly alone, not on a ship, but someone was standing against the rigging nearby, holding their breath. She squinted at the shadows, and then, when the figure looked more willing to collapse than step forward, she snapped her fingers and summoned a small, vibrant flame—a gesture managed with nonchalance, even though she'd been practicing it for weeks.

The light, which struggled against the sea breeze, illuminated the scarecrow shape of Lenos, Alucard's second mate. He squeaked, and she sighed and extinguished the fire, plunging them both back into comfortable darkness.

"Lenos," she said, trying to sound friendly. Had he seen what she'd done with the ship and the sea? The look on his face was one of caution, if not outright fear, but that was his usual expression around her. After all, he'd been the one to start the rumor that she was the Sarows, haunting the *Spire*.

The man stepped forward, and she saw that he was holding something out for her. His coat.

A refusal rose to her lips, automatic, but then good sense made her reach out and take it. She'd survived magic doors and evil queens; she'd be damned if she died of catching cold.

He let go of the coat the instant her fingers found purchase, as if afraid of being burned, and she shrugged it on, the lining still warm from Lenos's body. She turned up the collar and shoved her hands into the pockets, flexing her fingers for warmth.

"Are you afraid of me?" she asked in Arnesian.

"A little," he admitted, looking away.

"Because you don't trust me?"

He shook his head. "Not that," he mumbled. "You're just different from us. . . ."

She gave him a crooked smile. "So I've been told."

"Not cause you're a, well, you know, a girl. S'not that."

"Because I'm the Sarows, then? You really think that?"

He shrugged. "S'not that, not exactly. But you're *aven*."

Lila frowned. The word he used was *blessed*. But Lila had learned that there was no English equivalent. In Arnesian *blessed* wasn't always a good thing. Some said it meant *chosen*. Others said *favored*. But some said *cursed*. *Other*. *Apart*.

"*Aven* can be a good thing, too," she said, "so long as they're on your side."

"Are you on our side?" he asked quietly.

Lila was on her own side. But she supposed she was on the *Spire*'s side, too. "Sure."

He wrapped his arms around himself and turned his attention past her to the water. A fog was rolling in, and as he stared intently at it, Lila wondered what he saw in the mist.

"I grew up in this little place called Casta," he said. "On the southern cliffs. Castans think that sometimes magic chooses people."

"Like Master Kell," she said, adding, "the black-eyed prince."

Lenos nodded. "Yes, magic chose Master Kell. But what he is—*Antari*—that's only one kind of *aven*. Maybe the strongest, but it depends on your definition of strong. The priests are another. Some people think that *they're* the strongest, because they have just enough of every element to use them all in balance, so they can heal and grow and make life. There used to be all kinds of *aven*. Ones who could master all the elements. Ones who could only master one, but were so powerful, they could change the tides, or the wind, or the seasons. Ones who could hear what magic had to say. *Aven* isn't just one thing, because magic isn't just one thing. It's everything, old and new and always changing. The Castans think that when someone *aven* appears, it's for a reason. It's because the magic is trying to tell us something. . . ."

He trailed off. Lila stared at him. It was the most Lenos had ever said to her. The most she'd ever heard him say to *anyone,* for that matter.

"So you think I'm here for a reason?" she asked.

Lenos rocked from heel to toe. "We're all here for a reason, Bard. Some reasons are just bigger than others. So I guess I'm not scared of who you are, or even what you are. I'm scared of *why* you are."

He shivered and turned away.

"Wait," she said, shrugging out of his coat. "Here."

He reached for it, and to Lila's relief, when their hands nearly brushed, he didn't jerk back. She watched the man retreat across the dock, then rolled her neck and made her way below.

She found her own coat hanging on her cabin door, along with an unopened bottle of purple wine, and a note that read *Solase.*

Sorry.

Lila sighed and took up the bottle, her thoughts churning and her body aching for sleep.

And then she heard the call go up overhead.

"*Hals!*" shouted a voice from the deck above.

Land.

IV

The bells rang out a dozen times, and then a dozen more. They went on and on until Kell lost count, far past the hours in a day, a week, a month.

The persistent sound could only mean one thing: the royals had arrived.

Kell stood on his balcony and watched them come. It had been six years since London last played host to the *Essen Tasch,* but he still remembered watching the procession of ships and people, trying to imagine where they'd come from, what they'd seen. He couldn't go to the world, but on these rare occasions, it seemed to come to him.

Now, as he watched the ships drift up the Isle (as far as Rhy's floating stadiums would allow), he found himself wondering which one Lila would choose for herself. There were a handful of smaller, private crafts, but most were massive vessels, luxury boats designed to transport wealthy merchants and nobles from Faro and Vesk to the festivities in the Arnesian capital. All ships bore a mark of origin, on either sail or side, the painted symbol of their crown. That, along with a scroll of approval, would grant them access to the docks for the length of the *Essen Tasch*.

Would Lila prefer an elegant silver wood ship, like the one bearing the Faroan mark? Or something bolder, like the vibrantly painted Veskan vessel now approaching? Or a proud

Arnesian craft, with dark polished wood and crisp sails? Come to think of it, did Lila even know *how* to sail? Probably not, but if anyone could make the strange seem ordinary, the impossible look easy, it was Delilah Bard.

"What are you smirking at?" asked Rhy, appearing beside him.

"Your stadiums are making a mess of the river."

"Nonsense," said Rhy. "I've had temporary docks erected on the northern and southern banks on both sides of the city. There's plenty of room."

Kell nodded at the Isle. "Tell that to our guests."

Below, the other vessels had parted to make way for the Veskan fleet as it came up the river, stopping only when it reached the barricade. The Veskan royal barge, a splendid rig made of redwood with dark sails bearing the royal emblem of the crow in flight against a white moon, was flanked by two military ships.

Minutes later the Faroans' imperial vessel followed, its ships all skeletal and silver-white, the crest of the black tree scorched into their sails.

"We should get going," said the prince. "We'll have to be there to welcome them."

"*We?*" echoed Kell, even though the king had already made it clear that his presence was required. Not because Kell was family, he thought bitterly, but because he was *aven*. A symbol of Arnesian power.

"They'll want to see you," the king had said, and Kell had understood. When Maxim said *you* he didn't mean Kell the *person*. He meant Kell the *Antari*. He bristled. Why did he feel like a trophy? Or worse, a trinket—

"Stop that," chided Rhy.

"Stop what?"

"Whatever's going through your head that has you frowning even more than usual. You'll give us both wrinkles." Kell sighed.

"Come," pressed Rhy. "There's no way I'm facing them on my own."

"Which one are you afraid of? Lord Sol-in-Ar?"

"Cora."

"The Veskan princess?" Kell laughed. "She's just a child."

"She *was* just a child—and a nightmarish one at that—but I've heard she's grown into something truly fearsome."

Kell shook his head. "Come on, then," he said, slinging his arm around the prince's shoulder. "I'll defend you."

"My hero."

The Red Palace had five halls: the Grand, an extravagant three-story ballroom made of polished wood and sculpted crystal; the Gold, a sprawling reception hall, all stone and precious metal; the Jewel, seated at the palace heart and made entirely of glass; the Sky on the roof, its mosaic floor glittering under the sun and stars; and the Rose. The last of these, positioned near the front of the palace and accessed through its own hall and doors, possessed a stately elegance. It had been built in a wing of the palace with nothing overhead, and light shone through windows set into the ceiling. The walls and floor were royal marble, pale stone threaded with garnet and gold, crafted by mineral mages for the crown's use alone. In place of columns, bouquets of flowers in massive urns cut parallel lines through the chamber. Between these columns, a gold runner ran from doorway to dais and throne.

The Rose Hall was where the crown held court with its people, and where it intended to greet its neighboring royals.

If they ever showed up.

Kell and Rhy stood on either side of the thrones, Rhy leaning against his father's chair, Kell at attention beside the queen's.

Master Tieren stood at the foot of the dais, but he wouldn't meet Kell's gaze. Was it his imagination, or had the *Aven Essen* been avoiding him? The royal guards stood statuesque in their gleaming armor, while a select assembly of *ostra* and *vestra* milled about, having drifted into clusters to chat. It had been more than an hour since the royal ships had docked and an escort had been sent to accompany them to the palace. Sparkling wine sat on trays, going flat with the wait.

Rhy shifted from foot to foot, clearly tense. This was, after all, his first time at the helm of a royal affair, and while he'd always been one for details, they usually centered around his clothing, or his hair. The *Essen Tasch* was on another scale entirely. Kell watched him fidget with the gleaming gold seal of the Maresh—a chalice and rising sun—over his heart. He'd produced a second one, for Kell, which he had reluctantly pinned on the breast of his red coat.

King Maxim fiddled with a coin, something Kell only saw him do when he couldn't sit still. Like his father before him, Maxim Maresh was a metalworker, a strong magician in his own right, though he had little need of it now. Still, Kell had heard the stories of Maxim's youth, tales of the "steel prince" who forged armies and melted hearts, and he knew that even now the king traveled twice a year to the borders to stoke the fires of his men.

"I hope nothing has happened to our guests," said King Maxim.

"Perhaps they got lost," mused Rhy.

"We could only be so lucky," murmured Kell.

Queen Emira shot them both a look, and Kell almost laughed. It was such simple, motherly scorn.

At last, the trumpets sounded, and the doors swung open.

"Finally," muttered Rhy.

"Prince Col and Princess Cora," announced a servant, his voice echoing through the hall, "of the House Taskon, ruling family of Vesk."

The Taskon siblings entered, flanked by a dozen attendants.

They were striking, dressed loosely in green and silver, with elegant cloaks trailing behind. Col was eighteen now, Cora two years his junior.

"Your Majesties," said Prince Col, a burly youth, in heavily accented Arnesian.

"We are welcomed to your city," added Princess Cora with a curtsy and a cherubic smile.

Kell shot Rhy a look that said, *Honestly? This is the girl you're so afraid of?*

Rhy shot him one back that said, *You should be, too.*

Kell gave Princess Cora another, more appraising glance. The princess hardly looked strong enough to hold a wine flute. Her cascades of honey-blond hair were done up in an elaborate braid that circled her head like a crown, woven through with emeralds.

She was slight for a Veskan—tall, yes, but narrow-waisted, willowy in a way that would have better suited the Arnesian court. Rhy had been allowed to accompany his mother to the *Essen Tasch* in Vesk three years before, so he'd seen her grow. But Kell, confined to the city, had only seen the tournament on years when Arnes was called to host. When the Games were held there six years ago, Prince Col had come, along with one of his other brothers.

The last time Kell had seen *Cora,* twelve years ago, she'd been a small child.

Now her pale blue eyes traveled up, landed on his two-toned gaze, and stuck. He was so accustomed to people avoiding his eyes, their own glancing off, finding safer ground, that the intensity caught him off guard, and he fought the sudden urge to look away.

Meanwhile an attendant carried a large object, shrouded in heavy green cloth, to the throne dais, and set it down on the step. Whisking the cloth away with a dramatic flair, the attendant revealed a bird inside a cage—not a multicolored mimic, or a songbird, both favored by the Arnesian court, but something more . . . *predatory*. It was massive and silvery grey, save for its head, which had a plume and collar of black. Its beak looked razor sharp.

"A thank you," announced Prince Col, "for inviting us into your home." Col shared Cora's coloring, but nothing else. Where she was tall, he was taller. Where she was narrow, he was built like an ox. A handsome one, but still, there was something bullish about his attitude and expression.

"Gratitude," said the king, nodding to Master Tieren, who strode forward and lifted the cage. It would go to the sanctuary, Kell supposed, or be set free. A palace was no place for wild animals.

Kell tracked the exchange out of the corner of his eye, his attention still leveled on the princess, whose gaze was still leveled on him, too, as if transfixed by his black eye. She looked like the kind of girl who would point to something—or some*one*—and say, "I want one of those." The thought was almost amusing until he remembered Astrid's words—*I would own you, flower boy*—and then the humor turned cold. Kell took a slight, almost imperceptible step back.

"Our home shall be yours," King Maxim was saying. It all felt like a script.

"And if the gods favor us," said Prince Col with a grin, "so shall your tournament."

Rhy bristled, but the king simply laughed. "We shall see about that," he said with a hearty smile that Kell knew was false. The king didn't care for Prince Col, or any of the Veskan royal family for that matter. But the real danger lay with Faro. With Lord Sol-in-Ar.

As if on cue, the trumpets sounded again, and the Veskan entourage took up their glasses of wine and stepped aside.

"Lord Sol-in-Ar, Regent of Faro," announced the attendant as the doors opened.

Unlike the Veskans, whose entourage surrounded them, Sol-in-Ar strode in at the front, his men filing behind him in formation. They were all dressed in Faroan style, a single piece of fabric intricately folded around them, the tail end cast back over one shoulder like a cape. His men all wore rich purple, accented in black and white, while Sol-in-Ar wore white, the very edges of the fabric trimmed in indigo.

Like all ranking Faroans, he was clean-shaven, affording a full view of the beads set into his face, but unlike most, who favored glass or precious gems, Lord Sol-in-Ar's ornamentation appeared to be white gold, diamond-shaped slivers that traced curved paths from temples to throat. His black hair was trimmed short, and a single larger teardrop of white gold stood out against his forehead, just above his brows, marking him as royal.

"How do they choose?" Rhy had wondered aloud, years before, holding a ruby to his forehead. "I mean, Father says the *number* of gems is a social signifier, but apparently the color is a mystery. I doubt it's arbitrary—if it were the Veskans, maybe, but nothing about the Faroans seems arbitrary—which means the colors must mean *something*."

"Does it matter?" Kell had asked wearily.

"Of course it matters," snapped Rhy. "It's like knowing there's a language you don't speak, and having no one willing to teach it to you."

"Maybe it's private."

Rhy tipped his head and furrowed his brow to keep the ruby from falling. "How do I look?"

Kell had snorted. "Ridiculous."

But there was nothing ridiculous about Lord Sol-in-Ar. He was tall—several inches taller than the men of his guard—with a chiseled jaw and rigid gate. His skin was the color of charcoal, his eyes pale green, and sharp as cut glass. Older brother to the king of Faro, commander of the Faroan fleet, responsible for the unification of the once dispersed territories, and considered to be the majority of the actual thinking behind the throne.

And unable to rule, for lack of magic. He more than made up for it with his military prowess and keen eye for order, but Kell knew the fact made Rhy uneasy.

"Welcome, Lord Sol-in-Ar," said King Maxim.

The Faroan regent nodded, but did not smile. "Your city shines," he said simply. His accent was heavy and smooth, like a river stone. He flicked his hand, and two attendants carried forward a pair of potted saplings, their bark an inky black. The same trees that marked the Faroan royal seal, just as the bird was the symbol of Vesk. Kell had heard of the Faroan birch, rare trees said to have medicinal—even magical—properties.

"A gift," he said smoothly. "So that good things may grow."

The king and queen bowed their heads in thanks, and Lord Sol-in-Ar's gaze swept across the dais, passing Rhy and landing for only a moment on Kell before he bowed and stepped back. With that, the king and queen descended their thrones, taking up glasses of sparkling wine as they did. The rest of the room moved to echo the motion, and Kell sighed.

Standing there on display was painful enough.

Now came the truly unfortunate task of socializing.

Rhy was clearly steeling himself against the princess, who had apparently spent their last encounter trying to steal kisses and weave flowers in his hair. But Rhy's worrying turned out to be for nothing—she had her sights set on other prey. *Kings,* swore Kell in his head, gripping his wine flute as she approached.

"Prince Kell," she said, flashing a childlike grin. He didn't bother to point out that she should address him as *Master,* not *Prince.* "You will dance with me, at the evening balls."

He wasn't sure if her Arnesian was simply limited, or if she meant to be so direct. But Rhy shot him a look that said he'd spent months preparing for this tournament, that it was a display of politics and diplomacy, that they would all be making sacrifices, and that he'd rather stab himself than let Kell put the empire's peace in jeopardy by denying the princess a dance.

Kell managed a smile, and bowed. "Of course, Your Highness," he answered, adding in Veskan, *"Gradaich an'ach."*

It is my pleasure.

Her smile magnified as she bobbed away to one of her attendants.

Rhy leaned over. "Looks like I'm not the one who needs protecting after all. You know . . ." He sipped his wine. "It would be an interesting match. . . ."

Kell kept his smile fixed. "I will stab you with this pin."

"You would suffer."

"It would be worth—" He was cut off by the approach of Lord Sol-in-Ar.

"Prince Rhy," said the regent, nodding his head. Rhy straightened, and then bowed deeply.

"Lord Sol-in-Ar," he said. *"Hasanal rasnavoras ahas."*

Your presence honors our kingdom.

The regent's eyes widened in pleased surprise. *"Amun shahar,"* he said before shifting back to Arnesian. "Your Faroan is excellent."

The prince blushed. He had always had an ear for languages. Kell knew a fair amount of Faroan, too, thanks to Rhy preferring to have someone to practice on, but he said nothing.

"You make the effort to learn our tongue," said Rhy. "It is only respectful to reciprocate." And then, with a disarming smile, he added, "Besides, I've always found the Faroan language to be beautiful."

Sol-in-Ar nodded, his gaze shifting toward Kell.

"And you," said the regent. "You must be the Arnesian *Antari.*"

Kell bowed his head, but when he looked up, Sol-in-Ar was still examining him, head to toe, as if the mark of his magic were drawn not only in his eye, but across every inch of his being.

When at last his attention settled on Kell's face, he frowned faintly, the drop of metal on his forehead glinting.

"*Namunast,*" he murmured. *Fascinating.*

The moment Sol-in-Ar was gone, Kell finished his wine in a single gulp, and then retreated through the open doors of the Rose Hall before anyone could stop him.

He'd had more than enough royals for one day.

V

The river was turning red.

When the *Night Spire* first hit the mouth of the Isle, Lila could make out only the slightest tint to the water, and that only visible at night. Now, with the city fast approaching, the water glowed like a ruby lit from within, the red light visible even at midday. It was like a beacon, leading them into London.

At first, she'd thought the river's light was steady, even, but she noticed now—after months of training herself to see and feel and think about magic as a living thing—that it pulsed beneath the surface, like lightning behind layers of clouds.

She leaned on the rail and turned the shard of pale stone between her fingers. She'd only had it since facing the Dane twins in White London, but the edges were starting to wear smooth. She willed her hands to still, but there was too much nervous energy, and nowhere for it to go.

"We'll be there by dusk," said Alucard beside her. Lila's pulse fluttered. "If there's anything you want to tell me about your departure from the city, now's the time. Well, actually, any time over the last four months would have been the time, now is really up against a wall, but—"

"Don't start," she grumbled, tucking the stone shard back into her pocket.

"We all have demons, Bard. But if yours are waiting there—"

"My demons are all dead."

"Then I envy you." Silence fell between them. "You're still mad at me."

She straightened. "You tried to seduce me, for *information*."

"You can't hold that against me forever."

"It was *last night*."

"Well I was running out of options, and I figured it was worth a shot."

Lila rolled her eyes. "You really know how to make a girl feel special."

"I thought I was in trouble precisely for making you feel special."

Lila huffed, blowing the hair out of her eyes. She returned to watching the river, and was surprised when Alucard stayed, leaning his elbows on the rail beside her.

"Are *you* excited to go back?" she asked.

"I quite like London," he said. Lila waited for him to go on, but he didn't. Instead, he began to rub his wrists.

"You do that," said Lila, nodding at his hands, "whenever you're thinking."

He stopped. "Good thing I don't make a habit of deep thought." Elbows still resting on the rail, he turned his hands palm up, the cuffs of his tunic riding up so Lila could see the marks across his wrists. The first time she'd noticed them, she thought they were only shadows, but up close she realized they were *scars*.

He folded his arms in and drew a flask from inside his coat. It was made of glass, the pale-pink liquid sloshing inside. Alucard had never seemed all that fond of sobriety, but the closer they got to the city, the more he drank.

"I'll be sober again by the time we dock," he said, reading her look. His free hand drifted toward his wrist again.

"It's a tell," she said. "Your wrists. That's why I brought it up. People should always know their tells."

"And what is yours, Bard?" he asked, offering her the flask.

Lila took it but didn't drink. Instead she cocked her head. "You tell me."

Alucard twisted toward her and squinted, as if he could see the answer in the air around her. His blue eyes widened in mock revelation. "You tuck your hair behind your ear," he said. "But only on the right side. Whenever you're nervous. I'm guessing it's to keep yourself from fidgeting."

Lila gave him a grudging smile. "You got the gesture, but missed the motive."

"Enlighten me."

"People have a tendency to hide behind their features when they're nervous," she said. "I tuck my hair behind my ear to show my opponent—mark, adversary, what have you—that I'm not hiding. I look them in the eyes, and I let them look *me* in the eyes."

Alucard raised a brow at that. "Well, *eye*."

The flask shattered in Lila's hand. She hissed, first in shock, and then in pain as the liquor burned her palm. She dropped the flask and it fell in pieces to the deck.

"What did you say?" she whispered.

Alucard ignored the question. He tutted and flicked his wrist, the broken shards rising into the air above his fingers. Lila brought her bloody palm to her chest, but Alucard held out his other hand.

"Let me," he said, taking her wrist and turning it over gently to expose the shallow cuts. Glass glittered in her palm, but as his lips moved, the flecks and fragments rose to join the larger pieces in the air. With a twitch of his fingers, he brushed the shards away, and they fell soundless over the side of the boat.

"Alucard," she growled. "What did you say?"

Her hand was still resting upturned in his. "Your tell," he said, inspecting the cuts. "It's slight. You try to pass it off by cocking your head, steadying your gaze, but you're really doing it to make up for the gap in sight." He drew a black swatch of fabric from his sleeve, and began to wrap her hand. She let him. "And the hair," he added, tying the makeshift bandage in a knot. "You only tuck it behind your ear on the *right* side, to mislead people." He let go of her hand. "It's so subtle, I doubt many notice."

"You did," she muttered.

Alucard reached out, tipped her chin up with his knuckle, and looked her in the eyes. Eye.

"I'm extraordinarily perceptive," he said.

Lila clenched her fists, focusing on the pain that blossomed there.

"You're an incredible thief, Lila," he said, "especially con—"

"Don't you dare say *considering*," she snapped, pulling out of his grip. He respected her enough not to look away. "I am an incredible thief, Alucard. This," she said, gesturing to her eye, "is not a weakness. It hasn't been for a very long time. And even if it were, I more than make up for it."

Alucard smiled. A small, genuine smile. "We all have scars," he said, and before she could stop herself, she glanced at his wrists. "Yes," he said, catching the look, "even charming captains." He pushed up his cuffs again, revealing smooth, tan skin interrupted only by the silvered bands around both wrists. They were strangely uniform. In fact, they almost looked like—

"Manacles," he confirmed.

Lila frowned. "From what?"

Alucard shrugged. "A bad day." He took a step away, and leaned back against a stack of crates. "Do you know what Arnesians do to the pirates they catch?" he asked casually. "The ones who try to escape?"

Lila crossed her arms. "I thought you said you weren't a pirate."

"I'm not." He waved his hand. "Not anymore. But youth makes fools of us all. Let's just say I was in the wrong place at the wrong time on the wrong side."

"What do they do . . . ?" asked Lila, curious despite herself.

Alucard's gaze drifted toward the river. "The jailers use an efficient system of dissuasion. They keep all the prisoners in manacles, put them on before even hearing your plea. They're heavy things, fused together at the wrist, but not so bad, as irons go. But if you make too much of a fuss, or put up a fight, then they simply heat the metal up. Not too much. The first time it's really just a warning. But if it's your second or third offense, or if you're foolish enough to try to escape, it's much worse." Alucard's eyes had somehow gone sharp and empty at the same time, as if he were focusing, just on something else, something far away. His voice had a strangely even quality as he spoke. "It's a simple enough method. They take a metal bar from the fires, and touch it to the iron cuff until it gets hot. The worse the offense, the longer they hold the rod to the cuffs. Most of the time they stop when you start screaming, or when they see the skin begin to burn. . . ."

In Lila's mind, she saw Alucard Emery, not in his polished captain's coat, but bruised and beaten, his brown hair plastered to his face with sweat, hands bound as he tried to pull back from the heated iron. Tried to charm his way out of the mess. But it obviously hadn't worked, and she imagined the sound of him begging, the smell of charred flesh, the scream. . . .

"The trouble is," Alucard was saying, "that metal heats much faster than it cools, so the punishment doesn't end when they take away the rod."

Lila felt ill. "I'm sorry," she said, even though she hated those words, hated the pity that went with them.

"I'm not," he said, simply. "Every good captain needs his scars. Keeps the men in line."

He said it so casually, but she could see the strains of memory on his face. She had the strangest urge to reach out and touch his wrist, as if heat might still be rising from the skin.

Instead she asked, "Why did you become a pirate?"

He shot her that coy smile. "Well, it seemed like the best of several bad ideas."

"But it didn't work."

"How perceptive."

"Then how did you escape?"

The sapphire winked above his eye. "Who says I did?"

Just then, the call went through the crew.

"London!"

Lila twisted, and saw the city rising like a fire in the fading light.

Her heart raced, and Alucard stood up straight, the tunic sleeves sliding down over his wrists.

"Well then," he said, his rakish smile back in place. "It seems we have arrived."

VI

The *Night Spire* docked at dusk.

Lila helped tie off the lines and settle the ramps, her attention straying to the dozens of elegant ships that filled the Isle's banks. The Red London berths were a tangle of energy and people, chaos and magic, laughter and twilight. Despite the February chill, the city radiated warmth. In the distance, the royal palace rose like a second sun over the settling dark.

"Welcome back," said Alucard, brushing his shoulder against hers as he hauled a chest onto the dock. She started when she saw Esa sitting on top, purple eyes wide, tail flicking.

"Shouldn't she stay on the boat?" The cat's ear twitched, and Lila felt that whatever pleasant inclinations the cat was forming toward her, she'd just lost them.

"Don't be ridiculous," said Alucard. "The ship's no place for a cat." Lila was about to point out that the cat had been aboard the ship as long as she had when he added, "I believe in keeping my valuables with me."

Lila perked up. Were cats so precious here? Or rare? She hadn't ever seen another one, but in the little time she was ashore, she hadn't exactly been looking. "Oh yeah?"

"I don't like that look," Alucard said, twisting chest and cat away.

"What look?" asked Lila innocently.

"The look that says Esa might conveniently go missing if I tell you what she's worth." Lila snorted. "But if you must know, she's only priceless because I keep my heart inside her, so no one can steal it." He smiled when he said it, but Esa didn't even blink.

"Is that so?"

"In truth," he said, setting the chest onto a cart, "she was a gift."

"From who?" asked Lila before she could catch herself.

Alucard smirked. "Oh, are you suddenly ready to share? Shall we begin trading questions and answers?"

Lila rolled her eyes and went to help the men haul more chests ashore. A couple of hands would stay with the *Spire,* while the rest took up at an inn. The cart loaded, Alucard presented his papers to a guard in gleaming armor, and Lila let her gaze wander over the other ships. Some were intricate, others simple, but all were, in their way, impressive.

And then, two boats down, she saw a figure descend from an Arnesian rig. A *woman*. And not the kind Lila knew to frequent ships. She was dressed in trousers and a collarless coat, a sword slung on a belt at her waist.

The woman began to make her way down the dock toward the *Spire,* and there was something animal about the way she moved. *Prowled.* She was taller than Lila, taller than Alucard for that matter, with features as pointed as a fox's and a mane—there was no better word for it—of wild auburn hair, large chunks not braided exactly but twisted around themselves so she looked half lion and half snake. Perhaps Lila should have felt threatened, but she was too busy being awestruck.

"Now *there's* a captain not to cross," Alucard whispered in her ear.

"Alucard Emery," said the woman when she reached them. Her voice had a slight sea rasp, and her Arnesian was full of edges. "Haven't seen you on London land in quite a while. Here for the tournament, I assume."

"You know me, Jasta. Can't turn down the chance to make a fool of myself."

She chuckled, a sound like rusted bells. "Some things never change."

He flashed a mock frown. "Does that mean you won't be betting on me?"

"I'll see if I can spare a few coins," she said. And with that, Jasta continued on, weapons chiming like coins.

Alucard leaned on Lila. "Word of advice, Bard. Never challenge that one to a drinking contest. Or a sword fight. Or anything you might lose. Because you will."

But Lila was barely listening. She couldn't tear her gaze from Jasta as the woman stalked away down the docks, a handful of wolfish men falling in step behind her.

"I've never seen a female captain."

"Not many in Arnes proper, but it's a big world," said Alucard. "It's more common where she's from."

"And where's that?"

"Jasta? She's from Sonal. Eastern side of the empire. Up against the Veskan edge, which is why she looks . . ."

"Larger than life."

"Exactly. And don't you go looking for a new rig. If you'd pulled the stunt you did to get onto *her* ship, she would have cut your throat and dumped you overboard."

Lila smiled. "Sounds like my kind of captain."

"Here we are," said Alucard when they reached the inn.

The name of the place was Is Vesnara Shast, which translated to *The Wandering Road*. What Lila didn't know, not until she saw Lenos's unease, was that the Arnesian word for *road—shast—* was the same as the word for *soul*. She found the alternate name a bit unsettling, and the inn's atmosphere did nothing to ease the feeling.

It was a crooked old structure—she hadn't noticed, in her short time in Red London last fall, that most of the buildings felt new—that looked like boxes stacked rather haphazardly on top of each other. It actually reminded her a bit of her haunts back in Grey London. Old stones beginning to settle, floors beginning to slouch.

The main room was crammed with tables, each of which in turn was crammed with Arnesian sailors, and most appeared well in their cups, despite the fact it was barely sundown. A single hearth burned on the far wall, a wolfhound stretched in front, but the room was stuffy from bodies.

"Living the life of luxury, aren't we?" grumbled Stross.

"We've got beds," said Tav, ever the optimist.

"Are we sure about that?" asked Vasry.

"Did someone replace my hardened crew with a bunch of whining children?" chided Alucard. "Shall I go find you a teat to gnaw on, Stross?"

The first mate grumbled but said nothing more as the captain handed out the keys. Four men to a room. But despite the cramped quarters, and the fact that the inn looked like it was far exceeding capacity, Alucard had managed to snare a room of his own.

"Captain's privilege," he said.

As for Lila, she was bunked with Vasry, Tav, and Lenos.

The group dispersed, hauling their chests up to their chambers. The Wandering Road was, as the name suggested, wandering, a tangled mess of halls and stairs that seemed to defy several laws of nature at once. Lila wondered if there was some kind of spell on the inn, or if it was simply peculiar. It was the kind of place where you could easily get lost, and she could only imagine it got more confusing as the night and drink wore on. Alucard called it *eccentric*.

Her room had four bodies, but only two beds.

"This'll be cozy," said Tav.

"No," said Lila in decisive, if broken, Arnesian. "I don't share beds—"

"*Tac?*" teased Vasry, dropping his chest on the floor. "Surely we can work something ou—"

"—because I have a habit of stabbing people in my sleep," she finished coolly.

Vasry had the decency to pale a little.

"Bard can have a bed," said Tav. "I'll take the floor. And Vasry, what are the odds of you actually spending your nights here with us?"

Vasry batted his long, black lashes. "A point."

So far, Lenos had said nothing. Not when they got their key, not when they climbed the stairs. He hugged the wall, obviously unnerved to be sharing quarters with the Sarows. Tav was the most resilient, but if she played her cards right, she could probably have the room to herself by tomorrow.

It wasn't a bad room. It was roughly the same size as her cabin, which was roughly the same size as a closet, but when she looked out the narrow window, she could see the city, and the river, and the palace arcing over it.

And the truth was, it felt good to be back.

She pulled on her gloves, and a cap, and dug a parcel out of her chest before heading out. She closed the door just as Alucard stepped out of a room across the hall. Esa's white tail curled around his boot.

"Where are you off to?" he asked.

"Night Market."

He raised a sapphire-studded brow. "Barely back on London soil, and already off to spend your coins?"

"What can I say?" said Lila evenly. "I'm in need of a new dress."

Alucard snorted but didn't press the issue, and though he trailed her down to the stairs, he didn't follow her out.

For the first time in months, Lila was truly alone. She drew a breath and felt her chest loosen as she cast off Bard, the best thief aboard the *Night Spire,* and became simply a stranger in the thickening dark.

She passed several scrying boards advertising the *Essen Tasch,* white chalk dancing across the black surface as it spelled out details about the various ceremonies and celebrations. A couple of children hovered around the edges of a puddle, freezing and unfreezing it. A Veskan man lit a pipe with a snap of his fingers. A Faroan woman somehow changed the color of her scarf simply by running it through her fingers.

Wherever Lila looked, she saw signs of magic.

Out on the water, it was a strange enough sight—not as strange as it would have been in Grey London, of course—but here, it was everywhere. Lila had forgotten the way Red London glittered with it, and the more time she spent here, the more she realized that Kell really *didn't* belong. He didn't fit in with the clashes of color, the laughter and jostle and sparkle of magic. He was too understated.

This was a place for performers. And that suited Lila just fine.

It wasn't late, but winter darkness had settled over the city by the time she neared the Night Market. The stretch of stalls along the bank seemed to *glow,* lit not only by the usual lanterns and torches, but by pale spheres of light that followed the market-goers wherever they went. At first, it looked like they themselves were glowing, not head to toe, but from their core, as if their very life force had suddenly become visible. The effect was unsettling, hundreds of tiny lights burning against cloak fronts. But as she drew closer, she realized the light was coming from something in their hands.

"Palm fire?" asked a man at the mouth of the market, holding up a glass sphere filled with pale light. It was just warm enough to fog the air around its edges.

"How much?"

"Four lin."

It wasn't cheap, but her fingers were chilled, even with the gloves, and she was fascinated by the sphere, so she paid the man and took the orb, marveling at the soft, diffuse heat that spread through her hands and up her arms.

She cradled the palm fire, smiling despite herself. The market air still smelled of flowers, but also of burning wood, and cinnamon, and fruit. She'd been such an outsider last fall—she was still an outsider, of course, but now she knew enough to cover it. Jumbled letters that had meant nothing to her months before now began to form words. When the merchants called out their wares, she could glean their meaning, and when the music seemed to take shape on the air, as if by magic, she knew that was exactly what it was, and the thought didn't set her off balance. If anything, she'd felt off balance all her life, and now her feet were firmly planted.

Most people wandered from stall to stall, sampling mulled wine and skewered meat, fondling velvet-lined hoods and magical tokens, but Lila walked with her head up, humming to herself as she wove between the tents and stalls toward the other end of the market. There would be time to wander later, but right now, she had an errand.

Down the bank, the palace loomed like a low red moon. And there, sandwiched between two other tents at the far edge of the market, near the palace steps, she found the stall she was looking for.

The last time she'd been here, she hadn't been able to read the sign mounted above the entrance. Now she knew enough Arnesian to decipher it.

IS POSTRAN.
The Wardrobe.

Simple, but clever—just as in English, the word *postran* referred both to clothing and the place where it was kept.

Tiny bells had been threaded through the curtain of fabric that served as a door, and they rang softly as Lila pushed the cloth aside. Stepping into the stall was like crossing the threshold into a well-warmed house. Lanterns burned in the corners, emitting not only rosy light, but a glorious amount of heat. Lila scanned the tent. Once the back wall had been covered with faces, but now it was lined with winter things—hats, scarves, hoods, and a few accessories that seemed to merge all three.

A round woman, her brown hair wrestled into a braided bun, knelt before one of the tables, reaching for something beneath.

"*An esto,*" she called at the sound of the bells, then muttered quiet curses at whatever had escaped. "Aha!" she said at last, shoving a bauble back into her pocket before pushing to her feet. "*Solase,*" she said, brushing herself off as she turned. "*Kers . . .*" But then she trailed off, and burst into a smile.

It had been four months since Lila had stepped into Calla's tent to admire the masks along the wall. Four months since the merchant woman had given her a devil's face, and a coat, and a pair of boots, the beginnings of a new identity. A new life.

Four months, but Calla's eyes lit up instantly with recognition. "Lila," she said, stretching out the *i* into several *e*s.

"Calla," said Lila. *"As esher tan ves."*

I hope you are well.

The woman smiled. "Your Arnesian," she said in English, "it is improving."

"Not fast enough," said Lila. "Your High Royal is impeccable as always."

"*Tac,*" she chided, smoothing the front of her dark apron.

Lila felt a peculiar warmth toward the woman, a fondness that should have made her nervous, but she couldn't bring herself to smother the feeling.

"You have been gone."

"At sea," answered Lila.

"You have docked along with half the world, it seems," said Calla, crossing to the front of her stall and fastening the curtain shut. "And just in time for the *Essen Tasch*."

"It's not a coincidence."

"You come to watch, then," she said.

"My captain is competing," answered Lila.

Calla's eyes widened. "You sail with Alucard Emery?"

"You know of him?"

Calla shrugged. "Reputations, they are loud things." She waved her hand in the air, as if dismissing smoke. "What brings you to my stall? Time for a new coat? Green perhaps, or blue. Black is out of fashion this winter."

"I hardly care," said Lila. "You'll never part me from my coat."

Calla chuckled and ran a questing finger along Lila's sleeve. "It's held up well enough." And then she tutted. "Saints only know what you've been doing in it. Is that a *knife* tear?"

"I snagged it on a nail," she lied.

"*Tac,* Lila, my work is not so fragile."

"Well," she conceded, "it might have been a small knife."

Calla shook her head. "First storming castles, and now fighting on the seas. You are a very peculiar girl. *Anesh,* Master Kell is a peculiar boy, so what do I know."

Lila colored at the implication. "I have not forgotten my debt," she said. "I've come to pay it." With that, she produced a small wooden box. It was an elegant thing, inlaid with glass. Inside, the box was lined with black silk, and divided into basins. One held fire pearls, another a spool of silver wire, violet stone clasps and tiny gold feathers, delicate as down. Calla drew in a small, sharp breath at the treasure.

"*Mas aven,*" she whispered. And then she looked up. "Forgive me for asking, but I trust no one will come looking for these?" There was surprisingly little judgment in the question. Lila smiled.

"If you know of Alucard Emery, then you know he sails a royal ship. These were confiscated from a vessel on our waters. They were mine, and now they are yours."

Calla's short fingers trailed over the trinkets. And then she closed the lid, and tucked the box away. "They are too much," she said. "You will have a credit."

"I'm glad to hear that," said Lila. "Because I've come to ask a favor."

"It's not a favor if you've purchased and paid. What can I do?"

Lila reached into her coat and pulled out the black mask Calla had given her months before, the one that had solidified her nickname of Sarows. It was worn by salt air and months of use; cracks traced across the black leather, the horns had lost some of their upward thrust, and the cords that fastened it were in danger of breaking.

"What on earth have you been doing with this?" chided Calla, her lips pursing with something like motherly disapproval.

"Will you mend it?"

Calla shook her head. "Better to start fresh," she said, setting the mask aside.

"No," insisted Lila, reaching for it. "I'm fond of this one. Surely you can reinforce it."

"For what?" asked Calla archly. "Battle?"

Lila chewed her lip, and the merchant seemed to read the answer. "*Tac,* Lila, there is eccentricity, and there is *madness.* You cannot mean to compete in the *Essen Tasch.*"

"What?" teased Lila. "Is it *unladylike?*"

Calla sighed. "Lila, when we first met, I gave you your pick of all my wares, and you chose a devil's mask and a man's coat. This has nothing to do with what is proper, it's only that it's dangerous. *Anesh,* so are you." She said it as though it were a compliment, albeit a grudging one. "But you are not on the roster."

"Don't worry about that," said Lila with a smirk.

Calla started to protest, and then stopped herself and shook her head. "No, I do not want to know." She stared down at the devil's mask. "I should not help you with this."

"You don't have to," said Lila. "I could find someone else."

"You *could,*" said Calla, "but they wouldn't be as good."

"Nowhere *near* as good," insisted Lila.

Calla sighed. "*Stas reskon,*" she murmured. It was a phrase Lila had heard before. *Chasing danger.*

Lila smiled, thinking of Barron. "A friend once told me that if there was trouble to be found, I'd find it."

"We would be friends, then, your friend and I."

"I think you would," said Lila, her smile faltering. "But he is gone."

Calla set the mask aside. "Come back in two days. I will see what I can do."

"*Rensa tav,* Calla."

"Do not thank me yet, strange girl."

Lila turned to go, but hesitated when she reached the curtain. "I have only just returned," she said carefully, "so I've not had time to ask after the princes." She glanced back. "How are they?"

"Surely you can go and see for yourself."

"I can't," said Lila. "That is, I shouldn't. Kell and I, what we had . . . it was a temporary arrangement."

The woman gave her a look that said she didn't believe that, not as far as she could throw it. Lila assumed that was the end of things, so she turned again, but Calla said, "He came to me, after you were gone. Master Kell."

Lila's eyes widened. "What for?"

"To pay the debt for your clothes."

Her mood darkened. "I can pay my own debts," she snapped, "and Kell knows it."

Calla smiled. "That is what I told him. And he went away. But a week later, he came back, and made the same offer. He comes every week."

"Bastard," mumbled Lila, but the merchant shook her head.

"Don't you see?" said Calla. "He wasn't coming to pay your debt. He was coming to see if you'd returned to pay it yourself." Lila felt her face go hot. "I do not know why you two are circling each other like stars. It is not *my* cosmic dance. But I do know that you come asking after one another, when only a few strides and a handful of stairs divide you."

"It's complicated," said Lila.

"As esta narash," she murmured to herself, and Lila now knew enough to know what she said. *All things are.*

VII

Kell strolled the Night Market for the first time in weeks.

He'd taken to avoiding such public appearances, his moments of defiance too rare compared to those of self-consciousness. *Let them think what they want* was a thought that visited him with far less frequency and force than *They see you as a monster.*

But he was in need of air and Rhy, for once in his life, was too busy to entertain him. Which was fine. In the growing madness of the approaching games, Kell simply wanted to move, to wander, and so he found himself strolling through the market under the heavy cover of the crowds. The influx of strangers in the city afforded him shelter. There were so many foreigners here for the locals to look at, they were far less likely to notice him. Especially as Kell had taken Rhy's advice and traded his stark black high coat for a dusty blue one more in fashion, and pulled a winter hood up over his reddish hair.

Hastra walked beside him in common clothes. He hadn't tried to ditch his guard tonight, and in return, the young man had agreed to change his red and gold cloak and armor for something less conspicuous, even if the royal sword still hung sheathed at his side.

Now, as initial hesitation gave way to relief, Kell found himself *enjoying* the market for the first time in ages, moving through the crowd with a blissful degree of anonymity. It made him impatient to don the competitor's mask, to become someone else entirely.

Kamerov.

Hastra vanished and reappeared a few minutes later with a cup of spiced wine, offering it to Kell.

"Where is yours?" asked Kell, taking the cup.

Hastra shook his head. "Isn't proper, sir, to drink on guard."

Kell sighed. He didn't care for the idea of drinking alone, but he was in dire need of the wine. His first stop hadn't been to the market. It had been to the docks.

And there he'd found the inevitable: dark hull, silver trim, blue sails.

The *Night Spire* had returned to London.

Which meant that Alucard Emery was here. Somewhere.

Kell had half a mind to sink the ship, but that would only cause trouble, and if Rhy found out, he'd probably throw a tantrum or stab himself out of spite.

So he had settled for glaring at the *Spire,* and letting his imagination do the rest.

"Are we on a mission, sir?" Hastra had whispered (the young guard was taking his new role as confidant and accomplice very seriously).

"We are," muttered Kell, feigning severity.

He'd lingered in the shadowed overhang of a shop and scowled at the ship for several long and uneventful minutes before announcing that he needed a drink.

Which was how Kell ended up in the market, sipping his wine and absently scanning the crowds.

"Where's Staff?" he asked. "Did he get tired of being left behind?"

"Actually, I think he's been sent to see to Lord Sol-in-Ar."

See to? thought Kell. Was the king that nervous about the Faroan lord?

He set off again through the market, with Hastra a few strides behind.

The crowds grew thicker as Kell walked, swirling around him

like a tide. Faroans with their bright, intricately folded fabrics and jeweled skin. Veskans adorned by silver and gold bands, tall and made taller by their manes of hair. And of course, Arnesians, in their rich cowls and cloaks.

And then, some Kell couldn't place. A few fair enough to be Veskans, but in Arnesian clothes. A dark-skinned figure with a coil of Veskan braids.

The nightmare floated to the surface of his mind—so many strange faces, so many almost familiar ones—but he forced it down. A stranger brushed his arm as they crossed paths, and Kell found his hands going into his pockets to check for missing things, even though there was nothing there to steal.

So many people, he thought. Lila would pick every pocket here.

Just as he thought it, he caught sight of a shadow amid the color and light.

A thin figure.

A black coat.

A sharp smile.

Kell caught his breath, but by the time he blinked, the shadow was gone. Just another phantom made by the crowd. A trick of the eye.

Still, the glimpse, even false, made him feel unsteady, and his pace slowed enough to interrupt the foot traffic around him.

Hastra was there again at his side. "Are you all right, sir?"

Kell waved off his concern. "I'm fine," he said. "But we'd better head back."

He set off toward the palace end of the market, stopping only when he reached Calla's stall. "Wait here," he told Hastra before ducking inside.

Calla's shop was always changing, it seemed, to suit the city's festive needs. His gaze wandered over the various winter accessories that now lined the walls and covered the tables.

"*Avan!*" called the merchant as she appeared from a curtained area near the back of the tent, holding a piece of black leather in one hand. Calla was short and round, with the shrewd eye of a businesswoman and the warmth of a wood fire. Her face lit up when she saw him. "Master Kell!" she said, folding herself into deep curtsy.

"Come now, Calla," he said, guiding her up, "there's no need for that."

Her eyes danced with even more mischief than usual. "What brings you to my shop tonight, *mas vares*?"

She said the words—*my prince*—with such kindness that he didn't bother correcting her. Instead he fidgeted with a box on the table, a pretty inlaid thing. "Oh, I found myself in the market, and thought I would come and see that you are well."

"You do me too much honor," she said, smile widening. "And if you were coming to see about that debt," she went on, eyes bright, "you should know that it has recently been paid."

Kell's chest tightened. "What? *When?*"

"Indeed," continued Calla. "Only a few minutes ago."

Kell didn't even say good-bye.

He lunged out of the tent and into the churning market, scanning the currents of people streaming past.

"Sir," asked Hastra, clearly worried. "What's wrong?"

Kell didn't answer. He turned in a slow circle, scouring the crowd for the thin shadow, the black coat, the sharp smile.

She'd been real. She'd been *here*. And of course, she was already gone.

Kell knew he was beginning to draw attention, even with the cover of the masses. A few Arnesians started to whisper. He could feel their gazes.

"Let's go," he said, forcing himself back toward the palace. But as he walked, heart pounding, he replayed the moment in his mind, the glimpse of a ghost.

But it *hadn't* been a ghost. Or a trick of the eye.

Delilah Bard was back in London.

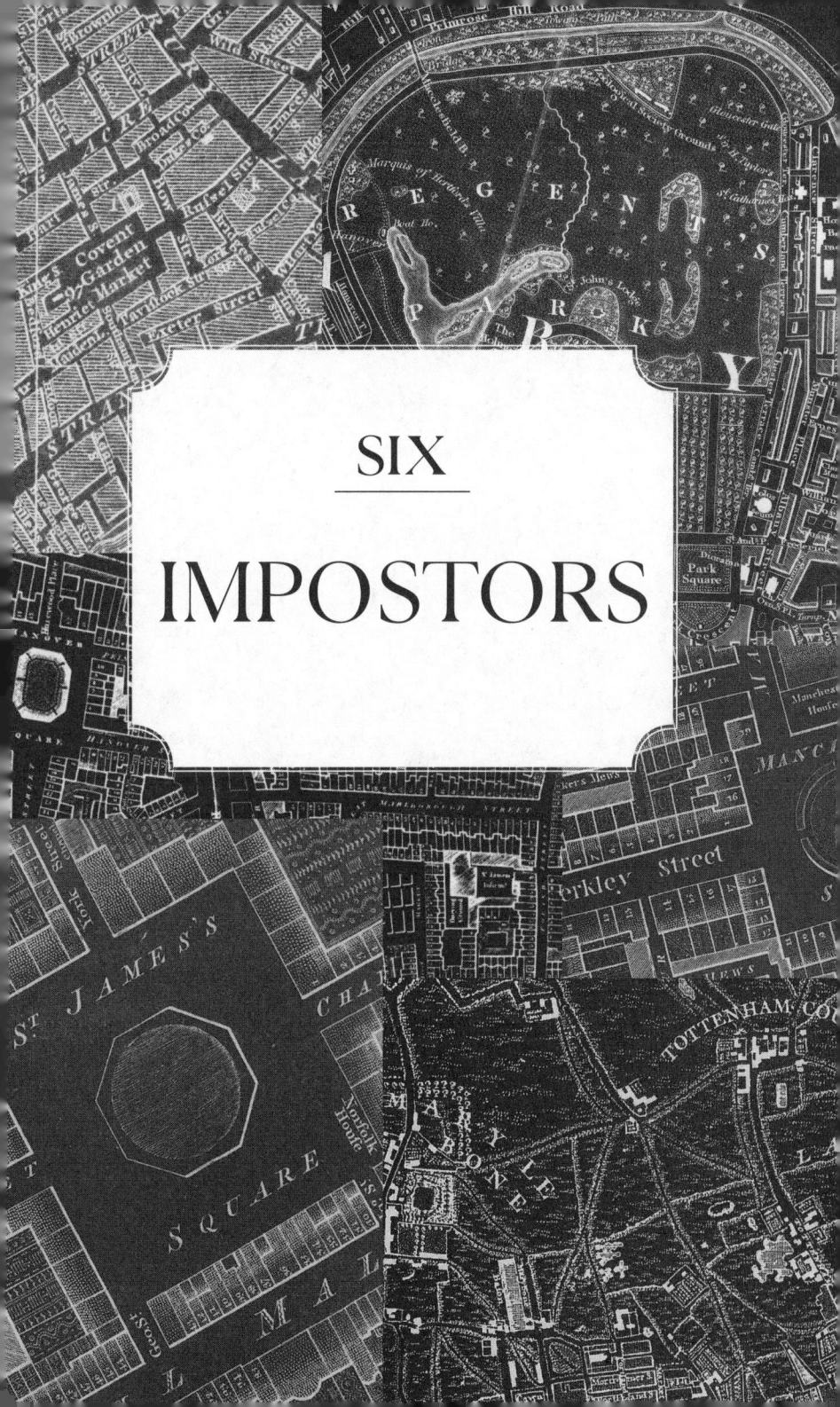

SIX

IMPOSTORS

I

White London.

Holland knew the stories by heart.

He'd grown up with them—stories of a bad king, a mad king, a curse; of a good king, a strong king, a savior. Stories of why the magic went away, and who would bring it back. And every time a new ruler the throne with blood and the dregs of power in their veins, the people would say *now*. Now the magic will come back. Now the world will wake. Now it will get better, now we will get stronger.

The stories ran in the veins of every Londoner. Even when the people grew thin and pale, even when they began to rot inside and out, even when they had no food, no strength, no power, the stories survived. And when Holland was young, he believed them, too. Even believed, when his eye went black, that *he* might be the hero. The good king. The strong king. The savior.

But on his knees before Athos Dane, Holland had seen the stories for what they were: desperate tales for starving souls.

And yet.

And yet.

Now he stood in the square at the heart of the city, with his name on every tongue and a god's power running in his veins. Everywhere he stepped, the frost withdrew. Everything he touched regained its color. All around him, the city was thawing (the day the Siljt unfroze, the people went mad. Holland had led uprisings, had witnessed riots, but never in his life had he seen *celebration*). Of course, there was tension. The people had starved too long, survived only on violence and greed. He couldn't blame them. But they would learn. Would see. Hope, faith, change: these were fragile things, and they had to be tended.

"*Køt!*" they called out—*King*—while the voice in his head, that constant companion, hummed with pleasure.

The day was bright, the air alive, and the people crowded to see Holland's latest feat, held at bay by the Iron Guard. Ojka stood beside him, her hair on fire in the sun, a knife in hand.

King! King! King!

It was called the Blood Square, where they stood. An execution site, the stones beneath his boots stained black and streaked where desperate fingers had scrounged at the spilled life in case it held a taste of magic. Eight years ago, the Danes had dragged him from a fast death here, and granted him a slow one.

The Blood Square.

It was time to give the name another meaning.

Holland held out his hands, and Ojka brought the blade to rest against his palms. The crowd quieted in anticipation.

"My king?" said Ojka, her yellow eye asking for permission. So many times the hand had been his, but not the will. This time the hand was his servant's, the will his own.

Holland nodded, and the blade bit down. Blood welled and spilled to the ruined stones, and where it struck, it broke the surface of the world, like a stone cast in a pool. The ground rippled, and behind his eyes Holland saw the square reborn. Clean, and whole. As the ripples spread, they swallowed the stains, mended the cracks, turned the broken pavers to polished marble, the abandoned basin of a well to a fountain, the fallen columns to vaulting archways.

We can do more, said the god in his head.

And before Holland could sort the *oshoc*'s thoughts from his own, the magic was spreading.

The archways of the Blood Square rippled and reformed, melting from stone into water before hardening to glass. Beyond them, the streets shuddered, and the ground beneath the crowd's feet dissolved from rock into rich, dark soil. The people fell to their knees, sinking to the loamy earth and digging their fingers in up to the wrists.

Enough, Osaron, thought Holland. He closed his bloody hands, but the ripples went on, the shells of ruined buildings collapsing into sand, the fountain overflowing not with water but with amber-colored wine.

The pillars morphed into apple trees, their trunks still marbled stone, and Holland's chest began to ache, his heart pounding as the magic poured like blood from his veins, each beat forcing more power into the world.

Enough!

The ripples died.

The world fell still.

The magic tapered off, the square a shimmering monstrosity of elements, the edges a wavering shore. The people were caked with earth, and wet from the fountain's rain, their faces bright, their eyes wide—not with hunger, but with awe.

"King! King! King!" they all called, while in his head, Osaron's own word echoed.

More. More. More.

II

Red London.

Back at the Wandering Road, the crowd had thinned, but the wolfhound was still sprawled in the exact same position by fire. Lila couldn't help but wonder if it was alive. She crossed to the hearth, and knelt slowly, hand hovering over the creature's chest.

"I already checked," said a voice behind her. Lila looked up to see Lenos fidgeting nervously. "He's okay."

Lila straightened. "Where is everybody?"

Lenos cocked his head toward a corner table. "Stross and Tav have got a game going."

The men were playing Sanct, and from what she could tell, they hadn't been playing long, because neither looked that angry and both still had all their weapons and most of their clothes. Lila wasn't a fan of the game, mostly because after four months of watching the sailors win and lose, she felt no closer to understanding the rules well enough to play, let alone cheat.

"Vasry went out," Lenos continued as Lila ambled toward the table. "Kobis went to bed."

"And Alucard?" she asked, trying to keep her tone flat with disinterest. She took up Stross's drink and downed it, ignoring the first mate's muttered protests.

Stross threw down a card with a hooded figure holding two

chalices. "Too late," he said to her, keeping his eyes on the table and the cards. "Captain said he was retiring."

"Awfully early," mused Lila.

Tav chuckled and mumbled something, but she couldn't decipher it. He was from somewhere at the edge of the empire, and the more he drank, the less intelligible his accent became. And since Lila's default when she didn't understand something was to keep her mouth shut, she simply walked away. After a few steps she stopped and turned back to Lenos, drawing the palm fire from her coat. The light was already fading, and she hadn't thought to ask if there was a way to restore it, or if it was a one-time-use kind of charm, which seemed wasteful.

"Here," she said, tossing Lenos the orb.

"What's this for?" he asked, surprised.

"Keeps the shadows at bay," she said, heading for the stairs. Lenos stood there, staring down at the orb, perplexed by either the sphere itself or the fact that the Sarows had just given him a gift.

Why *had* she given it to him?

Getting soft, grumbled a voice in her head. Not Kell's, or Barron's. No, this voice was all hers.

As Lila climbed the stairs, she produced a narrow bottle of wine she'd nicked, not from the inn or the market—she knew better than to steal from warded tents—but from Alucard's own stash aboard the *Spire*.

The captain's room sat across from hers, the doors facing like duelers. Which seemed fitting. But when she reached the doors, she paused between them, presented with the question of which she'd come for, and which she planned to open.

Lila hovered there in the hall.

She wasn't sure *why* she was drawn to his room more than hers. Perhaps because she was restless, being back in this city for the first time, a place at once strange and familiar. Perhaps because she wanted to slip back into the comfort of English. Perhaps because she wanted to learn more about the tournament, and Alucard's participation. Or perhaps out of simple habit. This was how they spent most nights at sea, after all, a bottle of wine and a magical fire, each trying to pry secrets from the other without giving up any of their own. Had Lila become so accustomed to the dance that she actually missed it?

Hang this, she thought. What a waste of life, to stand around and think so much on every little thing. What did it matter why she wanted to see the captain? She simply did.

And so, casting motive aside, she reached out to knock, only to stop when she heard footsteps from within, coming briskly toward the door.

Her thief's sense twitched, and her body moved before her mind, boots silently retreating one stride, then two, before sliding smoothly behind the corner of the hallway's nearest bend. She had no reason to hide, but she'd been doing it so long, the gesture came naturally. Besides, hiding was simply seeing without being seen, and that gave her the upper hand. Nothing to be lost by it, and often something to be gained.

An instant later, the door swung open and Alucard Emery stepped into the hall.

The first thing she noticed was his silence. The captain of the *Night Spire* normally made a certain amount of noise. His jewelry jangled and his weapons clanked, his steel-heeled boots announced every step, and even when his attire was quiet, Alucard himself usually hummed. Lila had mentioned it once, and he simply said he'd never been a fan of quiet. She'd thought him incapable of it, but as he made his way down the hall, his steps marked only by the gentle creak of the floorboards, she realized that, before, he'd always *meant* to be loud.

Another aspect of the role he was playing, now cast aside, replaced by . . . what?

He was fully dressed, but not in his usual clothes. Alucard had always favored fine, flashy things, but now he looked less like a pirate captain and more like an elegant shadow. He'd traded the blue coat he'd worn ashore for a charcoal half cloak, a simple silver scarf at his throat. He wore no obvious weapons and the sapphire was gone from his brow, along with all the rings from his fingers save one, the thick silver band shaped like a feather. His brassy brown hair was combed back beneath a black cap, and Lila's first thought was that, pared down, he looked younger, almost boyish.

But where was he going? And why was he going in disguise?

Lila trailed him down the stairs of the inn and out into the night, close enough to keep track and far enough away to avoid notice. She might have spent the last four months as a privateer, but she had spent *years* as a shadow. She knew how to blend into the dark, how to tail a mark, how to breathe and move with the current of the night instead of against it, and Alucard's steps might have been light, but hers were silent.

She'd expected him to head for the market, overflowing with people, or the web of streets that traced lines of light away from the river. Instead he hugged its banks, following the red glow of the Isle and the main concourse past the palace to a bridge on the far side. It was made of pale stone and accented with copper: copper railings, and copper pillars, and sculpted copper canopies. The whole thing formed a kind of shining tunnel. Lila hesitated at its base—the entire length of the bridge beneath the canopies was well lit, the metal reflecting and magnifying the light, and though people were strewn along it, mostly in pairs and groups, collars turned up against the cold, few actually seemed to be making their way across to the opposite bank. Blending in would be nearly impossible.

A few merchants had set up stalls beneath the lanterns, haloed by mist and candlelight, and Lila hung back to see if Alucard was heading for one of those, but he made his way briskly across, eyes ahead, and Lila was forced to either follow or be left behind. She set off after him, fighting to keep her pace leisurely, ignoring the glittering stalls and the patterned metal ceiling, but not so pointedly as to give away her purpose. It was a wasted effort in the end—Alucard never once looked back.

Walking beneath the copper canopies, she saw that they were dappled to look like trees, starlight shining through the leaves, and Lila thought, once more, what a strange world she'd stumbled into, and how glad she was to be there.

Alucard crossed the entire length of the bridge and descended a grand set of stairs to the southern bank of the Isle. Lila had only been on this side once, when she and Kell took Rhy to the sanctuary, and she'd never given much thought to what else lined this other, darker half of the city. Shops and taverns, she would have guessed, perhaps a shadier version of the northern bank. She would have been wrong. This half of London was quiet by comparison; the sanctuary rose solemnly from a bend in the river, and beyond a boundary of bank-side shops and inns, the city gave way to gardens and orchards and, beyond these, to manor homes.

Lila's old stomping grounds in Mayfair and Regent Park paled in comparison to this London's southern bank. Elegant carriages pulled by magnificent steeds dotted street after street of grand estates, high-walled and furnished with marble and glass and gleaming metal. The evening mist itself seemed to glitter with wealth.

Ahead, Alucard had quickened his pace, and Lila picked hers up to match. Far fewer people were on these streets, which made tailing him a good deal harder, but his attention was fixed on the road ahead. As far as Lila could tell, there was nothing to see here. No deals to do. No trouble to get into. Nothing but houses, half the windows dark.

Finally Alucard turned off the road, stepping through an intricate gate and into a courtyard lined with shrubbery and bordered by trees, their branches winter-bare.

When Lila caught up, she saw that the curling metalwork of

the gate formed an ornate *E*. And then she looked inside, and caught her breath. The floor of the courtyard was a mosaic of glittering blue and silver stone. She hovered in the shadow of the gate as Alucard made his way up the walk, and watched as, halfway to the door, he paused to collect himself. He dragged his cap from his head and shoved it into the satchel on his shoulder, tousled his hair, flexed his hands, muttered something she couldn't hear, and then picked up again, his stride calm and confident as he hopped up a short set of steps, then rang a bell.

A moment later, one of the two front doors swung open, and a steward appeared. On seeing Alucard, he bowed. "Lord Emery," he said, stepping aside. "Welcome home."

Lila stared in disbelief.

Alucard wasn't visiting the master of the house.

He *was* the master of the house.

Before he could step inside, a girl appeared in the doorway, squealed with delight, and threw her arms around his neck.

"Luc!" she cried as he swung her into the air. The girl couldn't be more than twelve or thirteen, and she had his wavy brown curls and dark eyes.

"Anisa." He broke into a smile Lila had never seen before, not on him. It wasn't the proud grin of a captain or the mischievous smirk of a rake, but the absolute adoration of an older brother. She'd never had any siblings, so she didn't *understand* the look, but she recognized the simple, blind love, and it twisted something in her.

And then, as suddenly as the girl had launched herself forward, she pulled away, affecting the mock frown Lila had seen on Alucard's own mouth so many times.

"Where is Esa?" demanded the girl, and Lila tensed, not at the question itself, but the fact she'd asked it in *English*. No one spoke that tongue in Red London, not unless they were trying to impress the royalty. Or they *were* royalty.

Alucard chuckled. "Of course," he said, crossing the threshold.

"Three years away from home, and your first question is about the cat. . . ." They disappeared inside, and Lila found herself staring at the front door as it closed.

Alucard Emery, captain of the *Night Spire,* tournament magician, and . . . Red London royal? Did anyone know? Did *everyone* know? Lila knew she should be surprised, but she wasn't. She'd known from the moment she met Alucard aboard the *Night Spire* that he was playing a part; it was just a matter of uncovering the man behind it. Now she knew the truth, and the truth gave her a card to play. And when it came to men like Alucard Emery, any advantage was worth taking.

A decorative wall circled the house, and Lila managed to hoist herself up with the help of a low branch. Perched on top, she could see through the great glass windows, many of which were unshuttered. Her silhouette blended into the tracery of trees at her back as she skirted the house, following the glimpses of Alucard and his sister as they made their way into a grand room with tall windows and a blazing hearth, and a pair of glass doors on the far wall leading to an expansive garden. She dropped into a crouch atop the wall as a man came into view. He had Alucard's coloring, and his jaw was the same square cut, but it looked hard without Alucard's smile. The man looked older by several years.

"Berras," said Alucard by way of greeting. The windows were cracked open, and the word reached Lila through the parted glass.

The man, Berras, strode forward, and for an instant it looked as though he might strike Alucard, but before he could, the girl lunged in front of her brother like a shield—there was something terribly practiced about the gesture, as if she'd done it many times before—and Berras stilled his hand in midair. On one of his fingers Lila saw a duplicate of Alucard's feather ring before his hand fell back to his side.

"Go, Anisa," he ordered.

The girl hesitated, but Alucard gave her a gentle smile and a nod, and she backed out of the room. The moment they were alone, Berras snapped.

"Where is Kobis?"

"I pushed him overboard," said Alucard. Disgust spilled across the man's face, and Alucard rolled his eyes. "Saints, Berras, it was a joke. Your moody little spy is safely housed at an inn with the rest of my crew."

Berras sneered faintly at the mention of the *Spire*'s men.

"That look does nothing for you, Brother," said the captain. "And the *Night Spire* sails for the crown. To insult my post is to insult House Maresh, and we wouldn't want to do *that*."

"Why are you *here*?" growled Berras, taking up a goblet. But before he could drink, Alucard flicked his wrist and the wine abandoned its cup, rising in a ribbon, coiling in on itself as it did. Between one instant and the next, it had hardened into a block of ruby-colored ice.

Alucard plucked the crystal from the air and considered it absently. "I'm in town for the tournament. I only came to make sure my family was well. How foolish of me to think I'd find a welcome." He tossed the frozen cube into the hearth, and turned to go.

Berras didn't speak, not until Alucard was at the garden doors.

"I would have let you rot in that jail."

A small, bitter smile touched the edge of Alucard's mouth. "Good thing it wasn't up to you."

With that, he stormed out. Lila straightened atop the wall, and rounded the perimeter to find Alucard standing on a broad balcony overlooking the grounds. Beyond the wall she could make out the arc of the palace, the diffused glow of the river.

Alucard's face was a mask of icy calm, bordering on disinterest, but his fingers gripped the balcony's edge, knuckles white.

Lila didn't make a sound, and yet Alucard sighed and said, "It isn't polite to spy."

Dammit. She'd forgotten about his gift for seeing the magic in people. It would make a handy skill for a thief, and Lila wondered, not for the first time, if there was a way to steal talents the way one did trinkets.

She stepped off the low wall onto the edge of the patio rail before dropping soundlessly to the terrace beside him.

"Captain," she said, half greeting and half apology.

"Still simply looking after your interests?" he asked. But he didn't sound angry.

"You're not upset," she observed.

Alucard raised a brow, and she found herself missing the familiar wink of blue. "I suppose not. Besides, my excursions were fairly innocuous compared to yours."

"You followed me?" snapped Lila.

Alucard chuckled. "You hardly have a right to sound affronted."

Lila shook her head, silently grateful she hadn't decided to march into the palace and surprise Kell. Truth be told, she still hadn't decided when she would see him. *If* she would see him. But when—and if—she did, she certainly didn't want Alucard there spying on them. Kell was somebody here, a royal, a saint, even if she could only think of him as the silly smuggler who frowned too much and nearly got them both killed.

"What are you grinning about?"

"Nothing," said Lila, leveling her expression. "So . . . *Luc,* huh?"

"It's a nickname. Surely they have those, wherever you're from. And for the record, I prefer Alucard. Or Captain Emery."

"Does the crew know?"

"Know what?"

"That you're . . ." She gestured to the estate, searching for the word.

"It's hardly a secret, Bard. Most Arnesians have heard of the House of Emery."

He gave her a look that said, *Odd, isn't it, that you haven't.*
"Haven't you heard them calling me *vestra*?"

Lila had. "I just assumed it was a slur. Like *pilse*."

Alucard laughed soundlessly. "Maybe it is, to them. It means *royal*."

"Like a *prince*?"

He gave a humorless laugh. "What a disappointment I must be to you. I know you wanted a pirate. You should have conned your way aboard a different ship. But don't worry. There are many doors between my person and the throne. And I have no desire to see them opened."

Lila chewed her lip. "But if everyone knows, then why sneak about like a thief?"

His gaze drifted back to the garden wall. "Because there are other people in this city, Bard. Some I don't care to see. And some I'd rather not see me."

"What's this?" she teased. "The great Alucard Emery has enemies?"

"Comes with the trade, I fear."

"It's hard to imagine you meeting someone you couldn't charm."

His eyes narrowed. "You say that like it's not a compliment."

"Perhaps it's not."

An uncomfortable silence began to settle.

"Nice house," said Lila.

It was the wrong thing to have said. His expression hardened. "I hope you'll forgive me for not inviting you in and introducing you to my esteemed family. It might be tricky to explain the sudden presence of a girl in a man's suit with the ability to speak the royal tongue but not the grace to use the front door."

Lila bit back a reply. She felt dismissed, but as she stepped up onto the balcony's edge, Alucard said, "Wait," and there was something in his voice that she barely recognized, because she'd never heard it from him before. Sincerity. She twisted back, and she saw him haloed by the light from the room behind, framed by the doorway. He was little more than a silhouette, a simplified portrait of a nobleman.

A picture of what someone should be, not what they were.

Then Alucard stepped forward, away from the light and into the shadows with her. This version of him looked real. Looked right. And Lila understood—when he said *Wait,* what he meant was, *Wait for me.*

"I suppose we should both be getting back," he added, aiming for indifference but falling short.

"Shouldn't you say good-bye?"

"I've never been a fan of farewells. Or hellos, for that matter. Unnecessary punctuation. Besides, they'll see me again."

Lila looked back at the house. "Won't Anisa be upset?"

"Oh, I imagine so. I'm afraid I'm accustomed to her disappointment."

"But what about—"

"No more questions, Lila," he said. "I'm tired."

The last protests cooled to ash on her tongue as Alucard stepped up onto the banister beside her, and then, in a single, effortless stride, onto the low wall.

It was narrow, but he moved with sure-footed ease atop it. He didn't even look down to check his steps.

"I grew up here," he said, reading her surprise. "If there's a way in or out, I've tried it."

They slipped along the garden wall and down into the courtyard, hugging the shadows until they were safely beyond the gate.

Alucard set off down the street without looking back, but Lila cast a glance at the grand estate.

The truth was, Lila understood why Alucard did it. Why he traded safety and boredom for adventure. She didn't know what it felt like to be safe, and she'd never had the luxury of being bored, but it was like she'd once told Kell. People either stole to stay alive or to feel alive. She had to imagine that they ran away for the same reasons.

Lila jogged to catch up, and fell in step beside the captain, the street quiet save for the sounds of their boots. She cheated a sideways glance, but Alucard's gaze was straight ahead, and far away.

She used to hate people like him, people who gave up something good, shucked warm meals and solid roofs as if they didn't matter.

But then Barron died and Lila realized that in a way she'd done the same thing. Run away from what could have been a good life. Or at least a happy one. Because it wasn't enough to be happy, not for Lila. She wanted *more*. Wanted an adventure. She used to think that if she stole enough, the want would fade, the hunger would go away, but maybe it wasn't that simple. Maybe it wasn't a matter of what she didn't have, of what she wasn't, but what she *was*. Maybe she wasn't the kind of person who stole to *stay* alive. Maybe she just did it for the thrill. And that scared her, because it meant she didn't need to do it, couldn't justify it, could have stayed at the Stone's Throw, could have saved Barron's life. . . . It was a slippery slope, that kind of thinking, one that ended in a cliff, so Lila backed away.

She was who she was.

And Alucard Emery?

Well, he was a man with secrets of his own.

And she couldn't fault him that.

III

Kell ducked and dodged, moving like shadow and light across the Basin.

He relished his burning muscles, his pounding heart; he'd slept poorly and woken worse, his thoughts still churning around the news of Lila's return. It made sense, didn't it? If she'd taken up with an Arnesian crew, most of them had docked back in London for the tournament.

Only two days until the *Essen Tasch*.

A blade swung high, and Kell lunged back out of its reach.

Two days, and still no sign of her. Some small, irrational part had been convinced that he'd be able to *feel* her return, be tuned to it the way he'd been to the Stone's Throw, and the Setting Sun, and the Scorched Bone. The fixed points in the worlds. Then again, maybe he *was* tuned to her. Maybe she was the small, invisible force that had drawn him out into the city in the first place.

But he'd missed her, and with the city so overrun, how was he supposed to find her again?

Just follow the knives, said a voice in his head. *And the bodies they're lodged in.*

He smiled to himself. And then, with a small pang, he wondered how long she'd been in London. And why she hadn't come to see him sooner. Their paths had only crossed for a few days, but he and Rhy and Tieren, they were the only people she knew in this world, or at least, the only people she'd known four months ago. Perhaps she'd gone off and made a wealth of friends—but he doubted it.

The next blow nearly found skin, and Kell jerked away just in time.

Focus, he chided himself. *Breathe.*

The silver mask was perfectly contoured to his face, shielding everything but air and sight. He'd put it on, wanting to get used to its size and weight, and quickly found himself relishing the difference, slipping into the comfort of anonymity, persona. So long as he wore the mask, Kell wasn't Kell.

He was *Kamerov.*

What would Lila think about that? Lila, Lila, he'd even considered using blood magic to find her—he still had her kerchief—but stopped himself before he drew the knife. He'd gone months without stooping so low. Besides, he wasn't some pup, chasing after a master or a bone. Let her come to him. But why *hadn't* she come to—

Metal flashed, too close, and he swore and rolled, regaining his feet.

He'd traded a dozen enemies for only one, but unlike the dummies he'd trained against, this one was very much alive. Hastra shifted back and forth, in full armor, trying to avoid Kell's blows. The young guard had been surprisingly willing to run around the Basin armed with only a small shield and a dull blade while Kell honed his agility and practiced turning elements into weapons.

The armor . . . he thought, wind whipping around him, *is designed to crack . . .* He leaped, pushed off a wall, slammed a gust of air into Hastra's back. *. . . when struck.* Hastra stumbled forward and spun to face him. *The first to ten hits . . .* He continued reciting the rules as water swirled around his hand. *. . . wins the match . . .* The water split, circling both hands. *. . . unless one of the competitors . . .* Both streams shot forward, freezing before they hit. . . . *is unable to continue* . . . Hastra could only block one shard, and the second caught him in the armored thigh and shattered into drops of ice. . . . *or admits defeat.*

Kell broke into a smile behind his mask, and when the breathless guard pulled off his helmet, he was grinning, too. Kell tugged off his silver mask, his damp hair standing on end.

"Is this what you've been doing down here all these weeks, Master Kell?" asked Hastra breathlessly. "Practicing for the tournament?"

Kell hesitated, and then said, "I suppose." After all, he had been training; he simply hadn't known what he was training *for*.

"Well it's paying off, sir," said the guard. "You make it look easy."

Kell laughed. The truth was, his whole body ached, and even while his blood sang for a fight, his power felt thin. Drained. He'd grown too used to the efficiency of blood magic, but elements took more will to wield. The fatigue from using blood spells hit him all at once, but this kind of fighting wore him down. Perhaps he'd actually get a sound night's sleep before the tournament.

Hastra crossed the training room gingerly, as if treading on hallowed ground, and stood by the Basin's archway, considering the equipment table with its bowl of water, its containers of earth and sand and oil.

"Do *you* have an element?" asked Kell, slicking back his hair.

Hastra's smile softened. "Little of this, little of that, sir."

Kell frowned. "What do you mean?"

"Parents wanted me to be a priest," said the young guard, scratching his head. "But I thought that didn't sound like nearly as much fun. Spend all day meditating in that musty stone structure—"

"You can *balance*?" cut in Kell, amazed. Priests were chosen not for their strength in one element, but for their tempered ability to manage all, not as Kell did, with sheer power, but with the evenness needed to nurture life. Balancing the elements was a sacred skill. Even Kell struggled with balance; just as a strong wind could uproot a sapling, an *Antari*'s power held too much force for the subtle arts. He could impact things already grown, but life was fragile at the start, and required a gentle touch.

The young guard shrugged, and then brightened a little. "You want to see?" he asked, almost bashful.

Kell looked around "Right now?"

Hastra grinned and dug a hand in his pocket, fetching out a small seed. When Kell raised a brow, the guard chuckled. "You never know when you might need to impress a lady," he said. "Lots of people puff up their chest and go for the flash and the bang. But I can't tell you how many nights have started with a seed and ended, well . . ." Hastra seemed to ramble whenever he got nervous, and Kell apparently made him very nervous. "Then again I doubt you'd have to try as hard to impress them, sir."

Hastra scanned the elements on the table. In one small bowl was some loose dirt: not the rich soil of the orchards and gardens, but the rocky kind found beneath pavers in the street. It wasn't the most elegant thing to train with—and when given the choice, Kell would go for rocks over dirt—but it was abundant. Kell watched as Hastra scooped up a palmful of earth, and made a small indent with his finger before dropping in the seed. He then dipped his other hand into the bowl of water, and pressed it down over the dirt, packing the seed and soil between his palms into a ball. Hastra closed his eyes, and his lips began to move. Kell felt a subtle warmth in the air between them, a sensation he knew well from his time with Tieren.

And then, still murmuring, Hastra began to slowly open his hands, the mound of damp earth cupped like an egg between them.

Kell watched, transfixed, as a pale green stem crept up through the moistened earth. The stem grew an inch, then two, twisting up into the air. Leaves began to unfurl, their surface a dark purple, before a white spherical bloom emerged.

Hastra trailed off, looking pleased.

"What is it?" asked Kell.

"Acina," said the guard. "Its leaves are good for pain."

"That's amazing."

The young guard shrugged. "My mum and dad were not happy when I chose to be a guard instead."

"I can imagine." Kell wanted to tell Hastra that he was wasted here. That his talent was far too precious to be thrown away in favor of a sword and some armor. But then, if a person's value alone should determine their place, what argument did Kell have for wanting more?

"But that's just because they don't know," continued Hastra sunnily. "They probably think I'm doing street patrol in the *sha*. They'll be proud, when they hear I'm guarding you, sir. Besides, I made a deal with my father," he added. "I'll join the sanctuary, eventually. But I've wanted to be a royal guard as long as I can remember. I knew I wouldn't be happy, not until I tried. Can't think of a worse thing, than wondering what would have been. So I thought, why not have both? The sanctuary will still have me, when I'm good and ready."

"And if you die before then?"

Hastra's cheery mood didn't dampen. "Then someone else will get my gift. And hopefully they'll be less stubborn. That's what my mother says." He leaned in conspiratorially. "I tend the courtyards, though, when no one's looking."

Kell smiled. The palace grounds *had* looked suspiciously lush, for this time of year. Hastra straightened, his gaze flicking to the stairs. "We should go—"

"We still have time," Kell assured him, getting to his feet.

"How do you know?" asked Hastra. "We can't hear the bells down here, and there are no windows to gauge the light."

"Magic," said Kell, and then, when Hastra's eyes widened, he gestured to the hourglass sitting on the table with his other tools. "And that."

There was still sand in the glass, and Kell wasn't ready to face the world above just yet. "Let's go again."

Hastra took up his position. "Yes, sir."

"Call me Kamerov," said Kell, slipping the helmet back over his head.

IV

Sessa Av!

The words ran across the tops of the scrying boards throughout London.

Two days!

The city was counting down.

Two days until the Essen Tasch!

Two days, and Lila Bard had a problem.

She'd hoped there'd be an obvious chink in the system, a way to threaten or bribe her way onto the tournament roster, or snag a wild card spot, but apparently the champions had all been chosen *weeks* ago. There were twelve names on that list, and two alternates, which meant if Lila Bard wanted a chance to play—and she *did*—she was going to have to steal a name.

Lila had nicked plenty of things in her time, but an identity wasn't one of them. Sure, she'd taken up pseudonyms, played a variety of made-up parts, but she'd never impersonated anyone *real*.

And of course, she couldn't simply impersonate them. She'd have to *replace* them.

Not worth it, warned a voice in her head, that pesky, pragmatic one that sounded too much like Kell. Maybe it was madness. Maybe she should just take her place in the stands and cheer for her captain, earn a few extra coins in the betting pools. It wouldn't be an unpleasant way to spend the week. And after all, what place did she have in the ring? She'd only been practicing a few months.

But.

There was that one word, lodged in her skin like a splinter.

But.

But she was restless.

But she wanted a thrill.

But it would be a challenge.

And when it came to magic, Lila wasn't just a quick study. She was a *natural*.

Master Tieren had told her months ago that something powerful lay inside her, waiting to be woken. Well, Lila had poked it with a stick, and it was wide awake—a living, humming thing as restless as she was.

And restlessness had always made her reckless.

Still, there was that pesky matter of the roster.

Lila had spent the day wandering Red London, learning everything she could about the *Essen Tasch* and its competitors. She'd passed enough time in taverns and brothels and public houses to know where you were most likely to find answers to questions without ever asking. Sure, you could always garnish pockets, but often if you sat in one place long enough, you'd learn more than anyone you paid would tell you. And everyone seemed to be talking about the tournament.

Alucard, apparently, was one of the Arnesian favorites, along with a woman named Kisimyr, the tournament's previous victor, and a man named Jinnar. But names were names. She needed to *see* the lineup before they took the stage. If there were no good marks, she told herself, she would let it go, stick to the stands with the rest of the crew. If there were no good marks. But she had to see. Had to know.

Frustrated, Lila finished her drink and pushed off her stool and headed back to the inn.

Somewhere on the way, her feet changed course, and by the

time she focused on where she was, she found herself standing across the main road from the royal palace, staring up. She wasn't surprised. All day her legs had been tugging her here. All day she'd found her gaze drifting to the gleaming structure.

Go in, said a voice.

Lila snorted. What would she do? Walk up the front steps? She'd done it once before, but that had been as a guest, with a stolen invitation. The doors had been cast open then, but now they were closed, a dozen guards in polished armor and red capes standing sentinel.

What would she say to them? *I'm here to see the black-eyed prince.* Her English might get her through the front door, but then what? Would the king and queen recognize her as the scrawny girl who'd helped Kell save their city? Lila suspected *Rhy* would remember her. She found herself warming at the thought of the prince—not as he was under the control of Astrid Dane, or bleeding to death on a sanctuary cot, but after, surrounded by pillows, dark circles below his amber eyes. Tired and kind and flirting through the pain.

And Kell?

How fared the black-eyed prince? Would he welcome her in? Hand her a drink and ask after her travels, or frown and ask if she was ready to leave, return to her own world where she belonged?

Lila squinted up in the dusk—the high balconies of the palace reduced to haloes of light in the cold evening—and thought she could make out a shadow standing on one of the tallest patios. It was too far to tell, that distance where everything was reduced to vague shapes, and the mind could twist them into anything. Still, the shadow seemed to curl over before her eyes, as if leaning on the rail, and in that moment the smudge of darkness became a magician in a high-collared coat. Lila stood and watched until the shape dissolved, swallowed up by the thickening night.

Her attention drifted down and landed on a pair of elegant black scrying boards that rose like columns before the palace steps. Months ago, Kell's face had shown up on these, first with the word *missing* at the top, and later with the word *wanted*. Now the ghostly chalk announced a variety of events in the hours leading up to the tournament itself—damn, there were a lot of parties—but one in particular caught her eye. Something called *Is Gosar Noche*.

The Banner Night.

She caught sight of the notice just before the board erased itself, and had to stand there for ten minutes waiting for the message to cycle back around. When it did, she read as quickly as she could, trying to make sense of the Arnesian script.

From what she could tell, competitors from all three empires were being summoned to the palace the following night—the night before the tournament—for a royal reception. And to select their banner, whatever that meant.

Wasn't this what she'd wanted?

An excuse to walk right into the Red Palace.

All she needed was a name.

The bells rang, and Lila swore under her breath. A whole day gone, she thought grimly as she trudged back to the Wandering Road, and no closer to her goal.

"There you are," said the captain's voice as soon as she stepped inside.

A handful of Alucard's men were gathered in the front room. They weren't dressed for the ship or the dock or the tavern inn. Tav, Stross, and Vasry wore fine hooded half-cloaks that gathered at the wrists, collar and cuff fastened with polished silver clasps. Alucard himself was dressed in an elegant coat, midnight blue with silver lining, his curls clasped back beneath a hat that dipped and curved like the sea. One hand rested on the hilt of his short sword, the silver feather ring glinting in the low light. Aside from the sapphire still sparkling in his right brow, he didn't look like the *casero* of the *Night Spire*. And yet, if he didn't look like a pirate, he didn't look entirely like a princeling, either. He looked polished, but also sharp, like a well-kept knife.

"Where have you been, Bard?"

She shrugged. "Exploring."

"We nearly left without you."

Her brow crinkled. "Where are you going?"

Alucard flashed a grin. "To a party," he said. Only the word for *party* in Arnesian wasn't that simple. Lila was learning that so many Arnesian words had meanings that shifted to fit their context. The word Alucard used was the broadest: *tasura,* which meant *party,* or *event,* or *function,* or *gathering,* and whose meaning ranged from celebratory to nefarious.

"I hate parties," she said, heading for the stairs.

But Alucard wasn't so easily dissuaded. He caught up, and took her elbow—gingerly, and only for an instant, as he knew how dangerous it was to touch Lila when she didn't want to be touched. "This one I think you'll enjoy," he murmured in English.

"Why's that?"

"Because I know how fascinated you are by the upcoming games."

"And?"

"And it's an unofficial tradition," he said, "for the local competitors to share a drink before the tournament begins." Lila's interest sharpened. "It's a bit of posturing, I admit," he added, gesturing to the others, "but I was hoping you would come."

"Why me?"

"Because it's a chance to size up the competition," said Alucard. "And you've got the sharpest eyes," he added with a wink.

Lila tried to hide her excitement. "Well," she said. "If you insist."

Alucard smiled and produced a silver scarf from his pocket.

"What's this for?" she asked as he tied it loosely around her throat.

"Tonight you're part of my entourage."

Lila laughed outright, a biting sound that stung the other men. "Your *entourage*." *What next?* She wondered. *Squire?*

"Think of it as the name for a crew on land."

"I hope you don't expect me to call you *Master*," she said, adjusting the knot.

"Saints, no, that word has no place except in bed. And *Lord* makes my skin crawl. *Captain* will do." He gestured at the waiting men. "Shall we?"

Lila's smile sharpened as she nodded at the door. "Lead the way, Captain."

The sign above the tavern door said *Is Casnor Ast.*

The Setting Sun.

Lila's steps slowed, then stopped. It was the strangest thing, but she couldn't shake the feeling she'd been there before. She hadn't, of course. She'd only stayed in Red London a few days after the ordeal with the Danes before taking up with the *Spire*'s crew—just long enough to heal and answer questions—and been confined to the palace the entire time.

But standing there, on the threshold, the place felt so *familiar*. When she closed her eyes, she almost felt like she was at . . . it couldn't be. Lila blinked, and looked around at the surrounding streets, trying to layer the image of this city on top of another, the one she'd lived in her entire life. And as the images merged, she realized that she knew exactly where she was. Where she would be. On this corner, back in Grey London, the exact same distance from the river, stood another tavern, one she knew too well.

The Stone's Throw.

What were the odds? Taverns were as plentiful as problems,

but two occupying the same exact place? Even from the outside, they looked nothing alike, and yet this place tugged on her bones with the same peculiar gravity she'd always felt back home. *Home.* She'd never thought of the Stone's Throw that way when she was there, but now it was the only word that fit. Only it wasn't the *building* she longed for. Not really.

She thrust her hand into her pocket, and curled her fingers around the silver pocket watch that hung like a weight in the bottom of the silk-lined fold.

"*Kers la,* Bard?"

She looked up, and realized that Alucard was holding the door open for her. She shook her head.

"*Skan,*" she said. *Nothing.*

Stepping inside, the power hit her in a wave. She couldn't see magic as Alucard did, but she could still feel it, filling the air like steam as it wafted off the gathered magicians. Not all the competitors traveled with a full entourage. Some—like the tan woman on the back wall, her black hair twisted into ropes and studded with gold—were the center of their own universe, while others sat in small groups or wandered the room alone, an aura of power drifting in their wake.

Meanwhile, the déjà vu continued. She did her best to shake it off and focus. After all, she wasn't just here to be part of Alucard's tableau. There was the issue of finding a mark, of performing her own little magic trick. The tavern was full of magicians, and Delilah Bard was going to make one of them disappear.

Someone boomed a greeting to Alucard, and the entourage came to a halt as the two clasped wrists. Tav went to round up drinks, while Stross surveyed the room with keen appraisal. She guessed he'd been brought along for the same reason she had, to size up the competition.

Vasry, meanwhile, eyed the room as if it were a feast.

"That's the reigning champion, Kisimyr," he whispered to

Lila in Arnesian as the woman with the roped hair strode toward Alucard, boots ringing out on the worn wood floor. The man who'd greeted Alucard retreated a few steps as she approached.

"Emery," she said with a feline grin and a heady accent. "You really don't know how to stay out of trouble." She wasn't from London. She was speaking Royal, but her words all ran together—not in the serpentine way of the Faroan tongue, more like she'd hacked off all the edges and taken out the space between. She had a low, resonant voice, and when she spoke, it sounded like rumbling thunder.

"Not when trouble is more fun," said Alucard with a bow. Kisimyr's grin widened as the two fell to quiet conversation—there was something sharp about that grin, and paired with the rest of her face, the slanted brow and straight-on gaze, it read like a taunt. A challenge. The woman exuded confidence. Not arrogance, exactly—that was usually unfounded, and everything about Kisimyr said she'd just *love* an excuse to show you what she could do.

Lila liked that, found herself mimicking the features, wondering what kind of whole they'd add up to on her own face.

She didn't know if she wanted to fight the woman or be her friend, but she certainly wouldn't be *replacing* her. Lila's attention shifted, trailing across a pair of brawny figures, and a very pretty girl in blue with cascades of dark hair, not to mention a fair number of curves. No good matches there. She continued to scan the room as Alucard's entourage made its way toward a corner booth.

Kisimyr had retreated into the folds of her own group, and she was talking to a young, dark-skinned man beside her. He was fine-boned and wiry, with bare arms and gold earrings running the length of both ears to match the ones in Kisimyr's.

"Losen," said Alucard softly. "Her protégé."

"Will they have to compete against each other?"

He shrugged. "Depends on the draw."

A man with a stack of paper appeared at Kisimyr's elbow.

"Works for the Scryer, that one," said Stross. "Best avoid him, unless you want to find yourself on the boards."

Just then, the tavern doors flung open, and a young man blew in—quite literally—on a gust of wind. It swirled around him and through the tavern, shuddering candle flames and rocking lanterns. Alucard twisted in his seat, then rolled his eyes with a smile. "Jinnar!" he said, and Lila couldn't tell by the way he said it if that was a name or a curse.

Even next to the broad Veskans and the jewel-marked Faroans she'd met in Sasenroche, the newcomer was one of the most striking men Lila had ever seen. Wisp-thin, like a late shadow, his skin had the rich tan of an Arnesian and his silver hair shot up in a vertical shock. Below silver brows, the irises of his eyes were *black*, shining like a cat's in the low tavern light, and framed by thick silver lashes. He had a jackal's grin, not sharp but wide. It only got wider when he saw Alucard.

"Emery!" he called, tugging the cloak from his shoulders and crossing the room, the two gestures wound together in a seamless motion. Beneath the cloak, his clothes weren't just close fitting; they were molded to his body, ornamented by silver cuffs that circled his throat and ran the lengths of his forearms.

Alucard stood. "They let you out in public?"

The young man threw his arm around the captain's shoulder. "Only for the *Essen Tasch*. You know that old Tieren has a soft spot for me."

He spoke so fast Lila could barely follow, but her attention prickled at the mention of London's head priest.

"Jin, meet my crew. At least, the ones I like best."

The man's eyes danced over the table, flitting across Lila for only a moment—it felt like a cool breeze—before returning to Alucard. Up close, his black gaze was even more unsettling.

"What are we calling you these days?"

"Captain will do."

"How very official. Though I suppose it's not as bad as a *vestra* title." He dipped into an elaborate gesture that vaguely resembled a bow, if a bow were paired with a rude hand gesture. "His Eminence Alucard, second son of the Royal House of Emery."

"You're embarrassing yourself."

"No, I'm embarrassing *you*," said Jin, straightening. "There's a difference."

Alucard offered him a seat, but Jin declined, perching instead on the shoulder of Alucard's own chair, light as a feather. "What have I missed?"

"Nothing, yet."

Jin looked around. "Going to be a strange one."

"Oh?"

"Air of mystery around it all this year."

"Is that an element joke?"

"Hah," said Jin, "I didn't even think about that."

"I thought you kept a list of wind jokes," teased Alucard. "I certainly do, just for you. I've broken them down into chills, gales, steam. . . ."

"Just like your sails," jabbed Jin, hopping down from the chair. "So full of air. But I'm serious," he said, leaning in. "I haven't even seen half the competition. Hidden away for effect perhaps. And the pomp surrounding everything! I was at Faro three years back, and you know how much they like their gold, but it was a pauper's haunt compared to this affair. I'm telling you, the air of spectacle's run away with it. Blame the prince. Always had a flare for drama."

"Says the man floating three inches off the ground."

Lila looked down, and started slightly when she saw that Jinnar was, in fact, hovering. Not constantly, but every time he moved, he took a fraction too long to settle, as if gravity didn't have the same hold on him as it did on everyone else. Or maybe, as if something else were lifting him up.

"Yes, well," Jin said with a shrug, "I suppose I'll fit in splendidly. As will you," he added, flicking the silver feather on Alucard's hat. "Now if you'll excuse me, I should make the rounds and the welcomes. I'll be back."

And with that, he was gone. Lila turned to Alucard, bemused. "Is he always like that?"

"Jinnar? He's always been a bit . . . enthusiastic. But don't let his childish humor fool you. He is the best wind mage I've ever met."

"He was *levitating*," said Lila. She'd seen plenty of magicians *doing* magic. But Jinnar *was* magic.

"Jinnar belongs to a particular school of magic, one that believes not only in using an element, but in becoming one with it." Alucard scratched his head. "It's like when children are learning to play renna and they have to carry the ball with them everywhere, to get comfortable with it. Well, Jin never set the ball down."

Lila watched the wind mage flit around the room, greeting Kisimyr and Losen, as well as the girl in blue. And then he stopped to perch on the edge of a couch, and began talking to a man she hadn't noticed yet. Or rather, she *had* noticed him, but she'd taken him for the cast-off member of someone else's entourage, dressed as he was in a simple black coat with an iridescent pin shaped like an *S* at his throat. He'd made his way through the gathering earlier, hugging the edges of the room and clutching a glass of white ale. The actions held more discomfort than stealth, and he'd eventually retreated to a couch to sip his drink in peace.

Now Lila squinted through the smoke and shadow-filled room as Jin shook his hand. The man's skin was fair, his hair dark—darker than Lila's—and shorter, but his bones were sharp. *How tall is he?* she wondered, sizing up the cut of his shoulders, the length of his arms. A touch of cool air brushed her cheek, and she blinked, realizing Jin had returned.

He was sitting again on the back of Alucard's chair, having appeared without so much as a greeting.

"Well," asked Alucard, tipping his head back, "is everyone here?"

"Nearly." Jinnar pulled the competition roster from his pocket. "No sign of Brost. Or the Kamerov fellow. Or Zenisra."

"Praise the saints," muttered Alucard at this last name.

Jin chuckled. "You make more enemies than most make bedfellows."

The sapphire in Alucard's brow twinkled. "Oh, I make plenty of those, too." He nodded at the man on the couch. "And the shadow?"

"Tall, dark, and quiet? Name's Stasion Elsor. Nice enough fellow. Shy, I think."

Stasion Elsor, thought Lila, turning the name over on her tongue.

"Or smart enough to keep his cards close to his chest."

"Maybe," said Jin. "Anyhow, he's a first-timer, comes from Besa Nal, on the coast."

"My man Stross hails from that region."

"Yes, well, hopefully Stasion's stage manner is stronger than his tavern one."

"It's not always about putting on a show," chided Alucard.

Jin cackled. "You're one to talk, Emery." With that, he dismounted the chair, and blew away.

Alucard got to his feet. He looked at the drink in his hand, as if he wasn't sure how it had gotten there. Then he finished it in a single swallow. "I suppose I better say my hellos," he said, setting down the empty glass. "I'll be back."

Lila nodded absently, her attention already returning to the man on the couch. Only he wasn't there anymore. She searched the room, eyes landing on the door just in time to see Stasion Elsor vanishing through it. Lila finished her own drink, and shoved herself up to her feet.

"Where are you going?" asked Stross.

She flashed him a sharp-edged smile and turned up the collar of her coat. "To find some trouble."

V

They were nearly the same height. That was the first thing she noticed as she fell in step behind him. Elsor was a touch taller, and a fraction broader in the shoulders, but he had a narrow waist and long legs. As Lila followed, she first matched his stride, and then began to mimic it.

So close to the river, the streets were crowded enough to cloak her pursuit, and she began to feel less like a thief with a mark and more like a cat with its prey.

There were so many chances to turn back. But she kept going.

Lila had never really bought into fate, but like most people who disavowed religion, she could summon a measure of belief when it was necessary.

Elsor wasn't from London. He didn't have an entourage. As she closed the gap, she wondered how many people had even noticed him back at the tavern, besides Jinnar. The light in the Sun had been low. Had anyone gotten a good look at his face?

Once the tournament began, they'd have no faces anyway.

Madness, warned a voice, but what did she have to lose? Alucard and the *Spire*? Caring, belonging, it was all so overrated.

Elsor put his hands in his pockets.

Lila put her hands in her pockets.

He rolled his neck.

She rolled her neck.

She had a variety of knives on her, but she didn't plan on killing him, not if it could be helped. Stealing an identity was one thing; stealing a life was another, and though she'd certainly killed her fair share, she didn't take it lightly. Still, for her plan to work, *something* had to happen to Stasion Elsor.

He rounded a corner onto a narrow street that led to the docks. The street was jagged and empty, dotted only by darkened shops and a scattering of bins and crates.

Elsor was no doubt an excellent magician, but Lila had the element of surprise and no problem playing dirty.

A metal bar leaned against a door, winking in the lantern light.

It scraped the stones as Lila lifted it, and Elsor spun around. He was fast, but she was faster, pressed into the doorway by the time his eyes found the place she'd been.

Flame sparked in the man's palm, and he held the light aloft, shadows dancing down the street. A fireworker.

It was the last sign Lila needed.

Her lips moved, magic prickling through her as she summoned a couplet of Blake. Not a song of fire, or water, but earth. A planter on the windowsill above him slid off the edge and came crashing down. It missed him by inches, shattering against the street, and Elsor spun to face the sound a second time. As he did, Lila closed the gap and raised the pipe, feeling a little less guilty.

Fool me twice, she thought, swinging the bar.

His hands came up, too slow to stop the blow, but fast enough to graze the front of her jacket before he collapsed to the street with the sound of dead weight and the hiss of doused flame.

Lila patted the drops of fire on her coat and frowned. Calla wouldn't be happy.

She set the bar against the wall, and knelt to consider Stasion Elsor—up close, the angles of his face were even sharper. Blood ran from his forehead, but his chest was rising and falling, and Lila felt rather proud of her restraint as she dragged his arm around her shoulders and struggled to her feet under the load. With his head lolling forward, and his dark hair covering the wound at his temple, he almost looked like a man too deep in his cups.

Now what? she thought, and at the same exact moment a voice behind her said, "What now?"

Lila spun, dropping Elsor and drawing her dagger at the same time. With a flick of her wrist the dagger became two, and as she struck metal against metal, the two blades lit, fire licking up their edges.

Alucard stood at the mouth of the narrow road, arms crossed. "Impressive," he said, sounding decidedly *unimpressed*. "Tell me, are you planning to burn me, or stab me, or both?"

"What are you doing here?" she hissed.

"I really think I should be the one asking that."

She gestured to the body. "Isn't it obvious?"

Alucard's gaze flicked from the knives down to the metal bar and the crumpled form at Lila's feet. "No, not really. Because you couldn't *possibly* be foolish enough to kill a competitor."

Lila snapped the knives back together, putting out the flames. "I didn't kill him."

Alucard let out a low groan. "Saints, you actually have a death wish." He gripped his hat. "What were you *thinking*?"

Lila looked around. "There're plenty of transports coming and going. I was going to stash him away on one of them."

"And what do you plan to do when he wakes up, turns the boat around, and makes it back in time to have you arrested and still compete?" When Lila didn't answer—she hadn't exactly gotten that far—Alucard shook his head. "You've got a real gift for taking things, Bard. You're not nearly as good at getting rid of them."

Lila held her ground. "I'll figure it out." Alucard was muttering curses in a variety of languages under his breath. "And were you *following* me?"

Alucard threw up his hands. "You've assaulted a competitor—I can only imagine with the daft notion of taking his place—and you honestly have the gall to be affronted at *my* actions? Did you even *think* what this would mean for *me*?" He sounded vaguely hysterical.

"This has nothing to do with you."

"This has everything to do with me!" he snapped. "I am your captain! You are my crew." The barb struck with unexpected force. "When the authorities find out a sailor aboard my ship sabotaged a competitor, what do you think they'll assume? That you were mad enough to do something so stupid on your own, or that *I* put you up to it?" He was pale with fury, and the air around them hummed. Indignation flickered through Lila, followed swiftly by guilt. The combination turned her stomach.

"Alucard—" she started.

"Did he see your face?"

Lila crossed her arms. "I don't think so."

Alucard paced, muttering, and then dropped to his knee beside Elsor. He rolled the man over and began digging through his pockets.

"Are you *robbing* him?" she asked, incredulous.

Alucard said nothing as he spread the contents of Elsor's coat across the frozen stones. An inn key. A few coins. A handful of folded pages. Tucked in the center of these, Lila saw, was his formal invitation to the *Essen Tasch*. Alucard plucked the iridescent pin from the collar of the man's coat, then shook his head and gathered up the items. He got to his feet, shoving the articles into Lila's hands. "When this goes badly, and it *will*, you won't take the *Spire* with you. Do you understand, Bard?"

Lila nodded tightly.

"And for the record," he said, "this is a terrible idea. You *will* get caught. Maybe not right away. But eventually. And when you do, I won't protect you."

Lila raised a brow. "I'm not asking you to. Believe it or not, Alucard, I can protect myself."

He looked down at the unconscious man between them. "Does that mean you *don't* need my help disposing of this man?"

Lila tucked her hair behind her ear. "I'm not sure I *need* it, but I'd certainly appreciate it." She knelt to take one of Elsor's arms, and Alucard reached for the other, but halfway there, he stopped and seemed to reconsider. He folded his arms, his eyes dark and his mouth a grim line.

"What is it now?" asked Lila, straightening.

"This is an expensive secret Bard," he said. "I'll keep it, in trade for another."

Dammit, thought Lila. She'd made it months at sea without sharing a thing she didn't want to. "I'll give you one question," she said at last. "One answer."

Alucard had asked the same ones over and over and over: *Who are you,* and *What are you,* and *Where did you come from?* And the answers she'd told him over and over and over weren't even lies. *Delilah Bard. One of a kind. London.*

But standing there on the docks that night, Alucard didn't ask any of those questions.

"You say you're from London . . ." He looked her in the eyes. "But you don't mean *this* one, do you?"

Lila's heart lurched, and she felt herself smile, even though this was the one question she couldn't answer with a lie. "No," she said. "Now help me with this body."

Alucard proved disturbingly adept at making someone disappear.

Lila leaned against a set of boxes at the transport end of the docks—devoted to the ships coming and going instead of the ones set in for the length of the tournament—and turned Elsor's *S* pin over in her fingers. Elsor himself sat on the ground, slumped against the crates, while Alucard tried to convince a pair of rough-looking men to take on a last-minute piece of cargo. She only caught snippets of the conversation, most of them Alucard's, tuned as she was to his Arnesian.

"Where do you put in . . . that's what, a fortnight this time of year . . . ?"

Lila pocketed the pin and sifted through Elsor's papers, holding them up to the nearest lantern light. The man liked to draw. Small pictures lined the edges of every scrap of paper, save the formal invitation. That was a lovely thing, edged in gold—it reminded her of the invite to Prince Rhy's birthday ball—marred only by a single fold down the center. Elsor had also been carrying a half-written letter, and a few sparse notes on the other competitors. Lila smiled when she saw his one-word note on Alucard Emery:

Performer.

She folded the pages and tucked them into her coat. Speaking of coats—she crouched and began to peel the unconscious man out of his. It was fine, a dark charcoal grey with a low, stiff collar and a belted waist. For a moment she considered trading, but couldn't bring herself to part with Calla's masterpiece, so instead she took a wool blanket from a cart and wrapped it around Elsor so he wouldn't freeze.

Lastly she produced a knife and cut a lock of hair from the man's head, tying it in a knot before dropping it in her pocket.

"I don't want to know," muttered Alucard, who was suddenly standing over her, the sailors a step behind. He nodded to the man on the ground. "*Ker tas naster,*" he grumbled. *There's your man.*

One of the sailors toed Elsor with his boot. "Drunk?"

The other sailor knelt, and clapped a pair of irons around Elsor's wrists, and Lila saw Alucard flinch reflexively.

"Mind him," he said as they hauled the man to his feet.

The sailor shrugged and mumbled something so garbled Lila couldn't tell where one word ended and the next began. Alucard only nodded as they turned and began to haul him toward the ship.

"That's it?" asked Lila.

Alucard frowned. "You know the most valuable currency in life, Bard?"

"What?"

"A favor." His eyes narrowed. "I now owe those men. And you owe me." He kept his eyes trained on the sailors as they hauled the unconscious Elsor aboard. "I've gotten rid of your problem, but it won't *stay* gone. That's a criminal transport. Once it sets out, it's not authorized to turn around until it reaches Delonar. And he's not on the charter, so by the time it docks, they'll know they're carrying an innocent man. So no matter what happens, you better not be here when he gets back."

The meaning in the words was clear, but she still had to ask. "And the *Spire*?"

Alucard looked at her, jaw set. "It only has room for one criminal." He let out a low breath, which turned to fog before his mouth. "But I wouldn't worry."

"Why's that?"

"Because you'll get caught long before we sail away."

Lila managed a grim smirk as Stasion Elsor and the sailors vanished below deck. "Have a little faith, Captain."

But the truth was, she had no idea what she was going to do when this fell apart, no idea if she'd just damned herself by accident, or worse, on purpose. Sabotaged another life. Just like at the Stone's Throw.

"Let's get something straight," said Alucard as they walked

away from the docks. "My help ends here. Alucard Emery and Stasion Elsor have no business with each other. And if we chance to meet in the ring, I won't spare you."

Lila snorted. "I should hope not. Besides, I still have a few tricks up my sleeve."

"I suppose you do," he said, finally glancing toward her. "After all, if you run far enough, no one can catch you."

She frowned, remembering his question, her answer.

"How long have you known?" she asked.

Alucard managed a ghost of a smile, framed by the doorway of their inn. "Why do you think I let you on my ship?"

"Because I was the best thief?"

"Certainly the strangest."

Lila didn't bother with sleep; there was too much to do. She and Alucard vanished into their respective rooms without even so much as a *good night,* and when she left a few hours later with Elsor's things bundled under her arm, Alucard didn't follow, even though she *knew* he was awake.

One problem at a time, she told herself as she climbed the stairs of the Coach and Castle Inn, the room key hanging from her fingers. A brass tag on the end held the name of the place and the room—*3.*

She found Elsor's room and let herself in.

She'd raided the man's pockets and studied his papers, but if there was anything else to learn before she donned the role at nightfall, she figured she'd find it here.

The room was simple. The bed was made. A looking glass leaned by the window and a silver folding frame sat on the narrow sill, a portrait of Elsor on one side, and a young woman on the other.

Rifling through a trunk at the foot of the bed, she found a few more pieces of clothing, a notebook, a short sword, a pair of gloves. These last were peculiar, designed to cover the tops of the hands but expose the palms and fingertips. Perfect for a fireworker, she thought, pocketing them.

The notebook held mostly sketches—including several of the young woman—as well as a few scribbled notes and a travel ledger. Elsor was scrupulous, and by all evidence, he had indeed come alone. Several letters and slips were tucked into the notebook, and Lila studied his signature, practicing first with her fingers and then a stub of a pencil until she'd gotten it right.

She then began to empty the trunk, tossing the contents onto the bed one by one. A set of boxes near the bottom held an elongated hat that curled down over the brow, and a canvas that unfolded to reveal a set of toiletries.

And then, in a box at the back of the trunk, she found Elsor's mask.

It was carved out of wood, and vaguely resembled a ram, with horns that hugged the sides of one's head and curled against one's cheeks. The only real facial coverage was a nose plate. That wouldn't do. She returned it to the bottom of the chest, and closed the lid.

Next she tried on each piece of clothing, testing her measurements against Elsor's. As she'd hoped, they weren't too far off. An examination of a pair of trousers confirmed she was an inch or two shorter than the man, but wedging some socks in the heels of her boots gave her the extra measure of height.

Lastly, Lila took up the portrait from the sill, and examined the man's face. He was wearing a hat like the one discarded on the bed, and dark hair spilled out beneath it, framing his angled face with near-black curls.

Lila's own hair was several shades lighter, but when she doused it with water from the basin, it looked close. Not a permanent solution, of course, especially in winter, but it helped her focus as she drew out one of her knives.

She returned the portrait to the sill, studying it as she took up a chunk of hair and sawed at it with the blade. It had grown long in the months at sea, and there was something liberating about shearing it off again. Strands tumbled to the floor as she shortened the back and shaped the front, the abusive combination of cold and steel giving the ends a slight curl.

Digging through Elsor's meager supplies, she found a comb as well as a tub of something dark and glossy. It smelled like tree nuts, and when she worked it into her hair, she was relieved to see it hold the curl.

His charcoal coat lay on the bed, and she shrugged it on. Taking up the hat from the bed, she set it gingerly on her styled head, and turned toward her reflection. A stranger, not quite Elsor but certainly not Bard, stared back at her. Something was missing. The pin. She dug in the pockets of his coat and pulled out the iridescent collar pin, fastening it at her throat. Then she cocked her head, adjusting her posture and mannerisms until the illusion came into sharper focus.

Lila broke into a grin.

This, she thought, adding Elsor's short sword to her waist, *is almost as fun as being a pirate.*

"*Avan, ras Elsor,*" said a portly woman when she descended the stairs. The innkeeper.

Lila nodded, wishing she'd had a chance to hear the man speak. Hadn't Alucard said that Stross was from the same part of the empire? His accent had rough edges, which Lila tried to mimic as she murmured, "*Avan.*"

The illusion held. No one else paid her any mind, and Lila strode out into the morning light, not as a street thief, or a sailor, but a magician, ready for the *Essen Tasch.*

SEVEN

INTERSECTIONS

I

The day before the *Essen Tasch,* the Night Market roused itself around noon.

Apparently the lure of festivities and foreigners eager to spend money was enough to amend the hours. With time to kill before the Banner Night, Lila wandered the stalls, her coins jingling in Elsor's pockets; she bought a cup of spiced tea and some kind of sweet bun, and tried to make herself comfortable in her new persona.

She didn't dare go back to the Wandering Road, where she'd have to trade Elsor for Bard or else be recognized. Once the tournament began, it wouldn't matter. Identities would disappear behind personas. But today she needed to be seen. Recognized. Remembered.

It wasn't hard. The stall owners were notorious gossips—all she had to do was strike up conversation as she shopped, drop a hint, a detail, once or twice a name, purposefully skirt the topic of the tournament, leave a parcel behind so someone trotted after her calling out, "Elsor! Master Elsor!"

By the time she reached the palace edge of the market, the work was done, word weaving through the crowd. *Stasion Elsor. One of the competitors. Handsome fellow. Too thin. Never seen him before. What can he do? Guess we'll see.* She felt their eyes on her as she shopped, caught the edges of their whispered conversation, and tried to smother her thief's instinct to shake the gaze and disappear.

Not yet, she thought as the sun finally began to sink.

One thing was still missing.

"Lila," said Calla when she entered. "You're early."

"You didn't set a time."

The merchant stopped, taking in Lila's new appearance.

"How do I look?" she asked, shoving her hands in Elsor's coat.

Calla sighed. "Even less like a woman than usual." She plucked the hat off Lila's head and turned it over in her hands.

"This is not bad," said Calla, before noticing Lila's shorn hair. She took a piece between her fingers. "But what is *this*?"

Lila shrugged. "I wanted a change."

Calla tutted, but she didn't prod. Instead, she disappeared through a curtain, and emerged a moment later with a box.

Inside was Lila's mask.

She lifted it, and staggered at the weight. The interior had been lined with dark metal, so cleanly made and shaped that it looked poured instead of hammered. Calla hadn't disposed of the leather demon mask, not entirely, but she'd taken it apart and made something new. The lines were clean, the angles sharp. Where simple black horns had once corkscrewed up over the head, now they curled back in an elegant way. The brow was sharper, jutting forward slightly like a visor, and the bottom of the mask, which had once ended on her cheekbones, now dipped lower at the sides, following the lines of her jaw. It was still a monster's face, but it was a new breed of demon.

Lila slid the mask over her head. She was still wondering at the beautiful, monstrous thing when Calla handed her something else. It was made of the same black leather, and lined with the same dark metal, and it shaped a kind of crown, or a smile, the sides taller than the center. Lila turned it over in her hands, wondering what it was for, until Calla retrieved it, swept around behind her, and fastened the plate around her throat.

"To keep your head on your shoulders," said the woman, who then proceeded to clasp the sides of the neck guard to small, hidden hinges on the tapered sides of the mask. It was like a jaw, and when Lila looked at her reflection, she saw her features nested within the two halves of the monster's skull.

She broke into a devilish grin, her teeth glinting within the mouth of the helmet.

"You," said Lila, "are brilliant."

"*Anesh*," said Calla with a shrug, though Lila could see that the merchant was proud.

She had the sudden and peculiar urge to *hug* the woman, but she resisted.

The hinged jaw allowed her to raise the mask, which she did, the demon's head resting on top of her own like a crown, the jaw still circling her throat. "How do I look?" she asked.

"Strange," said Calla. "And dangerous."

"Perfect."

Outside, the bells began to toll, and Lila's smile widened.

It was time.

Kell crossed to the bed and examined the clothes—a set of black trousers and a high-collared black shirt, both trimmed with gold. On top of the shirt sat the gold pin Rhy had given him for the royal reception. His coat waited, thrown over the back of a chair, but he left it there. It was a traveler's charm, and tonight he was confined to the palace.

The clothes on the bed were Rhy's choice, and they weren't simply a gift.

They were a message.

Tomorrow, you can be *Kamerov*.

Tonight, you are *Kell*.

Hastra had appeared earlier, only to confiscate his mask, on Rhy's orders.

Kell had been reluctant to relinquish it.

"You must be excited," Hastra had said, reading his hesitation, "about the tournament. Don't imagine you get to test your mettle very often."

Kell had frowned. "This isn't a game," he'd said, perhaps too sternly. "It's about keeping the kingdom safe." He felt a twinge of guilt as he watched Hastra go pale.

"I've sworn an oath to protect the royal family."

"I'm sorry then," said Kell ruefully, "that you're stuck protecting *me*."

"It's an honor, sir." There was nothing in his tone but pure, simple truth. "I would defend you with my life."

"Well," said Kell, surrendering Kamerov's mask. "I hope you never have to."

The young guard managed a small, embarrassed smile. "Me too, sir."

Kell paced his room and tried to put tomorrow from his mind. First he had to survive tonight.

A pitcher and bowl sat on the sideboard, and Kell poured water into the basin and pressed his palms to the sides until it steamed. Once clean, he dressed in Rhy's chosen attire, willing to humor his brother. It was the least he could do—though Kell wondered, as he slipped on the tunic, how long Rhy would be calling in this payment. He could picture the prince a decade from now, telling Kell to fetch him tea.

"Get it yourself," he would say, and Rhy would tut and answer, "Remember Kamerov?"

Kell's evening clothes were tight, formfitting in the style Rhy favored, and made of a black fabric so fine it caught the light instead of swallowing it. The cut and fit forced him to stand at full height, erasing his usual slouch. He fastened the gold buttons, the cuffs and collar—saints, how many clasps did it take to clothe a man?—and lastly the royal pin over his heart.

Kell checked himself in his mirror, and stiffened.

Even with his fair skin and auburn hair, even with the black eye that shone like polished rock, Kell looked *regal*. He stared at his reflection for several long moments, mesmerized, before tearing his gaze away.

He looked like a prince.

Rhy stood before the mirror, fastening the gleaming buttons of his tunic. Beyond the shuttered balcony, the sounds of celebration were rising off the cold night like steam. Carriages and laughter, footsteps and music.

He was running late, and he knew it, but he couldn't seem to get his nerves under control, wrangle his fears. It was getting dark, and the darkness leaned against the palace, and against him, the weight settling on his chest.

He poured himself a drink—his third—and forced a smile at his reflection.

Where was the prince who relished such festivities, who loved nothing better than to be the contagious joy at the center of the room?

Dead, thought Rhy, drily, before he could stop himself, and he was glad, not for the first time, that Kell could not read his mind as well as feel his pain. Luckily, other people still seemed to look at Rhy and see what he'd been instead of what he was. He didn't know if that meant he was good at hiding the difference, or that they weren't paying attention to begin with. Kell looked, and Rhy was sure he saw the change, but he had the sense not to say anything. There was nothing to be said. Kell had given Rhy a life—*his* life—and it wasn't his fault if Rhy didn't like it as much as his own. He'd lost that one, forfeited by his own foolishness.

He downed the drink, hoping it would render him in better spirits, but it dulled the world without ever touching his thoughts.

He touched the gleaming buttons and adjusted his crown for the dozenth time, shivering as a gust of cold air brushed against his neck.

"I fear you haven't enough gold," came a voice from the balcony doors.

Rhy stiffened. "What are guards for," he said slowly, "when they let even pirates pass?"

The man took a step forward, and then another, silver on him ringing like muffled chimes. "*Privateer*'s the term these days."

Rhy swallowed and turned to face Alucard Emery. "As for the gold," he said evenly, "it is a fine balance. The more I wear, the more likely one is to try and rob me of it."

"Such a dilemma," said Alucard, stealing another stride. Rhy took him in. He was dressed in clothes that had clearly never seen the sea. A dark blue suit, accented by a silver cloak, his rich brown hair groomed and threaded with gems to match. A single sapphire sparkled over his right eye. Those eyes, like night lilies caught in moonlight. He used to smell like them, too. Now he smelled like sea breeze and spice, and other things Rhy could not place, from lands he'd never seen.

"What brings a rogue like you to my chambers?" he asked.

"A rogue," Alucard rolled the word over his tongue. "Better a rogue than a bored royal."

Rhy felt Alucard's eyes wandering slowly, hungrily, over him, and he blushed. The heat started in his face and spread down, through his collar, his chest, beneath shirt and belt. It was disconcerting; Rhy might not have magic, but when it came to conquests, he was used to holding the power—things happened at his whim, and at his pleasure. Now he felt that power falter, slip. In all of Arnes, there was only one person capable of flustering the prince, of reducing him from a proud royal to a nervous youth, and that was Alucard Emery. Misfit. Rogue. Privateer. And royal. Removed from the throne by a stretch of tangled bloodlines, sure, but still. Alucard Emery could have had a crest and a place in court. Instead, he fled.

"You've come for the tournament," said Rhy, making small talk.

Alucard pursed his lips at the attempt. "Among other things."

Rhy hesitated, unsure what to say next. With anyone else, he would have had a flirtatious retort, but standing there, a mere stride away from Alucard, he felt short of breath, let alone words. He turned away, fidgeting with his cuffs. He heard the chime of silver and a moment later, Alucard snaked an arm possessively around his shoulders and brought his lips to the prince's neck, just below his ear. Rhy actually *shivered*.

"You are far too familiar with your prince," he warned.

"So you confess it, then?" His brushed his lips against Rhy's throat. "That you are mine."

He bit the lobe of Rhy's ear, and the prince gasped, back arching. Alucard always did know what to say—what to do—to tilt the world beneath his feet.

Rhy turned to say something, but Alucard's mouth was already there on his. Hands tangled in hair, clutched at coats. They were a collision, spurred by the force of three years apart.

"You missed me," said Alucard. It was not a question, but there *was* a confession in it, because everything about Alucard—the tension in his back, the ways his hips pressed into Rhy's, the race of his heart and the tremor in his voice—said that the missing had been mutual.

"I'm a prince," said Rhy, striving for composure. "I know how to keep myself entertained."

The sapphire glinted in Alucard's brow. "*I* can be very entertaining." He was already leaning in as he spoke, and Rhy found himself closing the distance, but at the last moment Alucard tangled his fingers in Rhy's hair and pulled his head back, exposing the prince's throat. He pressed his lips to the slope below Rhy's jaw.

Rhy clenched his teeth, fighting back a groan, but his stillness must have betrayed him; he felt Alucard smile against his skin. The man's fingers drifted to his tunic, deftly unbuttoning his collar so his kisses could continue downward, but Rhy felt him hesitate at the sight of the scar over his heart. "Someone has wounded you," he whispered into Rhy's collarbone. "Shall I make it better?"

Rhy pulled Alucard's face back to his, desperate to draw his attention from the mark, and the questions it might bring. He bit Alucard's lip, and delighted in the small victory of the gasp it earned him as—

The bells rang out.

The Banner Night.

He was late. They were late.

Alucard laughed softly, sadly. Rhy closed his eyes and swallowed.

"*Sanct,*" he cursed, hating the world that waited beyond his doors, and his place in it.

Alucard was already pulling away, and for an instant all Rhy wanted to do was pull him back, hold fast, terrified that if he let go, Alucard would vanish again, not just from the room but from London, from *him,* slip out into the night and the sea as he'd done three years before. Alucard must have seen the panic in his eyes, because he turned back, and drew Rhy in, and pressed his lips to Rhy's one last time, a gentle, lingering kiss.

"Peace," he said, pulling slowly free. "I am not a ghost." And then he smiled, and smoothed his coat, and turned away. "Fix your crown, my prince," he called back as he reached the door. "It's crooked."

II

Kell was halfway down the stairs when he was met by a short *ostra* with a trimmed beard and a frazzled look. Parlo, the prince's shadow since the tournament preparations first began.

"Master Kell," he said, breathless. "The prince is not with you?"

Kell cocked his head. "I assumed he was already downstairs."

Parlo shook his head. "Could something be wrong?"

"Nothing's wrong," said Kell with certainty.

"Well then, it's about to be. The king is losing patience, most of the guests are here, and the prince has not yet made an entrance."

"Perhaps that's exactly what he's trying to make." Parlo looked sick with panic. "If you're worried, why don't you go to his room and fetch him?" The *ostra* paled even further, as if Kell had just suggested something unfathomable. Obscene.

"Fine," grumbled Kell, turning back up the stairs. "*I'll* do it."

Tolners and Vis were standing outside Rhy's room. Kell was a few strides shy of the chamber when the doors burst open and a figure came striding out. A figure that most certainly *wasn't* Rhy. The guards' eyes widened at the sight of him. The man obviously hadn't gone in that way. Kell pulled up short as they nearly collided, and even though it had been years—too few, in Kell's estimation—he recognized the man at once.

"Alucard Emery," he said coldly, exhaling the name like a curse.

A slow smile spread across the man's mouth, and it took all Kell's restraint not to physically remove it. "Master Kell," said Alucard, cheerfully. "What an unexpected pleasure, running into you here." His voice had a natural undercurrent of laughter in it, and Kell could never tell if he was being mocked.

"I don't see how it's unexpected," said Kell, "as *I* live here. What *is* unexpected is running into *you,* since I thought I made myself quite clear the last time we met."

"Quite," echoed Alucard.

"Then what were you doing in my brother's chambers?"

Alucard raised a single studded brow. "Do you want a detailed account? Or will a summary suffice?"

Kell's fingernails dug into his palms. He could feel blood. Spells came to mind, a dozen different ways to wipe the smug look from Emery's face.

"Why are you here?" he growled.

"I'm sure you've heard," said Alucard, hands in his pockets. "I'm competing in the *Essen Tasch*. As such, I was invited to the royal palace for the Banner Night."

"Which is happening downstairs, *not* in the prince's room. Are you lost?" He didn't wait for Alucard to answer. "Tolners," he snapped. The guard stepped forward. "Escort Master Emery to the Rose Hall. Make sure he doesn't wander."

Tolners motioned, as if to take hold of Alucard's sleeve, and found himself propelled suddenly backward into the wall. Alucard never took his hands from his pockets, and his smile never wavered as he said, "I'm sure I can find my way."

He set off in the direction of the stairs, but as he passed Kell, the latter caught his elbow. "Do you remember what I told you, before banishing you from this city?"

"Vaguely. Your threats all seem to run together."

"I said," snarled Kell through clenched teeth, "that if you

break my brother's heart a second time, I will cut yours out. I stand by that promise, Alucard."

"Still fond of growling, aren't you, Kell? Ever the loyal dog, nipping at heels. Maybe one day you'll actually bite." With that he pulled free and strode away, his silver blue cloak billowing behind him.

Kell watched him go.

The moment Alucard was out of sight, he slammed his fist into the wall, hard enough to crack the inlaid wooden panel. He swore in pain and frustration, and an echoing curse came from within Rhy's chambers, but this time, Kell didn't feel bad for causing his brother a little pain. Blood stained his palm where his nails had sliced into the skin, and Kell pressed it to the broken decoration.

"*As Sora,*" he muttered. *Unbreak.*

The crack in the wood began to withdraw, the pieces of wood blending back together. He kept his hand there, trying to loosen the knot in his chest.

"Master Kell . . ." started Vis.

"What?" he snapped, spinning on the guards. The air in the hall churned around him. The floorboards trembled. The men looked pale. "If you see that man near Rhy's rooms again, arrest him."

Kell took a steadying breath, and was reaching for the prince's door when it swung inward to reveal Rhy, settling the gold band atop his head. When he saw the gathering of guards, and Kell at their center, he cocked his head.

"What?" he said. "I'm not *that* late." Before anyone else could speak, Rhy set off down the hall. "Don't just stand there, Kell," he called back. "We have a party to host."

"You're in a mood," said the prince as they passed into the dignified splendor of the Rose Hall.

Kell said nothing, trying to salvage the man he'd seen earlier in his bedroom mirror. He scanned the hall, his attention snagging almost instantly on Alucard Emery, who stood socializing with a group of magicians.

"Honestly, Kell," chided Rhy, "if looks could kill."

"Maybe *looks* can't," he said, flexing his fingers.

Rhy smiled and nodded his head at a cluster of guests. "You knew he was coming," he said through set teeth.

"I didn't realize you'd be giving him such an intimate welcome," snapped Kell in return. "How could you be so foolish—"

"I didn't invite him in—"

"—after everything that's happened."

"*Enough,*" hissed the prince, loud enough to turn the nearest heads.

Kell would have shrunk from the attention, but Rhy spread his arms, embracing it.

"Father," he called across the hall, "if I may do the honors."

King Maxim lifted his glass in reply, and Rhy stepped lithely up onto the nearest stone planter, and the gathering fell quiet.

"*Avan!*" he said, voice echoing through the hall. "*Glad'ach. Sasors,*" he added to the guests from Vesk and Faro. "I am Prince Rhy Maresh," he continued, slipping back into Arnesian. "Maxim and Emira, the illustrious king and queen of Arnes, my father and mother, have given me the honor of hosting this tournament. And it *is* an honor." He lifted a hand, and a wave of royal servants appeared, carrying trays laden with crystal goblets, candied fruits, smoked meat, and a dozen other delicacies. "Tomorrow you shall be introduced as champions. Tonight, I ask you to enjoy yourselves as honored guests and friends. Drink, feast, and claim your sigil. In the morning, the Games begin!"

Rhy bowed, and the crowd of gathered magicians and royals applauded as he hopped down from his perch. The tide of people shifted, some toward the banquets, others toward the banner tables.

"Impressive," observed Kell.

"Come on," said Rhy without meeting his eye. "*One* of us needs a drink."

"Stop."

Lila had just started up the palace steps, the demon's mask beneath her arm, when she heard the order.

She stiffened, her fingers reaching reflexively for the knife at her back as a pair of guards in gleaming armor blocked her path. Her pulse pounded, urging her to fight or flee, but Lila forced herself to hold her ground. They weren't drawing weapons.

"I'm here for the Banner Night," she said, drawing Elsor's royal verification from her coat. "I was told to report to the palace."

"You want the Rose Hall," explained the first guard, as if Lila had a damn clue where *that* was. The other guard pointed at a second, smaller set of stairs. Lila had never noticed the other entrances to the palace—there were two, flanking the main steps, and both were tame by comparison—but now that they'd been pointed out, the flow of traffic up and around those steps compared to the empty grand entrance was obvious. As was the fact that the doors to the Rose Hall had been flung open, while the palace's main entrance was firmly shut.

"*Solase,*" she said, shaking her head. "I must be more nervous than I thought." The guards smiled.

"I will lead you," said one, as if she might honestly go astray a second time. The guard ushered her over to right set of stairs and up before handing her off to an attendant, who led her through the entryway and into the Rose Hall.

It was an impressive space, less ballroom than throne room, undoubtedly refined without being ostentatious—how far she'd come, she thought wryly, to find massive urns of fresh-cut flowers and sumptuous red and gold tapestries *restrained*.

A familiar captain stood near the mouth of the hall, dressed in silver and midnight blue. He saw Lila, and his face passed through several reactions before settling on cool appraisal.

"Master Elsor."

"Master Emery." Lila gave a flourish and a bow, stiffening her posture into angles.

Alucard shook his head. "I honestly don't know whether to be impressed or unnerved."

Lila straightened. "The two aren't mutually exclusive."

He nodded at the Sarows mask under her arm. "Do you *want* to be found out?"

Lila shrugged. "There are many shadows in the night." She caught sight of the mask tucked beneath his own arm. Made of dark blue scales, their edges tipped with silver, the mask ran from hairline to cheekbone. Once on, it would leave his charmer's smile exposed, and do nothing to tame the crown of brassy curls that rose above. The mask itself looked purely aesthetic, its scales offering neither anonymity nor protection.

"What are you supposed to be?" she asked in Arnesian. "A fish?"

Alucard made a noise of mock affront. "*Obviously*," he said, brandishing the helmet, "I'm a dragon."

"Wouldn't it make more sense for you to be a fish?" challenged Lila. "After all, you do live on the sea, and you are rather slippery, and—"

"I'm a dragon," he interjected. "You're just not being very imaginative."

Lila grinned, partly in amusement, and partly in relief as they fell into a familiar banter. "I thought House Emery's sigil was a feather. Shouldn't you be a bird?"

Alucard rapped his fingers on the mask. "My family is full of birds," he said, the words laced with spite. "My father was a vulture. My mother was a magpie. My oldest brother is a crow. My sister, a sparrow. I have never really been a bird."

Lila resisted the urge to say he might have been a peacock. It didn't seem the time.

"But our house symbol," he went on, "it represents *flight,* and birds are not the only things that fly." He held up the dragon mask. "Besides, I am not competing for House Emery. I am competing for myself. And if you could see the rest of my outfit, you wouldn't—"

"Do you have wings? Or a tail?"

"Well, no, those would get in the way. But I do have more scales."

"So does a fish."

"Go away," he snapped, but there was humor in his voice, and soon they fell into an easy laugh, and then remembered where they were. *Who* they were.

"Emery!" called Jinnar, appearing at the captain's elbow.

His mask—a silver crown that curled like spun sugar, or perhaps a swirl of air—hung from his fingertips. His feet were firmly on the floor tonight, but she could practically feel the hum of energy coming off him, see it blur his edges. Like a hummingbird. How would she fight a hummingbird? How would she fight any of them?

"And who's this?" asked Jinnar, glancing at Lila.

"Why, Jinnar," said Alucard drolly, "don't you recognize our Master Elsor?"

The magician's black eyes narrowed. Lila raised a challenging brow. Jinnar had met the *real* Stasion Elsor back in the tavern. Now his black eyes swept over her, confused, and then suspicious. Lila's fingers twitched, and Alucard's hand came to rest on her shoulder—whether it was to show solidarity or keep her from drawing a weapon, she didn't know.

"Master Elsor," said Jinnar slowly. "You look different tonight. But then again," he added, eyes flicking to Alucard, "the light was so low in the tavern, and I haven't seen you since."

"An easy mistake to make," said Lila smoothly. "I'm not overly fond of displays."

"Well," chimed in Alucard brightly. "I do hope you'll overcome that once we take the stage."

"I'm sure I'll find my stride," retorted Lila.

"I'm sure you will."

A beat of silence hung between them, remarkable considering the din of the gathering crowd. "Well, if you'll excuse me," said Alucard, breaking the moment, "I've yet to properly harass Brost, and I'm determined to meet this Kamerov fellow . . ."

"It was nice to meet you . . . again," said Jinnar, before following Alucard away.

Lila watched them go, then began to weave through the crowd, trying to keep her features set in resignation, as if mingling with dozens of imperial magicians was commonplace. Along one wall, tables were laden with swatches of fabric and pitchers of ink, and magicians turned through pages of designs as they declared their banners—a crow on green, a flame on white, a rose on black—pennants that would wave from the stands the following day.

Lila plucked a crystal goblet from a servant's tray, weighing it in her fingers before remembering she wasn't here as a thief. She caught Alucard's eye, and toasted him with a wink. As she lapped the hall, taking in the main floor and the gallery above and sipping sweet wine, she counted the bodies to occupy her mind and keep her composure.

Thirty-six magicians, herself included, twelve from each of the three empires, and all marked by a mask on top of their head or under their arm or slung over their shoulder.

Two dozen servants, give or take (it was hard to tell, dressed alike as they were, and always moving).

Twelve guards.

Fifteen *ostra,* judging by their haughty expressions.

Six *vestra,* going by their royal pins.

Two blond Veskans wearing crowns instead of masks, each with an entourage of six, and a tall Faroan with an expressionless face and an entourage of eight.

The Arnesian king and queen in splendid red and gold.

Prince Rhy in the gallery above.

And, standing beside him, Kell.

Lila held her breath. For once, Kell's auburn hair was swept back from his face, revealing both the crisp blue of his left eye and the glossy black of his right. He wasn't wearing his usual coat, in *any* of its forms. Instead he was dressed head to toe in elegant black, a gold pin over his heart.

Kell had told her once that he felt more like possession than a prince, but standing at Rhy's side, one hand around his glass and the other on the rail as he gazed down on the crowd, he looked like he belonged.

The prince said something, and Kell's face lit up in a silent laugh.

Where was the bloodied boy who'd collapsed on her bedroom floor?

Where was the tortured magician, veins turning black as he fought a talisman's pull?

Where was the sad, lonely royal who'd stood on the docks and watched her walk away?

That last one she could almost see. There, at the edge of his mouth, the corner of his eye.

Lila felt her body moving toward him, drawn as if by gravity, several steps lost before she caught herself. She wasn't Lila Bard tonight. She was Stasion Elsor, and while the illusion seemed to be holding well enough, she knew it would crumble in front of Kell. And in spite of that, part of her still wanted to catch his eye, relish his moment of surprise, watch it dissolve into recognition, and—hopefully—welcome. But she couldn't imagine he'd be glad to see her, not here, mingling with the throngs of competitors. And in truth, Lila savored the sensation of watching without being watched. It made her feel like a predator, and in a room of magicians, that was something.

"I don't believe we've met," came a voice behind her in accented English.

She turned to find a young man, tall and slender, with reddish brown hair and dark lashes circling grey eyes. He had a silver-white mask tucked beneath his arm, and he shifted it to his other side before extending a gloved hand.

"Kamerov," he said genially. "Kamerov Loste."

So this was the elusive magician, the one neither Jinnar nor Alucard had managed to find. She didn't see what all the fuss was about.

"Stasion Elsor," she answered.

"Well, Master Elsor," he said with a confident smile, "perhaps we will meet in the arena."

She raised a brow and began to move away.

"Perhaps."

III

"I took the liberty of designing your pennant," said Rhy, resting his elbows on the gallery's marble banister. "I hope you don't mind."

Kell cringed. "Do I even want to know what's on it?"

Rhy tugged the folded piece of fabric from his pocket, and handed it over. The cloth was red, and when he unfolded it, he saw the image of a rose in black and white. The rose had been mirrored, folded along the center axis and reflected, so the design was actually *two* flowers, surrounded by a coil of thorns.

"How subtle," said Kell tonelessly.

"You could at least pretend to be grateful."

"And you couldn't have picked something a little more . . . I don't know . . . imposing? A serpent? A great beast? A bird of prey?"

"A bloody handprint?" retorted Rhy. "Oh, what about a glowing black eye?"

Kell glowered.

"You're right," continued Rhy, "I should have just drawn a frowning face. But then everyone would *know* it's you. I thought this was rather fitting."

Kell muttered something unkind as he shoved the banner into his pocket.

"You're welcome."

Kell surveyed the Rose Hall. "You think anyone will notice

that I'm—well, that Kamerov Loste is missing from the festivities?"

Rhy took a sip of his drink. "I doubt it," he said. "But just in case..."

He nodded the drink at a lean figure moving through the crowd. Kell was halfway through a sip of wine when he saw the man, and nearly choked on it. The figure was tall and slim, with trimmed auburn hair. He was dressed in elegant black trousers and a silver high-collared tunic, but it was the mask tucked under his arm that caught Kell's eye.

A single piece of sculpted silver-white metal, polished to a high shine.

His mask. Or rather, *Kamerov*'s.

"Who on earth is *that*?"

"That, my dear brother, is Kamerov Loste. At least for tonight."

"Dammit, Rhy, the more people you tell about this plan, the more likely it is to fail."

The prince waved a hand. "I've paid our actor handsomely to play the part tonight, and as far as he's concerned it's because the real Kamerov doesn't care for public displays. This is the only event where all thirty-six competitors are expected to show their faces, Kamerov included. Besides, Castars is discreet."

"You *know* him?"

Rhy shrugged. "Our paths have crossed."

"Stop," said Kell. "Please. I don't want to hear about your romantic interludes with the man currently posing as me."

"Don't be obscene. I haven't been with him since he agreed to take up this particular role. And that right there is a testament to my respect for you."

"How flattering."

Rhy caught the man's eye, and a few moments later, having toured the room, the false Kamerov Loste—well, Kell supposed they were both false, but the copy of the copy—ascended the stairs to the gallery.

"Prince Rhy," said the man, bowing with a little more flourish than Kell would have used. "And Master Kell," he added reverently.

"Master Loste," said Rhy cheerfully.

The man's eyes, both grey, drifted to Kell. Up close, he saw that they were the same height and build. Rhy had been thorough.

"I wish you luck in the coming days," said Kell.

The man's smile deepened. "It is an *honor* to fight for Arnes."

"A bit over the top, isn't he?" asked Kell as the impostor returned to the floor.

"Oh, don't be bitter," said Rhy. "The important thing is that Kamerov has a *face*. Specifically a face that isn't *yours*."

"He doesn't have the coat."

"No, unfortunately for us, you can't pull coats *out* of that coat of yours, and I figured you'd be unwilling to part with it."

"You'd be right." Kell was just turning away when he saw the shadow moving across the floor, a figure dressed in black with the edge of a smirk and a demon's mask. It almost looked like the one he'd seen on Lila the night of Rhy's masquerade. The night Astrid had taken Kell prisoner, taken Rhy's body for her own. Lila had appeared like a specter on the balcony, dressed in black and wearing a horned mask. She'd worn it then, and later, as they fled with Rhy's dying body between them, and in the sanctuary room as Kell fought to resurrect him. She'd worn it in her hair as they stood in the stone forest at the steps of the White London castle, and it had hung from her bloody fingers when it was over.

"Who is that?" he asked.

Rhy followed his gaze. "Someone who clearly shares your taste for monochrome. Beyond that . . ." Rhy tugged a folded paper from his pocket, and skimmed the roster. "It's not Brost, he's huge. I've met Jinnar. Must be Stasion."

Kell squinted, but the resemblance was already fading. The hair was too short, too dark, the mask different, the smile replaced by hard lines. Kell shook his head.

"I know it's mad, but for a second I thought it was . . ."

"Saints, you're seeing her in everyone and everything now, Kell? There's a word for that."

"Hallucination?"

"Infatuation."

Kell snorted. "I'm not infatuated," he said. "I just . . ." He just wanted to see her. "Our paths crossed one time. Months ago. It happens."

"Oh yes, your relationship with Miss Bard is positively ordinary."

"Be quiet."

"Crossing worlds, killing royals, saving cities. The marks of every good courtship."

"We weren't courting," snapped Kell. "In case you forgot, she left."

He didn't mean to sound wounded. It wasn't that she left *him*, it was simply that she left. And he couldn't follow, even if he'd wanted to. And now she was *back*.

Rhy straightened. "When this is over, we should take a trip."

Kell rolled his eyes. "Not this again."

And then he saw Master Tieren's white robes moving through the hall below. All night—all week, all month—the *Aven Essen* had been avoiding him.

"Hold this," he said, passing the prince his drink.

Before Rhy could argue, Kell was gone.

Lila slipped out before the crowd could thin, the demon mask hanging from one hand and her chosen pennant from the other.

Two silver knives crossed against a ground of black. She was in the foyer when she heard the sound of steps behind her. Not crisp boots on marble, but soft, well-worn shoes.

"Delilah Bard," said a calm, familiar voice.

She stopped mid-stride, then turned. The head priest of the London Sanctuary stood, holding a silver goblet in both hands, his fingers laced. His white robes were trimmed with gold, his silver-white hair groomed but simple around his sharp blue eyes.

"Master Tieren," she said, smiling even as her heart pounded in warning. "Is the *Aven Essen* supposed to drink?"

"I don't see why not," he said. "The key to all things, be they magical or alcoholic, is moderation." He considered the glass. "Besides, this is water."

"Ah," said Lila, cheating a step back, the mask behind her back. She wasn't entirely sure what to do. Normally her two options upon being cornered were turn and run or fight, but neither seemed appropriate when it came to Master Tieren. Some small part of her thrilled at being recognized, and she honestly couldn't imagine drawing a knife on Kell's mentor.

"That's quite an outfit you're wearing," observed the *Aven Essen,* advancing. "If you wanted an audience with Prince Rhy and Master Kell, I'm sure you could simply have called for one. Was a disguise really necessary?" And then, reading her expression, "But this disguise wasn't simply a way into the palace, was it?"

"Actually, I'm here as a competitor."

"No, you're not," he said simply.

Lila bristled. "How would you know?"

"Because I selected them myself."

Lila shrugged. "One of them must have dropped out."

He gave her a long, appraising look.

Was he reading her thoughts? *Could* he? That was the hardest part of being plunged into a world where magic was possible. It made you wonder if *everything* was. Lila was neither a skeptic nor a believer; she relied on her gut and the world she could see. But the world she could see had gotten considerably stranger.

"Miss Bard, what trouble have you gotten into now?" Before she could answer, he went on, "But that isn't the right question, is it? Judging by your appearance, the right question would be, where is Master Elsor?"

Lila cracked a smile. "He's alive and well," she said. "Well, he's alive. Or at least he was, the last time I checked." The priest let out a short exhale. "He's fine, Master Tieren. But he won't be able to make the *Essen Tasch,* so I'll be filling in."

There was another brief sigh, heavy with disapproval.

"You're the one who encouraged me," challenged Lila.

"I told you to tend your waking power, not cheat your way into an international tournament."

"You told me that I had magic in me. Now you don't think I have what it takes?"

"I don't *know* what you have, Lila. And neither do you. And while I'm glad to hear that your stay in our world has so far been fruitful, what you need is time and practice and a good deal of discipline."

"Have a little faith, Master Tieren. Some people believe that necessity is the key to flourishing."

"Those people are fools. And you have a dangerous disregard for your own life, and the lives of others."

"So I've been told." She cheated another step back. She was in the doorway now. "Are you going to try to stop me?"

He shot her a hard blue look. "Could I?"

"You could try. Arrest me. Expose me. We can make a show of it. But I don't think that's what you want. The real Stasion Elsor is on his way to Delonar, and won't be back in time to compete. Besides, this tournament, it's important, isn't it?" She drew a finger down the doorframe. "For diplomatic relations. There are people here from Vesk and Faro. What do you think they'd do if they knew where I really came from? What would that say about the doors between worlds? What would that say about *me*? It gets messy rather fast, doesn't it, Master Tieren? But more than that, I think you're curious to see what a Grey London girl can do."

Tieren fixed her with his gaze. "Has anyone ever told you that you're too sharp for your own good?"

"Too sharp. Too loud. Too reckless. I've heard it all. It's a wonder I'm still alive."

"Indeed."

Lila's hand fell from the door. "Don't tell Kell."

"Oh, trust me, child, that's the last thing I'll do. When you get caught, I plan on feigning ignorance about *all* of this." He lowered his voice, and added, mostly to himself, "This tournament will be the death of me." And then he cleared his throat. "Does he know you're here?"

Lila bit her lip. "Not yet."

"Do you plan to tell him?"

Lila looked to the Rose Hall beyond the priest. She did, didn't she? So what was stopping her? The uncertainty? So long as she knew and he didn't, she was in control. The moment he found out, the balance would shift. Besides, if Kell found out she was competing—if he found out what she'd *done* to compete—she'd never see the inside of an arena. Hell, she'd probably never see anything again but the inside of a cell, and even if she wasn't arrested, she'd certainly never hear the end of it.

She stepped out onto the landing, Tieren in her wake.

"How are they?" she asked, looking out at the city.

"The princes? They seem well enough. And yet . . ." Tieren sounded genuinely concerned.

"What is it?" she prompted.

"Things have not been the same since the Black Night. Prince Rhy is himself, and yet he isn't. He takes to the streets less often, and garners more trouble when he does."

"And Kell?"

Tieren hesitated. "Some think him responsible for the shadow that crossed our city."

"That's not fair," snapped Lila. "We saved the city."

Tieren gave a shrug as if to say, such is the nature of fear and doubt. They breed too easily. Kell and Rhy had seemed happy on that balcony, but she could see it, the fraying edges of the disguise. The darkness just beyond.

"You better go," said the *Aven Essen*. "Tomorrow will be . . . well, it will be something."

"Will you cheer for me?" she asked, forcing herself to keep her voice light.

"I'll pray you don't get yourself killed."

Lila smirked and started down the steps. She was halfway to the street when she heard someone say, "Wait."

But it wasn't Tieren. The voice was younger, one she hadn't heard in four months. Sharp and low, with a touch of strain, as if he were out of breath, or holding back.

Kell.

She hesitated on the stairs, head bowed, fingers aching where they gripped the helmet. She was about to turn around, but he spoke again, calling a name. It wasn't hers.

"Tieren," said Kell. "Please wait."

Lila swallowed, her back to the head priest and the black-eyed prince.

It took all of her strength to start walking again.

And when she did, she didn't look back.

"What is it, Master Kell?" asked Tieren.

Kell felt the words dry up in his throat. Finally, he managed a single petulant sentence. "You've been avoiding me."

The old man's eyes glittered, but he didn't deny the claim. "I have many talents, Kell," he said, "but believe it or not, deception has never been among them. I suspect it's why I've never won a game of Sanct. . . ."

Kell raised a brow. He couldn't picture the *Aven Essen* playing in the first place. "I wanted to thank you. For letting Rhy, and for letting me—"

"I haven't let you do anything," cut in Tieren. Kell cringed. "I simply haven't stopped you, because if I've learned one thing about you both, it's that if you want to do a thing, you'll do it, the world be damned."

"You think I'm being selfish."

"No, Master Kell." The priest rubbed his eyes. "I think you're being human."

Kell didn't know if that was a slight coming from the *Aven Essen*, who was supposed to think him *blessed*.

"I sometimes think I've gone mad."

Tieren sighed. "Truth be told, I think everyone is mad. I think Rhy is mad for putting this scheme together, madder still for planning it so well." His voice fell a measure. "I think the king and queen are mad for blaming one son above the other."

Kell swallowed. "Will they never forgive me?"

"Which would you rather have? Their forgiveness, or Rhy's life?"

"I shouldn't have to choose," he snapped.

Tieren's gaze drifted away to the steps and the Isle and the glittering city. "The world is neither fair nor right, but it has a way of balancing itself. Magic teaches us that much. But I want you to promise me something."

"What?"

That shrewd blue gaze swiveled back. "That you'll be careful."

"I'll do my best. You know I don't wish to cause Rhy pain, but—"

"I'm not asking you to mind Rhy's life, you stupid boy. I'm

asking you to mind your own." Master Tieren brought his hand to Kell's face, a familiar calm transferring like heat.

Just then, Rhy appeared, looking cheerfully drunk. "There you are!" he called, wrapping his arm around Kell's shoulders and hissing in his ear. "*Hide.* Princess Cora is hunting princes. . . ."

Kell let Rhy drag him back inside, casting one last glance at Tieren, who stood on the steps, his back to the palace and his eyes on the night.

IV

"What are we doing here?"

"Hiding."

"Surely we could have hidden in the palace."

"Really, Kell. You've no imagination."

"Is it going to sink?"

The bottle sloshed in Rhy's hand. "Don't be ridiculous."

"I think it's a valid question," retorted Kell.

"They told me it couldn't be done," Rhy said, toasting the arena.

"Couldn't, or shouldn't?" asked Kell, treading on the stadium floor as if it were made of glass. "Because if it's the latter—"

"You're such a nag—ow." Rhy stubbed his foot on something, a dull pain echoing through Kell's toes.

"Here," he grumbled, summoning a palmful of fire.

"No." Rhy lunged at him, forcing his hand closed and dousing the light. "We are sneaking. Sneaking is meant to be done in the dark."

"Well then, watch where you're going."

Rhy must have decided they'd gone far enough, because he slumped onto the polished stone floor of the arena. In the moonlight, Kell could see his brother's eyes, the circlet of gold in his hair, the bottle of spiced wine as he pulled out the stopper.

Kell lowered himself to the ground beside the prince and

rested against a something—a platform, a wall, a set of stairs? He tipped his head back and marveled at the stadium, what little he could see—the stands soon to be filled, the ruse soon to play out, and the idea that the whole thing could actually work.

"Are you sure about this?" asked Kell.

"A little late to change our minds," mused the prince.

"I'm serious, Rhy. There's still time."

The prince took a sip of wine and set the bottle down between them, clearly considering his answer. "Do you remember what I told you?" he asked gently. "After that night. About why I took the pendant from Holland."

Kell nodded. "You wanted strength."

"I still want it," Rhy whispered. "Every day. I wake up wanting to be a stronger person. A better prince. A worthy king. That want, it's like a fire in my chest. And then, there are these moments, these horrible, icy moments when I remember what I did . . ." His hand drifted to his heart. "To myself. To you. To my kingdom. And it hurts. . . ." His voice trembled. "More than dying ever did. There are days when I don't feel like I deserve this." He tapped the soul seal. "I deserve to be . . ." He trailed off, but Kell could feel his brother's pain, as though it were a physical thing.

"I guess what I'm trying to say," said Rhy, "is that I need this, too." His eyes finally found Kell's. "Okay?"

Kell swallowed. "Okay." He took up the bottle.

"That said, do try not to get us both killed."

Kell groaned, and Rhy chuckled.

"To clever plans," said Kell, toasting his brother. "And dashing princes."

"To masked magicians," said Rhy, swiping the wine.

"To mad ideas."

"To the *Essen Tasch*."

"Wouldn't it be amazing," murmured Rhy later, when the bottle was empty, "if we got away with it?"

"Who knows," said Kell. "We just might."

Rhy stumbled into his room, waving off Tolner's questions about where he'd been and shutting the door in the guard's face. It was dark, and he made it three unsteady strides before knocking his shin against a low table, and swearing roundly.

The room swam, a mess of shadows lit only by the pale light of the low-burning fire in the hearth and the candles in the corners, only half of which had been lit. Rhy retreated until his back found the nearest wall, and waited for the room to settle.

Downstairs, the party had finally dissipated, the royals retreating to their wings, the nobles to their homes. Tomorrow. Tomorrow the tournament would finally be here.

Rhy knew Kell's true hesitation, and it wasn't getting caught, or starting trouble; it was the fear of causing him pain. Every day Kell moved like Rhy was made of glass, and it was driving them both mad. But once the tournament started, once he saw that Rhy was fine, that he could take it, survive it—hell, he could survive *anything,* wasn't that the point?—then maybe Kell would finally let go, stop holding his breath, stop trying to protect him, and just *live.*

Because Rhy didn't need his protection, not anymore, and he'd only told a partial truth when he said they both needed this.

The whole truth was, Rhy needed it *more.*

Because Kell had given him a gift he did not want, could never repay.

He'd always envied his brother's strength.

And now, in a horrible way, it was his.

He was immortal.

And he *hated* it.

And he hated that he hated it. Hated that he'd become the thing he never wanted to be, a burden to his brother, a source of pain and suffering, a prison. Hated that if he'd had a choice, he would have said no. Hated that he was grateful he hadn't had a choice, because he wanted to live, even if he didn't deserve to.

But most of all, Rhy hated the way his living changed how *Kell* lived, the way his brother moved through life as if it were suddenly fragile. The black stone, and whatever lived inside it, and for a time in Kell, had changed his brother, woken something restless, something reckless. Rhy wanted to shout, to shake Kell and tell him not to shy away from danger on his account, but charge toward it, even if it meant getting hurt.

Because Rhy deserved that pain.

He could see his brother suffocating beneath the weight of it. Of him.

And he hated it.

And this gesture—this foolish, mad, dangerous gesture—was the best he could do.

The most he could do.

The room had steadied, and suddenly, desperately, Rhy needed another drink.

A sideboard stood along the wall, an ornate thing of wood and inlaid gold. Short glass goblets huddled beside a tray with a dozen different bottles of fine liquor, and Rhy squinted in the dimness, surveying the selection before reaching for the thin vial at the back, hidden by the taller, brighter bottles. The tonic in the vial was milky white, the stopper trailing a thin stem.

One for calm. Two for quiet. Three for sleep.

That's what Tieren said when he prescribed it.

Rhy's fingers trembled as he reached for the vial, jostling the other glasses.

It was late, and he didn't want to be alone with his thoughts. He could call for someone—he'd never had trouble finding company—but he wasn't in the mood to smile and laugh and charm. If Gen and Parrish were here, they'd play Sanct with him, help him keep the thoughts at bay. But Gen and Parrish were dead, and it was Rhy's fault.

You shouldn't be alive.

He shook his head, trying to clear the voices, but they clung.

You let everyone down.

"Stop," he growled under his breath. He hated the darkness, the wave of shadows that always caught up with him. He'd hoped the party would wear him down, help him sleep, but his tired body did nothing to quiet his raging thoughts.

You are weak.

He let three drops fall into an empty glass, followed by a splash of honeyed water.

A failure.

Rhy tossed back the contents (*Murderer*) and began to count, in part to mark the effects and in part to drown out the voices. He stood at the bar, staring down into the empty glass and measuring seconds until his thoughts and vision began to blur.

Rhy pushed away from the sideboard, and nearly fell as the room tipped around him. He caught himself against the bedpost and closed his eyes (*You shouldn't be alive*), tugging off his boots and feeling his way into bed. He curled around himself as the thoughts beat on: of Holland's voice, of the amulet, distorted now, twisting into memories of the night Rhy died.

He didn't remember everything, but he remembered Holland holding out the gift.

For strength.

He remembered standing in his chambers, slipping the pendant's cord over his head, being halfway down the hall, and then—nothing. Nothing until a searing heat tore through his chest, and he looked down to see his hand wrapped around the hilt of a dagger, the blade buried between his ribs.

He remembered the pain, and the blood, and the fear, and

finally the quiet and the dark. The surrender of letting go, of sinking down, away, and the shock of being dragged back, the force of it like falling, a terrible, jarring pain when he hit the ground. Only he wasn't falling down. He was falling up. Surging back to the surface of himself, and then, and then.

And then the tonic finally took hold, the memories silenced as the past and present both mercifully faded and Rhy slipped feverishly down into sleep.

V

White London.

Holland paced the royal chamber.

It was as vast and vaulting as the throne room, with broad windows to every side. Built into the castle's western spire, it overlooked the entire city. From here he could see the glow from the Sijlt dance like moonlight against the low clouds, see lamps burn pale but steady, diffused by windowpanes and low mist, see the city—*his* city—sleep and wake, rest and stir, and return to life.

His head snapped up as something landed on the sill—power surged reflexively to the surface—but it was just a bird. White and grey with a pale gold crest, and eyes that shone as black as Holland's. He exhaled.

A *bird*.

How long had it been since he'd seen one? Animals had fled with the magic long ago, rooting out the distant places where the world wasn't dying, burrowing down to reach the retreating life. Any creature foolish enough to stray within reach was slaughtered for sustenance or spellwork, or both. The Danes had kept two horses, pristine white beasts, and even those had fallen in the days after their deaths, when the city plunged into chaos and slaughter for the crown. Holland had missed those early days, of course. He'd spent them clinging to life in a garden a world away.

But here, now, was a bird.

He didn't realize he was reaching toward it until it ruffled and took wing, his fingertips grazing its feathers before it was out of reach.

A single bird. But it was a sign. The world was changing.

Osaron could summon many things, but not this. Nothing with a heartbeat, nothing with a soul. Holland supposed that was for the best. After all, if Osaron could make a body of his own, he would have no need for Holland. And as much as Holland needed Osaron's magic, the thought of the *oshoc* moving freely sent a shiver through him. No, Holland was not only Osaron's partner, he was Osaron's prison.

And his prisoner was growing restless.

More.

The voice echoed in his head.

Holland took up a book and began to read, but he was only two pages in when the paper shuddered, as if caught by a wind, and the whole thing—from parchment to cover—turned to glass in his hands.

"This is childish," he murmured, setting the ruined book aside and splaying his hands across the sill.

More.

He felt a tremor beneath his palms and looked down to find tendrils of fog sprawling over the stone and leaving frost, flowers, ivy, fire in their wake.

Holland wrenched his hands away as if burned.

"Stop this," he said, turning his gaze on the looking glass, a tall, elegant mirror between two windows. He looked at his reflection and saw Osaron's impatient, impetuous gaze.

We could do more.
We could be more.
We could have more.
We could have anything.
And instead . . .

The magic slithered forth, snaked out from Holland's own hands, a hundred wisp-thin lines that swept and arced around him, threading from wall to wall and ceiling to floor until he stood in the center of a cage.

Holland shook his head and dispelled the illusion. "This is my world," he said. "It is not a canvas for your whims."

You have no vision, sulked Osaron from the reflection.

"I have vision," replied Holland. "I have seen what happened to *your* world."

Osaron said nothing, but Holland could feel his restlessness. Could feel the *oshoc* pacing the edges of the *Antari*'s self, wearing grooves into his mind. Osaron was as old as the world, and as wild.

Holland closed his eyes and tried to force calm like a blanket over them both. He needed sleep. A large bed sat in the very center of the room, elegant but untouched. Holland didn't sleep. Not well. Athos had spent too many years carving—cutting, burning, breaking—the distrust of peace into his body. His muscles refused to unclench; his mind wouldn't unwind; the walls he'd built hadn't been built to come down. Athos might be dead, but Holland couldn't shake the fear that when his eyes closed, Osaron's might open. Couldn't bear the thought of surrendering control again.

He'd stationed guards beyond his room to make sure he didn't wander, but every time he woke, the chamber looked different. A spray of roses climbing the window, a chandelier of ice, a carpet of moss or some exotic fabric—some small change wrought in the night.

We had a deal.

He could feel the *oshoc*'s will warring with his own, growing stronger every day, and though Holland was still in control, he didn't know for how much longer. Something would have to be sacrificed. Or someone.

Holland opened his eyes, and met the *oshoc*'s gaze.

"I want to make a new deal."

In the mirror, Osaron inclined his head, waiting, listening.

"I will find you another body."

Osaron's expression soured. *They are too weak to sustain me. Even Ojka would crumble under my true touch.*

"I will find you a body as strong as mine," said Holland carefully.

Osaron looked intrigued. *An* Antari?

Holland pressed on. "*And* his world. To make your own. And in return, you will leave this world to me. Not as it was, but as it can be. Restored."

Another body, another world, mused Osaron. *So keen to be rid of me?*

"You want more freedom," said Holland. "I am offering it."

Osaron turned the offer over. Holland tried to keep his mind calm and clear, knowing the *oshoc* would feel his feelings and know his thoughts. *You offer me an* Antari *vessel. You know I cannot take such a body without permission.*

"That is my concern," said Holland. "Accept my offer, and you will have a new body and a new world to do with as you please. But you will not take *this* world. You will not ruin it."

Hmmm, the sound was a vibration through Holland's head. *Very well,* said the *oshoc* at last. *Bring me another body, and the deal is struck. I will take their world instead.*

Holland nodded.

But, added Osaron, *if they cannot be persuaded, I will keep your body as my own.*

Holland growled. Osaron waited.

Well? A slow smile crept over the reflection. *Do you still wish to make the deal?*

Holland swallowed, and looked out his window as a second bird soared past.

"I do."

EIGHT

THE ESSENTASCH

I

Kell sat up, a scream still lodged in his throat.

Sweat traced the lines of his face as he blinked away the nightmare.

In his dreams, Red London was burning. He could still smell the smoke now that he was awake, and it took him a moment to realize that it wasn't simply an echo, trailing him out of sleep. The bedsheets were singed where he was gripping them—he had somehow summoned fire in his sleep. Kell stared down at his hands, the knuckles white. It had been years since his control had faltered.

Kell threw off the covers, and he was halfway to his feet when he heard the cascade of sound beyond the windows, the trumpets and bells, the carriages and shouts.

The tournament.

His blood hummed as he dressed, turning his coat inside out several times—assuring himself that Kamerov's silver jacket hadn't been swallowed up by the infinite folds of fabric—before returning it to its royal red and heading downstairs.

He put in a cursory appearance at breakfast, nodding to the king and queen and wishing Rhy luck as a flurry of attendants swirled around the prince with final plans, notes, and questions.

"Where do you think you're going?" asked the king as Kell palmed a sweet bun and turned toward the door.

"Sir?" he asked, glancing back.

"This is a royal event, Kell. You are expected to attend."

"Of course." He swallowed. Rhy shot him a look that said, *I've gotten you this far. Don't blow it now.* And if he did? Would Rhy have to call Castars back in to make another appearance? It would be too risky, trading the roles again in time for the fights, and Kell had a feeling Castars's charm wouldn't save him in the ring. Kell fumbled for an excuse. "It's just . . . I didn't think it wise for me to stand with the royal family."

"And why is that?" demanded King Maxim. The queen's gaze drifted in his direction, glancing off his shoulder, and Kell had to bite back the urge to point out that he *wasn't* actually a member of the royal family, as the last four months had made abundantly clear. But Rhy's look was a warning.

"Well," said Kell, scrambling for an explanation, "for the prince's safety. It's one thing to put me on display with dignitaries and champions in the company of royals, Your Highness, but you've said yourself that I'm a target." The prince gave a small, encouraging nod, and Kell pressed on. "Is it really wise to put me so close to Rhy in such a public forum? I was hoping to stake out a less conspicuous place, in case I'm needed. Somewhere with a good view of the royal podium, but not upon it."

The king's gaze narrowed in thought. The queen's gaze returned to her tea.

"Well thought," said Maxim grudgingly. "But keep Staff or Hastra with you at all times," he warned. "No wandering off."

Kell managed a smile. "There's nowhere I'd rather be."

And with that, he slipped out.

"The king *does* know about your role," said Hastra as they walked down the hall. "Doesn't he?"

Kell shot the young guard a glance. "Of course," he said, casually. And then, on a whim, he added, "But the queen does not. Her nerves couldn't handle the strain."

Hastra nodded knowingly. "She hasn't been the same, has she?" he whispered. "Not since that night."

Kell straightened, and quickened his step. "None of us have."

When they reached the steps into the Basin, Kell paused. "You know the plan?"

"Yes, sir," said Hastra. He flashed an excited smile and disappeared.

Kell shrugged off his coat and turned it inside out as he descended into the Basin, where he'd already drawn a shortcut on the glassy stone wall. His mask was sitting in its box atop the table, along with a note from his brother.

Keep this—and your head—on your shoulders.

Kell shrugged Kamerov's silver jacket on and opened the box. The mask waited within, its surface polished to mirror clarity, sharpening Kell's reflection until it looked like it belonged to someone else.

Beside the box sat a piece of rolled red fabric, and when Kell smoothed it out, he saw it was a new pennant. The two roses had been replaced by twin lions, black and white and lined with gold against the crimson ground.

Kell smiled and tugged the mask on over his head, his reddish hair and two-toned eyes vanishing behind the silvery surface.

"Master Kamerov," said Staff when he stepped out into the morning air. "Are you ready?"

"I am," he answered in Arnesian, the edges of his voice muffled and smoothed by the metal.

They started up the steps, and when they reached the top, Kell waited while the guard vanished, then reappeared a moment later to confirm the path was clear. Or rather, covered. The steps were sheltered by the palace's foundation, running from river to street, and market stalls crowded the banks, obstructing the path. By the time Kell stepped out of the palace's shadow, slipped between the tents and onto the main road, the *Antari* royal was left behind. Kamerov Loste had taken his place.

He might have been a different man, but he was still tall, lean, and dressed in silver, from mask to boot, and the eyes of the crowd quickly registered the magician in their midst. But after the first wave, Kell didn't cringe from the attention. Instead of trying to embody Rhy, he embodied a version of himself—one who didn't fear the public eye, one who had power, and nothing to hide—and soon he fell into an easy, confident stride.

As he made his way with the crowd toward the central stadium, Staff hung back, blending in with the other guards who lined the road at regular intervals and walked among the throngs of people.

Kell smiled as he mounted the bridge path from the banks to the largest of the three floating arenas. Last night he'd imagined feeling the ground move beneath him, but that might have been the wine, because this morning as he reached the archway to the arena floor, it felt solid as earth beneath his feet.

Half a dozen other men and women, all Arnesian, were already gathered in the corridor—the magicians from Faro and Vesk must be assembled in their own halls—waiting to make their grand entrance. Like Kell, they were decked out in their official tournament attire, with elegant coats or cloaks and, of course, helmets.

He recognized Kisimyr's coiled hair behind a catlike mask, Losen a step behind her, as if he were an actual shadow. Beside them was Brost's massive form, his features barely obscured by the simple strip of dark metal over his eyes. And there, behind a mask of scales trimmed in blue, stood Alucard.

The captain's gaze drifted over Kell, and he felt himself tense, but of course, where Kell saw a foe, Alucard would have seen only a stranger in a silver mask. And one who'd obviously introduced himself at the Banner Night, because Alucard tipped his head with an arrogant smile.

Kell nodded back, secretly hoping their paths might cross in the ring.

Jinnar appeared on a gust of wind against Kell's back, slipping past him with a breezy chuckle before knocking shoulders with Alucard.

More footsteps sounded in the tunnel, and Kell turned to see the last few Arnesians join the group, the dark shape of Stasion Elsor at the rear. He was long and lean, his face entirely hidden by a demon's mask. For an instant, Kell's breath caught, but Rhy was right: Kell was determined to see Lila Bard in every black-clad form, every smirking shadow.

Stasion Elsor's eyes were shadowed by the mask, but up close, the demon's face was different, the horns arcing back and a skeletal jawbone collaring mouth and throat. A lock of hair a shade darker than Lila's traced a line like a crack between the magician's shaded brown eyes. And though his mouth was visible between the demon's teeth, Stasion didn't smile, only stared at Kell. Kamerov.

"*Fal chas*," said Kell. *Good luck.*

"And you," replied Stasion simply, his voice nearly swallowed by the sudden flare of trumpets.

Kell twisted back to the archways as the gate swung open, and the ceremonies began.

II

"See, Parlo?" said Rhy, stepping out onto the stadium's royal balcony. "I told you it wouldn't sink."

The attendant hugged the back wall, looking ill. "So far, so good, Your Highness," he said, straining to be heard over the trumpets.

Rhy turned his smile on the waiting crowd. Thousands upon thousands had piled into the central stadium for the opening ceremonies. Above, the canvas birds dipped and soared on their silk tethers, and below, the polished stone of the arena floor stood empty save for three raised platforms. Poles mounted on each hung massive banners, each with an empire's seal.

The Faroan Tree.

The Veskan Crow.

The Arnesian Chalice.

Atop each platform, twelve shorter poles stood with banners furled, waiting for their champions.

Everything was perfect. Everything was ready.

As the trumpets trailed off, a cold breeze rustled Rhy's curls, and he touched the band of gold that hugged his temples. More gold glittered in his ears, at his throat, at collar and cuff, and as it caught the light, Alucard's voice pressed against his skin.

I fear you haven't enough. . . .

Rhy stopped fidgeting. Behind him, the king and queen sat

enthroned on gilded chairs, flanked by Lord Sol-in-Ar and the Taskon siblings. Master Tieren stood to the side.

"Shall I, Father?"

The king nodded, and Rhy stepped forward until he was front and center on the platform, overlooking the arena. The royal balcony sat not at the very top of the stadium, but embedded in the center of one sloping side, an elegant box halfway between the competitors' entrances and directly across from the judge's own platform.

The crowd began to hush, and Rhy grinned and held up a gold ring the size of a bracelet. When he spoke, the spelled metal amplified his words. The same charmed rings—albeit copper and steel—had been sent to taverns and courtyards across the city so that all could hear. During the matches, commentators would use the rings to keep the city apprised on various victories and defeats, but at this moment, the city's attention belonged to Rhy.

"Good morning, to all who have gathered."

A ripple of pleased surprise went through the gathered crowd when they realized he was speaking Arnesian. The last time the tournament had been held in London, Rhy's father had stood above his people and spoken High Royal, while a translator on a platform below offered the words in the common tongue.

But this wasn't just an affair of state, as his father claimed. It was a celebration for the people, the city, the empire. And so Rhy addressed his people, his city, his empire, in *their* tongue.

He went a step further, too: the platform below, where the translators of not only Arnes but also Faro and Vesk were supposed to stand, was empty. The foreigners frowned, wondering if the absence was some kind of slight. But their expressions became buoyant when Rhy continued.

"*Glad-ach!*" he said, addressing the Veskans. "*Anagh cael tach.*" And then, just as seamlessly, he slid into the serpentine tongue of Faro. "*Sasors noran amurs.*"

He let the words trail off, savoring the crowd's reaction. Rhy had always had a way with languages. About time he put some of them to use.

"My father, King Maxim, has given me the honor of overseeing this year's tournament."

This time as he spoke, his words echoed from other corners of the stadium, his voice twisting into the other two neighboring tongues. An illusion, one Kell had helped him design, using a variety of voice and projection spells. His father insisted that strength was the *image* of strength. Perhaps the same was true for magic.

"For more than fifty years, the Element Games have brought us together through good sport and festival, given us cause to toast our Veskan brothers and sisters and embrace our Faroan friends. And though only one magician—one nation—can claim this year's title, we hope that the Games will continue to celebrate the bond between our great empires!" Rhy tipped his head and flashed a devilish smile. "But I doubt you're all here for the politics. I imagine you're here to see some *magic*."

A cheer of support went through the masses.

"Well then, I present to you your magicians."

A column of glossy black fabric unfurled from the base of the royal platform, the end weighted so it stretched taut. A matching banner unspooled from the opposite side of the arena.

"From Faro, our venerable neighbor to the south, I present the twins of wind and fire, Tas-on-Mir and Tos-an-Mir; the wave whisperer Ol-ran-Es; the unparalleled Ost-ra-Gal. . . ."

As Rhy read each name, it appeared in white script against the dark silk banner beneath him.

"From Vesk, our noble neighbors to the north, I present the mountainous Otto, the unmovable Vox, the ferocious Rul . . ."

And as each name was called, the magician strode forward across the arena floor, and took their place on the podium.

"And finally, from our great empire of Arnes, I present your champion, the fire cat, Kisimyr"—a thunderous cheer went through the crowd—"the sea king, Alucard; the windborne Jinnar..."

And as each magician took their place, their chosen banner unfurled above their head.

"And Kamerov, the silver knight."

It was a dance, elaborate and elegant and choreographed to perfection.

The crowd rumbled with applause as the last of the Arnesian pennants snapped in the cool morning air, a set of twin blades above Stasion Elsor.

"Over the next five days and nights," continued Rhy, "these thirty-six magicians will compete for the title and the crown." He touched his head. "You can't have this one," he added with a wink, "it's mine." A ripple of laughter went through the stands. "No, the tournament crown is something far more spectacular. Incomparable riches; unmatchable renown; glory to one's name, one's house, and one's kingdom."

All traces of writing vanished from the curtains of black fabric, and the lines of the tournament grid appeared in white.

"For the first round, our magicians have been paired off." As he said it, names wrote themselves into the outer edges of the bracket. Murmurs went through the crowd and the magicians themselves stirred as they saw their opponents' names for the first time.

"The eighteen victors," continued Rhy, "will be paired off again, and the nine that advance will be placed into groups of three, where they will face off one-on-one. From each group, only the one with the highest standing will emerge to battle in the final match. Three magicians will enter, and only one will leave victorious. So tell me," finished Rhy, twirling the golden ring between his fingers, "are you ready to see some magic?"

The noise in the stadium rose to a deafening pitch, and the prince smiled. He might not have been able to summon fire, or draw rain, or make trees grow, but he still knew how to make an impact. He could feel the audience's excitement, as if it were beating inside him. And then he realized it wasn't only their excitement he was feeling.

It was also Kell's.

All right, brother, he thought, balancing the gold ring on his thumb like a coin.

"The time has come to marvel, and cheer, and choose your champions. And so, without further delay . . ." Rhy flicked the gold circle up into the air, and as he did, fireworks exploded overhead. Each explosion of light had been paired with its own midnight blue burst of smoke, an illusion of night that reached only as far as the firework and set it off against the winter grey sky.

He caught the ring and held it up again, his voice booming over the fireworks and the crowd's cheers.

"Let the Games begin!"

III

Lila had lost her mind. That was the only explanation. She was standing on a platform, surrounded by men and women who practically shook with power, the explosion of fireworks above and the roar of the crowd to every side, wearing a stranger's stolen clothes and about to compete in a tournament in the name of an empire she didn't serve in a world she wasn't even from.

And she was grinning like a fool.

Alucard jostled her shoulder, and she realized the other magicians were descending the platform, filing back toward the corridor from which they'd entered.

She followed the procession out of the arena and across the bridge-tunnel framework—she honestly couldn't tell what was holding the stadium up, but whatever it was, she seemed to be walking on it—and back to the solid ground of the city's southern banks.

Once on land, the gaps between the magicians began to stretch as they walked at their own pace toward the tents, and Lila and Alucard found themselves with room to move and speak.

"You still look like a fish," whispered Lila.

"And you still look like a girl playing dress-up," snapped Alucard. A few silent strides later he added, "You'll be happy to know I had a small sum sent back to our friend's home, claiming it was a competitor's bonus."

"How generous," said Lila. "I'll pay you back with my *winnings*."

Alucard lowered his voice. "Jinnar will hold his peace, but there's nothing I can do about Master Tieren. You'd best avoid him, since he certainly knows what Stasion Elsor looks like."

Lila waved her hand. "Don't worry about that."

"You can't *kill* the *Aven Essen*."

"I wasn't planning on it," she shot back. "Besides, Tieren already knows."

"*What?*" His storm-dark eyes narrowed behind his scaled mask. "And since when do you call the London *Aven Essen* by his first name? I'm pretty sure that's some kind of blasphemy."

Lila's mouth quirked. "*Master* Tieren and I have a way of crossing paths."

"All part of your mysterious past, I'm sure. No, it's fine, don't bother telling me anything useful, I'm only your captain and the man who helped you send an innocent man off into saints know what so you could compete in a tournament you're in no way qualified to be in."

"Fine," she said. "I won't. And I thought you weren't associating with Stasion Elsor."

Alucard frowned, his mouth perfectly exposed beneath the mask. He appeared to be sulking.

"Where are we going?" she asked to break the silence.

"The tents," said Alucard, as if that explained everything. "First match is in an hour."

Lila summoned the bracket in her mind, but it proved unnecessary, since every scrying board they passed seemed to be showing the grid. Every pairing had a symbol beside it marking the arena—a dragon for the east, a lion for the west, a bird for the one in the center—as well as an order. According to the grid, Kisimyr was set to face off against her own protégé, Losen, Alucard against a Veskan named Otto, Jinnar against a Faroan with a string of syllables. And Lila? She read the name across from Stasion's. *Sar Tanak*. A crow to the left of the name indicated that Sar was Veskan.

"Any idea which one is Sar?" asked Lila, nodding to the towering blond men and women walking ahead.

"Ah," said Alucard, gesturing to a figure on the other side of the procession. "*That* would be Sar."

Lila's eyes widened as the shape stepped forward. *"That?"* The Veskan stood six feet tall and was built like a rock slab. She was a woman, as far as Lila could tell, her features stony behind her hawkish mask, straw hair scraped into short braids that stuck out like feathers. She looked like the kind of creature to carry an ax.

What had Alucard said about Veskans worshipping mountains?

Sar *was* a mountain.

"I thought magic had nothing to do with physical size."

"The body is a vessel," explained Alucard. "The Veskans believe that the larger the vessel, the more power it can hold."

"*Great,*" Lila muttered to herself.

"Cheer up," said Alucard as they neared another scrying board. He nodded to their names, positioned on opposite sides of the grid. "At least our paths probably won't cross."

Lila's steps slowed. "You mean I have to beat all these people, just for the chance to take you on?"

He tipped his head. "You could have begged that privilege any night aboard the *Spire,* Bard. If you wanted a swift and humiliating death."

"Oh, is that so?"

They crossed in front of the palace as they chatted, and Lila discovered that, on the far side, in place of the gardens that usually ran from palace wall to copper bridge, stood three tents, great circular things sporting empire colors. Lila was secretly glad the tents weren't floating, too. She'd found her sea legs, of course, but had enough to worry about in the *Essen Tasch* without the prospect of drowning.

"And be glad you don't have Kisimyr in your bracket," continued Alucard as a guard held open the curtained flap that served as the main entrance of their tent. "Or Brost. You got off light."

"No need to sound so relieved. . . ." said Lila, trailing off as she took in the splendor of the Arnesian tent's interior. They were standing in a kind of common area at the center, the rest of the tent segmented into twelve pie-like wedges. Fabric billowed down from the peaked ceiling—just the way it did in the royal palace rooms—and everything was soft and plush and trimmed with gold. For the first time in her life, Lila's awe wasn't matched by the desire to pocket anything—she was either growing too accustomed to wealth or, more likely, had enough charges on her plate without adding theft.

"Believe it or not," Alucard whispered, "one of us would like to see you live."

"Maybe I'll surprise you."

"You always do." He looked around, spotting his banner on one of the twelve curtained rooms. "And now, if you'll excuse me, I have a match to prepare for."

Lila waved. "I'll be sure to pick up your pennant. It's the one with a fish on it, right?"

"Har har."

"Good luck."

Lila unfastened her helmet as she passed into the private tent marked by a black flag with crossed knives.

"Bloody hell," she muttered as she tugged off the mask, the devil's jaw tangling in her hair. And then she looked up. And stopped. The room was many things—simple, elegant, softened by couches and tables and billowing fabric—but it was *not* empty.

A woman stood in the middle of the space, dressed in white and gold, holding a tray of tea. Lila jumped, fighting the urge to draw a weapon.

"*Kers la?*" she snapped, her helmet still resting on her head.

The woman frowned slightly. "*An tas arensor.*"

"I don't need an attendant," answered Lila, still in Arnesian, and still fighting with the helmet.

The woman set down the tray, came forward, and, in one effortless motion, disentangled the knot, freeing Lila from the devil's jaws. She lifted the helmet from Lila's head and set it on the table.

Lila had decided not to thank her for the unwarranted help, but the words still slipped out.

"You're welcome," answered the woman.

"I don't need you," repeated Lila.

But the woman held her ground. "All competitors are assigned an attendant."

"Well then," said Lila brusquely, "I dismiss you."

"I don't think you can."

Lila rubbed her neck. "Do you speak High Royal?"

The woman slid effortlessly into English. "It suits my station."

"As a servant?"

A smile nicked the corner of the woman's mouth. "As a priest." *Of course,* thought Lila. Master Tieren chose the competitors. It made sense that he would supply the attendants, too. "The prince insists that all competitors be provided an attendant, to see to their various needs."

Lila raised a brow. "Like what?"

The woman shrugged and gestured to a chair.

Lila tensed. There was a *body* in it. It had no head.

The woman crossed to the form, and Lila realized it wasn't a headless corpse after all, but a set of armor, not polished like the kind worn by the royal guards, but simple and white. Lila found herself reaching for the nearest piece. When she lifted it, she marveled at its lightness. It didn't seem like it would do much to protect her. She tossed it back onto the chair, but the attendant caught it before it fell.

"Careful," she said, setting the piece down gently. "The plates are fragile."

"What good is fragile armor?" asked Lila. The woman looked at her as though she had asked a very stupid question. Lila hated that kind of look.

"This is your first *Essen Tasch*," she said. It wasn't an inquiry. Without waiting for confirmation, the woman bent to a chest beside the chair and drew out a spare piece of armor. She held it up for Lila to see, and then threw it against the ground. When it met the floor, the plate cracked, and as it did, there was a flash of light. Lila winced at the sudden brightness; in the flare's wake, the armor plate was no longer white, but dark grey.

"This is how they keep score," explained the attendant, retrieving the spent armor. "A full set of armor is twenty-eight pieces. The first magician to break ten wins the match."

Lila reached down and took up the ruined plate. "Anything else I should know?" she asked, turning it over in her hands.

"Well," said the priest, "you cannot strike blows with your body, only your elements, but I'm sure you already knew that."

Lila hadn't. A trumpet sounded. The first matches were about to begin.

"Do you have a name?" she asked, handing the plate back.

"Ister."

"Well, Ister . . ." Lila backed away toward the curtain. "Do you just . . . stand here until I need you?"

The woman smiled and dug a volume from a pocket. "I have a book."

"Let me guess, a religious text?"

"Actually," said Ister, perching on the low couch, "it's about pirates."

Lila smiled. The priestess was growing on her.

"Well," said Lila, "I won't tell the *Aven Essen*."

Ister's smile tilted. "Who do you think gave it to me?" She turned the page. "Your match is at four, Master Stasion. Don't be late."

"Master Kamerov," came a cheerful voice as Kell stepped into his tent.

"Hastra."

The young guard's armor and cape were gone, and in their place he wore a simple white tunic trimmed in gold. A scarf, marked with the same gold trim, wrapped loosely around his face and throat, masking all but his aquiline nose and warm brown eyes. A curl escaped the wrap, and when he pulled the scarf down around his neck, Kell saw that he was grinning.

Saints, he looked young, like a sanctuary novice.

Kell didn't bother removing his helmet. It was too dangerous, and not only because he could be recognized; the mask was a constant reminder of the ruse. Without its weight, he might forget who he was, and who he wasn't.

Reluctantly he shed the silver coat and left it on a chair while Hastra fitted the plates of armor over his long-sleeved tunic.

In the distance, trumpets sounded. The first three matches were about to begin. There was no telling how long the opening rounds would take. Some might last an hour. Others would be over in minutes. Kell was the third match in the western arena. His first opponent was a Faroan wind mage named Tas-on-Mir.

He went over these details in his mind as the plates of armor were fastened and tightened. He didn't realize Hastra had finished until the young guard spoke.

"Are you ready, sir?"

A mirror stood before one curtained wall, and Kell considered himself, heart pounding. *You must be excited,* Hastra had said, and Kell *was*. At first, he'd thought it madness—and honestly, if he thought about it too hard, he knew it was still madness—but he couldn't help it. Logic be damned, wisdom be damned, he was excited.

"This way," said Hastra, revealing a second curtained door at the outside edge of the private tent. It was almost as if the addition had been designed with Kell's deception in mind. Perhaps it *was*. Saints, how long had Rhy been planning this charade? Perhaps Kell hadn't given his wayward brother enough credit. And perhaps Kell himself wasn't paying enough attention. He *had* been spending too much time in his rooms, or in the Basin, and he had taken to assuming that just because he could sense Rhy's body, he also knew his brother's mind. Obviously, he was mistaken.

Since when are you so invested in empire politics?
I'm invested in my kingdom, Brother.

Rhy had changed, that much Kell *had* noticed. But he had only seen his brother's varying moods, the way his temper darkened at night. This was different. This was *clever*.

But just to be safe, Kell took up his knife, discarded along with his coat, and pulled back one of the tent's many tapestries. Hastra watched as he nicked the soft flesh of his forearm and touched his fingers to the welling blood. On the canvas wall, he drew a small symbol, a vertical line, with a small horizontal mark on top leading to the right, and another on the bottom, leading to the left. Kell blew on it until it was dry, then let the tapestry swing back into place, hiding the symbol from sight.

Hastra didn't ask. He simply wished him luck, then hung back in the tent as Kell left; within several strides, a royal guard—Staff—fell in step beside him. They walked in silence, the crowds on the street—men and women who cared less for the matches than the festivities surrounding them—parting around him. Here and there children waved banners, and Kell caught sight of tangled lions amid the other pennants.

"Kamerov!" shouted someone, and soon the chant was being carried on the air—*Kamerov, Kamerov, Kamerov*—the name trailing behind him like a cape.

IV

"Alucard! Alucard! Alucard!" chanted the crowd.

Lila had missed the beginning of the fight, but it didn't matter; her captain was winning.

The eastern arena was filled to capacity, the lower levels shoulder to shoulder, while the upper tiers afforded worse views but a little more air. Lila had opted for one of the highest tiers open to the public, balancing the desire to study the match with the need to maintain anonymity. Stasion's black hat perched on her brow, and she leaned her elbows on the railing and watched dark earth swirl around Alucard's fingers. She imagined she could see his smile, even from this height.

Prince Rhy, who'd appeared a few minutes before, cheeks flushed from traveling between the stadiums, now stood on the royal balcony and watched with rapt attention, the stern-looking Faroan noble at his shoulder.

Two poles rose above the royal platform, each bearing a pennant to mark the match. Alucard's was a silver feather—or a drop of flame, she couldn't tell—against a backdrop of dark blue. She held a copy in one hand. The other pennant bore a set of three stacked white triangles on forest green. Alucard's opponent, a Veskan named Otto, wore an ancient-looking helmet with a nose plate and a domed skull.

Otto had chosen fire to Alucard's earth, and both were now dancing and dodging each other's blows. The smooth stone of the arena floor was dotted with obstacles, rock formations offering cover as well as the chance for ambush, and they must have been warded, since Alucard never made them move.

Otto was surprisingly quick on his feet for a man nearly seven feet tall, but his skill was one of blunt force, while Alucard's was sleight of hand—Lila couldn't think of it any other way. Most magicians, just like most ordinary fighters, gave away their attack by moving in the same direction as their magic. But Alucard could stand perfectly still while his element moved, or in this case, could dodge one way and send his power another, and through that simple, effective method, had scored eight hits to Otto's two.

Alucard was a showman, adding flourish and flare, and Lila had been on the receiving end of his games enough times to see that he was now playing with the Veskan, shifting into a defensive mode to prolong the fight and please the crowd.

A cheer rose from the western arena, where Kisimyr was going up against her protégé, Losen, and moments later the words on the nearest bracket board shifted, Losen's name vanishing and Kisimyr's writing itself into the advancing spot. In the arena below, flames circled Otto's fists. The hardest thing about fire was putting force behind it, giving it weight as well as heat. The Veskan was throwing his own weight behind the blows, instead of using the fire's strength.

"Magic is like the ocean," Alucard had told her in her first lesson. "When waves go the same way, they build. When they collide, they cancel. Get in the way of your magic, and you break the momentum. Move with it, and . . ."

The air around Lila began to tingle pleasantly.

"Master Tieren," she said without turning.

The *Aven Essen* stepped up beside her. "Master Stasion," he said casually. "Shouldn't you be getting ready?"

"I fight last," she said, shooting him a glance. "I wanted to see Alucard's match."

"Supporting friends?"

She shrugged. "Studying opponents."

"I see...."

Tieren gave her an appraising look. Or perhaps it was disapproving. He was a hard man to read, but Lila liked him. Not just because he didn't try to stop her, but because she could ask him questions, and he clearly didn't believe in protecting a person by keeping them in the dark. He'd entrusted her with a difficult task once, he'd kept her secrets twice, and he'd let her choose her own path at every turn.

Lila nodded at the royal box. "The prince seems keen on this match," she ventured, as down below Otto narrowly escaped a blow. "But who is the Faroan?"

"Lord Sol-in-Ar," said Tieren, "the older brother of the king."

Lila frowned. "Shouldn't being the eldest make *him* the king?"

"In Faro, the descent of the crown is not determined by the order of birth, but by the priests. Lord Sol-in-Ar has no affinity for magic. Thus, he cannot be king."

Lila could hear the distaste in Tieren's voice, and she could tell it wasn't for Sol-in-Ar, but for the priests who deemed him unworthy.

She didn't buy into all that nonsense about magic sorting the strong from the weak, making some kind of spiritual judgment. No, that was too much like fate, and Lila didn't put much stock in that. A person chose their path. Or they made a new one.

"How do you know so much?" she asked.

"I've spent my life studying magic."

"I didn't think we were talking about magic."

"We were talking about people," he said, his eyes following the match, "and people are the most variable and important component in the equation of magic. Magic itself is, after all, a constant, a pure and steady source, like water. People, and the world they shape—they are the conduits of magic, determining its nature, coloring its energy, the way a dye does water. You of all people should be able to see that magic changes in the hands of men. It is an element to be shaped. As for my interest in Faro and Vesk, the Arnesian empire is vast. It is not, however, the extent of the world, and last time I endeavored to check, magic existed beyond its borders. I'm glad of the *Essen Tasch,* if only for that reminder, and for the chance to see how magic is treated in other lands."

"I hope you've written this all down somewhere," she said. "For posterity and all."

He tapped the side of his head. "I keep it someplace safe." Lila snorted. Her attention drifted back to Sol-in-Ar. Men talked, and men at sea talked more than most. "Is it true what they say?"

"I wouldn't know, Master Elsor. I don't stay apprised."

She doubted he was half as naive as he seemed. "That Lord Sol-in-Ar wants to overthrow his brother and start a war?"

Tieren brought his hand down on her shoulder, his grip surprisingly firm. "Mind that tongue of yours," he said quietly. "There are too many ears for such careless remarks."

They watched the rest of the match in silence. It didn't last long.

Alucard was a blur of light, his helmet winking in the sun as he spun behind a boulder and around the other side. Lila watched, mesmerized, as he lifted his hands, and the earth around him shot forward.

Otto pulled his fire around him like a shell, shielding front and back and every side. Which was great, except he obviously couldn't *see* through the blaze, so he didn't notice the moment the earth changed direction and flew up into the air, pulling itself together into clods before it fell, not with ordinary force, but raining down in a blur. The crowd gasped, and the Veskan looked up too late. His hands shot skyward, and so did the fire, but not fast enough; three of the missiles found their mark, colliding with shoulder and forearm and knee hard enough to shatter the armor plates.

In a burst of light, the match was over.

An official—a priest, judging by his white robes—held a gold ring to his lips and said, "Alucard Emery advances!"

The crowd thundered with applause, and Lila looked up at the royal platform, but the prince was gone. She glanced around, already knowing that Tieren was, too. Trumpets sounded from the central arena. Lila saw that Jinnar had advanced. She scanned the list for the central arena's next match.

Tas-on-Mir, read the top name, and just below it, *Kamerov*.

The magic sang in Kell's blood as the crowd roared in the arena above. Saints, had every single person in Red London turned up to witness the opening rounds?

Jinnar passed him in the tunnel on the way out of his match. It didn't even look like he'd broken a sweat.

"*Fal chas!*" called the black-eyed magician, peeling off the remains of his armor. By the looks of it, he'd only broken three plates.

"*Rensa tav,*" answered Kell automatically as his chest hummed with nervous energy. What was he thinking? What was he doing here? This was all a mistake . . . and yet, his muscles and bones still ached for a fight, and beyond the tunnel, he could hear them calling the name—*Kamerov! Kamerov! Kamerov!*—and even though it wasn't his, it still sent a fresh burst of fire through his veins.

His feet drifted forward of their own accord to the mouth of the tunnel, where two attendants waited, a table between them.

"The rules have been well explained?" asked the first.

"And you are ready, willing, and able?" prompted the second.

Kell nodded. He'd seen enough tournament matches to know the way things worked, and Rhy had insisted on running through each and every one of them again, just to make sure. As the tournament went on, the rules would shift to allow for longer, harder matches. The *Essen Tasch* would become far more dangerous then, for Kell and Rhy both. But the opening rounds were simply meant to separate the good from the very good, the skilled from the masters.

"Your element?" prompted the first.

A selection of glass spheres sat on the table, much like the ones that Kell had once used to try to teach Rhy magic. Each sphere contained an element: dark earth, tinted water, colored dust to give the wind shape, and in the case of fire, a palmful of oil to create the flame. Kell's hand drifted over the orbs as he tried to decide which one he should pick. As an *Antari,* he could wield any of them. As Kamerov, he would have to choose. His hand settled on a sphere containing water, stained a vivid blue so it would be visible to the spectators once he entered the arena.

The two attendants bowed, and Kell stepped out into the arena, ushered forth on a wave of noise. He squinted up through his visor. It was a sunny winter day, the cold biting but the light bright, glinting off the arena's spires and the metallic thread in the banners that waved from every direction. The lions on Kell's pennant winked at him from all around the arena, while Tas-on-Mir's silver-blue spiral stood out here and there against its black ground (her twin sister, Tos-an-Mir, sported the inverse, black on silver-blue).

The drama and spectacle had always seemed silly from afar, but standing here, on the arena floor instead of up in the stands, Kell felt himself getting caught up in the show. The chanting, cheering crowd pulsed with energy, with magic. His heart thrummed, his body eager for the fight, and he looked up past the crowds to the royal platform where Rhy had taken his place beside the king, looking down. Their eyes met, and even though Rhy couldn't possibly see Kell's through his mask, he still felt the look pass between them like a taut string being plucked.

Do try not to get us both killed.

Rhy gave a single, almost imperceptible nod from the balcony, and Kell wove between the stone obstacles to the center of the arena.

Tas-on-Mir had already entered the ring. She was clothed, like all Faroans, in a single piece of wrapped fabric, its details lost beneath her armor. A simple helmet did more to frame her face than mask it, and silver-blue gems shone like beads of sweat along her brow and down her cheeks. In one hand, she held an orb filled with red powder. A wind mage. Kell's mind raced. Air was one of the easiest elements to move, and one of the hardest to fight, but force came easy, and precision did not.

A priest in white robes stood on a plinth atop the lowest balcony to officiate the match. He motioned, and the two came forward, nodded to the royal platform, and then faced each other, each holding out their sphere. The sand in Tas-on-Mir's orb began to swirl, while the water in Kell's sloshed lazily.

Then either silence fell across the stadium, or Kell's pulse drowned out everything—the crowds, the flapping pennants, the distant cheers from other matches. Somewhere in that void of noise, the spheres fell, and the first sound that reached Kell's ears was the crystalline sound of them shattering against the arena floor.

For an instant, the blood in Kell's veins quickened and the world around him slowed. And then, just as suddenly, it snapped back into motion. The Faroan's wind leaped up and began to coil around her. The dark water swirled around Kell's arms before pooling above his palms.

The Faroan jerked, and the red-tinted wind shot forth with spear-like force. Kell lunged back just in time to dodge one blow, and he missed the second as it smashed against his side, shattering a plate and showering the arena in light.

The blow knocked Kell's breath away; he stole a glance up at

Rhy in the royal box, and saw him gripping his chair and gritting his teeth. At a glance, it could have passed for concentration, but Kell knew it for what it was, an echo of his own pain. He uttered a silent apology, then dove behind the nearest mound of rock, narrowly escaping another hit. He rolled and came to his feet, grateful the armor was designed to respond only to attacks, not self-inflicted force.

Up above, Rhy gave him a withering look.

Kell considered the two pools of water still hovering above his hands, and imagined Holland's voice echoing around the arena, tangled in the wind. Taunting.

Fight.

Shielded by the rock, he held up one hand, and the watery sphere above his fingers began to unravel into two streams and then four, and then eight. The cords circled the arena from opposite sides, stretching thinner and thinner, into ribbons and then threads and then filaments, crisscrossing into a web.

In response, the red wind picked up, sharpening the way his water had, a dozen razors of air; Tas-on-Mir was trying to force him out. Kell winced as a sliver of wind nicked his cheek. His opponent's voice began to carry on the air from a dozen places, and to the rest of the arena it would look like Kell was fighting blind, but Kell could *feel* the Faroan—the blood and magic pulsing beneath her skin, the tension against the threads of water as he pulled them taut. Where . . . where . . . *there.* He spun, launching himself not to the side but *up.* He mounted the boulder, the second orb freezing the instant before it left his hand. It splintered as it hurtled toward Tas-on-Mir, who managed to summon a shield out of her wind before the shards could hit. But she was so focused on the attack from the front that she'd forgotten the web of water, which had reformed in the span of a second into a block of ice behind her. It crashed into her back, shattering the three plates that guarded her spine.

The crowd erupted as the Faroan fell forward to her hands and knees, and the water sailed back to Kell's side and twined around his wrists.

It had been a feint. The same one he'd used on Holland. But unlike the *Antari,* Tas-on-Mir didn't stay down. A moment later she was back on her feet, the red wind whipping around her as the broken plates fell away.

Three down, thought Kell. *Seven to go.*

He smiled behind his mask, and then they both became a blur of light, and wind, and ice.

Rhy's knuckles tightened on the arms of his chair.

Below, Kell ducked and dodged the Faroan's blows.

Even as Kamerov, he was incredible. He moved around the arena with staggering grace, barely touching the ground. Rhy had only seen his brother fight in scuffles and brawls. Was this what he'd looked like when he'd faced Holland? Or Athos Dane? Or was this the product of the months spent in the Basin, driven by his own demons?

Kell landed another hit, and Rhy found himself fighting back a laugh—at this, at the absurdity of what they were doing, at the very real pain in his side, at the fact that he couldn't make it stop. The fact that he wouldn't, even if he could. There was a kind of control in letting go, giving in.

"Our magicians are strong this year," he said to his father.

"But not *too* strong," said the king. "Tieren has chosen well. Let us hope the priests of Faro and Vesk have done the same."

Rhy's brow crinkled. "I thought the whole point of this was to show our strength."

His father gave him a chiding look. "Never forget, Rhy, that you are watching a *game.* One with three strong but equal players."

"And what if, one year, Vesk and Faro played to *win*?"

"Then we would know."

"Know what?"

The king's gaze returned to the match. "That war is near."

In the arena below, Kell rolled, then rose. The dark water swirled and swerved around him, slipping under and around the Faroan's wall of air before slamming into her chest. The armor there shattered into light with the blow, and the crowd burst into applause.

Kell's face was hidden, but Rhy knew he was smiling.

Show-off, he thought, just before Kell dodged too slowly and let a knifelike gust of wind get through, the blow slamming against his ribs. Light erupted in front of Rhy's eyes, and behind them as he caught his breath. Pain burned across his skin, and he tried to imagine he could draw it in, away from Kell, and ground it in himself.

"You look pale," observed the king.

Rhy sank back against the chair. "I'm fine." And he was. The pain made him feel alive. His heart pounded in his chest, racing alongside his brother's.

King Maxim got to his feet and looked around. "Where is Kell?" he asked. His voice had taken to hardening around the name in a way that turned Rhy's stomach.

"I'm sure he's around," he answered, gazing down at the two fighters in the ring. "He's been looking forward to the tournament. Besides, isn't that what Staff and Hastra are for? Keeping track of him?"

"They've grown soft in their duties."

"When will you stop punishing him?" snapped Rhy. "He's not the only one who did wrong."

Maxim's eyes darkened. "And *he*'s not the future king."

"What does that have to do with it?"

"Everything," said his father, leaning close and lowering his voice. "You think I do this out of spite? Some ill-borne malice? This is meant to be a lesson, Rhy. Your people will suffer when you err, and you will suffer when your people do."

"Believe me," muttered Rhy, rubbing an echo of pain across his ribs. "I'm suffering."

Below, Kell ducked and spun. Rhy could tell the fight was coming to an end. The Faroan was outmatched—she'd been outmatched from the beginning—and her motions were slowing, while Kell's only grew faster, more confident.

"Do you really think his life's in danger?"

"It's not *his* life I'm worried about," said the king. But Rhy knew that wasn't true. Not entirely. Kell's power made him a target. Vesk and Faro believed that he was blessed, the jewel in the Arnesian crown, the source of power that kept the empire strong. It was a myth Rhy was pretty certain the Arnesian crown perpetuated, but the dangerous thing about legends was that some people took them to heart, and those who thought Kell's magic guarded the empire might also think that by eliminating him, they could hobble the kingdom. Others thought that if they could steal him, the strength of Arnes would be theirs.

But Kell wasn't some talisman . . . was he?

When they were children, Rhy looked at Kell and saw only his brother. As they grew older, his vision changed. Some days he thought he saw a darkness. Other times he thought he saw a god. Not that he would ever tell Kell that. He knew Kell hated the idea of being chosen.

Rhy thought there were worse things to be.

Kell took another hit down in the arena, and Rhy felt the nerves sing down his arm.

"Are you sure you're all right?" pressed his father, and Rhy realized his knuckles had gone white on the chair.

"Perfectly," he said, swallowing the pain as Kell delivered the final two blows, back to back, ending the match. The crowd erupted in applause as the Faroan staggered to her feet and nodded, the motion stiff, before retreating from the ring.

Kell turned his attention to the royal balcony and bowed deeply.

Rhy raised his hand, acknowledging the victory, and the figure in silver and white vanished into the tunnel.

"Father," said Rhy, "if you don't forgive Kell, you will lose him."

There was no answer.

Rhy turned toward his father, but the king was already gone.

V

People always said that waiting was the worst part, and Lila agreed. So much so, in fact, that she rarely waited for anything. Waiting left too much room for questions, for doubt. It weakened a person's resolve—which was probably why, as she stood in the tunnel of the western arena *waiting* for her match, she started to feel like she'd made a terrible mistake.

Dangerous.
Reckless.
Foolish.
Mad.

A chorus of doubt so loud her boots took a step back of their own accord.

In one of the other stadiums, the crowds cheered as an Arnesian emerged victorious.

Lila retreated another step.

And then she caught sight of the flag—*her* flag—in the stands, and her steps ground to a halt.

I am Delilah Bard, she thought. *Pirate, thief, magician.*

Her fingertips began to thrum.

I have crossed worlds and taken ships. Fought queens and saved cities.

Her bones shuddered and her blood raced.

I am one of a kind.

The summoning trumpets blared, and with them, Lila forced

herself forward through the archway, her orb hanging from her fingers. Iridescent oil sloshed inside, ready to be lit.

As soon as she took the field, the anxiety bled away, leaving a familiar thrill in its wake.

Dangerous.
Reckless.
Foolish.
Mad.

The voices started up again, but they couldn't stop her now. The waiting was over. There was no turning back, and that simple fact made it easier to go forward.

The stands let out a cheer as Lila entered the arena. From the balcony, the stadium had looked considerable. From the floor, it looked *massive*.

She scanned the crowd—there were so many people, so many eyes on her. As a thief in the night, Lila Bard knew that staying out of the light was the surest way to stay alive, but she couldn't help it, she *relished* this kind of trick. Standing right in front of a mark while you pocketed their coins. Smiling while you stole. Looking them in the eye and daring them to see past the ruse. Because the best tricks were the ones pulled off not while the mark's back was turned, but while they were watching.

And Lila wanted to be seen.

Then she saw the Veskan.

Sar entered the arena, crossing the wide space in a matter of strides before coming to a stop in the center. Standing still, she looked like she'd grown straight out of the stone floor, a towering oak of a woman. Lila had never thought of herself as short, but next to the Veskan, she felt like a twig.

The bigger they are, thought Lila, *the harder they fall. Hopefully.*

At least the armor plates were sized to fit, giving Lila a bigger target. Sar's mask was made of wood and metal twined together into some kind of beast, with horns and a snout and slitted eyes through which Sar's own blue ones shone through. In her hand hung an orb full of earth.

Lila's teeth clenched.

Earth was the hardest element—almost any blow would break a plate—but it was also given in the smallest quantity. Air was everywhere, which meant fire was, too, if you could wrangle it into shape.

Sar bowed, her shadow looming over Lila.

The Veskan's flag rippled overhead, a cloudless blue marked by a single yellow *X*. Between Sar's letter and Lila's knives, the crowd was a sea of crossed lines. Most were silver on black, but Lila thought that probably had less to do with rumors of Stasion Elsor's skill, and more to do with the fact he was Arnesian. The locals would always take the majority. Right now, their loyalty was by default. But Lila could earn it. She imagined an entire stadium of black and silver flags.

Don't get ahead of yourself.

The arena floor was dotted with obstacles, boulders and columns and low walls all made from the same dark stone as the floor, so that the competitors and their elements stood out against the charcoal backdrop.

The trumpets trailed off, and Lila's gaze rose to the royal balcony, but the prince wasn't there. Only a young man wearing a green cape and a crown of polished wood and threaded silver—one of the Veskan royals—and Master Tieren. Lila winked and, even though the *Aven Essen* probably couldn't see, his bright eyes still seemed to narrow in disapproval.

A tense quiet fell over the crowd, and Lila twisted back to see a man in white and gold robes on the judge's platform that cantilevered over the arena. His hand was up, and for a second she wondered if he was summoning magic, until she realized he was only summoning silence.

Sar held out her sphere, the earth rising and rattling inside with nervous energy.

Lila swallowed and lifted her own, the oil disturbingly still by comparison.

Tyger Tyger, burning bright . . .

Her fingers tightened on the orb, and the surface of the oil burst into flame. The effect was impressive, but it wouldn't last, not with so little air in the sphere. She didn't wait—the instant the man in white began to lower his hand, Lila smashed the orb against the ground, sending up a burst of air-starved flame. The force of it jolted Lila and surprised the audience, who seemed to think it was all in the spirit of spectacle.

Sar crushed her own orb between her hands, and just like that, the match was underway.

"Focus," scolded Alucard.

"I am *focusing*," said Lila, *holding her hands on either side of the oil.*

"You're not. Remember, magic is like the ocean."

"Yeah, yeah," grumbled Lila, "waves."

"When waves go the same way," *he lectured, ignoring her commentary,* "they build. When they collide, they cancel."

"Right, so I want to build the wave—"

"No," said Alucard. "Just let the power pass through you."

Esa brushed against her. The Spire *rocked slightly with the sea. Her arms ached from holding them aloft, a bead of oil in each palm. It was her first lesson, and she was already failing.*

"You're not trying."

"Go to hell."

"Don't fight it. Don't force it. Be an open door."

"What happened to waves?" *muttered Lila.*

Alucard ignored her. "All elements are inherently connected," *he rambled on while she struggled to summon fire.* "There's no hard line between one and the next. Instead, they exist on a spectrum, bleeding into one another. It's about finding which part of that *spectrum pulls at you the strongest. Fire bleeds into air, which bleeds into water, which bleeds into earth, which bleeds into metal, which bleeds into bone."*

"And magic?"

He crinkled his brow, as if he didn't understand. "Magic is in everything."

Lila flexed her hands, focusing on the tension in her fingers, because she needed to focus on something. "Tyger Tyger, burning bright . . ." Nothing.

"You're trying too hard."

Lila let out an exasperated sound. "I thought I wasn't trying hard enough!"

"It's a balance. And your grip is too tight."

"I'm not even touching it."

"Of course you are. You're just not using your hands. You're exerting force. But force isn't the same as will. You're seizing a thing, when you need only cradle it. You're trying to control the element. But it doesn't work like that, not really. It's more of a . . . conversation. Question and answer, call and response."

"Wait, so is it waves, or doors, or conversations?"

"It can be anything you like."

"You're a wretched teacher."

"I warned you. If you're not up to it—"

"Shut up. I'm concentrating."

"You can't glare magic into happening."

Lila took a steadying breath. She tried to focus on the way fire felt, imagined the heat against her palms, but that didn't work, either. Instead she drew up the memories of Kell, of Holland, of the way the air changed when they did magic, the prickle, the pulse. She thought of holding the black stone, summoning its power, the vibration between her blood and bones and something else, something deeper. Something strange and impossible, and at the same time, utterly familiar.

Her fingertips began to burn, not with heat, but something stranger, something warm and cool, rough and smooth and alive.

Tyger Tyger, burning bright, *she whispered silently, and an instant later, the fire came to life against her palms. She didn't need to see what she'd done. She could feel it—not only the heat, but the power swimming beneath it.*

Lila was officially a magician.

Lila was still trying to wrangle the fire into shape when Sar's first ball of earth—it was basically a rock—slammed into her shoulder. The burst of light was sharp and fleeting as the plate broke. The pain lingered.

There was no time to react. Another mass came hurtling toward her, and Lila spun out of Sar's line of attack, ducking behind a pillar an instant before the earth shattered against it, raining pebbles onto the arena floor. Thinking she had time before the next attack, Lila continued around the pillar, prepared to strike, and was caught in the chest by a spear of earth, crushing the central plate. The blow slammed her back into a boulder, and her spine struck the rock with brutal force, two more plates shattering as she gasped and fell to her hands and knees.

Four plates lost in a matter of seconds.

The Veskan made a chuckling sound, low and guttural, and before Lila could even get upright, let alone retaliate, another ball of earth struck her in the shin, cracking a fifth plate and sending her back to her knees.

Lila rolled to her feet, swearing viciously, the words lost beneath the cheers and chants and snapping pennants. A puddle of fire continued to burn on the oil-slicked ground. Lila shoved against it with her will, sending a river of flame toward Sar. It barely grazed the Veskan, the heat licking harmlessly against the armor. Lila cursed and dove behind a barrier.

The Veskan said something taunting, but Lila continued to hide.

Think, think, think.

She'd spent all day watching the matches, making note of the moves everyone made, the way they played. She'd scraped together secrets, the chinks in a player's armor, the tells in their game.

And she'd learned one very important thing.

Everyone played *by the rules*. Well, as far as Lila could tell, there weren't that many, aside from the obvious: no touching. But these competitors, they were like performers. They didn't play dirty. They didn't fight like it really mattered. Sure, they wanted to win, wanted to take the glory and the prize, but they didn't fight like their *lives* were on the line. There was too much bravado, and too little fear. They moved with the confidence of knowing a bell would chime, a whistle would blow, the match would end, and they would still be safe.

Real fights didn't work that way.

Delilah Bard had never been in a fight that didn't matter.

Her eyes flicked around the arena and landed on the judge's platform. The man himself had stepped back, leaving the ledge open. It stood above the arena, but not by much. She could reach it.

Lila drew the fire in and tight, ready to strike. And then she turned, mounted the wall, and jumped. She made it, just barely, the crowd gasping in surprise as she landed on the platform and spun toward Sar.

And sure enough, the Veskan hesitated.

Hitting the crowds was clearly not allowed. But there was no rule about standing in front of them. That hitched moment was all Lila needed. Sar didn't attack, and Lila did, a comet of fire launching from each hand.

Don't fight it, don't force it, be an open door.

But Lila didn't feel like an open door. She felt like a magnifying glass, amplifying whatever strange magic burned inside her so that when it met the fire, the force was its own explosion.

The comets twisted and arced through the air, colliding into Sar from different angles. One she blocked. The other crashed against her side, shattering the three plates that ran from hip to shoulder.

Lila grinned like a fool as the crowd erupted. A flash of gold above caught her eye. At some point, the prince had arrived to watch. Alucard stood in the stands below him, and on her own level, the judge in white was storming forward. Before he could call foul, Lila leaped from the platform back to the boulder. Unfortunately, Sar had recovered, both from her surprise and the hit, and as Lila's foot hit the outcropping, a projectile of earth slammed into her shoulder, breaking a sixth piece of armor and knocking her off the edge.

As she fell back, she flipped with feline grace and landed in a crouch.

Sar braced herself for an attack as soon as Lila's boots struck stone, which was why Lila launched the fire *before* she landed. The meteor caught the Veskan's shin, shattering another plate.

Four to six.

Lila was catching up.

She rolled behind a barrier to recover as Sar stretched out her thick fingers, and the earth strewn across the arena shuddered and drew itself back toward her.

Lila saw a large clod of dirt and dropped to one knee, fingers curling around the earth the moment before Sar's invisible force took hold and pulled, hard enough to draw the element, and Lila with it. She didn't let go, boots sliding along the smooth stone floor as Sar reeled her in without realizing it, Lila herself still hidden by the various obstacles. The boulders and columns and walls ended, and the instant they did, Sar saw Lila, saw her let go of the ball of earth, now coated in flame. It careened back toward the Veskan, driven first by her pull and then by Lila's will, crashing into her chest and shattering two more plates.

Good. Now they were even.

Sar attacked again, and Lila dodged casually—or at least, she meant to, but her boot held fast to the floor, and she looked down to see a band of earth turned hard and dark as rock and fused to the ground. Sar's teeth flashed in a grin behind her mask, and it was all Lila could do to get her arms up in time to block the next attack.

Pain rang through her like a tuning fork as the plates across her stomach, hip, and thigh all shattered. Lila tasted blood, and hoped she'd simply bitten her tongue. She was one plate shy of losing the whole damn thing, and Sar was gearing up to strike again, and the earth that pinned her boot was still holding firm.

Lila couldn't pull her foot free, and her fire was scattered across the arena, dying right along with her chances. Her heart raced and her head spun, the noise in the arena drowning everything as Sar's ultimate attack crashed toward Lila.

There was no point in blocking, so she threw out her hands, heat scorching the air as she drew the last of her fire into a shield.

Protect me, she thought, abandoning poetry and spell in favor of supplication.

She didn't expect it to work.

But it did.

A wave of energy swept down her arms, meeting the meager flame, and an instant later, the fire *exploded* in front of her. A *wall* of flame erupted, dividing the arena and rendering Sar a shadow on the opposite side, her earthen attack burning to ash.

Lila's eyes widened behind her mask.

She'd never spoken to the magic, not directly. Sure, she'd cursed at it, and grumbled, and asked a slew of rhetorical questions. But she'd never commanded it, not the way Kell did with blood. Not the way she had with the stone, before she discovered the cost.

If the fire claimed a price, she couldn't feel it yet. Her pulse was raging in her head as her muscles ached and her thoughts raced, and the wall of flame burned merrily before her. Fire licked her outstretched fingers, the heat brushing her skin but never settling long enough to burn.

Lila didn't try to be a wave, or a door. She simply *pushed,* not with force, but with will, and the wall of fire shot forward, barreling toward Sar. To Lila, the whole thing seemed to take forever. She didn't understand why Sar was standing still, not until time snapped back into focus, and she realized that the wall's appearance, its transformation, had been the work of an instant.

The fire twisted in on itself, like a kerchief drawn through a hand, as it launched toward Sar, compressing, gaining force and heat and speed.

The Veskan was many things, but she wasn't fast—not as fast as Lila, and definitely not as fast as fire. She got her arms up, but she couldn't block the blast. It shattered every remaining plate across her front in a blaze of light.

Sar tumbled backward, the wood of her mask singed, and at last the earth crumbled around Lila's boot, releasing her.

The match was over.

And she had *won.*

Lila's legs went weak, and she fought the urge to sink to the cold stone floor.

Sweat streamed down her neck, and her hands were scraped raw. Her head buzzed with energy, and she knew that as soon as the high faded, everything would hurt like hell, but right now, she felt incredible.

Invincible.

Sar got to her feet, took a step toward her, and held out a hand that swallowed Lila's when she took it. Then the Veskan vanished into her tunnel, and Lila turned toward the royal platform to offer the prince a bow.

The gesture caught halfway when she saw Kell at Rhy's shoulder, looking windblown and flushed. Lila managed to finish the bow, one hand folded against her heart. The prince applauded. Kell only cocked his head. And then she was ushered out on a wave of cheers and the echo of "Stasion! Stasion! Stasion!"

Lila crossed the arena with slow, even steps, escaping into the darkened corridor.

And there she sank to her knees and laughed until her chest hurt.

VI

"You missed quite a match," said Rhy. Stasion Elsor had vanished, and the stadium began to empty. The first round was over. Thirty-six had become eighteen, and tomorrow, eighteen would become nine.

"Sorry," said Kell. "It's been a busy day."

Rhy swung his arm around his brother's shoulders, then winced. "Did you have to let that last blow through?" he whispered beneath the sounds of the crowd.

Kell shrugged. "I wanted to give the people a show." But he was smiling.

"You better put that grin away," chided Rhy. "If anyone sees you beaming like that, they'll think you've gone mad."

Kell tried to wrestle his features into their usual stern order, and lost. He couldn't help it. The last time he'd felt this alive, someone was trying to kill him.

His body ached in a dozen different places. He'd lost six plates to the Faroan's ten. It was far harder than he'd thought it would be, using only one element. Normally he let the lines between them blur, drawing on whichever he needed, knowing he could reach for any, and they would answer. In the end, it had taken half Kell's focus not to break the rules.

But he'd done it.

Rhy's arm fell away, and he nodded at the arena floor where

the Arnesian had been. "That one might give the others a run for their money."

"I thought the odds were in *Alucard*'s favor."

"Oh, they still are. But this one's something. You should see his next match, if you can find the time."

"I'll check my schedule."

A man cleared his throat. "Your Highness. Master Kell." It was Rhy's guard, Tolners. He led their escort out of the stadium, and Staff fell in step behind them on the way to the palace. It had only been hours since Kell left, but he felt like a different man. The walls weren't as suffocating, and even the looks didn't bother him as much.

It had felt so good to fight. The exhilaration was paired with a strange relief, a loosening in his limbs and chest, like a craving sated. For the first time in months, he was able to stretch his power. Not all the way, of course, and every moment he was constantly aware of the need for discretion, disguise, but it was *something*. Something he'd desperately needed.

"You're coming tonight, of course," said Rhy as they climbed the stairs to the royal hall. "To the ball?"

"Another one?" complained Kell. "Doesn't it get tiresome?"

"The politics are exhausting, but the company can be pleasant. And I can't hide you from Cora forever."

"Talk of exhausting," muttered Kell as they reached their hall. He stopped at his room, while Rhy continued toward the doors with the gold inlaid *R* at the end.

"The sacrifices we make," Rhy called back.

Kell rolled his eyes as the prince disappeared. He brought his hand to his own door, and paused. A bruise was coming out against his wrist, and he could feel the other places he'd been hit coloring beneath his clothes.

He couldn't wait for tomorrow's match.

He pushed open the door, and he was already shrugging out

of his coat when he saw the king standing at his balcony doors, looking out through the frosted glass. Kell's spirits sank.

"Sir," he said gingerly.

"Kell," said the king in way of greeting. His attention went to Staff, who stood in the doorway. "Please wait outside." And then, to Kell, "Sit."

Kell lowered himself onto a sofa, his bruises suddenly feeling less like victories, and more like traitors.

"Is something wrong?" asked Kell when they were alone.

"No," said the king. "But I've been thinking about what you said this morning."

This morning? This morning was years away. "About what, sir?"

"About your proximity to Rhy during the *Essen Tasch*. With so many foreigners flooding the city, I'd prefer if you kept to the palace."

Kell's chest tightened. "Have I done something wrong? Am I being punished?"

King Maxim shook his head. "I'm not doing this to punish you. I'm doing it to protect Rhy."

"Your Majesty, *I'm* the one who protects Rhy. If anything were to—"

"But Rhy doesn't need your protection," cut in the king, "not anymore. The only way to keep him safe is to keep *you* safe." Kell's mouth went dry. "Come, Kell," continued the king, "you can't care that much. I haven't seen you at the tournament all day."

Kell shook his head. "That's not the point. This isn't—"

"The central arena is visible from the palace balconies. You can watch the tournament from here." The king set a golden ring the size of his palm on the table. "You can even listen to it."

Kell opened his mouth, but the protests died on his tongue. He swallowed and clenched his hands. "Very well, sir," he said, pushing to his feet. "Am I banished from the balls, too?"

"No," said the king, ignoring the edge in Kell's voice. "We keep track of all those who come and go. I see no reason to keep you from those, so long as you are careful. Besides, we wouldn't want our guests to wonder where you were."

"Of course," murmured Kell.

As soon as the king was gone, Kell crossed into the small room off the main chamber and shut the door. Candles came to life on the shelf walls, and by their light he could see the back of the door, its wood marked by a dozen symbols, each a portal to another place in London. It would be so easy to go. They could not keep him. Kell drew his knife and cut a shallow line against his arm. When the blood welled, he touched his fingers to the cut, but instead of tracing an existing symbol, he drew a fresh mark on a bare stretch of wood: a vertical bar with two horizontal accents, one on top leading right, one on bottom leading left.

The same symbol he'd made in Kamerov's tent that morning.

Kell had no intention of missing the tournament, but if a lie would ease the king's mind, so be it. As far as breaking the king's trust, it didn't matter. The king hadn't trusted him in months.

Kell smiled grimly at the door, and went to join his brother.

VII

White London.

Ojka stood beneath the trees, wiping the blood from her knives.

She'd spent the morning patrolling the streets of Kosik, her old stomping ground, where trouble still flared like fire through dry fields. Holland said it was to be expected, that change would always bring unrest, but Ojka was less forgiving. Her blades found the throats of traitors and disbelievers, silencing their dissent one voice at a time. They didn't deserve to be a part of this new world.

Ojka holstered the weapons and breathed deeply. The castle grounds, once littered with statues, were now filled with trees, each blossoming despite the winter chill. For as long as Ojka could remember, her world had smelled like ash and blood, but now it smelled of fresh air and fallen leaves, of forests and raging fires, of life and death, of sweet and damp and clean, of promise, of change, of power.

Her hand drifted to the nearest tree, and when she placed her palm flat against the trunk she could feel a pulse. She didn't know if it was hers, or the king's, or the tree's. Holland had told her that it was the pulse of the world, that when magic behaved the way it should, it belonged to no one and everyone, nothing and everything. It was a shared thing.

Ojka didn't understand that, but she wanted to.

The bark was rough, and when she chipped away a piece with

her nail, she was surprised to see the wood beneath mottled with the silver threads of spellwork. A bird cawed overhead, and Ojka drew nearer, but before she could examine the tree, she felt the pulse of heat behind her eye, the king's voice humming through her head, resonant and welcome.

Come to me, he said.

Ojka's hand fell away from the tree.

She was surprised to find her king alone.

Holland was sitting forward on his throne, elbows on knees and head bowed over a silver bowl, its surface brimming with twisting smoke. She held her breath when she realized he was in the middle of a spell. The king's hands were raised to either side of the bowl, his face a mask of concentration. His mouth was a firm line, but shadows wove through both of his eyes, coiling through the black of the left one before overtaking the green of the right. The shadows were alive, snaking through his sight as the smoke did in the bowl, where it coiled around something she couldn't see. Lines of light traced themselves like lightning through the darkness, and Ojka's skin prickled with the strength of the magic before the spell finished, the air around her shivered, and everything went still.

The king's hands fell away from the bowl, but several long moments passed before the living darkness retreated from the king's right eye, leaving a vivid emerald in its wake.

"Your Majesty," said Ojka carefully.

He did not look up.

"Holland."

At that, his head rose. For an instant his two-toned gaze was still strangely empty, his focus far away, and then it sharpened, and she felt the weight of his attention settle on her.

"Ojka," he said, in his smooth, reverberating way.

"You summoned me."

"I did."

He stood and gestured to the floor beside the dais.

That was when she saw the bodies.

There were two of them, swept aside like dirt, and to be fair, they looked less like corpses than like crumbling piles of ash, flesh withered black on bone frames, bodies contorted as if in pain, what was left of hands raised to what was left of throats. One looked much worse than the other. She didn't know what had happened to them. Wasn't sure she *wanted* to know. And yet she felt compelled to ask. The question tumbled out, her voice tearing the quiet.

"Calculations," answered the king, almost to himself. "I was mistaken. I thought the collar was too strong, but it is not. The people were just too weak."

Dread spread through Ojka like a chill as her attention returned to the silver bowl. "Collar?"

Holland reached inside the bowl—for an instant, something in him seemed to recoil, resist the motion, but the king persisted—and as he did, shadow spilled over his skin, up his fingers, his hands, his wrists, becoming a pair of black gloves, smooth and strong, their surfaces subtly patterned with spellwork. Protection from whatever waited in the dark.

From the depths of the silver bowl, the king withdrew a circlet of dark metal, hinged on one side, symbols etched and glowing on its surface. Ojka tried to read the markings, but her vision kept slipping, unable to find purchase. The space inside the circlet seemed to swallow light, energy, the air within turning pale and colorless and as thin as paper. There was something *wrong* with the metal collar, wrong in a way that bent the world around it, and that wrongness plucked at Ojka's senses, made her feel dizzy and ill.

Holland turned the circlet over in his gloved hands, as if inspecting a piece of craftsmanship. "It must be strong enough," he said.

Ojka braved a step forward. "You summoned me," she repeated, her attention flicking from the corpses to the king.

"Yes," he said, looking up. "I need to know if it works."

Fear prickled through her, the old, instinctual bite of panic, but she held her ground. "Your Majesty—"

"Do you trust me?"

Ojka tensed. Trust. Trust was a hard-won thing in a world like theirs. A world where people starved for magic and killed for power. Ojka had stayed alive so long by blade and trick and bald distrust, and it was true that things were changing now, because of Holland, but fear and caution still whispered warnings.

"Ojka." He considered her levelly, with eyes of emerald and ink.

"I trust you," she said, forcing the words out, making them real, before they could climb back down her throat.

"Then come here." Holland held up the collar as if it were a crown, and Ojka felt herself recoil. No. She had earned this place beside him. She had earned her power. Been strong enough to survive the transfer, the test. She had proven herself worthy. Beneath her skin, the magic tapped out its strong and steady beat. She wasn't ready to let go, to relinquish the power and return to being an ordinary cutthroat. *Or worse,* she thought, glancing at the bodies.

Come here.

This time the command rang through her head, pulled on muscle, bone, magic.

Ojka's feet moved forward, one step, two, three, until she was standing right before the king. *Her* king. He had given her so much, and he had yet to claim his price. No boon came without a cost. She would have paid him in deed, in blood. If this was the cost—whatever this was—then so be it.

Holland lowered the collar. His hands were so sure, his eyes so steady. She should have bowed her head, but instead, she held his gaze, and there she found balance, found calm. There she felt safe.

And then the metal closed around her throat.

The first thing she felt was the sharp cold of metal on skin. Surprise, but not pain. Then the cold sharpened into a knife. It slid under her skin, tore her open, magic spilling like blood from the wounds.

Ojka gasped and staggered to her knees as ice shot through her head and down into her chest, frozen spikes splaying out through muscle and flesh, bone and marrow.

Cold. Gnawing and rending, and then gone.

And in its wake—nothing.

Ojka's doubled over, fingers clamped uselessly around the metal collar as she let out an animal groan. The world looked wrong—pale and thin and empty—and she felt severed from it, from herself, from her king.

It was like losing a limb: none of the pain, but all of the wrongness, a vital piece of her cut away so fast she could feel the space where it had been, where it should be. And then she realized what it was. The loss of a sense. Like sight, or sound, or touch.

Magic.

She couldn't feel its hum, couldn't feel its strength. It had been everywhere, a constant presence from her bones to the air around her body, and it was suddenly, horribly . . . gone.

The veins on her hands were beginning to lighten, from black to pale blue, and in the reflection of the polished stone floor, she could see the dark emblem of the king's mark retreating across her brow and cheek, withdrawing until it was nothing but a smudge in the center of her yellow eyes.

Ojka had always had a temper, quick to flame, her power surging with her mood. But now, as panic and fear tore through her, nothing rose to match it. She couldn't stop shaking, couldn't drag herself from the shock and terror and fear. She was weak. Empty. Flesh and blood and nothing more. And it was *terrible*.

"Please," she whispered to the throne room floor while Holland stood over her, watching. "Please, my king. I have always . . . been loyal. I will always . . . be loyal. Please . . ."

Holland knelt before her and took her chin in his gloved hand, guiding it gently up. She could see the magic swirling in his eyes, but she couldn't feel it in his touch.

"Tell me," he said. "What do you feel?"

The word escaped in a shudder. "I . . . I can't . . . feel . . . anything."

The king smiled grimly then.

"Please," whispered Ojka, hating the word. "You chose me. . . ."

The king's thumb brushed her chin. "I chose you," he said, his fingers slipping down her throat. "And I still do."

An instant later, the collar was gone.

Ojka gasped, magic flooding back like air into starved veins. A welcome pain, bright and vivid and alive. She tipped her head against the cold stone.

"Thank you," she whispered, watching the mark trace its way through her eye, across her brow and cheek. "Thank you."

It took her several long seconds to get to her feet, but she forced herself up as Holland returned the horrible collar to its silver bowl, the gloves melting from his fingers into shadow around the metal.

"Your Majesty," said Ojka, hating the quiver in her voice. "Who is the collar for?"

Holland brought his fingers to his heart, his expression unreadable.

"An old friend."

If that is for a friend, she thought, *what does Holland do to enemies?*

"Go," he said, returning to his throne. "Recover your strength. You're going to need it."

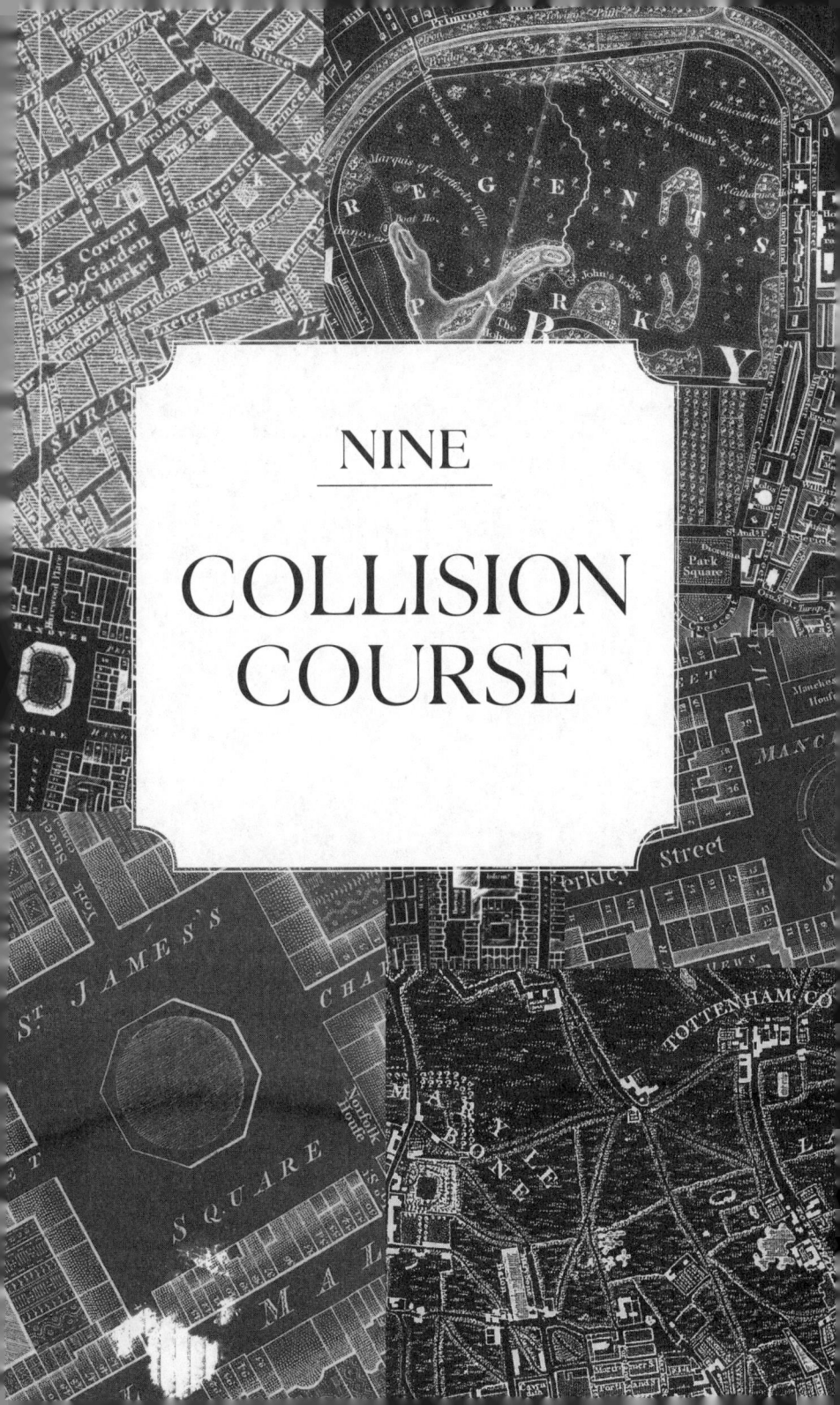

NINE

COLLISION COURSE

I

When Lila woke up the next day, it took her a moment to remember where she was, and, more importantly, why everything hurt.

She remembered retreating to Elsor's room the night before, resisting the urge to collapse onto his bed still fully dressed. She'd somehow gotten back into her own clothes, her own room at the Wandering Road, though she didn't remember much of the journey. It was now well into morning. Lila couldn't recall the last time she'd slept so long, or so deeply. Wasn't sleep supposed to make you feel rested? She only felt exhausted.

Her boot was trapped beneath something that turned out to be Alucard's cat. Lila didn't know how the creature had gotten into her room. She didn't care. And the cat didn't seem to care about her either. She barely moved when Lila dragged her foot free, and sat up.

Every part of her protested.

It wasn't just the wear and tear of the match—she'd gotten in some bad fights before, but nothing felt like this. The only thing that even came close was the aftermath of the black stone. The talisman's repercussions had been hollowing and sudden, where this was subtle but deep. Proof that magic wasn't an inexhaustible resource.

Lila dragged herself off the cot, stifling a grunt of pain, grateful that the room was empty. She tugged off her clothes as gingerly as possible, wincing at the bruises that had started to blossom across her ribs. The thought of fighting again today made her cringe, and yet some part of her thrilled at the idea. Admittedly, it was a very small part of her.

Dangerous.
Reckless.
Foolish.
Mad.

The words were beginning to feel more like badges of pride than blows.

Downstairs, the main room was sparsely populated, but she spotted Alucard at a table along the wall. She crossed the room, boots scuffing until she reached him and sank into a chair.

He was looking over a paper, and he didn't look up when she put her head down on the table with a soft thud.

"Not much of a morning person?"

She grumbled something unkind. He poured her a cup of rich black tea, spices weaving through the steam.

"Such a useless time of day," she said, dragging herself upright and taking the cup. "Can't sleep. Can't steal."

"There *is* more to life."

"Like what?"

"Like eating. And drinking. And dancing. You missed quite a ball last night."

She groaned at the thought. It was too early to imagine herself as Stasion Elsor performing in an arena, let alone in a palace. "Do they celebrate *every* night?"

"Believe it or not, some people actually come to the tournament *just* for the parties."

"Doesn't it get tiresome, all that . . ." She waved her hand, as if the whole thing could be summed up with a single gesture. In truth, Lila had only been to one ball in her entire life, and that night had started with a demon's mask and a glorious new coat, and ended with both covered in a prince's blood and the stony remains of a foreign queen.

Alucard shrugged, offering her some kind of pastry. "I can think of less pleasant ways to pass a night."

She took the bread-thing and nibbled on the corner. "I keep forgetting you're a part of that world."

His look cooled. "I'm not."

The breakfast was reviving; her vision started to focus, and as it did, her attention narrowed on the paper in his hands. It was a copy of the bracket, the eighteen victors now paired off into nine new sets. She'd been so tired, she hadn't even checked.

"What does the field look like today?"

"Well, *I* have the luxury of going up against one of my oldest friends, not to mention the best wind magician I've ever met—"

"Jinnar?" asked Lila, suddenly interested. That would be quite a match.

Alucard nodded grimly, "And you've only got to face . . ." He trailed his finger across the page. ". . . Ver-as-Is."

"What do you know about him?" she asked.

Alucard's brow furrowed. "I'm sorry, have you mistaken me for a comrade? The last time I checked we were on opposite sides of the bracket."

"Come on, Captain. If I die in this, you'll have to find yourself a new thief."

The words were out before she remembered she'd already lost her place aboard the *Night Spire*. She tried a second time. "My witty banter is one of a kind. You know you'll miss it when I'm gone." Again, it was the wrong thing to say, and a heavy silence settled in its wake. "Fine," she said, exasperated. "Two more questions, two more answers, in exchange for whatever you know."

Alucard's lips quirked. He folded the roster and set it aside, lacing his fingers with exaggerated patience. "When did you first come to our London?"

"Four months ago," she said. "I needed a change of scenery."

She meant to stop there, but the words kept coming. "I got pulled into something I didn't expect, and once it started, I wanted to see it through. And then it was over, and I was here, and I had a chance to start fresh. Not every past is worth holding onto."

That got a look of interest, and she expected him to continue down his line of inquiry, but instead he changed directions.

"What were you running from, the night you joined my crew?"

Lila frowned, her gaze escaping down to the cup of black tea. "Who said I was running?" she murmured. Alucard raised a brow, patient as a cat. She took a long, scalding sip, let it burn all the way down before she spoke. "Look, everyone talks about the unknown like it's some big scary thing, but it's the *familiar* that's always bothered me. It's heavy, builds up around you like rocks, until it's walls and a ceiling and a cell."

"Is that why you were so determined to take Stasion's spot?" he asked icily. "Because my company had become a burden?"

Lila set her cup down. Swallowed the urge to apologize. "You had your two questions, Captain. It's my turn."

Alucard cleared his throat. "Very well. Ver-as-Is. Obviously Faroan, and not a nice fellow, from what I've heard. An earth mage with a temper. You two should get along splendidly. It's the second round, so you're allowed to use a second element, if you're able."

Lila rapped her fingers on the table. "Water."

"Fire and water? That's an unusual pairing. Most dual magicians pick adjacent elements. Fire and water are on opposite sides of the spectrum."

"What can I say, I've always been contrary." She winked her good eye. "And I had such a good teacher."

"Flatterer," he muttered.

"Arse."

He touched his breast, as if offended. "You're up this afternoon," he said, pushing to his feet, "and I'm up soon." He didn't seem thrilled.

"Are you worried?" she asked. "About your match?"

Alucard took up his tea cup. "Jinnar's the best at what he does. But he only does one thing."

"And you're a man of many talents."

Alucard finished his drink and set the cup back on the table. "I've been told." He shrugged on his coat. "See you on the other side."

The stadium was *packed*.

Jinnar's banner flew, sunset purple on a silver ground, Alucard's silver on midnight blue.

Two Arnesians.

Two favorites.

Two friends.

Rhy was up on the royal platform, but Lila saw no sign of the king or queen, or Kell for that matter, though she spotted Alucard's siblings on a balcony below. Berras scowled while Anisa clapped and cheered and waved her brother's pennant.

The arena was a blur of motion and light, and the entire crowd held its breath as the two favorites danced around each other. Jinnar moved like air, Alucard like steel.

Lila fidgeted with the sliver of pale stone—turning the White London keepsake over in her fingers as she watched, trying to keep up with the competitors' movements, read the lines of attack, predict what they would do, and understand how they did it.

It was a close match.

Jinnar was a thing of beauty when it came to wind, but Alucard was right; it was his only element. He could render it into a wall or a wave, use it to cut like a knife, and with its help he could practically fly. But Alucard held earth and water, and everything they made between them—blades as solid as metal, shields of stone and ice—and in the end, his two elements triumphed over Jinnar's one, and Alucard won, breaking ten plates of armor to Jinnar's seven.

The black-eyed magician withdrew, a smile visible through the metal wisps of his mask, and Alucard tipped his scale-plated chin to the royal platform and offered a deep bow to the prince before disappearing into the corridor.

The audience started to file out, but Lila lingered. The walk to the arena had loosened her limbs, but she wasn't keen on moving again, not before she had to, so she hung back, watching the crowds ebb and flow as some left for other matches, and others came. The blue and silver pennants disappeared, replaced by a flaming red cat on a golden ground—that was Kisimyr's banner—and a pair of lions on red.

Kamerov.

Lila pocketed the shard of white stone and settled in. *This should be interesting.*

She had Kisimyr pinned as a fireworker, but the Arnesian champion came out—prowled, really, that mane of black hair spilling out in ropes below her feline mask—holding spheres of water and earth.

To the crowd's delight, Kamerov appeared with the same.

An equal match, then, at least as far the elements went. It wasn't even Lila's fight—thank god it wasn't her fight—but she felt her pulse tick up in excitement.

The orbs fell, and the match crashed into motion.

They were well paired—it took almost five full minutes for Kisimyr to land the first hit, a glancing blow to Kamerov's thigh. It took another eight for Kamerov to land the second.

Lila's eyes narrowed as she watched, picking up on something even before she knew what it was.

Kisimyr moved in a way that was elegant, but almost animal. But Kamerov . . . there was something *familiar* about the fluid way he fought. It was graceful, almost effortless, the flourishes tacked on in a way that looked unnecessary. Before the tournament, she'd truly only seen a handful of fights using magic. But it was like déjà vu, watching him down there on the arena floor.

Lila rapped her fingers on the rail and leaned forward.

Why did he seem so familiar?

Kell ducked, and rolled, and dodged, trying to pace his speed to Kisimyr's, which was hard because she was *fast*. Faster than his first opponent, and stronger than anyone he'd fought, save Holland. The champion matched him measure for measure, point for point. That first blow had been a mistake, clumsy, clumsy—but saints, he felt good. Alive.

Behind Kisimyr's mask, Kell caught the hint of a smile, and behind his own, he grinned back.

Earth hovered in a disk above his right hand, water swirling around his left. He twisted out from behind the shelter of a pillar, but she was already gone. Behind him. Kell spun, throwing the disk. Too slow. The two collided, attacked, and dove apart, as if they were fighting with swords instead of water and earth. Thrust. Parry. Strike.

A spear of hardened earth passed inches from Kell's armored cheek as he rolled, came up onto one knee, and attacked with both elements at the same time.

Both connected, blinding them in light.

The crowd went wild, but Kisimyr didn't even hesitate.

Her water, tinted red, had been orbiting her in a loop. Kell's attack had brought him close, into her sphere, and now she pushed hard against part of the circle, and it shot forward without breaking the ring, freezing as it did into an icy spike.

Kell jumped back, but not fast enough; the ice slammed into his shoulder, shattering the plate and piercing the flesh beneath.

The crowd gasped.

Kell hissed in pain and pressed his palm against the wound. When he drew his hand away from his shoulder, blood stained his fingers, jewel-red. Magic whispered through him—*As Travars. As Orense. As Osaro. As Hasari. As Steno. As Staro*—and his lips nearly formed a spell, but he caught himself just in time, wiped the blood on his sleeve instead, and attacked again.

Lila's eyes widened.

The rest of the crowd was fixated on Kamerov, but she happened to look up right after the blow and saw Prince Rhy in the royal box, his face contorted in pain. He hid it quickly, wiped the tension from his features, but his knuckles gripped the banister, head bowed, and Lila saw, and *understood*. She'd been there that night, when the princes were bound together, blood to blood, pain to pain, life to life.

Her attention snapped back to the arena.

It was suddenly obvious. The height, the posture, the fluid motions, the impossible grace.

She broke in a savage grin.

Kell.

It was him. It had to be. She had met Kamerov Loste at the Banner Night, had marked his grey eyes, his foxlike smile. But she'd also marked his height, the way he moved, and there was no question, no doubt in her mind—the man in the arena wasn't the one who'd wished her luck in the Rose Hall. It was the man she'd fought beside in three different Londons. The one she'd stolen from and threatened and saved. It was Kell.

"What are you smiling about?" asked Tieren, appearing at her side.

"Just enjoying the match," she said.

The *Aven Essen* made a small, skeptical hum.

"Tell me," she added, keeping her eyes on the fight. "Did you at least try to dissuade him from this madness? Or do you simply plan to feign ignorance with him, too?"

There was a pause, and when Tieren answered, his voice was even. "I don't know what you're talking about."

"Sure you don't, *Aven Essen*." She turned toward him. "I bet if Kamerov down there were to take off his helmet, he'd look like the man he was on the Banner Night, and not a certain black-eyed—"

"This kind of talk makes me wish I'd turned you in," said the priest, cutting her off. "Rumors are dangerous things, *Stasion*, especially when they stem from someone guilty of her own crimes. So I'll ask you again," he said. "What are you smiling about?"

Lila held his eyes, her features set.

"Nothing," she said, turning back to the match. "Nothing at all."

II

In the end, Kamerov won.

Kell won.

It had been a staggeringly close match between the reigning champion and the so-called silver knight. The crowd looked dizzy from holding its breath, the arena a mess of broken stone and black ice, half the obstacles cracked or chipped or in ruins.

The way he'd moved. The way he'd fought. Even in their short time together, Lila had never seen him fight like that. A single point—he'd won by a single point, unseated the champion, and all she could think was, *He's holding back.*

Even now he's holding back.

"Stasion! Stasion!"

Lila dragged her thoughts away from Kell; she had her own, more pressing concerns.

Her second match was about to begin.

She was standing in the middle of the western arena, the stands awash in silver and black, the Faroan's pale-green pennant only an accent in the crowd.

Across from her stood the man himself, Ver-as-Is, an orb of tinted earth in each palm. Lila considered the magician—he was lithe, his limbs long and thin and twined with muscle, his skin the color of char, and his eyes an impossibly pale green, the same as his flag. Set deep into his face, they seemed to glow. But it was the *gold* that most caught her interest.

Most of the Faroans she'd seen wore gems on their skin, but Ver-as-Is wore gold. Beneath his mask, which concealed only the top half of his head, beads of the precious metal traced the lines of his face and throat in a skeletal overlay.

Lila wondered if it was a kind of status symbol, a display of wealth.

But displaying your wealth was just *asking* to be robbed of it, and she wondered how hard it would be to remove the beads.

How did they stay on? Glue? Magic? No, she noticed the ornaments on Ver-as-Is hadn't been stuck in place, exactly—they'd been *buried,* each one embedded in the skin. The modification was expertly done, the flesh around the beads barely raised, creating the illusion that the metal had grown straight from his face. But she could see the faint traces of scarring, where flesh and foreign object met.

That would certainly make robbing difficult.

And messy.

"*Astal,*" said the judge in white and gold. *Prepare.*

The crowd stilled, holding its breath.

The Faroan lifted his orbs, waiting for her to do the same.

Lila held out her spheres—fire and water—said a quick prayer, and let go.

※

Alucard filled two glasses from the decanter on the table.

The glass was halfway to Lila's lips when he said, "I wouldn't drink that if I were you."

She stopped and peered at the contents. "What is this?"

"Avise wine . . . mostly."

"Mostly," she echoed. She squinted, and sure enough, she could see particles of something swirling in the liquid. "What have you put in it?"

"Red sand."

"I assume you contaminated my favorite drink for a reason?"

"Indeed."

He set his own glass back on the table.

"Tonight, you're going to learn to influence two elements simultaneously."

"I can't believe you ruined a bottle of avise wine."

"I told you magic was a conversation—"

"You also said it was an ocean," said Lila. "And a door, and once I think you even called it a cat—"

"Well, tonight we're calling it a conversation. We're simply adding another participant. The same power, different lines."

"I've never been able to pat my head and rub my stomach at the same time."

"Well then, this should be interesting."

Lila gasped for breath.

Ver-as-Is was circling, and her body screamed, still aching from the day before. And yet, tired as she was, the magic was there, under her skin, pulsing to get out.

They were even, six to six.

Sweat ran into her eyes as she ducked, dodged, leaped, struck. A lucky blow took out the plate on the Faroan's bicep. Seven to six.

Water spun before her in a shield, turning to ice every time Ver-as-Is struck. It shattered beneath his blows, but better the shield than her precious plates.

The ruse didn't work for long. After the second block, he caught on and followed up his first attack with another. Lila lost two more plates in a matter of seconds. Seven to eight.

She could feel her strength ebbing, and the Faroan only seemed to get stronger. Faster.

Fire and water was proving to be a wretched choice. They couldn't touch; every time they did, they canceled, turning to steam or smoke—

And that gave her an idea.

She maneuvered to the nearest boulder, one low enough to scale, and brought the two forces together in her hands. White smoke billowed forth, filling the arena, and in its cover she turned and vaulted up onto the rock. From above, she could see the swirl of air made by Ver-as-Is as he turned, trying to find her. Lila focused, and the steam separated; the water became mist and then ice, freezing around him, while her fire surged up into the air and then rained down. Ver-as-Is got his earth into an arcing shield, but not before she broke two of his plates. Nine to eight.

Before she could savor the advantage, a spike of earth shot through the air at her and she leaped backward off the boulder.

And straight into a trap.

Ver-as-Is was there, inside her guard, four earthen spears hurtling toward her. There was no way to avoid the blows, no *time*. She was going to lose, but it wasn't just about the match, not in this moment, because those spears were sharp, as sharp as the ice that had pierced Kell's shoulder.

Panic spiked through her, the way it had so many times when a knife came too close and she felt the balance tip, the kiss of danger, the brush of death.

No. Something surged inside her, something simple and instinctual, and in that moment, the whole world *slowed*.

It was magic—it had to be—but unlike anything she'd ever done. For an instant, the space inside the arena seemed to *change*, slowing her pulse and drawing out the fractions of time within the second, stretching the moment—not much, just long enough for her to dodge, and roll, and strike. One of Ver-as-Is's spears still grazed her arm, breaking the plate and drawing blood, but it didn't matter, because Ver-as-Is's body took an instant—that same, stolen instant—too long to move, and her ice hit him in the side, shattering his final plate.

And just like that, the moment snapped closed, and everything caught up. She hadn't noticed the impossible quiet of that suspended second until it collapsed. In its wake, the world was chaos. Her arm was stinging, and the crowd had exploded into cheers, but Lila couldn't stop staring at Ver-as-Is, who was looking down at himself, as if his body had betrayed him. As if he knew that what had just happened wasn't possible.

But if Lila had broken the rules, no one else seemed to notice. Not the judge, or the king, or the cheering stands.

"Victory goes to Stasion Elsor," announced the man in white and gold.

Ver-as-Is glowered at her, but he didn't call foul. Instead he turned and stormed away. Lila watched him go. She felt something wet against her lip, and tasted copper. When she reached her fingers through the jaws of her mask and touched her nose, they came away red. Her head was spinning. But that was all right; it had been a tough fight.

And she had won.

She just wasn't sure how.

III

Rhy was perched on the edge of Kell's bed, rubbing his collar while Hastra tried to wrap Kell's shoulder. It was healing, but not fast enough for a ball. "Suck it up, Brother," he chided the prince. "Tomorrow will be worse."

He'd won. It had been close—so close—and not just because beating Kisimyr by anything more than a hair would raise suspicions. No, she was good, she was excellent, maybe even the best. But Kell wasn't ready to stop fighting yet, wasn't ready to give up the freedom and the thrill and go back to being a trinket in a box. Kisimyr was strong, but Kell was desperate, and hungry, and he'd scored the tenth point.

He'd made it to the final nine.

Three groups of three, squaring off against each other, one at a time, only the holder of the highest points advancing. It wouldn't be enough to win. Kell would have to win by more than a single hit.

And he'd drawn the bad card. Tomorrow, he'd have to fight not one, but both matches. He pitied the prince, but there was no going back now.

Kell had told Rhy about the king's request that he keep to the palace. Of course, he'd told him *after* sneaking out to the match.

"He's going to have a fit if he finds out," Rhy warned.

"Which is why he won't," said Kell. Rhy looked unconvinced.

For all his rakish play, he'd never been good at disobeying his father. Up until recently, neither had Kell.

"Speaking of tomorrow," said Rhy from the bed, "you need to start losing."

Kell stiffened, sending a fresh jab of pain through his shoulder. "What? Why?"

"Do you have any idea how hard this was to plan? To pull off? It's honestly a miracle we haven't been found out—"

Kell got to his feet, testing his shoulder. "Well that's a vote of confidence—"

"And I'm not going to let you blow it by *winning*."

"I have no intention of winning the tournament. We're only to the nines." Kell felt like he was missing something. The look on Rhy's face confirmed it.

"Top thirty-six becomes eighteen," said Rhy slowly. "Top eighteen becomes nine."

"Yes, I can do math," said Kell, buttoning his tunic.

"Top nine becomes three," continued Rhy. "And what happens to those three, wise mathematician Kell?"

Kell frowned. And then it hit him. "Oh."

"Oh," Rhy parroted, hopping down from the bed.

"The Unmasking Ceremony," said Kell.

"Yes, that," said his brother.

The *Essen Tasch* had few rules when it came to fighting, and fewer still when it came to the guises worn during those fights. Competitors were free to maintain their personas for most of the tournament, but the Unmasking Ceremony required the three finalists to reveal themselves to the crowds and kings, to remove their masks and keep them off for the final match, and the subsequent crowning.

Like many of the tournament's rituals, the origin of the Unmasking Ceremony was fading from memory, but Kell knew the story hailed from the earliest days of the peace, when an assassin tried to use the tournament, and the anonymity it afforded, to kill the Faroan royal family. The assassin slew the winning magician and donned his helmet, and when the kings and queens of the three empires invited him onto their dais to receive the prize, he struck, killing the Faroan queen and gravely wounding a young royal before he was stopped. The fledgling peace might have been shattered then and there, but no one was willing to claim the assassin, who died before he could confess. In the end, the peace between the kingdoms held, but the Unmasking Ceremony was born.

"You *cannot* advance beyond the nines," said Rhy, definitively.

Kell nodded, heart sinking.

"Cheer up, Brother," said the prince, pinning the royal seal over his breast. "You've still two matches to fight. And who knows, maybe someone will even beat you fairly."

Rhy went for the door, and Kell fell in step behind him.

"Sir," said Hastra, "a word."

Kell stopped. Rhy paused in the doorway and looked back. "Are you coming?"

"I'll catch up."

"If you don't show, I'm likely to do something foolish, like throw myself at Aluc—"

"I won't miss the stupid ball," snapped Kell.

Rhy winked and shut the door behind him.

Kell turned to his guard. "What is it, Hastra?"

The guard looked profoundly nervous. "It's just . . . while you were competing, I came back to the palace to check on Staff. The king was passing through, and he stopped and asked me how you'd spent the day. . . ." Hastra hesitated, leaving the obvious unspoken: the king wouldn't have asked such a thing if he'd known of Kell's ruse. Which meant he didn't.

Kell stiffened. "And what did you say?" he asked, bracing himself.

Hastra's gaze went to the floor. "I told him that you hadn't left the palace."

"You lied to the king?" asked Kell, his voice carefully even.

"It wasn't really a lie," said Hastra slowly, looking up. "Not in the strictest sense."

"How so?"

"Well, I told him that *Kell* didn't leave the palace. I said nothing about *Kamerov*...."

Kell stared at the young man in amazement. "Thank you, Hastra. Rhy and I, we shouldn't have put you in that position."

"No," said Hastra, with surprising firmness, and then quickly, "but I understand why you did."

The bells started ringing. The ball had begun. Kell felt a sharp pain in his shoulder, and strongly suspected Rhy of making a point.

"Well," he said, heading for the door, "you won't have to lie much longer."

That night, Lila had half a mind to go to the ball. Now that she knew the truth, she wanted to see Kell's face without the mask, as if she might be able to see the deception written in the lines of his frown.

Instead, she ended up wandering the docks, watching the ships bob up and down, listening to the hush of water against their hulls. Her mask hung from her fingertips, its jaws wide.

The docks themselves were strangely empty—most of the sailors and dockworkers must have ventured to the pubs and parties, or at least the Night Market. Men at sea loved land more than anyone on shore, and they knew how to make the best of it.

"That was quite a match today," said a voice. A moment later Alucard appeared, falling in step beside her.

She thought of their words that morning, of the hurt in his voice when he asked why she'd done it, stolen Elsor's identity, put herself—put them *all*—at risk. And there it was again, that treacherous desire to apologize, to ask for her place back on his ship, or at least in his graces.

"Following me again?" she asked. "Shouldn't you be celebrating?"

Alucard tipped his head back. "I had no taste for it tonight. Besides," he said, his gaze falling, "I wanted to see what you did that was so much better than balls."

"You wanted to make sure I didn't get into trouble."

"I'm not your father, Bard."

"I should hope not. Fathers shouldn't try to seduce their daughters to learn their secrets."

He shook his head ruefully. "It was *one time*."

"When I was younger," she said absently, "I used to walk the docks back in London—my London—looking at all the ships that came in. Some days I imagined what mine would look like. Other days I just tried to imagine one that would take me away."

Alucard was staring at her. "What?"

"That's the first time you've ever volunteered a piece of information."

Lila smiled crookedly. "Don't get used to it."

They walked in silence for a few moments, Lila's pockets jingling. The Isle shone red beside them, and in the distance, the palace glowed.

But Alucard had never been good with silence. "So this is what you do instead of dancing," he said. "Haunt the docks like some sailor's ghost?"

"Well, only when I get bored of doing *this*." She pulled a fist from her pocket and opened it to reveal a collection of jewelry, coins, trinkets.

Alucard shook his head, exasperated. "Why?"

Lila shrugged. Because it was familiar, she might say, and she was good at it. Plus, the contents of people's pockets were far more interesting in *this* London. She'd found a dream stone, a fire pebble, and something that looked like a compass, but wasn't. "Once a thief, always a thief."

"What's this?" he asked, plucking the sliver of white stone from amid the tangle of stolen gems.

Lila tensed. "That's mine," she said. "A souvenir."

He shrugged and dropped the shard back onto the pile. "You're going to get caught."

"Then I better have my fun while I still can," she said, pocketing the lot. "And who knows, maybe the crown will pardon me, too."

"I wouldn't hold your breath." Alucard had begun rubbing his wrists and, realizing it, stopped and smoothed his coat. "Well, you may content yourself with haunting docks and robbing passersby, but I'd rather have a hot drink and a bit of finery, so . . ." He gave a sweeping bow. "Can I trust you to stay out of trouble, at least until tomorrow?"

Lila only smirked. "I'll try."

Halfway back toward the Wandering Road, Lila knew she was being followed.

She could hear their steps, smell their magic on the air, feel her heart pick up in that old familiar way. So when she glanced back and saw someone in the narrow road, she wasn't surprised.

She didn't run.

She should have, should have cut onto a main road when she first noticed them, put herself in public view. Instead, Lila did the one thing she'd promised Alucard she'd try not to do.

She found trouble.

When she reached the next turn in the road, an alley, she took it. Something glinted at the far end, and Lila took a step toward it before she realized what it was.

A knife.

She twisted out of the way as it came sailing toward her. She was fast, but not quite fast enough—the blade grazed her side before clattering to the ground.

Lila pressed her palm against her waist.

The cut was shallow, barely bleeding, and when her gaze flicked back up, she saw a man, his edges blurring into the dark. Lila spun, but the entrance to the alley was being blocked by another shape.

She shifted her stance, trying to keep her eyes on both at once. But as she stepped into the deeper shadow of the alley wall, a hand grasped her shoulder and she lurched forward as a third figure stepped out of the dark.

Nowhere to run. She took a step toward the shape at the alley's mouth, hoping for a drunken sailor, or a thug.

And then she saw the gold.

Ver-as-Is wasn't wearing his helmet, and without it she could see the rest of the pattern that traced up above his eyes and into his hairline.

"Elsor," he hissed, his Faroan accent turning the name into a serpentine sound.

Shit, thought Lila. But all she said was, "You again."

"You cheating scum," he continued in slurring Arnesian. "I don't know how you did it, but I saw it. I *felt* it. There was no way you could have—"

"Don't be sore," she interrupted. "It was just a ga—"

She was cut off as a fist connected with her wounded side and she doubled over, coughing. The blow hadn't come from Ver-as-Is, but one of the others, their gemmed faces masked by dark cloth. Lila's grip tightened on the metal-lined mask in her hand and she struck, slamming the helmet into the nearest man's forehead. He cried out and staggered back, but before Lila could strike again, they were on her, six hands to her two, slamming her into the alley wall. She stumbled forward as one wrenched her arm behind her back. Lila dropped to one knee on instinct and rolled, throwing the man over her shoulder, but before she could stand a boot cracked across her jaw. The darkness exploded into shards of fractured light, and an arm wrapped around her throat from behind, hauling her to her feet.

She scrambled for the knife she kept against her back, but the man caught her wrist and twisted it viciously up.

Lila was trapped. She waited for the surge of power she'd felt in the arena, waited for the world to slow and her strength to return, but nothing happened.

So she did something unexpected—she laughed.

She didn't feel like laughing—pain roared through her shoulder, and she could barely breathe—but she did it anyway, and was rewarded by confusion spreading like a stain across Ver-as-Is's face.

"You're pathetic," she spat. "You couldn't beat me one-on-one, so you come at me with three? All you do is prove how weak you really are."

She reached for magic, for fire or earth, even for bone, but nothing came. Her head pounded, and blood continued to trickle from the wound at her side.

"You think yours are the only people who can spell metal?" Ver-as-Is hissed, bringing the knife to her throat.

Lila met his gaze. "You're really going to kill me, just because you lost a match."

"No," he said. "Like for like. You cheated. So will I."

"You've already lost!" she snapped. "What's the fucking point?"

"A country is not a man, but a man is a country," he said, and then, to his men, "Get rid of him."

The other two began to drag her toward the docks.

"Can't even do it yourself," she chided. If the jab landed, he didn't let it show, just turned and began to walk away.

"Ver-as-Is," she called after him. "I'll give you a choice."

"Oh?" He glanced back, pale-green eyes widening with amusement.

"You can let me go right now, and walk away," she said, slowly. "Or I will kill you all."

He smiled. "And if I let you go, I suppose we will part as friends?"

"Oh no," she said, shaking her head. "I'm going to kill *you* either way. But if your men let me go now, I won't kill them as well."

For a moment, she thought she felt the arm at her throat loosen. But then it was back, twice as tight. *Shit,* she thought, as Ver-as-Is came toward her, spinning the knife in his hand.

"If only words were weapons . . ." he said, bringing the blade down. The handle crashed against her temple, and everything went black.

IV

Lila woke like a drowning person breaking the surface of water.

Her eyes shot open, but the world stayed pitch-black. She opened her mouth to shout, and realized it was already open, a cloth gag muffling the sound.

There was a throbbing ache in the side of her head that sharpened with every motion, and she thought she might be sick. She tried to sit up, and she quickly discovered that she couldn't.

Panic flooded through her, the need to retch suddenly replaced by the need to breathe. She was in a box. A very small box.

She went still, and she exhaled shakily when the box didn't shift or sway. As far as she could tell, she was still on land. Unless, of course, she was *under* it.

The air felt suddenly thinner.

She couldn't tell if the box was *actually* a coffin, because she couldn't see the dimensions. She was lying on her side in the darkness. She tried again to move and realized why she couldn't—her hands and feet had both been tied together, her arms wrenched behind her back. Her wrists ached from the coarse rope that circled them, her fingers numb, the knots tight enough that her skin was already rubbing raw. The slightest attempt to twist free caused a shudder of needle-sharp pain.

I will kill them, she thought. *I will kill them all.* She didn't say the words aloud because of the gag . . . and the fact that there wasn't much air in the box. The knowledge made her want to gasp.

Stay calm.
Stay calm.
Stay calm.

Lila wasn't afraid of many things. But she wasn't fond of small, dark spaces. She tried to survey her body for knives, but they were gone. Her collected trinkets were gone. Her shard of stone was gone. Anger burned through Lila like fire.

Fire.

That's what she needed. *What could go wrong with fire in a wooden box?* she wondered drily. Worst case, she would simply burn herself alive before she could get out. But if she was going to escape—and she *was* going to escape, if only to kill Ver-as-Is and his men—then she needed to be free of the rope. And rope burned.

So Lila tried to summon fire.

Tyger Tyger, burning bright . . .

Nothing. Not even a spark. It couldn't be the knife wound; that had dried, and the spell dried with it. That was how it worked. *Was* that how it worked? It seemed like it should work that way.

Panic. More panic. Clawing panic.

She closed her eyes, and swallowed, and tried again.

And again.

And again.

"Focus," said Alucard.

"Well it's a little hard, considering." Lila was standing in the middle of his cabin, blindfolded. The last time she'd seen him, he was sitting in his chair, ankle on knee, sipping a dark liquor. Judging by the sound of a bottle being lifted, a drink being poured, he was still there.

"Eyes open, eyes shut," he said, "it makes no difference."

Lila strongly disagreed. With her eyes open, she could summon fire. And with her eyes shut, well, she couldn't. Plus, she felt like a fool. "What exactly is the point of this?"

"The point, Bard, is that magic is a sense."

"Like sight," she snapped.

"Like sight," said Alucard. "But not sight. You don't need to see it. Just feel it."

"Feeling is a sense, too."

"Don't be flippant."

Lila felt Esa twine around her leg, and resisted the urge to kick the cat. "I hate this."

Alucard ignored her. "Magic is all and none. It's sight, and taste, and scent, and sound, and touch, and it's also something else entirely. It is the power in all powers, and at the same time, it is its own. And once you know how to sense its presence, you will never be without it. Now stop whining and focus."

Focus, thought Lila, struggling to stay calm. She could feel the magic, tangled in her pulse. She didn't need to see it. All she needed to do was reach it.

She squeezed her eyes shut, trying to trick her mind into thinking that the darkness was a choice. She was an open door. She was in control.

Burn, she thought, the word striking like a match inside her. She snapped her fingers and felt the familiar heat of fire licking the air above her skin. The rope caught, illuminating the dimensions of the box—small, very small, too small—and when she turned her head, a grisly face stared back at her, which resolved into the demon's mask right before Lila was thrown by searing pain. When the fire hovered above her fingers, it didn't hurt, but now, as it ate through the ropes, it *burned*.

She bit back a scream as the flame licked her wrists before finally snapping the rope. As soon as her hands were free, she rolled over the fire, plunging herself back into darkness. She tugged the gag off and sat up to reach her ankles, smacking her head against the top of the box and swearing roundly as she fell back. Maneuvering carefully, she managed to reach the ropes at her feet and unknot them.

Limbs free, she pushed against the lid of the box. It didn't budge. She swore and brought her palms together, a tiny flame sparking between them. By its light she could see that the box had no latches. It was a cargo crate. And it was nailed shut. Lila doused the light, and let her aching head rest against the floor of the crate. She took a few steadying breaths—*Emotion isn't strength,* she told herself, reciting one of Alucard's many idioms—and then she pressed her palms to the wooden walls of the crate, and *pushed*.

Not with her hands, but with her *will*. Will against wood, will against nail, will against air.

The box shuddered.

And *exploded*.

Metal nails ground free, boards snapped, and the air within the box shoved everything *out*. She covered her head as debris rained back down on her, then got to her feet, dragging in air. The flesh of her wrists was angry and raw, her hands shaking from pain and fury as she fought to get her bearings.

She'd been wrong. She was in a cargo hold. On a ship. But judging by the boat's steadiness, it was still docked. Lila stared down at the remains of the crate. The irony of the situation wasn't lost on her; after all, she'd tried to do the same thing to Stasion Elsor. But she liked to believe that if she'd actually put him in a crate, she would have given him air holes.

The devil's mask winked at her from the wreckage, and she

dug it free, pulling it down over her head. She knew where Ver-as-Is was staying. She'd seen his crew at the Sun Streak, an inn on the same street as the Wandering Road.

"Hey," called a man, as she climbed to the deck. "What do you think you're doing?"

Lila didn't slow. She crossed the ship briskly and descended the plank to the dock, ignoring the shouts from the deck, ignoring the morning sun and the distant sound of cheers.

Lila had warned Ver-as-Is what would happen.

And she was a girl of her word.

"What part of *you need to lose* don't you understand?"

Rhy was pacing Kell's tent, looking furious.

"You shouldn't be here," said Kell, rubbing his sore shoulder.

He hadn't meant to win. He'd just wanted it to be a good match. A close match. It wasn't his fault that 'Rul the Wolf' had stumbled. It wasn't his fault that the nines favored close combat. It wasn't his fault that the Veskan had *clearly* had a little too much fun the night before. He'd seen the man fight, and he'd been brilliant. Why couldn't he have been brilliant *today*?

Kell ran a hand through his sweat-slicked hair. The silver helmet sat, cast off, on the cushions.

"This is not the kind of trouble we need, Kell."

"It was an accident."

"I don't want to hear it."

Hastra stood against the wall, looking as if he wanted to disappear. Up in the central arena, they were still cheering Kamerov's name.

"Look at me," snapped Rhy, pulling Kell's jaw up so their eyes met. "You need to start losing *now*." He started pacing again, his voice low even though he'd had Hastra clear the tent. "The nines is a point game," he continued. "Top score in your group advances. With any luck, one of the others will take their match by a landslide, but as far as you're concerned, Kamerov is going *out*."

"If I lose by too much, it will look suspicious."

"Well you need to lose by *enough*," said Rhy. "The good news is, I've seen your next opponent, and he's good enough to beat you." Kell soured. "Fine," amended Rhy, "he's good enough to beat *Kamerov*. Which is exactly what he's going to do."

Kell sighed. "Who am I up against?"

Rhy finally stopped pacing. "His name is Stasion Elsor. And with any luck, he'll slaughter you."

Lila locked the door behind her.

She found her knives in a bag at the foot of the bed, along with the trinkets and the shard of stone. The men themselves were still asleep. By the looks of it—the empty bottles, the tangled sheets—they'd had a late night. Lila chose her favorite knife, the one with the knuckled grip, and approached the beds, humming softly.

How do you know when the Sarows is coming?
(Is coming is coming is coming aboard?)

She killed his two companions in their beds, but Ver-as-Is she woke, right before she slit his throat. She didn't want him to beg; she simply wanted him to see.

A strange thing happened when the Faroans died. The gems that marked their dark skin lost their hold and tumbled free. The gold beads slid from Ver-as-Is's face, hitting the floor like rain. Lila picked up the largest one and pocketed it as payment before she left. Back the way she'd come with her coat pulled tight and her head down, fetching the mask from the bin where she'd stashed it. Her wrists still burned, and her head still ached, but she felt much better now, and as she made her way toward the Wandering Road, breathing in the cool air, letting sunlight warm her skin, a stillness washed over her—the calm that came from taking control, from making a threat and following through. Lila felt like herself again. But underneath it all was a twinge, not of guilt or regret, but the nagging pinch that she was forgetting something.

When she heard the trumpets, it hit her.

She craned her neck, scouring the sky for the sun, and finding only clouds. But she knew. Knew it was late. Knew *she* was late. Her stomach dropped like a stone, and she slammed the helmet on and *ran*.

Kell stood in the center of the arena, waiting.

The trumpets rang out a second time. He squared his shoulders to the opposite tunnel, waiting for his opponent to emerge.

But no one came.

The day was cold, and his breath fogged in front of his mask. A minute passed, then two, and Kell found his attention flicking to the royal platform where Rhy stood, watching, waiting. Behind him, Lord Sol-in-Ar looked impassive, Princess Cora bored, Queen Emira lost in thought.

The crowd was growing restless, their attention slipping.

Kell's excitement tensed, tightened, wavered.

His banner—the mirrored lions on red—waved above the podium and in the crowd. The other banner—crossed knives on black—snapped in the breeze.

But Stasion Elsor was nowhere to be found.

"You're very late," said Ister as Lila surged into the Arnesian tent.

"I know," she snapped.

"You'll never—"

"Just *help me*, priest."

Ister sent a messenger to the stadium and enlisted two more attendants, and the three rushed to get Lila into her armor, a flurry of straps and pads and plates.

Christ. She didn't even know who she was set to fight.

"Is that blood?" asked one attendant, pointing to her collar.

"It's not mine," muttered Lila.

"What happened to your wrists?" asked another.

"Too many questions, not enough work."

Ister appeared with a large tray, the surface of which was covered in weapons. No, not weapons, exactly, only the hilts and handles.

"I think they're missing something."

"This is the nines," said Ister. "You have to supply the rest." She plucked a hilt up from the tray and curled her fingers around it. The priest's lips began to move, and Lila watched as a gust of wind whipped up and spun tightly around and above the hilt until it formed a kind of blade.

Lila's eyes widened. The first two rounds had been fought at a distance, attacks lobbed across the arena like explosives. But weapons meant hand-to-hand combat, and close quarters were Lila's specialty. She swiped two dagger hilts from the tray and slid them underneath the plates on her forearms.

"*Fal chas*," said Ister, just before the trumpets blared in warning, and Lila cinched the demon's jaw and took off, the final buckles on her mask still streaming behind her.

Kell cocked his head at Rhy, wondering what the prince would do. If Elsor didn't show, he would be forced to forfeit. If he was forced to forfeit, Kell would have the points to advance. Kell *couldn't* advance. He watched the struggle play out across Rhy's face, and then the king whispered something in his ear. The prince seemed to grow paler as he raised the gold ring to his mouth, ready to call the match. But before he could speak, an attendant appeared at the edge of the platform and spoke rapidly. Rhy hesitated, and then, mercifully, the trumpets rang.

Moments later Stasion hurried into the stadium looking . . . disheveled. But when he saw Kell, he broke into a smile, his teeth shining white behind his devil's mask. There was no warmth in that look. It was a predator's grin.

The crowds burst into excited applause as Kamerov Loste and Stasion Elsor took their places at the center of the arena.

Kell squinted through his visor at Elsor's mask. Up close it was a nightmarish thing.

"*Tas renar,*" said Kell. *You are late.*

"I'm worth the wait," answered Stasion. His voice caught Kell off guard. Husky and smooth, and sharp as a knife. And yet, undeniably female.

He knew that voice.

Lila.

But this wasn't Lila. This *couldn't* be Lila. She was a human, a Grey-worlder—a Grey-worlder unlike any other, yes, but a Grey-worlder all the same—and she didn't know how to do magic, and she would definitely never be crazy enough to enter the *Essen Tasch.*

As soon as the thought ran through his head, Kell's argument crumbled. Because if anyone was bullheaded enough to do something this stupid, this rash, this suicidal, it was the girl who'd picked his pocket that night in Grey London, who'd followed him through a door in the worlds—a door she should never have survived—and faced the black stone and the white royals and death itself with a sharpened smile.

The same sharpened smile that glinted now, between the lips of the demon's face.

"*Wait,*" said Kell.

The word was a whisper, but it was too late. The judge had already signaled, and Lila let go of her spheres. Kell dropped his own an instant later, but she was already on the attack.

Kell hesitated, but she didn't. He was still trying to process her presence when she iced the ground beneath his feet, then struck out at close range with a dagger made of flame. Kell lunged away, but not far enough, and a moment later he was on his back, light bursting from the plate across his stomach, and Lila Bard kneeling over him.

He stared up into her mismatched brown eyes.

Did she know it was him behind the silver mask?

"Hello," she said, and in that one word, he knew that she did. Before he could say anything, Lila pushed herself off again. Kell quickly rolled backward, leveraging himself into a fighting crouch.

She had two knives now (of *course* she had chosen the blades—one made of fire, one made of ice), and she was twirling them casually. Kell had chosen nothing. (It was a bold move, one Kamerov would make, and one designed to sink him. But not this fast.) He lashed his water into a whip and struck, but Lila rolled out of reach and threw her icy blade. Kell dodged, and in that distracted moment she tried to strike again, but this time his earth caught hold of her boot and his whip lashed out. Lila got her fire knife up to block his blow, the water whip breaking around the blade, but the whip's end managed to find her forearm, shattering a plate.

Lila was still pinned in place, but she was smirking, and an instant later her ice blade hit Kell from behind. He staggered forward as a second plate broke and he lost his hold on her foot.

And then the real fight began.

They sparred, a blur of elements and limbs, hits marked only by a flare of light. They came together, lunged apart, matching each other blow for blow.

"Have you lost your mind?" he growled as their elements crashed together.

"Nice to see you, too," she answered, ducking and spinning behind him.

"You have to stop," he ordered, narrowly dodging a fireball.

"You first," she chided, diving behind a column.

Water slashed, and fire burned, and earth rumbled.

"This is madness."

"I'm not the only one in disguise." Lila drew near, and he thought she'd go in for a strike, but at the last second she changed her mind, touched the fire blade to her empty palm, and *pushed*.

For an instant, the air around them faltered. Kell saw pain flash across Lila's face behind the mask, but then a wall of flame *erupted* toward him, and it was all he could do to will his water up into a wave over his head. Steam poured forth as the two elements collided. And then Lila did something completely unexpected. She reached out and froze the water over Kell's head. *His* water.

The audience gasped, and Kell swore, as the sheet of ice cracked and splintered and came crashing down on top of him. It wasn't against the rules—they'd both chosen water—but it was a rare thing, to claim your opponent's element for yourself, and overpower them.

A rarer thing still, to be overpowered.

Kell could have escaped, could have drawn the fight out another measure, maybe two. But he had to lose. So he held his ground and let the ceiling of ice fall, shattering the plates across his shoulders and back, and sending up flares of light.

And just like that, it was over.

Delilah Bard had won.

She came to a stop beside him, offered him her hand.

"Well played, *mas vares*," she whispered.

Kell stood there, dazed. He knew he should bow to her, to the crowd, and go, but his feet wouldn't move. He watched as Lila tipped her mask up to the stands, and the king, then watched as she gave him one last devilish grin and slipped away. He gave a rushed bow to the royal platform and sprinted after her, out of the stadium and into the tents, throwing open the curtain marked by the two crossed blades.

An attendant stood waiting, the only figure in an otherwise empty tent.

"Where is she?" he demanded, even though he knew the answer.

The devil's mask sat on the cushions, discarded along with the rest of the armor.

Lila was already gone.

V

Lila leaned back against Elsor's door, gasping for air.

She'd caught him off guard, that much was sure, and now Kell knew. Knew she'd been in London for days, knew she'd been there, right beside him, in the tournament. Her heart was pounding in her chest; she felt like a cat who'd finally caught its mouse, and then let it go. For now.

The high began to settle with her pulse. Her head was throbbing, and when she swallowed, she tasted blood. She waited for the wave of dizziness to pass, and when it didn't, she let her body sink to the wooden floor, Kell's voice ringing in her ears.

That familiar, exasperated tone.

This is madness.

So superior, as if they weren't *both* breaking all the rules. As if he weren't playing a part, just like her.

You have to stop.

She could picture his frown behind that silver mask, the crease deepening between those two-toned eyes.

What would he do now?

What would *she* do?

Whatever happened, it was worth it.

Lila got to her knees, frowning as a drop of blood hit the wooden floorboards. She touched her nose, then wiped the streak of red on her sleeve and got up.

She began to strip off Elsor's clothes, ruined from Ver-as-Is's assault and the subsequent match. Slowly she peeled away the weapons, and the fabric, then stared at herself in the mirror, half clothed, her body a web of fresh bruises and old scars.

A fire burned low in the hearth, a basin of cold water on the chest. Lila took her time getting clean and dry and warm, rinsing the darkening grease from her hair, the blood from her skin.

She looked around the room, trying to decide what to wear. And then she had an idea.

A novel, dangerous idea, which was, of course, her favorite kind.

Maybe it's time, she thought, *to go to a ball.*

"Rhy!" called Kell, the crowd parting around him. He'd shed the helmet and switched the coat, but his hair was still slicked with sweat, and he felt breathless.

"What are you doing here?" asked the prince. He was walking back to the palace, surrounded by an entourage of guards.

"It was her!" hissed Kell, falling in step beside him.

All around them, people cheered and waved, hoping to get so much as a glance or a smile from the prince. "Who was her?" Rhy asked, indulging the crowd.

"Stasion Elsor," he whispered. "It was *Lila.*"

Rhy's brow furrowed. "I know it's been a long day," he said, patting Kell's shoulder, "but obviously—"

"I know what I saw, Rhy. She spoke to me."

Rhy shook his head, the smile still fixed on his mouth. "That makes no sense. Tieren selected the players weeks ago."

Kell looked around, but Tieren was conveniently absent. "Well, he didn't select me."

"No, but *I* did." They reached the palace steps, and the crowd hung back as they climbed.

"I don't know what to tell you—I don't know if she *is* Elsor, or if she's just posing as him, but the person I just fought back there, that wasn't some magician from the countryside. That was Delilah Bard."

"Is that why you lost so easily?" asked the prince as they reached the top of the steps.

"You told me to lose!" snapped Kell as the guards held open the doors. His words echoed through the too-quiet foyer, and Kell's stomach turned when he glanced up and saw the king standing in the center of the room. Maxim took one look at Kell and said, "Upstairs. *Now*."

"I thought I made myself clear," said the king when they were in his room.

Kell was sitting in his chair beside the balcony, being chastised like a child while Hastra and Staff stood silently by. Rhy had been told to wait outside and was currently kicking up a fuss in the hall.

"Did I not instruct you to stay within the palace walls?" demanded Maxim, voice thick with condescension.

"You did, but—"

"Are you deaf to my wishes?"

"No, sir."

"Well I obviously didn't make myself clear when I asked you as your father, so now I command you as your *king*. You are hereby *confined* to the palace until further notice."

Kell straightened. "This isn't *fair*."

"Don't be a child, Kell. I wouldn't have asked if it wasn't for your own good." Kell scoffed, and the king's eyes darkened. "You mock my command?"

He stilled. "No. But we both know this isn't about what's good for *me*."

"You're right. It's about what's good for our kingdom. And if you are loyal to this crown, and to this family, you will confine yourself to this palace until the tournament is over. Am I understood?"

Kell's chest tightened. "Yes, sir," he said, his voice barely a whisper.

The king spun on Staff and Hastra. "If he leaves this palace again, you will both face charges, do you understand?"

"Yes, Your Majesty," they answered grimly.

With that the king stormed out.

Kell put his head in his hands, took a breath, then swiped everything from the low table before him, scattering books and shattering a bottle of avise wine across the inlaid floor.

"What a waste," muttered Rhy, sagging into the opposite chair.

Kell sank back and closed his eyes.

"Hey, it's not so bad," pressed Rhy. "At least you're already out of the competition."

That sank Kell's spirits even lower. His fingers drifted to the tokens around his neck, as he struggled to suppress the urge to *leave. Run.* But he couldn't, because whatever the king believed, Kell *was* loyal, to his crown, to his family. To *Rhy.*

The prince sat forward, seemingly oblivious to the storm in Kell's head. "Now," he said, "what shall we wear to the party?"

"Hang the party," grumbled Kell.

"Come now, Kell, the party never did anything to you. Besides, what if a certain young woman with a penchant for crossdressing decides to show? You wouldn't want to miss that."

Kell dragged his head up off the cushions. "She shouldn't be competing."

"Well, she made it this far. Maybe you're not giving her enough credit."

"I let her win."

"Did everyone else do the same?" asked Rhy, amused. "And I have to say, she looked like she was holding her own."

Kell groaned. She *was*. Which made no sense. Then again, nothing about Lila ever did. He got to his feet. "Fine."

"There's a good sport."

"But no more red and gold," he said, turning his coat inside out. "Tonight I'm wearing black."

Calla was humming and fastening pins in the hem of a skirt when Lila came in.

"Lila!" she said cheerfully. "*Avan*. What can I help you with this night? A hat? Some cuffs?"

"Actually . . ." Lila ran her hand along a rack of coats, then sighed, and nodded at the line of dresses. "I need one of those." She felt a vague dread, staring at the puffy, impractical garments, but Calla broke into a delighted smile. "Don't look so surprised," she said. "It's for Master Kell."

That only made the merchant's smile widen. "What is this occasion?"

"A tournament ball." Lila started to reach for one of the dresses, but Calla rapped her fingers. "No," she said firmly. "No black. If you are going to do this, you are going to do it right."

"What is wrong with black? It's the perfect color."

"For hiding. For blending into shadows. For storming castles. Not for balls. I let you go to the last one in black, and it has bothered me all winter."

"If that's true, you don't have enough things to worry about."

Calla *tsk*ed and turned toward the collection of dresses. Lila's gaze raked over them, and she cringed at a yolk-yellow skirt, a velvety purple sleeve. They looked like pieces of ripe fruit, like decadent desserts. Lila wanted to look powerful, not *edible*.

"Ah," said Calla, and Lila braced herself as the woman drew a dress from the rack and presented it to her. "How about this one?"

It wasn't black, but it wasn't confectionary either. The gown was a dark green, and it reminded Lila of the woods at night, of slivers of moonlight cutting through leaves.

The first time she had fled home—if it could be called that—she was ten. She headed into St. James's Park and spent the whole night shivering in a low tree, looking up through the limbs at the moon, imagining she was somewhere else. In the morning she dragged herself back and found her father passed out drunk in his room. He hadn't even bothered looking for her.

Calla read the shadows in her face. "You don't like it?"

"It's pretty," said Lila. "But it doesn't suit me." She struggled for the words. "Maybe who I was once, but not who I am now."

Calla nodded and put the dress back. "Ah, here we go." She reached for another gown and pulled it from the rack. "What about this?" The dress was . . . hard to describe. It was something between blue and grey, and studded with drops of silver. Thousands of them. The light danced across the bodice and down the skirts, causing the whole thing to shimmer darkly.

It reminded her of the sea and the night sky. It reminded her of sharp knives and stars and freedom.

"That," breathed Lila, "is perfect."

She didn't realize how complicated the dress was until she tried to put it on. It had resembled a pile of nicely stitched fabric draped over Calla's arm, but in truth it was the most intricate contraption Lila had ever faced.

Apparently the style that winter was structure. Hundreds of fasteners and buttons and clasps. Calla cinched and pulled and straightened and somehow got the dress onto Lila's body.

"*Anesh*," said Calla when it was finally done.

Lila cast a wary glance in the mirror, expecting to see herself at the center of an elaborate torture device. Instead, her eyes widened in surprise.

That bodice transformed Lila's already narrow frame into something with curves, albeit modest ones. It supplied her with a waist. It couldn't help much when it came to bosom, as Lila didn't have anything to work with, but thankfully the winter trend was to emphasize shoulders, not bust. The dress came all the way up to her throat, ending in a collar that reminded Lila vaguely of her helmet's jawline. The thought of the demon's mask gave her strength.

That's all this was, really: another disguise.

To Calla's dismay, Lila insisted on keeping her slim-cut pants on beneath the skirts, along with her boots, claiming no one would be able to tell.

"Please tell me this is easier to take off than it was to put on."

Calla raised a brow. "You do not think Master Kell knows how?"

Lila felt her cheeks burning. She should have disabused the merchant of her assumption months ago, but that assumption—that Kell and Lila were somehow... engaged, or at least entangled—was the reason Calla had first agreed to help her. And matters of pride aside, the merchant was dreadfully handy.

"There is the release," said Calla, tapping two pins at the base of the corset.

Lila reached back, fingering the laces of the corset, wondering if she could hide one of her knives there.

"Sit," urged the merchant.

"I honestly don't know if I can."

The woman *tsk*ed and nodded to a stool, and Lila lowered herself onto it. "Do not worry. The dress won't break."

"It's not the dress I'm worried about," she grumbled. No wonder so many of the women she stole from seemed faint; they obviously couldn't breathe, and Lila was fairly certain their corsets hadn't been *nearly* as tight as this one.

For god's sake, thought Lila. *I've been in a dress for five minutes and I'm already whining.*

"You close your eyes."

Lila stared, skeptical.

"*Tac,* you must trust."

Lila had never been good at trust, but she'd come this far, and now that she was in the dress, she was committed to following through. So she closed her eyes and let the woman dab something between lash and brow and then against her lips.

Lila kept her eyes closed as she felt a brush running through her hair, fingers tousling the strands.

Calla hummed as she worked, and Lila felt something in her sag, sadden. Her mother had been dead a very long time, so long she could barely remember the feeling of her hands smoothing her hair, the sound of her voice.

Tyger Tyger, burning bright.

Lila felt her palms begin to burn and, worried that she'd accidentally set fire to her dress, pressed them together and opened her eyes, focusing on the rug of the tent and the faint pain of pins sliding against her scalp.

Calla had set a handful of the hairpins in Lila's lap. They were polished silver, and she recognized them from the chest she'd brought ashore.

"These you bring back," said Calla as she finished. "I like them."

"I'll bring it all back," said Lila, getting to her feet. "I have no use for a dress like this beyond tonight."

"Most women believe that a dress need only matter for one night."

"Those women are wasteful," said Lila, rubbing her wrists. They were still chafed raw from the ropes that morning. Calla saw, and said nothing, only fastened broad silver bracelets over both. *Gauntlets,* thought Lila, even though the first word to come to mind was *chains.*

"One final touch."

"Oh for god's sake, Calla," she complained. "I think this is more than enough."

"You are a very strange girl, Lila."

"I was raised far away."

"Yes, well, that will explain some of it."

"Some of what?" asked Lila.

Calla gestured at her. "And I suppose where you were raised, women dressed as men and wore weapons like jewelry."

"... I've always been unique."

"Yes, well, it is no wonder you and Kell attract. Both unique. Both ... a bit ..." Suddenly, conveniently, the language seemed to fail her.

"Mean?" offered Lila.

Calla smiled. "No, no, not mean. Guard up. But tonight," she said, fastening a silver brim-veil into Lila's hair, "you bring his guard down."

Lila smiled, despite herself. "That's the idea."

VI

White London.

The knife glinted in Ojka's hand.

The king stood behind her, waiting. "Are you ready?"

Her fingers tightened on the blade as fear hummed through her. Fear, and power. She had survived the marking, the blood fever, even that collar. She would survive this.

"*Kosa,*" she said, the answer barely a whisper. *Yes.*

"Good."

They were standing in the castle courtyard, the gates closed and only the statues of the fallen twins bearing witness as the king's gaze warmed her spine and the winter wind bit at her face. Life was returning to the city, coloring it like a bruise, but the cold had lingered at the edges. Especially at night. The sun was warm, and things grew beneath it, but when it sank, it took all the heat with it. The king said that this was normal, that a healthy world had seasons of warmth and light, and others of shadow.

Ojka was ready for heat.

That was the first thing she had felt, back when the blood fever came. Glorious heat. She'd seen the burnt-up shells of her failed predecessors, but she'd welcomed the fire.

She'd believed, then, in Holland's power. In her potential.

She'd still believed, even when the king's collar had closed around her throat.

And now, he was asking her to believe again. Believe in his magic. In the magic he had given her. She had done the blood spells. Summoned ice and fire. Mended some things and broken others. Drawn doors within her world. This would be no different. It was still within her reach.

She stared down at the knife, hilt against one palm, edge pressed to the other. She had her orders. And yet she hesitated.

"My king," she said, still facing the courtyard wall. "It is not cowardice that makes me ask, but . . ."

"I know your mind, Ojka," said Holland. "You wonder why I ask this errand of you. Why I do not go myself. The truth is, I cannot."

"There is nothing you cannot do."

"All things come at a cost," he said. "To restore this world— *our* world—I had to sacrifice something of myself. If I left now, I am not certain I would be able to return."

So that was where the power came from. A spell. A deal. She had heard the king speaking to himself as if to someone else, had seen what lurked in the shadow of his eye, even thought she'd seen his reflection move when he did not.

How much had Holland sacrificed already?

"Besides . . ." She felt his hands come to rest on her shoulders, heat and magic flaring through her with his touch. "I gave you power so you could use it."

"Yes, my king," she whispered.

Her right eye pulsed as he folded his broad frame around her narrower one, shaping his body to hers. His arms shadowed her own, tracing from shoulders to elbows to wrists, his hands coming to rest against hers. "You will be fine, Ojka, so long as you are strong enough."

And if I am not?

She didn't think she'd said the words aloud, but the king heard her either way.

"Then you will be lost, and so will I." The words were cold, but not the way he said them. His voice was as it always was, a stone worn smooth, with a weight that made her knees weaken. He brought his lips to her ear. "But I believe in you." With that, he guided her knife hand with his own, dragging the blade against her skin. Blood welled, dark as ink, and he pressed something against her bloody palm. A coin, as red as her hair, with a gold star in the center.

"You know what I ask of you," he said, guiding her wounded hand and the coin within to the cold stone wall. "You know what you must do."

"I will not let you down, my king."

"I hope not," said Holland, withdrawing from her, taking the heat with him.

Ojka swallowed and focused on the place where her searing palm met the cold stones as she said the command, just as he'd taught her. *"As Travars."*

Her marked eye sang in her skull, her blood shuddering with the words. Where her hand met stone, shadow blossomed out into a door. She meant to step forward, step through, but she never had the chance.

The darkness ripped her forward. The world tore. And so did she.

A rending in her muscles. A breaking in her bones.

Her skin burned and her blood froze and everything was pain.

It lasted forever and an instant, and then there was nothing.

Ojka crumpled to her knees, shuddering with the knowledge that somehow she had failed. She wasn't strong enough. Wasn't worthy. And now she was gone, ripped away from her world, her purpose, her king. This calm, this settling feeling, this must be death.

And yet.

Death was not supposed to have edges, and this did. She

could feel them, even with her eyes closed. Could feel where her body ended, and the world began. Could death be a world unto itself? Did it have music?

Ojka's eyes drifted open, and she drew in a breath when she saw the cobbled street beneath her, the night sky tinged with red. Her veins burned darkly across her skin. Her eye pulsed with power. The crimson coin still dug into her palm, and her knife glinted on the stones a few feet away.

And the understanding hit her in a wave.

She'd done it.

A sound escaped her throat, something tangled up in shock and triumph as she staggered to her feet. Everything hurt, but Ojka relished the pain. It meant she was alive, she had *survived*. She had been tried, tested, and found able.

My king? she thought, reaching through the darkness of space and the walls between worlds. Worlds that *she* had crossed.

For a long moment, there was no answer. Then, incredibly, she heard his voice, paired with the thrumming of her pulse in her head.

My messenger.

It was the most beautiful sound. A thread of light in the darkness.

I am here, she thought, wondering where exactly *here* was. Holland had told her about this world. That red glow, that must be the river. And that beacon of light, the palace. She could hear the sounds of people, feel their energy as she readjusted her pale cloak and shifted her red hair in front of her marked eye. *What now?*

There was another pause, and when the king's voice came again, it was smooth and even.

Find him.

TEN

CATASTROPHE

I

Red London.

The city glittered from the palace steps, a stretch of frost and fog and magic.

Lila took it in, and then turned and presented Elsor's invitation. The stairs were filled with foreigners and nobles, and the guards didn't bother to look at the name on the slip, simply saw the royal seal and ushered her inside.

It had been four months since she'd last set foot in the heart of the royal palace.

She had seen the Rose Hall, of course, before the tournament, but that had been separate, impersonal. The palace itself felt like a grand house. A royal *home*. The entry hall was once again lined with heaping flower bouquets, but they had been arranged into a path, ushering Lila left through the foyer and past another set of large doors that must have been shut before, but were now thrown open, like wings. She stepped through into a massive ballroom of polished wood and cut glass, a honeycomb of light.

They called this one the Grand Hall.

Lila had been in another ballroom, the night of the Masquerade—the Gold Hall—and it was impressive, with its stonework and metal. This had all of the splendor, the opulence, and then something *more*. Dozens of chandeliers hung from the vaulted ceiling several stories up and lit the space with refracted candlelight. Columns rose from the oak floor, adorned with spiral staircases that broke off onto walkways and led to galleries and alcoves set into the walls overhead.

In the center of the ballroom, raised on a dais, a quartet of musicians played. Their instruments varied, but they were all made from polished wood and strung with golden wire, and the players themselves were brushed with gold. They stood perfectly still, save for only the most necessary movements of their fingers.

What had Jinnar said about Prince Rhy? *A flair for drama.*

Lila scanned the cavernous ballroom, and caught sight of the prince moving between tables on the opposite side of the hall. There, by the balcony doors, she saw Alucard, bowing to a lovely Faroan in purple silk. *Flirt.*

She skirted the room, wondering how long it would take her to spot Kell in such a crowd. But within moments, she saw him, not on the dance floor or mingling among the tables, but overhead. He stood alone on one of the lower balconies, his lanky form draped over the rail. His tousled auburn hair glinted beneath the chandeliers, and he rolled a glass between his palms, seeming troubled. From this angle, she couldn't see his eyes, but she imagined she could see the crease between them.

He looked as though he were looking for someone.

And Lila had a feeling that someone was *her.*

She retreated into the safety of the column's shadow, and for a few moments, she watched Kell watch the crowd. But she hadn't put on a dress for the sake of wearing it, so she finally finished her drink, set the empty glass on the nearest table, and stepped out into the light.

As she did, a girl appeared at Kell's side. The princess from Vesk. Her hand touched Kell's shoulder, and Lila frowned. Was she even old enough to flirt like that? Christ, she looked like a *child.* Slim but round-faced, pretty but dimpled—*soft*—with a wreath of wood and silver atop her straw-blond braid.

Kell gave the princess a look, but he didn't recoil from the touch, and she must have taken his stillness as an invitation, because she slipped her arm through his, and rested her head against his shoulder. Lila found her fingers itching for a knife, but then to her surprise, Kell's gaze drifted past the girl, down to the ballroom, and landed on *her*.

Kell tensed visibly.

So did Lila.

She watched as he said something to the princess and drew his arm free. The girl looked put out, but he didn't give her a second glance—didn't take his gaze from Lila—as he descended the stairs and came toward her, eyes dark, fists clenched at his side.

He opened his mouth, and Lila braced herself for an attack. But instead of yelling, Kell exhaled, held out his hand, and said, "Dance with me."

It wasn't a question. It was barely a request.

"I don't know how to dance," she said.

"I do," he said simply, as if the act didn't require two. But he was standing there, waiting, and eyes were beginning to turn their way, so she took his hand, and let him lead her out onto the shadowed edge of the ballroom floor. When the music kicked up, Kell's fingers tightened around hers, his other hand found her waist, and they began to move; well, Kell began to move, and Lila moved with him, forcing herself to follow his lead, to trust in it.

She hadn't been this close to him in months. Her skin hummed where he touched her. Was that normal? If magic coursed through everyone and everything, was this what it felt like when it found itself again?

They danced in silence for several long moments, spinning together and apart, a slower version of their cadence in the ring. And then, out of nowhere, Lila asked, "Why?"

"Why what?"

"Why did you ask me to dance?"

He *almost* smiled. A ghost. A trick of the light. "So you couldn't run away again before I said hello."

"Hello," said Lila.

"Hello," said Kell. "Where have you been?"

Lila smirked. "Why, did you miss me?"

Kell opened his mouth. Closed it. Opened it again before finally managing to answer, "Yes."

The word was low, and the sincerity caught her off guard. A blow beneath her ribs. "What," she fumbled, "the life of a royal no longer to your tastes?" But the truth was, she'd missed him, too. Missed his stubbornness and his moods and his constant frown. Missed his eyes, one crisp blue, the other glossy black.

"You look . . ." he started, then trailed off.

"Ridiculous?"

"Incredible."

Lila frowned. "You don't," she said, seeing the shadows under his eyes, the sadness in them. "What's wrong, Kell?"

He tensed slightly, but he didn't let go. He took a breath, as if formulating a lie, but when he exhaled, the truth came out. "Ever since that night, I haven't felt . . . I thought competing would help, but it only made it worse. I feel like I'm suffocating. I know you think it's madness, that I have everything I need, but I watched a king wither and die inside a castle." He looked down, as if he could see the problem through his shirt. "I don't know what's happening to me."

"Life," she said, as they spun around the floor. "And death."

"What do you mean?"

"Everyone thinks I have a death wish, you know? But I don't want to die—dying is easy. No, I want to *live,* but getting close to death is the only way to feel alive. And once you do, it makes you realize that everything you were doing before wasn't *actually* living. It was just making do. Call me crazy, but I think we do the best living when the stakes are high."

"You're crazy," said Kell.

She laughed softly. "Who knows? Maybe the world's gone crooked. Maybe you're still possessed. Or maybe you just got a taste of what it really means to be alive. Take it from someone who's had her fair share of close calls. You almost died, Kell. So now you know what it feels like to *live*. To fear for that life. To fight for it. And once you know, well, there's no going back."

His voice was unsteady. "What do I do?"

"I'm the wrong person to ask," she said. "I just run away."

"Running sounds good."

"Then run," she said. He stifled a laugh, but she was serious. "The thing about freedom, Kell? It doesn't come naturally. Almost no one has it handed to them. I'm free because I fought for it. You're supposed to be the most powerful magician in all the worlds. If you don't want to be here, then go."

The music picked up, and they came together, drew apart.

"I made Rhy a promise," said Kell as they turned, carried along by the dance. "That I would stand at his side when he was king."

She shrugged. "Last time I checked, he's not on the throne yet. Look, I stay here because I have nothing to go back to. There's no reason that once you leave, you can't return. Maybe you simply need to stretch your legs. Live a little. See the world. Then you can come back and settle down, and you and Rhy can live happily ever after."

He snorted.

"But, Kell . . ." she said, sobering, ". . . don't do what I did."

"You're going to have to be more specific."

She thought of Barron, the silver watch in the bottom of her coat. "If you decide to leave—when you decide to leave—don't do it without saying good-bye."

The music struck its final notes, and Kell spun Lila into his arms. Their bodies tangled, and both held their breath. The last time they'd embraced, they were bruised and bloody and about to be arrested. That had felt real; this felt like a fantasy.

Over Kell's shoulder, Lila saw the Princess of Vesk at the edge of the room, surrounded by gentlemen, and staring daggers at *her*. Lila flashed a smile and let Kell lead her off the floor, between a pair of columns.

"So, Kamerov?" she said as they found a quiet place to talk.

His grip tightened on her. "No one knows. They *can't*."

She shot him a withering look. "Do I really strike you as the telling type?" she asked. Kell said nothing, only examined her with that strange two-toned gaze, as if he expected her to disappear. "So . . ." she said, plucking a glass of sparkling wine from a passing tray, "did you kill the real Kamerov?"

"What? Of course not. He's a fiction." His brow furrowed. "Did *you* kill the real Elsor?"

Lila shook her head. "He's on a boat headed for Denolar. Or was it Delo—"

"*Delonar?*" snapped Kell, shaking his head. "Saints, what were you thinking?"

"I don't know," she said, honestly. "I don't understand what I am, how I'm alive, what I can do. I guess I just wanted to see."

"You didn't have to enter the most visible tournament in the three empires to test your fledgling abilities."

"But it's been fun."

"Lila," he said softly, and for once, his voice didn't sound angry. Tense, yes, but not mad. Had he ever said her name like that? It sounded almost like longing.

"Yes?" she asked, her breath tight.

"You have to withdraw."

And just like that, the warmth between them shattered, replaced by the Kell she remembered, stubborn and righteous.

"No, I don't," she said.

"You can't possibly continue."

"I've made it this far. I'm not dropping out."

"Lila—"

"What are you going to do, Kell? Have me arrested?"

"I should."

"But I'm not Stasion Elsor," she said, gesturing down to the ball gown. "I'm Delilah Bard." Truth really was the best disguise. His frown deepened. "Come on, don't be a sore loser."

"I threw the match," he snapped. "And even if I hadn't, you *can't* move on."

"I can, and I will."

"It's too dangerous. If you defeat Rul, you'll be in the final three. You'll be unmasked. This ruse of yours might work from a distance, but do you honestly think no one will notice who you are—and who you're not—if you show your face? Besides, I saw you in the ring today—"

"When I *won*?"

"When you *faltered*."

"I've made it this far."

"I felt your power slip. I saw the pain written on your face."

"That had nothing to do with our match—"

"What happens if you lose control?"

"I won't."

"Do you remember the cardinal rule of magic?" he pressed. *"Power in Balance, Balance in Power."* He lifted her hand, frowning at the veins on the back. They were darker than they should have been. "I don't think you're balancing. You're taking and using, and it's going to catch up with you."

Lila stiffened with annoyance. "Which is it, Kell? Are you angry at me, or worried about me, or happy to see me? Because I can't keep up."

He sighed. "I'm all of those things. Lila, I . . ." But he trailed off as he caught sight of something behind her. She watched the light go out of his eyes, his jaw clench.

"Ah, there you are, Bard," came a familiar voice, and she turned to see Alucard striding over. "Saints, is that a *dress* you're in? The crew will never believe it."

"You've got to be kidding me," growled Kell.

Alucard saw him, and stopped. He made a sound halfway between a chuckle and a cough. "Sorry, I didn't mean to interrupt—"

"It's fine, Captain," said Lila at the same time Kell growled, "Go away, Emery."

Lila and Kell looked at each other, confused.

"You *know* him?" demanded Kell.

Alucard straightened. "Of course she does. Bard works for me aboard the *Night Spire*."

"I'm his best thief," said Lila.

"Bard," chided Alucard, "we don't call it thieving in the presence of the crown."

Kell, meanwhile, appeared to be losing his mind. "No," he muttered, running a hand through his copper hair. "No. No. There are *dozens*."

"Kell?" she asked, moving to touch his arm.

He shook her off. "*Dozens* of ships, Lila! And you had to climb aboard *his*."

"I'm sorry," she shot back, bristling, "I was under the impression that I was free to do as I pleased."

"To be fair," added Alucard, "I think she was planning to steal it and slit my throat."

"Then why didn't you?" snarled Kell, spinning on her. "You're always so eager to slash and stab, why couldn't you have stabbed *him*?"

Alucard leaned in. "I think she's growing fond of me."

"*She* can speak for herself," shot Lila. She twisted toward Kell. "Why are you so upset?"

"Because Alucard Emery is a worthless noble with too much charm and too little honor, and you chose to go with *him*." The words cut through the air as Rhy rounded the corner.

"What on earth are you all shouting about . . ." The prince trailed off as he saw Kell, Lila, and Alucard huddled there.

"Lila!" he said cheerfully. "So you aren't a figment of my brother's imagination after all."

"Hello, Rhy," she said with a crooked smile. She turned toward Kell, but he was already storming out of the ballroom.

The prince sighed. "What have you done now, Alucard?"

"Nothing," said the captain, innocently.

Rhy turned to go after Kell, but Lila stepped ahead of him. "I'll take care of it."

Kell shoved open a pair of patio doors. For a moment he just stood there, letting the icy air press against his skin. And then, when the biting cold wasn't enough to douse his frustration, he plunged out into the winter night.

A hand caught his as he stepped onto the balcony, and he knew without turning back that it was hers. Lila's fingertips burned with heat, and his skin caught the spark. He didn't look back.

"Hello," she said.

"Hello," he said, the word a rasp.

He continued forward onto the balcony, her hand loosely twined with his. The cold wind stilled around them as they reached the edge.

"Of all the ships, Lila."

"Are you going to tell me why you hate him?" she asked.

Kell didn't answer. Instead he looked down at the Isle. After a few moments, he said, "The House of Emery is one of the oldest families in Arnes. They have long ties with the House of Maresh. Reson Emery and King Maxim were close friends. Queen Emira is Reson's cousin. And Alucard is Reson's second son. Three years ago, he left, in the middle of the night. No word. No warning. Reson Emery came to King Maxim for help finding him. And Maxim came to me."

"Did you use your blood magic, the way you did to find Rhy, and me?"

"No," said Kell. "I told the king and queen that I couldn't locate him, but the truth was, I never tried."

Lila's brow furrowed. "Why on earth not?"

"Isn't it obvious?" said Kell. "Because I'm the one who told him to go. And I wanted him to stay gone."

"Why? What did he do to you?"

"Not *me*," said Kell, jaw clenched.

Lila's eyes brightened in understanding. "Rhy."

"My brother was seventeen when he fell for your *captain*. And then Emery broke his heart. Rhy was devastated. I didn't need a magical tattoo to know my brother's pain on that front." He ran his free hand through his hair. "I told Alucard to disappear, and he did. But he didn't stay gone. No, he turned up a few months later when he was dragged back to the capital for crimes against the crown. Piracy, of all things. The king and queen turned the charge over, as a favor to the house of Emery. Gave Alucard the *Night Spire,* installed him in the name of the crown, and sent him on his way. And I told him that if he *ever* set foot in London again, I would kill him. I thought this time he would actually listen."

"But he came back."

Kell's fingers tightened around hers. "He did." Her pulse beat against his, strong and steady. He didn't want to let go. "Alucard has always been careless when it comes to precious things."

"I didn't choose him," she said, drawing Kell back from the edge. "I just chose to run."

She started to let go, but he wasn't ready. He pulled her toward him, their bodies nested against the cold. "Do you think you'll ever stop running?"

She tensed against him. "I don't know how."

Kell's free hand drifted up her bare arm to the nape of her neck. He tipped his head and rested his forehead against hers.

"You could just . . ." he whispered, "stay."

"Or you could go," she countered, "with me."

The words were a breath of fog against his lips, and Kell found himself leaning in to her warmth, her words.

"Lila," he said, the name aching in his chest.

He wanted to kiss her.

But she kissed him first.

The last time—the only time—it had been nothing but a ghost of lips against his, there and gone, so little to it, a kiss stolen for luck.

This was different.

They crashed into each other as if propelled by gravity, and he didn't know which of them was the object and which the earth, only that they were colliding. This kiss was Lila pressed into a single gesture. Her brazen pride and her stubborn resolve, her recklessness and her daring and her hunger for freedom. It was all those things, and it took Kell's breath away. Knocked the air from his lungs. Her mouth pressed hard against his, and her fingers wove through his hair as his sank down her spine, tangling in the intricate folds of her dress.

She forced him back against the railing, and he gasped, the shock of icy stone mixing with the heat of her body against him. He could feel her heart racing, feel the energy crackling through her, through him. They turned, caught up in another dance, and then he had her up against the frost-laced wall. Her breath hitched, and her nails dug into his skull. She sank her teeth into his bottom lip, drawing blood, and gave a wicked laugh, and still he kissed her. Not out of desperation or hope or for luck, but simply because he wanted to. Saints, he wanted to. He kissed her until the cold night fell away and his whole body sang with heat. He kissed her until the fire burned up the panic and the anger and the weight in his chest, until he could breathe again, and until they were both breathless.

And when they broke free, he could feel her smile on his lips.

"I'm glad you came back," he whispered.

"Me, too," she said. And then she looked him in the eyes, and added, "But I'm not dropping out of the tournament."

The moment cracked. Shattered. Her smile was fixed and sharp, and the warmth was gone.

"*Lila—*"

"*Kell,*" she mimicked, pulling free.

"There are consequences to this game."

"I can handle them."

"You're not listening," he said, exasperated.

"No," she snapped. "*You're* not." She licked the blood from her lips. "I don't need saving."

"Lila," he started, but she was already out of reach.

"Have a little faith," she said as she opened the door. "I'll be fine."

Kell watched her go, hoping she was right.

II

Ojka crouched on the palace patio, tucked into the shadow where the balcony met the wall, her hood up to hide her crimson hair. Inside this strange river castle, they appeared to be having some kind of celebration. Light danced across the stones, and music seeped through the doors. The cold air bit at Ojka's skin, but she didn't mind. She was used to cold—*real* cold—and the winter in this London was gentle by comparison.

Beyond the frosted glass, men and women ate and drank, laughed and spun around an ornate dance floor. None of them had markings. None of them had scars. All across the hall, magic was being used in petty ways, to light braziers and sculpt ice statues, to enchant instruments and entertain guests.

Ojka hissed, disgusted by the waste of power. A fresh language rune burned against her wrist, but she didn't need to speak this tongue to know how much they took for granted. Squandering life while her people starved in a barren world.

Before Holland, she reminded herself. Things were changing now; the world was mending, flourishing, but would it ever look like *this*? Months ago it would have been impossible to imagine. Now it was simply difficult. Hers was a world being slowly roused by magic. This was a world long graced.

Could a polished rock ever truly resemble a jewel?

She had the sudden, pressing urge to set fire to something.

Ojka, came a gentle chiding voice in her head, soft and teasing as a lover's whisper. She brought her fingers to her eye, the knot in the tether between her and her king. Her king, who could hear her thoughts, feel her desires—could he feel them *all?*—as if they were one.

I would not do it, Your Highness, she thought. *Not unless it pleased you. Then I would do anything.*

She felt the line between them slacken as the king drifted back into his own mind. Ojka turned her attention back to the ball.

And then she saw him.

Tall and thin, dressed in black, circling the floor with a pretty girl done up in green. Beneath a circlet of silver and wood, the girl's hair was fair , but Kell's was red. Not as red as Ojka's, no, but the copper still caught the light. One of his eyes was pale, the other as black as hers, as Holland's.

But he was *nothing* like her king. Her king was beautiful and powerful and perfect. This *Kell* was nothing but a skinny boy.

And yet, she knew him at first sight, not only because Holland knew him, but because he shone to her like a flame in the dark. Magic radiated like heat off the edges of his form, and when his dark eye drifted lazily across the bank of windows, past shadow and snow and Ojka, she *felt* the gaze. It rippled through her, and she braced herself, sure he would see her, feel her, but he didn't even notice. She wondered if the glass was mirrored instead of clear, so that everyone inside saw only themselves. Smiles reflecting back again and again while outside, the darkness waited, held at bay.

Ojka adjusted her balance on the balcony's rail. She'd made it this far by a series of ice steps forged on the palace wall, but the building itself must have been warded against intrusion; the one and only time she'd tried to slip inside through a pair of upstairs doors, she'd been rebuffed, not loudly, or painfully, but *forcefully.* The spellwork was fresh, the magic strong.

The only way in appeared to be the front doors, but Holland had warned her not to make a scene.

She pulled on the tether in her mind, and felt him take hold of the rope.

I have found him. She didn't bother explaining. She simply looked. She was the king's eyes. What she saw, so would he. *Shall I force him out?*

No, came the king's voice in her head. It hummed so beautifully in her bones. *Kell is stronger than he looks. If you try to force him and fail, he will not come. He must come. Be patient.*

Ojka sighed. *Very well.* But her mind was not at ease, and her king could tell. A soothing calm passed through her with his words, his will.

You are not only my eyes, he said. *You are my hands, my mouth, my will. I trust you to behave as I say I would.*

I will, she answered. *And I will not fail.*

III

"You look like hell."

Alucard's words rang through her head, the only thing he'd said that morning when she wished him luck.

"You say the sweetest things," she'd grumbled before escaping into her own tent. But the truth was, Lila *felt* like hell. She hadn't been able to find sleep in Elsor's room, so she'd gone back to the Wandering Road, with its cramped quarters and familiar faces. But every time she closed her eyes, she was back in that damn crate, or on the balcony with Kell—in the end she'd spent most of the night staring up at the candlelight as it played across the ceiling, while Tav and Lenos snored (who knew where Vasry was) and Kell's words played over and over in her head.

She closed her eyes, felt herself sway slightly.

"Master Elsor, are you well?"

She jerked back to attention. Ister was fitting the last of the armor plates on her leg.

"I'm fine," she muttered, trying to focus on Alucard's lessons.

Magic is a conversation.

Be an open door.

Let the waves through.

Right now, she felt like a rocky coastline.

She looked down at her wrist. The skin was already healing where the ropes had cut, but when she turned her hands over, her veins were dark. Not black, like the Dane twins, but not as light as they should be, either. Concern rippled through her, followed swiftly by annoyance.

She was fine.

She would be fine.

She'd come this far.

Delilah Bard was *not* a quitter.

Kell had beat the Veskan, Rul, by only two points, and lost to her by four. He was out of the running, but Lila could lose by a point and still advance. Besides, Alucard had already won his second match, securing his place in the final three alongside a magician named Tos-an-Mir, one of the famous Faroan twins. If Lila won, she'd finally get a chance to fight him. The prospect made her smile.

"What is that?" asked Ister, nodding down at the shard of pale stone in her hand. Lila had been rubbing it absently. Now she held it up to the tent's light. If she squinted, she could almost see the edge of Astrid's mouth, frozen in what could be a laugh, or a scream.

"A reminder," said Lila, tucking the chipped piece of statue into the coat slung over a cushion. It was a touch morbid, perhaps, but it made Lila feel better, knowing that Astrid was gone, and would stay gone. If there *was* a kind of magic that could bring back an evil queen turned to stone, she hoped it required a full set of pieces. This way, she could be certain that one was missing.

"Of what?" asked Ister.

Lila took up the dagger hilts and slid them into her forearm plates. "That I'm stronger than my odds," she said, striding out of the tent.

That I have crossed worlds, and saved cities.

She entered the stadium tunnel.

That I have defeated kings and queens.

She adjusted the helmet and strode out into the arena, awash in the cheers.

That I have survived impossible things.

Rul stood in the center of the floor, a towering shape.

That I am Delilah Bard . . .

She held out her spheres, her vision blurring for an instant before she let them go.

And I am unstoppable.

Kell stood on the balcony of his room, the gold ring on the rail between his hands, the sounds of the stadium reverberating through the metal.

The eastern arena floated just beside the palace, its ice dragons bobbing in the river around it, their bellies red. With the help of a looking scope, Kell could see down into the stadium, the two fighters like spots of white against the dark stone floor. Lila in her dark devil's mask. Rul with the steel face of a canine, his own wild hair jutting out like a ruff. His pennant was a blue wolf against a white ground, but the crowd was awash of silver blades on black.

Hastra stood behind him in the balcony doors, and Staff by the ones in the bedroom.

"You know him, don't you?" asked Hastra. "Stasion Elsor?"

"I'm not sure," murmured Kell.

Far below, the arena cheered. The match had started.

Rul favored earth and fire, and the elements swirled around him. He'd brought a handle and hilt into the ring; the earth swirled around the handle, hardening into a rock shield, while the fire formed a curving sword. Lila's own daggers came to life as they had the day before, one fire and the other ice. For an instant the two stood there, sizing each other up.

Then they collided.

Lila landed the first blow, getting in under Rul's sword, then spinning behind him and driving the fire dagger into the plate on the back of his leg. He twisted around, but she was already up and out, readying another strike.

Rul was taller by at least a foot, and twice as broad, but he was faster than a man his size had any right to be, and when she tried to find her way beneath his guard again, she failed, losing two plates in the effort.

Lila danced backward, and Kell could imagine her sizing the man up, searching for an in, a weakness, a chink. And somehow she found one. And then another.

She didn't fight like Rul, or Kisimyr, or Jinnar. She didn't fight like anyone Kell had ever seen. It wasn't that she was *better*—though she was certainly fast, and clever—it was just that she fought in the ring the way he imagined she did on the streets back in Grey London. Like everything was on the line. Like the other person was the only thing standing between her and freedom.

Soon she was ahead, six to five.

And then, suddenly, Rul struck.

She was rushing toward him, mid-stride when he turned the rock shield and threw it like a disk. It caught Lila in the chest, hard enough to throw her back into the nearest column. Light burst from the shattered plates on her stomach, shoulders, and spine, and Lila crumpled to the stone floor.

The crowd gasped, and the voice in the gold ring announced the damage.

Four plates.

"*Get up*," growled Kell as he watched her stagger to her feet, one hand gripping her ribs. She took a step and nearly fell, obviously shaken, but Rul was still on the attack. The massive disk flew back into his hand, and in a single fluid move he spun and launched it again, adding momentum to the force of magic.

Lila must have seen the attack, noticed the stone careening toward her, yet to Kell's horror, she didn't dodge. Instead she dropped both daggers and threw her *hands* up instead of her forearms to block the blow.

It was madness.

It wouldn't work—couldn't work—and yet, somehow the rock shield *slowed*.

Shock went through the crowd as they realized Stasion Elsor wasn't a dual magician after all. He had to be a *triad*.

The shield dragged through the air, as if fighting a current, and came to a stop inches from Lila's outstretched hands. It hovered there, suspended.

But Kell knew it wasn't simply hanging.

Lila was *pushing* against it. Trying to overpower Rul's element the way she had with his. But he'd let her then, he'd *stopped* fighting; Rul, momentarily stunned, now redoubled his efforts. Lila's boots slid back along the stone ground as she pushed on the disk with all her force.

The arena itself seemed to tremble, and the wind picked up as the magicians fought will to will.

Between Lila and Rul, the earthen disk shuddered. Through the looking scope, Kell could see her limbs shaking, her body curved forward with the strain.

Let go! He wanted to shout. But Lila kept pushing.

You stubborn fool, he thought as Rul summoned a burst of strength, lifted his fiery sword, and threw it. The blade went wide, but the flame must have snagged Lila's attention because she faltered, just enough, and the still-suspended rock shield stuttered forward and caught her in the leg. A glancing blow, but hard enough.

The tenth plate shattered.

The match was over.

The crowd erupted, and Rul let out a howl of victory, but Kell's attention was still on Lila, who stood there, arms at her side, head tipped back, looking strangely peaceful.

Until the moment she swayed, and collapsed.

IV

Kell was already moving through his room when the judge's voice spilled through the ring, calling for a medic.

He'd warned her. Over and over, he'd warned her.

Kell had his knife in his hand before he reached the door to the second chamber, Hastra on his heels. Staff tried to block the way, but Kell was faster, stronger, and he was in the alcove before the guards could stop him.

"*As Staro,*" he said, sealing the door shut behind him and drawing the symbol while Staff pounded on the wood.

"*As Tascen.*"

The palace fell away, replaced by the tournament tent.

"*The victory goes to Rul,*" announced the judge as Kell surged out of Kamerov's quarters and into Lila's. He got there as two attendants lowered her onto a sofa, a third working to undo her helmet. They started at the sight of him and went pale.

"Out," said Kell. "All of you."

The first two retreated instantly, but the third—a female priest—ignored him as she freed the hinged pieces of the demon's mask from Lila's head and set them aside. Beneath, her face was ghostly white, dark veins tracing her temples and twin streams of blackish red running from her nose. The priest rested a hand against her face, and a moment later her eyes fluttered open. A dozen oaths bubbled up, but Kell held his tongue. He held it as she drew a stilted breath and dragged herself into a sitting position, held it as she rolled her head and flexed her fingers, and lifted a cloth to her nose.

"You can go, Ister," she said, wiping away the blood.

Kell held his tongue as long as he could, but the moment the priest was gone, he lost it.

"I warned you!" he shouted. Lila winced, touching a hand to her temple.

"I'm fine," she muttered.

Kell made a stifled sound. "You collapsed in the ring!"

"It was a hard match," she said getting to her feet, trying and failing to hide her unsteadiness.

"How could you be so stupid?" he snapped, his voice rising. "You're bleeding black. You play with magic as if it were a game. You don't even understand the rules. Or worse, you decide there are none. You go stomping through the world, doing whatever the hell you please. You're careless. Senseless. Reckless."

"Keep it down, you two," said Rhy, striding in, Vis and Tolners at his back. "Kell, *you* shouldn't be here."

Kell ignored him and addressed the guards. "Lock her up."

"For what?" growled Lila.

"Calm down, Kell," said Rhy.

"For being an impostor."

Lila scoffed. "Oh, you're one to tal—"

Kell slammed her back into the tent pole, crushing her mouth with his hand. "Don't you *dare*." Lila didn't fight back. She went still as stone, mismatched eyes boring into him. There was a wildness to them, and he thought she might actually be afraid, or at least shocked. And then he felt the knife pressed against his side.

And the look in her eyes said that if it weren't for Rhy, she would have stabbed him.

The prince held up his hand. "*Stasion*," he said, addressing Lila as he took Kell's shoulder. "Please." She lowered the knife, and Rhy wrenched Kell backward with Tolners' help.

"You never listen. You never *think*. Having power is a responsibility, Lila, one you clearly don't deserve."

"Kell," warned Rhy.

"Why are you defending her?" he snapped, rounding on his brother. "Why am I the only one in this fucking world to be held accountable for my actions?"

They just stared at him, the prince and the guards, and Lila, she had the nerve to smile. It was a grim, defiant smile, marred by the dark blood still streaking her face.

Kell threw up his hands and stormed out.

He heard the sound of Rhy's boots on the cobbles coming after him, but Kell needed space, needed air, and before he knew what he was doing, he had the knife free from its sheath, the coins free from his collar.

The last thing he heard before he pressed his bloody fingers to the nearest wall was Rhy's voice calling for him to stop, but then the spell was on Kell's lips, and the world was falling away, taking everything with it.

V

One moment Kell was there, and the next he was gone, nothing but a dab of blood on the wall to mark his passing.

Rhy stood outside the tent, staring at the place where his brother had been, his chest aching not from physical pain but the sudden, horrible realization that Kell had purposefully gone where Rhy couldn't follow.

Tolners and Vis appeared like shadows behind him. A crowd was gathering, oblivious to the quarrel in the tent, oblivious to everything but the presence of a prince in their midst. Rhy knew he should be wrestling his features into form, fixing his smile, but he couldn't. He couldn't tear his eyes from the streak of blood.

Maxim strode into sight, Kell's guards on his heels. The crowd parted around the king, who smiled and nodded and waved even as he took Rhy's arm and guided him back toward the palace, talking about the final round and the three champions and the evening events, filling the silence with useless chatter until the doors of the palace closed behind them.

"What happened?" snapped the king, dragging him into a private chamber. "Where is Kell?"

Rhy slumped into a chair. "I don't know. He was in his rooms, but when he saw the match go south, he went down to the tents. He was just worried, Father."

"About what?" *Not about what,* Rhy thought. *Who.* But he

couldn't exactly tell the king about the girl parading as Stasion Elsor, the same girl who'd dragged the Black Night across the city at Kell's side (and saved the world, too, of course, but that wouldn't matter), so instead he simply said, "We had a fight."

"Where is he now?"

"I don't know." Rhy put his head in his hands, fatigue folding over him.

"Get up," ordered his father. "Go get ready."

Rhy dragged his head up. "For what?"

"Tonight's festivities, of course."

"But Kell—"

"Is *not here*," said the king, his voice as heavy as a stone. "He may have abandoned his duties, but you have not. You *will* not." Maxim was already heading for the door. "When Kell returns, he will be dealt with, but in the meantime, you are still the Prince of Arnes. And as such, you will act like it."

Kell sagged back against the cold stone wall as the bells of Westminster rang out the hour.

His heart pounded frantically with what he'd done.

He'd *left*. Left Red London. Left Rhy. Left Lila. Left a city—and a mess—in his wake.

All of it only a step away. A world apart.

If you don't want to be here, then go.

Run.

He hadn't meant to—he'd just wanted a moment of peace, a moment to *think*—and now he was here, fresh blood dripping to the icy street, his brother's voice still echoing in his head. Guilt pulled at him, but he shoved it away. This was no different from the hundreds of trips he'd made abroad, each and every one placing him out of reach.

This time it had simply been *his* choice.

Kell straightened and set off down the street. He didn't know where he was going, only that the first step had not been enough; he needed to keep moving before the guilt caught up. Or the cold. Grey London's winter had a bitter dampness to it, and he pulled his coat tight, and bent his head, and walked.

Five minutes later, he was standing outside the Five Points.

He could have gone anywhere, but he always ended up there. Muscle memory, that was the only real explanation. His feet carried him along the paths worn into the world, the cosmic slope, a gravitational bend drawing things of mass and magic to the fixed point.

Inside, a familiar face looked up from behind the bar. Not Barron's wide brow and dark beard, but Ned Tuttle's large eyes, his long jaw, his broad, surprised, *delighted* smile.

"Master Kell!"

At least the young Enthusiast didn't launch himself over the counter when Kell came in. He only dropped three glasses and knocked over a bottle of port. The glasses Kell let fall, but the port he stopped an inch above the floor, the gesture lost on all but Ned himself.

He slid onto a stool, and a moment later a glass of dark whisky appeared before him. Not magic, just Ned. When he finished the first glass in a single swig, the bottle appeared at his elbow.

The Enthusiast pretended to busy himself with the handful of other patrons while Kell drank. On the third glass, he slowed down; after all, it wasn't his body alone he was trashing. But how many nights had Kell borne Rhy's drinking; how many mornings had he woken with the stale taste of wine and elixirs coating his tongue?

Kell tipped a little more into his tumbler.

He could feel the eyes of the patrons drifting toward him, and he wondered if they were being drawn by magic or rumor. Could they feel the pull, the tip of gravity, or was it simply word of mouth? What had Ned told them? Anything? Everything?

Right then, Kell didn't care. He just wanted to smother the feelings before they could smother him. Blot out the image of Lila's bloody face before it ruined the memory of her mouth against his.

It was only a matter of time before Ned reappeared, but when he did, it wasn't with questions or mindless chatter. Instead, the lanky young man poured himself a drink from the same bottle, folded his arms on the edge of the counter, and set something down in front of Kell. It glinted in the lamplight.

A Red London lin.

The coin Kell had left behind on his last visit.

"I believe this is yours," he said.

"It is."

"It smells like tulips."

Kell tilted his head; the room tilted with it. "The King of England always said roses."

Ned gaped. "George the fourth said that?"

"No, the third," said Kell absently, adding, "the fourth is an ass."

Ned nearly choked on his drink, letting out a simple, startled laugh. Kell flicked his fingers, and the Red London lin leaped up onto its side and began to spin in lazy circles. Ned's eyes widened. "Will I ever be able to do that?"

"I hope not," said Kell, glancing up. "You shouldn't be able to do anything."

The man's narrow features contorted. "Why's that?"

"A long time ago, this world—your world—had magic of its own."

Ned leaned in, a child waiting for the monster in the story. "What happened?"

Kell shook his head, the whisky muddling his thoughts. "A lot of very bad things." The coin made its slow revolutions. "It's all about balance, Ned." Why couldn't Lila understand? "Chaos needs order. Magic needs moderation. It's like a fire. It doesn't have self-control. It feeds off whatever you give it, and if you give it too much, it burns and burns until there's nothing left.

"Your world had fire, once," said Kell. "Not much—it was too far from the source—but enough to burn. We cut it off before it could, and what was left began to dwindle. Eventually, it went out."

"But how do you know we would have burned?" asked Ned, eyes fever bright.

Kell knocked the coin over with a brush of his fingers. "Because too little of something is just as dangerous as too much." He straightened on his stool. "The point is, magic shouldn't exist here anymore. It shouldn't be *possible*."

"Impossibility is a thing that begs to be disproven," said Ned brightly. "Perhaps it hasn't been possible for years, perhaps it's not even possible right now, but that doesn't mean it *can't* be. It doesn't mean it *won't* be. You say the magic guttered, the flame went out. But what if it simply needed to be stoked?"

Kell poured himself another drink. "Maybe you're right."

But I hope you're wrong, he thought. *For all our sakes.*

Rhy was *not* in the mood.

Not in the mood to be at the ball.

Not in the mood to play host.

Not in the mood to smile and joke and pretend that everything was all right. His father cast warning looks his way, and his mother stole glances, as if she thought he would break. He wanted to yell at both of them, for driving his brother away.

Instead, he stood between the king and queen while the three champions cast off their masks.

First came the Veskan, Rul, his rough hair trailing down his jaw, still preening from his victory over Elsor.

Then Tos-an-Mir, one half of the favored Faroan twins, her gems tracing fiery patterns from brow to chin.

And of course, Alucard Emery. Rogue, rake, royal, and renewed darling of the Arnesian empire.

Rhy congratulated Lord Sol-in-Ar and Prince Col on the excellent showing, marveled aloud at the balanced field—an Arnesian, a Faroan, and a Veskan in the finals! What were the odds?—and then retreated to a pillar to drink in peace.

Tonight's festivities were being held in the Jewel Hall, a ballroom made entirely of glass. For a place so open, it made Rhy feel entombed.

All around him, people drank. People danced. Music played.

Across the ballroom, Princess Cora flirted with half a dozen Arnesian nobles, all while casting glances in search of Kell.

Rhy closed his eyes and focused on his brother's pulse, the echo of his own; he tried to reach through that beat and convey . . . what? That he was angry? That he was sorry? That he couldn't do any of this without Kell? That he didn't blame him for leaving? That he *did*?

Come home, he thought selfishly. *Please.*

Refined applause rang through the glass chamber, and he dragged his eyes open and saw the three champions returning in fresh attire, their masks tucked under their arms, their faces on display.

The wolfish Rul went straight for the nearest table of food, where his Veskan comrades were already deep in their cups.

Tos-an-Mir maneuvered the crowd, trailed by her sister, Tas-on-Mir, the first magician to fall to Kell. Rhy could only tell them apart by the gems set into their dark skin, Tos-an-Mir's a fiery orange where Tas-on-Mir's were pearlescent blue.

Alucard was the center of his own private universe. Rhy watched as a pretty *ostra* brought her painted lips to Alucard's ear to whisper something, and felt his grip tighten on his glass.

Someone slouched against the pillar beside him. A slim figure dressed in black. Lila looked better than she had that afternoon: still drawn, with shadows like bruises beneath her eyes, and yet spry enough to swipe two fresh glasses from a passing tray. She offered one to Rhy. He took it absently. "You came back."

"Well," she said, tipping her drink toward the ballroom, "you do know how to throw a party."

"To London," clarified Rhy.

"Ah," she said. "That."

"Are you all right?" he asked, thinking of her match that afternoon.

She swallowed, kept her eyes on the crowd. "I don't know."

A silence formed around them, a raft of quiet in the sea of sound.

"I'm sorry," she said at last, the words so soft Rhy almost didn't hear.

He rolled his shoulder toward her. "For what?"

"I don't really know. It seemed like the right thing to say."

Rhy took a long drink and considered this strange girl, her sharp edges, her guarded face. "Kell only has two faces," he said.

Lila raised a brow. "*Only* two? Don't most people have one?"

"On the contrary, Miss Bard—and you are Bard again, judging by your clothes? I assume Stasion has been left somewhere to recuperate? Most people have far more than two. I myself have an entire wardrobe." He didn't smile when he said it. His gaze drifted past his parents, the Arnesian nobles, Alucard Emery. "But Kell has only two. The one he wears for the world at large, and the one he wears for those he loves." He sipped his wine. "For us."

Lila's expression hardened. "Whatever he feels for me, it isn't love."

"Because it isn't soft and sweet and doting?" Rhy rocked back, stretching against the pillar. "Do you know how many times he's nearly beat me senseless out of love? How many times I've done the same? I've seen the way he looks at those he hates . . ." He shook his head. "There are very few things my brother cares about, and even fewer people."

Lila swallowed. "What do you think he's doing?"

Rhy considered his wine. "Judging by the way this is going to my head," he said, lifting the glass, "I'd say he's drowning his feelings, just like me."

"He'll come back."

Rhy closed his eyes. "I wouldn't."

"Yes," said Lila, "you would."

"Ned," said Kell in the early hours of the morning, "you wanted to give me something, the last time I was here. What was it?"

Ned looked down and shook his head. "Oh, it was nothing."

But Kell had seen the excitement in the man's eyes, and even though he couldn't take whatever it was, he still wanted to know. "Tell me."

Ned chewed his lip, then nodded. He reached beneath the counter and drew out a carved piece of wood. It was roughly the length of a hand, from palm to fingertip, the length etched with a pattern and the end pointed.

"What is it?" asked Kell, curious and confused.

Ned dragged the Red London lin toward him and balanced the point of the carved stick on top. When he let go, the wood didn't fall. It stood, perfectly upright, the carved point balancing on the coin.

"Magic," said Ned with a tired smile. "That's what I thought, anyway. I know now it's not really magic. A clever trick with magnets, that's all." He nudged the wood with his finger and it wavered, then righted. "But when I was young, it made me believe. Even when I found out it was a trick, I still *wanted* to believe. After all, just because this wasn't magic, that didn't mean nothing was." He plucked the stick from its perch and set it on the counter, stifling a yawn.

"I should go," said Kell.

"You can stay." It was very late—or very early—and the Five Points had long since emptied.

"No," said Kell simply. "I can't."

Before Ned could insist—before he could offer to keep the tavern open, before he could give Kell the room at the top of the stairs—the one with the green door and the wall still warped from his first encounter with Lila, when he'd pinned her to the wood, the one marked by Kell's finding spell and stained with Barron's blood—Kell got to his feet and left.

He turned up the collar of his coat, stepped out into the dark, and began to walk again. He walked the bridges and the streets of Lila's London, the parks and the paths. He walked until his muscles hurt and the pleasant buzz of whisky burned off and he was left with only that stubborn ache in his chest and the nagging pressure of guilt, of need, of duty.

And even then, he walked.

He couldn't stop walking. If he stopped, he would think, and if he thought too hard, he would go home.

He walked for hours, and only when his legs felt like they would give way unless he stopped, did he finally sink onto a bench along the Thames and listen to the sounds of Grey London, similar to and yet so different from his own.

The river had no light. It was a stretch of black, turning purple with the first hints of morning.

He turned the options over in his mind like a coin.

Run.

Run home.

Run.

Run home.

Run.

VI

Red London.

Ojka paced the palace shadows, furious with herself.

She'd lost him. She didn't know how he'd gotten away, only that he had. She'd spent the day searching for him in the crowds, waiting for night to fall, had returned to her post on the balcony, but the ballroom was dark, the celebration somewhere else. A steady stream of men and women poured up and down the steps, vanished and emerged, but none of them were Kell.

In the thickest hours of the night she saw a pair of guards, men in splendid red and gold, leaning in the shadow of the palace steps, talking softly. Ojka drew her blade. She couldn't decide if she should cut their throats and steal their armor, or torture them for information. But before she could do either, she heard a name pass between them.

Kell.

As she drew close, the language rune began to burn against her skin, and their words took shape.

". . . saying he's gone . . ." continued one.

"What do you mean, *gone*? As in taken?"

"Run off. Glad, too. Always gave me the creeps. . . ."

Ojka hissed, retreating down the banks. He wasn't gone. He couldn't be *gone*.

She knelt on the cold earth and drew a piece of parchment

from her pocket, spreading it over the ground. Next she dug her fingers into the dirt and ripped up a clod, crushing it in her palm.

This wasn't blood magic. Just a spell she'd used a hundred times in Kosik, hunting down those who owed her coin, or life.

"*Køs øchar,*" she said as the earth tumbled onto the parchment. As it fell, it traced the lines of the city, the river, the streets.

Ojka dusted off her hands.

"*Køs Kell,*" she said. But the map didn't change. The earth didn't stir. Wherever Kell was, he wasn't in London. Ojka clenched her teeth, and stood, dreading her king's reaction even as she drew upon the bond.

He is gone, she thought, and a moment later she was met by Holland—not only his voice, but his displeasure.

Explain.

He is not in this world, she said. *He is gone.*

A pause and then, *Did he go alone?*

Ojka hesitated. *I believe so. The royal family is still here.*

The silence that followed made her ill. She imagined Holland sitting on his throne, surrounded by the bodies that had failed him. She would not be one of those.

At last, the king spoke.

He will come back.

How do you know? asked Ojka.

He will always come home.

Rhy was a wreck. He'd stayed up through the night, through the darkness, through the memories, resisting the urge to take something to bring sleep without knowing where Kell was, and what might happen to his brother if he did. Instead the prince had tossed and turned for half the night before throwing the blankets off and pacing the room until dawn finally broke over the city.

The final match of the *Essen Tasch* was mere hours away. Rhy didn't care about the tournament. He didn't care about Faro and Vesk and politics. He only cared about his brother.

And Kell was still gone.

Still gone.

Still gone.

The darkness swarmed in Rhy's head.

The palace was coming to life around him. Soon he'd have to don the crown, and the smile, and play prince. He ran his hands through his hair, wincing in pain as a dark curl snagged on one of his rings. Rhy cursed. And then stopped pacing.

His eyes danced across the room—pillows and blankets and sofas, so many *soft* things—before landing on the royal pin. He'd cast it off with his tunic after the ball, and now it glinted in the first of the morning's light.

He tested the tip against his thumb, biting his lip as it drew blood. Rhy watched the bead well and spill down his palm, his heart racing. Then he brought the pin to the crook of his arm.

Maybe it was the lingering alcohol. Or maybe it was the gnawing panic of knowing that he couldn't reach Kell, or the guilt of understanding just how much his brother had given up, or the selfish need for him to give up more, to come back, to come home, that made Rhy press the point of the pin into the smooth flesh on the inside of his forearm, and begin to write.

Kell hissed at the sudden burning in his skin.

He was used to dull aches, shallow pains, echoes of Rhy's various mishaps, but this was sharp and bright, deliberate in a way that a glancing blow to the ribs or a banged knee never was. The pain dragged itself along the inside of his left arm, and he forced up the sleeve, expecting to see blood staining his tunic, angry red marks across his skin, but there was nothing. The pain stopped, and then started again, drawing itself down his arm in waves. No, *lines*.

He stared down at the skin, trying to make sense of the searing pain.

And then, suddenly, he understood.

He couldn't see the lines, but when he closed his eyes, he could feel them trace their way over his skin the way Rhy used to trace letters with his fingertip, writing out secret messages on Kell's arm. It was a game they'd played when they were young, stuck side by side at some event or a boring dinner.

This wasn't a game, not now. And yet Kell could feel the letters blazing down his arm, marked with something far sharper than a fingernail.

S
S-O
S-O-R
S-O-R-R
S-O-R-R-Y.

Kell was on his feet by the second *R,* cursing at himself for leaving as he drew the coins from around his throat and abandoned the ashen dawn of one London for the vibrant morning of another.

As he made his way to the palace, he thought of everything he wanted to say to the king, but when he climbed the grand stairs and stepped into the foyer, the royal family was already there. So were the Veskan prince and princess, the Faroan lord.

Rhy's gaze met Kell's, and his expression blazed with relief, but Kell kept his guard up as he stepped forward. He could feel the storm coming, the energy in the air thick with everything unsaid. He was braced for the fight, the harsh words, the accusations, the orders, but when the king spoke, his voice was warm.

"Ah, there he is. We were about to leave without you."

Kell couldn't hide his surprise. He'd assumed he would be bound to the palace, perhaps indefinitely. Not welcomed back without the slightest reprimand. He hesitated, meeting the king's gaze. It was steady, but he could see the warning in it.

"Sorry I'm late," he said, straining to keep his voice airy. "I was on an errand, and I lost track of time."

"You're here now," said the king, bringing a hand to Kell's shoulder. "That is what matters." The hand squeezed, hard, and for an instant Kell thought he wouldn't let go. But then the procession set out, and Maxim's hand fell away, and Rhy came to Kell's side, whether out of solidarity or desperation, he didn't know.

The central arena was filled to capacity, onlookers spilling out into the streets despite the early hour. In a clever touch, the dragons of the eastern arena and the lions of the western one had been moved, and were now converging on the central stadium, icy beasts in the river, lions posted on the stone supports, and the central's birds in flight overhead. The stadium floor was a tangle of obstacles, columns and boulders and rock shelves, and the stands above swarmed with life and color; Alucard's pennant with its silver feather waved from every side, dotted here and there with Rul's blue wolf, and Tos-an-Mir's black spiral.

When the three magicians finally emerged from their respective tunnels and took their places in the center of the floor, the roar was deafening; Kell and Rhy both cringed at the noise.

In the broad light of morning, the prince looked terrible (Kell could only assume he looked the same). Dark circles stood out beneath Rhy's pale eyes, and he held his left arm gingerly, shielding the letters freshly scarred into his skin. To every side, the stadium was alive with energy and noise, but the royal box was perilously quiet, the air heavy with things unsaid.

The king kept his eyes on the arena floor. The queen finally shot a glance at Kell, but it was laced with scorn. Prince Col seemed to sense the tension, and watched it all with hawkish blue eyes, while Cora seemed oblivious to the dangerous mood, still sulking from Kell's subtle rebuff.

Only Lord Sol-in-Ar appeared immune to the atmosphere of dissent. If anything his mood had improved.

Kell scanned the masses below. He didn't realize he was searching for Lila, not until he found her in the crowd. It should have been impossible in such a massive space, but he could feel the shift of gravity, the pull of her presence, and his eyes found hers across the stadium. From here he couldn't see her features, couldn't tell if her lips were moving, but he imagined them forming the word *hello.*

And then Rhy stepped forward, managing to muster a shadow of his usual charm as he brought the gold amplifier to his lips.

"Welcome!" he called out. "*Glad'ach! Sasors!* What a tournament it has been. It is only fitting that our three great empires find themselves here, represented equally by three great champions. From Faro, a twin by birth, without equal in the ring, the fiery Tos-an-Mir." Whistles filled the air as the Faroan bowed, her gold mask winking in the light. "From Vesk, a beast of a fighter, a wolf of a man, Rul!" In the arena, Rul himself let out a howl, and the Veskans in the crowd took up the call. "And of course, from our own Arnes, the captain of the sea, the prince of power, Alucard!"

The applause was thunderous, and even Kell brought his hands together, albeit slowly, and without much noise.

"The rules of this final round are simple," continued Rhy, "because there are few. This is no longer a game of points. A magician's armor is composed of twenty-eight plates, some broad targets, others small and hard to hit. Today, the last one with plates unbroken wins the crown. So cheer your three magicians, because only one will leave this ring the champion!"

The trumpets blared, the orbs fell, and Rhy retreated into the platform's shadow as the match began

Below, the magicians became a blur of elements: Rul's earth and fire; Tos-an-Mir's fire and air; Alucard's earth, air, and water. *Of course he's a triad,* thought Kell grimly.

It took less than a minute for Alucard to land the first blow on Rul's shoulder. It took more than five for Rul to land the second on Alucard's shin. Tos-an-Mir seemed content to let the two men strike each other from the books, until Alucard landed an icy blow to the back of her knees, and then she joined the fray.

The air in the royal booth was suffocating. Rhy was silent, slumped tiredly in the shadow of the balcony's awning, while Kell stood vigilantly beside the king, whose gaze never wavered from the match.

Below, Tos-an-Mir moved like a gold-masked shadow, dancing on the air, while Rul loped and lunged in his predatory lupine way. Alucard still moved with a noble's poise, even as his elements arced and crashed around him in a storm. The sounds of the fight were lost beneath the swell of cheers, but every point was marked by an explosion of light, a burst of brightness that only drove the crowd to a higher pitch.

And then, mercifully, the tension in the royal booth began to ease. The mood lightened, like the air after a storm, and Kell felt dizzy with relief. Attendants brought tea. Prince Col made a joke, and Maxim laughed. The queen complimented Lord Sol-in-Ar's magician.

By the end of the hour, Rul was out of plates, sitting on the stone floor looking dazed while Alucard and Tos-an-Mir danced around each other, crashing together like swords before breaking apart. And then, slowly but surely, Alucard Emery began to lose. Kell felt his spirits lift, though Rhy knocked his shoulder when he went so far as to cheer for one of Tos-an-Mir's hits. He rallied, closing the gap, and they fell into a stalemate.

At last, she got behind Alucard and under his guard. She moved to shatter the last of the his plates with a knifelike gust, but at the last instant, he twisted out of its path and a lash of water split her final piece of armor.

And just like that, it was over.

Alucard Emery had officially won.

Kell let out a groan as the stadium erupted into noise, raining down cheers and roses and silver pennants, and filling the air with a name.

"Alucard! Alucard! Alucard!"

And even though Rhy had the good taste not to whoop and shout like the rest of the crowd, Kell could see him beaming proudly as he stepped forward to formally announce the victor of the *Essen Tasch*.

Sanct, thought Kell. Emery was about to become even more insufferable.

Lord Sol-in-Ar addressed Tos-an-Mir and the crowd in Faroan, Princess Cora praised Rul and the gathered Veskans, and at last Prince Rhy dismissed the stands with promise of parties and closing ceremonies, the rest of the day a cause for celebration.

The king smiled and even clapped Kell on the back as the Maresh family made their way back to the palace, a train of cheerful subjects in their wake.

And as they climbed the palace stairs, and stepped inside the flower-strewn hall, it seemed as if everything would be all right.

And then Kell saw the queen hold Rhy back on the landing with a word, a question, and by the time he turned back to see why they'd stopped, the doors were swinging shut, blocking out the morning light and the sounds of the city. In the dim foyer, Kell caught the glint of metal as the king shed the illusion of kindness and said only two words, not even directed at Kell, but at the six guards that were circling loosely.

Two words that made Kell wish he'd never come back.

"Arrest him."

VII

Lila lifted her glass with the rest of the *Night Spire* as they toasted their captain.

The crew was gathered around on table and chair in the Wandering Road, and it was like they were back on the ship after a good night's take, laughing and drinking and telling stories before she and the captain retreated below.

Alucard Emery was bruised, bloody, and undoubtedly exhausted, but that didn't stop him from celebrating. He was standing atop a table in the center of the room, buying drinks and giving speeches about birds and dragons, Lila didn't really know, she'd stopped listening. Her head was still pounding and her bones ached with every motion. Tieren had given her something to soothe the pain and restore her strength, insisting as well on a diet of solid food and real sleep. Both of which seemed about as likely as getting out of London without a price on her head. She'd taken the tonic, made vague promises about the rest.

"Balance," he'd instructed, pressing the vial into her hand, "is not solely about magic. Some of it is simply common sense. The body is a vessel. If it's not handled carefully, it will crack. Everyone has limits. Even you, Miss Bard."

He'd turned to go, but she'd called him back.

"Tieren." She had to know, before she gave up another life. "You told me once that you saw something in me. Power."

"I did."

"What is it?" she'd asked. "What am I?"

Tieren had given her one of his long, level looks. "You are asking whether or not I believe you to be an *Antari*."

Lila had nodded.

"That I cannot answer," said Tieren simply. "I do not know."

"I thought you were supposed to be wise," she'd grumbled.

"Whoever told you that?" But then his face turned sober. "You are *something*, Delilah Bard. As to what, I cannot say. But one way or another, I imagine we'll find out."

Somewhere a glass shattered, and Lila's attention snapped back to the tavern, and Alucard up on the table.

"Hey, Captain," called out Vasry. "I have a question! What are you planning to do with all those winnings?"

"Buy a better crew," said Alucard, the sapphire winking again at his brow.

Tav swung an arm around Lila's shoulders. "Where you been, Bard? Hardly seen you!"

"I get enough of you all aboard the *Spire*," she grumbled.

"You talk tough," said Vasry, eyes glassy from drink, "but you're soft at heart."

"Soft as a knife."

"You know, a knife's only a bad thing if you're on the wrong side."

"Good thing you're one of us."

Her chest tightened. They didn't know—about her ruse, about the real Stasion Elsor somewhere on the sea, about the fact that Alucard had cut her from the crew.

Her eyes found Lenos across the table, and there was something in that look of his that made her think *he* knew. Knew she was leaving, at least, even if he didn't know the why of it.

Lila got to her feet. "I need some air," she muttered, but when she made it out the door, she didn't stop.

She was halfway to the palace before she realized it, and then she kept going until she climbed the steps and found Master

Tieren on the landing and saw in his eyes that something was wrong.

"What is it?" she asked.

The *Aven Essen* swallowed. "It's Kell."

The royal prison was reserved for special cases.

At the moment, Kell appeared to be the only one. His cell was bare except for a cot and a pair of iron rings set into the wall. The rings were clearly meant to hold chains, but at present there were none, only the cuffs clamped around his wrists, the bindings cold and cut with magic. Every piece of metal in the cell was incised with marks, enchanted to dull and dampen power. He should know. He'd helped to spell them.

Kell sat on the cot, ankles crossed, his head tipped back against the cold stone wall. The prison was housed in the base of the palace, one pillar over from the Basin where he trained, but unlike the Basin the walls were reinforced, and none of the river's red light seeped through. Only the winter chill.

Kell shivered slightly; they'd taken his coat, along with the traveling tokens around his neck, hung them on the wall beyond the cell. He hadn't fought the men off. He'd been too stunned to move as the guards closed in, slamming the iron cuffs around his wrists. By the time he believed what was happening, it was too late.

In the hours since, Kell's anger had cooled and hardened.

Two guards stood outside the cell, watching him with a mixture of fear and wonder, as if he might perform a trick. He closed his eyes, and tried to sleep.

Footsteps sounded on the stairs. Who would it be?

Tieren had already come. Kell had only one question for the old man.

"Did you know about Lila?"

The look in Tieren's eyes told him all he needed to know.

The footsteps drew closer, and Kell looked up, expecting the king, or Rhy. But instead Kell beheld the queen.

Emira stood on the opposite side of the bars, resplendent in her royal red and gold, her face a careful mask. If she was glad to see him caged—or saddened at all by the sight—it didn't show. He tried to meet her eyes, but they escaped to the wall behind his head.

"Do you have everything you need?" she asked, as if he were a guest in a plush palace wing, and not a cell. A laugh tried to claw its way up Kell's throat. He swallowed it and said nothing.

Emira brought a hand to the bars, as if testing their strength. "It shouldn't have come to this."

She turned to go, but Kell sat forward. "Do you hate me, my queen?"

"Kell," she said softly, "how could I?" Something in him softened. Her dark eyes finally found his. And then she said, "You gave me back my son."

The words cut. There had been a time when she insisted that she had two sons, not one. If he had not lost all her love, he had lost that.

"Did you ever know her?" asked Kell.

"Who?" asked the queen.

"My real mother."

Emira's features tightened. Her lips pursed.

A door crashed open overhead.

"Where is he?" Rhy came storming down the stairs.

Kell could hear him coming a mile away, could feel the prince's anger twining through his own, molten hot where Kell's ran cold. Rhy reached the prison, took one look at Kell behind the cell bars, and blanched.

"Let him out *now*," demanded the prince.

The guards bowed their heads, but held their places, gauntleted hands at their sides.

"Rhy," started Emira, reaching for her son's arm.

"Get off me, Mother," he snapped, turning his back on her. "If you won't let him out," he told the guards, "then I order you to let me in."

Still they did not move.

"What are the charges?" he snarled.

"Treason," said Emira, at the same time the guard answered, "Disobeying the king."

"I disobey the king all the time," said Rhy. "You haven't arrested *me*." He offered up his hands. Kell watched them bicker, focusing on the cold, letting it spread like frost, overtaking everything. He was so tired of caring.

"This will not stand." Rhy gripped the bar, exposing his gold sleeve. Blood had soaked through, dotting the fabric where he'd carved the word.

Emira paled. "Rhy, you're hurt!" Her eyes immediately went to Kell, so full of accusation. "What—"

More boots sounded on the stairs and a moment later the king was there, his frame filling the doorway. Maxim took one look at his wife and son, and said, "Get out."

"How could you do this?" demanded Rhy.

"He broke the law," said the queen.

"He is my brother."

"He is not—"

"*Go,*" bellowed the king. The queen fell silent, and Rhy's hands slumped back to his side as he looked to Kell, who nodded grimly. "Go."

Rhy shook his head and went, Emira a silent specter in his wake, and Kell was left to face the king alone.

The prince stormed past Lila in a blur.

A few seconds later she heard a crash, and she turned to see Rhy gripping the nearest sideboard, a shattered vase at his feet. Water wicked into the rug and spread across the stone floor, flowers strewn amid the broken glass. Rhy's crown was gone, his curls wild. His shoulders were shaking with anger, and his knuckles were white on the shelf.

Lila knew she should probably go, slip away before Rhy noticed her, but her feet were already carrying her toward the prince. She stepped over the mess of petals, the shards of glass.

"What did that vase ever do to you?" she asked, tipping her shoulder against the wall.

Rhy looked up, his amber eyes rimmed with red.

"An innocent bystander, I'm afraid," he said. The words came out hollow, humorless.

He ducked his head and let out a shuddering sigh. Lila hesitated. She knew she should probably bow, kiss his hand, or swoon—at the very least explain what she was doing there, in the private palace halls, as close to the prison as anyone would let her—but instead she flicked her fingers, producing a small blade. "Who do I need to kill?"

Rhy let out a stifled sound, half sob, half laugh, and sank onto his haunches, still gripping the wooden edge of the table. Lila crouched beside him, then shifted gingerly and put her back to the sideboard. She stretched out her legs, scuffed black boots sinking into the plush carpet.

A moment later, Rhy slumped onto the carpet beside her. Dried blood stained his sleeve, but he folded his forearm against his stomach. He obviously didn't want to talk about it, so she didn't ask. There were more pressing questions.

"Did your father really arrest Kell?"

Rhy swallowed. Nodded.

"Christ," she muttered. "What now?"

"The king will let him go, when his temper cools."

"And then?"

Rhy shook his head. "I honestly don't know."

Lila let her head fall back against the sideboard, then winced.

"It's my fault, you know," said the prince, rubbing his bloodied arm. "I asked him to come back."

Lila snorted. "Well, I told him to leave. I guess we're both at fault." She took a deep breath and shoved herself up to her feet. "Come on?"

"Where are we going?"

"We got him in there," she said. "We're going to get him out."

✤

"This isn't what I wanted," said the king.

He took up the keys and unlocked Kell's cell, then stepped inside and unfastened the iron cuffs. Kell rubbed his wrists but made no other move as the king retreated through the open cell door, pulled up a chair, and sat down.

Maxim looked tired. Wisps of silver had appeared at his temples, and they shone in the lantern light. Kell crossed his arms and waited for the monarch to meet his eye.

"Thank you," said the king.

"For what?"

"For not leaving."

"I did."

"I meant here."

"I'm in a cell," said Kell drily.

"We both know it wouldn't stop you."

Kell closed his eyes, and heard the king slump back in his chair.

"I will admit I lost my temper," said Maxim.

"You had me *arrested*," growled Kell, his voice so low the king might have missed it, had there been any other noises in the cell. Instead the words rang out, echoed.

"You disobeyed me."

"I did." Kell forced his eyes open. "I have been loyal to this crown, to this family, my entire life. I have given everything I have, everything I am, and you treat me like . . ." His voice faltered. "I can't keep doing this. At least when you treated me like a son, I could pretend. But now . . ." He shook his head. "The queen treats me as a traitor, and you treat me as a prisoner."

The king's look darkened. "You made this prison, Kell. When you tied your life to Rhy's."

"Would you have had him die?" snapped Kell. "I saved his life. And before you go blaming me for putting it in danger, we both know he managed that much himself. When will you stop punishing me alone for a family's worth of fault?"

"You both put this *whole kingdom* in danger with your folly. But at least Rhy is trying to atone. To prove that he deserves my trust. All you've done—"

"*I brought your son back from the dead!*" shouted Kell, lunging to his feet. "I did it knowing it would bind our lives, knowing what it would mean for me, what I would become, knowing that the resurrection of his life would mean the end of mine, and I did it anyway, because he is my brother and your son and the future King of Arnes." Kell gasped for breath, tears streaming down his face. "What more could I possibly do?"

They were both on their feet now. Maxim caught his elbow and forced him close. Kell tried to pull free, but Maxim was built like a tree, and his massive hand gripped the back of Kell's neck.

"I can't *keep atoning*," Kell whispered into the king's shoulder. "I gave him my life, but you cannot ask me to stop living."

"Kell," he said, voice softening. "I am sorry. But I cannot let you go." The air lodged in Kell's chest. The king's grip loosened, and he tore free. "This is bigger than you and Rhy. Faro and Vesk—"

"I do not care about their superstitions!"

"You should. People *act* on them, Kell. Our enemies scour the world for another *Antari*. Our allies would have you for themselves. The Veskans are convinced you are the key to our kingdom's power. Sol-in-Ar thinks you are a weapon, an edge to be turned against foes."

"Little do these people know I'm just a *pawn,*" spat Kell, retreating from the king's grip.

"This is the card you've been dealt," said Maxim. "It is only a matter of time before someone tries to take you for themselves, and if they cannot have your strength, I believe they will try to snuff it out. The Veskans are right, Kell. If you die, so does Arnes."

"I am not the key to this kingdom!"

"But you are the key to my son. My heir."

Kell felt ill.

"Please," begged Maxim. "Hear reason." But Kell was sick of reason, sick of excuses. "We all must sacrifice."

"No," snarled Kell. "I am done making sacrifices. When this is over, and the lords and ladies and royals are all gone, I am *leaving.*"

"I cannot let you go."

"You said it yourself, Your Majesty. You do not have the power to stop me." And with that, Kell turned his back on the king, took his coat from the wall, and walked out.

When Kell was a child, he used to stand in the royal courtyard, with its palace orchard, and close his eyes and listen—to the music, to the wind, to the river—and imagine he was somewhere else.

Somewhere without buildings, without palaces, without people.

He stood there now, among the trees—trees caught in the throes not only of winter, but of spring, summer, fall—and squeezed his eyes shut, and listened, waiting for the old sense of calm to find him. He waited. And waited. And—

"Master Kell."

He turned to see Hastra waiting a few paces back. Something was off, and at first Kell couldn't place it; then he realized that Hastra wasn't wearing the uniform of a royal guard. Kell knew it was because of him. One more failure to add to the stack. "I'm sorry, Hastra. I know how much you wanted this."

"I wanted an adventure, sir. And I've had one. It's not so bad. Rhy spoke to the king, and he's agreed to let me train with Master Tieren. Better the sanctuary than a cell." And then his eyes widened. "Oh, sorry."

Kell only shook his head. "And Staff?"

Hastra grimaced. "Afraid you're stuck with him. Staff's the one who fetched the king when you first left."

"Thank you, Hastra," he said. "If you're half as good a priest as you were a royal guard, the *Aven Essen* better watch his job."

Hastra broke into a grin, and slipped away. Kell listened to the sounds of his steps retreating across the courtyard, the distant sound of the courtyard doors closing, and turned his attention back to the trees. The wind picked up, and the rustling of the leaves was almost loud enough to drown out the sounds of the palace, to help him forget the world that waited back inside the doors.

I am leaving, he thought. *You do not have the power to stop me.*

"Master Kell."

"What now?" he asked, turning back. His brow furrowed. "Who are you?"

A woman stood there, between two of the trees, hands clasped behind her back and head bowed as if she'd been waiting for some time, though Kell hadn't even heard her approach. Her red hair floated like a flame above her crisp white cape, and he wondered why she felt so strange and so familiar at the same time. As if they'd already met, though he was sure they hadn't.

And then the woman straightened and looked up, revealing her face. Fair skin, and red lips, and a scar beneath two different-colored eyes, one yellow and the other impossibly black.

Both eyes narrowed, even as a smile passed her lips.

"I've been looking everywhere for you."

VIII

The air caught in Kell's chest. An *Antari*'s mark was confined to the edges of one's eye, but the black of the woman's iris spilled over like tears down her cheek, inky lines running into her red hair. It was unnatural.

"Who are you?"

"My name," she said, "is Ojka."

"*What* are you?" he asked.

She cocked her head. "I am a messenger." She was speaking Royal, but her accent was thick, and he could see the language rune jutting from her cuff. So she was from White London.

"You're an *Antari*?" But that wasn't possible. Kell was the last of those. His head spun. "You can't be."

"I am only a messenger."

Kell shook his head. Something was wrong. She didn't *feel* like an *Antari*. The magic felt stranger, darker. She took a step forward, and he found himself stepping back. The trees thickened overhead, from spring to summer.

"Who sent you?"

"My king."

So someone had clawed his way to the White London throne. It was only a matter of time.

She stole another slow step forward, and Kell kept his distance, slipping from summer to fall.

"I'm glad I found you," she said. "I've been looking."

Kell's gaze flicked past her, to the palace doors. "Why?"

She caught the look, and smiled. "To deliver a message."

"If you have a message for the crown," he said, "deliver it yourself."

"My message is not for the crown," she pressed. "It is for *you*."

A shiver went through him. "What could you have to say to me?"

"My king needs your help. My city needs your help."

"Why me?" he asked.

Her expression shifted, saddened. "Because it's all your fault."

Kell pulled back, as if struck. "What?"

She continued toward him, and he continued back, and soon they stood in winter, a nest of bare branches scratching in the wind. "It *is* your fault. You struck down the Danes. You killed our last true *Antari*. But *you* can help us. Our city needs you. Please come. Meet with my king. Help him rebuild."

"I cannot simply leave," he said, the words automatic.

"Can't you?" asked the messenger, as if she'd heard his thoughts.

I am leaving.

The woman—Ojka—gestured to a nearby tree, and Kell noticed the spiral, already drawn in blood. A door.

His eyes went to the palace.

Stay.

You made this prison.

I cannot let you go.

Run.

You are an Antari.

No one can stop you.

"Well?" asked Ojka, holding out her hand, the veins black against her skin. "Will you come?"

🙢

"What do you mean he's been released?" snapped Rhy.

He and Lila were standing in the royal prison, staring past a guard at the now empty cell. He'd been ready to storm the men and free Kell with Lila's help, but there was no Kell to free. *"When?"*

"King's orders," said the guard. "Not ten minutes ago. Can't have gotten far."

Rhy laughed, a sick, hysterical sound clawing up his throat, and then he was gone again, racing back up the stairs to Kell's rooms with Lila in tow.

He reached Kell's room and flung open the doors, but the chamber was empty.

He fought to quell the rising panic as he backed out into the hall.

"What are you two doing?" asked Alucard, coming up the stairs.

"What are *you* doing here?" asked Rhy.

"Looking for you," said Alucard at the same time Lila asked, "Have you seen Kell?"

Alucard raised a brow. "We make a point of avoiding each other."

Rhy let out an exasperated sound and surged past the captain, only to collide with a young man on the stairs. He almost didn't recognize the guard without his armor. "Hastra," he said, breathlessly. "Have *you* seen Kell?"

Hastra nodded. "Yes, sir. I just left him in the courtyard."

The prince wilted with relief. He was about to start off down the stairs again when Hastra added, "There's someone with him now. I think. A woman."

Lila prickled visibly. "What kind of woman?"

"You think?" asked Alucard.

Hastra looked a little dazed. "I . . . I can't remember her face." A crease formed between his brows. "It's strange, I've always been so good with faces. . . . There was something about her face though . . . something off . . ."

"Hastra," said Alucard, his voice tense. "Open your hands."

Rhy hadn't even noticed that the young guard's hands were clenched at his sides.

Hastra looked down, as if he hadn't noticed, either, then held them out and uncurled his fingers. One hand was empty. The other clutched a small disk, spellwork scrawled across its surface.

"Huh," said the guard. "That's odd."

But Rhy was already tearing down the hall, Lila a stride behind him, leaving Alucard in their wake.

Kell reached out and took Ojka's hand.

"Thank you," she said, voice flooding with happiness and relief as her fingers tightened around his. She pressed her free hand to the blood-marked tree.

"*As Tascen*," she said, and a moment later, the palace courtyard was gone, replaced by the streets of Red London. Kell looked around. It took him a moment to register where they were . . . but it wasn't where they *were* that mattered, but where they *would* be.

In this London, it was only a narrow road, flanked by a tavern and a garden wall.

But in White London, it was the castle gate.

Ojka pulled a trinket from beneath her white cloak, then pressed her still-bloody hand to the winter ivy clinging to the wall stones. She paused and looked to Kell, waiting for his permission, and Kell found himself glancing back through the streets, the royal palace still visible in the distance. Something rippled through him—guilt, panic, hesitation—but before he could pull back, Ojka said the words, and the world folded in around them. Red London disappeared, and Kell felt himself stepping forward, out of the street, and into the stone forest that stood before the castle.

Only it wasn't a stone forest, not anymore.

It was just an ordinary one, filled with trees, bare winter branches giving way to a crisp blue sky. Kell started—since when did White London have such a color? This wasn't the world he remembered, wasn't the world she'd spoken of, one damaged and dying.

This world wasn't broken at all.

Ojka stood near the gate, steadying herself against the wall. When she looked up, a feline smile curled across her face.

Kell had only a moment to process the changes—the grass beneath his feet, the sunlight, the sound of birds—and to realize he'd made a terrible mistake, before he heard footsteps, and spun to find himself face to face with the *king*.

He stood across from Kell, shoulders back and head high, revealing two eyes: one emerald, and the other black.

"Holland?"

The word came out as a question, because the man in front of him bore almost no resemblance to the Holland Kell had known, the one he had fought—had defeated, had cast into the abyss—four months ago. The last time Kell had seen Holland, he had been a few dragging pulses from death.

That Holland couldn't be standing here.

That Holland could never have survived.

But it *was* Holland before him, and he hadn't just survived.

He'd been *transformed*.

There was healthy color in his cheeks, the glow that only came in the prime of life, and his hair—which, despite his age, had always been a charcoal grey—was now straight and black and glossy, carving sharp lines where it fell against his temples and brow. And when Kell met Holland's gaze, the man— magician—king—*Antari*—actually *smiled,* a gesture that did more to transform his face than the new clothes and the aura of health.

"Hello, Kell," said Holland, and a small part of him was relieved to find that the *Antari*'s voice, at least, was still familiar. It wasn't loud, had never been loud, but it was commanding, edged by that subtle gravel that made it sound like he'd been shouting. Or screaming.

"You shouldn't be here," said Kell.

Holland raised a single, black brow. "Neither should you."

Kell felt the shadow at his back, the shift of weight just before a lunge. He was already reaching for his knife, but he was too late, and his fingers only found the hilt before something cold and heavy clamped around his throat, and the world exploded in pain.

Rhy burst through the courtyard doors, calling his brother's name. There was no sign of him before the line of trees, no answer but the echo of Rhy's own voice. Lila and Alucard were somewhere behind him, the pounding of boots lost beneath his raging pulse.

"Kell?" he called out again, surging into the orchard. He dug his nails into the wound at his arm, the pain a tether he tried to pull on as he passed the line of spring blossoms.

And then, halfway between the lines of summer green and autumn gold, Rhy collapsed with a scream.

One moment he was on his feet, and the next he was on his hands and knees, crying out in pain as something sharp and jagged tore through him.

"Rhy?" came a voice nearby as the prince folded in on himself, a sob tearing its way free.

Rhy.
Rhy.
Rhy.

His name echoed through the courtyard, but he was drowning in his own blood; he was sure he would see it painting the stones. His vision blurred, sliding out of focus as he fell, the way he had so many times when the darkness came, bringing forth the memories and the dreams.

This was a bad dream.

His mouth was filling with blood.

It had to be a bad dream.

He tried to get to his feet.

It—

He collapsed again with a scream as the pain ripped through his chest and buried itself between his ribs.

"Rhy?" shouted the voice.

He tried to answer, but his jaw locked. He couldn't breathe. Tears were streaming down his face and the pain was too real, too familiar, a blade driven through flesh and muscle, scraping against bone. His heart raced, and then stuttered, skipped a beat, and his vision went black and he was back on the cot in the sanctuary again, falling through darkness, crashing down into—

Nothing.

Lila had run straight for the courtyard wall, sprinting through the strange orchard and out the other side. But there was no sign of them, no blood on the stones, no mark. She backed away, trying to think of where else to look. Then she heard the scream.

Rhy.

She found the prince on the ground, clawing at his chest. He was sobbing, pressing his arm to his ribs as if he'd been stabbed, but there was no blood. Not here. It hit her like a blow.

Whatever was happening to Rhy wasn't happening to Rhy at all.

It was happening to *Kell.*

Alucard appeared, and went ashen at the sight of the prince. He called to the guards before folding to his knees as Rhy let out another sob. "What's happening to him?" asked Alucard.

Rhy's lips were stained with blood, and Lila didn't know if he'd bitten them through, or if the damage was worse.

"Kell..." gasped the prince, shuddering in pain. "Something's... wrong... can't..."

"What does Kell have to do with this?" asked the captain.

Two royal guards appeared, the queen behind them, looking pale with fear.

"Where is Kell?" she cried as soon as she saw the prince.

"Get back!" called the guards when a handful of nobles tried to come near.

"Call for the king!"

"Hold on," pleaded Alucard, talking to Rhy.

Lila backed away as the prince curled in on himself. She started searching the trees for a sign of Kell, of the woman, of the way they had gone.

Rhy rolled onto his side, tried to rise, failed, and began coughing blood onto the orchard ground.

"Someone find Kell!" demanded the queen, her voice on the edge of hysteria.

Where had he gone?

"What can I do, Rhy?" whispered Alucard. "What can I do?"

Kell surfaced with the pain.

He was breaking into pieces, some vital part being torn away. Pain radiated from the metal collar at his throat, cutting off air, blood, thought, power. He tried desperately to summon magic, but nothing came. He gasped for air—it felt as if he were drowning, the taste of blood pooling in his mouth even though it was empty.

The forest was gone, the room around him barren. Kell

shivered—his coat and shirt were gone—the bare skin of his back and shoulders pressed against something cold and metal. He couldn't move; he was standing upright, but not by his own strength. His body was being held in a kind of frame, his arms forced wide to either side, his hands bound to the vertical bars of the structure. He could feel a horizontal bar against his shoulders, a vertical one against his head and spine.

"A relic," said an even voice, and Kell dragged his vision into focus and saw Holland standing before him. "From my predecessors."

The *Antari*'s gaze was steady, his whole form still, as if sculpted from stone instead of flesh, but his black eye swirled, silvery shadows twisting through it like serpents in oil.

"What have you done?" choked Kell.

Holland tipped his head. "What *should* I have done?"

Kell set his teeth, forced himself to think beyond the collar's icy pain. "You should . . . have stayed in Black London. You should . . . have died."

"And let my people die, too? Let my city plunge into yet another war, let my world sink farther and farther toward death, knowing I could save it?" Holland shook his head. "No. My world has sacrificed enough for yours."

Kell opened his mouth to speak, but the pain knifed through him, sharpening over his heart. He looked down and saw the seal fracturing. No. *No.*

"Holland," he gasped. "Please. You have to take this collar off."

"I will," said Holland slowly. "When you agree."

Panic tore through him. "To what?"

"When I was in Black London—after *you* sent me there—I made a deal. My body for *his* power."

"*His?*"

But there could be only one thing waiting in that darkness to make a deal. The same *thing* that had crushed a world, that had tried to escape in a shard of stone. The same thing that had torn a path through his city, tried to devour Kell's soul.

"You *fool*," he snarled. "You're the one . . . who told me that to let dark magic in was to lose . . ." His teeth were chattering. "That you were either the master . . . or the servant. And look . . . what you've done. You may be free of Athos's spell . . . but you've just traded one master for another."

Holland took Kell by the jaw and slammed his head back against the metal beam. Pain rang through his skull. The collar tightened, and the seal above his heart cracked and split.

"Listen to me," begged Kell, the second pulse faltering in his chest. "I know this magic."

"You knew a shadow. A sliver of its power."

"That power destroyed one world already."

"And healed another," said Holland.

Kell couldn't stop shaking. The pain was fading, replaced by something worse. A horrible, deadening cold. "Please. Take this off. I won't fight back. I—"

"You've had your perfect world," said Holland. "Now I want *mine*."

Kell swallowed, closed his eyes, tried to keep his thoughts from fraying.

Let me in.

Kell blinked. The words had come from Holland's mouth, but the voice wasn't his. It was softer, more resonant, and even as it spoke, Holland's face began to change. Shadow bled from one eyes into the other, consuming the emerald green and staining it black. A wisp of silver smoke curled through those eyes, and someone—something—looked out, but it wasn't Holland.

"*Hello,* Antari."

Holland's expression continued to shift, the features of his face rearranging from hard edges into soft, almost gentle ones. The lines of his forehead and cheeks smoothed to polished stone, and his mouth contorted into a beatific smile. And when the creature spoke, it had two voices; one filling the air, a smoother version of Holland's own, while the other echoed in Kell's head, low and rich as smoke. That second voice twined behind Kell's eyes, and spread through his mind, searching.

"*I can save you,*" it said, plucking at his thoughts. "*I can save your brother. I can save everything.*" The creature reached up and touched a strand of Kell's sweat-slicked hair, as if fascinated. "*Just let me in.*"

"You are a monster," growled Kell.

Holland's fingers tightened around Kell's throat. "*I am a god.*" Kell felt the creature's will pressing against his own, felt it forcing its way into his mind with icy fingers and cold precision.

"Get out of my head." Kell slammed forward against the binds with all his strength, cracking his forehead against Holland's. Pain lanced through him, hot and bright, and blood trickled down his nose, but the thing in Holland's body only smiled.

"*I am in everyone's head,*" it said. "*I am in everything. I am as old as creation itself. I am life and death and power. I am inevitable.*"

Kell's heart was pounding, but Rhy's was slipping. One beat for every two. And then three. And then—

The creature flashed its teeth. "*Let me in.*"

But Kell couldn't. He thought of his world, of setting this creature loose upon it wearing his skin. He saw the palace crumble and the river go dark, saw the bodies fall to ash in the streets, the color bleed out until there was only black, and saw himself standing at the center, just as he had in every nightmare. Helpless.

Tears streamed down his face.

He couldn't. He couldn't do that. He couldn't *be* that.

I'm sorry, Rhy, he thought, knowing he'd just damned them both.

"No," he said aloud, the word scraping his throat.

But to his surprise, the monster's smile widened. "*I was hoping you would say that.*"

Kell didn't understand the creature's joy, not until it stepped back and held up its hands. *"I like this skin. And now that you have refused me, I get to keep it."*

Something shifted in the creature's eyes, a pulse of light, a sliver of green, flaring, fighting, only to be swallowed again by the darkness. The monster shook its head almost ruefully. *"Holland, Holland . . ."* it purred.

"Bring him back," demanded Kell. "We are not done." But the creature kept shaking its head as it reached for Kell's throat. He tried to pull away, but there was no escape.

"You were right, Antari," it said, running its fingertips along the metal collar. *"Magic is either a servant or a master."*

Kell fought against the metal frame, the cuffs cutting into his wrists. "Holland!" he shouted, the word echoing through the stone room. "Holland, you bastard, fight back!"

The demon only stood and watched, its black eyes amused, unblinking.

"Show me you're not weak!" screamed Kell. "Prove you're not still a slave to someone else's will! Did you really come all the way back to lose like this? Holland!"

Kell sagged back against the metal frame, wrists bloody and voice hoarse as the monster turned and walked away.

"Wait, demon," choked Kell, straining against the pressing darkness, the cold, the fading echo of Rhy's pulse.

The creature glanced back. *"My name,"* it said, *"is Osaron."*

Kell fought against the metal frame as his vision blurred, refocused, and then began to tunnel. "Where are you going?"

The demon held something up for him to see, and Kell's heart lurched. It was a single crimson coin, marked by a gold star in its center. A Red London lin.

"*No,*" he pleaded, twisting against the cuffs until they shredded his skin and blood streamed down his wrists. "Osaron, you can't."

The demon only smiled. "But who will stop me now?"

IX

Lila paced the orchard.

She had to do something.

The courtyard was brimming with guards, the palace in a frenzy. Tieren was trying to coax answers from Hastra, and several rows away, Alucard was still curled over Rhy, murmuring something too soft for her to hear. It sounded like a soothing whisper. Or a prayer. She had heard men praying at sea, not to God, but to the world, to magic, to anything that might be listening. A higher power, a different name. Lila hadn't believed in God for a very long time—she'd given up praying when it was clear that no one would answer—and while she was willing to admit that magic *existed,* it didn't seem to listen, or at least, it didn't seem to care. Lila took a strange pleasure in that, because it meant the power was her own.

God wasn't going to help Rhy.

But Lila could.

She marched back through the orchard.

"Where are you going?" demanded Alucard, looking up from the prince.

"To fix this," she said. And with that she took off, sprinting through the courtyard doors. She didn't stop, not for the attendants or the guards who tried to bar her way. She ducked and spun, surging past them and through the palace doors and down the steps.

Lila knew what she had to do, though she had no idea if it would work. It was madness to try, but she didn't have a choice. That wasn't true. The old Lila would have pointed out that she always had a choice, and that she'd live a hell of a lot longer if she chose herself.

But when it came to Kell, there was a debt. A bond. Different from the one that bound him and Rhy, but just as solid.

Hold on, she thought.

Lila pressed through the crowded streets and away from the festivities. In her mind she tried to draw a map of White London, what little she'd seen of it, but she couldn't remember much besides the castle, and Kell's warning to never cross over exactly where you wanted to be.

When she finally found herself alone, she pulled the shard of Astrid Dane from her back pocket. Then she rolled up her sleeve and withdrew her knife.

This is madness, she thought. *Sheer and utter madness.*

She knew the difference between elemental and *Antari*. Yes, she had survived before, but she had been with Kell, under the protection of his magic. And now she was alone.

What am I? she'd asked Tieren.

What am I? she'd wondered every night at sea, every day since she'd first found herself here in this city, in this world.

Now Lila swallowed and drew the knife's blade across her forearm. It bit into flesh, and a thin ribbon of red rose and spilled over. She smeared the wall with her blood and clutched the shard of stone.

Whatever I am, she thought, pressing her hand to the wall, *let it be enough.*

ACKNOWLEDGMENTS

Here we are again. The end of another book. I'm always surprised to have made it this far. It might have taken you days, or weeks, or even months to read *A Gathering of Shadows,* but it took me years to write, edit, and see this book to publication. That duration renders this moment surreal. Even harder is remembering who to thank.

To my mother and father, for telling me I could be whatever I wanted, whether that was a designer, an interrogator, or a fantasy author.

To my editor, Miriam, for being a killer editor, a stalwart champion, and an ace GIF user. And for being a friend and companion on this particularly wondrous adventure.

To my agent, Holly, for proving time and again that you are magic.

To my former publicist, Leah, and my new publicist, Alexis, and to Patty Garcia, for keeping me afloat.

To art director Irene Gallo and cover designer Will Staehle, for making things look so fierce.

To my beta reader, Patricia, for sticking with me through thick and thin and strange and dark.

To my Nashville crew, especially Courtney and Carla, Ruta, Paige, Lauren, Sarah, Ashley, Sharon, David, and so, so many more, for being the warmest community in all the land.

To my wee Scottish flatmate, Rachel, for being an utter delight, and not making fun of me when I talked to myself or vanished for long stretches into the deadline pit.

To my new housemate, Jenna, because you have no idea what you're in for.

To my readers, who are, without question, the best readers in the entire world (sorry everyone else's readers).

To everyone else: So many of you have stood at my side, championed my work, cheered on good days and been present on bad, and taken this journey with me stride for stride. I can never thank you all, but please know that if you're reading this, you matter. You've made an impact on my life and my series, and for that, I'm incredibly grateful.

(I also want to point out that I made it nine books without invoking the dreaded cliffhanger.)

Turn the page for a preview of the next
Shades of Magic novel

Available now from Tor Books

Copyright © 2017 by Victoria Schwab

I

Delilah Bard—always a thief, recently a magician, and one day, hopefully, a pirate—was running as fast as she could.

Hold on, Kell, she thought as she sprinted through the streets of Red London, still clutching the shard of stone that had once been part of Astrid Dane's mouth. A token stolen in another life, when magic and the idea of multiple worlds were new to her. When she had only just discovered that people could be possessed, or bound like rope, or turned to stone.

Fireworks thundered in the distance, met by cheers and chants and music, all the sounds of a city celebrating the end of the *Essen Tasch,* the tournament of magic. A city oblivious to the horror happening at its heart. And back at the palace, the prince of Arnes—Rhy—was dying, which meant that somewhere, a world away, so was Kell.

Kell. The name rang through her with all the force of an order, a plea.

Lila reached the road she was looking for and staggered to a stop, knife already out, blade pressing to the flesh of her hand. Her heart pounded as she turned her back on the chaos and pressed her bleeding palm—and the stone still curled within it—to the nearest wall.

Twice before Lila had made this journey, but always as a passenger.

Always using Kell's magic.

Never her own.

And never alone.

But there was no time to think, no time to be afraid, and certainly no time to wait.

Chest heaving and pulse high, Lila swallowed and said the words, as boldly as she could. Words that belonged only on the lips of a blood magician. An *Antari*. Like Holland. Like Kell.

"*As Travars.*"

The magic sang up her arm, and through her chest, and then the city lurched around her, gravity twisting as the world gave way.

Lila thought it would be easy or, at least, *simple*.

Something you either survived, or did not.

She was wrong.

II

A world away, Holland was drowning.

He fought to the surface of his own mind, only to be forced back down into the dark water by a will as strong as iron. He fought, and clawed, and gasped for air, strength leaching out with every violent thrash, every desperate struggle. It was worse than dying, because dying gave way to death, and this did not.

There was no light. No air. No strength. It had all been taken, severed, leaving only darkness and, somewhere beyond the crush, a voice shouting his name.

Kell's voice—

Too far away.

Holland's grip faltered, slipped, and he was sinking again.

All he had ever wanted was to bring the magic back—to see his world spared from its slow, inexorable death—a death caused first by the fear of another London, and then by the fear of his own.

All Holland wanted was to see his world restored.

Revived.

He knew the legends—the dreams—of a magician powerful enough to do it. Strong enough to breathe air back into its starved lungs, to quicken its dying heart.

For as long as Holland could remember, that was all he'd wanted.

And for as long as Holland could remember, he had wanted the magician to be *him*.

Even before the darkness bloomed across his eye, branding him with the mark of power, he'd wanted it to be him. He'd stood on the banks of the Sijlt as a child, skating stones across the frozen surface, imagining that he would be the one to crack the ice. Stood in the Silver Wood as a grown man, praying for the strength to protect his home. He'd never wanted to be *king,* though in the stories the magician always was. He didn't want to rule the world. He only wanted to save it.

Athos Dane had called this arrogance, that first night, when Holland was dragged, bleeding and half conscious, into the new king's chambers. Arrogance and pride, he'd chided, as he carved his curse into Holland's skin.

Things to be broken.

And Athos had. He'd broken Holland one bone, one day, one order at a time. Until all Holland wanted, more than the ability to save his world, more than the strength to bring the magic back, more than *anything,* was for it to end.

It was cowardice, he knew, but cowardice came so much easier than hope.

And in that moment by the bridge, when Holland lowered his guard and let the spoiled princeling Kell drive the metal bar through his chest, the first thing he felt—the first and last and *only* thing he felt—was relief.

That it was finally over.

Only it wasn't.

It is a hard thing, to kill an *Antari.*

When Holland woke, lying in a dead garden, in a dead city, in a dead world, the first thing he felt then was pain. The second thing was freedom. Athos Dane's hold was gone, and Holland was alive—broken, but alive.

And stranded.

Trapped in a wounded body in a world with no door at the mercy of another king. But this time, he had a *choice.*

A chance to set things right.

He'd stood, half dead, before the onyx throne, and spoken to the king carved in stone, and traded freedom for a chance to save his London, to see it bloom again. Holland made the deal, paid with his own body and soul. And with the shadow king's power, he had finally brought the magic back, seen his world bloom into color, his people's hope revived, his city restored.

He'd done everything he could, given up everything he had, to keep it safe.

But it still was not enough.

Not for the shadow king, who always wanted more, who grew stronger every day and craved chaos, magic in its truest form, power without control.

Holland was losing hold of the monster in his skin.

And so he'd done the only thing he could.

He'd offered Osaron another vessel.

"Very well . . . " said the king, the demon, the god. *"But if they cannot be persuaded, I will keep your body as my own."*

And Holland agreed—how could he not?

Anything for London.

And Kell—spoiled, childish, headstrong Kell, broken and powerless and snared by that damned collar—had still refused.

Of course he had refused.

Of course—

The shadow king had smiled then, with Holland's own mouth, and he had fought, with everything he could summon, but a deal was a deal and the deal was done and he felt Osaron surge up—that single, violent motion—and Holland was shoved down, into the dark depths of his own mind, forced under by the current of the shadow king's will.

Helpless, trapped within a body, within a deal, unable to do anything but watch, and feel, and drown.

"Holland!"

Kell's voice cracked as he strained his broken body against the frame, the way *Holland* had once, when Athos Dane first bound him. Broke him. The cage leached away most of Kell's power; the collar around his throat cut off the rest. There was a terror in Kell's eyes, a desperation that surprised him.

"Holland, you bastard, fight back!"

He tried, but his body was no longer his, and his mind, his tired mind, was sinking down, down—

Give in, said the shadow king.

"Show me you're not weak!" Kell's voice pushed through. "Prove you're not still a slave to someone else's will!"

You cannot fight me.

"Did you really come all the way back to lose like this?"

I've already won.

"Holland!"

Holland hated Kell, and in that moment, the hatred was almost enough to drive him up, but even if he wanted to rise to the other *Antari*'s bait, Osaron was unyielding.

Holland heard his own voice, then, but of course it wasn't his. A twisted imitation by the monster wearing his skin. In Holland's hand, a crimson coin, a token to another London, Kell's London, and Kell was swearing and throwing himself against his bonds until his chest heaved and his wrists were bloody.

Useless.

It was all useless.

Once again he was a prisoner in his own body. Kell's voice echoed through the dark.

You've just traded one master for another.

They were moving now, Osaron guiding Holland's body. The door closed behind them, but Kell's screams still hurled themselves against the wood, shattering into broken syllables and strangled cries.

Ojka stood in the hall, sharpening her knives. She looked up, revealing the crescent scar on one cheek, and her two-toned eyes, one yellow, the other black. An *Antari* forged by their hands—by their mercy.

"Your Majesty," she said, straightening.

Holland tried to rise up, tried to force his voice across their—*his*—lips, but when speech came, the words were Osaron's.

"Guard the door. Let no one pass."

A flicker of a smile across the red slash of Ojka's mouth. "As you wish."

The palace passed in a blur, and then they were outside, passing the statues of the Dane twins at the base of the stairs, moving swiftly beneath a bruised sky through a garden now flanked by trees instead of bodies.

What would become of it, without Osaron, without *him*? Would the city continue to flourish? Or would it collapse, like a body stripped of life?

Please, he begged silently. *This world needs me.*

"*There is no point,*" said Osaron aloud, and Holland felt sick to be the thought in their head instead of the word. "*It is already dead,*" continued the king. "*We will start over. We will find a world worthy of our strength.*"

They reached the garden wall and Osaron drew a dagger from the sheath at their waist. The bite of steel on flesh was nothing, as if Holland had been cut off from his very senses, buried too deep to feel anything but Osaron's grip. But as the shadow king's fingers streaked through the blood and lifted Kell's coin to the wall, Holland struggled up one last time.

He couldn't win back his body—not yet—not all of it—but perhaps he didn't need everything.

One hand. Five fingers.

He threw every ounce of strength, every shred of will, into that one limb, and halfway to the wall, it stopped, hovering in the air.

Blood trickled down his wrist. Holland knew the words to break a body, to turn it to ice, or ash, or stone.

All he had to do was guide his hand to his own chest.

All he had to do was shape the magic—

Holland could feel the annoyance ripple through Osaron. Annoyance, but not rage, as if this last stand, this great protest, was nothing but an itch.

How tedious.

Holland kept fighting, even managed to guide his hand an inch, two.

Let go, Holland, warned the creature in his head.

Holland forced the last of his will into his hand, dragging it another inch.

Osaron sighed.

It did not have to be this way.

Osaron's will hit him like a wall. His body didn't move, but his mind slammed backward, pinned beneath a crushing pain. Not the pain he'd felt a hundred times, the kind he'd learned to exist beyond, outside, the kind he might escape. This pain was rooted in his very core. It lit him up, sudden and bright, every nerve burning with such searing heat that he screamed and screamed and screamed inside his head, until the darkness finally—mercifully—closed over him, forcing him under and down.

And this time, Holland didn't try to surface.

This time, he let himself drown.

III

Kell kept throwing himself against the metal cage long after the door slammed shut and the bolt slid home. His voice still echoed against the pale stone walls. He had screamed himself hoarse. But still, no one came. Fear pounded through him, but what scared Kell most was the loosening in his chest—the unhinging of a vital link, the spreading sense of loss.

He could hardly feel his brother's pulse.

Could hardly feel anything but the pain in his wrists and a horrible numbing cold. He twisted against the metal frame, fighting the restraints, but they held fast. Spell work was scrawled down the sides of the contraption, and despite the quantity of Kell's blood smeared on the steel, there was the collar circling his throat, cutting off everything he needed. Everything he had. Everything he *was*. The collar cast a shadow over his mind, an icy film over his thoughts, cold dread and sorrow and, through it all, an absence of hope. Of strength. *Give up*, it whispered through his blood. *You have nothing. You are nothing. Powerless.*

He'd never been powerless.

He didn't know how to be powerless.

Panic rose in place of magic.

He had to get out.

Out of this cage.

Out of this collar.

Out of this world.

Rhy had carved a word into his own skin to bring Kell home, and he'd turned around and left again. Abandoned the prince, the crown, the city. Followed a woman in white through a door in the world because she told him he was needed, told him he could help, told him it was his fault, that he had to make it right.

Kell's heart faltered in his chest.

No—not *his* heart. Rhy's. A life bound to his with magic he no longer *had*. The panic flared again, a breath of heat against the numbing cold, and Kell clung to it, pushing back against the collar's hollow dread. He straightened in the frame, clenched his teeth and *pulled* against his cuffs until he felt the crack of bone inside his wrist, the tear of flesh. Blood fell in thick red drops to the stone floor, vibrant but useless. He bit back a scream as metal dragged over—and into—skin. Pain knifed up his arm, but he kept pulling, metal scraping muscle and then bone before his right hand finally came free.

Kell slumped back with a gasp and tried to wrap his bloody, limp fingers around the collar, but the moment they touched the metal, a horrible pins-and-needles cold seared up his arm, swam in his head.

"*As Steno,*" he pleaded. *Break.*

Nothing happened.

No power rose to meet the word.

Kell let out a sob and sagged against the frame. The room tilted and tunneled, and he felt his mind sliding toward darkness, but he forced his body to stay upright, forced himself to swallow the bile rising in his throat. He curled his skinned and splintered hand around his still-trapped arm, and began to pull.

It was minutes—but it felt like hours, years—before Kell finally tore himself free.

He stumbled forward out of the frame, and swayed on his feet. The metal cuffs had cut deep into his wrists—too deep—and the pale stone beneath his feet was slick with red.

Is this yours? whispered a voice.

A memory of Rhy's young face twisted in horror at the sight of Kell's ruined forearms, the blood streaked across the prince's chest. *Is this all yours?*

Now the collar dripped red as Kell frantically pulled on the metal.

His fingers ached with cold as he found the clasp and clawed at it, but still it held. His focus blurred. He slipped in his own blood and went down, catching himself with broken hands. Kell cried out, curling in on himself even as he screamed at his body to rise.

He had to get up.

He had to get back to Red London.

He had to stop Holland—stop *Osaron*.

He had to save Rhy.

He had to, he had to, he had to—but in that moment, all Kell could do was lie on the cold marble, warmth spreading in a thin red pool around him.

ABOUT THE AUTHOR

Jenna Maurice

VICTORIA "V. E." SCHWAB is the #1 *New York Times* bestselling author of more than twenty books, including the acclaimed novel *The Invisible Life of Addie LaRue*, the Shades of Magic series, the Villains series, and the Monsters of Verity duology. Her work has received critical acclaim; been featured in *The New York Times, Entertainment Weekly, The Washington Post,* and more; been translated into more than a dozen languages; and been optioned for television and film. When she's not haunting Paris streets or trudging up English hillsides, she lives in Edinburgh, Scotland, and is usually tucked into the corner of a coffee shop, dreaming up monsters.

veschwab.com
Twitter: @veschwab
Instagram: @veschwab

PRAISE FOR THE SHADES OF MAGIC SERIES

"Addictive and immersive, this series is a must-read."
—*Entertainment Weekly*

"Schwab has given us a gem of a tale that is original in its premise and compelling in its execution. This is a book to treasure."
—Deborah Harkness, *New York Times* bestselling author, on *A Darker Shade of Magic*

"Feels like a priceless object, brought from another, better world of fantasy books." —*io9* on *A Darker Shade of Magic*

"Compulsively readable . . . A world worth getting lost in."
—NPR

"This is how fantasy should be done. . . . A series that redefines epic." —*Publishers Weekly* (starred review)

"If you haven't picked up the Shades of Magic series before, do so. *A Darker Shade of Magic* is good; *A Gathering of Shadows* is better; *A Conjuring of Light* blows them both away." —*Culturess*

PRAISE FOR V. E. SCHWAB AND *THE INVISIBLE LIFE OF ADDIE LaRUE*

"The most joyous evocation of unlikely immortality."
—Neil Gaiman, *New York Times* bestselling author

"Completely absorbed me enough to make me forget the real world." —Jodi Picoult, *New York Times* bestselling author

"One of the most propulsive, compulsive, and captivating novels in recent memory." —*The Washington Post*

"This evocative and clever tale will leave you smiling, filled with love and longing for more magical moments in everyday life."
—CNN, Best Books of October 2020

"Schwab is simply one of the most skilled writers working in her genre." —*Tor.com*

TOR BOOKS BY V. E. SCHWAB

STANDALONES
The Invisible Life of Addie LaRue

THE VILLAINS SERIES
Vicious
Vengeful

THE SHADES OF MAGIC SERIES
A Darker Shade of Magic
A Gathering of Shadows
A Conjuring of Light

A DARKER SHADE OF MAGIC

V. E. SCHWAB

TOR PUBLISHING GROUP
NEW YORK

This is a work of fiction. All of the characters, organizations, and events portrayed in this novel are either products of the author's imagination or are used fictitiously.

A DARKER SHADE OF MAGIC

Copyright © 2015 by Victoria Schwab

All rights reserved.

A Tor Book
Published by Tom Doherty Associates / Tor Publishing Group
120 Broadway
New York, NY 10271

www.tor-forge.com

Tor® is a registered trademark of Macmillan Publishing Group, LLC.

The Library of Congress has cataloged the hardcover edition as follows:

Names: Schwab, Victoria, author.
Title: A darker shade of magic / V. E. Schwab.
Description: First edition. | New York : Tor, a Tom Doherty Associates book, 2015.
Identifiers: LCCN 2015004143 (print) | ISBN 9780765376459 (hardcover) | ISBN 9781466851375 (ebook)
Subjects: LCSH: Magic—Fiction. | Quantum theory—Fiction. | Other subjects: FICTION / Fantasy / Historical. | LCGFT: Science fiction. | Fantasy fiction.
Classification: LCC PS3619.C4848 D37 2015 (print) | DDC 813/.6—dc23
LC record available at https://lccn.loc.gov/2015004143

ISBN 978-1-250-89121-1 (second trade paperback)

Our books may be purchased in bulk for promotional, educational, or business use. Please contact your local bookseller or the Macmillan Corporate and Premium Sales Department at 1-800-221-7945, extension 5442, or by e-mail at MacmillanSpecialMarkets@macmillan.com.

Second Tor Paperback Edition: 2023

Printed in the United States of America

0 9 8 7 6 5 4 3

For the ones who dream of stranger worlds

Such is the quandary when it comes to magic, that it is not an issue of strength but of balance. For too little power, and we become weak. Too much, and we become something else entirely.

—TIEREN SERENSE,
head priest of the London Sanctuary

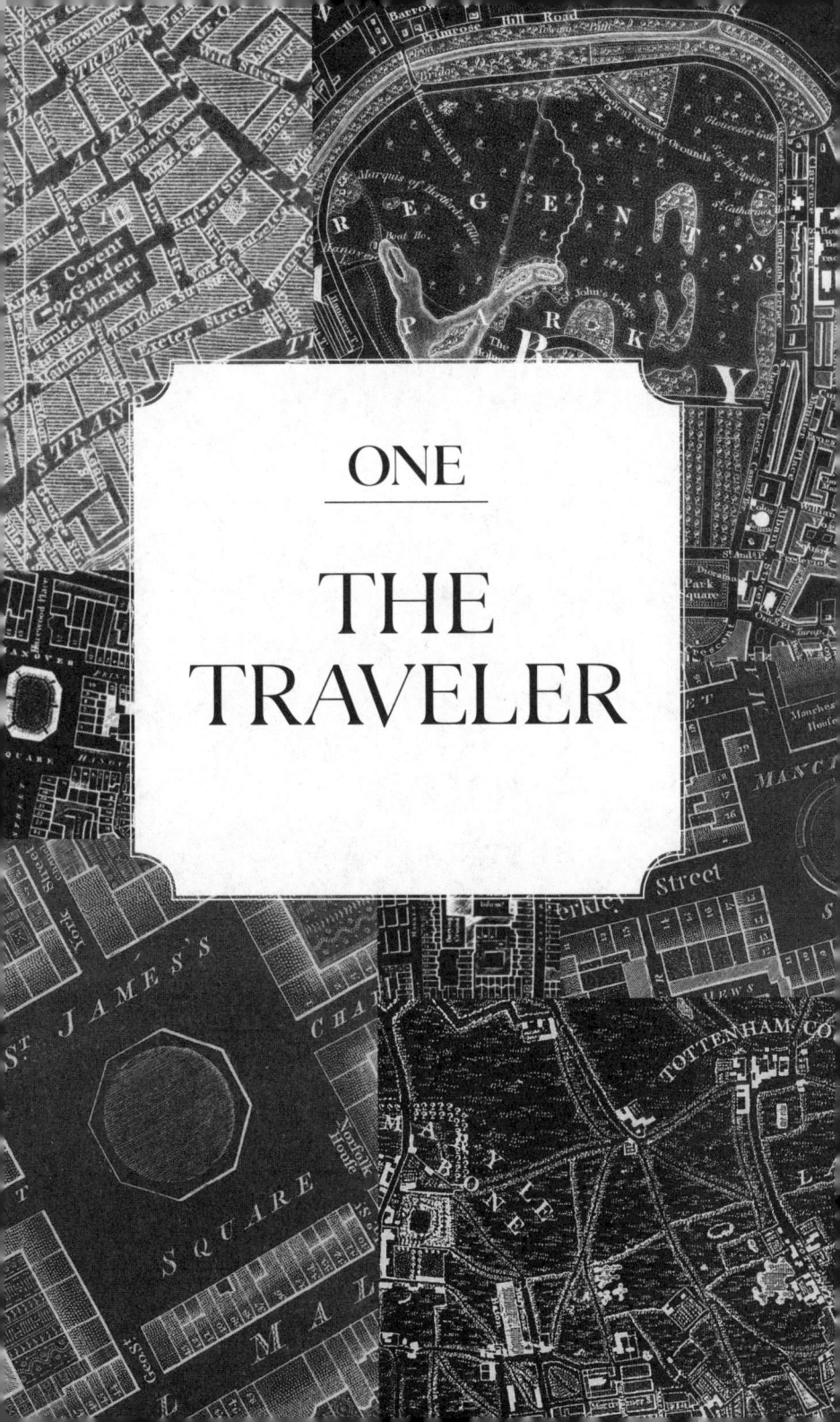

ONE

THE TRAVELER

I

Kell wore a very peculiar coat.

It had neither one side, which would be conventional, nor two, which would be unexpected, but *several,* which was, of course, impossible.

The first thing he did whenever he stepped out of one London and into another was take off the coat and turn it inside out once or twice (or even three times) until he found the side he needed. Not *all* of them were fashionable, but they each served a purpose. There were ones that blended in and ones that stood out, and one that served no purpose but of which he was just particularly fond.

So when Kell passed through the palace wall and into the anteroom, he took a moment to steady himself—it took its toll, moving between worlds—and then shrugged out of his red, high-collared coat and turned it inside out from right to left so that it became a simple black jacket. Well, a simple black jacket elegantly lined with silver thread and adorned with two gleaming columns of silver buttons. Just because he adopted a more modest palette when he was abroad (wishing neither to offend the local royalty nor to draw attention) didn't mean he had to sacrifice style.

Oh, kings, thought Kell as he fastened the buttons on the coat. He was starting to think like Rhy.

On the wall behind him, he could just make out the ghosted symbol made by his passage. Like a footprint in sand, already fading.

He'd never bothered to mark the door from *this* side, simply because he never went back this way. Windsor's distance from London was terribly inconvenient considering the fact that, when traveling between worlds, Kell could only move between a place in one and the same *exact* place in another. Which was a problem because there was no Windsor Castle a day's journey from *Red* London. In fact, Kell had just come through the stone wall of a courtyard belonging to a wealthy gentleman in a town called Disan. Disan was, on the whole, a very pleasant place.

Windsor was not.

Impressive, to be sure. But not pleasant.

A marble counter ran against the wall, and on it a basin of water waited for him, as it always did. He rinsed his bloody hand, as well as the silver crown he'd used for passage, then slipped the cord it hung on over his head, and tucked the coin back beneath his collar. In the hall beyond, he could hear the shuffle of feet, the low murmur of servants and guards. He'd chosen the anteroom specifically to avoid them. He knew very well how little the Prince Regent liked him being here, and the last thing Kell wanted was an audience, a cluster of ears and eyes and mouths reporting the details of his visit back to the throne.

Above the counter and the basin hung a mirror in a gilded frame, and Kell checked his reflection quickly—his hair, a reddish brown, swept down across one eye, and he did not fix it, though he did take a moment to smooth the shoulders of his coat—before passing through a set of doors to meet his host.

The room was stiflingly warm—the windows latched despite what looked like a lovely October day—and a fire raged oppressively in the hearth.

George III sat beside it, a robe dwarfing his withered frame and a tea tray untouched before his knees. When Kell came in, the king gripped the edges of his chair.

"Who's there?" he called out without turning. "Robbers? Ghosts?"

"I don't believe ghosts would answer, Your Majesty," said Kell, announcing himself.

The ailing king broke into a rotting grin. "Master Kell," he said. "You've kept me waiting."

"No more than a month," he said, stepping forward.

King George squinted his blind eyes. "It's been longer, I'm sure."

"I promise, it hasn't."

"Maybe not for *you*," said the king. "But time isn't the same for the mad and the blind."

Kell smiled. The king was in good form today. It wasn't always so. He was never sure what state he'd find his majesty in. Perhaps it had seemed like more than a month because the last time Kell visited, the king had been in one of his moods, and Kell had barely been able to calm his fraying nerves long enough to deliver his message.

"Maybe it's the year that has changed," continued the king, "and not the month."

"Ah, but the year is the same."

"And what year is that?"

Kell's brow furrowed. "Eighteen nineteen," he said.

A cloud passed across King George's face, and then he simply shook his head and said, "Time," as if that one word could be to blame for everything. "Sit, sit," he added, gesturing at the room. "There must be another chair here somewhere."

There wasn't. The room was shockingly sparse, and Kell was certain the doors in the hall were locked and unlocked from without, not within.

The king held out a gnarled hand. They'd taken away his

rings, to keep him from hurting himself, and his nails were cut to nothing.

"My letter," he said, and for an instant Kell saw a glimmer of George as he once was. Regal.

Kell patted the pockets of his coat and realized he'd forgotten to take the notes out before changing. He shrugged out of the jacket and returned it for a moment to its red self, digging through its folds until he found the envelope. When he pressed it into the king's hand, the latter fondled it and caressed the wax seal—the red throne's emblem, a chalice with a rising sun—then brought the paper to his nose and inhaled.

"Roses," he said wistfully.

He meant the magic. Kell never noticed the faint aromatic scent of Red London clinging to his clothes, but whenever he traveled, someone invariably told him that he smelled like freshly cut flowers. Some said tulips. Others stargazers. Chrysanthemums. Peonies. To the king of England, it was always roses. Kell was glad to know it was a pleasant scent, even if he couldn't smell it. He could smell Grey London (smoke) and White London (blood), but to him, Red London simply smelled like home.

"Open it for me," instructed the king. "But don't mar the seal."

Kell did as he was told, and withdrew the contents. For once, he was grateful the king could no longer see, so he could not know how brief the letter was. Three short lines. A courtesy paid to an ailing figurehead, but nothing more.

"It's from my queen," explained Kell.

The king nodded. "Go on," he commanded, affecting a stately countenance that warred with his fragile form and his faltering voice. *"Go on."*

Kell swallowed. "'Greetings to his majesty, King George III,'" he read, "'from a neighboring throne.'"

The queen did not refer to it as the *red* throne, or send greetings from *Red* London (even though the city was in fact quite crimson, thanks to the rich, pervasive light of the river), because she did not think of it that way. To her, and to everyone else who inhabited only one London, there was little need to differentiate among them. When the rulers of one conversed with those of another, they simply called them *others,* or *neighbors,* or on occasion (and particularly in regard to White London) less flattering terms.

Only those few who could move among the Londons needed a way to keep them straight. And so Kell—inspired by the lost city known to all as Black London—had given each remaining capital a color.

Grey for the magic-less city.

Red, for the healthy empire.

White, for the starving world.

In truth, the cities themselves bore little resemblance to one another (and the countries around and beyond bore even less). The fact they were all called *London* was its own mystery, though the prevailing theory was that one of the cities had taken the name long ago, before the doors were all sealed and the only things allowed through were letters between kings and queens. As to which city had first laid claim to the name, none could agree.

"'We hope to learn that you are well,'" continued the queen's letter, "'and that the season is as fair in your city as it is in ours.'"

Kell paused. There was nothing more, save a signature. King George wrung his hands.

"Is that all it says?" he asked.

Kell hesitated. "No," he said, folding the letter. "That's only the beginning."

He cleared his throat and began to pace as he pulled his

thoughts together and put them into the queen's voice. "Thank you for asking after our family, she says. The King and I are well. Prince Rhy, on the other hand, continues to impress and infuriate in equal measure, but has at least gone the month without breaking his neck or taking an unsuitable bride. Thanks be to Kell alone for keeping him from doing either, or both."

Kell had every intention of letting the queen linger on his own merits, but just then the clock on the wall chimed five, and Kell swore under his breath. He was running late.

"Until my next letter," he finished hurriedly, "stay happy and stay well. With fondness. Her Highness Emira, Queen of Arnes."

Kell waited for the king to say something, but his blind eyes had a steady, faraway look, and Kell feared he had lost him. He set the folded note on the tea tray and was halfway to the wall when the king spoke up.

"I don't have a letter for her," he murmured.

"That's all right," said Kell softly. The king hadn't been able to write one for years. Some months he tried, dragging the quill haphazardly across the parchment, and some months he insisted on having Kell transcribe, but most months he simply told Kell the message and Kell promised to remember.

"You see, I didn't have the time," added the king, trying to salvage a vestige of his dignity. Kell let him have it.

"I understand," he said. "I'll give the royal family your regards."

Kell turned again to go, and again the old king called out to stop him.

"Wait, wait," he said. "Come back."

Kell paused. His eyes went to the clock. Late, and getting later. He pictured the Prince Regent sitting at his table in St. James, gripping his chair and quietly stewing. The thought made Kell smile, so he turned back toward the king as the latter pulled something from his robe with fumbling fingers.

It was a coin.

"It's fading," said the king, cupping the metal in his weathered hands as if it were precious and fragile. "I can't feel the magic anymore. Can't smell it."

"A coin is a coin, Your Majesty."

"Not so and you know it," grumbled the old king. "Turn out your pockets."

Kell sighed. "You'll get me in trouble."

"Come, come," said the king. "Our little secret."

Kell dug his hand into his pocket. The first time he had visited the king of England, he'd given him a coin as proof of who he was and where he came from. The story of the other Londons was entrusted to the crown and handed down heir to heir, but it had been years since a traveler had come. King George had taken one look at the sliver of a boy and squinted and held out his meaty hand, and Kell had set the coin in his palm. It was a simple lin, much like a grey shilling, only marked with a red star instead of a royal face. The king closed his fist over the coin and brought it to his nose, inhaling its scent. And then he'd smiled, and tucked the coin into his coat, and welcomed Kell inside.

From that day on, every time Kell paid his visit, the king would insist the magic had worn off the coin, and make him trade it for another, one new and pocket-warm. Every time Kell would say it was forbidden (it was, expressly), and every time the king would insist that it could be their little secret, and Kell would sigh and fetch a fresh bit of metal from his coat.

Now he plucked the old lin out of the king's palm and replaced it with a new one, folding George's gnarled fingers gently over it.

"Yes, yes," cooed the ailing king to the coin in his palm.

"Take care," said Kell as he turned to go.

"Yes, yes," said the king, his focus fading until he was lost to the world, and to his guest.

Curtains gathered in the corner of the room, and Kell pulled the heavy material aside to reveal a mark on the patterned wallpaper. A simple circle, bisected by a line, drawn in blood a month ago. On another wall in another room in another palace, the same mark stood. They were as handles on opposite sides of the same door.

Kell's blood, when paired with the token, allowed him to move *between* the worlds. He needn't specify a place because wherever he was, that's where he'd be. But to make a door *within* a world, both sides had to be marked by the same exact symbol. Close wasn't close enough. Kell had learned that the hard way.

The symbol on the wall was still clear from his last visit, the edges only slightly smeared, but it didn't matter. It had to be redone.

He rolled up his sleeve and freed the knife he kept strapped to the inside of his forearm. It was a lovely thing, that knife, a work of art, silver from tip to hilt and monogrammed with the letters *K* and *L*.

The only relic from another life.

A life he didn't know. Or at least, didn't remember.

Kell brought the blade to the back of his forearm. He'd already carved one line today, for the door that brought him this far. Now he carved a second. His blood, a rich ruby red, welled up and over, and he returned the knife to its sheath and touched his fingers to the cut and then to the wall, redrawing the circle and the line that ran through it. Kell guided his sleeve down over the wound—he'd treat all the cuts once he was home—and cast a last glance back at the babbling king before pressing his palm flat to the mark on the wall.

It hummed with magic.

"As Tascen," he said. *Transfer.*

The patterned paper rippled and softened and gave way under his touch, and Kell stepped forward and through.

II

Between one stride and the next, dreary Windsor became elegant St. James. The stuffy cell of a room gave way to bright tapestries and polished silver, and the mad king's mumblings were replaced by a heavy quiet and a man sitting at the head of an ornate table, gripping a goblet of wine and looking thoroughly put out.

"You're late," observed the Prince Regent.

"Apologies," said Kell with a too-short bow. "I had an errand."

The Prince Regent set down his cup. "I thought *I* was your errand, Master Kell."

Kell straightened. "My orders, Your Highness, are to see to the *king* first."

"I wish you wouldn't indulge him," said the Prince Regent, whose name was also George (Kell found the Grey London habit of sons taking father's names both redundant and confusing) with a dismissive wave of his hand. "It gets his spirits up."

"Is that a bad thing?" asked Kell.

"For him, yes. He'll be in a frenzy later. Dancing on the tables talking of magic and other Londons. What trick did you do for him this time? Convince him he could fly?"

Kell had only made that mistake once. He learned on his next visit that the King of England had nearly walked out a window. On the third floor. "I assure you I gave no demonstrations."

Prince George pinched the bridge of his nose. "He cannot hold his tongue the way he used to. It's why he is confined to quarters."

"Imprisoned, then?"

Prince George ran his hand along the table's gilded edge. "Windsor is a perfectly respectable place to be kept."

A respectable prison is still a prison, thought Kell, withdrawing a second letter from his coat pocket. "Your correspondence."

The prince forced him to stand there as he read the note (he never commented on the way it smelled of flowers), and then as he withdrew a half-finished reply from the inside pocket of his coat and completed it. He was clearly taking his time in an effort to spite Kell, but Kell didn't mind. He occupied himself by drumming his fingers on the edge of the gilded table. Each time he made it from pinky to forefinger, one of the room's many candles went out.

"Must be a draft," he said absently while the Prince Regent's grip tightened on his quill. By the time he finished the note, he'd broken two and was in a bad mood, while Kell found his own disposition greatly improved.

He held out his hand for the letter, but the Prince Regent did not give it to him. Instead, he pushed up from his table. "I'm stiff from sitting. Walk with me."

Kell wasn't a fan of the idea, but since he couldn't very well leave empty-handed, he was forced to oblige. But not before pocketing the prince's latest unbroken quill from the table.

"Will you go straight back?" asked the prince as he led Kell down a hall to a discreet door half concealed by a curtain.

"Soon," said Kell, trailing by a stride. Two members of the royal guard had joined them in the hall and now slunk behind like shadows. Kell could feel their eyes on him, and he wondered how much they'd been told about their guest. The royals were always expected to know, but the understanding of those in their service was left to their discretion.

"I thought your only business was with me," said the prince.

"I'm a fan of your city," responded Kell lightly. "And what I do is draining. I'll go for a walk and get some air, then make my way back."

The prince's mouth was a thin grim line. "I fear the air is not as replenishing here in the city as in the countryside. What is it you call us . . . *Grey* London? These days that is far too apt a name. Stay for dinner." The prince ended nearly every sentence with a period. Even the questions. Rhy was the same way, and Kell thought it must simply be a by-product of never being told *no*.

"You'll fare better here," pressed the prince. "Let me revive you with wine and company."

It seemed a kind enough offer, but the Prince Regent didn't do things out of kindness.

"I cannot stay," said Kell.

"I insist. The table is set."

And who is coming? wondered Kell. What did the prince want? To put him on display? Kell often suspected that he would like to do as much, if for no other reason than that the younger George found secrets cumbersome, preferring spectacle. But for all his faults, the prince wasn't a fool, and only a fool would give someone like Kell a chance to stand out. Grey London had forgotten magic long ago. Kell wouldn't be the one to remind them of it.

"A lavish kindness, your highness, but I am better left a specter than made a show." Kell tipped his head so that his copper hair tumbled out of his eyes, revealing not only the crisp blue of the left one but the solid black of the right. A black that ran edge to edge, filling white and iris both. There was nothing human about that eye. It was pure magic. The mark of a blood magician. Of an *Antari*.

Kell relished what he saw in the Prince Regent's eyes when they tried to hold Kell's gaze. Caution, discomfort . . . and fear.

"Do you know why our worlds are kept separate, Your Highness?" He didn't wait for the prince to answer. "It is to keep yours safe. You see, there was a time, ages ago, when they were not so separate. When doors ran between your world and mine, and others, and anyone with a bit of power could pass through. Magic itself could pass through. But the thing about magic," added Kell, "is that it preys on the strong-minded and the weak-willed, and one of the worlds couldn't stop itself. The people fed on the magic and the magic fed on them until it ate their bodies and their minds and then their souls."

"Black London," whispered the Prince Regent.

Kell nodded. He hadn't given that city its color mark. Everyone—at least everyone in Red London and White, and those few in Grey who knew anything at all—knew the legend of Black London. It was a bedtime story. A fairy tale. A *warning*. Of the city—and the world—that wasn't, anymore.

"Do you know what Black London and yours have in common, Your Highness?" The Prince Regent's eyes narrowed, but he didn't interrupt. "Both lack temperance," said Kell. "Both hunger for power. The only reason your London still exists is because it was cut off. It learned to forget. You do not want it to remember." What Kell didn't say was that Black London had a wealth of magic in its veins, and Grey London hardly any; he wanted to make a point. And by the looks of it, he had. This time, when he held out his hand for the letter, the prince didn't refuse, or even resist. Kell tucked the parchment into his pocket along with the stolen quill.

"Thank you, as ever, for your hospitality," he said, offering an exaggerated bow.

The Prince Regent summoned a guard with a single snap of his fingers. "See that Master Kell gets where he is going." And then, without another word, he turned and strode away.

The royal guards left Kell at the edge of the park. St. James Palace loomed behind him. Grey London lay ahead. He took a deep breath and tasted smoke on the air. As eager as he was to get back home, he had some business to attend to, and after dealing with the king's ailments and the prince's attitude, Kell could use a drink. He brushed off his sleeves, straightened his collar, and set out toward the heart of the city.

His feet carried him through St. James Park, down an ambling dirt path that ran beside the river. The sun was setting, and the air was crisp if not clean, a fall breeze fluttering the edges of his black coat. He came upon a wooden footbridge that spanned the stream, and his boots sounded softly as he crossed it. Kell paused at the arc of the bridge, Buckingham House lantern-lit behind him and the Thames ahead. Water sloshed gently under the wooden slats, and he rested his elbows on the rail and stared down at it. When he flexed his fingers absently, the current stopped, the water stilling, smooth as glass, beneath him.

He considered his reflection.

"You're not *that* handsome," Rhy would say whenever he caught Kell gazing into a mirror.

"I can't get enough of myself," Kell would answer, even though he was never looking at himself—not *all* of himself anyway—only his eye. His right one. Even in Red London, where magic flourished, the eye set him apart. Marked him always as *other*.

A tinkling laugh sounded off to Kell's right, followed by a grunt, and a few other, less distinct noises, and the tension went out of his hand, the stream surging back into motion beneath him. He continued on until the park gave way to the streets of London, and then the looming form of Westminster. Kell had a fondness for the abbey, and he nodded to it, as if to an old friend. Despite the city's soot and dirt, its clutter and its poor, it had something Red London lacked: a resistance to change. An appreciation for the enduring, and the effort it took to make something so.

How many years had it taken to construct the abbey? How many more would it stand? In Red London, tastes turned as often as seasons, and with them, buildings went up and came down and went up again in different forms. Magic made things simple. *Sometimes,* thought Kell, *it made things* too *simple.*

There had been nights back home when he felt like he went to bed in one place and woke up in another.

But here, Westminster Abbey always stood, waiting to greet him.

He made his way past the towering stone structure, through the streets, crowded with carriages, and down a narrow road that hugged the dean's yard, walled by mossy stone. The narrow road grew narrower still before it finally stopped in front of a tavern.

And here Kell stopped, too, and shrugged out of his coat. He turned it once more from right to left, exchanging the black affair with silver buttons for a more modest, street-worn look: a brown high-collared jacket with fraying hems and scuffed elbows. He patted the pockets and, satisfied that he was ready, went inside.

III

The Stone's Throw was an odd little tavern.

Its walls were dingy and its floors were stained, and Kell knew for a fact that its owner, Barron, watered down the drinks, but despite it all, he kept coming back.

It fascinated him, this place, because despite its grungy appearance and grungier customers, the fact was that, by luck or design, the Stone's Throw was *always there.* The name changed, of course, and so did the drinks it served, but at this very spot in Grey, Red, and White London alike, stood a tavern. It wasn't a *source,* per se, not like the Thames, or Stonehenge, or the dozens of lesser-known beacons of magic in the world, but it was *something.* A phenomenon. A fixed point.

And since Kell conducted his affairs in the tavern (whether the sign read the Stone's Throw, or the Setting Sun, or the Scorched Bone), it made Kell himself a kind of fixed point, too.

Few people would appreciate the poetry. Holland might. If Holland appreciated anything.

But poetry aside, the tavern was a perfect place to do business. Grey London's rare believers—those whimsical few who clung to the idea of magic, who caught hold of a whisper or a whiff—gravitated here, drawn by the sense of something else, something more. Kell was drawn to it, too. The difference was that *he* knew what was tugging at them.

Of course, the magically inclined patrons of the Stone's Throw weren't drawn only by the subtle, bone-deep pull of power, or the promise of something different, something more. They were also drawn by *him*. Or at least, the rumor of him. Word of mouth was its own kind of magic, and here, in the Stone's Throw, word of *the magician* passed men's lips as often as the diluted ale.

He studied the amber liquid in his own cup.

"Evening, Kell," said Barron, pausing to top off his drink.

"Evening, Barron," said Kell.

It was as much as they ever said to each other.

The owner of the Stone's Throw was built like a brick wall—if a brick wall decided to grow a beard—tall and wide and impressively steady. No doubt Barron had seen his share of strange, but it never seemed to faze him.

Or if it did, he knew how to keep it to himself.

A clock on the wall behind the counter struck seven, and Kell pulled a trinket from his now-worn brown coat. It was a wooden box, roughly the size of his palm and fastened with a simple metal clasp. When he undid the clasp and slid the lid off with his thumb, the box unfolded into a game board with five grooves, each of which held an element.

In the first groove, a lump of earth.

In the second, a spoon's worth of water.

In the third, in place of air, sat a thimble of loose sand.

In the fourth, a drop of oil, highly flammable.

And in the fifth, final groove, a bit of bone.

Back in Kell's world, the box and its contents served not only as a toy, but as a test, a way for children to discover which elements they were drawn to, and which were drawn to them. Most quickly outgrew the game, moving on to either spellwork or larger, more complicated versions as they honed their skills. Because of both its prevalence and its limitations, the element set could be found in almost every household in Red London, and most likely in the villages beyond, (though Kell could not be certain). But here, in a city without magic, it was truly rare, and Kell was certain his client would approve. After all, the man was a Collector.

In Grey London, only two kinds of people came to find Kell. Collectors and Enthusiasts.

Collectors were wealthy and bored and usually had no interest in magic itself—they wouldn't know the difference between a healing rune and a binding spell—and Kell enjoyed their patronage immensely.

Enthusiasts were more troublesome. They fancied themselves true magicians, and wanted to purchase trinkets, not for the sake of owning them or for the luxury of putting them on display, but for *use*. Kell did not like Enthusiasts—in part because he found their aspirations wasted, and in part because serving them felt so much closer to treason—which is why, when a young man came to sit beside him, and Kell looked up, expecting his Collector client and finding instead an unknown Enthusiast, his mood soured considerably.

"Seat taken?" asked the Enthusiast, even though he was already sitting.

"Go away," said Kell evenly.

But the Enthusiast did not leave.

Kell knew the man was an Enthusiast—he was gangly and awkward, his jacket a fraction too short for his build, and when he brought his long arms to rest on the counter and the fabric inched up, Kell could make out the end of a tattoo. A poorly drawn power rune meant to bind magic to one's body.

"Is it true?" the Enthusiast persisted. "What they say?"

"Depends on who's talking," said Kell, closing the box, sliding the lid and clasp back into place, "and what's being said." He had done this dance a hundred times. Out of the corner of his blue eye he watched the man's lips choreograph his next move. If he'd been a Collector, Kell might have cut him some slack, but men who waded into waters claiming they could swim should not need a raft.

"That you bring *things*," said the Enthusiast, eyes darting around the tavern. "*Things* from other places."

Kell took a sip of his drink, and the Enthusiast took his silence for assent.

"I suppose I should introduce myself," the man went on. "Edward Archibald Tuttle, the third. But I go by Ned." Kell raised a brow. The young Enthusiast was obviously waiting for him to respond with an introduction of his own, but as the man clearly already had a notion of who he was, Kell bypassed the formalities and said, "What do you want?"

Edward Archibald—*Ned*—twisted in his seat, and leaned in conspiratorially. "I'm looking for a bit of earth."

Kell tipped his glass toward the door. "Check the park."

The young man managed a low, uncomfortable laugh. Kell finished his drink. *A bit of earth.* It seemed like a small request. It wasn't. Most Enthusiasts knew that their own world held little power, but many believed that possessing a piece of *another* world would allow them to tap into its magic.

And there was a time when they would have been right. A time when the doors stood open at the sources, and power flowed between the worlds, and anyone with a bit of magic in their veins and a token from another world could not only tap into that power, but could also move with it, step from one London to another.

But that time was gone.

The doors were gone. Destroyed centuries ago, after Black London fell and took the rest of its world with it, leaving nothing but stories in its wake. Now only the *Antari* possessed enough power to make new doors, and even then only they could pass through them. *Antari* had always been rare, but none knew *how* rare until the doors were closed, and their numbers began to wane. The source of *Antari* power had always been a mystery (it followed no bloodline) but one thing was certain: the longer the worlds were kept apart, the fewer *Antari* emerged.

Now, Kell and Holland seemed to be the last of a rapidly dying breed.

"Well?" pressed Ned. "Will you bring me the earth or not?"

Kell's eyes went to the tattoo on the Enthusiast's wrist. What so many Grey-worlders didn't seem to grasp was that a spell was only as strong as the person casting it. How strong was this one?

A smiled tugged at the corner of Kell's lips as he nudged the game box in the man's direction. "Know what that is?"

Ned lifted the child's game gingerly, as if it might burst into flames at any moment (Kell briefly considered igniting it, but restrained himself). He fiddled with the box until his fingers found the clasp and the board fell open on the counter. The elements glittered in the flickering pub light.

"Tell you what," said Kell. "Choose one element. Move it from its notch—without touching it, of course—and I'll bring you your dirt."

Ned's brow furrowed. He considered the options, then jabbed a finger at the water. "That one."

At least he wasn't fool enough to try for the bone, thought Kell. Air, earth, and water were the easiest to will—even Rhy, who showed no affinity whatsoever, could manage to rouse those. Fire was a bit trickier, but by far, the hardest piece to move was the bit of bone. And for good reason. Those who could move bones could move bodies. It was strong magic, even in Red London.

Kell watched as Ned's hand hovered over the game board. He began to whisper to the water under his breath in a language that might have been Latin, or gibberish, but surely wasn't the King's English. Kell's mouth quirked. Elements had no tongue, or rather, they could be spoken to in any. The words themselves were less important than the focus they brought to the speaker's mind, the connection they helped to form, the *power* they tapped into. In short, the language did not matter, only the *intention* did. The Enthusiast could have spoken to the water in plain English (for all the good it would do him) and yet he muttered on in his invented language. And as he did, he moved his hand clockwise over the small board.

Kell sighed, and propped his elbow on the counter and rested his head on his hand while Ned struggled, face turning red from the effort.

After several long moments, the water gave a single ripple (it could have been caused by Kell yawning or the man gripping the counter) and then went still.

Ned stared down at the board, veins bulging. His hand closed into a fist, and for a moment Kell worried he'd smash the little game, but his knuckles came down beside it, hard.

"Oh well," said Kell.

"It's rigged," growled Ned.

Kell lifted his head from his hand. "Is it?" he asked. He flexed his fingers a fraction, and the clod of earth rose from its groove and drifted casually into his palm. "Are you certain?" he added as a small gust caught up the sand and swirled it into the air, circling his wrist. "Maybe it is"—the water drew itself up into a drop and then turned to ice in his palm—"or maybe it's not. . . ." he added as the oil caught fire in its groove.

"Maybe . . ." said Kell as the piece of bone rose into the air, ". . . you simply lack any semblance of power."

Ned gaped at him as the five elements each performed their own small dance around Kell's fingers. He could hear Rhy's chiding: *Show-off.* And then, as casually as he'd willed the pieces up, he let them fall. The earth and ice hit their grooves with a thud and a clink while the sand settled soundlessly in its bowl and the flame dancing on the oil died. Only the bone was left, hovering in the air between them. Kell considered it, all the while feeling the weight of the Enthusiast's hungry gaze.

"How much for it?" he demanded.

"Not for sale," answered Kell, then corrected himself, "Not for you."

Ned shoved up from his stool and turned to go, but Kell wasn't done with him yet.

"If I brought you your dirt," he said, "what would you give me for it?"

He watched the Enthusiast freeze in his steps. "Name your price."

"My price?" Kell didn't smuggle trinkets between worlds for the *money*. Money changed. What would he do with shillings in Red London? And pounds? He'd have better luck burning them than trying to buy anything with them in the White alleys. He supposed he could spend the money here, but what ever would he spend it *on*? No, Kell was playing a different game. "I don't want your money," he said. "I want something that matters. Something you don't want to lose."

Ned nodded hastily. "Fine. Stay here and I'll—"

"Not tonight," said Kell.

"Then when?"

Kell shrugged. "Within the month."

"You expect me to sit here and *wait*?"

"I don't *expect* you to do anything," said Kell with a shrug. It was cruel, he knew, but he wanted to see how far the Enthusiast was willing to go. And if his resolve held firm and he were here next month, decided Kell, he would bring the man his bag of earth. "Run along now."

Ned's mouth opened and closed, and then he huffed, and trudged off, nearly knocking into a small, bespectacled man on his way out.

Kell plucked the bit of bone out of the air and returned it to its box as the bespectacled man approached the now-vacant stool.

"What was that about?" he asked, taking the seat.

"Nothing of bother," said Kell.

"Is that for me?" asked the man, nodding at the game box.

Kell nodded and offered it to the Collector, who lifted it gingerly from his hand. He let the gentleman fiddle with it, then proceeded to show him how it worked. The Collector's eyes widened. "Splendid, splendid."

And then the man dug into his pocket and withdrew a folded kerchief. It made a thud when he set it on the counter. Kell reached out and unwrapped the parcel to find a glimmering silver box with a miniature crank on the side.

A *music* box. Kell smiled to himself.

They had music in Red London, and music boxes, too, but most of theirs played by enchantment, not cog, and Kell was rather taken by the effort that went into the little machines. So much of the Grey world was clunky, but now and then its lack of magic led to ingenuity. Take its music boxes. A complex but elegant design. So many parts, so much work, all to create a little tune.

"Do you need me to explain it to you?" asked the Collector.

Kell shook his head. "No," he said softly. "I have several."

The man's brow knit. "Will it still do?"

Kell nodded and began to fold the kerchief over the trinket to keep it safe.

"Don't you want to hear it?"

Kell did, but not here in the dingy little tavern, where the sound could not be savored. Besides, it was time to go home.

He left the Collector at the counter, tinkering with the child's game—marveling at the way that neither the melted ice nor the sand spilled out of their grooves, no matter how he shook the box—and stepped out into the night. Kell made his way toward the Thames, listening to the sounds of the city around him, the nearby carriages and faraway cries, some in pleasure, some in pain (though they were still nothing compared to the screams that carried through White London). The river soon came into sight, a streak of black in the night as church bells rang out in the distance, eight of them in all.

Time to go.

He reached the brick wall of a shop that faced the water, and stopped in its shadow, pushing up his sleeve. His arm had started to ache from the first two cuts, but he drew out his knife and carved a third, touching his fingers first to the blood and then to the wall.

One of the cords around his throat held a red lin, like the one King George had returned to him that afternoon, and he took hold of the coin and pressed it to the blood on the bricks.

"Well, then," he said. "Let's go home." He often found himself speaking to the magic. Not commanding, simply conversing. Magic was a living thing—that, everyone knew—but to Kell it felt like more, like a friend, like family. It was, after all, a part of him (much more than it was a part of most) and he couldn't help feeling like it knew what he was saying, what he was feeling, not only when he summoned it, but always, in every heartbeat and every breath.

He was, after all, *Antari*.

And *Antari* could speak to blood. To life. To magic itself. The first and final element, the one that lived in all and was of none.

He could feel the magic stir against his palm, the brick wall warming and cooling at the same time with it, and Kell hesitated, waiting to see if it would answer without being asked.

But it held, waiting for him to give voice to his command. Elemental magic may speak any tongue, but *Antari* magic—true magic, blood magic—spoke one, and only one. Kell flexed his fingers on the wall.

"As Travars," he said. *Travel.*

This time, the magic listened, and obeyed. The world rippled, and Kell stepped forward through the door and into darkness, shrugging off Grey London like a coat.

TWO

RED ROYAL

I

"Sanct!" announced Gen, throwing a card down onto the pile, faceup. On its front, a hooded figure with a bowed head held up a rune like a chalice, and in his chair, Gen grinned triumphantly.

Parrish grimaced and threw his remaining cards facedown on the table. He could accuse Gen of cheating, but there was no point. Parrish himself had been cheating for the better part of an hour and still hadn't won a single hand. He grumbled as he shoved his coins across the narrow table to the other guard's towering pile. Gen gathered up the winnings and began to shuffle the deck. "Shall we go again?" he asked.

"I'll pass," answered Parrish, shoving to his feet. A cloak—heavy panels of red and gold fanning like rays of sun—spilled over his armored shoulders as he stood, the layered metal plates of his chest piece and leg guards clanking as they slid into place.

"*Ir chas era,*" said Gen, sliding from Royal into Arnesian. The common tongue.

"I'm not bitter," grumbled Parrish back. "I'm broke."

"Come on," goaded Gen. "Third time's the charm."

"I have to piss," said Parrish, readjusting his short sword.

"Then go piss."

Parrish hesitated, surveying the hall for signs of trouble. The hall was devoid of trouble—or any other forms of activity—but full of pretty things: royal portraits, trophies, tables (like the one they'd been playing on), and, at the hall's end, a pair of ornate doors. Made of cherrywood, the doors were carved with the royal emblem of Arnes, the chalice and rising sun, the grooves filled with melted gold, and above the emblem, the threads of metallic light traced an *R* across the polished wood.

The doors led to Prince Rhy's private chambers, and Gen and Parrish, as part of Prince Rhy's private guard, had been stationed outside of them.

Parrish was fond of the prince. He was spoiled, of course, but so was every royal—or so Parrish assumed, having served only the one—but he was also good-natured and exceedingly lenient when it came to his guard (hell, he'd given Parrish the deck of cards himself, beautiful, gilded-edge things) and sometimes, after a night of drinking, would shed his Royal and its pretentions and converse with them in the common tongue (his Arnesian was flawless). If anything, Rhy seemed to feel guilty for the persistent presence of the guards, as if surely they had something better to do with their time than stand outside his door and be vigilant (and in truth, most nights it was more a matter of discretion than vigilance).

The best nights were the ones when Prince Rhy and Master Kell set out into the city, and he and Gen were allowed to follow at a distance or relieved of their duties entirely and allowed to stay for company rather than protection (everyone knew that Kell could keep the prince safer than any of his guard). But Kell was still away—a fact that had put the ever-restless Rhy in a mood—and so the prince had withdrawn early to his chambers, and Parrish and Gen had taken up their watch, and Gen had robbed Parrish of most of his pocket money.

Parrish scooped up his helmet from the table, and went to relieve himself; the sound of Gen counting his coins followed him out. Parrish took his time, feeling he was owed as much after losing so many lin, and when he finally ambled back to the prince's hall, he was distressed to find it empty. Gen was nowhere to be seen. Parrish frowned; leniency went only so far. Gambling was one thing, but if the prince's chambers were caught unguarded, their captain would be furious.

The cards were still on the table, and Parrish began to clean them up when he heard a male voice in the prince's chamber and stopped. It was not a strange thing to hear, in and of itself—Rhy was prone to entertaining and made little secret of his varied tastes, and it was hardly Parrish's place to question his proclivities.

But Parrish recognized the voice at once; it did not belong to one of Rhy's pursuits. The words were English, but accented, the edges rougher than an Arnesian tongue.

It was a voice like a shadow in the woods at night. Quiet and dark and cold.

And it belonged to Holland. The *Antari* from afar.

Parrish paled a little. He worshipped Master Kell—a fact Gen gave him grief for daily—but Holland terrified him. He didn't know if it was the evenness in the man's tone or his strangely faded appearance or his haunted eyes—one black, of course, the other a milky green. Or perhaps it was the way he seemed to be made more of water and stone than flesh and blood and soul. Whatever it was, the foreign *Antari* had always given Parrish the shivers.

Some of the guards called him Hollow behind his back, but Parrish never dared.

"What?" Gen would tease. "Not like he can hear you through the wall between worlds."

"You don't know," Parrish would whisper back. "Maybe he can."

And now Holland was in Rhy's room. Was he supposed to be there? Who had let him in?

Where was *Gen?* wondered Parrish as he took up his spot in front of the door. He didn't mean to eavesdrop, but there was a narrow gap between the left side of the door and the right, and when he turned his head slightly, the conversation reached him through the crack.

"Pardon my intrusion," came Holland's voice, steady and low.

"It's none at all," answered Rhy casually. "But what business brings you to me instead of to my father?"

"I have been to your father for business already," said Holland. "I come to you for something else."

Parrish's cheeks reddened at the seductiveness in Holland's tone. Perhaps it would be better to abandon his post than listen in, but he held his ground, and heard Rhy slump back onto a cushioned seat.

"And what's that?" asked the prince, mirroring the flirtation.

"It is nearly your birthday, is it not?"

"It is nearly," answered Rhy. "You should attend the celebrations, if your king and queen will spare you."

"They will not, I fear," replied Holland. "But my king and queen are the reason I've come. They've bid me deliver a gift."

Parrish could hear Rhy hesitate. "Holland," he said, the sound of cushions shifting as he sat forward, "you know the laws. I cannot take—"

"I know the laws, young prince," soothed Holland. "As to the gift, I picked it out here, in your own city, on my masters' behalf."

There was a long pause, followed by the sound of Rhy standing. "Very well," he said.

Parrish heard the shuffle of a parcel being passed and opened.

"What is it for?" asked the prince after another stretch of quiet.

Holland made a sound, something between a smile and a laugh, neither of which Parrish had borne witness to before. "For strength," he said.

Rhy began to say something else, but at the same instant, a set of clocks went off through the palace, marking the hour and masking whatever else was said between the *Antari* and the prince. The bells were still echoing through the hall when the door opened and Holland stepped out, his two-toned eyes landing instantly on Parrish.

Holland guided the door shut and considered the royal guard with a resigned sigh. He ran a hand through his charcoal hair.

"Send away one guard," he said, half to himself, "and another takes his place."

Before Parrish could think of a response, the *Antari* dug a coin from his pocket and flicked it into the air toward him.

"I wasn't here," said Holland as the coin rose and fell. And by the time it hit Parrish's palm, he was alone in the hall, staring down at the disk, wondering how it got there, and certain he was forgetting something. He clutched the coin as if he could catch the slipping memory, and hold on.

But it was already gone.

II

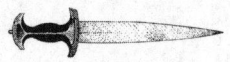

Even at night, the river shone red.

As Kell stepped from the bank of one London onto the bank of another, the black slick of the Thames was replaced by the warm, steady glow of the Isle. It glittered like a jewel, lit from within, a ribbon of constant light unraveling through Red London. A source.

A vein of power. An artery.

Some thought magic came from the mind, others the soul, or the heart, or the will.

But Kell knew it came from the blood.

Blood was magic made manifest. There it thrived. And there it poisoned. Kell had seen what happened when power warred with the body, watched it darken in the veins of corrupted men, turning their blood from crimson to black. If red was the color of magic in balance—of harmony between power and humanity—then black was the color of magic without balance, without order, without restraint.

As an *Antari,* Kell was made of both, balance and chaos; the blood in his veins, like the Isle of Red London, ran a shimmering, healthy crimson, while his right eye was the color of spilled ink, a glistening black.

He wanted to believe that his strength came from his blood alone, but he could not ignore the signature of dark magic that marred his face. It gazed back at him from every looking glass and every pair of ordinary eyes as they widened in awe or fear. It hummed in his skull whenever he summoned power.

But his blood never darkened. It ran true and red. Just as the Isle did.

Arcing over the river, in a bridge of glass and bronze and stone, stretched the royal palace. It was known as the Soner Rast. The "Beating Heart" of the city. Its curved spires glittered like beads of light.

People flocked to the river palace day and night, some to bring cases to the king or queen, but many simply to be near the Isle that ran beneath. Scholars came to the river's edge to study the source, and magicians came hoping to tap into its strength, while visitors from the Arnesian countryside only wanted to gaze upon the palace and river alike, and to lay flowers—from lilies to shooting stars, azaleas to moondrops—all along the bank.

Kell lingered in the shadow of a shop across the road from the riverside and looked up at the palace, like a sun caught in constant rise over the city, and for a moment, he saw it the way visitors must. With wonder.

And then a flicker of pain ran through his arm, and he came back to his senses. He winced, slipped the traveling coin back around his neck, and made his way toward the Isle, the banks of the river teeming with life.

The Night Market was in full swing.

Vendors in colored tents sold wares by the light of river and lantern and moon, some food and others trinkets, the magic and mundane alike, to locals and to pilgrims. A young woman held a bushel of starflowers for visitors to set on the palace steps. An old man displayed dozens of necklaces on a raised arm, each adorned with a burnished pebble, tokens said to amplify control over an element.

The subtle scent of flowers was lost beneath the aroma of

cooking meat and freshly cut fruit, heavy spices and mulled wine. A man in dark robes offered candied plums beside a woman selling scrying stones. A vendor poured steaming tea into short glass goblets across from another vibrant stall displaying masks and a third offering tiny vials of water drawn from the Isle, the contents still glowing faintly with its light. Every night of the year, the market lived and breathed and thrived. The stalls were always changing, but the energy remained, as much a part of the city as the river it fed on. Kell traced the edge of the bank, weaving through the evening fair, savoring the taste and smell of the air, the sound of laughter and music, the thrum of magic.

A street mage was doing fire tricks for a cluster of children, and when the flames burst up from his cupped hands into the shape of a dragon, a small boy stumbled back in surprise and fell right into Kell's path. He caught the boy's sleeve before he hit the street stones, and hoisted him to his feet.

The boy was halfway through mumbling a *thankyousirsorry* when he looked up and caught sight of Kell's black eye beneath his hair, and the boy's own eyes—both light brown—went wide.

"Mathieu," scolded a woman as the boy tore free of Kell's hand and fled behind her cloak.

"Sorry, sir," she said in Arnesian, shaking her head. "I don't know what's gotten—"

And then she saw Kell's face, and the words died. She had the decency not to turn and flee like her son, but what she did was much worse. The woman bowed in the street so deeply that Kell thought she would fall over.

"*Aven,* Kell," she said, breathless.

His stomach twisted, and he reached for her arm, hoping to make her straighten before anyone else could see the gesture, but he was only halfway to her, and already too late.

"He was . . . not l-looking," she stammered, struggling to find the words in English, the royal tongue. It only made Kell cringe more.

"It was my fault," he said gently in Arnesian, taking her elbow and urging her up out of the bow.

"He just . . . he just . . . he did not recognize you," she said, clearly grateful to be speaking the common tongue. "Dressed as you are."

Kell looked down at himself. He was still wearing the brown and fraying coat from the Stone's Throw, as opposed to his uniform. He hadn't forgotten; he'd simply wanted to enjoy the fair, just for a few minutes, as one of the pilgrims or locals. But the ruse was at an end. He could feel the news ripple through the crowd, the mood shifting like a tide as the patrons of the Night Market realized who was among them.

By the time he let go of the woman's arm, the crowd was parting for him, the laughter and shouting reduced to reverent whispers. Rhy knew how to deal with these moments, how to twist them, how to own them.

Kell wanted only to disappear.

He tried to smile, but knew it must look like a grimace, so he bid the woman and her son good night, and made his way quickly down the river's edge, the murmurings of the vendors and patrons trailing him as he went. He didn't look back, but the voices followed all the way to the flower-strewn steps of the royal palace.

The guards did not move from their posts, acknowledging him with only a slight tilt of their heads as he ascended the stairs. He was grateful that most of them did not bow—only Rhy's guard Parrish seemed unable to resist, but at least he had the decency to be discreet. As Kell climbed the steps, he shrugged off his coat and turned it inside out from right to left.

When he slid his arms into the sleeves again, they were no longer tattered and soot-stained. Instead, they were lovely, polished, the same shimmering red as the Isle running beneath the palace.

A red reserved for royalty.

Kell paused at the top step, fastened the gleaming gold buttons, and went in.

III

He found them in the courtyard, taking a late tea under the cloudless night and the fall canopy of trees.

The king and queen were sitting at a table, while Rhy was stretched on a sofa, rambling on again about his birthday and the slew of festivities intended to surround it.

"It's called a birth*day*," chided King Maxim—a towering man with broad shoulders and bright eyes and a black beard—without looking up from a stack of papers he was reading. "Not a birth*days* and certainly not a birth*week*."

"Twenty years!" countered Rhy, waving his empty teacup. "Twenty! A few days of celebration hardly seems excessive." His amber eyes glittered mischievously. "And besides, half of them are for the people, anyway. Who am I to deny them?"

"And the other half?" asked Queen Emira, her long dark hair threaded with gold ribbon and gathered in a heavy braid behind her.

Rhy flashed his winning smile. "You're the one determined to find me a match, Mother."

"Yes," she said, absently straightening the teaware, "but I'd rather not turn the palace into a brothel to do it."

"Not a brothel!" said Rhy, running his fingers through his rich black hair and upsetting the circle of gold that rested there.

"Merely an efficient way of assessing the many necessary attributes of— Ah, Kell! Kell will support my thinking."

"I think it's a horrible idea," said Kell, striding toward them.

"Traitor!" said Rhy with mock affront.

"But," he added, approaching the table, "he'll do it anyway. You might as well throw the party here at the palace, where we can all keep him out of trouble. Or at least minimize it."

Rhy beamed. "Sound logic, sound logic," he said, mimicking his father's deep voice.

The king set aside the paper he was holding and considered Kell. "How was your trip?"

"Longer than I would have liked," said Kell, sorting through his coats and pockets until he found the Prince Regent's letter.

"We were beginning to worry," said Queen Emira.

"The king was not well and the prince was worse," said Kell, offering the note. King Maxim took it and set it aside, unread.

"Sit," urged the queen. "You look pale."

"Are you well?" asked the king.

"Quite, sir," said Kell, sinking gratefully into a chair at the table. "Only tired." The queen reached out and brought her hand to Kell's cheek. Her complexion was darker than his— the royal family bore a rich tan that, when paired with their honey eyes and black hair, made them look like polished wood. With fair skin and reddish hair, Kell felt perpetually out of place. The queen brushed a handful of copper strands off his forehead. She always went looking for the truth in his right eye, as if it were a scrying board, something to be gazed into, seen past. But what she saw, she never shared. Kell took her hand and kissed it. "I'm fine, Your Majesty." She gave him a weary look, and he corrected himself. "Mother."

A servant appeared bearing tea, sweet and laced with mint, and Kell took a long drink and let his family talk, his mind wandering in the comfort of their noise.

When he could barely keep his eyes open, he excused himself. Rhy pushed up from the sofa with him. Kell wasn't surprised. He had felt the prince's gaze on him since he'd first taken his seat. Now, as the two bid their parents good night, Rhy trailed Kell into the hall, fiddling with the circle of gold nested in his black curls.

"What did I miss?" asked Kell.

"Not much," said Rhy. "Holland paid a visit. He only just left."

Kell frowned. Red London and White kept in much closer contact than Red and Grey, but their communication still held a kind of routine. Holland was off schedule by nearly a week.

"What have you come back with tonight?" asked Rhy.

"A headache," said Kell, rubbing his eyes.

"You know what I mean," countered the prince. "What did you bring through that door?"

"Nothing but a few lins." Kell spread his arms wide. "Search me if you like," he added with a smirk. Rhy had never been able to figure out Kell's coat and its many sides, and Kell was already turning back down the hall, considering the matter done, when Rhy surprised him by reaching not for his pockets but for his shoulders, and pushing him back against the wall. Hard. A nearby painting of the king and queen shuddered, but did not fall. The guards dotting the hall looked up but did not move from their posts.

Kell was a year older than Rhy but built like an afternoon shadow, tall and slim, while Rhy was built like a statue, and nearly as strong.

"Do not lie," warned Rhy. "Not to me."

Kell's mouth became a hard line. Rhy had caught him, two years before. Not caught in the *act,* of course, but snagged him in another, more devious way. Trust. The two had been drinking on one of the palace's many balconies one summer night, the glow of the Isle beneath them and the stretch of sky above, and the truth had stumbled out. Kell had told his brother about the deals he struck in Grey London, and in White, and even on occasion in Red, about the various things he'd smuggled, and Rhy had stared at him, and listened, and when he spoke, it wasn't to lecture Kell on all the ways it was wrong, or illegal. It was to ask *why*.

"I don't know," said Kell, and it had been the truth.

Rhy had sat up, eyes bleary from drink. "Have we not provided?" he'd asked, visibly upset. "Is there anything you want for?"

"No," Kell had answered, and that had been a truth and a lie at the same time.

"Are you not loved?" whispered Rhy. "Are you not welcomed as family?"

"But I'm *not* family, Rhy," Kell had said. "I'm not truly a Maresh, for all that the king and queen have offered me that name. I feel more like a possession than a prince."

At that, Rhy had punched him in the face.

For a week after, Kell had two black eyes instead of one, and he'd never spoken like that again, but the damage was done. He'd hoped Rhy would prove too drunk to remember the conversation, but he'd remembered everything. He hadn't told the king or queen, and Kell supposed he owed Rhy that, but now, every time he traveled, he had to endure Rhy's questioning and with it, the reminder that what he was doing was foolish and wrong.

Rhy let go of Kell's shoulders. "Why do you insist on keeping up these pursuits?"

"They amuse me," said Kell, brushing himself off.

Rhy shook his head. "Look, I've turned a blind eye to your childish rebellion for quite a while now, but those doors were shut for a reason," he warned. "Transference is *treason*."

"They're only trinkets," said Kell, continuing down the hall. "There's no real danger in it."

"There's plenty," said Rhy, matching his stride. "Like the danger that awaits you if our parents ever learn—"

"Would you tell them?" asked Kell.

Rhy sighed. Kell watched him try to answer several ways before he finally said, "There is nothing I would not give you."

Kell's chest ached. "I know."

"You are my brother. My closest friend."

"I know."

"Then put an end to this foolishness, before I do."

Kell managed a small, tired smile. "Careful, Rhy," he said. "You're beginning to sound like a king."

Rhy's mouth quirked. "One day I will be. And I need you there beside me."

Kell smiled back. "Believe me. There's no place I'd rather be." It was the truth.

Rhy patted his shoulder and went to bed. Kell shoved his hands into his pockets and watched him go. The people of London—and of the country beyond—loved their prince. And why shouldn't they? He was young and handsome and kind. Perhaps he played the part of rake too often and too well, but behind the charismatic smile and the flirtatious air was a sharp mind and a good intent, the desire to make everyone around him happy. He had little gift for magic—and even less focus for it—but what he lacked in power he more than made up for in charm. Besides, if Kell had learned anything from his trips to White London, it was that magic made rulers worse, not better.

He continued down the hall to his own rooms, where a dark set of oak doors led onto a sprawling chamber. The Isle's red glow poured through the open doors of a private balcony, tapestry billowed and dipped in fabric clouds from the high ceiling, and a luxurious canopied bed, filled with feather and lined with silk, stood waiting. Beckoning. It took all of Kell's will not to collapse into it. Instead, he crossed through the chamber and into a second smaller room lined with books—a variety of tomes on magic, including what little he could find on *Antari* and their blood commands, the majority destroyed out of fear in the Black London purge—and closed the door behind him. He snapped his fingers absently and a candle perching on the edge of a shelf sparked to life. In its light he could make out a series of marks on the back of the door. An inverted triangle, a set of lines, a circle—simple marks, easy enough to re-create, but specific enough to differentiate. Doors to different places in Red London. His eyes went to the one in the middle. It was made up of two crossed lines. X *marks the spot,* he thought to himself, pressing his fingers to the most recent cut on his arm—the blood still wet—then tracing the mark.

"*As Tascen,*" he said tiredly.

The wall gave way beneath his touch, and his private library became a cramped little room, the lush quiet of his royal chambers replaced by the din of the tavern below and the city beyond, much nearer than it had been a mere moment before.

Is Kir Ayes—the Ruby Fields—was the name that swung above the tavern's door. The place was run by an old woman named Fauna; she had the body of a gran, the mouth of a sailor, and the temper of a drunk. Kell had cut a deal with her when he was young (she was still old then, always old), and the room at the top of the stairs became his.

The room itself was rough and worn and several strides too small, but it belonged entirely to him. Spellwork—and not strictly legal at that—marked the window and the door, so that no one else could find the room, or perceive that it was there. At first glance, the chamber looked fairly empty, but a closer inspection would reveal that the space under the cot and the drawers in the dresser were filled with boxes and in those boxes were treasures from every London.

Kell supposed that *he* was a Collector, too.

The only items on display were a book of poems, a glass ball filled with black sand, and a set of maps. The poems were by a man named Blake, and had been given to Kell by a Collector in Grey London the year before, the spine already worn to nothing. The glass ball was a trinket from White London, said to show one's dreams in the sands, but Kell had yet to try it.

The maps were a reminder.

The three canvases were tacked side by side, the sole decoration on the walls. From a distance, they could have passed for the *same* map—the same outline of the same island country—but up close, only the word *London* could be found on all three. Grey London. Red London. White London. The map on the left was of Great Britain, from the English Channel up through the tips of Scotland, every facet rendered in detail. By contrast, the map on the right held almost none. Makt, the country called itself, the capital city held by the ruthless Dane twins, but the territory beyond was in constant flux. The map in the middle Kell knew best, for it was home. Arnes. The country's name was written in elegant script down the length of the island, though in truth, the land on which London stood was only the tip of the royal empire.

Three very different Londons, in three very different countries, and Kell was one of the only living souls to have seen them all. The great irony, he supposed, was that he had never seen the worlds *beyond* the cities. Bound to the service of his king and crown, and constantly kept within reach, he had never been more than a day's journey from one London or another.

Fatigue ate at Kell's body as he stretched and shrugged off his coat. He dug through the pockets until he found the Collector's parcel, which he set carefully on the bed, gingerly undoing the wrapping to reveal the tiny silver music box inside. The room's lanterns grew brighter as he held up the trinket to the light, admiring it. The ache in his arm drew him back, and he set the music box aside and turned his attention to the dresser.

A basin of water and a set of jars waited there, and Kell rolled up the sleeve of his black tunic and set to work on his forearm. He moved with expert hands, and in minutes he'd rinsed the skin and applied a salve. There was a blood command for healing—*As Hasari*—but it wasn't meant for *Antari* to use on themselves, especially not for minor wounds, as it took more energy than it afforded health. As it was, the cuts on his arm were already beginning to mend. *Antari* healed quickly, thanks to the amount of magic in their veins, and by morning the shallow marks would be gone, the skin smooth. He was about to pull down his sleeve when the small shiny scar captured his attention. It always did. Just below the crook of his elbow, the lines were so blurred that the symbol was almost unreadable.

Almost.

Kell had lived in the palace since he was five. He first noticed the mark when he was twelve. He had spent weeks searching for the rune in the palace libraries. *Memory.*

He ran his thumb over the scar. Contrary to its name, the symbol wasn't meant to help one remember. It was meant to make one forget.

Forget a moment. A day. A life. But magic that bound a person's body or mind was not only forbidden—it was a capital offense. Those accused and convicted were stripped of their power, a fate some found worse than death in a world ruled by magic. And yet, Kell bore the mark of such a spell. Worse, he suspected that the king and queen themselves had sanctioned it.

K.L.

The initials on his knife. There were so many things he didn't understand—would never understand—about the weapon, its monogram, and the life that went with it. (Were the letters English? Or Arnesian? The letters could be found in both alphabets. What did the *L* stand for? Or even the *K,* for that matter? He knew nothing of the letters that had formed his name—*K.L.* had become *Kay-Ell* and *Kay-Ell* had become *Kell.*) He was only a child when he was brought to the palace. Had the knife always been his? Or had it been his father's? A token, something to take with him, something to help him remember who he'd been? Who *had* he been? The absence of memory ate at him. He often caught himself staring at the center map on the wall, wondering where he'd come from. *Who* he'd come from.

Whoever they were, they hadn't been *Antari*. Magic might live in the blood, but not in the bloodline. It wasn't passed from parent to child. It chose its own way. Chose its shape. The strong sometimes gave birth to the weak, or the other way around. Fire wielders were often born from water mages, earth movers from healers. Power could not be cultivated like a crop, distilled through generations. If it could, *Antari* would be sewn and reaped. They were ideal vessels, capable of controlling any element, of drawing any spell, of using their own blood to command the world around them. They were tools, and in the wrong hands, weapons. Perhaps the lack of inheritance was nature's way of balancing the scales, of maintaining order.

In truth, none knew what led to the birth of an *Antari*. Some believed that it was random, a lucky throw of dice. Others claimed that *Antari* were divine, destined for greatness. Some scholars, like Tieren, believed that *Antari* were the result of transference between the worlds, magic of different kinds intertwining, and that that was why they were dying out. But no matter the theory on how they came to be, most believed that *Antari* were sacred. Chosen by magic or blessed by it, perhaps. But certainly *marked* by it.

Kell brought his fingers absently to his right eye.

Whatever one chose to believe, the fact remained that *Antari* had grown even more rare, and therefore more precious. Their talent had always made them something to be coveted, but now their scarcity made them something to be gathered and guarded and kept. Possessed. And whether or not Rhy wanted to admit it, Kell belonged to the royal collection.

He took up the silver music box, winding the tiny metal crank.

A valuable trinket, he thought, *but a trinket all the same.* The song started, tickling his palm like a bird, but he didn't set down the box. Instead, he held it tight, the notes whispering out as he fell back onto the stiff cot and considered the small beautiful contraption.

How had he ended up on this shelf? What had happened when his eye turned black? Was he born that way and hidden, or did the mark of magic manifest? Five years. Five years he'd been someone else's son. Had they been sad to let him go? Or had they gratefully offered him up to the crown?

The king and queen refused to tell him of his past, and he'd learned to stop voicing his questions, but fatigue wore away his walls, and let them through.

What life had he forgotten?

Kell's hand fell away from his face as he chided himself. How much could a child of five really have to remember? Whoever he'd been before he was brought to the palace, that person didn't matter anymore.

That person didn't exist.

The music box's song faltered and came to a stop, and Kell rewound it again, and closed his eyes, letting the Grey London melody and the Red London air drag him down to sleep.

THREE

GREY THIEF

I

Lila Bard lived by a simple rule: if a thing was worth having, it was worth taking.

She held the silver pocket watch up to the faint glow of the streetlamp, admiring the metal's polished shine, wondering what the engraved initials—*L.L.E.*—on the back might stand for. She'd nicked the watch off a gentleman, a clumsy collision on a too-crowded curb that had led to a swift apology, a hand on the shoulder to distract from a hand on the coat. Lila's fingers weren't just fast; they were light. A tip of the top hat and a pleasant good night, and she was the proud new owner of a timepiece, and he was on his way and none the wiser.

She didn't care about the object itself, but she cared a great deal for what it bought her: freedom. A poor excuse for it, to be sure, but better than a prison or a poorhouse. She ran a gloved thumb over the crystal watch face.

"Do you have the time?" asked a man at her shoulder.

Lila's eyes flicked up. It was a constable.

Her hand went to the brim of her top hat—stolen from a dozing chauffeur the week before—and she hoped the gesture passed for a greeting and not a nervous slip, an attempt to hide her face.

"Half past nine," she murmured deeply, tucking the watch into the vest pocket under her cloak, careful not to let the constable catch sight of the various weapons glittering beneath it.

Lila was tall and thin, with a boyish frame that helped her pass for a young man, but only from a distance. Too close an inspection, and the illusion would crumble.

Lila knew she should turn and go while she could, but when the constable searched for something to light his pipe and came up empty, she found herself fetching up a sliver of wood from the street. She put one boot up on the base of the lamppost and stepped lithely up to light the stick in the flame. Lantern light glanced off her jawline, lips, cheekbones, the edges of her face exposed beneath the top hat. A delicious thrill ran through her chest, spurned on by the closeness of danger, and Lila wondered, not for the first time, if something was wrong with her. Barron used to say so, but Barron was a bore.

Looking for trouble, he'd say. *You're gonna look till you find it.*

Trouble is the looker, she'd answer. *It keeps looking till it finds you. Might as well find it first.*

Why do you want to die?

I don't, she'd say. *I just want to live.*

She stepped down from the lamppost, her face plunging back into her hat's shadow as she handed the constable the burning sliver of wood. He offered a muttered thanks and lit the pipe, gave a few puffs, and seemed about to go, but then he paused. Lila's heart gave a nervous flutter as he considered her again, this time more carefully. "You ought to be mindful, sir," he said at last. "Out alone at night. Likely to get your pocket picked."

"Robbers?" asked Lila, struggling to keep her voice low. "Surely not in Eaton."

"Aye." The constable nodded and pulled a folded sheet of paper from his coat. Lila reached out and took it, even though she knew at first glance what it was. A WANTED poster. She stared down at a sketch that was little more than a shadowy outline wearing a mask—a haphazard swatch of fabric over the eyes—and a broad brim hat. "Been picking pockets, even robbed a few gentlemen and a lady outright. Expect that mess, of course, but not 'round here. A right audacious crook, this one."

Lila fought back a smile. It was true. Nicking spare change in South Bank was one thing, stealing silver and gold from the carriage-bound in Mayfair quite another, but thieves were fools to stay in slums. The poor kept up their guards. The rich strutted around, assuming they'd be safe, so long as they stayed in the good parts of town. But Lila knew there were no good parts. Only smart parts and stupid parts, and she was quick enough to know which one to play.

She handed back the paper and tipped the stolen top hat to the constable. "I'll mind my pockets, then."

"Do," urged the constable. "Not like it used to be. Nothing is . . ." He ambled away, sucking on his pipe and muttering about the way the world was falling apart or some such—Lila couldn't hear the rest over the thudding pulse in her ears.

The moment he was out of sight, Lila sighed and slumped back against the lamppost, dizzy with relief. She dragged the top hat from her head and considered the mask and the broad brim cap stuffed inside. She smiled to herself. And then she put the hat back on, pushed off the post, and made her way to the docks, whistling as she walked.

II

The *Sea King* wasn't nearly as impressive as the name suggested.

The ship leaned heavily against the dock, its paint stripped by salt, its wooden hull half rotted in some places, and fully rotted in others. The whole thing seemed to be sinking very, very slowly into the Thames.

The only thing keeping the boat up appeared to be the dock itself, the state of which wasn't much better, and Lila wondered if one day the side of the ship and the boards of the dock would simply rot together or crumble away into the murky bay.

Powell claimed that the *Sea King* was as sturdy as ever. *Still fit for the high seas,* he swore. Lila thought it was hardly fit for the sway of the London port's swells.

She put a boot up on the ramp, and the boards groaned underfoot, the sound rippling back until it seemed like the whole boat was protesting her arrival. A protest she ignored as she climbed aboard, loosening the cloak's knot at her throat.

Lila's body ached for sleep, but she carried out her nightly ritual, crossing the dock to the ship's bow and curling her fingers around the wheel. The cold wood against her palms, the gentle roll of the deck beneath her feet, it all felt *right*. Lila Bard knew in her bones that she was meant to be a pirate. All she needed was a working ship. And once she had one . . . A breeze caught up her coat, and for a moment she saw herself far from the London port, far from any land, plowing forward across the high seas. She closed her eyes and tried to imagine the feel of the sea breeze rushing through her threadbare sleeves. The beat of the ocean against the ship's sides. The thrill of freedom—true freedom—and adventure. She tipped her chin up as an imaginary spray of salty water tickled her chin. She drew a deep breath and smiled at the taste of the sea air. By the time she opened her eyes, she was surprised to find the *Sea King* just as it had been. Docked and dead.

Lila pushed off the rail and made her way across the deck, and for the first time all night, as her boots echoed on the wood, she felt something like safe. She knew it *wasn't* safe, knew nowhere in the city was, not a plush carriage in Mayfair and certainly not a half-rotten ship on the dodgy end of the docks, but it felt a little something like it. Familiar . . . was that it? Or maybe simply hidden. That was as close to safe as it got. No eyes watched her cross the deck. None saw her descend the steep set of steps that ran into the ship's bones and bowels. None followed her through the dank little hall, or into the cabin at the end.

The knot at her throat finally came loose, and Lila pulled the cloak from her shoulders and tossed it onto a cot that hugged one of the cabin walls. It fell fluttering to the bed, soon followed by the top hat, which spilled its disguise like jewels onto the dark fabric. A small coal stove sat in the corner, the embers barely enough to warm the room. Lila stirred them up and used the stick to light a couple of tallow candles scattered around the cabin. She then tugged off her gloves and lobbed them onto the cot with the rest. Finally, she slid off her belt, freeing holster and dagger both from the leather strap. They weren't her only weapons, of course, but they were the only ones she bothered to take off. The knife was nothing special, just wickedly sharp—she tossed it onto the bed with the rest of the discarded things—but the pistol was a gem, a flintlock revolver that had fallen out of a wealthy dead man's hand and into hers the year before. Caster—for all good weapons deserved a name—was a beauty of a gun, and she slipped him gently, almost reverently, into the drawer of her desk.

The thrill of the night had gone cold with the walk to the docks, excitement burned to ash, and Lila found herself slouching into a chair. It protested as much as everything else on the ship, groaning roundly as she kicked her boots up onto the desk, the worn wooden surface of which was piled with maps, most rolled, but one spread and pinned in place by stones or stolen trinkets. It was her favorite one, that map, because none of the places on it were labeled. Surely, someone knew what kind of map it was, and where it led, but Lila didn't. To her, it was a map to anywhere.

A large slab of mirror sat propped on the desk, leaning back against the hull wall, its edges fogged and silvering. Lila found her gaze in the glass and cringed a little. She ran her fingers through her hair. It was ragged and dark and scraped against her jaw.

Lila was nineteen.

Nineteen, and every one of the years felt carved into her. She poked at the skin under her eyes, tugged at her cheeks, ran a finger along her lips. It had been a long time since anyone had called her pretty.

Not that Lila wanted to be pretty. Pretty wouldn't serve her well. And lord knew she didn't envy the *ladies* with their cinched corsets and abundant skirts, their falsetto laughs and the ridiculous way they used them. The way they swooned and leaned on men, feigning weakness to savor their strength.

Why anyone would ever *pretend* to be weak was beyond her.

Lila tried to picture herself as one of the ladies she'd stolen from that night—so easy to get tangled up in all that fabric, so easy to stumble and be caught—and smiled. How many ladies had flirted with *her*? Swooned and leaned and pretended to marvel at *her* strength?

She felt the weight of the night's take in her pocket.

Enough.

It served them right, for playing weak. Maybe they wouldn't be so quick to swoon at every top hat and take hold of every offered hand.

Lila tipped her head back against the back of the chair. She could hear Powell in his quarters, acting out his own nightly routine of drinking and cursing and muttering stories to the bowed walls of the rotting ship. Stories of lands he'd never visited. Maidens he'd never wooed. Treasures he'd never plundered. He was a liar and a drunkard and a fool—she'd seen him be all three on any given night in the Barren Tide—but he had an extra cabin and she had need of one, and they had reached an agreement. She lost a cut of every night's take to his hospitality, and in return he forgot that he was renting the room to a wanted criminal, let alone a girl.

Powell rambled on within his room. He carried on for hours, but Lila was so used to the noise that soon it faded in with the other groans and moans and murmurings of the old *Sea King*.

Her head had just started to slump when someone knocked on her door three times. Well, someone knocked twice, but was clearly too drunk to finish the third, dragging their hand down the wood. Lila's boots slid from the desk and landed heavily on the floor.

"What is it?" she called, getting to her feet as the door swung open. Powell stood there, swaying from drink and the gentle rock of the boat.

"Liiiila," he sang her name. "Liiiiilaaaaaa."

"What?"

A bottle sloshed in one hand. He held out the other, palm up. "My cut."

Lila shoved her hand into her pocket and came out with a handful of coins. Most of them were faded, but a few bits of silver glinted in the mix, and she picked them out and dropped them into Powell's palm. He closed his fist and jingled the money.

"It's not enough," he said as she returned the coppers to her pocket. She felt the silver watch in her vest, warm against her ribs, but didn't pull it out. She wasn't sure why. Maybe she'd taken a liking to the timepiece after all. Or maybe she was afraid that if she started offering such pricey goods, Powell would come to expect them.

"Slow night," she said, crossing her arms. "I'll make up the difference tomorrow."

"You're trouble," slurred Powell.

"Indeed," she said, flashing a grin. Her tone was sweet but her teeth were sharp.

"Maybe more trouble than you're worth," he slurred. "Certainly more than you're worth tonight."

"I'll get you the rest tomorrow," she said, hands slipping back to her side. "You're drunk. Go to bed." She started to turn away, but Powell caught her elbow.

"I'll take it tonight," he said with a sneer.

"I said I don't—"

The bottle tumbled from Powell's other hand as he forced her back into the desk, pinning her with his hips.

"Doesn't have to be coin," he whispered, dragging his eyes down her shirtfront. "Must be a girl's body under there somewhere." His hands began to roam, and Lila drove her knee into his stomach and sent him staggering backward.

"Shouldn't a done that," growled Powell, face red. His fingers fumbled with his buckle. Lila didn't wait. She went for the pistol in the drawer, but Powell's head snapped up and he lunged and caught her wrist, dragging her toward him. He threw her bodily back onto the cot, and she landed on the hat and the gloves and the cloak and the discarded knife.

Lila scrambled for the dagger as Powell charged forward. He grabbed her knee as her fingers wrapped around the leather sheath. He jerked her toward him as she drew the blade free, and when he caught her other hand with his, she used his grip to pull herself to her feet and drive the knife into his gut.

And just like that, all the struggle went out of the cramped little room.

Powell stared down at the blade jutting out of his front, eyes wide with surprise, and for a moment it looked like he might carry on despite it, but Lila knew how to use a knife, knew where to cut to hurt and where to cut to kill.

Powell's grip on her tightened. And then it went slack. He swayed and frowned, and then his knees buckled.

"Shouldn't a done that," she echoed, pulling the knife free before he could collapse forward onto it.

Powell's body hit the floor and stayed there. Lila stared down at it a moment, marveling at the stillness, the quiet broken only by her pulse and the hush of the water against the hull of the ship. She toed the man with her boot.

Dead.

Dead . . . and making a mess.

Blood was spreading across the boards, filling in the cracks and dripping through to lower parts of the ship. Lila needed to do something. *Now.*

She crouched, wiped her blade on Powell's shirt, and recovered the silver from his pocket. And then she stepped over his body, retrieved the revolver from its drawer, and got dressed. When the belt was back around her waist and the cloak around her shoulders, she took up the bottle of whiskey from the floor.

It hadn't broken when it fell. Lila pulled the cork free with her teeth and emptied the contents onto Powell, even though there was probably enough alcohol in his blood to burn without it.

She took up a candle and was about to touch it to the floor when she remembered the map. The one to anywhere. She freed it from the desk and tucked it under her cloak, and then, with a last look around the room, she set fire to the dead man and the boat.

Lila stood on the dock and watched the *Sea King* burn.

She stared up at it, face warmed by the fire that danced on her chin and cheeks the way the lamp light had before the constable. *It's a shame,* she thought. She'd rather liked the rotting ship. But it wasn't hers. No, hers would be much better.

The *Sea King* groaned as the flames gnawed its skin and then its bones, and Lila watched the dead ship begin to sink. She stayed until she could hear the far-off cries and the sound of boots, too late, of course, but coming all the same.

And then she sighed and went in search of another place to spend the night.

III

Barron was standing on the steps of the Stone's Throw, staring absently toward the docks when Lila strolled up, the top hat and the map both tucked under her arm. When she followed his gaze, she could see the dregs of the fire over the building tops, the smoke ghosted against the cloudy night.

Barron pretended not to notice her at first. She couldn't blame him. The last time he'd seen her, almost a year before, he'd kicked her out for thieving—not from him, of course, from a patron—and she'd stormed off, damning him and his little tavern inn alike.

"Where you going, then?" he'd rumbled after her like thunder. It was as close as he'd ever come to shouting.

"To find an adventure," she'd called without looking back.

Now she scuffed her boots along the street stones. He sucked on a cigar. "Back so soon?" he said without looking up. She climbed the steps, and slouched against the tavern door. "You find adventure already? Or it find you?"

Lila didn't answer. She could hear the clink of cups inside and the chatter of drunk men getting drunker. She hated that noise, hated most taverns altogether, but not the Stone's Throw. The others all repulsed her, *repelled* her, but this place dragged at her like gravity, a low and constant pull. Even when she didn't mean to, she always seemed to end up here. How many times in the last year had her feet carried her back to these steps? How many times had she almost gone inside? Not that Barron needed to know about that. She watched him tip his head back and stare up at the sky as if he could see something there besides clouds.

"What happened to the *Sea King*?" he asked.

"It burned down." A defiant flutter of pride filled her chest when his eyes widened a fraction in surprise. She liked surprising Barron. It wasn't an easy thing to do.

"Did it now?" he asked lightly.

"You know how it is," said Lila with a shrug. "Old wood goes up so easy."

Barron gave her a long look, then exhaled a smoke-filled breath. "Powell should've been more careful with his brig."

"Yeah," said Lila. She fiddled with the brim of the top hat.

"You smell like smoke."

"I need to rent a room." The words stuck in her throat.

"Funny," said Barron, taking another puff. "I distinctly remember you suggesting that I take my tavern and all its many—albeit modest—rooms and shove each and every one of them up my—"

"Things change," she said as she plucked the cigar from his mouth and took a drag.

He studied her in the lamplight. "You okay?"

Lila studied the smoke as it poured through her lips. "I'm always okay."

She handed back the cigar and dug the silver watch out of her vest pocket. It was warm and smooth, and she didn't know why she liked it so much, but she did. Maybe because it was a choice. Taking it had been a choice. Keeping it had been one, too. And maybe the choice started as a random one, but there was something to it. Maybe she'd kept it for a reason. Or maybe she'd only kept it for this. She held it out to Barron. "Will this buy me a few nights?"

The owner of the Stone's Throw considered the watch. And then he reached out and curled Lila's fingers over it.

"Keep it," he said casually. "I know you're good for the coin."

Lila slid the trinket back into her pocket, thankful for its weight as she realized she was back to nothing. Well, almost nothing. A top hat, a map to anywhere—or nowhere—a handful of knives, a flintlock, a few coins, and a silver watch.

Barron pushed the door open, but when she turned to go inside, he barred her path. "No one here's a mark. You got that?"

Lila nodded stiffly. "I'm not staying long," she said. "Just till the smoke clears."

The sound of glass breaking reached them beyond the doorway, and Barron sighed and went inside, calling over his shoulder, "Welcome back."

Lila sighed and looked up, not at the sky but at the upper windows of the dingy little tavern. It was hardly a pirate ship, a place for freedom and adventure.

Just till the smoke clears, she echoed to herself.

Maybe it wasn't so bad. After all, she hadn't come back to the Stone's Throw with her tail tucked between her legs. She was in hiding. A wanted man. She smiled at the irony of the term.

A piece of paper flapped on a post beside the door. It was the same notice the constable had showed her, and she smiled at the figure in the broad-brimmed hat and mask staring out at her beneath the word WANTED. The Shadow Thief, they called her. They'd drawn her even taller and thinner than she actually was, stretched her into a wraith, black-clad and fearsome. The stuff of fairy tales. And legends.

Lila winked at the shadow before going in.

FOUR

WHITE THRONE

I

"Perhaps it should be a masquerade instead."

"Focus."

"Or maybe a costume ball. Something with a bit of flare."

"Come on, Rhy. Pay attention."

The prince sat in a high-backed chair, gold-buckled boots kicked up on the table, rolling a glass ball between his hands. The orb was part of a larger, more intricate version of the game Kell had pawned off in the Stone's Throw. In place of pebbles or puddles or piles of sand nesting on the little board, there were five glass balls, each containing an element. Four still sat in the dark wood chest on the table, its inside lined with silk and its edges capped in gold. The one in Rhy's hands held a handful of earth, and it tipped side to side with the motion of his fingers. "Costumes with layers, ones that can be taken off . . ." he went on.

Kell sighed.

"We can all start the night in full-dress and end in—"

"You're not even trying."

Rhy groaned. His boots hit the floor with a thud as he straightened and held the glass ball up between them. "Fine," he said. "Observe my magical prowess." Rhy squinted at the dirt trapped inside the glass and, attempting to focus, spoke to the earth under his breath in low murmuring English. But the earth did not move. Kell watched a crease appear between Rhy's eyes as he focused and whispered and waited and grew increasingly irritated. At last, the dirt shifted (albeit halfheartedly) within the glass.

"I did it!" exclaimed Rhy.

"You shook it," said Kell.

"I wouldn't dare!"

"Try again."

Rhy made a sound of dismay as he slumped in his chair. "Sanct, Kell. What's wrong with me?"

"Nothing is wrong," insisted Kell.

"I speak eleven languages," said Rhy. "Some for countries I have never seen, nor am likely to set foot in, yet I cannot coax a clod of dirt to move, or a drop of water to rise from its pool." His temper flared. "It's maddening!" he growled. "Why is the language of magic so hard for my tongue to master?"

"Because you cannot win the elements over with your charm or your smile or your status," said Kell.

"They disrespect me," said Rhy with a dry smile.

"The earth beneath your feet does not care you will be king. Nor the water in your cup. Nor the air you breathe. You must speak to them as equal, or even better, as supplicant."

Rhy sighed and rubbed his eyes. "I know. I know. I only wish . . ." he trailed off.

Kell frowned. Rhy looked genuinely upset. "Wish what?"

Rhy's gaze lifted to meet Kell's, the pale gold glittering even as a wall went up behind them. "I wish I had a drink," he said, burying the matter. He shoved up from his chair and crossed the chamber to pour himself one from a sideboard against the wall. "I do try, Kell. I want to be good, or at least better. But we can't all be . . ." Rhy took a sip and waved his hand at Kell.

The word he assumed Rhy was looking for was *Antari*. The word he used was *"You."*

"What can I say?" said Kell, running his hand through his hair. "I'm one of a kind."

"Two of a kind," corrected Rhy.

Kell's brow creased. "I've been meaning to ask; what was Holland doing here?"

Rhy shrugged and wandered back toward the chest of elements. "The same thing he always is. Delivering mail." Kell considered the prince. Something was off. Rhy was a notorious fidgeter whenever he was lying, and Kell watched him shift his weight from foot to foot and tap his fingers against the open lid of the chest. But rather than press the issue, Kell let it drop and, instead, reached down and plucked another of the glass balls from the chest, this one filled with water. He balanced it in his palm, fingers splayed.

"You're trying too hard." Kell bid the water in the glass to move, and it moved, swirling first loosely within the orb and then faster and tighter, creating a small, contained cyclone.

"That's because it *is* hard," said Rhy. "Just because *you* make it look easy doesn't mean it is."

Kell wouldn't tell Rhy that he didn't even need to speak in order to move the water. That he could simply think the words, feel them, and the element listened, and answered. Whatever flowed through the water—and the sand, and the earth, and the rest—flowed through him, too, and he could will it, as he would a limb, to move for him. The only exception was blood. Though it flowed as readily as the rest, blood itself did not obey the laws of elements—it could not be manipulated, told to move, or forced to still. Blood had a will of its own, and had to be addressed not as an object, but as an equal, an adversary. Which was why *Antari* stood apart. For they alone held dominion not only over elements, but also over blood. Where elemental invocation was designed simply to help the mind focus, to find a personal synchronicity with the magic—it was meditative, a chant as much as a summoning—the *Antari* blood commands were, as the term suggested, *commands*. The words Kell spoke to open doors or heal wounds with his blood were *orders*. And they had to be given in order to be obeyed.

"What's it like?" asked Rhy out of nowhere.

Kell dragged his attention away from the glass, but the water kept spinning inside it. "What's what like?"

"Being able to travel. To see the other Londons. What are *they* like?"

Kell hesitated. A scrying table sat against one wall. Unlike the smooth black panels of slate that broadcast messages throughout the city, the table served a different purpose. Instead of stone, it held a shallow pool of still water, enchanted to project one's ideas, memories, images from their mind onto the surface of the water. It was used for reflection, yes, but also to share one's thoughts with others, to help when words failed to convey, or simply fell short.

With the table, Kell could show him. Let Rhy see the other Londons as he saw them. A selfish part of Kell wanted to share them with his brother, so that he wouldn't feel so alone, so that someone else would see, would know. But the thing about people, Kell had discovered, is that they didn't *really* want to know. They thought they did, but knowing only made them miserable. Why fill up a mind with things you can't use? Why dwell on places you can't go? What good would it do Rhy, who, for all the privileges his royal status might grant him, could never set foot in another London?

"Uneventful," said Kell, returning his glass to the chest. As soon as his fingers left its surface, the cyclone fell apart, the water sloshing and settling to a stop. Before Rhy could ask any more questions, Kell pointed at the glass in the prince's hand and told him to try again.

Rhy tried again—and failed again—to move the earth within

the glass. He made a frustrated noise and knocked the sphere away across the table. "I'm rubbish at this, and we both know it."

Kell caught the glass ball as it reached the table's edge and tumbled over. "Practice—" he started.

"Practice won't do a damned thing."

"Your problem, Rhy," chided Kell, "is that you don't want to learn magic to learn magic. You only want to learn it because you think it will help you lure people into your bed."

Rhy's lips twitched. "I don't see how that's a *problem*," he said, "And it would. I've seen the way the girls—and boys—fawn over your pretty black eye, Kell." He shoved to his feet. "Forget the lesson. I'm in no mood for learning. Let's go out."

"Why?" asked Kell. "So you can use *my* magic to lure people into *your* bed?"

"A fine idea," said Rhy. "But no. We must go out, you see, because we're on a mission."

"Oh?" asked Kell.

"Yes. Because unless you plan to wed me yourself—and don't get me wrong, I think we'd make a dashing pair—I must try and find a mate."

"And you think you'll find one traipsing around the city?"

"Goodness, no," said Rhy with a crooked grin. "But who knows what fun I'll find while failing."

Kell rolled his eyes and put the orbs away. "Moving on," he said.

"Let's be done with this," whined Rhy.

"We shall be done," said Kell. "As soon as you can contain a flame."

Of all the elements, fire was the only one Rhy had shown a . . . well, *talent* was too strong a word, but perhaps an *ability* for. Kell cleared the wooden table and set a sloped metal dish before the prince, along with a piece of white chalk, a vial of oil, and an odd little device like a pair of crossed pieces of blackened wood joined by a hinge in the middle. Rhy sighed and drew a binding circle on the table around the dish using the chalk. He then emptied the vial onto the plate, the oil pooling in the center, no bigger than a ten-lin coin. Finally, he lifted the device, which fit easily in his palm. It was a fire starter. When Rhy closed his hand around it and squeezed, the two stems scraped together, and a spark fell from the hinge to the pool of oil, and caught.

A small blue flame danced across the surface of the coin-size pool, and Rhy cracked his knuckles, rolled his neck, and pushed up his sleeves.

"Before the light goes out," urged Kell.

Rhy shot him a look, but brought his hands to either side of the chalk-binding circle, palms in, and began to speak to the fire not in English, but in Arnesian. It was a more fluid, coaxing tongue that leant itself to magic. The words poured out in a whisper, a smooth, unbroken line of sound that seemed to take shape in the room around them.

And to their mutual amazement, it worked. The flame in the dish turned white and grew, enveloping what was left of the oil and continuing to burn without it. It spread, coating the surface of the plate and flaring up into the air before Rhy's face.

"Look!" said Rhy, pointing at the light. "Look, I did it!"

And he had. But even though he'd stopped speaking to the flame, it kept growing.

"Don't lose focus," said Kell as the white fire spread, licking the edges of the chalk circle.

"What?" challenged Rhy as the fire twisted and pressed against the binding ring. "No word of praise?" He looked away from the fire and toward Kell, his fingers brushing along the table as he turned. "Not even a—"

"*Rhy,*" warned Kell, but it was too late. Rhy's hand had skimmed the circle, smudging the line of chalk. The fire tore free.

It flared up across the table, sudden and hot, and Rhy nearly toppled backward in his chair trying to get out of its way.

In a single motion, Kell had freed his knife, drawn it across his palm, and pressed his bloodied hand to the tabletop. *"As Anasae,"* he ordered—*dispel*. The enchanted fire died instantly, vanishing into air. Kell's head spun.

Rhy stood there, breathless. "I'm sorry," he said guiltily. "I'm sorry, I shouldn't have . . ."

Rhy hated it when Kell was forced to use blood magic, because he felt personally responsible—he often was—for the sacrifice that came with it. He had caused Kell a great deal of pain once, and had never quite forgiven himself for it. Now Kell took up a cloth and wiped his wounded hand. "It's fine," he said, tossing aside the rag. "I'm fine. But I think we're done for today."

Rhy nodded shakily. "I could use another drink," he said. "Something strong."

"Agreed," said Kell with a tired smile.

"Hey, we haven't been to the Aven Stras in ages," said Rhy.

"We can't go there," said Kell. What he meant was, *I can't let* you *go there*. Despite its name, the Aven Stras—"Blessed Waters"—had become a haunt for the city's unsavory sorts.

"Come on," said Rhy, already returned to his sporting self. "We'll get Parrish and Gen to dig up some uniforms and we'll all go as—"

Just then a man cleared his throat, and Rhy and Kell both turned to find King Maxim standing in the doorway.

"Sir," they said in unison.

"Boys," he said. "How are your studies going?"

Rhy gave Kell a weighted look, and Kell raised a brow, but said only, "They've come and gone. We just finished."

"Good," said the king, producing a letter.

Kell didn't realize how much he badly he wanted that drink

with Rhy until he saw the envelope, and he knew he wouldn't get it. His heart sank, but he didn't let it show.

"I need you to carry a message," said the king. "To our strong neighbor."

Kell's chest tightened with the familiar mixture of fear and excitement that was inextricable when it came to White London.

"Of course, sir," he said.

"Holland delivered a letter yesterday," explained the king. "But couldn't stay to collect the response. I told him I would send it back with you."

Kell frowned. "All is well, I hope," he said carefully. He rarely knew the contents of the royal messages he carried, but he could usually glean the tone—the correspondences with Grey London had devolved to mere formality, the cities having little in common, while the dialogue with White was constant and involved and left a furrow in the king's brow. Their "strong neighbor" (as the king called the other city) was a place torn by violence and power, the name at the end of the royal letters changing with disturbing frequency. It would have been too easy to discontinue correspondence and leave White London to its decay, but the Red crown couldn't. Wouldn't.

They felt responsible for the dying city.

And they were.

After all, it had been *Red* London's decision to seal itself off, leaving White London—which sat between Red and Black—trapped and forced to fight back the dark plague on its own, to seal itself in, and the corrupted magic out. It was a decision that haunted centuries of kings and queens, but at the time, White London was strong—stronger even than Red—and the Red crown believed (or *claimed* to believe) it was the only way they would all survive. They were right and wrong. Grey London receded into quiet obliviousness. Red not only survived but flourished. But White was forever changed. The city, once glorious, fell to chaos and conquering. Blood and ash.

"All is as well as it can be," said the king as he handed Kell the note and turned back toward the door. Kell moved to follow when Rhy caught his arm.

"Promise," the prince whispered under his breath. "Promise you'll come back empty-handed this time."

Kell hesitated. "I promise," he said, wondering how many times he had said those words, how empty they'd become.

But as he pulled a pale piece of silver from beneath his collar, he hoped that this time they might prove true.

II

Kell stepped through the door in the world and shivered. Red London had vanished, taking the warmth with it; his boots hit cold stone, and his breath blossomed in the air before his lips, and he pulled his coat—the black one with the silver buttons—tightly around his shoulders.

Priste ir Essen. Essen ir Priste.

"Power in Balance. Balance in Power." Equal parts motto, mantra, and prayer, the words ran beneath the royal emblem in Red London, and could be found in shops and homes alike. People in Kell's world believed that magic was neither an infinite resource nor a base one. It was meant to be used but not abused, wielded with reverence as well as caution.

White London had a very different notion.

Here, magic was not seen as equal. It was seen as something to be *conquered. Enslaved. Controlled.* Black London had let magic in, let it take over, let it consume. In the wake of the city's fall, White London had taken the opposite approach, seeking to bind power in any way they could. *Power in Balance* became *Power in Dominance.*

And when the people fought to control the magic, the magic resisted them. Shrank away into itself, burrowed down into the earth and out of reach. The people clawed the surface of the world, digging up what little magic they could still grasp, but it was thin and only growing thinner, as were those fighting for it. The magic seemed determined to starve its captors out. And slowly, surely, it was succeeding.

This struggle had a side effect, and that effect was the reason Kell had named White London *white*: every inch of the city, day or night, summer or winter, bore the same pall, as though a fine coat of snow—or ash—had settled over everything. And everyone. The magic here was bitter and mean, and it bled the world's life and warmth and color, leaching it out of everything and leaving only the pale and bloated corpse behind.

Kell looped the White London coin—a weighty iron thing—around his neck, and tucked it back beneath his collar. The crisp blackness of his coat made him stand out against the faded backdrop of the city streets, and he shoved his blood-streaked hand into his pocket before the rich red sight of it gave anyone ideas. The pearl-toned surface of the half-frozen river—here called neither the Thames, nor the Isle, but the Sijlt—stretched at his back, and across it, the north side of the city reached to the horizon. In front of him, the south side waited, and several blocks ahead, the castle lunged into the air with knifelike spires, its stone mass dwarfing the buildings on every side.

He didn't waste time, but made his way directly toward it.

Being lanky, Kell had a habit of slouching, but walking through the streets of White London, he pulled himself to his full height and kept his chin up and his shoulders back as his boots echoed on the cobblestones. His posture wasn't the only thing that changed. At home, Kell masked his power. Here he knew better. He let his magic fill the air, and the starving air ate it up, warming against his skin, wicking off in tendrils of fog. It was a fine line to walk. He had to show his strength while still holding fast to it. Too little, and he'd be seen as prey. Too much, and he'd be seen as a prize.

In *theory,* the people of the city knew Kell, or of him, and knew that he was under the protection of the white crown. And in *theory,* no one would be foolish enough to defy the Dane twins. But hunger—for energy, for life—did things to people. Made *them* do things.

And so Kell kept his guard up and watched the sinking sun as he walked, knowing that White London was at its most docile in the light of day. The city changed at night. The quiet—an unnatural, heavy, held-breath kind of silence—broke and gave way to noise, sounds of laughter, of passion—some thought it a way to summon power—but mostly those of fighting, and killing. A city of extremes. Thrilling, maybe, but deadly. The streets would have been stained dark with blood long ago if the cutthroats didn't drink it all.

With the sun still up, the lowly and the lost lingered in doorways, and hung out of windows, and loitered in the gaps between buildings. And all of them watched Kell as he passed, gaunt stares and bony edges. Their clothes had the same faded quality as the rest of the city. So did their hair, their eyes, and their skin, the surface of which was covered in markings. Brands and scars, mutilations meant to bind what magic they could summon to their bodies. The weaker they were, the more scars they made on themselves, ruining their flesh in a frantic attempt to hold on to what little power they had.

In Red London, such markings would be seen as base, tainting not only body but also magic by binding it to them. Here, only the strong could afford to scorn the marks, and even then, they did not see them as defiling—merely desperate. But even those above such brands relied on amulets and charms (Holland alone went without any jewelry, save the broach that marked him as a servant of the throne). Magic did not come willingly here. The language of elements had been abandoned when they ceased to listen (the only element that could be summoned was a perverted kind of energy, a bastard of fire and something darker, corrupted). What magic *could* be had was taken, forced into shape by amulets and spells and bindings. It was never enough, never filling.

But the people did not leave.

The power of the Sijlt—even in its half-frozen state—tethered them to the city, its magic the only remaining flicker of warmth.

And so they stayed, and life went on. Those who had not (yet) fallen victim to the gnawing hunger for magic went about their daily work, and minded their own, and did their best to forget about the slow way their world was dying. Many clung to the belief that the magic would return. That a strong enough ruler would be able to force the power back into the veins of the world and revive it.

And so they waited.

Kell wondered if the people of White London truly believed that Astrid and Athos Dane were strong enough, or if they were simply waiting for the next magician to rise up and overthrow them. Which someone would, eventually. Someone always did.

The quiet got heavier as the castle came into sight. Grey and Red London both had palaces for their rulers.

White London had a *fortress*.

A high wall surrounded the castle, and between the vaulting citadel and its outer wall stood an expansive stone courtyard, running like a moat around the looming structure and brimming with marble forms. The infamous Krös Mejkt, the "Stone Forest," was made up not of trees but of statues, all of them people. It was rumored the figures hadn't always been stone, that the forest was actually a graveyard, kept by the Danes to commemorate those they killed, and remind any who passed through the outer wall of what happened to traitors in the twins' London.

Passing under the entryway and through the courtyard, Kell approached the massive stone steps. Ten guards flanked the stairs of the fortress, still as the statues in the forest. They were nothing but puppets, stripped by King Athos of everything but the breath in their lungs and the blood in their veins and his order in their ears. The sight of them made Kell shiver. In Red London, using magic to control, possess, or bind the body and mind of another person was forbidden. Here, it was yet another sign of Athos and Astrid's strength, their might—and therefore *right*—to rule.

The guards stood motionless; only their empty eyes followed him as he approached and passed through the heavy doors. Beyond, more guards lined the walls of an arching antechamber, still as stone save for their shifting gazes. Kell crossed the room and into a second corridor, this one empty. It wasn't until the doors closed behind him that Kell let himself exhale and lower his guard a fraction.

"I wouldn't do that just yet," said a voice from the shadows. A moment later a shape stepped out of them. Torches lined the walls, burning but never burning out, and in their flickering light Kell saw the man.

Holland.

The *Antari*'s skin was nearly colorless, and charcoal hair swept across his forehead, ending just above his eyes. One of them was a greyish green, but the other was glossy and black. And when that eye met Kell's, it felt like two stones sparking against each other.

"I've come with a letter," said Kell.

"Have you?" Holland said drily. "I thought you'd come for tea."

"Well, I'll take that, too, I suppose, while I'm here."

Holland's mouth quirked in something that wasn't a smile.

"Athos or Astrid?" he asked, as if it were a riddle. But riddles had right answers, and when it came to the Dane twins, there was none. Kell could never decide which one he would rather face. He didn't trust the siblings, not together, and certainly not apart.

"Astrid," he said, wondering if he'd chosen well.

Holland gave no indication, only nodded, and led the way.

The castle was built like a church (and maybe it had been one, once), its skeleton vast and hollow. Wind whistled through the halls, and their steps echoed over the stone. Well, *Kell's* steps did. Holland moved with the terrifying grace of a predator. A white half-cloak draped over one of his shoulders, billowing behind him as he walked. It was held together by a clasp, a silver circular broach, etched with markings that at a distance looked like nothing more than decoration.

But Kell knew the story of Holland and the silver clasp.

He hadn't heard it from the *Antari*'s lips, of course, but had bought the truth off a man at the Scorched Bone, traded the full story for a Red London lin several years before. He couldn't understand why Holland—arguably the most powerful person in the city, and perhaps the world—would serve a pair of glorified cutthroats like Astrid and Athos. Kell had himself been to the city a handful of times before the last king fell, and he had seen Holland at the ruler's side, but as an ally, not a servant. He had been different then, younger and more arrogant, yes, but there was also something else, something more, a light in his eyes. A *fire*. And then, between one visit and the next, the fire was gone, and so was the king, replaced by the Danes. Holland was still there, at their side as if nothing had changed. But *he* had changed, gone cold and dark, and Kell wanted to know what had happened—what had *really* happened.

So he went looking for an answer. And he found it, as he

found most things—and most found him—in the tavern that never moved.

Here it was called the Scorched Bone.

The storyteller clutched the coin as if for warmth as he hunched on his stool and spun the tale in Maktahn, the guttural native tongue of the harsh city.

"*Ön vejr tök...*" he began under his breath. *The story goes...*

"Our throne is not something you're born to. It's not held by blood. But taken by it. Someone cuts their way to the throne and holds it as long as they can—a year, maybe two—until they fall, and someone else rises. Kings come and go. It is a constant cycle. And usually, it is a simple enough matter. The murderer takes the place of the murdered.

"Seven years ago," the man continued, "when the last king was killed, several tried to claim his crown, but in the end, it came down to three. Astrid, Athos, and Holland."

Kell's eyes widened. While he knew Holland had served the prior crown, he had not known of his aspirations to be king. Though it made sense; Holland was *Antari* in a world where power meant everything. He should have been the obvious victor. Still, the Dane twins proved nearly as powerful as they were ruthless and cunning. And together, they defeated him. But they didn't kill him. Instead, they *bound* him.

At first Kell thought he'd misunderstood—his Maktahn wasn't as flawless as his Arnesian—and he made the man repeat the word. *Vöxt.* "Bound."

"It's that clasp," said the man in the Scorched Bone, tapping his chest. "The silver circle."

It was a binding spell, he explained. And a dark one at that. Made by Athos himself. The king had an unnatural gift for controlling others—but the seal didn't make Holland a mindless slave, like the guards that lined the castle halls. It didn't make him think or feel or want. It only made him *do*.

"The pale king is clever," added the man, fiddling with his coin. "*Terrible,* but clever."

Holland stopped abruptly, and Kell forced his mind and his gaze back to the castle hall and the door that now waited in front of them. He watched as the White *Antari* brought his hand to the door, where a circle of symbols was burned into the wood. He drew his fingers deftly across them, touching four in sequence; a lock yielded within, and he led Kell through.

The throne room was just as sprawling and hollow as the rest of the castle, but it was circular and made of brilliant white stone, from the rounded walls and the arching ribs of the ceiling to the glittering floors and the twin thrones on the raised platform in its center. Kell shivered, despite the fact the room wasn't cold. It only *looked* like ice.

He felt Holland slip away, but did not turn his attention from the throne, or the woman sitting on it.

Astrid Dane would have blended right in, if it weren't for her veins.

They stood out like dark threads on her hands and at her temples; the rest of her was a study in white. So many tried to hide the fact they were fading, covering their skin or painting it up to look healthier. The queen of White London did not. Her long colorless hair was woven back into a braid, and her porcelain skin bled straight into the edges of her tunic. Her entire outfit was fitted to her like armor; the collar of her shirt was high and rigid, guarding her throat, and the tunic itself ran from chin to wrist to waist, less out of a sense of modesty, Kell was sure, than protection. Below a gleaming silver belt, she wore fitted pants that tapered into tall boots (rumor had it that a man once spat at her for refusing to wear a dress; she'd cut off his lips). The only bits of color were the pale blue of her eyes and the greens and reds of the talismans that hung from her neck and wrists and were threaded through her hair.

Astrid had draped herself over one of the two thrones, her long thin body like taut wire under her clothes. Sinewy, but far from weak. She fiddled with a pendant at her neck, its surface like frosted glass, its edges as red as freshly drawn blood. *Strange,* thought Kell, *to see something so bright in White London.*

"I smell something sweet," she said. She'd been gazing up at the ceiling. Now her eyes wandered down and landed on Kell. "Hello, flower boy."

The queen spoke in English. Kell knew that she hadn't studied the language, that she—like Athos—relied on spellwork instead. Somewhere under her close-fitting clothes, a translation rune was scarred into her skin. Unlike the desperate tattoos made by the power hungry, the language rune was a soldier's response to a politician's problem. Red London treated English as a mark of high society, but White London found little use for it. Holland had told Kell once that this was a land of warriors, not diplomats. They valued battle more than ballrooms and saw no value in a tongue that their own people did not understand. Rather than waste years learning the common tongue between kings, those who took the throne simply took the rune as well.

"Your Majesty," said Kell.

The queen drew herself up into a sitting position. The laziness of her motions was a farce. Astrid Dane was a serpent, slow only until she chose to strike. "Come closer," she said. "Let me see how you've grown."

"I've been grown for some time," said Kell.

She drew a nail down the arm of the throne. "Yet you do not fade."

"Not yet," he said, managing a guarded smile.

"Come to me," she said again, holding out her hand. "Or I will come to you."

Kell was not sure if it was a promise or a threat, but he had no choice regardless, and so he stepped forward into the serpent's nest.

III

The whip cracked through the air, the forked end splitting open the skin of the boy's back. He did not scream—Athos wished he would—but a gasp of pain whistled through his clenched teeth.

The boy was pinned against a square metal frame like a moth, his arms spread wide, wrists bound to each of the two vertical bars that formed the square's sides. His head hung forward, sweat and blood trickling down the lines of his face, dripping from his chin.

The boy was sixteen, and he had not bowed.

Athos and Astrid had ridden through the streets of White London on their pale steeds, surrounded by their empty-eyed soldiers, relishing the fear in their people's eyes, and with it, their obedience. Knees hit stone. Heads bowed low.

But one boy—Athos later learned his name was Beloc, the word coughed through bloody lips—stood there, his head barely tipped forward. The eyes of the crowd had gone to him, a visceral ripple rolling through them—shock, yes, but underneath it, amazement bordering on approval. Athos had pulled his horse to a stop and gazed down at the boy, considering his moment of stubborn youthful defiance.

Athos had been a boy once, of course. He had done foolish, headstrong things. But he had learned many lessons in the struggle for the White crown, and many more since taking it as his own, and he knew above all that defiance was like a weed, something to be ripped out at the roots.

On her steed, his sister watched, amused, as Athos tossed a coin to the boy's mother, who stood beside him.

"*Öt vosa rijke,*" he said. "For your loss."

That night, the empty-eyed soldiers came, broke down the doors of Beloc's small house, and dragged the boy kicking and screaming and hooded into the street, his mother held back by a spell scrawled across the stone walls, unable to do anything but wail.

The soldiers dragged the boy all the way to the palace and delivered him, bloody and beaten, to the glittering white floor in front of Athos's throne.

"Look at this," Athos chided his men. "You've hurt him." The king stood and looked down at the boy. "That's my job."

Now the whip split air and flesh again, and this time, at last, Beloc screamed.

The whip cascaded from Athos's palm like liquid silver, pooling on the ground beside his boot. He began to coil it around his hand.

"Do you know what I see in you?" He wound the silver rope and slid it into a holster at his waist. "A fire."

Beloc spit blood on the floor between them. Athos's lips twisted. He strode across the chamber, caught hold of the boy's face by his jaw, and slammed his head back against the wood of the frame. Beloc groaned in pain, the sound muffled by Athos's hand over his mouth. The king brought his lips to the boy's ear.

"It burns through you," he whispered against the boy's cheek. "I cannot wait to carve it out."

"*Nö kijn avost,*" growled Beloc when the king's hand fell away. *I don't fear death.*

"I believe you," said Athos smoothly. "But I'm not going to

kill you. Though, I'm sure," he added, turning away, "you'll wish I had."

A stone table stood nearby. On it sat a metal chalice filled with ink, and beside it, a very sharp blade. Athos took up both and brought them to Beloc's pinned body. The boy's eyes widened as he realized what was about to happen, and he tried to fight against his binds, but they did not give.

Athos smiled. "You have heard then, about the marks I make."

The whole city knew of Athos's penchant—and his prowess—for binding spells. Marks that stripped away a person's freedom, their identity, their soul. Athos took his time readying the knife, letting the boy's fear fill the room as he swirled the metal through the ink, coating it. The length of the blade was grooved, the ink filling the notch as if it were a pen. When it was ready, the king drew the stained knife out, the gesture seductively slow, cruel. He smiled, and brought the tip to the boy's heaving chest.

"I'm going to let you keep your mind," said Athos. "Do you know why?" The blade's tip bit in, and Beloc gasped. "So I can watch the war play in your eyes every time your body obeys my will instead of yours."

Athos pressed down, and Beloc bit back a scream as the knife carved its way across his flesh, down his collar, over his heart. Athos whispered something low and constant as he drew the lines of the binding spell. Skin broke, and blood welled and spilled into the blade's path, but Athos seemed unbothered, his eyes half closed as he guided the knife.

When it was over, he set the blade aside and stepped back to admire his work.

Beloc was slumped against his binds, chest heaving. Blood and ink ran down his skin.

"Stand up straight," commanded Athos, satisfaction washing over him as he watched Beloc try to resist, his muscles shuddering against the instruction before giving in and dragging his wounded body up into a semblance of posture. Hatred burned through the boy's eyes, bright as ever, but his body now belonged to Athos.

"What is it?" asked the king.

The question wasn't directed at the boy, but at Holland, who had appeared in the doorway. The *Antari*'s eyes slid over the scene—the blood, the ink, the tortured commoner—his expression lodged between distant surprise and disinterest. As if the sight meant nothing to him.

Which was a lie.

Holland liked to play at being hollow, but Athos knew it was a ruse. He might have feigned numbness, but he was hardly immune to sensation. To pain.

"*Ös-vo tach?*" asked Holland, nodding at Beloc. *Are you busy?*

"No," answered Athos, wiping his hands on a dark cloth. "I think we're done for now. What is it?"

"He is here."

"I see," said Athos, setting aside the towel. His white cloak hung on a chair, and he took it up and slung it around his shoulders in one fluid motion, fastening the clasp at his throat. "Where is he now?"

"I delivered him to your sister."

"Well then," said Athos, "let's hope we're not too late."

Athos turned toward the door, but as he did, he caught Holland's gaze wandering back to the boy strapped against the metal frame.

"What should I do with him?" he asked.

"Nothing," said Athos. "He'll still be here when I get back."

Holland nodded, but before he could turn to go, Athos brought a hand to his cheek. Holland did not pull away, did not even stiffen under the king's touch. "Jealous?" he asked. Holland's two-toned eyes held Athos's, the green and the black both steady, unblinking. "He suffered," added Athos softly. "But not like you." He brought his mouth closer. "No one suffers as beautifully as you."

There it was, in the corner of Holland's mouth, the crease of his eye. Anger. Pain. Defiance. Athos smiled, victorious.

"We better go," he said, hand falling away. "Before Astrid swallows our young guest whole."

IV

Astrid beckoned.

Kell wished he could set the letter on the narrow table that sat between the thrones and go, keep his distance, but the queen sat there holding out her hand for it, for him.

He drew King Maxim's letter from his pocket and offered it to her, but when she reached to take it, her hand slid past the paper and closed around his wrist. He pulled back on instinct, but her grip only tightened. The rings on her fingers glowed, and the air crackled as she mouthed a word and lightning danced up Kell's arm, followed almost instantly by pain. The letter tumbled from his hand as the magic in his blood surged forward, willing him to act, to *react,* but he fought the urge. It was a game. Astrid's game. She *wanted* him to fight back, so he willed himself not to, even when her power—the closest thing to an element she could summon, something sharp, electric, and unnatural—forced a leg to buckle beneath him.

"I like it when you kneel," she said softly, letting go of his wrist. Kell pressed his hands flat against the cool stone floor and took a shaky breath. Astrid swiped the letter from the ground and set it on the table before sinking back into her throne.

"I should keep you," she added, tapping a finger thoughtfully against the pendant that hung from her throat.

Kell rose slowly to his feet. An aching pain rolled up his arm in the energy's wake. "Why's that?" he asked.

Her hand fell from the charm. "Because I do not like things that don't belong to me," she said. "I do not trust them."

"Do you trust *anything*?" he countered, rubbing his wrist. "Or any*one,* for that matter?"

The queen considered him, her pale lips curling at the edges. "The bodies in my floor all trusted someone. Now I walk on them to tea."

Kell's gaze drifted down to the granite beneath his feet. There were rumors, of course, about the bits of duller white that studded the stone.

Just then the door swung open behind him, and Kell turned to see King Athos striding in, Holland trailing several steps behind. Athos was a reflection of his sister, only faintly distorted by his broader shoulders and shorter hair. But everything else about him, from complexion to wiry muscle to the wanton cruelty they shared, was an exact replica.

"I heard we had company," he said cheerfully.

"Your Highness," said Kell with a nod. "I was just leaving."

"Already?" said the king. "Stay and have a drink."

Kell hesitated. Turning down the Prince Regent's invitation was one thing; turning down Athos Dane's was quite another.

Athos smiled at his indecision. "Look at how he worries, sister."

Kell did not realize she had risen from her seat until he felt her there beside him, running a finger down the silver buttons of his coat. *Antari* or not, the Danes made him feel like a mouse in the company of snakes. He willed himself not to pull away from the queen's touch a second time, lest it provoke her.

"I want to keep him, brother," said Astrid.

"I fear our neighboring crown would not be pleased," said Athos. "But he'll stay for a drink. Won't you, Master Kell?"

Kell felt himself nodding slowly, and Athos's smile spread, teeth glinting like knifepoints. "Splendid." He snapped his fingers and a servant appeared, turning his dead eyes up to his master. "A chair," ordered Athos, and the servant fetched one and set it behind Kell's knees before retreating, quiet as a ghost.

"Sit," commanded Athos.

Kell did not. He watched the king ascend the dais and approach the table between the thrones. On it sat a decanter of golden liquid and two empty glass goblets. Athos lifted one of the glasses, but did not pour from the decanter. Instead, he turned toward Holland.

"Come here."

The other *Antari* had retreated to the far wall, fading into it despite the near black of his hair and the true black of his eye. Now he came forward with his slow and silent steps. When he reached Athos, the king held out the empty goblet and said, "Cut yourself."

Kell's stomach turned. Holland's fingers drifted for an instant toward the clasp at his shoulder before making their way to his exposed side of his half-cloak. He rolled up his sleeve, revealing the tracery of his veins, but also a mess of scars. *Antari* healed faster than most. The cuts must have been deep.

He drew a knife from his belt and raised arm and blade both over the goblet.

"Your Majesty," said Kell hastily. "I have no taste for blood. Could I trouble you for something else?"

"Of course," said Athos lightly. "It's no trouble at all."

Kell was halfway through a shaky sigh of relief when Athos turned back to Holland, who'd begun to lower his arm. The king frowned. "I thought I said cut."

Kell cringed as Holland raised his arm over the goblet and drew the knife across his skin. The cut was shallow, a graze, just deep enough to draw blood. It welled and spilled in a thin ribbon into the glass.

Athos smiled and held Holland's gaze. "We haven't got all night," he said. "Press down harder."

Holland's jaw clenched, but he did as he was told. The knife bit into his arm, deep, and the blood flowed, a rich dark red, into the glass. When the goblet was full, Athos passed it to his sister and ran a finger along Holland's cheek.

"Go clean up," he said softly, gently, the way a parent would to a child. Holland withdrew, and Kell realized that he'd not only taken his seat, but was now gripping the arms of his chair with whitening knuckles. He forced his fingers free as Athos plucked the second glass from the table and poured the pale gold liquid into it.

He held it up for Kell to see, then drank to show the glass and contents alike were safe before pouring a new measure and offering it to Kell. The gesture of a man used to sabotage.

Kell took the glass and drank too fast and too deep in an effort to calm his nerves. As soon as the goblet was empty, Athos filled it again. The drink itself was light and sweet and strong, and went down easily. Meanwhile, the Danes shared their cup, Holland's blood turning their lips a vibrant red as they drank. *Power lies in the blood,* thought Kell as his own began to warm.

"It's amazing," he said, forcing himself to drink his second portion slower than his first.

"What is?" asked Athos, sinking into his throne.

Kell nodded at the goblet of Holland's blood. "That you manage to keep your clothes so white." He finished his second glass, and Astrid laughed and poured him a third.

V

Kell should have stopped at one drink.

Or two.

He thought he'd stopped at three, but he couldn't be entirely sure. He hadn't felt the full effects of the drink until he'd gotten to his feet, and the white stone floor had tilted dangerously beneath him. Kell knew that it was foolish, drinking as much as he had, but the sight of Holland's blood had rattled him. He couldn't get the *Antari*'s expression out of his mind, the look that crossed his face just before the knife bit down. Holland's visage was a perpetual mask of menacing calm, but just for an instant it had cracked. And Kell had done nothing. Had not pleaded—or even pressed—for Athos to yield. It wouldn't have done any good, but still. They were both *Antari*. Luck alone cast Holland here in ruthless White and Kell in vibrant Red. What if their fortunes had been reversed?

Kell took a shaky breath, the air fogging before his lips. The cold was doing little to clear his head, but he knew he couldn't go home, not yet, not like this, so he made his wandering way through the streets of White London.

This, too, was foolish. Reckless. He was always being reckless.

Why? he thought, suddenly angry at himself. Why did he always do this? Step out of safety and into shadow, into risk, into danger? *Why?* he heard Rhy begging on the roof that night.

He didn't know. He wished he did, but he didn't. All he knew was that he wanted to stop. The anger bled away, leaving something warm and steady. Or maybe that was the drink.

It had been a good drink, whatever it was. A strong drink. But not the kind of strong that made you weak. No, no, the kind of strong that made you strong. That made your blood sing. That made . . . Kell tipped his chin to look at the sky, and nearly lost his balance.

He needed to focus.

He was fairly sure he was heading in the general direction of the river. The air was biting against his lips, and it was getting dark—when had the sun gone down?—and in the dregs of light, the city was starting to stir around him. Silence cracking into noise.

"Pretty thing," whispered an old woman from a doorway in Maktahn. "Pretty skin. Pretty bones."

"This way, Master," called another.

"Come inside."

"Rest your feet."

"Rest your bones."

"Pretty bones."

"Pretty blood."

"Drink your magic."

"Eat your life."

"Come inside."

Kell tried to focus, but he couldn't seem to hold his thoughts together. As soon as he managed to gather a few, a breeze would blow through his head and scatter them, leaving him dazed and a little dizzy. Danger prickled at the edge of his senses. He closed his eyes, but every time he did, he saw Holland's blood running into the glass, so he forced them open and looked up.

He hadn't meant to head for the tavern. His feet had set out on their own. His body had made its way. Now he found himself staring at the sign over the door of the Scorched Bone.

Despite being a fixed point, the tavern in White London didn't *feel* like the others. It still pulled at him, but the air smelled like blood as well as ash, and the street stones were cold beneath his boots. They tugged at his warmth. His power. His feet tried to carry him forward, but he willed them to stay.

Go home, thought Kell.

Rhy was right. Nothing good could come of these deals. Nothing good enough. It wasn't worth it. The baubles he traded for, they brought him no peace. It was just a silly game. And it was time to stop.

He held on to that thought as he drew the knife from its holster and brought it to his forearm.

"It's you," came a voice behind him.

Kell turned, the blade sliding back to his side.

A woman stood there at the mouth of the alley, her face hidden by the hood of a threadbare blue cloak. If they'd been in any other London, the blue might have been the color of sapphires or the sea. Here it was the faintest shade, like the sky through layers and layers of clouds.

"Do I know you?" he asked, squinting into the dark.

She shook her head. "But I know you, *Antari*."

"No, you don't," he said with a fair amount of certainty.

"I know what you *do*. When you're not at the castle."

Kell shook his head. "I am not making deals tonight."

"Please," she said, and he realized that she was clutching an envelope. "I don't want you to bring me anything." She held out the letter. "I only want you *take* it."

Kell's brow crinkled. A letter? The worlds had been sealed off from one another for centuries. Who could she be writing *to*?

"My family," said the woman, reading the question in his eyes.

"Ages ago, when Black London fell, and the doors were sealed, we were divided. Over the centuries our families have tried to keep the thread . . . but I'm the only one left. Everyone here is dead but myself, and everyone there is dead but one. Olivar. He's the only family I have and he's on that side of the door and he's dying and I just want . . ." She brought the letter to her chest. "We are all that's left."

Kell's head was still swimming. "How did you even hear," he asked, "that Olivar was ill?"

"The other *Antari*," she explained, glancing around as if she feared someone would hear. "Holland. He brought me a letter."

Kell couldn't picture Holland deigning to smuggle *anything* between Londons, let alone correspondences between commoners.

"He didn't want to," added the woman. "Olivar gave him everything he had to buy the letter's passage and even then"—she brought her hand to her collar as if reaching for a necklace, and finding only skin—"I paid the rest."

Kell frowned. That seemed even less in Holland's nature. Not that he was selfless, but Kell doubted that he was greedy in this way, doubted that he cared about that kind of payment. Then again, everyone had secrets, and Holland wore his so close that Kell was forced to wonder how much he truly knew of the *Antari*'s character.

The woman thrust out the letter again. *"Nijk shöst,"* she said. *"Please,* Master Kell."

He tried to focus, to think. He'd promised Rhy . . . but it was only a letter. And technically, under the laws set out by the crowns of all three Londons, letters were a necessary exemption from the rule of no transference. Sure, they only meant letters between the *crowns* themselves, but still . . .

"I can pay you in advance," she pressed. "You needn't come

back to close the deal. This is the last and only letter. Please." She dug in her pocket and retrieved a small parcel wrapped in cloth, and before Kell could say yes or no, she pushed the note and payment both into his hands. A strange feeling shot through him as the fabric of the parcel met his skin. And then the woman was pulling away.

Kell looked down at the letter, an address penned onto the envelope, and then to the parcel. He went to unwrap it, and the woman shot forward and caught his hand.

"Don't be a fool," she whispered, glancing around the alley. "They'll cut you for a coin in these parts." She folded his fingers over the package. "Not here," she warned. "But it's enough, I swear. It must be." Her hands slipped away. "It's all I can give."

Kell frowned down at the object. The mystery of it was tempting, but there were too many questions, too many pieces that didn't make sense, and he looked up and started to refuse. . . .

But there was no one to refuse.

The woman was gone.

Kell stood there, at the mouth of the Scorched Bone, feeling dazed. What had just happened? He'd finally mustered the resolve to make no deals, and the deal had come to him. He stared down at the letter and the payment, whatever it was. And then, in the distance, someone screamed, and the sound jarred Kell back to the darkness and the danger. He shoved the letter and parcel both into the pocket of his coat, and drew his knife across his arm, trying to ignore the dread that welled with his blood as he summoned the door home.

FIVE

BLACK STONE

I

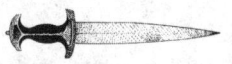

The silver jingled in Lila's pocket as she made her way back to the Stone's Throw.

The sun had barely set on the city, but she'd already managed a fair take that day. It was risky, picking pockets by anything but night—especially with her particular disguise, which required a blurred eye or low light—but Lila had to shoulder the risk if she was going to rebuild. A map and a silver watch did not a ship buy or a fortune make.

Besides, she liked the weight of coins in her pocket. They sang like a promise. Added swagger to her step. A pirate without a ship, that's what she was, through and through. And one day, she'd have the ship, and then she'd sail away and be done with this wretched city once and for all.

As Lila strolled down the cobblestones, she began making a mental list (as she often did) of all the things she'd need to be a proper privateer. A pair of good leather sea boots, for one. And a sword and scabbard, of course. She had the pistol, Caster—beauty that it was—and her knives, all sharp enough to cut, but every pirate had a sword and scabbard. At least the ones she'd met . . . and the ones she'd read about in books. Lila had never had much time for reading, but she *could* read—it was a good skill for a thief, and she turned out to be a quick study—and on the occasion that she nicked books, she nicked only the ones about pirates and adventures.

So, a pair of good boots, a sword, and scabbard. Oh, and a hat. Lila had the black, broad-brim one, but it wasn't very flashy. Didn't even have a feather, or a ribbon, or—

Lila passed a boy perched on a stoop a few doors shy of the Stone's Throw, and slowed, her thoughts trailing off. The boy was ragged and thin, half her age and as dirty as a chimney broom. He was holding out his hands, palms skyward, and Lila reached into her pocket. She didn't know what made her do it—good spirits, maybe, or the fact that the night was young—but she dropped a few coppers into the kid's cupped hands as she walked by. She didn't stop, didn't talk, and didn't acknowledge his thanks, but she did it all the same.

"Careful now," said Barron when she reached the tavern steps. She hadn't heard him come out. "Someone might think you've got a heart under all that brass."

"No heart," said Lila, pulling aside her cloak to reveal the holstered pistol and one of her knives. "Just these."

Barron sighed and shook his head, but she caught the edge of a smile, and behind it, something like pride. It made her squirm.

"Got anything to eat?" she asked, toeing the step with her worn-out boot.

He tipped his head toward the door, and she was about to follow him inside for a pint and a bowl of soup—she could spare that much coin, if he'd take it—when she heard a scuffle behind her. She turned to see a cluster of street rats—three of them, no older than she was—hustling the ragged boy. One of the rats was fat and one of them was skinny and one of them was short, and all of them were obviously scum. Lila watched as the short one barred the boy's path. The fat one shoved him up against the wall. The skinny one snatched the copper coins from his fingers. The boy barely fought back. He just looked down at his hands with a kind of grim resignation. They had been empty moments before, and they were empty again.

Lila's fists clenched as the three thugs vanished down a side road.

"Lila," warned Barron.

They weren't worth the work, Lila knew that. She robbed from the rich for a reason: they had more to steal. These boys probably didn't have anything worth taking besides what they'd already picked off of the boy in the street. A few coins Lila obviously hadn't minded parting with. But that wasn't the *point*.

"I don't like that look," said Barron when she didn't come inside.

"Hold my hat." She thrust the top hat into his hands, but reached in as she did and pulled the nested disguise from its depths.

"They're not worth it," he said. "And in case you didn't notice, there were three of them, and one of you."

"So little faith," she said, snapping the soft broad-brim hat into form. "And besides, it's the principle of the thing, Barron."

The tavern owner sighed. "Principle or not, Lila, one of these days, you're going to get yourself killed."

"Would you miss me?" she asked.

"Like an itch," he shot back.

She gave him the edge of a grin and tied the mask over her eyes. "Look after the kid," she said, pulling the brim of the hat down over her face. Barron grunted as she hopped down from the step.

"Hey, you," she heard Barron calling to the boy huddled on the nearby stoop, still staring at his empty hands. "Come over here...."

And then she was off.

II

7 Naresk Vas.

That was the address written on the envelope.

Kell had sobered considerably, and decided to go straight to the point of delivery and be done with the peculiar business of the letter. Rhy need never know. Kell would even drop the trinket—whatever it was—in his private room at the Ruby Fields before heading back to the palace so that he could, in good conscience, return empty-handed.

It seemed like a good plan, or at least, like the best of several bad ones.

But as he reached the corner of Otrech and Naresk, and the address on the paper came into sight, Kell slowed, and stopped, and then took two steps sideways into the nearest shadow.

Something was wrong.

Not in an obvious way, but under his skin, in his bones.

Naresk Vas looked empty, but it wasn't.

That was the thing about magic. It was everywhere. In everything. In *everyone*. And while it coursed like a low and steady pulse, through the air and the earth, it beat louder in the bodies of living things. And if Kell tried—if he *reached*—he could feel it. It was a sense, not as strong as sight or sound or smell, but there all the same, its presence now drifting toward him from the shadows across the street.

Which meant that Kell was not alone.

He held his breath and hung back in the alley, eyes fixed on the address across the street. And then, sure enough, he saw something *move*. A hooded figure hovered in the dark between 7 and 9 Naresk Vas. Kell couldn't see anything about him except the glint of a weapon at his side.

For a second, Kell—still a little off from his time with the Danes—thought it might be Olivar, the man whose letter he was holding. But it *couldn't* be Olivar. The woman said the man was dying, and even if he were well enough to meet Kell on the street, he couldn't *know* to meet him there, not when Kell himself had only just accepted the task. Which meant it wasn't Olivar. But if it wasn't him, who was it?

Danger prickled at the edges of Kell's skin.

He dragged the letter from his pocket, studying the address, then held his breath as he broke the seal and pulled the letter free. He bit back a curse.

Even in the dark, he could see that the paper was blank.

Nothing but a piece of folded parchment.

Kell's mind reeled. He'd been set up.

If they—whoever they were—weren't after the letter, then . . .

Sanct. Kell's hand went to the parcel still in his pocket. The *payment*. When his fingers curled around the folded cloth, that strange sensation ran up his arm again. What had he taken?

What had he done?

Just then, the shadow across the street looked up.

The paper in Kell's hand had caught the lantern light, just for a moment, but a moment was all it took. The shadow charged forward toward Kell.

And Kell turned, and ran.

III

Lila trailed the group of thugs through the winding London streets, waiting for them to go their separate ways. Barron was right: the odds weren't great against all three, but she had her sights set on one. And as the three broke into two and the two at last diverged, she followed her mark.

It was the thin one she was after, the rat who'd taken the coins off skin-and-bones back on the step. She hugged the shadows as she trailed him through the maze of narrowing roads, the stolen copper rattling in his pocket, a sliver of wood between his teeth. Finally, he turned off down an alley, and Lila slipped after, unheard, unseen, unnoticed.

As soon as they were alone, she closed the gap between them in a single stride and brought her knife up to the skinny rat's throat, pressing down hard enough to draw blood.

"Empty the pockets," she growled in a husky voice.

He didn't move. "Yer making a mistake," he said, shifting the wooden pick in his mouth.

She shifted her grip so the knife bit into his throat. "Am I?"

And then she heard the shuffle of steps rushing up behind her and ducked just in time to dodge a fist. Another one of the rats stood there, the short sod, one meaty hand clenched, the other gripping a metal bar. And then, an instant later, the fat one finally caught up, red-cheeked and breathless.

"It's *you*," he said, and for an instant Lila thought he recognized her. Then she realized he recognized the sketch in the WANTED ad. "The Shadow Thief."

The skinny one spit out his chewing stick and broke into a grin. "Looks like we caught ourselves a prize, gents."

Lila hesitated. She knew she could win against one street rat, and thought she might even be able to win against two, but three? Maybe, if they'd stand still, but they kept shifting so she couldn't see all of them at once. She heard the snick of a switchblade, the tap of the metal bar against the street stones. She had the gun in her holster and the knife in her hand, and another in her boot, but she wouldn't be fast enough to level all three boys.

"Did the poster say dead or alive?" asked the short one.

"You know, I don't think it specified," said the skinny one, wiping the blood from his throat.

"I think it said dead," added the fat one.

"Even if it said alive," reasoned the skinny one, "I don't suppose they'd mind if he were missing pieces." He lunged for her and she lunged away, accidentally stepping into the fat one's reach. He grabbed for her and she slashed, drawing blood before the short one got his hands on her. But when his arms circled her chest, she felt his grip stiffen.

"What's this now?" he hissed. "Our boy's a—"

Lila didn't wait. She slammed her boot into his foot, hard, and he gasped and let go. Only an instant, but it was enough for Lila to do the thing she knew she had to do, the one thing she *hated* to do.

She ran.

IV

Kell could hear the footsteps, first one set and then two and then three—or maybe the third was just the pumping of his heart—as he raced through the alleys and side streets. He didn't stop, didn't breathe, not until he reached the Ruby Fields. Fauna met his gaze as he passed within, her grey brow furrowing—he almost never came by the front door—but she didn't stop him, didn't ask. The footsteps had fallen away a few blocks back, but he still checked the markings on the stairs as he climbed toward the room at the top, and on the room's door—charms bound to the building itself, to wood and stone, designed to keep the room hidden from all eyes but his.

Kell shut the door and sagged back against the wood as candles flickered to life around the narrow room.

He'd been set up, but by who? And for *what*?

He wasn't sure he *wanted* to know, but he needed to, and so he dragged the stolen parcel from his pocket. It was wrapped in a swatch of faded grey fabric, and when he unfolded the cloth, a rough-cut stone tumbled out into his palm.

It was small enough to nest in a closed fist, and as black as Kell's right eye, and it sang in his hand, a low, deep vibration that called on his own power like a tuning fork. Like to like. Resonating. Amplifying. His pulse quickened.

Part of him wanted to drop the stone. The other part wanted to grip it tighter.

When Kell held it up to the candlelight, he saw that one side was jagged, as if broken, but the other was smooth, and on that smooth face a symbol glowed faintly.

Kell's heart lurched when he saw it.

He'd never seen the stone before, but he recognized the mark.

It was written in a language few could speak and fewer still could use. A language that ran through his veins with his blood and pulsed in his black eye.

A language he had come to think of simply as *Antari*.

But the language of magic hadn't always belonged to *Antari* alone. No, there were stories. Of a time when others could speak directly to magic (even if they couldn't command it by blood). Of a world so bonded to power that every man, woman, and child became fluent in its tongue.

Black London. The language of magic had belonged to them.

But after the city fell, every relic had been destroyed, every remnant in every world forcibly erased as part of a cleansing, a purge—a way to ward against the plague of power that had devoured it.

That was the reason there were no books written in *Antari*. What few texts existed now were piecemeal, the spells collected and transcribed phonetically and passed down, the original language eradicated.

It made him shiver now, to see it drawn as it was meant to be, not in letters, but in rune.

The only rune he knew.

Kell possessed a single book on the *Antari* tongue, entrusted to him by his tutor, Tieren. It was a leather journal filled with blood commands—spells that summoned light or darkness, encouraged growth, broke enchantments—all of them sounded out and explained, but on its cover, there was a symbol.

"What does it mean?" he'd asked the tutor.

"It's a word," explained Tieren. "One that belongs to every world and none. It is the word for 'magic.' It refers to its existence, and its creation...." Tieren brought a finger to the rune. "If magic had a name, it would be this," he said, tracing the symbol's lines. *"Vitari."*

Now Kell ran his thumb over the stone's rune, the word echoing in his head.

Vitari.

Just then, footsteps fell on the stairs, and Kell stiffened. No one should be able to see those stairs, let alone use them, but he could hear the boots. How had they followed him here?

And that's when Kell saw the pattern on the swatch of pale fabric that had once been wrapped around the stone and now lay unfolded on his bed. There were symbols scrawled across it. A tracing spell.

Sanct.

Kell shoved the stone in his pocket and lunged for the window as the small door behind him burst open violently. He mounted the sill and jumped out, and down, hitting the street below hard and rolling to his feet as the intruders came crashing into his room.

Someone had set him up. Someone wanted him to bring a forbidden relic out of White London and into *his* city.

A figure leaped through the window in his wake, and Kell spun to face the shadows on his heels. He expected two of them, but found only one. The hooded stranger slowed, and stopped.

"Who are you?" demanded Kell.

The shadow didn't answer him. It strode forward, reaching

for the weapon at its hip, and in the low alley light Kell saw an X scarred the back of his hand. The mark of cutthroats and traitors. A knife-for-hire. But when the man drew his weapon, Kell froze. It was no rusted dagger, but a gleaming half-sword, and he knew the sigil on its hilt. The chalice and rising sun. The symbol of the royal family. It was the blade wielded by members of the royal guard. And only by them.

"Where did you get that?" growled Kell, anger rolling through him.

The cutthroat flexed his fingers around his half-sword. It began to glow dully, and Kell tensed. The swords of the royal guards weren't just beautiful or sharp; they were *enchanted*. Kell himself had helped create the spellwork that ran through the metal, spellwork that dampened a magician's power with only one cut. The blades were designed to put a stop to conflicts before they began, to remove the threat of magical retaliation. Because of their potential, and the fear of that potential in the wrong hands, the royal guards were told to keep the blade on them at *all* times. If one of them had lost their sword, they'd likely lost their life as well.

"*Sarenach*," said the cutthroat. *Surrender*. The command caught Kell by surprise. Knives-for-hire took loot and blood, not prisoners.

"Put down that sword," ordered Kell. He tried to will the weapon from the cutthroat's grip, but it was warded. Another fail-safe to keep the blade from falling into the wrong hands. Which it already had. Kell swore and drew his own knife from its holster. It was a good foot shorter than the royal blade.

"Surrender," said the cutthroat again, his voice strangely even. He tilted up his chin and Kell caught a glimmer of magic in the man's eyes. A compulsion spell? Kell had only a moment to note the use of forbidden magic before the man lunged, the glowing weapon slicing through the air toward him. He jerked back, dodging the sword as a second figure appeared at the other end of the alley.

"Surrender," said the second man.

"One at a time," snapped Kell. He threw his hand into the air, and the street stones shuddered and then shot upward in a wall of rock and dirt, barring the second attacker's path.

But the first kept coming, kept slashing, and Kell scrambled backward out of the sword's arc. He almost made it; the blade caught his arm, slicing through fabric but narrowly missing his skin. He lunged away as the weapon cut again, but this time it found flesh, slashing across his ribs. Pain tore through Kell's chest as blood welled and spilled down his stomach. The man pressed forward and Kell retreated a step and tried to will the street stones to rise between them. They shuddered and laid still.

"Surrender," ordered the cutthroat in his too-even tone.

Kell pressed his hand to his shirtfront, trying to stem the blood as he dodged another slice. "No." He spun the dagger in his hand, took it by the tip, and threw as hard as he could. The blade found its mark, and buried itself in the cutthroat's shoulder. But to Kell's horror, the man didn't drop his weapon. He kept coming. Pain didn't even register on his face as he pulled the knife free and cast it aside.

"Surrender the stone," he said, dead-eyed.

Kell's hand closed protectively around the talisman in his pocket. It hummed against his palm, and Kell realized as he held it that even if he could give it away—which he couldn't, he wouldn't, not without knowing what it was for and who was after it—he didn't *want* to let it go. Couldn't bear the thought of parting with it. Which was absurd. And yet, something in him ached to keep it.

The cutthroat came at him again.

Kell tried to take another step back, but his shoulders met the makeshift barricade.

There was nowhere to run.

Darkness glittered in the cutthroat's eyes and his blade sang through the air, and Kell threw out his empty hand and ordered, *"Stop,"* as if that would do a damned thing.

And yet, somehow, it did.

The word echoed through the alley, and between one reverberation and the next, the night changed around him. Time seemed to slow, and so did the cutthroat, and so did Kell, but the stone clutched in his hand surged to life. Kell's own magic had bled out through the wound across his ribs, but the stone sang with power, and thick black smoke poured between his fingers. It shot up Kell's arm and across his chest and down his outstretched hand, and rushed forward through the air toward the cutthroat. When the smoke reached him, it did not strike him, did not force him off his feet. Instead, it twisted and coiled around the cutthroat's body, spreading over his legs, up his arms, around his chest. And everywhere it touched, as soon as it touched, it *froze,* catching the cutthroat between one stride and the next, one breath and the next.

Time snapped back into motion, and Kell gasped, his pulse pounding in his ears and the stone singing in his grip.

The stolen royal blade hung mid-slash, inches from his face. The cutthroat himself stood motionless, his coat caught mid-billow behind him. Through the sheet of shadowy ice or stone or whatever it was, Kell could see the cutthroat's stiff form, eyes open and empty. Not the blank gaze of the compelled, but the vacancy of the dead.

Kell stared down at the stone still thrumming in his hand, at the glowing symbol on its face.

Vitari.

It is the word for magic. It refers to its existence, and its creation.

Could it also mean the *act* of creating?

There was no blood command for *create*. The golden rule of magic said that it couldn't *be* created. The world was made of give and take, and magic could be strengthened and weakened, but it could not be manifested out of nothing. And yet . . . he reached out to touch the frozen man.

Had the power somehow been summoned by his blood? But he hadn't given a blood command, hadn't done anything but say "Stop."

The stone had done the rest.

Which was impossible. Even with the strongest elemental magic, one had to focus on the form they wanted it to take. But Kell hadn't envisioned the frozen shell, which meant the stone didn't simply follow an order. It *interpreted*. It *created*. Was this the way magic had worked in Black London? Without walls, without rules, without anything but want and will?

Kell forced himself to return the talisman to his pocket. His fingers didn't want to relinquish it. It took all his focus to let go, and the moment the stone slipped from his hand back into his coat, a dizzy chill ran through him, and the world rocked. He felt weak as well as wounded. Drained. *It isn't something for nothing after all,* thought Kell. But it was still something. Something powerful. Something dangerous.

He tried to straighten, but pain tore across his stomach, and he groaned, slumping back against the alley wall. Without his power, he couldn't will the wound closed, couldn't even keep his own blood in his veins. He needed to catch his breath, needed to clear his mind, needed to *think,* but just then the stones at his back began to shake, and he pushed off the wall an instant before it crumbled to reveal the second hooded figure.

"Surrender," said the man in the same even tone as his counterpart.

Kell could not.

He didn't trust the stone—even as he itched to take hold of it again—didn't know how to control it, but neither could he surrender it, so Kell lunged forward, recovering his own knife from the ground, and when the man came at him, he buried it in his attacker's chest. For a second, Kell worried the man wouldn't go down, feared the compulsion would keep him on his feet as it had the other one. Kell forced the blade deep and wrenched it up through organ and bone, and at last the man's knees buckled. For one brief moment, the compulsion broke, and the light flooded back into his eyes. And then it was gone.

It wasn't the first time Kell had killed someone, but he still felt ill as he pulled the knife free and the man crumpled, dead, at his feet.

The alley swayed and Kell clutched his stomach, fighting for breath as pain rolled through him. And then he heard another set of steps in the distance and forced himself upright. He stumbled past the bodies, the frozen and the fallen both, and ran.

V

Kell couldn't stop the blood.

It soaked through his shirtfront, the fabric clinging to him as he ran—stumbled—through the narrow maze of streets that gathered, weblike, in the corners of Red London.

He clutched at his pocket to make sure the stone was safe, and a thrum ran through his fingers as they felt it there. He should have run for the river, should have pitched the talisman into the glittering Isle and let it sink. He should have, but he hadn't, and that left him with a problem.

And the problem was catching up.

Kell cut a corner too sharp and skidded into the wall, biting back a gasp as his wounded side collided with the bricks. He couldn't keep running, but he had to get away. Somewhere he wouldn't be followed.

Somewhere he *couldn't* be followed.

Kell dragged himself to a stop and reached for the Grey London pendant at his neck, ripping the cord over his head.

Footsteps echoed, heavy and too close, but Kell held his ground and pressed his hand to his blood-soaked ribs, wincing. He brought his palm and the coin in it against the alley stones and said, *"As Travars."*

He felt the word pass his lips and shiver against his hand at the same time.

But nothing happened. The wall stayed where it was, and so did Kell.

Pain tore white-hot through his side from the royal blade, the spellwork cutting him off from his power. *No,* pleaded Kell silently. Blood magic was the strongest kind in the world. It couldn't be disabled, not by a simple piece of spellwork. It was stronger. It *had* to be stronger. Kell closed his eyes.

"As Travars," he said again.

He shouldn't have to say anything else, shouldn't have to force it, but he was tired and bleeding and fighting to focus his eyes, let alone his power, and so he added *"Please."*

He swallowed and brought his forehead to rest against the stones and heard the steps getting closer and closer and said, again, *"Please let me through."*

The stone hummed in his pocket, a whispered promise of power, of aid, and he was about draw it out and call upon its strength, when the wall finally shuddered and gave way beneath his touch.

The world vanished and an instant later reappeared, and Kell collapsed to the cobblestoned street, the subtle, steady light of Red London replaced by the dank, smoke-filled Grey London night. He stayed a moment on his hands and knees, and actually considered losing consciousness right there in the alley, but finally managed to get to his feet. When he did, the city slanted dangerously around him. He took two steps, and promptly collided with a man in a mask and a broad brim hat. Distantly, Kell knew it was strange, to be wearing a disguise, but he was hardly in a position to judge appearances, given his current state.

"Sorry," he mumbled, pulling his coat close around him to hide the blood.

"Where'd you come from?" asked the man, and Kell looked up and realized that under that disguise it wasn't a man at all. It was a woman. Not even that. A girl. All stretched out like a shadow, like Kell, but one even later in the day. Too long, too thin. But she was *dressed* like a man, boots and britches and a cloak (and under that, a few glinting weapons). And, of course, the mask and the hat. She seemed out of breath, as though she'd been running. *Strange,* thought Kell again.

He swayed a little on his feet.

"You all right there, gent?" asked the girl in disguise.

Footsteps sounded in the street beyond the alley, and Kell tensed, forcing himself to remember that he was safe now, safe here. The girl cast a quick glance back before returning her attention to him. He took a step toward her, and his legs nearly buckled beneath him. She went to catch him, but he caught himself against the wall first.

"I'll be okay," he whispered shakily.

The girl tipped her chin up, and there was something strong and defiant in her eyes and the lines of her jaw. A challenge. And then she smiled. Not with her whole mouth, just the edges, and Kell thought—in a far-off, woozy way—that under different circumstances, they might have been friends.

"There's blood on your face," she said.

Where wasn't *there blood?* Kell brought his hand to his cheek, but his hand was damp with it, too, so it wasn't much help. The girl came closer. She drew a small, dark kerchief from her pocket and reached out, dabbing his jaw with it before pressing the fabric into his hand.

"Keep it," she said. And then she turned and strode away.

Kell watched the strange girl go, then slumped back against the alley wall.

He tipped his head back and stared up at the Grey London sky, starless and bleak over the tops of the buildings. And then he reached into his pocket for the Black London stone, and froze.

It wasn't there.

He dug furiously through his pockets, every one of them, but it was no good. The talisman was gone. Breathless and bleeding and exhausted, Kell looked down at the kerchief clutched in his hand.

He couldn't believe it.

He'd been robbed.

SIX

THIEVES MEET

I

A London away, the city bells struck eight.

The sound came from the sanctuary at the city's edge, but it rang out over the glittering Isle and through the streets, pouring in open windows and out open doors and down alleys until it reached the Ruby Fields and, just beyond, the frozen figure of a man in the dark.

A man with an X on the back of his hand and a stolen royal sword still raised above his head. A man trapped in ice, or stone, or something stranger.

As the bells trailed off, a jagged crack formed in the shell over the man's face. And then another, down his arm. And a third, along the blade. Small fissures that deepened quickly, spreading like fingers through the casing.

"*Stop,*" the young *Antari* had ordered his attacker, and the attacker had not listened, but the magic had. It had poured out of the black stone in the *Antari*'s hand, coiled around the man, and hardened into a shell.

And now, the shell was breaking.

Not as a shell *should* break, the surface fracturing and the shards crumbling away, raining down upon the street. No, this shell broke apart and yet never let go of the man beneath. Instead, it clung to him as it melted, not down his body, but *into* it. Seeping in through his clothes and his skin until it was gone—or not gone. *Absorbed.*

The once-frozen man shuddered, then took a breath. The royal half-sword slipped from his fingers and clattered to the stones as the last shimmering drops of magic glistened like oil on his skin before sinking in, the veins darkening, tracing over him like ink. The man's head hung forward, eyes open, but empty. And fully black, pupils blown and spreading through irises and into whites.

The compulsion spell already cast on him had stripped the man's resistance and allowed the other magic to slip right in, through vein and brain and muscle, taking hold of everything it touched, the once-red core of life now burning pure and dark.

Slowly, the man—or rather now, the thing inside him—lifted his head. His black eyes shone, slick against the dry dark as he surveyed the alley. The body of the second cutthroat lay nearby, but he was already quite dead, the light snuffed out. Nothing to salvage. Nothing to burn. There wasn't much life left in his own body, either—just enough flame to feed on—but it would do for now.

He rolled his shoulders and began to walk, haltingly at first, as a man unused to his body. And then faster, surer. His posture straightened, and his legs strode toward the lights of the nearest building. The man's mouth drew into a smile. It was late, but the lanterns were lit in the windows, and laughter, high and sweet and promising, filled the air like the sound of bells.

II

Lila hummed as she made her way back to the Stone's Throw.

As she walked, she began to divest herself of the disguise; the mask came off first, followed by the broad-brim hat. She'd forgotten she was wearing them when she ran into the drunk fellow back in the alley, but he'd been so deep in his cups that he'd hardly seemed to notice. Just as he'd hardly seemed to notice her hand in his coat as she held up the kerchief, or her fingers curling around the contents of his pocket as she pressed the dark cloth into his palm. An easy mark.

Truth be told, she was still cross with herself for running—or rather, for falling into a trap and *needing* to run—from the trio of street rats. *But,* she thought, closing her hand around the satisfying weight in her cloak pocket, *the outing hadn't been a total waste.*

As the tavern came into sight, she pulled the trinket from her cloak and paused beneath a lamppost to get a closer look at the take. When she did, her heart sank. She'd hoped for metal, something silver, or gold, but the lump was stone. Not a gem or a jewel, either. Not even a bit of crystal. It looked like a river rock—glossy and black—one side smooth and the other jagged, like it had been smashed or chipped off from a larger piece of stone. What kind of gent walked around with rocks in his pocket? And broken ones at that?

And yet, she thought she could feel something, a kind of prickle where her skin met the stone's surface. Lila held it up to the light, and squinted at it a moment before dismissing the sensation and deeming the rock worthless—a sentimental trifle at best. Her mood soured as she shoved it back in her pocket and climbed the steps of the Stone's Throw.

Even though the tavern was bustling, Barron looked up when she came in, eyes going from her face to the disguise tucked under her arm. She thought she saw a flicker of concern, and it made her cringe. She wasn't his family. He wasn't hers. She didn't need his worry, and he didn't need her weight.

"Run into trouble?" he asked as she passed up the counter and went straight for the stairs.

She wasn't about to own up to being snared in the alley or running away from the fight, and her take had been a total bust, so she simply shrugged. "Nothing I couldn't handle."

The scrawny boy from the steps sat on a corner stool, eating a bowl of stew. Lila realized she was hungry—that is to say, hungrier than usual, Lila hadn't felt *full* in years—but she was tired, too, and relieved to find that the call of her bones to bed was louder than that of her stomach to table. Besides, she hadn't retrieved the coins. She had the silver, of course, but she had to save it if she was ever going to get out of this tavern, out of this city. Lila knew too well how the cycle went, thieves stealing only enough to stay thieves.

She had no intention of contenting herself to such meager victories. And now that she'd been made—she cursed the thought of three street rats discovering what three dozen constables hadn't, that their wanted man wasn't a man at all—stealing would only get harder. She needed larger scores, and she needed them soon.

Her stomach growled, and she knew Barron would give her

something for nothing if she could bring herself to ask for it, but she couldn't. She *wouldn't.*

Lila Bard might have been a thief but she wasn't a beggar.

And when she left—and she would—she had every intention of leaving behind the coin she owed him, down to the last farthing. She set off up the stairs.

At the top of the narrow steps stood a little landing with a green door. She remembered slamming that same door, shoving past Barron and down the steps, leaving only a tantrum in her wake. She remembered the fight—she'd stolen from a patron, and Barron had put her to task for it. What was worse, he'd wanted rent but barred her from paying him room and board with any "borrowed" coin. He'd wanted only honest money, and she had no way to get it, so he'd offered to pay her to help him run the tavern. She'd shot him down. Saying yes would have meant staying, and staying would have meant settling. In the end it'd been easier to hang the place and run. *Not away,* Lila had told herself. No, Lila had been running toward something. Something better. And even if she hadn't reached it yet, she would.

"This isn't a life!" she'd shouted, the handful of things she owned shoved under her arm. "This isn't anything. It's not enough. It's not fucking enough."

She hadn't adopted the disguise yet, hadn't been bold enough to rob outright.

There has to be more, she'd thought. *I have to be more.*

She'd grabbed the broad-brim hat from a hook near the door as she'd stormed out. It hadn't been hers.

Barron hadn't tried to stop her. He'd only gotten out of her way.

A life worth having is a life worth taking.

It had been almost a year—eleven months, two weeks, and a

handful of days—since she'd stormed away from the little room and the Stone's Throw, swearing she was done with both.

And yet here she was again. She reached the top of the stairs—each protesting her arrival as much as she did—and let herself in.

The sight of the room filled her with a mix of revulsion and relief. Bone-tired, she dug the rock from her pocket and dropped it with a thud onto a wooden table by the door.

Barron had set her top hat on the bed, and Lila sank down beside it to unlace her boots. They were worn to nearly nothing, and she cringed at the thought of how much it would cost to buy a decent pair. It wasn't an easy thing to steal. Relieving a man of his pocket watch was one thing. Relieving him of his shoes was quite another.

She was halfway through the strings on the first boot when she heard a sound of strain, like an *oof,* and looked up to find a man standing in her bedroom.

He hadn't come through the door—it was locked—and yet there he was, one bloody hand braced against the wall. Lila's kerchief was balled up between his palm and the wooden boards, and she thought she could make out a mark of some sort ghosted into the paneling beneath.

His hair hung down into his eyes, but she recognized him at once.

It was the fellow from the alley. The drunk one.

"Give it back," he said, breathing heavily. He had a faint accent, one she couldn't place.

"How the bloody hell did you get in?" she asked, rising to her feet.

"You have to give it back." Here, in the light of the close little room, she could see the shirt matted to his chest, the sheen of sweat across his brow. "You shouldn't . . . have taken . . . it. . . ."

Lila's eyes flicked to the stone where it sat on the table, and his gaze followed and stuck. They lunged for it at the same time. Or rather, Lila lunged for it. The stranger pushed off the wall in that general direction, swayed sharply, and then collapsed at her feet. His head bounced a little when it hit the floor.

Great, thought Lila, staring down at his body. She toed his shoulder with her boot, and when he didn't move, she knelt and rolled him over. He looked like he'd had a hell of a night. His black tunic was stuck to his skin; at first she thought it was sweat, but when she touched it, her fingers came away red. She considered searching his pockets and dumping his body out the window, but then she noticed the faint rise and fall of his chest through his stained shirt and realized he was not, in fact, dead.

Yet.

Up close, the stranger wasn't nearly as old as she'd first thought. Beneath a bit of soot and blood, his skin was smooth, and his face still held some boyish angles. He looked to be a year or two older than Lila herself, but not much more. She brushed the coppery hair from his forehead, and his eyelids fluttered and began to drift open.

Lila pulled back sharply. One of his eyes was a lovely blue. The other was pitch black. Not black-irised like some of the men she'd seen from the Far East, but a pure, *unnatural* black, running edge to edge, uninterrupted by color or white.

His gaze began to focus, and Lila reached for the nearest thing—a book—and struck him with it. His head lolled and his body went slack, and when he showed no signs of waking, she set the book aside, and took hold of his wrists.

He smells like flowers, she thought absently as she dragged his body across the floor.

III

When Kell came to, he was tied to a bed.

Coarse rope wound over his wrists, pinning them to the headboard behind him. His head was pounding, and dull pain spread through his ribs when he tried to move, but at least the bleeding had stopped, and when he reached for his power, he was relieved to feel it rise to meet him. The royal blade's spell had worn off.

After a few moments of self-assessment, Kell realized he wasn't alone in the room. Dragging his head up off the pillow, he found the thief perched in a chair at the foot of the bed, winding up a silver timepiece and watching him over her knees. She'd done away with her disguise, and Kell was surprised by the face beneath. Her dark hair was cut short along her jaw, which ended at a pointed chin. She looked young, but sharp, bony in a starved-bird kind of way. The only roundness came from her eyes, both brown, but not quite the same shade. He opened his mouth, intending to start their conversation with a question, like, *Will you untie me?* or *Where is the stone?* but instead found himself saying, "One of your eyes is lighter than the other."

"And one of your eyes is black," she shot back. She sounded cautious, but not frightened. Or, if she was, she was very good at hiding it. "What are you?" she asked.

"A monster," said Kell hoarsely. "You'd better let me go."

The girl gave a small, mocking laugh. "Monsters don't faint in the presence of ladies."

"Ladies don't dress like men and pick pockets," retorted Kell.

Her smile only sharpened. "What are you really?"

"Tied to your bed," said Kell matter-of-factly.

"And?"

His brow furrowed. "And in trouble."

That, at least, garnered a sliver of surprise. "Aside from the obvious being tied to my bed?"

"Yes," said Kell, struggling to sit up a little despite the binds so he could look her in the eye. "I need you to let me go and give me back the thing you stole." He scanned the room, hoping to catch sight of the stone, but it no longer sat on the table. "I won't turn you in," he added. "We'll pretend this never happened, but I *need* it."

He hoped she would glance, inch, even lean in the direction of the talisman, but she stayed perfectly still, her gaze unwavering. "How did you get in here?" she asked.

Kell chewed his cheek. "You wouldn't believe me," he said dismissively.

She shrugged. "I suppose we'll find out."

He hesitated. She hadn't flinched at the sight of his eye, and she hadn't turned him in or called for help when he marched bloodstained through a wall and into her room. The Grey world knew so little of magic, had forgotten so much, but there was something in the girl's gaze, a challenge that made him wonder if she would prove him wrong. If she *could*.

"What is your name?" he asked.

"Don't change the subject."

"I'm not," he said, twining his fingers around the ropes binding him to the bed. "I want only to know my captor."

She considered him a moment before answering. "Delilah

Bard," she said. "But Lila will do." *Lila*. A soft name but she used it like a knife, slashing out on the first syllable, the second barely a whisper of metal through air. "And my captive?"

"Kell," he said. "My name is Kell, and I come from another London, and I got into your room using magic."

Sure enough, her lips quirked. "Magic," she echoed drily.

"Yes," he said. "Magic." This time when he said the word, his grip tightened on the ropes and they caught fire and burned instantly to ash. A bit showy, perhaps, but it had the desired effect. Lila stiffened visibly in her chair as Kell sat fully upright on the bed. A wave of dizziness rolled over him, and he paused there, rubbing his wrists while he waited for the room to right itself.

"Specifically," he said, "I used magic to make a door."

He patted himself down and discovered that his knife was missing. She'd disarmed him. He frowned and swung his legs slowly off the bed, boots coming to rest against the floor. "When you picked my pocket in the alley, you gave me your kerchief. I was able to use it to make a door, one that led from me to you." Which was, incidentally, *much* harder than it sounded. Doors were meant to lead to places, not people. It was only the second time Kell had ever successfully used his magic to find his way to someone. Not to mention, he had been bleeding power with every step. It had been too much. The last dregs of magic had gotten him here, and then . . .

"Another London," said Lila.

"Yes."

"And you made a door."

"Yes."

"Using magic."

"Yes." He met her eyes then, expecting confusion, skepticism, disbelief, and finding something else. She was staring at him blankly—no, *not* blankly. Her gaze was intense. Assessing.

Kell hoped she wouldn't ask for another demonstration. His power was only just trickling back, and he needed to save it.

She lifted a finger to the wall, where the ghosted echo of his door still lingered. "I guess that explains the mark."

Kell frowned a little. Most people here couldn't see the echoes of spellwork, or at least, they didn't notice them. The marks, like most magic, passed beneath the spectrum of their senses.

"And the rock?" she asked.

"Magic," he said. *Black magic. Strong magic. Dead magic.* "Bad magic."

Finally, Lila slipped. For the briefest moment, her eyes flicked to a chest along the wall. Kell didn't hesitate. He lunged for the top drawer, but before his fingers met the wood, a knife found his throat. It had come out of nowhere. A pocket. A sleeve. A thin blade resting just below his chin. Lila's smile was as sharp as its metal edge.

"Sit down before you fall down, magic boy."

Lila lowered the knife, and Kell sank slowly onto the foot of the bed. And then, she surprised him a second time by producing the talisman, not from the top drawer of the chest as she'd hinted, but out of thin air. One moment her palm was empty, and the next the stone was simply there, her sleight of hand flawless. Kell swallowed, thinking. He could strip the knife from her grip, but she probably had another, and worse, she had the stone. She was human and knew nothing of magic, but if she made a request, the stone might very well answer. Kell thought of the cutthroat, encased in rock.

Lila ran her thumb over the talisman. "What's so bad about it?"

He hesitated, choosing his words. "It should not exist."

"What is it worth?"

"Your life," said Kell, clenching his fists. "Because trust me, whoever's after me will kill you in a blink to take it back."

Lila's gaze went to the window. "Were you followed?"

Kell shook his head. "No," he said slowly. "They can't follow me here."

"Then I have nothing to worry about." Her attention returned to the talisman. Kell could see the curiosity burning through her, and he wondered if the stone pulled at her the way it had at him.

"Lila," he said slowly. "Please put it down."

She squinted at the symbol on its face, as if somehow that would help her read it. "What does it mean?" Kell did not answer. "If you tell me, I will give it back."

Kell did not believe her but answered anyway. "It's the symbol for magic," he said. *"Vitari."*

"A magic stone called 'magic'? Not very original. What does it do?"

"I don't know." It was a kind of truth.

"I don't believe you."

"I don't care."

Lila frowned. "I'm beginning to think you don't want it back."

"I don't," said Kell, and it was mostly true, though a part of him wanted nothing more than to hold it again. "But I need it. And I answered your question."

Lila considered the stone. "A magic stone called magic," she mused, turning it over in her palm. "Which leads me to believe that it, what? *Makes* magic? Or makes things *out of* magic?" She must have seen the answer in Kell's worried face, because she smiled triumphantly. "A source of power, then . . ." She appeared to be having a conversation with herself. "Can it make anything? I wonder how it wor—"

Kell went for the talisman. His hand made it halfway there before Lila's knife slashed through the air and across his palm. He gasped as blood dripped to the floor.

"I warned you," she said, wagging the knife like a finger.

"Lila," he said wearily, cradling his hand to his chest. "Please. Give it back."

But Kell knew she wouldn't. There was a glint of mischief in her eye—a look, he knew, he had worn himself—as her fingers curled around the stone. What would she summon? What *could* she summon, this gangly little human? She held both hands ceremoniously out before her, and Kell watched, half in curiosity and half in concern, as smoke plumed out between her fingers. It wrapped around her free hand, twisting and hardening until she was holding a beautiful sword in a polished scabbard.

Her eyes widened with shock and pleasure.

"It worked," she whispered, half to herself.

The hilt shone the same glossy black of Kell's eye and the stolen stone, and when she pulled the sword free of its sheath, the metal glinted—black as well—in the candlelight, and solid as any hammered steel. Lila let out a delighted sound. Kell let out a breath of relief at the sight of the sword—it could have been worse—and watched as she set it against the wall.

"So you see," said Kell carefully. "Now hand it over." She didn't realize—couldn't realize—that this kind of magic was *wrong,* or that the stone was feeding on her energy. "Please. Before you hurt yourself."

Lila gave him a derisive glare and fondled the stone. "Oh no," she said. "I'm just getting started."

"Lila . . . ," began Kell, but it was too late. Black smoke was already pouring between her knuckles, much more of it than before, and taking shape in the room between them. This time, instead of a weapon, it pulled itself into the form of a young man. Not just any young man, Kell realized as the features smoothed from smoke into flesh.

It was *Kell.*

The resemblance was nearly flawless, from the coat with its

fraying hem to the reddish hair that fell across his face, obscuring his black eye. Only this Kell had no blue eye. Both glistened as hard and black as the rock in Lila's hand. The apparition didn't move, not at first, only stood there waiting.

The Kell that *was* Kell glared at the Kell that wasn't. "What do you think you're doing?" The question was directed at Lila.

"Just having a bit of fun," she said.

"You can't go around *making people*."

"Obviously I can," she said.

And then, the black-eyed Kell began to *move*. He shrugged off his coat and tossed it onto the nearest chair. And then, Kell watched with horror as his echo began to unfasten his tunic, one button at a time.

Kell gave a small, strangled laugh. "You've got to be kidding me." Lila only smiled and rolled the stone in her palm as the Kell that wasn't Kell slid slowly, teasingly, out of his tunic and stood there, bare chested. His fingers began to undo the belt at his waist.

"Okay, enough," said Kell. "Dispel it."

She sighed. "You're no fun."

"This *isn't* fun."

"Maybe not for you," she said with a smirk as the other Kell continued his striptease, sliding the belt from its loops.

But Lila didn't see what he saw: the once-blank face of the echo was beginning to *change*. It was a subtle shift in the magic, a hollow thing starting to fill.

"Lila," insisted Kell. "Listen to me. Dispel it *now*."

"Fine, fine," she said, meeting the black-eyed Kell's gaze. "Um . . . how do I do that?"

"You willed him into being," said Kell, getting to his feet. "Now will him *away*."

Lila's brow creased, and the phantom stopped divesting himself of clothes but did not disappear.

"Lila."

"I'm trying," she said, tightening her grip on the stone.

At that, the phantom Kell's face contorted, shifting rapidly from vacant to aware to *angry*. It was as if he *knew* what was happening. His eyes flicked from Lila's face to her hand and back to her face. And then he *lunged*. He moved so fast, an instant, a blink, and he was upon her. The stone tumbled from Lila's grip as the Kell that wasn't Kell slammed her back against the wall. His mouth opened to speak, but before he could, his hands dissolved—*he* dissolved—suddenly back into smoke, and then into nothing, and Lila found herself face-to-face with the Kell that *was* Kell, his bloody hand raised to the place where the illusion had been, his command—*As Anasae*—still echoing through the room.

Lila swayed on her feet and caught herself on the chest of drawers, her brief possession of the stone clearly taking its toll, the way it had on Kell. She managed to drag in a single shaky breath before he closed his bleeding hand around her throat.

"Where is my knife?" he growled.

"Top drawer," she said, gasping.

Kell nodded but didn't let her go. Instead, he grabbed her wrist and pinned it back to the wall beside her head.

"What are you doing?" she snapped, but Kell didn't answer. He focused on the wood, and it began to crack and warp, peeling away and growing up around her wrist. Lila struggled, but in an instant it was done. When Kell let go, the wall did not. He retrieved the stone from the floor as Lila twisted and fought against the makeshift bind.

"What the bloody hell . . . ?" She tried to pull free of the wooden cuff as Kell forced himself to pocket the stone. "You've ruined the wall. How am I supposed to pay for this? How am I supposed to *explain* this?"

Kell went to the drawer. There he found most of the contents of his pockets—thankfully she'd only raided the black coat he'd been wearing—and his knife.

"You can't leave me here like this," she muttered.

Kell refilled his pockets and ran a thumb over the familiar letters on his blade before returning it to the holster against his forearm. And then he heard the sound of metal sliding free of leather behind him as Lila fetched another dagger from a sheath at her back.

"I wouldn't throw that if I were you," he said, crossing to the window.

"Why's that?" she growled.

"Because," he said, sliding up the glass. "You're going to need it to saw yourself free."

And with that Kell stepped up onto the sill, and through.

It was a longer drop than he had hoped for, but he landed in a crouch, the air in the alley rushing up to ease his fall. The window had seemed the safest route, since Kell wasn't actually sure where in Grey London he was, or even what kind of house he'd been kept in. From the street, he realized it was not a house at all, but a tavern, and when he rounded the corner, he saw the sign swaying in the evening air. It swung from shadow into lamplight and then back to shadow, but Kell knew at a glimpse what it said.

THE STONE'S THROW.

He shouldn't have been surprised to see it—all roads seemed to lead here—but it still threw him. *What are the odds?* he thought, even though he knew that the thing about magic was that it bent the odds. But still.

Kell had a strange feeling about the girl, but he pushed it aside.

She didn't matter. He had the stone.

Now he just had to figure out what to do about it.

IV

It took Lila the better part of an hour to hack, slash, and saw herself free. By the time the wood finally gave way under her knife, the blade's edge was irreparably dulled, a portion of the wall was destroyed, and she was desperately in need of a stiff drink. Her coins had not multiplied, but savings be damned: tonight she needed the drink.

She rubbed the pain out of her wrist, tossed the dulled knife onto the bed, and fetched her second, still-sharp dagger from the floor, where she had dropped it. A steady stream of oaths crossed her lips as she wiped Kell's blood from the blade, and a steady stream of questions filled her head as she sheathed it, but she pushed them all down and dug her revolver out of the drawer, slotting it into its holster—if she'd had it on her at the time, she'd have blown a hole in Kell's head.

She was still quietly cursing and pulling her cloak about her shoulders when something caught her eye. The sword, the one she'd summoned, was still propped up against the wall. The bastard hadn't stopped to dispense of *that* on his way out. Now she lifted it carefully, beautiful thing that it was, and admired the glittering black hilt. It was everything she'd imagined it would be. Down to the details carved into the grip. The scabbard hummed beneath her fingers, just as the rock had when she'd held it. She *wanted* to keep the blade, wanted to keep *holding* it, with a strange, bone-deep sense of longing that she didn't trust. Lila knew what it felt like to want something, knew the way it whispered and sang and screamed in your bones. And this felt like that, but wasn't. An impostor of longing.

She remembered the way she had felt when she lost the rock, the sudden, gutting dizziness that followed, like all the energy had gone out of her limbs. Stolen when she wasn't looking. In a strange way, it reminded Lila of a pickpocket, a sly piece of sleight of hand. That was the way it worked. A proper trick took *two* hands, one you paid attention to, the other you failed to notice. Lila had been so focused on the one in front of her face, waving something shiny, that she hadn't noticed the other stealing from her pocket.

Bad magic, Kell had called it.

No, thought Lila now. *Clever magic.*

And *clever* was more dangerous than *bad* any day of the week. Lila knew that much. And so, much as it pained her to do it, she went to the open window and cast the sword out. *Good riddance,* she thought as she watched it tumble to the alley stones below.

Her gaze drifted up to the rooftops and the chimneystacks, and she wondered where Kell had gone. She wondered, but the question spawned a dozen others, and knowing she would never learn the answers to any of them, she slammed the window shut and went to find that drink.

A man stumbled through the front door of the Stone's Throw and nearly fell down the front stairs. *Tricky buggers,* he thought groggily. Surely, they hadn't been there when he entered the tavern only a few hours earlier. Or if they had, they'd gone and changed, rearranged somehow. Maybe there were more of them now. Or fewer. He tried to count them, but his vision blurred and he gave up, swaying on his feet.

The man's name was Booth, and he had to piss.

The thought rose up out of the fog and there it was, bright as a light. Booth scuffed his boots along the cobblestones to the nearest alley (he had the decency not to relieve himself on the steps, even if they *had* come out of nowhere).

He half walked, half tumbled into the narrow gap between the buildings, realizing only then how dark it was—he couldn't see his own hand, even if he'd been sober enough to look for it—but his eyes kept drifting shut anyway, so it didn't really matter.

Booth leaned his forehead against the cool stones of the tavern wall as he pissed, humming softly to himself, a shanty about women and wine and . . . something else that probably began with *w,* though he couldn't remember now. He let the melody wander off as he refastened his pants, but as he turned back toward the mouth of the alley, his boot caught something on the ground. It skidded away with a scrape before fetching up against the wall, and he might have left it there had a gust of wind not blown the nearest lantern on its hook, sending a flash of brightness into the darkened alley.

The shard of light glinted off metal, and Booth's eyes widened. He might have been several pints along, but greed was a sobering thing, and as the light vanished again, he found himself on his hands and knees on the damp alley floor, grasping in the shadows until his fingers finally curled around the prize.

Booth struggled to his feet and toddled a few steps nearer to the lantern light, and there realized that he was holding the casing of a sword, the weapon still safe within. The hilt glittered, not silver or gold or steel, but black. Black as oil, and smooth as rock. He wrapped his fingers around the grip and drew the weapon from its sheath, letting out a low groan of appreciation. The metal of the blade was as glossy and dark as the hilt. A strange sword, and rare by the looks of it. Booth weighed it in his meaty hands. It would fetch a pretty penny. A *very* pretty penny. Only in the right places, of course. Couldn't be thought stolen, of course. Finders keepers ... finders sellers, that is, and such, of course.

Funny thing, though.

His fingertips, where they curled around the hilt, had started to prickle. *That is a bit peculiar,* he thought, in that calm and distant way that comes with thorough intoxication. He wasn't worried, not at first. But then he tried to loosen his hold on the weapon and couldn't. He told his fingers to let go, but they remained firmly around the sword's gleaming black hilt.

Booth shook his hand, first slowly, then vigorously, but couldn't seem to free his fingers from the weapon. And then, quite suddenly, the prickle became a jolt, hot and cold and foreign at once, a very *unpleasant* feeling. It spread up his arm, beneath his skin, and when he stumbled back a step, toward the light at the mouth of the alley, he saw that the veins on the back of his hand, over his wrist and up his forearm, were turning *black*.

He shook his hand harder and nearly lost his balance, but still, he couldn't seem to release the sword. It wouldn't let him.

"Let go," he grumbled, unsure of whether he was speaking to his own hand or the weapon locked within it.

In response, the hand holding the sword—which did not seem to belong to him anymore at all—tightened on the hilt. Booth gasped as his fingers turned the blade slowly back toward his own stomach. "What the devil," he swore, grappling with himself, his free hand fighting to hold the other at bay. But it wasn't enough—the thing taking hold was stronger than the rest—and with a single clean thrust, Booth's hand, the one with the sword, drove it into his gut and buried it to the hilt.

He doubled over in the alley with a groan, hand still fixed to the grip. The black sword glowed with a dark internal light, and then began to *dissolve*. The gleaming weapon melted, not down, but in. Through the wound, and into Booth's body. Into his blood. His heartbeat faltered and then redoubled, steady and strong in his veins as the magic spread. His body shuddered, then stilled.

For a long moment, Booth—what remained of him—crouched there on the alley floor, motionless, hands to his stomach, where the blade had driven in, and where now, only an inky black stain, like melted wax, remained in its wake. And then, slowly, his arms slipped to his sides, the veins running over them now a true black. The color of true magic. His head drifted up, and he blinked two black eyes and looked around, then down at himself, considering his form. He flexed his fingers, carefully, testing.

And then, slowly, steadily, he got to his feet.

SEVEN

THE FOLLOWER

I

Lila could have simply gone down into the belly of the Stone's Throw, but she owed Barron enough already—he wouldn't take her coin, either because he thought she needed it or because it wasn't hers to begin with—and she needed the fresh air to clear her head.

Other Londons.

Men walking through magical doors.

Stones that made something out of nothing.

It was all the stuff of stories.

Of *adventures*.

All of it at her fingertips. And then gone. And Lila left feeling empty, hungry, and hollow in a new and terrifying way. Or maybe it was the same kind of hunger she'd always felt, and now the missing thing had a name: *magic*. She wasn't sure. All she knew was that, holding the stone, she'd felt something. And looking into Kell's ruined eye, she'd felt something. And when the magic spun the wood of the wall around her wrist, she'd felt something. Again the questions surged, and again she shoved them down, and took in the night air—thick with soot and heavy with impending rain—and trudged through the web of streets, and across Westminster to the Barren Tide.

The Barren Tide sat near just north of the bridge on the southern side, tucked between Belvedere and York in a crevice of a street called Mariner's Walk, and she'd taken to stopping in on some of her more successful nights before heading back to Powell (the way she'd seen it, it left one less coin for him to skim). She liked the pub because it was full of dark wood and fogging glass, rough edges and rougher fare. Not a smart place to pick pockets, but a fine place to blend in, to disappear. She had little fear of being recognized, either as a girl (the light was always kept low, and her hood kept up) or as a wanted thief (most of the patrons were wanted for *something*).

Her weapons were in easy reach, but she didn't think she'd need them. At the Barren Tide, people tended to mind their own business. On the not-so-rare occasion that a fight broke out, the regulars were more concerned for the safety of their drinks (they'd sooner save a pitcher from a shaking table than step in to help the man whose falling body shook it), and Lila imagined someone could cry for help in the middle of the room and earn little more than a tip of the cup and a raised brow.

Not a place for all nights, to be sure. But a place for tonight.

It wasn't until Lila was firmly stationed at the bar, fingers curled around a pint, that she let the questions take her mind and run free—the *why*s and *how*s and most of all *what now*s, because she knew she couldn't simply go back to not knowing and not seeing and not wondering—and she was so wrapped up in them, she didn't notice that a man had sat down beside her. Not until he spoke.

"Are you frightened?"

His voice was deep and smooth and foreign, and Lila looked up. "Excuse me?" she said, almost forgetting to keep her voice low.

"You're clutching your drink," explained the man, pointing at the fingers wrapped knuckles-white around her glass. Lila relaxed, but only a little.

"Long night," she said, bringing the warm beer to her lips.

"And yet still young," mused the man, taking a sip from his tumbler. Even in the Barren Tide, whose belly filled each night with a motley crew, the man seemed out of place. In the low light of the pub, he looked strangely ... faded. His clothes were dark grey, and he wore a simple short cloak held by a silver clasp. His skin was pale, made paler by the dark wood bar beneath his hands, his hair a strange, colorless shade just shy of black. When he spoke, his voice was steady without being sweet, empty in a way that gave her chills, and his accent had gravel in it.

"Not from around here, are you?" she asked.

The corner of his mouth tugged up at that. "No." He ran a finger absently around the rim of his glass. Except it didn't feel absent. None of his motions did. He moved with a slow precision that made Lila nervous.

There was something about him, odd and jarringly familiar at the same time. She couldn't see it, but she *felt* it. And then it struck her. That feeling. It was the same one she had looking into Kell's black eye, holding the stone, bound to the wall. A shiver. A tingle. A whisper.

Magic.

Lila tensed, and hoped it didn't show as she lifted the pint to her lips.

"I suppose we should be introduced," said the stranger, turning in his seat so she could see his face. Lila nearly choked on her drink. There was nothing amiss in the angle of his jaw or the set of his nose or the line of his lips. But his *eyes*. One was greyish green. The other was pitch-black. "My name is Holland."

A chill ran through her. He was the same as Kell, and yet entirely different. Looking into Kell's eye had been like looking through a window into a new world. Strange and confusing, but not frightening. Looking into Holland's eye made her skin crawl. Dark things swirled just beneath the smooth black depths. One word whispered through her mind. *Run*.

She didn't trust herself to lift her glass again, in case her hands shook, so she nudged it away and casually dug a shilling from her pocket.

"Bard," she said, by way of introduction and farewell.

She was about to push away from the counter when the man caught her wrist, pinning it to the weathered wood between them. A shiver ran up her arm at his touch, and the fingers of her free hand twitched, tempted toward the dagger under her cloak, but she resisted. "And your first name, miss?"

She tried to pull free, but his grip was made of stone. He didn't even appear to be trying. "Delilah," she growled. "Lila, if you like. Now let me go unless you want to lose your fingers."

Again his lips tugged into something that wasn't quite a smile.

"Where is he, Lila?"

Her heart lurched. "Who?"

Holland's grip tightened in warning. Lila winced.

"Do not lie. I can smell his magic on you."

Lila held his gaze. "Perhaps because he used it to cuff me to a wall after I robbed him blind and tied him to a bed. If you're looking for your friend, don't look at me. We met on bad terms and parted on worse."

Holland's grip loosened, and Lila let out an inward sigh of relief. But it died an instant later when Holland was suddenly on his feet. He took her roughly by the arm and dragged her toward the door.

"What in bloody hell are you doing?" she snapped, boots scraping against the worn floor as she tried and failed to gain purchase. "I told you, we are not friends."

"We'll see," said Holland, driving her forward.

The patrons of the Barren Tide never even looked up from

their drinks. *Bastards,* thought Lila as she was shoved roughly out into the street.

The moment the pub door closed behind them, Lila went for the revolver at her belt, but for someone whose movements seemed so slow, Holland was fast—*impossibly* fast—and by the time she pulled the trigger, she'd fired into nothing but air. Before the shot even finished sounding, Holland reappeared, this time at her back. She felt him there, felt the air shift the barest moment before one of his hands closed around her throat, pinning her shoulders against his chest. The other hand wrapped around the fingers on her pistol and brought the barrel to rest against her temple. The whole thing had taken less than a breath.

"Divest yourself of weapons," he instructed. "Or I will do it for you."

His grip wasn't crushing; if anything, his hold was casual, confident, and Lila had been around cutthroats long enough to know that the ones you truly had to fear were the ones who gripped their guns loosely, like they'd been born holding them. Lila used her free hand to dig the knife out of her belt and drop it to the ground. She freed a second from her back. A third she usually kept in her boot, but it was sitting on her bed, ruined. Holland's hand slid from her throat to her shoulder, but he cocked the pistol in warning.

"What, no cannons?" he asked drily.

"You're mad," growled Lila. "Your friend Kell, he's long gone."

"Do you think?" asked Holland. "Let's find out."

The air around them began to crackle with energy. With *magic*. And Holland was right: she could *smell* it. Not flowers, as with Kell (flowers and something else, something grassy and clean). Instead, Holland's power smelled metallic, like heated steel. It singed the air.

She wondered if Kell would be able to smell it, too. If that's what Holland wanted.

There was something else in that magic—not a smell, but a sense all the same—something sharp, like anger, like hate. A fierceness that didn't show in the lines of Holland's face. No, his face was startlingly calm. Terrifyingly calm.

"Scream," he said.

Lila frowned. "What do you—"

The question was cut off by pain. A bolt of energy, like bottled lightning, shot up her arm where he gripped it, dancing over her skin and electrifying her nerves, and she cried out before she could stop herself. And then, almost as quickly as the pain came, it vanished, leaving Lila breathless and shaking.

"You . . . bastard," she snarled.

"Call his name," instructed Holland.

"I can assure you . . . he's not . . . going to come," she said, stumbling over the words. "Certainly not . . . for *me*. We—"

Another wave of pain, this one brighter, sharper, and Lila clenched her jaw against the scream and waited for the pain to pass, but this time it didn't; it only worsened, and through it she could hear Holland say calmly, "Perhaps I should start breaking bones?"

She tried to say no, but when she opened her mouth to answer, all she heard was a cry, and then, as if encouraged, the pain worsened. She called Kell's name then, for all the good it would do her. He wouldn't come. Maybe if she tried, this madman would realize that and let her go. Find another form of bait. The pain finally petered out, and Lila realized she was on her knees, one hand gripping the cold stone street, the other wrenched up behind her, still in Holland's grip. She thought she was going to be sick.

"Better," said Holland.

"Go to hell," she spat.

He jerked her up to her feet and back against him, and brought the gun beneath her chin. "I've never used a revolver," he said in her ear. "But I know how they work. Six shots, yes? You've fired one. That leaves five more, if the gun was full. Do you think I could fire the rest without killing you? Humans die so easily, but I bet, if I'm clever . . ." He let the gun slide down her body, pausing at her shoulder, her elbow, before trailing down her side to her thigh and coming to rest against her knee. "The sooner he comes, the sooner I will let you go. *Call his name.*"

"He won't come," she whispered bitterly. "Why do you refuse to believe—"

"Because I know our friend," said Holland. He lifted his gun-wielding hand—Lila shuddered with relief as the kiss of metal left her skin—and wrapped his arm casually around her shoulders. "He is near. I can hear his boots on the street stones. Close your eyes. Can you hear him?"

Lila squeezed her eyes shut, but all she could hear was the thud of her heart and the thought racing through her mind. *I don't want to die. Not here. Not now. Not like this.*

"Bring him to me," whispered Holland. The air began to hum again.

"Don't—" Lila's bones lit up with pain. It shot from her skull to her weathered boots and back, and she screamed. And then, suddenly, the agony stopped and the sound died on her lips and Holland let go. She crumpled forward to the cobbled street, the stones scraping against her knees and palms as she caught herself.

Through the pounding in her head, she heard Holland's voice say, "There you are."

She dragged her head up and saw Kell standing in the road, the strange magical boy in his black coat, looking breathless and angry.

Lila couldn't believe it.

He'd come back.

But *why* had he come back?

Before she could ask, he looked straight at her—one eye black and one blue and both wide—and said a single word.

"Run."

II

Kell had been standing on the bridge, leaning against the rail and trying to make sense of how and why he'd been set up—the false letter, the humble plea, the compelled cutthroats—when he caught the scent of magic on the air. Not a faint tendril, either, but a flare. A beacon of light in a darkened city. And a signature he would know anywhere. Heated steel and ash.

Holland.

Kell's feet carried him toward it; it wasn't until he stepped off the south edge of the bridge that he heard the first scream. He should have stopped right then, should have thought things through. It was a blunt and obvious trap—the only reason Holland would send up a flare of power was if he wanted to be noticed, and the only person in Grey London who would notice him was Kell—but he still broke into a sprint.

Were you followed? Lila had asked him.

No. They can't follow me here.

But Kell had been wrong. No one in the worlds could follow him . . . except for Holland. He was the only one who could, and had, which meant that he was after the stone. It also meant that Kell should be running *away* from the signature and the scream, not toward them.

The voice cried out again, and this time he was near enough to recognize the source of the cry being raked across the heavy air.

Lila.

Why would Holland go after *her*?

But Kell knew the answer. It sat like a weight in his chest. Holland would go after Lila because of *him*. Because in a world with so little magic, every trace stood out. And Lila would have traces—both his magic, and the stone's—written all over her. Kell knew how to cover his. Lila couldn't possibly. She'd be like a torch.

It's her own fault, thought Kell, even as he ran toward the scream. *Her own damn fault.*

He raced down the street, ignoring the burn across his ribs and the voice in his head that told him to leave her, to get away while he still could.

A blunt and obvious trap.

He cut down along the river, through an alley, around a bend, and came to a staggering halt on a narrow street just in time to hear Lila's scream cut off, to see her body sagging forward to the cobblestones. Holland stood over her, but his eyes were trained on Kell.

"There you are," he said, as if he were happy to see the other *Antari*.

Kell's mind spun. Lila looked up.

"Run," he told her, but she just kept staring at him. "Lila, *go.*"

Her eyes focused then, and she staggered to her feet, but Holland caught her by the shoulder and pressed a pistol to the base of her neck.

"No, Lila," he said in his calm, infuriating way. "Stay."

Kell's hands curled into fists. "What is this about, Holland?"

"You know quite well. You have something that isn't yours."

The stone hung heavy in his pocket. No, it wasn't his. But it wasn't Holland's, either. And it certainly didn't belong to the White throne. Had the power-hungry Danes possessed the talisman, they never would have relinquished it, let alone sent it away. But who *would*? Who *did*?

With its power, Astrid and Athos would be nearly invincible, yes, but a commoner could use the stone's magic to become a king. In a world starving for power, why would anyone go to such lengths to be rid of it?

Fear, thought Kell. Fear of the magic, and fear of what would happen if it fell into the twins' hands. Astrid and Athos must have learned of the stone and its escape, and sent Holland to retrieve it.

"Give me the stone, Kell."

His mind spun. "I don't know what you're talking about."

Holland gave him a withering look. His fingers tightened almost imperceptibly around Lila, and power crackled across her skin. She bit back a scream and fought to stay on her feet.

"Stop," demanded Kell. Holland did.

"Will you make me repeat myself?" he asked.

"Just let her go," said Kell.

"The stone first," said Holland.

Kell swallowed as he drew the talisman from his coat. It sang through his fingertips, wanting to be used. "You can try and take it from me," he said, "as soon as you let her go." Even as the words left Kell's lips, he regretted them.

The corner of Holland's mouth curled grimly up. He withdrew his hand, one finger at a time, from Lila's arm. She staggered forward and spun on him.

"Fly away, little bird," he said, his gaze still trained on Kell.

"Go," snapped Kell.

He could feel Lila's eyes hanging on him, but he wasn't foolish enough to let his own stray from Holland—not now—and he let out a small breath when he finally heard her boots echoing on the street stones. *Good,* he thought. *Good.*

"That was foolish," said Holland, tossing the revolver aside as if it were beneath him. "Tell me, are you are as arrogant as you seem, or only as naïve?"

"Holland, please—"

The *Antari*'s gaze darkened. "You look at me, Kell, and think we are alike. That we are the same, even, one person on two divergent paths. Perhaps you think our power bonds us. Allow me to correct your misapprehension. We may share an ability, you and I, but that does not make us equals."

He flexed his fingers, and Kell had the sneaking suspicion that this was going to end badly. Holland had fought against the Danes. Holland had spilled blood and life and magic. Holland had nearly claimed the White throne as his own.

Kell must seem like a spoiled child to the other *Antari*.

But Kell still had the stone. It was bad magic, forbidden magic, but it was something. It called to him, and he tightened his grip, the jagged side digging into his palm. Its power pressed at his edges, wanting to be let in, and he resisted, keeping a wall between the talisman's energy and his own. He didn't need much. He only needed to summon something inanimate—something that would stop Holland without turning on them both.

A cage, he thought. And then commanded. *A cage.*

The stone hummed in his hand, and black smoke began to pour between his fingers, and—

But Holland didn't wait.

A gust of wind ripped through the air and slammed Kell forcefully into the door of a shop behind him. The stone tumbled from his grip, the wisps of black smoke dissolving back into nothing as the talisman hit the street. Before Kell could lunge for it, the metal nails of another door shuddered free and sang through the air, driving into his coat and pinning him to the wood. Most of the nails found fabric, but one of them found flesh, and Kell gasped in pain as the spike drove through his arm and into the door behind him.

"Hesitation is the death of advantage," mused Holland as Kell fought in vain against the metal pinnings. He willed them to move, but Holland willed them to stay, and Holland's will proved stronger.

"What are you doing here?" asked Kell through gritted teeth.

Holland sighed. "I thought it would be obvious," he said, stepping toward the stone. "I'm cleaning up a mess."

As Holland made his way toward the talisman, Kell fought to focus on the metal pinning him. The nails began to tremble as his will pushed against the other *Antari*'s. They slid free an inch—Kell clenched his jaw as the one in his arm shifted—Holland's attention wavering as he knelt to fetch the stone from the ground.

"Don't," warned Kell.

But Holland ignored him. He took up the talisman and straightened, weighing it in his palm. His will and attention were both centered on the stone now, and this time when Kell focused, the nails holding him shuddered and slid free. They drew themselves out of the wall—and out of his coat and his flesh—and clattered to the ground just as Holland held the stone up to the nearest lamplight.

"Drop it," ordered Kell, clutching his wounded arm.

Holland didn't.

Instead, he cocked his head and considered the small black stone. "Have you figured out yet how it works?" And then, as Kell lunged forward, Holland's thin fingers folded over it. Such a small gesture, slow, casual, but the moment his fist closed, black smoke poured between his fingers and swept around Kell. It happened so fast. One moment he was surging forward, and the next his legs froze mid-step. When he looked down, he saw shadows swirling around his boots.

"Stay," commanded Holland as the smoke turned to steel,

heavy black chains that grew straight out of the street and clanged as they locked around Kell's ankles, bolting him in place. When he reached for them, they burned his hands, and he pulled back, hissing in pain.

"Conviction is key," observed Holland, running his thumb over the stone's surface. "*You* believe that magic is an equal. A companion. A friend. But it is not. The stone is proof. You are either magic's master, or its slave."

"Put it down," said Kell. "No good will come of it."

"You're right," said Holland, still clutching the stone. "But I have my orders."

More smoke poured forth from the talisman, and Kell braced himself, but the magic didn't settle, didn't take shape. It swirled and curled around them, as if Holland hadn't yet decided what to do with it. Kell summoned a gust of air, hoping to dispel it, but the wind passed straight through, billowing Holland's cloak but leaving the dark magic untouched.

"Strange," said Holland as much to himself as to Kell. "How one small rock can do so much." His fingers tightened around the stone then, and the smoke coiled around Kell. Suddenly it was everywhere, Blotting out his vision and forcing its way into his nose and mouth, down his throat, choking him, smothering him.

And then it was gone.

Kell coughed and gasped for breath, and looked down at himself, unhurt.

For an instant, he thought the magic had failed.

And then he tasted blood.

Kell brought his fingers toward his lips, but stopped when he saw that his entire palm was wet with red. His wrists and arms felt damp, too.

"What . . . ," he started, but couldn't finish. His mouth filled with copper and salt. He doubled over and retched before losing his balance and collapsing to his hands and knees in the street.

"Some people say magic lives in the mind, others the heart," said Holland quietly, "but you and I both know it lives in the blood."

Kell coughed again, and fresh red dotted the ground. It dripped from his nose and mouth. It poured from his palms and wrists. Kell's head spun and his heart raced as he bled out onto the street. He wasn't bleeding from a wound. He was just *bleeding*. The cobblestones beneath him were quickly turning slick. He couldn't stop it. He couldn't even get to his feet. The only person who could break the spell was staring down at him with a resignation that bordered on disinterest.

"Holland . . . listen to me," pleaded Kell. "You can . . ." he fought to focus. "The stone . . . it can make . . ."

"Save your breath."

Kell swallowed and forced the words out. "You can use the stone . . . to *break your seal.*"

The White *Antari* raised a charcoal brow, and then shook his head. "This *thing*," he said, tapping the silver circle at his shoulder, "is not what's binding me." He knelt before Kell, careful to avoid the spreading blood. "It's only the iron." He pulled aside his collar to reveal the mark scorched into the skin over his heart. "*This* is the brand." The skin was silvery, the mark strangely fresh, and even though Kell couldn't see Holland's back, he knew the symbol went all the way through. *A soul seal.* A spell burned not only into one's body, but into one's life.

Unbreakable.

"It never fades," said Holland, "but Athos still reapplies the mark now and then. When he thinks I'm wavering." He looked down at the stone in his hand. "Or when he's bored." His fingers tightened around it, and Kell coughed up more blood.

Desperately, he reached for the coin pendants around his

neck, but Holland got there first. He dug them out from under Kell's collar and snapped the cords with a swift tug, tossing the tokens away down the alley. Kell's heart sank as he heard the sound of them bouncing into the dark. His mind spun over the blood commands, but he couldn't seem to hold the words in his head, let alone shape them. Every time one rose up, it fell apart, broken by the thing killing him from the inside. Every time he tried to make a word, more blood filled his mouth. He coughed and clutched at syllables, only to choke on them.

"*As . . . An . . .*" he stammered, but the magic forced blood up his throat, blocking the word.

Holland clucked his tongue. "My will against yours, Kell. You will never win."

"Please," Kell gasped, breath ragged. The dark stain beneath him was spreading too fast. "Don't . . . do this."

Holland gave him a pitying look. "You know I don't have a choice."

"*Make one.*" The metallic smell of blood filled Kell's mouth and nose. His vision faltered again. One arm buckled beneath him.

"Are you afraid of dying?" asked Holland, as if genuinely curious. "Don't worry. It's really quite hard to kill *Antari*. But I can't have—"

He was cut off by a glint of metal in the air and the ringing sound of it striking bone as it connected with his skull. Holland went down hard, the stone tumbling from his grip and skittering several feet into the dark. Kell managed to focus his eyes enough to see Lila standing there, clutching an iron bar with both hands.

"Am I late?"

Kell let out a small dazed laugh that quickly dissolved into wracking coughs. Fresh blood stained his lips. The spell hadn't broken. The chains around his ankles began to tighten, and he gasped. Holland wasn't attacking him, but the magic still was.

He tried desperately to tell Lila, but he couldn't find the air. And thankfully, he didn't need it. She was ahead of him. She snatched up the stone, swiped it across the bloody ground, and then held it out in front of her like a light.

"*Stop,*" she ordered. Nothing.

"*Go away.*" The magic faltered.

Kell pressed his hands flat into the pool of blood beneath him. "*As Anasae,*" he said, and coughed, the command finally passing his lips without Holland's will to force it down.

And this time, the magic listened.

The spells broke. The chains dissolved to nothing around his legs, and Kell's lungs filled with air. Power flooded through what little blood was left in his veins. It felt like there was nearly none.

"Can you stand?" asked Lila. She helped him to his feet, and the whole world swayed, his sight plunging into black for several horrible seconds. He felt her grip on him tighten.

"Keep it together," she said.

"Holland . . ." he murmured, his voice sounding strange and faraway in his own ears. Lila looked back at the man sprawled on the ground. Her hand closed over the stone, and smoke poured out.

"Wait . . ." said Kell shakily, but the chains were already taking shape, first in smoke and then in the same dark metal he'd only just escaped. They seemed to grow straight out of the street and coil around Holland's body, his waist and wrists and ankles, pinning him to the damp ground as he had pinned Kell. It wouldn't hold him long, but it was better than nothing. At first, Kell marveled that Lila could summon something so specific. Then he remembered she didn't need to have power. She needed only to *want* a thing. The stone did the rest.

"No more magic," he warned as she shoved the stone into her pocket, the strain showing on her face. Her grip had vanished for a moment, and when he took a step forward, he nearly collapsed, but Lila was there again to catch him.

"Steady now," she said, pulling his arm around her narrow shoulders. "I had to find my gun. Stay with me."

Kell clung to consciousness as long as he could. But the world was dangerously quiet, the distance between his thoughts and his body growing further apart. He couldn't feel the pain in his arm where the nail had struck—couldn't feel much of anything, which scared him more than the pressing dark. Kell had fought before, but never like this, never for his life. He'd gotten into his fair share of scrapes (most of them Rhy's fault) and had had his fair share of bruises, but he'd always walked away intact. He'd never been seriously hurt, never struggled to keep his own heart beating. Now he feared that if he stopped fighting, if he stopped forcing his feet forward and his eyes open, that he might actually die. He didn't want to die. Rhy would never forgive him if he died.

"Stay with me," echoed Lila.

Kell tried to focus on the ground beneath his boots. On the rain that had started to fall. On Lila's voice. The words themselves began to blur together, but he held on to the sound as he fought to keep the darkness at bay. He held on as she helped him over the bridge that seemed to go on and on forever, and through the streets that wound and tipped around them. He held on as hands—Lila's and then another's—dragged him through a doorway and up a flight of old stairs and into a room, stripping off his blood-soaked clothes.

He held on until he felt a cot beneath him and Lila's voice stopped and the thread was gone.

And then he finally, gratefully, plummeted down into black.

III

Lila was soaked to the bone.

Halfway across the bridge, the sky had finally opened up—not a drizzle, as London often seemed to favor, but a downpour. Within moments, they had been soaked through. It certainly didn't make dragging the half-conscious Kell any easier. Lila's arms ached from holding him up—she nearly fumbled him twice—and by the time she reached the back door of the Stone's Throw, Kell was barely conscious and Lila was shivering and all she could think was that she should have kept running.

She hadn't lived this long and stayed this free by stopping to help every fool who got himself into trouble. It was all she could do to keep herself *out* of trouble, and whatever else Holland was, he was clearly trouble.

But Kell had come back.

He didn't have to—didn't have any reason to—but he had, all the same, and the weight of it clung to her when she fled, slowing her down before finally dragging her boots to a stop. Even as she turned around, raced back, a small part of her had hoped that she'd be too late. Hoped they'd already be gone. But the rest of her wanted get there in time, if only to know *why*.

Why had he come back?

Lila asked him that very question as she was dragging him to his feet. But Kell didn't answer. His head lolled against her collar. What the hell had happened? What had Holland done to him?

Lila couldn't even tell if Kell was still bleeding—she didn't see an obvious wound—but he was covered in blood and it made her wish she'd struck Holland a second time for good measure. Kell made a soft sound, between a gasp and a groan, and Lila started talking, worried that he might die on her and it would somehow be her fault, even though she'd come back.

"Stay with me," she'd said, wrapping his arm around her shoulders. With his body so close to hers, all she could think of was the smell. Not of blood—that didn't bother her—but of the *other* scents, the ones that clung to Kell, and to Holland. Flowers and earth and metal and ash.

I can smell his magic on you.

Is that what it was? The scent of magic? She had noticed Kell's in a passing way, when she first dragged his body across her bedroom floor. Now, with his arm draped around her, the scent was overpowering. The trace of Holland's burning steel lingered in the air. And even though the stone was safely in her pocket, she could smell it, too, its scent washing over the alley. Like sea and wood smoke. Salt and darkness. She felt a moment of pride for the strength of her senses until she remembered that she hadn't smelled Kell's flowers or the stone's smoke on herself as she made her way to the Barren Tide, or as she sat at the counter, and Holland had tracked her there by both.

But the rain fell heavy and steady, and soon she could smell nothing but water on stones. Maybe her nose wasn't strong enough. Maybe the scent of magic was still there, beneath the rain—she didn't know if it *could* be expunged, or at least dampened—but she hoped the storm would help cover their trail.

She was halfway up the stairs, Kell's boots leaving red-tinged water in their wake, when a voice stopped her.

"What in *God's name* are you doing?"

Lila twisted around to see Barron, and Kell nearly slipped from her grasp. She caught him round the middle at the last instant, narrowly saving him from a tumble down the steps. "Long story. Heavy body."

Barron cast a backward glance at the tavern, shouted something to the barmaid, and charged up the steps, a rag thrown over his shoulder. Together they hoisted Kell's soaking body up the remaining stairs and into the little room at the top.

Barron held his tongue as they stripped away Kell's wet coat and stained shirt, and laid him down on Lila's bed. He didn't ask her where she'd found this stranger, or why there was no wound to explain the bloody trail he'd left on the tavern's stairs (though the gash across his ribs was still quite angry). When Lila scoured the room for something to burn (in case the rain had not been enough to hide their scent, in case it still lingered here from earlier that night) and came up empty, Barron didn't ask, only went to fetch some herbs from the kitchen below.

He watched silently as she held a bowl of them over a candle and let the room fill with an earthy smell that had nothing to do with Kell or Holland or magic. He stayed as she dug through the pockets of Kell's coat (which turned out to be several coats somehow folded into one) in search of something—anything—that might help mend him (he was a magician, after all, and it stood to reason that magicians carried around magic). And Barron said nothing when at last she dug the black stone from her pocket and dropped it in a small wooden box, setting a handful of warm herbs inside before shoving the lot into the bottom drawer of her chest.

It wasn't until Lila slumped down into the chair at the foot of the bed and began to clean her pistol that Barron finally spoke.

"What are you doing with this man?" His eyes were dark and narrow.

Lila looked up from her gun. "You know him?"

"In a way," said Barron archly.

"You know what he is then?" she asked.

"Do *you*?" challenged Barron.

"In a way," she retorted. "First I took him for a mark."

Barron ran a hand through his hair, and Lila realized for the first time that it was thinning. "Christ, Lila," he muttered. "What did you take?"

Her gaze flicked to the bottom drawer of the chest, then drifted back to Kell. He looked deathly pale against the dark blanket on her bed, and he wasn't moving, save for the faint rise and fall of his chest.

She took him in, the magical young man in her bed, first so guarded, now exposed. Vulnerable. Her eyes trailed up the lines of his stomach, over his wounded ribs, across his throat. They wandered down his arms, bare but for the knife strapped to his forearm. She hadn't touched it this time.

"What happened?" asked Barron.

Lila wasn't entirely sure how to answer that. It had been a very strange night.

"I stole something, and he came looking for it," she said quietly, unable to draw her eyes from Kell's face. He looked younger asleep. "Took it back. I thought that was the end of that. But someone else came looking for him. Found me instead . . ." She trailed off, then picked up. "He saved my life," she said, half to herself, brow crinkling. "I don't know why."

"So you brought him here."

"I'm sorry," said Lila, turning toward Barron. "I didn't have anywhere else to go." The words stung even as she said them. "As soon as he wakes—"

Barron was shaking his head. "I'd rather you here than dead.

The person who did this"—he waved a hand at Kell's body—"are *they* dead?"

Lila shook her head.

Barron frowned. "Best tell me what they look like, so I know not to let them in."

Lila described Holland as best she could. His faded appearance. His two-toned eyes. "He feels like Kell," she added. "If that makes sense. Like—"

"Magic," said Barron matter-of-factly.

Lila's eyes widened. "How do you . . . ?"

"Running a tavern, you meet all kinds. Running *this* tavern, you meet all kinds, and then some."

Lila realized she was shivering, and Barron went in search of another tunic for Kell while she changed. He came back with an extra towel, a small pile of clothes, and a steaming bowl of soup. Lila felt ill and grateful at the same time. Barron's kindness was like a curse, because she knew she had done nothing to deserve it. It wasn't fair. Barron did not owe her anything. Yet she owed him so much. Too much. It drove her mad.

Still, her hunger had finally caught up with her fatigue, and the cold in her skin was quickly becoming the cold in her bones, so she took the soup and mumbled a thank-you and added the cost to the coin she already owed, as if this kind of debt could ever be paid.

Barron left them and went below. Outside, the night wore on. The rain wore on, too.

She didn't remember sitting down, but she woke up an hour or so later in her wooden chair with a blanket tossed over her shoulders. She was stiff, and Kell was still asleep.

Lila rolled her neck and sat forward.

"Why did you come back?" she asked again, as if Kell might answer in his sleep.

But he didn't. Didn't mumble. Didn't toss or turn. He just lay there, so pale and so still that now and then Lila would hold a piece of glass to his lips to make sure he hadn't died. His bare chest rose and fell, and she noticed that, present injuries aside, he had so few scars. A faint line at his shoulder. A much fresher one across his palm. A ghosted mark in the crook of his elbow.

Lila had too many scars to count, but she could count Kell's. And she did. Several times.

The tavern below had quieted, and Lila got to her feet and burned a few more herbs. She turned her silver watch and waited for Kell to wake. Sleep dragged at her bones, but every time she thought of rest, she imagined Holland stepping through her wall, the way Kell had. Pain echoed through her arm where he'd gripped her, a small jagged burn the only relic, and her fingers went to the Flintlock at her hip.

If she had another shot, she wouldn't miss.

EIGHT

AN ARRANGEMENT

I

Kell woke up in Lila's bed for the second time that night.

Though at least this time, he discovered, there were no ropes. His hands rested at his sides, bound by nothing but the rough blanket that had been cast over him. It took him a moment to remember that it was Lila's room, Lila's bed, to piece together the memory of Holland and the alley and the blood, and afterward, Lila's grip and her voice, as steady as the rain. The rain had stopped falling now, and low morning light was creeping into the sky, and for a moment all Kell wanted was to be home. Not in the shoddy room in the Ruby Fields, but at the palace. He closed his eyes and could almost hear Rhy pounding on his door, telling him to get dressed because the carriages were waiting, and so were the people.

"Get ready or be left behind," Rhy would say, bursting into the room.

"Then leave me," Kell would groan.

"Not a chance," Rhy would answer, wearing his best prince's grin. "Not today."

A cart clattered past outside, and Kell blinked, Rhy fading back into nothing.

Were they worried about him yet, the royal family? Did they have any idea what was happening? How could they? Even Kell did not know. He knew only that he had the stone, and that he needed to be rid of it.

He tried to sit up, but his body cried out, and he had to bite his tongue to keep from voicing it. His skin, his muscle, his very bones . . . everything ached in a steady, horrible way, as if he were nothing but a bruise. Even the beat of his heart in his chest and the pulse of his blood through his veins felt sore, strained. He felt like death. It was as close as he had ever come, and closer than he ever wished to be. When the pain—or at least the novelty of it—lessened, he forced himself upright, bracing a hand against the headboard.

He fought to focus his vision, and when he managed, he found himself looking squarely into Lila's eyes. She was sitting in that same chair at the foot of the bed, her pistol in her lap.

"Why did you do it?" she asked, the question primed on her tongue, as if she'd been waiting.

Kell squinted. "Do what?"

"Come back," she said, the words low. "Why did you come back?" Two words hung in the air, unsaid but understood. *For me.*

Kell fought to drag his thoughts together, but even they were as stiff and sore as the rest of him. "I don't know."

Lila seemed unimpressed by the answer, but she only sighed and returned her weapon to the holster at her waist. "How are you feeling?"

Like hell, thought Kell. But then he looked down at himself and realized that, despite his aching body, the wound at his arm, where the nail had driven through, as well as the one across his stomach from the cutthroat's stolen sword, were nearly healed. "How long was I asleep?"

"A few hours," said Lila.

Kell ran a hand gingerly over his ribs. That didn't make

sense. Cuts this deep took days to mend, not hours. Not unless he had a—

"I used this," said Lila, tossing a circular tin his way. Kell plucked it out of the air, wincing a little as he did. The container was unmarked, but he recognized it at once. The small metal tin contained a healing salve. Not just any healing salve, but one of his own, the royal emblem of the chalice and rising sun embossed on its lid. He'd misplaced it weeks ago.

"Where did you get this?" he asked.

"In a pocket in your coat," said Lila, stretching. "By the way, did you *know* that your coat is more than one coat? I'm pretty sure I went through five or six to find that."

Kell stared at her, slack-jawed.

"What?" she asked.

"How did you know what it was for?"

Lila shrugged. "I didn't."

"What if it had been *poison*?" he snapped.

"There's really no winning with you," she snapped back. "It smelled fine. It seemed fine." Kell groaned. "And obviously I tested it on myself first."

"You did *what*?"

Lila crossed her arms. "I'm not repeating myself just so you can gape and glare." Kell shook his head, cursing under his breath as she nodded at a pile of clothes at the foot of the bed. "Barron brought those for you."

Kell frowned (saints, even his brow hurt when it furrowed). He and Barron had a *business* agreement. He was pretty sure it didn't cover shelter and personal necessities. He would owe him for the trouble—and it *was* trouble. Both of them knew it.

Kell could feel Lila's eyes hanging on him as he reached for the clean tunic and shrugged it gingerly over his shoulders. "What is it?" he asked.

"You said no one would follow you."

"I said no one *could,*" corrected Kell. "Because no one can, except for Holland." Kell looked at his hands and frowned. "I just never thought—"

"One is not the same thing as none, Kell," said Lila. And then she let out a breath and ran a hand through her cropped dark hair. "But I suppose you didn't exactly have all your wits about you." Kell looked up in surprise. Was she actually excusing him? "And I did hit you with a book."

"What?"

"Nothing," said Lila, waving her hand. "So this Holland. He's like you?"

Kell swallowed, remembering Holland's words in the alley—*We may share an ability, you and I, but that does not make us equals—* and the dark, almost disdainful look that crossed his face when he said it. He thought of the brand burned into the other *Antari*'s skin, and the patchwork of scars on his arms, and the White king's smug smile as Holland pressed the knife into his skin. No, Holland was nothing like Kell, and Kell was nothing like Holland.

"He can also move between worlds," explained Kell. "In that way, we are alike."

"And the eye?" questioned Lila.

"A mark of our magic," said Kell. "*Antari.* That is what we are called. Blood magicians."

Lila chewed her lip. "Are there any others I should know about?" she asked, and Kell thought he saw a sliver of something—fear?—cross her features, buried almost instantly behind the stubborn set of her jaw.

Kell shook his head slowly. "No," he said, "We are the only two."

He expected her to look relieved, but her expression only grew graver. "Is that why he didn't kill you?"

"What do you mean?"

Lila sat forward in her chair. "Well, if he'd wanted to kill you, he could have. Why bleed you dry? For the fun of it? He didn't seem to be enjoying himself."

She was right. Holland could have slit his throat. But he hadn't.

It's really quite hard to kill Antari. Holland's words echoed in Kell's head. *But I can't have—*

Can't have what? wondered Kell. Ending an *Antari*'s life might be hard, but it wasn't impossible. Had Holland been fighting against his orders, or following them?

"Kell?" pressed Lila.

"Holland never enjoys himself," he said under his breath. And then he looked up sharply. "Where is the stone now?"

Lila gave him a long weighing look and then said, "I have it."

"Then give it back," demanded Kell, surprising himself with his own urgency. He told himself it would be safest on his person, but in truth, he wanted to *hold* it, couldn't shake the sense that if he did, his aching muscles would be soothed and his weak blood strengthened.

She rolled her eyes. "Not this again."

"Lila, listen to me. You've no idea what—"

"Actually," she cut in, getting to her feet, "I'm starting to get a decent idea of what it can do. If you want it back, tell me the rest."

"You wouldn't understand," said Kell automatically.

"Try me," she challenged.

Kell squinted at her, this strange girl. Lila Bard did seem to have a way of figuring things out. She was still alive. That said something. *And* she'd come back for him. He didn't know why—cutthroats and thieves weren't usually known for their moral compasses—but he did know that without her, he would be in a far worse state.

"Very well," said Kell, swinging his legs off the bed. "The stone is from a place known as Black London."

"You mentioned other Londons," she said, as if the concept were curious, but not entirely impossible. She didn't faze easily. "How many are there?"

Kell ran a hand through his auburn hair. It stuck up at odd angles from rain and sleep. "There are four worlds," he said. "Think of them as different houses built on the same foundation. They have little in common, save for their geography, and the fact that each has a version of this city straddling this river on this island country, and in each, that city is called London."

"That must be confusing."

"It isn't, really, when you live in only one of them and never need think of the others. But as someone who moves between, I use color to keep them straight. Grey London, which is yours. Red London, which is mine. White London, which is Holland's. And Black London, which is no one's."

"And why's that?"

"Because it fell," said Kell, rubbing the back of his neck where the pendant cords had snapped. "Lost to darkness. The first thing about magic that you have to understand, Lila, is that it is not inanimate. It is alive. Alive in a different way than you or I, but still very much alive."

"Is that why it got angry?" she asked. "When I tried to get rid of it?"

Kell frowned. He'd never seen magic *that* alive.

"Nearly three centuries ago," he said slowly, working out the math (it seemed further away, the effect of being so long referred to as simply "the past"), "the four worlds were twined together; magic and those who wielded it able to move between them with relative ease through any one of the many sources."

"Sources?"

"Pools of immense natural power," explained Kell. "Some small, discreet—a copse of trees in the Far East, a ravine on the Continent—others vast, like your Thames."

"The Thames?" said Lila with a derisive snort. "A source of magic?"

"Perhaps the greatest source in the world," said Kell. "Not that you'd know it here, but if you could see it as it is in *my* London..." Kell trailed off. "As I was saying, the doors between the worlds were open, and the four cities of London intermingled. But even with constant transference, they were not entirely equal in their power. If true magic were a fire, then Black London sat closest to the heat." By this logic, White London stood second in strength, and Kell knew it must have, though he could not imagine it now. "It was believed that the power there not only ran strong in the blood, but pulsed like a second soul through everything. And at some point, it grew too strong and overthrew its host.

"The world sits in balance," said Kell, "humanity in one hand, magic in the other. The two exist in every living thing, and in a perfect world, they maintain a kind of harmony, neither exceeding the other. But most worlds are not perfect. In Grey London—your London—humanity grew strong and magic weak. But in Black London, it was the other way around. The people there not only held magic in their bodies, they let magic into their minds, and it took them as its own, burning up their lives to fuel its power. They became vessels, conduits, for its will, and through them, it twisted whim into reality, blurring the lines, breaking them down, creating and destroying and corrupting everything."

Lila said nothing, only listened and paced.

"It spread like a plague," continued Kell, "and the other three remaining worlds retreated into themselves and locked their doors to prevent the spread of sickness." He did not say that it had been *Red* London's retreat, its sealing off of itself, that forced the other cities to follow, and left White London pinned between their closed doors and Black London's seething magic. He did not say that the world caught between was forced to fight the darkness back alone. "With the sources restricted, and the doors locked, the remaining three cities were isolated and began to diverge, each becoming as they are now. But what became of Black London and the rest of its world, we can only guess. Magic requires a living host—it can thrive only where life does, too—so most assume that the plague burned through its hosts and eventually ran out of kindling, leaving only charred remains. None know for sure. Over time, Black London became a ghost story. A fairy tale. Told so many times that some don't even think it real."

"But the stone . . . ?" said Lila, still pacing.

"The stone shouldn't exist," said Kell. "Once the doors were sealed, every relic from Black London was tracked down and destroyed as a precaution."

"Obviously not *every* relic," observed Lila.

Kell shook his head. "White London supposedly undertook the task with even more fervor than we did. You must understand, they feared the doors would not hold, feared the magic would break through and consume them. In their cleanse, they did not stop at objects and artifacts. They slit the throats of everyone they even suspected of possessing—of having come in contact with—Black London's corrupted magic." Kell brought his fingers to his blackened eye. "It is said that some mistook *Antari*'s marks for such corruption and dragged them from their houses in the night. An entire generation slaughtered before they realized that, without the doors, such magicians would be their only way of reaching out." Kell's hand fell away. "But no, obviously not *every* relic was destroyed." He wondered if that was how it had been broken, if they'd tried, and failed and buried it, wondered if someone new had dug it up. "The stone shouldn't exist and it can't be allowed to exist. It's—"

Lila stopped pacing. "Evil?"

Kell shook his head. "No," he said. "It is *Vitari*. In a way, I suppose it is pure. But it is pure potential, pure power, pure *magic*."

"And no humanity," said Lila. "No harmony."

Kell nodded. "Purity without balance is its own corruption. The damage this talisman could manage in the wrong hands . . ." *In* anyone's *hands,* he thought. "The stone's magic is the magic of a ruined world. It cannot stay here."

"Well," said Lila, "what do you intend to do?"

Kell closed his eyes. He didn't know who had come across the stone, or how, but he understood their fear. The memory of it in Holland's hands—and the thought of it in Athos's or Astrid's—turned his stomach. His own skin sang for the talisman, thirsted for it, and that scared him more than anything. Black London fell because of magic like this. What horror would it bring to the Londons that remained? To the starving White, or the ripened Red, or the defenseless Grey?

No, the stone had to be destroyed.

But how? It wasn't like other relics. It wasn't a thing to be tossed in a fire or crushed beneath an ax. It looked as though someone had tried, but the broken edge did not seem to diminish its function, which meant that even if he did succeed in shattering it, it might only make more pieces, rendering every shard its own weapon. It was no mere token; the stone had a life—and a will—of its own, and had shown so more than once. Only strong magic would be able to unmake such a thing, but as the talisman was magic itself, he doubted that magic could ever be made to destroy it.

Kell's head ached with the realization that it could not be ruined—it had to be disposed of. Sent away, somewhere it could do no damage. And there was only one place it would be safe, and everyone safe from it.

Kell knew what he had to do. Some part of him had known since the moment the stone had passed into his hands.

"It belongs in Black London," he said. "I have to take it back."

Lila cocked her head. "But how can you? You don't know what's left of it, and even if you did, you said the world was sealed off."

"I don't know what's left of it, no, but *Antari* magic was originally used to make the doors between the worlds. And *Antari* magic would have been used to seal them shut. And so it stands to reason that *Antari* magic could open them again. Or at least create a crack."

"Then why haven't you?" challenged Lila, a glint in her eye. "Why hasn't anyone? I know you're a rare breed, but you cannot tell me that in the centuries since you locked yourselves out, no *Antari* has been curious enough to try and get back in."

Kell considered her defiant smile, and was grateful, for humanity's sake, that she lacked the magic to try. As for Kell, of course he'd been curious. Growing up, a small part of him never believed Black London was *real,* or that it had ever been—the doors had been sealed for so long. What child didn't wish to know if his bedtime stories were the stuff of fiction or of truth? But even if he'd *wanted* to break the seal—and he didn't, not enough to risk the darkness on the other side—he'd never had a way.

"Maybe some were curious enough," said Kell. "But an *Antari* needs *two* things to make a door: the first is blood, the second is a token from the place they want to go. And as I told you, the tokens were all destroyed."

Lila's eyes widened. "But the stone is a token."

"The stone is a token," echoed Kell.

Lila gestured to the wall where Kell had first come in. "So you open a door to Black London, and what? Throw the stone in? What on earth have you been waiting for?"

Kell shook his head. "I can't make a door from here to there."

Lila let out an exasperated noise. "But you just said—"

"The other Londons sit between," he explained. A small book rested on the table by the bed. He brushed his thumb over the pages. "The worlds are like pieces of paper," he said, "stacked one on top of the other." That's how he'd always thought of it. "You have to move in order." He pinched a few pages between his fingers. "Grey London," he said, letting one fall back to the stack. "Red London." He let go of a second. "White London." The third page fluttered as it fell. "And Black." He let the rest of the pages fall back to the book.

"So you'll have to go *through*," said Lila.

It sounded so simple when she put it like that. But it wouldn't be. No doubt the crown was searching for him in Red London, and saints only knew who else (had Holland compelled others there? Were they searching, too?), and without his pendants, he'd have to hunt down a new trinket to get from there to White London. And once he made it that far—*if* he made it that far—and assuming the Danes weren't on him in an instant, *and* assuming he was able to overcome the seal and open a door to Black London, the stone couldn't simply be thrown in. Doors didn't work that way. Kell would have to go with it. He tried not to think about that.

"So," said Lila, eyes glittering. "When do we go?"

Kell looked up. "*We* don't."

Lila was leaning back against the wall, just beside the place he'd cuffed her to the wood—the board was ripped and ruined where she'd hacked herself free—as if reminding him, both of his actions, and of hers.

"I want to come," she insisted. "I won't tell you where the stone is. Not until you agree to let me."

Kell's hands curled into fist. "Those binds you summoned up for Holland won't hold. *Antari* magic is strong enough to dispel them, and once he wakes, it won't take him long to realize that and free himself and start hunting us down again. Which means I don't have time for games."

"It's not a game," she said simply.

"Then what is it?"

"A chance." She pushed off the wall. "A way out." Her calm shifted, and for a moment Kell glimpsed the things beneath. The want, the fear, the desperation.

"You want out," he said, "but you have no idea what you're getting *into*."

"I don't care," she said. "I want to come."

"You can't," he said, pushing to his feet. A shallow wave of dizziness hit him, and he braced himself against the bed, waiting for it to pass.

She gave a mocking laugh. "You're in no shape to go alone."

"You *can't* come, Lila," he said again. "Only *Antari* can move between the worlds."

"That rock of mine—"

"It's not yours."

"It is right now. And you said yourself, it's pure magic. It *makes* magic. It will let me through." She said it as if she were certain.

"What if it won't?" he challenged. "What if it isn't all-powerful? What if it's only a trinket to conjure up small spells?" But she didn't seem to believe him. He wasn't sure he believed himself. He had held the stone. He had felt its power, and it felt limitless. But he did not wish for Lila to test it. "You cannot know for sure."

"That's my risk to take, not yours."

Kell stared at her. "Why?" he asked.

Lila shrugged. "I'm a wanted man."

"You're not a man."

Lila flashed a hollow smile. "The authorities don't know that yet. Probably why I'm still wanted instead of hanged."

Kell refused to let it go. "Why do you really want to do this?"

"Because I'm a fool."

"*Lila*—"

"Because I can't stay here," she snapped, the smile gone from her face. "Because I want to see the world, even if it's not mine. And because I will save your life."

Madness, thought Kell. Absolute madness. She wouldn't make it through the door. And even if the stone worked, even if she somehow did, what then? Transference was treason, and Kell was fairly certain that law extended to people, particularly fugitives. Smuggling a music box was one thing, but smuggling a thief was quite another. *And smuggling a relic of Black London?* chided a voice in Kell's head. He rubbed his eyes. He could feel hers fixed on him. Treason aside, the fact remained that she was a Grey-worlder; she didn't belong in his London. It was too dangerous. It was mad, and he'd be mad to let her try . . . but Lila was right about one thing. Kell did not feel strong enough to do this alone. And worse, he did not want to. He was afraid—more afraid than he wanted to admit—about the task ahead of him, and the fate that waited at its end. And someone would need to tell the Red throne—tell his mother and father and Rhy—what had happened. He could not bring this danger to their doorstep, but he could leave Lila there to tell them of it.

"You don't know anything about these worlds," he said, but the fight was bleeding out of his voice.

"Sure I do," countered Lila cheerfully. "There's Dull London, Kell London, Creepy London, and Dead London," she recited, ticking them off on her fingers. "See? I'm a fast learner."

You're also human, thought Kell. A strange, stubborn, cut-throat human, but human all the same. Light, thin and watered down by rain, was beginning to creep into the sky. He couldn't afford to stand here, waiting her out.

"Give me the stone," he said, "and I'll let you come."

Lila bit back a sharp laugh. "I think I'll hold on to it until we're through."

"And if you don't survive?" challenged Kell.

"Then you can raid my corpse," she said drily. "I doubt I'll care."

Kell stared at her, at a loss. Was her bravado a front, or did she truly have so little to lose? But she had a life, and a life was a thing that could always be lost. How could she fear nothing, even death?

Are you afraid of dying? Holland had asked him in the alley. And Kell was. Had always been, ever since he could remember. He feared *not living,* feared ceasing to exist. Lila's world may believe in Heaven and Hell, but his believed in dust. He was taught early that magic reclaimed magic, and earth reclaimed earth, the two dividing when the body died, the person they had combined to be simply forfeit, lost. Nothing lasted. Nothing remained.

Growing up, he had nightmares in which he suddenly broke apart, one minute running through the courtyard or standing on the palace steps, the next scattered into air and ash. He'd wake sweat-soaked and gasping, Rhy shaking his shoulder.

"Aren't you afraid of dying?" he asked Lila now.

She looked at him as if it were a strange question. And then she shook her head. "Death comes for everyone," she said simply. "I'm not afraid of dying. But I am afraid of dying *here*." She swept her hand over the room, the tavern, the city. "I'd rather die on an adventure than live standing still."

Kell considered her for a long moment. And then he said, "Very well."

Lila's brow crinkled distrustfully. "What do you mean, 'very well'?"

"You can come," clarified Kell.

Lila broke into a grin. It lit up her face in a whole new way, made her look young. Her eyes went to the window. "The sun is almost up," she said. "And Holland's likely looking for us by now. Are you well enough to go?" she asked.

It's really quite hard to kill Antari.

Kell nodded as Lila pulled the cloak around her shoulders and holstered her weapons, moving with brisk, efficient motions, as if afraid that if she took too long, he would revoke the offer. He only stood there, marveling.

"Don't you want to say good-bye?" he asked, gesturing at the floorboards and somewhere beneath them, Barron.

Lila hesitated, considering her boots and the world below them. "No," she said softly, her voice uncertain for the first time since they'd met.

He didn't know how Lila's and Barron's threads were tangled, but he let the issue lie. He did not blame her. After all, he had no plans to detour to the palace, to see his brother one last time. He told himself that it was too dangerous, or that Rhy would not let him go, but it was as much the truth that Kell could not bring himself to say good-bye.

Kell's coat was hanging on the chair, and he crossed to it and turned it inside out from left to right, exchanging the worn black for ruby red.

Interest flickered like a light behind Lila's eyes but never truly showed, and he supposed she'd seen the trick herself when she went searching through his pockets in the night.

"How many coats do you suppose there are inside that one?" she asked casually, as if inquiring about the weather, and not a complex enchantment.

"I'm not exactly sure," said Kell, digging in a gold-embroidered pocket and sighing inwardly with relief as his fingers skimmed a spare coin. "Every now and then I think I've found them all, and then I stumble on a new one. And sometimes, old ones get lost. A couple of years ago I came across a short coat, an ugly green thing with patched elbows. But I haven't seen it since." He drew the Red London lin from the coat and kissed it. Coins made perfect door keys. In theory, anything from a world would do—most of what Kell wore came from Red London—but coins were simple, solid, specific, and guaranteed to work. He couldn't afford to muddy this up, not when a second life was on his hands (and it was, no matter what she claimed).

While he'd been searching for the token, Lila had emptied the money from her own pockets—a rather eclectic assortment of shillings, pennies, and farthings—and piled them on the dresser by her bed. Kell reached out and plucked a halfpenny off its stack to replace the Grey token he'd lost, while Lila chewed her lip and stared down at the coins a moment, hands thrust into the inner pockets of her cloak. She was fiddling with something there, and a few moments later she pulled out an elegant silver watch and set it beside the pile of coins.

"I'm ready," she said, tearing her eyes from the timepiece.

I'm not, thought Kell, shrugging on his coat and crossing to the door. Another, smaller wave of dizziness hit, but it passed sooner than the last as he opened the door.

"Wait," said Lila. "I thought we'd go the way you came. By the wall."

"Walls aren't always where they ought to be," answered Kell. In truth, the Stone's Throw was one of the only places where the walls *didn't* change, but that made it no safer. The Setting Sun might have sat on the same foundation in Red London, but it was also the place where Kell did business, and one of the first places someone might come looking for him.

"Besides, we don't know what—or who—" he amended, remembering the attackers under their compulsion, "is waiting on the other side. Better get closer to where we're going before we go there. Understand?"

Lila looked as though she didn't, but nodded all the same.

The two crept down the stairs, past a small landing that branched off down a narrow hall studded with rooms. Lila paused beside the nearest door and listened. A low rumbling snore came through the wood. Barron. She touched the door briefly, then pushed past Kell and down the remaining stairs without looking back. She slid the bolt on the back entrance and hurried into the alley. Kell followed her out, stopping long enough to raise his hand and will the metal lock back into place behind them. He listened to the *shhk* of metal sliding home, then turned to find Lila waiting, her back purposely to the tavern, as if her present were already her past.

II

The rain had ended and left the streets dreary and damp, but despite the wet ground and the October chill, London was beginning to drag itself awake. The sound of rickety carts filled the air, met with the smell of fresh bread and new fires, and merchants and buyers began the slow revival of work, pinning back the doors and shutters of shops and readying their businesses for the day. Kell and Lila made their way through the rousing city, moving briskly in the thin dawn light.

"You're sure you have the stone?" pressed Kell.

"Yes," said Lila, lips quirking. "And if you're thinking of stealing it back, I would advise against it, as you'd have to search me, and magic or no, I'm willing to bet my knife could find your heart before your hand could find the rock." She said it with such casual confidence that Kell suspected she might be right, but he had no desire to find out. Instead, he turned his attention to the streets around them, trying to picture them as if they were a world away. "We're nearly there."

"Where's there?" she asked.

"Whitbury Street," he said.

He'd crossed through at Whitbury before (it put him near his rooms at the Ruby Fields, which meant that he could drop any newly acquired items before reporting to the palace). But more important, the row of shops on Whitbury did not sit *di-*

rectly on top of the Ruby Fields, but sat a short two blocks shy. He'd learned long ago never to walk into a world exactly where you wanted to be. If trouble were waiting, you'd land right on top of it.

"There's an inn in Red London," he explained, trying not to think about the last time he was there. About the tracing spell and the attack and the corpses of the men in the alley beyond. Corpses *he'd* made. "I keep a room there," he went on. "It will have what I need to make a door to White London." Lila didn't pick up on his use of *I* instead of *we,* or if she did, she didn't bother to correct him. In fact, she seemed lost in her own thoughts as they wove through the network of back streets. Kell kept his chin up, his senses tuned.

"I'm not going to run into myself, am I?" asked Lila, breaking the silence.

Kell glanced her way. "What are you talking about?"

She kicked a loose stone. "Well, I mean, it's another world, isn't it? Another version of London? Is there another version of me?"

Kell frowned. "I've never met *anyone* like you."

He hadn't meant it as a compliment, but Lila took it that way, flashing him a grin. "What can I say," she said, "I'm one of a kind."

Kell managed an echo of her smile, and she gasped. "What's that on your face?"

The smile vanished. "What?"

"Never mind," she said, laughing. "It's gone." Kell only shook his head—he didn't grasp the joke—but whatever it was, it seemed to delight Lila, and she chuckled to herself all the way to Whitbury.

As they turned onto the pleasant little lane, Kell came to a stop on the curb between two shop fronts. One belonged to a dentist and the other a barber (in Red London, it was an herbalist and stonesmith), and if Kell squinted he could still see traces of his blood on the brick wall in front of him, the surface sheltered by a narrow overhang. Lila was staring intently at the wall. "Is this where they are? Your rooms?"

"No," he said, "but this is where we go through."

Lila's fists clenched and unclenched at her side. He thought she must be frightened, but when she glanced his way, her eyes were bright, the edge of a smile on her lips.

Kell swallowed and stepped up to the wall, and Lila joined him. He hesitated.

"What are we waiting for?"

"Nothing," said Kell. "It's just . . ." He slipped out of his coat and wrapped it around her shoulders, as if the magic could be so easily deceived. As if it wouldn't know the difference between human and *Antari*. He doubted his coat would make a difference—either the stone would let her through or it wouldn't—but he still relinquished it.

In response, Lila fetched her kerchief—the one she'd given him when she picked his pocket and reclaimed when he passed out on her floor—and tucked it into his back pocket.

"What are you doing?" he asked.

"Seems right somehow," she said. "You gave me something of yours. I give you something of mine. Now we're linked."

"It doesn't work that way," he said.

Lila shrugged. "Can't hurt."

Kell supposed she was right. He slid his knife free and drew the blade across his palm, a thin line of blood welling up. He dabbed it with his fingers and made a mark on the wall.

"Take out the stone," he said.

Lila eyed him distrustfully.

"You'll *need* it," he pressed.

She sighed and pulled her broad-brim hat from a fold in her coat. It was crumpled, but with a flick of her wrist it unfolded, and she reached into the hat's bowl like a magician and drew out the black rock. Something in Kell twisted at the sight of it, an ache in his blood, and it took all his strength not to reach for the talisman. He bit back the urge and thought for the first time that perhaps it was better if he didn't hold it.

Lila closed her fingers around the stone, and Kell closed his fingers around Lila's, and as it was he could *feel* the talisman humming through the flesh and bone of her hand. He tried not to think about the way it sang to him.

"Are you sure?" he asked one last time.

"It will work," said Lila. Her voice sounded less certain now than it had been, less like she believed and more like she *wanted* to, so Kell nodded. "You said yourself," she added, "that everyone has a mix of humanity and magic in them. That means I do, too." She turned her gaze up to his. "What happens now?"

"I don't know," he said truthfully.

Lila drew closer, so close their ribs were touching and he could feel her heart racing through them. She was so good at hiding it, her fear. It didn't show in her eyes, or the lines of her face, but her pulse betrayed her. And then Lila's lips tugged into a grin, and Kell wondered if it was fear she felt after all, or something else entirely.

"I'm not going to die," she said. "Not till I've seen it."

"Seen what?"

Her smile widened. "Everything."

Kell smiled back. And then Lila brought her free hand to his jaw and tugged his mouth toward hers. The kiss was there and then gone, like one of her smiles.

"What was that for?" he asked, dazed.

"For luck," she said, squaring her shoulders to the wall. "Not that I need it."

Kell stared at her a moment and then forced himself to turn

toward the bloodstained bricks. He tightened his hand over hers, and he brought his fingers to the mark.

"*As Travars,*" he said.

The wall gave way, and the traveler and the thief stepped forward and through.

III

Barron woke to a noise.

It was the second time that morning.

Noise was a fairly common thing in a tavern; the volume of it ebbed and flowed depending on the hour, at some times thunderous, at others murmuring, but it was always there, in some measure. Even when the pub was closed, the Stone's Throw was never truly silent. But Barron knew every kind of noise his tavern made, from the creak of the floorboards to the groan of the doors to the wind through the hundreds of cracks in the old walls.

He knew them all.

And this one was different.

Barron had owned the tavern at the seam—for that was how he thought of the aching old building—for a very long time. Long enough to understand the strange that drifted past and in like debris. Long enough for the strange to seem normal. And while he was not a part of that strange, having no interest or affinity for the practicing of that strangeness others called magic, he had come to develop a sense of sorts, where the strange was concerned.

And he listened to it.

Just as he listened now to the noise above his head. It wasn't loud, not at all, but it was out of place and brought with it a feeling, under his skin and in his bones. A feeling of wrongness. Of danger. The hair on his arm prickled, and his heart, always steady, began to beat faster in warning.

The noise came again, and he recognized the groan of footsteps on the old wooden floor. He sat up in his bed. Lila's room sat directly over his own. But the footsteps did not belong to Lila.

When someone spends enough time under your roof (as Lila had beneath his), you come to know the kind of noise they make—not only their voices but the way they move through a space—and Barron knew the sound of Lila's tread when she wanted to be heard, and the sound of her tread when she didn't, and this was neither. And besides, he had first woken to the sound of Lila and Kell leaving not long before (he had not stopped her, had long since learned that it was futile to try, and had long since resolved to be instead an anchor, there and ready when she wandered back, which she invariably did).

But if Lila was not moving about her room, who was?

Barron got to his feet, the shivery feeling of wrong worsening as he tugged the suspenders from his waist up onto his broad shoulders and pulled on his boots.

A shotgun hung on the wall by the door, half rusted from disuse (on the occasion trouble brewed downstairs, Barron's hulking form was usually enough to quash it). Now he took hold of the gun by the barrel and pulled it down from its mount. He drew open the door, cringing as it groaned, and set off up the stairs to Lila's room.

Stealth, he knew, was useless. Barron had never been a small man, and the steps creaked loudly under his boots as he climbed. When he reached the short green door at the top of the stairs, he hesitated and pressed his ear to the wood. He heard nothing, and for a brief moment, he doubted himself. Thought he'd slept too lightly after Lila's departure and simply dreamt the threat out of concern. His grip, which had been knuckles white on the shotgun, began to loosen, and he let out a breath and thought of going back to bed. But then he heard the metallic sound of coins tumbling, and the doubt gutted like a candle. He threw open the door, shotgun raised.

Lila and Kell were both gone, but the room was not empty: a man stood beside the open window, weighing Lila's silver pocket watch in the palm of his hand. The lantern on the table burned with an odd pale light that made the man look strangely colorless, from his charcoal hair to his pale skin to his faded grey clothes. When his gaze drifted up casually from the timepiece and settled on Barron—he seemed entirely unfazed by the gun—the tavern owner saw that one of his eyes was green. The other was pitch black.

Lila had described the man to him and given him a name.

Holland.

Barron did not hesitate. He pulled the trigger, and the shotgun blasted through the room with a deafening sound that left his ears ringing. But when the plume of smoke cleared, the colorless intruder stood exactly where he'd been before the blast, unharmed. Barron stared in disbelief. The air in front of Holland glittered faintly, and it took Barron a moment to grasp that it was full of shot pellets. The tiny metal beads hung suspended in front of Holland's chest. And then they fell, clattering to the floor like hail.

Before Barron could squeeze off the second shot, Holland's fingers twitched, and the weapon went flying out of Barron's hands and across the narrow room, crashing against the wall. He lunged for it, or at least he meant to, but his body refused, remaining firmly rooted to the spot, not out by fear, but something stronger. *Magic.* He willed his limbs to move, but the impossible force willed them still.

"Where are they?" asked Holland. His voice was low and cold and hollow.

A bead of sweat rolled down Barron's cheek as he fought the magic, but it was no use. "Gone," he said, his voice a low rumble.

Holland frowned, disappointed. He drew a curved knife from his belt. "I noticed that." He crossed the room with even, echoing steps, and brought the blade up slowly to Barron's throat. It was very cold, and very sharp. "Where have they gone?"

Up close, Kell smelled of lilies and grass. Holland smelled of ash and blood and metal.

Barron met the magician's eyes. They were so like Kell's. And so different. Looking into them, he saw anger and hatred and pain, things that never spread, never touched the rest of his face. "Well?" he pressed.

"No idea," growled Barron. It was the truth. He could only hope they were far away.

Holland's mouth turned down. "Wrong answer."

He drew the blade across, and Barron felt a searing heat at his throat, and then nothing.

NINE

FESTIVAL & FIRE

I

Red London welcomed Kell home as if nothing were wrong. It had not rained here, and the sky was streaked with wisps of cloud and crimson light, as if a reflection of the Isle. Carriages rolled in rumbling fashion over street stones on their well-worn paths, and the air was filled with the sweet steam of spice and tea and, farther off, the sounds of building celebration.

Had it really been only a matter of hours since Kell had fled, wounded and confused, away from this world and into another? The simple, assuring calm, the rightness of this place, set him off-balance and made him doubt, if only for a moment, that anything could be amiss. But he knew the peace was superficial—somewhere in the palace that bridged the river, his presence had surely been missed; somewhere in the city, two men lay dead, and more with empty eyes were likely looking for him and his prize—but here, on what had been Whitbury and was now Ves Anash, the light of the river spilling in from one side and the morning sun from the other, Red London seemed oblivious to the danger it was in, the danger he was dragging through it.

A small black stone capable of creating anything and razing everything. He shuddered at the thought and tightened his grip on Lila's hand, only to realize it was not there.

He spun, hoping to find her standing next to him, hoping

they'd been pulled apart only a step or two in the course of their passage. But he was alone. The echo of *Antari* magic glowed faintly on the wall, marking the way he'd come with Lila.

But Lila was gone.

And with her, the stone.

Kell slammed his hand against the wall, splitting open the cut that had just begun to close. Blood trickled down his wrist, and Kell swore and went to search for a cloth in his coat, forgetting that he'd draped it over Lila's shoulders. He was halfway through swearing again when he remembered Lila's kerchief. The one she'd given him in exchange, tucked into his back pocket.

Seems right somehow, she'd said. *You gave me something of yours. I give you something of mine. Now we're linked.*

Linked, thought Kell. His mind spun as he dragged the square of fabric free. Would it work? Not if she'd somehow been torn apart or trapped between the worlds (there were stories, of non-*Antari* who tried to open doors and got stuck). But if she'd never come through, or if she was here somewhere—alive or dead—it might.

He brought the bloodstained kerchief to the wall and pressed his hand flat against the echo of his recent mark.

"*As Enose,*" he commanded the magic. "*As Enose* Delilah Bard."

Lila opened her eyes and saw red.

Not a bold red, splashed like paint over the buildings, but a subtle, pervasive tint, like she was looking through a pane of colored glass. Lila tried to blink away the color, but it lingered. When Kell called his city *Red* London, she assumed he'd picked the color for some arbitrary—or at least ordinary—reason.

Now she could see that he meant it literally. She drew a breath and tasted flowers on the air. Lilies and marigolds and stargazers. The scent was overpowering, verging on sickly sweet, like perfume—no wonder it clung to Kell. After a few moments, it calmed a little (so did the tint), as her senses adjusted to her new surroundings, but when she drew too deep a breath, it assaulted her again.

Lila coughed and lay still. She was on her back in an alley, in front of a rather pretty red door (painted, not tinted). A loose street stone dug into her spine through the coat. Kell's coat. It was spread beneath her on the ground, billowing out like wings.

But Kell was not there.

She tightened her fingers to make sure she could move them, and felt the black stone nested in her palm, still humming. *It worked,* she thought, letting out an amazed exhale as she sat up. It had actually *worked*.

Not perfectly—if it had worked perfectly, she and Kell would be standing in the same place—but she was here, which was to say *there*. Somewhere *new*.

She'd done it.

Delilah Bard had finally escaped, sailed away. Not with a ship, but with a stone.

As for where she was *exactly*, she hadn't the faintest idea. She got to her feet and realized that the red tint wasn't coming from the sky, but from the ground. The world to her right was considerably redder than the world to her left. And, she realized, senses tuning, considerably louder. Not just the usual noise of peddlers and carts, for the Londons seemed to have that in common, but the din of a growing crowd, all cheers and shouts and celebration. Part of her knew she should stay still and wait for Kell to find her, but the other part was already moving toward the swell of light and color and sound.

Kell had found her once, she reasoned. He could do it again.

She tucked the black stone into the hidden pocket of her worn cloak (the dizziness upon letting go was brief and shallow) then scooped up Kell's coat, dusted it off, and pulled it on over the top. She expected it to be bulky, if not outright unruly, but to her surprise, the coat fit perfectly, its silver buttons lying smooth and even on the rich black fabric.

Strange, thought Lila, shoving her hands into its pockets. *Not the strangest thing by far, but still strange.*

She wove through the streets, which were like her London in their narrow, twisting fashion and yet so different. Instead of rough stone and soot-stained glass, the shops were built of dark wood and smooth rock, colored glass, and shining metal. They looked strong and strangely delicate at once, and running through them all, through *everything,* was an energy (she could think of no other word). She walked in the direction of the crowd, marveling at the change wrought in the world, a world whose bones were shared with hers, but whose body was a new, glorious thing.

And then she turned a corner and saw the source of the commotion. Scores of people had gathered along a major road, bustling in anticipation. They had the air of commoners, and yet their dress was so much finer than Lila had ever seen on the commoners at home. Their style itself was not so foreign—the men wore elegant coats with high collars, the woman waist-cinched dresses under capes—but the materials flowed on them like melted metal, and threads of gold ran through hair and hat and cuff.

Lila pulled Kell's silver-buttoned coat close around her, thankful she could hide the threadbare cloak beneath. In the cracks between the jostling crowd, she could make out the red river beyond, right where the Thames should have been, its strange light washing over the banks.

The Thames? A source of magic?

Perhaps the greatest source in the world. Not that you'd know it here, but if you could see it as it is in my *London . . .*

It was indeed magnificent. And yet, Lila was drawn less to the water and more to the ships blanketing it. Vessels of all shapes and sizes, from brigs and galleys to schooners and frigates, bobbed on the red waves, their sails billowing. Dozens of emblems marked the fabric on their masts and flanks, but over them all, red and gold banners had been hung. They glittered, taunting her. *Come aboard,* they seemed to say. *I can be yours.* Had Lila been a man, and the ships fair maidens guiding up their skirts, she could not have wanted them more. *Hang the fine dresses,* she thought. *I'll take a ship.*

But though the mismatched fleet was enough to draw a gasp of approval from *Lila's* lips, it was neither the gorgeous ships nor the impossible red river that held the crowd's attention.

A procession was marching down the avenue.

Lila reached the edge of the crowd as a row of men paraded past clothed in swaths of dark fabric that wound around their bodies as if their limbs were spools. The men held fire in their palms, and when they danced and spun, the fire arced around them, tracing their paths and lingering in the air behind them. Their lips moved as they did, the words buried under the sounds of the parade, and Lila found herself pressing forward into the crush to get a better view. Too soon the men were gone, but in their wake a line of women came into view. Dressed in flowing gowns, they executed a more fluid version of the same dance, but with water. Lila watched, wide-eyed; it behaved like ribbon in their hands, twisting and curling through the air, as if by magic.

Of course, thought Lila, *it* is *by magic.*

The water dancers gave way to earth, and then metal and finally, wind, the last made visible by colored dust blown from palms into the air.

Every dancer was dressed in their own way, but all had ribbons of red and gold tied off along their arms and legs, trailing behind them like comet tails as they moved through the city.

Music rose in the dancers' wake, strong as drums but sweet as strings, drawing notes Lila had never heard from instruments she had never seen. The musicians continued on, but the music lingered in the air, hanging over the crowd like a tent ceiling, as if sound itself could be made physical. It was hypnotic.

And then came the knights atop their mounts, armor shining in the sun and red cloaks billowing behind them. The horses themselves were glorious beasts, not speckled but solid whites and greys and glossy blacks *almost as beautiful,* thought Lila, *as the ships.* Their eyes were like polished stones, some brown, others blue, or green. Their glistening manes ran black or silver or gold, and they moved with a grace that didn't match their size or pace.

The knights all held banners like jousting poles, a golden sun rising against a red sky.

Just then a huddle of young boys cut in front of Lila on their way past, trailing ribbons from their arms and legs, and she hooked one around the collar.

"What's all this about?" she asked the squirming child.

The child's eyes went wide, and he spit out a string of words in a tongue she did not recognize. It certainly wasn't English.

"Can you understand me?" she asked, drawing out the words, but the boy only shook his head, wriggled in her grip, and spat out foreign words until she let him go.

Another, louder cheer rippled through the gathered crowd, and she looked up to see an open carriage approaching. It was pulled by a set of white horses and flanked by an armored guard. The carriage ran banners that were more ornate and more elaborate: here the sun she'd seen on so many flags rose over a chalice, as if the contents of the cup were morning light. The cup itself was marked by an ornate *M*, all of it woven in shades of gold thread against red silk.

In the carriage stood a man and a woman, holding hands, crimson cloaks pouring from their shoulders and pooling on the polished carriage floor. They were tan, both of them, with sun-kissed skin and black hair that showed off the gleaming gold crowns nested there. (*Royalty,* thought Lila. Of course. It was a different world. A different king and queen. But there was *always* royalty.)

And there between the king and queen, one boot up on the seat like a conqueror, stood a young man, a thin crown glinting in his dark, tousled locks, a cloak of pure gold spilling over his broad shoulders. A prince. He raised his hand in a wave to the crowd, and they devoured the gesture.

"*Vares Rhy!*" A shout went up from the other side of the parade, quickly taken up and carried on by a dozen other voices. "*Vares Rhy! Vares Rhy!*"

The prince flashed a dazzling smile and, several feet to Lila's left, a young woman actually swooned. Lila scoffed at the girl's silliness, but when she turned back to the parade, she caught the prince looking at *her*. Intensely. Lila felt her face go hot. He didn't smile, didn't wink, only held her gaze for a long, long moment, brow crinkling faintly as if he knew she didn't belong, as if he looked at her and saw something else. Lila knew she should probably bow, or at least avert her eyes, but she stared stubbornly back. And then the moment passed. The prince broke into a fresh smile and turned back toward his subjects, and the carriage continued on, leaving ribbons and dancers and excited citizens in its wake.

Lila dragged herself back to her senses. She didn't realize how far she'd pressed forward with the rest of the crowd until she heard the cluster of girls chattering at her elbow.

"Where was he?" murmured one of them. Lila started, relieved to hear *someone* speaking her language.

"*Ser asina gose,*" said another, then, in heavily accented English, "You sound good."

"*Rensa tav,*" said the first. "I'm practicing for tonight. You should as well, if you want a dance." She rose up onto her toes to wave at the disappearing prince.

"Your partner in dance," said a third in broken English, "is appears to be missing."

The first girl frowned. "He is always in the procession. I do hope he is well."

"*Mas aven,*" said the second, rolling her eyes. "Elissa is in love with the black-eyed prince."

Lila frowned. Black-eyed prince?

"You cannot deny he is dashing. In a haunted kind of way."

"*Anesh.* In a *frightening* kind of way."

"*Tac.* He is nothing compared to Rhy."

"Excuse me," cut in Lila. The trio of girls twisted toward her. "What is all this?" she asked, waving her hand at the parade. "What's it for?"

The one who spoke in broken English let out an amazed laugh, as though Lila must be joking.

"*Mas aven,*" said the second. "Where are you from that you do not know? It is Prince Rhy's birthday, of course."

"Of course," echoed Lila.

"Your accent is remarkable," said the one who'd been searching for her black-eyed prince. Elissa. "Who is your tutor?"

Now it was Lila's turn to laugh. The girls only stared at her. But then trumpets—at least they sounded roughly like trumpets—began to sound from the direction the royals and the rest of the festival had come, and the crowd, now in the procession's wake, moved toward the music, taking the cluster of girls with it. Lila stepped out of the throng and brought her hand to her pocket, checking to make sure the black rock was still there. It was. It hummed, wanting to be held, but she resisted the urge. It may be clever, but so was she.

Without the procession blocking her view, Lila could fully see the glittering river on the other side of the road. It shone with an impossible red light, as if lit from beneath. A *source*, Kell had called the river, and Lila could see why. It *vibrated* with power, and the royal procession must have crossed a bridge, for now it trailed down the opposite bank to far-off chants and cheers. Lila's eyes trailed along the water until they reached a massive, vaulting structure that could only be the palace. It sat not on the banks of the river, like parliament, but *over* the river itself, spanning the water like a bridge. It seemed carved out of glass, or crystal, its joints fused with copper and stone. Lila took in the structure with hungry eyes. The palace looked like a jewel. No, a crown of jewels, better sized to a *mountain* than a head.

The trumpets were issuing from the steps, where servants in red and gold half-cloaks were pouring out, carrying trays of food and drink for the masses.

The scent on the air—of strange food and drink and magic—was utterly intoxicating. Lila felt her head swimming with it as she stepped into the street.

The crowds were thinning, and between the emptying road and the red river, a market had blossomed like a hedge of roses. A portion of the masses had gone with the royal parade, but the rest had taken to the market, and Lila followed.

"*Crysac!*" called a woman, holding up fiery red gems. "*Nissa lin.*"

"*Tessane!*" urged another, with what looked like a steaming metal teapot. "*Cas tessane.*" He waved two fingers in the air. "*Sessa lin.*"

Everywhere merchants announced their wares in their strange tongue. Lila tried to pick up terms here and there, to pair the shouted words with the items held aloft—*cas* seemed to mean hot, and *lin,* she guessed, was a kind of coin—but everything was bright and colorful and humming with power, and she could hardly focus long enough to keep track of anything.

She pulled Kell's coat tighter about her shoulders and wandered the booths and stalls with hungry eyes. She had no money, but she had quick fingers. She passed a stall marked ESSENIR, and saw within a table piled high with polished stones of every color—not simple reds or blues, but perfect imitations of nature: fire yellow, summer grass green, night blue. The merchant's back was to her, and she couldn't help herself.

Lila reached for the nearest charm, a lovely blue-green stone the color of the open sea—at least, the color she imagined it must be, the color she'd seen it painted—with small white marks, like breaking waves. But when her fingers curled around it, a hot pain seared across her skin.

She gasped, more from the shock of being burned than the heat itself, and pulled back sharply, hand singing. Before she could retreat, the merchant caught her by the wrist.

"*Kers la?*" he demanded. When she didn't answer—couldn't answer—he started shouting faster and louder, the words blurring together in her ears.

"Unhand me," she demanded.

The merchant's brow furrowed at the sound of her voice. "What you think?" he said, in guttural English. "You get free by speaking fancy?"

"I haven't the faintest idea what you're talking about," snapped Lila. "Now let *go.*"

"Speak *Arnesian.* Speak English. Doesn't matter. Still *gast.* Still thief."

"I am not a *gast*," growled Lila.

"*Viris gast.* Fool thief. Tries to steal from enchanted tent."

"I didn't know it was enchanted," countered Lila, reaching for the dagger at her waist.

"*Pilse,*" growled the merchant, and Lila had a feeling she'd just been insulted. And then the merchant raised his voice. "*Strast!*" he shouted, and Lila twisted in his grip to see armored guards at the edge of the market. "*Strast!*" he called again, and one of the men cocked his head and turned toward them.

Shit, thought Lila, wrenching free of the merchant's grip, only to stumble back into another set of hands. They tightened on her shoulders and she was about to draw her knife when the merchant went pale.

"*Mas aven,*" he said, hunching forward into a bow.

The hands holding Lila vanished, and she spun to find Kell standing there, frowning his usual frown and staring past her at the merchant.

"What is the meaning of this?" he asked, and Lila didn't know which surprised her more: his sudden appearance, the way he spoke to the merchant—his voice cool, dismissive—or the way the merchant looked at him, with a mixture of awe and fear.

Kell's auburn hair was pushed back, his black eye on display in the red morning light.

"*Aven vares.* If I knew she was with y-you . . ." stammered the merchant before lapsing back into Arnesian, or whatever the language was called. Lila was surprised to hear the tongue pour out of Kell's mouth in response as he tried to calm the merchant. And then she caught that word again, *gast,* on the merchant's tongue and lunged for him. Kell hauled her back.

"Enough," Kell snarled in her ear. "*Solase,*" he said to the merchant, apologetically. "She's a *foreigner.* Uncivilized, but harmless."

Lila shot him a dark look.

"Anesh, mas vares," said the merchant, bowing even lower. "Harmful enough to steal . . ." With his head down, the merchant didn't see Kell look back over his shoulder at the guard weaving through the market toward them. He didn't see the way Kell stiffened. But Lila did.

"I will buy whatever she tried to take," said Kell hastily, digging a hand in the pocket of his coat, unconcerned by the fact Lila was still wearing it.

The merchant straightened and started shaking his head. *"An. An.* I cannot be taking money from you."

The guard was getting closer, and Kell clearly didn't want to be there when he arrived, because he fetched a coin from the coat and set it on the table with a snap.

"For your trouble," he said, turning Lila away. *"Vas ir."*

He didn't wait for the merchant's answer, only shoved Lila through the crowd, away from the stall and the guard about to reach it.

"Uncivilized?" growled Lila as Kell clasped her shoulder and guided her out of the market.

"Five minutes!" said Kell, sliding his coat from her shoulders and back onto his own, flicking up the collar. "You can't keep your hands to yourself for five minutes! Tell me you haven't already gone and sold off the stone."

Lila let out an exasperated noise. "Unbelievable," she snapped as he led her out of the throngs and away from the river, toward one of the narrower streets. "I'm so glad you're all right, Lila," she parroted. "Thank God using the stone didn't rip you into a thousand thieving pieces."

Kell's hand loosened on her shoulder. "I can't believe it worked."

"Don't sound so excited," shot Lila drily.

Kell came to a stop and turned her toward him. "I'm not," he said. His blue eye looked troubled, his black unreadable. "I'm glad you're unhurt, Lila, but the doors between worlds are meant to be locked to all but *Antari,* and the fact that the stone granted you passage only proves how dangerous it is. And every moment it's here, in *my* world, I'm terrified."

Lila found her eyes going to the ground. "Well, then," she said. "Let's get it out of here."

A small grateful smile crossed Kell's lips. And then Lila dug the stone out of her pocket and held it up, and Kell let out a dismayed sound and swallowed her hand with his, hiding the stone from sight. Something flickered through his eyes when he touched her, but she didn't think it was *her* touch that moved him. The stone gave a strange little shudder in her hand, as if it felt Kell and wanted to be with him. Lila felt vaguely insulted.

"Sanct!" he swore at her. "Just hold it up for all to see, why don't you."

"I thought you wanted it back!" she shot back, exasperated. "There's no winning with you."

"Just keep it," he hissed. "And for king's sake, keep it out of sight."

Lila shoved it back into her cloak and said a very many unkind things under her breath.

"And on the topic of language," said Kell, "you cannot speak so freely here. English is not a common tongue."

"I noticed that. Thanks for the warning."

"I told you the worlds would be different. But you're right, I should have warned you. Here English is a tongue used by the elite, and those who wish to mingle with them. Your very use of it will cause you to stand out."

Lila's eyes narrowed. "What would you have me do? *Not* speak?"

"The thought had crossed my mind," said Kell. Lila scowled. "But as I doubt that's possible for you, I'd ask that you simply keep your voice down." He smiled, and Lila smiled back, resisting the urge to break his nose.

"Now that that's settled . . ." He turned to go.

"Pilse," she grumbled, hoping it meant something foul indeed as she fell into step behind him.

II

Aldus Fletcher was not an honest man.

He ran a pawnshop in an alley by the docks, and each day, men came off the boats, some with things they wanted, others with things they wanted to be rid of. Fletcher provided for both. And for the locals, too. It was a truth widely known in the darker corners of Red London that Fletcher's shop was the place for anything you shouldn't have.

Now and again *honest* folk wandered in, of course, wanting to find or dispose of smoking pipes and instruments, scrying boards and rune stones and candlesticks, and Fletcher didn't mind padding the shop with their wares as well, in case the royal guard came to inspect. But his true trade lay in risk and rarity.

A smooth stone panel hung on the wall beside the counter, big as a window but black as pitch. On its surface, white smoke shifted and shimmered and spread itself like chalk, announcing the full itinerary of the prince's birthday celebrations. An echo of Rhy's smiling face ghosted itself on the scrying board above the notice. He beamed and winked as beneath his throat the message hovered:

The king and queen invite
you to celebrate the prince's

twentieth year on the palace steps
following the annual parade.

After a few seconds, the message and the prince's face both dissolved and, for a moment, the scrying board went dark, then came back to life and began to cycle through a handful of other announcements.

"*Erase es ferase?*" rumbled Fletcher in his deep voice. *Coming or going?*

The question was lobbed at a boy—and he *was* a boy, the stumble of his first beard growing patchily in—who stood considering a table of trinkets by the door. *Coming* meant a buyer, *going* meant a seller.

"Neither," murmured the boy. Fletcher kept an eye on the youth's wandering hands, but he wasn't too worried; the shop was warded against thieving. It was a slow day, and Fletcher almost wished the boy would try. He could use a little entertainment. "Just looking," he added nervously.

Fletcher's shop didn't usually get lookers. People came with a purpose. And they had to make that purpose known. Whatever the boy was after, he didn't want it badly enough to say.

"You let me know," said Fletcher, "if you can't find what it is you're looking for."

The boy nodded, but kept cheating glances at Fletcher. Or rather, at Fletcher's arms, which were resting on the counter. The air outside was heavy for a morning so late in the harvest season (one might have thought that, given his clientele, the shop would run thieves' hours, dusk till dawn, but Fletcher had found that the best crooks knew how to play off crime as casual), and Fletcher had his sleeves rolled up to the elbows, exposing a variety of marks and scars on his sun-browned forearms. Fletcher's skin was a map of his life. And a hard-lived life at that.

"S'true what they say?" the boy finally asked.

"About what?" said Fletcher, raising a thick brow.

"'Bout you." The boy's gaze went to the markings around Fletcher's wrists. The limiters circled both his hands like cuffs, scarred into flesh and something deeper. "Can I see them?"

"Ah, these?" asked Fletcher, holding up his hands.

The markings were a punishment, given only to those who defied the golden rule of magic.

"Thou shalt not use thy power to control another," he recited, flashing a cold and crooked grin. For such a crime, the crown showed little mercy. The guilty were *bound,* branded with limiters designed to tourniquet their power.

But Fletcher's were broken. The marks on the inside of his wrists were marred, obscured, like fractured links in a metal chain. He had gone to the ends of the world to break those binds, had traded blood and soul and years of life, but here he was. Free again. Of a sort. He was still bound to the shop and the illusion of impotence—an illusion he maintained lest the guards learn of his recovery and return to claim more than his magic. It helped, of course, that he'd bought favor with a few of them. Everyone—even the rich and the proud and the royal—wanted things they shouldn't have. And those things were Fletcher's specialty.

The boy was still staring at the marks, wide-eyed and pale. *"Tac."* Fletcher brought his arms back to rest on the counter. "Time for looking's over. You going to buy something or not?"

The boy scurried out, empty-handed, and Fletcher sighed and tugged a pipe from his back pocket. He snapped his fingers, and a small blue flame danced on the end of his thumb, which he used to light the leaves pressed into the bowl. And then he drew something from his shirt pocket and set it on the wooden counter.

It was a chess piece. A small, white rook to be exact. A marker of a debt he'd yet to pay but would.

The rook had once belonged to the young *Antari* whelp, Kell, but it had come to Fletcher's shop several years before as part of the pot in a round of Sanct.

Sanct was the kind of game that grew. A mix of strategy and luck and a fair bit of cheating, it could be over in minutes or last for hours. And the final hand of the night had been going on for nearly two. They were the last players, Fletcher and Kell, and as the night had grown, so had the pot. They weren't playing for coins, of course. The table was piled high with tokens and trinkets and rare magic. A vial of hope sand. A water blade. A coat that concealed an infinite number of sides.

Fletcher had played every card but three: a pair of kings with a saint among them. He was sure he'd won. And then Kell played three saints. The problem was, there were only three saints in the whole deck, and Fletcher had one in his hand. But as Kell laid out his hand, the card in Fletcher's shimmered and changed from a saint to a servant, the lowest card in the deck.

Fletcher turned red as he watched it. The royal brat had slipped an enchanted card into the set and played Fletcher as well as the game. And that was the best and worst thing about Sanct. Nothing was off-limits. You didn't have to win fair. You only had to win.

Fletcher had no choice but to lay out his ruined hand, and the room broke into raucous comments and jeers. Kell only smiled and shrugged and got to his feet. He plucked a trinket from the top of the pile—a chess piece from another London—and tossed it to Fletcher.

"No hard feelings," he said with a wink before he took the lot and left.

No hard feelings.

Fletcher's fingers tightened on the small stone statue. The

bell at the front of the shop rang as another customer stepped in, a tall, thin man with a greying beard and a hungry glint in his eye. Fletcher pocketed the rook and managed a grim smile.

"*Erase es ferase?*" he asked.

Coming or going?

III

Kell could *feel* the stone in Lila's pocket as they walked.

There had been a moment when his fingers closed over hers and his skin had brushed the talisman, when all he wanted was to take it from her. It felt like everything would be all right if he could simply hold it. Which was an absurd notion. Nothing would be all right so long as the stone existed. Still, it pulled at his senses, and he shivered and tried not to think about it as he led Lila through Red London, away from the noise and toward the Ruby Fields.

Rhy's celebrations would last all day, drawing the majority of the city—its people and its guard—to the banks of the river and the red palace.

Guilt rolled through him. He should have been a part of the procession, should have ridden in the open carriage with the royal family, should have been there to tease and chide his brother for the way he relished the attention.

Kell was sure that Rhy would sulk for weeks about his absence. And then he remembered that he'd never have the chance to apologize. The thought cut like a knife, even though he told himself it had to be this way, that when the time came, Lila would explain. And Rhy? Rhy would forgive him.

Kell kept his collar up and his head down, but he still felt eyes on him as they moved through the streets. He kept looking over his shoulder, unable to shake the feeling of being followed. Which he was, of course, by Lila, who looked at him with increasing scrutiny as they wove through the streets.

Something was clearly bothering her, but she held her tongue, and for a while Kell wondered if she was biding his order or simply biding her time. And then, when the appearance of a pair of royal guards, helmets tucked casually under their arms, sent Kell—and by necessity Lila—retreating hastily into a recessed doorway, she finally broke her silence.

"Tell me something, Kell," she said as they stepped back onto the curb when the men were gone. "The commoners treat you like a noble yet you hide from the guards like a thief. Which is it?"

"Neither," he answered, silently willing her to let the matter go.

But Lila wouldn't. "Are you some kind of valiant criminal?" she pressed. "A Robin Hood, all hero to the people and outlaw to the crown?"

"No."

"Are you wanted for something?"

"Not exactly."

"In my experience," observed Lila, "a person is either wanted or they're not. Why would you hide from the guards if you're not?"

"Because I thought they might be looking for me."

"And why would they be doing that?"

"Because I'm missing."

He heard Lila's steps slow. "Why would they care?" she asked, coming to a stop. "Who are you?"

Kell turned to face her. "I told you—"

"No," she said, eyes narrowing. "Who are you *here*? Who are you to *them*?"

Kell hesitated. All he wanted was to cross through his city as quickly as possible, retrieve a White London token from his rooms, and get the wretched black stone out of this world. But

Lila didn't look like she planned on moving until he answered her. "I belong to the royal family," he said.

In the matter of hours he'd known Lila, he'd learned that she didn't surprise easily, but at this claim, her eyes finally went wide with disbelief. "You're a *prince*?"

"No," he said firmly.

"Like the pretty fellow in the carriage? Is he your brother?"

"His name is Rhy, and no." Kell cringed when he said it. "Well . . . not exactly."

"So *you're* the black-eyed prince. I have to admit, I never took you for a—"

"I'm not a prince, Lila."

"I suppose I can see it, you are rather arrogant and—"

"I'm *not a*—"

"But what's a member of the royal family doing—"

Kell pushed her back against the brick wall of the alley. "I'm not a *member* of the royal family," he snapped. "I *belong* to them."

Lila's forehead crinkled. "What do you mean?"

"They own me," he said, cringing at the words. "I'm a possession. A trinket. So you see, I grew up in the palace, but it is not my home. I was raised by the royals, but they are not my family, not by blood. I have worth to them and so they keep me, but that is not the same as belonging."

The words burned when he spoke them. He knew he wasn't being fair to the king and queen, who treated him with warmth if not love, or to Rhy, who had always looked on him as a brother. But it was true, wasn't it? As much as it pained him. For all his caring, and for theirs, the fact remained he was a weapon, a shield, a tool to be used. He was not a prince. He was not a son.

"You poor thing," said Lila coldly, pushing him away. "What do you want? Pity? You won't find it from me."

Kell clenched his jaw. "I didn't—"

"You have a house if not a home," she spat. "You have people who care for you if not about you. You may not have everything you want, but I'd wager you have everything you could ever *need,* and you have the audacity to claim it all forfeit because it is not love."

"I—"

"Love doesn't keep us from freezing to death, Kell," she continued, "or starving, or being knifed for the coins in our pocket. Love doesn't buy us anything, so be glad for what you have and who you have because you may want for things but you *need* for nothing."

She was breathless by the time she finished, her eyes bright and her cheeks flushed.

And for the first time, Kell saw Lila. Not as she wanted to be, but as she was. A frightened, albeit clever, girl trying desperately to stay alive. One who had likely frozen and starved and fought—and almost certainly killed—to hold on to some semblance of a life, guarding it like a candle in a harsh wind.

"Say something," she challenged.

Kell swallowed, clenched his hands into fists at his sides, and looked at her hard. "You're right," he said.

The admission left him strangely gutted, and in that moment, he just wanted to go home (and it was a home, far more of one than Lila probably had). To let the queen touch his cheek, and the king his shoulder. To swing his arm around Rhy's neck and toast to his birthday and listen to him ramble and laugh.

It ached, how badly he wanted it.

But he couldn't.

He had made a mistake. He had put them all in danger, and he had to make it right.

Because it was his duty to protect them.

And because he loved them.

Lila was still staring, waiting for the catch in his words, but there was none.

"You're right," he said again. "I'm sorry. Compared to your life, mine must seem a jewel—"

"Don't you dare pity me, magic boy," growled Lila, a knife in her hand. And just like that, the scared street rat was gone, and the cutthroat was back. Kell smiled thinly. There was no winning these battles with Lila, but he was relieved to see her back in threatening form. He broke her gaze and looked up at the sky, the red of the Isle reflecting off the low clouds. A storm was coming. Rhy would sulk at that, too, spiteful of anything that might dampen the splendor of his day.

"Come on," said Kell, "we're almost there."

Lila sheathed her blade and followed, this time with fewer daggers in her eyes.

"This place we're headed," she said. "Does it have a name?"

"Is Kir Ayes," said Kell. "The Ruby Fields." He had not told Lila yet that her journey would end here. That it had to. For his peace of mind and for her safety.

"What are you hoping to find there?"

"A token," said Kell. "Something that will grant us passage to White London." He parsed through the shelves and drawers in his mind, the various trinkets from the various cities glittering behind his eyes. "The inn itself," he went on, "is run by a woman named Fauna. You two should get along splendidly."

"Why's that?"

"Because you're both—"

He was about to say *hard as tacks,* but then he rounded the corner and came to a sharp stop, the words dying on his tongue.

"Is that the Ruby Fields?" asked Lila at his shoulder.

"It is," said Kell quietly. "Or, it was."

There was nothing left but ash and smoke.

The inn, and everything in it, had been burned to the ground.

IV

It had been no ordinary fire.

Ordinary fires didn't consume metal as well as wood. And ordinary fires spread. This one hadn't. It had traced the edges of the building and burned in a near-perfect inn-shaped blaze, only a few tendrils scorching the street stones that circled the building.

No, this was spellwork.

And it was fresh. Warmth still wafted off the ruins as Kell and Lila waded through them, searching for something—*anything*—that might have survived. But nothing had.

Kell felt sick.

This kind of fire burned hot and fast, and the edges suggested a binding circle. It wouldn't simply have contained the flames. It would have contained everything. Everyone. How many people had been trapped inside? How many corpses now in the wreckage, reduced to bone, or merely ash?

And then Kell thought, selfishly, of his room.

Years of collecting—music boxes and lockets, instruments and ornaments, the precious and the simple and the strange—all gone.

Rhy's warning—*give up this foolishness before you're caught*—echoed in his head, and for an instant, Kell was glad that he'd been robbed of the bounty before it could be discovered. And then the weight of it sank in. Whoever did this, they hadn't *robbed* him—at least, that hadn't been the point. But they'd stripped him of his loot to cut him off. An *Antari* could not travel without tokens. They were trying to corner him, to make sure that if he managed to flee back into Red London, he would have nothing at his disposal.

It was a measure of thoroughness that reeked of Holland's own hand. The same hand that had ripped the London coins from Kell's throat and cast them away into the dark.

Lila toed the melted remains of a kettle. "What now?"

"There's nothing here," said Kell, letting a handful of ash slide through his fingers. "We'll have to find another token." He brushed the soot from his hands, thinking. He wasn't the only person in Red London with a trinket, but the list was short, as he'd been far more willing to trade in artifacts from the novel, harmless Grey than the warped and violent White. The king himself had a token, passed down over the years. Fauna had one, a trinket as part of their deal (though Fauna, he feared, was now buried somewhere in the rubble).

And Fletcher had one.

Kell cringed inwardly.

"I know a man," he said, which wasn't the half of it, but was certainly simpler than explaining that Fletcher was a petty criminal who'd lost a bounty to him in a game of Sanct when Kell was several years younger and several shades more arrogant, and Kell had gifted him the White London trinket as either a peace offering (if he felt like lying to himself) or a jab (if he was being honest). "Fletcher. He keeps a shop by the docks. He'll have a token."

"Yes, well, let's hope they haven't burned *his* shop down as well."

"I'd like to see them tr—" The words died in Kell's throat. Someone was coming. Someone who smelled of dried blood and burning metal. Kell lunged for Lila, and she got out half a word of protest before he clamped one hand over her mouth and shoved the other into her pocket. His fingers found the stone and folded over it, and power surged through his body, coursed through his blood. Kell caught his breath as a shudder ran through him, but there was no time to dwell on the sensation—at once thrilling and terrifying—and no time to hesitate. *Conviction,* Holland had said, *conviction is key,* so Kell did not waffle, did not waver.

"*Conceal us,*" he ordered the talisman.

And the stone obliged. It sang to life, its power ringing through him as—between one heartbeat and the next—black smoke enveloped Kell and Lila both. It settled over them like a shadow, a veil; when he brought his fingers to it, they met something that was more than air and less than cloth. When Kell looked down at Lila, he could see her, and when she looked up, she could clearly see him, and the world around them was still perfectly visible, albeit tinted by the spell. Kell held his breath and hoped the stone had done its task. He didn't have a choice. There was no time to run.

Just then Holland appeared at the mouth of the side street.

Kell and Lila both tensed at the sight of him. He looked slightly crumpled from his time on the alley floor. His wrists were red and raw beneath his wrinkled half-cloak. His silver clasp was tarnished, his collar flecked with mud, and his expression as close to anger as Kell had ever seen it. A small crease between his brows. A tightness in his jaw.

Kell could feel the stone shudder in his hand, and he wondered if Holland was drawn to it, or if it was drawn to Holland.

The other *Antari* was holding something—a flattened crystal, the size and shape of a playing card—up to his lips, and speaking into it in his low even way.

"*Öva sö taro,*" he said in his native tongue. *He is in the city.*

Kell couldn't hear the other person's answer, but after a pause, Holland answered, *"Kösa"*—*I'm sure*—and slipped the crystal back into his pocket. The *Antari* tipped his shoulder against the wall and studied the charred ruins of the inn. He stood there, as if lost in thought.

Or waiting.

The steadiness of his gaze made Lila fidget ever so slightly against Kell, and he tightened his grip over her mouth.

Holland squinted. Perhaps in thought. Perhaps at them. And then he spoke.

"They screamed while the building was burning," he said in English, his voice too loud to be meant only for himself. "All of them screamed by the end. Even the old woman."

Kell gritted his teeth.

"I know you're here, Kell," continued Holland. "Even the burned remains cannot hide your scent. And even the stone's magic cannot hide the stone. Not from me. It calls to me the way it does to you. I would find you anywhere, so end this foolishness and face me."

Kell and Lila stood frozen in front of him, only a few short strides separating them.

"I'm in no mood for games," warned Holland, his usual calm now flecked by annoyance. When neither Kell nor Lila moved, he sighed and drew a silver pocket watch from his cloak. Kell recognized it as the one Lila had left behind for Barron. He felt her stiffen against him as Holland tossed the timepiece in their direction; it bounced along the blackened street, skidding to a stop at the edge of the inn's charred remains. From here Kell could see that it was stained with blood.

"He died because of you," said Holland, addressing Lila. "Because you ran. You were a coward. Are you still?"

Lila struggled to get free of Kell's arms, but he held her there with all his strength, pinning her against his chest. He felt tears slide over his hand at her mouth, but he didn't let go. "No," he said breathlessly into her ear. "Not here. Not like this."

Holland sighed. "You will die a coward's death, Delilah Bard." He drew a curved blade from beneath his cloak. "When this is over," he said, "you will both wish you had come out."

He lifted his empty hand, and a wind caught up the ashes of the ruined inn, whipping them into the air overhead. Kell looked up at the cloud of it above them and said a prayer under his breath.

"Last chance," said Holland.

When he was met by silence, he lowered his hand, and the ash began to fall. And Kell saw what would happen. It would drift down, and settle on the veil, exposing them, and Holland would be upon them both in an instant. Kell's mind spun as his grip tightened on the stone, and he was about to summon its power again when the ash met their veil . . . and passed through.

It sank straight through the impossible cloth, and then through them, as though they were not there. As though they were not real. The crease between Holland's two-toned eyes deepened as the last of the ash settled back to the ruins, and Kell took a (very small) measure of comfort from the *Antari*'s frustration. He may be able to *sense* them, but he could not *see* them.

Finally, when the wind was gone and the ground lay still, and Kell and Lila remained concealed by the power of the stone, Holland's certainty faltered. He sheathed the curved blade and took a step back, turned, and strode away, cloak billowing behind him.

The moment he was gone, Kell's grip on Lila loosened, and she wrenched free of him and the spell and shot forward to the silver watch on the street.

"Lila," he called.

She didn't seem to hear him, and he didn't know if it was

because she'd abandoned their protective shroud or because her world had narrowed to the size and shape of a small bloodied watch. He watched her sink to one knee and take up the timepiece with shaking fingers.

He went to Lila's side and brought his hand to her shoulder, or tried, but it went straight through. So he was right. The veil didn't simply make them invisible. It made them incorporeal.

"Reveal me," he ordered the stone. Energy rippled through him, and a moment later, the veil dissolved. Kell marveled a moment at how easy it had been as he knelt beside her—the magic had come effortlessly—but this was the first time it had willingly undone itself. They could not afford to stay there, exposed, so Kell took her arm and silently summoned the magic to conceal them once more. It obeyed, the shadow veil settling again over them both.

Lila shook under his touch, and he wanted to tell her it was all right, that Holland might have taken the timepiece and left Barron's life, but he did not want to lie. Holland was many things—most of them well hidden—but he was not sentimental. If he had ever been compassionate, or at least merciful, Athos had bled it out of him long ago, carved it out along with his soul.

No, Holland was ruthless.

And Barron was dead.

"Lila," said Kell gently. "I'm sorry."

Her fingers curled tightly around the timepiece as she rose to her feet. Kell rose with her, and even though she would not look him in the eye, he could see the anger and pain written in the lines of her face.

"When this is over," she said, tucking the watch into a fold of her cloak. "I want to be the one to slit his throat." And then she straightened and let out a small, shuddering breath. "Now," she said, "which way to Fletcher?"

TEN

ONE WHITE ROOK

I

Booth was beginning to fall apart.

In this grim grey London, the drunkard's body hadn't lasted long at all—much to the displeasure of the thing burning its way through him. It wasn't the magic's fault; there was so little to hold on to here, so little to feed on. The people had only a candle's light of life inside them, not the fire to which the darkness was accustomed. So little heat, so easily extinguished. The moment he got inside, he burned them up to nothing, blood and bone to husk and ash in no time at all.

Booth's black eyes drifted down to his charred fingers. With such poor kindling, he couldn't seem to spread, couldn't last long in any body.

Not for lack of trying. After all, he'd left a trail of discarded shells along the docks.

Burned through the place they all called Southwark in a mere hour.

But his current body—the one he'd taken in the tavern alley—was now coming undone. The black stain across his shirtfront pulsed, trying to keep the last of the life from bleeding out. Perhaps he shouldn't have stabbed the drunkard first, but it seemed the fastest way in.

But the failing shell and the lack of prospects had left him with a predicament. He appeared to be rotting.

Bits of skin flaked off with every step. The people in the street looked at him and moved away, out of reach, as if whatever was eating him was contagious. Which, of course, it was. Magic was a truly beautiful disease. But only when the hosts were strong enough. Pure enough. The people here were not.

He walked on through the city—shuffled, hobbled, really, at this point—the power in this shell only embers now, and quickly cooling.

And in his desperation, he found himself drawn on—drawn *back*—to the place where he had started: the Stone's Throw. He wondered at the pull of the odd little tavern. It was a flicker of warmth in the cold, dead city. A glimmer of light, of life, of magic.

If he could get there, he might find a fire yet.

He was so consumed by the need to reach the tavern that he did not notice the man standing by its door, nor the carriage fast approaching as he stepped off the curb and into the street.

Edward Archibald Tuttle stood outside the Stone's Throw, frowning at the time.

It should be open by now, but the bolts were still thrown, the windows shuttered, and everything within seemed strangely still. He checked his pocket watch. It was after noon. How odd. *Suspicious,* he thought. *Nefarious, even.* His mind spun over the possibilities, all of them dark.

His family insisted that he had too vivid an imagination, but he held that the rest of the world simply lacked the sight, the sense for magic, which he, obviously, possessed. Or at least endeavored to possess. Or, truly, had begun to fear he would never possess, had begun to think (though he would not admit it) did not exist.

Until he found the traveler. The renowned magician known only as Kell.

That single—and singular—meeting had rekindled his belief, stoked the fires hotter than they had ever been.

And so Edward had done as he was told, and returned to the Stone's Throw in hopes of finding the magician a second time and receiving his promised bag of earth. To that end, he had come yesterday, and to that end, he would come again tomorrow, and the next, until the illustrious figure returned.

While he waited, Ned—for that was what his friends and family called him—spun stories in his head, trying to imagine how the eventual meeting would take shape, how it would unfold. The details changed, but the end remained the same: in every version, the magician Kell would tip his head and consider Ned with his black eye.

"Edward Archibald Tuttle," he'd say, "May I call you Ned?"

"All my friends do."

"Well, Ned, I see something special in you. . . ."

He'd then insist upon being Ned's mentor, or even better, his partner. After that, the fantasy usually devolved into praise.

Ned had been playing out yet another of these daydreams while he stood on the steps of the Stone's Throw, waiting. His pockets were weighed with trinkets and coins, anything the magician might want in exchange for his prize. But the magician had not come, and the tavern was all locked up, and Ned—after whispering something that was equal parts spell and prayer and nonsense and trying unsuccessfully to will the bolt from its place—was about to pause his pursuit for the moment and go pass a few hours in an open establishment, when he heard a crash behind him in the street.

Horses whinnied and wheels clattered to a halt. Several

crates of apples tumbling out of a cart as the driver pulled back sharply on the reins. He looked more frightened than his horses.

"What's the matter?" asked Ned, striding over.

"Bloody hell," the driver was saying. "I've hit him. I've hit someone."

Ned looked around. "I don't think you've hit anything."

"Is he under the cart?" went on the driver. "Oh God. I didn't see him."

But when he knelt to inspect the space beneath the carriage, the spokes of its wheels, Ned saw nothing but a stretch of soot—it was, strangely enough, vaguely person-shaped—across the stones, already blowing away. One small mound seemed to move, but then it crumbled inward and was gone. *Strange,* he thought with a frown. *Ominous.* He held his breath and reached out toward the smear of charcoal dust, expecting it to spring to life. His fingers met the ash and . . . nothing happened. He rubbed the soot between his thumb and forefinger, disappointed.

"Nothing there, sir," he said, getting to his feet.

"I swear," said the driver. "There was someone here. Right here."

"Must have been mistaken."

The driver shook his head, mumbling, then climbed down from the cart and reloaded the crates, looking under the cart a few more times, just in case.

Ned held his fingers up to the light, wondering at the soot. He had felt something—or *thought* he had—a prickle of warmth, but the feeling had quickly faded to nothing. He sniffed the soot once and sneezed roundly, then wiped the ash on his pant leg and wandered off down the street.

II

Kell and Lila made their way to the docks, invisible to passersby. But not only invisible. *Intangible.* Just as the ash had passed through them at the ruined inn, and Kell's hand through Lila's shoulder, so did the people on the street. They could neither feel nor hear them. It was as if, beneath the veil, Kell and Lila were not part of the world around them. As if they existed outside of it. And just as the world could not touch them, they could not touch the world. When Lila absently tried to pocket an apple from a cart, her hand went through the fruit as sure as the fruit went through her hand. They were as ghosts in the bustling city.

This was strong magic, even in a London rich with power. The stone's energy thrummed through Kell, twining with his own like a second pulse. A voice in the back of his head warned him against the thing coursing through his body, but he pushed the voice away. For the first time since he'd been wounded, Kell didn't feel dizzy and weak, and he clung to the strength as much as to the stone itself as he led Lila toward the docks.

She'd been quiet since they left the remains of the inn, holding on to Kell with one hand and the timepiece with the other. When she finally spoke, her voice was low and sharp.

"Before you go thinking Barron and I were blood, we weren't," she said as they walked side by side. "He wasn't my family. Not really." The words rang stiff and hollow, and the way she clenched her jaw and rubbed her eyes (when she thought he wasn't looking) told another story. But Kell let Lila keep her lie.

"Do you have any?" he asked, remembering her biting remarks about his situation with the crown. "Family, that is?"

Lila shook her head. "Mum's been dead since I was ten."

"No father?"

Lila gave a small humorless laugh. "My *father*." She said it like it was a bad word. "The last time I saw *him,* he tried to sell my flesh to pay his tab."

"I'm sorry," said Kell.

"Don't be," said Lila, managing the sharp edge of a smile. "I cut the man's throat before he could get his belt off." Kell tensed. "I was fifteen," she went on casually. "I remember wondering at the amount of blood, the way it kept spilling out of him. . . ."

"First time you killed someone?" asked Kell.

"Indeed," she said, her smile turning rueful. "But I suppose the nice thing about killing is that it gets easier."

Kell's brow furrowed. "It shouldn't."

Lila's eyes flicked up to his. "Have *you* ever killed anyone?" she asked.

Kell's frown deepened. "Yes."

"And?"

"And what?" he challenged. He expected her to ask who or where or when or how. But she didn't. She asked why.

"Because I had no choice," he said.

"Did you enjoy it?" she asked.

"Of course not."

"I did." There was a streak of bitterness woven through the admission. "I mean, I didn't enjoy the blood, or the gurgling sound he made as he died, or the way the body looked when it was over. Empty. But the moment I decided to do it, and the moment after that when the knife bit in and I knew that I'd done it, I felt"—Lila searched for the words—"powerful." She considered Kell then. "Is that what magic feels like?" she asked honestly.

Maybe in White London, thought Kell, where power was held like a knife, a weapon to be used against those in your way.

"No," he said. "That's not magic, Lila. That's just murder. Magic is . . ." But he trailed off, distracted by the nearest scrying board, which had suddenly gone dark.

Up and down the streets, the black notice boards affixed to lampposts and storefronts went blank. Kell slowed. All morning they had been running notices of Rhy's celebrations, a cycling itinerary of the day's—and week's—parades and public feasts, festivals and private dances. When the boards first went dark, Kell assumed that they were simply changing over stories. But then they all began to flash the same alarming message. A single word:

MISSING

The letters flashed, bold and white, at the top of every board, and beneath it, a picture of *Kell*. Red hair and black eye and silver-buttoned coat. The image moved faintly, but didn't smile, only stared out at the world. A second word wrote itself beneath the portrait:

REWARD

Sanct.

Kell slammed to a stop, and Lila, who'd been half a step behind, ran into him.

"What's the matter?" she asked, pushing off his arm. And then she saw it, too. "Oh . . ."

An old man stopped a few feet away to read the board, oblivious to the fact that the missing man stood just behind his shoulder. Beneath the wavering image of Kell's face, an empty circle drew itself in chalk. The instructions beside it read:

If seen, touch here.

Kell swore under his breath. Being hunted by Holland was bad enough, but now the whole city would be on alert. And they couldn't stay invisible forever. He wouldn't be able to lift a token, let alone use it, as long as they were under the veil.

"Come on." He picked up his pace, dragging Lila with him until they reached the docks. All around, his face stared back at them, frowning slightly.

When they reached Fletcher's shop, the door was shut and locked, a small sign hanging on its front that read RENACHE. *Away.*

"Do we wait?" asked Lila.

"Not out here," said Kell. The door was bolted three ways, and likely charmed as well, but they didn't need to be let in. They passed straight through the wood, the way they had half a dozen people on the street.

Only once they were safe within the shop did Kell will the magic to release the veil. Again it listened and obeyed without protest, the magic thinning and then dissolving entirely. *Conviction,* he mused as the spell slid from his shoulders, the room coming into sharper focus around him. Holland had been right. It was about staying in control. And Kell had.

Lila let go of his hand and turned back to face him. She froze.

"Kell," she said carefully.

"What is it?" he asked.

"Put down the stone."

He frowned, looked down at the talisman in his grip, and caught his breath. The veins on the back of his hand were dark, so dark that they stood out like ink against his flesh, the lines tracing up toward his elbow. The power he'd felt pulsing through him was *actually* pulsing through him, turning his blood black. He had been so focused on his renewed strength, and on the spell itself, on staying hidden, that he had not felt—had not wanted to feel—the warmth of the magic spreading up his arm like poison. But he should have noticed, should have known—that was the thing. Kell *knew* better. He knew how dangerous the stone was, and yet, even now, staring down at his darkened veins, that danger felt strangely faraway. A persistent calm pressed through him stride for stride with the stone's magic, telling him that everything would be all right, so long as he kept holding—

A knife buried itself in the post beside his head, and the room snapped back into focus.

"Have you gone deaf?" growled Lila, freeing another blade. "I said *put it down*."

Before the calm could close over him again, Kell willed himself to release the stone. At first, his fingers stayed clasped around the talisman as warmth—and in its wake, a kind of numbness—seeped through him. He brought his free, untainted hand to his darkening wrist and gripped hard, willing his resisting fingers to uncurl, to release the stone.

And finally, reluctantly, they did.

The stone tumbled from his grip, and Kell's knee instantly buckled beneath him. He caught himself on a table's edge, gasping for breath as his vision swam and the room tilted. He hadn't felt the stone leeching his energy, but now that it was gone, it was like someone had doused his fire. Everything went cold.

The talisman glinted on the wooden floor, a streak of blood against the jagged edge where Kell had gripped too hard. Even in its wake, it took all Kell's will not to take it up again. Shaking and chilled, he still longed to hold it. There were men who lurked in dens and in the dark corners of London, chasing highs like this, but Kell had never been one of them, never craved the raw power. Never needed to. Magic wasn't something he lusted for; it was something he simply *had*. But now his veins felt starved of it, and starving *for* it.

Before he could lose battle for control, Lila knelt beside the stone. "Clever little thing," she said, reaching for it.

"Don't—" started Kell, but she'd already used her handkerchief to sweep it up.

"Someone's got to hold on to it," she said, slipping the talisman into her pocket. "And I'd wager I'm the better choice right now."

Kell clutched the table as the magic withdrew, the veins in his arm lightening little by little.

"Still with us?" asked Lila.

Kell swallowed and nodded. The stone was a poison, and they had to be rid of it. He steadied himself. "I'm all right."

Lila raised a brow. "Yes. You are the very image of health."

Kell sighed and slumped into a chair. On the docks outside, the celebrations were in full swing. Fireworks punctuated the music and cheers, the noise dulled, but not much, by the walls of the shop.

"What's he like?" asked Lila, looking in a cabinet. "The prince."

"Rhy?" Kell ran a hand through his hair. "He's . . . charming and spoiled, generous and fickle and hedonistic. He would flirt with a nicely upholstered chair, and he never takes anything seriously."

"Does he get into as much trouble as you do?"

Kell cracked a smile. "Oh, much more. Believe it or not, I'm the responsible one."

"But you two are close."

Kell's smile fell, and he nodded once. "Yes. The king and queen may not be my parents, but Rhy is my brother. I would die for him. I would kill for him. And I have."

"Oh?" asked Lila, admiring a hat. "Do tell."

"It's not a pleasant story," said Kell, sitting forward.

"Now I want to hear it even more," said Lila.

Kell considered her and sighed, looking down at his hands. "When Rhy was thirteen, he was abducted. We were playing some stupid game in the palace courtyard when he was taken. Though, knowing Rhy, he might have gone willingly at first. Growing up, he was always too trusting."

Lila set the hat aside. "What happened?"

"Red London is a good place," insisted Kell. "The royals here are kind, and just, and most of the subjects are happy. But," he continued, "I have been to all three Londons, and I can say this: there is no version that does not suffer in one way or another."

He thought of the opulence, the glittering wealth, and what it must look like to those without. Those who had been stripped of power for crimes, and those never blessed with much to begin with. Kell could not help wondering, What would have become of Rhy Maresh if he were not a royal? Where would he be? But of course, Rhy could survive on his charm and his smile. He would always get by.

"My world is a world made of magic," he said. "The gifted reap the blessings, and the royal family wants to believe that those who are not gifted do as well. That their generosity and their care extend to every citizen." He found Lila's eyes. "But I have seen the darker parts of this city. In your world, magic is a rarity. In mine, the lack of it is just as strange. And those without gifts are often looked down upon as unworthy of them, and treated as less for it. The people here believe that magic chooses its path. That it judges, and so can they. *Aven essen,* they call it. *Divine balance.*"

But by that logic, the magic had *chosen* Kell, and he did not believe that. Someone else could just have easily woken or been born with the *Antari* mark, and been brought into the lush red folds of the palace in his stead.

"We live brightly," said Kell. "For better or worse, our city burns with life. With light. And where there's light . . . well. Several years ago, a group began to form. They called themselves the Shadows. Half a dozen men and women—some with power, some without—who believed the city burned its power too brightly and with too little care, squandering it. To them, Rhy was not a boy, but a symbol of everything wrong. And so they took him. I later learned they meant to hang his body from the palace doors. Saints be thanked, they never got the chance.

"I was fourteen when it happened, a year Rhy's senior and still coming into my power. When the king and queen learned of their son's abduction, they sent the royal guard across the city. Every scrying board in every public square and private home burned with the urgent message to find the stolen prince. And I knew they would not find him. I knew it in my bones and in my blood.

"I went to Rhy's rooms—I remember how empty the palace was, with all the guards out searching—and found the first thing I knew was truly his, a small wooden horse he'd carved, no bigger than a palm. I had made doors using tokens before, but never one like this, never to a person instead of a place. But there is an *Antari* word for *find,* and so I thought it would work. It had to. And it did. The wall of his room gave way to the bottom of a boat. Rhy was lying on the floor. And he wasn't breathing."

Air hissed between Lila's teeth, but she didn't interrupt.

"I had learned the blood commands for many things," said Kell. "*As Athera.* To grow. *As Pyrata.* To burn. *As Illumae.* To light. *As Travars.* To Travel. *As Orense.* To open. *As Anasae.* To dispel. *As Hasari.* To heal. So I tried to heal him. I cut my hand and pressed it to his chest and said the words. And it didn't work." Kell would never shake the image of Rhy lying on the damp deck floor, pale and still. It was one of the only times in his life that he looked small.

"I didn't know what to do," continued Kell. "I thought maybe I hadn't used enough blood. So I cut my wrists."

He could feel Lila's unwavering stare as he looked down at his hands now, palms up, considering the ghosted scars.

"I remember kneeling over him, the dull ache spreading up my arms as I pressed my palms against him and said the words over and over and over. *As Hasari. As Hasari. As Hasari.* What I didn't realize then was that a healing spell—even a blood command—takes time. It was already working, had been since the first invocation. A few moments later, Rhy woke up." Kell broke into a sad smile. "He looked up and saw me crouching over him, bleeding, and the first thing he said wasn't 'What happened?' or 'Where are we?' He touched the blood on his chest and said, 'Is it yours? Is it all yours?' and when I nodded, he burst into tears, and I took him home."

When he found Lila's gaze, her dark eyes were wide.

"But what happened to the Shadows?" she asked, when it was clear that he was done. "The ones who took him? Were they in the boat? Did you go back for them? Did you send the guards?"

"Indeed," said Kell. "The king and queen tracked down every member of the Shadows. And Rhy pardoned them all."

"*What?*" gasped Lila. "After they tried to kill him?"

"That's the thing about my brother. He's headstrong and

thinks with every part of his body but his brain most days, but he's a *good* prince. He possesses something many lack: *empathy*. He forgave his captors. He understood why they did it, and he felt their suffering. And he was convinced that if he showed them mercy, they wouldn't try to harm him again." Kell's eyes went to the floor. "And I made sure they couldn't."

Lila's brow crinkled as she realized what he was saying. "I thought you said—"

"I said *Rhy* forgave them." Kell pushed to his feet. "I never said I did."

Lila stared at him, not with shock or horror, but a measure of respect. Kell rolled his shoulders and smoothed his coat. "I guess we better start looking."

She blinked once, twice, obviously wanting to say more, but Kell made it as clear as he could that this particular discussion was over. "What are we looking for?" she finally asked.

Kell surveyed the packed shelves, the overflowing cabinets and cupboards.

"A white rook."

III

For all the digging he'd done through the ruins of the Ruby Fields, Kell had failed to notice the alley where he'd been attacked—and where he'd left two bodies behind—only hours before. If he'd ventured there, he would have seen that one of those bodies—the cutthroat previously encased in stone—was missing.

That same cutthroat now made his way down the curb, humming faintly as he relished the warmth of the sun and the far-off sounds of celebration.

His body wasn't doing very well. Better than the other shell, of course, the drunkard in the duller London; that one hadn't lasted long at all. This one had fared better, much better, but now it was all burnt up inside and beginning to blacken without, the darkness spreading through its veins and over its skin like a stain. He looked less like a man now, and more like a charred piece of wood.

But that was to be expected. After all, he had been busy.

The night before, the lights of the pleasure house had burned bright and luring in the dark, and a woman stood waiting for him in the doorway with a painted smile and hair the color of fire, of life.

"*Avan, res nastar,*" she purred in the smooth Arnesian tongue.

She drew up her skirts as she said it, flashing a glimpse of knee. "Won't you come in?"

And he had, the cutthroat's coins jingling in his pocket.

She'd led him down a hall—it was dark, much darker than it had been outside—and he'd let her lead, enjoying the feel of her hand—or in truth, her pulse—in his. She never looked him in the eyes, or she might have seen that they were darker than the hall around them. Instead, she focused on his lips, his collar, his belt.

He was still learning the nuances of his new body, but he managed to press his cracking lips to the woman's soft mouth. Something passed between them—the ember of a pure black flame—and the woman shivered.

"*As Besara,*" he whispered in her ear. *Take.*

He slid the dress from her shoulders and kissed her deeper, his darkness passing over her tongue and through her head, intoxicating. Power. Everybody wanted it, wanted to be closer to magic, to its source. And she welcomed it. Welcomed *him*. Nerves tingled as the magic took them, feasting on the current of life, the blood, the body. He'd taken the drunkard, Booth, by force, but a willing host was always better. Or at least, they tended to last longer.

"*As Herena,*" he cooed, pressing the woman's body back onto the bed. *Give.*

"*As Athera,*" he moaned as he took her, and she took him in. *Grow.*

They moved together like a perfect pulse, one bleeding into the other, and when it was over, and the woman's eyes floated open, they reflected his, both a glossy black. The thing inside her skin pulled her rouged lips into a crooked smile.

"*As Athera,*" she echoed, sliding up from the bed. He rose and followed, and they set out—one mind in two bodies—first through the pleasure house, and then through the night.

Yes, he had been busy.

He could feel himself spreading through the city as he made his way toward the waiting red river, the pulse of magic and life laid out like a promised feast.

IV

Fletcher's shop was built like a maze, arranged in a way that only the snake himself would understand. Kell had spent the last ten minutes turning through drawers and had uncovered a variety of weapons and charms, and a fairly innocuous parasol, but no white rook. He groaned and tossed the parasol aside.

"Can't you just find the damned thing using magic?" asked Lila.

"The whole place is warded," answered Kell. "Against locator spells. And against thieving, so put that back."

Lila dropped the trinket she was about to palm back on the counter. "So," she said, considering the contents of a glass case, "you and Fletcher are friends?"

Kell pictured Fletcher's face the night he'd lost the pot. "Not exactly."

Lila raised a brow. "Good," she said. "More fun to steal from enemies."

Enemies was a fair word. The strange thing was, they could have been partners.

"A smuggler and a fence," he'd said. "We'd make a perfect team."

"I'll pass," said Kell. But when the game of Sanct had been in its last hand, and he'd known that he had won, he'd baited

Fletcher with the one thing he wouldn't refuse. *"Anesh,"* he'd conceded. "If you win, I'll work for you."

Fletcher had smiled his greedy smile and drawn his last card.

And Kell had smiled back and played his hand and won everything, leaving Fletcher with nothing more than a bruised ego and a small white rook.

No hard feelings.

Now Kell turned over half the store, searching for the token and glancing every few moments at the door while his own face watched them from the scrying board on the wall.

MISSING

Meanwhile, Lila had stopped searching and was staring at a framed map. She squinted and tilted her head, frowning as if something were amiss.

"What is it?" asked Kell.

"Where's Paris?" she asked, pointing to the place on the continent where it should be.

"There is no Paris," said Kell, rummaging through a cupboard. "No France. No England, either."

"But how can there be a London without an England?"

"I told you, the city's a linguistic oddity. Here London is the capital of Arnes."

"So Arnes is simply your name for England."

Kell laughed. "No," he said, shaking his head as he crossed to her side. "Arnes covers more than half of your Europe. The island—your England—is called the *raska*. The *crown*. But it's only the tip of the empire." He traced the territory lines with his fingertip. "Beyond our country lies Vesk, to the north, and Faro, to the south."

"And beyond them?"

Kell shrugged. "More countries. Some grand, some small. It's a whole world, after all."

Her gaze trailed over the map, eyes bright. A small private smile crossed her lips. "Yes, it is."

She pulled away and wandered into another room. And then moments later, she called, "Aha!"

Kell started. "Did you find it?" he called back.

She reappeared, holding up her prize, but it wasn't the rook. It was a knife. Kell's spirits sank.

"No," she said, "but isn't this clever?" She held it up for Kell to see. The hilt of the dagger wasn't simply a grip; the metal curved around over the knuckles in a wavering loop before rejoining the stock.

"For hitting," explained Lila, as if Kell couldn't grasp the meaning of the metal knuckles. "You can stab them, or you can knock their teeth out. Or you can do both." She touched the tip of the blade with her finger. "Not at the same time, of course."

"Of course," echoed Kell, shutting a cabinet. "You're very fond of weapons."

Lila stared at him blankly. "Who isn't?"

"And you already have a knife," he pointed out.

"So?" asked Lila, admiring the grip. "No such thing as too many knives."

"You're a violent sort."

She wagged the blade. "We can't all turn blood and whispers into weapons."

Kell bristled. "I don't whisper. And we're not here to loot."

"I thought that's *exactly* why we're here."

Kell sighed and continued to look around the shop. He'd turned over the whole thing, including Fletcher's cramped little room at the back, and come up empty. Fletcher wouldn't have sold it . . . or would he? Kell closed his eyes, letting his senses wander, as if maybe he could feel the foreign magic. But the space was practically humming with power, overlapping tones that made it impossible to parse the foreign and forbidden from the merely forbidden.

"I've got a question," said Lila, her pockets jingling suspiciously.

"Of course you do." Kell sighed, opening his eyes. "And I thought I said no thieving."

She chewed her lip and dug a few stones and a metal contraption even Kell didn't recognize the use of out of her pocket, setting them on a chest. "You said the worlds were cut off. So how does this man—Fletcher—have a piece of White London?"

Kell sifted through a desk he swore he'd searched, then felt under the lip for hidden drawers. "Because I gave it to him."

"Well, what were *you* doing with it?" Her eyes narrowed. "Did you steal it?"

Kell frowned. He had. "No."

"Liar."

"I didn't take it for myself," said Kell. "Few people in your world know about mine. Those that do—Collectors and Enthusiasts—are willing to pay a precious sum for a piece of it. A trinket. A token. In my world, most know about yours—a few people are as intrigued by your mundaneness as you are by our magic—but everyone knows about the *other* London. White London. And for a piece of *that* world, some would pay dearly."

A wry smile cut across Lila's mouth. "You're a smuggler."

"Says the pickpocket," snapped Kell defensively.

"I know I'm a thief," said Lila, lifting a red lin from the top of the chest and rolling it over her knuckles. "I've accepted that. It's not my fault that you haven't." The coin vanished. Kell opened his mouth to protest, but the lin reappeared an instant later in her other palm. "I don't understand, though. If you're a royal—"

"I'm *not*—"

Lila gave him a withering look. "If you *live* with royals and you *dine* with them and you *belong* to them, surely you don't want for money. Why risk it?"

Kell clenched his jaw, thinking of Rhy's plea to stop his foolish games. "You wouldn't understand."

Lila quirked a brow. "Crime isn't that complicated," she said. "People steal because taking something gives them something. If they're not in it for the money, they're in it for control. The act of taking, of breaking the rules, makes them feel powerful. They're in it for the sheer defiance." She turned away. "Some people steal to stay alive, and some steal to feel alive. Simple as that."

"And which are you?" asked Kell.

"I steal for freedom," said Lila. "I suppose that's a bit of both." She wandered into a short hallway between two rooms. "So that's how you came across the black rock?" she called back. "You made a deal for it?"

"No," said Kell. "I made a mistake. One I intend to fix, if I can find the damned thing." He slammed a drawer shut in frustration.

"Careful," said a gruff voice in Arnesian. "You might break something."

Kell spun to find the shop's owner standing there, shoulder tipped against a wardrobe, looking vaguely bemused.

"Fletcher," said Kell.

"How did you get in?" asked Fletcher.

Kell forced himself to shrug as he shot a glance toward Lila, who'd had the good sense to stay in the hallway and out of sight. "I guess your wards are wearing thin."

Fletcher crossed his arms. "I doubt that."

Kell stole a second glance toward Lila, but she was no longer in the hall. A spike of panic ran through him, one that worsened a moment later when she reappeared behind Fletcher. She moved with silent steps, a knife glittering in one hand.

"Tac," said Fletcher, lifting his hand beside his head. "Your friend is very rude." As he said it, Lila froze mid-stride. The strain showed in her face as she tried to fight the invisible force holding her in place, but it was no use. Fletcher had the rare and dangerous ability to control *bones,* and therefore *bodies*. It was an ability that had earned him the binding scars he was so proud of breaking.

Lila, for one, seemed unimpressed. She muttered some very violent things, and Fletcher splayed his fingers. Kell heard a sound like cracking ice, and Lila let out a stifled cry, the knife tumbling from her fingers.

"I thought you preferred to work alone," said Fletcher conversationally.

"Let her go," ordered Kell.

"Are you going to make me, *Antari*?"

Kell's fingers curled into fists—the shop was warded a dozen ways, against intruders and thieves and, with Kell's luck, anyone who meant Fletcher harm—but the shop owner himself gave a low chuckle and dropped his hand, and Lila went stumbling to her hands and knees, clutching her wrist and swearing vehemently.

"Anesh," he said casually. "What brings you back to my humble shop?"

"I gave you something once," said Kell. "I'd like to borrow it."

Fletcher gave a derisive snort. "I am not in the business of borrowers."

"I'll buy it then."

"And if it's not for sale?"

Kell forced himself to smile. "You of all people know," he said, "that *everything* is for sale."

Fletcher parroted the smile, cold and dry. "I won't sell it to you, but I might sell it to her"—his gaze glanced to Lila, who had gotten to her feet and retreated to the nearest wall to lurk and curse—"for the right price."

"She doesn't speak Arnesian," said Kell. "She hasn't the faintest idea what you're saying."

"Oh?" Fletcher grabbed his crotch. "I bet I can make her understand," he said, shaking himself in her direction.

Lila's eyes narrowed. "Burn in hell, you fu—"

"I wouldn't bother with her," cut in Kell. "She bites."

Fletcher sighed and shook his head. "What kind of trouble are you in, *Master Kell*?"

"None."

"You must be in some, to come here. And besides," said Fletcher, smile sharpening. "They don't put your face up on the boards for nothing."

Kell's eyes flicked to the scrying board on the wall, the one that had been painted with his face for the last hour. And then he paled. The circle at the bottom, the one that said *If seen touch here* was pulsing bright green.

"What have you done?" growled Kell.

Fletcher only smiled.

"No hard feelings," he said darkly, right before the shop doors burst open, and the royal guard poured in.

V

Kell had only an instant to arrange his features, to force panic into composure, before the guards were there, five in all, filling up the room with movement and noise.

He couldn't run—there was nowhere to run *to*—and he didn't want to hurt them, and Lila... Well, he had no idea where Lila was. One moment she'd been right there against the wall, and the next she'd vanished (though Kell had seen her fingers go into the pocket of her coat the instant before she disappeared, and he could feel the subtle hum of the stone's magic in the air, the way Holland must have felt it at the Ruby Fields).

Kell forced himself to stay still, to feign calm, even though his heart was racing in his chest. He tried to remind himself that he wasn't a criminal, that the royals were likely only worried by his disappearance. He hadn't done anything wrong, not in the eyes of the *crown*. Not that they *knew* of. Unless, in his absence, Rhy had told the king and queen of his transgressions. He wouldn't—Kell *hoped* he wouldn't—but even if he had, Kell was *Antari,* a member of the royal family, someone to be respected, even feared. He coated himself in that knowledge as he leaned back lazily, almost arrogantly, against the table behind him.

When the members of the royal guard saw him standing

there, alive and unconcerned, confusion spread across their features. Had they expected a body? A brawl? Half went to kneel, and half brought hands to rest on the hilts of their swords, and one stood there, frowning, in the middle.

"Ellis," said Kell, nodding at the head of the royal guard.

"Master Kell," said Ellis, stepping forward. "Are you well?"

"Of course."

Ellis fidgeted. "We've been worried about you. The whole palace has been."

"I didn't mean to worry anyone," he said, considering the guard around him. "As you can see, I'm perfectly all right."

Ellis looked around, then back at Kell. "It's just . . . sir . . . when you did not return from your errand abroad . . ."

"I was delayed," said Kell, hoping that would quell the questions.

Ellis frowned. "Did you not see the signs? They're posted everywhere."

"I only just returned."

"Then, forgive me," countered Ellis, gesturing to the shop. "But what are you doing *here*?"

Fletcher frowned. Though he spoke only Arnesian, he clearly understood the royal tongue well enough to know he was being insulted.

Kell forced a thin smile. "Shopping for Rhy's present."

A nervous laugh passed through the guard.

"You'll come with us, then?" asked Ellis, and Kell understood the words that went unsaid. *Without a fight.*

"Of course," said Kell, rising to his full height and smoothing his jacket.

The guards looked relieved. Kell's mind spun as he turned to Fletcher and thanked him for his help.

"*Mas marist,*" answered the shop's owner darkly. *My pleasure.* "Just doing my civic duty."

"I'll be back," said Kell in English (which garnered a raised brow from the royal guard), "as soon as I am through. To find what I was looking for." The words were directed at Lila. He could still feel her in the room, feel the stone even as it hid her. It whispered to him.

"Sir," said Ellis, gesturing to the door. "After you."

Kell nodded and followed him out.

The moment she heard the guards burst in, Lila had the good sense to close her hand over the stone and say *"Conceal me."*

And the stone had obeyed once more.

She'd felt a flutter up her arm, just beneath her skin, a lovely sensation—had it felt that nice the last time she'd used the talisman?—and then the veil had settled over her again and she was gone. Just as before, she could see herself, but no one else could see her. Not the guards, not Fletcher, not even Kell, whose two-toned eyes leveled on her but seemed to make out only the place she'd been, and not the place she was.

But though he could not see her, she could see him, and in his face she read a flicker of worry, disguised by his voice but not his posture, and under it a warning, threaded through the false calm of his words.

Stay, it seemed to urge, even before he said the words, lobbed at the room but clearly meant for her. So she stayed and waited and watched as Kell and four of the five members of the guard poured out into the street. Watched as a single guard hung back, his face hidden beneath the lowered visor of his helmet.

Fletcher was saying something to him, gesturing at his palm in the universal sign for payment. The guard nodded, and his hand went to his belt as Fletcher turned to watch Kell through the window.

Lila saw it coming.

Fletcher never did.

Instead of reaching for a purse, the guard went for a blade. The metal glinted once in the shop's low light, and then it was under Fletcher's chin, drawing a silent red line across his throat.

A closed carriage, pulled by royal white horses, gold and red ribbons still woven through their manes from the earlier parade, was waiting for Kell in front of the shop.

As Kell made his way to it, he shrugged out of his coat and turned it left to right, sliding his arms back into the now-red sleeves of his royal attire. His thoughts spun over what to tell the king and queen—not the truth, of course. But the king himself had a White London token, an ornament that sat on a shelf in his private chamber, and if Kell could get it, and get back to Lila and the stone . . . Lila and the stone loose in the city—it was a troubling thought. But hopefully she would stay put, just a little while. Stay out of trouble.

Ellis walked a half step behind Kell, three more guards trailing in his wake. The last had stayed behind to talk to Fletcher, and most likely settle the matter of the reward (though Kell was fairly sure Fletcher hated him enough to turn him in even without the added prospect of money).

Down the river toward the palace, the day's celebrations were dying down—no, not dying, *shifting*—to make way for the evening's festivities. The music had softened, and the crowds along the docks and up the market stretch had thinned, migrating to the city's various pubs and inns to continue toasting Rhy's name.

"Come, sir," said Ellis, holding the carriage door open for him. Instead of seats that faced each other, this carriage had two sets of benches both facing forward; two of the guards took the seat behind, and one went up to sit with the driver, while Ellis slid onto the front bench beside Kell and pulled the carriage door closed. "Let's get you home."

Kell's chest ached at the thought of it. He had tried not to let himself think of home, of how badly he wanted to be there, not since the stone—and the grim task of its disposal—had fallen to him. Now all he wanted was to see Rhy, to embrace him one last time, and he was secretly glad of the chance.

He let out a shaky breath and sank back onto the bench as Ellis drew the carriage curtains.

"I'm sorry about this, sir," he said, and Kell was about to ask what for when a hand clamped a cloth over his mouth, and his lungs filled with something bitter and sweet. He tried to wrench free, but armored gloves closed over his wrists and held him back against the bench, and within moments, everything went dark.

Lila sucked in a breath, unheard beneath the veil, as the guard let go of Fletcher's shoulder and he fell forward, thudding in a lifeless mass against the worn floorboards of the shop.

The guard stood there, unfazed by the murder and seemingly oblivious to the fact he was now splattered with someone else's blood. He surveyed the room, his gaze drifting past her, but through the slot in his helmet, Lila thought she saw an odd shimmer in his eyes. Something like magic. Satisfied that there was no one else to dispose of, the guard returned his blade to its sheath, turned on his heel, and left the shop. A dull bell followed him out, and a few moments later, Lila heard a carriage shudder to life and rumble away down the street.

Fletcher's body lay sprawled on the floor of his shop, blood soaking through his wiry blond hair and staining the boards beneath his chest. His smug expression was gone, replaced by surprise, the emotion preserved by death like an insect in amber. His eyes were open and empty, but something pale had tumbled from his shirt pocket and was now caught between his body and the floor.

Something that looked very much like a white rook.

Lila looked around to make sure she was alone, then did away with the concealment spell. It was easy enough, undoing the magic, but letting go of the stone itself proved considerably more difficult; it took her a long moment, and when she finally managed to pull free and drop the talisman back into her pocket, the whole room tilted. A shudder passed through her, stealing warmth and something more. In the magic's wake, she felt . . . *empty*. Lila was used to hunger, but the stone left her feeling starved in a bone-deep way. Hollow.

Bloody rock, she thought, tucking the toe of her boot under Fletcher's dead shoulder and turning him over, his blank stare now directed up at the ceiling, and at her.

She knelt, careful to avoid the spreading red slick as she picked up the blood-flecked chess piece.

Lila swore with relief and straightened, weighing it appraisingly. At first glance, it looked rather ordinary, and yet, when she curled her fingers around the stone—or bone, or whatever it was carved out of—she could almost feel the difference between its energy and that of the London around her. It was subtle, and perhaps she was imagining it, but the rook felt like a draft in a warm room. Just cold enough to seem out of place.

She shrugged off the sensation and tucked the chess piece into her boot (she didn't know how magic worked, but it didn't seem a wise idea to keep the two talismans close together, not until they were needed, and she wasn't touching the thieving little rock again unless she absolutely had to). She wiped Fletcher's blood off on her pants.

All things considered, Lila was feeling rather accomplished.

After all, she had the Black London stone *and* the White London token. Now all she needed was Kell.

Lila turned toward the door and hesitated. He'd told her to stay put, but as she looked down at Fletcher's fresh corpse, she feared he'd walked into trouble of his own. She'd been in Red London only a day, but it didn't seem like the place where royal guards went around slitting people's throats. Maybe Kell would be fine. But if he wasn't?

Her gut said to go, and years of stealing to survive had taught her to listen when it spoke. Besides, she reasoned, no one in the city was looking for *her*.

Lila made for the door, and she was almost to it when she saw the knife again, the one she'd been so keen on, sitting on top of the chest where she'd left it. Kell had warned her against thieving in the shop, but the owner was dead and it was just sitting there, unappreciated. She took it up and ran a finger gingerly along the blade. It really was a lovely knife. She eyed the door, wondering if the wards protecting the shop from thieves had died with their maker. Might as well test it. Carefully, she opened the door, set the weapon on the floor, and used the toe of her boot to kick the knife over the threshold. She cringed, waiting for the backlash—a current of energy, a wave of pain, or even the knife's stubborn return shop-side—but none came.

Lila smiled greedily and stepped out onto the street. She fetched up the knife and slid it into her belt and went to find—and most likely *rescue*—Kell from whatever mess he'd gotten himself into now.

VI

Parrish and Gen milled around the festival, helmets in one hand and mugs of wine in the other. Parrish had won back his coin—really, between the constant cards and the odd gambles, the two seemed to trade the pocket money back and forth without much gain or loss—and, being the better of the two sports, offered to buy Gen a drink.

It was, after all, a celebration.

Prince Rhy had been kind enough to give the two closest members of his private guard a few hours off, to enjoy the festivities with the masses gathered along the Isle. Parrish, prone to worry, had hesitated, but Gen had reasoned that on this day of all days, Rhy would be suitably well attended without them. At least for a little while. And so the two had wandered into the fray of the festival.

The celebration hugged the river, the market triple its usual size, its banks overflowing with patrons and cheer, music and magic. Every year, the festivities seemed to grow grander, once a simple hour or two of merriment, now a full day of revelry (followed by several more days of recovery, the excitement tapering off slowly until life returned to normal). But on this, the main day, the morning parade gave way to an afternoon of food and drink and good spirits, and finally, an evening ball.

This year it was to be a masquerade.

The great steps of the palace were already being cleared, the flowers gathered up and taken in to line the entry hall. Orbs of crisp light were being hung like low stars both outside the palace and within, and dark blue carpets unrolled, so that for the evening, the royal grounds would seem to float not on the river as a rising sun, but far above, a moon surrounded by the dazzling night sky. All over London, the young and beautiful and elite were climbing into their carriages, practicing their Royal under their breath as they rode to the palace in their masks and dresses and capes. And once there, they would worship the prince as though he were divine, and he would drink in their adoration as he always did, with relish and good cheer.

The masquerade within the palace walls was an invitation-only affair, but out on the riverbanks, the party was open to all and would go on in its own fashion until after midnight before finally dying down, the remnants wandering home with the merry revelers.

Parrish and Gen would soon be recalled to the prince's side, but for now they were leaning against a tent pole in the market, watching the crowds and enjoying themselves immensely. Now and then, Parrish would knock Gen's shoulder, a silent nudge to keep a sharp eye on the crowd. Even though they weren't officially on duty, they (or at least, Parrish) took enough pride in their jobs to wear their royal armor (though it didn't hurt that ladies seemed to enjoy a man in arms) and watch for signs of trouble. Most of the afternoon, trouble had come in the form of someone celebrating Rhy's day with a little too much enthusiasm, but now and then a fight broke out, and a weapon or a flash of magic was cause for intervention.

Gen appeared to be having a perfectly pleasant time, but Parrish was getting restless. His partner insisted that it was because Parrish had stopped at one drink, but he didn't think that was it. There was an energy in the air, and even though he knew the buzz was most likely coming from the festival itself, it still made him nervous. It wasn't just that there was *more* power than usual. It felt *different*. He rolled his empty cup between his hands and tried to set his mind at ease.

A troupe of fire workers was putting on a show nearby, twisting flames into dragons and horses and birds, and as Parrish watched them, the light from their enchanted fire blurred his vision. As it came back into focus, he caught the gaze of a woman just beyond, a lovely one with red lips and golden hair and a voluptuous, only half-concealed bosom. He dragged his gaze from her chest up to her eyes, and then frowned. They weren't blue or green or brown.

They were black.

Black as a starless sky or a scrying board.

Black as Master Kell's right eye.

He squinted to make sure, then called to Gen. When his compatriot didn't answer, he turned and saw the guard watching a young man—no, a *girl* in men's clothes, and strange dull clothes at that—weaving through the crowd toward the palace.

Gen was frowning at her faintly, as if she looked odd, out of place, and she did, but not as odd as the woman with black eyes. Parrish grabbed Gen's arm and dragged his attention forcefully away.

"*Kers?*" growled Gen, nearly spilling his wine. *What?*

"That woman there in blue," said Parrish, turning back to the crowd. "Her eyes . . ." But he trailed off. The black-eyed woman was gone.

"Smitten, are you?"

"It's not that. I swear her eyes—they were *black*."

Gen raised a brow and took a sip from his cup.

"Perhaps you've done a little too much celebrating after all," he said, clapping the other guard on the arm. Over his shoulder, Parrish watched the girl in boy's clothes disappear into a tent before Gen frowned and added, "Looks like you're not the only one."

Parrish followed his gaze and saw a man, his back to them, embracing a woman in the middle of the market. The man's hands were wandering a bit too much, even for a celebration day, and the woman didn't seem to be enjoying herself. She brought her hands to the man's chest, as if to push away, but he responded by kissing her deeper. Gen and Parrish abandoned their post and made their way toward the couple. And then, abruptly, the woman stopped struggling. Her hands fell to her sides and her head lolled, and when the man released her a moment later, she swayed on her feet and slumped into a seat. The man, meanwhile, simply turned and walked away, half walking, half stumbling through the crowd.

Parrish and Gen both followed, closing the gap in a slow, steady way so as not to cause alarm. The man appeared and disappeared through the crowd before finally cutting between tents toward the riverbank. The guards picked up their pace and reached the gap right after the man vanished through.

"You there," called Gen, taking the lead. He always did. "Stop."

The man heading for the Isle now slowed to a halt.

"Turn around," ordered Gen when he was nearly to him, one hand on his sword.

The man did. Parrish's eyes widened as they snagged on the stranger's face. Two pools, shining and black as river stones at night, sat where eyes should be, the skin around them veined with black. When the man tugged his mouth into a smile, flecks drifted off like ash.

"Asan narana," he said in a language that wasn't Arnesian. He held out his hand, and Parrish recoiled when he saw that it was entirely black, the fingertips tapering into charred bone points.

"What in king's name—" started Gen, but he didn't have a chance to finish because the man smiled and thrust his blackened hand through the armor and into the guard's chest.

"Dark heart," he said, this time in Royal.

Parrish stood frozen with shock and horror as the man, or whatever he was, withdrew his hand, what was left of his fingers wet with blood. Gen crumpled to the ground, and Parrish's shock shattered into motion. He charged forward, drawing his royal short sword, and thrust the blade into the stomach of the black-eyed monster.

For an instant, the creature looked amused. And then Parrish's sword began to glow as the spellwork on the enchanted blade took effect and severed the man from his magic. His eyes went wide, the black retreating from them, and from his veins, until he looked more or less like an ordinary man again (albeit a dying one). He drew in a rattling breath and gripped Parrish's armor—he bore an *X,* the mark of cutthroats, on the back of his hand—and then he crumbled to ash around Parrish's blade.

"Sanct," he swore, staring at the mound of soot as it began to blow away.

And then, out of nowhere, pain blossomed in his back, white-hot, and he looked down to see the tip of a sword protruding from his chest. It slid out with a horrible, wet sound, and Parrish's knees buckled as his attacker rounded him.

He took a shuddering breath, his lungs filling with blood, and looked up to see Gen looming over him, the blood-slicked blade hanging at his side.

"Why?" whispered Parrish.

Gen gazed down at him with two black eyes and a grim smile. *"Asan harana,"* he said. "Noble heart."

And then he raised the sword above his head and swung it down.

ELEVEN

MASQUERADE

I

The palace rose like a second sun over the Isle as the day's light sank low behind it, haloing its edges with gold. Lila made her way toward the glowing structure, weaving through the crowded market—it had become a rather raucous festival as the day and drink wore on—her mind spinning over the matter of how to get *into* the palace once she'd reached it. The stone pulsed in her pocket, luring her with its easy answer, but she'd made a decision not to use the magic again, not unless she had no other choice. It took too much, and did so with the quiet cunning of a thief. No, if there were another way in, she'd find it.

And then, as the palace neared and the front steps came into sight, Lila saw her opportunity.

The main doors were flung open, silky blue carpet spilling like night water down the stairs, and on them ascended a steady stream of partygoers. They appeared to be attending a ball.

Not just a ball, she realized, watching the river of guests.

A *masquerade*.

Every man and woman wore a disguise. Some masks were simple stained leather, some far more ornate, adorned by horns or feathers or jewels, some fell only across the eyes, and others revealed nothing at all. Lila broke into a wicked grin. She wouldn't need to be a member of society to get in. She need never show her face.

But there was another thing that every guest appeared to have: an *invitation*. That, she feared, would be harder to obtain. But just then, as if by a stroke of luck, or providence, Lila heard the high sweet sound of laughter, and turned to see three girls no older than she being helped out of a carriage, their dresses full and their smiles wide as they chattered and chirped and settled themselves on the street. Lila recognized them instantly from the morning parade, the girls who had been swooning over Rhy and the "black-eyed prince," whom Lila now knew to be Kell. The girls who had been practicing their English. Of *course*. Because English was the language of the royals, and those who mingled with them. Lila's smiled widened. Perhaps Kell was right: in any other setting, her accent would cause her to stand out. But here, here it would help her blend in, help her *belong*.

One of the girls—the one who'd prided herself on her English—produced a gold-trimmed invitation, and the three pored over it for several moments before she tucked it beneath her arm. Lila approached.

"Excuse me," she said, bringing a hand to rest at the girl's elbow. "What time does the masquerade begin?"

The girl didn't seem to remember her. She gave Lila a slow appraising look—the kind that made her want to free a few teeth from the girl's head—before smiling tightly. "It's starting now."

Lila parroted the smile. "Of course," she said as the girl pulled free, oblivious to the fact she was now short an invitation.

The girls set off toward the palace steps, and Lila considered her prize. She ran a thumb over the paper's gilded edges and ornate Arnesian script. Her eyes drifted up again, taking in the procession to the palace doors, but she didn't join it. The men and women ascending the stairs practically glittered in their jewel-tone gowns and dark, elegant suits. Lush cloaks spilled over their shoulders and threads of precious metal shone in their hair. Lila looked down at herself, her threadbare cloak and worn brown boots, and felt shabbier than ever. She tugged her own mask—nothing but a crumpled strip of black fabric—from her pocket. Even with an invitation and a healthy grasp of the English language, she'd never be let in, not looking like this.

She shoved the mask back in her cloak pocket and looked around at the market stalls that stood nearby. Farther down the booths were filled with food and drink, but here, at the edge nearest the palace, the stalls sold other wares. Charms, yes, but also canes and shoes and other fineries. Fabric and light spilled out of the mouth of the nearest tent, and Lila straightened and stepped inside.

A hundred faces greeted her from the far wall, the surface of which was covered in masks. From the austere to the intricate, the beautiful to the grotesque, the faces squinted and scowled and welcomed her in turn. Lila crossed to them and reached out to free one from its hook. A black half-mask with two horns spiraling up from the temples.

"*A tes fera, kes ile?*"

Lila jumped, and saw a woman standing at her side. She was small and round, with half a dozen braids coiled like snakes around her head, a mask nested in them like a hairpin.

"I'm sorry," said Lila slowly. "I don't speak Arnesian."

The woman only smiled and laced her hands in front of her broad stomach. "Ah, but your English is superb."

Lila sighed with relief. "As is yours," she said.

The woman blushed. It was obviously a point of pride. "I am a servant of the ball," she replied. "It is only fitting." She then gestured to the mask in Lila's hands. "A little dark, don't you think?"

Lila looked the mask in the eyes. "No," she said. "I think it's perfect."

And then Lila turned the mask over and saw a string of numbers that must have been the price. It wasn't written in shillings or pounds, but Lila was sure that, regardless of the kind of coin, she couldn't afford it. Reluctantly, she returned the mask to its hook.

"Why set it back, if it is perfect?" pressed the woman.

Lila sighed. She would have stolen it had the merchant not been standing there. "I don't have any money," she said, thrusting a hand into her pocket. She felt the silver of the watch and swallowed. "But I do have this. . . ." She pulled the timepiece from her pocket and held it out, hoping the woman wouldn't notice the blood (she'd tried to wipe most of it off).

But the woman only shook her head. *"An, an,"* she said, folding Lila's fingers back over the watch. "I cannot take your payment. No matter its shape."

Lila's brow furrowed. "I don't understand—"

"I saw you this morning. In the market." Lila's thoughts turned back to the scene, to her almost being arrested for stealing. But the woman wasn't speaking of the theft. "You and Master Kell, you are . . . friends, yes?"

"Of a sort," said Lila, blushing when that drew a secretive smile from the woman. "No," she amended, "No, I don't mean . . ." But the woman simply patted her hand.

"Ise av eran," she said lightly. "It's not my place to"—she paused, searching for a word—"pry. But Master Kell is *aven—blessed*—a jewel in our city's crown. And if you are his, or he is yours, my shop is yours as well."

Lila cringed. She hated charity. Even when people thought they were giving something freely, it always came with a chain, a weight that set everything off-balance. Lila would rather steal a thing outright than be indebted to kindness. But she needed the clothes.

The woman seemed to read the hesitation in her eyes. "You are not from here, so you do not know. Arnesians pay their debts in many ways. Not all of them with coin. I need nothing from you now, so you will pay me back another time, and in your own way. Yes?"

Lila hesitated. And then bells began to ring in the palace, loud enough to echo through her, and she nodded. "Very well," she said.

The merchant smiled. *"Ir chas,"* she said. "Now, let us find you something fitting."

"Hmm." The merchant woman—who called herself Calla—chewed her lip. "Are you certain you wouldn't prefer something with a corset? Or a train?"

Calla had tried to lead Lila to a rack of dresses, but her eyes had gone straight to the men's coats. Glorious things, with strong shoulders and high collars and gleaming buttons.

"No," said Lila, lifting one from the rack. "This is *exactly* what I want."

The merchant looked at her with strange fascination, but little—or, at the very least, well-concealed—judgment, and said, "*Anesh*. If you're set on that direction, I will find you some boots."

A few minutes later, Lila found herself in a curtained corner of the tent, holding the nicest clothes she'd ever touched, let alone owned. *Borrowed,* she corrected herself. Borrowed until paid for.

Lila pulled the artifacts from her various pockets—the black stone, the white rook, the bloodstained silver watch, the invitation—and set them on the floor before tugging off her boots and shrugging out of her old worn cloak. Calla had given her a new black tunic—it fit so well that she wondered if there was some kind of tailoring spell on it—and a pair of close-fitting pants that still hung a little loosely on her bony frame. She'd insisted on keeping her belt, and Calla had the decency not to gawk at the number of weapons threaded through it as she handed her the boots.

Every pirate needed a good pair of boots, and these were gorgeous things, sculpted out of black leather and lined with something softer than loose cotton, and Lila let out a rare gleeful sound as she pulled them on. And then there was the coat. It was an absolute dream, high-collared and lovely and black—*true* black, velvety and rich—with a fitted waist and a built-in half-cloak that gathered at glassy red clasps on either side of her throat and spilled over her shoulders and down her back. Lila ran her fingers admiringly over the glossy jet-black buttons that cascaded down its front. She'd never been one for baubles and fineries, never wanted anything more than salt air and a solid boat and an empty map, but now that she was standing in a foreign stall in a faraway land, clothed in rich fabrics, she was beginning to see the appeal.

At last, she lifted up the waiting mask. So many of the faces that hung around the stall were lovely, delicate things made of feather and lace and garnished with glass. But this one was beautiful in a different way, an opposite way. It reminded Lila less of dresses and finery, and more of sharpened knives and ships on the seas at night. It looked *dangerous*. She brought it to rest against her face and smiled.

There was a silver-tinted looking glass propped in the corner, and she admired her reflection in it. She looked little like the shadow of a thief on the WANTED posters back home, and nothing like the scrawny girl hoarding coppers to escape a dingy life. Her polished boots glistened from knee to toe, lengthening her legs. Her coat broadened her shoulders and hugged her waist. And her mask tapered down her cheeks, the black horns curling up over her head in a way that was at once elegant and monstrous. She gave herself a long, appraising look, the way the girl had in the street, but there was nothing to scoff at now.

Delilah Bard looked like a king.

No, she thought, straightening. She looked like a *conqueror.*

"Lila?" came the merchant woman's voice beyond the curtain. She pronounced the name as though it were full of *e*'s. "Does it fit?" Lila slid the trinkets into the new silk-lined pockets of her coat and emerged. The heels of her boots clicked proudly on the stone ground—and yet, she had tested the tread and knew that if she moved on the balls of her feet, the steps would be silent—and Calla smiled, a mischievous twinkle in her eyes, even as she *tsk*ed.

"*Mas aven,*" she said. "You look more ready to storm a city than seduce a man."

"Kell will love it," assured Lila, and the way she said his name, infusing it with a subtle softness, an intimacy, made the merchant woman ruffle cheerfully. And then the bells chimed again through the city, and Lila swore to herself. "I must go," she said. "Thank you again."

"You'll pay me back," said Calla simply.

Lila nodded. "I will."

She was to the mouth of the tent when the merchant woman added, "Look after him."

Lila smiled grimly and tugged up the collar of her coat. "I will," she said again before vanishing into the street.

II

Colors blossomed over Kell's head, blurs of red and gold and rich dark blue. At first they were nothing more than broad streaks, but as his vision came into focus, he recognized them as palace draperies, the kind that hung from the ceilings in each of the royal bedrooms, drawing sky-like patterns out of cloth.

Squinting up, Kell realized he must be in Rhy's room.

He knew this because the ceiling in his own was decorated like midnight, billows of near-black fabric studded with silver thread, and the queen's ceiling was like noon, cloudless and blue, and the king's was like dusk with its bands of yellow and orange. Only Rhy's was draped like this. Like dawn. Kell's head spun, and he closed his eyes and took a deep breath as he tried to piece his thoughts together.

He was lying on a couch, his body sinking into the soft cushions beneath him. Music played beyond the walls of the room, an orchestra, and woven through it, the sounds of laughter and revelry. Of course. Rhy's birthday ball. Just then, someone cleared his throat, and Kell dragged his eyes back open and turned his head to see Rhy himself sitting across from him.

The prince was draped in a chair, one ankle across his knee, sipping tea and looking thoroughly annoyed.

"Brother," said Rhy, tipping his cup. He was dressed in all black, his coat and pants and boots adorned with dozens of gold buttons. A mask—a gaudy thing, decorated with thousands of tiny sparkling gold scales—rested on top of his head in place of his usual crown.

Kell went to push the hair out of his eyes and quickly discovered that he could not. His hands were cuffed behind his back.

"You've got to be joking . . ." He shuffled himself up into a sitting position. "Rhy, why in king's name am I wearing these?" The cuffs weren't like those ordinary manacles found in Grey London, made of metal links. Nor were they like the binds in White, which caused blinding pain upon resistance. No, these were sculpted out of a solid piece of iron and carved with spellwork designed to dampen magic. Not as severe as the royal swords, to be sure, but effective.

Rhy set his teacup on an ornate side table. "I couldn't very well have you running away again."

Kell sighed and tipped his head back against the couch. "This is preposterous. I suppose that's why you had me drugged, too? Honestly, Rhy."

Rhy crossed his arms. He was clearly sulking. Kell dragged his head up and looked around, noticing that there were two members of the royal guard in the room with them, still dressed in formal armor, their helmets on, their visors down. But Kell knew Rhy's personal guard well enough to recognize them, armor or none, and these were not them.

"Where are Gen and Parrish?" asked Kell.

Rhy shrugged lazily. "Having a little too much fun, I imagine."

Kell shifted on the couch, trying to free himself from the cuffs. They were too tight. "Don't you think you're blowing this a little out of proportion?"

"Where have you been, brother?"

"Rhy," said Kell sternly. "Take these off."

Rhy's boot slid from his knee and came to rest firmly on the ground. He straightened in his seat, squaring himself to Kell. "Is it true?"

Kell's brow furrowed. "Is what true?"

"That you have a piece of Black London?"

Kell stiffened. "What are you talking about?"

"Is it true?" persisted the prince.

"Rhy," said Kell slowly. "Who told you that?" No one knew, none except those who wanted the stone gone and those who wanted it reclaimed.

Rhy shook his head sadly. "What have you brought into our city, Kell? What have you brought upon it?"

"Rhy, I—"

"I warned you this would happen. I told you that if you carried on with your deals, you would be caught and that even I could not protect you then."

Kell's blood ran cold.

"Do the king and queen know?"

Rhy's eyes narrowed. "No. Not yet."

Kell let out a small sigh of relief. "They don't need to. I'm doing what I have to do. I'm taking it back, Rhy. All the way back to the fallen city."

Rhy's brow crinkled. "I can't let you do that."

"Why not?" demanded Kell. "It is the only place the talisman belongs."

"Where is it now?"

"Safe," said Kell, hoping that was true.

"Kell, I can't help you if you won't let me."

"I'm taking care of it, Rhy. I promise you I am."

The prince was shaking his head. "Promises are not enough," he said. "Not anymore. Tell me where the stone is."

Kell froze. "I never told you it was a stone."

Heavy silence fell between them. Rhy held his gaze. And

then, finally, his lips drew into a small, dark smile, twisting his face in a way that made it look like someone else's.

"Oh, Kell," he said. He leaned forward, resting his elbows on his knees, and Kell caught sight of something under the collar of his shirt and stiffened. It was a pendant. A glass necklace with blood-red edges. He knew it, had seen it before only days earlier.

On Astrid Dane.

Kell lunged to his feet, but the guards were upon him, holding him back. Their motions were too even, their grip too crushing. Compelled. Of course. No wonder their visors were down. Compulsion showed in the eyes.

"Hello, flower boy." The words came from Rhy's mouth in a voice that was, and wasn't, his.

"Astrid," hissed Kell. "Have you compelled everyone in this palace?"

A low chuckle escaped Rhy's lips. "Not yet, but I'm working on it."

"What have you done with my brother?"

"I've only borrowed him." Rhy's fingers curled under his shirt collar and drew out the pendant. There was only one thing it could be: a possession charm. "*Antari* blood," she said proudly. "Allows the spell to exist in both worlds."

"You will pay for this," growled Kell. "I will—"

"You will what? Hurt me? And risk hurting your dear prince? I doubt it." Again, that cold smile, so foreign to Rhy's face, spread across his lips. "Where is the stone, Kell?"

"What are you doing here?"

"Isn't it obvious?" Rhy's hand swept across the room. "I'm branching out."

Kell pulled against his binds, the metal digging into his wrists. The dampening cuffs were strong enough to mute elemental abilities and prevent spellwork, but they couldn't prevent *Antari* magic. If he could only—

"Tell me where you've hidden the stone."

"Tell me why you are wearing my brother's body," he shot back, trying to buy time.

Astrid sighed from within the prince's shell. "You know so little of war. Battles may be fought from the outside in, but wars are won from the inside out." She gestured down at Rhy's body. "Kingdoms and crowns are taken from within. The strongest fortress can withstand any attack from *beyond* its walls, and yet even it is not fortified against an attack from behind them. Had I marched upon your palace from the steps, would I have made it this far? But now, now no one will see me coming. Not the king, nor the queen, nor the people. I am their beloved prince, and will be so until the moment I choose not to be."

"I know," said Kell. "I know what and who you are. What will you do, Astrid? Kill me?"

Rhy's face lit up with a strange kind of glee. "No"—the word slid over his tongue—"but I'm sure you'll wish I had. Now"—Rhy's hand lifted Kell's chin—"where is my stone?"

Kell looked into his brother's amber eyes, and beyond them, to the thing lurking in his brother's body. He wanted to beg Rhy, to plead with him to fight against the spell. But it wouldn't work. As long as *she* was in there, he wasn't.

"I don't know where it is," said Kell.

Rhy's smile spread, wolfish and sharp. "You know. . . ." Rhy's mouth formed the words, and Rhy held up his hand, considering his long fingers, the knuckles adorned with glittering rings. Those same hands began twisting the rings so that their jeweled settings were on the inside. "A little piece of me was hoping you would say that."

And then Rhy's fingers curled into a fist and connected with Kell's jaw.

Kell's head cracked to the side, and he nearly stumbled, but the guards tightened their grips and held him on his feet. Kell tasted blood, but Rhy just smiled that horrible smile and rubbed his knuckles. "This is going to be fun."

III

Lila ascended the palace stairs, the half-cloak of her new coat billowing behind her. The shimmering midnight carpet rippled faintly with every upward step, as though it were truly water. Other guests climbed the stairs in pairs or small groups, but Lila did her best to mimic their lofty arrogance—shoulders back, head high—as she ascended alone. She might not be of money, but she'd stolen enough from those who were to copy their manners and their mannerisms.

At the top, she presented the invitation to a man in black and gold who bowed and stepped aside, allowing her into a foyer blanketed in flowers. More flowers than Lila had ever seen. Roses and lilies and peonies, daffodils and azaleas, and scores more she could not recognize by sight. Clusters of tiny white blossoms like snowflakes, and massive stems that resembled sunflowers if sunflowers were sky blue. The room filled with the fragrance of them all, and yet it did not overwhelm her. Perhaps she was simply getting used to it.

Music poured through a second, curtained doorway, and the mystery of what lay beyond drew Lila forward through the gallery of flowers. And then, just as she reached out to pull the curtain aside, a second servant appeared from the other side and barred her path. Lila tensed, worried that somehow her disguise and invitation were not enough, that she would be discovered as an impostor, an outsider. Her fingers twitched toward the knife under her coat.

And then the man smiled and said in stiff English, "I am presenting whom?"

"Excuse me?" asked Lila, keeping her voice low, gruff.

The attendant's brow crinkled. "What title and name should I announce you under, sir?"

"Oh." Relief swept over her, and her hand slid back to her side. A smile spread across her lips. "Captain Bard," she said, "of the *Sea King*." The attendant looked uncertain, but turned away and said the words without protest.

Her name echoed and was swallowed by the room before she'd even stepped inside.

When she did, her mouth fell open.

The vivid glamour of the world outside paled in comparison to the world within. It was a palace of vaulting glass and shimmering tapestry and, woven through it all like light, *magic*. The air was alive with it. Not the secret, seductive magic of the stone, but a loud, bright, encompassing thing. Kell had told Lila that magic was like an extra sense, layered on top of sight and smell and taste, and now she understood. It was everywhere. In everything. And it was intoxicating. She could not tell if the energy was coming from the hundreds of bodies in the room, or from the room itself, which certainly reflected it. *Amplified* it like sound in an echoing chamber.

And it was strangely—*impossibly*—familiar.

Beneath the magic, or perhaps because of it, the space itself was alive with color and light. She'd never set foot inside St. James, but it couldn't possibly have compared to the splendor of this. Nothing in her London could. Her world felt truly grey by comparison, bleak and empty in a way that made Lila want to kiss the stone for freeing her from it, for bringing her here, to this glittering jewel of a place. Everywhere she looked, she saw wealth. Her fingers itched, and she resisted the urge to start picking pockets, reminding herself that the cargo in her own was too precious to risk being caught.

The curtained doorway led onto a landing, a set of stairs sloping down and away onto the hall's polished floor, the stone itself lost beneath boots and twirling skirts.

At the base of the stairs stood the king and queen, greeting each of their guests. Standing there, dressed in gold, they looked unbearably elegant. Lila had never been so near to royalty—she didn't count Kell—and knew she should slip away as soon as possible, but she couldn't resist the urge to flaunt her disguise. And besides, it would be rude not to greet her hosts. *Reckless,* growled a voice in her head, but Lila only smiled and descended the stairs.

"Welcome, Captain," said the king, his grip firm around Lila's hand.

"Your Majesty," she said, struggling to keep her voice from drifting up. She nodded her mask toward him, careful not to jab him with her horns.

"Welcome," echoed the queen as Lila kissed her outstretched hand. But as she pulled away, the queen added, "We have not met before."

"I am a friend of Kell's," said Lila as casually as possible, her gaze still on the floor.

"Ah," said the queen. "Then welcome."

"Actually," Lila went on, "Your Highness, I am looking for him. Do you know where he might be?"

The queen considered her blankly and said, "He is not here." Lila frowned, and the queen added, "But I am not worried." Her tone was strangely steady, as if she were reciting a line that wasn't hers. The bad feeling in Lila's chest grew worse.

"I'm sure he'll turn up," said Lila, sliding her hand free of the queen's.

"Everything will be okay," said the king, his voice similarly hollow.

"It will," added the queen.

Lila frowned. Something was wrong. She lifted her gaze, risking impertinence to look the queen in the eye, and saw there a subtle gleam. The same shimmer she'd seen in the eyes of the guard after he'd slit Fletcher's throat. Some kind of *spell*. Had no one else noticed? Or had no one else been brazen enough to stare so baldly at the crown?

The next guest cleared his throat at Lila's back, and she broke the queen's gaze. "I'm sorry to have kept you," she said quickly, shifting past the royal hosts and into the ballroom. She skirted the crowd of dancers and drinkers, looking for signs of the prince, but judging by the eagerness in the air, the way eyes constantly darted toward doors and sets of stairs, he'd yet to make an appearance.

She slipped away, through a pair of doors at the edge of the ballroom, and found herself in a corridor. It was empty, save for a guard and a young woman wrapped in a rather amorous embrace and too occupied to notice as Lila slid past and vanished through another set of doors. And then another. Navigating the streets of London had taught her a fair amount about the mazelike flow of places, the way wealth gathers in the heart and tapers to the corners. She moved from hall to hall, winding around the palace's beating heart without straying too far. Everywhere she went, she found guests and guards and servants, but no sign of Kell or the prince or any break in the maze. Until, finally, she came upon a set of spiral stairs. They were elegant but narrow, clearly not meant for public use. She cast a last glance back in the direction of the ball and then ascended the steps.

The floor above was quiet in a private way, and she knew she must be getting close, not only because of that silence, but also because the stone in her pocket was beginning to hum. As if it could *feel* Kell near and wished to be nearer. Again, Lila tried not to be offended.

She found herself in a new set of halls, the first of which was empty, the second of which was not. Lila rounded the corner and caught her breath. She pressed herself back into a shadowed nook, narrowly missing the eyes of a guard. He was standing in front of a set of ornate doors, and he was not alone. In fact, while every other door in the hall stood unmanned, the one at the end was guarded by no fewer than three armed and armored men.

Lila swallowed and slid her newest knife from her belt. She hesitated. For the second time in as many days, she found herself one against three. It had yet to end well. Her grip tightened on the knife as she scrounged for a plan that wasn't sure to end in a grave. The stone took up its murmuring rhythm again, and she was reluctantly about to draw it from her coat when she stopped and noticed something.

The hall was studded with doors, and while the farthest one was guarded, the nearest one stood ajar. It led onto a luxurious bedroom, and at the back of it, a balcony, curtains fluttering in the evening air.

Lila smiled and returned the knife to her belt.

She had an idea.

IV

Kell spat blood onto Rhy's lovely inlaid floor, marring the intricate pattern. If Rhy himself were here, he would not be happy. But Rhy wasn't here.

"The stone, my rose." Astrid's sultry tone poured between Rhy's lips. "Where is it?"

Kell struggled to get to his knees with his arms still pinned behind his back. "What do you want with it?" he growled as the two guards dragged him to his feet.

"To take the throne, of course."

"You already have a throne," observed Kell.

"In a dying London. And do you know why it dies? Because of you. Because of this city and its cowardly retreat. It made of us a shield, and now it thrives while we perish. It seems only just that I should take it, as reparation. Retribution."

"So you would, what?" asked Kell. "Abandon your brother to the decaying corpse of your world so you can enjoy the splendors of this one?"

A cold, dry laugh escaped Rhy's throat. "Not at all. That would make me a very poor sister. Athos and I will rule together. Side by side."

Kell's eyes narrowed. "What do you mean?"

"We are going to restore balance to the worlds. Reopen the doors. Or rather, tear them down, create one that stays open, so that anyone—*everyone*—can move between. A merger, if you will, of our two illustrious Londons."

Kell paled. Even when the doors had been unlocked, they had been *doors*. And they were kept closed. An open door between the worlds wouldn't only be dangerous. It would be *unstable*.

"The stone is not strong enough to do that," he said, trying to sound sure. But he wasn't. The stone had made a door for Lila. But making a pinprick in a piece of cloth was very different from tearing the fabric in half.

"Are you certain?" teased Astrid. "Perhaps you are right. Perhaps your half of the stone is not enough."

Kell's blood went cold. "My half?"

Rhy's mouth curled into a smile. "Haven't you noticed that it is broken?"

Kell reeled. "The jagged edge."

"Athos found it like that, in two pieces. He likes to find treasure, you see. Always has. Growing up, we used to scavenge the rocks along the coast, searching for anything of value. A habit he never lost. His searching merely became a bit more sophisticated. A bit more pointed. Of course, we knew of the Black London purge, of the eradication of artifacts, but he was so sure there must be something—*anything*—to help save our dying world."

"And he found it," said Kell, digging his wrists into the metal cuff. The edges were smooth, not sharp, and dull pain spread up his arm, but the skin refused to break. He stared down at the blood from his lip on Rhy's floor, but the guards were holding him up, their grip unyielding.

"He scoured," continued Astrid in Rhy's tongue. "Found a few useless things secreted away—a notebook, a piece of cloth—and then, lo and behold, he found the stone. Broken in two, yes, but, as I'm sure you've noticed, its state has not stopped it from working. It is magic, after all. It may divide, but it does not weaken. The two halves remain connected, even when they are apart. Each half is strong enough on its own, strong enough to change the world. But they want each other, you see. They are drawn together through the wall. If a drop of your blood is enough to make a door, think what two halves of the stone could do."

It could tear down the wall itself, thought Kell. Tear reality apart.

Rhy's fingers rapped along the back of a chair. "It was my idea, I confess, giving you the stone, allowing you to carry it across the line."

Kell grimaced as he twisted his wrists against the iron binding them. "Why not use Holland?" he asked, trying to buy more time. "To smuggle the stone here? He obviously delivered that necklace to Rhy."

Astrid drew Rhy's lips into a smile and ran a finger lightly over Kell's cheek. "I wanted you." Rhy's hand continued up and tangled in Kell's hair as Astrid leaned in, pressed her stolen cheek to Kell's bloody one, and whispered in his ear, "I told you once, that I would own your life." Kell wrenched back, and Rhy's hand fell away.

"Besides," she said with a sigh. "It made sense. If things went wrong, and Holland was caught, the guilt would lie on our crown, and we would not have another chance. If things went wrong and *you* were caught, the guilt would lie on your head. I know of your hobbies, Kell. You think the Scorched Bone keeps secrets? *Nothing* goes unnoticed in my city." Rhy's tongue clicked. "A royal servant with a bad habit of smuggling things across borders. Not so hard to believe. And if things went *right,* and I succeeded in taking this castle, this kingdom, I couldn't have you out there, unaccounted for, fighting against me. I wanted you here, where you belong. At my feet."

Dark energy began to crackle in Rhy's palm, and Kell braced himself, but Astrid couldn't seem to control it, not with Rhy's crude skills. The lightning shot to the left, striking the metal post of the prince's bed.

Kell forced himself to chuckle thinly. "You should have picked a better body," he said. "My brother has never had a gift for magic."

Astrid rolled Rhy's wrist, considering his fingers. "No matter," she said. "I have an entire family to choose from."

Kell had an idea. "Why don't you try on someone a little stronger?" he goaded.

"Like you?" asked Astrid coolly. "Would you like me to take *your* body for a spin?"

"I'd like to see you try," said Kell. If he could get her to take off the necklace, to put it on him instead . . .

"I could," she whispered. "But possession doesn't work on *Antari*," she added drily. Kell's heart sank. "I know that, and so do you. Nice try, though." Kell watched as his brother turned and lifted a knife from a nearby table. "Now, *compulsion*," he said—she said—admiring the glinting edge. "That's another matter."

Rhy's fingers tightened on the blade, and Kell pulled back, but there was nowhere to go. The guards gripped him, vise-tight, as the prince strode over lazily and raised the knife, slicing the buttons off Kell's shirt and pushing the collar aside to reveal the smooth, fair flesh over his heart.

"So few scars . . ." Rhy's fingers brought the knifepoint to Kell's skin. "We'll fix that."

"Stop right there," came a voice at the balcony.

Kell twisted, and saw Lila. She was dressed differently, in a black coat and a horned mask, and she was standing atop the banister, bracing herself in the balcony's doorframe and pointing her pistol at the prince's chest.

"This is a family matter," warned Astrid with Rhy's voice.

"I've heard enough to know you're not really family." Lila cocked the gun and leveled it on Rhy. "Now step away from Kell."

Rhy's mouth made a grim smile. And then his hand flew out. This time the lightning found its mark, striking Lila square in the chest. She gasped and lost her grip on the doorframe, her boots slipping off the banister rail as she stumbled back and plunged into the dark.

"Lila!" shouted Kell as she disappeared over the rail. He jerked free of the guards, the cuff finally cutting into his wrist enough to draw blood. In an instant, he had curled his fingers around the metal and spat out the command to unlock the cuff.

"As Orense." Open.

His shackles fell away, and the rest of Kell's power flooded back. The guards lunged at him, but his hands came up and the men went flying backward, one into the wall and the other into the metal frame of Rhy's bed. Kell freed his dagger and spun on the prince, ready for a fight.

But Rhy only gazed at him, amused. "What do you plan to do now, Kell? You won't hurt me, not as long as I'm wearing your brother."

"But I will." It was Lila's voice again, followed instantly by the sound of a gun. Pain and surprise both flashed across Rhy's face, and then one of his legs crumpled beneath him, blood darkening the fabric around his calf. Lila was standing outside, not on the banister as she'd been before, but in the air above it, feet resting on a plume of black smoke. Relief poured over Kell, followed instantly by horror. She hadn't just walked into danger. She'd brought the stone with her.

"You'll have to try harder than that to kill me," she said, hopping down from the smoke platform and onto the balcony. She strode into the chamber.

Rhy got to his feet. "Is that a challenge?" The guards were recovering, too, one moving behind Lila, the other hovering behind Kell.

"Run," he said to Lila.

"Nice to see you, too," she snapped, shoving the talisman back in her pocket. He saw the weakness sweep over her in the magic's wake, but only in her eyes and jaw. She was good at hiding it.

"You shouldn't have come here," growled Kell.

"No," echoed Rhy. "You shouldn't have. But you're here now. And you've brought me a gift." Lila's hand pressed against her coat, and Rhy's mouth curled into that horrible smile. Kell readied himself for an attack, but instead, Rhy's hand brought the blade to his own chest and rested the tip between his ribs, just under his heart. Kell stiffened. "Give me the stone, or I will kill the prince."

Lila frowned, eyes flicking between Rhy and Kell, uncertain.

"You wouldn't kill him," challenged Kell.

Rhy raised a dark brow. "Do you really believe that, flower boy, or do you only hope it's true?"

"You chose his body because he's part of your plan. You won't—"

"Never presume to know your enemy." Rhy's hand pressed down on the knife, the tip sinking between his ribs. "I have a closetful of kings."

"*Stop,*" demanded Kell as blood spread out from the knife's tip. He tried commanding the bones in Rhy's arm to still, but Astrid's own powerful will inside the prince's body made Kell's grip tenuous.

"How long can you stay my hand?" challenged Astrid. "What happens when your focus starts to slip?" Rhy's amber eyes went to Lila. "He doesn't want me to hurt his brother. You best give me the stone before I do."

Lila hesitated, and Rhy's free hand curled around the possession charm and drew it over his head, holding it loosely in his palm. "The stone, Lila."

"Don't do this," said Kell, and he didn't know if he meant the words for Astrid or Lila or both.

"The *stone*."

"Astrid, please," whispered Kell, his voice wavering.

At that, Rhy's mouth twisted into a triumphant smile. "You are mine, Kell, and I will break you. Starting with your heart."

"Astrid."

But it was too late. Rhy's body twisted toward Lila, and a single word left his mouth—*catch*—before he cast the pendant into the air and drove the knife into his chest.

V

It happened so fast, the pendant moving at the same time as the blade. Kell saw Lila lunge out of the charm's reach, and he twisted back in time to see Rhy burying the knife between his ribs.

"No!" screamed Kell, surging forward.

The necklace skidded along the floor and fetched up against a guard's boot, and Rhy crumpled forward, the blade driven in to the hilt as Kell scrambled to his side and pulled the knife free.

Rhy—and it *was* Rhy now—let out a choked sound, and Kell pressed his blood-streaked fingers to his brother's chest. Rhy's shirtfront was already wet, and he shuddered under Kell's touch. Kell had just began to speak, to command the magic to heal the prince, when a guard slammed into him from the side and they both went down on the inlaid floor.

Several feet away Lila was grappling with the other guard while Kell's attacker clutched the talisman in one hand and tried to wrap the other around Kell's throat. Kell kicked and fought and dragged himself free, and when the guard (and Astrid within) charged forward, he threw up his hand. The metal armor—and the body inside—went flying backward, not into the wall, but into the banister at the balcony, which crumbled under the force and sent the guard's body over and down. It landed with a crash on the courtyard stones below, the sound followed instantly by screams, and Kell ran to the patio to see a dozen of the ball's dancers circling the body. One of them, a woman in a lovely green gown, reached out curiously for the pendant, now discarded on the courtyard stones.

"Stop!" called Kell, but it was too late. The moment the woman's fingers curled around it, he could see her change, the possession rippling through her in a single drawn-out shiver before her head flicked up at him, mouth drawing into a cold grim smile. She turned on her heel and plunged into the palace.

"Kell!" called Lila, and he spun, taking in the room for the first time as it was, in disarray. The remaining guard lay motionless on the floor, a dagger driven through the visor of his helmet, and Lila crouched over Rhy, her mask lifted and her tangled hands pressing against the prince's chest. She was covered in blood, but it wasn't hers. Rhy's shirt was soaked through.

"*Rhy,*" said Kell, the word a sob, a shuddering breath as he knelt over his brother. He drew his dagger and slashed his hand, cutting deep. "Hold on, Rhy." He pressed his wounded palm to the prince's chest—it was rising and falling in staccato breaths—and said, *"As Hasari."*

Heal.

Rhy coughed up blood.

The courtyard below had exploded into activity, voices pouring up through the broken balcony. Footsteps were sounding through the halls, fists banging on the chamber doors, which Kell now saw were scrawled with spellwork. Locking charms.

"We have to go," said Lila.

"As Hasari," said Kell again, putting pressure on the wound. There was so much blood. Too much.

"I'm sorry," murmured Rhy.

"Shut up, Rhy," said Kell.

"Kell," ordered Lila.

"I'm not leaving him," he said simply.

"So take him with us." Kell hesitated. "You said the magic needs time to work. We can't wait. Bring him with us if you will, but we need to *go*."

Kell swallowed. "I'm sorry," he said, just before forcing himself—and Rhy—to his feet. The prince gasped in pain. "I'm sorry."

They couldn't go by the door. Couldn't parade the wounded prince in front of a palace full of people there to celebrate his birthday. And, somewhere among them, Astrid Dane. But there was a private hall between Rhy's room and Kell's, one they'd used since they were boys, and now he half dragged, half carried his brother toward a concealed door, and then through it. He led the prince and Lila down the narrow corridor, the walls of which were covered with an assortment of odd marks—bets and challenges and personal scores kept by tallies, the tasks themselves long forgotten. A trail through their strange and sheltered youth.

Now they left a trail of blood.

"Stay with me," said Kell. "Stay with me. Rhy. Listen to my voice."

"Such a nice voice," said Rhy quietly, his head lolling forward.

"*Rhy.*"

Kell heard armored bodies break into the prince's room as they reached his own, and he shut the door to the hall and pressed his bloodied hand to the wood and said, *"As Staro."* *Seal.*

As the word left his lips, metalwork spread out from his fingers, tracing back and forth over the door and binding it shut.

"We can't keep running from bedroom to bedroom," snapped Lila. "We have to get out of this palace!"

Kell knew that. Knew they had to get away. He led them to the private study at the far edge of his room, the one with the blood markings on the back of the door. Shortcuts to half a dozen places in the city. The one that led to the Ruby Fields was useless now, but the others would work. He scanned the options until he found the one—the only one—he knew would be safe.

"Will this work?" asked Lila.

Kell wasn't sure. Doors *within* worlds were harder to make but easier to use; they could only be created by *Antari,* but others could—*hypothetically*—pass through. Indeed, Kell had led Rhy through a portal once before—the day he found him on the boat—but there had been only two of them then, and now there were three.

"Don't let go," said Kell. He drew fresh blood over the mark and held Rhy and Lila as closely as he could, hoping the door—and the magic—would be strong enough to lead them all to sanctuary.

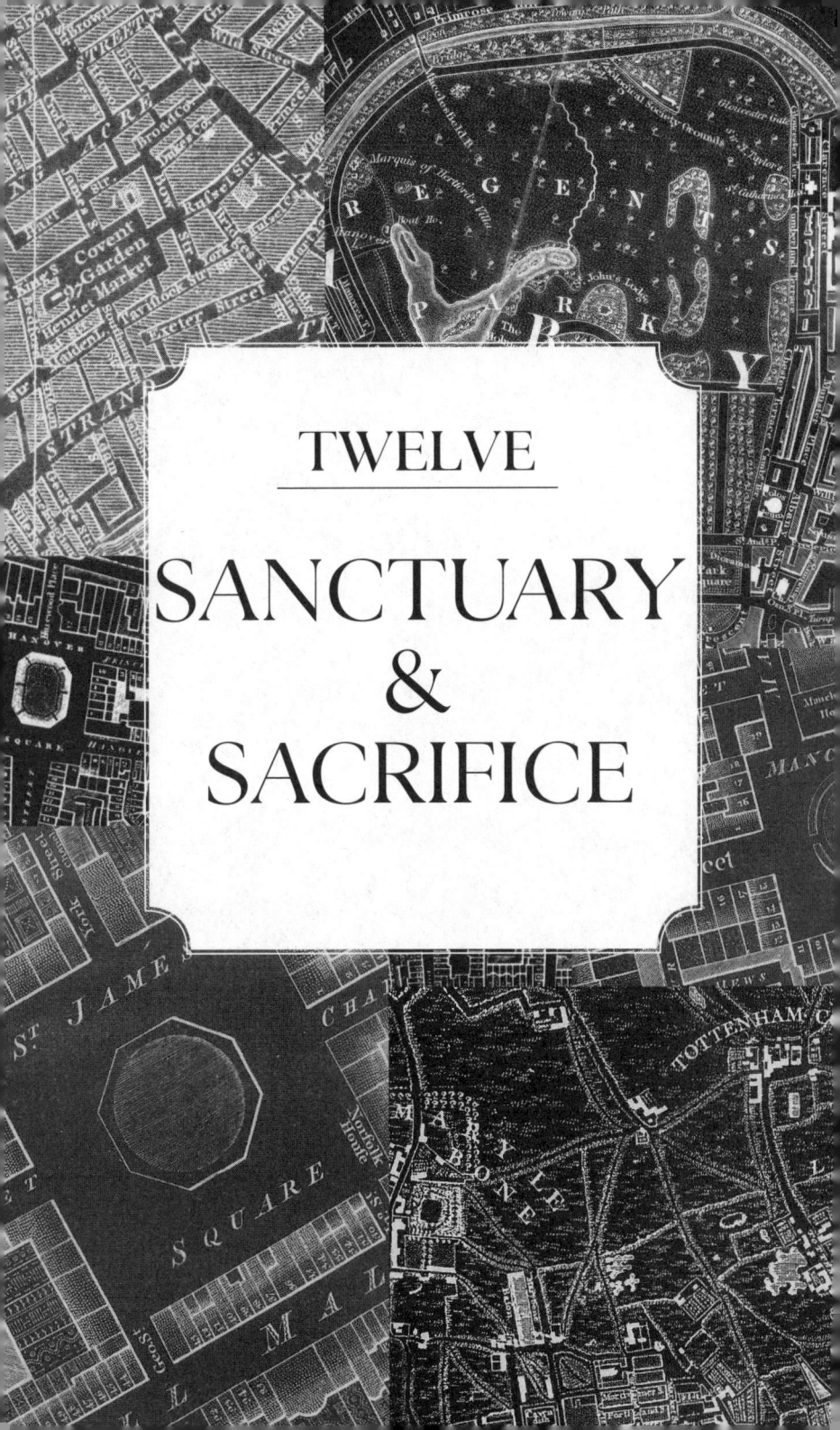

TWELVE

SANCTUARY & SACRIFICE

I

The London Sanctuary sat at a bend in the river near the edge of the city, a stone structure with the simple elegance of a temple and an air just as reverent. It was a place where men and women came to study magic as much as worship it. Scholars and masters here spent their lives striving to comprehend—and connect with—the essence of power, the origin, the source. To understand the element of magic. The entity in all, and yet of none.

As a child, Kell had spent as much time in the sanctuary as he had in the palace, studying under—and being studied by—his tutor, Master Tieren, but though he visited now and then, he had not been back to stay in years (not since Rhy began to throw tantrums at Kell's every absence, insisting that the latter be not only a fixture, but also a family member). Still, Tieren insisted that he would always have a room there, and so Kell had kept the door drawn on his wall, marked by a simple circle of blood with an *X* drawn through.

The symbol of sanctuary.

Now he and Lila—with a bloody Rhy between them—stumbled through, out of the grandeur and current chaos of the palace and into a simple stone room.

Candlelight flickered against the smooth rock walls, and the chamber itself was narrow and high-ceilinged and sparsely furnished. The sanctuary scorned distraction, the private chambers supplied with only the essential. Kell may have been *aven—blessed*—but Tieren insisted on treating him as he would any other student (a fact for which Kell was grateful). As such, his room held neither more nor less than any other: a wooden desk along one wall and a low cot along another, with a small table beside it. On the table, burning, as it always burned, sat an infinite candle. The room had no windows and only one door, and the air held the coolness of underground places, of crypts.

A circle was etched into the floor, symbols scrawled around the edges. An enhancing sphere meant for meditation. Rhy's blood trailed a path across it as Kell and Lila dragged him to the cot and laid him down as gently as possible.

"Stay with me," Kell kept saying, but Rhy's quiet "sure" and "all right" and "as you wish" had given way to silence and shallow breaths.

How many *As Hasari*s had Kell said? The words had once more become a low chant on his lips, in his head, in his heartbeat, but Rhy was not healing. How long until the magic worked? It had to work. Fear clawed its way up Kell's throat. He should have looked at Astrid's weapon. Should have paid attention to the metal and the markings on it. Had she done something to block his magic? *Why wasn't it working?*

"Stay with me," he murmured. Rhy had stopped moving. His eyes were closed, and the strain had gone out of his jaw.

"Kell," Lila said softly. "I think it's too late."

"No," he said, gripping the cot. "It's not. The magic just needs time. You don't understand how it works."

"Kell."

"It just needs time." Kell pressed both hands to his brother's chest and stifled a cry. It neither rose nor fell. He couldn't feel a heartbeat underneath the ribs. "I can't . . ." he said, gasping as if he, too, were starved of air. "I can't . . ." Kell's voice wavered

as his fingers tangled in his brother's bloody shirt. "I can't give up."

"It's over," said Lila. "There's nothing you can do."

But that wasn't true. There was still something. All the warmth went out of Kell's body. But so did the hesitation, and the confusion, and the fear. He knew what to do. Knew what he *had* to do. "Give me the stone," he said.

"No."

"Lila, give me the bloody stone before it's too late."

"It's *already* too late. He's—"

"*He's not dead!*" snapped Kell. He held out a stained and shaking hand. "Give it to me."

Lila's hand went to her pocket and hovered there. "There's a reason I'm holding it, Kell," she said.

"Dammit, Lila. *Please.*"

She let out a shaky breath and withdrew the stone. He ripped it from her fingers, ignoring the pulse of power up his arm as he turned back to Rhy's body.

"You told me yourself, nothing good comes out of this," said Lila as Kell set the stone over Rhy's unbeating heart and pressed his palm down on top of it. "I know you're upset, but you can't think that this . . ."

But he couldn't hear her. Her voice dissolved, along with everything else, as Kell focused on the magic coursing in his veins.

Save him, he ordered the stone.

Power sang through his blood, and smoke poured out from under his fingers. It snaked up his arm and around Rhy's ribs, turning to blackened rope as it tangled around them. Tying them together. Binding them. But Rhy still lay there, unmoving.

My life is his life, thought Kell. *His life is mine. Bind it to mine and bring him back.*

He could feel the magic, hungry and wanting, pushing against him, trying to tap in to his body, his power, his life force. And this time, he let it in.

As soon as he did, the black rope tightened, and Kell's heart lurched in his chest. It skipped a beat, and Rhy's heart caught it, thudding once beneath Kell's touch. For an instant, all he felt was relief, joy.

Then, *pain*.

Like being torn apart, one nerve at a time. Kell screamed as he doubled forward over the prince, but he didn't let go. Rhy's back arched under his hand, the dark coils of magic cinching around them. The pain only worsened, carved itself in burning strokes over Kell's skin, his heart, his life.

"Kell!" Lila's voice broke through the fog, and he saw her rushing forward a step and then two, already reaching out to stop him, to pull him free of the spell. *Stop,* he thought. He didn't say it, didn't raise a finger, but the magic was in his head and it heard his will. It rushed through him and the smoke rushed out and slammed Lila backward. She hit the stone wall hard and crumpled to the floor.

Something in Kell stirred, distant and hushed. *Wrong,* it whispered. *This is . . .* But then another wave of pain sent him reeling. Power pounded through his veins, and his head came to rest against his brother's ribs as the pain tore through him, skin and muscle, bone and soul.

Rhy gasped, and so did Kell, his heart skipping once more in his chest.

And then it stopped.

II

The room went deathly still.

Kell's hand slipped from Rhy's ribs, and his body tumbled from the cot to the stone floor with a sickening thud. Lila's ears were still ringing from the force of her head meeting the wall as she pushed herself to her hands and knees, and then to her feet.

Kell wasn't moving. Wasn't breathing.

And then, after a moment that seemed to last hours, he drew a deep, shuddering breath. And so did Rhy.

Lila swore with relief as she knelt over Kell. His shirt was open, his stomach and chest streaked with blood, but under that, a black symbol, made up of concentric circles, was branded into his skin, directly over his heart. Lila looked up at the cot. The same mark was scrawled over Rhy's bloody chest.

"What have you done?" she whispered. She didn't know that much about magic, but she was fairly certain that bringing someone back from the dead was solidly in the *bad* column. If all magic came at a price, what had this cost Kell?

As if in answer, his eyes floated open. Lila was relieved to see that one of them was still blue. There had been an instant, during the spell, when both had gone solid black.

"Welcome back," she said.

Kell groaned, and Lila helped him up into a sitting position on the cold stone floor. His attention went to the bed, where

Rhy's chest rose and fell in a slow but steady motion. His eyes went from the mark on the prince's skin to the mirrored mark on his own, which he touched, wincing faintly.

"What did you do?" asked Lila.

"I bound Rhy's life to mine," he said hoarsely. "As long as I survive, so will he."

"That seems like a dangerous spell."

"It's not a spell," he said softly. She didn't know if he lacked the strength to speak louder or was afraid of waking his brother. "It's called a soul seal. Spells can be broken. A soul seal cannot. It's a piece of permanent magic. But *this*," he added, grazing the mark, "this is . . ."

"Forbidden?" ventured Lila.

"Impossible," said Kell. "This kind of magic, it doesn't exist."

He seemed dazed and distant as he got to his feet, and Lila tensed when she saw that he was still gripping the stone. Black veins traced up his arm. "You need to let go of that now."

Kell looked down, as if he'd forgotten he was holding it. But when he managed to unclench his fingers, the talisman didn't fall out. Threads of black spun out from the rock, winding down his fingers and up his wrist. He stared down at the stone for several long moments. "It appears I can't," he said at last.

"Isn't that bad?" pressed Lila.

"Yes," he said, and his calm worried her more than anything. "But I didn't have a choice. . . . I had to . . ." He trailed off, turning toward Rhy.

"Kell, are you all right?" It seemed an absurd question, given the circumstances, and Kell gave her a look that said as much, so Lila added, "When you were doing that spell, you weren't *you*."

"Well, I am now."

"Are you sure about that?" she asked, gesturing at his hand. "Because that's new." Kell frowned. "That rock is bad magic;

you said it yourself. It feeds on energy. On people. And now it's strapped itself to you. You can't tell me that doesn't worry you."

"Lila," he said darkly. "I couldn't let him die."

"But what you've done instead—"

"I did what I had to do," he said. "I suppose it doesn't matter. I am already lost."

Lila scowled. "What do you mean by that?"

Kell's eyes softened a little. "Someone has to return the stone to Black London, Lila. It's not just a matter of opening a door and casting the object through. I have to *take it there*. I have to walk through with it." Kell looked down at the stone binding itself to his hand. "I never expected to make it back."

"Christ, Kell," growled Lila. "If you're not going to bother staying alive, then what's the damn point? Why tether Rhy's life to yours if you're just going to throw it away?"

Kell cringed. "So long as I live, so will he. And I didn't say I planned on dying."

"But you just said—"

"I said I'm not coming *back*. The seals on Black London were designed less to keep anyone from going in, and more to keep anyone from getting out. I can't strip the spells. And even if I could, I wouldn't. And with the spells intact, even if I manage to make a door *into* Black London, the seals will never let me back *out*."

"And you weren't going to mention *any* of this. You were just going to let me follow you on a one-way trip to—"

"You said you wanted an adventure," snapped Kell, "and no, I never intended to let you—"

Just then the door swung open. Kell and Lila fell silent, their argument echoing on the walls of the narrow stone chamber.

An old man was standing in the doorway wearing a black robe, one hand against the doorframe, the other holding up a sphere of pale white light. He wasn't old in a withered way. In fact, he stood straight and broad-shouldered, his age belied only by his white hair and the deep creases on his face, made deeper by the shadows cast from the light in his palm. Kell pulled his coat around himself and buried his damaged hand in his pocket.

"Master Tieren," he said casually, as if the informality of his voice could cover up the fact that he and Lila were streaked with blood and standing in front of the body of a nearly dead prince.

"Kell," said the man, frowning deeply. *"Kers la? Ir vanesh mer...."* And then he trailed off and looked at Lila. His eyes were pale and startlingly blue; they seemed to go straight through her. His brow furrowed, and then he began speaking again, this time in English. As if he could tell, with a single glance, that she did not understand, did not belong. "What brings you here?" he asked, addressing both of them.

"You said I would always have a room," answered Kell wearily. "I'm afraid I had need of it."

He stepped aside so that Master Tieren could see the wounded prince.

The man's eyes went wide, and he touched his fingers to his lips in a small prayer-like gesture. "Is he . . . ?"

"He's alive," said Kell, hand drifting to his collar to hide the mark. "But the palace is under attack. I cannot explain everything, not now, but you must believe me, Tieren. It has been taken by traitors. They are using forbidden magic, possessing the bodies and minds of those around them. No one is safe—*nowhere* is safe—and no one is to be trusted." He was breathless by the time he finished.

Tieren crossed to Kell in a handful of slow strides. He took Kell's face in his hands, the gesture strangely intimate, and looked into his eyes as he had Lila's, as if he could see past them. "What have you done to yourself?"

Kell's voice caught in his throat. "Only what I had to." His coat had fallen open, and the man's gaze drifted down to the blackened mark over Kell's heart. "Please," he said, sounding frightened. "I would not have brought danger into these halls, but I had no choice."

The man's hands fell away. "The sanctuary is warded against darkness. The prince will be safe within these walls."

Relief swept across Kell's features. Tieren turned to consider Lila a second time.

"You are not from here," he said by way of introduction.

Lila held out her hand. "Delilah Bard."

The man took it, and something like a shiver, but warmer, passed beneath her skin, a calm spreading through her in its wake. "My name is Master Tieren," he said. "I am the *onase aven*—that is to say, the head priest—of the London Sanctuary. And a healer," he added, as if to explain the sensation. Their hands fell apart, and Tieren went to the prince's side and brought his bony fingers to rest feather-light on top of Rhy's chest. "His injuries are severe."

"I know," said Kell shakily. "I can feel them as if they were my own."

Lila tensed, and Tieren's expression darkened. "Then I will do what I can to ease his pain, and yours."

Kell nodded gratefully. "It's my fault," he said. "But I will set things right." Tieren opened his mouth to speak, but Kell stopped him. "I cannot tell you," he said. "I must ask for your trust as well as your discretion."

Tieren's mouth became a thin line. "I will lead you to the tunnels," he said. "From there you will be able to find your way. Whichever way you need."

Kell had been silent since leaving the small room. He hadn't been able to look at his brother, hadn't been able to say goodbye, had only swallowed and nodded and turned away, following Master Tieren out. Lila trailed behind, picking Rhy's dried blood from the cuffs of her new coat (she supposed she would have had to get her hands—and sleeves—dirty sooner or later). As they made their way through the bowels of the sanctuary, she watched Kell and the way his gaze hung on Tieren, as if willing the priest to say something. But the priest kept his mouth shut and his eyes ahead, and eventually Kell's step began to trail, until he and Lila were side by side in the head priest's wake.

"The clothing suits you," he said quietly. "Do I want to know how you came by it?"

Lila tilted her head. "I didn't steal it, if that's what you're asking. I bought it from a woman in the market named Calla."

Kell smiled faintly at the name. "And how did you pay for it?"

"I haven't yet," retorted Lila. "But that doesn't mean I won't." Her gaze dropped away. "Though I don't know when I'll have the chance . . ."

"You will," said Kell. "Because you're staying here."

"Like hell I am," shot Lila.

"The sanctuary will keep you safe."

"I will not be left behind."

Kell shook his head. "You were never meant to go farther. When I said yes, I did so with the intent to leave you here, in my city, to deliver word of my fate to the king and queen." Lila drew a breath, but he held up his uninjured hand. "And to keep you safe. White London is no place for a Grey-worlder. It's no place for *anyone*."

"I'll be the judge of that," she said. "I'm going with you."

"Lila, this isn't some *game*. Enough people have died, and I—"

"You're right, it's not a game," pressed Lila. "It's *strategy*. I heard what the queen said about the stone being broken in two. You need to dispose of *both* pieces, and as of right now, you only have one. The White king has the other, right? Which means we have our work cut out for us. And it is *we,* Kell. Two of them means there should be two of us as well. You can take the king, and I'll handle the queen."

"You're no match for Astrid Dane."

"Tell me, do you underestimate everyone, or just me? Is it because I'm a girl?"

"It's because you're a *human,*" he snapped. "Because you may be the bravest, boldest soul I've ever met, but you're still too much flesh and blood and too little power. Astrid Dane is made of magic and malice."

"Yes, well, that's all well and good for her, but she's not even *in* her body, is she? She's here, having a grand time in Red London. Which means she should make an easy target." Lila gave him the sharpest edge of a grin. "And I may be human, but I've made it this far."

Kell frowned deeply.

It is amazing, thought Lila, *that he doesn't have more wrinkles.*

"You have," he said. "But no farther."

"The girl has power in her," offered Tieren without looking back.

Lila brightened. "See?" she preened. "I've been telling you that all along."

"What *kind* of power?" asked Kell, raising a brow.

"Don't sound so skeptical," Lila shot back.

"Unnurtured," said Tieren. "Untended. Unawakened."

"Well, come on then, *onase aven,*" she said, holding out her hands. "Wake it up."

Tieren glanced back and offered her a ghost of a smile. "It

shall awake on its own, Delilah Bard. And if you nurture it, it will grow."

"She comes from the other London," said Kell. Tieren showed no surprise. "The one without magic."

"No London is truly without magic," observed the priest.

"And human or not," added Lila sharply, "I'd like to remind you that you're still alive because of me. *I'm* the reason that White queen's not wearing you like a coat. *And* I've got something you need."

"What's that?"

Lila pulled the white rook from her pocket. "The key."

Kell's eyes widened a fraction in surprise, and then narrowed. "Do you honestly think you could keep it from me, if I wished to take it?"

In an instant, Lila had the rook in one hand and her knife in the other. The brass knuckles of the handle glinted in the candlelight while the stone hummed low and steady, as if whispering to Kell.

"Try it," she sneered.

Kell stopped walking and looked at her. "What is *wrong* with you?" he asked, sounding honestly baffled. "Do you care so little about your life that you would throw it all away for a few hours of adventure and a violent death?"

Lila frowned. She'd admit that, in the beginning, all she wanted was an adventure, but that wasn't why she was insisting now. The truth was, she'd seen the change in Kell, seen the shadow sweep across his eyes when he summoned that clever cursed magic, seen how hard it was for him to return to his senses after. Every time he used the stone, he seemed to lose a bigger piece of himself. So no, Lila wasn't going with him just to satisfy some thirst for danger. And she wasn't going with him just to keep him company. She was going because they'd come this far, and because she feared he wouldn't succeed, not alone.

"My life is mine to spend," she said. "And I will not spend it here, no matter how nice your city is, or how much safer it might be. We had a deal, Kell. And you now have Tieren to guard your story and heal your brother. I'm of no use to him. Let me be of use to you."

Kell looked her in the eyes. "You will be trapped there," he said. "When it is over."

Lila shivered. "Perhaps," she said, "or perhaps I will go with you to the end of the world. After all, you've made me curious."

"Lila—" His eyes were dark with pain and worry, but she only smiled.

"One adventure at a time," she said.

They reached the edge of the tunnel, and Tieren pushed open a pair of metal gates. The red river glowed up at them from below. They were standing on its northern bank, the palace shimmering in the distance, still surrounded by starry light, as if nothing were amiss.

Tieren brought his hand to Kell's shoulder and murmured something in Arnesian before adding in English, "May the saints and source of all be with you both."

Kell nodded and gripped the priest's hand with his unwounded one before stepping out into the evening. But as Lila went to follow, Tieren caught her arm. He squinted at her as if searching for a secret.

"What?" asked Lila.

"How did you lose it?" he asked.

Lila frowned. "Lose what?"

His weathered fingers drifted up beneath her chin. "Your eye."

Lila pulled her face from his grip, her hand going to the darker of her two brown eyes. The one made of glass. Few people ever noticed. Her hair cut a sharp line across her face, and even when she did look someone in the eye, they rarely held the gaze for long enough to mark the difference. "I don't remember," she said. It wasn't a lie. "I was a child, and it was an accident, I'm told."

"Hm," said Tieren pensively. "Does Kell know?"

Her frown deepened. "Does it matter?"

After a long moment, the old man tilted his head. "I suppose not," he said.

Kell was looking back at Lila, waiting for her.

"If the darkness takes him," said Tieren under his breath, "you must end his life." He looked at her. Through her. "Do you think you can?"

Lila didn't know whether he wanted to know if she had the strength, or the will.

"If he dies," she said, "so will Rhy."

Tieren sighed. "Then the world will be as it should," he said, sadly. "Instead of as it is."

Lila swallowed, and nodded, and went to join Kell.

"To White London, then?" she asked when she reached him, holding out the rook. Kell did not move. He was staring out at the river and the palace arching over it. She thought he might be taking in his London, his home, saying his good-byes, but then he spoke.

"The bones are the same in every world," he said, gesturing to the city, "but the rest of it will be different. As different as this world is from yours." He pointed across the river, and toward the center of London. "Where we're going, the castle is there. Athos and Astrid will be there, too. Once we cross through, stay close. Do not leave my side. It is night here, which means it is night in White London, too, and the city is full of shadows." Kell looked at Lila. "You can still change your mind."

Lila straightened and tugged up the collar of her coat. She smiled. "Not a chance."

III

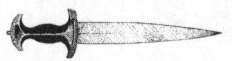

The palace was in a state of upheaval.

Guests were spilling, confused and concerned, down the great stairs, ushered out by the royal guards. Rumors spread like fire through the crowd, rumors of violence and death and wounded royalty. Words like *treason* and *coup* and *assassin* filled the air, only feeding the frenzy.

Someone claimed that a guard had been murdered. Another claimed to have seen that guard fall from the prince's balcony to the courtyard below. Another still said that a woman in a green gown had stolen a necklace from the gruesome scene and rushed into the palace. Another insisted he'd seen her thrust the pendant into the hands of another guard and then collapse at his feet. The guard had not even called for help. He'd simply stormed away toward the royal chambers.

There the king and queen had withdrawn, their strange calm only adding to the guests' confusion. The guard had vanished into their room, and a moment later, the king had apparently burst forth, his steadiness cast off as he shouted about treason. He claimed that the prince had been stabbed and that Kell was to blame, demanding the *Antari*'s arrest. And just like that, the confusion shattered into to panic, chaos billowing like smoke through the night.

By the time Gen's boots approached the palace, the stairs

were crowded with worried guests. The thing inside Gen's armor turned its black eyes up at the dancing lights and jostling bodies. It wasn't the mayhem that drew him there. It was the scent. Someone had used strong magic, beautiful magic, and he meant to find out who.

He set off up the stairs, pressing past the flustered guests. No one seemed to notice that his armor was rent, peeled back over the heart, a stain like black wax across his front. Nor did they notice the blood—Parrish's blood—splashed across the metal.

When he reached the top of the stairs, he drew a deep breath and smiled; the night hung heavy with panic and power, the energy filling his lungs, stoking him like coals. He could smell the magic now. He could *taste* it.

And he was hungry.

He'd chosen his latest shell quite well; the guards, in their commotion, let him pass. It wasn't until he was inside, through the flower-lined antechamber and striding across the emptied ballroom, that a helmeted figure stopped him.

"Gen," demanded the guard, "where have you . . ." But the words died in the guard's throat when he saw the man's eyes. *"Mas aven—"*

The oath was cut off by Gen's sword, sliding through armor and between ribs. The guard dragged in a single, shuddering breath and tried to cry out, but the sword cut sideways and up, and the air died in his throat. Easing the body down, the thing wearing Gen's skin resheathed his weapon and removed the guard's helmet, sliding it over his own head. When he pulled the visor down, his black eyes were nothing but a glint through the metal slit.

Footsteps sounded through the palace, and shouted orders echoed overhead. He straightened. The air was full of blood and magic, and he went to find its source.

The stone still sang in Kell's hand, but not quite the way it had before. Now the melody, the thrum of power, seemed to be singing *in* his bones instead of over them. Every moment, he felt it in his heartbeat and in his head. With it came a strange quiet, a calm, one he trusted even less than the initial surge of power. The calm told him everything would be well. It cooed and soothed and steadied his heart and made Kell forget that anything was wrong, made him forget that he was holding the stone at all. That was the worst part. It was bound to his hand, and yet it hung at the outside of his senses; he had to fight to remember it was there with him. *Inside* of him. Every time he remembered, it was like waking from a dream, full of panic and fear, only to be dragged down into sleep again. In those brief moments of clarity, he wanted to claw free, break or tear or cut the stone from his skin. But he didn't, because competing with that urge to cast it off was the equal, opposite desire to hold it close, to cling to its warmth as if he were dying of cold. He *needed* its strength. Now more than ever.

Kell didn't want Lila to see how scared he was, but he thought she saw it anyway.

They had woven back toward the city center, the streets mostly deserted on this side of the river, but had yet to cross any of the bridges that arced back and forth over the Isle. It was too dangerous, too exposed. Especially since, halfway there, Kell's face had reappeared on the scrying boards that lined the streets.

Only this time, instead of saying:

MISSING

It now said:

WANTED

For *treason, murder,* and *abduction.*

Kell's chest tightened at the accusations, and he held fast to the fact that Rhy was safe—as safe as he could possibly be. His fingers went to the brand over his heart; if he focused, he could feel the echo of Rhy's heartbeat, the pulse a fraction of time after his own.

He looked around, trying to picture the streets not only as they were here, but as they would be in White London, superimposing the images in his mind.

"This will have to do," he said.

Where they stood now, at the mouth of an alley across from a string of ships—Lila had surveyed them with an appraising eye—they would stand before a bridge in the next city. A bridge that led to a street that ended at the walls of the White Castle. As they'd walked, Kell had described to Lila the dangers of the other London, from its twin rulers to its starving, power-hungry populace. And then he had described the castle and the bones of his plan, because bones were all he had right now.

Bones and hope. Hope that they would make it, that he would be able to hold on to himself long enough to beat Athos and retrieve the second half of the stone and then—

Kell closed his eyes and took a low, steadying breath. *One adventure at a time.* Lila's words echoed in his mind.

"What are we waiting for?"

Lila was leaning against the wall. She tapped the bricks. "Come on, Kell. Door time." And her casual air, her defiant energy, the way, even now, she didn't seem concerned or afraid, only *excited* him, gave him strength.

The gash across his palm, though now partially obscured by the black stone, was still fresh. He touched the cut with his finger and drew a mark on the brick wall in front of them. Lila took his hand, palm to palm with the stone singing between them, and offered him the white rook, and he brought it to the blood on the wall, swallowing his nerves.

"As Travars," he commanded, and the world softened and darkened around them as they stepped forward and through the newly hewn doorway.

Or at least, that's how it should have happened.

But halfway through the stride, a force jarred Kell backward, tearing Lila's hand from his as it ripped him out of the place between worlds and back onto the hard stone street of Red London. Kell blinked up at the night, dazed, and then realized he was not alone. Someone was standing over him. At first, the figure was no more than a shadow, rolling up his sleeves. And then Kell saw the silver circle glittering at his collar.

Holland looked down at him and frowned.

"Leaving so soon?"

IV

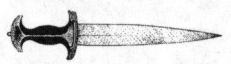

Lila's black boots landed on the pale street. Her head spun a little from the sudden change, and she steadied herself against the wall. She heard the sound of Kell's steps behind her.

"Well, that's an improvement," she said, turning. "At least we're in the same place this—"

But he wasn't there.

She was standing on the curb in front of a bridge, the White Castle rising in the distance across the river, which was neither grey nor red, but a pearly, half-frozen stretch of water, shining dully in the thickening night. Lanterns along the river burned with a pale blue fire that cast the world in a strange, colorless way, and Lila, in her crisp black clothes, stood out as much a light in the dark.

Something shone near her feet, and she looked down to find the white rook on the ground, its pale surface still dotted with Kell's blood. But no Kell. She picked up the token and pocketed it, trying to swallow her rising nerves.

Nearby, a starved dog was watching her with empty eyes.

And then, quickly, Lila became aware of other eyes. In windows and doorways, and in the shadows between pools of sickly light. Her hand went to the knife with the metal knuckles.

"Kell?" she called out under her breath, but there was no answer. Maybe it was like last time. Maybe they'd simply been separated, and he was making his way toward her now. Maybe, but Lila had felt the strange pull as they stepped through, had felt his hand vanish from hers too soon.

Footsteps echoed, and she turned in a slow circle but saw no one.

Kell had warned her of this world—he'd called it *dangerous*—but so much of Lila's own world had fit that term, so she hadn't given it much stock. After all, he'd grown up in a palace and she'd grown up on the streets, and Lila thought she knew a good bit more about bad alleys and worse men than Kell. Now, standing here, alone, Lila was beginning to think she hadn't given him enough credit. Anyone—even a highborn—could see the danger here. Could smell it. Death and ash and winter air.

She shivered. Not only from cold, but from fear. A simple bone-deep sense of *wrong*. It was like looking into Holland's black eye. For the first time, Lila wished she had more than knives and the Flintlock.

"*Övos norevjk,*" came a voice to her right, and she spun to see a man, bald, every inch of exposed skin, from the crown of his head down to his fingers, covered in tattoos. Whatever he was speaking, it didn't sound like Arnesian. It was gruff and guttural, and even though she didn't know the words, she could grasp the tone, and she didn't like it.

"*Tovach ös mostevna,*" said another, appearing to her left, his skin like parchment.

The first man chuckled. The second *tsk*ed.

Lila pulled the knife free. "Stay back," she ordered, hoping her gesture would make up for any language barrier.

The men exchanged a look and then withdrew their own jagged weapons.

A cold breeze cut through, and Lila fought down a shiver. The men broke into rotting grins. She lowered her knife. And then, in one smooth move, she drew the pistol from her belt, raised it, and shot the first man between the eyes. He went down like a sack of stones, and Lila smiled before she realized how loud the gunshot sounded. She hadn't noticed how quiet the city was until the shot rang out, the blast carrying down the streets. All around them, doors began to open. Shadows moved. Whispers and murmurs came from corners of the street—first one, then two, then half a dozen.

The second man, the one with papery skin, looked at the dead one, and then at Lila. He started talking again in a low threatening growl, and Lila was glad she didn't speak his tongue. She didn't want to know what he was saying.

Slivers of dark energy crackled through the air around the man's blade. She could feel people moving behind her, the shadows taking shape into people, gaunt and grey.

Come on, Kell, she thought as she raised the gun again. *Where are you?*

V

"Let me pass," said Kell.

Holland only raised a brow.

"Please," said Kell. "I can end this."

"Can you?" challenged Holland. "I do not think you have it in you." His gaze went to Kell's hand, the dark magic twining around it. "I warned you, magic is not about balance. It is about dominance. You control it, or it controls you."

"I am still in control," said Kell through gritted teeth.

"No," said Holland. "You're not. Once you let the magic in, you've already lost."

Kell's chest tightened. "I don't want to fight you, Holland."

"You do not have a choice." Holland wore a sharpened ring on one hand and used it now to cut a line across his palm. Blood dripped to the street. *"As Isera,"* he said softly. *Freeze.*

The dark drops hit the ground and turned to black ice, shooting forward across the street. Kell tried to step back, but the ice moved too fast, and within seconds he was standing on top of it, fighting for balance.

"Do you know what makes you weak?" said Holland. "You've never had to be strong. You've never had to try. You've never had to fight. And you've certainly never had to fight for your *life*. But tonight that changes, Kell. Tonight, if you do not fight, you *will* die. And if you—"

Kell didn't wait for him to finish. A sudden gust of wind whipped forward, nearly knocking Kell off-balance as it cycloned toward Holland. It surrounded the *Antari,* swallowing him from sight. The wind whistled, but through it Kell could hear a low, haunting sound. And then he realized it was a laugh.

Holland was laughing.

A moment later, Holland's blood-streaked hand appeared, parting the cyclone wall, and then the rest of him stepped through, the column of wind crumbling around him. "Air cannot be made sharp," he chided. "Cannot hurt. Cannot kill. You should choose your elements with more care. Watch."

Holland moved with such smooth swiftness, it was hard to follow his motions, let alone keep up. In a single fluid move, he dropped to a knee and touched the ground and said *"As Steno."*

Break.

The paving stone beneath his palm shattered into a dozen sharpened shards, and as he stood, the shards came with him, hovering in the air the way the nails had done in the alley. He flicked his wrist, and the shards shot forward through the air toward Kell. The stone against his palm sang with warning, and he barely had time to throw up his hand, the talisman shining in it, and say, "Stop."

The smoke poured forth and caught the slivers in their path, crushing them to dust. Power shot through Kell with the command, followed instantly by something darker, colder. He gasped at the sensation. He could feel the magic climbing over his skin, and under it, and he willed it to stop, pushed back with all his strength as the smoke dissolved.

Holland was shaking his head. "Go ahead, Kell. Use the stone. It will consume you faster, but you might just win."

Kell swore under breath and summoned another cyclone, this one in front of him. He snapped the fingers of the hand without the stone. A flame appeared in his palm, and when he touched it to the twisting air, it took it, engulfing the wind in fire. The burning cyclone scorched across the ground, melting the ice as it charged toward Holland, who threw out his hand and summoned the ground up into a shield, and then, the instant the flame was gone, sent the stone wall surging toward Kell. He threw up his hands, fighting for control over the rocks, and realized too late that they were only a distraction for the arcing wave of water that struck him from behind.

The surge from the river slammed Kell to his hands and knees, but before he could recover, it swept him up and coiled around him. In moments, Kell was trapped by the swell, gasping for air before it swallowed him entirely. He fought, pinned by the force of the water.

"Astrid wanted you alive," said Holland, drawing the curved blade from beneath his cloak. "She insisted upon it." His free hand curled into a fist, and the water tightened, crushing the air from Kell's lungs. "But I'm sure she will understand if I have no choice but to kill you in order to retrieve the stone."

Holland strode toward him with measured steps over the icy ground, the curved blade hanging at his side, and Kell twisted and thrashed, scouring for something, anything he could use. He reached for the knife in Holland's grip, but the metal was warded, and it didn't even quiver. Kell was running out of air, and Holland was nearly to him. And then through the wall of water he saw the rippling image of the ship supplies, the pile of boards and poles and the dark metal of chains coiled on posts by the bridge.

Kell's fingers twitched, and the nearest set of chains flew forward, wrapping around Holland's wrist, jarring his focus. The water lost its shape and fell apart, and Kell stumbled forward to the ground, soaking wet and gasping for breath. Holland was still trying to free himself, and Kell knew he couldn't afford to hesitate. Another set of chains, from another post, snaked around the *Antari*'s leg and up his waist. Holland moved to throw the curved blade, but a third set of chains caught his arm and drew taut. It wouldn't hold, not for long. Kell willed a metal pole up from the dock floor and through the air, the bar hovering a foot or so behind Holland.

"I can't let you win," said Kell.

"Then you'd better kill me," growled Holland. "If you don't, it will never end."

Kell drew the knife from his forearm and lifted it as if to strike.

"You're going to have to try harder than that," said Holland as Kell's hand froze, the bones held still by the other *Antari*'s will. It was exactly what Kell was hoping for. The moment Holland's focus was on the knife, Kell attacked, not from the front, but from behind, willing the metal bar forward with all his strength.

It soared through the air and found its mark, striking Holland in the back with enough force to pierce through cloak and skin and bone. It protruded from Holland's chest, the metal and blood obscuring the seal scarred over his heart. The silver circle clasp broke and tumbled away, the half-cloak sliding off Holland's shoulders as his knees folded.

Kell staggered to his feet as Holland collapsed onto the damp street. A horrible sadness rolled through him as he crossed to the *Antari*'s body. They had been two of a kind, a dying breed. Now he was the only one. And soon, there would be none. Perhaps that was how it should be. How it *needed* to be.

Kell wrapped his fingers around the bloody metal bar and pulled it free of Holland's chest. He tossed the pole aside, the dull sound of it clanging down the road like a faltering heartbeat. Kell knelt beside Holland's body as blood began to pool beneath it. When he felt for a pulse, he found one there. But it was shallow, fading.

"I'm sorry," he said. It felt stupid and useless to say, but the sharpness had gone out of his anger, and his sadness, his fear, his loss—they had all dulled into a steady ache, one he felt he might never shake as he reached under the *Antari*'s collar and found a White London token on a cord around his neck.

Holland *knew*. He'd seen the attack coming, and he hadn't stopped it. The instant before the metal struck him from behind, Holland had stopped fighting. It was only a second, a fraction of a breath, but it had been enough to give Kell the edge, the opening. And in the sliver of time after the metal pierced his body, and before he fell, it wasn't anger or pain that crossed his face. It was relief.

Kell snapped the cord and straightened, but couldn't bring himself to leave the *Antari* there, in the street. He looked from the token to the waiting wall and then dragged Holland's body to its feet.

VI

The first thing Kell saw when he stepped into White London was Lila brandishing two knives, both of them bloody. She'd managed to cut a path through several men—their bodies littered the street—but four or five were circling her, and more hung back and watched with hungry eyes and whispered in their guttural tongue.

"Pretty red blood."

"Smells like magic."

"Open her up."

"See what's inside."

Kell lowered Holland's body to the ground, and stepped forward.

"*Vös rensk torejk!*" he boomed, rumbling the ground for good measure. *Back away from her.*

A ripple went through the crowd when they saw him—some fled, but others, too curious, took only a step or two back. The moment Lila saw him, her eyes narrowed.

"You are *very, very* late," she growled. Her usual calm had cracked, and underneath she looked tense with fear. "And why are you wet?" Kell looked down at his dripping clothes. He ran his hands along them, willing the water out, and a moment later, he stood, dry except for the puddle at his boots.

"I hit a snag," he said, gesturing back toward Holland. But several dark-eyed citizens were already beginning to investigate the body. One pulled out a knife and pressed it to the dying *Antari*'s wrist.

"Stop," ordered Kell, slamming the assailants backward with a gust of wind. He hauled the *Antari* up over his shoulder.

"Leave him," spat Lila. "Let them pick his bones clean."

But Kell shook his head.

"If you don't," she said. "They'll pick *ours*."

Kell turned and saw the men and women closing in around them.

The people of White London knew the orders, knew the Danes would take the head of any who touched their guest from afar, but it was night, and the lure of fresh magic and Holland's defenseless state—"Let me make a crown from him," murmured one; "I bet there's still blood left," said another—seemed to tip them off their senses. Lila and Kell moved backward until their heels met the bridge.

"Lila?" said Kell as they backed onto it.

"Yeah?" she said, her voice low and tight.

"Run."

She didn't hesitate, but turned and took off sprinting across the bridge. Kell's hand shot up, and with it, a wall of stone, a barricade to buy them time. And then he, too, was running. As fast as he could, with Holland's body over his narrow shoulder and the black magic surging in his veins.

Kell was halfway across the bridge—and Lila nearly to the other side—when the commoners finally tore down the wall and surged after them onto the structure. The moment he reached the opposite bank, Kell sank to the ground and touched his bloody hand to the floor of the bridge.

"As Steno," he commanded, just as Holland had, and instantly,

the bridge began to crumble, plunging stone and bodies down into the icy Sijlt. Kell fought for breath, his pulse thudding his ears. Lila was standing over him, glaring at Holland's body.

"Is he dead?"

"Close enough," said Kell, getting to his feet, hauling the *Antari*'s body with him.

"I hope you made him suffer," she spat, turning toward the looming castle.

No, thought Kell as they set off. *He suffered long enough.*

He could feel the people watching as they moved through the streets, but no one came out of their houses. They were too near the castle now, and the castle had eyes. Soon, it loomed before them, the stone citadel behind its high wall, the archway like a gaping mouth, leading onto the darkened courtyard and its statues.

The stone hummed against Kell's palm, and he realized it wasn't calling only to him now. It was calling to its other half. Beside him, Lila drew yet another blade from beneath her coat. But this one wasn't an ordinary knife. It was a royal half-sword from Red London.

Kell's mouth fell open. "Where did you get that?" he asked.

"Nicked it off the guard who tried to kill me," she said, admiring the weapon. He could see the markings scrawled across the blade. Metal that disabled magic. "Like I said, you can never have too many knives."

Kell held out his hand. "Can you spare it?"

Lila considered him a moment, then shrugged and handed it over. Kell fingered the grip as she drew out her pistol and began to reload it.

"Are you ready?" she asked, spinning the chamber.

Kell gazed through the gate at the waiting castle. "No."

At that, she offered him the sharpest edge of a grin. "Good," she said. "The ones who think they're ready always end up dead."

Kell managed a ghost of a smile. "Thank you, Lila."

"For what?"

But Kell didn't answer, only stepped forward into the waiting dark.

THIRTEEN

THE WAITING KING

I

A cloud of black smoke hung in the air of the white throne room, a patch of night against the pale backdrop. Its edges frayed and curled and faded, but its center was smooth and glossy, like the fragment of stone in Athos's hand, or the surface of a scrying board, which was exactly what the king had summoned with it.

Athos Dane sat on his throne, his sister's body in her own chair beside him, and turned the stone over in his hand as he watched the shifting image of Kell and his companion pass into the courtyard of his castle.

Where the stone's other half had gone, so had its gaze.

The farthest London had been little more than a blur, but as Kell and his companion traveled nearer, the image in the surface had grown crisp and clear. Athos had watched the events unfold across the various cities—Kell's flight, the girl's cunning, his servant's failure, and his sister's foolishness, the wounded prince, and the slaughtered *Antari*.

His fingers tightened on the talisman.

Athos had watched it all unfold with a mixture of amusement and annoyance and, admittedly, excitement. He bristled at the loss of Holland, but a spike of pleasure ran through him at the thought of killing Kell.

Astrid would be furious.

Athos rolled his head and considered his sister's body, propped up on its throne, the charm pulsing at her throat. A London away, she might still be wreaking havoc, but here she sat, still and pale as the sculpted stone beneath her. Her hands draped on the arms of the chair, and wisps of white hair ribboned over her closed eyes. Athos *tsk*ed at his sister.

"*Ös vosa nochten,*" he said. "You should have let me go to the masquerade instead. Now my plaything is dead, and yours has made an awful mess. What do you have to say for yourself?"

Of course, she did not answer.

Athos rapped his long fingers on the edge of his throne, thinking. If he broke the spell and woke her, she would only complicate things. No, he had given her the chance to deal with Kell in her own way, and she had failed. It was his turn now.

Athos smiled and rose to his feet. His fingers tightened on the stone, and the image of Kell dissolved into smoke and then into nothing. Power thrummed through the king, the magic hungry for more, but he held it in place, feeding it only what it needed. It was a thing to be controlled, and Athos had never been a lenient master.

"Do not worry yourself, Astrid," he said to the spellbound queen. "I will make things right."

And then he smoothed his hair, readjusted the collar of his white cloak, and went to greet his guests.

II

The White London fortress rose in a column of sharp light out of the shadowed stone courtyard. Lila slipped into the forest of statues to fulfill her part of the plan while Kell made his way toward the waiting steps. He laid Holland's body on a stone bench and ascended the stairs, one hand curled around the royal blade, the other around the Black London talisman.

Go ahead, Kell, Holland had goaded. *Use the stone. It will consume you faster, but you might just win.*

He wouldn't. He vowed not to. His recent use in battle had only spurred the darkness on. Black threads now coiled up past his elbow and toward his shoulder, and Kell couldn't afford to lose any more of himself. As it was, every heartbeat seemed to spread the poison more.

His pulse thudded in his ears as he climbed the steps. Kell wasn't foolish enough to think he could sneak up on Athos—not here. He had to know that Kell was coming, yet he let him approach his doors without assault. The ten empty-eyed guards that usually flanked the stairs were gone, the way cleared for Kell. The unhindered path was itself a challenge. An act of arrogance befitting White London's king.

Kell would rather have faced an army than the unmanned doors and whatever waited on the other side. Every forward step that went unchecked, unobstructed, only made him more nervous for the next. By the time he reached the landing at the top, his hands were trembling and his chest was tight.

He brought his shaking fingertips to the doors and forced a last breath of cold air into his lungs. And then he pushed. The castle doors opened under his touch, requiring neither force nor magic, and Kell's shadow spilled forward into the corridor. He took a step over the threshold, and the torches of the chamber lit with pale fire, trailing up against the vaulted ceilings and down the hall and revealing the faces of the dozen guards who lined it.

Kell sucked in a breath, bracing himself, but the soldiers did not move.

"They won't lay a hand on you," came a silvery voice. "Not unless you try to flee." Athos Dane stepped out of the shadows, dressed in his usual pristine white, his faded features rendered colorless by the torchlight. "The pleasure of killing you will be mine. And mine alone."

Athos held the other half of the black stone loosely in one hand, and a thrum of power spiked through Kell's body at the sight of it.

"Astrid will sulk, of course," continued Athos. "She wanted you as a pet, but I have always maintained that you were more trouble alive than dead. And I think recent events would serve as evidence of that."

"It's over, Athos," said Kell. "Your plan failed."

Athos smiled grimly. "You are like Holland," he said. "Do you know why he could not take the crown? He never relished war. He saw bloodshed and battle as means to an end. A destination. But *I* have always relished the journey. And I promise you, I'm going to savor this."

His fingers tightened over his half of the stone, and smoke poured forth. Kell didn't hesitate. He willed the armor—and the guards within—from their places against the wall and into a barricade between himself and the king. But it was not enough. The smoke went over, and under, and through, and reached for Kell, trying to twine around his arms. He willed the wall of guards forward into Athos, and sliced at the smoke with the royal sword. But the king did not drop the stone, and the magic was clever and moved around Kell's blade, catching hold of his wrists and turning instantly into forged chains that ran not down to the floor but out to the walls on either side of the antechamber hall.

The metal pulled taut, forcing Kell's arms wide as Athos vaulted over the guards and landed smoothly, effortlessly in front of him. The chains cinched, cutting into Kell's already wounded wrists, and his stolen sword tumbled from his fingers as Athos produced a silver whip. It uncoiled from his hand, cascading to the floor, its forked tip licking the stone.

"Shall we see how well you suffer?"

As Athos went to raise the whip, Kell wrapped his fingers around the chains. The blood on his palm was nearly dry, but he grabbed the metal hard enough to reopen the gash.

"*As Orense,*" he said an instant before the whip cracked through the air, and the chains released Kell just in time for him to dodge the forked silver. He rolled, fetching up the discarded blade, and pressed his bleeding palm to the floor stones, remembering Holland's attack.

"*As Steno,*" he said. The floor stone cracked into a dozen sharp shards under his fingers. Kell rose, the jagged pieces rising with him, and when he cast his hand out, they shot forward toward the king. Athos casually held up his hand in response, the stone clutched within, and a shield took shape in front of him, the slivers of rock shattering uselessly against it.

Athos smiled darkly. "Oh, yes," he said, lowering the shield. "I'm going to enjoy this."

Lila wove through the forest of statues, their heads bowed in surrender, hands up in plea.

She circled the vaulting fortress—it looked like a cathedral, if a cathedral were built on stilts and had no stained glass, only steel and stone. Still, the fortress was long and narrow like a church with one main set of doors on the north side, and three smaller, albeit still impressive, entrances at the south, east, and west sides. Lila's heart hammered as she approached the south entrance, the path to the stairs lined by stone supplicants.

She would have preferred to scale the walls and go in by an upper window, something more discreet than marching up the stairs, but she had no rope and no hook, and even if she'd had the necessary outfittings for such a jaunt, Kell had warned her against it.

The Danes, he had told her, trusted no one, and the castle was as much trap as it was a king's seat. "The main doors face north," he'd said, "I'll go by those. You enter through the south doors."

"Isn't that dangerous?"

"In this place," he'd answered, "everything is dangerous. But if the doors deny you, at least the fall won't be as steep."

So Lila had agreed to go by the doors despite her nagging fear that they were traps. It was all a trap. She reached the south stairs and pulled her horned mask down over her eyes before scaling the steps. At the top, the doors gave way without resistance, and again Lila's gut told her to go, to run the other way, but for the first time in her life, she ignored the warning and stepped inside. The space beyond the doors was dark, but the moment she crossed the threshold, lanterns flared to light, and Lila froze. Dozens of guards lined the walls like living suits of armor. Their heads twisted toward the open door, toward her, and she steeled herself against the impending assault.

But it never came.

Kell had told her that White London was a throne taken—and held—by force, and that this type of ascension didn't usually inspire loyalty. The guards here were clearly bound by magic, trapped under some kind of control spell. But that was the problem with forcing people to do things they didn't want to do. You had to be so specific. They had no choice but to follow orders, but they probably weren't inclined to go above and beyond them.

A slow smile drew across her lips.

Whatever order King Athos had given his guards, it didn't seem to extend to her. Their empty eyes followed her as she moved down the hall as calmly as possible. As if she belonged there. As if she had not come to kill their queen. She wondered, as she moved past them, how many wanted her to succeed.

The halls in the red palace had been labyrinthine, but here there was a simple grid of lines and intersections, further proof that the castle had once been something like a church. One hall gave onto another before putting her out in front of the throne room, just as Kell had said it would.

But Kell had also said the hall would be empty.

And it was not.

A boy stood in front of the throne room door. He was younger than Lila, and thin in a wiry way, and unlike the guards with their empty eyes, his were dark and bruised and feverish. When he saw her coming, he drew his sword.

"*Vösk,*" he ordered.

Lila's brow furrowed.

"*Vösk,*" he said again. "*Ös reijkav vösk.*"

"Hey, you," she said curtly. "Move."

The boy started speaking low and urgently in his own language. Lila shook her head and drew the knife with the brass knuckles from its sheath. "Get out of my way."

Feeling she had made herself understood, Lila strode forward toward the door. But the boy lifted his sword, put himself squarely in her path, and said, *"Vösk."*

"Look," she snapped. "I have no idea what you're saying. . . ."

The young guard looked around, exasperated.

"But I would strongly advise you to go and pretend this interaction never took place and—hey, what the bloody hell do you think you're doing?"

The boy had shaken his head and muttered something under his breath, and then he brought his sword to his own arm, and began to cut.

"Hey," Lila said again as the boy gritted his teeth and drew a second line, and then a third. *"Stop that."*

She went to catch his wrist, but he stopped cutting the pattern and looked her in the eyes, and said, *"Leave."*

For a moment, Lila thought she'd heard him wrong. And then she realized he was speaking English. When she looked down, she saw that he'd carved some kind of symbol into his skin.

"Leave," he said again. *"Now."*

"Get out of my way," countered Lila.

"I can't."

"Boy—" she warned.

"I can't," he said again. "I have to guard the door."

"Or what?" challenged Lila.

"There is no *or what*." He pulled aside the collar of his shirt to show a mark, angry and black, scarred into his skin. "He ordered me to guard the door, so I must guard it."

Lila frowned. The mark was different from Kell's, but she understood what it must be: some kind of seal. "What happens if you step aside?" she asked.

"I can't."

"What happens if I cut you down?"

"I'll die."

He said both things with sad and equal certainty. *What a mad world,* thought Lila.

"What's your name?" she asked.

"Beloc."

"How old are you?"

"Old enough." There was a proud tilt to his jaw, and a fire in his eyes she recognized. A defiance. But he was still young. Too young for this.

"I don't want to hurt you, Beloc," she said. "Don't make me."

"I wish I didn't have to."

He squared himself to her, holding his sword with both hands, his knuckles white. "You'll have to go through me."

Lila growled and gripped her knife.

"Please," he added. "Please go through me."

Lila gave him a long hard look. "How?" she said at last.

His brows went up in question.

"How do you want to die?" she clarified.

The fire in his eyes wavered for an instant, and then he recovered, and said, "Quickly."

Lila nodded. She lifted her knife, and he lowered his sword just a fraction, just enough. And then he closed his eyes and began to whisper something to himself. Lila didn't hesitate. She knew how to use a knife, how to wound, and how to kill. She closed the gap between them and drove the blade between Beloc's ribs and up before he'd even finished his prayer. There were worse ways to go, but she still swore under her breath at Athos and Astrid and the whole forsaken city as she lowered the boy's body to the floor.

She wiped her blade on the hem of her shirt and sheathed the knife as she stepped up to the waiting doors of the throne room. A circle of symbols was etched into the wood, twelve marks in all. She brought her hand to the dial, remembering Kell's instructions.

"Think of it as a clockface," he'd said, drawing the motion in the air. "One, seven, three, nine." Now she drew it with her finger, touching the symbol at the first hour, then drawing her fingertip down and across the circle to the seventh, around and up to the three, and straight through the middle to the nine.

"Are you certain you've got it?" Kell had asked, and Lila had sighed and blown the hair out of her eyes.

"I told you, I'm a fast learner."

At first, nothing happened. And then something passed between her fingers and the wood, and a lock slid within.

"Told you," she murmured, pushing the door open.

III

Athos was laughing. It was a horrible sound.

The hall around them was in disarray, the hollow guards in a heap, the hangings torn, and the torches scattered on the ground, still burning. A bruise blossomed beneath Kell's eye, and Athos's white cloak was singed and flecked with blackish blood.

"Shall we go again?" said Athos. Before the words had even left his lips, a bolt of dark energy shot out like lightning from the front of the king's shield. Kell threw up his hand, and the floor shot up between them, but he wasn't fast enough. The electricity slammed into him and hurled him backward into the front doors of the castle hard enough to split the wood. He coughed, breathless and dizzy from the blow, but he had no chance to recover. The air crackled and came alive, and another bolt struck him so hard that the doors splintered and broke, and Kell went tumbling back into the night.

For an instant, everything went black, and then his vision came back, and he was falling.

The air sprang up to catch him, or at least muffle the fall, but he still hit the stone courtyard at the base of the stairs hard enough to crack bone. The royal blade went skittering away several feet. Blood dripped from Kell's nose to the stones.

"We both hold swords," chided Athos as he descended the

stairs, his white cloak billowing regally behind him. "Yet you choose to fight with a pin."

Kell struggled to his feet, cursing. The king seemed unaffected by the black stone's magic. His veins had always been dark, and his eyes remained their usual icy blue. He was clearly in control, and for the first time Kell wondered if Holland had been right. If there was no such thing as balance, only victors and victims. Had he already lost? The dark magic hummed through his body, begging to be used.

"You're going to die, Kell," said Athos when he reached the courtyard. "You might as well die trying."

Smoke poured from Athos's stone and shot forward, the tendrils of darkness turning to glossy black knifepoints as they surged toward Kell. He threw up his empty hand and tried to will the blades to stop, but they were made of magic, not metal, and they didn't yield, didn't slow. And then, the instant before wall of knives shredded Kell, his other hand—the one bound to the stone—flew up, as if on its own, and the order echoed through his mind.

Protect me.

No sooner had the thought formed than it became real. Shadow wrapped around him, colliding with the knife-tipped smoke. Power surged through Kell's body, fire and ice water and energy all at once, and he gasped as the darkness spread farther beneath his skin and over it, ribboning out from the stone, past his arm and across his chest as the wall of magic deflected the attack and turned it back on Athos.

The king dodged, striking the blades aside with a wave of his stone. Most rained down on the courtyard floor, but one found its mark and buried itself in Athos's leg. The king hissed and dug the knifepoint out. He cast it aside and smiled darkly as he straightened. "That's more like it."

Lila's steps echoed through the throne room. The space was cavernous and circular and as white as snow, interrupted only by a ring of pillars around the edges and the two thrones on the platform in the middle, sitting side by side and carved out of a single piece of pale stone. One of the thrones sat empty.

The other one held Astrid Dane.

Her hair—so blond, it seemed colorless—was coiled like a crown around her head, wisps as fine as spider silk falling onto her face, which tipped forward as if she'd dozed off. Astrid was deathly pale and dressed in white, but not the soft whites of a fairytale queen, no velvet or lace. No, this queen's clothes wrapped around her like armor, tapering sharply along her collar and down her wrists, and where others would have worn dresses, Astrid Dane wore tightly fitted pants that ran into crisp white boots. Her long fingers curled around the arms of the throne, half the knuckles marked by rings, though the only true color on her came from the pendant hanging around her neck, the edges rimmed with blood.

Lila stared at the motionless queen. Her pendant looked exactly like the one Rhy had been wearing in Red London when he wasn't Rhy. A possession charm.

And by the looks of it, Astrid Dane was still under its spell.

Lila took a step forward, cringing as her boots echoed through the hollow room with unnatural clarity. *Clever,* thought Lila. The throne room's shape wasn't just an aesthetic decision. It was designed to carry sound. Perfect for a paranoid ruler. But despite the sound of Lila's steps, the queen never stirred. Lila continued forward, half expecting guards to burst forth from hidden corners—of which there were none—and rush to Astrid's aid.

But no one came.

Serves you right, thought Lila. Hundreds of guards, and the only one to raise a sword wanted to fall on it. Some queen.

The pendant glittered against Astrid's chest, pulsing faintly with light. Somewhere in another city, in another world, she had taken another body—maybe the king or queen or the captain of the guard—but here, she was defenseless.

Lila smiled grimly. She would have liked to take her time, make the queen pay—for Kell's sake—but she knew better than to test her luck. She slid her pistol from its holster. One shot. Quick and easy and over.

She raised the weapon, leveled it at the queen's head, and fired.

The shot rang out through the throne room, followed instantly by a ripple of light, a rumble like thunder, and a blinding pain in Lila's shoulder. It sent her staggering back, the gun tumbling from her hand. She gripped her arm with a gasp, cussing roundly as blood seeped through her shirt and coat. She'd been shot.

The bullet had clearly ricocheted, but off of what?

Lila squinted at Astrid on her throne and realized that the air around the woman in white wasn't as empty as it seemed; it rippled in the gunshot's wake, the direct assault revealing air that shivered and shone, flecked with glassy shards of light. With *magic.* Lila gritted her teeth as her hand fell from her wounded shoulder (and her torn coat) to her waist. She retrieved her knife, still flecked with Beloc's blood, and inched closer until she was standing squarely in front of the throne. Her breath bounced against the nearly invisible barrier and brushed back against her own cheeks.

She raised the knife slowly, bringing the tip of the blade forward until it met the edge of the spell. The air crackled around the knifepoint, glinting like frost, but did not give. Lila swore under her breath as her gaze shifted down through the air, over the queen's body, before landing on the floor at her feet. There, her eyes narrowed. On the stone at the base of the throne were symbols. She couldn't read them, of course, but the way they wove together, the way they wove around the entire throne and the queen made it clear they were important. Links in the chain of a spell.

And links could be broken.

Lila crouched and brought the blade to the nearest symbol's edge. She held her breath and dragged the knife along the ground, scratching away at the marking from her side until she'd erased a narrow band of ink or blood or whatever the spell had been written in (she didn't want to know).

The air around the throne lost its shimmer and dimmed, and as Lila stood, wincing, she knew that whatever enchantment had been protecting the queen was gone.

Lila's fingers shifted on her knife.

"Good-bye, Astrid," she said, plunging the blade forward toward the queen's chest.

But before the tip could tear the white tunic, a hand caught Lila's wrist. She looked down to see Astrid Dane's pale blue eyes staring up at her. Awake. The queen's mouth drew into a thin, sharp smile.

"Bad little thief," she whispered. And then Astrid's grip tightened, and searing pain tore up Lila's arm. She heard someone screaming, and it took her a moment to realize the sound was coming from her throat.

Blood streaked Athos's cheek.

Kell gasped for breath.

The king's white cloak was torn, and shallow gashes marred Kell's leg, his wrist, his stomach. Half the statues in the courtyard around them lay toppled and broken as the magic clashed, striking against itself like flint.

"I will take that black eye of yours," said Athos, "and wear it around my neck."

He lashed out again, and Kell countered, will to will, stone to stone. But Kell was fighting two fights, one with the king, and the other with himself. The darkness kept spreading, claiming more of him with every moment, every motion. He could not win; at this rate, he would either lose the fight or lose himself. Something had to give.

Athos's magic found a fissure in Kell's shadow-drawn shield and hit him hard, cracking his ribs. Kell coughed, tasting blood as he fought to focus his vision on the king. He had to do something, and he had to do it soon. The royal half-sword glittered on the ground nearby. Athos lifted the stone to strike again.

"Is that all you have?" Kell goaded through gritted teeth. "The same, tired tricks? You lack your sister's creativity."

Athos's eyes narrowed. And then he held out the stone and summoned something new.

Not a wall, or a blade, or a chain. No, the smoke coiled around him, shaping itself into a sinister curving shadow. A massive silver serpent with black eyes, its forked tongue flicking the air as it rose, taller than the king himself.

Kell forced himself to give a low, derisive laugh, even though it hurt his broken ribs. He fetched the royal half-sword from the ground. It was chipped and slick with dust and blood, but he could still make out the symbols running down its metal length. "I've been waiting for you to do that," he said. "Create something strong enough to kill me. Since you clearly cannot do it yourself."

Athos frowned. "What does it matter, the shape your death takes? It is still at my hand."

"You said you wanted to kill me yourself," countered Kell.

"But I suppose this is as close as you can come. Go ahead and hide behind the stone's magic. Call it your own."

Athos let out a low growl. "You're right," he said. "Your death should—and will—be mine."

He tightened his fingers around the stone, clearly intending to dispel the serpent. The snake, which had been slithering around the king, now stopped its course, but it did not dissolve. Instead, it turned its glossy black eyes on Athos, the way Kell's mirror image had on Lila in her room. Athos glared up at the serpent, willing it away. When it did not obey his thought, he gave voice to the command.

"You submit to *me*," ordered Athos as the serpent flicked its tongue. "You are my creation, and I am your—"

He never had the chance to finish.

The serpent reared back and struck. Its fanged jaws closed over the stone in Athos's hand, and before the king could even scream, the snake had enveloped him. Its silver body coiled around his arms and chest, and then around his neck, snapping it with an audible crack.

Kell sucked in a breath as Athos Dane's head slumped forward, the terrifying king reduced to nothing but a rag doll corpse. The serpent uncoiled, and the king's body tumbled forward to the broken ground. And then the serpent turned its shining black eyes on Kell. It slithered toward him with frightening speed, but Kell was ready.

He drove the royal half-sword up into the serpent's belly. It pierced the snake's rough skin, the spellwork on the metal glowing for an instant before the creature's thrashing broke the blade in two. The snake shuddered and fell, dispelled to nothing but a shadow at Kell's feet.

A shadow, and in the midst of it, a broken piece of black stone.

IV

Lila's back hit the pillar hard.

She crumpled to the stone floor of the throne room, and blood ran into her false eye as she struggled to push herself to her hands and knees. Her shoulder cried out with pain, but so did the rest of her. She tried not to think about it. Astrid, meanwhile, seemed to be having a grand time. She was smiling lazily at Lila, like a cat with a kitchen mouse.

"I am going to cut that smile off your face," growled Lila as she staggered to her feet.

She had been in a lot of fights with a lot of people, but she'd never fought anyone like Astrid Dane. The woman moved with both jarring speed and awkward grace, one moment slow and smooth, the next striking so fast that it was all Lila could do to stay on her feet. Stay alive.

Lila knew she was going to lose.

Lila knew she was going to *die*.

But she'd be damned if it counted for nothing.

Judging by the rumbling of the castle grounds around them, Kell had his hands full. The least she could do was keep the number of Danes he had to fight to one. Buy him a little time.

Honestly, what had happened to her? The Lila Bard of south London looked out for herself. That Lila would never waste her life on someone else. She'd never choose right over wrong so long as wrong meant staying alive. She'd never have turned back to help the stranger who helped her. Lila spit a mouthful of blood and straightened. Perhaps she never should have stolen the damned stone, but even here, and now, facing death in the form of a pale queen, she didn't regret it. She'd wanted freedom. She'd wanted adventure. And she didn't think she minded dying for it. She only wished dying didn't hurt so much.

"You've gotten in the way long enough," said Astrid, raising her hands in front of her.

Lila's mouth quirked. "I do seem to have a talent for that."

Astrid began to speak in that guttural tongue Lila had heard in the streets. But in the queen's mouth, the words sounded different. Strange and harsh and beautiful, they poured from her lips, rustling like a breeze through rotting leaves. They reminded Lila of the music blanketing the crowd in Rhy's parade, sound made physical. *Powerful*.

And Lila wasn't foolish enough to stand there and listen to it. Her pistol, now empty, lay discarded several feet away, her newest knife at the foot of the throne. She still had one dagger at her back and she went for it, sliding the weapon free. But before the blade could leave her fingers, Astrid finished the incantation, and a wave of energy slammed into Lila, knocking the wind out of her lungs as she hit the floor and slid several feet.

She rolled up into a crouch, gasping for air. The queen was toying with her.

Astrid's fingers rose as she prepared to strike again, and Lila knew it was her only chance. Her fingers tightened on the dagger, and she threw it, hard and fast and straight, at the queen's heart. It flew right at Astrid, but instead of dodging, she simply reached out and plucked the metal out of the air. With her bare hand. Lila's heart sank as the queen snapped the blade in two and tossed the pieces aside, all without interrupting her spell.

Shit, thought Lila, right before the stone floor beneath her began to rumble and shake. She fought to keep her footing and very nearly missed the wave of broken stone cresting over her head. Pebbles rained from above, and she dove out of the way just as the whole thing came crashing down. She was fast, but not fast enough. Pain tore up her right side, her leg, from heel to knee, which was trapped beneath the rubble, pale stone flecked with fragments of whitened rock.

No, not whitened rock, realized Lila with horror.

Bones.

Lila scrambled to free her leg, but Astrid was there, wrenching her onto her back and kneeling on her chest. Astrid reached down and ripped the horned mask from Lila's facs, tossing it aside. She took hold of Lila's jaw and wrenched her face up to hers.

"Pretty little thing," said the queen. "Under all that blood."

"Burn in hell," spat Lila.

Astrid only smiled. And then the nails of her other hand sank into Lila's wounded shoulder. Lila bit back a scream and thrashed under the queen's grip, but it was no use.

"If you're going to kill me," she snapped, "just do it already."

"Oh, I will," said Astrid, withdrawing her fingers from Lila's throbbing shoulder. "But not yet. When I have finished with Kell, I shall come back for you, and I shall take my time divesting you of your life. And when I'm done, I'll add you to my floor." She held up her hand between them, showing Lila her fingertips, now stained with blood. It was such a vivid red against the queen's pale skin. "But first . . ." Astrid brought a bloody finger to the place between Lila's eyes, tracing a pattern there.

Lila fought as hard as she could to get free, but Astrid was an unmovable force on top of her, pinning her down as she drew a bloody mark on her own pale forehead.

Astrid began to speak, low and fast and in that other tongue. Lila struggled frantically now, and tried to scream, attempting to interrupt the spell, but the queen's long fingers clamped over her mouth, and Astrid's spell spilled out, taking shape in the air around them. A spike of ice shot through Lila, her skin prickling as the magic rippled over her. And above her, the queen's face began to *change*.

Her chin sharpened, and her cheeks warmed from porcelain to a healthier hue. Her lips reddened, and her eyes darkened from blue to brown—two different shades—and her hair, once as white as snow and wound about her head, now fell down onto her face, chestnut brown and chopped in a sharp line along her jaw. Even her clothes rippled and shifted and took on an all-too-familiar form. The queen smiled a knifelike grin, and Lila gazed up in horror not at Astrid Dane, but at the mirror image of herself.

When Astrid spoke, Lila's own voice poured out. "I better go," she said. "I'm sure Kell could use a hand."

Lila swung a last, desperate punch, but Astrid caught her wrist as if it were nothing more than a nuisance, and pinned it against the floor. She bent her head over Lila's, bringing her lips to her ear. "Don't worry," she whispered. "I'll give him your regards."

And then Astrid slammed Lila's head back against the ruined floor, and Lila's world went dark.

Kell stood in the stone courtyard, surrounded by broken statues, a dead king, and a jagged piece of black stone. He was bleeding, and broken, but he was still alive. He let the ruined royal sword slip through this fingers and clatter to the ground and drew a shuddering breath, the cold air burning his lungs and fogging in front of his bloody lips. Something was moving through him, warm and cool, lulling and dangerous. He wanted to stop fighting, wanted to give in, but he couldn't. It wasn't over yet.

Half of the stone pulsed against his palm. The other half glinted on the ground where the serpent had dropped it. It called to him, and Kell's body moved of its own accord toward the missing piece. The stone guided his fingers down to the splintered ground and closed them around the fragment of rock waiting there. The moment the two pieces met, Kell felt words form on his lips.

"*As Hasari*," he said, the command spilling out on its own in a voice that was and wasn't his. In his hand, the two halves of the stone began to *heal*. The pieces fused back together, the cracks untracing themselves until the surface was a smooth, unblemished black, and in its wake an immense power—clear, beautiful, and sweet—poured through Kell's body, bringing with it a sense of right. A sense of *whole*. It filled him with calm. With quiet. The simple steady rhythm of magic pulled him down like sleep. All Kell wanted to do was to let go, to disappear into the power and darkness and peace.

Give in, said a voice in his head. His eyes drifted shut, and he swayed on his feet.

And then he heard Lila's voice calling his name.

The stillness rippled as Kell forced his eyes open, and he saw her descending the stairs. She seemed far away. Everything seemed far away.

"Kell," she said again as she reached him. Her eyes took in the scene—the ruined courtyard; Athos's corpse; his own, battered form—and the talisman, now whole.

"It's over," she said. "It's time to let it go."

He looked down at the talisman in his hand, at the way the black threads had thickened and become like rope, wrapping around his body.

"Please," said Lila. "I know you can do this. I know you can hear me." She held out her hand, eyes wide with worry. Kell frowned, power still coursing through him, distorting his vision, his thoughts.

"Please," she said again.

"Lila," he said softly, desperately. He reached out and steadied himself on her shoulder.

"I'm here," she whispered. "Just give me the stone."

He considered the talisman. And then his fingers closed over it, and smoke whispered out. He didn't have to speak. The magic was in his head now, and it knew what he wanted. Between one instant and the next, the smoke became a knife. He stared down at the metal's glinting edge.

"Lila," he said again.

"Yes, Kell?"

His fingers tightened on it. "Catch."

And then he drove the blade into her stomach.

Lila let out a gasp of pain. And then her whole body shuddered, rippled, and became someone else's. It stretched into the form of Astrid Dane, dark blood blossoming against her white clothes.

"How . . ." she growled, but Kell willed her body still, her jaw shut. No words—no spell—would save her now. He wanted to kill Astrid Dane. But more than that, he wanted her to *suffer*. For his brother. His prince. Because in that moment, staring into her wide blue eyes, all he could see was Rhy.

Rhy wearing her talisman.

Rhy flashing a smile that was too cruel and too cold to be his own.

Rhy curling his fingers around Kell's throat and whispering in his ear with someone else's words.

Rhy thrusting a knife into his stomach.

Rhy—*his* Rhy—crumpling to the stone floor.

Rhy bleeding.

Rhy dying.

Kell wanted to *crush* her for what she'd done. And in his hands, the want became a will, and the darkness began to spread out from the knife buried in her stomach. It crawled over her clothes and under her skin, and turned everything it touched to pale white stone. Astrid tried to open her mouth, to speak or to scream, but before any sound could escape her clenched teeth, the stone had reached her chest, her throat, her faded red lips. It overtook her stomach, trailed down her legs and over her boots before running straight into the pitted ground. Kell stood there, staring at the statue of Astrid Dane, her eyes frozen wide with shock, lips drawn into a permanent snarl. She looked like the rest of the courtyard now.

But it wasn't enough.

As much as he wanted to leave her there in the broken garden with her brother's corpse, he couldn't. Magic, like everything, faded. Spells were broken. Astrid could be free again one day. And he couldn't let that happen.

Kell gripped her white stone shoulder. His fingers were bloody, like the rest of him, and the *Antari* magic came as easily as air. *"As Steno,"* he said.

Deep cracks formed across the queen's face, jagged fissures carving down her body, and when his fingers tightened, the stone statue of Astrid Dane shattered under his touch.

V

Kell shivered, the strange calm settling over him again.

It was heavier this time. And then someone called his name, just as they had moments earlier, and he looked up to see Lila clutching her shoulder as she half ran, half limped down the stairs, bruised and bloody, but alive. Her black mask hung from her bloody fingers.

"You all right?" she asked when she reached him.

"Never better," he said, even though it was taking every ounce of his strength to focus his eyes on her, his mind on her.

"How did you know?" she asked, looking down at the rubble of the queen. "How did you know she wasn't me?"

Kell managed an exhausted smile. "Because she said *please*."

Lila stared at him, aghast. "Is that a joke?"

Kell shrugged slightly. It took a lot of effort. "I just knew," he said.

"You just knew," she echoed.

Kell nodded. Lila took him in with careful eyes, and he wondered what he must look like in that moment.

"You look terrible," she said. "You better get rid of that rock."

Kell nodded.

"I could come with you."

Kell shook his head. "No. Please. I don't want you to." It was the honest answer. He didn't know what waited on the other side, but whatever it was, he would face it alone.

"Fine," said Lila, swallowing. "I'll stay here."

"What will you do?" he asked.

Lila forced a shrug. "Saw some nice ships on the dock when we were running for our lives. One of them will do."

"Lila . . ."

"I'll be okay," she said tightly. "Now, hurry up before someone notices we've killed the monarchs."

Kell tried to laugh, and something shot through him, like pain but darker. He doubled over, his vision blurring.

"Kell?" Lila dropped to her knees beside him. "What is it? What's happening?"

No, he pleaded with his body. *No. Not now.* He was so close. So close. All he had to do was—

Another wave sent him to his hands and knees.

"Kell!" demanded Lila. "Talk to me."

He tried to answer, tried to say something, anything, but his jaw locked shut, his teeth grinding together. He fought the darkness, but the darkness fought back. And it was winning.

Lila's voice was getting further and further away. "Kell . . . can you hear me? Stay with me. Stay with me."

Stop fighting, said a voice in his head. *You've already lost.*

No, thought Kell. *No. Not yet.* He managed to bring his fingers to the shallow gash across his stomach, and began to draw a mark on the cracked stone. But before he could press his stone-bound hand against it, a force slammed him backward to the ground. The darkness twined around him and dragged him down. He fought against the magic, but it was already inside him, coursing through his veins. He tried to tear free of its hold, to push it away, but it was too late.

He took one last gasp of air, and then the magic dragged him under.

Kell couldn't move.

Shadows wove around his limbs and held like stone, pinning him still. The more he fought, the tighter they coiled, leeching the last of his strength. Lila's voice was far, far away and then gone, and Kell was left in a world filled with only darkness.

A darkness that was everywhere.

And then, somehow, it wasn't. It drew itself together, coiling in front of him, coalescing until it was first a shadow and then a man. He was shaped like Kell, from his height and his hair to his coat, but every inch of him was the smooth and glossy black of the recovered stone.

"Hello, Kell," said the darkness, the words not in English or Arnesian or Maktahn, but the native tongue of magic. And finally, Kell understood. This was *Vitari*. The thing that had been pulling at him, pushing to get in, making him stronger while weakening his will and feeding on his life.

"Where are we?" he asked, his voice hoarse.

"We are in you," said *Vitari*. "We are *becoming* you."

Kell struggled uselessly against the dark ropes. "Get out of my body," he growled.

Vitari smiled his shadowy black smile and took a step toward Kell.

"You've fought well," he said. "But the time for fighting is over." He closed the gap and brought a hand to Kell's chest. "You were made for me, *Antari*," he said. "A perfect vessel. I will wear your skin forever."

Kell twisted under his touch. He had to fight. He'd come so far. He couldn't give up now.

"It's too late," said *Vitari*. "I already have your heart." At that, his fingertips pressed down, and Kell gasped as *Vitari*'s hand passed *into* his chest. He felt *Vitari*'s fingers close around his beating heart, felt it lurch, darkness spilling across his tattered shirtfront like blood.

"It's over, Kell," said the magic. "You're mine."

Kell's body shuddered on the ground. Lila took his face in her hands. It was burning up. The veins on his throat and at his temple had darkened to black, and the strain showed in the lines of his jaw, but he wasn't moving, wouldn't open his eyes.

"Fight this!" she shouted as his body spasmed. "You've come all this way. You can't just *give up*."

His back arched against the ground, and Lila pushed open Kell's shirt and saw black spreading over his heart.

"Dammit," she swore, trying to pry the stone out of his hand. It wouldn't budge.

"If you die," she snapped, "what happens to Rhy?"

Kell's back hit the ground, and he let out a labored breath.

Lila had recovered her weapons, and now she freed her knife, weighing it in her palm. She didn't want to have to kill him. But she could. And she didn't want to cut off his hand, but she certainly would.

A groan escaped between his lips.

"Don't you fucking give up, Kell. Do you hear me?"

Kell's heart stuttered, skipping a beat.

"I asked so nicely," said *Vitari*, his hand still buried in Kell's chest. "I gave you the chance to give in. You made me use force."

Heat spread through Kell's limbs, leaving a strange cold in its wake. He heard Lila's voice. Far away and stretched so thin, the words, an echo of an echo, barely reached him. But he heard a name. *Rhy*.

If he died, so would Rhy. He couldn't stop fighting.

"I'm not going to kill you, Kell. Not exactly."

Kell squeezed his eyes shut, darkness folding over him.

"Isn't there a word for this?" Lila's voice echoed through his head. *"What is it? Come on, Kell. Say the blasted word."*

Kell forced himself to focus. Of course. Lila was right. There was a word. *Vitari* was pure magic. And all magic was bound by rules. By order. *Vitari* was a creation, but everything that could be created could also be destroyed. *Dispelled.*

"As Anasae," said Kell. He felt a glimmer of power. But nothing happened.

Vitari's free hand closed around his throat.

"Did you really think that would work?" sneered the magic in Kell's shape, but there was something in his voice and in the way he tensed. *Fear.* It could work. It would work. It had to.

But *Antari* magic was a verbal pact. He'd never been able to summon it with thought alone, and here, in his head, everything was thought. Kell had to *say* the word. He focused, reaching with his fading senses until he could feel his body, not as it was here in this illusion, this mental plane, but as it was in truth, stretched on the bitterly cold ground of the broken courtyard, Lila crouching over it. Over him. He clung to that chill, focusing on the way it pressed into his back. He struggled to feel his fingers, wrapped around the stone so hard that they ached. He focused on his mouth, clenched shut in pain, and forced it to unlock. Forced his lips to part.

To form the words. *"As An—"*

His heart faltered as *Vitari*'s fingers tightened around it.

"No," growled the magic, the fear bold now, twisting his impatience into anger. And Kell understood his fear. *Vitari* wasn't simply a spell. He was the *source* of all the stone's power. Dispelling him would dispel the talisman itself. It would all be over.

Kell fought to hold on to his body. To himself. He forced air into his lungs and out his mouth.

"*As Anas—*" he managed before Vitari's hand shifted from heart to lungs, crushing the air out of them.

"You can't," said the magic desperately. "I am the only thing keeping your brother alive."

Kell hesitated. He didn't know if that was true, if the bond he'd made with his brother *could* be broken. But he did know that Rhy would never forgive him for what he'd done, and it wouldn't even matter unless they both made it through.

Kell summoned the last of his strength and focused not on *Vitari* trying to crush his life, or on the darkness sweeping through him, but on Lila's voice and the cold ground and his aching fingers and his bloody lips as they formed the words.

"*As Anasae.*"

VI

Across Red London, the bodies fell.

Men and women who'd been kissed or taken, wooed or forced, those who had let the magic in and those who had had it thrust upon them, all of them fell as the black flame inside them gutted and went out. Dispelled.

Everywhere, the magic left a trail of bodies.

In the streets, they staggered and collapsed. Some crumbled to ash, all burned up, and some were reduced to husks, empty inside, and a lucky few crumpled, gasping and weak but still alive.

In the palace, the magic dressed as Gen had just reached the royal chambers, his blackening hand on the door, when the darkness died and took him with it.

And in the sanctuary, far from the castle walls, on a bare cot in a candlelit room, the prince of Red London shivered and fell still.

FOURTEEN

THE FINAL DOOR

I

Kell opened his eyes and saw stars.

They floated high above the castle walls, nothing but pricks of pale white light in the distance.

The stone slipped from his fingers, hitting the ground with a dull clink. There was nothing to it now, no hum, no urge, no promise. It was just a piece of rock.

Lila was saying something, and for once she didn't sound angry, not as angry as usual, but he couldn't hear her over the pounding of his heart as he brought one shaking hand to the collar of his shirt. He didn't really want to see. Didn't want to know. But he tugged his collar down anyway and looked at the skin over his heart, the place where the seal had bonded Rhy's life to his own.

The black tracery of the magic was gone.

But the scar of it wasn't. The seal itself was still intact. Which meant it hadn't only been tethered to *Vitari*. It had been tethered to *him*.

Kell let out a small sobbing sound of relief.

And finally, the world around him came back into focus. The cold stone of the courtyard and Athos's corpse and the shards of Astrid, and Lila, with her arms flung around his shoulders for an instant—and only an instant, gone before he could appreciate their presence.

"Miss me?" whispered Kell, his throat raw.

"Sure," she said, her eyes red. She toed the talisman with her boot. "Is it dead?" she asked.

Kell picked up the stone, feeling nothing but its weight.

"You can't kill magic," said Kell, getting slowly to his feet. "Only dispel it. But it's gone."

Lila chewed her lip. "Do you still have to send it back?"

Kell considered the hollow rock and nodded slowly. "To be safe," he said. But maybe, now that he was finally free of its grip, he didn't have to be the one to go with it. Kell scanned the courtyard until he saw Holland's body. In the fight the *Antari* had fallen from the stone bench, and now lay stretched on the ground, his blood-soaked cloak the only sign that Holland wasn't merely sleeping.

Kell got to his feet, every inch of him protesting, and went to Holland's side. He knelt and took one of the *Antari*'s hands in his. Holland's skin was going cold, the pulse at his wrist weak, and getting weaker, his heart dragging itself through the final beats. But he was still alive.

It's really quite hard to kill Antari, he had once said. It appeared he was right.

Kell felt Lila hovering behind him. He didn't know if this would work, if one *Antari* could command for another, but he pressed his fingers to the wound at Holland's chest and drew a single line on the ground beside his body. And then he touched the hollow stone to the blood and set it on the line, bringing Holland's hand to rest on top of it.

"Peace," he said softly, a parting word for a broken man. And then he pressed his hand on top of Holland's and said, *"As Travars."*

The ground beneath the *Antari* gave way, bending into shadow. Kell pulled back as the darkness, and whatever lay beyond, swallowed Holland's body and the stone, leaving only blood-streaked ground behind.

Kell stared at the stained earth, unwilling to believe that it had actually worked. That he had been spared. That he was alive. That he could go *home*.

He swayed on his feet, and Lila caught him.

"Stay with me," she said.

Kell nodded, dizzy. The stone had masked the pain, but in its absence, his vision blurred with it. Rhy's wounds layered on top of his own, and when he tried to bite back a groan, he tasted blood.

"We have to go," said Kell. Now that the city was absent a ruler—or two—the fighting would start again. Someone would claw their bloody way to the throne. They always did.

"Let's get you home," said Lila. Relief poured over him in a wave before the hard reality caught up.

"Lila," he said, stiffening. "I don't know if I can take you with me." The stone had guaranteed her passage through the worlds, made a door for her where none should be. Without it, the chances of the world allowing her through . . .

Lila seemed to understand. She looked around and wrapped her arms around herself. She was bruised and bleeding. How long would she last here alone? Then again, it was Lila. She'd probably survive anything.

"Well," she said. "We can try."

Kell swallowed.

"What's the worst that could happen?" she added as they made their way to the courtyard wall. "I get pulled into a hundred little pieces between worlds?" She said it with a wry smile, but he could see the fear in her eyes. "I'm prepared to stay. But I want to try and leave."

"If it doesn't work—"

"Then I'll find my way," said Lila.

Kell nodded and led her to the courtyard wall. He made a mark on the pale stones and dug the Red London coin from his pocket. And then he pulled Lila close, wrapped his broken body around hers, and tipped his forehead against hers.

"Hey, Lila," he said softly into the space between them.

"Yeah?"

He pressed his mouth to hers for one brief moment, the warmth there and then gone. She frowned up at him, but did not pull away.

"What was that for?" she asked.

"For luck," he said. "Not that you need it."

And then he pressed his hand against the wall and thought of home.

II

Red London took shape around Kell, heavy with night. It smelled of earth and fire, of blooming flowers and spiced tea, and underneath it all, of home. Kell had never been so happy to be back. But his heart sank when he realized that his arms were empty.

Lila wasn't with him.

She hadn't made it back.

Kell swallowed and looked down at the token in his bloody hand. And then he threw it as hard as he could. He closed his eyes and took a deep breath, trying to steady himself.

And then he heard a voice. Her voice.

"Never thought I'd be so happy to smell the flowers."

Kell blinked and spun to see Lila standing there. Alive, and in one piece.

"It's not possible," he said.

The edge of her mouth quirked up. "It's nice to see you, too."

Kell threw his arms around her. And for a second, only a second, she didn't pull away, didn't threaten to stab him. For a second, and only a second, she hugged him back.

"What are you?" he asked, amazed.

Lila only shrugged. "Stubborn."

They stood there a moment, leaning on each other, one

keeping the other on their feet, though neither was sure which needed more supporting. Both knew only that they were happy to be here, to be alive.

And then he heard the sounds of boots and swords, and saw the flares of light.

"I think we're being attacked," whispered Lila into the collar of his coat.

Kell lifted his head from her shoulder to see a dozen members of the guard surrounding them, blades drawn. Through their helmets, their eyes looked at him with fear and rage. He could feel Lila tense against him, feel her itching to reach for a pistol or a knife.

"Don't fight," he whispered as he slid his arms slowly from her back. He took her hand and turned toward his family's men. "We surrender."

The guards forced Kell and Lila to their knees before the king and queen, and held them there despite Lila's muttered oaths. Their wrists were bound in metal behind them, the way Kell's had been earlier that night in Rhy's chambers. Had it really been only hours? They weighed on Kell like years.

"Leave us," ordered King Maxim.

"Sir," protested one of the royal guard, shooting a glance at Kell. "It is not safe to—"

"I said get out," he boomed.

The guard withdrew, leaving only Kell and Lila on their knees in the emptied ballroom, the king and queen looming over them. King Maxim's eyes were feverish, his skin blotching with anger. At his side, Queen Emira looked deathly pale.

"What have you done?" demanded the king.

Kell cringed, but he told them the truth. Of Astrid's possession charm, and the Dane twins' plan, but also of the stone, and of the way he came by it (and of its preceding habit). He told them of its discovery, and of trying to return it to the only place it would be safe. And the king and queen listened, less with disbelief than with horror, the king growing redder and the queen growing paler with every explanation.

"The stone is gone now," finished Kell. "And the magic with it."

The king slammed his fist against a banister. "The Danes will pay for what they've—"

"The Danes are dead," said Kell. "I killed them myself."

Lila cleared her throat.

Kell rolled his eyes. "With Lila's help."

The king seemed to notice Lila for the first time. "Who are you? What madness have you added to these plots?"

"My name is Delilah Bard," she shot back. "We met, just earlier this evening. When I was trying to save your city, and you were standing there, all blank-eyed under some kind of spell."

"*Lila,*" snapped Kell in horror.

"I'm half the reason your city is still standing."

"*Our* city?" questioned the queen. "You're not from here, then?"

Kell tensed. Lila opened her mouth, but before she could answer, he said, "No. She's from afar."

The king's brow furrowed. "How *far* afar?"

And before Kell could answer, Lila threw her shoulders back. "My ship docked a few days ago," she announced. "I came to London because I heard that your son's festivities were not to be missed, and because I had business with a merchant named Calla in the market on the river. Kell and I have crossed paths once or twice before, and when it was clear that he needed help, I gave it." Kell stared at Lila. She gave him a single raised brow and added, "He promised me a reward, of course."

The king and queen stared at Lila, too, as if trying to decide which piece of her story sounded *least* plausible (it was either the fact that she owned a ship, or the fact that a foreigner spoke such flawless English), but at last the queen's composure faltered.

"Where is our *son*?" she pleaded. The way she said it, as if they had only one, made Kell flinch.

"Is Rhy alive?" demanded the king.

"Thanks to Kell," cut in Lila. "We've spent the last day trying to save your kingdom, and you don't even—"

"He's alive," said Kell, cutting her off. "And he will live," he added, holding the king's gaze. "As long as I do." There was a faint challenge in the line.

"What do you mean?"

"Sir," said Kell, breaking the gaze. "I did only what I had to do. If I could have given him my life, I would have. Instead, I could only share it." He twisted in his bonds, the edge of the scar visible under his collar. The queen drew in a breath. The king's face darkened.

"Where is he, Kell?" asked the king, his voice softening.

Kell's shoulders loosened, the weight sliding from them. "Release us," he said. "And I will bring him home."

III

"Come in."

Kell had never been so glad to hear his brother's voice. He opened the door and stepped into Rhy's room, trying not to picture the way it had been when he last left it, the prince's blood streaked across the floor.

It had been three days since that night, and all signs of the chaos had since been erased. The balcony had been repaired, the blood polished out of the inlaid wood, the furniture and fabrics made new.

Now Rhy lay propped up in his bed. There were circles under his eyes, but he looked more bored than ill, and that was progress. The healers had fixed him up as best they could (they'd fixed Kell and Lila, too), but the prince wasn't mending as quickly as he should have been. Kell knew why, of course. Rhy hadn't simply been wounded, as they had been told. He'd been *dead*.

Two attendants stood at a table nearby, and a guard sat in a chair beside the door, and all three watched Kell as he entered. Part of Rhy's dark mood came from the fact that the guard was neither Parrish nor Gen. Both had been found dead—one by sword, and the other by the black fever, as it was quickly named, that had raged through the city—a fact that troubled Rhy as much as his own condition.

The attendants and the guard watched Kell with new caution as he approached the prince's bed.

"They will not let me up, the bastards," grumbled Rhy, glaring at them. "If I cannot leave," he said to them, "then be so kind as to leave yourselves." The weight of loss and guilt, paired with the nuisance of injury and confinement, had put Rhy in a foul humor. "By all means," he added as his servants rose, "stand guard outside. Make me feel like more of a prisoner than I already do."

When they were gone, Rhy sighed and slumped back against the pillows.

"They mean only to help," said Kell.

"Perhaps it wouldn't be so bad," he said, "if they were prettier to look at." But the boyish jab rang strangely hollow. His eyes found Kell's, and his look darkened. "Tell me everything," he said. "But start with this." He touched the place over his heart, where he wore a scar that matched Kell's own. "What foolish thing have you done, my brother?"

Kell looked down at the rich red linens on the bed and pulled aside his collar to show the mirroring scar. "I did only what you would have done, if you were me."

Rhy frowned. "I love you, Kell, but I had no interest in matching tattoos."

Kell smiled sadly. "You were dying, Rhy. I saved your life."

He couldn't bring himself to tell Rhy the whole truth: that the stone hadn't only saved his life but had restored it.

"How?" demanded the prince. "At what cost?"

"One I paid," said Kell. "And would pay again."

"Answer me without circles!"

"I bound your life to mine," said Kell, "As long as I live, so shall you."

Rhy's eyes widened. "You did what?" he whispered, horrified. "I should get out of this bed and wring your neck."

"I wouldn't," advised Kell. "Your pain is mine and mine is yours."

Rhy's hands curled into fists. "How could you?" he said, and Kell worried that the prince was bitter about being tethered to him. Instead, Rhy said, "How could you carry that weight?"

"It is as it is, Rhy. It cannot be undone. So please, be grateful, and be done with it."

"How can I be done with it?" scorned Rhy, already slipping back into a more playful tone. "It is carved into my chest."

"Lovers like men with scars," said Kell, cracking a smile. "Or so I've heard."

Rhy sighed and tipped his head back, and the two fell into silence. At first, it was an easy quiet, but then it began to thicken, and just when Kell was about to break it, Rhy beat him to the act.

"What have I done?" he whispered, amber eyes cast up against the gossamer ceiling. "What have I done, Kell?" He rolled his head so he could see his brother. "Holland brought me that necklace. He said it was a gift, and I believed him. Said it was from this London, and I believed him."

"You made a mistake, Rhy. Everybody makes them. Even royal princes. I've made many. It's only fair that you make one."

"I should have known better. I *did* know better," he added, his voice cracking.

He tried to sit up, and winced. Kell urged him back down. "Why did you take it?" he asked when the prince was settled.

For once, Rhy would not meet his gaze. "Holland said it would bring me strength."

Kell's brow furrowed. "You are already strong."

"Not like you. That is, I know I'll never be like you. But I have no gift for magic, and it makes me feel weak. One day I'm going to be king. I wanted to be a strong king."

"Magic does not make people strong, Rhy. Trust me. And you have something better. You have the people's love."

"It's easy to be loved. I want to be respected, and I thought . . ." Rhy's voice was barely a whisper. "I took the necklace. All that matters is that I took it." Tears began to escape, running into his black curls. "And I could have ruined everything. I could have lost the crown before I ever wore it. I could have doomed my city to war or chaos or collapse."

"What sons our parents have," said Kell gently. "Between the two of us, we'll tear the whole world down."

Rhy let out a stifled sound between a laugh and a sob. "Will they ever forgive us?"

Kell mustered a smile. "I am no longer in chains. That speaks to progress."

The king and queen had sent word across the city, by guard and scrying board alike, that Kell was innocent of all charges. But the eyes in the street still hung on him, wariness and fear and suspicion woven through the reverence. Maybe when Rhy was well again and could speak to his people directly, they would believe he was all right and that Kell had had no hand in the darkness that had fallen over the palace that night. Maybe, but Kell doubted it would ever be as simple as it had been before.

"I meant to tell you," said Rhy. "Tieren came to visit. He brought some—"

He was interrupted by a knock at the door. Before either Rhy or Kell could answer, Lila stormed into the room. She was still wearing her new coat—patches sewn over the spots where it had been torn by bullet and blade and stone—but she'd been bathed at least, and a gold clasp held the hair out of her eyes. She still looked a bit like a starved bird, but she was clean and fed and mended.

"I don't like the way the guards are looking at me," she said before glancing up and seeing the prince's gold eyes on her. "I'm sorry," she added. "I didn't mean to intrude."

"Then what did you mean to do?" challenged Kell.

Rhy held up his hand. "You are surely not an intrusion," he said, pushing himself up in the bed. "Though I fear you've met me rather out of my usual state of grace. Do you have a name?"

"Delilah Bard," she said. "We've met before. And you looked worse."

Rhy laughed silently. "I apologize for anything I might have done. I was not myself."

"I apologize for shooting you in the leg," said Lila. "I was myself entirely."

Rhy broke into his perfect smile.

"I like this one," he said to Kell. "Can I borrow her?"

"You can try," said Lila, raising a brow. "But you'll be a prince without his fingers."

Kell grimaced, but Rhy only laughed. The laughter quickly dissolved into wincing, and Kell reached out to steady his brother, even as the pain echoed in his own chest.

"Save your flirting for when you're well," he said.

Kell pushed to his feet and began to usher Lila out.

"Will I see more of you, Delilah Bard?" called the prince.

"Perhaps our paths will cross again."

Rhy's smile went crooked. "If I have any say in it, they will."

Kell rolled his eyes but thought he caught Lila actually blushing as he guided her out and shut the door, leaving the prince to rest.

IV

"I could try and take you back," Kell was saying. "To your London."

He and Lila were walking along the river's edge, past the evening market—where people's eyes still hung too heavy and too long—and farther on toward the docks. The sun was sinking behind them, casting long shadows in front of them like paths.

Lila shook her head and pulled the silver watch from her pocket. "There's nothing for me there," she said, snapping the timepiece open and shut. "Not anymore."

"You don't belong here, either," he said simply.

She shrugged. "I'll find my way." And then she tipped her chip up and looked him in the eyes. "Will you?"

The scar over his heart twinged dully, a ghost of pain, and he rubbed his shoulder. "I'll try." He dug a hand in the pocket of his coat—the black one with the silver buttons—and withdrew a small parcel. "I got you something."

He handed it over and watched Lila undo the wrappings of the box, then slide the lid off. It fell open in her hand, revealing a small puzzle board and a handful of elements. "For practice," he said. "Tieren says you've got some magic in you. Better find it."

They paused on a bench, and he showed her how it worked,

and she chided him for showing off, and then she put the box away and said thank you. It seemed to be a hard phrase for her to say, but she managed. They got to their feet, neither willing to walk away just yet, and Kell looked down at Delilah Bard, a cutthroat and a thief, a valiant partner and a strange, terrifying girl.

He would see her again. He knew he would. Magic bent the world. Pulled it into shape. There were fixed points. Most of the time those points were places. But sometimes, rarely, they were people. For someone who never stood still, Lila still felt like a pin in Kell's world. One he was sure to snag on.

He didn't know what to say, so he simply said, "Stay out of trouble."

She flashed him a smile that said she wouldn't, of course.

And then she tugged up her collar, shoved her hands into her pockets, and strolled away.

Kell watched her go.

She never once looked back.

Delilah Bard was finally free.

She thought of the map back in London—Grey London, her London, old London—the parchment she'd left in the cramped little room at the top of the stairs in the Stone's Throw. The map to anywhere. Isn't that what she had now?

Her bones sang with the promise of it.

Tieren had said there was something in her. Something untended. She didn't know what shape it would take, but she was keen to find out. Whether it was the kind of magic that ran through Kell, or something different, something new, Lila knew one thing:

The world was hers.

The *worlds* were hers.

And she was going to take them all.

Her eyes wandered over the ships on the far side of the river, their gleaming sides and carved masts tall and sharp enough to pierce the low clouds. Flags and sails flapped in the breeze in reds and golds, but also greens and purples and blues.

Boats with royal banners, and boats without. Boats from other lands across other seas, from near and far, wide and away.

And there, tucked between them, she saw a proud, dark ship, with polished sides and a silver banner and sails the color of night, a black that hinted at blue when it caught the light just so.

That one, thought Lila with a smile.

That one'll do.

ACKNOWLEDGMENTS

We think of authors as solitary creatures hunched over work in cramped but empty rooms, and while it's true that writing is a pursuit most often done alone, a book is the result not of one mind, or pair of hands, but of many. To thank every soul would be impossible, but there are some I *cannot* forget to mention. They are as much responsible for this book as I am.

To my editor, Miriam, my partner in crime, for loving Kell and Lila and Rhy as much as I do, and for helping me pave the foundation of this series with blood, shadow, and stylish outfits. A great editor doesn't have all the answers, but they ask the right questions, and you are a *truly* great editor.

To my agent, Holly, for being such a wonderful advocate of this strange little fantasy, even when I pitched it as *pirates, thieves, sadist kings, and violent magic-y stuff.* And to my film agent, Jon, for matching Holly's passion stride for stride. No one could ask for better champions.

To my mother, for wandering the streets of London with me in Kell's footsteps, and to my father, for taking me seriously when I said I was writing a book about cross-dressing thieves and magical men in fabulous coats. In fact, to both of my parents, for never scoffing when I said I wanted to be a writer.

To Lady Hawkins, for traipsing with me through the streets

of Edinburgh, and to Edinburgh, for being its magical self. My bones belong to you.

To Patricia, for knowing this book as well as I do, and for always being willing and able eyes, no matter how rough the pages.

To Carla and Courtney, the best cheerleaders—and the best *friends*—a neurotic, caffeine-addicted author could ask for.

To the Nashville creative community—Ruta, David, Lauren, Sarah, Sharon, Rae Ann, Dawn, Paige, and so many others—who welcomed me home with love and charm and margaritas.

To Tor, and to Irene Gallo, Will Staehle, Leah Withers, Becky Yeager, Heather Saunders, and everyone else who has helped to make this book ready for the world.

And to my readers, both the loyal and the new, because without you, I'm just a girl talking to myself in public.

This is for you.

Turn the page for a preview of the next
Shades of Magic novel

Available now from Tor Books

Copyright © 2016 by Victoria Schwab

I

The Arnesian Sea.

Delilah Bard had a way of finding trouble.

She'd always thought it was better than letting trouble find *her,* but floating in the ocean in a two-person skiff with no oars, no view of land, and no real resources save the ropes binding her wrists, she was beginning to reconsider.

The night was moonless overhead, the sea and sky mirroring the starry darkness to every side; only the ripple of water beneath the rocking boat marked the difference between up and down. That infinite reflection usually made Lila feel like she was perched at the center of the universe.

Tonight, adrift, it made her want to scream.

Instead, she squinted at the twinkleof lights in the distance, the reddish hue alone setting the craft's lanterns apart from the starlight. And she watched as the ship—*her* ship—moved slowly but decidedly *away.*

Panic crawled its way up her throat, but she held her ground.

I am Delilah Bard, she thought, as the ropes cut into her skin. *I am a thief and a pirate and a traveler. I have set foot in three different worlds, and lived. I have shed the blood of royals and held magic in my hands. And a ship full of men cannot do what I can. I don't need any of you.*

I am one of a damned kind.

Feeling suitably empowered, she set her back to the ship, and gazed out at the sprawling night ahead.

It could be worse, she reasoned, just before she felt cold water licking her boots and looked down to see that there was a hole in the boat. Not a large hole by any stretch, but the size was little comfort; a small hole could sink a boat just as effectively, if not as fast.

Lila groaned and looked down at the coarse rope cinched tight around her hands, doubly grateful that the bastards had left her legs free, even if she was trapped in an abominable *dress*. A full-skirted, flimsy green contraption with too much gossamer and a waist so tight she could hardly breathe and *why in god's name* must women *do* this to themselves?

The water inched higher in the skiff, and Lila forced herself to focus. She drew what little breath her outfit would allow and took stock of her meager, quickly dampening inventory: a single cask of ale (a parting gift), three knives (all concealed), half a dozen flares (bequeathed by the men who'd set her adrift), the aforementioned dress (damn it to hell), and the contents of that dress's skirts and pockets (necessary, if she was to prevail).

Lila took up one of the flares—a device like a firework that, when struck against any surface, produced a stream of colored light. Not a burst, but a steady beam strong enough to cut the darkness like a knife. Each flare was supposed to last a quarter of an hour, and the different colors had their own code on the open water: yellow for a sinking ship, green for illness aboard, white for unnamed distress, and red for pirates.

She had one of each, and her fingers danced over their ends as she considered her options. She eyed the rising water and settled on the yellow flare, taking it up with both hands and striking it against the side of the little boat.

Light burst forth, sudden and blinding. It split the world in two, the violent gold-white of the flare and the dense black nothing around it. Lila spent half a minute cursing and blinking back tears at the brightness as she angled the flare up and away from her face. And then she began to count. Just as her eyes were finally adjusting, the flare faltered, flickered, and went out. She scanned the horizon for a ship but saw none, and the water in the boat continued its slow but steady rise up the calf of her boot. She took up a second flare—white for distress—and struck it on the wood, shielding her eyes. She counted the minutes as they ticked by, scouring the night beyond the boat for signs of life.

"Come on," she whispered. "Come on, come on, come on . . ." The words were lost beneath the hiss of the flare as it died, plunging her back into darkness.

Lila gritted her teeth.

Judging by the level of the water in the little boat, she had only a quarter of an hour—one flare's worth of time—before she was well and truly in danger of sinking.

Then something snaked along the skiff's wooden side. Something with teeth.

If there is a god, she thought, *a celestial body, a heavenly power, or anyone above—or below—who might just like to see me live another day, for pity's or entertainment's sake, now would be a good time to intercede.*

And with that, she took up the red flare—the one for pirates—and struck it, bathing the night around her in an eerie crimson light. It reminded her for an instant of the Isle River back in London. Not *her* London—if the dreary place had ever been hers—or the terrifyingly pale London responsible for Athos and Astrid and Holland, but *his* London. Kell's London.

He flashed up in her vision like a flare, auburn hair and that constant furrow between his eyes: one blue, one black. *Antari.* Magic boy. Prince.

Lila stared straight into the flare's red light until it burned the image out. She had more pressing concerns right now. The water was rising. The flare was dying. Shadows were slithering against the boat.

Just as the red light of the pirate's flare began to peter out, she saw it.

It began as nothing—a tendril of mist on the surface of the sea—but soon the fog drew itself into the phantom of a ship. The polished black hull and shining black sails reflected the night to every side, the lanterns aboard small and colorless enough to pass for starlight. Only when it drew close enough for the flare's dying red light to dance across the reflective surfaces did the ship come into focus. And by then, it was nearly on top of her.

By the flare's sputtering glow, Lila could make out the ship's name, streaked in shimmering paint along the hull. *Is Ranes Gast.*

The Copper Thief.

Lila's eyes widened in amazement and relief. She smiled a small, private smile, and then buried the look beneath something more fitting—an expression somewhere between grateful and beseeching, with a dash of wary hope.

The flare guttered and went out, but the ship was beside her now, close enough for her to see the faces of the men leaning over the rail.

"*Tosa!*" she called in Arnesian, getting to her feet, careful not to rock the tiny, sinking craft. *Help.* Vulnerability had never come naturally, but she did her best to imitate it as the men looked down at her, huddled there in her little waterlogged boat with her bound wrists and her soggy green dress. She felt ridiculous.

"*Kers la?*" asked one, more to the others than to her. *What is this?*

"A gift?" said another.

"You'd have to share," muttered a third.

A few of the other men said less pleasant things, and Lila tensed, glad that their accents were too full of mud and ocean spray for her to understand all the words, even if she gleaned their meaning.

"What are you doing down there?" asked one of them, his skin so dark his edges smudged into the night.

Her Arnesian was still far from solid, but four months at sea surrounded by people who spoke no English had certainly improved it.

"*Sensan,*" answered Lila—*sinking*—which earned a laugh from the gathering crew. But they seemed in no hurry to haul her up. Lila held her hands aloft so they could see the rope. "I could use some help," she said slowly, the wording practiced.

"Can see that," said the man.

"Who throws away a pretty thing?" chimed in another.

"Maybe she's all used up."

"Nah."

"Hey, girl! You got all your bits and pieces?"

"Better let us see!"

"What's with all the shouting?" boomed a voice, and a moment later a rail-thin man with deep-set eyes and receding black hair came into sight at the side of the ship. The others shied away in deference as he took hold of the wooden rail and looked down at Lila. His eyes raked over her, the dress, the rope, the cask, the boat.

The captain, she wagered.

"You seem to be in trouble," he called down. He didn't raise his voice, but it carried nonetheless, his Arnesian accent clipped but clear.

"How perceptive," Lila called back before she could stop herself. The insolence was a gamble, but no matter where she was, the one thing she knew was how to read a mark. And sure enough, the thin man smiled.

"My ship's been taken," she continued, "and my new one won't last long, and as you can see—"

He cut her off. "Might be easier to talk if you come up here?"

Lila nodded with a wisp of relief. She was beginning to fear they'd sail on and leave her to drown. Which, judging by the crew's lewd tones and lewder looks, might actually be the better option, but down here she had nothing and up there she had a chance.

A rope was flung over the side; the weighted end landed in the rising water near her feet. She took hold and used it to guide her craft against the ship's side, where a ladder had been lowered; but before she could hoist herself up, two men came down and landed in the boat beside her, causing it to sink *considerably* faster. Neither of them seemed bothered. One proceeded to haul up the cask of ale, and the other, much to Lila's dismay, began to haul up *her*. He threw her over his shoulder, and it took every ounce of her control—which had never been plentiful—not to bury a knife in his back, especially when his hands began to wander up her skirt.

Lila dug her nails into her palms, and by the time the man finally set her down on the ship's desk beside the waiting cask ("Heavier than she looks," he muttered, "and only half as soft . . .") she'd made eight small crescents in her skin.

"Bastard," growled Lila in English under her breath. He gave her a wink and murmured something about being soft where it mattered, and Lila silently vowed to kill him. Slowly.

And then she straightened and found herself standing in a circle of sailors.

No, not sailors, of course.

Pirates.

Grimy, sea stained and sun bleached, their skin darkened and their clothes faded, each and every one of them had a knife tattooed across his throat. The mark of the pirates of the *Copper*

Thief. She counted seven surrounding her, five tending to the rigging and sails, and assumed another half dozen below deck. Eighteen. Round it up to twenty.

The rail-thin man broke the circle and stepped forward.

"*Solase,*" he said, spreading his arms. "What my men have in balls, they lack in manners." He brought his hands to the shoulders of her green dress. There was blood under his nails. "You are shaking."

"I've had a bad night," said Lila, hoping, as she surveyed the rough crew, that it wasn't about to get worse.

The thin man smiled, his mouth surprisingly full of teeth. "*Anesh,*" he said, "but you are in better hands now."

Lila knew enough about the crew of the *Copper Thief* to know that was a lie, but she feigned ignorance. "Whose hands would those be?" she asked, as the skeletal figure took her fingers and pressed his cracked lips to her knuckles, ignoring the rope still wound tightly around her wrists. "Baliz Kasnov," he said. "Illustrious captain of the *Copper Thief.*"

Perfect. Kasnov was a legend on the Arnesian sea. His crew was small but nimble, and they had a penchant for boarding ships and slitting throats in the darkest hours before dawn, slipping away with their cargo and leaving the dead behind to rot. He may have looked starved, but he was an alleged glutton for treasure, especially the consumable kind, and Lila knew that the *Copper Thief* was sailing for the northern coast of a city named Sol in hopes of ambushing the owners of a particularly large shipment of fine liquor. "Baliz Kasnov," she said, sounding out the name as if she'd never heard it.

"And you are?" he pressed.

"Delilah Bard," she said. "Formerly of the *Golden Fish.*"

"Formerly?" prompted Kasnov as his men, obviously bored by the fact she was still clothed, began to tap into the cask. "Well, Miss Bard," he said, linking his arm through hers conspiratorially.

"Why don't you tell me how you came to be in that little boat? The sea is no place for a fair young lady such as yourself."

"*Vaskens*," she said—*pirates*—as if she had no idea the word applied to present company. "They stole my ship. It was a gift, from my father, for my wedding. We were meant to sail toward Faro—we set out two nights ago—but they came out of nowhere, stormed the *Golden Fish* . . ." She'd practiced this speech, not only the words but the pauses. "They . . . they killed my husband. My captain. Most of my crew." Here Lila let herself lapse into English. "It happened so fast—" She caught herself, as if the slip were accidental.

But the captain's attention snagged, like a fish on a hook. "Where are you from?"

"London," said Lila, letting her accent show. A murmur went through the group. She pressed on, intent on finishing her story. "The *Fish* was small," she said, "but precious. Laden down with a month's supplies. Food, drink . . . money. As I said, it was a gift. And now it's gone."

But it wasn't really, not yet. She looked back over the rail. The ship was a smudge of light on the far horizon. It had stopped its retreat and seemed to be waiting. The pirates followed her gaze with hungry eyes.

"How many men?" asked Kasnov.

"Enough," she said. "Seven? Eight?"

The pirates smiled greedily, and Lila knew what they were thinking. They had more than twice that number, and a ship that hid like a shadow in the dark. If they could catch the fleeing bounty . . . she could feel Baliz Kasnov's deep-set eyes scrutinizing her. She stared back at him and wondered, absently, if he could do any magic. Most ships were warded with a handful of spells—things to make their lives safer and more convenient—but she had been surprised to find that most of the men she met at sea had little inclination for the elemental arts. Alucard said that magical proficiency was a valued skill, and that true affinity would usually land one gainful employment on land. Magicians at sea almost always focused on the elements of relevance—water and wind—but few hands could turn the tide, and in the end most still favored good old-fashioned steel. Which Lila could certainly appreciate, having several pieces currently hidden on her person.

"Why did they spare you?" asked Kasnov.

"Did they?" challenged Lila.

The captain licked his lips. He'd already decided what to do about the ship, she could tell; now he was deciding what to do about her. The Copper Thieves had no reputation for mercy.

"Baliz . . ." said one of the pirates, a man with skin darker than the rest. He clasped the captain's shoulder and whispered in his ear. Lila could only make out a few of the muttered words. *Londoners. Rich.* And *ransom.*

A slow smile spread across the captain's lips. "*Anesh*," he said with a nod. And then, to the entire gathered crew, "Sails up! Course south by west! We have a golden fish to catch."

The men rumbled their approval.

"My lady," said Kasnov, leading Lila toward the steps. "You've had a hard night. Let me show you to my chamber, where you'll surely be more comfortable."

Behind her, she heard the sounds of the cask being opened and the ale being poured, and she smiled as the captain led her belowdecks.

Kasnov didn't linger, thank God.

He deposited her in his quarters, the rope still around her wrists, and vanished again, locking the door behind him. To her relief, she'd only seen three men belowdecks. That meant fifteen aboard the *Copper Thief*.

Lila perched on the edge of the captain's bed and counted to ten, twenty, then thirty, as the steps sounded above and the ship banked toward her own fleeing vessel. They hadn't even bothered to search her for weapons, which Lila thought a bit presumptuous as she dug a blade from her boot and, with a single practiced gesture, spun it in her grip and slashed the ropes. They fell to the floor as she rubbed her wrists, humming to herself. A shanty about the Sarows, a phantom said to haunt wayward ships at night.

How do you know when the Sarows is coming?
(Is coming is coming is coming aboard?)

Lila took the waist of her dress in two hands, and ripped; the skirt tore away, revealing close-fitting black pants—holsters pinning a knife above each knee—that tapered into her boots. She took the blade and slid it up the corset at her back, slicing the ribbons so she could breathe.

When the wind dies away but still sings in your ears,
(In your ears in your head in your blood in your bones.)

She tossed the green skirt onto the bed and slit it open from hem to tattered waist. Hidden among the gossamer were half a dozen thin sticks that passed for boning and looked like flares, but were neither. She slid her blade back into her boot and freed the tapers.

When the current goes still but the ship, it drifts along,
(Drifts on drifts away drifts alone.)

Overhead, Lila heard a thud, like dead weight. And then another, and another, as the ale took effect. She took up a piece of black cloth, rubbed charcoal on one side, and tied it over her nose and mouth.

When the moon and the stars all hide from the dark,
(For the dark is not empty at all at all.)
(For the dark is not empty at all.)

The last thing Lila took from deep within the folds of the green skirt was her mask. A black leather face-piece, simple but for the horns that curled with strange and frightening grace over the brow. Lila settled the mask on her nose and tied it in place.

How do you know when the Sarows is coming?
(Is coming is coming is coming aboard?)

A looking glass, half-silvered with age, leaned in the corner of the captain's cabin, and she caught her reflection as footsteps sounded on the stairs.

Why you don't and you don't and you won't see it coming,
(You won't see it coming at all.)

Lila smiled behind the mask. And then she turned and pressed her back against the wall. She struck a taper against the wood, the way she had the flares—but unlike flares, no light poured forth, only clouds of pale smoke.

An instant later, the captain's door burst open, but the pirates were too late. She tossed the pluming taper into the room and heard footsteps stumble, and men cough, before the drugged smoke brought them down.

Two down, thought Lila, stepping over their bodies.
Thirteen to go.

ABOUT THE AUTHOR

Jenna Maurice

VICTORIA "V. E." SCHWAB is the #1 *New York Times* bestselling author of more than twenty books, including the acclaimed Shades of Magic series, the Villains series, and the Monsters of Verity duology. Her work has received critical acclaim; been featured in *The New York Times, Entertainment Weekly, The Washington Post,* and more; been translated into more than a dozen languages; and been optioned for television and film. When she's not haunting Paris streets or trudging up English hillsides, she lives in Edinburgh, Scotland, and is usually tucked into the corner of a coffee shop, dreaming up monsters.

veschwab.com
Twitter: @veschwab
Instagram: @veschwab